CHARLES DICKENS

Little Dorrit

Edited with an Introduction and Notes by
HARVEY PETER SUCKSMITH

OXFORD
UNIVERSITY PRESS

OXFORD

UNIVERSITY PRESS

Great Clarendon Street, Oxford OX2 6DP

Oxford University Press is a department of the University of Oxford.
It furthers the University's objective of excellence in research, scholarship,
and education by publishing worldwide in

Oxford New York

Athens Auckland Bangkok Bogotá Buenos Aires Calcutta
Cape Town Chennai Dar es Salaam Delhi Florence Hong Kong Istanbul
Karachi Kuala Lumpur Madrid Melbourne Mexico City Mumbai
Nairobi Paris São Paulo Shanghai Singapore Taipei Tokyo Toronto Warsaw

with associated companies in Berlin Ibadan

Oxford is a registered trade mark of Oxford University Press
in the UK and in certain other countries

Published in the United States
by Oxford University Press Inc., New York

First published by Oxford University Press 1979
First issued as a World's Classics paperback 1982
Reissued as an Oxford World's Classics paperback 1999
Reissued 2008

British Library Cataloguing in Publication Data

Data available

Library of Congress Cataloging in Publication Data
Dickens, Charles, 1812–1870.
Little Dorrit.
(Oxford world's classics)
Bibliography: p.
I. Sucksmith, Harvey Peter. II. Title.
PR4562.A2S9 1982 823'.8 81–18975

ISBN 978–0–19–953821–8

4

Printed in Great Britain by
Clays Ltd, St Ives plc

GENERAL CONTENTS

EXTRA ILLUSTRATIONS

INTRODUCTION

SINCE *Little Dorrit*, Dickens's eleventh novel, first appeared in monthly parts, from December 1855 to June 1857, the book's critical fortunes have varied enormously. Nevertheless, today's wide acclaim would seem to vindicate the immediate popularity of the serialized version (to judge by its extensive sales) or Bernard Shaw's high praise for its social vision rather than the hostility of some contemporary reviews or the reservations of the later nineteenth and early twentieth centuries. Certainly, it may now be safely said that *Little Dorrit* ranks with *Bleak House* as one of Dickens's most ambitious achievements and one of the greatest works of English literature.

One sign of a great work of fiction is its marvellous fusion of the general with the specific, and *Little Dorrit* demonstrates, in a most remarkable manner, the incarnation of universal truth in particular fact. No other novel of Dickens, for instance, is more extensively grounded in facts, for the author drew on the experiences of a lifetime. The very surname 'Dorrit' was derived from 'Dorrett' on a tombstone at Rochester, scene of his earlier years, while the French, Swiss and Italian scenes are drawn from his own impressions of the Continent in 1844–6 and 1853, some of these already recorded in *Pictures from Italy* (1846). Again, Dickens not only composed the novel with the disasters of the Crimean War (1854–6) in mind, but many details from that period as well as from personal, social and political life found their way into the book.

Critics have often dismissed Dickens as a mere caricaturist and he does display so striking and intense an imagination that the reader, unaware of the many solid facts which underlie his fiction, may suspect he is given to exaggeration. Yet, like many other masters of satire, Dickens saw that life frequently caricatures itself, and the more we excavate the substantial basis of his novels, and no more so than in *Little Dorrit*, the more we come to appreciate his exactness and even restraint.

Contemporary agitation and journalism, for example, confirm his picture of a miserable Victorian Sunday in London, and during June and July 1855, about the time he was engaged on the novel's third chapter, there was rioting for three days in Hyde Park against a bill to prevent Sunday trading. Writing of his childhood during the 1830s and 1840s, Augustus Hare in *The Story of My Life* (1896) indicates the sort of extreme measures that might well be involved in a nineteenth-century puritan upbringing. Hare, like Arthur Clennam in the novel, was reared by a foster mother who subjected him to the strictest Sabbatarian regime, tormented his imagination with the terrors of hell, and strove to break his will through austere discipline and ferocious punishments. Again, Rigaud may seem unlikely and melodramatic to us, yet he was based on a real psychopathic killer, Pierre-François Lacenaire, who was even more theatrical and flamboyant than Dickens's character. Guillotined for a particularly cold-blooded double murder in 1836, Lacenaire, who shows many of Rigaud's traits, was work-shy with genteel pretensions and took to a life of theft, extortion, forgery and murder for gain. He dressed well, affecting an elegant air and scrupulous politeness, and admired the Romantic theatre whose over-acting he imitated.

In his preface, Dickens rightly defends himself against the charge that the Barnacles, the Circumlocution Office, Merdle and the financial scandal are exaggerations. He cites the railway-share mania of the forties which culminated in the fall of Hudson the 'Railway King' in 1849, the Royal British Bank's failure in 1856, and the Tipperary Bank scandal touched off by the swindler John Sadleir's suicide on 16 February 1856. With regard to Circumlocution, Dickens cites the proceedings before the Roebuck Committee on the conduct of the Crimean War which presented its report in June 1855. Indeed, elements of black farce and burlesque were present in the real events which provide the context of Dickens's satire: the lack of splints and bandages at the Battle of Alma, for example, or the aged, British Commander-in-Chief Lord Raglan's habit of referring to the enemy as 'the French', in fact his principal ally. On 27 June 1855, Dickens delivered a scathing speech before the Administrative Reform Association which he had joined in May, and on 15 June his friend Layard had asserted in the Commons that 'the manner in which merit and efficiency have been sacrificed, in public appointments, to party and family influences, and to a blind adherence to routine . . . threatens . . . to involve the country in grave disasters.' The novel presents this incident, with characteristic irony, in the passage which begins, 'Sometimes, angry spirits attacked the Circumlocution Office' (p. 89). With respect to the Barnacles, Dickens might well have cited the Northcote–Trevelyan report on the civil service (1853) which revealed that 'the idle, and useless, the fool of the family, the consumptive, the hypochondriac, those who have a tendency to insanity are the sort of young men "provided for" in a public office.'

Yet the temptation to rush to the other extreme and regard *Little Dorrit* as animated social history should be resisted. Rhetoric (the novel's opening paragraphs are an instance), as well as an impassioned conviction of the truth, helps to explain the substantiality of the Dickens world, and the author of *Hard Times* was well aware that a novel is not simply a matter of hard facts but of their presentation through the imagination. Indeed, Dickens's vision is not historical in the narrow sense at all. It is intuitive and prophetic. It works on the specific in order to liberate its universal possibilities and eternal significance.

Thus, the date of the main action in *Little Dorrit* is specified as the 1820s; but, by deliberately telescoping periods, events and personages, Dickens combines a sense of the particular and definite with something less precise and more general. For example, the age of the Reform Bill (1832) and that of the early 1850s sometimes merge, helped by parallel situations or attitudes and key figures who play a similar role in both eras. Certainly, reactionaries in each period, alarmed at the power of the press, talked about 'mob' like the people at Mrs. Gowan's dinner; Augustus Stiltstalking suggests the austere Duke of Wellington who had directly opposed Chartism in 1848 and parliamentary reform before 1832; while the cavalry had in fact charged at Bristol in 1831 and quite disastrously at Balaclava in 1854. John Barnacle's 'idea of conciliating the mob' surely refers to Lord John Russell, who had steered the Reform Bill through Parliament and recently (1854) introduced a new reform bill. And William Barnacle and Tudor Stiltstalking's 'ever memorable coalition' (p. 263) reflects both the one between Russell and the Earl of Aberdeen, which made the ministry of 1852–5 possible, and another 'memorable' one involving Russell which had sustained the Grey ministry of the early 1830s.

Again, in Lord Decimus Tite Barnacle, Dickens is hinting strongly at Lord Palmerston, who became Prime Minister in January 1855 and continued to obstruct administrative reform. In April and May, Dickens lampooned Palmerston in *Household Words*, and compared him in a June speech to Shakespeare's Julius Caesar. This, together with Palmerston's famous *Civis Romanus* speech of 1850, no doubt accounts for the name 'Decimus' with its suggestion of patrician arrogance and ambition. *Little Dorrit* satirizes many of Palmerston's traits, as Dickens saw them— his glib and evasive management of Parliament, *laissez-faire* policies and obstructionist tactics (pp. 339–40)—while avoiding an absolute identification and keeping the character generalized.

Dickens is not preoccupied with particular politicians, with patent law, or imprisonment for debt, George Hudson or John Sadleir, or the mismanagement of the Crimean War. He is concerned rather with the stifling of creativity, the world as a prison, the calamity which greed and fraud combine to produce, the callous inefficiency of a political and bureaucratic machine in the hands of those who think themselves superior and not responsible to their fellow men. And Dickens continues to be widely read because his genuine myth-making faculty touches his creations with an archetypal power which remains true to man's experience. The swindler, rack-renter, kill-joy and psychopathic criminal are still loose in our society, bureaucracy grows increasingly inhuman, inventors are still frustrated and unhonoured, Barnacles still cling tenaciously, yet Dickens has stamped their perennial likenesses indelibly on our minds.

Little Dorrit illustrates the imaginative process by which the central vision and effects in a great novel select, shape, and assimilate its subject-matter. In this respect, what is interesting about Mr. Merdle is not his factual origin in John Sadleir but what Dickens omits to tell us about the swindler's gestation. There are important similarities between Merdle's history and that of 'The Forger' in Samuel Warren's *Passages from the Diary of a Late Physician* (1830) which Dickens had read, about twenty years earlier. But the vital element which Dickens borrowed from Warren was the ironic machinery of the sickness which turns out to be the criminal's guilt. It is this imaginative idea, together with Merdle's gesture of taking himself into custody and his jailor of a butler, which enables the swindler to be assimilated into the central motifs of ironic deception and society as a prison.

The handling of autobiographical material in *Little Dorrit* also shows how Dickens transmutes particular facts into art by giving them ironic distance and a universal application which is part of the novel's central meaning. The Marshalsea scenes, based on his father's imprisonment there, and the Flora Finching incidents, which sprang from his re-encounter with his youthful love, Maria Beadnell (now Winter), shortly before he began *Little Dorrit*, may derive conviction and power from their traumatic source. Yet these highly personal episodes become great impersonal art only through Dickens's imagination and skill. His father's imprisonment, a blow to his own private genteel aspirations, is trans-formed into the grand ironic and impersonal concept of a shabby society which, for all its genteel pretensions, is a prison. The pain of an old unhappy love is exorcized by an ironic discovery which not only exposes one corner of the world of illusions, a theme of the novel, but touches every mature man's experience, as Dickens points out in a letter (5 July 1856): 'We have all had our Floras . . . It is a wonderful gratification to find that everybody knows her.' Certainly, in the first great scene with Flora (pp. 125–9), the manuscript and corrected proofs show with what artistry Dickens worked to increase the power and clarity of the ironic effect and vision.

A superficial reader might suppose that *Little Dorrit* marks a return to Dickens's earlier episodic manner; but this would be a failure to grasp the book's complex unity and ultimate meaning. True, the mystery of Arthur's parentage is awkward and absurdly complicated, as Dickens's memoranda show, and Miss Wade's narrative is not completely integrated with the novel, as Dickens acknowledged. Admittedly too, Dickens experienced great difficulty at first in organizing his extremely hetero-geneous material into a coherent whole. The original idea for the work, which appears in his notes as 'The man who comfortably charges every-thing on Providence' (p. 694), proved a false start, and the way to the novel's unified social vision was only opened up when Dickens came to grasp that a whole interconnected scheme of things, not one person, was responsible for the condition he deplored. The change of title from 'Nobody's Fault' to 'Little Dorrit' reflects this progress in Dickens's understanding as well as the emergence of a more hopeful counter-theme to balance the pessimistic prison motif. Phiz's design for the cover of the monthly numbers graphically demonstrates this interconnectedness and unity of vision.

Dickens imposes unity and coherence on the novel in many different ways. He uses form to bind his material together, to give it meaningful shape and direction, and to stress development. Thus, the opening scenes of the two books, 'Poverty' and 'Riches', with their panoramic views, prison motifs and travellers, and the closing scenes which involve release from prison are obviously meant as parallels and the question prompted: Is a significant comparison or contrast implied? Again, a note by Dickens (p. 704) shows that parallel scenes, here and elsewhere, were deliberately planned. Moreover, a sense of crisis, aroused by careful foreshadowing, as we also see from the notes, culminates in a series of disasters which might be called a 'compound catastrophe' since its various elements are engineered by a single fault, deception, on which the catastrophe is making what amounts to a single comment.

The well-known prison symbolism also helps to unify the novel. Further notes (pp. 694, 704) show that the development of this motif was carefully designed, and in no other novel of Dickens does one symbol play so ubiquitous a role. This central idea expands relentlessly to include actual jails like the Marshalsea and the one in Marseilles, analogous institutions like quarantine, London's housing, or the Alpine Convent, and the many mental and moral prisons of the novel. It infuses the verbal imagery, from the various birds in cages to Mr. Chivery's prison of reticence (pp. 250–1) and the public at the Circumlocution Office treated like 'troublesome Convicts' (p. 453). Relentlessly too, the prison-taint spreads everywhere, touching even Amy Dorrit and infecting Arthur Clennam. But perhaps its most terrible manifestation is that ultimate prison, described by Dr. Haggage (p. 53), ironically after delivering Amy, that second womb with its dreadful peace into which those defeated by life regress. Finally, Dickens tells us that this 'lower world' is itself a prison, barred by the sun's rays (pp. 636–7). And it is from this cosmic standpoint that we should regard the idea of society as a prison, since Dickens suggests here that all specific and 'sublunary' things in the *Little Dorrit* world are part of a greater whole and a greater truth.

Yet if society or the world as a prison appears to be the novel's central motif, what does this really mean? Certainly it involves the stifling of the creative will, a concept that does justice to much in *Little Dorrit*—but not all. The idea of deception also pervades the novel and lies at its thematic core, Dickens himself stressing the universal self-deceit: '. . . for we all know how we all deceive ourselves' (p. 120). A more comprehensive view of the theme, therefore, might hold that society is a prison of deception in which deceit and delusion are the walls separating the prisoners. Isolation and ignorance, the ideas shared by prison and deception and thus enabling them to be yoked together, are stressed very early in the novel. The first chapter concludes with Rigaud's separation from Cavalletto and the Italian's frantic ignorance of Rigaud's fate. Two chapters later, Arthur discovers that his mother, isolated in her room, is even ignorant of the season. By the third paragraph of chapter vi, Dickens is emphasizing the ideas of prison and deception, isolation and ignorance in an ironic context (p. 48).

The characters of *Little Dorrit* embody and illustrate this central theme, since each form of deception they represent is a kind of prison. Mrs. General, for instance, presides over a typical mid-Victorian world where appearances have to be kept up. As the key figure of the educationalist, she insists that any inconvenient truths be safely confined under layers of varnish or locked in cupboards, instructing her pupils to constrain genuine responses behind a hypocritical and conformist *persona* (p. 377). A *persona*, of course, may imprison the living truth within a daily existence of lies, and an over-valuation of the social mask may foster grave public dangers. Indeed, no other writer has so devastatingly exposed the 'persona-culture' of Victorian England and its shortcomings. If Casby's patriarchal pose, which deceives his tenants so long, seems rather wooden, this is apt; for a mask is rigid and false, and there are few closer prisons than the posture which must be sustained. The comparison with a mere stuffed suit of clothes and glimpses of a mean furtive life betray the fraudulent Merdle, a graven image worshipped by his deceived adorers. Yet, as his complaint and habitual gesture reveal, Merdle is isolated, and imprisoned, by guilt. So is Mrs. Clennam. She also practices deception but her paralysis is an imprisoning self-deceit from which she is released by shock. Other prisoners of self-deception range from Henry Gowan, captive of his own cynical, false judgements, to Miss Wade and Mr. F's Aunt, shut up for life in the most secure prison of all, that of insane delusions, paranoia in the first case, paranoid schizophrenia in the second. Prejudice, tinged with paranoid suspicion, is widespread in the novel, forming part of the Barnacle syndrome. The minds of Mrs. Gowan, Lord Lancaster Stiltstalking, Lord Decimus Tite Barnacle, and Barnacle Junior are closely restricted by political or social fantasies, bogus reactionary ideas, and a delusion of snobbish superiority (which even kindly Mr. Meagles helps to foster). Again, Mr. Tite Barnacle, whose home on the squalid fringes of a fashionable district is compared to a bottle, appears corked up with the bad smell of his own genteel pretensions. Rigaud is also trapped in a false genteel posture which he appears to mistake for reality. The same is true of William Dorrit, though here the prison image and genteel delusion are carried to the most splendid peak of development. The Marshalsea jailbird has been affecting gentility for a quarter of a century when fate, that double-dealer, steps in, allowing the dream to become reality only to clap the ex-prisoner within the hallucination that he is once more back in the genteel pose of the Father of the Marshalsea. This is a case of prison within prison, of delusion within delusion. Life has become a nightmare in which all sense of reality and freedom is lost.

Social institutions contribute their share to this prison-like world of deception. The nation's political life is stifled in the parliamentary panto-mime which is a mere front for snobbery and jobbery. The economic sphere is sustained by idols with clay feet, while capital is either sucked upwards into a vicious and fruitless spiral of investment or drawn down-wards through the heartless and wasteful vortex of insolvency and ex-tortion. Administration is a crippling sham routine. Circumlocution's agents, like their victims, are caught in an endless and insane paper-chase, entangling a nation's best efforts in a fatal mesh of red tape (pp. 87–104). 'The sheets of foolscap paper,' a Barnacle proudly tells Parliament, that Circumlocution 'had devoted to the public service would pave the footways on both sides of Oxford Street from end to end . . . while of tape—red tape—it had used enough to stretch, in graceful festoons, from Hyde Park Corner to the General Post Office' (p. 433).

At first, even love appears to offer no way out. Thus, Flora is forever trapped in a bogus romantic posture, which properly belongs to girlhood, though here, as with John Chivery, satire softens into a gentle comedy. Arthur seems doomed to frustration, disappointment and despair; yet love, for him, is a journey from deception and imprisonment to deliver-ance from both jail and delusion.

It is with Amy's loving care that the counter-theme develops. In a prison of collective deception, love offers the only way out to truth and freedom. Arthur's release from the Marshalsea, in contrast to William Dorrit's, is a matter also of illumination and union. Here, the Victorian idealization of woman as utterly pure and selfless helps the presentation of Amy as an *anima*-like redeemer of man, through whom the healing voice of Nature speaks to Arthur and the ocean is freed at last from the sun's fiery dominion:

the ocean was no longer to be seen lying asleep in the heat, but its thousand sparkling eyes were open, and its whole breadth was in joyful animation . . . Clennam, listening to the voice as it read to him, heard in it all that great Nature was doing, heard in it all the soothing songs she sings to man. (p. 679)

Again, Arthur's characteristic Victorian manliness in rejecting Amy's fortune and the situation which can be resolved only by the loss of her wealth are used by Dickens to indicate that salvation lies in the renunci-ation of life's material things. For the progress of these lovers marks the stages in a ritual and their union carries more than a suggestion of the *hieros gamos*, the archetype of the sacred marriage through which the world is offered a chance of redemption. For when the material cosmos turns to a transient illusion, the eternal truth of myth alone can give an enduring meaning to life: 'They went quietly down into the roaring streets, inseparable and blessed; and as they passed along in sunshine and in shade, the noisy and the eager, and the arrogant and the froward and the vain, fretted, and chafed, and made their usual uproar' (p. 688). Love transcends the world by bringing inner peace in the midst of external strife. Love threads its way through light and darkness, weaving the opposites together into a larger pattern of meaning. Love is, indeed, the truth that sets us free.

HARVEY PETER SUCKSMITH

In addition to the acknowledgements in the Clarendon edition I should again like to thank the general editors of that edition, James Kinsley and Kathleen Tillotson.

H.P.S.

NOTE ON THE TEXT

ISSUED in monthly parts from 1 December 1855 to 1 June 1857, and in one volume without change except for a list of errata, including correction of 'Rigaud' to 'Blandois' in No. XV (made in the second issue of the 1857 edition). Later editions in Dickens's lifetime (in 1859, 1861, and 1868) show a progressive deterioration and very little correction; and almost all modern editions have been based on the last and worst of these. The present text, that of the editor's Clarendon *Little Dorrit*, 1979, is based on the corrected issue of the first, one-volume edition of 1857. This has been emended in over 100 places from the author's manuscript (in the Forster collection, Victoria and Albert Museum) where it contains an obviously correct reading overlooked by Dickens in reading proof, or when the printer has overlooked a correction in proof. Many proofs are in the Forster collection and a few also in the Dexter collection, British Library.

A CHRONOLOGY OF CHARLES DICKENS

1812	(7 Feb.) Born at Landport, Hants, to John and Elizabeth Dickens
1815–17	London
1817–22	Chatham, Kent; early education
1823–	London
1824	John Dickens in Marshalsea Debtors' Prison; Dickens employed in Warren's blacking-warehouse
1824–7	At Wellington House Academy
1827–8	Employed as solicitors' clerk
?1829–?1831	Shorthand reporter, at Doctors' Commons; on *Mirror of Parliament*; on *True Sun*
1833–4	First stories published in *Monthly Magazine*
1834	(Aug.)–1836 (Nov.) Reporter on *Morning Chronicle*; sketches published, collected as *Sketches by Boz*, two series Feb. and Dec. 1836
1836	(April)–1837 (Nov.) *Pickwick Papers* (monthly)
1836	(2 April) Marries Catherine Hogarth; lives at Furnival's Inn
1837	(Jan.)–1839 (Jan.) Edits *Bentley's Miscellany*; *Oliver Twist* (monthly —published complete Nov. 1838)
1837	(April)–1839 (Dec.) At 48 Doughty Street. Mary Hogarth dies there, May 1837
1838	(April)–1839 (Oct.) *Nicholas Nickleby* (monthly)
1839	(Dec.) Moves to 1 Devonshire Terrace
1840–1	*Master Humphrey's Clock* (weekly), including *The Old Curiosity Shop* and *Barnaby Rudge*; also monthly, April 1840–Nov. 1841
1842	(Jan.–June) In North America. *American Notes* (Oct.)
1843	(Jan.)–1844 (July) *Martin Chuzzlewit* (monthly) (Dec.) *A Christmas Carol*
1844	(July)–1845 (June) Living in Italy (Dec.) *The Chimes*
1845	(Sept.) First performance by the Amateurs; others in 1846–8, 1850–1 (Oct.)–1846 (March) Planning, editing and contributing to *Daily News* (Dec.) *The Cricket on the Hearth*
1846	(May) *Pictures from Italy* (June–Nov.) Living in Switzerland (Oct.)–1848 (April) *Dombey and Son* (monthly) (Nov.)–1847 (Feb.) Living in Paris (Dec.) *The Battle of Life*
1847	(Nov.) Miss Coutts's 'Home for Homeless Women' opened

1848   (Dec.) *The Haunted Man*

1849   (May)–1850 (Nov.) *David Copperfield* (monthly)

1850   (March) Starts *Household Words* (weekly), editing and contributing
            regularly

1851   (Oct.) Moves to Tavistock House

1852   (March)–1853 (Sept.) *Bleak House* (monthly)

1854   *Hard Times* (weekly)

1855   (Dec.)–1857 (June) *Little Dorrit* (monthly)

1856   (March) Buys Gad's Hill Place, Kent

1858   (April) Begins Public Readings
            (May) Separates from Mrs. Dickens

1859   (April–Nov.) *A Tale of Two Cities* (weekly and monthly)
            (May) *All the year Round* begins
            (June) *Household Words* ends

1860   *The Uncommercial Traveller*
            (Oct.) Final removal to Gad's Hill
            (Dec.)–1861 (Aug.) *Great Expectations* (weekly)

1864   (May)–1865 (Nov.) *Our Mutual Friend* (monthly)

1867   (Nov.)–1868 (April) Public reading tour in USA

1869   (April) Breakdown in provincial reading tour

1870   (Jan.–March) Farewell season of Public readings in London
            (April–Sept.) *The Mystery of Edwin Drood* (monthly; unfinished)
            (9 June) Dies at Gad's Hill

LITTLE DORRIT.

BY

CHARLES DICKENS.

WITH ILLUSTRATIONS BY H. K. BROWNE.

LONDON:

BRADBURY AND EVANS, 11, BOUVERIE STREET.

1857.

PREFACE

I HAVE been occupied with this story, during many working hours of two years. I must have been very ill employed, if I could not leave its merits and demerits as a whole, to express themselves on its being read as a whole. But, as it is not unreasonable to suppose that I may have held its various threads with a more continuous attention than any one else can have given to them during its desultory publication, it is not unreasonable to ask that the weaving may be looked at in its completed state, and with the pattern finished.

If I might offer any apology for so exaggerated a fiction as the Barnacles and the Circumlocution Office, I would seek it in the common experience of an Englishman, without presuming to mention the unimportant fact of my having done that violence to good manners, in the days of a Russian war, and of a Court of Enquiry at Chelsea. If I might make so bold as to defend that extravagant conception, Mr. Merdle, I would hint that it originated after the Railroad-share epoch, in the times of a certain Irish bank, and of one or two other equally laudable enterprises. If I were to plead anything in mitigation of the preposterous fancy that a bad design will sometimes claim to be a good and an expressly religious design, it would be the curious coincidence that it has been brought to its climax in these pages, in the days of the public examination of late Directors of a Royal British Bank. But, I submit myself to suffer judgment to go by default on all these counts, if need be, and to accept the assurance (on good authority) that nothing like them was ever known in this land.

Some of my readers may have an interest in being informed whether or no any portions of the Marshalsea Prison are yet standing. I did not know, myself, until the sixth of this present month, when I went to look. I found the outer front courtyard, often mentioned in this story, meta-morphosed into a butter-shop; and I then almost gave up every brick of the jail for lost. Wandering, however, down a certain adjacent "Angel Court, leading to Bermondsey," I came to "Marshalsea Place:" the houses in which I recognised, not only as the great block of the former prison, but as preserving the rooms that arose in my mind's-eye when I became Little Dorrit's biographer. The smallest boy I ever conversed with, carrying the largest baby I ever saw, offered a supernaturally intelligent explanation of the locality in its old uses, and was very nearly correct. How this young Newton (for such I judge him to be) came by his information, I don't know; he was a quarter of a century too young to know anything about it of himself. I pointed to the window of the room where Little Dorrit was born, and where her father lived so long, and asked him what was the name of the

lodger who tenanted that apartment at present? He said "Tom Pythick."
I asked him who was Tom Pythick? and he said, "Joe Pythick's uncle."

A little further on, I found the older and smaller wall, which used to
enclose the pent-up inner prison where nobody was put, except for ceremony. But, whosoever goes into Marshalsea Place, turning out of Angel
Court, leading to Bermondsey, will find his feet on the very paving-stones
of the extinct Marshalsea jail; will see its narrow yard to the right and to
the left, very little altered if at all, except that the walls were lowered when
the place got free; will look upon the rooms in which the debtors lived;
and will stand among the crowding ghosts of many miserable years.

In the Preface to Bleak House I remarked that I had never had so many
readers. In the Preface to its next successor, Little Dorrit, I have still to
repeat the same words. Deeply sensible of the affection and confidence that
have grown up between us, I add to this Preface, as I added to that, May
we meet again!

LONDON,
   May, 1857.

CONTENTS

BOOK THE FIRST. POVERTY

THE END OF THE FIRST BOOK

BOOK THE SECOND. RICHES

CONTENTS

LIST OF ILLUSTRATIONS

BOOK THE FIRST. POVERTY

CHAPTER I

SUN AND SHADOW

THIRTY years ago, Marseilles lay burning in the sun, one day.

A blazing sun upon a fierce August day was no greater rarity in southern France then, than at any other time, before or since. Everything in Marseilles, and about Marseilles, had stared at the fervid sky, and been stared at in return, until a staring habit had become universal there. Strangers were stared out of countenance by staring white houses, staring white walls, staring white streets, staring tracts of arid road, staring hills from which verdure was burnt away. The only things to be seen not fixedly staring and glaring were the vines drooping under their load of grapes. These did occasionally wink a little, as the hot air barely moved their faint leaves.

There was no wind to make a ripple on the foul water within the harbor, or on the beautiful sea without. The line of demarcation between the two colors, black and blue, showed the point which the pure sea would not pass; but it lay as quiet as the abominable pool, with which it never mixed. Boats without awnings were too hot to touch; ships blistered at their moorings; the stones of the quays had not cooled, night or day, for months. Hindoos, Russians, Chinese, Spaniards, Portuguese, Englishmen, Frenchmen, Genoese, Neapolitans, Venetians, Greeks, Turks, descendants from all the builders of Babel, come to trade at Marseilles, sought the shade alike—taking refuge in any hiding-place from a sea too intensely blue to be looked at, and a sky of purple, set with one great flaming jewel of fire.

The universal stare made the eyes ache. Towards the distant line of Italian coast, indeed, it was a little relieved by light clouds of mist, slowly rising from the evaporation of the sea; but it softened nowhere else. Far away the staring roads, deep in dust, stared from the hill-side, stared from the hollow, stared from the interminable plain. Far away the dusty vines overhanging wayside cottages, and the monotonous wayside avenues of parched trees without shade, drooped beneath the stare of earth and sky. So did the horses with drowsy bells, in long files of carts, creeping slowly towards the interior; so did their recumbent drivers, when they were awake, which rarely happened; so did the exhausted laborers in the fields. Everything that lived or grew, was oppressed by the glare; except the lizard, passing swiftly over rough stone walls, and the cicala, chirping his dry hot chirp, like a rattle. The very dust was scorched brown, and something quivered in the atmosphere as if the air itself were panting.

Blinds, shutters, curtains, awnings, were all closed and drawn to keep out the stare. Grant it but a chink or keyhole, and it shot in like a white-hot arrow. The churches were the freest from it. To come out of the twilight of pillars and arches—dreamily dotted with winking lamps, dreamily peopled with ugly old shadows piously dozing, spitting, and begging—was to plunge into a fiery river, and swim for life to the nearest strip of shade. So, with people lounging and lying wherever shade was, with but little hum of tongues or barking of dogs, with occasional jangling of discordant church bells, and rattling of vicious drums, Marseilles, a fact to be strongly smelt and tasted, lay broiling in the sun one day.

In Marseilles that day there was a villanous prison. In one of its chambers, so repulsive a place that even the obtrusive stare blinked at it, and left it to such refuse of reflected light as it could find for itself, were two men. Besides the two men, a notched and disfigured bench, immoveable from the wall, with a draught-board rudely hacked upon it with a knife, a set of draughts, made of old buttons and soup bones, a set of dominoes, two mats, and two or three wine bottles. That was all the chamber held, exclusive of rats and other unseen vermin, in addition to the seen vermin, the two men.

It received such light as it got, through a grating of iron bars, fashioned like a pretty large window, by means of which it could be always inspected from the gloomy staircase on which the grating gave. There was a broad strong ledge of stone to this grating, where the bottom of it was let into the masonry, three or four feet above the ground. Upon it, one of the two men lolled, half sitting and half lying, with his knees drawn up, and his feet and shoulders planted against the opposite sides of the aperture. The bars were wide enough apart to admit of his thrusting his arm through to the elbow; and so he held on negligently, for his greater ease.

A prison taint was on everything there. The imprisoned air, the imprisoned light, the imprisoned damps, the imprisoned men, were all deteriorated by confinement. As the captive men were faded and haggard, so the iron was rusty, the stone was slimy, the wood was rotten, the air was faint, the light was dim. Like a well, like a vault, like a tomb, the prison had no knowledge of the brightness outside; and would have kept its polluted atmosphere intact, in one of the spice islands of the Indian Ocean.

The man who lay on the ledge of the grating was even chilled. He jerked his great cloak more heavily upon him by an impatient movement of one shoulder, and growled, "To the devil with this Brigand of a Sun that never shines in here!"

He was waiting to be fed; looking sideways through the bars, that he might see the further down the stairs, with much of the expression of a wild beast in similar expectation. But his eyes, too close together, were not so nobly set in his head as those of the king of beasts are in his, and they were sharp rather than bright—pointed weapons with little surface to betray them. They had no depth or change; they glittered, and they opened and shut. So far, and waiving their use to himself, a clockmaker could have made a better pair. He had a hook nose, handsome after its kind, but too high between the eyes, by probably just as much as his eyes were too near to one another. For the rest, he was large and tall in frame, had thin lips, where his thick moustache showed them at all, and a quantity of dry hair, of no definable color, in its shaggy state, but shot with red. The hand with which he held the grating (seamed all over the back with ugly scratches newly healed) was unusually small and plump; would have been unusually white, but for the prison grime.

The other man was lying on the stone floor, covered with a coarse brown coat.

"Get up, pig!" growled the first. "Don't sleep when I am hungry."

"It's all one, master," said the pig, in a submissive manner, and not without cheerfulness; "I can wake when I will, I can sleep when I will. It's all the same."

As he said it, he rose, shook himself, scratched himself, tied his brown coat loosely round his neck by the sleeves (he had previously used it as a coverlet), and sat down upon the pavement yawning, with his back against the wall opposite to the grating.

"Say what the hour is," grumbled the first man.

"The mid-day bells will ring—in forty minutes." When he made the little pause, he had looked round the prison-room, as if for certain information.

"You are a clock. How is it that you always know?"

"How can I say! I always know what the hour is, and where I am. I was brought in here at night, and out of a boat, but I know where I am. See here! Marseilles Harbor;" on his knees on the pavement, mapping it all out with a swarthy forefinger; "Toulon (where the galleys are), Spain over there, Algiers over *there*. Creeping away to the left here, Nice. Round by the Cornice to Genoa. Genoa Mole and Harbor. Quarantine Ground. City there; terrace-gardens blushing with the bella donna. Here, Porto Fino. Stand out for Leghorn. Out again for Civita Vecchia. So away to——hey! there's no room for Naples;" he had got to the wall by this time; "but it's all one; it's in there!"

He remained on his knees, looking up at his fellow prisoner with a lively look for a prison. A sunburnt, quick, lithe, little man, though rather thickset. Ear-rings in his brown ears, white teeth lighting up his grotesque brown face, intensely black hair clustering about his brown throat, a ragged red shirt open at his brown breast. Loose, seamanlike trousers, decent shoes, a long red cap, a red sash round his waist, and a knife in it.

"Judge if I come back from Naples as I went! See here, my master! Civita Vecchia, Leghorn, Porto Fino, Genoa, Cornice, Off Nice (which is in there), Marseilles, you and me. The apartment of the jailer and his keys is where I put this thumb; and here at my wrist, they keep the national razor in its case—the guillotine locked up."

The other man spat suddenly on the pavement, and gurgled in his throat.

Some lock below gurgled in *its* throat immediately afterwards, and then a door clashed. Slow steps began ascending the stairs; the prattle of a sweet little voice mingled with the noise they made; and the prison-keeper appeared, carrying his daughter, three or four years old, and a basket.

"How goes the world this forenoon, gentlemen? My little one, you see, going round with me to have a peep at her father's birds. Fie, then! Look at the birds, my pretty, look at the birds."

He looked sharply at the birds himself, as he held the child up at the grate, especially at the little bird, whose activity he seemed to mistrust. "I have brought your bread, Signor John Baptist," said he (they all spoke in French, but the little man was an Italian); "and if I might recommend you not to game—"

"You don't recommend the master!" said John Baptist, showing his teeth as he smiled.

"Oh! but the master wins," returned the jailer, with a passing look of no particular liking at the other man, "and you lose. It's quite another thing. You get husky bread and sour drink by it; and he gets sausage of Lyons, veal in savory jelly, white bread, strachino cheese, and good wine by it. Look at the birds, my pretty!"

"Poor birds!" said the child.

The fair little face, touched with divine compassion, as it peeped shrinkingly through the grate, was like an angel's in the prison. John Baptist rose and moved towards it, as if it had a good attraction for him. The other bird remained as before, except for an impatient glance at the basket.

"Stay!" said the jailer, putting his little daughter on the outer ledge of the grate, "she shall feed the birds. This big loaf is for Signor John Baptist. We must break it to get it through into the cage. So, there's a tame bird, to kiss the little hand! This sausage in a vine-leaf is for Monsieur Rigaud. Again—this veal in savory jelly is for Monsieur Rigaud. Again—these three white little loaves are for Monsieur Rigaud. Again, this cheese—again, this wine—again, this tobacco—all for Monsieur Rigaud. Lucky bird!"

The child put all these things between the bars into the soft, smooth, well-shaped hand, with evident dread—more than once drawing back her own, and looking at the man with her fair brow roughened into an expression half of fright and half of anger. Whereas, she had put the lump of coarse bread into the swart, scaled, knotted hands of John Baptist (who had scarcely as much nail on his eight fingers and two thumbs as would have made out one for Monsieur Rigaud), with ready confidence; and, when he kissed her hand, had herself passed it caressingly over his face. Monsieur Rigaud, indifferent to this distinction, propitiated the father by laughing and nodding at the daughter as often as she gave him anything; and, so soon as he had all his viands about him in convenient nooks of the ledge on which he rested, began to eat with an appetite.

When Monsieur Rigaud laughed, a change took place in his face, that was more remarkable than prepossessing. His moustache went up under his nose, and his nose came down over his moustache, in a very sinister and cruel manner.

"There!" said the jailer, turning his basket upside down to beat the crumbs out, "I have expended all the money I received; here is the note of it, and *that's* a thing accomplished. Monsieur Rigaud, as I expected yesterday, the President will look for the pleasure of your society at an hour after mid-day, to-day."

"To try me, eh?" said Rigaud, pausing, knife in hand and morsel in mouth.

"You have said it. To try you."

"There is no news for me?" asked John Baptist, who had begun, contentedly, to munch his bread.

The jailer shrugged his shoulders.

"Lady of mine! Am I to lie here all my life, my father?"

"What do I know!" cried the jailer, turning upon him with southern quickness, and gesticulating with both his hands and all his fingers, as if he were threatening to tear him to pieces. "My friend, how is it possible for one to tell how long you are to lie here? What do I know, John Baptist Cavalletto? Death of my life! There are prisoners here sometimes, who are not in such a devil of a hurry to be tried."

He seemed to glance obliquely at Monsieur Rigaud in this remark; bu Monsieur Rigaud had already resumed his meal, though not with quite so quick an appetite as before.

"Adieu, my birds!" said the keeper of the prison, taking his pretty child in his arms, and dictating the words with a kiss.

"Adieu, my birds!" the pretty child repeated.

Her innocent face looked back so brightly over his shoulder, as he walked away with her, singing her the song of the child's game:

> "Who passes by this road so late?
> Compagnon de la Majolaine!
> Who passes by this road so late?
> Always gay!"

that John Baptist felt it a point of honor to reply at the grate, and, in good time and tune, though a little hoarsely:

"Of all the king's knights 'tis the flower,
        Compagnon de la Majolaine!
Of all the king's knights 'tis the flower,
        Always gay!"

Which accompanied them so far down the few steep stairs, that the prison-keeper had to stop at last for his little daughter to hear the song out, and repeat the Refrain while they were yet in sight. Then the child's head disappeared, and the prison-keeper's head disappeared, but the little voice prolonged the strain until the door clashed.

Monsieur Rigaud, finding the listening John Baptist in his way before the echoes had ceased (even the echoes were the weaker for imprisonment, and seemed to lag), reminded him with a push of his foot that he had better resume his own darker place. The little man sat down again upon the pavement, with the negligent ease of one who was thoroughly accustomed to pavements; and placing three hunks of coarse bread before himself, and falling to upon a fourth, began contentedly to work his way through them, as if to clear them off were a sort of game.

Perhaps he glanced at the Lyons sausage, and perhaps he glanced at the veal in savory jelly, but they were not there long, to make his mouth water; Monsieur Rigaud soon dispatched them, in spite of the President and tribunal, and proceeded to suck his fingers as clean as he could, and to wipe them on his vine-leaves. Then, as he paused in his drink to contemplate his fellow-prisoner, his moustache went up, and his nose came down.

"How do you find the bread?"

"A little dry, but I have my old sauce here," returned John Baptist, holding up his knife.

"How sauce?"

"I can cut my bread so—like a melon. Or so—like an omelette. Or so—like a fried fish. Or so—like Lyons sausage," said John Baptist, demonstrating the various cuts on the bread he held, and soberly chewing what he had in his mouth.

"Here!" cried Monsieur Rigaud. "You may drink. You may finish this."

It was no great gift, for there was mighty little wine left; but Signor Cavalletto, jumping to his feet, received the bottle gratefully, turned it upside down at his mouth, and smacked his lips.

"Put the bottle by with the rest," said Rigaud.

The little man obeyed his orders, and stood ready to give him a lighted match; for he was now rolling his tobacco into cigarettes, by the aid of little squares of paper which had been brought in with it.

"Here! You may have one."

"A thousand thanks, my master!" John Baptist said it in his own language, and with the quick conciliatory manner of his own countrymen.

Monsieur Rigaud arose, lighted a cigarette, put the rest of his stock into

a breast-pocket, and stretched himself out at full length upon the bench.
Cavalletto sat down on the pavement, holding one of his ankles in each
hand, and smoking peacefully. There seemed to be some uncomfortable
attraction of Monsieur Rigaud's eyes to the immediate neighbourhood of
that part of the pavement where the thumb had been in the plan. They
were so drawn in that direction, that the Italian more than once followed
them to and back from the pavement in some surprise.

"What an infernal hole this is!" said Monsieur Rigaud, breaking a long
pause. "Look at the light of day. Day? The light of yesterday week, the
light of six months ago, the light of six years ago. So slack and dead!"

It came languishing down a square funnel that blinded a window in the
staircase wall, through which the sky was never seen—nor anything else.

"Cavalletto," said Monsieur Rigaud, suddenly withdrawing his gaze
from this funnel, to which they had both involuntarily turned their eyes,
"you know me for a gentleman?"

"Surely, surely!"

"How long have we been here?"

"I, eleven weeks, to-morrow night at midnight. You, nine weeks and
three days, at five this afternoon."

"Have I ever done anything here? Ever touched the broom, or spread
the mats, or rolled them up, or found the draughts, or collected the
dominoes, or put my hand to any kind of work?"

"Never!"

"Have you ever thought of looking to me to do any kind of work?"

John Baptist answered with that peculiar back-handed shake of the right
forefinger which is the most expressive negative in the Italian language.

"No! You knew from the first moment when you saw me here, that I was
a gentleman?"

"ALTRO!" returned John Baptist, closing his eyes and giving his head a
most vehement toss. The word being, according to its Genoese emphasis, a
confirmation, a contradiction, an assertion, a denial, a taunt, a compliment,
a joke, and fifty other things, became in the present instance, with a
significance beyond all power of written expression, our familiar English
"I believe you!"

"Haha! You are right! A gentleman I am! And a gentleman I'll live,
and a gentleman I'll die! It's my intent to be a gentleman. It's my game.
Death of my soul, I play it out wherever I go!"

He changed his posture to a sitting one, crying with a triumphant air:

"Here I am! See me! Shaken out of destiny's dice-box into the company
of a mere smuggler;—shut up with a poor little contraband trader, whose
papers are wrong, and whom the police lay hold of, besides, for placing his
boat (as a means of getting beyond the frontier) at the disposition of other
little people whose papers are wrong; and he instinctively recognises my
position, even by this light and in this place. It's well done! By Heaven!

I win, however the game goes."

Again his moustache went up, and his nose came down.

"What's the hour, now?" he asked, with a dry hot pallor upon him, rather difficult of association with merriment.

"A little half-hour after mid-day."

"Good! The President will have a gentleman before him soon. Come! Shall I tell you on what accusation? It must be now, or never, for I shall not return here. Either I shall go free, or I shall go to be made ready for shaving. You know where they keep the razor."

Signor Cavalletto took his cigarette from between his parted lips, and showed more momentary discomfiture than might have been expected.

"I am a"—Monsieur Rigaud stood up to say it—"I am a cosmopolitan gentleman. I own no particular country. My father was Swiss—Canton de Vaud. My mother was French by blood, English by birth. I myself was born in Belgium. I am a citizen of the world."

His theatrical air, as he stood with one arm on his hip, within the folds of his cloak, together with his manner of disregarding his companion and addressing the opposite wall instead, seemed to intimate that he was rehearsing for the President, whose examination he was shortly to undergo, rather than troubling himself merely to enlighten so small a person as John Baptist Cavalletto.

"Call me five-and-thirty years of age. I have seen the world. I have lived here, and lived there, and lived like a gentleman everywhere. I have been treated and respected as a gentleman universally. If you try to prejudice me, by making out that I have lived by my wits—how do your lawyers live—your politicians—your intriguers—your men of the Exchange?"

He kept his small smooth hand in constant requisition, as if it were a witness to his gentility, that had often done him good service before.

"Two years ago I came to Marseilles. I admit that I was poor; I had been ill. When your lawyers, your politicians, your intriguers, your men of the Exchange, fall ill, and have not scraped money together, *they* become poor. I put up at the Cross of Gold,—kept then by Monsieur Henri Barronneau —sixty-five at least, and in a failing state of health. I had lived in the house some four months, when Monsieur Henri Barronneau had the misfortune to die;—at any rate, not a rare misfortune, that. It happens without any aid of mine, pretty often."

John Baptist having smoked his cigarette down to his fingers' ends, Monsieur Rigaud had the magnanimity to throw him another. He lighted the second at the ashes of the first, and smoked on, looking sideways at his companion, who, pre-occupied with his own case, hardly looked at him.

"Monsieur Barronneau left a widow. She was two-and-twenty. She had gained a reputation for beauty, and (which is often another thing) was beautiful. I continued to live at the Cross of Gold. I married Madame Barronneau. It is not for me to say whether there was any great disparity in such a match. Here I stand, with the contamination of a jail upon me; but it is possible that you may think me better suited to her than her former husband was."

He had a certain air of being a handsome man—which he was not; and a certain air of being a well-bred man—which he was not. It was mere swagger and challenge; but in this particular, as in many others, blustering assertion goes for proof, half over the world.

"Be it as it may, Madame Barronneau approved of me. *That* is not to prejudice me I hope?"

His eye happening to light upon John Baptist with this enquiry, that little man briskly shook his head in the negative, and repeated in an argumentative tone under his breath, altro, altro, altro, altro—an infinite number of times.

"Now came the difficulties of our position. I am proud. I say nothing in defence of pride, but I am proud. It is also my character to govern. I can't submit; I must govern. Unfortunately, the property of Madame Rigaud was settled upon herself. Such was the insane act of her late husband. More unfortunately still, she had relations. When a wife's relations interpose against a husband who is a gentleman, who is proud, and who must govern, the consequences are inimical to peace. There was yet another source of difference between us. Madame Rigaud was unfortunately a little vulgar. I sought to improve her manners and ameliorate her general tone; she (supported in this likewise by her relations) resented my endeavours. Quarrels began to arise between us; and, propagated and exaggerated by the slanders of the relations of Madame Rigaud, to become notorious to the neighbours. It has been said that I treated Madame Rigaud with cruelty. I may have been seen to slap her face—nothing more. I have a light hand; and if I have been seen apparently to correct Madame Rigaud in that manner, I have done it almost playfully."

If the playfulness of Monsieur Rigaud were at all expressed by his smile at this point, the relations of Madame Rigaud might have said that they would have much preferred his correcting that unfortunate woman seriously.

"I am sensitive and brave. I do not advance it as a merit to be sensitive and brave, but it is my character. If the male relations of Madame Rigaud had put themselves forward openly, I should have known how to deal with them. They knew that, and their machinations were conducted in secret; consequently, Madame Rigaud and I were brought into frequent and unfortunate collision. Even when I wanted any little sum of money for my personal expenses, I could not obtain it without collision—and I too, a man whose character it is to govern! One night, Madame Rigaud and myself were walking amicably—I may say like lovers—on a height over-hanging the sea. An evil star occasioned Madame Rigaud to advert to her relations; I reasoned with her on that subject, and remonstrated on the want of duty and devotion manifested in her allowing herself to be influenced by their jealous animosity towards her husband. Madame Rigaud retorted, I retorted. Madame Rigaud grew warm; I grew warm, and provoked her. I admit it. Frankness is a part of my character. At length, Madame Rigaud, in an access of fury that I must ever deplore, threw herself upon me with screams of passion (no doubt those that were overheard at some distance), tore my clothes, tore my hair, lacerated my hands, trampled and trod the dust, and finally leaped over, dashing herself to death upon the rocks below. Such is the train of incidents which malice has perverted into my endeavouring to force from Madame Rigaud a relinquishment of her rights; and, on her persistence in a refusal to make the concession I required, struggling with her —assassinating her!"

He stepped aside to the ledge where the vine-leaves yet lay strewn about, collected two or three, and stood wiping his hands upon them, with his back to the light.

"Well," he demanded after a silence, "have you nothing to say to all that?"

"It's ugly," returned the little man, who had risen, and was brightening his knife upon his shoe, as he leaned an arm against the wall.

"What do you mean?"

John Baptist polished his knife in silence.

"Do you mean that I have not represented the case correctly?"

"Al-tro!" returned John Baptist. The word was an apology now, and stood for, "Oh, by no means!"

"What then?"

"Presidents and tribunals are so prejudiced."

"Well!" cried the other, uneasily flinging the end of his cloak over his shoulder with an oath, "Let them do their worst!"

"Truly I think they will," murmured John Baptist to himself, as he bent his head to put his knife in his sash.

Nothing more was said on either side, though they both began walking to and fro, and necessarily crossed at every turn. Monsieur Rigaud sometimes half stopped, as if he were going to put his case in a new light, or make some irate remonstrance; but Signor Cavalletto continuing to go slowly to and fro at a grotesque kind of jog-trot pace, with his eyes turned downward, nothing came of these inclinings.

Bye-and-bye the noise of the key in the lock arrested them both. The sound of voices succeeded, and the tread of feet. The door clashed, the voices and the feet came on, and the prison-keeper slowly ascended the stairs, followed by a guard of soldiers.

"Now, Monsieur Rigaud," said he, pausing for a moment at the grate, with his keys in his hand, "have the goodness to come out."

"I am to depart in state, I see?"

"Why, unless you did," returned the jailer, "you might depart in so many pieces that it would be difficult to get you together again. There's a crowd, Monsieur Rigaud, and it doesn't love you."

He passed on out of sight, and unlocked and unbarred a low door in the corner of the chamber. "Now," said he, as he opened it and appeared within, "come out."

There is no sort of whiteness in all the hues under the sun, at all like the whiteness of Monsieur Rigaud's face as it was then. Neither is there any expression of the human countenance at all like that expression, in every little line of which the frightened heart is seen to beat. Both are conventionally compared with death; but the difference is the whole deep gulf between the struggle done, and the fight at its most desperate extremity.

He lighted another of his paper cigars at his companion's; put it tightly between his teeth; covered his head with a soft slouched hat; threw the end of his cloak over his shoulder again; and walked out into the side gallery on which the door opened, without taking any further notice of Signor Cavalletto. As to that little man himself, his whole attention had become absorbed in getting near the door, and looking out at it. Precisely as a beast might approach the opened gate of his den and eye the freedom beyond, he passed those few moments in watching and peering, until the door was closed upon him.

There was an officer in command of the soldiers; a stout, serviceable, profoundly calm man, with his drawn sword in his hand, smoking a cigar. He very briefly directed the placing of Monsieur Rigaud in the midst of the party, put himself with consummate indifference at their head, gave the word "march!" and so they all went jingling down the staircase. The door clashed—the key turned—and a ray of unusual light, and a breath of unusual air, seemed to have passed through the jail, vanishing in a tiny wreath of smoke from the cigar.

Still, in his captivity, like a lower animal—like some impatient ape, or roused bear of the smaller species—the prisoner, now left solitary, had jumped upon the ledge, to lose no glimpse of this departure. As he yet stood clasping the grate with both hands, an uproar broke upon his hearing; yells, shrieks, oaths, threats, execrations, all comprehended in it, though (as in a storm) nothing but a raging swell of sound distinctly heard.

Excited into a still greater resemblance to a caged wild animal by his anxiety to know more, the prisoner leaped nimbly down, ran round the chamber, leaped nimbly up again, clasped the grate and tried to shake it, leaped down and ran, leaped up and listened, and never rested until the noise, becoming more and more distant, had died away. How many better prisoners have worn their noble hearts out so; no man thinking of it; not even the beloved of their souls realising it; great kings and governors, who had made them captive, careering in the sunlight jauntily, and men

cheering them on. Even the said great personages dying in bed, making
exemplary ends and sounding speeches; and polite history, more servile
than their instruments, embalming them!

At last, John Baptist, now able to choose his own spot within the compass
of those walls, for the exercise of his faculty of going to sleep when he would,
lay down upon the bench, with his face turned over on his crossed arms,
and slumbered. In his submission, in his lightness, in his good humour,
in his short-lived passion, in his easy contentment with hard bread and
hard stones, in his ready sleep, in his fits and starts altogether, a true son
of the land that gave him birth.

The wide stare stared itself out for one while; the sun went down in
a red, green, golden glory; the stars came out in the heavens, and the fire-
flies mimicked them in the lower air, as men may feebly imitate the goodness of a better order of beings; the long dusty roads and the interminable
plains were in repose—and so deep a hush was on the sea, that it scarcely
whispered of the time when it shall give up its dead.

CHAPTER II

FELLOW TRAVELLERS

"No more of yesterday's howling, over yonder, to-day, sir; is there?"

"I have heard none."

"Then you may be sure there *is* none. When these people howl, they
howl to be heard."

"Most people do, I suppose."

"Ah! But these people are always howling. Never happy otherwise."

"Do you mean the Marseilles people?"

"I mean the French people. They're always at it. As to Marseilles, we
know what Marseilles is. It sent the most insurrectionary tune into the
world that was ever composed. It couldn't exist without allonging and
marshonging to something or other—victory or death, or blazes, or something."

The speaker, with a whimsical good humour upon him all the time,
looked over the parapet-wall with the greatest disparagement of Marseilles;
and taking up a determined position, by putting his hands in his pockets,
and rattling his money at it, apostrophised it with a short laugh.

"Allong and marshong, indeed. It would be more creditable to you,
I think, to let other people allong and marshong about their lawful business,
instead of shutting 'em up in quarantine!"

"Tiresome enough," said the other. "But we shall be out to-day."

"Out to-day!" repeated the first. "It's almost an aggravation of the enormity, that we shall be out to-day. Out! What have we ever been in for?'

"For no very strong reason I must say. But as we come from the East, and as the East is the country of the plague—"

"The plague!" repeated the other. "That's my grievance. I have had the plague continually, ever since I have been here. I am like a sane man shut up in a madhouse; I can't stand the suspicion of the thing. I came here as well as ever I was in my life; but to suspect me of the plague is to give me the plague. And I have had it—and I have got it."

"You bear it very well, Mr. Meagles," said the second speaker, smiling.

"No. If you knew the real state of the case, that's the last observation you would think of making. I have been waking up, night after night, and saying, *now* I have got it, *now* it has developed itself, *now* I am in for it, *now* these fellows are making out their case for their precautions. Why, I'd as soon have a spit put through me, and be stuck upon a card in a collection of beetles, as lead the life I have been leading here."

"Well, Mr. Meagles, say no more about it, now it's over," urged a cheerful feminine voice.

"Over!" repeated Mr. Meagles, who appeared (though without any ill-nature) to be in that peculiar state of mind in which the last word spoken by anybody else is a new injury. "Over! and why should I say no more about it because it's over!"

It was Mrs. Meagles who had spoken to Mr. Meagles; and Mrs. Meagles was, like Mr. Meagles, comely and healthy, with a pleasant English face which had been looking at homely things for five-and-fifty years or more, and shone with a bright reflection of them.

"There! Never mind, Father, never mind!" said Mrs. Meagles. "For goodness sake content yourself with Pet."

"With Pet?" repeated Mr. Meagles in his injured vein. Pet, however, being close behind him, touched him on the shoulder, and Mr. Meagles immediately forgave Marseilles from the bottom of his heart.

Pet was about twenty. A fair girl with rich brown hair hanging free in natural ringlets. A lovely girl, with a frank face, and wonderful eyes; so large, so soft, so bright, set to such perfection in her kind good head. She was round and fresh and dimpled and spoilt, and there was in Pet an air of timidity and dependence which was the best weakness in the world, and gave her the only crowning charm a girl so pretty and pleasant could have been without.

"Now, I ask you," said Mr. Meagles in the blandest confidence, falling back a step himself, and handing his daughter a step forward to illustrate his question: "I ask you simply as between man and man, you know, DID you ever hear of such damned nonsense as putting Pet in quarantine?"

"It has had the result of making even quarantine enjoyable."

"Come!" said Mr. Meagles, "that's something, to be sure. I am obliged to you for that remark. Now Pet, my darling, you had better go along with

Mother and get ready for the boat. The officer of health, and a variety of humbugs in cocked hats, are coming off to let us out of this at last; and all we jail-birds are to breakfast together in something approaching to a Christian style again, before we take wing for our different destinations. Tattycoram, stick you close to your young mistress."

He spoke to a handsome girl with lustrous dark hair and eyes, and very neatly dressed, who replied with a half curtsey as she passed off in the train of Mrs. Meagles and Pet. They crossed the bare scorched terrace, all three together, and disappeared through a staring white archway. Mr. Meagles's companion, a grave dark man of forty, still stood looking towards this archway after they were gone; until Mr. Meagles tapped him on the arm.

"I beg your pardon," said he, starting.

"Not at all," said Mr. Meagles.

They took one silent turn backward and forward in the shade of the wall, getting, at the height on which the quarantine barracks are placed, what cool refreshment of sea breeze there was, at seven in the morning. Mr. Meagles's companion resumed the conversation.

"May I ask you," he said, "what is the name of—"

"Tattycoram?" Mr. Meagles struck in. "I have not the least idea."

"I thought," said the other, "that—"

"Tattycoram?" suggested Mr. Meagles again.

"Thank you—that Tattycoram was a name; and I have several times wondered at the oddity of it."

"Why, the fact is," said Mr. Meagles, "Mrs. Meagles and myself are, you see, practical people."

"That, you have frequently mentioned in the course of the agreeable and interesting conversations we have had together walking up and down on these stones," said the other, with a half smile breaking through the gravity of his dark face.

"Practical people. So one day, five or six years ago now, when we took Pet to church at the Foundling—you have heard of the Foundling Hospital in London? Similar to the Institution for the Found Children in Paris?"

"I have seen it."

"Well! One day when we took Pet to church there to hear the music—because, as practical people, it is the business of our lives to show her everything that we think can please her—Mother (my usual name for Mrs. Meagles) began to cry so, that it was necessary to take her out. 'What's the matter, Mother?' said I, when we had brought her a little round; 'you are frightening Pet, my dear.' 'Yes, I know that, Father,' says Mother, 'but I think it's through my loving her so much, that it ever came into my head.' 'That ever what came into your head, Mother?' 'O dear, dear!' cried Mother, breaking out again, 'when I saw all those children ranged tier above tier, and appealing from the father none of them has ever known on earth, to the great father of us all in Heaven, I thought, does any wretched mother ever come here, and look among those young faces, wondering which is the poor child she brought into this forlorn world, never through all its life to know her love, her kiss, her voice, even her name!' Now that was practical in Mother, and I told her so. I said, 'Mother, that's what I call practical in you, my dear.'"

The other, not unmoved, assented.

"So I said next day: now, Mother, I have a proposition to make that I think you'll approve of. Let us take one of those same children to be a little maid to Pet. We are practical people. So if we should find her temper a little defective, or any of her ways a little wide of ours, we shall know what we have to take into account. We shall know what an immense deduction must be made from all the influences and experiences that have formed us— no parents, no child-brother or sister, no individuality of home, no Glass Slipper, or Fairy Godmother. And that's the way we came by Tatty-coram."

"And the name itself—"

"By George!" said Mr. Meagles, "I was forgetting the name itself. Why, she was called in the Institution, Harriet Beadle—an arbitrary name, of course. Now, Harriet we changed into Hatty, and then into Tatty, because, as practical people, we thought even a playful name might be a new thing to her, and might have a softening and affectionate kind of effect, don't you see? As to Beadle, that I needn't say was wholly out of the question. If there is anything that is not to be tolerated on any terms, anything that is a type of jack-in-office insolence and absurdity, anything that represents in coats, waistcoats, and big sticks, our English holding-on by nonsense, after every one has found it out, it is a beadle. You haven't seen a beadle lately?"

"As an Englishman, who has been more than twenty years in China, no."

"Then," said Mr. Meagles, laying his forefinger on his companion's breast with great animation, "don't you see a beadle, now, if you can help it. Whenever I see a beadle in full fig, coming down a street on a Sunday at the head of a charity school, I am obliged to turn and run away, or I should hit him. The name of Beadle being out of the question, and the originator of the Institution for these poor foundlings having been a blessed creature of the name of Coram, we gave that name to Pet's little maid. At one time she was Tatty, and at one time she was Coram, until we got into a way of mixing the two names together, and now she is always Tattycoram."

"Your daughter," said the other, when they had taken another silent turn to and fro, and after standing for a moment at the wall glancing down at the sea, had resumed their walk, "is your only child, I know, Mr. Meagles. May I ask you—in no impertinent curiosity, but because I have had so much pleasure in your society, may never in this labyrinth of a world exchange a quiet word with you again, and wish to preserve an accurate remembrance of you and yours—may I ask you, if I have not gathered from your good wife that you have had other children?"

"No. No," said Mr. Meagles. "Not exactly other children. One other child."

"I am afraid I have inadvertently touched upon a tender theme."

"Never mind," said Mr. Meagles. "If I am grave about it, I am not at all sorrowful. It quiets me for a moment, but does not make me unhappy. Pet had a twin sister who died when we could just see her eyes—exactly like Pet's—above the table, as she stood on tiptoe holding by it."

"Ah! indeed, indeed?"

"Yes, and being practical people, a result has gradually sprung up in the minds of Mrs. Meagles and myself which perhaps you may—or perhaps you may not—understand. Pet and her baby sister were so exactly alike, and so completely one, that in our thoughts we have never been able to separate them since. It would be of no use to tell us that our dead child was a mere infant. We have changed that child according to the changes in the child spared to us, and always with us. As Pet has grown, that child has grown; as Pet has become more sensible and womanly, her sister has become more sensible and womanly, by just the same degrees. It would be as hard to convince me that if I was to pass into the other world to-morrow, I should not, through the mercy of God, be received there by a daughter just like Pet, as to persuade me that Pet herself is not a reality at my side."

"I understand you," said the other, gently.

"As to her," pursued her father, "the sudden loss of her little picture and playfellow, and her early association with that mystery in which we all have our equal share, but which is not often so forcibly presented to a child, has necessarily had some influence on her character. Then, her mother and I were not young when we married, and Pet has always had a sort of grown-up life with us, though we have tried to adapt ourselves to her. We have been advised more than once when she has been a little ailing, to change climate and air for her as often as we could—especially at about this time of her life—and to keep her amused. So, as I have no need to stick at a bank-desk now (though I have been poor enough in my time I assure you, or I should have married Mrs. Meagles long before), we go trotting about the world. This is how you found us staring at the Nile, and the Pyramids, and the Sphinxes, and the Desert, and all the rest of it; and this is how Tattycoram will be a greater traveller in course of time than Captain Cook."

"I thank you," said the other, "very heartily for your confidence."

"Don't mention it," returned Mr. Meagles, "I am sure you are quite welcome. And now Mr. Clennam, perhaps I may ask you whether you have yet come to a decision where to go next?"

"Indeed, no. I am such a waif and stray everywhere, that I am liable to be drifted where any current may set."

"It's extraordinary to me—if you'll excuse my freedom in saying so—that you don't go straight to London," said Mr. Meagles, in the tone of a confidential adviser.

"Perhaps I shall."

"Aye! But I mean with a will."

"I have no will. That is to say," he colored a little, "next to none that I can put in action now. Trained by main force; broken, not bent; heavily ironed with an object on which I was never consulted and which was never mine; shipped away to the other end of the world before I was of age, and exiled there until my father's death there, a year ago; always grinding in a mill I always hated; what is to be expected from *me* in middle-life? Will, purpose, hope? All those lights were extinguished before I could sound the words."

"Light 'em up again!" said Mr. Meagles.

"Ah! Easily said. I am the son, Mr. Meagles, of a hard father and mother. I am the only child of parents who weighed, measured, and priced everything: for whom what could not be weighed, measured and priced, had no existence. Strict people as the phrase is, professors of a stern religion, their very religion was a gloomy sacrifice of tastes and sympathies that were never their own, offered up as a part of a bargain for the security of their possessions. Austere faces, inexorable discipline, penance in this world and terror in the next—nothing graceful or gentle anywhere, and the void in my cowed heart everywhere—this was my childhood, if I may so misuse the word as to apply it to such a beginning of life."

"Really though?" said Mr. Meagles, made very uncomfortable by the picture offered to his imagination. "That was a tough commencement. But come! You must now study, and profit by all that lies beyond it, like a practical man."

"If the people who are usually called practical, were practical in your direction—"

"Why, so they are!" said Mr. Meagles.

"Are they indeed?"

"Well, I suppose so," returned Mr. Meagles, thinking about it. "Eh? One can but *be* practical, and Mrs. Meagles and myself are nothing else."

"My unknown course is easier and more hopeful than I had expected to find it then," said Clennam, shaking his head with his grave smile. "Enough of me. Here is the boat!"

The boat was filled with the cocked hats to which Mr. Meagles entertained a national objection; and the wearers of those cocked hats landed and came up the steps, and all the impounded travellers congregated together. There was then a mighty production of papers on the part of the cocked hats, and a calling over of names, and great work of signing, sealing, stamping, inking, and sanding, with exceedingly blurred, gritty, and undecipherable results. Finally, everything was done according to rule, and the travellers were at liberty to depart whithersoever they would.

They made little account of stare and glare, in the new pleasure of recovering their freedom, but flitted across the harbor in gay boats, and re-assembled at a great hotel, whence the sun was excluded by closed lattices, and where bare paved floors, lofty ceilings, and resounding corridors, tempered the intense heat. There, a great table in a great room, was soon profusely covered with a superb repast; and the quarantine quarters became bare indeed, remembered among dainty dishes, southern fruits, cooled wines, flowers from Genoa, snow from the mountain tops, and all the colors of the rainbow flashing in the mirrors.

"But I bear those monotonous walls no ill-will now," said Mr. Meagles. "One always begins to forgive a place as soon as it's left behind; I dare say a prisoner begins to relent towards his prison, after he is let out."

They were about thirty in company, and all talking; but necessarily in groups. Father and Mother Meagles sat with their daughter between them, the last three on one side of the table: on the opposite side sat Mr. Clennam; a tall French gentleman with raven hair and beard, of a swart and terrible, not to say genteelly diabolical aspect, but who had shown himself the mildest of men; and a handsome young Englishwoman, travelling quite alone, who had a proud observant face, and had either withdrawn herself from the rest or been avoided by the rest—nobody, herself excepted perhaps, could have quite decided which. The rest of the party were of the usual materials. Travellers on business, and travellers for pleasure; officers from India on leave; merchants in the Greek and Turkey trades; a clerical English husband in a meek strait-waistcoat, on a wedding trip with his young wife; a majestic English mama and papa, of the patrician order, with a family of three growing up daughters, who were keeping a journal for the confusion of their fellow creatures; and a deaf old English mother tough in travel, with a very decidedly grown up daughter indeed, which daughter went sketching about the universe in the expectation of ultimately toning herself off into the married state.

The reserved Englishwoman took up Mr. Meagles in his last remark.

"Do you mean that a prisoner forgives his prison?" said she, slowly and with emphasis.

"That was my speculation, Miss Wade. I don't pretend to know positively how a prisoner might feel. I never was one before."

"Mademoiselle doubts," said the French gentleman in his own language, "its being so easy to forgive?"

"I do."

Pet had to translate this passage to Mr. Meagles, who never by any accident acquired any knowledge whatever of the language of any country into which he travelled. "Oh!" said he. "Dear me! But that's a pity, isn't it?"

"That I am not credulous?" said Miss Wade.

"Not exactly that. Put it another way. That you can't believe it easy to forgive."

"My experience," she quietly returned, "has been correcting my belief in many respects, for some years. It is our natural progress, I have heard."

"Well, well! But it's not natural to bear malice, I hope?" said Mr. Meagles cheerily.

"If I had been shut up in any place to pine and suffer, I should always hate that place and wish to burn it down, or raze it to the ground. I know no more."

"Strong, sir?" said Mr. Meagles to the Frenchman; it being another of his habits to address individuals of all nations in idiomatic English, with a perfect conviction that they were bound to understand it somehow. "Rather forcible in our fair friend, you'll agree with me, I think?"

The French gentleman courteously replied, "Plait-il?" To which Mr. Meagles returned with much satisfaction, "You are right. My opinion."

The breakfast beginning bye-and-bye to languish, Mr. Meagles made the company a speech. It was short enough and sensible enough, considering that it was a speech at all, and hearty. It merely went to the effect that as they had all been thrown together by chance, and had all preserved a good understanding together, and were now about to disperse, and were not likely ever to find themselves all together again, what could they do better than bid farewell to one another, and give one another Godspeed, in a simultaneous glass of cool champagne all round the table? It was done, and with a general shaking of hands the assembly broke up for ever.

The solitary young lady all this time had said no more. She rose with the rest, and silently withdrew to a remote corner of the great room, where she sat herself on a couch in a window, seeming to watch the reflection of the water, as it made a silver quivering on the bars of the lattice. She sat, turned away from the whole length of the apartment, as if she were lonely of her own haughty choice. And yet it would have been as difficult as ever to say, positively, whether she avoided the rest, or was avoided.

The shadow in which she sat, falling like a gloomy veil across her forehead, accorded very well with the character of her beauty. One could hardly see the face, so still and scornful, set off by the arched dark eyebrows, and the folds of dark hair, without wondering what its expression would be if a change came over it. That it could soften or relent, appeared next to impossible. That it could deepen into anger or any extreme of defiance, and that it must change in that direction when it changed at all, would have been its peculiar impression upon most observers. It was dressed and trimmed into no ceremony of expression. Although not an open face, there was no pretence in it. I am self-contained and self-reliant; your opinion is nothing to me; I have no interest in you, care nothing for you, and see and hear you with indifference— this it said plainly. It said so in the proud eyes, in the lifted nostril, in the handsome, but compressed and even cruel mouth. Cover either two of those channels of expression, and the third would have said so still. Mask them all, and the mere turn of the head would have shown an unsubduable nature.

Pet had moved up to her (she had been the subject of remark among her family and Mr. Clennam, who were now the only other occupants of the room), and was standing at her side.

"Are you"—she turned her eyes, and Pet faltered—"expecting any one to meet you here, Miss Wade?"

"I? No."

"Father is sending to the Poste Restante. Shall he have the pleasure of directing the messenger to ask if there are any letters for you?"

"I thank him, but I know there can be none."

"We are afraid," said Pet, sitting down beside her, shyly and half tenderly, "that you will feel quite deserted when we are all gone."

"Indeed!"

"Not," said Pet, apologetically and embarrassed by her eyes, "not, of course, that we are any company to you, or that we have been able to be so, or that we thought you wished it."

"I have not intended to make it understood that I did wish it."

"No. Of course. But—in short," said Pet, timidly touching her hand as it lay impassive on the sofa between them, "will you not allow Father to render you any slight assistance or service? He will be very glad."

"Very glad," said Mr. Meagles, coming forward with his wife and Clennam. "Anything short of speaking the language, I shall be delighted to undertake, I am sure."

"I am obliged to you," she returned, "but my arrangements are made, and I prefer to go my own way in my own manner."

"*Do* you?" said Mr. Meagles, to himself, as he surveyed her with a puzzled look. "Well! There's character in that, too."

"I am not much used to the society of young ladies, and I am afraid I may not show my appreciation of it as others might. A pleasant journey to you. Good bye!"

She would not have put out her hand, it seemed, but that Mr. Meagles put out his so straight before her, that she could not pass it. She put hers in it, and it lay there just as it had lain upon the couch.

"Good bye!" said Mr. Meagles. "This is the last good bye upon the list, for Mother and I have just said it to Mr. Clennam here, and he only waits to say it to Pet. Good bye! We may never meet again."

"In our course through life we shall meet the people who are coming to meet *us*, from many strange places and by many strange roads," was the composed reply; "and what it is set to us to do to them, and what it is set to them to do to us, will all be done."

There was something in the manner of these words that jarred upon Pet's ear. It implied that what was to be done was necessarily evil, and it caused her to say in a whisper, "O, Father!" and to shrink childishly in her spoilt way, a little closer to him. This was not lost on the speaker.

"Your pretty daughter," she said, "starts to think of such things. Yet," looking full upon her, "you may be sure that there are men and women already on their road, who have their business to do with *you*, and who will do it. Of a certainty they will do it. They may be coming hundreds, thousands, of miles over the sea there; they may be close at hand now; they may be coming, for anything you know, or anything you can do to prevent it, from the vilest sweepings of this very town."

With the coldest of farewells, and with a certain worn expression on her beauty that gave it, though scarcely yet in its prime, a wasted look, she left the room.

Now, there were many stairs and passages that she had to traverse in passing from that part of the spacious house to the chamber she had secured for her own occupation. When she had almost completed the journey, and was passing along the gallery in which her room was, she heard an angry sound of muttering and sobbing. A door stood open, and within she saw the attendant upon the girl she had just left; the maid with the curious name.

She stood still, to look at this maid. A sullen, passionate girl! Her rich black hair was all about her face, her face was flushed and hot, and as she sobbed and raged, she plucked at her lips with an unsparing hand.

"Selfish brutes!" said the girl, sobbing and heaving between whiles. "Not caring what becomes of me! Leaving me here hungry and thirsty and tired, to starve, for anything they care! Beasts! Devils! Wretches!"

"My poor girl, what is the matter?"

She looked up suddenly, with reddened eyes, and with her hand suspended, in the act of pinching her neck, freshly disfigured with great scarlet blots. "It's nothing to you what's the matter. It don't signify to any one."

"O yes it does; I am sorry to see you so."

"You are not sorry," said the girl. "You are glad. You know you are glad. I never was like this but twice, over in the quarantine yonder; and both times you found me. I am afraid of you."

"Afraid of me?"

"Yes. You seem to come like my own anger, my own malice, my own—whatever it is—I don't know what it is. But I am ill-used, I am ill-used, I am ill-used!" Here the sobs and the tears, and the tearing hand, which had all been suspended together, since the first surprise, went on together anew.

The visitor stood looking at her with a strange attentive smile. It was wonderful to see the fury of the contest in the girl, and the bodily struggle she made as if she were rent by the Demons of old.

"I am younger than she is by two or three years, and yet it's me that looks after her, as if I was old, and it's she that's always petted and called Baby! I detest the name. I hate her. They make a fool of her, they spoil her. She thinks of nothing but herself, she thinks no more of me than if I was a stock or a stone!" So the girl went on.

"You must have patience."

"I *won't* have patience!"

"If they take much care of themselves, and little or none of you, you must not mind it."

"I *will* mind it!"

"Hush! Be more prudent. You forget your dependent position."

"I don't care for that. I'll run away. I'll do some mischief. I won't bear it; I can't bear it; I shall die if I try to bear it!"

The observer stood with her hand upon her own bosom, looking at the girl, as one afflicted with a diseased part might curiously watch the dissection and exposition of an analogous case.

The girl raged and battled with all the force of her youth and fulness of life, until by little and little her passionate exclamations trailed off into broken murmurs as if she were in pain. By corresponding degrees she sunk into a chair, then upon her knees, then upon the ground beside the bed, drawing the coverlet with her, half to hide her shamed head and wet hair in it, and half, as it seemed, to embrace it, rather than have nothing to take to her repentant breast.

"Go away from me, go away from me! When my temper comes upon me, I am mad. I know I might keep it off if I only tried hard enough, and sometimes I do try hard enough, and at other times I don't and won't. What have I said! I knew, when I said it, it was all lies. They think I am being taken care of somewhere, and have all I want. They are nothing but good to me. I love them dearly; no people could ever be kinder to a thankless creature than they always are to me. Do, do go away, for I am afraid of you. I am afraid of myself when I feel my temper coming, and I am as much afraid of you. Go away from me, and let me pray and cry myself better!"

The day passed on; and again the wide stare stared itself out; and the hot night was on Marseilles; and through it the caravan of the morning, all dispersed, went their appointed ways. And thus ever, by day and night, under the sun and under the stars, climbing the dusty hills and toiling along the weary plains, journeying by land and journeying by sea, coming and going so strangely, to meet and to act and react on one another, move all we restless travellers through the pilgrimage of life.

CHAPTER III

HOME

It was a Sunday evening in London, gloomy, close and stale. Maddening church bells of all degrees of dissonance, sharp and flat, cracked and clear, fast and slow, made the brick and mortar echoes hideous. Melancholy streets in a penitential garb of soot, steeped the souls of the people who were condemned to look at them out of windows, in dire despondency. In every thoroughfare, up almost every alley, and down almost every turning, some doleful bell was throbbing, jerking, tolling, as if the Plague were in the city and the dead-carts were going round. Everything was bolted and barred that could by possibility furnish relief to an overworked people. No pictures, no unfamiliar animals, no rare plants or flowers, no natural or artificial wonders of the ancient world—all *taboo* with that enlightened strictness, that the ugly South sea gods in the British Museum might have supposed themselves at home again. Nothing to see but streets, streets, streets. Nothing to breathe but streets, streets, streets. Nothing to change the brooding mind, or raise it up. Nothing for the spent toiler to do, but to compare the monotony of his seventh day with the monotony of his six days, think what a weary life he led, and make the best of it—or the worst, according to the probabilities.

At such a happy time, so propitious to the interests of religion and morality, Mr. Arthur Clennam, newly arrived from Marseilles by way of Dover, and by Dover coach the Blue-eyed Maid, sat in the window of a coffee-house on Ludgate Hill. Ten thousand responsible houses sur- rounded him, frowning as heavily on the streets they composed, as if they were every one inhabited by the ten young men of the Calender's story, who blackened their faces and bemoaned their miseries every night. Fifty thousand lairs surrounded him where people lived so unwholesomely, that fair water put into their crowded rooms on Saturday night, would be corrupt on Sunday morning; albeit my lord, their county member, was amazed that they failed to sleep in company with their butcher's meat. Miles of close wells and pits of houses, where the inhabitants gasped for air, stretched far away towards every point of the compass. Through the heart of the town a deadly sewer ebbed and flowed, in the place of a fine fresh river. What secular want could the million or so of human beings whose daily labor, six days in the week, lay among these Arcadian objects, from the sweet sameness of which they had no escape between the cradle and the grave—what secular want could they possibly have upon their seventh day? Clearly they could want nothing but a stringent policeman.

Mr. Arthur Clennam sat in the window of the coffee-house on Ludgate Hill, counting one of the neighbouring bells, making sentences and bur- dens of songs out of it in spite of himself, and wondering how many sick people it might be the death of in the course of a year. As the hour approached, its changes of measure made it more and more exasperating. At the quarter, it went off into a condition of deadly lively importunity, urging the populace in a voluble manner to Come to church, Come to church, Come to church! At the ten minutes, it became aware that the congregation would be scanty, and slowly hammered out in low spirits, They *won't* come, they *won't* come, they *won't* come! At the five minutes, it abandoned hope, and shook every house in the neighbourhood for three hundred seconds, with one dismal swing per second, as a groan of despair.

"Thank Heaven!" said Clennam, when the hour struck, and the bell stopped.

But its sound had revived a long train of miserable Sundays, and the procession would not stop with the bell, but continued to march on. "Heaven forgive me," said he, "and those who trained me. How I have hated this day!"

There was the dreary Sunday of his childhood, when he sat with his hands before him, scared out of his senses by a horrible tract which commenced business with the poor child by asking him in its title, why he was going to Perdition? —a piece of curiosity that he really in a frock and drawers was not in a condition to satisfy—and which, for the further attraction of his infant mind, had a parenthesis in every other line with some such hiccupping reference as 2 Ep. Thess. c. iii. v. 6 & 7. There was the sleepy Sunday of his boyhood, when, like a military deserter, he was marched to chapel by a picquet of teachers three times a day, morally handcuffed to another boy; and when he would willingly have bartered two meals of indigestible sermon for another ounce or two of inferior mutton at his scanty dinner in the flesh. There was the interminable Sunday of his nonage; when his mother, stern of face and unrelenting of heart, would sit all day behind a bible—bound like her own construction of it in the hardest, barest, and straitest boards, with one dinted ornament on the cover like the drag of a chain, and a wrathful sprinkling of red upon the edges of the leaves—as if it, of all books! were a fortification against sweetness of temper, natural affection, and gentle intercourse. There was the resentful Sunday of a little later, when he sat glowering and glooming through the tardy length of the day, with a sullen sense of injury in his heart, and no more real knowledge of the beneficent history of the New Testament, than if he had been bred among idolaters. There was a legion of Sundays, all days of unserviceable bitterness and mortification, slowly passing before him.

"Beg pardon, sir," said a brisk waiter, rubbing the table. "Wish see bedroom?"

"Yes. I have just made up my mind to do it."

"Chaymaid!" cried the waiter. "Gelen box num seven wish see room!"

"Stay!" said Clennam, rousing himself. "I was not thinking of what I said; I answered mechanically. I am not going to sleep here. I am going home."

"Deed, sir? Chaymaid! Gelen box num seven, not go sleep here, gome."

He sat in the same place as the day died, looking at the dull houses opposite, and thinking, if the disembodied spirits of former inhabitants were ever conscious of them, how they must pity themselves for their old places of imprisonment. Sometimes a face would appear behind the dingy glass of a window, and would fade away into the gloom as if it had seen enough of life and had vanished out of it. Presently the rain began to fall in slanting lines between him and those houses, and people began to collect under cover of the public passage opposite, and to look out hopelessly at the sky as the rain dropped thicker and faster. Then wet umbrellas began to appear, draggled skirts, and mud. What the mud had been doing with itself, or where it came from, who could say? But it seemed to collect in a moment, as a crowd will, and in five minutes to have splashed all the sons and daughters of Adam. The lamplighter was going his rounds now; and as the fiery jets sprang up under his touch, one might have fancied them astonished at being suffered to introduce any show of brightness into such a dismal scene.

Mr. Arthur Clennam took up his hat, and buttoned his coat, and walked out. In the country, the rain would have developed a thousand fresh scents, and every drop would have had its bright association with some beautiful form of growth or life. In the city, it developed only foul stale smells, and was a sickly, lukewarm, dirt-stained, wretched addition to the gutters.

He crossed by Saint Paul's and went down, at a long angle, almost to the water's edge, through some of the crooked and descending streets which lie (and lay more crookedly and closely then) between the river and Cheapside. Passing, now the mouldy hall of some obsolete Worshipful Company, now the illuminated windows of a Congregationless Church that seemed to be waiting for some adventurous Belzoni to dig it out and discover its history; passing silent warehouses and wharves, and here and there a narrow alley leading to the river, where a wretched little bill, Found Drowned, was weeping on the wet wall; he came at last to the house he sought. An old brick house, so dingy as to be all but black, standing by itself within a gateway. Before it, a square courtyard where a shrub or two and a patch of grass were as rank (which is saying much), as the iron railings enclosing them were rusty; behind it, a jumble of roofs. It was a double house, with long, narrow, heavily-framed windows. Many years ago, it had had it in its mind to slide down sideways; it had been propped up, however, and was leaning on some half dozen gigantic crutches: which gymnasium for the neighbouring cats, weather-stained, smoke-blackened, and overgrown with weeds, appeared in these latter days to be no very sure reliance.

"Nothing changed," said the traveller, stopping to look round. "Dark and miserable as ever. A light in my mother's window, which seems never to have been extinguished since I came home twice a year from school, and dragged my box over this pavement. Well, well, well!"

He went up to the door, which had a projecting canopy in carved work, of festooned jack-towels and children's heads with water on the brain, designed after a once popular monumental pattern; and knocked.

A shuffling step was soon heard on the stone floor of the hall, and the door was opened by an old man: bent and dried, but with keen eyes.

He had a candle in his hand, and he held it up for a moment to assist his keen eyes. "Ah, Mr. Arthur?" he said, without any emotion, "you are come at last? Step in."

Mr. Arthur stepped in and shut the door.

"Your figure is filled out, and set," said the old man, turning to look at him with the light raised again, and shaking his head; "but you don't come up to your father in my opinion. Nor yet your mother."

"How is my mother?"

"She is as she always is now. Keeps her room when not actually bedridden, and hasn't been out of it fifteen times in as many years, Arthur." They had walked into a spare, meagre, dining room. The old man had put the candlestick upon the table, and, supporting his right elbow with his left hand, was smoothing his leathern jaws while he looked at the visitor. The visitor offered his hand. The old man took it coldly enough, and seemed to prefer his jaws; to which he returned, as soon as he could.

"I doubt if your mother will approve of your coming home on the Sabbath, Arthur," he said, shaking his head warily.

"You wouldn't have me go away again?"

"Oh! I? I? I am not the master. It's not what I would have. I have stood between your father and mother for a number of years. I don't pretend to stand between your mother and you."

"Will you tell her that I have come home?"

"Yes Arthur, yes. Oh to be sure! I'll tell her that you have come home. Please to wait here. You won't find the room changed." He took another candle from a cupboard, lighted it, left the first on the table, and went upon his errand. He was a short, bald old man, in a high shouldered black coat and waistcoat, drab breeches and long drab gaiters. He might, from his dress, have been either clerk or servant, and in fact had long been both. There was nothing about him in the way of decoration but a watch, which was lowered into the depths of its proper pocket by an old black ribbon, and had a tarnished copper key moored above it, to show where it was sunk. His head was awry, and he had a one-sided, crab-like way with him, as if his foundations had yielded at about the same time as those of the house, and he ought to have been propped up in a similar manner.

"How weak am I," said Arthur Clennam, when he was gone, "that I could shed tears at this reception! I, who have never experienced anything else; who have never expected anything else."

He not only could, but did. It was the momentary yielding of a nature that had been disappointed from the dawn of its perceptions, but had not quite given up all its hopeful yearnings yet. He subdued it, took up the candle and examined the room. The old articles of furniture were in their old places; the Plagues of Egypt, much the dimmer for the fly and smoke plagues of London, were framed and glazed upon the walls. There was the old cellaret with nothing in it, lined with lead, like a sort of coffin in compartments; there was the old dark closet, also with nothing in it, of which he had been many a time the sole contents, in days of punishment, when he had regarded it as the veritable entrance to that bourne to which the tract had found him galloping. There was the large, hard-featured clock on the sideboard, which he used to see bending its figured brows upon him with a savage joy when he was behind-hand with his lessons, and which, when it was wound up once a week with an iron handle, used to sound as if it were growling in ferocious anticipation of the miseries into which it would bring him. But, here was the old man come back, saying, "Arthur, I'll go before and light you."

Arthur followed him up the staircase, which was panelled off into spaces like so many mourning tablets, into a dim bed-chamber, the floor of which had gradually so sunk and settled, that the fireplace was in a dell. On a black bier-like sofa in this hollow, propped up behind with one great angular black bolster, like the block at a state execution in the good old times, sat his mother in a widow's dress.

She and his father had been at variance from his earliest remembrance. To sit speechless himself in the midst of rigid silence, glancing in dread from the one averted face to the other, had been the peacefullest occupation of his childhood. She gave him one glassy kiss, and four stiff fingers muffled in worsted. This embrace concluded, he sat down on the opposite side of her little table. There was a fire in the grate, as there had been night and day for fifteen years. There was a kettle on the hob, as there had been night and day for fifteen years. There was a little mound of damped ashes on the top of the fire, and another little mound swept together under the grate, as there had been night and day for fifteen years. There was a smell of black dye in the airless room, which the fire had been drawing out of the crape and stuff of the widow's dress for fifteen months, and out of the bier-like sofa for fifteen years.

"Mother, this is a change from your old active habits."

"The world has narrowed to these dimensions, Arthur," she replied, glancing round the room. "It is well for me that I never set my heart upon its hollow vanities."

The old influence of her presence and her stern strong voice, so gathered about her son, that he felt conscious of a renewal of the timid chill and reserve of his childhood.

"Do you never leave your room, mother?"

"What with my rheumatic affection, and what with its attendant debility or nervous weakness—names are of no matter now—I have lost the use of my limbs. I never leave my room. I have not been outside this door for—

tell him for how long," she said, speaking over her shoulder.

"A dozen year next Christmas," returned a cracked voice out of the dimness behind.

"Is that Affery?" said Arthur, looking towards it.

The cracked voice replied that it was Affery: and an old woman came forward into what doubtful light there was, and kissed her hand once; then subsided again into the dimness.

"I am able," said Mrs. Clennam, with a slight motion of her worsted-muffled right hand towards a chair on wheels, standing before a tall writing-cabinet close shut up, "I am able to attend to my business duties, and I am thankful for the privilege. It is a great privilege. But no more of business on this day. It is a bad night, is it not?"

"Yes, mother."

"Does it snow?"

"Snow, mother? And we only yet in September?"

"All seasons are alike to me," she returned, with a grim kind of luxuriousness. "I know nothing of summer and winter, shut up here. The Lord has been pleased to put me beyond all that." With her cold grey eyes and her cold grey hair, and her immoveable face, as stiff as the folds of her stony head-dress,—her being beyond the reach of the seasons, seemed but a fit sequence to her being beyond the reach of all changing emotions.

On her little table lay two or three books, her handkerchief, a pair of steel spectacles newly taken off, and an old-fashioned gold watch in a heavy double case. Upon this last object her son's eyes and her own now rested together.

"I see that you received the packet I sent you on my father's death, safely, mother."

"You see."

"I never knew my father to show so much anxiety on any subject, as that his watch should be sent straight to you."

"I keep it here as a remembrance of your father."

"It was not until the last, that he expressed the wish. When he could only put his hand upon it, and very indistinctly say to me 'your mother.' A moment before, I thought him wandering in his mind, as he had been for many hours—I think he had no consciousness of pain in his short illness—when I saw him turn himself in his bed and try to open it."

"Was your father, then, not wandering in his mind when he tried to open it?"

"No. He was quite sensible at that time."

Mrs. Clennam shook her head; whether in dismissal of the deceased or opposing herself to her son's opinion, was not clearly expressed.

"After my father's death I opened it myself, thinking there might be for anything I knew, some memorandum there. However, as I need not tell you, mother, there was nothing but the old silk watch-paper worked in

beads, which you found (no doubt) in its place between the cases, where
I found and left it."

Mrs. Clennam signified assent; then added "no more of business on this
day," and then added, "Affery, it is nine o'clock."

Upon this, the old woman cleared the little table, went out of the room,
and quickly returned with a tray, on which was a dish of little rusks and a
small precise pat of butter, cool, symmetrical, white, and plump. The old
man who had been standing by the door in one attitude during the whole
interview, looking at the mother up-stairs as he had looked at the son
down-stairs, went out at the same time, and, after a longer absence,
returned with another tray on which was the greater part of a bottle of port
wine (which, to judge by his panting, he had brought from the cellar), a
lemon, a sugar basin, and a spice box. With these materials and the aid of
the kettle, he filled a tumbler with a hot and odorous mixture, measured
out and compounded with as much nicety as a physician's prescription.
Into this mixture, Mrs. Clennam dipped certain of the rusks and ate them;
while the old woman buttered certain other of the rusks, which were to
be eaten alone. When the invalid had eaten all the rusks and drunk all the
mixture, the two trays were removed; and the books and the candle,
watch, handkerchief, and spectacles were replaced upon the table. She
then put on the spectacles and read certain passages aloud from a book
—sternly, fiercely, wrathfully—praying that her enemies (she made them by
her tone and manner expressly hers) might be put to the edge of the sword,
consumed by fire, smitten by plagues and leprosy, that their bones might
be ground to dust, and that they might be utterly exterminated. As she
read on, years seemed to fall away from her son like the imaginings of a
dream, and all the old dark horrors of his usual preparation for the sleep of
an innocent child to overshadow him.

She shut the book and remained for a little time with her face shaded by
her hand. So did the old man, otherwise still unchanged in attitude; so,
probably, did the old woman in her dimmer part of the room. Then the
sick woman was ready for bed.

"Good night, Arthur. Affery will see to your accommodation. Only
touch me, for my hand is tender." He touched the worsted muffling of her
hand—that was nothing; if his mother had been sheathed in brass there
would have been no new barrier between them—and followed the old man
and woman down-stairs.

The latter asked him, when they were alone together among the heavy
shadows of the dining room, would he have some supper?

"No, Affery, no supper."

"You shall if you like," said Affery. "There's her to-morrow's partridge
in the larder—her first this year; say the word and I'll cook it."

No, he had not long dined, and could eat nothing.

"Have something to drink, then," said Affery; "you shall have some of her bottle of port, if you like. I'll tell Jeremiah that you ordered me to bring it you."

No; nor would he have that, either.

"It's no reason, Arthur," said the old woman, bending over him to whisper, "that because I am afeared of my life of 'em, you should be. You've got half the property, haven't you?"

"Yes, yes."

"Well then, don't *you* be cowed. You're clever, Arthur, an't you?"

He nodded, as she seemed to expect an answer in the affirmative.

"Then stand up against them! She's awful clever, and none but a clever one durst say a word to her. *He's* a clever one—oh he's a clever one!—and he gives it her when he has a mind to't, he does!"

"Your husband does?"

"Does? It makes me shake from head to foot, to hear him give it her. My husband, Jeremiah Flintwinch, can conquer even your mother. What can he be but a clever one to do that!"

His shuffling footstep coming towards them caused her to retreat to the other end of the room. Though a tall hard-favoured sinewy old woman, who in her youth might have enlisted in the Foot Guards without much fear of discovery, she collapsed before the little keen-eyed crab-like old man.

"Now Affery," said he, "now woman, what are you doing? Can't you find Master Arthur something or another to pick at?"

Master Arthur repeated his recent refusal to pick at anything.

"Very well, then," said the old man; "make his bed. Stir yourself." His neck was so twisted, that the knotted ends of his white cravat usually dangled under one ear; his natural acerbity and energy, always contending with a second nature of habitual repression, gave his features a swollen and suffused look; and altogether, he had a weird appearance of having hanged himself at one time or other, and of having gone about ever since halter and all, exactly as some timely hand had cut him down.

"You'll have bitter words together to-morrow, Arthur; you and your mother," said Jeremiah. "Your having given up the business on your father's death—which she suspects, though we have left it to you to tell her—won't go off smoothly."

"I have given up everything in life for the business, and the time came for me to give up that."

"Good!" cried Jeremiah, evidently meaning Bad. "Very good! only don't expect me to stand between your mother and you, Arthur. I stood between your mother and your father, fending off this, and fending off that, and getting crushed and pounded betwixt 'em; and I've done with such work."

"You will never be asked to begin it again for me, Jeremiah."

"Good, I'm glad to hear it; because I should have had to decline it, if I had been. That's enough—as your mother says—and more than enough of such matters on a Sabbath night. Affery, woman, have you found what you want yet?"

She had been collecting sheets and blankets from a press, and hastened to gather them up, and to reply, "yes, Jeremiah." Arthur Clennam helped her by carrying the load himself, wished the old man good night, and went up-stairs with her to the top of the house.

They mounted up and up, through the musty smell of an old close house, little used, to a large garret bedroom. Meagre and spare, like all the other rooms, it was even uglier and grimmer than the rest, by being the place of banishment for the worn-out furniture. Its moveables were ugly old chairs with worn-out seats, and ugly old chairs without any seats; a threadbare patternless carpet, a maimed table, a crippled wardrobe, a lean set of fire-irons like the skeleton of a set deceased, a washing stand that looked as if it had stood for ages in a hail of dirty soap-suds, and a bedstead with four bare atomies of posts, each terminating in a spike, as if for the dismal accommodation of lodgers who might prefer to impale themselves. Arthur opened the long low window, and looked out upon the old blasted and blackened forest of chimneys, and the old red glare in the sky which had seemed to him once upon a time but a nightly reflection of the fiery environment that was presented to his childish fancy in all directions, let it look where it would.

He drew in his head again, sat down at the bedside, and looked on at Affery Flintwinch making the bed.

"Affery, you were not married when I went away."

She screwed her mouth into the form of saying "No," shook her head, and proceeded to get a pillow into its case.

"How did it happen?"

"Why, Jeremiah, o' course," said Affery, with an end of the pillow-case between her teeth.

"Of course he proposed it, but how did it all come about? I should have thought that neither of you would have married; least of all should I have thought of your marrying each other."

"No more should I," said Mrs. Flintwinch, tying the pillow tightly in its case.

"That's what I mean. When did you begin to think otherwise?"

"Never begun to think otherwise at all," said Mrs. Flintwinch.

Seeing, as she patted the pillow into its place on the bolster, that he was still looking at her, as if waiting for the rest of her reply, she gave it a great poke in the middle, and asked, "How could I help myself?"

"How could you help yourself from being married?"

"O' course," said Mrs. Flintwinch. "It was no doing o' mine. I'd never thought of it. I'd got something to do, without thinking, indeed! She kept me to it when she could go about, and she could go about then."

"Well?"

"Well?" echoed Mrs. Flintwinch. "That's what I said myself. Well! What's the use of considering? If them two clever ones has made up their minds to it, what's left for *me* to do? Nothing."

"Was it my mother's project, then?"

"The Lord bless you, Arthur, and forgive me the wish!" cried Affery, speaking always in a low tone. "If they hadn't been both of a mind in it, how could it ever have been? Jeremiah never courted me; tan't likely that he would, after living in the house with me and ordering me about for as many years as he'd done. He said to me one day, he said, 'Affery,' he said, 'now I am going to tell you something. What do you think of the name of Flintwinch?' 'What do I think of it?' I says. 'Yes,' he said; 'because you're going to take it,' he said. 'Take it?' I says. 'Jere-*mi*-ah?' Oh, he's a clever one!"

Mrs. Flintwinch went on to spread the upper sheet over the bed, and the blanket over that, and the counterpane over that, as if she had quite concluded her story.

"Well?" said Arthur again.

"Well?" echoed Mrs. Flintwinch again. "How could I help myself? He said to me, 'Affery, you and me must be married, and I'll tell you why. She's failing in health, and she'll want pretty constant attendance up in her room, and we shall have to be much with her, and there'll be nobody about now but ourselves when we're away from her, and altogether it will be more convenient. She's of my opinion,' he said, 'so if you'll put your bonnet on, next Monday morning at eight, we'll get it over.'" Mrs. Flintwinch tucked up the bed.

"Well?"

"Well?" repeated Mrs. Flintwinch, "I think so! I sits me down and says it. Well!—Jeremiah then says to me, 'As to banns, next Sunday being the third time of asking (for I've put 'em up a fortnight), is my reason for naming Monday. She'll speak to you about it herself, and now she'll find you prepared, Affery.' That same day she spoke to me, and she said, 'So, Affery, I understand that you and Jeremiah are going to be married. I am glad of it, and so are you, with reason. It is a very good thing for you, and very welcome under the circumstances to me. He is a sensible man, and a trustworthy man, and a persevering man, and a pious man.' What could I say when it had come to that? Why, if it had been—a Smothering instead of a Wedding," Mrs. Flintwinch cast about in her mind with great pains for this form of expression, "I couldn't have said a word upon it, against them two clever ones."

"In good faith, I believe so."

"And so you may, Arthur."

"Affery, what girl was that in my mother's room just now?"

"Girl?" said Mrs. Flintwinch in a rather sharp key.

"It was a girl, surely, whom I saw near you—almost hidden in the dark corner?"

"Oh! She? Little Dorrit? *She's* nothing; she's a whim of—hers." It was a peculiarity of Affery Flintwinch that she never spoke of Mrs. Clennam by name. "But there's another sort of girls than that about. Have you forgot your old sweetheart? Long and long ago, I'll be bound."

"I suffered enough from my mother's separating us, to remember her. I recollect her very well."

"Have you got another?"

"No."

"Here's news for you, then. She's well to do now, and a widow. And if you like to have her, why you can."

"And how do you know that, Affery?"

"Them two clever ones have been speaking about it.—There's Jeremiah on the stairs!" She was gone in a moment.

Mrs. Flintwinch had introduced into the web that his mind was busily weaving, in that old workshop where the loom of his youth had stood, the last thread wanting to the pattern. The airy folly of a boy's love had found its way even into that house, and he had been as wretched under its hopelessness as if the house had been a castle of romance. Little more than a week ago, at Marseilles, the face of the pretty girl from whom he had parted with regret, had had an unusual interest for him, and a tender hold upon him, because of some resemblance, real or imagined, to this first face that had soared out of his gloomy life into the bright glories of fancy. He leaned upon the sill of the long low window, and looking out upon the blackened forest of chimneys again, began to dream. For, it had been the uniform tendency of this man's life—so much was wanting in it to think about, so much that might have been better directed and happier to speculate upon—to make him a dreamer, after all.

CHAPTER IV

MRS. FLINTWINCH HAS A DREAM

WHEN Mrs. Flintwinch dreamed, she usually dreamed unlike the son of her old mistress, with her eyes shut. She had a curiously vivid dream that night, and before she had left the son of her old mistress many hours. In fact it was not at all like a dream, it was so very real in every respect. It happened in this wise.

The bed-chamber occupied by Mr. and Mrs. Flintwinch was within a few paces of that to which Mrs. Clennam had been so long confined. It was not on the same floor, for it was a room at the side of the house, which was approached by a steep descent of a few odd steps, diverging from the main staircase nearly opposite to Mrs. Clennam's door. It could scarcely be said to be within call, the walls, doors, and panelling of the old place were so cumbrous; but it was within easy reach, in any undress, at any hour of the night, in any temperature. At the head of the bed, and within a foot of Mrs. Flintwinch's ear, was a bell, the line of which hung ready to Mrs. Clennam's hand. Whenever this bell rang, up started Affery, and was in the sick room before she was awake.

Having got her mistress into bed, lighted her lamp, and given her good night, Mrs. Flintwinch went to roost as usual, saving that her lord had not yet appeared. It was her lord himself who became—unlike the last theme in the mind, according to the observation of most philosophers—the subject of Mrs. Flintwinch's dream.

It seemed to her that she awoke, after sleeping some hours, and found Jeremiah not yet abed. That she looked at the candle she had left burning, and, measuring the time like King Alfred the Great, was confirmed by its wasted state in her belief that she had been asleep for some considerable period. That she arose thereupon, muffled herself up in a wrapper, put on her shoes, and went out on the staircase much surprised, to look for Jeremiah.

The staircase was as wooden and solid as need be, and Affery went straight down it without any of those deviations peculiar to dreams. She did not skim over it, but walked down it, and guided herself by the bannisters on account of her candle having died out. In one corner of the hall, behind the house-door, there was a little waiting-room, like a well-shaft, with a long narrow window in it as if it had been ripped up. In this room, which was never used, a light was burning.

Mrs. Flintwinch crossed the hall, feeling its pavement cold to her stockingless feet, and peeped in between the rusty hinges of the door, which stood a little open. She expected to see Jeremiah fast asleep or in a fit, but he was calmly seated in a chair, awake, and in his usual health. But what—hey?—Lord forgive us!—Mrs. Flintwinch muttered some ejaculation to this effect, and turned giddy.

For, Mr. Flintwinch awake, was watching Mr. Flintwinch asleep. He sat on one side of a small table, looking keenly at himself on the other side with his chin sunk on his breast, snoring. The waking Flintwinch had his full front face presented to his wife; the sleeping Flintwinch was in profile. The waking Flintwinch was the old original; the sleeping Flintwinch was the double. Just as she might have distinguished between a tangible object and its reflection in a glass, Affery made out this difference with her head going round and round.

If she had had any doubt which was her own Jeremiah, it would have been resolved by his impatience. He looked about him for an offensive weapon, caught up the snuffers, and, before applying them to the cabbage-headed candle, lunged at the sleeper as though he would have run him through the body.

"Who's that? What's the matter?" cried the sleeper, starting.

Mr. Flintwinch made a movement with the snuffers, as if he would have enforced silence on his companion by putting them down his throat; the companion coming to himself, said, rubbing his eyes, "I forgot where I was."

"You have been asleep," snarled Jeremiah, referring to his watch, "two hours. You said you would be rested enough if you had a short nap."

"I have had a short nap," said Double.

"Half-past two o'clock in the morning," muttered Jeremiah. "Where's your hat? Where's your coat? Where's the box?"

"All here," said Double, tying up his throat with sleepy carefulness in a shawl. "Stop a minute. Now give me the sleeve—not that sleeve, the other one. Ha! I'm not as young as I was." Mr. Flintwinch had pulled him into his coat with vehement viciousness. "You promised me a second glass after I was rested."

"Drink it!" returned Jeremiah, "and—choke yourself, I was going to say—but go, I mean." At the same time he produced the identical port-wine bottle, and filled a wine-glass.

"Her port-wine, I believe?" said Double, tasting it as if he were in the Docks, with hours to spare. "Her health."

He took a sip.

"Your health!"

He took another sip.

"His health!"

He took another sip.

"And all friends round Saint Paul's." He emptied and put down the wine-glass half-way through this ancient civic toast, and took up the box. It was an iron box some two feet square, which he carried under his arms pretty easily. Jeremiah watched his manner of adjusting it, with jealous eyes; tried it with his hands, to be sure that he had a firm hold of it; bade him for his life be careful what he was about; and then stole out on tiptoe to open the door for him. Affery, anticipating the last movement, was on the staircase. The sequence of things was so ordinary and natural, that, standing there, she could hear the door open, feel the night air, and see the stars outside.

But now came the most remarkable part of the dream. She felt so afraid of her husband, that being on the staircase, she had not the power to retreat to her room (which she might easily have done before he had fastened the door), but stood there staring. Consequently when he came

up the staircase to bed, candle in hand, he came full upon her. He looked
astonished, but said not a word. He kept his eyes upon her, and kept
advancing; and she, completely under his influence, kept retiring before
him. Thus, she walking backward and he walking forward, they came into
their own room. They were no sooner shut in there, than Mr. Flintwinch
took her by the throat, and shook her until she was black in the face.

"Why, Affery, woman—Affery!" said Mr. Flintwinch. "What have you
been dreaming of? Wake up, wake up! What's the matter?"

"The—the matter, Jeremiah?" gasped Mrs. Flintwinch, rolling her
eyes.

"Why, Affery, woman—Affery! You have been getting out of bed in
your sleep, my dear! I come up, after having fallen asleep myself, below,
and find you in your wrapper here, with the nightmare. Affery, woman,"
said Mr. Flintwinch, with a friendly grin on his expressive countenance,
"if you ever have a dream of this sort again, it'll be a sign of your being in
want of physic. And I'll give you such a dose, old woman—such a dose!"

Mrs. Flintwinch thanked him and crept into bed.

END OF No. I

CHAPTER V

FAMILY AFFAIRS

As the city clocks struck nine on Monday morning, Mrs. Clennam was
wheeled by Jeremiah Flintwinch of the cut-down aspect, to her tall
cabinet. When she had unlocked and opened it, and had settled herself at
its desk, Jeremiah withdrew—as it might be, to hang himself more effect-
ually—and her son appeared.

"Are you any better this morning, mother?"

She shook her head, with the same austere air of luxuriousness that she
had shown over-night when speaking of the weather. "I shall never be
better any more. It is well for me, Arthur, that I know it and can bear it."

Sitting with her hands laid separately upon the desk, and the tall cabinet
towering before her, she looked as if she were performing on a dumb church
organ. Her son thought so (it was an old thought with him), while he took
his seat beside it.

She opened a drawer or two, looked over some business papers, and put
them back again. Her severe face had no thread of relaxation in it, by which
any explorer could have been guided to the gloomy labyrinth of her
thoughts.

"Shall I speak of our affairs, mother? Are you inclined to enter upon
business?"

"Am I inclined, Arthur? Rather, are you? Your father has been dead a year and more. I have been at your disposal, and waiting your pleasure, ever since."

"There was much to arrange before I could leave; and when I did leave, I travelled a little for rest and relief."

She turned her face towards him, as not having heard or understood his last words.

"For rest and relief."

She glanced round the sombre room, and appeared from the motion of her lips to repeat the words to herself, as calling it to witness how little of either it afforded her.

"Besides, mother, you being sole executrix, and having the direction and management of the estate, there remained little business, or I might say none, that I could transact, until you had had time to arrange matters to your satisfaction."

"The accounts are made out." she returned, "I have them here. The vouchers have all been examined and passed. You can inspect them when you like, Arthur; now, if you please."

"It is quite enough, mother, to know that the business is completed. Shall I proceed then?"

"Why not!" she said, in her frozen way.

"Mother, our House has done less and less for some years past, and our dealings have been progressively on the decline. We have never shown much confidence, or invited much; we have attached no people to us; the track we have kept is not the track of the time; and we have been left far behind. I need not dwell on this to you, mother. You know it necessarily."

"I know what you mean," she answered, in a qualified tone.

"Even this old house in which we speak," pursued her son, "is an instance of what I say. In my father's earlier time, and in his uncle's time before him, it was a place of business—really a place of business, and business resort. Now, it is a mere anomaly and incongruity here, out of date and out of purpose. All our consignments have long been made to Rovinghams' the commission-merchants; and although, as a check upon them, and in the stewardship of my father's resources, your judgment and watchfulness have been actively exerted, still those qualities would have influenced my father's fortunes equally, if you had lived in any private dwelling: would they not?"

"Do you consider," she returned, without answering his question, "that a house serves no purpose, Arthur, in sheltering your infirm and afflicted—justly infirm and righteously afflicted—mother?"

"I was speaking only of business purposes."

"With what object?"

"I am coming to it."

"I foresee," she returned, fixing her eyes upon him, "what it is. But the Lord forbid that I should repine under any visitation. In my sinfulness I merit bitter disappointment, and I accept it."

"Mother, I grieve to hear you speak like this, though I have had my apprehensions that you would—"

"You knew I would. You knew *me*," she interrupted.

Her son paused for a moment. He had struck fire out of her, and was surprised. "Well!" she said, relapsing into stone. "Go on. Let me hear."

"You have anticipated, mother, that I decide, for my part, to abandon the business. I have done with it. I will not take upon myself to advise you; you will continue it, I see. If I had any influence with you, I would simply use it to soften your judgment of me in causing you this disappointment: to represent to you that I have lived the half of a long term of life, and have never before set my own will against yours. I cannot say that I have been able to conform myself, in heart and spirit, to your rules; I cannot say that I believe my forty years have been profitable or pleasant to myself, or any one; but I have habitually submitted, and I only ask you to remember it."

Woe to the suppliant, if such a one there were or ever had been, who had any concession to look for in the inexorable face at the cabinet. Woe to the defaulter whose appeal lay to the tribunal where those severe eyes presided. Great need had the rigid woman of her mystical religion, veiled in gloom and darkness, with lightnings of cursing, vengeance, and destruction, flashing through the sable clouds. Forgive us our debts as we forgive our debtors, was a prayer too poor in spirit for her. Smite thou my debtors, Lord, wither them, crush them; do Thou as I would do, and Thou shalt have my worship: this was the impious tower of stone she built up to scale Heaven.

"Have you finished, Arthur, or have you anything more to say to me? I think there can be nothing else. You have been short, but full of matter!"

"Mother, I have yet something more to say. It has been upon my mind, night and day, this long time. It is far more difficult to say than what I have said. That concerned myself; this concerns us all."

"Us all! Who are us all?"

"Yourself, myself, my dead father."

She took her hands from the desk; folded them in her lap; and sat looking towards the fire, with the impenetrability of an old Egyptian sculpture.

"You knew my father infinitely better than I ever knew him; and his reserve with me yielded to you. You were much the stronger, mother, and directed him. As a child, I knew it as well as I know it now. I knew that your ascendancy over him was the cause of his going to China to take care of the business there, while you took care of it here (though I do not even now know whether these were really terms of separation that you agreed upon); and that it was your will that I should remain with you until I was twenty, and then go to him as I did. You will not be offended by my recalling this, after twenty years?"

"I am waiting to hear why you recall it."

He lowered his voice, and said, with manifest reluctance, and against his will:

"I want to ask you, mother, whether it ever occurred to you to suspect—"

At the word Suspect, she turned her eyes momentarily upon her son, with a dark frown. She then suffered them to seek the fire as before; but with the frown fixed above them, as if the sculptor of old Egypt had indented it in the hard granite face, to frown for ages.

"—that he had any secret remembrance which caused him trouble of mind—remorse? Whether you ever observed anything in his conduct suggesting that; or ever spoke to him upon it, or ever heard him hint at such a thing?"

"I do not understand what kind of secret remembrance you mean to infer that your father was a prey to," she returned, after a silence. "You speak so mysteriously."

"Is it possible, mother," her son leaned forward to be the nearer to her while he whispered it, and laid his hand nervously upon her desk, "is it possible, mother, that he had unhappily wronged any one, and made no reparation?"

Looking at him wrathfully, she bent herself back in her chair to keep him further off, but gave him no reply.

"I am deeply sensible, mother, that if this thought has never at any time flashed upon you, it must seem cruel and unnatural in me, even in this confidence, to breathe it. But I cannot shake it off. Time and change (I have tried both before breaking silence), do nothing to wear it out. Remember, I was with my father. Remember, I saw his face when he gave the watch into my keeping, and struggled to express that he sent it as a token you would understand, to you. Remember, I saw him at the last with the pencil in his failing hand, trying to write some word for you to read, but to which he could give no shape. The more remote and cruel this vague suspicion that I have, the stronger the circumstances that could give it any semblance of probability to me. For Heaven's sake let us examine sacredly whether there is any wrong entrusted to us to set right. No one can help towards it, mother, but you."

Still so recoiling in her chair that her overpoised weight moved it, from time to time, a little on its wheels, and gave her the appearance of a phantom of fierce aspect gliding away from him, she interposed her left arm, bent at the elbow with the back of her hand towards her face, between herself and him, and looked at him in a fixed silence.

"In grasping at money and in driving hard bargains—I have begun, and I must speak of such things now, mother—some one may have been grievously deceived, injured, ruined. You were the moving power of all this machinery before my birth; your stronger spirit has been infused into all my father's dealings, for more than two score years. You can set these doubts at rest, I think, if you will really help me to discover the truth. Will you, mother?"

He stopped in the hope that she would speak. But her grey hair was not more immoveable in its two folds, than were her firm lips.

"If reparation can be made to any one, if restitution can be made to any one, let us know it and make it. Nay, mother, if within my means, let *me* make it. I have seen so little happiness come of money; it has brought within my knowledge so little peace to this house, or to any one belonging to it; that it is worth less to me than to another. It can buy me nothing that will not be a reproach and misery to me, if I am haunted by a suspicion that it darkened my father's last hours with remorse, and that it is not honestly and justly mine."

There was a bell-rope hanging on the panelled wall, some two or three yards from the cabinet. By a swift and sudden action of her foot, she drove her wheeled chair rapidly back to it and pulled it violently—still holding her arm up in its shield-like posture, as if he were striking at her, and she warding off the blow.

A girl came hurrying in, frightened.

"Send Flintwinch here!"

In a moment the girl had withdrawn, and the old man stood within the door. "Oh! You're hammer and tongs already, you two?" he said, coolly stroking his face. "I thought you would be. I was pretty sure of it."

"Flintwinch!" said the mother, "look at my son. Look at him!"

"Well! I *am* looking at him," said Flintwinch.

She stretched out the arm with which she had shielded herself, and as she went on, pointed at the object of her anger.

"In the very hour of his return almost—before the shoe upon his foot is dry—he asperses his father's memory to his mother! Asks his mother to become, with him, a spy upon his father's transactions through a lifetime! Has misgivings that the goods of this world, which we have painfully got together early and late, with wear and tear and toil and self-denial, are so much plunder; and asks to whom they shall be given up, as reparation and restitution!"

Although she said this raging, she said it in a voice so far from being beyond her control, that it was even lower than her usual tone. She also spoke with great distinctness.

"Reparation!" said she. "Yes truly! It is easy for him to talk of reparation, fresh from journeying and junketting in foreign lands, and living a life of vanity and pleasure. But let him look at me, in prison, and in bonds here. I endure without murmuring, because it is appointed that I shall so make reparation for my sins. Reparation! Is there none in this room? Has there been none here this fifteen years?"

Thus was she always balancing her bargain with the Majesty of heaven,

Mr. Flintwinch mediates as a friend of the Family

posting up the entries to her credit, strictly keeping her set-off, and claiming her due. She was only remarkable in this, for the force and emphasis with which she did it. Thousands upon thousands do it, according to their varying manner, every day.

"Flintwinch, give me that book!"

The old man handed it to her from the table. She put two fingers between the leaves, closed the book upon them, and held it up to her son in a threatening way.

"In the days of old, Arthur, treated of in this Commentary, there were pious men, beloved of the Lord, who would have cursed their sons for less than this: who would have sent them forth, and sent whole nations forth, if such had supported them, to be avoided of God and man, and perish, down to the baby at the breast. But I only tell you that if you ever renew that theme with me, I will renounce you; I will so dismiss you through that doorway, that you had better have been motherless from your cradle. I will never see or know you more. And if, after all, you were to come into this darkened room to look upon me lying dead, my body should bleed, if I could make it, when you came near me."

In part relieved by the intensity of this threat, and in part (monstrous as the fact is) by a general impression that it was in some sort a religious proceeding, she handed back the book to the old man, and was silent.

"Now," said Jeremiah; "premising that I'm not going to stand between you two, will you let me ask (as I *have* been called in, and made a third) what is all this about?"

"Take your version of it," returned Arthur, finding it left to him to speak, "from my mother. Let it rest there. What I have said, was said to my mother only."

"Oh!" returned the old man. "From your mother? Take it from your mother? Well! But your mother mentioned that you had been suspecting your father. That's not dutiful, Mr. Arthur. Who will you be suspecting next?"

"Enough," said Mrs. Clennam, turning her face so that it was addressed for the moment to the old man only. "Let no more be said about this."

"Yes, but stop a bit, stop a bit," the old man persisted. "Let us see how we stand. Have you told Mr. Arthur, that he mustn't lay offences at his father's door? That he has no right to do it? That he has no ground to go upon?"

"I tell him so now."

"Ah! Exactly," said the old man. "You tell him so now. You hadn't told him so before, and you tell him so now. Ay, ay! That's right! You know I stood between you and his father so long, that it seems as if death had made no difference, and I was still standing between you. So I will, and so in fairness I require to have that plainly put forward. Arthur, you please to hear that you have no right to mistrust your father, and have no ground to go upon."

He put his hands to the back of the wheeled chair, and muttering to himself, slowly wheeled his mistress back to her cabinet. "Now," he resumed, standing behind her: "in case I should go away leaving things half done, and so should be wanted again when you come to the other half and get into one of your flights, has Arthur told you what he means to do about the business?"

"He has relinquished it."

"In favour of nobody, I suppose?"

Mrs. Clennam glanced at her son, leaning against one of the windows. He observed the look, and said, "To my mother, of course. She does what she pleases."

"And if any pleasure," she said after a short pause, "could arise for me out of the disappointment of my expectations, that my son in the prime of his life would infuse new youth and strength into it, and make it of great profit and power, it would be in advancing an old and faithful servant. Jeremiah, the captain deserts the ship, but you and I will sink or float with it."

Jeremiah, whose eyes glistened as if they saw money, darted a sudden look at the son, which seemed to say, "I owe *you* no thanks for this; *you* have done nothing towards it!" and then told the mother that he thanked her, and that Affery thanked her, and that he would never desert her, and that Affery would never desert her. Finally, he hauled up his watch from its depths, said "Eleven. Time for your oysters!" and with that change of subject, which involved no change of expression or manner, rang the bell.

But Mrs. Clennam, resolved to treat herself with the greater rigor for having been supposed to be unacquainted with reparation, refused to eat her oysters when they were brought. They looked tempting; eight in number, circularly set out on a white plate on a tray covered with a white napkin, flanked by a slice of buttered French roll, and a little compact glass of cool wine and water; but she resisted all persuasions, and sent them down again—placing the act to her credit, no doubt, in her Eternal Day-book.

This refection of oysters was not presided over by Affery, but by the girl who had appeared when the bell was rung; the same who had been in the dimly-lighted room last night. Now that he had an opportunity of observing her, Arthur found that her diminutive figure, small features, and slight spare dress, gave her the appearance of being much younger than she was. A woman, probably of not less than two and twenty, she might have been passed in the street for little more than half that age. Not that her face was very youthful, for in truth there was more consideration and care in it than naturally belonged to her utmost years; but she was so little and light, so noiseless and shy, and appeared so conscious of being out of place among the three hard elders, that she had all the manner and much of the appearance of a subdued child.

In a hard way, and in an uncertain way that fluctuated between patronage and putting down, the sprinkling from a watering-pot and hydraulic pressure, Mrs. Clennam showed an interest in this dependant. Even in the moment of her entrance upon the violent ringing of the bell, when the mother shielded herself with that singular action from the son, Mrs. Clennam's eyes had had some individual recognition in them, which seemed reserved for her. As there are degrees of hardness in the hardest metal, and shades of color in black itself, so, even in the asperity of Mrs. Clennam's demeanour towards all the rest of humanity and towards Little Dorrit,[1] there was a fine gradation.

Little Dorrit let herself out to do needlework. At so much a day—or at so little—from eight to eight, Little Dorrit was to be hired. Punctual to the moment, Little Dorrit appeared; punctual to the moment, Little Dorrit vanished. What became of Little Dorrit between the two eights, was a mystery.

Another of the moral phenomena of Little Dorrit. Besides her consideration money, her daily contract included meals. She had an extraordinary repugnance to dining in company; would never do so, if it were possible to escape. Would always plead that she had this bit of work to begin first, or that bit of work to finish first; and would, of a certainty, scheme and plan—not very cunningly it would seem, for she deceived no one—to dine alone. Successful in this; happy in carrying off her plate anywhere, to make a table of her lap, or a box, or the ground, or even as was supposed, to stand on tip-toe, dining moderately at a mantelshelf; the great anxiety of Little Dorrit's day was set at rest.

It was not easy to make out Little Dorrit's face; she was so retiring, plied her needle in such removed corners, and started away so scared if encountered on the stairs. But it seemed to be a pale transparent face, quick in expression, though not beautiful in feature, its soft hazel eyes excepted. A delicately bent head, a tiny form, a quick little pair of busy hands, and a shabby dress—it must needs have been very shabby to look at all so, being so neat—were Little Dorrit as she sat at work.

For these particulars or generalities concerning Little Dorrit, Mr. Arthur was indebted in the course of the day to his own eyes and to Mrs. Affery's tongue. If Mrs. Affery had had any will or way of her own, it would probably have been unfavourable to Little Dorrit. But as "them two clever ones"—Mrs. Affery's perpetual reference, in whom her personality was swallowed up —were agreed to accept Little Dorrit as a matter of course, she had nothing for it but to follow suit. Similarly, if the two clever ones had agreed to murder Little Dorrit by candle-light, Mrs. Affery, being required to hold the candle, would no doubt have done it.

In the intervals of roasting the partridge for the invalid chamber, and preparing a baking-dish of beef and pudding for the dining-room, Mrs. Affery made the communications above set forth; invariably putting her head in at the door again after she had taken it out, to enforce resistance to the two clever ones. It appeared to have become a perfect passion with Mrs. Flintwinch, that the only son should be pitted against them.

In the course of the day too, Arthur looked through the whole house. Dull and dark he found it. The gaunt rooms, deserted for years upon years, seemed to have settled down into a gloomy lethargy from which nothing could rouse them again. The furniture, at once spare and lumbering, hid in the rooms rather than furnished them, and there was no color in all the house; such color as had ever been there, had long ago started away on lost sunbeams—got itself absorbed, perhaps, into flowers, butterflies, plumage of birds, precious stones, what not. There was not one straight floor, from the foundation to the roof; the ceilings were so fantastically clouded by smoke and dust, that old women might have told fortunes in them, better than in grouts of tea; the dead-cold hearths showed no traces of having ever been warmed, but in heaps of soot that had tumbled down the chimneys, and eddied about in little dusky whirlwinds when the doors were opened. In what had once been a drawing-room, there were a pair of meagre mirrors, with dismal processions of black figures carrying black garlands, walking round the frames; but even these were short of heads and legs, and one undertaker-like Cupid had swung round on his own axis and got upside down, and another had fallen off altogether. The room Arthur Clennam's deceased father had occupied for business purposes, when he first remembered him, was so unaltered that he might have been imagined still to keep it invisibly, as his visible relict kept her room upstairs; Jeremiah Flintwinch still going between them negociating. His picture, dark and gloomy, earnestly speechless on the wall, with the eyes intently looking at his son as they had looked when life departed from them, seemed to urge him awfully to the task he had attempted; but as to any yielding on the part of his mother, he had now no hope, and as to any other means of setting his distrust at rest, he had abandoned hope a long time. Down in the cellars, as up in the bed-chambers, old objects that he well remembered were changed by age and decay, but were still in their old places; even to empty beer-casks hoary with cobwebs, and empty wine-bottles with fur and fungus choking up their throats. There, too, among unused bottle-racks and pale slants of light from the yard above, was the strong room stored with old ledgers which had as musty and corrupt a smell as if they were regularly balanced, in the dead small hours, by a nightly resurrection of old book-keepers.

The baking-dish was served up in a penitential manner, on a shrunken cloth at an end of the dining table, at two o'clock; when he dined with Mr. Flintwinch, the new partner. Mr. Flintwinch informed him that his

mother had recovered her equanimity now, and that he need not fear her
again alluding to what had passed in the morning, "And don't you lay
offences at your father's door, Mr. Arthur," added Jeremiah, "once for
all, don't do it! Now, we have done with the subject."

Mr. Flintwinch had been already re-arranging and dusting his own
particular little office, as if to do honor to his accession to new dignity. He
resumed this occupation when he was replete with beef, had sucked up all
the gravy in the baking-dish with the flat of his knife, and had drawn
liberally on a barrel of small beer in the scullery. Thus refreshed, he
tucked up his shirt-sleeves and went to work again; and Mr. Arthur,
watching him as he set about it, plainly saw that his father's picture, or
his father's grave, would be as communicative with him as this old man.

"Now, Affery, woman," said Mr. Flintwinch, as she crossed the hall.
"You hadn't made Mr. Arthur's bed when I was up there last. Stir yourself.
Bustle."

But Mr. Arthur found the house so blank and dreary, and was so unwilling to assist at another implacable consignment of his mother's
enemies (perhaps himself among them) to mortal disfigurement and
immortal ruin, that he announced his intention of lodging at the coffee-
house where he had left his luggage. Mr. Flintwinch taking kindly to the
idea of getting rid of him, and his mother being indifferent, beyond considerations of saving, to most domestic arrangements that were not bounded
by the walls of her own chamber, he easily carried this point without new
offence. Daily business hours were agreed upon, which his mother, Mr.
Flintwinch, and he, were to devote together to a necessary checking of
books and papers; and he left the home he had so lately found, with a
depressed heart.

But Little Dorrit?

The business hours, allowing for intervals of invalid regimen of oysters
and partridges, during which Clennam refreshed himself with a walk,
were from ten to six for about a fortnight. Sometimes Little Dorrit was
employed at her needle, sometimes not, sometimes appeared as a humble
visitor: which must have been her character on the occasion of his arrival.
His original curiosity augmented every day, as he watched for her, saw
or did not see her, and speculated about her. Influenced by his predominant
idea, he even fell into a habit of discussing with himself the possibility of
her being in some way associated with it. At last he resolved to watch Little
Dorrit and know more of her story.

CHAPTER VI

THIRTY years ago there stood, a few doors short of the church of Saint George, in the Borough of Southwark, on the left hand side of the way going southward, the Marshalsea Prison. It had stood there many years before, and it remained there some years afterwards; but it is gone now, and the world is none the worse without it.

It was an oblong pile of barrack building, partitioned into squalid houses standing back to back, so that there were no back rooms; environed by a narrow paved yard, hemmed in by high walls duly spiked at top. Itself a close and confined prison for debtors, it contained within it a much closer and more confined jail for smugglers. Offenders against the revenue laws, and defaulters to excise or customs, who had incurred fines which they were unable to pay, were supposed to be incarcerated behind an iron-plated door, closing up a second prison, consisting of a strong cell or two, and a blind alley some yard and a half wide, which formed the mysterious termination of the very limited skittle-ground in which the Marshalsea debtors bowled down their troubles.

Supposed to be incarcerated there, because the time had rather out-grown the strong cells and the blind alley. In practice they had come to be considered a little too bad, though in theory they were quite as good as ever; which may be observed to be the case at the present day with other cells that are not at all strong, and with other blind alleys that are stone-blind. Hence the smugglers habitually consorted with the debtors (who received them with open arms), except at certain constitutional moments when somebody came from some Office, to go through some form of overlooking something, which neither he nor anybody else knew anything about. On those truly British occasions, the smugglers, if any, made a feint of walking into the strong cells and the blind alley, while this somebody pretended to do his something; and made a reality of walking out again as soon as he hadn't done it—neatly epitomising the administration of most of the public affairs in our right little, tight little, island.

There had been taken to the Marshalsea Prison, long before the day when the sun shone on Marseilles and on the opening of this narrative, a debtor with whom this narrative has some concern.

He was, at that time, a very amiable and very helpless middle-aged gentleman, who was going out again directly. Necessarily, he was going out again directly, because the Marshalsea lock never turned upon a debtor who was not. He brought in a portmanteau with him, which he doubted its being worth while to unpack; he was so perfectly clear—like all the rest of them, the turnkey on the lock said—that he was going out again directly.

He was a shy, retiring man; well-looking, though in an effeminate style; with a mild voice, curling hair, and irresolute hands—rings upon the fingers in those days—which nervously wandered to his trembling lip a hundred times, in the first half-hour of his acquaintance with the jail. His principal anxiety was about his wife.

"Do you think, sir," he asked the turnkey, "that she will be very much shocked, if she should come to the gate to-morrow morning?"

The turnkey gave it as the result of his experience that some of 'em was and some of 'em wasn't. In general, more no than yes. "What like is she, you see?" he philosophically asked: "that's what it hinges on."

"She is very delicate and inexperienced indeed."

"That," said the turnkey, "is agen her."

"She is so little used to go out alone," said the debtor, "that I am at a loss to think how she will ever make her way here, if she walks."

"P'raps," quoth the turnkey, "she'll take a ackney coach."

"Perhaps." The irresolute fingers went to the trembling lip. "I hope she will. She may not think of it."

"Or p'raps," said the turnkey, offering his suggestions from the top of his well-worn wooden stool, as he might have offered them to a child for whose weakness he felt a compassion, "p'raps she'll get her brother, or her sister, to come along with her."

"She has no brother or sister."

"Niece, nevy, cousin, serwant, young 'ooman, greengrocer.—Dash it! One or other on 'em," said the turnkey, repudiating beforehand the refusal of all his suggestions.

"I fear—I hope it is not against the rules—that she will bring the children."

"The children?" said the turnkey. "And the rules? Why, lord set you up like a corner pin, we've a reg'lar playground o' children here. Children? Why, we swarm with 'em. How many a you got?"

"Two," said the debtor, lifting his irresolute hand to his lip again, and turning into the prison.

The turnkey followed him with his eyes. "And you another," he observed to himself, "which makes three on you. And your wife another, I'll lay a crown. Which makes four on you. And another coming, I'll lay half-a-crown. Which'll make five on you. And I'll go another seven and sixpence to name which is the helplessest, the unborn baby or you!"

He was right in all his particulars. She came next day with a little boy of three years old, and a little girl of two, and he stood entirely corroborated.

"Got a room now; haven't you?" the turnkey asked the debtor after a week or two.

"Yes, I have got a very good room."

"Any little sticks a coming, to furnish it?" said the turnkey.

"I expect a few necessary articles of furniture to be delivered by the carrier, this afternoon."

"Missis and little 'uns a coming, to keep you company?" asked the turnkey.

"Why, yes, we think it better that we should not be scattered, even for a few weeks."

"Even for a few weeks, *of* course," replied the turnkey. And he followed him again with his eyes, and nodded his head seven times when he was gone.

The affairs of this debtor were perplexed by a partnership, of which he knew no more than that he had invested money in it; by legal matters of assignment and settlement, conveyance here and conveyance there, suspicion of unlawful preference of creditors in this direction, and of mysterious spiriting away of property in that; and as nobody on the face of the earth could be more incapable of explaining any single item in the heap of confusion than the debtor himself, nothing comprehensible could be made of his case. To question him in detail, and endeavour to reconcile his answers; to closet him with accountants and sharp practitioners, learned in the wiles of insolvency and bankruptcy; was only to put the case out at compound interest of incomprehensibility. The irresolute fingers fluttered more and more ineffectually about the trembling lip on every such occasion, and the sharpest practitioners gave him up as a hopeless job.

"Out?" said the turnkey, "*he*'ll never get out. Unless his creditors take him by the shoulders and shove him out."

He had been there five or six months, when he came running to this turnkey one forenoon to tell him, breathless and pale, that his wife was ill.

"As anybody might a known she would be," said the turnkey.

"We intended," he returned, "that she should go to a country lodging only to-morrow. What am I to do! Oh, good Heaven, what am I to do!"

"Don't waste your time in clasping your hands and biting your fingers," responded the practical turnkey, taking him by the elbow, "but come along with me."

The turnkey conducted him—trembling from head to foot, and constantly crying under his breath, What was he to do! while his irresolute fingers bedabbled the tears upon his face—up one of the common staircases in the prison, to a door on the garret story. Upon which door the turnkey knocked with the handle of his key.

"Come in!" cried a voice inside.

The turnkey opening the door, disclosed in a wretched, ill-smelling little room, two hoarse, puffy, red-faced personages seated at a ricketty table, playing at all-fours, smoking pipes, and drinking brandy.

"Doctor," said the turnkey, "here's a gentleman's wife in want of you without a minute's loss of time!"

The doctor's friend was in the positive degree of hoarseness, puffiness, red-facedness, all-fours, tobacco, dirt, and brandy; the doctor in the comparative—hoarser, puffier, more red-faced, more all-foury, tobaccoer, dirtier, and brandier. The doctor was amazingly shabby, in a torn and darned rough-weather sea-jacket, out at elbows and eminently short of buttons (he had been in his time the experienced surgeon carried by a passenger ship), the dirtiest white trousers conceivable by mortal man, carpet slippers, and no visible linen. "Childbed?" said the doctor. "I'm the boy!" With that the doctor took a comb from the chimney-piece and stuck his hair upright—which appeared to be his way of washing himself—produced a professional chest or case, of most abject appearance, from the cupboard where his cup and saucer and coals were, settled his chin in the frowsy wrapper round his neck, and became a ghastly medical scarecrow.

The doctor and the debtor ran down-stairs, leaving the turnkey to return to the lock, and made for the debtor's room. All the ladies in the prison had got hold of the news, and were in the yard. Some of them had already taken possession of the two children, and were hospitably carrying them off; others were offering loans of little comforts from their own scanty store; others were sympathising with the greatest volubility. The gentlemen prisoners, feeling themselves at a disadvantage, had for the most part retired, not to say sneaked, to their rooms; from the open windows of which, some of them now complimented the doctor with whistles as he passed below, while others, with several stories between them, interchanged sarcastic references to the prevalent excitement.

It was a hot summer day, and the prison rooms were baking between the high walls. In the debtor's confined chamber, Mrs. Bangham, charwoman and messenger, who was not a prisoner (though she had been once), but was the popular medium of communication with the outer world, had volunteered her services as fly-catcher and general attendant. The walls and ceiling were blackened with flies. Mrs. Bangham, expert in sudden device, with one hand fanned the patient with a cabbage leaf, and with the other set traps of vinegar and sugar in gallipots; at the same time enunciating sentiments of an encouraging and congratulatory nature, adapted to the occasion.

"The flies trouble you don't they, my dear?" said Mrs. Bangham. "But p'raps they'll take your mind off of it, and do you good. What between the buryin' ground, the grocer's, the waggon-stables, and the paunch trade, the Marshalsea flies get very large. P'raps they're sent as a consolation, if we only know'd it. How are you now, my dear? No better? No my dear, it ain't to be expected; you'll be worse before you're better, and you know it, don't you? Yes. That's right! And to think of a sweet little cherub being born inside the lock! Now ain't it pretty, ain't *that* something to carry you through it pleasant? Why, we ain't had such a thing happen here, my dear, not for I couldn't name the time when. And you a crying too?" said Mrs.

Bangham, to rally the patient more and more. "You! Making yourself so famous! With the flies a falling into the gallipots by fifties! And everything a going on so well! And here if there ain't," said Mrs. Bangham as the door opened, "if there ain't your dear gentleman along with Doctor Haggage! And now indeed we *are* complete, I *think!*"

The doctor was scarcely the kind of apparition to inspire a patient with a sense of absolute completeness, but as he presently delivered the opinion, "We are as right as we can be, Mrs. Bangham, and we shall come out of this like a house a-fire;" and as he and Mrs. Bangham took possession of the poor, helpless pair, as everybody else and anybody else had always done; the means at hand were as good on the whole as better would have been. The special feature in Dr. Haggage's treatment of the case, was his determination to keep Mrs. Bangham up to the mark. As thus:

"Mrs. Bangham," said the doctor, before he had been there twenty minutes, "go outside⁴ and fetch a little brandy, or we shall have you giving in."

"Thank you sir. But none on my accounts," said Mrs. Bangham.

"Mrs. Bangham," returned the doctor, "I am in professional attendance on this lady, and don't choose to allow any discussion on your part. Go outside⁴ and fetch a little brandy, or I foresee that you'll break down."

"You're to be obeyed sir," said Mrs. Bangham, rising. "If you was to put your own lips to it, I think you wouldn't be the worse, for you look but poorly, sir."

"Mrs. Bangham," returned the doctor, "I am not your business, thank you, but you are mine. Never you mind *me*, if you please. What you have got to do, is, to do as you are told, and to go and get what I bid you."

Mrs. Bangham submitted; and the doctor, having administered her potion, took his own. He repeated the treatment every hour, being very determined with Mrs. Bangham. Three or four hours passed; the flies fell into the traps by hundreds; and at length one little life, hardly stronger than theirs, appeared among the multitude of lesser deaths.

"A very nice little girl indeed," said the doctor; "little, but well-formed. Halloa, Mrs. Bangham! You're looking queer! You be off, ma'am, this minute, and fetch a little more brandy, or we shall have you in hysterics."

By this time, the rings had begun to fall from the debtor's irresolute hands, like leaves from a wintry tree. Not one was left upon them that night, when he put something that chinked into the doctor's greasy palm. In the meantime Mrs. Bangham had been out an errand to a neighbouring establishment decorated with three golden balls, where she was very well known.

"Thank you," said the doctor, "thank you. Your good lady is quite composed. Doing charmingly."

"I am very happy and very thankful to know it," said the debtor, "though I little thought once, that—"

"That a child would be born to you in a place like this?" said the doctor.
"Bah, bah, sir, what does it signify? A little more elbow-room is all we
want here. We are quiet here; we don't get badgered here; there's no
knocker here, sir, to be hammered at by creditors and bring a man's heart
into his mouth. Nobody comes here to ask if a man's at home, and to say
he'll stand on the door mat till he is. Nobody writes threatening letters
about money, to this place. It's freedom, sir, it's freedom! I have had
to-day's practice at home and abroad, on a march, and aboard ship, and
I'll tell you this: I don't know that I have ever pursued it under such quiet
circumstances, as here this day. Elsewhere, people are restless, worried,
hurried about, anxious respecting one thing, anxious respecting another.
Nothing of the kind here, sir. We have done all that—we know the worst of
it; we have got to the bottom, we can't fall, and what have we found?
Peace. That's the word for it. Peace." With this profession of faith, the
doctor, who was an old jail-bird, and was more sodden than usual, and had
the additional and unusual stimulus of money in his pocket, returned to his
associate and chum in hoarseness, puffiness, red-facedness, all-fours,
tobacco, dirt, and brandy.

Now, the debtor was a very different man from the doctor, but he had
already begun to travel, by his opposite segment of the circle, to the same
point. Crushed at first by his imprisonment, he had soon found a dull
relief in it. He was under lock and key; but the lock and key that kept him
in, kept numbers of his troubles out. If he had been a man with strength of
purpose to face those troubles and fight them, he might have broken the
net that held him, or broken his heart; but being what he was, he languidly
slipped into this smooth descent, and never more took one step upward.

When he was relieved of the perplexed affairs that nothing would make
plain, through having them returned upon his hands by a dozen agents in
succession who could make neither beginning, middle, nor end of them, or
him, he found his miserable place of refuge a quieter refuge than it had been
before. He had unpacked the portmanteau long ago; and his elder children
now played regularly about the yard, and everybody knew the baby, and
claimed a kind of proprietorship in her.

"Why, I'm getting proud of you," said his friend the turnkey, one day.
"You'll be the oldest inhabitant soon. The Marshalsea wouldn't be like the
Marshalsea now, without you and your family."

The turnkey really was proud of him. He would mention him in laudatory terms to new comers, when his back was turned. "You took notice
of him," he would say, "that went out of the Lodge just now?"

New comer would probably answer yes.

"Brought up as a gentleman, he was, if ever a man was. Ed'cated at
no end of expense. Went into the Marshal's house once, to try a new piano
for him. Played it, I understand, like one o'clock—beautiful! As to languages
—speaks anything. We've had a Frenchman here in his time, and it's my

opinion he knowed more French than the Frenchman did. We've had an Italian here in his time, and he shut *him* up in about half a minute. You'll find some characters behind other locks, I don't say you won't; but if you want the top sawyer, in such respects as I've mentioned, you must come to the Marshalsea."

When his youngest child was eight years old, his wife, who had long been languishing away—of her own inherent weakness, not that she retained any greater sensitiveness as to her place of abode than he did—went upon a visit to a poor friend and old nurse in the country, and died there. He remained shut up in his room for a fortnight afterwards; and an attorney's clerk, who was going through the Insolvent Court, engrossed an address of condolence to him, which looked like a Lease, and which all the prisoners signed. When he appeared again, he was greyer (he had soon begun to turn grey); and the turnkey noticed that his hands went often to his trembling lips again, as they had used to do when he first came in. But he got pretty well over it in a month or two; and in the meantime the children played about the yard as regularly as ever, but in black.

Then Mrs. Bangham, long popular medium of communication with the outer world, began to be infirm, and to be found oftener than usual comatose on pavements, with her basket of purchases spilt, and the change of her clients ninepence short. His son began to supersede Mrs. Bangham, and to execute commissions in a knowing manner, and to be of the prison prisonous and of the streets streety.

Time went on, and the turnkey began to fail. His chest swelled, and his legs got weak, and he was short of breath. The well-worn wooden stool was "beyond him," he complained. He sat in an arm-chair with a cushion, and sometimes wheezed so, for minutes together, that he couldn't turn the key. When he was overpowered by these fits, the debtor often turned it for him.

"You and me," said the turnkey, one snowy winter's night, when the Lodge, with a bright fire in it, was pretty full of company, "is the oldest inhabitants. I wasn't here myself, above seven year before you. I shan't last long. When I'm off the lock for good and all, you'll be the Father of the Marshalsea."

The turnkey went off the lock of this world, next day. His words were remembered and repeated; and tradition afterwards handed down from generation to generation—a Marshalsea generation might be calculated as about three months—that the shabby old debtor with the soft manner and the white hair, was the Father of the Marshalsea.

And he grew to be proud of the title. If any impostor had arisen to claim it, he would have shed tears in resentment of the attempt to deprive him of his rights. A disposition began to be perceived in him, to exaggerate the number of years he had been there; it was generally understood that you must deduct a few from his account; he was vain, the fleeting generations of debtors said.

All new comers were presented to him. He was punctilious in the exaction of this ceremony. The wits would perform the office of introduction with overcharged pomp and politeness, but they could not easily overstep his sense of its gravity. He received them in his poor room (he disliked an introduction in the mere yard, as informal—a thing that might happen to anybody), with a kind of bowed-down beneficence. They were welcome to the Marshalsea, he would tell them. Yes, he was the Father of the place. So the world was kind enough to call him; and so he was, if more than twenty years of residence gave him a claim to the title. It looked small at first, but there was very good company there—among a mixture —necessarily a mixture—and very good air.

It became a not unusual circumstance for letters to be put under his door at night, enclosing half-a-crown, two half-crowns, now and then at long intervals even half-a-sovereign, for the Father of the Marshalsea. "With the compliments of a collegian taking leave." He received the gifts as tributes, from admirers, to a public character. Sometimes these correspondents assumed facetious names, as the Brick, Bellows, Old Gooseberry, Wide Awake, Snooks, Mops, Cutaway, the Dogs-meat Man; but he considered this in bad taste, and was always a little hurt by it.

In the fulness of time, this correspondence showing signs of wearing out, and seeming to require an effort on the part of the correspondents to which in the hurried circumstances of departure many of them might not be equal, he established the custom of attending collegians of a certain standing, to the gate, and taking leave of them there. The collegian under treatment, after shaking hands, would occasionally stop to wrap up something in a bit of paper, and would come back again, calling "Hi!"

He would look round surprised. "Me?" he would say, with a smile.

By this time the collegian would be up with him, and he would paternally add, "What have you forgotten? What can I do for you?"

"I forgot to leave this," the collegian would usually return, "for the Father of the Marshalsea."

"My good sir," he would rejoin, "he is infinitely obliged to you." But, to the last, the irresolute hand of old would remain in the pocket into which he had slipped the money, during two or three turns about the yard, lest the transaction should be too conspicuous to the general body of collegians.

One afternoon he had been doing the honors of the place to a rather large party of collegians, who happened to be going out, when, as he was coming back, he encountered one from the poor side who had been taken in execution for a small sum a week before, had "settled" in the course of that afternoon, and was going out too. The man was a mere Plasterer, in his working dress; had his wife with him, and a bundle; and was in high spirits.

"God bless you, sir," he said in passing.

"And you," benignantly returned the Father of the Marshalsea.

They were pretty far divided, going their several ways, when the

Plasterer called out, "I say!—sir!" and came back to him.

"It an't much," said the Plasterer, putting a little pile of halfpence in his hand, "but it's well meant."

The Father of the Marshalsea had never been offered tribute in copper yet. His children often had, and with his perfect acquiescence it had gone into the common purse, to buy meat that he had eaten, and drink that he had drunk; but fustian splashed with white lime, bestowing halfpence on him, front to front, was new.

"How dare you!" he said to the man, and feebly burst into tears.

The Plasterer turned him towards the wall, that his face might not be seen; and the action was so delicate, and the man was so penetrated with repentance, and asked pardon so honestly, that he could make him no less acknowledgment than, "I know you meant it kindly. Say no more."

"Bless your soul, sir," urged the Plasterer, "I did indeed. I'd do more by you than the rest of 'em do, I fancy."

"What would you do?" he asked.

"I'd come back to see you, after I was let out."

"Give me the money again," said the other, eagerly, "and I'll keep it, and never spend it. Thank you for it, thank you! I shall see you again?"

"If I live a week you shall."

They shook hands and parted. The collegians, assembled in Symposium in the Snuggery that night, marvelled what had happened to their Father; he walked so late in the shadows of the yard, and seemed so downcast.

CHAPTER VII

THE CHILD OF THE MARSHALSEA

THE baby whose first draught of air had been tinctured with Doctor Haggage's brandy, was handed down among the generations of collegians, like the tradition of their common parent. In the earlier stages of her existence, she was handed down in a literal and prosaic sense; it being almost a part of the entrance footing of every new collegian to nurse the child who had been born in the college.

"By rights," remarked the turnkey, when she was first shown to him, "I ought to be her godfather."

The debtor irresolutely thought of it for a minute, and said, "Perhaps you wouldn't object to really being her godfather?"

"Oh! *I* don't object," replied the turnkey, "if you don't."

Thus it came to pass that she was christened one Sunday afternoon, when the turnkey, being relieved, was off the lock; and that the turnkey went up to the font of Saint George's church, and promised and vowed and renounced on her behalf, as he himself related when he came back, "like a good 'un."

This invested the turnkey with a new proprietary share in the child, over and above his former official one. When she began to walk and talk, he became fond of her; bought a little arm-chair and stood it by the high fender of the lodge fireplace; liked to have her company when he was on the lock; and used to bribe her with cheap toys to come and talk to him. The child, for her part, soon grew so fond of the turnkey, that she would come climbing up the lodge-steps of her own accord at all hours of the day. When she fell asleep in the little arm-chair by the high fender, the turnkey would cover her with his pocket handkerchief; and when she sat in it dressing and undressing a doll—which soon came to be unlike dolls on the other side of the lock, and to bear a horrible family resemblance to Mrs. Bangham—he would contemplate her from the top of his stool, with exceeding gentleness. Witnessing these things, the collegians would express an opinion that the turnkey, who was a bachelor, had been cut out by nature for a family man. But the turnkey thanked them, and said, "No, on the whole it was enough for him to see other people's children there."

At what period of her early life, the little creature began to perceive that it was not the habit of all the world to live locked up in narrow yards surrounded by high walls with spikes at the top, would be a difficult question to settle. But she was a very, very, little creature indeed, when she had somehow gained the knowledge, that her clasp of her father's hand was to be always loosened at the door which the great key opened; and that while her own light steps were free to pass beyond it, his feet must never cross that line. A pitiful and plaintive look, with which she had begun to regard him when she was still extremely young, was perhaps a part of this discovery.

With a pitiful and plaintive look for everything indeed, but with something in it for only him that was like protection, this Child of the Marshalsea and child of the Father of the Marshalsea, sat by her friend the turnkey in the Lodge, kept the family room, or wandered about the prison-yard, for the first eight years of her life. With a pitiful and plaintive look for her wayward sister; for her idle brother; for the high blank walls; for the faded crowd they shut in; for the games of the prison children as they whooped and ran, and played at hide and seek, and made the iron bars of the inner gateway "Home."

Wistful and wondering, she would sit in summer weather by the high fender in the Lodge, looking up at the sky through the barred window, until bars of light would arise, when she turned her eyes away, between her and her friend, and she would see him through a grating, too.

"Thinking of the fields," the turnkey said once, after watching her, "ain't you?"

"Where are they?" she enquired.

"Why, they're—over there, my dear," said the turnkey, with a vague flourish of his key. "Just about there."

"Does anybody open them, and shut them? Are they locked?"

The turnkey was discomfited. "Well!" he said. "Not in general."

"Are they very pretty, Bob?" She called him Bob, by his own particular request and instruction.

"Lovely. Full of flowers. There's buttercups, and there's daisies, and there's"—the turnkey hesitated, being short of floral nomenclature—"there's dandelions, and all manner of games."

"Is it very pleasant to be there, Bob?"

"Prime," said the turnkey.

"Was father ever there?"

"Hem!" coughed the turnkey. "Oh yes, he was there, sometimes."

"Is he sorry not to be there now?"

"N—not particular," said the turnkey.

"Nor any of the people?" she asked, glancing at the listless crowd within. "O are you quite sure and certain, Bob?"

At this difficult point of the conversation Bob gave in, and changed the subject to hard-bake: always his last resource when he found his little friend getting him into a political, social, or theological corner. But this was the origin of a series of Sunday excursions that these two curious companions made together. They used to issue from the Lodge on alternate Sunday afternoons with great gravity, bound for some meadows or green lanes that had been elaborately appointed by the turnkey in the course of the week; and there she picked grass and flowers to bring home, while he smoked his pipe. Afterwards, there were tea-gardens, shrimps, ale, and other delicacies; and then they would come back hand in hand, unless she was more than usually tired, and had fallen asleep on his shoulder.

In those early days, the turnkey first began profoundly to consider a question which cost him so much mental labor, that it remained undetermined on the day of his death. He decided to will and bequeath his little property of savings to his godchild, and the point arose how could it be so "tied up" as that only she should have the benefit of it? His experience on the lock gave him such an acute perception of the enormous difficulty of "tying up" money with any approach to tightness, and contrariwise of the remarkable ease with which it got loose, that through a series of years he regularly propounded this knotty point to every new insolvent agent and other professional gentleman who passed in and out.

"Supposing," he would say, stating the case with his key, on the professional gentleman's waistcoat; "supposing a man wanted to leave his property to a young female, and wanted to tie it up so that nobody else should ever be able to make a grab at it; how would you tie up that property?"

"Settle it strictly on herself," the professional gentleman would complacently answer.

"But look here," quoth the turnkey. "Supposing she had, say a brother, say a father, say a husband, who would be likely to make a grab at that property when she came into it—how about that?"

"It would be settled on herself, and they would have no more legal claim on it than you," would be the professional answer.

"Stop a bit," said the turnkey. "Supposing she was tender-hearted, and they came over her. Where's your law for tying it up then?"

The deepest character whom the turnkey sounded, was unable to produce his law for tying such a knot as that. So, the turnkey thought about it all his life, and died intestate after all.

But that was long afterwards, when his god-daughter was past sixteen. The first half of that space of her life was only just accomplished, when her pitiful and plaintive look saw her father a widower. From that time the protection that her wondering eyes had expressed towards him, became embodied in action, and the Child of the Marshalsea took upon herself a new relation towards the Father.

At first, such a baby could do little more than sit with him, deserting her livelier place by the high fender, and quietly watching him. But this made her so far necessary to him that he became accustomed to her, and began to be sensible of missing her when she was not there. Through this little gate, she passed out of childhood into the care-laden world.

What her pitiful look saw, at that early time, in her father, in her sister, in her brother, in the jail; how much, or how little of the wretched truth it pleased God to make visible to her; lies hidden with many mysteries. It is enough that she was inspired to be something which was not what the rest were, and to be that something, different and laborious, for the sake of the rest. Inspired? Yes. Shall we speak of the inspiration of a poet or a priest, and not of the heart impelled by love and self-devotion to the lowliest work in the lowliest way of life!

With no earthly friend to help her, or so much as to see her, but the one so strangely assorted; with no knowledge even of the common daily tone and habits of the common members of the free community who are not shut up in prisons; born and bred, in a social condition, false even with a reference to the falsest condition outside the walls; drinking from infancy of a well whose waters had their own peculiar stain, their own unwholesome and unnatural taste; the Child of the Marshalsea began her womanly life.

No matter through what mistakes and discouragements, what ridicule (not unkindly meant, but deeply felt) of her youth and little figure, what humble consciousness of her own babyhood and want of strength, even in the matter of lifting and carrying; through how much weariness and hopelessness, and how many secret tears; she drudged on, until recognised as useful, even indispensable. That time came. She took the place of eldest of the three, in all things but precedence; was the head of the fallen family; and bore, in her own heart, its anxieties and shames.

At thirteen, she could read and keep accounts—that is, could put down in words and figures how much the bare necessaries that they wanted would cost, and how much less they had to buy them with. She had been, by snatches of a few weeks at a time, to an evening school outside, and got her sister and brother sent to day-schools by desultory starts, during three or four years. There was no instruction for any of them at home; but she knew well—no one better—that a man so broken as to be the Father of the Marshalsea, could be no father to his own children.

To these scanty means of improvement, she added another of her own contriving. Once, among the heterogeneous crowd of inmates there appeared a dancing-master. Her sister had a great desire to learn the dancing-master's art, and seemed to have a taste that way. At thirteen years old, the Child of the Marshalsea presented herself to the dancing-master, with a little bag in her hand and preferred her humble petition.

"If you please, I was born here, sir."

"Oh! You are the young lady, are you?" said the dancing-master, surveying the small figure and uplifted face.

"Yes, sir."

"And what can I do for you?" said the dancing-master.

"Nothing for me, sir, thank you," anxiously undrawing the strings of the little bag; "but if, while you stay here, you could be so kind as to teach my sister cheap—"

"My child, I'll teach her for nothing," said the dancing-master, shutting up the bag. He was as good-natured a dancing-master as ever danced to the Insolvent Court, and he kept his word. The sister was so apt a pupil, and the dancing-master had such abundant leisure to bestow upon her (for it took him a matter of ten weeks to set to his creditors, lead off, turn the Commissioners, and right and left back to his professional pursuits), that wonderful progress was made. Indeed the dancing-master was so proud of it, and so wishful to display it before he left, to a few select friends among the collegians, that at six o'clock on a certain fine morning a minuet de la cour came off in the yard—the college-rooms being of too confined proportions for the purpose—in which so much ground was covered, and the steps were so conscientiously executed, that the dancing-master, having to play the kit besides, was thoroughly blown.

The success of this beginning, which led to the dancing-master's continuing his instruction after his release, emboldened the poor child to try again. She watched and waited months, for a seamstress. In the fulness of time a milliner came in, and to her she repaired on her own behalf.

"I beg your pardon, ma'am," she said, looking timidly round the door of the milliner whom she found in tears and in bed; "but I was born here."

Everybody seemed to hear of her as soon as they arrived; for the milliner sat up in bed, drying her eyes, and said, just as the dancing-master had said:

"Oh! *You* are the child, are you?"

"Yes, ma'am."

"I am sorry I haven't got anything for you," said the milliner, shaking her head.

"It's not that, ma'am. If you please I want to learn needlework."

"Why should you do that," returned the milliner, "with me before you? It has not done me much good."

"Nothing—whatever it is—seems to have done anybody much good who comes here," she returned in all simplicity; "but I want to learn, just the same."

"I am afraid you are so weak, you see," the milliner objected.

"I don't think I am weak, ma'am."

"And you are so very, very, little, you see," the milliner objected.

"Yes, I am afraid I am very little indeed," returned the Child of the Marshalsea; and so began to sob over that unfortunate defect of hers, which came so often in her way. The milliner—who was not morose or hard-hearted, only newly insolvent—was touched, took her in hand with good-will, found her the most patient and earnest of pupils, and made her a cunning workwoman in course of time.

In course of time, and in the very self-same course of time, the Father of the Marshalsea gradually developed a new flower of character. The more Fatherly he grew as to the Marshalsea, and the more dependant he became on the contributions of his changing family, the greater stand he made by his forlorn gentility. With the same hand that had pocketed a collegian's half-crown half an hour ago, he would wipe away the tears that streamed over his cheeks if any reference were made to his daughters' earning their bread. So, over and above her other daily cares, the Child of the Marshalsea had always upon her, the care of preserving the genteel fiction that they were all idle beggars together.

The sister became a dancer. There was a ruined uncle in the family group—ruined by his brother, the Father of the Marshalsea, and knowing no more how than his ruiner did, but accepting the fact as an inevitable certainty—on whom her protection devolved. Naturally a retired and simple man, he had shown no particular sense of being ruined, at the time when that calamity fell upon him, further than that he left off washing himself when the shock was announced, and never took to that luxury any more. He had been a very indifferent musical amateur in his better days; and when he fell with his brother, resorted for support to playing a clarionet as dirty as himself in a small Theatre Orchestra. It was the theatre in which his niece became a dancer; he had been a fixture there a long time when she took her poor station in it; and he accepted the task of serving as her escort and guardian, just as he would have accepted an illness, a legacy, a feast, starvation—anything but soap.

To enable this girl to earn her few weekly shillings, it was necessary for the Child of the Marshalsea to go through an elaborate form with the Father.

"Fanny is not going to live with us, just now, father. She will be here a good deal in the day, but she is going to live outside with uncle."

"You surprise me. Why?"

"I think uncle wants a companion, father. He should be attended to, and looked after."

"A companion? He passes much of his time here. And you attend to him and look after him, Amy, a great deal more than ever your sister will. You all go out so much; you all go out so much."

This was to keep up the ceremony and pretence of his having no idea that Amy herself went out by the day to work.

"But we are always very glad to come home, father; now, are we not? And as to Fanny, perhaps besides keeping uncle company and taking care of him, it may be as well for her not quite to live here, always. She was not born here as I was, you know, father."

"Well, Amy, well. I don't quite follow you, but it's natural I suppose that Fanny should prefer to be outside, and even that you often should, too. So, you and Fanny and your uncle, my dear, shall have your own way. Good, good. I'll not meddle; don't mind me."

To get her brother out of the prison; out of the succession to Mrs. Bangham in executing commissions, and out of the slang interchange with very doubtful companions, consequent upon both; was her hardest task. At eighteen he would have dragged on from hand to mouth, from hour to hour, from penny to penny, until eighty. Nobody got into the prison from whom he derived anything useful or good, and she could find no patron for him but her old friend and godfather.

"Dear Bob," said she, "what is to become of poor Tip?" His name was Edward, and Ted had been transformed into Tip, within the walls.

The turnkey had strong private opinions as to what would become of poor Tip, and had even gone so far with the view of averting their fulfilment, as to sound Tip in reference to the expediency of running away and going to serve his country. But, Tip had thanked him, and said he didn't seem to care for his country.

"Well my dear," said the turnkey, "something ought to be done with him. Suppose I try and get him into the law?"

"That would be so good of you, Bob!"

The turnkey had now two points to put to the professional gentlemen as they passed in and out. He put this second one so perseveringly, that a stool and twelve shillings a week were at last found for Tip in the office of an attorney in a great National Palladium called the Palace Court; at that time one of a considerable list of everlasting bulwarks to the dignity and safety of Albion, whose places know them no more.

Tip languished in Clifford's Inn for six months, and at the expiration of that term, sauntered back one evening with his hands in his pockets, and incidentally observed to his sister that he was not going back again.

"Not going back again?" said the poor little anxious Child of the Marshalsea, always calculating and planning for Tip, in the front rank of her charges.

"I am so tired of it," said Tip, "that I have cut it."

Tip tired of everything. With intervals of Marshalsea lounging, and Mrs. Bangham succession, his small second mother, aided by her trusty friend, got him into a warehouse, into a market garden, into the hop trade, into the law again, into an auctioneer's, into a brewery, into a stockbroker's, into the law again, into a coach office, into a waggon office, into the law again, into a general dealer's, into a distillery, into the law again, into a wool house, into a dry goods house, into the Billingsgate trade, into the foreign fruit trade, and into the docks. But whatever Tip went into, he came out of tired, announcing that he had cut it. Wherever he went, this foredoomed Tip appeared to take the prison walls with him, and to set them up in such trade or calling; and to prowl about within their narrow limits in the old slip-shod, purposeless, down-at-heel way; until the real immoveable Marshalsea walls asserted their fascination over him, and brought him back.

Nevertheless, the brave little creature did so fix her heart on her brother's rescue, that while he was ringing out these doleful changes, she pinched and scraped enough together to ship him for Canada. When he was tired of nothing to do, and disposed in its turn to cut even that, he graciously consented to go to Canada. And there was grief in her bosom over parting with him, and joy in the hope of his being put in a straight course at last.

"God bless you, dear Tip. Don't be too proud to come and see us, when you have made your fortune."

"All right!" said Tip, and went.

But not all the way to Canada; in fact, not further than Liverpool. After making the voyage to that port from London, he found himself so strongly impelled to cut the vessel, that he resolved to walk back again. Carrying out which intention, he presented himself before her at the expiration of a month, in rags, without shoes, and much more tired than ever.

At length, after another interval of successorship to Mrs. Bangham, he found a pursuit for himself, and announced it.

"Amy, I have got a situation."

"Have you really and truly, Tip?"

"All right. I shall do now. You needn't look anxious about me any more, old girl."

"What is it, Tip?"

"Why, you know Slingo by sight?"

"Not the man they call the dealer?"

"That's the chap. He'll be out on Monday, and he's going to give me a berth."

"What is he a dealer in, Tip?"

"Horses. All right! I shall do now, Amy."

She lost sight of him for months afterwards, and only heard from him once. A whisper passed among the elder collegians that he had been seen at a mock auction in Moorfields, pretending to buy plated articles for massive silver, and paying for them with the greatest liberality in bank notes; but it never reached her ears. One evening she was alone at work—standing up at the window, to save the twilight lingering above the wall—when he opened the door and walked in.

She kissed and welcomed him; but was afraid to ask him any question. He saw how anxious and timid she was, and appeared sorry.

"I am afraid, Amy, you'll be vexed this time. Upon my life I am!"

"I am very sorry to hear you say so, Tip. Have you come back?"

"Why—yes."

"Not expecting this time that what you had found would answer very well, I am less surprised and sorry than I might have been, Tip."

"Ah! But that's not the worst of it."

"Not the worst of it?"

"Don't look so startled. No, Amy, not the worst of it. I have come back, you see; but—*don't* look so startled—I have come back in what I may call a new way. I am off the volunteer list altogether. I am in now, as one of the regulars."

"Oh! Don't say you are a prisoner, Tip! Don't, don't!"

"Well, I don't want to say it," he returned in a reluctant tone; "but if you can't understand me without my saying it, what am I to do? I am in for forty pound odd."

For the first time in all those years, she sunk under her cares. She cried, with her clasped hands lifted above her head, that it would kill their father if he ever knew it; and fell down at Tip's graceless feet.

It was easier for Tip to bring her to her senses, than for her to bring *him* to understand that the Father of the Marshalsea would be beside himself if he knew the truth. The thing was incomprehensible to Tip, and altogether a fanciful notion. He yielded to it in that light only, when he submitted to her entreaties, backed by those of his uncle and sister. There was no want of precedent for his return; it was accounted for to the father in the usual way; and the collegians, with a better comprehension of the pious fraud than Tip, supported it loyally.

This was the life, and this the history, of the Child of the Marshalsea, at twenty-two. With a still surviving attachment to the one miserable yard and block of houses as her birthplace and home, she passed to and fro in it shrinkingly now, with a womanly consciousness that she was pointed out to every one. Since she had begun to work beyond the walls, she had found it necessary to conceal where she lived, and to come and go as secretly as she could, between the free city and the iron gates, outside of which she had never slept in her life. Her original timidity had grown with this concealment, and her light step and her little figure shunned the thronged streets while they passed along them.

Worldly wise in hard and poor necessities, she was innocent in all things else. Innocent, in the mist through which she saw her father, and the prison, and the turbid living river that flowed through it and flowed on.

This was the life, and this the history, of Little Dorrit; now going home upon a dull September evening, observed at a distance by Arthur Clennam. This was the life, and this the history, of Little Dorrit; turning at the end of London Bridge, recrossing it, going back again, passing on to Saint George's church, turning back suddenly once more, and flitting in at the open outer gate and little courtyard of the Marshalsea.

CHAPTER VIII

THE LOCK

ARTHUR CLENNAM stood in the street, waiting to ask some passer-by what place that was. He suffered a few people to pass him in whose faces there was no encouragement to make the enquiry, and still stood pausing in the street, when an old man came up and turned into the courtyard.

He stooped a good deal, and plodded along in a slow preoccupied manner, which made the bustling London thoroughfares no very safe resort for him. He was dirtily and meanly dressed, in a threadbare coat, once blue, reaching to his ankles and buttoned to his chin, where it vanished in the pale ghost of a velvet collar. A piece of red cloth with which that phantom had been stiffened in its lifetime was now laid bare, and poked itself up, at the back of the old man's neck, into a confusion of grey hair and rusty stock and buckle which altogether nearly poked his hat off. A greasy hat it was, and a napless; impending over his eyes, cracked and crumpled at the brim, and with a wisp of pocket handkerchief dangling out below it. His trousers were so long and loose, and his shoes so clumsy and large, that he shuffled like an elephant; though how much of this was gait, and how much trailing cloth and leather, no one could have told. Under one arm he carried a limp and worn-out case, containing some wind instrument; in the same hand he had a pennyworth of snuff in a little packet of whitey-brown paper, from which he slowly comforted his poor old blue nose with a lengthened-out pinch, as Arthur Clennam looked at him.

To this old man, crossing the courtyard, he preferred his enquiry, touching him on the shoulder. The old man stopped and looked round, with the expression in his weak grey eyes of one whose thoughts had been far off, and who was a little dull of hearing also.

"Pray, sir," said Arthur, repeating his question, "what is this place?"

"Aye! This place?" returned the old man, staying his pinch of snuff on its road, and pointing at the place without looking at it. "This is the Marshalsea, sir."

"The debtors' prison?"

"Sir," said the old man, with the air of deeming it not quite necessary to insist upon that designation, "the debtors' prison."

He turned himself about, and went on.

"I beg your pardon," said Arthur, stopping him once more, "but will you allow me to ask you another question? Can any one go in here?"

"Any one can *go in*," replied the old man; plainly adding by the significance of his emphasis, "but it is not every one who can go out."

"Pardon me once more. Are you familiar with the place?"

"Sir," returned the old man, squeezing his little packet of snuff in his hand, and turning upon his interrogator as if such questions hurt him, "I am."

"I beg you to excuse me. I am not impertinently curious, but have a good object. Do you know the name of Dorrit here?"

"My name, sir," replied the old man most unexpectedly, "is Dorrit."

Arthur pulled off his hat to him. "Grant me the favor of half a dozen words. I was wholly unprepared for your announcement, and hope that assurance is my sufficient apology for having taken the liberty of addressing you. I have recently come home to England after a long absence. I have seen at my mother's—Mrs. Clennam in the city—a young woman working at her needle, whom I have only heard addressed or spoken of as Little Dorrit. I have felt sincerely interested in her, and have had a great desire to know something more about her. I saw her, not a minute before you came up, pass in at that door."

The old man looked at him attentively. "Are you a sailor, sir?" he asked. He seemed a little disappointed by the shake of the head that replied to him. "Not a sailor? I judged from your sunburnt face that you might be. Are you in earnest, sir?"

"I do assure you that I am, and do entreat you to believe that I am, in plain earnest."

"I know very little of the world, sir," returned the other, who had a weak and quavering voice. "I am merely passing on, like the shadow over the sun-dial. It would be worth no man's while to mislead me; it would really be too easy—too poor a success, to yield any satisfaction. The young woman whom you saw go in here is my brother's child. My brother is William Dorrit; I am Frederick. You say you have seen her at your mother's (I know your mother befriends her), you have felt an interest in her, and you wish to know what she does here. Come and see."

He went on again, and Arthur accompanied him.

"My brother," said the old man, pausing on the step, and slowly facing round again, "has been here many years; and much that happens even among ourselves, out of doors, is kept from him for reasons that I needn't enter upon now. Be so good as to say nothing of my niece's working at her needle. Be so good as to say nothing that goes beyond what is said among us. If you keep within our bounds, you cannot well be wrong. Now! Come and see."

Arthur followed him down a narrow entry, at the end of which a key was turned, and a strong door was opened from within. It admitted them into a lodge or lobby, across which they passed, and so through another door and a grating into the prison. The old man always plodding on before, turned round, in his slow, stiff, stooping manner, when they came to the turnkey on duty, as if to present his companion. The turnkey nodded; and the companion passed in without being asked whom he wanted.

The night was dark; and the prison lamps in the yard, and the candles in the prison windows faintly shining behind many sorts of wry old curtain and blind, had not the air of making it lighter. A few people loitered about, but the greater part of the population was within doors. The old man taking the right-hand side of the yard, turned in at the third or fourth doorway, and began to ascend the stairs. "They are rather dark, sir, but you will not find anything in the way."

He paused for a moment before opening a door on the second story. He had no sooner turned the handle, than the visitor saw Little Dorrit, and saw the reason of her setting so much store by dining alone.

She had brought the meat home that she should have eaten herself, and was already warming it on a gridiron over the fire, for her father, clad in an old grey gown and a black cap, awaiting his supper at the table. A clean cloth was spread before him, with knife, fork, and spoon, salt-cellar, pepper-box, glass, and pewter ale-pot. Such zests as his particular little phial of cayenne pepper, and his pennyworth of pickles in a saucer, were not wanting.

She started, coloured deeply, and turned white. The visitor, more with his eyes than by the slight impulsive motion of his hand, entreated her to be reassured and to trust him.

"I found this gentleman," said the uncle, "—Mr. Clennam, William, son of Amy's friend—at the outer gate, wishful, as he was going by, of paying his respects, but hesitating whether to come in or not. This is my brother William, sir."

"I hope," said Arthur, very doubtful what to say, "that my respect for your daughter may explain and justify my desire to be presented to you, sir."

"Mr. Clennam," returned the other, rising, taking his cap off in the flat of his hand, and so holding it, ready to put on again, "you do me honor.

You are welcome, sir." With a low bow. "Frederick, a chair. Pray sit down, Mr. Clennam."

He put his black cap on again as he had taken it off, and resumed his own seat. There was a wonderful air of benignity and patronage in his manner. These were the ceremonies with which he received the collegians.

"You are welcome to the Marshalsea, sir. I have welcomed many gentlemen to these walls. Perhaps you are aware—my daughter Amy may have mentioned—that I am the Father of this place."

"I—so I have understood," said Arthur, dashing at the assertion.

"You know, I dare say, that my daughter Amy was born here. A good girl, sir, a dear girl, and long a comfort and support to me. Amy, my dear, put the dish on; Mr. Clennam will excuse the primitive customs to which we are reduced here. Is it a compliment to ask you if you would do me the honor, sir, to—"

"Thank you," returned Arthur. "Not a morsel."

He felt himself quite lost in wonder at the manner of the man, and that the probability of his daughter's having had a reserve as to her family history, should be so far out of his mind.

She filled his glass, put all the little matters on the table ready to his hand, and then sat beside him while he ate his supper. Evidently in observance of their nightly custom, she put some bread before herself, and touched his glass with her lips; but Arthur saw she was troubled and took nothing. Her look at her father, half admiring him and proud of him, half-ashamed for him, all devoted and loving, went to his inmost heart.

The Father of the Marshalsea condescended towards his brother as an amiable, well-meaning man; a private character, who had not arrived at distinction. "Frederick," said he, "you and Fanny sup at your lodgings to-night, I know. What have you done with Fanny, Frederick?"

"She is walking with Tip."

"Tip—as you may know—is my son, Mr. Clennam. He has been a little wild, and difficult to settle, but his introduction to the world was rather"— he shrugged his shoulders with a faint sigh, and looked round the room —"a little adverse. Your first visit here, sir?"

"My first."

"You could hardly have been here since your boyhood without my knowledge. It very seldom happens that anybody—of any pretensions— any pretensions—comes here without being presented to me."

"As many as forty or fifty in a day have been introduced to my brother," said Frederick, faintly lighting up with a ray of pride.

"Yes!" the Father of the Marshalsea assented. "We have even exceeded that number. On a fine Sunday in term time, it is quite a Levee—quite a Levee. Amy, my dear, I have been trying half the day to remember the name of the gentleman from Camberwell who was introduced to me last Christmas week, by that agreeable coal-merchant who was remanded for six months."

"I don't remember his name, father."

"Frederick, do *you* remember his name?"

Frederick doubted if he had ever heard it. No one could doubt that Frederick was the last person upon earth to put such a question to, with any hope of information.

"I mean," said his brother, "the gentleman who did that handsome action with so much delicacy. Ha! Tush! The name has quite escaped me. Mr. Clennam, as I have happened to mention a handsome and delicate action, you may like, perhaps, to know what it was."

"Very much," said Arthur, withdrawing his eyes from the delicate head beginning to droop, and the pale face with a new solicitude stealing over it.

"It is so generous, and shows so much fine feeling, that it is almost a duty to mention it. I said at the time that I always would mention it on every suitable occasion, without regard to personal sensitiveness. A—well —a—it's of no use to disguise the fact—you must know, Mr. Clennam, that it does sometimes occur that people who come here, desire to offer some little—Testimonial—to the Father of the place."

To see her hand upon his arm in mute entreaty half repressed, and her timid little shrinking figure turning away, was to see a sad, sad sight.

"Sometimes," he went on in a low, soft voice, agitated, and clearing his throat every now and then; "sometimes—hem—it takes one shape and sometimes another; but it is generally—ha—Money. And it is, I cannot but confess it, it is too often—hem—acceptable. This gentleman that I refer to, was presented to me, Mr. Clennam, in a manner highly gratifying to my feelings, and conversed not only with great politeness, but with great—ahem—information." All this time, though he had finished his supper, he was nervously going about his plate with his knife and fork, as if some of it were still before him. "It appeared from his conversation that he had a garden, though he was delicate of mentioning it at first, as gardens are—hem—are not accessible to me. But it came out, through my admiring a very fine cluster of geranium—beautiful cluster of geranium to be sure— which he had brought from his conservatory. On my taking notice of its rich color, he showed me a piece of paper round it, on which was written 'For the Father of the Marshalsea,' and presented it to me. But this was— hem—not all. He made a particular request, on taking leave, that I would remove the paper in half-an-hour. I—ha—I did so; and I found that it contained—ahem—two guineas. I assure you, Mr. Clennam, I have received—hem—Testimonials in many ways, and of many degrees of value, and they have always been—ha—unfortunately acceptable; but I never was more pleased than with this—ahem—this particular Testimonial."

Arthur was in the act of saying the little he could say on such a theme, when a bell began to ring, and footsteps approached the door. A pretty girl of a far better figure, and much more developed than Little Dorrit, though looking much younger in the face when the two were observed together, stopped in the doorway on seeing a stranger; and a young man who was with her, stopped too.

"Mr. Clennam, Fanny. My eldest daughter and my son, Mr. Clennam. The bell is a signal for visitors to retire, and so they have come to say good night; but there is plenty of time, plenty of time. Girls, Mr. Clennam will excuse any household business you may have together. He knows, I dare say, that I have but one room here."

"I only want my clean dress from Amy, father," said the second girl.

"And I my clothes," said Tip.

Amy opened a drawer in an old piece of furniture that was a chest of drawers above, and a bedstead below, and produced two little bundles, which she handed to her brother and sister. "Mended and made up?" Clennam heard the sister ask in a whisper. To which Amy answered "Yes." He had risen now, and took the opportunity of glancing round the room. The bare walls had been colored green, evidently by an unskilled hand, and were poorly decorated with a few prints. The window was curtained, and the floor carpeted; and there were shelves, and pegs, and other such conveniences, that had accumulated in the course of years. It was a close, confined room, poorly furnished; and the chimney smoked to boot, or the tin screen at the top of the fireplace was superfluous; but constant pains and care had made it neat, and even, after its kind, comfortable.

All the while the bell was ringing, and the uncle was anxious to go. "Come Fanny, come Fanny," he said, with his ragged clarionet-case under his arm; "the lock, child, the lock!"

Fanny bade her father good night, and whisked off airily. Tip had already clattered down-stairs. "Now, Mr. Clennam," said the uncle, looking back as he shuffled out after them, "the lock, sir, the lock."

Mr. Clennam had two things to do before he followed; one, to offer his testimonial to the Father of the Marshalsea, without giving pain to his child; the other to say something to that child, though it were but a word, in explanation of his having come there.

"Allow me," said the Father, "to see you down-stairs."

She had slipped out after the rest, and they were alone. "Not on any account," said the visitor, hurriedly. "Pray allow me to—" chink, chink, chink.

"Mr. Clennam," said the Father, "I am deeply, deeply—" But his visitor had shut up his hand to stop the chinking, and had gone down-stairs with great speed.

He saw no Little Dorrit on his way down, or in the yard. The last two or three stragglers were hurrying to the Lodge, and he was following, when he caught sight of her, in the doorway of the first house from the entrance. He turned back hastily.

"Pray forgive me," he said, "for speaking to you here; pray forgive me

for coming here at all! I followed you to-night. I did so, that I might
endeavour to render you and your family some service. You know the
terms on which I and my mother are, and may not be surprised that I have
preserved our distant relations at her house, lest I should unintentionally
make her jealous, or resentful, or do you any injury in her estimation.
What I have seen here, in this short time, has greatly increased my heartfelt
wish to be a friend to you. It would recompense me for much disappointment if I could hope to gain your confidence."

She was scared at first, but seemed to take courage while he spoke to her.

"You are very good, sir. You speak very earnestly to me. But I—but I
wish you had not watched me."

He understood the emotion with which she said it, to arise in her father's
behalf; and he respected it, and was silent.

"Mrs. Clennam has been of great service to me; I don't know what we
should have done without the employment she has given me; I am afraid
it may not be a good return to become secret with her; I can say no more
to-night, sir. I am sure you mean to be kind to us. Thank you, thank you."

"Let me ask you one question before I leave. Have you known my
mother long?"

"I think two years, sir.—The bell has stopped."

"How did you know her first? Did she send here for you?"

"No. She does not even know that I live here. We have a friend, father
and I—a poor laboring man, but the best of friends—and I wrote out that
I wished to do needlework, and gave his address. And he got what I wrote
out displayed at a few places where it cost nothing, and Mrs. Clennam
found me that way, and sent for me. The gate will be locked, sir!"

She was so tremulous and agitated, and he was so moved by compassion
for her, and by deep interest in her story as it dawned upon him, that he
could scarcely tear himself away. But the stoppage of the bell, and the
quiet in the prison, were a warning to depart; and with a few hurried words
of kindness he left her gliding back to her father.

But he had remained too late. The inner gate was locked, and the Lodge
closed. After a little fruitless knocking with his hand, he was standing there
with the disagreeable conviction upon him that he had to get through the
night, when a voice accosted him from behind.

"Caught, eh?" said the voice. "You won't go home till morning.—
Oh! It's you, is it, Mr. Clennam?"

The voice was Tip's; and they stood looking at one another in the prison-
yard, as it began to rain.

"You've done it," observed Tip; "you must be sharper than that, next
time."

"But you are locked in too," said Arthur.

"I believe I am!" said Tip, sarcastically. "About! But not in your way.
I belong to the shop, only my sister has a theory that our governor must

never know it. I don't see why, myself."

"Can I get any shelter?" asked Arthur. "What had I better do?"

"We had better get hold of Amy, first of all," said Tip, referring any difficulty to her, as a matter of course.

"I would rather walk about all night—it's not much to do—than give that trouble."

"You needn't do that, if you don't mind paying for a bed. If you don't mind paying, they'll make you up one on the Snuggery table, under the circumstances. If you'll come along, I'll introduce you there."

As they passed down the yard, Arthur looked up at the window of the room he had lately left, where the light was still burning. "Yes, sir," said Tip, following his glance. "That's the governor's. She'll sit with him for another hour reading yesterday's paper to him, or something of that sort; and then she'll come out like a little ghost, and vanish away without a sound."

"I don't understand you."

"The governor sleeps up in the room, and she has a lodging at the turnkey's. First house there," said Tip, pointing out the doorway into which she had retired. "First house, sky parlor. She pays twice as much for it as she would for one twice as good outside. But she stands by the governor, poor dear girl, day and night."

This brought them to the tavern-establishment at the upper end of the prison, where the collegians had just vacated their social evening club. The apartment on the ground-floor in which it was held, was the Snuggery in question; the presidential tribune of the chairman, the pewter-pots, glasses, pipes, tobacco-ashes, and general flavor of members, were still as that convivial institution had left them on its adjournment. The Snuggery had two of the qualities popularly held to be essential to grog for ladies, in respect that it was hot and strong; but in the third point of analogy, requiring plenty of it, the Snuggery was defective: being but a cooped-up apartment.

The unaccustomed visitor from outside, naturally assumed everybody here to be prisoners—landlord, waiter, barmaid, potboy, and all. Whether they were or not, did not appear; but they all had a weedy look. The keeper of a chandler's shop in a front parlor, who took in gentlemen boarders, lent his assistance in making the bed. He had been a tailor in his time, and had kept a phaeton, he said. He boasted that he stood up litigiously for the interests of the college; and he had undefined and undefinable ideas that the Marshal intercepted a "Fund," which ought to come to the collegians. He liked to believe this, and always impressed the shadowy grievance on new comers and strangers; though he could not, for his life, have explained what Fund he meant, or how the notion had got rooted in his soul. He had fully convinced himself, notwithstanding, that his own proper share of the Fund was three and ninepence a week; and that in this amount he, as an individual collegian, was swindled by the Marshal, regularly every Monday.

Apparently, he helped to make the bed, that he might not lose an opportunity of stating this case; after which unloading of his mind, and after announcing (as it seemed he always did, without anything coming of it), that he was going to write a letter to the papers and show the Marshal up, he fell into miscellaneous conversation with the rest. It was evident from the general tone of the whole party, that they had come to regard insolvency as the normal state of mankind, and the payment of debts as a disease that occasionally broke out.

In this strange scene, and with these strange spectres flitting about him, Arthur Clennam looked on at the preparations, as if they were part of a dream. Pending which, the long-initiated Tip, with an awful enjoyment of the Snuggery's resources, pointed out the common kitchen fire maintained by subscription of collegians, the boiler for hot water supported in like manner, and other premises generally tending to the deduction that the way to be healthy, wealthy, and wise, was to come to the Marshalsea.

The two tables put together in a corner, were, at length, converted into a very fair bed; and the stranger was left to the Windsor chairs, the presidential tribune, the beery atmosphere, sawdust, pipe-lights, spittoons and repose. But the last item was long, long, long, in linking itself to the rest. The novelty of the place, the coming upon it without preparation, the sense of being locked up, the remembrance of that room up-stairs, of the two brothers, and above all of the retiring childish form, and the face in which he now saw years of insufficient food, if not of want, kept him waking and unhappy.

Speculations, too, bearing the strangest relations towards the prison, but always concerning the prison, ran like nightmares through his mind while he lay awake. Whether coffins were kept ready for people who might die there, where they were kept, how they were kept, where people who died in the prison were buried, how they were taken out, what forms were observed, whether an implacable creditor could arrest the dead? As to escaping, what chances there were of escape? Whether a prisoner could scale the walls with a cord and grapple, how he would descend upon the other side: whether he could alight on a housetop, steal down a staircase, let himself out at a door, and get lost in the crowd? As to Fire in the prison, if one were to break out while he lay there?

And these involuntary starts of fancy were, after all, but the setting of a picture in which three people kept before him. His father, with the stedfast look with which he had died, prophetically darkened forth in the portrait; his mother, with her arm up, warding off his suspicion; Little Dorrit, with her hand on the degraded arm, and her drooping head turned away.

What if his mother had an old reason she well knew for softening to this poor girl! What if the prisoner now sleeping quietly—Heaven grant it!—by the light of the great Day of Judgment should trace back his fall to her. What if any act of hers, and of his father's, should have even remotely brought the grey heads of those two brothers so low!

A swift thought shot into his mind. In that long imprisonment here, and in her own long confinement to her room, did his mother find a balance to be struck? I admit that I was accessory to that man's captivity. I have suffered for it in kind. He has decayed in his prison; I in mine. I have paid the penalty.

When all the other thoughts had faded out, this one held possession of him. When he fell asleep, she came before him in her wheeled chair, warding him off with this justification. When he awoke, and sprang up causelessly frightened, the words were in his ears, as if her voice had slowly spoken them at his pillow, to break his rest: "He withers away in his prison; I wither away in mine; inexorable justice is done; what do I owe on this score!"

END OF No. II

CHAPTER IX

LITTLE MOTHER

THE morning light was in no hurry to climb the prison wall and look in at the snuggery windows; and when it did come, it would have been more welcome if it had come alone, instead of bringing a rush of rain with it. But the equinoctial gales were blowing out at sea, and the impartial south-west wind, in its flight, would not neglect even the narrow Marshalsea. While it roared through the steeple of Saint George's Church, and twirled all the cowls in the neighbourhood, it made a swoop to beat the Southwark smoke into the jail; and, plunging down the chimneys of the few early collegians who were yet lighting their fires, half suffocated them.

Arthur Clennam would have been little disposed to linger in bed, though his bed had been in a more private situation, and less affected by the raking out of yesterday's fire, the kindling of to-day's under the collegiate boiler, the filling of that Spartan vessel at the pump, the sweeping and sawdusting of the common room, and other such preparations. Heartily glad to see the morning, though little rested by the night, he turned out as soon as he could distinguish objects about him, and paced the yard for two heavy hours before the gate was opened.

The walls were so near to one another, and the wild clouds hurried over them so fast, that it gave him a sensation like the beginning of sea-sickness to look up at the gusty sky. The rain, carried aslant by flaws of wind, blackened that side of the central building which he had visited last night, but left a narrow dry trough under the lee of the wall, where he walked up and down among waifs of straw and dust and paper, the waste droppings of the pump, and the stray leaves of yesterday's greens. It was as haggard a view of life as a man need look upon.

Nor was it relieved by any glimpse of the little creature who had brought him there. Perhaps she glided out of her doorway and in at that where her father lived, while his face was turned from both; but he saw nothing of her. It was too early for her brother; to have seen him once, was to have seen enough of him to know that he would be sluggish to leave whatever frowsy bed he occupied at night; so, as Arthur Clennam walked up and down, waiting for the gate to open, he cast about in his mind for future rather than for present means of pursuing his discoveries.

At last the lodge-gate turned, and the turnkey, standing on the step, taking an early comb at his hair, was ready to let him out. With a joyful sense of release he passed through the Lodge, and found himself again in the little outer courtyard where he had spoken to the brother last night.

There was a string of people already straggling in, whom it was not difficult to identify as the nondescript messengers, go-betweens, and errand-bearers of the place. Some of them had been lounging in the rain until the gate should open; others, who had timed their arrival with greater nicety, were coming up now, and passing in with damp whitey-brown paper bags from the grocers, loaves of bread, lumps of butter, eggs, milk, and the like. The shabbiness of these attendants upon shabbiness, the poverty of these insolvent waiters upon insolvency, was a sight to see. Such threadbare coats and trousers, such fusty gowns and shawls, such squashed hats and bonnets, such boots and shoes, such umbrellas and walking-sticks, never were seen in Rag Fair. All of them wore the cast-off clothes of other men and women; were made up of patches and pieces of other people's individuality, and had no sartorial existence of their own proper. Their walk was the walk of a race apart. They had a peculiar way of doggedly slinking round the corner, as if they were eternally going to the pawn-brokers. When they coughed, they coughed like people accustomed to be forgotten on door-steps and in draughty passages, waiting for answers to letters in faded ink, which gave the recipients of those manuscripts great mental disturbance, and no satisfaction. As they eyed the stranger in passing, they eyed him with borrowing eyes—hungry, sharp, speculative as to his softness if they were accredited to him, and the likelihood of his standing something handsome. Mendicity on commission stooped in their high shoulders, shambled in their unsteady legs, buttoned and pinned and darned and dragged their clothes, frayed their button-holes, leaked out of their figures in dirty little ends of tape, and issued from their mouths in alcoholic breathings.

As these people passed him standing still in the courtyard, and one of them turned back to enquire if he could assist him with his services, it came into Arthur Clennam's mind that he would speak to Little Dorrit again before he went away. She would have recovered her first surprise, and might feel easier with him. He asked this member of the fraternity (who had two red herrings in his hand, and a loaf and a blacking-brush under his arm), where was the nearest place to get a cup of coffee at. The nondescript replied in encouraging terms, and brought him to a coffee-shop in the street within a stone's throw.

"Do you know Miss Dorrit?" asked the new client.

The nondescript knew two Miss Dorrits; one who was born inside— That was the one! That was the one? The nondescript had known her many years. In regard of the other Miss Dorrit, the nondescript lodged in the same house with herself and uncle.

This changed the client's half-formed design of remaining at the coffee-shop until the nondescript should bring him word that Little Dorrit had issued forth into the street. He entrusted the nondescript with a confidential message to her, importing that the visitor who had waited on her father last night, begged the favor of a few words with her at her uncle's lodging; he obtained from the same source full directions to the house, which was very near; dismissed the nondescript gratified with half-a-crown; and having hastily refreshed himself at the coffee-shop, repaired with all speed to the clarionet-player's dwelling.

There were so many lodgers in this house, that the door-post seemed to be as full of bell-handles as a cathedral organ is of stops. Doubtful which might be the clarionet-stop, he was considering the point, when a shuttle-cock flew out of the parlor-window, and alighted on his hat. He then observed that in the parlor-window was a blind with the inscription, MR. CRIPPLES'S ACADEMY; also in another line, EVENING TUITION; and behind the blind was a little white-faced boy, with a slice of bread and butter, and a battledore. The window being accessible from the footway, he looked in over the blind, returned the shuttlecock, and put his question.

"Dorrit?" said the little white-faced boy (Master Cripples in fact). "*Mr.* Dorrit? Third bell and one knock."

The pupils of Mr. Cripples appeared to have been making a copy-book of the street door, it was so extensively scribbled over in pencil. The frequency of the inscriptions, "Old Dorrit," and "Dirty Dick," in combination, suggested intentions of personality on the part of Mr. Cripples's pupils. There was ample time to make these observations, before the door was opened by the poor old man himself.

"Ha!" said he, very slowly remembering Arthur, "you were shut in last night?"

"Yes, Mr. Dorrit. I hope to meet your niece here presently."

"Oh!" said he, pondering. "Out of my brother's way? True. Would you come up-stairs and wait for her?"

"Thank you."

Turning himself, as slowly as he turned in his mind whatever he heard or said, he led the way up the narrow stairs. The house was very close, and had an unwholesome smell. The little staircase windows looked in at the back windows of other houses as unwholesome as itself, with poles and lines thrust out of them, on which unsightly linen hung: as if the inhabitants were angling for clothes, and had had some wretched bites not worth attending to. In the back garret—a sickly room, with a turn-up bedstead in it, so hastily and recently turned up that the blankets were boiling over, as it were, and keeping the lid open—a half-finished breakfast of coffee and toast, for two persons, was jumbled down anyhow on a ricketty table.

There was no one there. The old man, mumbling to himself, after some consideration, that Fanny had run away, went to the next room to fetch her back. The visitor, observing that she held the door on the inside, and that when the uncle tried to open it, there was a sharp adjuration of "Don't, stupid!" and an appearance of loose stocking and flannel, concluded that the young lady was in an undress. The uncle, without appearing to come to any conclusion, shuffled in again, sat down in his chair, and began warming his hands at the fire. Not that it was cold, or that he had any waking idea whether it was or not.

"What did you think of my brother, sir ?" he asked, when he, bye and bye, discovered what he was doing, left off, reached over to the chimney-piece, and took his clarionet case down.

"I was glad," said Arthur, very much at a loss, for his thoughts were on the brother before him; "to find him so well and cheerful."

"Ha!" muttered the old man, "Yes, yes, yes, yes, yes!"

Arthur wondered what he could possibly want with the clarionet case. He did not want it at all. He discovered, in due time, that it was not the little paper of snuff (which was also on the chimney-piece), put it back again, took down the snuff instead, and solaced himself with a pinch. He was as feeble, spare, and slow in his pinches as in everything else, but a certain little trickling of enjoyment of them played in the poor worn nerves about the corners of his eyes and mouth.

"Amy, Mr. Clennam. What do you think of her?"

"I am much impressed, Mr. Dorrit, by all that I have seen of her and thought of her."

"My brother would have been quite lost without Amy," he returned. "We should all have been lost without Amy. She is a very good girl, Amy. She does her duty."

Arthur fancied that he heard in these praises, a certain tone of custom which he had heard from the father last night, with an inward protest and feeling of antagonism. It was not that they stinted her praises, or were insensible to what she did for them; but that they were lazily habituated to her, as they were to all the rest of their condition. He fancied that although they had before them, every day, the means of comparison between her and one another and themselves, they regarded her as being in her necessary place; as holding a position towards them all which belonged to her, like her name or her age. He fancied that they viewed her, not as having risen away from the prison atmosphere, but as appertaining to it; as being vaguely what they had a right to expect, and nothing more.

Her uncle resumed his breakfast, and was munching toast sopped in coffee, oblivious of his guest, when the third bell rang. That was Amy, he said, and went down to let her in; leaving the visitor with as vivid a picture on his mind of his begrimed hands, dirt-worn face, and decayed figure, as if he were still drooping in his chair.

She came up after him, in the usual plain dress, and with the usual timid manner. Her lips were a little parted, as if her heart beat faster than usual.

"Mr. Clennam, Amy," said her uncle, "has been expecting you some time."

"I took the liberty of sending you a message."

"I received the message, sir."

"Are you going to my mother's this morning? I think not, for it is past your usual hour."

"Not to-day, sir. I am not wanted to-day."

"Will you allow me to walk a little way in whatever direction you may be going? I can then speak to you as we walk, both without detaining you here, and without intruding longer here myself."

She looked embarrassed, but said, if he pleased. He made a pretence of having mislaid his walking-stick, to give her time to set the bedstead right, to answer her sister's impatient knock at the wall, and to say a word softly to her uncle. Then he found it, and they went down-stairs; she first, he following, the uncle standing at the stair-head, and probably forgetting them before they had reached the ground floor.

Mr. Cripples's pupils, who were by this time coming to school, desisted from their morning recreation of cuffing one another with bags and books, to stare with all the eyes they had at a stranger who had been to see Dirty Dick. They bore the trying spectacle in silence, until the mysterious visitor was at a safe distance; when they burst into pebbles and yells, and likewise into reviling dances, and in all respects buried the pipe of peace with so many savage ceremonies, that if Mr. Cripples had been the chief of the Cripplewayboo tribe with his war-paint on, they could scarcely have done greater justice to their education.

In the midst of this homage, Mr. Arthur Clennam offered his arm to Little Dorrit, and Little Dorrit took it. "Will you go by the Iron Bridge," said he, "where there is an escape from the noise of the street?" Little Dorrit· answered, if he pleased, and presently ventured to hope that he would "not mind" Mr. Cripples's boys, for she had herself received her education, such as it was, in Mr. Cripples's evening academy. He returned, with the best will in the world, that Mr. Cripples's boys were forgiven out of the bottom of his soul. Thus did Cripples unconsciously become a master of the ceremonies between them, and bring them more naturally together than Beau Nash might have done if they had lived in his golden days, and he had alighted from his coach and six for the purpose.

The morning remained squally, and the streets were miserably muddy, but no rain fell as they walked towards the Iron Bridge. The little creature seemed so young in his eyes, that there were moments when he found himself thinking of her, if not speaking to her, as if she were a child. Perhaps he seemed as old in her eyes as she seemed young in his.

"I am sorry to hear you were so inconvenienced last night, sir, as to be locked in. It was very unfortunate."

It was nothing, he returned. He had had a very good bed.

Oh yes! she said quickly; she believed there were excellent beds at the coffee-house. He noticed that the coffee-house was quite a majestic hotel to her, and that she treasured its reputation.

"I believe it is very expensive," said Little Dorrit, "but my father has told me that quite beautiful dinners may be got there. And wine," she added timidly.

"Were you ever there?"

"Oh no! Only into the kitchen, to fetch hot-water."

To think of growing up with a kind of awe upon one as to the luxuries of that superb establishment, the Marshalsea hotel!

"I asked you last night," said Clennam, "how you had become acquainted with my mother. Did you ever hear her name before she sent for you?"

"No, sir."

"Do you think your father ever did?"

"No, sir."

He met her eyes raised to his with so much wonder in them (she was scared when that encounter took place, and shrunk away again), that he felt it necessary to say:

"I have a reason for asking, which I cannot very well explain; but you must, on no account, suppose it to be of a nature to cause you the least alarm or anxiety. Quite the reverse. And you think that at no time of your father's life was my name of Clennam ever familiar to him?"

"No, sir."

He felt, from the tone in which she spoke, that she was glancing up at him with those parted lips; therefore he looked before him, rather than make her heart beat quicker still by embarrassing her afresh.

Thus they emerged upon the Iron Bridge, which was as quiet after the roaring streets, as though it had been open country. The wind blew roughly, the wet squalls came rattling past them, skimming the pools on the road and pavement, and raining them down into the river. The clouds raced on furiously in the lead-colored sky, the smoke and mist raced after them, the dark tide ran fierce and strong in the same direction. Little Dorrit seemed the least, the quietest, and weakest of Heaven's creatures.

"Let me put you in a coach," said Arthur Clennam, very nearly adding, "my poor child."

She hurriedly declined, saying that wet or dry made little difference to her; she was used to go about in all weathers. He knew it to be so, and was touched with more pity; thinking of the slight figure at his side, making its nightly way through the damp, dark, boisterous streets, to such a place of rest.

"You spoke so feelingly to me last night, sir, and I found afterwards that you had been so generous to my father, that I could not resist your message, if it was only to thank you; especially as I wished very much to say to you—" she hesitated and trembled, and tears rose in her eyes, but did not fall.

"To say to me—?"

"That I hope you will not misunderstand my father. Don't judge him, sir, as you would judge others outside the gates. He has been there so long! I never saw him outside, but I can understand that he must have grown different in some things since."

"My thoughts will never be unjust or harsh towards him, believe me."

"Not," she said, with a prouder air, as the misgiving evidently crept upon her that she might seem to be abandoning him, "Not that he has anything to be ashamed of for himself, or that I have anything to be ashamed of for him. He only requires to be understood. I only ask for him that his life may be fairly remembered. All that he said was quite true. It all happened just as he related it. He is very much respected. Everybody who comes in, is glad to know him. He is more courted than any one else. He is far more thought of than the Marshal is."

If ever pride were innocent, it was innocent in Little Dorrit when she grew boastful of her father.

"It is often said that his manners are a true gentleman's, and quite a study. I see none like them in that place, but he is admitted to be superior to all the rest. This is quite as much why they make him presents, as because they know him to be needy. He is not to be blamed for being in need, poor love. Who could be in prison a quarter of a century, and be prosperous!"

What affection in her words, what compassion in her repressed tears, what a great soul of fidelity within her, how true the light that shed false brightness round him!

"If I have found it best to conceal where my home is, it is not because I am ashamed of him. God forbid! Nor am I so much ashamed of the place itself as might be supposed. People are not bad because they come there. I have known numbers of good, persevering, honest people, come there through misfortune. They are almost all kind-hearted to one another. And it would be ungrateful indeed in me, to forget that I have had many quiet, comfortable hours there; that I had an excellent friend there when I was quite a baby, who was very fond of me; that I have been taught there, and have worked there, and have slept soundly there. I think it would be almost cowardly and cruel not to have some little attachment for it, after all this."

She had relieved the faithful fulness of her heart, and modestly said, raising her eyes appealingly to her new friend's, "I did not mean to say so much, nor have I ever but once spoken about this before. But it seems to set it more right than it was last night. I said I wished you had not followed me, sir. I don't wish it so much now, unless you should think—indeed I don't wish it at all, unless I should have spoken so confusedly, that—that you can scarcely understand me, which I am afraid may be the case."

He told her with perfect truth that it was not the case; and putting himself between her and the sharp wind and rain, sheltered her as well as he could.

"I feel permitted now," he said, "to ask you a little more concerning your father. Has he many creditors?"

"Oh! a great number."

"I mean detaining creditors, who keep him where he is?"

"Oh yes! a great number."

"Can you tell me—I can get the information, no doubt, elsewhere, if you cannot—who is the most influential of them?"

Little Dorrit said, after considering a little, that she used to hear long ago of Mr. Tite Barnacle as a man of great power. He was a commissioner, or a board, or a trustee, "or something." He lived in Grosvenor Square, she thought, or very near it. He was under Government—high in the Circumlocution Office. She appeared to have acquired, in her infancy, some awful impression of the might of this formidable Mr. Tite Barnacle of Grosvenor Square, or very near it, and the Circumlocution Office, which quite crushed her when she mentioned him.

"It can do no harm," thought Arthur, "if I see this Mr. Tite Barnacle."

The thought did not present itself so quietly but that her quickness intercepted it. "Ah!" said Little Dorrit, shaking her head with the mild despair of a lifetime. "Many people used to think once of getting my poor father out, but you don't know how hopeless it is."

She forgot to be shy at the moment, in honestly warning him away from the sunken wreck he had a dream of raising; and looked at him with eyes which assuredly, in association with her patient face, her fragile figure, her spare dress, and the wind and rain, did not turn him from his purpose of helping her.

"Even if it could be done," said she—"and it never never can be done now—where could father live, or how could he live? I have often thought that if such a change could come, it might be anything but a service to him now. People might not think so well of him outside as they do there. He might not be so gently dealt with outside, as he is there. He might not be so fit himself for the life outside, as he is for that."

Here for the first time she could not restrain her tears from falling; and
the little thin hands he had watched when they were so busy, trembled as
they clasped each other.

"It would be a new distress to him even to know that I earn a little
money, and that Fanny earns a little money. He is so anxious about us,
you see, feeling helplessly shut up there. Such a good, good father!"

He let the little burst of feeling go by before he spoke. It was soon gone.
She was not accustomed to think of herself, or to trouble any one with her
emotions. He had but glanced away at the piles of city roofs and chimneys
among which the smoke was rolling heavily, and at the wilderness of masts
on the river, and the wilderness of steeples on the shore, indistinctly mixed
together in the stormy haze, when she was again as quiet as if she had been
plying her needle in his mother's room.

"You would be glad to have your brother set at liberty?"

"Oh very, very glad, sir!"

"Well, we will hope for him at least. You told me last night of a friend
you had?"

His name was Plornish, Little Dorrit said.

And where did Plornish live? Plornish lived in Bleeding Heart Yard.
He was "only a plasterer," Little Dorrit said, as a caution to him not to
form high social expectations of Plornish. He lived at the last house in
Bleeding Heart Yard, and his name was over a little gateway.

Arthur took down the address and gave her his. He had now done all
he sought to do for the present, except that he wished to leave her with a
reliance upon him, and to have something like a promise from her that she
would cherish it.

"There is one friend!" he said, putting up his pocket-book. "As I take
you back—you are going back?"

"Oh yes! going straight home."

"As I take you back," the word home jarred upon him, "let me ask you
to persuade yourself that you have another friend. I make no professions,
and say no more."

"You are truly kind to me, sir. I am sure I need no more."

They walked back through the miserable muddy streets, and among the
poor, mean shops, and were jostled by the crowds of dirty hucksters usual to
a poor neighbourhood. There was nothing, by the short way, that was
pleasant to any of the five senses. Yet it was not a common passage through
common rain, and mire, and noise, to Clennam, having this little, slender,
careful creature on his arm. How young she seemed to him, or how old he
to her; or what a secret either to the other, in that beginning of the destined
interweaving of their stories, matters not here. He thought of her having
been born and bred among these scenes, and shrinking through them now,
familiar yet misplaced; he thought of her long acquaintance with the
squalid needs of life, and of her innocence; of her old solicitude for others,

Little Mother

and her few years and her childish aspect.

They were come into the High Street, where the prison stood, when a voice cried, "Little mother, little mother!" Little Dorrit stopping and looking back, an excited figure of a strange kind bounced against them (still crying "little mother"), fell down, and scattered the contents of a large basket, filled with potatoes, in the mud.

"Oh, Maggy," said Little Dorrit, "what a clumsy child you are!"

Maggy was not hurt, but picked herself up immediately, and then began to pick up the potatoes, in which both Little Dorrit and Arthur Clennam helped. Maggy picked up very few potatoes, and a great quantity of mud; but they were all recovered, and deposited in the basket. Maggy then smeared her muddy face with her shawl, and presenting it to Mr. Clennam as a type of purity, enabled him to see what she was like.

She was about eight-and-twenty, with large bones, large features, large feet and hands, large eyes, and no hair. Her large eyes were limpid and almost colorless; they seemed to be very little affected by light, and to stand unnaturally still. There was also that attentive listening expression in her face, which is seen in the faces of the blind; but she was not blind, having one tolerably serviceable eye. Her face was not exceedingly ugly, though it was only redeemed from being so by a smile; a good-humoured smile, and pleasant in itself, but rendered pitiable by being constantly there. A great white cap, with a quantity of opaque frilling that was always flapping about, apologised for Maggy's baldness; and made it so very difficult for her old black bonnet to retain its place upon her head, that it held on round her neck like a gipsy's baby. A commission of haberdashers could alone have reported what the rest of her poor dress was made of; but it had a strong general resemblance to sea-weed, with here and there a gigantic tea-leaf. Her shawl looked particularly like a tea-leaf, after long infusion.

Arthur Clennam looked at Little Dorrit, with the expression of one saying, "May I ask who this is?" Little Dorrit, whose hand this Maggy, still calling her little mother, had begun to fondle, answered in words. (They were under a gateway into which the majority of the potatoes had rolled.)

"This is Maggy, sir."

"Maggy, sir," echoed the personage presented. "Little mother!"

"She is the grand-daughter—" said Little Dorrit.

"Grand-daughter," echoed Maggy.

"Of my old nurse, who has been dead a long time. Maggy, how old are you?"

"Ten, mother," said Maggy.

"You can't think how good she is, sir," said Little Dorrit, with infinite tenderness.

"Good *she* is," echoed Maggy, transferring the pronoun in a most expressive way from herself, to her little mother.

"Or how clever," said Little Dorrit. "She goes on errands as well as any one." Maggy laughed. "And is as trustworthy as the Bank of England." Maggy laughed. "She earns her own living entirely. Entirely, sir!" said Little Dorrit in a lower and triumphant tone. "Really does!"

"What is her history?" asked Clennam.

"Think of that, Maggy!" said Little Dorrit, taking her two large hands and clapping them together. "A gentleman from thousands of miles away, wanting to know your history!"

"*My* history?" cried Maggy. "Little mother."

"She means me," said Little Dorrit, rather confused; "she is very much attached to me. Her old grandmother was not so kind to her as she should have been; was she, Maggy?"

Maggy shook her head, made a drinking vessel of her clenched left hand, drank out of it, and said, "Gin." Then beat an imaginary child, and said, "Broom-handles and pokers."

"When Maggy was ten years old," said Little Dorrit, watching her face while she spoke, "she had a bad fever, sir, and she has never grown any older ever since."

"Ten years old," said Maggy, nodding her head. "But what a nice hospital! So comfortable, wasn't it? Oh so nice it was. Such a Ev'nly place!"

"She had never been at peace before, sir," said Little Dorrit, turning towards Arthur for an instant and speaking low, "and she always runs off upon that."

"Such beds there is there!" cried Maggy. "Such lemonades! Such oranges! Such d'licious broth and wine! Such Chicking! Oh, AIN'T it a delightful place to go and stop at!"

"So Maggy stopped there as long as she could," said Little Dorrit, in her former tone of telling a child's story; the tone designed for Maggy's ear, "and at last, when she could stop there no longer, she came out. Then, because she was never to be more than ten years old, however long she lived—"

"However long she lived," echoed Maggy.

"And because she was very weak; indeed was so weak that when she began to laugh she couldn't stop herself—which was a great pity—"

(Maggy mighty grave of a sudden.)

"Her grandmother did not know what to do with her, and for some years was very unkind to her indeed. At length, in course of time, Maggy began to take pains to improve herself, and to be very attentive and very industrious; and by degrees was allowed to come in and out as often as she liked, and got enough to do to support herself, and does support herself. And that," said Little Dorrit, clapping the two great hands together again, "is Maggy's history, as Maggy knows!"

Ah! But Arthur would have known what was wanting to its completeness, though he had never heard the words Little mother; though he had never seen the fondling of the small spare hand; though he had had no sight for the tears now standing in the colorless eyes; though he had had no hearing for the sob that checked the clumsy laugh. The dirty gateway with the wind and rain whistling through it, and the basket of muddy potatoes waiting to be spilt again or taken up, never seemed the common hole it really was, when he looked back to it by these lights. Never, never!

They were very near the end of their walk, and they now came out of the gateway to finish it. Nothing would serve Maggy but that they must stop at a grocer's window, short of their destination, for her to show her learning. She could read after a sort; and picked out the fat figures in the tickets of prices, for the most part correctly. She also stumbled, with a large balance of success against her failures, through various philanthropic recommendations to Try our Mixture, Try our Family Black, Try our Orange-flavoured Pekoe, challenging competition at the head of Flowery Teas; and various cautions to the public against spurious establishments and adulterated articles. When he saw how pleasure brought a rosy tint into Little Dorrit's face when Maggy made a hit, he felt that he could have stood there making a library of the grocer's window until the rain and wind were tired.

The courtyard received them at last, and there he said good bye to Little Dorrit. Little as she had always looked, she looked less than ever when he saw her going into the Marshalsea lodge passage, the little mother attended by her big child.

The cage door opened, and when the small bird, reared in captivity, had tamely fluttered in, he saw it shut again; and then he came away.

CHAPTER X

CONTAINING THE WHOLE SCIENCE OF GOVERNMENT

THE Circumlocution Office was (as everybody knows without being told) the most important Department under government. No public business of any kind could possibly be done at any time, without the acquiescence of the Circumlocution Office. Its finger was in the largest public pie, and in the smallest public tart. It was equally impossible to do the plainest right and to undo the plainest wrong, without the express authority of the Circumlocution Office. If another Gunpowder Plot had been discovered half an hour before the lighting of the match, nobody would have been justified in saving the parliament until there had been half a score of boards, half a bushel of minutes, several sacks of official memoranda, and a family-vault-full of ungrammatical correspondence, on the part of the Circumlocution Office.

This glorious establishment had been early in the field, when the one sublime principle involving the difficult art of governing a country, was first distinctly revealed to statesmen. It had been foremost to study that bright revelation, and to carry its shining influence through the whole of the official proceedings. Whatever was required to be done, the Circumlocution Office was beforehand with all the public departments in the art of perceiving—HOW NOT TO DO IT.

Through this delicate perception, through the tact with which it invariably seized it, and through the genius with which it always acted on it, the Circumlocution Office had risen to overtop all the public departments; and the public condition had risen to be—what it was.

It is true that How not to do it was the great study and object of all public departments and professional politicians all round the Circumlocution Office. It is true that every new premier and every new government, coming in because they had upheld a certain thing as necessary to be done, were no sooner come in than they applied their utmost faculties to discovering, How not to do it. It is true that from the moment when a general election was over, every returned man who had been raving on hustings because it hadn't been done, and who had been asking the friends of the honorable gentleman in the opposite interest on pain of impeachment to tell him why it hadn't been done, and who had been asserting that it must be done, and who had been pledging himself that it should be done, began to devise, How it was not to be done. It is true that the debates of both Houses of Parliament the whole session through, uniformly tended to the protracted deliberation, How not to do it. It is true that the royal speech at the opening of such session virtually said, My lords and gentlemen, you have a considerable stroke of work to do, and you will please to retire to your respective chambers, and discuss, How not to do it. It is true that the royal speech, at the close of such session, virtually said, My lords and gentlemen, you have through several laborious months been considering with great loyalty and patriotism, How not to do it, and you have found it out; and with the blessing of Providence upon the harvest (natural, not political), I now dismiss you. All this is true, but the Circumlocution Office went beyond it.

Because the Circumlocution Office went on mechanically, every day, keeping this wonderful, all-sufficient wheel of statesmanship, How not to do it, in motion. Because the Circumlocution Office was down upon any ill-advised public servant who was going to do it, or who appeared to be by any surprising accident in remote danger of doing it, with a minute, and a memorandum, and a letter of instructions, that extinguished him. It was this spirit of national efficiency in the Circumlocution Office that had gradually led to its having something to do with everything. Mechanicians, natural philosophers, soldiers, sailors, petitioners, memorialists, people with grievances, people who wanted to prevent grievances, people who wanted to redress grievances, jobbing people, jobbed people, people who couldn't get rewarded for merit, and people who couldn't get punished for demerit, were all indiscriminately tucked up under the fools-cap paper of the Circumlocution Office.

Numbers of people were lost in the Circumlocution Office. Unfortunates with wrongs, or with projects for the general welfare (and they had better have had wrongs at first, than have taken that bitter English recipe for certainly getting them), who in slow lapse of time and agony had passed safely through other public departments; who, according to rule, had been bullied in this, over-reached by that, and evaded by the other; got referred at last to the Circumlocution Office, and never reappeared in the light of day. Boards sat upon them, secretaries minuted upon them, commissioners gabbled about them, clerks registered, entered, checked, and ticked them off, and they melted away. In short, all the business of the country went through the Circumlocution Office, except the business that never came out of it; and *its* name was Legion.

Sometimes, angry spirits attacked the Circumlocution Office. Some-times, parliamentary questions were asked about it, and even parliamentary motions made or threatened about it, by demagogues so low and ignorant as to hold that the real recipe of government was, How to do it. Then would the noble lord, or right honorable gentleman, in whose department it was to defend the Circumlocution Office, put an orange in his pocket, and make a regular field-day of the occasion. Then would he come down to that House with a slap upon the table, and meet the honorable gentleman foot to foot. Then would he be there to tell that honorable gentleman that the Circumlocution Office not only was blameless in this matter, but was commendable in this matter, was extollable to the skies in this matter. Then would he be there to tell that honorable gentleman, that, although the Circumlocution Office was invariably right and wholly right, it never was so right as in this matter. Then would he be there to tell that honorable gentleman that it would have been more to his honor, more to his credit, more to his good taste, more to his good sense, more to half the dictionary of commonplaces, if he had left the Circumlocution Office alone, and never approached this matter. Then would he keep one eye upon a coach or crammer from the Circumlocution Office sitting below the bar, and smash the honorable gentleman with the Circumlocution Office account of this matter. And although one of two things always happened; namely, either that the Circumlocution Office had nothing to say and said it, or that it had something to say of which the noble lord, or right honorable gentleman, blundered one half and forgot the other; the Circumlocution Office was always voted immaculate, by an accommodating majority.

Such a nursery of statesmen had the department become in virtue of a long career of this nature, that several solemn lords had attained the reputation of being quite unearthly prodigies of business, solely from having practised, How not to do it, at the head of the Circumlocution

Office. As to the minor priests and acolytes of that temple, the result of all this was that they stood divided into two classes, and, down to the junior messenger, either believed in the Circumlocution Office as a heaven-born institution, that had an absolute right to do whatever it liked; or took refuge in total infidelity, and considered it a flagrant nuisance.

The Barnacle family had for some time helped to administer the Circumlocution Office. The Tite Barnacle Branch, indeed, considered themselves in a general way as having vested rights in that direction, and took it ill if any other family had much to say to it. The Barnacles were a very high family, and a very large family. They were dispersed all over the public offices, and held all sorts of public places. Either the nation was under a load of obligation to the Barnacles, or the Barnacles were under a load of obligation to the nation. It was not quite unanimously settled which; the Barnacles having their opinion, the nation theirs.

The Mr. Tite Barnacle who at the period now in question usually coached or crammed the statesman at the head of the Circumlocution Office, when that noble or right honorable individual sat a little uneasily in his saddle, by reason of some vagabond making a tilt at him in a newspaper, was more flush of blood than money. As a Barnacle he had his place, which was a snug thing enough; and as a Barnacle he had of course put in his son Barnacle Junior, in the office. But he had intermarried with a branch of the Stiltstalkings, who were also better endowed in a sanguineous point of view than with real or personal property, and of this marriage there had been issue, Barnacle Junior, and three young ladies. What with the patrician requirements of Barnacle Junior, the three young ladies, Mrs. Tite Barnacle née Stiltstalking, and himself, Mr. Tite Barnacle found the intervals between quarter day and quarter day rather longer than he could have desired; a circumstance which he always attributed to the country's parsimony.

For Mr. Tite Barnacle, Mr. Arthur Clennam made his fifth enquiry one day at the Circumlocution Office; having on previous occasions awaited that gentleman successively in a hall, a glass case, a waiting-room, and a fire-proof passage where the department seemed to keep its wind. On this occasion Mr. Barnacle was not engaged, as he had been before, with the noble prodigy at the head of the department; but was absent. Barnacle Junior, however, was announced as a lesser star, yet visible above the office horizon.

With Barnacle Junior, he signified his desire to confer; and found that young gentleman singeing the calves of his legs at the parental fire, and supporting his spine against the mantel-shelf. It was a comfortable room, handsomely furnished in the higher official manner; and presenting stately suggestions of the absent Barnacle, in the thick carpet, the leather-covered desk to sit at, the leather-covered desk to stand at, the formidable

easy chair and hearth-rug, the interposed screen, the torn-up papers,
the dispatch-boxes with little labels sticking out of them, like medicine
bottles or dead game, the pervading smell of leather and mahogany, and
a general bamboozling air of How not to do it.

The present Barnacle, holding Mr. Clennam's card in his hand, had a
youthful aspect, and the fluffiest little whisker, perhaps, that ever was
seen. Such a downy tip was on his callow chin, that he seemed half fledged
like a young bird; and a compassionate observer might have urged, that
if he had not singed the calves of his legs, he would have died of cold.
He had a superior eye-glass dangling round his neck, but unfortunately
had such flat orbits to his eyes, and such limp little eyelids, that it wouldn't
stick in when he put it up, but kept tumbling out against his waistcoat
buttons with a click that discomposed him very much.

"Oh, I say. Look here! My father's not in the way, and won't be in the
way to-day," said Barnacle Junior. "Is this anything that I can do?"

(Click! Eye-glass down. Barnacle Junior quite frightened and feeling
all round himself, but not able to find it.)

"You are very good," said Arthur Clennam. "I wish however to see
Mr. Barnacle."

"But I say. Look here! You haven't got any appointment, you know,"
said Barnacle Junior.

(By this time he had found the eye-glass, and put it up again.)

"No," said Arthur Clennam. "That is what I wish to have."

"But I say. Look here! Is this public business?" asked Barnacle
Junior.

(Click! Eye-glass down again. Barnacle Junior in that state of search
after it, that Mr. Clennam felt it useless to reply at present.)

"Is it," said Barnacle Junior, taking heed of his visitor's brown face,
"anything about—Tonnage—or that sort of thing?"

(Pausing for a reply, he opened his right eye with his hand, and stuck
his glass in it, in such inflammatory manner that his eye began watering
dreadfully.)

"No," said Arthur, "it is nothing about tonnage."

"Then look here. Is it private business?"

"I really am not sure. It relates to a Mr. Dorrit."

"Look here, I tell you what! You had better call at our house, if you
are going that way. Twenty-four, Mews Street, Grosvenor Square. My
father's got a slight touch of the gout, and is kept at home by it."

(The misguided young Barnacle evidently going blind on his eye-glass
side, but ashamed to make any further alteration in his painful arrangements.)

"Thank you. I will call there now. Good morning." Young Barnacle
seemed discomfited at this, as not having at all expected him to go.

"You are quite sure," said Barnacle Junior, calling after him when he got to the door, unwilling wholly to relinquish the bright business idea he had conceived; "that it's nothing about Tonnage?"

"Quite sure."

With which assurance, and rather wondering what might have taken place if it *had* been anything about tonnage, Mr. Clennam withdrew to pursue his enquiries.

Mews Street, Grosvenor Square, was not absolutely Grosvenor Square itself, but it was very near it. It was a hideous little street of dead wall, stables, and dunghills, with lofts over coach-houses inhabited by coachmen's families, who had a passion for drying clothes, and decorating their window-sills with miniature turnpike-gates. The principal chimneysweep of that fashionable quarter lived at the blind end of Mews Street; and the same corner contained an establishment much frequented about early morning and twilight, for the purchase of wine-bottles and kitchenstuff. Punch's shows used to lean against the dead wall in Mews Street, while their proprietors were dining elsewhere; and the dogs of the neighbourhood made appointments to meet in the same locality. Yet there were two or three small airless houses at the entrance end of Mews Street, which went at enormous rents on account of their being abject hangers-on to a fashionable situation; and whenever one of these fearful little coops was to be let (which seldom happened, for they were in great request), the house agent advertised it as a gentlemanly residence in the most aristocratic part of town, inhabited solely by the élite of the beau monde.

If a gentlemanly residence coming strictly within this narrow margin, had not been essential to the blood of the Barnacles, this particular branch would have had a pretty wide selection among let us say ten thousand houses, offering fifty times the accommodation for a third of the money. As it was, Mr. Barnacle, finding his gentlemanly residence extremely inconvenient and extremely dear, always laid it, as a public servant, at the door of the country, and adduced it as another instance of the country's parsimony.

Arthur Clennam came to a squeezed house, with a ramshackle bowed front, little dingy windows, and a little dark area like a damp waistcoatpocket, which he found to be number twenty-four, Mews Street, Grosvenor Square. To the sense of smell, the house was like a sort of bottle filled with a strong distillation of mews; and when the footman opened the door, he seemed to take the stopper out.

The footman was to the Grosvenor Square footmen, what the house was to the Grosvenor Square houses. Admirable in his way, his way was a back and a bye way. His gorgeousness was not unmixed with dirt; and both in complexion and consistency, he had suffered from the closeness of his pantry. A sallow flabbiness was upon him, when he took the stopper out, and presented the bottle to Mr. Clennam's nose.

"Be so good as to give that card to Mr. Tite Barnacle, and to say that

I have just now seen the younger Mr. Barnacle who recommended me to call here."

The footman (who had as many large buttons with the Barnacle crest upon them, on the flaps of his pockets, as if he were the family strong box, and carried the plate and jewels about with him buttoned up) pondered over the card a little; then said "Walk in." It required some judgment to do it without butting the inner hall-door open, and in the consequent mental confusion and physical darkness slipping down the kitchen stairs. The visitor, however, brought himself up safely on the door-mat.

Still the footman said "Walk in," so the visitor followed him. At the inner hall-door, another bottle seemed to be presented and another stopper taken out. This second vial appeared to be filled with concentrated provisions, and extract of Sink from the pantry. After a skirmish in the narrow passage, occasioned by the footman's opening the door of the dismal dining-room with confidence, finding some one there with consternation, and backing on the visitor with disorder, the visitor was shut up, pending his announcement, in a close back parlor. There he had an opportunity of refreshing himself with both the bottles at once, looking out at a low blinding back wall three feet off, and speculating on the number of Barnacle families within the bills of mortality who lived in such hutches of their own free flunkey choice.

Mr. Barnacle would see him. Would he walk up-stairs? He would, and he did; and in the drawing-room, with his leg on a rest, he found Mr. Barnacle himself, the express image and presentment of How not to do it.

Mr. Barnacle dated from a better time, when the country was not so parsimonious, and the Circumlocution Office was not so badgered. He wound and wound folds of white cravat round his neck, as he wound and wound folds of tape and paper round the neck of the country. His wristbands and collar were oppressive, his voice and manner were oppressive. He had a large watch-chain and bunch of seals, a coat buttoned up to inconvenience, a waistcoat buttoned up to inconvenience, an unwrinkled pair of trousers, a stiff pair of boots. He was altogether splendid, massive, overpowering, and impracticable. He seemed to have been sitting for his portrait to Sir Thomas Lawrence all the days of his life.

"Mr. Clennam?" said Mr. Barnacle. "Be seated."

Mr. Clennam became seated.

"You have called on me, I believe," said Mr. Barnacle, "at the Circumlocution—" giving it the air of a word of about five and twenty syllables, "Office."

"I have taken that liberty."

Mr. Barnacle solemnly bent his head as who should say "I do not deny that it is a liberty; proceed to take another liberty, and let me know your business."

"Allow me to observe that I have been for some years in China, am quite a stranger at home, and have no personal motive or interest in the enquiry I am about to make."

Mr. Barnacle tapped his fingers on the table, and, as if he were now sitting for his portrait to a new and strange artist, appeared to say to his visitor, "If you will be good enough to take me with my present lofty expression, I shall feel obliged."

"I have found a debtor in the Marshalsea prison of the name of Dorrit, who has been there many years. I wish to investigate his confused affairs, so far as to ascertain whether it may not be possible, after this lapse of time, to ameliorate his unhappy condition. The name of Mr. Tite Barnacle has been mentioned to me as representing some highly influential interest among his creditors. Am I correctly informed?"

It being one of the principles of the Circumlocution Office never, on any account whatever, to give a straightforward answer, Mr. Barnacle said, "Possibly."

"On behalf of the Crown, may I ask, or as a private individual?"

"The Circumlocution Department, sir," Mr. Barnacle replied, "may have possibly recommended—possibly—I cannot say—that some public claim against the insolvent estate of a firm or copartnership to which this person may have belonged, should be enforced. The question may have been, in the course of official business, referred to the Circumlocution Department for its consideration. The Department may have either originated, or confirmed, a Minute making that recommendation."

"I assume this to be the case, then."

"The Circumlocution Department," said Mr. Barnacle, "is not responsible for any gentleman's assumptions."

"May I enquire how I can obtain official information as to the real state of the case?"

"It is competent," said Mr. Barnacle, "to any member of the—Public," mentioning that obscure body with reluctance, as his natural enemy, "to memorialise the Circumlocution Department. Such formalities as are required to be observed in so doing, may be known on application to the proper branch of that Department."

"Which is the proper branch?"

"I must refer you," returned Mr. Barnacle, ringing the bell, "to the Department itself for a formal answer to that enquiry."

"Excuse my mentioning—"

"The Department is accessible to the—Public." Mr. Barnacle was always checked a little by that word of impertinent signification, "if the—Public approaches it according to the official forms; if the—Public does not approach it according to the official forms, it, the —Public has itself to blame."

Mr. Barnacle made him a severe bow, as a wounded man of family, a wounded man of place, and a wounded man of a gentlemanly residence, all rolled into one; and he made Mr. Barnacle a bow, and was shot out into Mews Street by the flabby footman.

Having got to this pass, he resolved, as an exercise in perseverance, to betake himself again to the Circumlocution Office, and try what satisfaction he could get there. So he went back to the Circumlocution Office, and once more sent up his card to Barnacle Junior by a messenger who took it very ill indeed that he should come back again, and who was eating mashed potatoes and gravy behind a partition by the hall fire.

He was re-admitted to the presence of Barnacle Junior, and found that young gentleman singeing his knees now, and gaping his weary way on to four o'clock.

"I say. Look here. You stick to us in a devil of a manner," said Barnacle Junior, looking over his shoulder.

"I want to know—"

"Look here. Upon my soul you mustn't come into the place saying you want to know, you know," remonstrated Barnacle Junior, turning about and putting up the eye-glass.

"I want to know," said Arthur Clennam, who had made up his mind to persistence in one short form of words, "the precise nature of the claim of the Crown against a prisoner for debt named Dorrit."

"I say. Look here. You really are going it at a great pace, you know. Egad you haven't got an appointment," said Barnacle Junior, as if the thing were growing serious.

"I want to know," said Arthur. And repeated his case.

Barnacle Junior stared at him until his eye-glass fell out, and then put it in again and stared at him until it fell out again. "You have no right to come this sort of move," he then observed with the greatest weakness. "Look here. What do you mean? You told me you didn't know whether it was public business or not."

"I have now ascertained that it is public business," returned the suitor, "and I want to know"—and again repeated his monotonous enquiry.

Its effect upon young Barnacle was to make him repeat in a defenceless way, "Look here! Upon my SOUL you mustn't come into the place, saying you want to know, you know!" The effect of that upon Arthur Clennam was to make him repeat his enquiry in exactly the same words and tone as before. The effect of that upon young Barnacle was to make him a wonderful spectacle of failure and helplessness.

"Well, I tell you what. Look here. You had better try the Secretarial Department," he said at last, sidling to the bell and ringing it. "Jenkinson," to the mashed potatoes messenger, "Mr. Wobbler!"

Arthur Clennam, who now felt that he had devoted himself to the storming of the Circumlocution Office, and must go through with it, accompanied the messenger to another floor of the building, where that functionary pointed out Mr. Wobbler's room. He entered that apartment, and found two gentlemen sitting face to face at a large and easy desk, one of whom was polishing a gun-barrel on his pocket-handkerchief, while the other was spreading marmalade on bread with a paper-knife.

"Mr. Wobbler?" enquired the suitor.

Both gentlemen glanced at him, and seemed surprised at this assurance.

"So he went," said the gentleman with the gun-barrel, who was an extremely deliberate speaker, "down to his cousin's place, and took the Dog with him by rail. Inestimable Dog. Flew at the porter fellow when he was put into the dog-box, and flew at the guard when he was taken out. He got half-a-dozen fellows into a Barn, and a good supply of Rats, and timed the Dog. Finding the Dog able to do it immensely, made the match, and heavily backed the Dog. When the match came off, some devil of a fellow was bought over, sir, Dog was made drunk, Dog's master was cleaned out."

"Mr. Wobbler?" enquired the suitor.

The gentleman who was spreading the marmalade returned, without looking up from that occupation, "What did he call the Dog?"

"Called him Lovely," said the other gentleman. "Said the Dog was the perfect picture of the old aunt from whom he has expectations. Found him particularly like her when hocussed."

"Mr. Wobbler?" said the suitor.

Both gentlemen laughed for some time. The gentleman with the gun-barrel, considering it on inspection in a satisfactory state, referred it to the other; receiving confirmation of his views, he fitted it into its place in the case before him, and took out the stock and polished that, softly whistling.

"Mr. Wobbler?" said the suitor.

"What's the matter?" then said Mr. Wobbler, with his mouth full.

"I want to know——" and Arthur Clennam again mechanically set forth what he wanted to know.

"Can't inform you," observed Mr. Wobbler, apparently to his lunch. "Never heard of it. Nothing at all to do with it. Better try Mr. Clive, second door on the left in the next passage."

"Perhaps he will give me the same answer."

"Very likely. Don't know anything about it," said Mr. Wobbler.

The suitor turned away and had left the room, when the gentleman with the gun called out "Mister! Hallo!"

He looked in again.

"Shut the door after you. You're letting in a devil of a draught here!"

A few steps brought him to the second door on the left in the next passage. In that room he found three gentlemen; number one doing nothing particular, number two doing nothing particular, number three doing nothing particular. They seemed, however, to be more directly concerned than the others had been in the effective execution of the great principle of the office, as there was an awful inner apartment with a double door, in which the Circumlocution Sages appeared to be assembled in council, and out of which there was an imposing coming of papers, and into which there was an imposing going of papers, almost constantly; wherein another gentleman, number four, was the active instrument.

"I want to know," said Arthur Clennam,—and again stated his case in the same barrel-organ way. As number one referred him to number two, and as number two referred him to number three, he had occasion to state it three times before they all referred him to number four. To whom he stated it again.

Number four was a vivacious, well-looking, well-dressed, agreeable young fellow—he was a Barnacle, but on the more sprightly side of the family—and he said in an easy way, "Oh! you had better not bother yourself about it, I think."

"Not bother myself about it?"

"No! I recommend you not to bother yourself about it."

This was such a new point of view that Arthur Clennam found himself at a loss how to receive it.

"You can if you like. I can give you plenty of forms to fill up. Lots of 'em here. You can have a dozen, if you like. But you'll never go on with it," said number four.

"Would it be such hopeless work? Excuse me; I am a stranger in England."

"*I* don't say it would be hopeless," returned number four, with a frank smile. "I don't express an opinion about that; I only express an opinion about you. *I* don't think you'd go on with it. However, of course, you can do as you like. I suppose there was a failure in the performance of a contract, or something of that kind, was there?"

"I really don't know."

"Well! That you can find out. Then you'll find out what Department the contract was in, and then you'll find out all about it there."

"I beg your pardon. How shall I find out?"

"Why, you'll—you'll ask till they tell you. Then you'll memorialise that Department (according to regular forms which you'll find out) for leave to memorialise this Department. If you get it (which you may after a time), that memorial must be entered in that Department, sent to be registered in this Department, sent back to be signed by that Department, sent back to be counter-signed by this Department, and then it will begin to be regularly before that Department. You'll find out when the business passes through each of these stages, by asking at both Departments till they tell you."

"But surely this is not the way to do the business," Arthur Clennam could not help saying.

This airy young Barnacle was quite entertained by his simplicity in supposing for a moment that it was. This light in hand young Barnacle knew perfectly that it was not. This touch and go young Barnacle had "got up" the Department in a private secretaryship, that he might be ready for any little bit of fat that came to hand; and he fully understood the Department to be a politico diplomatico hocus pocus piece of machinery, for the assistance of the nobs in keeping off the snobs. This dashing young Barnacle, in a word, was likely to become a statesman, and to make a figure.

"When the business is regularly before that Department, whatever it is," pursued this bright young Barnacle, "then you can watch it from time to time through that Department. When it comes regularly before this Department, then you must watch it from time to time through this Department. We shall have to refer it right and left; and when we refer it anywhere, then you'll have to look it up. When it comes back to us at any time, then you had better look *us* up. When it sticks anywhere, you'll have to try to give it a jog. When you write to another Department about it, and then to this Department about it, and don't hear anything satisfactory about it, why then you had better—keep on writing."

Arthur Clennam looked very doubtful indeed. "But I am obliged to you, at any rate," said he, "for your politeness."

"Not at all," replied this engaging young Barnacle. "Try the thing, and see how you like it. It will be in your power to give it up at any time, if you don't like it. You had better take a lot of forms away with you. Give him a lot of forms!" With which instruction to number two, this sparkling young Barnacle took a fresh handful of papers from numbers one and three, and carried them into the sanctuary, to offer to the presiding Idols of the Circumlocution Office.

Arthur Clennam put his forms in his pocket gloomily enough, and went his way down the long stone passage and the long stone staircase. He had come to the swing doors leading into the street, and was waiting, not over patiently, for two people who were between him and them to pass out and let him follow, when the voice of one of them struck familiarly on his ear. He looked at the speaker and recognised Mr. Meagles. Mr. Meagles was very red in the face—redder than travel could have made him—and collaring a short man who was with him, said, "Come out, you rascal, come out!"

It was such an unexpected hearing, and it was also such an unexpected sight to see Mr. Meagles burst the swing-doors open, and emerge into the street with the short man, who was of an unoffending appearance, that Clennam stood still for the moment exchanging looks of surprise with the porter. He followed, however, quickly; and saw Mr. Meagles going down the street with his enemy at his side. He soon came up with his old travelling companion, and touched him on the back. The choleric face which Mr. Meagles turned upon him smoothed when he saw who it was, and he put out his friendly hand.

"How are you!" said Mr. Meagles. "How d'ye *do!* I have only just come over from abroad. I am glad to see you."

"And I am rejoiced to see you."

"Thank'ee. Thank'ee!"

"Mrs. Meagles and your daughter— ?"

"Are as well as possible," said Mr. Meagles. "I only wish you had come upon me in a more prepossessing condition as to coolness."

Though it was anything but a hot day, Mr. Meagles was in a heated state that attracted the attention of the passers by; more particularly as he leaned his back against a railing, took off his hat and cravat, and heartily rubbed his steaming head and face, and his reddened ears and neck, without the least regard for public opinion.

"Whew!" said Mr. Meagles, dressing again. "That's comfortable. Now I am cooler."

"You have been ruffled, Mr. Meagles. What is the matter?"

"Wait a bit, and I'll tell you. Have you leisure for a turn in the Park?"

"As much as you please."

"Come along, then. Ah! you may well look at him." He happened to have turned his eyes towards the offender whom Mr. Meagles had so angrily collared. "He's something to look at, that fellow is."

He was not much to look at, either in point of size or in point of dress; being merely a short, square, practical looking man, whose hair had turned grey, and in whose face and forehead there were deep lines of cogitation, which looked as though they were carved in hard wood. He was dressed in decent black, a little rusty, and had the appearance of a sagacious master in some handicraft. He had a spectacle-case in his hand, which he turned over and over while he was thus in question, with a certain free use of the thumb that is never seen but in a hand accustomed to tools.

"You keep with us," said Mr. Meagles, in a threatening kind of way, "and I'll introduce you presently. Now, then!"

Clennam wondered within himself, as they took the nearest way to the Park, what this unknown (who complied in the gentlest manner) could have been doing. His appearance did not at all justify the suspicion that he had been detected in designs on Mr. Meagles's pocket-handkerchief; nor had he any appearance of being quarrelsome or violent. He was a quiet, plain, steady man; made no attempt to escape; and seemed a little depressed, but neither ashamed nor repentant. If he were a criminal offender, he must surely be an incorrigible hypocrite; and if he were no offender, why should Mr. Meagles have collared him in the Circumlocution Office? He perceived that the man was not a difficulty in his own mind alone, but in Mr. Meagles's too; for such conversation as they had together on the short way to the Park was by no means well sustained, and Mr.

Meagles's eye always wandered back to the man, even when he spoke of something very different.

At length, they being among the trees, Mr. Meagles stopped short, and said:

"Mr. Clennam, will you do me the favor to look at this man? His name is Doyce, Daniel Doyce. You wouldn't suppose this man to be a notorious rascal; would you?"

"I certainly should not." It was really a disconcerting question, with the man there.

"No. You would not. I know you would not. You wouldn't suppose him to be a public offender; would you?"

"No."

"No. But he is. He is a public offender. What has he been guilty of? Murder, manslaughter, arson, forgery, swindling, housebreaking, highway robbery, larceny, conspiracy, fraud? Which should you say now?"

"I should say," returned Arthur Clennam, observing a faint smile in Daniel Doyce's face, "not one of them."

"You are right," said Mr. Meagles. "But he has been ingenious, and he has been trying to turn his ingenuity to his country's service. That makes him a public offender directly, sir."

Arthur looked at the man himself, who only shook his head.

"This Doyce," said Mr. Meagles, "is a smith and engineer. He is not in a large way, but he is well known as a very ingenious man. A dozen years ago, he perfects an invention (involving a very curious secret process) of great importance to his country and his fellow creatures. I won't say how much money it cost him, or how many years of his life he had been about it, but he brought it to perfection a dozen years ago. Wasn't it a dozen?" said Mr. Meagles, addressing Doyce. "He is the most exasperating man in the world; he never complains!"

"Yes. Rather better than twelve years ago."

"Rather better?" said Mr. Meagles, "you mean rather worse. Well, Mr. Clennam. He addresses himself to the Government. The moment he addresses himself to the Government, he becomes a public offender! Sir," said Mr. Meagles, in danger of making himself excessively hot again, "he ceases to be an innocent citizen, and becomes a culprit. He is treated, from that instant, as a man who has done some infernal action. He is a man to be shirked, put off, brow-beaten, sneered at, handed over by this highly-connected young or old gentleman to that highly-connected young or old gentleman, and dodged back again; he is a man with no rights in his own time, or his own property; a mere outlaw, whom it is justifiable to get rid of anyhow; a man to be worn out by all possible means."

It was not so difficult to believe, after the morning's experience, as Mr. Meagles supposed.

"Don't stand there, Doyce, turning your spectacle-case over and over," cried Mr. Meagles, "but tell Mr. Clennam what you confessed to me."

"I undoubtedly was made to feel," said the inventor, "as if I had committed an offence. In dancing attendance at the various offices, I was always treated, more or less, as if it was a very bad offence. I have frequently found it necessary to reflect, for my own self-support, that I really had not done anything to bring myself into the Newgate Calendar, but only wanted to effect a great saving and a great improvement."

"There!" said Mr. Meagles. "Judge whether I exaggerate! Now you'll be able to believe me when I tell you the rest of the case."

With this prelude, Mr. Meagles went through the narrative; the established narrative, which has become tiresome; the matter of course narrative which³ we all know by heart. How, after interminable attendance and correspondence, after infinite impertinences, ignorances, and insults, my lords made a Minute, number three thousand four hundred and seventy-two, allowing the culprit to make certain trials of his invention at his own expense. How the trials were made in the presence of a board of six, of whom two ancient members were too blind to see it, two other ancient members were too deaf to hear it, one other ancient member was too lame to get near it, and the final ancient member was too pig-headed to look at it. How there were more years; more impertinences, ignorances, and insults. How my lords then made a Minute, number five thousand one hundred and three, whereby they resigned the business to the Circumlocution Office. How the Circumlocution Office, in course of time, took up the business as if it were a bran new thing of yesterday, which had never been heard of before; muddled the business, addled the business, tossed the business in a wet blanket. How the impertinences, ignorances, and insults went through the multiplication table. How there was a reference of the invention to three Barnacles and a Stiltstalking, who knew nothing about it; into whose heads nothing could be hammered about it; who got bored about it, and reported physical impossibilities about it. How the Circumlocution Office, in a Minute, number eight thousand seven hundred and forty, "saw no reason to reverse the decision at which my lords had arrived." How the Circumlocution Office, being reminded that my lords had arrived at no decision, shelved the business. How there had been a final interview with the head of the Circumlocution Office that very morning, and how the Brazen Head had spoken, and had been, upon the whole, and under all the circumstances, and looking at it from the various points of view, of opinion that one of two courses was to be pursued in respect of the business: that was to say, either to leave it alone for evermore, or to begin it all over again.

"Upon which," said Mr. Meagles, "as a practical man, I then and there, in that presence, took Doyce by the collar, told him it was plain to me that he was an infamous rascal, and treasonable disturber of the government peace, and took him away. I brought him out at the office door by the

collar, that the very porter might know I was a practical man who appreciated the official estimate of such characters; and here we are!"

If that airy young Barnacle had been there, he would have frankly told
them perhaps that the Circumlocution Office had achieved its functions.
That what the Barnacles had to do, was to stick on to the national ship as
long as they could. That to trim the ship, lighten the ship, clean the ship,
would be to knock them off; that they could but be knocked off once; and
that if the ship went down with them yet sticking to it, that was the ship's
look out, and not theirs.

"There!" said Mr. Meagles, "now you know all about Doyce. Except,
which I own does not improve my state of mind, that even now you don't
hear him complain."

"You must have great patience," said Arthur Clennam, looking at him
with some wonder, "great forbearance."

"No," he returned, "I don't know that I have more than another man."

"By the Lord you have more than I have though!" cried Mr. Meagles.

Doyce smiled, as he said to Clennam, "You see, my experience of these
things does not begin with myself. It has been in my way to know a little
about them, from time to time. Mine is not a particular case. I am not
worse used than a hundred others, who have put themselves in the same
position—than all the others, I was going to say."

"I don't know that I should find that a consolation, if it were my case;
but I am very glad that you do."

"Understand me! I don't say," he replied in his steady, planning way,
and looking into the distance before him as if his grey eye were measuring
it, "that it's a recompense for a man's toil and hope; but it's a certain sort
of relief to know that I might have counted on this."

He spoke in that quiet deliberate manner, and in that undertone, which
is often observable in mechanics who consider and adjust with great
nicety. It belonged to him like his suppleness of thumb, or his peculiar
way of tilting up his hat at the back every now and then, as if he were
contemplating some half-finished work of his hand, and thinking about it.

"Disappointed?" he went on, as he walked between them under the
trees. "Yes. No doubt I am disappointed. Hurt? Yes. No doubt I am hurt.
That's only natural. But what I mean, when I say that people who put
themselves in the same position, are mostly used in the same way—"

"In England," said Mr. Meagles.

"Oh! of course I mean in England. When they take their inventions
into foreign countries, that's quite different. And that's the reason why
so many go there."

Mr. Meagles very hot indeed again.

"What I mean is, that however this comes to be the regular way of our
government, it is its regular way. Have you ever heard of any projector

or inventor who failed to find it all but inaccessible, and whom it did not discourage and illtreat?"

"I cannot say that I ever have."

"Have you ever known it to be beforehand in the adoption of any useful thing? Ever known it to set an example of any useful kind?"

"I am a good deal older than my friend here," said Mr. Meagles, "and I'll answer that. Never."

"But we all three have known, I expect," said the inventor, "a pretty many cases of its fixed determination to be miles upon miles, and years upon years, behind the rest of us; and of its being found out persisting in the use of things long superseded, even after the better things were well known and generally taken up?"

They all agreed upon that.

"Well then," said Doyce with a sigh, "as I know what such a metal will do at such a temperature, and such a body under such a pressure, so I may know (if I will only consider), how these great lords and gentlemen will certainly deal with such a matter as mine. I have no right to be surprised, with a head upon my shoulders, and memory in it, that I fall into the ranks with all who came before me. I ought to have let it alone. I have had warning enough, I am sure."

With that he put up his spectacle-case, and said to Arthur, "If I don't complain, Mr. Clennam, I can feel gratitude; and I assure you that I feel it towards our mutual friend. Many's the day, and many's the way, in which he has backed me."

"Stuff and nonsense," said Mr. Meagles.

Arthur could not but glance at Daniel Doyce in the ensuing silence. Though it was evidently in the grain of his character, and of his respect for his own case, that he should abstain from idle murmuring, it was evident that he had grown the older, the sterner, and the poorer for his long endeavour. He could not but think what a blessed thing it would have been for this man, if he had taken a lesson from the gentlemen who were so kind as to take the nation's affairs in charge, and had learnt, How not to do it.

Mr. Meagles was hot and despondent for about five minutes, and then began to cool and clear up.

"Come, come!" said he. "We shall not make this the better by being grim. Where do you think of going, Dan?"

"I shall go back to the factory," said Dan.

"Why then, we'll all go back to the factory, or walk in that direction," returned Meagles cheerfully. "Mr. Clennam won't be deterred by its being in Bleeding Heart Yard."

"Bleeding Heart Yard?" said Clennam. "I want to go there."

"So much the better," cried Mr. Meagles. "Come along!"

As they went along, certainly one of the party, and probably more than one, thought that Bleeding Heart Yard was no inappropriate destination for a man who had been in official correspondence with my lords and the Barnacles—and perhaps had a misgiving also that Britannia herself might come to look for lodgings in Bleeding Heart Yard, some ugly day or other, if she over-did the Circumlocution Office.

CHAPTER XI

LET LOOSE

A LATE, dull autumn night, was closing in upon the river Saone. The stream, like a sullied looking-glass in a gloomy place, reflected the clouds heavily; and the low banks leaned over here and there, as if they were half curious, and half afraid, to see their darkening pictures in the water. The flat expanse of country about Chalons lay a long heavy streak, occasionally made a little ragged by a row of poplar trees, against the wrathful sunset. On the banks of the river Saone it was wet, depressing, solitary; and the night deepened fast.

One man, slowly moving on towards Chalons, was the only visible figure in the landscape. Cain might have looked as lonely and avoided. With an old sheepskin knapsack at his back, and a rough, unbarked stick cut out of some Wood in his hand; miry, footsore, his shoes and gaiters trodden out, his hair and beard untrimmed; the cloak he carried over his shoulder, and the clothes he wore, soddened with wet; limping along in pain and difficulty; he looked as if the clouds were hurrying from him, as if the wail of the wind and the shuddering of the grass were directed against him, as if the low mysterious plashing of the water murmured at him, as if the fitful autumn night were disturbed by him.

He glanced here, and he glanced there, sullenly but shrinkingly; and sometimes stopped and turned about, and looked all round him. Then he limped on again, toiling and muttering:

"To the devil with this plain that has no end! To the devil with these stones that cut like knives! To the devil with this dismal darkness, wrapping itself about one with a chill! I hate you!"

And he would have visited his hatred upon it all with the scowl he threw about him, if he could. He trudged a little further; and looking into the distance before him, stopped again.

"I, hungry, thirsty, weary. You, imbeciles, where the lights are yonder, eating and drinking, and warming yourselves at fires! I wish I had the sacking of your town, I would repay you, my children!"

But the teeth he set at the town, and the hand he shook at the town, brought the town no nearer; and the man was yet hungrier, thirstier, and wearier, when his feet were on its jagged pavement, and he stood looking about him.

There was the hotel with its gateway, and its savory smell of cooking; there was the café, with its bright windows, and its rattling of dominoes; there was the dyer's, with its strips of red cloth on the doorposts; there was the silversmith's, with its ear-rings, and its offerings for altars; there was the tobacco dealer's, with its lively group of soldier customers coming out pipe in mouth; there were the bad odors of the town, and the rain and refuse in the kennels, and the faint lamps slung across the road, and the huge Diligence, and its mountain of luggage, and its six grey horses with their tails tied up, getting under weigh at the coach office. But no small cabaret for a straitened traveller being within sight, he had to seek one round the dark corner, where the cabbage leaves lay thickest, trodden about the public cistern at which women had not yet left off drawing water. There, in the back street he found one, the Break of Day. The curtained windows clouded the Break of Day, but it seemed light and warm, and it announced in legible inscriptions, with appropriate pictorial embellishment of billiard cue and ball, that at the Break of Day one could play billiards; that there one could find meat, drink, and lodging, whether one came on horseback, or came on foot; and that it kept good wines, liqueurs, and brandy. The man turned the handle of the Break of Day door, and limped in.

He touched his discolored slouched hat, as he came in at the door, to a few men who occupied the room. Two were playing dominoes at one of the little tables; three or four were seated round the stove, conversing as they smoked; the billiard-table in the centre was left alone for the time; the landlady of the Daybreak sat behind her little counter among her cloudy bottles of syrups, baskets of cakes, and leaden drainage for glasses, working at her needle.

Making his way to an empty little table, in a corner of the room behind the stove, he put down his knapsack and his cloak upon the ground. As he raised his head from stooping to do so, he found the landlady beside him.

"One can lodge here to-night, madame?"

"Perfectly!" said the landlady, in a high, sing-song, cheery voice.

"Good. One can dine—sup—what you please to call it?"

"Ah, perfectly!" cried the landlady as before.

"Dispatch then, madame, if you please. Something to eat, as quickly as you can; and some wine at once. I am exhausted."

"It is very bad weather, monsieur," said the landlady.

"Cursed weather."

"And a very long road."

"A cursed road."

His hoarse voice failed him, and he rested his head upon his hands until a bottle of wine was brought from the counter. Having filled and

emptied his little tumbler twice, and having broken off an end from the
great loaf that was set before him with his cloth and napkin, soup-plate,
salt, pepper, and oil, he rested his back against the corner of the wall,
made a couch of the bench on which he sat, and began to chew crust until
such time as his repast should be ready.

There had been that momentary interruption of the talk about the stove,
and that temporary inattention to and distraction from one another, which
is usually inseparable in such a company from the arrival of a stranger.
It had passed over by this time; and the men had done glancing at him,
and were talking again.

"That's the true reason," said one of them, bringing a story he had been
telling, to a close, "that's the true reason why they said that the devil was
let loose." The speaker was the tall Swiss belonging to the church, and
he brought something of the authority of the church into the discussion—
especially as the devil was in question.

The landlady, having given her directions for the new guest's entertainment to her husband, who acted as cook to the Break of Day, had resumed
her needlework behind her counter. She was a smart, neat, bright little
woman, with a good deal of cap and a good deal of stocking, and she struck
into the conversation with several laughing nods of her head, but without
looking up from her work.

"Ah Heaven, then!" said she. "When the boat came up from Lyons,
and brought the news that the devil was actually let loose at Marseilles,
some fly-catchers swallowed it. But I? No, not I."

"Madame, you are always right," returned the tall Swiss. "Doubtless
you were enraged against that man, madame?"

"Ah, yes, then!" cried the landlady, raising her eyes from her work,
opening them very wide, and tossing her head on one side. "Naturally,
yes."

"He was a bad subject."

"He was a wicked wretch," said the landlady, "and well merited what
he had the good fortune to escape. So much the worse."

"Stay, madame! Let us see," returned the Swiss, argumentatively
turning his cigar between his lips. "It may have been his unfortunate
destiny. He may have been the child of circumstances. It is always possible
that he had, and has, good in him if one did but know how to find it out.
Philosophical philanthropy teaches—"

The rest of the little knot about the stove murmured an objection to the
introduction of that threatening expression. Even the two players at
dominoes glanced up from their game, as if to protest against philosophical
philanthropy being brought by name into the Break of Day.

"Hold there, you and your philanthropy," cried the smiling landlady,
nodding her head more than ever. "Listen then. I am a woman, I. I know
nothing of philosophical philanthropy. But I know what I have seen, and

what I have looked in the face, in this world here, where I find myself. And I tell you this, my friend, that there are people (men and women both, unfortunately) who have no good in them—none. That there are people whom it is necessary to detest without compromise. That there are people who must be dealt with as enemies of the human race. That there are people who have no human heart, and who must be crushed like savage beasts and cleared out of the way. They are but few, I hope; but I have seen (in this world here where I find myself, and even at the little Break of Day) that there are such people. And I do not doubt that this man—whatever they call him, I forget his name—is one of them."

The landlady's lively speech was received with greater favor at the Break of Day, than it would have elicited from certain amiable white-washers of the class she so unreasonably objected to, nearer Great Britain.

"My faith! If your philosophical philanthropy," said the landlady, putting down her work, and rising to take the stranger's soup from her husband, who appeared with it at a side door, "puts anybody at the mercy of such people by holding terms with them at all, in words or deeds, or both, take it away from the Break of Day, for it isn't worth a sou."

As she placed the soup before the guest, who changed his attitude to a sitting one, he looked her full in the face, and his moustache went up under his nose, and his nose came down over his moustache.

"Well!" said the previous speaker, "let us come back to our subject. Leaving all that aside, gentlemen, it was because the man was acquitted on his trial, that people said at Marseilles that the devil was let loose. That was how the phrase began to circulate, and what it meant; nothing more."

"How do they call him?" said the landlady. "Biraud, is it not?"

"Rigaud, madame," returned the tall Swiss.

"Rigaud! To be sure!"

The traveller's soup was succeeded by a dish of meat, and that by a dish of vegetables. He ate all that was placed before him, emptied his bottle of wine, called for a glass of rum, and smoked his cigarette with his cup of coffee. As he became refreshed, he became overbearing; and patronised the company at the Daybreak in certain small talk, at which he assisted, as if his condition were far above his appearance.

The company might have had other engagements, or they might have felt their inferiority, but in any case they dispersed by degrees, and not being replaced by other company, left their new patron in possession of the Break of Day. The landlord was clinking about in his kitchen; the landlady was quiet at her work; and the refreshed traveller sat smoking by the stove, warming his ragged feet.

"Pardon me, madame—that Biraud."

"Rigaud, monsieur."

"Rigaud. Pardon me again—has contracted your displeasure, how?"

The landlady, who had been at one moment thinking within herself that this was a handsome man, at another moment that this was an ill-looking man, observed the nose coming down and the moustache going up, and strongly inclined to the latter decision. Rigaud was a criminal, she said, who had killed his wife.

"Aye, aye? Death of my life, that's a criminal indeed. But how do you know it?"

"All the world knows it."

"Hah! And yet he escaped justice?"

"Monsieur, the law could not prove it against him to its satisfaction. So the law says. Nevertheless, all the world knows he did it. The people knew it so well, that they tried to tear him to pieces."

"Being all in perfect accord with their own wives?" said the guest. "Haha!"

The landlady of the Break of Day looked at him again, and felt almost confirmed in her last decision. He had a fine hand though, and he turned it with a great show. She began once more to think that he was not ill-looking after all.

"Did you mention, madame—or was it mentioned among the gentlemen —what became of him?"

The landlady shook her head; it being the first conversational stage at which her vivacious earnestness had ceased to nod it, keeping time to what she said. It had been mentioned at the Daybreak, she remarked, on the authority of the journals, that he had been kept in prison for his own safety. However that might be, he had escaped his deserts, so much the worse.

The guest sat looking at her as he smoked out his final cigarette, and as she sat with her head bent over her work, with an expression that might have resolved her doubts, and brought her to a lasting conclusion on the subject of his good or bad looks if she had seen it. When she did look up, the expression was not there. The hand was smoothing his shaggy moustache.

"May one ask to be shown to bed, madame?"

Very willingly, monsieur. Hola, my husband! My husband would conduct him up-stairs. There was one traveller there, asleep, who had gone to bed very early indeed, being overpowered by fatigue; but it was a large chamber with two beds in it, and space enough for twenty. This the landlady of the Break of Day chirpingly explained, calling between whiles, Hola, my husband! out at the side door.

My husband answered at length, "It is I, my wife!" and presenting himself in his cook's cap, lighted the traveller up a steep and narrow staircase; the traveller carrying his own cloak and knapsack, and bidding the landlady good night with a complimentary reference to the pleasure of seeing her again to-morrow. It was a large room, with a rough splintery floor, unplastered rafters overhead, and two bedsteads on opposite sides. Here my husband put down the candle he carried, and with a sidelong look at his guest stooping over his knapsack, gruffly gave him the instruction, "The bed to the right!" and left him to his repose. The landlord, whether he was a good or a bad physiognomist, had fully made up his mind that the guest was an ill-looking fellow.

The guest looked contemptuously at the clean coarse bedding prepared for him, and, sitting down on the rush chair at the bedside, drew his money out of his pocket, and told it over in his hand. "One must eat," he muttered to himself, "but by Heaven I must eat at the cost of some other man to-morrow!"

As he sat pondering, and mechanically weighing his money in his palm, the deep breathing of the traveller in the other bed fell so regularly upon his hearing that it attracted his eyes in that direction. The man was covered up warm, and had drawn the white curtain at his head, so that he could be only heard, not seen. But the deep regular breathing, still going on while the other was taking off his worn shoes and gaiters, and still continuing when he had laid aside his coat and cravat, became at length a strong provocative to curiosity, and incentive to get a glimpse of the sleeper's face.

The waking traveller, therefore, stole a little nearer, and yet a little nearer, and a little nearer, to the sleeping traveller's bed, until he stood close beside it. Even then he could not see his face, for he had drawn the sheet over it. The regular breathing still continuing, he put his smooth white hand (such a treacherous hand it looked, as it went creeping from him!) to the sheet, and gently lifted it away.

"Death of my soul!" he whispered, falling back, "here's Cavalletto!"

The little Italian, previously influenced in his sleep perhaps by the stealthy presence at his bedside, stopped in his regular breathing, and with a long deep respiration opened his eyes. At first they were not awake, though open. He lay for some seconds looking placidly at his old prison companion, and then, all at once, with a cry of surprise and alarm, sprang out of bed.

"Hush! What's the matter! Keep quiet! It's I. You know me?" cried the other, in a suppressed voice.

But John Baptist, widely staring, muttering a number of invocations and ejaculations, tremblingly backing into a corner, slipping on his trousers, and tying his coat by the two sleeves round his neck, manifested an unmistakeable desire to escape by the door rather than renew the acquaintance. Seeing this, his old prison comrade fell back upon the door, and set his shoulders against it.

"Cavalletto! Wake, boy! Rub your eyes and look at me. Not the name you used to call me—don't use that—Lagnier, say Lagnier!"

John Baptist, staring at him with eyes opened to their utmost width, made a number of those national, back-handed shakes of the right fore-finger in the air, as if he were resolved on negativing beforehand everything that the other could possibly advance, during the whole term of his life.

"Cavalletto! Give me your hand. You know Lagnier the gentleman. Touch the hand of a gentleman!"

Submitting himself to the old tone of condescending authority, John Baptist, not at all steady on his legs as yet, advanced and put his hand in his patron's. Monsieur Lagnier laughed; and having given it a squeeze, tossed it up and let it go.

"Then you were—" faltered John Baptist.

"Not shaved? No. See here!" cried Lagnier, giving his head a twirl, "as tight on as your own."

John Baptist, with a slight shiver, looked all round the room as if to recall where he was. His patron took that opportunity of turning the key in the door, and then sat down upon his bed.

"Look!" he said, holding up his shoes and gaiters. "That's a poor trim for a gentleman, you'll say. No matter, you shall see how soon I'll mend it. Come and sit down. Take your old place!"

John Baptist, looking anything but re-assured, sat down on the floor at the bedside, keeping his eyes upon his patron all the time.

"That's well!" cried Lagnier. "Now we might be in the old infernal hole again, hey? How long have you been out?"

"Two days after you, my master."

"How do you come here?"

"I was cautioned not to stay there, and so I left the town at once, and since then I have changed about. I have been doing odds and ends at Avignon, at Pont Esprit, at Lyons; upon the Rhone, upon the Saone." As he spoke, he rapidly mapped the places out with his sunburnt hand on the floor.

"And where are you going?"

"Going, my master?"

"Aye!"

John Baptist seemed to desire to evade the question without knowing how. "By Bacchus!" he said at last, as if he were forced to the admission, "I have sometimes had a thought of going to Paris, and perhaps to England."

"Cavalletto. This is in confidence. I also am going to Paris, and per-haps to England. We'll go together."

The little man nodded his head, and showed his teeth; and yet seemed not quite convinced that it was a surpassingly desirable arrangement.

"We'll go together," repeated Lagnier. "You shall see how soon I will force myself to be recognised as a gentleman, and you shall profit by it. Is it agreed? Are we one?"

"Oh, surely, surely!" said the little man.

"Then you shall hear before I sleep—and in six words, for I want sleep —how I appear before you, I, Lagnier. Remember that. Not the other."

"Altro, altro! Not Ri——" Before John Baptist could finish the name, his comrade had got his hand under his chin and fiercely shut up his mouth.

"Death! what are you doing? Do you want me to be trampled upon and stoned? Do *you* want to be trampled upon and stoned? You would be. You don't imagine that they would set upon me, and let my prison chum go? Don't think it!"

There was an expression in his face as he released his grip of his friend's jaw, from which his friend inferred, that if the course of events really came to any stoning and trampling, Monsieur Lagnier, would so distin-guish him with his notice as to ensure his having his full share of it. He remembered what a cosmopolitan gentleman Monsieur Lagnier was, and how few weak distinctions he made.

"I am a man," said Monsieur Lagnier, "whom society has deeply wronged since you last saw me. You know that I am sensitive and brave, and that it is my character to govern. How has society respected those qualities in me? I have been shrieked at through the streets. I have been guarded through the streets against men, and especially women, running at me armed with any weapons they could lay their hands on. I have lain in prison for security, with the place of my confinement kept a secret, lest I should be torn out of it and felled by a hundred blows. I have been carted out of Marseilles in the dead of night, and carried leagues away from it packed in straw. It has not been safe for me to go near my house; and, with a beggar's pittance in my pocket, I have walked through vile mud and weather ever since, until my feet are crippled—look at them! Such are the humiliations that society has inflicted upon me, possessing the qualities I have mentioned, and which you know me to possess. But society shall pay for it."

All this he said in his companion's ear, and with his hand before his lips.

"Even here," he went on in the same way, "even in this mean drinking-shop, society pursues me. Madame defames me, and her guests defame me. I, too, a gentleman with manners and accomplishments to strike them dead! But the wrongs society has heaped upon me are treasured in this breast."

To all of which John Baptist, listening attentively to the suppressed hoarse voice, said from time to time, "Surely, surely!" tossing his head and shutting his eyes, as if there were the clearest case against society that perfect candor could make out.

"Put my shoes there," continued Lagnier. "Hang my cloak to dry there by the door. Take my hat." He obeyed each instruction, as it was given. "And this is the bed to which society consigns me, is it? Hah. *Very* well!"

As he stretched out his length upon it, with a ragged handkerchief bound round his wicked head, and only his wicked head showing above the bed-clothes, John Baptist was rather strongly reminded of what had so very nearly happened to prevent the moustache from any more going up as it did, and the nose from any more coming down as it did.

"Shaken out of destiny's dice-box again into your company, eh? By Heaven! So much the better for you. You'll profit by it. I shall need a long rest. Let me sleep in the morning."

John Baptist replied that he should sleep as long as he would, and wishing him a happy night, put out the candle. One might have supposed that the next proceeding of the Italian would have been to undress; but he did exactly the reverse, and dressed himself from head to foot, saving his shoes. When he had so done, he lay down upon his bed with some of its coverings over him, and his coat still tied round his neck, to get through the night.

When he started up, the Godfather Break of Day was peeping at its namesake. He rose, took his shoes in his hand, turned the key in the door with great caution, and crept down-stairs. Nothing was astir there but the smell of coffee, wine, tobacco, and syrups; and madame's little counter looked ghastly enough. But he had paid madame his little note at it over night, and wanted to see nobody—wanted nothing but to get on his shoes and his knapsack, open the door, and run away.

He prospered in his object. No movement or voice was heard when he opened the door; no wicked head tied up in a ragged handkerchief looked out of the upper window. When the sun had raised his full disc above the flat line of the horizon, and was striking fire out of the long muddy vista of paved road with its weary avenue of little trees, a black speck moved along the road and splashed among the flaming pools of rain-water, which black speck was John Baptist Cavalletto running away from his patron.

END OF No. III

CHAPTER XII

BLEEDING HEART YARD

In London itself, though in the old rustic road towards a suburb of note where in the days of William Shakespeare, author and stage-player, there were Royal hunting seats, howbeit no sport is left there now but for hunters of men, Bleeding Heart Yard was to be found. A place much changed in feature and in fortune, yet with some relish of ancient greatness about it. Two or three mighty stacks of chimneys, and a few large dark rooms which had escaped being walled and subdivided out of the recognition of their old proportions, gave the Yard a character. It was inhabited by poor people, who set up their rest among its faded glories, as Arabs of the desert pitch their tents among the fallen stones of the Pyramids; but there was a family sentimental feeling prevalent in the Yard, that it had a character.

As if the aspiring city had become puffed up in the very ground on which it stood, the ground had so risen about Bleeding Heart Yard that you got into it down a flight of steps which formed no part of the original approach, and got out of it by a low gateway into a maze of shabby streets, which went about and about, tortuously ascending to the level again. At this end of the Yard and over the gateway, was the factory of Daniel Doyce, often heavily beating like a bleeding heart of iron, with the clink of metal upon metal.

The opinion of the Yard was divided respecting the derivation of its name. The more practical of its inmates abided by the tradition of a murder; the gentler and more imaginative inhabitants, including the whole of the tender sex, were loyal to the legend of a young lady of former times closely imprisoned in her chamber by a cruel father for remaining true to her own true love, and refusing to marry the suitor he chose for her. The legend related how that the young lady used to be seen up at her window behind the bars, murmuring a love-lorn song, of which the burden was, "Bleeding Heart, Bleeding Heart, bleeding away," until she died. It was objected by the murderous party that this Refrain was notoriously the invention of a tambour-worker, a spinster and romantic, still lodging in the Yard. But, forasmuch as all favorite legends must be associated with the affections, and as many more people fall in love than commit murder—which it may be hoped, howsoever bad we are, will continue unto the end of the world to be the dispensation under which we shall live—the Bleeding Heart, Bleeding Heart, bleeding away story, carried the day by a great majority. Neither party would listen to the antiquaries who delivered learned lectures in the neighbourhood, showing the Bleeding Heart to have been the heraldic cognizance of the old family to whom the property had once belonged. And, considering that the hour-glass they turned from year to year was filled with the earthiest and coarsest sand, the Bleeding Heart Yarders had reason enough for objecting to be despoiled of the one little golden grain of poetry that sparkled in it.

Down into the Yard, by way of the steps, came Daniel Doyce, Mr. Meagles, and Clennam. Passing along the Yard, and between the open doors on either hand, all abundantly garnished with light children nursing heavy ones, they arrived at its opposite boundary, the gateway. Here Arthur Clennam stopped to look about him for the domicile of Plornish, plasterer: whose name, according to the custom of Londoners, Daniel Doyce had never seen or heard of to that hour.

It was plain enough, nevertheless, as Little Dorrit had said; over a lime-splashed gateway in the corner, within which Plornish kept a ladder and a barrel or two. The last house in Bleeding Heart Yard which she had described as his place of habitation, was a large house, let off to various tenants; but Plornish ingeniously hinted that he lived in the parlor, by means of a painted hand under his name, the forefinger of which hand (on which the artist had depicted a ring and a most elaborate nail of the genteelest form), referred all enquirers to that apartment.

Parting from his companions, after arranging another meeting with Mr. Meagles, Clennam went alone into the entry, and knocked with his knuckles at the parlor-door. It was opened presently by a woman with a child in her arms, whose unoccupied hand was hastily re-arranging the upper part of her dress. This was Mrs. Plornish, and this maternal action was the action of Mrs. Plornish during a large part of her waking existence.

Was Mr. Plornish at home? "Well, sir," said Mrs. Plornish, a civil woman, "not to deceive you, he's gone to look for a job."

Not to deceive you, was a method of speech with Mrs. Plornish. She would deceive you, under any circumstances, as little as might be; but she had a trick of answering in this provisional form.

"Do you think he will be back soon, if I wait for him?"

"I have been expecting him," said Mrs. Plornish, "this half-an-hour, at any minute of time. Walk in, sir."

Arthur entered the rather dark and close parlor (though it was lofty too), and sat down in the chair she placed for him.

"Not to deceive you, sir, I notice it," said Mrs. Plornish, "and I take it kind of you."

He was at a loss to understand what she meant; and by expressing as much in his looks, elicited her explanation.

"It an't many that comes into a poor place, that deems it worth their while to move their hats," said Mrs. Plornish. "But people think more of it than people think."

Clennam returned, with an uncomfortable feeling in so very slight a courtesy being unusual, Was that all! and stooping down to pinch the cheek of another young child who was sitting on the floor, staring at him, asked Mrs. Plornish how old that fine boy was?

"Four year just turned, sir," said Mrs. Plornish. "He *is* a fine little fellow, an't he, sir? But this one is rather sickly." She tenderly hushed the baby in her arms, as she said it. "You wouldn't mind my asking if it happened to be a job as you was come about, sir, would you?" added Mrs. Plornish, wistfully.

She asked it so anxiously, that if he had been in possession of any kind of tenement, he would have had it plastered a foot deep, rather than answer, No. But he was obliged to answer No; and he saw a shade of disappointment on her face, as she checked a sigh, and looked at the low fire. Then he saw, also, that Mrs. Plornish was a young woman, made somewhat slatternly in herself and her belongings by poverty; and so dragged at by poverty and the children together, that their united forces had already dragged her face into wrinkles.

"All such things as jobs," said Mrs. Plornish, "seems to me to have gone under ground, they do indeed." (Herein Mrs. Plornish limited her remark to the plastering trade, and spoke without reference to the Circumlocution Office and the Barnacle Family.)

"Is it so difficult to get work?" asked Arthur Clennam.

"Plornish finds it so," she returned. "He is quite unfortunate. Really he is."

Really he was. He was one of those many wayfarers on the road of life, who seem to be afflicted with supernatural corns, rendering it impossible for them to keep up even with their lame competitors. A willing, working, soft-hearted, not hard-headed fellow, Plornish took his fortune as smoothly as could be expected; but it was a rough one. It so rarely happened that anybody seemed to want him, it was such an exceptional case when his powers were in any request, that his misty mind could not make out how it happened. He took it as it came, therefore; he tumbled into all kinds of difficulties, and tumbled out of them; and, by tumbling through life, got himself considerably bruised.

"It's not for want of looking after jobs, I am sure," said Mrs. Plornish, lifting up her eyebrows, and searching for a solution of the problem between the bars of the grate; "nor yet for want of working at them, when they are to be got. No one ever heard my husband complain of work."

Somehow or other, this was the general misfortune of Bleeding Heart Yard. From time to time there were public complaints, pathetically going about, of labor being scarce—which certain people seemed to take extraordinarily ill, as though they had an absolute right to it on their own terms—but Bleeding Heart Yard, though as willing a Yard as any in Britain, was never the better for the demand. That high old family, the Barnacles, had long been too busy with their great principle to look into the matter; and indeed the matter had nothing to do with their watchfulness in out-generaling all other high old families except the Stiltstalkings.

While Mrs. Plornish spoke in these words of her absent lord, her lord returned. A smooth-cheeked, fresh-colored, sandy-whiskered man of thirty. Long in the legs, yielding at the knees, foolish in the face, flannel-jacketed, lime-whitened. "This is Plornish, sir."

"I came," said Clennam, rising, "to beg the favor of a little conversation with you, on the subject of the Dorrit family."

Plornish became suspicious. Seemed to scent a creditor. Said, "Ah, Yes. Well. He didn't know what satisfaction *he* could give any gentleman respecting that family. What might it be about, now?"

"I know you better," said Clennam, smiling, "than you suppose."

Plornish observed, not smiling in return, And yet he hadn't the pleasure of being acquainted with the gentleman, neither.

"No," said Arthur, "I know of your kind offices at second hand, but on the best authority. Through Little Dorrit.—I mean," he explained, "Miss Dorrit."

"Mr. Clennam, is it? Oh! I've heard of you, sir."

"And I of you," said Arthur.

"Please to sit down again, sir, and consider yourself welcome.—Why, yes," said Plornish, taking a chair, and lifting the elder child upon his knee, that he might have the moral support of speaking to a stranger over his head, "I have been on the wrong side of the lock myself, and in that way we come to know Miss Dorrit. Me and my wife, we are well acquainted with Miss Dorrit."

"Intimate!" cried Mrs. Plornish. Indeed, she was so proud of the acquaintance, that she had awakened some bitterness of spirit in the Yard, by magnifying to an enormous amount the sum for which Miss Dorrit's father had become insolvent. The Bleeding Hearts resented her claiming to know people of such distinction.

"It was her father that I got acquainted with first. And through getting acquainted with him, you see—why—I got acquainted with her," said Plornish tautologically.

"I see."

"Ah! And there's manners! There's polish! There's a gentleman to have run to seed in the Marshalsea Jail! Why, perhaps you are not aware," said Plornish, lowering his voice, and speaking with a perverse admiration of what he ought to have pitied or despised, "not aware that Miss Dorrit and her sister dursn't let him know that they work for a living. No!" said Plornish, looking with a ridiculous triumph first at his wife, and then all round the room. "Dursn't let him know it, they dursn't!"

"Without admiring him for that," Clennam quietly observed, "I am very sorry for him." The remark appeared to suggest to Plornish, for the first time, that it might not be a very fine trait of character after all. He pondered about it for a moment, and gave it up.

"As to me," he resumed, "certainly Mr. Dorrit is as affable with me, I am sure, as I can possibly expect. Considering the differences and distances betwixt us, more so. But it's Miss Dorrit that we were speaking of."

"True. Pray how did you introduce her at my mother's?"

Mr. Plornish picked a bit of lime out of his whisker, put it between his lips, turned it with his tongue like a sugar-plum, considered, found himself unequal to the task of lucid explanation, and appealing to his wife, said, "Sally, *you* may as well mention how it was, old woman."

"Miss Dorrit," said Sally, hushing the baby from side to side, and laying her chin upon the little hand as it tried to disarrange the gown again, "came here one afternoon with a bit of writing, telling that how she wished for needlework, and asked if it would be considered any ill-conwenience in case she was to give her address here." (Plornish repeated, her address here, in a low voice, as if he were making responses at church.) "Me and Plornish says, No, Miss Dorrit, no ill-conwenience," (Plornish repeated, no ill-conwenience,) "and she wrote it in, according. Which then me and Plornish says, Ho Miss Dorrit!" (Plornish repeated, Ho Miss Dorrit.) "Have you thought of copying it three or four times, as the way to make it known in more places than one? No, says Miss Dorrit, I have not, but I will. She copied it out according, on this table, in a sweet writing, and Plornish, he took it where he worked, having a job just then," (Plornish repeated, job just then,) "and likeways to the landlord of the Yard; through which it was that Mrs. Clennam first happened to employ Miss Dorrit." Plornish repeated, employ Miss Dorrit; and Mrs. Plornish having come to an end, feigned to bite the fingers of the little hand as she kissed it.

"The landlord of the Yard," said Arthur Clennam, "is——"

"He is Mr. Casby, by name, he is," said Plornish, "and Pancks, he collects the rents. That," added Mr. Plornish, dwelling on the subject, with a slow thoughtfulness that appeared to have no connexion with any specific object, and to lead him nowhere, "that is about what *they* are, you may believe me or not, as you think proper."

"Aye?" returned Clennam, thoughtful in his turn. "Mr. Casby, too! An old acquaintance of mine, long ago!"

Mr. Plornish did not see his road to any comment on this fact, and made none. As there truly was no reason why he should have the least interest in it, Arthur Clennam went on to the present purport of his visit; namely, to make Plornish the instrument of effecting Tip's release, with as little detriment as possible to the self-reliance and self-helpfulness of the young man, supposing him to possess any remnant of those qualities: without doubt a very wide stretch of supposition. Plornish, having been made acquainted with the cause of action from the Defendant's own mouth, gave Arthur to understand that the Plaintiff was "a Chaunter"—meaning, not a singer of anthems, but a seller of horses—and that he (Plornish) considered that ten shillings in the pound "would settle handsome," and that more would be a waste of money. The Principal and instrument soon drove off together to a stable-yard in High Holborn, where a remarkably fine grey gelding, worth, at the lowest figure, seventy-five guineas (not taking into account the value of the shot he had been made to swallow, for the improvement of his form), was to be parted with for a twenty-pound note, in consequence of his having run away last week with Mrs. Captain Barbary of Cheltenham, who wasn't up to a horse of his courage, and who, in mere spite, insisted on selling him for that ridiculous sum: or, in other words, on giving him away. Plornish, going up this yard alone and leaving his Principal outside, found a gentleman with tight drab legs, a rather old hat, a little hooked stick, and a blue neckerchief (Captain Maroon of

Gloucestershire, a private friend of Captain Barbary); who happened to be there, in a friendly way, to mention these little circumstances concerning the remarkably fine grey gelding, to any real judge of a horse and quick snapper-up of a good thing, who might look in at that address as per advertisement. This gentleman, happening also to be the Plaintiff in the Tip case, referred Mr. Plornish to his solicitor, and declined to treat with Mr. Plornish, or even to endure his presence in the yard, unless he appeared there with a twenty-pound note: in which case only, the gentleman would augur from appearances that he meant business, and might be induced to talk to him. On this hint, Mr. Plornish retired to communicate with his Principal, and presently came back with the required credentials. Then said Captain Maroon, "Now, how much time do you want to make up the other twenty in? Now, I'll give you a month." Then said Captain Maroon, when that wouldn't suit, "Now, I'll tell what I'll do with you. You shall get me a good bill at four months, made payable at a banking-house, for the other twenty!" Then said Captain Maroon, when *that* wouldn't suit, "Now, come! Here's the last I've got to say to you. You shall give me another ten down, and I'll run my pen clean through it." Then said Captain Maroon, when *that* wouldn't suit, "Now, I'll tell you what it is, and this shuts it up; he has used me bad, but I'll let him off for another five down and a bottle of wine; and if you mean done, say done, and if you don't like it, leave it." Finally said Captain Maroon, when *that* wouldn't suit either, "Hand over, then!"—And in consideration of the first offer, gave a receipt in full and discharged the prisoner.

"Mr. Plornish," said Arthur, "I trust to you, if you please, to keep my secret. If you will undertake to let the young man know that he is free, and to tell him that you were employed to compound for the debt by some one whom you are not at liberty to name, you will not only do me a service, but may do him one, and his sister also."

"The last reason, sir," said Plornish, "would be quite sufficient. Your wishes shall be attended to."

"A Friend has obtained his discharge, you can say if you please. A Friend who hopes that for his sister's sake, if for no one else's, he will make good use of his liberty."

"Your wishes, sir, shall be attended to."

"And if you will be so good, in your better knowledge of the family, as to communicate freely with me, and to point out to me any means by which you think I may be delicately and really useful to Little Dorrit, I shall feel under an obligation to you."

"Don't name it, sir," returned Plornish, "it'll be ekally a pleasure and a—it'll be ekally a pleasure and a—." Finding himself unable to balance his sentence after two efforts, Mr. Plornish wisely dropped it. He took Clennam's card, and appropriate pecuniary compliment.

He was earnest to finish his commission at once, and his Principal was in the same mind. So, his Principal offered to set him down at the Marshalsea Gate, and they drove in that direction over Blackfriars Bridge. On the way, Arthur elicited from his new friend, a confused summary of the interior life of Bleeding Heart Yard. They was all hard up there, Mr. Plornish said, uncommon hard up, to-be-sure. Well, he couldn't say how it was; he didn't know as anybody *could* say how it was; all he know'd was, that so it was. When a man felt, on his own back and in his own belly, that he was poor, that man (Mr. Plornish gave it as his decided belief) know'd well that poor he was somehow or another, and you couldn't talk it out of him, no more than you could talk Beef into him. Then you see, some people as was better off said, and a good many such people lived pretty close up to the mark themselves if not beyond it so he'd heerd, that they was "improvident" (that was the favorite word) down the Yard. For instance, if they see a man with his wife and children a going to Hampton Court in a Wan, perhaps once in a year, they says, "Hallo! I thought you was poor, my improvident friend!" Why, Lord, how hard it was upon a man! What was a man to do? He couldn't go mollancholly mad, and even if he did, you wouldn't be the better for it. In Mr. Plornish's judgment, you would be the worse for it. Yet you seemed to want to make a man mollancholly mad. You was always at it—if not with your right hand, with your left. What was they a doing in the Yard? Why, take a look at 'em and see. There was the girls and their mothers a working at their sewing, or their shoe-binding, or their trimming, or their waistcoat making, day and night and night and day, and not more than able to keep body and soul together after all—often not so much. There was pretty well all sorts of trader you could name, all wanting to work, and yet not able to get it. There was old people, after working all their lives, going and being shut up in the Workhouse, much worse fed and lodged and treated altogether, than—Mr. Plornish said manufacturers, but appeared to mean malefactors. Why, a man didn't know where to turn himself, for a crumb of comfort. As to who was to blame for it, Mr. Plornish didn't know who was to blame for it. He could tell you who suffered, but he couldn't tell you whose fault it was. It wasn't *his* place to find out, and who'd mind what he said, if he did find out? He only know'd that it wasn't put right by them what undertook that line of business, and that it didn't come right of itself. And in brief his illogical opinion was, that if you couldn't do nothing for him, you had better take nothing from him for doing of it; so far as he could make out, that was about what it come to. Thus, in a prolix, gently-growling, foolish way, did Plornish turn the tangled skein of his estate about and about, like a blind man who was trying to find some beginning or end to it; until they reached the prison gate. There, he left his Principal alone; to wonder, as he rode away, how many thousand Plornishes there might be within a day or two's journey of the Circumlocution Office, playing sundry curious variations on the same tune, which were not known by ear in that glorious institution.

CHAPTER XIII

PATRIARCHAL

THE mention of Mr. Casby again revived, in Clennam's memory, the smouldering embers of curiosity and interest which Mrs. Flintwinch had fanned on the night of his arrival. Flora Casby had been the beloved of his boyhood; and Flora was the daughter and only child of wooden-headed old Christopher (so he was still occasionally spoken of by some irreverent spirits who had had dealings with him, and in whom familiarity had bred its proverbial result perhaps), who was reputed to be rich in weekly tenants, and to get a good quantity of blood out of the stones of several unpromising courts and alleys.

After some days of enquiry and research, Arthur Clennam became convinced that the case of the Father of the Marshalsea was indeed a hopeless one, and sorrowfully resigned the idea of helping him to freedom again. He had no hopeful enquiry to make, at present, concerning Little Dorrit either; but he argued with himself that it might, for anything he knew it might, be serviceable to the poor child, if he renewed this acquaintance. It is hardly necessary to add, that beyond all doubt he would have presented himself at Mr. Casby's door, if there had been no Little Dorrit in existence; for we all know how we all deceive ourselves—that is to say, how people in general, our profounder selves excepted, deceive themselves —as to motives of action.

With a comfortable impression upon him, and quite an honest one in its way, that he was still patronising Little Dorrit in doing what had no reference to her, he found himself one afternoon at the corner of Mr. Casby's street. Mr. Casby lived in a street in the Gray's Inn Road, which had set off from that thoroughfare with the intention of running at one heat down into the valley, and up again to the top of Pentonville Hill; but which had run itself out of breath in twenty yards, and had stood still ever since. There is no such place in that part now; but it remained there for many years, looking with a baulked countenance at the wilderness patched with unfruitful gardens and pimpled with eruptive summer-houses, that it had meant to run over in no time.

"The house," thought Clennam, as he crossed to the door, "is as little changed as my mother's, and looks almost as gloomy. But the likeness ends outside. I know its staid repose within. The smell of its jars of old rose-leaves and lavender seems to come upon me even here."

When his knock, at the bright brass knocker of obsolete shape, brought a woman-servant to the door, those faded scents in truth saluted him like wintry breath that had a faint remembrance in it of the bygone spring. He stepped into the sober, silent, air-tight house—one might have fancied it to have been stifled by Mutes in the Eastern manner—and the door, closing again, seemed to shut out sound and motion. The furniture was formal, grave, and quaker-like, but well-kept; and had as prepossessing an aspect, as anything, from a human creature to a wooden stool, that is meant for much use and is preserved for little, can ever wear. There was a grave clock, ticking somewhere up the staircase; and there was a songless bird in the same direction, pecking at his cage as if he were ticking too. The parlor-fire ticked in the grate. There was only one person on the parlor-hearth, and the loud watch in his pocket ticked audibly.

The servant-maid had ticked the two words "Mr. Clennam" so softly that she had not been heard; and he consequently stood, within the door she had closed, unnoticed. The figure of a man advanced in life, whose smooth grey eyebrows seemed to move to the ticking as the firelight flickered on them, sat in an arm-chair, with his list shoes on the rug, and his thumbs slowly revolving over one another. This was old Christopher Casby—recognisable at a glance—as unchanged in twenty years and upwards, as his own solid furniture—as little touched by the influences of the varying seasons, as the old rose-leaves and old lavender in his porcelain jars.

Perhaps there never was a man, in this troublesome world, so trouble-some for the imagination to picture as a boy. And yet he had changed very little in his progress through life. Confronting him, in the room in which he sat, was a boy's portrait, which anybody seeing him would have identified as Master Christopher Casby, aged ten: though disguised with a haymaking rake, for which he had had, at any time, as much taste or use as for a diving-bell; and sitting (on one of his own legs) upon a bank of violets, moved to precocious contemplation by the spire of a village church. There was the same smooth face and forehead, the same calm blue eye, the same placid air. The shining bald head, which looked so very large because it shone so much; and the long grey hair at its sides and back, like floss silk or spun glass, which looked so very benevolent because it was never cut; were not, of course, to be seen in the boy as in the old man. Nevertheless, in the Sera-phic creature with the haymaking rake, were clearly to be discerned the rudiments of the Patriarch with the list shoes.

Patriarch was the name which many people delighted to give him. Various old ladies in the neighbourhood spoke of him as The Last of the Patriarchs. So grey, so slow, so quiet, so impassionate, so very bumpy in the head, Patriarch was the word for him. He had been accosted in the streets, and respectfully solicited to become a Patriarch for painters and for sculptors: with so much importunity, in sooth, that it would appear to be beyond the Fine Arts to remember the points of a Patriarch, or to invent one. Philanthropists of both sexes had asked who he was, and on being informed, "Old Christopher Casby, formerly Town-agent to Lord Decimus Tite Barnacle," had cried in a rapture of disappointment, "Oh! why, with that head, is he not a benefactor to his species! Oh! why, with that head, is he not a father to the orphan and a friend to the friendless!" With that head, however, he remained old Christopher Casby, proclaimed by common report rich in house property; and with that head, he now sat in his silent parlor. Indeed it would be the height of unreason to expect him to be sitting there without that head.

Arthur Clennam moved to attract his attention, and the grey eyebrows turned towards him.

"I beg your pardon," said Clennam, "I fear you did not hear me announced?"

"No, sir, I did not. Did you wish to see me, sir?"

"I wished to pay my respects."

Mr. Casby seemed a feather's weight disappointed by the last words, having perhaps prepared himself for the visitor's wishing to pay something else. "Have I the pleasure, sir," he proceeded—"take a chair, if you please —have I the pleasure of knowing—? Ah! truly, yes, I think I have! I believe I am not mistaken in supposing that I am acquainted with those features? I think I address a gentleman of whose return to this country I was informed by Mr. Flintwinch?"

"That is your present visitor."

"Really! Mr. Clennam?"

"No other, Mr. Casby."

"Mr. Clennam, I am glad to see you. How have you been since we met?"

Without thinking it worth while to explain that in the course of some quarter of a century he had experienced occasional slight fluctuations in his health and spirits, Clennam answered generally that he had never been better, or something equally to the purpose; and shook hands with the possessor of "that head," as it shed its patriarchal light upon him.

"We are older, Mr. Clennam," said Christopher Casby.

"We are—not younger," said Clennam. After this wise remark he felt that he was scarcely shining with brilliancy, and became aware that he was nervous.

"And your respected father," said Mr. Casby, "is no more! I was grieved to hear it, Mr. Clennam, I was grieved."

Arthur implied in the usual way that he felt infinitely obliged to him.

"There was a time," said Mr. Casby, "when your parents and myself were not on friendly terms. There was a little family misunderstanding among us. Your respected mother was rather jealous of her son, maybe; when I say her son, I mean your worthy self, your worthy self."

His smooth face had a bloom upon it, like ripe wall-fruit. What with his blooming face, and that head, and his blue eyes, he seemed to be delivering sentiments of rare wisdom and virtue. In like manner, his physiognomical expression seemed to teem with benignity. Nobody could have said where the wisdom was, or where the virtue was, or where the benignity was; but they all seemed to be somewhere about him.

"Those times, however," pursued Mr. Casby, "are past and gone, past and gone. I do myself the pleasure of making a visit to your respected mother occasionally, and of admiring the fortitude and strength of mind with which she bears her trials, bears her trials."

When he made one of these little repetitions, sitting with his hands crossed before him, he did it with his head on one side and a gentle smile, as if he had something in his thoughts too sweetly profound to be put into words. As if he denied himself the pleasure of uttering it, lest he should soar too high; and his meekness therefore preferred to be unmeaning.

"I have heard that you were kind enough on one of those occasions," said Arthur, catching at the opportunity as it drifted past him, "to mention Little Dorrit to my mother."

"Little—? Dorrit? That's the seamstress who was mentioned to me by a small tenant of mine? Yes, yes. Dorrit? That's the name. Ah, yes, yes! You call her Little Dorrit?"

No road in that direction. Nothing came of the cross-cut. It led no further.

"My daughter Flora," said Mr. Casby, "as you may have heard probably, Mr. Clennam, was married and established in life, several years ago. She had the misfortune to lose her husband when she had been married a few months. She resides with me again. She will be glad to see you, if you will permit me to let her know that you are here."

"By all means," returned Clennam. "I should have preferred the request, if your kindness had not anticipated me."

Upon this, Mr. Casby rose up in his list shoes, and with a slow, heavy step (he was of an elephantine build), made for the door. He had a long wide-skirted bottle-green coat on, and a bottle-green pair of trousers, and a bottle-green waistcoat. The Patriarchs were not dressed in bottle-green broadcloth, and yet his clothes looked patriarchal.

He had scarcely left the room, and allowed the ticking to become audible again, when a quick hand turned a latchkey in the house-door, opened it, and shut it. Immediately afterwards, a quick and eager short dark man bustled into the room with so much way upon him, that he was within a foot of Clennam before he could stop.

"Halloa!" he said.

Clennam saw no reason why he should not say "Halloa!" too.

"What's the matter?" said the short dark man.

"I have not heard that anything is the matter," returned Clennam.

"Where's Mr. Casby?" asked the short dark man, looking about.

"He will be here directly, if you want him."

"*I* want him?" said the short dark man. "Don't you?"

This elicited a word or two of explanation from Clennam, during the delivery of which the short dark man held his breath and looked at him. He was dressed in black, and rusty iron grey; had jet black beads of eyes; a scrubby little black chin; wiry black hair striking out from his head in prongs, like forks or hair-pins; and a complexion that was very dingy by nature, or very dirty by art, or a compound of nature and art. He had dirty hands and dirty broken nails, and looked as if he had been in the coals; he was in a perspiration, and snorted and sniffed and puffed and blew, like a little laboring steam-engine.

"Oh!" said he, when Arthur had told him how he came to be there. "Very well. That's right. If he should ask for Pancks, will you be so good as to say that Pancks is come in?" And so, with a snort and a puff, he worked out by another door.

Now, in the old days at home, certain audacious doubts respecting the last of the Patriarchs, which were afloat in the air, had, by some forgotten means, come in contact with Arthur's sensorium. He was aware of motes and specks of suspicion, in the atmosphere of that time; seen through which medium, Christopher Casby was a mere Inn signpost without any Inn—an invitation to rest and be thankful, when there was no place to put up at, and nothing whatever to be thankful for. He knew that some of these specks even represented Christopher as capable of harboring designs in "that head," and as being a crafty impostor. Other motes there were which showed him as a heavy, selfish, drifting Booby, who, having stumbled, in the course of his unwieldy jostlings against other men, on the discovery that to get through life with ease and credit, he had but to hold his tongue, keep the bald part of his head well polished, and leave his hair alone, had had just cunning enough to seize the idea and stick to it. It was said that his being town-agent to Lord Decimus Tite Barnacle was referable, not to his having the least business capacity, but to his looking so supremely benignant that nobody could suppose the property screwed or jobbed under such a man; also, that for similar reasons he now got more money out of his own wretched lettings, unquestioned, than anybody with a less knobby and less shining crown could possibly have done. In a word, it was represented (Clennam called to mind, alone in the ticking parlor) that many people select their models, much as the painters, just now mentioned, select theirs; and that, whereas in the Royal Academy some evil old ruffian of a Dog-stealer will annually be found embodying all the cardinal virtues, on account of his eyelashes, or his chin, or his legs (thereby planting thorns of confusion in the breasts of the more observant students of nature), so, in the great social Exhibition, accessories are often accepted in lieu of the internal character.

Calling these things to mind, and ranging Mr. Pancks in a row with them, Arthur Clennam leaned this day to the opinion, without quite deciding on it, that the last of the Patriarchs was the drifting Booby aforesaid, with the one idea of keeping the bald part of his head highly polished: and that, much as an unwieldy ship in the Thames river may sometimes be seen heavily driving with the tide, broadside on, stern first, in its own way and in the way of everything else, though making a great show of navigation, when all of a sudden, a little coaly steam-tug will bear down upon it, take it in tow, and bustle off with it; similarly, the cumbrous Patriarch had been taken in tow by the snorting Pancks, and was now following in the wake of that dingy little craft.

The return of Mr. Casby, with his daughter Flora, put an end to these meditations. Clennam's eyes no sooner fell upon the object of his old passion, than it shivered and broke to pieces.

Most men will be found sufficiently true to themselves to be true to an old idea. It is no proof of an inconstant mind, but exactly the opposite, when the idea will not bear close comparison with the reality, and the contrast is a fatal shock to it. Such was Clennam's case. In his youth he had ardently loved this woman, and had heaped upon her all the locked-up wealth of his affection and imagination. That wealth had been, in his desert home, like Robinson Crusoe's money; exchangeable with no one, lying idle in the dark to rust, until he poured it out for her. Ever since that memorable time, though he had, until the night of his arrival, as completely dismissed her from any association with his Present or Future as if she had been dead (which she might easily have been for anything he knew), he had kept the old fancy of the Past unchanged, in its old sacred place. And now, after all, the last of the Patriarchs coolly walked into the parlor, saying in effect, "Be good enough to throw it down and dance upon it. This is Flora."

Flora, always tall, had grown to be very broad too, and short of breath; but that was not much. Flora, whom he had left a lily, had become a peony; but that was not much. Flora, who had seemed enchanting in all she said and thought, was diffuse and silly. That was much. Flora, who had been spoiled and artless long ago, was determined to be spoiled and artless now. That was a fatal blow.

This is Flora!

"I am sure," giggled Flora, tossing her head with a caricature of her girlish manner, such as a mummer might have presented at her own funeral, if she had lived and died in classical antiquity, "I am ashamed to see Mr. Clennam, I am a mere fright, I know he'll find me fearfully changed, I am actually an old woman, it's shocking to be so found out, it's really shocking!"

He assured her that she was just what he had expected, and that time had not stood still with himself.

"Oh! But with a gentleman it's so different and really you look so amazingly well that you have no right to say anything of the kind, while, as to me you know—oh!" cried Flora with a little scream, "I am dreadful!"

The Patriarch, apparently not yet understanding his own part in the drama under representation, glowed with vacant serenity.

"But if we talk of not having changed," said Flora, who, whatever she said, never once came to a full stop, "look at Papa, is not Papa precisely what he was when you went away, isn't it cruel and unnatural of Papa to be such a reproach to his own child, if we go on in this way much longer people who don't know us will begin to suppose that I am Papa's Mama!"

That must be a long time hence, Arthur considered.

"Oh Mr. Clennam you insincerest of creatures," said Flora, "I see already you have not lost your old way of paying compliments, your old way when you used to pretend to be so sentimentally struck you know—at least I don't mean that, I—oh I don't know what I mean!" Here Flora tittered confusedly, and gave him one of her old glances.

The Patriarch, as if he now began to perceive that his part in the piece was to get off the stage as soon as might be, rose, and went to the door by which Pancks had worked out, hailing that Tug by name. He received an answer from some little Dock beyond, and was towed out of sight directly.

"You mustn't think of going yet," said Flora—Arthur had looked at his hat, being in a ludicrous dismay, and not knowing what to do; "you could never be so unkind as to think of going, Arthur—I mean Mr. Arthur—or I suppose Mr. Clennam would be far more proper—but I am sure I don't know what I'm saying—without a word about the dear old days gone for ever, however when I come to think of it I dare say it would be much better not to speak of them and it's highly probable that you have some much more agreeable engagement and pray let Me be the last person in the world to interfere with it though there *was* a time, but I am running into nonsense again."

Was it possible that Flora could have been such a chatterer, in the days she referred to? Could there have been anything like her present disjointed volubility, in the fascinations that had captivated him?

"Indeed I have little doubt," said Flora, running on with astonishing speed, and pointing her conversation with nothing but commas, and very few of them, "that you are married to some Chinese lady, being in China so long and being in business and naturally desirous to settle and extend your connexion nothing was more likely than that you should propose to a Chinese lady and nothing was more natural I am sure than that the Chinese lady should accept you and think herself very well off too, I only hope she's not a Pagodian dissenter."

"I am not," returned Arthur, smiling in spite of himself, "married to any lady, Flora."

"Oh good gracious me I hope you never kept yourself a bachelor so long on my account!" tittered Flora; "but of course you never did why should you, pray don't answer, I don't know where I'm running to, oh do tell me something about the Chinese ladies whether their eyes are really so long and narrow always putting me in mind of mother-of-pearl fish at cards and do they really wear tails down their backs and plaited too or is it only the men, and when they pull their hair so very tight off their foreheads don't they hurt themselves, and why do they stick little bells all over their bridges and temples and hats and things or don't they really do it!" Flora gave him another of her old glances. Instantly she went on again, as if he had spoken in reply for some time.

"Then it's all true and they really do! good gracious Arthur!—pray excuse me—old habit—Mr. Clennam far more proper—what a country to live in for so long a time, and with so many lanterns and umbrellas too how very dark and wet the climate ought to be and no doubt actually is, and the sums of money that must be made by those two trades where everybody carries them and hangs them everywhere, the little shoes too and the feet screwed back in infancy is quite surprising, what a traveller you are!"

In his ridiculous distress, Clennam received another of the old glances, without in the least knowing what to do with it.

"Dear dear," said Flora, "only to think of the changes at home Arthur —cannot overcome it, seems so natural, Mr. Clennam far more proper —since you became familiar with the Chinese customs and language which I am persuaded you speak like a Native if not better for you were always quick and clever though immensely difficult no doubt, I am sure the tea chests alone would kill *me* if I tried, such changes Arthur—I am doing it again, seems so natural, most improper—as no one could have believed, who could have ever imagined Mrs. Finching when I can't imagine it myself!"

"Is that your married name?" asked Arthur, struck, in the midst of all this, by a certain warmth of heart that expressed itself in her tone when she referred, however oddly, to the youthful relation in which they had stood to one another. "Finching?"

"Finching oh yes isn't it a dreadful name, but as Mr. F said when he proposed to me which he did seven times and handsomely consented I must say to be what he used to call on liking twelve months after all, he wasn't answerable for it and couldn't help it could he, Excellent man, not at all like you but excellent man!"

Flora had at last talked herself out of breath for one moment. One moment; for she recovered breath in the act of raising a minute corner of her pocket-handkerchief to her eye, as a tribute to the ghost of the departed Mr. F, and began again.

"No one could dispute, Arthur—Mr. Clennam—that it's quite right you should be formally friendly to me under the altered circumstances and indeed you couldn't be anything else, at least I suppose not you ought to know, but I can't help recalling that there *was* a time when things were very different."

"My dear Mrs. Finching," Arthur began, struck by the good tone again.

"Oh not that nasty ugly name, say Flora!"

"Flora. I assure you, Flora, I am happy in seeing you once more, and in finding that, like me, you have not forgotten the old foolish dreams, when we saw all before us in the light of our youth and hope."

"You don't seem so," pouted Flora, "you take it very coolly, but however I know you are disappointed in me, I suppose the Chinese ladies— Mandarinesses if you call them so—are the cause or perhaps I am the cause myself, it's just as likely."

"No, no," Clennam entreated, "don't say that."

"Oh I must you know," said Flora, in a positive tone, "what nonsense not to, I know I am not what you expected, I know that very well."

In the midst of her rapidity, she had found that out with the quick perception of a cleverer woman. The inconsistent and profoundly unreasonable way in which she instantly went on, nevertheless, to inter-weave their long-abandoned boy and girl relations with their present interview, made Clennam feel as if he were lightheaded.

"One remark," said Flora, giving their conversation, without the slightest notice and to the great terror of Clennam, the tone of a love-quarrel, "I wish to make, one explanation I wish to offer, when your Mama came and made a scene of it with my Papa and when I was called down into the little breakfast room where they were looking at one another with your Mama's parasol between them seated on two chairs like mad bulls what was I to do!"

"My dear Mrs. Finching," urged Clennam—"all so long ago and so long concluded, is it worth while seriously to——"

"I can't, Arthur," returned Flora, "be denounced as heartless by the whole society of China without setting myself right when I have the opportunity of doing so, and you must be very well aware that there was Paul and Virginia which had to be returned and which was returned without note of comment, not that I mean to say you could have written to me watched as I was but if it had only come back with a red wafer on the cover I should have known that it meant Come to Pekin Nankeen and What's the third place, barefoot."

"My dear Mrs. Finching, you were not to blame, and I never blamed you. We were both too young, too dependent and helpless, to do anything but accept our separation.—Pray think how long ago," gently remonstrated Arthur.

"One more remark," proceeded Flora with unslackened volubility, "I wish to make, one more explanation I wish to offer, for five days I had a cold in the head from crying which I passed entirely in the back drawing-room—there is the back drawing-room still on the first floor and still at the back of the house to confirm my words—when that dreary period had passed a lull succeeded years rolled on and Mr. F became acquainted with us at a mutual friend's, he was all attention he called next day he soon began to call three evenings a week and to send in little things for supper, it was not love on Mr. F's part it was adoration, Mr. F proposed with the full approval of Papa and what could I do?"

"Nothing whatever," said Arthur, with the cheerfulest readiness, "but what you did. Let an old friend assure you of his full conviction that you did quite right."

"One last remark," proceeded Flora, rejecting common-place life with a wave of her hand, "I wish to make, one last explanation I wish to offer, there *was* a time ere Mr. F first paid attentions incapable of being mistaken, but that is past and was not to be, dear Mr. Clennam you no longer wear a golden chain you are free I trust you may be happy, here is Papa who is always tiresome and putting in his nose everywhere where he is not wanted."

With these words, and with a hasty gesture fraught with timid caution—such a gesture had Clennam's eyes been familiar with in the old time—poor Flora left herself, at eighteen years of age, a long long way behind again; and came to a full stop at last.

Or rather, she left about half of herself at eighteen years of age behind, and grafted the rest on to the relict of the late Mr. F; thus making a moral mermaid of herself, which her once boy-lover contemplated with feelings wherein his sense of the sorrowful and his sense of the comical were curiously blended.

For example. As if there were a secret understanding between herself and Clennam of the most thrilling nature; as if the first of a train of post-chaises and four, extending all the way to Scotland, were at that moment round the corner; and as if she couldn't (and wouldn't) have walked into the Parish Church with him, under the shade of the family umbrella, with the Patriarchal blessing on her head, and the perfect concurrence of all mankind; Flora comforted her soul with agonies of mysterious signalling, expressing dread of discovery. With the sensation of becoming more and more lightheaded every minute, Clennam saw the relict of the late Mr. F enjoying herself in the most wonderful manner, by putting herself and him in their old places, and going through all the old performances—now, when the stage was dusty, when the scenery was faded, when the youthful actors were dead, when the orchestra was empty, when the lights were out. And still, through all this grotesque revival of what he remembered as having once been prettily natural to her, he could not but feel that it revived at sight of him, and that there was a tender memory in it.

The Patriarch insisted on his staying to dinner, and Flora signalled

"Yes!" Clennam so wished he could have done more than stay to dinner—so heartily wished he could have found the Flora that had been, or that never had been —that he thought the least atonement he could make for the disappointment he almost felt ashamed of, was to give himself up to the family desire. Therefore, he stayed to dinner.

Pancks dined with them. Pancks steamed out of his little dock at a quarter before six, and bore straight down for the Patriarch, who happened to be then driving, in an inane manner, through a stagnant account of Bleeding Heart Yard. Pancks instantly made fast to him and hauled him out.

"Bleeding Heart Yard?" said Pancks, with a puff and a snort. "It's a troublesome property. Don't pay you badly, but rents are very hard to get there. You have more trouble with that one place, than with all the places belonging to you."

Just as the big ship in tow gets the credit, with most spectators, of being the powerful object, so the Patriarch usually seemed to have said himself whatever Pancks said for him.

"Indeed?" returned Clennam, upon whom this impression was so efficiently made by a mere gleam of the polished head, that he spoke the ship instead of the Tug. "The people are so poor there?"

"*You* can't say, you know," snorted Pancks, taking one of his dirty hands out of his rusty iron-grey pockets to bite his nails, if he could find any, and turning his beads of eyes upon his employer, "whether they're poor or not. They say they are, but they all say that. When a man says he's rich, you're generally sure he isn't. Besides, if they *are* poor, you can't help it. You'd be poor yourself if you didn't get your rents."

"True enough," said Arthur.

"You're not going to keep open house for all the poor of London," pursued Pancks. "You're not going to lodge 'em for nothing. You're not going to open your gates wide and let 'em come free. Not if you know it, you an't."

Mr. Casby shook his head, in placid and benignant generality.

"If a man takes a room of you at half-a-crown a week, and when the week comes round hasn't got the half-crown, you say to that man, Why have you got the room, then? If you haven't got the one thing, why have you got the other? What have you been and done with your money? What do you mean by it? What are you up to? That's what *you* say to a man of that sort; and if you didn't say it, more shame for you!" Mr. Pancks here made a singular and startling noise, produced by a strong blowing effort in the region of the nose, unattended by any result but that acoustic one.

"You have some extent of such property about the east and north-east here, I believe?" said Clennam, doubtful which of the two to address.

"Oh pretty well," said Pancks. "You're not particular to east or north-east, any point of the compass will do for you. What you want is a good investment and a quick return. You take it where you can find it. You an't nice as to situation—not you."

There was a fourth and most original figure in the Patriarchal tent, who also appeared before dinner. This was an amazing little old woman, with a face like a staring wooden doll too cheap for expression, and a stiff yellow wig perched unevenly on the top of her head, as if the child who owned the doll had driven a tack through it anywhere so that it only got fastened on. Another remarkable thing in this little old woman was, that the same child seemed to have damaged her face in two or three places with some blunt instrument in the nature of a spoon; her countenance, and particularly the tip of her nose, presenting the phenomena of several dints, generally answering to the bowl of that article. A further remarkable thing in this little old woman was, that she had no name but Mr. F's Aunt.

She broke upon the visitor's view under the following circumstances: Flora said, when the first dish was being put on table, perhaps Mr. Clennam might not have heard that Mr. F had left her a legacy? Clennam in return implied his hope that Mr. F had endowed the wife whom he adored, with the greater part of his worldly substance, if not with all. Flora said, oh yes, she didn't mean that, Mr. F had made a beautiful will, but he had left her as a separate legacy, his Aunt. She then went out of the room to fetch the legacy, and, on her return, rather triumphantly presented "Mr. F's Aunt."

The major characteristics discoverable by the stranger in Mr. F's Aunt, were extreme severity and grim taciturnity; sometimes interrupted by a propensity to offer remarks, in a deep warning voice, which, being totally uncalled for by anything said by anybody, and traceable to no association of ideas, confounded and terrified the mind. Mr. F's Aunt may have thrown in these observations on some system of her own, and it may have been ingenious, or even subtle; but the key to it was wanted.

The neatly-served and well-cooked dinner (for everything about the Patriarchal household promoted quiet digestion) began with some soup, some fried soles, a butter-boat of shrimp sauce, and a dish of potatoes. The conversation still turned on the receipt of rents. Mr. F's Aunt, after regarding the company for ten minutes with a malevolent gaze, delivered the following fearful remark.

"When we lived at Henley, Barnes's gander was stole by tinkers."

Mr. Pancks courageously nodded his head and said, "All right, ma'am." But the effect of this mysterious communication upon Clennam, was absolutely to frighten him. And another circumstance invested this old lady with peculiar terrors. Though she was always staring, she never acknowledged that she saw any individual. The polite and attentive stranger would desire, say, to consult her inclinations on the subject of potatoes. His expressive action would be hopelessly lost upon her, and what could he do? No man could say, "Mr. F's Aunt, will you permit me?"

Every man retired from the spoon, as Clennam did, cowed and baffled.

There was mutton, a steak, and an apple-pie—nothing in the remotest way connected with ganders—and the dinner went on like a disenchanted feast, as it truly was. Once upon a time Clennam had sat at that table taking no heed of anything but Flora; now the principal heed he took of Flora was, to observe, against his will, that she was very fond of porter, that she combined a great deal of sherry with sentiment, and that if she were a little overgrown, it was upon substantial grounds. The last of the Patriarchs had always been a mighty eater, and he disposed of an immense quantity of solid food with the benignity of a good soul who was feeding some one else. Mr. Pancks, who was always in a hurry, and who referred at intervals to a little dirty note-book which he kept beside him (perhaps containing the names of the defaulters he meant to look up by way of dessert), took in his victuals much as if he were coaling; with a good deal of noise, a good deal of dropping about, and a puff and a snort occasionally, as if he were nearly ready to steam away.

All through dinner, Flora combined her present appetite for eating and drinking, with her past appetite for romantic love, in a way that made Clennam afraid to lift his eyes from his plate; since he could not look towards her without receiving some glance of mysterious meaning or warning, as if they were engaged in a plot. Mr. F's Aunt sat silently defying him with an aspect of the greatest bitterness, until the removal of the cloth and the appearance of the decanters, when she originated another observation—struck into the conversation like a clock, without consulting anybody.

Flora had just said "Mr. Clennam, will you give me a glass of port for Mr. F's Aunt?"

"The Monument near London Bridge," that lady instantly proclaimed, "was put up arter the Great Fire of London; and the Great Fire of London was not the fire in which your uncle George's workshops was burned down."

Mr. Pancks, with his former courage, said, "Indeed, ma'am? All right!" But appearing to be incensed by imaginary contradiction, or other ill-usage, Mr. F's Aunt, instead of relapsing into silence, made the following additional proclamation.

"I hate a fool!"

She imparted to this sentiment, in itself almost Solomonic, so extremely injurious and personal a character, by levelling it straight at the visitor's head, that it became necessary to lead Mr. F's Aunt from the room. This was quietly done by Flora; Mr. F's Aunt offering no resistance, but enquiring on her way out "What he come there for, then?" with implacable animosity.

When Flora returned, she explained that her legacy was a clever old lady, but was sometimes a little singular, and "took dislikes"—peculiarities

Mr. F's Aunt is conducted into retirement

of which Flora seemed to be proud rather than otherwise. As Flora's good nature shone in the case, Clennam had no fault to find with the old lady for eliciting it, now that he was relieved from the terrors of her presence; and they took a glass or two of wine in peace. Foreseeing then that the Pancks would shortly get under weigh, and that the Patriarch would go to sleep, he pleaded the necessity of visiting his mother, and asked Mr. Pancks in which direction he was going?

"Citywards, sir," said Pancks.

"Shall we walk together?" said Arthur.

"Quite agreeable," said Pancks.

Meanwhile Flora was murmuring in rapid snatches for his ear, that there *was* a time and that the past was a yawning gulf however and that a golden chain no longer bound him and that she revered the memory of the late Mr. F and that she should be at home to-morrow at half-past one and that the decrees of Fate were beyond recall and that she considered nothing so improbable as that he ever walked on the north-west side of Gray's Inn Gardens at exactly four o'clock in the afternoon. He tried at parting to give his hand in frankness to the existing Flora—not the vanished Flora, or the Mermaid—but Flora wouldn't have it, couldn't have it, was wholly destitute of the power of separating herself and him from their bygone characters. He left the house miserably enough; and so much more light-headed than ever, that if it had not been his good fortune to be towed away, he might, for the first quarter of an hour, have drifted anywhere.

When he began to come to himself, in the cooler air and the absence of Flora, he found Pancks at full speed, cropping such scanty pasturage of nails as he could find, and snorting at intervals. These, in conjunction with one hand in his pocket and his roughened hat hind side before, were evidently the conditions under which he reflected.

"A fresh night!" said Arthur.

"Yes, it's pretty fresh," assented Pancks. "As a stranger, you feel the climate more than I do, I dare say. Indeed I haven't got time to feel it."

"You lead such a busy life?"

"Yes, I have always some of 'em to look up, or something to look after. But I like business," said Pancks, getting on a little faster. "What's a man made for?"

"For nothing else?" said Clennam.

Pancks put the counter question, "What else?" It packed up, in the smallest compass, a weight that had rested on Clennam's life; and he made no answer.

"That's what I ask our weekly tenants," said Pancks. "Some of 'em will pull long faces to me, and say, Poor as you see us, master, we are always grinding, drudging, toiling, every minute we're awake. I say to them, What else are you made for? It shuts them up. They haven't a word to answer. What else are you made for? That clinches it."

"Ah dear, dear, dear!" sighed Clennam.

"Here am I," said Pancks, pursuing his argument with the weekly tenant. "What else do you suppose I think I am made for? Nothing. Rattle me out of bed early, set me going, give me as short a time as you like to bolt my meals in, and keep me at it. Keep me always at it, I'll keep you always at it, you keep somebody else always at it. There you are, with the Whole Duty of Man in a commercial country."

When they had walked a little further in silence, Clennam said: "Have you no taste for anything, Mr. Pancks?"

"What's taste?" dryly retorted Pancks.

"Let us say inclination."

"I have an inclination to get money, sir," said Pancks, "if you'll show me how." He blew off that sound again, and it occurred to his companion for the first time that it was his way of laughing. He was a singular man in all respects; he might not have been quite in earnest, but that the short, hard, rapid manner in which he shot out these cinders of principles, as if it were done by mechanical revolvency, seemed irreconcilable with banter.

"You are no great reader, I suppose?" said Clennam.

"Never read anything but letters and accounts. Never collect anything but advertisements relative to next of kin. If *that's* a taste, I have got that. You're not of the Clennams of Cornwall, Mr. Clennam."

"Not that I ever heard of."

"I know you're not. I asked your mother, sir. She has too much character to let a chance escape her."

"Supposing I had been of the Clennams of Cornwall?"

"You'd have heard of something to your advantage."

"Indeed! I have heard of little enough to my advantage, for some time."

"There's a Cornish property going a begging, sir, and not a Cornish Clennam to have it for the asking," said Pancks, taking his note-book from his breast pocket and putting it in again. "I turn off here. I wish you good night."

"Good night!" said Clennam. But the Tug suddenly lightened, and, untrammeled by having any weight in tow, was already puffing away into the distance.

They had crossed Smithfield together, and Clennam was left alone at the corner of Barbican. He had no intention of presenting himself in his mother's dismal room that night, and could not have felt more depressed and cast away if he had been in a wilderness. He turned slowly down Aldersgate Street, and was pondering his way along towards Saint Paul's, purposing to come into one of the great thoroughfares for the sake of their light and life, when a crowd of people flocked towards him on the same pavement, and he stood aside against a shop to let them pass. As they came up, he made out that they were gathered round a something that was carried on men's shoulders. He soon saw that it was a litter, hastily made of a shutter or some such thing; and a recumbent figure upon it, and the scraps of conversation in the crowd, and a muddy bundle carried by one man, and a muddy hat carried by another, informed him that an accident had occurred. The litter stopped under a lamp before it had passed him half a dozen paces, for some re-adjustment of the burden; and, the crowd stopping too, he found himself in the midst of the array.

"An accident going to the Hospital?" he asked an old man beside him, who stood shaking his head, inviting conversation.

"Yes," said the man, "along of them Mails. They ought to be prose-cuted and fined, them Mails. They come a racing out of Lad Lane and Wood Street at twelve or fourteen mile a hour, them Mails do. The only wonder is, that people an't killed oftener by them Mails."

"This person is not killed, I hope?"

"I don't know!" said the man, "it an't for the want of a will in them Mails, if he an't." The speaker having folded his arms, and set in comfort-ably to address his depreciation of them Mails to any of the bystanders who would listen, several voices, out of pure sympathy with the sufferer, confirmed him; one voice saying to Clennam, "They're a public nuisance, them Mails, sir;" another, "*I* see one on 'em pull up within half a inch of a boy, last night;" another, "*I* see one on 'em go over a cat, sir—and it might have been your own mother;" and all representing, by implication, that if he happened to possess any public influence, he could not use it better than against them Mails.

"Why, a native Englishman is put to it every night of his life, to save his life from them Mails," argued the first old man; "and *he* knows when they're a coming round the corner, to tear him limb from limb. What can you expect from a poor foreigner who don't know nothing about 'em!"

"Is this a foreigner?" said Clennam, leaning forward to look.

In the midst of such replies as "Frenchman, sir," "Porteghee, sir," "Dutchman, sir," "Prooshan, sir," and other conflicting testimony, he now heard a feeble voice asking, both in Italian and in French, for water. A general remark going round, in reply, of "Ah, poor fellow, he says he'll never get over it; and no wonder!" Clennam begged to be allowed to pass, as he understood the poor creature. He was immediately handed to the front, to speak to him.

"First, he wants some water," said he, looking round. (A dozen good fellows dispersed to get it.) "Are you badly hurt, my friend?" he asked the man on the litter, in Italian.

"Yes, sir; yes, yes, yes. It's my leg, it's my leg. But it pleases me to hear the old music, though I am very bad."

"You are a traveller? Stay! See the water! Let me give you some."

They had rested the litter on a pile of paving stones. It was at a con-venient height from the ground, and by stooping he could lightly raise the head with one hand, and hold the glass to the lips with the other. A little, muscular, brown man, with black hair and white teeth. A lively face, apparently. Ear-rings in his ears.

"That's well. You are a traveller?"

"Surely, sir."

"A stranger in this city?"

"Surely, surely, altogether. I am arrived this unhappy evening."

"From what country?"

"Marseilles."

"Why, see there! I also! Almost as much a stranger here as you, though born here, I came from Marseilles a little while ago. Don't be cast down." The face looked up at him imploringly, as he rose from wiping it, and gently replaced the coat that covered the writhing figure. "I won't leave you, till you shall be well taken care of. Courage! You will be very much better, half-an-hour hence."

"Ah! Altro, Altro!" cried the poor little man, in a faintly incredulous tone; and as they took him up, hung out his right hand to give the forefinger a back-handed shake in the air.

Arthur Clennam turned; and walking beside the litter, and saying an encouraging word now and then, accompanied it to the neighbouring hospital of Saint Bartholomew. None of the crowd but the bearers and he being admitted, the disabled man was soon laid on a table in a cool, methodical way, and carefully examined by a surgeon: who was as near at hand, and as ready to appear, as Calamity herself. "He hardly knows an English word," said Clennam; "is he badly hurt?" "Let us know all about it first," said the surgeon, continuing his examination with a business-like delight in it, "before we pronounce."

After trying the leg with a finger and two fingers, and one hand and two hands, and over and under, and up and down, and in this direction and in that, and approvingly remarking on the points of interest to another gentleman who joined him, the surgeon at last clapped the patient on the shoulder, and said, "He won't hurt. He'll do very well. It's difficult enough, but we shall not want him to part with his leg this time." Which Clennam interpreted to the patient, who was full of gratitude, and, in his demonstrative way, kissed both the interpreter's hand and the surgeon's, several times.

"It's a serious injury, I suppose?" said Clennam.

"Ye-es," replied the surgeon, with the thoughtful pleasure of an artist, contemplating the work upon his easel. "Yes, it's enough. There's a compound fracture above the knee, and a dislocation below. They are both of a beautiful kind." He gave the patient a friendly clap on the shoulder again, as if he really felt that he was a very good fellow indeed, and worthy of all commendation for having broken his leg in a manner interesting to science.

"He speaks French?" said the surgeon.

"Oh yes, he speaks French."

"He'll be at no loss here, then.—You have only to bear a little pain like a brave fellow, my friend, and to be thankful that all goes as well as it does," he added, in that tongue, "and you'll walk again to a marvel. Now, let us see whether there's anything else the matter, and how our ribs are."

There was nothing else the matter, and our ribs were sound. Clennam remained until everything possible to be done had been skilfully and promptly done—the poor belated wanderer in a strange land movingly besought that favor of him—and lingered by the bed to which he was in due time removed, until he had fallen into a doze. Even then he wrote a few words for him on his card, with a promise to return to-morrow, and left it to be given to him when he should awake.

All these proceedings occupied so long, that it struck eleven o'clock at night as he came out at the Hospital Gate. He had hired a lodging for the present in Covent Garden, and he took the nearest way to that quarter, by Snow Hill and Holborn.

Left to himself again, after the solicitude and compassion of his last adventure, he was naturally in a thoughtful mood. As naturally, he could not walk on thinking for ten minutes, without recalling Flora. She necessarily recalled to him his life, with all its misdirection and little happiness.

When he got to his lodging, he sat down before the dying fire, as he had stood at the window of his old room looking out upon the blackened forest of chimneys, and turned his gaze back upon the gloomy vista by which he had come to that stage in his existence. So long, so bare, so blank. No childhood; no youth, except for one remembrance; the one remembrance proved, only that day, to be a piece of folly.

It was a misfortune to him, trifle as it might have been to another. For, while all that was hard and stern in his recollection, remained Reality on being proved—was obdurate to the sight and touch, and relaxed nothing of its old indomitable grimness—the one tender recollection of his experience would not bear the same test, and melted away. He had foreseen this, on the former night, when he had dreamed with waking eyes; but he had not felt it then; and he had now.

He was a dreamer in such wise, because he was a man who had deep-rooted in his nature, a belief in all the gentle and good things his life had been without. Bred in meanness and hard dealing, this had rescued him to be a man of honorable mind and open hand. Bred in coldness and severity, this had rescued him to have a warm and sympathetic heart. Bred in a creed too darkly audacious to pursue, through its process of reversing the making of man in the image of his Creator to the making of his Creator in the image of an erring man, this had rescued him to judge not, and in humility to be merciful, and have hope and charity.

And this saved him still from the whimpering weakness and cruel selfishness of holding that because such a happiness or such a virtue had not come into his little path, or worked well for him, therefore it was not in the great scheme, but was reducible, when found in appearance, to the basest elements. A disappointed mind he had, but a mind too firm and healthy for such unwholesome air. Leaving himself in the dark, it could rise into the light, seeing it shine on others and hailing it.

Therefore, he sat before his dying fire, sorrowful to think upon the way by which he had come to that night, yet not strewing poison on the way by which other men had come to it. That he should have missed so much, and at his time of life should look so far about him for any staff to bear him company upon his downward journey and cheer it, was a just regret. He looked at the fire from which the blaze departed, from which the after-glow subsided, in which the ashes turned grey, from which they dropped to dust, and thought, "How soon I too shall pass through such changes, and be gone!"

To review his life, was like descending a green tree in fruit and flower, and seeing all the branches wither and drop off one by one, as he came down towards them.

"From the unhappy suppression of my youngest days, through the rigid and unloving home that followed them, through my departure, my long exile, my return, my mother's welcome, my intercourse with her since, down to the afternoon of this day with poor Flora," said Arthur Clennam, "what have I found!"

His door was softly opened, and these spoken words startled him, and came as if they were an answer:

"Little Dorrit."

CHAPTER XIV

LITTLE DORRIT'S PARTY

ARTHUR CLENNAM rose hastily, and saw her standing at the door. This history must sometimes see with Little Dorrit's eyes, and shall begin that course by seeing him.

Little Dorrit looked into a dim room, which seemed a spacious one to her, and grandly furnished. Courtly ideas of Covent Garden, as a place with famous coffee-houses, where gentlemen wearing gold-laced coats and swords had quarrelled and fought duels; costly ideas of Covent Garden, as a place where there were flowers in winter at guineas a-piece, pine-apples at guineas a pound, and peas at guineas a pint; picturesque ideas of Covent Garden, as a place where there was a mighty theatre, showing wonderful and beautiful sights to richly-dressed ladies and gentlemen, and which was for ever far beyond the reach of poor Fanny or poor uncle; desolate ideas of Covent Garden, as having all those arches in it, where the miserable children in rags among whom she had just now passed, like young rats, slunk and hid, fed on offal, huddled together for warmth, and were hunted about (look to the rats young and old, all ye Barnacles, for before God they are eating away our foundations, and will bring the roofs on our heads!); teeming ideas of Covent Garden, as a place of past and present mystery, romance, abundance, want, beauty, ugliness, fair country gardens, and foul street-gutters, all confused together,—made the room dimmer than it was, in Little Dorrit's eyes, as they timidly saw it from the door.

At first in the chair before the gone-out fire, and then turned round wondering to see her, was the gentleman whom she sought. The brown, grave gentleman, who smiled so pleasantly, who was so frank and considerate in his manner, and yet in whose earnestness there was something that reminded her of his mother, with the great difference that she was earnest in asperity and he in gentleness. Now he regarded her with that attentive and enquiring look before which Little Dorrit's eyes had always fallen, and before which they fell still.

"My poor child! Here at midnight?"

"I said Little Dorrit, sir, on purpose to prepare you. I knew you must be very much surprised."

"Are you alone?"

"No, sir, I have got Maggy with me."

Considering her entrance sufficiently prepared for by this mention of her name, Maggy appeared from the landing outside, on the broad grin. She instantly suppressed that manifestation, however, and became fixedly solemn.

"And I have no fire," said Clennam. "And you are—" He was going to say so lightly clad, but stopped himself in what would have been a reference to her poverty, saying instead, "And it is so cold."

Putting the chair from which he had risen, nearer to the grate, he made her sit down in it; and hurriedly bringing wood and coal, heaped them together and got a blaze. "Your foot is like marble, my child;" he had happened to touch it, while stooping on one knee at his work of kindling the fire; "put it nearer the warmth." Little Dorrit thanked him hastily. It was quite warm, it was very warm! It smote upon his heart to feel that she hid her thin, worn shoe.

Little Dorrit was not ashamed of her poor shoes. He knew her story, and it was not that. Little Dorrit had a misgiving that he might blame her father, if he saw them; that he might think, "why did he dine to-day, and leave this little creature to the mercy of the cold stones!" She had no belief that it would have been a just reflection; she simply knew, by experience, that such delusions did sometimes present themselves to people. It was a part of her father's misfortunes that they did.

"Before I say anything else," Little Dorrit began, sitting before the pale fire, and raising her eyes again to the face which in its harmonious look of interest, and pity, and protection, she felt to be a mystery far above her in degree, and almost removed beyond her guessing at; "may I tell you something, sir?"

"Yes, my child."

A slight shade of distress fell upon her, at his so often calling her a child. She was surprised that he should see it, or think of such a slight thing; but he said directly:

"I wanted a tender word, and could think of no other. As you just now gave yourself the name they give you at my mother's, and as that is the name by which I always think of you, let me call you Little Dorrit."

"Thank you, sir, I should like it better than any name."

"Little Dorrit."

"Little mother," Maggy (who had been falling asleep) put in, as a correction.

"It's all the same, Maggy," returned Little Dorrit, "all the same."

"Is it all the same, mother?"

"Just the same."

Maggy laughed, and immediately snored. In Little Dorrit's eyes and ears, the uncouth figure and the uncouth sound were as pleasant as could be. There was a glow of pride in her big child, overspreading her face, when it again met the eyes of the grave brown gentleman. She wondered what he was thinking of, as he looked at Maggy and her. She thought what a good father he would be. How, with some such look, he would counsel and cherish his daughter.

"What I was going to tell you, sir," said Little Dorrit, "is, that my brother is at large."

Arthur was rejoiced to hear it, and hoped he would do well.

"And what I was going to tell you, sir," said Little Dorrit, trembling in all her little figure and in her voice, "is, that I am not to know whose generosity released him—am never to ask, and am never to be told, and am never to thank that gentleman with all my grateful heart!"

He would probably need no thanks, Clennam said. Very likely he would be thankful himself (and with reason), that he had had the means and chance of doing a little service to her, who well deserved a great one.

"And what I was going to say, sir, is," said Little Dorrit, trembling more and more, "that if I knew him, and I might, I would tell him that he can never, never know how I feel his goodness, and how my poor good father would feel it. And what I was going to say, sir, is, that if I knew him, and I might—but I don't know him and I must not—I know that!—I would tell him that I shall never any more lie down to sleep, without having prayed to Heaven to bless him and reward him. And if I knew him, and I might, I would go down on my knees to him, and take his hand and kiss it, and ask not to draw it away, but to leave it—O to leave it for a moment—and let my thankful tears fall on it, for I have no other thanks to give him!"

Little Dorrit had put his hand to her lips, and would have kneeled to him; but he gently prevented her, and replaced her in her chair. Her eyes, and the tones of her voice, had thanked him far better than she thought. He was not able to say, quite as composedly as usual, "There, Little Dorrit; there, there, there! We will suppose that you did know this person, and that you might do all this, and that it was all done. And now tell me, who am quite another person—who am nothing more than the friend who begged you to trust him—why you are out at midnight, and what it is that brings you so far through the streets at this late hour, my slight, delicate," child was on his lips again, "Little Dorrit!"

"Maggy and I have been to-night," she answered, subduing herself with the quiet effort that had long been natural to her, "to the theatre where my sister is engaged."

"And oh ain't it a 'Ev'nly place," suddenly interrupted Maggy, who seemed to have the power of going to sleep and waking up whenever she chose. "Almost as good as a hospital. Only there ain't no Chicking in it."

Here she shook herself, and fell asleep again.

"We went there," said Little Dorrit, glancing at her charge, "because I like sometimes to know, of my own knowledge, that my sister is doing well; and like to see her there, with my own eyes, when neither she nor Uncle is aware. It is very seldom indeed that I can do that, because when I am not out at work I am with my father, and even when I am out at work I hurry home to him. But I pretend to-night that I am at a party."

As she made the confession, timidly hesitating, she raised her eyes to the face, and read its expression so plainly that she answered it.

"Oh no, certainly! I never was at a party in my life."

She paused a little under his attentive look, and then said, "I hope there is no harm in it. I could never have been of any use, if I had not pretended a little."

She feared that he was blaming her in his mind, for so devising to contrive for them, think for them, and watch over them, without their knowledge or gratitude; perhaps even with their reproaches for supposed neglect. But what was really in his mind, was the weak figure with its strong purpose, the thin worn shoes, the insufficient dress, and the pretence of recreation and enjoyment. He asked where the supposititious party was? At a place where she worked, answered Little Dorrit, blushing. She had said very little about it; only a few words to make her father easy. Her father did not believe it to be a grand party—indeed he might suppose that. And she glanced for an instant at the shawl she wore.

"It is the first night," said Little Dorrit, "that I have ever been away from home. And London looks so large, so barren, and so wild." In Little

Dorrit's eyes, its vastness under the black sky was awful; a tremor passed over her as she said the words.

"But this is not," she added, with the quiet effort again, "what I have come to trouble you with, sir. My sister's having found a friend, a lady she has told me of and made me rather anxious about, was the first cause of my coming away from home. And being away, and coming (on purpose) round by where you lived, and seeing a light in the window——"

Not for the first time. No, not for the first time. In Little Dorrit's eyes, the outside of that window had been a distant star, on other nights than this. She had toiled out of her way, tired and troubled, to look up at it, and wonder about the grave brown gentleman from so far off, who had spoken to her as a friend and protector.

"There were three things," said Little Dorrit, "that I thought I would like to say, if you were alone and I might come up-stairs. First, what I have tried to say, but never can—never shall——"

"Hush, hush! That is done with, and disposed of. Let us pass to the second," said Clennam, smiling her agitation away, making the blaze shine upon her, and putting wine and cake and fruit towards her on the table.

"I think," said Little Dorrit—"this is the second thing, sir—I think Mrs. Clennam must have found out my secret, and must know where I come from and where I go to. Where I live, I mean."

"Indeed?" returned Clennam, quickly. He asked her, after a short consideration, why she supposed so.

"I think," replied Little Dorrit, "that Mr. Flintwinch must have watched me."

And why, Clennam asked, as he turned his eyes upon the fire, bent his brows, and considered again; why did she suppose that?

"I have met him twice. Both times near home. Both times at night, when I was going back. Both times I thought (though that may easily be my mistake), that he hardly looked as if he had met me by accident."

"Did he say anything?"

"No; he only nodded and put his head on one side."

"The devil take his head!" mused Clennam, still looking at the fire; "it's always on one side."

He roused himself to persuade her to put some wine to her lips, and to touch something to eat—it was very difficult, she was so timid and shy—and then said, musing again:

"Is my mother at all changed to you?"

"Oh, not at all. She is just the same. I wondered whether I had better tell her my history. I wondered whether I might—I mean, whether you would like me to tell her. I wondered," said Little Dorrit, looking at him in a suppliant way, and gradually withdrawing her eyes as he looked at her, "whether you would advise me what I ought to do."

"Little Dorrit," said Clennam; and the phrase had already begun, between those two, to stand for a hundred gentle phrases, according to the varying tone and connexion in which it was used; "do nothing. I will have some talk with my old friend, Mrs. Affery. Do nothing, Little Dorrit— except refresh yourself with such means as there are here. I entreat you to do that."

"Thank you, I am not hungry. Nor," said Little Dorrit, as he softly put her glass towards her, "nor thirsty.—I think Maggy might like something, perhaps."

"We will make her find pockets presently for all there is here," said Clennam; "but before we awake her, there was a third thing to say."

"Yes. You will not be offended, sir ?"

"I promise that, unreservedly."

"It will sound strange. I hardly know how to say it. Don't think it unreasonable or ungrateful in me," said Little Dorrit, with returning and increasing agitation.

"No, no, no. I am sure it will be natural and right. I am not afraid that I shall put a wrong construction on it, whatever it is."

"Thank you. You are coming back to see my father again ?"

"Yes."

"You have been so good and thoughtful as to write him a note, saying that you are coming to-morrow ?"

"Oh, that was nothing! Yes."

"Can you guess," said Little Dorrit, folding her small hands tight in one another, and looking at him with all the earnestness of her soul looking steadily out of her eyes, "what I am going to ask you not to do ?"

"I think I can. But I may be wrong."

"No, you are not wrong," said Little Dorrit, shaking her head. "If we should want it so very, very badly that we cannot do without it, let *me* ask you for it."

"I will, —I will."

"Don't encourage him to ask. Don't understand him, if he does ask. Don't give it to him. Save him and spare him that, and you will be able to think better of him!"

Clennam said—not very plainly, seeing those tears glittering in her anxious eyes—that her wish should be sacred with him.

"You don't know what he is," she said; "you don't know what he really is. How can you, seeing him there all at once, dear love, and not gradually, as I have done! You have been so good to us, so delicately and truly good, that I want him to be better in your eyes than in anybody's. And I cannot bear to think," cried Little Dorrit, covering her tears with her hands, "I cannot bear to think, that you of all the world should see him in his only moments of degradation!"

"Pray," said Clennam, "do not be so distressed. Pray, pray, Little

Dorrit! This is quite understood now."

"Thank you, sir. Thank you! I have tried very much to keep myself from saying this; I have thought about it, days and nights; but when I knew for certain you were coming again, I made up my mind to speak to you. Not because I am ashamed of him," she dried her tears quickly, "but because I know him better than any one does, and love him, and am proud of him."

Relieved of this weight, Little Dorrit was nervously anxious to be gone. Maggy being broad awake, and in the act of distantly gloating over the fruit and cakes with chuckles of anticipation, Clennam made the best diversion in his power by pouring her out a glass of wine, which she drank in a series of loud smacks; putting her hand upon her windpipe after every one, and saying, breathless, with her eyes in a very prominent state, "Oh ain't it d'licious! Ain't it hospitally!" When she had finished the wine and these encomiums, he charged her to load her basket (she was never without her basket) with every eatable thing upon the table, and to take especial care to leave no scrap behind. Maggy's pleasure in doing this, and her little mother's pleasure in seeing Maggy pleased, was as good a turn as circumstances could have given to the late conversation.

"But the gates will have been locked long ago," said Clennam, suddenly remembering it. "Where are you going?"

"I am going to Maggy's lodging," answered Little Dorrit. "I shall be quite safe, quite well taken care of."

"I must accompany you there," said Clennam. "I cannot let you go alone."

"Yes, pray leave us to go there by ourselves. Pray do!" begged Little Dorrit.

She was so earnest in the petition, that Clennam felt a delicacy in obtruding himself upon her: the rather, because he could well understand that Maggy's lodging was of the obscurest sort. "Come, Maggy," said Little Dorrit, cheerily, "we shall do very well; we know the way, by this time, Maggy?"

"Yes, yes, little mother; we know the way," chuckled Maggy. And away they went. Little Dorrit turned at the door to say "God bless you!" She said it very softly, but perhaps she may have been as audible above—who knows!—as a whole cathedral choir.

Arthur Clennam suffered them to pass the corner of the street, before he followed at a distance; not with any idea of encroaching a second time on Little Dorrit's privacy, but to satisfy his mind by seeing her secure, in the neighbourhood to which she was accustomed. So diminutive she looked, so fragile and defenceless against the bleak damp weather, flitting along in the shuffling shadow of her charge, that he felt, in his compassion, and in his habit of considering her a child apart from the rest of the rough world, as if he would have been glad to take her up in his arms and carry her to her journey's end.

In course of time they came into the leading thoroughfare where the Marshalsea was, and then he saw them slacken their pace, and soon turn down a bye-street. He stopped, felt that he had no right to go further, and slowly left them. He had no suspicion that they ran any risk of being houseless until morning; had no idea of the truth, until long, long afterwards.

But, said Little Dorrit, when they stopped at a poor dwelling all in darkness, and heard no sound on listening at the door, "Now, this is a good lodging for you, Maggy, and we must not give offence. Consequently, we will only knock twice, and not very loud; and if we cannot wake them so, we must walk about till day."

Once, Little Dorrit knocked with a careful hand, and listened. Twice, Little Dorrit knocked with a careful hand, and listened. All was close and still. "Maggy, we must do the best we can, my dear. We must be patient, and wait for day."

It was a chill dark night, with a damp wind blowing, when they came out into the leading street again, and heard the clocks strike half-past one. "In only five hours and a half," said Little Dorrit, "we shall be able to go home." To speak of home, and to go and look at it, it being so near, was a natural sequence. They went to the closed gate, and peeped through into the courtyard. "I hope he is sound asleep," said Little Dorrit, kissing one of the bars, "and does not miss me."

The gate was so familiar, and so like a companion, that they put down Maggy's basket in a corner to serve for a seat, and keeping close together, rested there for some time. While the street was empty and silent, Little Dorrit was not afraid; but when she heard a footstep at a distance, or saw a moving shadow among the street lamps, she was startled, and whispered, "Maggy, I see some one. Come away!" Maggy would then wake up more or less fretfully, and they would wander about a little, and come back again.

As long as eating was a novelty and an amusement, Maggy kept up pretty well. But, that period going by, she became querulous about the cold, and shivered and whimpered. "It will soon be over, dear," said Little Dorrit, patiently. "Oh it's all very fine for you, little mother," returned Maggy, "but I'm a poor thing, only ten years old." At last, in the dead of the night, when the street was very still indeed, Little Dorrit laid the heavy head upon her bosom, and soothed her to sleep. And thus she sat at the gate, as it were alone; looking up at the stars, and seeing the clouds pass over them in their wild flight—which was the dance at Little Dorrit's party.

"If it really was a party!" she thought once, as she sat there. "If it was light and warm and beautiful, and it was our house, and my poor dear was its master, and had never been inside these walls. And if Mr. Clennam was one of our visitors, and we were dancing to delightful music, and were all as gay and lighthearted as ever we could be! I wonder—" Such a vista of wonder opened out before her, that she sat looking up at the stars, quite lost; until Maggy was querulous again, and wanted to get up and walk.

Three o'clock, and half-past three, and they had passed over London Bridge. They had heard the rush of the tide against obstacles; had looked down, awed, through the dark vapor on the river; had seen little spots of lighted water where the bridge lamps were reflected, shining like demon eyes, with a terrible fascination in them for guilt and misery. They had shrunk past homeless people, lying coiled up in nooks. They had run from drunkards. They had started from slinking men, whistling and signing to one another at bye corners, or running away at full speed. Though everywhere the leader and the guide, Little Dorrit, happy for once in her youthful appearance, feigned to cling to and rely upon Maggy. And more than once some voice, from among a knot of brawling or prowling figures in their path, had called out to the rest, to "let the woman and the child go by!"

So, the woman and the child had gone by, and gone on, and five had sounded from the steeples. They were walking slowly towards the east, already looking for the first pale streak of day, when a woman came after them.

"What are you doing with the child?" she said to Maggy.

She was young—far too young to be there, Heaven knows!—and neither ugly nor wicked-looking. She spoke coarsely, but with no naturally coarse voice; there was even something musical in its sound.

"What are you doing with yourself?" retorted Maggy, for want of a better answer.

"Can't you see, without my telling you?"

"I don't know as I can," said Maggy.

"Killing myself. Now I have answered you, answer me. What are you doing with the child?"

The supposed child kept her head drooped down, and kept her form close at Maggy's side.

"Poor thing!" said the woman. "Have you no feeling, that you keep her out in the cruel streets at such a time as this? Have you no eyes, that you don't see how delicate and slender she is? Have you no sense (you don't look as if you had much) that you don't take more pity on this cold and trembling little hand?"

She had stepped across to that side, and held the hand between her own two, chafing it. "Kiss a poor lost creature, dear," she said, bending her face, "and tell me where she's taking you."

Little Dorrit turned towards her.

"Why, my God!" she said, recoiling, "you're a woman!"

"Don't mind that!" said Little Dorrit, clasping one of the hands that had suddenly released hers. "I am not afraid of you."

"Then you had better be," she answered. "Have you no mother?"

"No."

"No father?"

"Yes, a very dear one."

"Go home to him, and be afraid of me. Let me go. Good night!"

"I must thank you first; let me speak to you as if I really was a child."

"You can't do it," said the woman. "You are kind and innocent; but you can't look at me out of a child's eyes. I never should have touched you, but that I thought you were a child." And with a strange, wild cry, she went away.

No day yet in the sky, but there was day in the resounding stones of the streets; in the waggons, carts, and coaches; in the workers going to various occupations; in the opening of early shops; in the traffic at markets; in the stir at the river-side. There was coming day in the flaring lights, with a feebler color in them than they would have had at another time; coming day in the increased sharpness of the air, and the ghastly dying of the night.

They went back again to the gate, intending to wait there now until it should be opened; but the air was so raw and cold, that Little Dorrit, leading Maggy about in her sleep, kept in motion. Going round by the church, she saw lights there, and the door open; and went up the steps and looked in.

"Who's that?" cried a stout old man, who was putting on a nightcap as if he were going to bed in a vault.

"It's no one particular, sir," said Little Dorrit.

"Stop!" cried the man. "Let's have a look at you!"

This caused her to turn back again, in the act of going out, and to present herself and her charge before him.

"I thought so!" said he. "I know *you*."

"We have often seen each other," said Little Dorrit, recognising the sexton, or the beadle, or the verger, or whatever he was, "when I have been at church here."

"More than that, we've got your birth in our Register, you know; you're one of our curiosities."

"Indeed?" said Little Dorrit.

"To be sure. As the child of the—by-the-bye, how did you get out so early?"

"We were shut out last night, and are waiting to get in."

"You don't mean it? And there's another hour good yet! Come into the Vestry. You'll find a fire in the Vestry, on account of the painters. I'm waiting for the painters, or I shouldn't be here, you may depend upon it. One of our curiosities mustn't be cold, when we have it in our power to warm her up comfortable. Come along."

He was a very good old fellow, in his familiar way; and having stirred

the Vestry fire, he looked round the shelves of registers for a particular
volume. "Here you are, you see," he said, taking it down and turning the
leaves. "Here you'll find yourself, as large as life. Amy, daughter of William
and Fanny Dorrit. Born, Marshalsea Prison, Parish of Saint George. And
we tell people that you have lived there, without so much as a day's or a
night's absence, ever since. Is it true?"

"Quite true, till last night."

"Lord!" But his surveying her with an admiring gaze suggested something else to him, to wit: "I am sorry to see, though, that you are faint
and tired. Stay a bit. I'll get some cushions out of the church, and you and
your friend shall lie down before the fire. Don't be afraid of not going in to
join your father when the gate opens. *I'll* call you."

He soon brought in the cushions, and strewed them on the ground.

"There you are, you see. Again as large as life. Oh, never mind thanking.
I've daughters of my own. And though they weren't born in the Marshalsea
Prison, they might have been, if I had been, in my ways of carrying on, of
your father's breed. Stop a bit. I must put something under the cushion
for your head. Here's a Burial volume. Just the thing! We have got Mrs.
Bangham in this book. But what makes these books interesting to most
people is—not who's in 'em, but who isn't—who's coming, you know, and
when. That's the interesting question."

Commendingly looking back at the pillow he had improvised, he left
them to their hour's repose. Maggy was snoring already, and Little Dorrit
was soon fast asleep, with her head resting on that sealed book of Fate,
untroubled by its mysterious blank leaves.

This was Little Dorrit's party. The shame, desertion, wretchedness,
and exposure, of the great capital; the wet, the cold, the slow hours, and
the swift clouds, of the dismal night. This was the party from which Little
Dorrit went home, jaded, in the first grey mist of a rainy morning.

END OF No. IV

CHAPTER XV

MRS. FLINTWINCH HAS ANOTHER DREAM

THE debilitated old house in the city, wrapped in its mantle of soot, and
leaning heavily on the crutches that had partaken of its decay and worn out
with it, never knew a healthy or a cheerful interval, let what would betide.
If the sun ever touched it, it was but with a ray, and that was gone in half an
hour; if the moonlight ever fell upon it, it was only to put a few patches on
its doleful cloak, and make it look more wretched. The stars, to be sure,
coldly watched it when the nights and the smoke were clear enough; and
all bad weather stood by it with a rare fidelity. You should alike find rain,

hail, frost, and thaw lingering in that dismal enclosure, when they had vanished from other places; and as to snow, you should see it there for weeks, long after it had changed from yellow to black, slowly weeping away its grimy life. The place had no other adherents. As to street noises, the rumbling of wheels in the lane merely rushed in at the gateway in going past, and rushed out again: making the listening Mistress Affery feel as if she were deaf, and recovered the sense of hearing by instantaneous flashes. So with whistling, singing, talking, laughing, and all pleasant human sounds. They leaped the gap in a moment, and went upon their way.

The varying light of fire and candle in Mrs. Clennam's room made the greatest change that ever broke the dead monotony of the spot. In her two narrow windows, the fire shone sullenly all day, and sullenly all night. On rare occasions, it flashed up passionately, as she did; but for the most part it was suppressed, like her, and preyed upon itself evenly and slowly. During many hours of the short winter days, however, when it was dusk there early in the afternoon, changing distortions of herself in her wheeled chair, of Mr. Flintwinch with his wry neck, of Mistress Affery coming and going, would be thrown upon the house wall that was over the gateway, and would hover there like shadows from a great magic lantern. As the room-ridden invalid settled for the night, these would gradually disappear: Mistress Affery's magnified shadow always flitting about, last, until it finally glided away into the air, as though she were off upon a witch-excursion. Then the solitary light would burn unchangingly, until it burned pale before the dawn, and at last died under the breath of Mistress Affery, as her shadow descended on it from the witch-region of sleep.

Strange, if the little sick-room fire were in effect a beacon fire, summoning some one, and that the most unlikely some one in the world, to the spot that *must* be come to. Strange, if the little sick-room light were in effect a watch-light, burning in that place every night until an appointed event should be watched out! Which of the vast multitude of travellers, under the sun and the stars, climbing the dusty hills and toiling along the weary plains, journeying by land and journeying by sea, coming and going so strangely, to meet and to act and re-act on one another, which of the host may, with no suspicion of the journey's end, be travelling surely hither?

Time shall show us. The post of honor and the post of shame, the general's station and the drummer's, a peer's statue in Westminster Abbey and a seaman's hammock in the bosom of the deep, the mitre and the workhouse, the woolsack and the gallows, the throne and the guillotine— the travellers to all are on the great high-road; but it has wonderful divergences, and only Time shall show us whither each traveller is bound.

On a wintry afternoon at twilight, Mrs. Flintwinch, having been heavy all day, dreamed this dream:

She thought she was in the kitchen getting the kettle ready for tea, and was warming herself with her feet upon the fender and the skirt of her gown tucked up, before the collapsed fire in the middle of the grate, bordered on either hand by a deep cold black ravine. She thought that as she sat thus, musing upon the question, whether life was not for some people a rather dull invention, she was frightened by a sudden noise behind her. She thought that she had been similiarly frightened once last week, and that the noise was of a mysterious kind—a sound of rustling, and of three or four quick beats like a rapid step; while a shock or tremble was communicated to her heart, as if the step had shaken the floor, or even as if she had been touched by some awful hand. She thought that this revived within her, certain old fears of hers that the house was haunted; and that she flew up the kitchen stairs, without knowing how she got up, to be nearer company.

Mistress Affery thought that on reaching the hall, she saw the door of her liege lord's office standing open, and the room empty. That she went to the ripped-up window, in the little room by the street door, to connect her palpitating heart, through the glass, with living things beyond and outside the haunted house. That she then saw, on the wall over the gateway, the shadows of the two clever ones in conversation above. That she then went up-stairs with her shoes in her hand, partly to be near the clever ones as a match for most ghosts, and partly to hear what they were talking about.

"None of your nonsense with me," said Mr. Flintwinch. "I won't take it from you."

Mrs. Flintwinch dreamed that she stood behind the door, which was just ajar, and most distinctly heard her husband say these bold words.

"Flintwinch," returned Mrs. Clennam, in her usual strong low voice, "there is a demon of anger in you. Guard against it."

"I don't care whether there's one or a dozen," said Mr. Flintwinch, forcibly suggesting in his tone that the higher number was nearer the mark. "If there was fifty, they should all say, None of your nonsense with me, I won't take it from you.—I'd make 'em say it, whether they liked it or not."

"What have I done, you wrathful man?" her strong voice asked.

"Done?" said Mr. Flintwinch. "Dropped down upon me."

"If you mean, remonstrated with you——"

"Don't put words in my mouth that I don't mean," said Jeremiah, sticking to his figurative expression with tenacious and impenetrable obstinacy: "I mean dropped down upon me."

"I remonstrated with you," she began again, "because——"

"I won't have it!" cried Jeremiah. "You dropped down upon me."

"I dropped down upon you, then, you ill-conditioned man," (Jeremiah chuckled at having forced her to adopt his phrase), "for having been need-lessly significant to Arthur that morning. I have a right to complain of it as almost a breach of confidence. You did not mean it——"

"I won't have it!" interposed the contradictory Jeremiah, flinging back the concession. "I did mean it."

"I suppose I must leave you to speak in soliloquy if you choose," she replied, after a pause that seemed an angry one. "It is useless my addressing myself to a rash and headstrong old man who has a set purpose not to hear me."

"Now, I won't take that from you either," said Jeremiah. "I have no such purpose. I have told you I did mean it. Do you wish to know why I meant it, you rash and headstrong old woman?"

"After all, you only restore me my own words," she said, struggling with her indignation. "Yes."

"This is why, then. Because you hadn't cleared his father to him, and you ought to have done it. Because, before you went into any tantrum about yourself, who are——"

"Hold there, Flintwinch!" she cried out in a changed voice: "you may go a word too far."

The old man seemed to think so. There was another pause, and he had altered his position in the room, when he spoke again more mildly:

"I was going to tell you why it was. Because, before you took your own part, I thought you ought to have taken the part of Arthur's father. Arthur's father! I had no particular love for Arthur's father. I served Arthur's father's uncle, in this house, when Arthur's father was not much above me—was poorer as far as his pocket went—and when his uncle might as soon have left me his heir as have left him. He starved in the parlor, and I starved in the kitchen; that was the principal difference in our positions; there was not much more than a flight of break-neck stairs between us. I never took to him in those times; I don't know that I ever took to him greatly at any time. He was an undecided, irresolute chap, who had had everything but his orphan life scared out of him when he was young. And when he brought you home here, the wife his uncle had named for him, I didn't need to look at you twice (you were a good-looking woman at that time) to know who'd be master. You have stood of your own strength ever since. Stand of your own strength now. Don't lean against the dead."

"I do *not*—as you call it—lean against the dead."

"But you had a mind to do it, if I had submitted," growled Jeremiah, "and that's why you drop down upon me. You can't forget that I didn't submit. I suppose you are astonished that I should consider it worth my while to have justice done to Arthur's father? Hey? It doesn't matter whether you answer or not, because I know you are, and you know you are. Come, then, I'll tell you how it is. I may be a bit of an oddity in point of temper, but this is my temper—I can't let anybody have entirely their own way. You are a determined woman, and a clever woman; and when you see your purpose before you, nothing will turn you from it. Who knows that better than I do?"

"Nothing will turn me from it, Flintwinch, when I have justified it to myself. Add that."

"Justified it to yourself? I said you were the most determined woman on the face of the earth (or I meant to say so), and if you are determined to justify any object you entertain, of course you'll do it."

"Man! I justify myself by the authority of these Books," she cried, with stern emphasis, and appearing from the sound that followed to strike the dead-weight of her arm upon the table.

"Never mind that," returned Jeremiah, calmly, "we won't enter into that question at present. However that may be, you carry out your purposes, and you make everything go down before them. Now, I won't go down before them. I have been faithful to you, and useful to you, and I am attached to you. But I can't consent, and I won't consent, and I never did consent, and I never will consent, to be lost in you. Swallow up everybody else, and welcome. The peculiarity of my temper is, ma'am, that I won't be swallowed up alive."

Perhaps this had originally been the mainspring of the understanding between them. Descrying thus much of force of character in Mr. Flintwinch, perhaps Mrs. Clennam had deemed alliance with him worth her while.

"Enough and more than enough of the subject," said she gloomily.

"Unless you drop down upon me again," returned the persistent Flintwinch, "and then you must expect to hear of it again."

Mistress Affery dreamed that the figure of her lord here began walking up and down the room, as if to cool his spleen, and that she ran away; but that, as he did not issue forth when she had stood listening and trembling in the shadowy hall a little time, she crept up-stairs again, impelled as before by ghosts and curiosity, and once more cowered outside the door.

"Please to light the candle, Flintwinch," Mrs. Clennam was saying, apparently wishing to draw him back into their usual tone. "It is nearly time for tea. Little Dorrit is coming, and will find me in the dark."

Mr. Flintwinch lighted the candle briskly, and said, as he put it down upon the table:

"What are you going to do with Little Dorrit? Is she to come to work here for ever? To come to tea here for ever? To come backwards and forwards here, in the same way, for ever?"

"How can you talk about 'for ever' to a maimed creature like me? Are we not all cut down like the grass of the field, and was not I shorn by the scythe many years ago; since when, I have been lying here, waiting to be gathered into the barn?"

"Aye, aye! But since you have been lying here—not near dead—nothing like it—numbers of children and young people, blooming women, strong men, and what not, have been cut down and carried; and still here are you, you see, not much changed after all. Your time and mine may be a long one yet. When I say for ever, I mean (though I am not poetical) through all our time." Mr. Flintwinch gave this explanation with great calmness, and calmly waited for an answer.

"So long as Little Dorrit is quiet, and industrious, and stands in need of the slight help I can give her, and deserves it; so long, I suppose, unless she withdraws of her own act, she' will continue to come here, I being spared."

"Nothing more than that?" said Flintwinch, stroking his mouth and chin.

"What should there be more than that! What could there be more than that!" she ejaculated, in her sternly wondering way.

Mrs. Flintwinch dreamed, that, for the space of a minute or two, they remained looking at each other with the candle between them, and that she somehow derived an impression that they looked at each other fixedly.

"Do you happen to know, Mrs. Clennam," Affery's liege lord then demanded in a much lower voice, and with an amount of expression that seemed quite out of proportion to the simple purpose of his words, "where she lives?"

"No."

"Would you—now, would you like to know?" said Jeremiah, with a pounce as if he had sprung upon her.

"If I cared to know, I should know already. Could I not have asked her, any day?"

"Then you don't care to know?"

"I do not."

Mr. Flintwinch, having expelled a long significant breath, said with his former emphasis, "For I have accidentally—mind! —found out."

"Wherever she lives," said Mrs. Clennam, speaking in one unmodulated hard voice, and separating her words as distinctly as if she were reading them off from separate bits of metal that she took up one by one, "she has made a secret of it, and she shall always keep her secret from me."

"After all, perhaps you would rather not have known the fact, anyhow?" said Jeremiah; and he said it with a twist, as if his words had come out of him in his own wry shape.

"Flintwinch," said his mistress and partner, flashing into a sudden energy that made Affery start, "why do you goad me? Look round this room. If it is any compensation for my long confinement within these narrow limits—not that I complain of being afflicted; you know I never complain of that— if it is any compensation to me for my long confinement to this room, that while I am shut up from all pleasant change, I am also shut up from the knowledge of some things that I may prefer to avoid knowing, why should you, of all men, grudge me that relief?"

"I don't grudge it to you," returned Jeremiah.

"Then say no more. Say no more. Let Little Dorrit keep her secret from me, and do you keep it from me also. Let her come and go, unobserved and unquestioned. Let me suffer, and let me have what alleviation belongs to my condition. Is it so much, that you torment me like an evil spirit?"

"I asked you a question. That's all."

"I have answered it. So, say no more. Say no more." Here the sound of the wheeled chair was heard upon the floor, and Affery's bell rang with a hasty jerk.

More afraid of her husband at the moment than of the mysterious sound in the kitchen, Affery crept away as lightly and as quickly as she could, descended the kitchen stairs almost as rapidly as she had ascended them, resumed her seat before the fire, tucked up her skirt again, and finally threw her apron over her head. Then the bell rang once more, and then once more, and then kept on ringing; in despite of which importunate summons, Affery still sat behind her apron, recovering her breath.

At last Mr. Flintwinch came shuffling down the staircase into the hall, muttering and calling "Affery woman!" all the way. Affery still remaining behind her apron, he came stumbling down the kitchen stairs, candle in hand, sidled up to her, twitched her apron off, and roused her.

"O Jeremiah!" cried Affery, waking. "What a start you gave me!"

"What have you been doing, woman?" enquired Jeremiah. "You've been rung for, fifty times."

"O Jeremiah," said Mistress Affery, "I have been a-dreaming!"

Reminded of her former achievement in that way, Mr. Flintwinch held the candle to her head, as if he had some idea of lighting her up for the illumination of the kitchen.

"Don't you know it's her tea-time?" he demanded, with a vicious grin, and giving one of the legs of Mistress Affery's chair a kick.

"Jeremiah? Tea-time? I don't know what's come to me. But I got such a dreadful turn, Jeremiah, before I went—off a-dreaming, that I think it must be that."

"Yoogh! Sleepy-Head!" said Mr. Flintwinch, "what are you talking about?"

"Such a strange noise, Jeremiah, and such a curious movement. In the kitchen here—just here."

Jeremiah held up his light and looked at the blackened ceiling, held down his light and looked at the damp stone floor, turned round with his light and looked about at the spotted and blotched walls.

"Rats, cats, water, drains," said Jeremiah.

Mistress Affery negatived each with a shake of her head. "No, Jeremiah; I have felt it before. I have felt it up-stairs, and once on the staircase as I was going from her room to ours in the night—a rustle and a sort of trembling touch behind me."

"Affery, my woman," said Mr. Flintwinch, grimly, after advancing his nose to that lady's lips as a test for the detection of spirituous liquors, "if you don't get tea pretty quick, old woman, you'll become sensible of a rustle and a touch that'll send you flying to the other end of the kitchen."

This prediction stimulated Mrs. Flintwinch to bestir herself, and to hasten up-stairs to Mrs. Clennam's chamber. But, for all that, she now began to entertain a settled conviction that there was something wrong in the gloomy house. Henceforth, she was never at peace in it after daylight departed; and never went up or down-stairs in the dark without having her apron over her head, lest she should see something.

What with these ghostly apprehensions, and her singular dreams, Mrs. Flintwinch fell that evening into a haunted state of mind, from which it may be long before this present narrative descries any trace of her recovery. In the vagueness and indistinctness of all her new experiences and perceptions, as everything about her was mysterious to herself, she began to be mysterious to others; and became as difficult to be made out to anybody's satisfaction, as she found the house and everything in it difficult to make out to her own.

She had not yet finished preparing Mrs. Clennam's tea, when the soft knock came to the door which always announced Little Dorrit. Mistress Affery looked on at Little Dorrit taking off her homely bonnet in the hall, and at Mr. Flintwinch scraping his jaws and contemplating her in silence, as expecting some wonderful consequence to ensue which would frighten her out of her five wits or blow them all three to pieces.

After tea, there came another knock at the door, announcing Arthur. Mistress Affery went down to let him in, and he said on entering, "Affery, I am glad it's you. I want to ask you a question." Affery immediately replied, "For goodness sake don't ask me nothing, Arthur! I am frightened out of one half of my life, and dreamed out of the other. Don't ask me nothing! I don't know which is which or what is what!"—and immediately started away from him, and came near him no more.

Mistress Affery having no taste for reading, and no sufficient light for needlework in the subdued room, supposing her to have the inclination, now sat every night in the dimness from which she had momentarily emerged on the evening of Arthur Clennam's return, occupied with crowds of wild speculations and suspicions respecting her mistress, and her husband, and the noises in the house. When the ferocious devotional exercises were engaged in, these speculations would distract Mistress Affery's eyes towards the door, as if she expected some dark form to appear at those propitious moments, and make the party one too many.

Otherwise, Affery never said or did anything to attract the attention of the two clever ones towards her in any marked degree, except on certain occasions, generally at about the quiet hours towards bed-time, when she would suddenly dart out of her dim corner, and whisper with a face of terror, to Mr. Flintwinch reading the paper near Mrs. Clennam's little table:

"There, Jeremiah! Now! What's that noise!"

Then the noise, if there were any, would have ceased, and Mr. Flintwinch would snarl, turning upon her as if she had cut him down that moment against his will, "Affery, old woman, you shall have a dose, old woman, such a dose! You have been dreaming again!"

CHAPTER XVI

NOBODY'S WEAKNESS

THE time being come for the renewal of his acquaintance with the Meagles family, Clennam, pursuant to contract made between himself and Mr. Meagles, within the precincts of Bleeding Heart Yard, turned his face on a certain Saturday towards Twickenham, where Mr. Meagles had a cottage-residence of his own. The weather being fine and dry, and any English road abounding in interest for him who had been so long away, he sent his valise on by the coach, and set out to walk. A walk was in itself a new enjoyment to him, and one that had rarely diversified his life afar off.

He went by Fulham and Putney, for the pleasure of strolling over the heath. It was bright and shining there; and when he found himself so far on his road to Twickenham, he found himself a long way on his road to a number of airier and less substantial destinations. They had risen before him fast, in the healthful exercise and the pleasant road. It is not easy to walk alone in the country without musing upon something. And he had plenty of unsettled subjects to meditate upon, though he had been walking to the Land's End.

First, there was the subject seldom absent from his mind, the question what he was to do henceforth in life; to what occupation he should devote himself, and in what direction he had best seek it. He was far from rich, and every day of indecision and inaction made his inheritance a source of greater anxiety to him. As often as he began to consider how to increase this inheritance, or to lay it by, so often his misgiving that there was some one with an unsatisfied claim upon his justice, returned; and that alone was a subject to outlast the longest walk. Again, there was the subject of his relations with his mother, which were now upon an equable and peaceful but never confidential footing, and whom he saw several times a week. Little Dorrit was a leading and a constant subject: for the circumstances of his life, united to those of her own story, presented the little creature to him as the only person between whom and himself there were ties of innocent reliance on one hand, and affectionate protection on the other; ties of compassion, respect, unselfish interest, gratitude, and pity. Thinking of her, and of the possibility of her father's release from prison by the unbarring hand of death—the only change of circumstance he could foresee that might enable him to be such a friend to her as he wished to be, by altering her whole manner of life, smoothing her rough road, and giving her a home— he regarded her, in that perspective, as his adopted daughter, his poor child of the Marshalsea hushed to rest. If there were a last subject in his thoughts, and it lay towards Twickenham, its form was so indefinite that it was little more than the pervading atmosphere in which these other subjects floated before him.

He had crossed the heath and was leaving it behind, when he gained upon a figure which had been in advance of him for some time, and which, as he gained upon it, he thought he knew. He derived this impression from some- thing in the turn of the head, and in the figure's action of consideration, as it went on at a sufficiently sturdy walk. But when the man—for it was a man's figure—pushed his hat up at the back of his head, and stopped to consider some object before him, he knew it to be Daniel Doyce.

"How do you do, Mr. Doyce?" said Clennam, overtaking him. "I am glad to see you again, and in a healthier place than the Circumlocution Office."

"Ha! Mr. Meagles's friend!" exclaimed that public criminal, coming out of some mental combinations he had been making, and offering his hand. "I am glad to see you, sir. Will you excuse me if I forget your name?"

"Readily. It's not a celebrated name. It's not Barnacle."

"No, no," said Daniel, laughing. "And now I know what it is. It's Clennam. How do you do, Mr. Clennam?"

"I have some hope," said Arthur, as they walked on together, "that we may be going to the same place, Mr. Doyce."

"Meaning Twickenham?" returned Daniel. "I am glad to hear it."

They were soon quite intimate, and lightened the way with a variety of conversation. The ingenious culprit was a man of great modesty and good sense; and, though a plain man, had been too much accustomed to combine what was original and daring in conception with what was patient and minute in execution, to be by any means an ordinary man. It was at first difficult to lead him to speak about himself, and he put off Arthur's advan- ces in that direction by admitting slightly, oh yes, he had done this, and he had done that, and such a thing was of his making, and such another thing was his discovery, but it was his trade, you see, his trade; until, as he gradually became assured that his companion had a real interest in his account of himself, he frankly yielded to it. Then it appeared that he was the son of a north-country blacksmith, and had originally been apprenticed by his widowed mother to a lock-maker; that he had "struck out a few little things" at the lock-maker's, which had led to his being released from his indentures with a present, which present had enabled him to gratify his ardent wish to bind himself to a working engineer, under whom he had labored hard, learned hard, and lived hard, seven years. His time being out, he had "worked in the shop" at weekly wages seven or eight years more; and had then betaken himself to the banks of the Clyde, where he had studied, and filed, and hammered, and improved his knowledge, theoretical and practical, for six or seven years more. There he had had an offer to go to Lyons, which he had accepted; and from Lyons had been engaged to go to Germany, and in Germany had had an offer to go to St. Petersburg, and there had done very well indeed—never better. However, he had naturally felt a preference for his own country, and a wish to gain distinction there, and to do whatever service he could do, there rather than elsewhere. And so he had come home. And so at home he had established himself in business, and had invented and executed, and worked his way on, until, after a dozen years of constant suit and service, he had been enrolled in the Great British Legion of Honor, the Legion of the Rebuffed of the Circumlocution Office, and had been decorated with the Great British Order of Merit, the Order of the Disorder of the Barnacles and Stiltstalkings.

"It is much to be regretted," said Clennam, "that you ever turned your thoughts that way, Mr. Doyce."

"True, sir, true to a certain extent. But what is a man to do? If he has the misfortune to strike out something serviceable to the nation, he must follow where it leads him."

"Hadn't he better let it go?" asked Clennam.

"He can't do it," said Doyce, shaking his head with a thoughtful smile. "It's not put into his head to be buried. It's put into his head to be made useful. You hold your life on the condition that to the last you shall struggle hard for it. Every man holds a discovery on the same terms."

"That is to say," said Arthur, with a growing admiration of his quiet companion, "you are not finally discouraged even now?"

"I have no right to be, if I am," returned the other. "The thing is as true as it ever was."

When they had walked a little way in silence, Clennam, at once to change the direct point of their conversation and not to change it too abruptly, asked Mr. Doyce if he had any partner in his business, to relieve him of a portion of its anxieties?

"No," he returned, "not at present. I had when I first entered on it, and
a good man he was. But he has been dead some years; and as I could not
easily take to the notion of another when I lost him, I bought his share for
myself and have gone on by myself ever since. And here's another thing,"
he said, stopping for a moment with a good-humoured laugh in his eyes,
and laying his closed right hand, with its peculiar suppleness of thumb, on
Clennam's arm, "no inventor can be a man of business, you know."

"No?" said Clennam.

"Why, so the men of business say," he answered, resuming the walk and
laughing outright. "I don't know why we unfortunate creatures should be
supposed to want common sense, but it is generally taken for granted that
we do. Even the best friend I have in the world, our excellent friend over
yonder," said Doyce, nodding towards Twickenham, "extends a sort of
protection to me, don't you know, as a man not quite able to take care of
himself?"

Arthur Clennam could not help joining in the good-humoured laugh,
for he recognised the truth of the description.

"So I find that I must have a partner who is a man of business and not
guilty of any inventions," said Daniel Doyce, taking off his hat to pass his
hand over his forehead, "if it's only in deference to the current opinion,
and to uphold the credit of the Works. I don't think he'll find that I have
been very remiss or confused in my way of conducting them; but that's for
him to say—whoever he is—not for me."

"You have not chosen him yet, then?"

"No, sir, no. I have only just come to a decision to take one. The fact is,
there's more to do than there used to be, and the Works are enough for me
as I grow older. What with the books and correspondence, and foreign
journeys for which a Principal is necessary, I can't do all. I am going to
talk over the best way of negociating the matter, if I find a spare half-hour
between this and Monday morning, with my—my Nurse and protector,"
said Doyce, with laughing eyes, again. "He is a sagacious man in business,
and has had a good apprenticeship to it."

After this, they conversed on indifferent subjects until they arrived at
their journey's end. A composed and unobtrusive self-sustainment was
noticeable in Daniel Doyce—a calm knowledge that what was true must
remain true, in spite of all the Barnacles in the family ocean, and would be
just the truth, and neither more nor less, when even that sea had run dry—
which had a kind of greatness in it, though not of the official quality.

As he knew the house well, he conducted Arthur to it by the way that
showed it to the best advantage. It was a charming place (none the worse
for being a little eccentric), on the road by the river, and just what the
residence of the Meagles family ought to be. It stood in a garden, no doubt
as fresh and beautiful in the May of the year, as Pet now was in the May of
her life; and it was defended by a goodly show of handsome trees and spread-

ing evergreens, as Pet was by Mr. and Mrs. Meagles. It was made out of an old brick house, of which a part had been altogether pulled down, and another part had been changed into the present cottage; so there was a hale elderly portion, to represent Mr. and Mrs. Meagles, and a young picturesque, very pretty portion, to represent Pet. There was even the later addition of a conservatory sheltering itself against it, uncertain of hue in its deep stained glass, and in its more transparent portions flashing to the sun's rays, now like fire and now like harmless water drops; which might have stood for Tattycoram. Within view was the peaceful river and the ferryboat, to moralise to all the inmates, saying: Young or old, passionate or tranquil, chafing or content, you, thus runs the current always. Let the heart swell into what discord it will, thus plays the rippling water on the prow of the ferry-boat ever the same tune. Year after year, so much allowance for the drifting of the boat, so many miles an hour the flowing of the stream, here the rushes, there the lilies, nothing uncertain or unquiet, upon this road that steadily runs away; while you, upon your flowing road of time, are so capricious and distracted.

The bell at the gate had scarcely sounded when Mr. Meagles came out to receive them. Mr. Meagles had scarcely come out, when Mrs. Meagles came out. Mrs. Meagles had scarcely come out, when Pet came out. Pet had scarcely come out, when Tattycoram came out. Never had visitors a more hospitable reception.

"Here we are, you see," said Mr. Meagles, "boxed up, Mr. Clennam, within our own home-limits, as if we were never going to expand—that is, travel—again. Not like Marseilles, eh? No allonging and marshonging here?"

"A different kind of beauty, indeed!" said Clennam, looking about him.

"But, Lord bless me!" cried Mr. Meagles, rubbing his hands with a relish, "it was an uncommonly pleasant thing being in quarantine, wasn't it? Do you know, I have often wished myself back again? We were a capital party."

This was Mr. Meagles's invariable habit. Always to object to everything while he was travelling, and always to want to get back to it when he was not travelling.

"If it was summer-time," said Mr. Meagles, "which I wish it was on your account, and in order that you might see the place at its best, you would hardly be able to hear yourself speak for birds. Being practical people, we never allow anybody to scare the birds; and the birds, being practical people, too, come about us in myriads. We are delighted to see you, Clennam (if you'll allow me, I shall drop the Mister); I heartily assure you, we are delighted."

"I have not had so pleasant a greeting," said Clennam—then he recalled what Little Dorrit had said to him in his own room, and faithfully added "except once—since we last walked to and fro, looking down at the Mediterranean."

"Ah!" returned Mr. Meagles. "Something like a look out, *that* was, wasn't it? I don't want a military government, but I shouldn't mind a little allonging and marshonging—just a dash of it—in this neighbourhood sometimes. It's Devilish still."

Bestowing this eulogium on the retired character of his retreat with a dubious shake of the head, Mr. Meagles led the way into the house. It was just large enough, and no more; was as pretty within as it was without, and was perfectly well-arranged and comfortable. Some traces of the migratory habits of the family were to be observed in the covered frames and furniture, and wrapped-up hangings; but it was easy to see that it was one of Mr. Meagles's whims to have the cottage always kept, in their absence, as if they were always coming back the day after to-morrow. Of articles collected on his various expeditions, there was such a vast miscellany that it was like the dwelling of an amiable Corsair. There were antiquities from Central Italy, made by the best modern houses in that department of industry; bits of mummy from Egypt (and perhaps Birmingham); model gondolas from Venice; model villages from Switzerland; morsels of tessellated pavement from Herculaneum and Pompeii, like petrified minced veal; ashes out of tombs, and lava out of Vesuvius; Spanish fans, Spezzian straw hats, Moorish slippers, Tuscan hair-pins, Carrara sculpture, Trastaverini scarves, Genoese velvets and filagree, Neapolitan coral, Roman cameos, Geneva jewellery, Arab lanterns, rosaries blest all round by the Pope himself, and an infinite variety of lumber. There were views, like and unlike, of a multitude of places; and there was one little picture-room devoted to a few of the regular sticky old Saints, with sinews like whipcord, hair like Neptune's, wrinkles like tattooing, and such coats of varnish that every holy personage served for a fly-trap, and became what is now called in the vulgar tongue a Catch-em-alive O. Of these pictorial acquisitions Mr. Meagles spoke in the usual manner. He was no judge, he said, except of what pleased himself; he had picked them up, dirt-cheap, and people *had* considered them rather fine. One man, who at any rate ought to know something of the subject, had declared that "Sage, Reading" (a specially oily old gentleman in a blanket, with a swan's-down tippet for a beard, and a web of cracks all over him like rich pie-crust), to be a fine Guercino. As for Sebastian del Piombo there, you would judge for yourself; if it were not his later manner, the question was, Who was it? Titian, that might or might not be—perhaps he had only touched it. Daniel Doyce said perhaps he hadn't touched it, but Mr. Meagles rather declined to overhear the remark.

When he had shown all his spoils, Mr. Meagles took them into his own snug room overlooking the lawn, which was fitted up in part like a dressing-room and in part like an office, and in which, upon a kind of counter-desk, were a pair of brass scales for weighing gold, and a scoop for shovelling out money.

"Here they are, you see," said Mr. Meagles. "I stood behind these two articles five-and-thirty years running, when I no more thought of gadding about than I now think of—staying at home. When I left the Bank for good, I asked for them, and brought them away with me. I mention it at once, or you might suppose that I sit in my counting-house (as Pet says I do), like the king in the poem of the four-and-twenty blackbirds, counting out my money."

Clennam's eyes had strayed to a natural picture on the wall, of two pretty little girls with their arms entwined. "Yes, Clennam," said Mr. Meagles in a lower voice. "There they both are. It was taken some seventeen years ago. As I often say to Mother, they were babies then."

"Their names?" said Arthur.

"Ah, to be sure! You have never heard any name but Pet. Pet's name is Minnie; her sister's, Lillie."

"Should you have known, Mr. Clennam, that one of them was meant for me?" asked Pet herself, now standing in the doorway.

"I might have thought that both of them were meant for you, both are still so like you. Indeed," said Clennam, glancing from the fair original to the picture and back, "I cannot even now say which is not your portrait."

"D'ye hear that, Mother?" cried Mr. Meagles to his wife, who had followed her daughter. "It's always the same, Clennam; nobody can decide. The child to your left is Pet."

The picture happened to be near a looking-glass. As Arthur looked at it again, he saw, by the reflection of the mirror, Tattycoram stop in passing outside the door, listen to what was going on, and pass away with an angry and contemptuous frown upon her face that changed its beauty into ugliness.

"But come!" said Mr. Meagles. "You have had a long walk, and will be glad to get your boots off. As to Daniel here, I suppose he'd never think of taking *his* boots off, unless we showed him a boot-jack."

"Why not?" asked Daniel, with a significant smile at Clennam.

"Oh! You have so many things to think about," returned Mr. Meagles, clapping him on the shoulder, as if his weakness must not be left to itself on any account. "Figures, and wheels, and cogs, and levers, and screws, and cylinders, and a thousand things."

"In my calling," said Daniel, amused, "the greater usually includes the less. But never mind, never mind! Whatever pleases you, pleases me."

Clennam could not help speculating, as he seated himself in his room by the fire, whether there might be in the breast of this honest, affectionate, and cordial Mr. Meagles, any microscopic portion of the mustard-seed that had sprung up into the great tree of the Circumlocution Office. His curious sense of a general superiority to Daniel Doyce, which seemed to be founded, not so much on anything in Doyce's personal character, as on the mere fact of his being an originator and a man out of the beaten track of other men, suggested the idea. It might have occupied him until he went down to dinner an hour afterwards, if he had not another question to consider, which had been in his mind so long ago as before he was in quarantine at Marseilles, and which had now returned to it, and was very urgent with it. No less a question than this: Whether he should allow himself to fall in love with Pet?

He was twice her age. (He changed the leg he had crossed over the other, and tried the calculation again, but could not bring out the total at less.) He was twice her age. Well! He was young in appearance, young in health and strength, young in heart. A man was certainly not old at forty; and many men were not in circumstances to marry, or did not marry, until they attained that time of life. On the other hand, the question was, not what he thought of the point, but what she thought of it.

He believed that Mr. Meagles was disposed to entertain a ripe regard for him, and he knew that he had a sincere regard for Mr. Meagles and his good wife. He could foresee that to relinquish this beautiful only child, of whom they were so fond, to any husband, would be a trial of their love which perhaps they never yet had had the fortitude to contemplate. But the more beautiful and winning and charming she, the nearer they must always be to the necessity of approaching it. And why not in his favor, as well as in another's?

When he had got so far, it came again into his head, that the question was, not what they thought of it but what she thought of it.

Arthur Clennam was a retiring man, with a sense of many deficiencies; and he so exalted the merits of the beautiful Minnie in his mind, and depressed his own, that when he pinned himself to this point, his hopes began to fail him. He came to the final resolution, as he made himself ready for dinner, that he would *not* allow himself to fall in love with Pet.

They were only five, at a round table, and it was very pleasant indeed. They had so many places and people to recall, and they were all so easy and cheerful together (Daniel Doyce either sitting out like an amused spectator at cards, or coming in with some shrewd little experiences of his own, when it happened to be to the purpose), that they might have been together twenty times, and not have known so much of one another.

"And Miss Wade," said Mr. Meagles, after they had recalled a number of fellow-travellers. "Has anybody seen Miss Wade?"

"I have," said Tattycoram.

She had brought a little mantle which her young mistress had sent for, and was bending over her, putting it on, when she lifted up her dark eyes, and made this unexpected answer.

"Tatty!" her young mistress exclaimed. "You seen Miss Wade?—where?"

"Here, Miss," said Tattycoram.

"How?"

An impatient glance from Tattycoram seemed, as Clennam saw it, to answer "With my eyes!" But her only answer in words was: "I met her near the church."

"What was she doing there I wonder!" said Mr. Meagles. "Not going to it, I should think."

"She had written to me first," said Tattycoram.

"Oh, Tatty!" murmured her mistress, "take your hands away. I feel as if some one else was touching me!"

She said it in a quick involuntary way, but half playfully, and not more petulantly or disagreeably than a favorite child might have done, who laughed next moment. Tattycoram set her full red lips together, and crossed her arms upon her bosom.

"Did you wish to know, sir," she said, looking at Mr. Meagles, "what Miss Wade wrote to me about?"

"Well, Tattycoram," returned Mr. Meagles, "since you ask the question, and we are all friends here, perhaps you may as well mention it, if you are so inclined."

"She knew, when we were travelling, where you lived," said Tattycoram, "and she had seen me not quite—not quite——"

"Not quite in a good temper, Tattycoram?" suggested Mr. Meagles, shaking his head at the dark eyes with a quiet caution. "Take a little time—count five-and-twenty, Tattycoram."

She pressed her lips together again, and took a long deep breath.

"So she wrote to me to say that if I ever felt myself hurt," she looked down at her young mistress, "or found myself worried," she looked down at her again, "I might go to her, and be considerately treated. I was to think of it, and could speak to her by the church. So I went there to thank her."

"Tatty," said her young mistress, putting her hand up over her shoulder that the other might take it, "Miss Wade almost frightened me when we parted, and I scarcely liked to think of her just now as having been so near me without my knowing it. Tatty, dear!"

Tatty stood for a moment, immovable.

"Hey?" cried Mr. Meagles. "Count another five-and-twenty, Tattycoram."

She might have counted a dozen, when she bent and put her lips to the caressing hand. It patted her cheek, as it touched the owner's beautiful curls, and Tattycoram went away.

"Now, there," said Mr. Meagles, softly, as he gave a turn to the dumb-waiter on his right hand, to twirl the sugar towards himself. "There's a girl who might be lost and ruined, if she wasn't among practical people.

Mother and I know, solely from being practical, that there are times when that girl's whole nature seems to roughen itself against seeing us so bound up in Pet. No father and mother were bound up in her, poor soul. I don't like to think of the way in which that unfortunate child, with all that passion and protest in her, feels when she hears the Fifth Commandment on a Sunday. I am always inclined to call out, Church, Count five-and-twenty, Tattycoram."

Besides his dumb-waiter, Mr. Meagles had two other not dumb waiters, in the persons of two parlor-maids, with rosy faces and bright eyes, who were a highly ornamental part of the table decoration. "And why not, you see?" said Mr. Meagles, on this head. "As I always say to Mother, why not have something pretty to look at, if you have anything at all?"

A certain Mrs. Tickit, who was Cook and Housekeeper when the family were at home, and Housekeeper only when the family were away, completed the establishment. Mr. Meagles regretted that the nature of the duties in which she was engaged, rendered Mrs. Tickit unpresentable at present, but hoped to introduce her to the new visitor to-morrow. She was an important part of the cottage, he said, and all his friends knew her. That was her picture up in the corner. When they went away, she always put on the silk gown and the jet-black row of curls represented in that portrait (her hair was reddish-grey in the kitchen), established herself in the breakfast-room, put her spectacles between two particular leaves of Doctor Buchan's Domestic Medicine, and sat looking over the blind all day until they came back again. It was supposed that no persuasion could be invented which would induce Mrs. Tickit to abandon her post at the blind, however long their absence, or to dispense with the attendance of Doctor Buchan: the lucubrations of which learned practitioner, Mr. Meagles implicitly believed she had never yet consulted to the extent of one word in her life.

In the evening, they played an old-fashioned rubber; and Pet sat looking over her father's hand, or singing to herself by fits and starts at the piano. She was a spoilt child; but how could she be otherwise? Who could be much with so pliable and beautiful a creature, and not yield to her endearing influence? Who could pass an evening in the house, and not love her for the grace and charm of her very presence in the room? This was Clennam's reflection, notwithstanding the final conclusion at which he had arrived up-stairs.

In making it, he revoked. "Why, what are you thinking of, my good sir?" asked the astonished Mr. Meagles, who was his partner. "I beg your pardon. Nothing," returned Clennam. "Think of something, next time; that's a dear fellow," said Mr. Meagles. Pet laughingly believed he had been thinking of Miss Wade. "Why of Miss Wade, Pet?" asked her father. "Why, indeed!" said Arthur Clennam. Pet colored a little, and went to the piano again.

As they broke up for the night, Arthur overheard Doyce ask his host if he could give him half-an-hour's conversation before breakfast in the morning? The host replying willingly, Arthur lingered behind a moment, having his own word to add on that topic.

"Mr. Meagles," he said, on their being left alone, "you remember when you advised me to go straight to London?"

"Perfectly well."

"And when you gave me some other good advice, which I needed at that time?"

"I won't say what it was worth," answered Mr. Meagles; "but of course I remember our being very pleasant and confidential together."

"I have acted on your advice; and having disembarrassed myself of an occupation that was painful to me for many reasons, wish to devote myself and what means I have, to another pursuit."

"Right! You can't do it too soon," said Mr. Meagles.

"Now, as I came down to-day, I found that your friend, Mr. Doyce, is looking for a partner in his business—not a partner in his mechanical knowledge, but in the ways and means of turning the business arising from it to the best account."

"Just so," said Mr. Meagles, with his hands in his pockets, and with the old business expression of face that had belonged to the scales and scoop.

"Mr. Doyce mentioned incidentally, in the course of our conversation, that he was going to take your valuable advice on the subject of finding such a partner. If you should think our views and opportunities at all likely to coincide, perhaps you will let him know my available position. I speak, of course, in ignorance of the details, and they may be unsuitable on both sides."

"No doubt, no doubt," said Mr. Meagles, with the caution belonging to the scales and scoop.

"But they will be a question of figures and accounts——"

"Just so, just so," said Mr. Meagles, with the arithmetical solidity belonging to the scales and scoop.

"—And I shall be glad to enter into the subject, provided Mr. Doyce responds, and you think well of it. If you will at present, therefore, allow me to place it in your hands, you will much oblige me."

"Clennam, I accept the trust with readiness," said Mr. Meagles. "And, without anticipating any of the points which you, as a man of business, have of course reserved, I am free to say to you that I think something may come of this. Of one thing you may be perfectly certain. Daniel is an honest man."

"I am so sure of it, that I have promptly made up my mind to speak to you."

"You must guide him, you know; you must steer him; you must direct him; he is one of a crotchetty sort," said Mr. Meagles, evidently meaning nothing more than that he did new things and went new ways; "but he is as honest as the sun, and so good night!"

Clennam went back to his room, sat down again before his fire, and made up his mind that he was glad he had resolved not to fall in love with Pet. She was so beautiful, so amiable, so apt to receive any true impression given to her gentle nature and her innocent heart, and make the man who should be so happy as to communicate it, the most fortunate and enviable of all men, that he was very glad indeed he had come to that conclusion.

But, as this might have been a reason for coming to the opposite conclusion, he followed out the theme again a little way in his mind. To justify himself, perhaps.

"Suppose that a man," so his thoughts ran, "who had been of age some twenty years or so; who was a diffident man, from the circumstances of his youth; who was rather a grave man, from the tenor of his life; who knew himself to be deficient in many little engaging qualities which he admired in others, from having been long in a distant region, with nothing softening near him; who had no kind sisters to present to her; who had no congenial home to make her known in; who was a stranger in the land; who had not a fortune to compensate, in any measure, for these defects; who had nothing in his favor but his honest love and his general wish to do right—suppose such a man were to come to this house, and were to yield to the captivation of this charming girl, and were to persuade himself that he could hope to win her; what a weakness it would be!"

He softly opened his window, and looked out upon the serene river. Year after year so much allowance for the drifting of the ferry-boat, so many miles an hour the flowing of the stream, here the rushes, there the lilies, nothing uncertain or unquiet.

Why should he be vexed or sore at heart? It was not his weakness that he had imagined. It was nobody's, nobody's within his knowledge, why should it trouble him? And yet it did trouble him. And he thought—who has not thought for a moment, sometimes—that it might be better to flow away monotonously, like the river, and to compound for its insensibility to happiness with its insensibility to pain.

CHAPTER XVII

NOBODY'S RIVAL

BEFORE breakfast in the morning, Arthur walked out to look about him. As the morning was fine, and he had an hour on his hands, he crossed the river by the ferry, and strolled along a footpath through some meadows. When he came back to the towing-path, he found the ferry-boat on the opposite side, and a gentleman hailing it and waiting to be taken over.

This gentleman looked barely thirty. He was well dressed, of a sprightly and gay appearance, a well-knit figure, and a rich dark complexion. As Arthur came over the stile and down to the water's edge, the lounger glanced at him for a moment, and then resumed his occupation of idly tossing stones into the water with his foot. There was something in his way of spurning them out of their places with his heel, and getting them into the required position, that Clennam thought had an air of cruelty in it. Most of us have more or less frequently derived a similar impression, from a man's manner of doing some very little thing: plucking a flower, clearing away an obstacle, or even destroying an insentient object.

The gentleman's thoughts were preoccupied, as his face showed, and he took no notice of a fine Newfoundland dog, who watched him attentively, and watched every stone too, in its turn, eager to spring into the river on receiving his master's sign. The ferry-boat came over, however, without his receiving any sign, and when it grounded his master took him by the collar and walked him into it.

"Not this morning," he said to the dog. "You won't do for ladies' company, dripping wet. Lie down."

Clennam followed the man and the dog into the boat, and took his seat. The dog did as he was ordered. The man remained standing, with his hands in his pockets, and towered between Clennam and the prospect. Man and dog both jumped lightly out as soon as they touched the other side, and went away. Clennam was glad to be rid of them.

The church clock struck the breakfast hour, as he walked up the little lane by which the garden-gate was approached. The moment he pulled the bell, a deep barking assailed him from within the wall.

"I heard no dog last night," thought Clennam. The gate was opened by one of the rosy maids, and on the lawn were the Newfoundland dog and the man.

"Miss Minnie is not down yet, gentlemen," said the blushing portress, as they all came together in the garden. Then she said to the master of the dog, "Mr. Clennam, sir," and tripped away.

"Odd enough, Mr. Clennam, that we should have met just now," said the man. Upon which the dog became mute. "Allow me to introduce myself—Henry Gowan. A pretty place this, and looks wonderfully well this morning!"

The manner was easy, and the voice agreeable; but still Clennam thought, that if he had not made that decided resolution to avoid falling in love with Pet, he would have taken a dislike to this Henry Gowan.

"It's new to you, I believe?" said this Gowan, when Arthur had extolled the place.

"Quite new. I made acquaintance with it only yesterday afternoon."

"Ah! Of course this is not its best aspect. It used to look charming in the spring, before they went away last time. I should like you to have seen it then."

But for that resolution so often recalled, Clennam might have wished him in the crater of Mount Etna, in return for this civility.

"I have had the pleasure of seeing it under many circumstances during the last three years, and it's—a Paradise."

It was (at least it might have been, always excepting for that wise resolution) like his dexterous impudence to call it a Paradise. He only called it a Paradise because he first saw her coming, and so made her out within her hearing to be an angel, Confusion to him!

And ah, how beaming she looked, and how glad! How she caressed the dog, and how the dog knew her! How expressive that heightened color in her face, that fluttered manner, her downcast eyes, her irresolute happiness! When had Clennam seen her look like this? Not that there was any reason why he might, could, would, or should have ever seen her look like this, or that he had ever hoped for himself to see her look like this; but still—when had he ever known her do it!

He stood at a little distance from them. This Gowan, when he had talked about a Paradise, had gone up to her and taken her hand. The dog had put his great paws on her arm and laid his head against her dear bosom. She had laughed and welcomed them, and made far too much of the dog, far, far, too much—that is to say, supposing there had been any third person looking on who loved her.

She disengaged herself now, and came to Clennam, and put her hand in his and wished him good morning, and gracefully made as if she would take his arm and be escorted into the house. This Gowan had no objection. No, he knew he was too safe.

There was a passing cloud on Mr. Meagles's good-humoured face, when they all three (four, counting the dog, and he was the most objectionable but one of the party) came in to breakfast. Neither it, nor the touch of uneasiness on Mrs. Meagles as she directed her eyes towards it, was unobserved by Clennam.

"Well, Gowan," said Mr. Meagles, even suppressing a sigh; "how goes the world with you this morning?"

"Much as usual, sir. Lion and I being determined not to waste anything of our weekly visit, turned out early, and came over from Kingston, my present head-quarters, where I am making a sketch or two." Then he told how he had met Mr. Clennam at the ferry, and they had come over together.

"Mrs. Gowan is well, Henry?" said Mrs. Meagles. (Clennam became attentive.)

"My mother is quite well, thank you." (Clennam became inattentive.) "I have taken the liberty of making an addition to your family dinner-party to-day, which I hope will not be inconvenient to you or to Mr. Meagles. I couldn't very well get out of it," he explained, turning to the latter. "The young fellow wrote to propose himself to me; and as he is well connected, I thought you would not object to my transferring him here."

"Who *is* the young fellow?" asked Mr. Meagles, with peculiar complacency.

"He is one of the Barnacles. Tite Barnacle's son, Clarence Barnacle, who is in his father's Department. I can at least guarantee that the river shall not suffer from his visit. He won't set it on fire."

"Aye, aye?" said Meagles. "A Barnacle is he? *We* know something of that family, eh Dan? By George, they are at the top of the tree, though! Let me see. What relation will this young fellow be to Lord Decimus now? His Lordship married, in seventeen ninety-seven, Lady Jemima Bilberry, who was the second daughter by the third marriage—no! There I am wrong! That was Lady Seraphina—Lady Jemima was the first daughter by the second marriage of the fifteenth Earl of Stiltstalking with The Honourable Clementina Toozellem. Very well. Now this young fellow's father married a Stiltstalking and *his* father married his cousin who was a Barnacle. The father of that father who married a Barnacle, married a Joddleby.—I am getting a little too far back, Gowan; I want to make out what relation this young fellow is to Lord Decimus."

"That's easily stated. His father is nephew to Lord Decimus."

"Nephew—to—Lord—Decimus," Mr. Meagles luxuriously repeated with his eyes shut, that he might have nothing to distract him from the full flavor of the genealogical tree. "By George, you are right, Gowan. So he is."

"Consequently, Lord Decimus is his great uncle."

"But stop a bit!" said Mr. Meagles, opening his eyes with a fresh discovery. "Then, on the mother's side, Lady Stiltstalking is his great aunt."

"Of course she is."

"Aye, aye, aye?" said Mr. Meagles, with much interest. "Indeed, indeed? We shall be glad to see him. We'll entertain him as well as we can, in our humble way; and we shall not starve him, I hope, at all events."

In the beginning of this dialogue, Clennam had expected some great harmless outburst from Mr. Meagles, like that which had made him burst out of the Circumlocution Office, holding Doyce by the collar. But his good friend had a weakness which none of us need go into the next street to find, and which no amount of Circumlocution experience could long subdue in him. Clennam looked at Doyce; but Doyce knew all about it beforehand, and looked at his plate, and made no sign, and said no word.

"I am much obliged to you," said Gowan, to conclude the subject. "Clarence is a great ass, but he is one of the dearest and best fellows that ever lived!"

It appeared, before the breakfast was over, that everybody whom this Gowan knew was either more or less of an ass, or more or less of a knave; but was, notwithstanding, the most loveable, the most engaging, the simplest, truest, kindest, dearest, best fellow that ever lived. The process by which this unvarying result was attained, whatever the premises, might have been stated by Mr. Henry Gowan thus: "I claim to be always book-keeping, with a peculiar nicety, in every man's case, and posting up a careful little account of Good and Evil with him. I do this so conscientiously, that I am happy to tell you I find the most worthless of men to be the dearest old fellow too; and am in a condition to make the gratifying report, that there is much less difference than you are inclined to suppose between an honest man and a scoundrel." The effect of this cheering discovery happened to be, that while he seemed to be scrupulously finding good in most men, he did in reality lower it where it was, and set it up where it was not; but that was its only disagreeable or dangerous feature.

It scarcely seemed, however, to afford Mr. Meagles as much satisfaction as the Barnacle genealogy had done. The cloud that Clennam had never seen upon his face before that morning, frequently overcast it again; and there was the same shadow of uneasy observation of him on the comely face of his wife. More than once or twice when Pet caressed the dog, it appeared to Clennam that her father was unhappy in seeing her do it; and, in one particular instance when Gowan stood on the other side of the dog, and bent his head at the same time, Arthur fancied that he saw tears rise to Mr. Meagles's eyes as he hurried out of the room. It was either the fact too, or he fancied further, that Pet herself was not insensible to these little incidents; that she tried, with a more delicate affection than usual, to express to her good father how much she loved him; that it was on this account that she fell behind the rest, both as they went to church and as they returned from it, and took his arm. He could not have sworn but that as he walked alone in the garden afterwards, he had an instantaneous glimpse of her in her father's room, clinging to both her parents with the greatest tenderness, and weeping on her father's shoulder.

The latter part of the day turning out wet, they were fain to keep the house, look over Mr. Meagles's collection, and beguile the time with conversation. This Gowan had plenty to say for himself, and said it in an off-hand and amusing manner. He appeared to be an artist by profession, and to have been at Rome some time; yet he had a slight, careless, amateur way with him—a perceptible limp, both in his devotion to art and his attainments—which Clennam could scarcely understand.

He applied to Daniel Doyce for help, as they stood together, looking out of window.

"You know Mr. Gowan?" he said in a low voice.

"I have seen him here. Comes here every Sunday, when they are at home."

"An artist, I infer from what he says?"

"A sort of a one," said Daniel Doyce, in a surly tone.

"What sort of a one?" asked Clennam, with a smile.

"Why, he has sauntered into the Arts at a leisurely Pall-Mall pace," said Doyce, "and I doubt if they care to be taken quite so coolly."

Pursuing his enquiries, Clennam found that the Gowan family were a very distant ramification of the Barnacles; and that the paternal Gowan, originally attached to a legation abroad, had been pensioned off as a Commissioner of nothing particular somewhere or other, and had died at his post with his drawn salary in his hand, nobly defending it to the last extremity. In consideration of this eminent public service, the Barnacle then in power had recommended the Crown to bestow a pension of two or three hundred a-year on his widow; to which the next Barnacle in power had added certain shady and sedate apartments in the Palace at Hampton Court, where the old lady still lived, deploring the degeneracy of the times, in company with several other old ladies of both sexes. Her son, Mr. Henry Gowan, inheriting from his father, the Commissioner, that very questionable help in life, a very small independence, had been difficult to settle; the rather as public appointments chanced to be scarce, and his genius, during his earlier manhood, was of that exclusively agricultural character which applies itself to the cultivation of wild oats. At last he had declared that he would become a Painter; partly because he had always had an idle knack that way, and partly to grieve the souls of the Barnacles-in-chief who had not provided for him. So it had come to pass successively, first, that several distinguished ladies had been frightfully shocked; then, that portfolios of his performances had been handed about o'nights, and declared with ecstacy to be perfect Claudes, perfect Cuyps, perfect phænomena; then, that Lord Decimus had bought his picture, and had asked the President and Council to dinner at a blow, and had said, with his own magnificent gravity, "Do you know, there appears to me to be really immense merit in that work?" and, in short, that people of condition had absolutely taken pains to bring him into fashion. But, somehow it had all failed. The prejudiced public had stood out against it obstinately. They had determined not to admire Lord Decimus's picture. They had determined to believe that in every service, except their own, a man must qualify himself, by striving early and late, and by working heart and soul, might and main. So now Mr. Gowan, like that worn-out old coffin which never was Mahomet's nor anybody else's, hung midway between two points: jaundiced and jealous as to the one he had left: jaundiced and jealous as to the other he couldn't reach.

Such was the substance of Clennam's discoveries concerning him, made that rainy Sunday afternoon and afterwards.

About an hour or so after dinner time, Young Barnacle appeared, attended by his eye-glass; in honor of whose family connexions, Mr. Meagles had cashiered the pretty parlor-maids for the day, and placed on duty in their stead two dingy men. Young Barnacle was in the last degree amazed and disconcerted at sight of Arthur, and had murmured involuntarily, "Look here!—Upon my soul, you know!" before his presence of mind returned.

Even then, he was obliged to embrace the earliest opportunity of taking his friend into a window, and saying, in a nasal way that was a part of his general debility:

"I want to speak to you, Gowan. I say. Look here. Who is that fellow?"

"A friend of our host's. None of mine."

"He's a most ferocious Radical, you know," said Young Barnacle.

"Is he? How do you know?"

"Egod, sir, he was Pitching into our people the other day, in the most tremendous manner. Went up to our place and Pitched into my father to that extent that it was necessary to order him out. Came back to our department and Pitched into me. Look here. You never saw such a fellow."

"What did he want?"

"Egod, sir," returned Young Barnacle, "He said he wanted to know, you know! Pervaded our department—without an appointment—and said he wanted to know!"

The stare of indignant wonder with which Young Barnacle accompanied this disclosure, would have strained his eyes injuriously but for the opportune relief of dinner. Mr. Meagles (who had been extremely solicitous to know how his uncle and aunt were) begged him to conduct Mrs. Meagles to the dining-room. And when he sat on Mrs. Meagles's right hand, Mr. Meagles looked as gratified as if his whole family were there.

All the natural charm of the previous day was gone. The eaters of the dinner, like the dinner itself, were lukewarm, insipid, over-done—and all owing to this poor little dull Young Barnacle. Conversationless at any time, he was now the victim of a weakness special to the occasion, and solely referable to Clennam. He was under a pressing and continual necessity of looking at that gentleman, which occasioned his eye-glass to get into his soup, into his wine-glass, into Mrs. Meagles's plate, to hang down his back like a bell-rope, and be several times disgracefully restored to his bosom by one of the dingy men. Weakened in mind by his frequent losses of this instrument, and its determination not to stick in his eye, and more and more enfeebled in intellect every time he looked at the mysterious Clennam, he applied spoons to his eye, forks, and other foreign matters connected with the furniture of the dinner-table. His discovery of these mistakes greatly increased his difficulties, but never released him from the necessity of looking at Clennam. And whenever Clennam spoke, this ill-starred young man was clearly seized with a dread that he was coming, by some artful device, round to that point of wanting to know, you know.

It may be questioned, therefore, whether anyone but Mr. Meagles had much enjoyment of the time. Mr. Meagles, however, thoroughly enjoyed Young Barnacle. As a mere flask of the golden water in the tale became a full fountain when it was poured out, so Mr. Meagles seemed to feel that this small spice of Barnacle imparted to his table the flavor of the whole family tree. In its presence, his frank, fine, genuine qualities paled; he was not so easy, he was not so natural, he was striving after something that did not belong to him, he was not himself. What a strange peculiarity on the part of Mr. Meagles, and where should we find such another case!

At last the wet Sunday wore itself out in a wet night; and Young Barnacle went home in a cab, feebly smoking; and the objectionable Gowan went away on foot, accompanied by the objectionable dog. Pet had taken the most amiable pains all day to be friendly with Clennam, but Clennam had been a little reserved since breakfast—that is to say, would have been, if he had loved her.

When he had gone to his own room, and had again thrown himself into the chair by the fire, Mr. Doyce knocked at the door, candle in hand, to ask him how and at what hour he purposed returning on the morrow? After settling this question, he said a word to Mr. Doyce about this Gowan —who would have run in his head a good deal, if he had been his rival.

"Those are not good prospects for a painter," said Clennam.

"No," returned Doyce.

Mr. Doyce stood, chamber-candlestick in hand, the other hand in his pocket, looking hard at the flame of his candle, with a certain quiet perception in his face that they were going to say something more.

"I thought our good friend a little changed, and out of spirits, after he came this morning?" said Clennam.

"Yes," returned Doyce.

"But not his daughter?" said Clennam.

"No," said Doyce.

There was a pause on both sides. Mr. Doyce, still looking at the flame of his candle, slowly resumed:

"The truth is, he has twice taken his daughter abroad, in the hope of separating her from Mr. Gowan. He rather thinks she is disposed to like him, and he has painful doubts (I quite agree with him, as I dare say you do), of the hopefulness of such a marriage."

"There——" Clennam choked, and coughed, and stopped.

"Yes, you have taken cold," said Daniel Doyce. But without looking at him.

——"There is an engagement between them, of course?" said Clennam airily.

"No. As I am told, certainly not. It has been solicited on the gentleman's part, but none has been made. Since their recent return, our friend has yielded to a weekly visit, but that is the utmost. Minnie would not deceive her father and mother. You have travelled with them, and I believe you know what a bond there is among them, extending even beyond this present life. All that there is between Miss Minnie and Mr. Gowan, I have no doubt we see."

"Ah! We see enough!" cried Arthur.

Mr. Doyce wished him Good Night, in the tone of a man who had heard a mournful, not to say despairing, exclamation, and who sought to infuse some encouragement and hope into the mind of the person by whom it had been uttered. Such tone was probably a part of his oddity, as one of a crotchetty band; for how could he have heard anything of that kind, without Clennam's hearing it, too?

The rain fell heavily on the roof, and pattered on the ground, and dripped among the evergreens, and the leafless branches of the trees. The rain fell heavily, drearily. It was a night of tears.

If Clennam had not decided against falling in love with Pet; if he had had the weakness to do it; if he had, little by little, persuaded himself to set all the earnestness of his nature, all the might of his hope, and all the wealth of his matured character, on that cast; if he had done this, and found that all was lost; he would have been, that night, unutterably miserable. As it was——

As it was, the rain fell heavily, drearily.

CHAPTER XVIII

LITTLE DORRIT'S LOVER

LITTLE DORRIT had not attained her twenty-second birthday without finding a lover. Even in the sallow Marshalsea, the ever young Archer shot off a few featherless arrows now and then from a mouldy bow, and winged a Collegian or two.

Little Dorrit's lover, however, was not a Collegian. He was the sentimental son of a turnkey. His father hoped, in the fulness of time, to leave him the inheritance of an unstained key; and had from his early youth familiarised him with the duties of his office, and with an ambition to retain the prison-lock in the family. While the succession was yet in abeyance, he assisted his mother in the conduct of a snug tobacco business round the corner of Horsemonger Lane (his father being a non-resident turnkey), which could usually command a neat connexion within the College walls.

Years agone, when the object of his affections was wont to sit in her little arm-chair by the high lodge-fender, Young John (family name, Chivery), a year older than herself, had eyed her with admiring wonder. When he had played with her in the yard, his favorite game had been to counterfeit locking her up in corners, and to counterfeit letting her out for real kisses. When he grew tall enough to peep through the keyhole of the great lock of the main door, he had divers times set down his father's dinner, or supper, to get on as it might on the outer side thereof, while he stood taking cold in one eye by dint of peeping at her through that airy perspective.

If Young John had ever slackened in his truth in the less penetrable days of his boyhood, when youth is prone to wear its boots unlaced and is happily unconscious of digestive organs, he had soon strung it up again and screwed it tight. At nineteen, his hand had inscribed in chalk on that part of the wall which fronted her lodging, on the occasion of her birthday, "Welcome sweet nursling of the Fairies!" At twenty-three, the same hand falteringly presented cigars on Sundays to the Father of the Marshalsea, and Father of the queen of his soul.

Young John was small of stature, with rather weak legs and very weak light hair. One of his eyes (perhaps the eye that used to peep through the keyhole) was also weak, and looked larger than the other, as if it couldn't collect itself. Young John was gentle likewise. But he was great of soul. Poetical, expansive, faithful.

Though too humble before the ruler of his heart to be sanguine, Young John had considered the subject of his attachment in all its lights and shades. Following it out to blissful results, he had descried, without self-commendation, a fitness in it. Say things prospered, and they were united. She, the child of the Marshalsea; he, the lock-keeper. There was a fitness in that. Say he became a resident turnkey. She would officially succeed to the chamber she had rented so long. There was a beautiful propriety in that. It looked over the wall, if you stood on tiptoe; and, with a trellis-work of scarlet beans and a canary or so, would become a very Arbour. There was a charming idea in that. Then, being all in all to one another, there was even an appropriate grace in the lock. With the world shut out (except that part of it which would be shut in); with its troubles and disturbances only known to them by hearsay, as they would be described by the pilgrims tarrying with them on their way to the Insolvent Shrine; with the Arbour above, and the Lodge below; they would glide down the stream of time, in pastoral domestic happiness. Young John drew tears from his eyes by finishing the picture with a tombstone in the adjoining churchyard, close against the prison wall, bearing the following touching inscription:

"Sacred to the Memory of JOHN CHIVERY, Sixty years Turnkey, and fifty years Head Turnkey, Of the neighbouring Marshalsea, Who departed this life, universally respected, on the thirty-first of December, One thousand eight hundred and eighty-six, Aged eighty-three years. Also of his truly beloved and truly loving wife, AMY, Whose maiden name was DORRIT, Who survived his loss not quite forty-eight hours, And who breathed her last in the Marshalsea aforesaid. There she was born, There she lived, There she died."

The Chivery parents were not ignorant of their son's attachment—indeed it had, on some exceptional occasions, thrown him into a state of mind that had impelled him to conduct himself with irascibility towards the customers, and damage the business—but they, in their turns, had worked it out to desirable conclusions. Mrs. Chivery, a prudent woman, had desired her husband to take notice that their John's prospects of the lock would certainly be strengthened by an alliance with Miss Dorrit, who had herself a kind of claim upon the College, and was much respected there. Mrs. Chivery had desired her husband to take notice that if, on the one hand, their John had means and a post of trust, on the other hand, Miss Dorrit had Family; and that her (Mrs. Chivery's) sentiment was, that two halves made a whole. Mrs. Chivery, speaking as a mother and not as a diplomatist, had then, from a different point of view, desired her husband to recollect that their John had never been strong, and that his love had fretted and worritted him enough as it was, without his being driven to do himself a mischief, as nobody couldn't say he wouldn't be if he was crossed. These arguments had so powerfully influenced the mind of Mr. Chivery, who was a man of few words, that he had, on sundry Sunday mornings, given his boy what he termed "a lucky touch," signifying that he considered such commendation of him to Good Fortune, preparatory to his that day declaring his passion and becoming triumphant. But Young John had never taken courage to make the declaration; and it was principally on these occasions that he had returned excited to the tobacco shop, and flown at the customers.

In this affair, as in every other, Little Dorrit herself was the last person considered. Her brother and sister were aware of it, and attained a sort of station by making a peg of it on which to air the miserably ragged old fiction of the family gentility. Her sister asserted the family gentility, by flouting the poor swain as he loitered about the prison for glimpses of his dear. Tip asserted the family gentility, and his own, by coming out in the character of the aristocratic brother, and loftily swaggering in the little skittle ground respecting seizures by the scruff of the neck, which there were looming probabilities of some gentleman unknown executing on some little puppy not mentioned. These were not the only members of the Dorrit family who turned it to account. No, no. The Father of the Marshalsea was supposed to know nothing about the matter, of course; his poor dignity could not see so low. But he took the cigars on Sundays, and was glad to get them; and sometimes even condescended to walk up and down the yard with the donor (who was proud and hopeful then), and benignantly to smoke one in his society. With no less readiness and condescension did he receive attentions from Chivery Senior, who always relinquished his arm-chair and newspaper to him, when he came into the Lodge during one of his spells of duty; and who had even mentioned to him, that if he would like at any time after dusk, quietly to step out into the fore-court and take a look at the street, there was not much to prevent him. If he did not avail himself of this latter civility, it was only because he had lost the relish for it; inasmuch as he took everything else he could get, and would say at times, "Extremely civil person, Chivery; very attentive man and very respectful. Young Chivery, too; really, almost with a delicate perception of one's position here. A very well conducted family indeed, the Chiveries. Their behaviour gratifies me."

The devoted Young John all this time regarded the family with reverence. He never dreamed of disputing their pretensions, but did homage to the miserable Mumbo Jumbo they paraded. As to resenting any affront from *her* brother, he would have felt, even if he had not naturally been of a most pacific disposition, that to wag his tongue or lift his hand against that sacred gentleman would be an unhallowed act. He was sorry that his noble mind should take offence; still, he felt the fact to be not incompatible with its nobility, and sought to propitiate and conciliate that gallant soul. Her father, a gentleman in misfortune—a gentleman of a fine spirit and courtly manners, who always bore with him—he deeply honored. Her sister, he considered somewhat vain and proud, but a young lady of infinite accomplishments, who could not forget the past. It was an instinctive testimony to Little Dorrit's worth, and difference from all the rest, that the poor young fellow honored and loved her for being simply what she was.

The tobacco business round the corner of Horsemonger Lane was carried on in a rural establishment one story high, which had the benefit of the air from the yards of Horsemonger Lane Jail, and the advantage of a retired walk under the wall of that pleasant establishment. The business was of too modest a character to support a life-size Highlander, but it maintained a little one on a bracket on the doorpost, who looked like a fallen Cherub that had found it necessary to take to a kilt.

From the portal thus decorated, one Sunday after an early dinner of baked viands, Young John issued forth on his usual Sunday errand; not empty-handed, but with his offering of cigars. He was neatly attired in a plum-colored coat, with as large a collar of black velvet as his figure could carry; a silken waistcoat, bedecked with golden sprigs; a chaste neckerchief much in vogue at that day, representing a preserve of lilac pheasants on a buff ground; pantaloons so highly decorated with side-stripes, that each leg was a three-stringed lute; and a hat of state, very high and hard. When the prudent Mrs. Chivery perceived that in addition to these adornments her John carried a pair of white kid gloves, and a cane like a little finger-post, surmounted by an ivory hand marshalling him the way that he should go; and when she saw him, in this heavy marching order, turn the corner to the right; she remarked to Mr. Chivery who was at home at the time, that she thought she knew which way the wind blew.

The Collegians were entertaining a considerable number of visitors that Sunday afternoon, and their Father kept his room for the purpose of receiving presentations. After making the tour of the yard, Little Dorrit's lover with a hurried heart went up-stairs, and knocked with his knuckles at the Father's door.

"Come in, come in!" said a gracious voice. The Father's voice, her father's, the Marshalsea's father's. He was seated in his black velvet cap, with his newspaper, three-and-sixpence accidentally left on the table, and two chairs arranged. Everything prepared for holding his Court.

"Ah, Young John! How do you do, how do you do?"

"Pretty well, I thank you, sir. I hope you are the same."

"Yes, John Chivery; yes. Nothing to complain of."

"I have taken the liberty, sir, of——"

"Eh?" The Father of the Marshalsea always lifted up his eyebrows at this point, and became amiably distraught and smilingly absent in mind.

"—A few cigars, sir."

"Oh!" (For the moment, excessively surprised.) "Thank you, Young John, thank you. But really, I am afraid I am too— No? Well then, I will say no more about it. Put them on the mantel-shelf, if you please, Young John. And sit down, sit down. You are not a stranger, John."

"Thank you, sir, I am sure.—Miss;" here Young John turned the great hat round and round upon his left-hand, like a slowly twirling mouse-cage; "Miss Amy quite well, sir?"

"Yes, John, yes; very well. She is out."

"Indeed, sir?"

"Yes, John. Miss Amy is gone for an airing. My young people all go out a good deal. But at their time of life, it's natural, John."

"Very much so, I am sure, sir."

"An airing. An airing. Yes." He was blandly tapping his fingers on the table, and casting his eyes up at the window. "Amy has gone for an airing on the Iron Bridge. She has become quite partial to the Iron Bridge of late, and seems to like to walk there better than anywhere." He returned to conversation. "Your father is not on duty at present, I think, John?"

"No, sir, he comes on later in the afternoon." Another twirl of the great hat, and then Young John said, rising, "I am afraid I must wish you good day, sir."

"So soon? Good day, Young John. Nay, nay," with the utmost condescension, "never mind your glove, John. Shake hands with it on. You are no stranger here, you know."

Highly gratified by the kindness of his reception, Young John descended the staircase. On his way down he met some Collegians bringing up visitors to be presented, and at that moment Mr. Dorrit happened to call over the bannisters with particular distinctness, "Much obliged to you for your little testimonial, John!"

Little Dorrit's lover very soon laid down his penny on the toll-plate of the Iron Bridge, and came upon it looking about him for the well-known and well-beloved figure. At first he feared she was not there; but as he walked on towards the Middlesex side, he saw her standing still, looking at the water. She was absorbed in thought, and he wondered what she might be thinking about. There were the piles of city roofs and chimneys, more free from smoke than on week-days; and there were the distant masts and steeples. Perhaps she was thinking about them.

Little Dorrit mused so long, and was so entirely preoccupied, that although her lover stood quiet for what he thought was a long time, and twice or thrice retired and came back again to the former spot, still she did not move. So, in the end, he made up his mind to go on, and seem to come upon her casually in passing, and speak to her. The place was quiet, and now or never was the time to speak to her.

He walked on, and she did not appear to hear his steps until he was close upon her. When he said "Miss Dorrit!" she started and fell back from him, with an expression in her face of fright and something like dislike that caused him unutterable dismay. She had often avoided him before—always, indeed, for a long, long while. She had turned away and glided off, so often, when she had seen him coming towards her, that the unfortunate Young John could not think it accidental. But he had hoped that it might be shyness, her retiring character, her foreknowledge of the state of his heart, anything short of aversion. Now, that momentary look had said, "You, of all people! I would rather have seen any one on earth, than you!"

It was but a momentary look, inasmuch as she checked it, and said in her soft little voice, "Oh, Mr. John! Is it you?" But she felt what it had been, as he felt what it had been; and they stood looking at one another equally confused.

"Miss Amy, I am afraid I disturbed you by speaking to you."

"Yes, rather. I—I came here to be alone, and I thought I was."

"Miss Amy, I took the liberty of walking this way, because Mr. Dorrit chanced to mention, when I called upon him just now, that you——"

She caused him more dismay than before by suddenly murmuring, "O, father, father!" in a heart-rending tone, and turning her face away.

"Miss Amy, I hope I don't give you any uneasiness by naming Mr. Dorrit. I assure you I found him very well, and in the best of spirits, and he showed me even more than his usual kindness; being so very kind as to say that I was not a stranger there, and in all ways gratifying me very much."

To the inexpressible consternation of her lover, Little Dorrit, with her hands to her averted face, and rocking herself where she stood, as if she were in pain, murmured, "O, father, how can you! O dear, dear father, how can you, can you, do it!"

The poor fellow stood gazing at her, overflowing with sympathy, but not knowing what to make of this, until, having taken out her handkerchief and put it to her still averted face, she hurried away. At first he remained stock still; then hurried after her.

"Miss Amy, pray! Will you have the goodness to stop a moment. Miss Amy, if it comes to that, let *me* go. I shall go out of my senses, if I have to think that I have driven you away like this."

His trembling voice and unfeigned earnestness brought Little Dorrit to a stop. "O, I don't know what to do," she cried, "I don't know what to do!"

To Young John, who had never seen her bereft of her quiet self-command, who had seen her from her infancy ever so reliable and self-suppressed, there was a shock in her distress, and in having to associate himself with it as its cause, that shook him from his great hat to the pavement. He felt it necessary to explain himself. He might be misunderstood—supposed to mean something, or to have done something, that had never entered into his imagination. He begged her to hear him explain himself, as the greatest favor she could show him.

"Miss Amy, I know very well that your family is far above mine. It were vain to conceal it. There never was a Chivery a gentleman that ever I heard of, and I will not commit the meanness of making a false representation on a subject so momentous. Miss Amy, I know very well that your high-souled brother, and likewise your spirited sister, spurn me from a heighth. What I have to do is to respect them, to wish to be admitted to their friendship, to look up at the eminence on which they are placed, from my lowlier station—for, whether viewed as tobacco or viewed as the lock, I well know it is lowly—and ever wish them well and happy."

There really was a genuineness in the poor fellow, and a contrast between the hardness of his hat and the softness of his heart (albeit, perhaps, of his head, too), that was moving. Little Dorrit entreated him to disparage neither himself nor his station, and, above all things, to divest himself of any idea that she supposed hers to be superior. This gave him a little comfort.

"Miss Amy," he then stammered, "I have had for a long time—ages they seem to me—Revolving ages—a heart-cherished wish to say something to you. May I say it?"

Little Dorrit involuntarily started from his side again, with the faintest shadow of her former look; conquering that, she went on at great speed half across the Bridge without replying.

"May I—Miss Amy, I but ask the question humbly —may I say it? I have been so unlucky already in giving you pain, without having any such intentions, before the holy Heavens! that there is no fear of my saying it unless I have your leave. I can be miserable alone, I can be cut up by myself; why should I also make miserable and cut up one, that I would fling myself off that parapet to give half a moment's joy to! Not that that's much to do, for I'd do it for twopence."

The mournfulness of his spirits, and the gorgeousness of his appearance, might have made him ridiculous, but that his delicacy made him respectable. Little Dorrit learnt from it what to do.

"If you please, John Chivery," she returned, trembling, but in a quiet way, "since you are so considerate as to ask me whether you shall say any more—if you please, no."

"Never, Miss Amy?"

"No, if you please. Never."

"Oh Lord!" gasped Young John.

"But perhaps, you will let me, instead, say something to you. I want to say it earnestly, and with as plain a meaning as it is possible to express. When you think of us, John —I mean my brother and sister, and me— don't think of us as being any different from the rest; for, whatever we once were (which I hardly know) we ceased to be long ago, and never can be any more. It will be much better for you, and much better for others, if you will do that, instead of what you are doing now."

Young John dolefully protested that he would try to bear it in mind, and would be heartily glad to do anything she wished.

"As to me," said Little Dorrit, "think as little of me as you can; the less, the better. When you think of me at all, John, let it only be as the child you have seen grow up in the prison, with one set of duties always occupying her; as a weak, retired, contented, unprotected girl. I particularly want you to remember, that when I come outside the gate, I am unprotected and solitary."

He would try to do anything she wished. But why did Miss Amy so much want him to remember that?

"Because," returned Little Dorrit, "I know I can then quite trust you not to forget to-day, and not to say any more to me. You are so generous that I know I can trust to you for that; and I do, and I always will. I am going to show you, at once, that I fully trust you. I like this place where we are speaking, better than any place I know;" her slight color had faded, but her lover thought he saw it coming back just then; "and I may be often here. I know it is only necessary for me to tell you so, to be quite sure that you will never come here again in search of me. And I am—quite sure!"

She might rely upon it, said Young John. He was a miserable wretch, but her word was more than a law for him.

"And good bye, John," said Little Dorrit. "And I hope you will have a good wife one day, and be a happy man. I am sure you will deserve to be happy, and you will be, John."

As she held out her hand to him with these words, the heart that was under the waistcoat of sprigs—mere slop-work, if the truth must be known—swelled to the size of the heart of a gentleman; and the poor common little fellow having no room to hold it, burst into tears.

"O don't cry;" said Little Dorrit piteously. "Don't, don't! Good bye, John. God bless you!"

"Good bye, Miss Amy. Good bye!"

And so he left her: first observing that she sat down on the corner of a seat, and not only rested her little hand upon the rough wall, but laid her face against it too, as if her head were heavy, and her mind were sad.

It was an affecting illustration of the fallacy of human projects, to behold her lover with the great hat pulled over his eyes, the velvet collar turned up as if it rained, the plum-colored coat buttoned to conceal the silken waistcoat of golden sprigs, and the little direction-post pointing inexorably home, creeping along by the worst back-streets, and composing, as he went, the following new inscription for a tombstone in Saint George's Churchyard:

"Here lie the mortal remains of JOHN CHIVERY, Never anything worth mentioning, Who died about the end of the year one thousand eight hundred and twenty-six, Of a broken heart, Requesting with his last breath that the word AMY might be inscribed over his ashes, Which was accordingly directed to be done, By his afflicted Parents."

END OF No. V

CHAPTER XIX

THE FATHER OF THE MARSHALSEA IN TWO OR THREE RELATIONS

THE brothers William and Frederick Dorrit, walking up and down the College-yard—of course on the aristocratic or Pump side, for the Father made it a point of his state to be chary of going among his children on the Poor side, except on Sunday mornings, Christmas Days, and other occasions of ceremony, in the observance whereof he was very punctual, and at which times he laid his hand upon the heads of their infants, and blessed those young Insolvents with a benignity that was highly edifying—the brothers, walking up and down the College-yard together, were a memorable sight. Frederick the free, was so humbled, bowed, withered, and faded; William the bond, was so courtly, condescending, and benevolently conscious of a position; that in this regard only, if in no other, the brothers were a spectacle to wonder at.

They walked up and down the yard, on the evening of Little Dorrit's Sunday interview with her lover on the Iron Bridge. The cares of state were over for that day, the Drawing Room had been well attended, several new presentations had taken place, the three-and-sixpence accidentally left on the table had accidentally increased to twelve shillings, and the Father of the Marshalsea refreshed himself with a whiff of cigar. As he walked up and down, affably accommodating his step to the shuffle of his brother, not proud in his superiority, but considerate of that poor creature, bearing with him, and breathing toleration of his infirmities in every little puff of smoke that issued from his lips and aspired to get over the spiked wall, he was a sight to wonder at.

His brother Frederick of the dim eye, palsied hand, bent form, and groping mind, submissively shuffled at his side, accepting his patronage as he accepted every incident of the labyrinthian world in which he had got lost. He held the usual screwed bit of whity-brown paper in his hand, from which he ever and again unscrewed a spare pinch of snuff. That falteringly taken, he would glance at his brother not unadmiringly, put his hands behind him, and shuffle on so at his side until he took another pinch, or stood still to look about him—perchance suddenly missing his clarionet.

The College visitors were melting away as the shades of night drew on, but the yard was still pretty full, the Collegians being mostly out, seeing their friends to the Lodge. As the brothers paced the yard, William the bond looked about him to receive salutes, returned them by graciously lifting off his hat, and, with an engaging air, prevented Frederick the free from running against the company, or being jostled against the wall. The Collegians as a body were not easily impressible, but even they, according to their various ways of wondering, appeared to find in the two brothers a sight to wonder at.

"You are a little low this evening, Frederick," said the Father of the Marshalsea. "Anything the matter?"

"The matter?" He stared for a moment, and then dropped his head and eyes again. "No, William, no. Nothing is the matter."

"If you could be persuaded to smarten yourself up a little, Frederick——"

"Aye, aye!" said the old man hurriedly. "But I can't be. I can't be. Don't talk so. That's all over."

The Father of the Marshalsea glanced at a passing Collegian with whom he was on friendly terms, as who should say, "An enfeebled old man, this; but he is my brother, sir, my brother, and the voice of Nature is potent!" and steered his brother clear of the handle of the pump by the threadbare sleeve. Nothing would have been wanting to the perfection of his character as a fraternal guide, philosopher, and friend, if he had only steered his brother clear of ruin, instead of bringing it upon him.

"I think, William," said the object of his affectionate consideration, "that I am tired, and will go home to bed."

"My dear Frederick," returned the other. "Don't let me detain you; don't sacrifice your inclinations to me."

"Late hours, and a heated atmosphere, and years I suppose," said Frederick, "weaken me."

"My dear Frederick," returned the Father of the Marshalsea, "do you think you are sufficiently careful of yourself? Do you think your habits are as precise and methodical as—shall I say as mine are? Not to revert again to that little eccentricity which I mentioned just now, I doubt if you take air and exercise enough, Frederick. Here is the parade, always at your service. Why not use it more regularly than you do?"

"Hah!" sighed the other. "Yes, yes, yes, yes."

"But it is of no use saying yes yes, my dear Frederick," the Father of the Marshalsea in his mild wisdom persisted, "unless you act on that assent. Consider my case, Frederick. I am a kind of example. Necessity and time have taught me what to do. At certain stated hours of the day, you will find me on the parade, in my room, in the Lodge, reading the paper, receiving company, eating and drinking. I have impressed upon Amy during many years, that I must have my meals (for instance) punctually. Amy has grown up in a sense of the importance of these arrangements, and you know what a good girl she is."

The brother only sighed again, as he plodded dreamily along, "Hah! Yes, yes, yes, yes."

"My dear fellow," said the Father of the Marshalsea, laying his hand upon his shoulder, and mildly rallying him—mildly, because of his weakness, poor dear soul; "you said that before, and it does not express much, Frederick, even if it means much. I wish I could rouse you, my good Frederick; you want to be roused."

"Yes, William, yes. No doubt," returned the other, lifting his dim eyes to his face. "But I am not like you."

The Father of the Marshalsea said, with a shrug of modest self-depreciation, "Oh! You might be like me, my dear Frederick; you might be, if you chose!" and forbore, in the magnanimity of his strength, to press his fallen brother further.

There was a deal of leave-taking going on in corners, as was usual on Sunday nights; and here and there in the dark, some poor woman, wife or mother, was weeping with a new Collegian. The time had been when the Father himself had wept, in the shades of that yard, as his own poor wife had wept. But it was many years ago; and now he was like a passenger aboard ship in a long voyage, who has recovered from sea-sickness, and is impatient of that weakness in the fresher passengers taken aboard at the last port. He was inclined to remonstrate, and to express his opinion that people who couldn't get on without crying, had no business there. In manner, if not in words, he always testified his displeasure at these interruptions of the general harmony; and it was so well understood, that delinquents usually withdrew if they were aware of him.

On this Sunday evening, he accompanied his brother to the gate with an air of endurance and clemency; being in a bland temper and graciously disposed to overlook the tears. In the flaring gaslight of the Lodge, several Collegians were basking: some taking leave of visitors, and some who had no visitors, watching the frequent turning of the key, and conversing with one another and with Mr. Chivery. The paternal entrance made a sensation of course; and Mr. Chivery, touching his hat (in a short manner though) with his key, hoped he found himself tolerable.

"Thank you, Chivery, quite well. And you?"

Mr. Chivery said in a low growl, "O! *he* was all right." Which was his general way of acknowledging enquiries after his health, when a little sullen.

"I had a visit from Young John to-day, Chivery. And very smart he looked, I assure you."

So Mr. Chivery had heard. Mr. Chivery must confess, however, that his wish was that the boy didn't lay out so much money upon it. For what did it bring him in? It only brought him in Wexation. And he could get that anywhere, for nothing.

"How vexation, Chivery?" asked the benignant father.

"No odds," returned Mr. Chivery. "Never mind. Mr. Frederick going out?"

"Yes, Chivery, my brother is going home to bed. He is tired, and not quite well. Take care, Frederick, take care. Good night, my dear Frederick!"

Shaking hands with his brother, and touching his greasy hat to the company in the Lodge, Frederick slowly shuffled out of the door which Mr. Chivery unlocked for him. The Father of the Marshalsea showed the amiable solicitude of a superior being that he should come to no harm.

"Be so kind as to keep the door open a moment, Chivery, that I may see him go along the passage and down the steps. Take care, Frederick! (He is very infirm). Mind the steps! (He is so very absent). Be careful how you cross, Frederick. (I really don't like the notion of his going wandering at large, he is so extremely liable to be run over.)"

With these words, and with a face expressive of many uneasy doubts and much anxious guardianship, he turned his regards upon the assembled company in the Lodge: so plainly indicating that his brother was to be pitied for not being under lock and key, that an opinion to that effect went round among the Collegians assembled.

But he did not receive it with unqualified assent; on the contrary, he said, No, gentlemen, no; let them not misunderstand him. His brother Frederick was much broken, no doubt, and it might be more comfortable to himself (the Father of the Marshalsea) to know that he was safe within the walls. Still, it must be remembered that to support an existence there during many years, required a certain combination of qualities—he did not say high qualities, but qualities—moral qualities. Now, had his brother Frederick that peculiar union of qualities? Gentlemen, he was a most excellent man, a most gentle, tender, and estimable man, with the simplicity of a child; but would he, though unsuited for most other places, do for that place? No; he said confidently, no! And, he said, Heaven forbid that Frederick should be there in any other character than in his present voluntary character! Gentlemen, whoever came to that College, to remain there a length of time, must have strength of character to go through a good deal and to come out of a good deal. Was his beloved brother Frederick that man? No. They saw him, even as it was, crushed. Misfortune crushed him. He had not power to recoil enough, not elasticity enough, to be a long time in such a place, and yet preserve his self-respect and feel conscious that he was a gentleman. Frederick had not (if he might use the expression) Power enough to see in any delicate little attentions and—and—Testimonials that he might under such circumstances receive, the goodness of human nature, the fine spirit animating the Collegians as a community, and at the same time no degradation to himself, and no depreciation of his claims as a gentleman. Gentlemen, God bless you!

Such was the homily with which he improved and pointed the occasion to the company in the Lodge, before turning into the sallow yard again, and going with his own poor shabby dignity past the Collegian in the dressing-gown who had no coat, and past the Collegian in the sea-side slippers who had no shoes, and past the stout greengrocer Collegian in the corduroy knee-breeches who had no cares, and past the lean clerk Collegian in buttonless black who had no hopes, up his own poor shabby staircase, to his own shabby room.

There, the table was laid for his supper, and his old grey gown was ready for him on his chair-back at the fire. His daughter put her little prayer-book in her pocket—had she been praying for pity on all prisoners and captives!—and rose to welcome him.

Uncle had gone home, then? she asked him, as she changed his coat and gave him his black velvet cap. Yes, uncle had gone home Had her father enjoyed his walk? Why, not much, Amy; not much. No? Did he not feel quite well?

As she stood behind him, leaning over his chair so lovingly, he looked with downcast eyes at the fire. An uneasiness stole over him that was like a touch of shame; and when he spoke, as he presently did, it was in an unconnected and embarrassed manner.

"Something, I—hem!—I don't know what, has gone wrong with Chivery. He is not—ha!—not nearly so obliging and attentive as usual to-night. It—hem!—it's a little thing, but it puts me out, my love. It's impossible to forget," turning his hands over and over, and looking closely at them, "that—hem!—that in such a life as mine, I am unfortunately dependent on these men for something, every hour in the day."

Her arm was on his shoulder, but she did not look in his face while he spoke. Bending her head, she looked another way.

"I—hem!—I can't think, Amy, what has given Chivery offence. He is generally so—so very attentive and respectful. And to-night he was quite—quite short with me. Other people there too! Why, good Heaven! if I was to lose the support and recognition of Chivery and his brother-officers, I might starve to death here."

While he spoke, he was opening and shutting his hands like valves; so conscious all the time of that touch of shame, that he shrunk before his own knowledge of his meaning.

"I—ha!—I can't think what it's owing to. I am sure I cannot imagine what the cause of it is. There was a certain Jackson here once, a turnkey of the name of Jackson (I don't think you can remember him, my dear, you were very young), and—hem!—and he had a—brother, and this—young brother paid his addresses to—at least, did not go so far as to pay his addresses to—but admired—respectfully admired—the—not the daughter, the sister—of one of us; a rather distinguished Collegian; I may say, very much so. His name was Captain Martin; and he consulted me on the question whether it was necessary that his daughter—sister—should hazard offending the turnkey brother by being too—ha!—too plain with the other brother. Captain Martin was a gentleman and a man of honor, and I put it to him first to give me his—his own opinion. Captain Martin (highly respected in the army) then unhesitatingly said, that it appeared to him that his—hem!—sister was not called upon to understand the young man too distinctly, and that she might lead him on—I am doubtful whether lead him on was Captain Martin's exact expression; indeed I think he said tolerate him—on her father's—I should say, brother's—account. I hardly know how I have strayed into this story. I suppose it has been through being unable to account for Chivery; but as to the connexion between the two, I don't see——"

His voice died away, as if she could not bear the pain of hearing him, and her hand gradually crept to his lips. For a little while, there was a dead silence and stillness; and he remained shrunk in his chair, and she remained with her arm round his neck, and her head bowed down upon his shoulder.

His supper was cooking in a saucepan on the fire, and, when she moved, it was to make it ready for him on the table. He took his usual seat, she took hers, and he began his meal. They did not, as yet, look at one another. By little and little he began; laying down his knife and fork with a noise, taking things up sharply, biting at his bread as if he were offended with it, and in other similar ways showing that he was out of sorts. At length he pushed his plate from him, and spoke aloud. With the strangest inconsistency.

"What does it matter whether I eat or starve? What does it matter whether such a blighted life as mine comes to an end, now, next week, or next year? What am I worth to any one? A poor prisoner, fed on alms and broken victuals; a squalid, disgraced wretch!"

"Father, father!" As he rose, she went on her knees to him, and held up her hands to him.

"Amy," he went on in a suppressed voice, trembling violently, and looking at her as wildly as if he had gone mad. "I tell you, if you could see me as your mother saw me, you wouldn't believe it to be the creature you have only looked at through the bars of this cage. I was young, I was accomplished, I was good-looking, I was independent—by God I was, child!—and people sought me out, and envied me. Envied me!"

"Dear father!" She tried to take down the shaking arm that he flourished in the air, but he resisted, and put her hand away.

"If I had but a picture of myself in those days, though it was ever so ill done, you would be proud of it, you would be proud of it. But I have no such thing. Now, let me be a warning! Let no man," he cried, looking haggardly about, "fail to preserve at least that little of the times of his prosperity and respect. Let his children have that clue to what he was. Unless my face, when I am dead, subsides into the long departed look—they say such things happen, I don't know—my children will have never seen me."

"Father, father!"

"O despise me, despise me! Look away from me, don't listen to me, stop me, blush for me, cry for me—Even you, Amy! Do it, do it! I do it to myself! I am hardened now, I have sunk too low to care long even for that."

"Dear father, loved father, darling of my heart!" She was clinging to him with her arms, and she got him to drop into his chair again, and caught at the raised arm, and tried to put it round her neck.

"Let it lie there, father. Look at me, father, kiss me, father! Only think of me, father, for one little moment!"

Still he went on in the same wild way, though it was gradually breaking down into a miserable whining.

"And yet I have some respect here. I have made some stand against it. I am not quite trodden down. Go out and ask who is the chief person in the place. They'll tell you it's your father. Go out and ask who is never trifled with, and who is always treated with some delicacy. They'll say, your father. Go out and ask what funeral here (it must be here, I know it can be nowhere else) will make more talk, and perhaps more grief, than any that has ever gone out at the gate. They'll say, your father's. Well then. Amy! Amy! Is your father so universally despised? Is there nothing to redeem him? Will you have nothing to remember him by, but his ruin and decay?

Will you be able to have no affection for him when he is gone, poor cast-away, gone?"

He burst into tears of maudlin pity for himself, and at length suffering her to embrace him, and take charge of him, let his grey head rest against her cheek, and bewailed his wretchedness. Presently he changed the subject of his lamentations, and clasping his hands about her as she embraced him, cried, O Amy, his motherless, forlorn child! O the days that he had seen her careful and laborious for him! Then he reverted to himself, and weakly told her how much better she would have loved him if she had known him in his vanished character, and how he would have married her to a gentleman who should have been proud of her as his daughter, and how (at which he cried again) she should first have ridden at his fatherly side on her own horse, and how the crowd (by which he meant in effect the people who had given him the twelve shillings he then had in his pocket) should have trudged the dusty roads respectfully.

Thus, now boasting, now despairing, in either fit a captive with the jail-rot upon him, and the impurity of his prison worn into the grain of his soul, he revealed his degenerate state to his affectionate child. No one else ever beheld him in the details of his humiliation. Little recked the Collegians who were laughing in their rooms over his late address in the Lodge, what a serious picture they had in their obscure gallery of the Marshalsea that Sunday night.

There was a classical daughter once—perhaps—who ministered to her father in his prison as her mother had ministered to her. Little Dorrit, though of the unheroic modern stock, and mere English, did much more, in comforting her father's wasted heart upon her innocent breast, and turning to it a fountain of love and fidelity that never ran dry or waned, through all his years of famine.

She soothed him; asked him for his forgiveness if she had been, or seemed to have been, undutiful; told him, Heaven knows truly, that she could not honor him more if he were the favorite of Fortune and the whole world acknowledged him. When his tears were dried, and he sobbed in his weakness no longer, and was free from that touch of shame, and had recovered his usual bearing, she prepared the remains of his supper afresh, and, sitting by his side, rejoiced to see him eat and drink. For, now he sat in his black velvet cap and old grey gown, magnanimous again; and would have comported himself towards any Collegian who might have looked in to ask his advice, like a great moral Lord Chesterfield, or Master of the ethical ceremonies of the Marshalsea.

To keep his attention engaged, she talked with him about his wardrobe; when he was pleased to say, that Yes, indeed, those shirts she proposed would be exceedingly acceptable, for those he had were worn out, and, being ready-made, had never fitted him. Being conversational and in a reasonable flow of spirits, he then invited her attention to his coat as it hung behind the door: remarking that the Father of the place would set an indifferent example to his children, already disposed to be slovenly, if he went among them out at elbows. He was jocular, too, as to the heeling of his shoes; but became grave on the subject of his cravat, and promised her that when she could afford it, she should buy him a new one.

While he smoked out his cigar in peace, she made his bed, and put the small room in order for his repose. Being weary then, owing to the advanced hour and his emotions, he came out of his chair to bless her and wish her Good night. All this time he had never once thought of *her* dress, her shoes, her need of anything. No other person upon earth, save herself, could have been so unmindful of her wants.

He kissed her many times with "Bless you, my love. Good night, my dear!"

But her gentle breast had been so deeply wounded by what she had seen of him, that she was unwilling to leave him alone, lest he should lament and despair again. "Father dear, I am not tired; let me come back presently, when you are in bed, and sit by you."

He asked her with an air of protection, if she felt solitary?

"Yes, father."

"Then come back by all means, my love."

"I shall be very quiet, father."

"Don't think of me, my dear," he said, giving her his kind permission fully. "Come back by all means."

He seemed to be dozing when she returned, and she put the low fire together very softly lest she should awake him. But he overheard her, and called out who was that?

"Only Amy, father."

"Amy, my child, come here. I want to say a word to you."

He raised himself a little in his low bed, as she kneeled beside it to bring her face near him; and put his hand between hers. O! Both the private father and the Father of the Marshalsea were strong within him then.

"My love, you have had a life of hardship here. No companions, no recreations, many cares I am afraid?"

"Don't think of that, dear. I never do."

"You know my position, Amy. I have not been able to do much for you; but all I have been able to do, I have done."

"Yes, my dear father," she rejoined, kissing him. "I know, I know."

"I am in the twenty-third year of my life here," he said, with a catch in his breath that was not so much a sob as an irrepressible sound of self approval, the momentary outburst of a noble consciousness. "It is all I could do for my children—I have done it. Amy, my love, you are by far the best loved of the three; I have had you principally in my mind—whatever I have done for your sake, my dear child, I have done freely and without murmuring."

Only the wisdom that holds the clue to all hearts and all mysteries, can surely know to what extent a man, especially a man brought down as this man had been, can impose upon himself. Enough, for the present place, that he lay down with wet eyelashes, serene, in a manner majestic, after bestowing his life of degradation as a sort of portion on the devoted child upon whom its miseries had fallen so heavily, and whose love alone had saved him to be even what he was.

That child had no doubts, asked herself no questions, for she was but too content to see him with a lustre round his head. Poor dear, good dear, truest, kindest, dearest, were the only words she had for him, as she hushed him to rest.

She never left him all that night. As if she had done him a wrong which her tenderness could hardly repair, she sat by him in his sleep, at times softly kissing him with suspended breath, and calling him in a whisper by some endearing name. At times she stood aside, so as not to intercept the low fire-light, and, watching him when it fell upon his sleeping face, wondered did he look now at all as he had looked when he was prosperous and happy; as he had so touched her by imagining that he might look once more in that awful time. At the thought of that time, she kneeled beside his bed again, and prayed "O spare his life! O save him to me! O look down upon my dear, long-suffering, unfortunate, much changed, dear dear father!"

Not until the morning came to protect him and encourage him, did she give him a last kiss and leave the small room. When she had stolen downstairs, and along the empty yard, and had crept up to her own high garret, the smokeless housetops and the distant country hills were discernible over the wall in the clear morning. As she gently opened the window, and looked eastward down the prison yard, the spikes upon the wall were tipped with red, then made a sullen purple pattern on the sun as it came flaming up into the heavens. The spikes had never looked so sharp and cruel, nor the bars so heavy, nor the prison space so gloomy and contracted. She thought of the sunrise on rolling rivers, of the sunrise on wide seas, of the sunrise on rich landscapes, of the sunrise on great forests where the birds were waking and the trees were rustling; and she looked down into the living grave on which the sun had risen, with her father in it, three and twenty years, and said, in a burst of sorrow and compassion, "No, no, I have never seen him in my life!"

CHAPTER XX

IF Young John Chivery had had the inclination, and the power, to write a satire on family pride, he would have had no need to go for an avenging illustration out of the family of his beloved. He would have found it amply in that gallant brother and that dainty sister, so steeped in mean experiences, and so loftily conscious of the family name; so ready to beg or borrow from the poorest, to eat of anybody's bread, spend anybody's money, drink from anybody's cup and break it afterwards. To have painted the sordid facts of their lives, and they throughout invoking the death's-head apparition of the family gentility to come and scare their benefactors, would have made Young John a satirist of the first water.

Tip had turned his liberty to hopeful account by becoming a billiard-marker. He had troubled himself so little as to the means of his release, that Clennam scarcely needed to have been at the pains of impressing the mind of Mr. Plornish on that subject. Whoever had paid him the compliment, he very readily accepted the compliment with *his* compliments, and there was an end of it. Issuing forth from the gate on these easy terms, he became a billiard-marker; and now occasionally looked in at the little skittle-ground in a green Newmarket coat (second-hand), with a shining collar and bright buttons (new), and drank the beer of the Collegians.

One solid stationary point in the looseness of this gentleman's character, was, that he respected and admired his sister Amy. The feeling had never induced him to spare her a moment's uneasiness, or to put himself to any restraint or inconvenience on her account; but, with that Marshalsea taint upon his love, he loved her. The same rank Marshalsea flavor was to be recognised in his distinctly perceiving that she sacrificed her life to her father, and in his having no idea that she had done anything for himself.

When this spirited young man, and his sister, had begun systematically to produce the family skeleton for the over-awing of the College, this narrative cannot precisely state. Probably at about the period when they began to dine on the College charity. It is certain that the more reduced and necessitous they were, the more pompously the skeleton emerged from its tomb; and that when there was anything particularly shabby in the wind, the skeleton always came out with the ghastliest flourish.

Little Dorrit was late on the Monday morning, for her father slept late, and afterwards there was his breakfast to prepare and his room to arrange. She had no engagement to go out to work, however, and therefore stayed with him until, with Maggy's help, she had put everything right about him, and had seen him off upon his morning walk (of twenty yards or so) to the coffee-house to read the paper. She then got on her bonnet and went out;

having been anxious to get out much sooner. There was, as usual, a cessation of the small-talk in the Lodge as she passed through it; and a Collegian who had come in on Saturday night, received the intimation from the elbow of a more seasoned Collegian, "Look out. Here she is!"

She wanted to see her sister, but when she got round to Mr. Cripples's she found that both her sister and her uncle had gone to the theatre where they were engaged. Having taken thought of this probability by the way, and having settled that in such case she would follow them, she set off afresh for the theatre, which was on that side of the river, and not very far away.

Little Dorrit was almost as ignorant of the ways of theatres as of the ways of gold mines, and when she was directed to a furtive sort of door, with a curious up-all-night air about it, that appeared to be ashamed of itself and to be hiding in an alley, she hesitated to approach it; being further deterred by the sight of some half dozen close-shaved gentlemen, with their hats very strangely on, who were lounging about the door, looking not at all unlike Collegians. On her applying to them, reassured by this resemblance, for a direction to Miss Dorrit, they made way for her to enter a dark hall— it was more like a great grimy lamp gone out than anything else—where she could hear the distant playing of music and the sound of dancing feet. A man so much in want of airing that he had a blue mould upon him, sat watching this dark place from a hole in a corner, like a spider; and he told her that he would send a message up to Miss Dorrit by the first lady or gentleman who went through. The first lady who went through had a roll of music, half in her muff and half out of it, and was in such a tumbled condition altogether, that it seemed as if it would be an act of kindness to iron her. But as she was very good-natured, and said "Come with me; I'll soon find Miss Dorrit for you," Miss Dorrit's sister went with her, drawing nearer and nearer, at every step she took in the darkness, to the sound of music and the sound of dancing feet.

At last they came into a maze of dust, where a quantity of people were tumbling over one another, and where there was such a confusion of unaccountable shapes of beams, bulk-heads, brick walls, ropes, and rollers, and such a mixing of gaslight and daylight, that they seemed to have got on the wrong side of the pattern of the universe. Little Dorrit, left to herself, and knocked against by somebody every moment, was quite bewildered when she heard her sister's voice.

"Why, good gracious, Amy, what ever brought you here!"

"I wanted to see you, Fanny dear; and as I am going out all day tomorrow, and knew you might be engaged all day to-day, I thought——"

"But the idea, Amy, of *you* coming behind! I never did!" As her sister said this in no very cordial tone of welcome, she conducted her to a more open part of the maze, where various golden chairs and tables were heaped together, and where a number of young ladies were sitting on anything they could find, chattering. All these young ladies wanted ironing, and all had a curious way of looking everywhere, while they chattered.

Just as the sisters arrived here, a monotonous boy in a Scotch cap put his head round a beam on the left, and said, "Less noise there, ladies!" and disappeared. Immediately after which, a sprightly gentleman with a quantity of long black hair looked round a beam on the right, and said, "Less noise there, darlings!" and also disappeared.

"The notion of you among professionals, Amy, is really the last thing I could have conceived!" said her sister. "Why, how did you ever get here?"

"I don't know. The lady who told you I was here, was so good as to bring me in."

"Like you quiet little things! You can make your way anywhere, I believe. *I* couldn't have managed it, Amy, though I know so much more of the world."

It was the family custom to lay it down as family law, that she was a plain domestic little creature, without the great and sage experiences of the rest. This family fiction was the family assertion of itself against her services. Not to make too much of them.

"Well! And what have you got on your mind, Amy? Of course you have got something on your mind, about me?" said Fanny. She spoke as if her sister, between two and three years her junior, were her prejudiced grandmother.

"It is not much; but since you told me of the lady who gave you the bracelet, Fanny——"

The monotonous boy put his head round the beam on the left, and said, "Look out there, ladies!" and disappeared. The sprightly gentleman with the black hair as suddenly put his head round the beam on the right, and said, "Look out there, darlings!" and also disappeared. Thereupon all the young ladies rose, and began shaking their skirts out behind.

"Well, Amy?" said Fanny, doing as the rest did; "what were you going to say?"

"Since you told me a lady had given you the bracelet you showed me, Fanny, I have not been quite easy on your account, and indeed want to know a little more, if you will confide more to me."

"Now, ladies!" said the boy in the Scotch cap. "Now, darlings!" said the gentleman with the black hair. They were every one gone in a moment, and the music and the dancing feet were heard again.

Little Dorrit sat down in a golden chair, made quite giddy by these rapid interruptions. Her sister and the rest were a long time gone; and during their absence a voice (it appeared to be that of the gentleman with the black hair) was continually calling out through the music, "One, two, three, four, five, six—go! One, two, three, four, five, six—go! Steady, darlings! One, two, three, four, five, six—go!" Ultimately the voice stopped, and they all came back again, more or less out of breath, folding themselves in their shawls, and making ready for the streets. "Stop a moment, Amy, and let them get away before us," whispered Fanny. They were soon left alone; nothing more important happening, in the meantime, than the boy looking round his old beam, and saying, "Everybody at eleven to-morrow, ladies!" and the gentleman with the black hair looking round his old beam, and saying, "Everybody at eleven to-morrow, darlings!" each in his own accustomed manner.

When they were alone, something was rolled up or by other means got out of the way, and there was a great empty well before them, looking down into the depths of which Fanny said, "Now, uncle!" Little Dorrit, as her eyes became used to the darkness, faintly made him out, at the bottom of the well, in an obscure corner by himself, with his instrument in its ragged case under his arm.

The old man looked as if the remote high gallery windows, with their little strip of sky, might have been the point of his better fortunes, from which he had descended, until he had gradually sunk down below there to the bottom. He had been in that place six nights a week for many years, but had never been observed to raise his eyes above his music-book, and was confidently believed to have never seen a play. There were legends in the place that he did not so much as know the popular heroes and heroines by sight, and that the low comedian had "mugged" at him in his richest manner fifty nights for a wager, and he had shown no trace of consciousness. The carpenters had a joke to the effect that he was dead without being aware of it; and the frequenters of the pit supposed him to pass his whole life, night and day and Sunday and all, in the orchestra. They had tried him a few times with pinches of snuff offered over the rails, and he had always responded to this attention with a momentary waking up of manner that had the pale phantom of a gentleman in it: beyond this he never, on any occasion, had any other part in what was going on than the part written out for the clarionet; in private life, where there was no part for the clarionet, he had no part at all. Some said he was poor, some said he was a wealthy miser; but he said nothing, never lifted up his bowed head, never varied his shuffling gait by getting his springless foot from the ground. Though expecting now to be summoned by his niece, he did not hear her until she had spoken to him three or four times; nor was he at all surprised by the presence of two nieces instead of one, but merely said, in his tremulous voice, "I am coming, I am coming!" and crept forth by some underground way which emitted a cellarous smell.

"And so, Amy," said her sister, when the three together passed out, at the door that had such a shame-faced consciousness of being different from other doors: the uncle instinctively taking Amy's arm as the arm to be relied on: "so, Amy, you are curious about me?"

She was pretty, and conscious, and rather flaunting; and the conde-scension with which she put aside the superiority of her charms, and of her worldly experience, and addressed her sister on almost equal terms, had a vast deal of the family in it.

"I am interested, Fanny, and concerned in anything that concerns you."

"So you are, so you are, and you are the best of Amys. If I am ever a little provoking, I am sure you'll consider what a thing it is to occupy my position and feel a consciousness of being superior to it. I shouldn't care," said the Daughter of the Father of the Marshalsea, "if the others were not so common. None of them have come down in the world as we have. They are all on their own level. Common."

Little Dorrit mildly looked at the speaker, but did not interrupt her. Fanny took out her handkerchief, and rather angrily wiped her eyes. "I was not born where you were, you know, Amy, and perhaps that makes a difference. My dear child, when we get rid of uncle, you shall know all about it. We'll drop him at the cook's shop where he is going to dine."

They walked on with him until they came to a dirty shop-window in a dirty street, which was made almost opaque by the steam of hot meats, vegetables, and puddings. But, glimpses were to be caught of a roast leg of pork bursting into tears of sage and onion in a metal reservoir full of gravy, of an unctuous piece of roast beef and blisterous Yorkshire pudding bubbling hot in a similar receptacle, of a stuffed fillet of veal in rapid cut, of a ham in a perspiration with the pace it was going at, of a shallow tank of baked potatoes glued together by their own richness, of a truss or two of boiled greens, and other substantial delicacies. Within, were a few wooden partitions, behind which such customers as found it more convenient to take away their dinners in their stomachs than in their hands, packed their purchases in solitude. Fanny, opening her reticule as they surveyed these things, produced from that repository a shilling and handed it to Uncle. Uncle, after not looking at it a little while, divined its object, and muttering "Dinner? Ha! Yes, yes, yes!" slowly vanished from them into the mist.

"Now, Amy," said her sister, "come with me, if you are not too tired to walk to Harley Street, Cavendish Square."

The air with which she threw off this distinguished address, and the toss she gave her new bonnet (which was more gauzy than serviceable) made her sister wonder; however, she expressed her readiness to go to Harley Street, and thither they directed their steps. Arrived at that grand destination, Fanny singled out the handsomest house, and knocking at the door enquired for Mrs. Merdle. The footman who opened the door, although he had powder on his head, and was backed up by two other footmen likewise powdered, not only admitted Mrs. Merdle to be at home, but asked Fanny to walk in. Fanny walked in, taking her sister with her; and they went up-stairs with powder going before and powder stopping behind, and were left in a spacious semicircular drawing-room, one of several drawing-rooms, where there was a parrot on the outside of a golden cage holding on by its beak with its scaly legs in the air, and putting itself into many strange upside-down postures. This peculiarity has been observed in birds of quite another feather, climbing upon golden wires.

The room was far more splendid than anything Little Dorrit had ever imagined, and would have been splendid and costly in any eyes. She looked in amazement at her sister and would have asked a question, but that Fanny with a warning frown pointed to a curtained doorway of communication with another room. The curtain shook next moment, and a lady, raising it with a heavily ringed hand, dropped it behind her again as she entered.

The lady was not young and fresh from the hand of Nature, but was young and fresh from the hand of her maid. She had large unfeeling handsome eyes, and dark unfeeling handsome hair, and a broad unfeeling handsome bosom, and was made the most of in every particular. Either because she had a cold, or because it suited her face, she wore a rich white fillet tied over her head and under her chin. And if ever there were an unfeeling handsome chin that looked as if, for certain, it had never been, in familiar parlance, "chucked" by the hand of man, it was the chin curbed up so tight and close by that laced bridle.

"Mrs. Merdle," said Fanny. "My sister, ma'am."

"I am glad to see your sister, Miss Dorrit. I did not remember that you had a sister."

"I did not mention that I had," said Fanny.

"Aye!" Mrs. Merdle curved the little finger of her left hand as who should say, "I have caught you. I know you didn't!" (All her action was usually with her left hand because her hands were not a pair; the left being much the whiter and plumper of the two.) Then she added: "Sit down," and composed herself voluptuously, in a nest of crimson and gold cushions, on an ottoman near the parrot.

"Also professional?" said Mrs. Merdle, looking at Little Dorrit through an eye-glass.

Fanny answered No. "No," said Mrs. Merdle, dropping her glass. "Has not a professional air. Very pleasant; but not professional."

"My sister, ma'am," said Fanny, in whom there was a singular mixture of deference and hardihood, "has been asking me to tell her, as between sisters, how I came to have the honor of knowing you. And as I had engaged to call upon you once more, I thought I might take the liberty of bringing her with me, when perhaps you would tell her. I wish her to know, and perhaps you will tell her."

"Do you think, at your sister's age——" hinted Mrs. Merdle.

"She is much older than she looks," said Fanny; "almost as old as I am."

"Society," said Mrs. Merdle, with another curve of her little finger, "is so difficult to explain to young persons (indeed is so difficult to explain to most persons), that I am glad to hear that. I wish Society was not so arbitrary, I wish it was not so exacting—Bird, be quiet!"

The parrot had given a most piercing shriek, as if its name were Society and it asserted its right to its exactions.

"But," resumed Mrs. Merdle, "we must take it as we find it. We know it is hollow and conventional and worldly and very shocking, but unless we are Savages in the Tropical seas (I should have been charmed to be one myself—most delightful life and perfect climate I am told), we must consult it. It is the common lot. Mr. Merdle is a most extensive merchant, his transactions are on the vastest scale, his wealth and influence are very great, but even he—Bird, be quiet!"

The parrot had shrieked another shriek; and it filled up the sentence so expressively that Mrs. Merdle was under no necessity to end it.

"Since your sister begs that I would terminate our personal acquaintance," she began again, addressing Little Dorrit, "by relating the circumstances that are much to her credit, I cannot object to comply with her request, I am sure. I have a son (I was first married extremely young) of two or three and twenty."

Fanny set her lips, and her eyes looked half triumphantly at her sister.

"A son of two or three and twenty. He is a little gay, a thing Society is accustomed to in young men, and he is very impressible. Perhaps he inherits that misfortune. I am very impressible myself, by nature. The weakest of creatures. My feelings are touched in a moment."

She said all this, and everything else, as coldly as a woman of snow; quite forgetting the sisters except at odd times, and apparently addressing some abstraction of Society. For whose behoof, too, she occasionally arranged her dress, or the composition of her figure upon the ottoman.

"So he is very impressible. Not a misfortune in our natural state, I dare say, but we are not in a natural state. Much to be lamented, no doubt, particularly by myself, who am a child of nature if I could but show it; but so it is. Society suppresses us and dominates us—Bird, be quiet!"

The parrot had broken into a violent fit of laughter, after twisting divers bars of his cage with his crooked bill, and licking them with his black tongue.

"It is quite unnecessary to say to a person of your good sense, wide range of experience, and cultivated feelings," said Mrs. Merdle, from her nest of crimson and gold—and there put up her glass to refresh her memory as to whom she was addressing,—"that the stage sometimes has a fascination for young men of that class of character. In saying the stage, I mean the people on it of the female sex. Therefore, when I heard that my son was supposed to be fascinated by a dancer, I knew what that usually meant in Society, and confided in her being a dancer at the Opera, where young men moving in Society are usually fascinated."

She passed her white hands over one another, observant of the sisters now; and the rings upon her fingers grated against each other, with a hard sound.

"As your sister will tell you, when I found what the theatre was, I was much surprised and much distressed. But when I found that your sister, by rejecting my son's advances (I must add, in an unexpected manner), had brought him to the point of proposing marriage, my feelings were of the profoundest anguish—acute."

She traced the outline of her left eyebrow, and put it right.

"In a distracted condition which only a mother—moving in Society— can be susceptible of, I determined to go myself to the theatre, and represent my state of mind to the dancer. I made myself known to your sister. I found her, to my surprise, in many respects different from my expectations; and certainly in none more so, than in meeting me with—what shall I say?—a sort of family assertion on her own part?" Mrs. Merdle smiled.

"I told you, ma'am," said Fanny, with a heightening color, "that although you found me in that situation, I was so far above the rest, that I considered my family as good as your son's; and that I had a brother who, knowing the circumstances, would be of the same opinion, and would not consider such a connexion any honor."

"Miss Dorrit," said Mrs. Merdle, after frostily looking at her through her glass, "precisely what I was on the point of telling your sister, in pursuance of your request. Much obliged to you for recalling it so accurately, and anticipating me. I immediately," addressing Little Dorrit, "(for I am the creature of impulse), took a bracelet from my arm, and begged your sister to let me clasp it on hers, in token of the delight I had in our being able to approach the subject, so far on a common footing." (This was perfectly true, the lady having bought a cheap and showy article on her way to the interview, with a general eye to bribery.)

"And I told you, Mrs. Merdle," said Fanny, "that we might be unfortunate, but were not common."

"I think, the very words, Miss Dorrit," assented Mrs. Merdle.

"And I told you, Mrs. Merdle," said Fanny, "that if you spoke to me of the superiority of your son's standing in Society, it was barely possible that you rather deceived yourself in your suppositions about my origin; and that my father's standing, even in the Society in which he now moved (what that was, was best known to myself), was eminently superior, and was acknowledged by every one."

"Quite accurate," rejoined Mrs. Merdle. "A most admirable memory."

"Thank you, ma'am. Perhaps you will be so kind as to tell my sister the rest."

"There is very little to tell," said Mrs. Merdle, reviewing the breadth of bosom which seemed essential to her having room enough to be unfeeling in, "but it is to your sister's credit. I pointed out to your sister the plain state of the case; the impossibility of the Society in which we moved, recognising the Society in which she moved—though charming, I have no doubt; the immense disadvantage at which she would consequently place

the family she had so high an opinion of, upon which we should find ourselves compelled to look down with contempt, and from which (socially
speaking) we should feel obliged to recoil with abhorrence. In short, I
made an appeal to that laudable pride in your sister."

"Let my sister know, if you please, Mrs. Merdle," Fanny pouted, with
a toss of her gauzy bonnet, "that I had already had the honor of telling your
son that I wished to have nothing whatever to say to him."

"Well, Miss Dorrit," assented Mrs. Merdle, "perhaps I might have
mentioned that before. If I did not think of it, perhaps it was because my
mind reverted to the apprehensions I had at the time, that he might
persevere and you might have something to say to him. I also mentioned
to your sister—I again address the non-professional Miss Dorrit—that
my son would have nothing in the event of such a marriage, and would be
an absolute beggar. (I mention that, merely as a fact which is part of the
narrative, and not as supposing it to have influenced your sister, except in
the prudent and legitimate way in which, constituted as our artificial system
is, we must all be influenced by such considerations.) Finally, after some
high words and high spirit on the part of your sister; we came to the complete understanding that there was no danger; and your sister was so
obliging as to allow me to present her with a mark or two of my appreciation
at my dressmaker's."

Little Dorrit looked sorry, and glanced at Fanny with a troubled face.

"Also," said Mrs. Merdle, "as to promise to give me the present pleasure
of a closing interview, and of parting with her on the best of terms. On
which occasion," added Mrs. Merdle, quitting her nest, and putting
something in Fanny's hand, "Miss Dorrit will permit me to say Farewell
with best wishes, in my own dull manner."

The sisters rose at the same time, and they all stood near the cage of the
parrot, as he tore at a claw-full of biscuit and spat it out, seemed to mock
them with a pompous dance of his body without moving his feet, and
suddenly turned himself upside down and trailed himself all over the outside of his golden cage, with the aid of his cruel beak and his black tongue.

"Adieu, Miss Dorrit, with best wishes," said Mrs. Merdle. "If we could
only come to a Millennium, or something of that sort, I for one might have
the pleasure of knowing a number of charming and talented persons from
whom I am at present excluded. A more primitive state of society would
be delicious to me. There used to be a poem when I learnt lessons, something about Lo the poor Indian whose something mind! If a few thousand
persons moving in Society, could only go and be Indians, I would put my
name down directly; but as, moving in Society, we can't be Indians,
unfortunately—Good morning!"

They came down-stairs with powder before them and powder behind,
the elder sister haughty and the younger sister humbled, and were shut
out into unpowdered Harley Street, Cavendish Square.

"Well?" said Fanny, when they had gone a little way without speaking. "Have you nothing to say, Amy?"

"Oh, I don't know what to say!" she answered, distressed. "You didn't like this young man, Fanny?"

"Like him? He is almost an idiot."

"I am so sorry—don't be hurt—but, since you ask me what I have to say, I am so very sorry, Fanny, that you suffered this lady to give you anything."

"You little Fool!" returned her sister, shaking her with the sharp pull she gave her arm. "Have you no spirit at all? But that's just the way! You have no self-respect, you have no becoming pride. Just as you allow yourself to be followed about by a contemptible little Chivery of a thing," with the scornfullest emphasis, "you would let your family be trodden on, and never turn."

"Don't say that, dear Fanny. I do what I can for them."

"You do what you can for them!" repeated Fanny, walking her on very fast. "Would you let a woman like this, whom you could see if you had any experience of anything to be as false and insolent as a woman can be—would you let her put her foot upon your family, and thank her for it?"

"No, Fanny, I am sure."

"Then make her pay for it, you mean little thing. What else can you make her do? Make her pay for it, you stupid child; and do your family some credit with the money!"

They spoke no more, all the way back to the lodging where Fanny and her uncle lived. When they arrived there, they found the old man practising his clarionet in the dolefullest manner in a corner of the room. Fanny had a composite meal to make, of chops, and porter, and tea; and indignantly pretended to prepare it for herself, though her sister did all that in quiet reality. When, at last, Fanny sat down to eat and drink, she threw the table implements about and was angry with her bread, much as her father had been last night.

"If you despise me," she said, bursting into vehement tears, "because I am a dancer, why did you put me in the way of being one? It was your doing. You would have me stoop as low as the ground before this Mrs. Merdle, and let her say what she liked and do what she liked, and hold us all in contempt, and tell me so to my face. Because I am a dancer!"

"O Fanny!"

"And Tip too, poor fellow. She is to disparage him just as much as she likes, without any check—I suppose because he has been in the law, and the docks, and different things. Why, it was your doing, Amy. You might at least approve of his being defended."

All this time the uncle was dolefully blowing his clarionet in the corner, sometimes taking it an inch or so from his mouth for a moment while he stopped to gaze at them, with a vague impression that somebody had said something.

"And your father, your poor father, Amy. Because he is not free, to show himself and to speak for himself, you would let such people insult him with impunity. If you don't feel for yourself because you go out to work, you might at least feel for him, I should think, knowing what he has undergone so long."

Poor Little Dorrit felt the injustice of this taunt rather sharply. The remembrance of last night added a barbed point to it. She said nothing in reply, but turned her chair from the table towards the fire. Uncle, after making one more pause, blew a dismal wail and went on again.

Fanny was passionate with the teacups and the bread as long as her passion lasted, and then protested that she was the wretchedest girl in the world, and she wished she was dead. After that, her crying became remorseful, and she got up and put her arms round her sister. Little Dorrit tried to stop her from saying anything, but she answered that she would, she must! Thereupon she said again, and again, "I beg your pardon, Amy," and "Forgive me, Amy," almost as passionately as she had said what she regretted.

"But indeed, indeed, Amy," she resumed, when they were seated in sisterly accord side by side, "I hope and I think you would have seen this differently, if you had known a little more of Society."

"Perhaps I might, Fanny," said the mild Little Dorrit.

"You see, while you have been domestic and resignedly shut up there, Amy," pursued her sister, gradually beginning to patronise, "I have been out, moving more in Society, and may have been getting proud and spirited —more than I ought to be perhaps?"

Little Dorrit answered "Yes. O yes!"

"And while you have been thinking of the dinner or the clothes, I may have been thinking, you know, of the family. Now, may it not be so, Amy?"

Little Dorrit again nodded "Yes," with a more cheerful face than heart.

"Especially as we know," said Fanny, "that there certainly is a tone in the place to which you have been so true, which does belong to it, and which does make it different from other aspects of Society. So kiss me once again, Amy dear, and we will agree that we may both be right, and that you are a tranquil, domestic, home-loving, good girl."

The clarionet had been lamenting most pathetically during this dialogue, but was cut short now by Fanny's announcement that it was time to go; which she conveyed to her uncle by shutting up his scrap of music, and taking the clarionet out of his mouth.

Little Dorrit parted from them at the door, and hastened back to the Marshalsea. It fell dark there sooner than elsewhere, and going into it that evening was like going into a deep trench. The shadow of the wall was on every object. Not least, upon the figure in the old grey gown and the black velvet cap, as it turned towards her when she opened the door of the dim room.

"Why not upon me too!" thought Little Dorrit, with the door yet in her hand. "It was not unreasonable in Fanny."

CHAPTER XXI

MR. MERDLE'S COMPLAINT

UPON that establishment of state, the Merdle establishment in Harley Street, Cavendish Square, there was the shadow of no more common wall than the fronts of other establishments of state on the opposite side of the street. Like unexceptionable Society, the opposing rows of houses in Harley Street were very grim with one another. Indeed, the mansions and their inhabitants were so much alike in that respect, that the people were often to be found drawn up on opposite sides of dinner-tables, in the shade of their own loftiness, staring at the other side of the way with the dullness of the houses.

Everybody knows how like the street, the two dinner-rows of people who take their stand by the street will be. The expressionless uniform twenty houses, all to be knocked at and rung at in the same form, all approachable by the same dull steps, all fended off by the same pattern of railing, all with the same impracticable fire-escapes, the same inconvenient fixtures in their heads, and everything without exception to be taken at a high valuation—who has not dined with these? The house so drearily out of repair, the occasional bow-window, the stuccoed house, the newly-fronted house, the corner house with nothing but angular rooms, the house with the blinds always down, the house with the hatchment always up, the house where the collector has called for one quarter of an Idea, and found nobody at home—who has not dined with these? The house that nobody will take, and is to be had a bargain—who does not know her? The showy house that was taken for life by the disappointed gentleman, and which doesn't suit him at all—who is unacquainted with that haunted habitation?

Harley Street, Cavendish Square, was more than aware of Mr. and Mrs. Merdle. Intruders there were in Harley Street, of whom it was not aware; but Mr. and Mrs. Merdle it delighted to honor. Society was aware of Mr. and Mrs. Merdle. Society had said "Let us license them; let us know them."

Mr. Merdle was immensely rich; a man of prodigious enterprise; a Midas without the ears, who turned all he touched to gold. He was in everything good, from banking to building. He was in Parliament, of course. He was in the City, necessarily. He was Chairman of this, Trustee of that, President of the other. The weightiest of men had said to projectors, "Now, what name have you got? Have you got Merdle?" And, the reply being in the negative, had said, "Then I won't look at you."

This great and fortunate man had provided that extensive bosom, which required so much room to be unfeeling enough in, with a nest of crimson and gold some fifteen years before. It was not a bosom to repose upon, but it was a capital bosom to hang jewels upon. Mr. Merdle wanted something to hang jewels upon, and he bought it for the purpose. Storr and Mortimer might have married on the same speculation.

Like all his other speculations, it was sound and successful. The jewels showed to the richest advantage. The bosom, moving in Society with the jewels displayed upon it, attracted general admiration. Society approving, Mr. Merdle was satisfied. He was the most disinterested of men,—did everything for Society, and got as little for himself, out of all his gain and care, as a man might.

That is to say, it may be supposed that he got all he wanted, otherwise with unlimited wealth he would have got it. But his desire was to the utmost to satisfy Society (whatever that was), and take up all its drafts upon him for tribute. He did not shine in company; he had not very much to say for himself; he was a reserved man, with a broad, overhanging, watchful head, that particular kind of dull red color in his cheeks which is rather stale than fresh, and a somewhat uneasy expression about his coat-cuffs as if they were in his confidence, and had reasons for being anxious to hide his hands. In the little he said, he was a pleasant man enough; plain, emphatic about public and private confidence, and tenacious of the utmost deference being shown by every one, in all things, to Society. In this same Society (if that were it which came to his dinners, and to Mrs. Merdle's receptions and concerts), he hardly seemed to enjoy himself much, and was mostly to be found against walls and behind doors. Also when he went out to it, instead of its coming home to him, he seemed a little fatigued, and upon the whole rather more disposed for bed; but he was always cultivating it nevertheless, and always moving in it, and always laying out money on it with the greatest liberality.

Mrs. Merdle's first husband had been a colonel, under whose auspices the bosom had entered into competition with the snows of North America, and had come off at little disadvantage in point of whiteness, and at none in point of coldness. The colonel's son was Mrs. Merdle's only child. He was of a chuckle-headed high-shouldered make, with a general appearance of being, not so much a young man as a swelled boy. He had given so few signs of reason, that a byeword went among his companions that his brain had been frozen up in a mighty frost which prevailed at Saint John, New Brunswick, at the period of his birth there, and had never thawed from that hour. Another byeword represented him as having in his infancy, through the negligence of a nurse, fallen out of a high window on his head, which had been heard by responsible witnesses to crack. It is probable that both these representations were of ex post facto origin; the young gentleman (whose expressive name was Sparkler) being monomaniacal in offering marriage to all manner of undesirable young ladies, and in remarking of every successive young lady to whom he tendered a matrimonial proposal that she was "a doosed fine gal—well educated too—with no biggodd nonsense about her."

A son-in-law, with these limited talents, might have been a clog upon another man; but Mr. Merdle did not want a son-in-law for himself; he wanted a son-in-law for Society. Mr. Sparkler having been in the Guards, and being in the habit of frequenting all the races, and all the lounges, and all the parties, and being well known, Society was satisfied with its son-in-law. This happy result Mr. Merdle would have considered well attained, though Mr. Sparkler had been a more expensive article. And he did not get Mr. Sparkler by any means cheap for Society, even as it was.

There was a dinner giving in the Harley Street establishment, while Little Dorrit was stitching at her father's new shirts by his side that night; and there were magnates from the Court and magnates from the City, magnates from the Commons and magnates from the Lords, magnates from the bench and magnates from the bar, Bishop magnates, Treasury magnates, Horse Guards magnates, Admiralty magnates,—all the magnates that keep us going, and sometimes trip us up.

"I am told," said Bishop magnate to Horse Guards, "that Mr. Merdle has made another enormous hit. They say a hundred thousand pounds."

Horse Guards had heard two.

Treasury had heard three.

Bar, handling his persuasive double eye-glass, was by no means clear but that it might be four. It was one of those happy strokes of calculation and combination, the result of which it was difficult to estimate. It was one of those instances of a comprehensive grasp, associated with habitual luck and characteristic boldness, of which an age presented us but few. But here was Brother Bellows, who had been in the great Bank case, and who could probably tell us more. What did Brother Bellows put this new success at?

Brother Bellows was on his way to make his bow to the bosom, and could only tell them in passing that he had heard it stated, with great appearance of truth, as being worth, from first to last, half-a-million of money.

Admiralty said Mr. Merdle was a wonderful man. Treasury said he was a new power in the country, and would be able to buy up the whole House of Commons. Bishop said he was glad to think that this wealth flowed into the coffers of a gentleman who was always disposed to maintain the best interests of Society.

Mr. Merdle himself was usually late on these occasions, as a man still detained in the clutch of giant enterprises when other men had shaken off their dwarfs for the day. On this occasion, he was the last arrival. Treasury said Merdle's work punished him a little. Bishop said he was glad to think that this wealth flowed into the coffers of a gentleman who accepted it with meekness.

Powder! There was so much Powder in waiting, that it flavored the dinner. Pulverous particles got into the dishes, and Society's meats had a seasoning of first-rate footmen. Mr. Merdle took down a countess who was secluded somewhere in the core of an immense dress, to which she was in the proportion of the heart to the overgrown cabbage. If so low a simile may be admitted, the dress went down the staircase like a richly brocaded Jack in the Green, and nobody knew what sort of small person carried it.

Society had everything it could want, and could not want, for dinner. It had everything to look at, and everything to eat, and everything to drink. It is to be hoped it enjoyed itself; for Mr. Merdle's own share of the repast might have been paid for with eighteenpence. Mrs. Merdle was magnificent. The chief butler was the next magnificent institution of the day. He was the stateliest man in company. He did nothing, but he looked on as few other men could have done. He was Mr. Merdle's last gift to Society. Mr. Merdle didn't want him, and was put out of countenance when the great creature looked at him; but inappeasable Society would have him—and had got him.

The invisible countess carried out the Green at the usual stage of the entertainment, and the file of beauty was closed up by the bosom. Treasury said, Juno. Bishop said, Judith.

Bar fell into discussion with Horse Guards concerning courts-martial. Brother Bellows and Bench struck in. Other magnates paired off. Mr. Merdle sat silent, and looked at the table-cloth. Sometimes a magnate addressed him, to turn the stream of his own particular discussion towards him; but Mr. Merdle seldom gave much attention to it, or did more than rouse himself from his calculations and pass the wine.

When they rose, so many of the magnates had something to say to Mr. Merdle individually, that he held little levees by the sideboard, and checked them off as they went out at the door.

Treasury hoped he might venture to congratulate one of England's world-famed capitalists and merchant-princes (he had turned that original sentiment in the house a few times, and it came easy to him) on a new achievement. To extend the triumphs of such men, was to extend the triumphs and resources of the nation; and Treasury felt—he gave Mr. Merdle to understand—patriotic on the subject.

"Thank you, my lord," said Mr. Merdle; "thank you. I accept your congratulations with pride, and I am glad you approve."

"Why, I don't unreservedly approve, my dear Mr. Merdle. Because," smiling Treasury turned him by the arm towards the sideboard and spoke banteringly, "it never can be worth your while to come among us and help us."

Mr. Merdle felt honored by the——

"No, no," said Treasury, "that is not the light in which one so distinguished for practical knowledge, and great foresight, can be expected to regard it. If we should ever be happily enabled, by accidentally possessing the control over circumstances, to propose to one so eminent to—to come among us, and give us the weight of his influence, knowledge, and character, we could only propose it to him as a duty. In fact, as a duty that he owed to Society."

Mr. Merdle intimated that Society was the apple of his eye, and that its claims were paramount to every other consideration. Treasury moved on, and Bar came up.

Bar, with his little insinuating Jury droop, and fingering his persuasive double eye-glass, hoped he might be excused if he mentioned to one of the greatest converters of the root of all evil into the root of all good, who had for a long time reflected a shining lustre on the annals even of our commercial country—if he mentioned, disinterestedly, and as, what we lawyers called in our pedantic way, *amicus curiæ*, a fact that had come by accident within his knowledge. He had been required to look over the title of a very considerable estate in one of the eastern counties—lying, in fact, for Mr. Merdle knew we lawyers loved to be particular, on the borders of two of the eastern counties. Now, the title was perfectly sound, and the estate was to be purchased by one who had the command of—Money (Jury droop and persuasive eye-glass), on remarkably advantageous terms. This had come to Bar's knowledge only that day, and it had occurred to him "I shall have the honor of dining with my esteemed friend Mr. Merdle this evening, and, strictly between ourselves, I will mention the opportunity." Such a purchase would involve not only great legitimate political influence, but some half-dozen church presentations of considerable annual value. Now, that Mr. Merdle was already at no loss to discover means of occupying even his capital, and of fully employing even his active and vigorous intellect, Bar well knew: but he would venture to suggest that the question arose in his mind, whether one who had deservedly gained so high a position and so European a reputation did not owe it—we would not say to himself, but we would say to Society, to possess himself of such influences as these; and to exercise them—we would not say for his own, or for his party's, but we would say for Society's—benefit.

Mr. Merdle again expressed himself as wholly devoted to that object of his constant consideration, and Bar took his persuasive eye-glass up the grand staircase. Bishop then came undesignedly sliding in the direction of the sideboard.

Surely the goods of this world, it occurred in an accidental way to Bishop to remark, could scarcely be directed into happier channels than when they accumulated under the magic touch of the wise and sagacious, who, while they knew the just value of riches (Bishop tried here to look as if he were rather poor himself), were aware of their importance, judiciously governed and rightly distributed, to the welfare of our brethren at large.

Mr. Merdle with humility expressed his conviction that Bishop couldn't mean him, and with inconsistency expressed his high gratification in Bishop's good opinion.

Bishop then—jauntily stepping out a little with his well-shaped right leg, as though he said to Mr. Merdle "don't mind the apron; a mere form!" —put this case to his good friend:

Whether it had occurred to his good friend, that Society might not unreasonably hope that one so blest in his undertakings, and whose example on his pedestal was so influential with it, would shed a little money in the direction of a mission or so to Africa?

Mr. Merdle signifying that the idea should have his best attention, Bishop put another case:

Whether his good friend had at all interested himself in the proceedings of our Combined Additional Endowed Dignitaries Committee, and whether it had occurred to him that to shed a little money in *that* direction might be a great conception finely executed?

Mr. Merdle made a similar reply, and Bishop explained his reason for enquiring.

Society looked to such men as his good friend to do such things. It was not that *he* looked to them, but that Society looked to them. Just as it was not Our Committee who wanted the Additional Endowed Dignitaries, but it was Society that was in a state of the most agonising uneasiness of mind until it got them. He begged to assure his good friend, that he was extremely sensible of his good friend's regard on all occasions for the best interests of Society; and he considered that he was at once consulting those interests, and expressing the feeling of Society, when he wished him continued prosperity, continued increase of riches, and continued things in general.

Bishop then betook himself up-stairs, and the other magnates gradually floated up after him until there was no one left below but Mr. Merdle. That gentleman, after looking at the table-cloth until the soul of the chief butler glowed with a noble resentment, went slowly up after the rest, and became of no account in the stream of people on the grand staircase. Mrs. Merdle was at home, the best of the jewels were hung out to be seen, Society got what it came for, Mr. Merdle drank twopennyworth of tea in a corner and got more than he wanted.

Among the evening magnates was a famous physician, who knew everybody, and whom everybody knew. On entering at the door, he came upon Mr. Merdle drinking his tea in a corner, and touched him on the arm.

Mr. Merdle started. "Oh! It's you!"

"Any better to-day?"

"No," said Mr. Merdle, "I am no better."

"A pity I didn't see you this morning. Pray come to me to-morrow, or let me come to you."

"Well!" he replied. "I will come to-morrow as I drive by."

Bar and Bishop had both been bystanders during this short dialogue, and as Mr. Merdle was swept away by the crowd, they made their remarks upon it to the Physician. Bar said, there was a certain point of mental strain beyond which no man could go; that the point varied with various textures of brain and peculiarities of constitution, as he had had occasion to notice in several of his learned brothers; but, the point of endurance passed by a line's breadth, depression and dyspepsia ensued. Not to intrude on the sacred mysteries of medicine, he took it, now (with the Jury droop and persuasive eye-glass), that this was Merdle's case? Bishop said that when he was a young man, and had fallen for a brief space into the habit of writing sermons on Saturdays, a habit which all young sons of the church should sedulously avoid, he had frequently been sensible of a depression, arising as he supposed from an overtaxed intellect, upon which the yolk of a new-laid egg, beaten up by the good woman in whose house he at that time lodged, with a glass of sound sherry, nutmeg, and powdered sugar, acted like a charm. Without presuming to offer so simple a remedy to the consideration of so profound a professor of the great healing art, he would venture to enquire whether the strain, being by way of intricate calculations, the spirits might not (humanly speaking) be restored to their tone by a gentle and yet generous stimulant?

"Yes," said the physician, "yes, you are both right. But I may as well tell you that I can find nothing the matter with Mr. Merdle. He has the constitution of a rhinoceros, the digestion of an ostrich, and the concentration of an oyster. As to nerves, Mr. Merdle is of a cool temperament, and not a sensitive man: is about as invulnerable, I should say, as Achilles. How such a man should suppose himself unwell without reason, you may think strange. But I have found nothing the matter with him. He may have some deep-seated recondite complaint. I can't say. I only say, that at present I have not found it out."

There was no shadow of Mr. Merdle's complaint on the bosom now displaying precious stones in rivalry with many similar superb jewel-stands; there was no shadow of Mr. Merdle's complaint on young Sparkler hovering about the rooms, monomaniacally seeking any sufficiently ineligible young lady with no nonsense about her; there was no shadow of Mr. Merdle's complaint on the Barnacles and Stiltstalkings, of whom whole colonies were present; or on any of the company. Even on himself, its shadow was faint enough as he moved about among the throng, receiving homage.

Mr. Merdle's complaint. Society and he had so much to do with one another in all things else, that it is hard to imagine his complaint, if he had one, being solely his own affair. Had he that deep-seated recondite complaint, and did any doctor find it out? Patience. In the meantime, the shadow of the Marshalsea wall was a real darkening influence, and could be seen on the Dorrit Family at any stage of the sun's course.

CHAPTER XXII

A PUZZLE

MR. CLENNAM did not increase in favor with the Father of the Marshalsea in the ratio of his increasing visits. His obtuseness on the great Testimonial question was not calculated to awaken admiration in the paternal breast, but had rather a tendency to give offence in that sensitive quarter, and to be regarded as a positive shortcoming in point of gentlemanly feeling. An impression of disappointment, occasioned by the discovery that Mr. Clennam scarcely possessed that delicacy for which, in the confidence of his nature, he had been inclined to give him credit, began to darken the fatherly mind in connexion with that gentleman. The father went so far as to say, in his private family circle, that he feared Mr. Clennam was not a man of high instincts. He was happy, he observed, in his public capacity as leader and representative of the College, to receive Mr. Clennam when he called to pay his respects; but he didn't find that he got on with him personally. There appeared to be something (he didn't know what it was) wanting in him. Howbeit, the father did not fail in any outward show of politeness, but, on the contrary, honored him with much attention; perhaps cherishing the hope that, although not a man of a sufficiently brilliant and spontaneous turn of mind to repeat his former testimonial unsolicited, it might still be within the compass of his nature to bear the part of a responsive gentleman, in any correspondence that way tending.

In the threefold capacity, of the gentleman from outside who had been accidentally locked in on the night of his first appearance, of the gentleman from outside who had enquired into the affairs of the Father of the Marshalsea with the stupendous idea of getting him out, and of the gentleman from outside who took an interest in the Child of the Marshalsea, Clennam soon became a visitor of mark. He was not surprised by the attentions he received from Mr. Chivery when that officer was on the lock, for he made little distinction between Mr. Chivery's politeness and that of the other turnkeys. It was on one particular afternoon that Mr. Chivery surprised him all at once, and stood forth from his companions in bold relief.

Mr. Chivery, by some artful exercise of his power of clearing the Lodge, had contrived to rid it of all sauntering Collegians; so that Clennam, coming out of the prison, should find him on duty alone.

"(Private) I ask your pardon, sir," said Mr. Chivery in a secret manner; "but which way might you be going?"

"I am going over the Bridge." He saw in Mr. Chivery, with some astonishment, quite an Allegory of Silence, as he stood with his key on his lips.

"(Private) I ask your pardon again," said Mr. Chivery, "but could you go round by Horsemonger Lane? Could you by any means find time to look in at that address?" handing him a little card, printed for circulation among the connexion of Chivery and Co. Tobacconists, Importers of pure Havannah Cigars, Bengal Cheroots, and fine-flavored Cubas, Dealers in Fancy Snuffs, &c. &c.

"(Private) It an't tobacco business," said Mr. Chivery. "The truth is, it's my wife. She's wishful to say a word to you, sir, upon a point respecting —yes," said Mr. Chivery, answering Clennam's look of apprehension with a nod, "respecting *her.*"

"I will make a point of seeing your wife directly."

"Thank you, sir. Much obliged. It an't above ten minutes out of your way. Please to ask for *Mrs.* Chivery!" These instructions, Mr. Chivery, who had already let him out, cautiously called through a little slide in the outer door, which he could draw back from within for the inspection of visitors, when it pleased him.

Arthur Clennam, with the card in his hand, betook himself to the address set forth upon it, and speedily arrived there. It was a very small establishment, wherein a decent woman sat behind the counter working at her needle. Little jars of tobacco, little boxes of cigars, a little assortment of pipes, a little jar or two of snuff, and a little instrument like a shoeing-horn for serving it out, composed the retail stock in trade.

Arthur mentioned his name, and his having promised to call, on the solicitation of Mr. Chivery. About something relating to Miss Dorrit, he believed. Mrs. Chivery at once laid aside her work, rose up from her seat behind the counter, and deploringly shook her head.

"You may see him now," said she, "if you'll condescend to take a peep."

With these mysterious words, she preceded the visitor into a little parlor behind the shop, with a little window in it commanding a very little dull back yard. In this yard, a wash of sheets and table-cloths tried (in vain, for want of air) to get itself dried on a line or two; and among those flapping articles was sitting in a chair, like the last mariner left alive on the deck of a damp ship without the power of furling the sails, a little woe-begone young man.

"Our John," said Mrs. Chivery.

Not to be deficient in interest, Clennam asked what he might be doing there?

"It's the only change he takes," said Mrs. Chivery, shaking her head afresh. "He won't go out, even in the back yard, when there's no linen;

but when there's linen to keep the neighbours' eyes off, he'll sit there, hours. Hours, he will. Says he feels as if it was groves!" Mrs. Chivery shook her head again, put her apron in a motherly way to her eyes, and reconducted her visitor into the regions of the business.

"Please to take a seat, sir," said Mrs. Chivery. "Miss Dorrit is the matter with Our John, sir; he's a breaking his heart for her, and I would wish to take the liberty to ask how it's to be made good to his parents when bust?"

Mrs. Chivery, who was a comfortable-looking woman, much respected about Horsemonger Lane for her feelings and her conversation, uttered this speech with fell composure, and immediately afterwards began again to shake her head and dry her eyes.

"Sir," said she in continuation, "you are acquainted with the family, and have interested yourself with the family, and are influential with the family. If you can promote views calculated to make two young people happy, let me, for Our John's sake, and for both their sakes, implore you so to do."

"I have been so habituated," returned Arthur, at a loss, "during the short time I have known her, to consider Little—I have been so habituated to consider Miss Dorrit in a light altogether removed from that in which you present her to me, that you quite take me by surprise. Does she know your son?"

"Brought up together, sir," said Mrs. Chivery. "Played together!"

"Does she know your son as her admirer?"

"Oh! bless you, sir," said Mrs. Chivery, with a sort of triumphant shiver, "she never could have seen him on a Sunday without knowing he was that. His cane alone would have told it long ago, if nothing else had. Young men like John don't take to ivory hands a pinting, for nothing. How did I first know it myself? Similarly."

"Perhaps Miss Dorrit may not be so ready as you, you see."

"Then she knows it, sir," said Mrs. Chivery, "by word of mouth."

"Are you sure?"

"Sir," said Mrs. Chivery, "sure and certain as in this house I am. I see my son go out with my own eyes when in this house I was, and I see my son come in with my own eyes when in this house I was, and I know he done it!" Mrs. Chivery derived a surprising force of emphasis from the foregoing circumstantiality and repetition.

"May I ask you how he came to fall into the desponding state which causes you so much uneasiness?"

"That," said Mrs. Chivery, "took place on that same day when to this house I see that John with these eyes return. Never been himself in this house since. Never was like what he has been since, not from the hour when to this house seven year ago me and his father, as tenants by the quarter, came!" An effect in the nature of an affidavit was gained for this speech, by Mrs. Chivery's peculiar power of construction.

"May I venture to enquire what is your version of the matter?"

"You may," said Mrs. Chivery, "and I will give it you in honor and in word as true as in this shop I stand. Our John has every one's good word and every one's good wish. He played with her as a child when in that yard a child she played. He has known her ever since. He went out upon the Sunday afternoon when in this very parlor he had dined, and met her, with appointment or without appointment, which I do not pretend to say. He made his offer to her. Her brother and sister is high in their views, and against our John. Her father is all for himself in his views, and against sharing her with any one. Under which circumstances she has answered our John, 'No, John, I cannot have you, I cannot have any husband, it is not my intentions ever to become a wife, it is my intentions to be always a sacrifice, farewell, find another worthy of you, and forget me!' This is the way in which she is doomed to be a constant slave, to them that are not worthy that a constant slave she unto them should be. This is the way in which our John has come to find no pleasure but in taking cold among the linen, and in showing in that yard, as in that yard I have myself shown you, a broken down ruin that goes home to his mother's heart!" Here the good woman pointed to the little window, whence her son might be seen sitting disconsolate in the tuneless groves; and again shook her head and wiped her eyes, and besought him, for the united sakes of both the young people, to exercise his influence towards the bright reversal of these dismal events.

She was so confident in her exposition of the case, and it was so undeniably founded on correct premises in so far as the relative positions of Little Dorrit and her family were concerned, that Clennam could not feel positive on the other side. He had come to attach to Little Dorrit an interest so peculiar—an interest that removed her from, while it grew out of, the common and coarse things surrounding her—that he found it disappointing, disagreeable, almost painful, to suppose her in love with young Mr. Chivery in the back yard, or any such person. On the other hand, he reasoned with himself that she was just as good and just as true, in love with him, as not in love with him; and that to make a kind of domesticated fairy of her, on the penalty of isolation at heart from the only people she knew, would be but a weakness of his own fancy, and not a kind one. Still, her youthful and ethereal appearance, her timid manner, the charm of her sensitive voice and eyes, the very many respects in which she had interested him out of her own individuality, and the strong difference between herself and those about her, were not in unison, and were determined not to be in unison, with this newly-presented idea.

He told the worthy Mrs. Chivery, after turning these things over in his mind—he did that, indeed, while she was yet speaking—that he might be relied upon to do his utmost at all times to promote the happiness of Miss

Dorrit, and to further the wishes of her heart if it were in his power to do so, and if he could discover what they were. At the same time, he cautioned her against assumptions and appearances; enjoined strict silence and secresy, lest Miss Dorrit should be made unhappy; and particularly advised her to endeavour to win her son's confidence, and so to make quite sure of the state of the case. Mrs. Chivery considered the latter precaution superfluous, but said she would try. She shook her head as if she had not derived all the comfort she had fondly expected from this interview, but thanked him nevertheless for the trouble he had kindly taken. They then parted good friends, and Arthur walked away.

The crowd in the street jostling the crowd in his mind, and the two crowds making a confusion, he avoided London Bridge, and turned off in the quieter direction of the Iron Bridge. He had scarcely set foot upon it, when he saw Little Dorrit walking on before him. It was a pleasant day, with a light breeze blowing, and she seemed to have that minute come there for air. He had left her in her father's room within an hour.

It was a timely chance, favorable to his wish of observing her face and manner when no one else was by. He quickened his pace; but, before he reached her, she turned her head.

"Have I startled you?" he asked.

"I thought I knew the step," she answered, hesitating.

"And did you know it, Little Dorrit? You could hardly have expected mine."

"I did not expect any. But when I heard a step, I thought it—sounded like yours."

"Are you going further?"

"No, sir, I am only walking here for a little change."

They walked together, and she recovered her confiding manner with him, and looked up in his face, as she said, after glancing around:

"It is so strange. Perhaps you can hardly understand it. I sometimes have a sensation as if it was almost unfeeling to walk here."

"Unfeeling?"

"To see the river, and so much sky, and so many objects, and such change and motion. Then to go back, you know, and find him in the same cramped place."

"Ah yes! But going back, you must remember that you take with you the spirit and influence of such things, to cheer him."

"Do I? I hope I may! I am afraid you fancy too much, sir, and make me out too powerful. If you were in prison, could I bring such comfort to you?"

"Yes, Little Dorrit. I am sure of it!"

He gathered from a tremor on her lip, and a passing shadow of great agitation on her face, that her mind was with her father. He remained silent for a few moments, that she might regain her composure. The Little

Dorrit, trembling on his arm, was less in unison than ever with Mrs. Chivery's theory, and yet was not irreconcilable with a new fancy which sprung up within him, that there might be some one else, in the hopeless— newer fancy still—in the hopeless unattainable distance.

They turned, and Clennam said, Here was Maggy coming! Little Dorrit looked up, surprised, and they confronted Maggy, who brought herself at sight of them to a dead stop. She had been trotting along, so preoccupied and busy, that she had not recognised them until they turned upon her. She was now in a moment so conscience-stricken, that her very basket partook of the change.

"Maggy, you promised me to stop near father."

"So I would, Little Mother, only he wouldn't let me. If he takes and sends me out I must go. If he takes and says, 'Maggy, you hurry away and back with that letter, and you shall have a sixpence if the answer's a good 'un,' I must take it. Lor, Little Mother, what's a poor thing of ten year old to do? And if Mr. Tip—if he happens to be a coming in as I come out, and if he says, 'Where are you a going, Maggy?' and if I says, 'I'm a going So and So,' and if he says, 'I'll have a Try too,' and if he goes into the George and writes a letter, and if he gives it me and says, 'Take that one to the same place, and if the answer's a good 'un I'll give you a shilling,' it ain't my fault, mother!"

Arthur read, in Little Dorrit's downcast eyes, to whom she foresaw that the letters were addressed.

"I'm a going So and So. There! That's where I am a going to," said Maggy. "I'm a going So and So. It an't you, Little Mother, that's got any-thing to do with it—it's you, you know," said Maggy, addressing Arthur. "You'd better come, So and So, and let me take and give 'em to you."

"We will not be so particular as that, Maggy. Give them me here," said Clennam, in a low voice.

"Well, then, come across the road," answered Maggy, in a very loud whisper. "Little Mother wasn't to know nothing of it, and she would never have known nothing of it if you had only gone, So and So, instead of bothering and loitering about. It ain't my fault. I must do what I am told. They ought to be ashamed of themselves for telling me."

Clennam crossed to the other side, and hurriedly opened the letters. That from the father, mentioned that most unexpectedly finding himself in the novel position of having been disappointed of a remittance from the City on which he had confidently counted, he took up his pen, being restrained by the unhappy circumstance of his incarceration during three and twenty years (doubly underlined), from coming himself, as he would otherwise certainly have done—took up his pen to entreat Mr. Clennam to advance him the sum of Three Pounds Ten Shillings upon his I. O. U., which he begged to enclose. That from the son, set forth that Mr. Clennam would, he knew, be gratified to hear that he had at length obtained permanent employment of a highly satisfactory nature, accompanied with every prospect of complete success in life; but that the temporary inability of his employer to pay him his arrears of salary to that date (in which condition said employer had appealed to that generous forbearance in which he trusted he should never be wanting towards a fellow-creature), combined with the fraudulent conduct of a false friend, and the present high price of provisions, had reduced him to the verge of ruin, unless he could by a quarter before six that evening raise the sum of eight pounds. This sum, Mr. Clennam would be happy to learn, he had, through the promptitude of several friends who had a lively confidence in his probity, already raised, with the exception of a trifling balance of one pound seventeen and fourpence; the loan of which balance, for the period of one month, would be fraught with the usual beneficent consequences.

These letters Clennam answered with the aid of his pencil and pocket-book, on the spot; sending the father what he asked for, and excusing himself from compliance with the demand of the son. He then commissioned Maggy to return with his replies, and gave her the shilling of which the failure of her supplemental enterprise would have disappointed her otherwise.

When he rejoined Little Dorrit, and they had begun walking as before, she said all at once:

"I think I had better go. I had better go home."

"Don't be distressed," said Clennam. "I have answered the letters. They were nothing. You know what they were. They were nothing."

"But I am afraid," she returned, "to leave him, I am afraid to leave any of them. When I am gone, they pervert—but they don't mean it—even Maggy."

"It was a very innocent commission that she undertook, poor thing. And in keeping it secret from you, she supposed, no doubt, that she was only saving you uneasiness."

"Yes, I hope so, I hope so. But I had better go home!"

"You are not afflicted because I, of all people, have had these letters," said Clennam with a reassuring smile. "I am in your confidence, dear Little Dorrit. I am like yourself."

"O, not like me, not like me! Very, very different from me! It was but the other day that my sister told me I had become so used to the prison that I had its tone and character. It must be so. I am sure it must be when I see these things. My place is there. I am better there. It is unfeeling in me to be here when I can do the least thing there. Good bye. I had far better stay at home!"

"Don't call it home, my child!" he entreated. "It is always painful to me to hear you call it home."

"But it is home! What else can I call home? Why should I ever forget it for a single moment?"

"You never do, dear Little Dorrit, in any good and true service."

"I hope not, O I hope not! But it is better for me to stay there; much better, much more dutiful, much happier. Please don't go with me, let me go by myself. Good bye. God bless you. Thank you, thank you."

He felt that it was better to respect her entreaty, and did not move while her slight form went quickly away from him. When it had fluttered out of sight, he turned his face towards the water, and stood thinking.

She would have been distressed at any time by this discovery of the letters; but so much so, and in that unrestrainable way?

No.

When she had seen her father begging with his threadbare disguise on, when she had entreated him not to give her father money, she had been distressed, but not like this. Something had made her keenly and additionally sensitive just now. Now, was there some one in the hopeless unattainable distance? Or had the suspicion been brought into his mind, by his own associations of the troubled river running beneath the bridge with the same river higher up, its changeless tune upon the prow of the ferry-boat, so many miles an hour the peaceful flowing of the stream, here the rushes, there the lilies, nothing uncertain or unquiet?

He thought of his poor child, Little Dorrit, for a long time there; he thought of her, going home; he thought of her in the night; he thought of her when the day came round again. And the poor child Little Dorrit thought of him—too faithfully, ah, too faithfully! —in the shadow of the Marshalsea wall.

END OF No. VI

CHAPTER XXIII

MACHINERY IN MOTION

MR. MEAGLES bestirred himself with such prompt activity in the matter of the negociation with Daniel Doyce which Clennam had entrusted to him, that he soon brought it into business train, and called on Clennam at nine o'clock one morning to make his report.

"Doyce is highly gratified by your good opinion," he opened the business by saying, "and desires nothing so much as that you should examine the affairs of the Works for yourself, and entirely understand them. He has handed me the keys of all his books and papers—here they are jingling in this pocket—and the only charge he has given me is, 'let Mr. Clennam have the means of putting himself on a perfect equality with me as to knowing whatever I know. If it should come to nothing after all, he will respect my confidence. Unless I was sure of that to begin with, I should have nothing to do with him.' And there, you see," said Mr. Meagles, "you have Daniel Doyce all over."

"A very honorable character."

"Oh yes, to be sure. Not a doubt of it. Odd, but very honorable. Very odd though. Now, would you believe, Clennam," said Mr. Meagles, with a hearty enjoyment of his friend's eccentricity, "that I had a whole morning in What's-his-name Yard——"

"Bleeding Heart?"

"A whole morning in Bleeding Heart Yard, before I could induce him to pursue the subject at all?"

"How was that?"

"How was that, my friend? I no sooner mentioned your name in connexion with it, than he declared off."

"Declared off, on my account?"

"I no sooner mentioned your name, Clennam, than he said 'that will never do!' What did he mean by that? I asked him. No matter, Meagles; that would never do. Why would it never do? You'll hardly believe it, Clennam," said Mr. Meagles, laughing within himself, "but it came out that it would never do, because you and he, walking down to Twickenham together, had glided into a friendly conversation, in the course of which he had referred to his intention of taking a partner, supposing at the time that you were as firmly and finally settled as Saint Paul's Cathedral. 'Whereas,' says he, 'Mr. Clennam might now believe, if I entertained his proposition, that I had a sinister and designing motive in what was open free speech. Which I can't bear,' says he, 'which I really am too proud to bear.'"

"I should as soon suspect——"

"Of course you would," interrupted Mr. Meagles, "and so I told him. But it took a morning to scale that wall; and I doubt if any other man than myself (he likes me of old), could have got his leg over it. Well, Clennam. This business-like obstacle surmounted, he then stipulated that before resuming with you I should look over the books, and form my own opinion. I looked over the books, and formed my own opinion. 'Is it, on the whole, for, or against?' says he. 'For,' says I. 'Then,' says he, 'you may now, my good friend, give Mr. Clennam the means of forming his opinion. To enable him to do which, without bias and with perfect freedom, I shall go out of town for a week.' And he's gone," said Mr. Meagles; "that's the rich conclusion of the thing."

"Leaving me," said Clennam, "with a high sense, I must say, of his candor and his——"

"Oddity," Mr. Meagles struck in. "I should think so!"

It was not exactly the word on Clennam's lips, but he forbore to interrupt his good-humoured friend.

"And now," added Mr. Meagles, "you can begin to look into matters as soon as you think proper. I have undertaken to explain where you may want explanation, but to be strictly impartial, and to do nothing more."

They began their perquisitions in Bleeding Heart Yard that same forenoon. Little peculiarities were easily to be detected by experienced eyes in Mr. Doyce's way of managing his affairs, but they almost always involved some ingenious simplification of a difficulty, and some plain road to the desired end. That his papers were in arrear, and that he stood in need of assistance to develop the capacity of his business, was clear enough; but all the results of his undertakings during many years were distinctly set forth, and were ascertainable with ease. Nothing had been done for the purposes of the pending investigation; everything was in its genuine working dress, and in a certain honest rugged order. The calculations and entries, in his own hand, of which there were many, were bluntly written, and with no very neat precision; but were always plain, and directed straight to the purpose. It occurred to Arthur that a far more elaborate and taking show of business—such as the records of the Circumlocution Office made perhaps —might be far less serviceable, as being meant to be far less intelligible.

Three or four days of steady application rendered him master of all the facts it was essential to become acquainted with. Mr. Meagles was at hand the whole time, always ready to illuminate any dim place with the bright little safety-lamp belonging to the scales and scoop. Between them, they agreed upon the sum it would be fair to offer for the purchase of a half share in the business, and then Mr. Meagles unsealed a paper in which Daniel Doyce had noted the amount at which he valued it; which was even something less. Thus, when Daniel came back, he found the affair as good as concluded.

"And I may now avow, Mr. Clennam," said he, with a cordial shake of the hand, "that if I had looked high and low for a partner, I believe I could not have found one more to my mind."

"I say the same," said Clennam.

"And I say of both of you," added Mr. Meagles, "that you are well matched. You keep him in check, Clennam, with your common sense, and you stick to the Works, Dan, with your——"

"Uncommon sense?" suggested Daniel, with his quiet smile.

"You may call it so, if you like—and each of you will be a right hand to the other. Here's my own right hand upon it, as a practical man, to both of you."

The purchase was completed within a month. It left Arthur in possession of private personal means not exceeding a few hundred pounds; but it opened to him an active and promising career. The three friends dined together on the auspicious occasion; the factory and the factory wives and children made holiday and dined too; even Bleeding Heart Yard dined and was full of meat. Two months had barely gone by in all, when Bleeding Heart Yard had become so familiar with short-commons again that the treat was forgotten there; when nothing seemed new in the partnership but the paint of the inscription on the door-posts, DOYCE AND CLENNAM; when it appeared even to Clennam himself, that he had had the affairs of the firm in his mind for years.

The little counting-house reserved for his own occupation, was a room of wood and glass at the end of a long low workshop, filled with benches, and vices, and tools, and straps, and wheels; which, when they were in gear with the steam engine, went tearing round as though they had a suicidal mission to grind the business to dust and tear the factory to pieces. A communication of great trapdoors in the floor and roof with the workshop above and the workshop below, made a shaft of light in this perspective, which brought to Clennam's mind the child's old picture-book, where similar rays were the witnesses of Abel's murder. The noises were sufficiently removed and shut out from the counting-house to blend into a busy hum, interspersed with periodical clinks and thumps. The patient figures at work were swarthy with the filings of iron and steel that danced on every bench and bubbled up through every chink in the planking. The workshop was arrived at by a step-ladder from the outer yard below, where it served as a shelter for the large grindstone where tools were sharpened. The whole had at once a fanciful and practical air in Clennam's eyes which was a welcome change; and, as often as he raised them from his first work of getting the array of business documents into perfect order, he glanced at these things with a feeling of pleasure in his pursuit that was new to him.

Raising his eyes thus one day, he was surprised to see a bonnet laboring up the step-ladder. The unusual apparition was followed by another bonnet. He then perceived that the first bonnet was on the head of Mr. F's Aunt, and that the second bonnet was on the head of Flora, who seemed to have propelled her legacy up the steep ascent with considerable difficulty.

Though not altogether enraptured by the sight of these visitors, Clennam lost no time in opening the counting-house door, and extricating them from the workshop; a rescue which was rendered the more necessary by Mr. F's Aunt already stumbling over some impediment, and menacing steam-power as an Institution with a stony reticule she carried.

"Good gracious, Arthur,—I should say Mr. Clennam, far more proper —the climb we have had to get up here and how ever to get down again without a fire-escape and Mr. F's Aunt slipping through the steps and bruised all over and you in the machinery and foundry way too only think, and never told us!"

Thus Flora, out of breath. Meanwhile, Mr. F's Aunt rubbed her esteemed insteps with her umbrella, and vindictively glared.

"Most unkind never to have come back to see us since that day, though naturally it was not to be expected that there should be any attraction at *our* house and you were much more pleasantly engaged, that's pretty certain, and is she fair or dark blue eyes or black I wonder, not that I expect that she should be anything but a perfect contrast to me in all particulars for I am a disappointment as I very well know and you are quite right to be devoted no doubt though what I am saying Arthur never mind I hardly know myself Good gracious!"

By this time he had placed chairs for them in the counting-house. As Flora dropped into hers, she bestowed the old look upon him.

"And to think of Doyce and Clennam, and who Doyce can be," said Flora; "delightful man no doubt and married perhaps or perhaps a daughter, now has he really? then one understands the partnership and sees it all, don't tell me anything about it for I know I have no claim to ask the question the golden chain that once was forged, being snapped and very proper."

Flora put her hand tenderly on his, and gave him another of the youthful glances.

"Dear Arthur—force of habit, Mr. Clennam every way more delicate and adapted to existing circumstances—I must beg to be excused for taking the liberty of this intrusion but I thought I might so far presume upon old times for ever faded never more to bloom as to call with Mr. F's Aunt to congratulate and offer best wishes, A great deal superior to China not to be denied and much nearer though higher up!"

"I am very happy to see you," said Clennam, "and I thank you, Flora, very much for your kind remembrance."

"More than I can say myself at any rate," returned Flora, "for I might have been dead and buried twenty distinct times over and no doubt whatever should have been before you had genuinely remembered Me or anything like it in spite of which one last remark I wish to make, one last explanation I wish to offer——"

"My dear Mrs. Finching," Arthur remonstrated in alarm.

"Oh not that disagreeable name, say Flora!"

"Flora, is it worth troubling yourself afresh to enter into explanations? I assure you none are needed. I am satisfied—I am perfectly satisfied."

A diversion was occasioned here, by Mr. F's Aunt making the following inexorable and awful statement:

"There's mile-stones on the Dover road!"

With such mortal hostility towards the human race did she discharge this missile, that Clennam was quite at a loss how to defend himself; the rather as he had been already perplexed in his mind by the honor of a visit from this venerable lady, when it was plain she held him in the utmost abhorrence. He could not but look at her with disconcertment, as she sat breathing bitterness and scorn, and staring leagues away. Flora, however, received the remark as if it had been of a most apposite and agreeable nature; approvingly observing aloud that Mr. F's Aunt had a great deal of spirit. Stimulated either by this compliment, or by her burning indignation, that illustrious woman then added, "Let him meet it if he can!" And, with a rigid movement of her stony reticule (an appendage of great size, and of a fossil appearance), indicated that Clennam was the unfortunate person at whom the challenge was hurled.

"One last remark," resumed Flora, "I was going to say I wish to make one last explanation I wish to offer, Mr. F's Aunt and myself would not have intruded on business hours Mr. F having been in business and though the wine trade still business is equally business call it what you will and business habits are just the same as witness Mr. F himself who had his slippers always on the mat at ten minutes before six in the afternoon and his boots inside the fender at ten minutes before eight in the morning to the moment in all weathers light or dark—would not therefore have intruded without a motive which being kindly meant it may be hoped will be kindly taken Arthur, Mr. Clennam far more proper, even Doyce and Clennam probably more business-like."

"Pray say nothing in the way of apology," Arthur entreated. "You are always welcome."

"Very polite of you to say so Arthur—cannot remember Mr. Clennam until the word is out, such is the habit of times for ever fled and so true it is that oft in the stilly night ere slumber's chain has bound people fond memory brings the light of other days around people—very polite but more polite than true I am afraid, for to go into the machinery business without so much as sending a line or a card to papa—I don't say me though there was a time but that is past and stern reality has now my gracious never mind —does not look like it you must confess."

Even Flora's commas seemed to have fled on this occasion; she was so much more disjointed and voluble than in the preceding interview.

"Though indeed," she hurried on, "nothing else is to be expected and why should it be expected and if it's not to be expected why should it be and I am far from blaming you or any one, When your mama and my papa worried us to death and severed the golden bowl—I mean bond but I dare say you know what I mean and if you don't you don't lose much and care just as little I will venture to add—when they severed the golden bond that bound us and threw us into fits of crying on the sofa nearly choked at least myself everything was changed and in giving my hand to Mr. F I know I did so with my eyes open but he was so very unsettled and in such low spirits that he had distractedly alluded to the river if not oil of something from the chemist's and I did it for the best."

"My good Flora, we settled that before. It was all quite right."

"It's perfectly clear you think so," returned Flora, "for you take it very coolly, if I hadn't known it to be China I should have guessed myself the Polar regions, dear Mr. Clennam you are right however and I cannot blame you but as to Doyce and Clennam papa's property being about here we heard it from Pancks and but for him we never should have heard one word about it I am satisfied."

"No no, don't say that."

"What nonsense not to say it Arthur—Doyce and Clennam—easier and less trying to me than Mr. Clennam—when I know it and you know it too and can't deny it.'"

"But I do deny it, Flora. I should soon have made you a friendly visit."

"Ah!" said Flora, tossing her head. "I dare say!" and she gave him another of the old looks. "However when Pancks told us I made up my mind that Mr. F's Aunt and I would come and call because when papa—which was before that—happened to mention her name to me and to say that you were interested in her I said at the moment Good gracious why not have her here then when there's anything to do instead of putting it out."

"When you say Her," observed Clennam, by this time pretty well bewildered, "do you mean Mr. F's——"

"My goodness, Arthur—Doyce and Clennam really easier to me with old remembrances—who ever heard of Mr. F's Aunt doing needlework and going out by the day!"

"Going out by the day! Do you speak of Little Dorrit?"

"Why yes of course," returned Flora; "and of all the strangest names I ever heard the strangest, like a place down in the country with a turnpike, or a favorite pony or a puppy or a bird or something from a seed-shop to be put in a garden or a flower-pot and come up speckled."

"Then, Flora," said Arthur, with a sudden interest in the conversation, "Mr. Casby was so kind as to mention Little Dorrit to you, was he? What did he say?"

"Oh you know what papa is," rejoined Flora, "and how aggravatingly he sits looking beautiful and turning his thumbs over and over one another till he makes one giddy if one keeps one's eyes upon him, he said when we were talking of you—I don't know who began the subject Arthur (Doyce and Clennam) but I am sure it wasn't me, at least I hope not but you really must excuse my confessing more on that point."

"Certainly," said Arthur. "By all means."

"You are very ready," pouted Flora, coming to a sudden stop in a captivating bashfulness, "that I must admit, Papa said you had spoken of her in an earnest way and I said what I have told you and that's all."

"That's all?" said Arthur, a little disappointed.

"Except that when Pancks told us of your having embarked in this business and with difficulty persuaded us that it was really you I said to Mr. F's Aunt then we would come and ask you if it would be agreeable to all parties that she should be engaged at our house when required for I know she often goes to your Mama's and I know that your Mama has a very touchy temper Arthur—Doyce and Clennam—or I never might have married Mr. F and might have been at this hour but I am running into nonsense."

"It was very kind of you, Flora, to think of this."

Poor Flora rejoined with a plain sincerity which became her better than her youngest glances, that she was glad he thought so. She said it with so much heart, that Clennam would have given a great deal to buy his old character of her on the spot, and throw it and the mermaid away for ever.

"I think, Flora," he said, "that the employment you can give Little Dorrit, and the kindness you can show her——"

"Yes and I will," said Flora, quickly.

"I am sure of it—will be a great assistance and support to her. I do not feel that I have the right to tell you what I know of her, for I acquired the knowledge confidentially, and under circumstances that bind me to silence. But I have an interest in the little creature, and a respect for her that I cannot express to you. Her life has been one of such trial and devotion, and such quiet goodness, as you can scarcely imagine. I can hardly think of her, far less speak of her without feeling moved. Let that feeling represent what I could tell you, and commit her to your friendliness with my thanks."

Once more he put out his hand frankly to poor Flora; once more poor Flora couldn't accept it frankly, found it worth nothing openly, must make the old intrigue and mystery of it. As much to her own enjoyment as to his dismay, she covered it with a corner of her shawl as she took it. Then, looking towards the glass front of the counting-house, and seeing two figures approaching, she cried with infinite relish, "Papa! Hush, Arthur, for Mercy's sake!" and tottered back to her chair with an amazing imitation of being in danger of swooning, in the dread surprise and maidenly flutter of her spirits.

The Patriarch meanwhile came inanely beaming towards the counting-house, in the wake of Pancks. Pancks opened the door for him, towed him in, and retired to his own moorings in a corner.

"I heard from Flora," said the Patriarch, with his benevolent smile, "that she was coming to call, coming to call. And being out, I thought I'd come also, thought I'd come also."

The benign wisdom he infused into this declaration (not of itself profound), by means of his blue eyes, his shining head, and his long white hair, was most impressive. It seemed worth putting down among the noblest sentiments enunciated by the best of men. Also, when he said to Clennam, seating himself in the proffered chair, "And you are in a new business, Mr. Clennam? I wish you well, sir, I wish you well!" he seemed to have done benevolent wonders.

"Mrs. Finching has been telling me, sir," said Arthur, after making his acknowledgments; the relict of the late Mr. F meanwhile protesting, with a gesture, against his use of that respectable name; "that she hopes occasionally to employ the young needlewoman you recommended to my mother. For which I have been thanking her."

The Patriarch turning his head in a lumbering way towards Pancks, that assistant put up the note-book in which he had been absorbed, and took him in tow.

"You didn't recommend her, you know," said Pancks; "how could you?

You knew nothing about her, you didn't. The name was mentioned to you, and you passed it on. That's what *you* did."

"Well!" said Clennam. "As she justifies any recommendation, it is much the same thing."

"You are glad she turns out well," said Pancks, "but it wouldn't have been your fault if she had turned out ill. The credit's not yours as it is, and the blame wouldn't have been yours as it might have been. You gave no guarantee. You knew nothing about her."

"You are not acquainted, then," said Arthur, hazarding a random question, "with any of her family?"

"Acquainted with any of her family?" returned Pancks. "How should you be acquainted with any of her family? You never heard of 'em. You can't be acquainted with people you never heard of, can you? You should think not!"

All this time the Patriarch sat serenely smiling; nodding or shaking his head benevolently, as the case required.

"As to being a reference," said Pancks, "you know in a general way, what being a reference means. It's all your eye, that is! Look at your tenants down the Yard here. They'd all be references for one another, if you'd let 'em. What would be the good of letting 'em? It's no satisfaction to be done by two men instead of one. One's enough. A person who can't pay, gets another person who can't pay, to guarantee that he can pay. Like a person with two wooden legs, getting another person with two wooden legs, to guarantee that he has got two natural legs. It don't make either of them able to do a walking-match. And four wooden legs are more troublesome to you than two, when you don't want any." Mr. Pancks concluded by blowing off that steam of his.

A momentary silence that ensued was broken by Mr. F's Aunt, who had been sitting upright in a cataleptic state since her last public remark. She now underwent a violent twitch, calculated to produce a startling effect on the nerves of the uninitiated, and with the deadliest animosity observed:

"You can't make a head and brains out of a brass knob with nothing in it. You couldn't do it when your Uncle George was living; much less when he's dead."

Mr. Pancks was not slow to reply, with his usual calmness, "Indeed, ma'am? Bless my soul! I'm surprised to hear it." Despite his presence of mind, however, the speech of Mr. F's Aunt produced a depressing effect on the little assembly; firstly, because it was impossible to disguise that Clennam's unoffending head was the particular temple of reason depreciated, and secondly, because nobody ever knew on these occasions whose Uncle George was referred to, or what spectral presence might be invoked under that appellation.

Therefore Flora said, though still not without a certain boastfulness and triumph in her legacy, that Mr. F's Aunt was "very lively to-day" and she thought they had better go. But, Mr. F's Aunt proved so lively as to take the suggestion in unexpected dudgeon and declare that she would not go; adding, with several injurious expressions, that if "He"—too evidently meaning Clennam—wanted to get rid of her, "let him chuck her out of winder;" and urgently expressing her desire to see "Him" perform that ceremony.

In this dilemma, Mr. Pancks, whose resources appeared equal to any emergency in the Patriarchal waters, slipped on his hat, slipped out at the counting-house door, and slipped in again a moment afterwards with an artificial freshness upon him, as if he had been in the country for some weeks. "Why, bless my heart, ma'am!" said Mr. Pancks, rubbing up his hair in great astonishment, "is that you? How do you *do*, ma'am? You are looking charming to-day! I am delighted to see you. Favor me with your arm, ma'am; we'll have a little walk together, you and me, if you'll honor me with your company." And so escorted Mr. F's Aunt down the private staircase of the counting-house, with great gallantry and success. The patriarchal Mr. Casby then rose with the air of having done it himself, and blandly followed: leaving his daughter, as she followed in her turn, to remark to her former lover in a distracted whisper (which she very much enjoyed), that they had drained the cup of life to the dregs; and further to hint mysteriously that the late Mr. F was at the bottom of it.

Alone again, Clennam became a prey to his old doubts in reference to his mother and Little Dorrit, and revolved the old thoughts and suspicions. They were all in his mind, blending themselves with the duties he was mechanically discharging, when a shadow on his papers caused him to look up for the cause. The cause was Mr. Pancks. With his hat thrown back upon his ears as if his wiry prongs of hair had darted up like springs and cast it off, with his jet-black beads of eyes inquisitively sharp, with the fingers of his right hand in his mouth that he might bite the nails, and with the fingers of his left hand in reserve in his pocket for another course, Mr. Pancks cast his shadow through the glass upon the books and papers.

Mr. Pancks asked, with a little enquiring twist of his head, if he might come in again? Clennam replied with a nod of his head in the affirmative. Mr. Pancks worked his way in, came alongside the desk, made himself fast by leaning his arms upon it, and started conversation with a puff and a snort.

"Mr. F's Aunt is appeased, I hope?" said Clennam.

"All right, sir," said Pancks.

"I am so unfortunate as to have awakened a strong animosity in the breast of that lady," said Clennam. "Do you know why?"

"Does *she* know why?" said Pancks.

"I suppose not."

"*I* suppose not," said Pancks.

He took out his note-book, opened it, shut it, dropped it into his hat, which was beside him on the desk, and looked in at it as it lay at the bottom of the hat: all with a great appearance of consideration.

"Mr. Clennam," he then began, "I am in want of information, sir."

"Connected with this firm?" asked Clennam.

"No," said Pancks.

"With what then, Mr. Pancks? That is to say, assuming that you want it of me."

"Yes, sir; yes, I want it of you," said Pancks, "if I can persuade you to furnish it. A, B, C, D. DA, DE, DI, DO. Dictionary order. Dorrit. That's the name, sir."

Mr. Pancks blew off his peculiar noise again, and fell to at his right-hand nails. Arthur looked searchingly at him; he returned the look.

"I don't understand you, Mr. Pancks."

"That's the name that I want to know about."

"And what do you want to know?"

"Whatever you can and will tell me." This comprehensive summary of his desires was not discharged without some heavy laboring on the part of Mr. Pancks's machinery.

"This is a singular visit, Mr. Pancks. It strikes me as rather extraordinary that you should come, with such an object, to me."

"It may be all extraordinary together," returned Pancks. "It may be out of the ordinary course, and yet be business. In short, it is business. I am a man of business. What business have I in this present world, except to stick to business? No business."

With his former doubt whether this dry hard personage were quite in earnest, Clennam again turned his eyes attentively upon his face. It was as scrubby and dingy as ever, and as eager and quick as ever, and he could see nothing lurking in it that was at all expressive of a latent mockery that had seemed to strike upon his ear in the voice.

"Now," said Pancks, "to put this business on its own footing, it's not my proprietor's."

"Do you refer to Mr. Casby as your proprietor?"

Pancks nodded. "My proprietor. Put a case. Say, at my proprietor's I hear name—name of young person Mr. Clennam wants to serve. Say, name first mentioned to my proprietor by Plornish in the Yard. Say, I go to Plornish. Say, I ask Plornish as a matter of business, for information. Say, Plornish, though six weeks in arrear to my proprietor, declines. Say, Mrs. Plornish declines. Say, both refer to Mr. Clennam. Put the case."

"Well?"

"Well, sir," returned Pancks, "say, I come to him. Say, here I am."

With those prongs of hair sticking up all over his head, and his breath coming and going very hard and short, the busy Pancks fell back a step (in Tug metaphor, took half a turn astern) as if to show his dingy hull complete, then forged ahead again, and directed his quick glance by turns into his hat where his note-book was, and into Clennam's face.

"Mr. Pancks, not to trespass on your ground of mystery, I will be as plain with you as I can. Let me ask two questions. First——"

"All right!" said Pancks, holding up his dirty forefinger with its broken nail. "I see! 'What's your motive?'"

"Exactly."

"Motive," said Pancks, "good. Nothing to do with my proprietor; not stateable at present, ridiculous to state at present; but good. Desiring to serve young person, name of Dorrit," said Pancks, with his forefinger still up as a caution. "Better admit motive to be good."

"Secondly, and lastly, what do you want to know?"

Mr. Pancks fished up his note-book before the question was put, and buttoning it with care in an inner breast pocket, and looking straight at Clennam all the time, replied with a pause and a puff, "I want supplementary information of any sort."

Clennam could not withhold a smile, as the panting little steam tug, so useful to that unwieldy ship the Casby, waited on and watched him as if it were seeking an opportunity of running in and rifling him of all it wanted, before he could resist its manœuvres; though there was that in Mr. Pancks's eagerness, too, which awakened many wondering speculations in his mind. After a little consideration, he resolved to supply Mr. Pancks with such leading information as it was in his power to impart to him; well knowing that Mr. Pancks, if he failed in his present research, was pretty sure to find other means of getting it.

He, therefore, first requesting Mr. Pancks to remember his voluntary declaration that his proprietor had no part in the disclosure, and that his own intentions were good (two declarations which that coaly little gentleman with the greatest ardor repeated), openly told him that as to the Dorrit lineage or former place of habitation he had no information to communicate, and that his knowledge of the family did not extend beyond the fact that it appeared to be now reduced to five members; namely, to two brothers, of whom one was single, and one a widower with three children. The ages of the whole family he made known to Mr. Pancks, as nearly as he could guess at them; and finally he described to him the position of the Father of the Marshalsea, and the course of time and events through which he had become invested with that character. To all this, Mr. Pancks, snorting and blowing in a more and more portentous manner as he became more interested, listened with great attention; appearing to derive the most agreeable sensations from the painfullest parts of the narrative, and particularly to be quite charmed by the account of William Dorrit's long imprisonment.

"In conclusion, Mr. Pancks," said Arthur, "I have but to say this. I have reasons beyond a personal regard, for speaking as little as I can of the Dorrit family, particularly at my mother's house" (Mr. Pancks nodded), "and for knowing as much as I can. So devoted a man of business as you are—eh ?"

For, Mr. Pancks had suddenly made that blowing effort with unusual force.

"It's nothing," said Pancks.

"So devoted a man of business as yourself has a perfect understanding of a fair bargain. I wish to make a fair bargain with you, that you shall enlighten me concerning the Dorrit family, when you have it in your power, as I have enlightened you. It may not give you a very flattering idea of my business habits, that I failed to make my terms beforehand," continued Clennam; "but I prefer to make them a point of honor. I have seen so much business done on sharp principles that, to tell you the truth, Mr. Pancks, I am tired of them."

Mr. Pancks laughed. "It's a bargain, sir," said he. "You shall find me stick to it."

After that, he stood a little while looking at Clennam, and biting his ten nails all round; evidently while he fixed in his mind what he had been told, and went over it carefully before the means of supplying a gap in his memory should be no longer at hand. "It's all right," he said at last, "and now I'll wish you good day, as it's collecting-day in the Yard. By-the-bye, though. A lame foreigner with a stick."

"Aye, aye. You do take a reference sometimes, I see ?" said Clennam.

"When he can pay, sir," replied Pancks. "Take all you can get, and keep back all you can't be forced to give up. That's business. The lame foreigner with the stick wants a top room down the Yard. Is he good for it ?"

"I am," said Clennam, "and I will answer for him."

"That's enough. What I must have of Bleeding Heart Yard," said Pancks, making a note of the case in his book, "is my bond. I want my bond, you see. Pay up, or produce your property! That's the watchword down the Yard. The lame foreigner with the stick represented that you sent him; but he could represent (as far as that goes) that the Great Mogul sent him. He has been in the Hospital, I believe ?"

"Yes. Through having met with an accident. He is only just now discharged."

"It's pauperizing a man, sir, I have been shown, to let him into a Hospital ?" said Pancks. And again blew off that remarkable sound.

"I have been shown so too," said Clennam, coldly.

Mr. Pancks, being by that time quite ready for a start, got under steam in a moment, and, without any other signal or ceremony, was snorting down the step-ladder and working into Bleeding Heart Yard, before he seemed to be well out of the counting-house.

Throughout the remainder of the day, Bleeding Heart Yard was in consternation, as the grim Pancks cruised in it; haranguing the inhabitants on their backslidings in respect of payment, demanding his bond, breathing notices to quit and executions, running down defaulters, sending a swell of terror on before him, and leaving it in his wake. Knots of people, impelled by a fatal attraction, lurked outside any house in which he was known to be, listening for fragments of his discourses to the inmates; and, when he was rumoured to be coming down the stairs, often could not disperse so quickly but that he would be prematurely in among them, demanding their own arrears, and rooting them to the spot. Throughout the remainder of the day, Mr. Pancks's What were they up to? and What did they mean by it? sounded all over the Yard. Mr. Pancks wouldn't hear of excuses, wouldn't hear of complaints, wouldn't hear of repairs, wouldn't hear of anything but unconditional money down. Perspiring and puffing and darting about in eccentric directions, and becoming hotter and dingier every moment, he lashed the tide of the Yard into a most agitated and turbid state. It had not settled down into calm water again, full two hours after he had been seen fuming away on the horizon at the top of the steps.

There were several small assemblages of the Bleeding Hearts at the popular points of meeting in the Yard that night, among whom it was universally agreed that Mr. Pancks was a hard man to have to do with; and that it was much to be regretted, so it was, that a gentleman like Mr. Casby should put his rents in his hands, and never know him in his true light. For (said the Bleeding Hearts), if a gentleman with that head of hair and them eyes took his rents into his own hands, ma'am, there would be none of this worritting and wearing, and things would be very different.

At which identical evening hour and minute, the Patriarch—who had floated serenely through the Yard in the forenoon before the harrying began, with the express design of getting up this trustfulness in his shining bumps and silken locks—at which identical hour and minute, that first-rate humbug of a thousand guns was heavily floundering in the little Dock of his exhausted Tug at home, and was saying, as he turned his thumbs:

"A very bad day's work, Pancks, very bad day's work. It seems to me, sir, and I must insist on making the observation forcibly, in justice to myself, that you ought to have got much more money, much more money."

CHAPTER XXIV

FORTUNE-TELLING

Little Dorrit received a call that same evening from Mr. Plornish, who, having intimated that he wished to speak to her, privately, in a series of coughs so very noticeable as to favor the idea that her father, as regarded her seamstress occupation, was an illustration of the axiom that there are no such stone-blind men as those who will not see, obtained an audience with her on the common staircase outside the door.

"There's been a lady at our place to-day, Miss Dorrit," Plornish growled, "and another one along with her as is a old wixen if ever I met with such. The way she snapped a person's head off, dear me!"

The mild Plornish was at first quite unable to get his mind away from Mr. F's Aunt. "For," said he, to excuse himself, "she is, I do assure you, the winegariest party!"

At length, by a great effort, he detached himself from the subject sufficiently to observe:

"But she's neither here nor there just at present. The other lady, she's Mr. Casby's daughter; and if Mr. Casby an't well off, none better, it an't through any fault of Pancks. For, as to Pancks, he does, he really does, he does indeed!"

Mr. Plornish, after his usual manner, was a little obscure, but conscientiously emphatic.

"And what she come to our place for," he pursued, "was to leave word that if Miss Dorrit would step up to that card—which it's Mr. Casby's house that is, and Pancks he has a office at the back, where he really does, beyond belief—she would be glad for to engage her. She was a old and a dear friend, she said particular, of Mr. Clennam, and hoped for to prove herself a useful friend to *his* friend. Them was her words. Wishing to know whether Miss Dorrit could come to-morrow morning, I said I would see you, Miss, and enquire, and look round there to-night to say yes, or, if you was engaged to-morrow, when."

"I can go to-morrow, thank you," said Little Dorrit. "This is very kind of you, but you are always kind."

Mr. Plornish, with a modest disavowal of his merits, opened the room-door for her re-admission, and followed her in with such an exceedingly bald pretence of not having been out at all, that her father might have observed it without being very suspicious. In his affable unconsciousness, however, he took no heed. Plornish, after a little conversation, in which he blended his former duty as a Collegian with his present privilege as a humble outside friend, qualified again by his low estate as a plasterer, took his leave; making the tour of the prison before he left, and looking on at a game of skittles, with the mixed feelings of an old inhabitant who had his private reasons for believing that it might be his destiny to come back again.

Early in the morning, Little Dorrit, leaving Maggy in high domestic trust, set off for the Patriarchal tent. She went by the Iron Bridge, though it cost her a penny, and walked more slowly in that part of her journey than in any other. At five minutes before eight, her hand was on the Patriarchal knocker, which was quite as high as she could reach.

She gave Mrs. Finching's card to the young woman who opened the door, and the young woman told her that "Miss Flora"—Flora having, on her return to the parental roof, re-invested herself with the title under which she had lived there—was not yet out of her bedroom, but she was to please to walk up into Miss Flora's sitting-room. She walked up into Miss Flora's sitting-room, as in duty bound, and there found a breakfast-table comfortably laid for two, with a supplementary tray upon it laid for one. The young woman, disappearing for a few moments, returned to say that she was to please to take a chair by the fire, and to take off her bonnet and make herself at home. But Little Dorrit being bashful, and not used to make herself at home on such occasions, felt at a loss how to do it; so she was still sitting near the door with her bonnet on, when Flora came in in a hurry, half-an-hour afterwards.

Flora was so sorry to have kept her waiting, and good gracious why did she sit out there in the cold when she had expected to find her by the fire reading the paper, and hadn't that heedless girl given her the message then, and had she really been in her bonnet all this time, and pray for goodness sake let Flora take it off! Flora, taking it off in the best-natured manner in the world, was so struck by the face disclosed, that she said, "Why, what a good little thing you are, my dear!" and pressed the face between her hands like the gentlest of women.

It was the word and the action of a moment. Little Dorrit had hardly time to think how kind it was, when Flora dashed at the breakfast-table, full of business, and plunged over head and ears into loquacity.

"Really so sorry that I should happen to be late on this morning of all mornings because my intention and my wish was to be ready to meet you when you came in and to say that any one that interested Arthur Clennam half so much must interest me and that I gave you the heartiest welcome and was so glad, instead of which they never called me and there I still am snoring I dare say if the truth was known and if you don't like either cold fowl or hot boiled ham which many people don't I dare say besides Jews and theirs are scruples of conscience which we must all respect though I must say I wish they had them equally strong when they sell us false articles for real that certainly ain't worth the money I shall be quite vexed," said Flora.

Little Dorrit thanked her, and said, shyly, bread and butter and tea was all she usually——

"Oh nonsense my dear child I can never hear of that," said Flora, turning on the urn in the most reckless manner, and making herself wink by splashing hot water into her eyes as she bent down to look into the tea-pot. "You are to come here on the footing of a friend and companion you know if you will let me take that liberty and I should be ashamed of myself indeed if you could come here upon any other, besides which Arthur Clennam spoke in such terms—you are tired my dear."

"No, ma'am."

"You turn so pale you have walked too far before breakfast and I dare say live a great way off and ought to have had a ride," said Flora, "dear dear is there anything that would do you good?"

"Indeed I am quite well, ma'am. I thank you again and again, but I am quite well."

"Then take your tea at once I beg," said Flora, "and this wing of fowl and bit of ham, don't mind me or wait for me because I always carry in this tray myself to Mr. F's Aunt who breakfasts in bed and a charming old lady too and very clever, Portrait of Mr. F behind the door and very like though too much forehead and as to a pillar with a marble pavement and balustrades and a mountain I never saw him near it nor not likely in the wine trade, excellent man but not at all in that way."

Little Dorrit glanced at the portrait, very imperfectly following the references to that work of art.

"Mr. F was so devoted to me that he never could bear me out of his sight," said Flora, "though of course I am unable to say how long that might have lasted if he hadn't been cut short while I was a new broom, worthy man but not poetical manly prose but not romance."

Little Dorrit glanced at the portrait again. The artist had given it a head that would have been, in an intellectual point of view, top-heavy for Shakespeare.

"Romance, however," Flora went on, busily arranging Mr. F's Aunt's toast, "as I openly said to Mr. F when he proposed to me and you will be surprised to hear that he proposed seven times once in a hackney coach once in a boat once in a pew once on a donkey at Tunbridge Wells and the rest on his knees, Romance was fled with the early days of Arthur Clennam, our parents tore us asunder we became marble and stern reality usurped the throne, Mr. F said very much to his credit that he was perfectly aware of it and even preferred that state of things accordingly the word was spoken the fiat went forth and such is life you see my dear and yet we do not break but bend, pray make a good breakfast while I go in with the tray."

She disappeared, leaving Little Dorrit to ponder over the meaning of her scattered words. She soon came back again; and at last began to take her own breakfast, talking all the while.

"You see my dear," said Flora, measuring out a spoonful or two of some brown liquid that smelt like brandy, and putting it into her tea, "I am obliged to be careful to follow the directions of my medical man though the flavor is anything but agreeable being a poor creature and it may be have never recovered the shock received in youth from too much giving way to crying in the next room when separated from Arthur, have you known him long?"

As soon as Little Dorrit comprehended that she had been asked this question—for which time was necessary, the galloping pace of her new patroness having left her far behind—she answered that she had known Mr. Clennam ever since his return.

"To be sure you couldn't have known him before unless you had been in China or had corresponded neither of which is likely," returned Flora, "for travelling-people usually get more or less mahogany and you are not at all so and as to corresponding what about? that's very true unless tea, so it was at his mother's was it really that you knew him first, highly sensible and firm but dreadfully severe—ought to be the mother of the man in the iron mask."

"Mrs. Clennam has been kind to me," said Little Dorrit.

"Really? I am sure I am glad to hear it because as Arthur's mother it's naturally pleasant to my feelings to have a better opinion of her than I had before, though what she thinks of me when I run on as I am certain to do and she sits glowering at me like Fate in a go-cart—shocking comparison really—invalid and not her fault—I never know or can imagine."

"Shall I find my work anywhere, ma'am?" asked Little Dorrit, looking timidly about; "can I get it?"

"You industrious little fairy," returned Flora, taking, in another cup of tea, another of the doses prescribed by her medical man, "there's not the slightest hurry and it's better that we should begin by being confidential about our mutual friend—too cold a word for me at least I don't mean that, very proper expression mutual friend—than become through mere formalities not you but me like the Spartan boy with the fox biting him, which I hope you'll excuse my bringing up for of all the tiresome boys that will go tumbling into every sort of company that boy's the tiresomest."

Little Dorrit, her face very pale, sat down again to listen. "Hadn't I better work the while?" she asked. "I can work and attend too. I would rather, if I may."

Her earnestness was so expressive of her being uneasy without her work, that Flora answered, "Well my dear whatever you like best," and produced a basket of white handkerchiefs. Little Dorrit gladly put it by her side, took out her little pocket-housewife, threaded her needle, and began to hem.

"What nimble fingers you have," said Flora, "but are you sure you are well?"

"Oh yes, indeed!"

Flora put her feet upon the fender, and settled herself for a thorough good romantic disclosure. She started off at score, tossing her head, sighing in the most demonstrative manner, making a great deal of use of her eyebrows, and occasionally, but not often, glancing at the quiet face that bent over the work.

"You must know my dear," said Flora, "but that I have no doubt you know already not only because I have already thrown it out in a general way but because I feel I carry it stamped in burning what's his names upon my brow that before I was introduced to the late Mr. F I had been engaged to Arthur Clennam—Mr. Clennam in public where reserve is necessary Arthur here—we were all in all to one another it was the morning of life it was bliss it was frenzy it was everything else of that sort in the highest degree, when rent asunder we turned to stone in which capacity Arthur went to China and I became the statue bride of the late Mr. F."

Flora, uttering these words in a deep voice, enjoyed herself immensely.

"To paint," said she, "the emotions of that morning when all was marble within and Mr. F's Aunt followed in a glass-coach which it stands to reason must have been in shameful repair or it never could have broken down two streets from the house and Mr. F's Aunt brought home like the fifth of November in a rush-bottomed chair I will not attempt, suffice it to say that the hollow form of breakfast took place in the dining-room down-stairs that papa partaking too freely of pickled salmon was ill for weeks and that Mr. F and myself went upon a continental tour to Calais where the people fought for us on the pier until they separated us though not for ever that was not yet to be."

The statue bride, hardly pausing for breath, went on, with the greatest complacency, in a rambling manner sometimes incidental to flesh and blood.

"I will draw a veil over that dreamy life, Mr. F was in good spirits his appetite was good he liked the cookery he considered the wine weak but palatable and all was well, we returned to the immediate neighbourhood of Number Thirty Little Gosling Street London Docks and settled down, ere we had yet fully detected the housemaid in selling the feathers out of the spare bed Gout flying upwards soared with Mr. F to another sphere."

His relict, with a glance at his portrait, shook her head and wiped her eyes.

"I revere the memory of Mr. F as an estimable man and most indulgent husband, only necessary to mention Asparagus and it appeared or to hint at any little delicate thing to drink and it came like magic in a pint bottle it was not ecstacy but it was comfort, I returned to papa's roof and lived secluded if not happy during some years until one day papa came smoothly blundering in and said that Arthur Clennam awaited me below, I went below and found him ask me not what I found him except that he was still unmarried still unchanged!"

The dark mystery with which Flora now enshrouded herself might have stopped other fingers than the nimble fingers that worked near her. They worked on, without pause, and the busy head bent over them watching the stitches.

"Ask me not," said Flora, "if I love him still or if he still loves me or what the end is to be or when, we are surrounded by watchful eyes and it may be that we are destined to pine asunder it may be never more to be reunited not a word not a breath not a look to betray us all must be secret as the tomb wonder not therefore even if I should seem comparatively cold to Arthur or Arthur should seem comparatively cold to me we have fatal reasons it is enough if we understand them hush!"

All of which Flora said with as much headlong vehemence as if she really believed it. There is not much doubt, that, when she worked herself into full mermaid condition, she did actually believe whatever she said in it.

"Hush!" repeated Flora, "I have now told you all, confidence is established between us hush, for Arthur's sake I will always be a friend to you my dear girl and in Arthur's name you may always rely upon me."

The nimble fingers laid aside the work, and the little figure rose and kissed her hand. "You are very cold," said Flora, changing to her own natural kind-hearted manner, and gaining greatly by the change. "Don't work to-day I am sure you are not well I am sure you are not strong."

"It is only that I feel a little overcome by your kindness, and by Mr. Clennam's kindness in confiding me to one he has known and loved so long."

"Well really my dear," said Flora, who had a decided tendency to be always honest when she gave herself time to think about it, "It's as well to leave that alone now, for I couldn't undertake to say after all, but it doesn't signify lie down a little!"

"I have always been strong enough to do what I want to do, and I shall be quite well directly," returned Little Dorrit, with a faint smile. "You have overpowered me with gratitude, that's all. If I keep near the window for a moment, I shall be quite myself."

Flora opened a window, sat her in a chair by it, and considerately retired to her former place. It was a windy day, and the air stirring on Little Dorrit's face soon brightened it. In a very few minutes she returned to her basket of work, and her nimble fingers were as nimble as ever.

Quietly pursuing her task, she asked Flora if Mr. Clennam had told her where she lived? When Flora replied in the negative, Little Dorrit said that she understood why he had been so delicate, but that she felt sure he would approve of her confiding her secret to Flora, and that she would therefore do so now with Flora's permission. Receiving an encouraging answer, she condensed the narrative of her life into a few scanty words about herself, and a glowing eulogy upon her father; and Flora took it all in with a natural tenderness that quite understood it, and in which there was no incoherence.

When dinner-time came, Flora drew the arm of her new charge through hers, led her down-stairs, and presented her to the Patriarch and Mr. Pancks, who were already in the dining-room waiting to begin. (Mr. F's Aunt was, for the time, laid up in ordinary in her chamber.) By those gentlemen she was received according to their characters; the Patriarch appearing to do her some inestimable service in saying that he was glad to see her, glad to see her; and Mr. Pancks blowing off his favorite sound as a salute.

In that new presence, she would have been bashful enough under any circumstances, and particularly under Flora's insisting on her drinking a glass of wine and eating of the best that was there; but her constraint was greatly increased by Mr. Pancks. The demeanour of that gentleman at first suggested to her mind that he might be a taker of likenesses, so intently did he look at her, and so frequently did he glance at the little note-book by his side. Observing that he made no sketch, however, and that he talked about business only, she began to have suspicions that he represented some creditor of her father's, the balance due to whom was noted in that pocket-volume. Regarded from this point of view, Mr. Pancks's puffings expressed injury and impatience, and each of his louder snorts became a demand for payment.

But, here again she was undeceived by anomalous and incongruous conduct on the part of Mr. Pancks himself. She had left the table half an hour, and was at work alone. Flora had "gone to lie down" in the next room, concurrently with which retirement a smell of something to drink had broken out in the house. The Patriarch was fast asleep, with his philanthropic mouth open, under a yellow pocket-handkerchief in the dining-room. At this quiet time, Mr. Pancks softly appeared before her, urbanely nodding.

"Find it a little dull, Miss Dorrit?" enquired Pancks, in a low voice.

"No, thank you, sir," said Little Dorrit.

"Busy, I see," observed Mr. Pancks, stealing into the room by inches. "What are those now, Miss Dorrit?"

"Handkerchiefs."

"Are they, though!" said Pancks. "I shouldn't have thought it." Not in the least looking at them, but looking at Little Dorrit. "Perhaps you wonder who I am. Shall I tell you? I am a fortune-teller."

Little Dorrit now began to think he was mad.

"I belong body and soul to my proprietor," said Pancks; "you saw my proprietor having his dinner below. But I do a little in the other way, sometimes; privately, very privately, Miss Dorrit."

Little Dorrit looked at him doubtfully, and not without alarm. "I wish you'd show me the palm of your hand," said Pancks. "I should like to have a look at it. Don't let me be troublesome."

He was so far troublesome that he was not at all wanted there, but she laid her work in her lap for a moment, and held out her left hand with the thimble on it.

"Years of toil, eh?" said Pancks, softly, touching it with his blunt fore-finger. "But what else are we made for? Nothing. Hallo!" looking into the lines. "What's this with bars? It's a College! And what's this with a grey gown and a black velvet cap? It's a father! And what's this with a clarionet? It's an uncle! And what's this in dancing-shoes? It's a sister! And what's this straggling about in an idle sort of a way? It's a brother! And what's this thinking for 'em all? Why, this is you, Miss Dorrit!"

Her eyes met his as she looked up wonderingly into his face, and she thought that although his were sharp eyes, he was a brighter and gentler-looking man than she had supposed at dinner. His eyes were on her hand again directly, and her opportunity of confirming or correcting the impression was gone.

"Now, the deuce is in it," muttered Pancks, tracing out a line in her hand with his clumsy finger, "if this isn't me in the corner here! What do I want here? What's behind me?"

He carried his finger slowly down to the wrist, and round the wrist, and affected to look at the back of the hand for what was behind him.

"Is it any harm?" asked Little Dorrit, smiling.

"Deuce a bit!" said Pancks. "What do you think it's worth?"

"I ought to ask you that. I am not the fortune-teller."

"True," said Pancks. "What's it worth? You shall live to see, Miss Dorrit."

Releasing the hand by slow degrees, he drew all his fingers through his prongs of hair, so that they stood up in their most portentous manner; and repeated slowly, "Remember what I say, Miss Dorrit. You shall live to see."

She could not help showing that she was much surprised, if it were only by his knowing so much about her.

"Ah! That's it!" said Pancks, pointing at her. "Miss Dorrit, not that, ever!"

More surprised than before, and a little more frightened, she looked to him for an explanation of his last words.

"Not that," said Pancks, making, with great seriousness, an imitation of a surprised look and manner, that appeared to be unintentionally grotesque. "Don't do that. Never on seeing me, no matter when, no matter where. I am nobody. Don't take on to mind me. Don't mention me. Take no notice. Will you agree, Miss Dorrit?"

"I hardly know what to say," returned Little Dorrit, quite astounded. "Why?"

"Because I am a fortune-teller. Pancks the gipsy. I haven't told you so much of your fortune yet, Miss Dorrit, as to tell you what's behind me on that little hand. I have told you you shall live to see. Is it agreed, Miss Dorrit?"

"Agreed that I—am—to——"

"To take no notice of me away from here, unless I take on first. Not to mind me when I come and go. It's very easy. I am no loss, I am not handsome, I am not good company, I am only my proprietor's grubber. You need do no more than think, 'Ah! Pancks the gipsy at his fortune-telling —he'll tell the rest of my fortune one day—I shall live to know it.' Is it agreed, Miss Dorrit?"

"Ye-es," faltered Little Dorrit, whom he greatly confused, "I suppose so, while you do no harm."

"Good!" Mr. Pancks glanced at the wall of the adjoining room, and stooped forward. "Honest creature, woman of capital points, but heedless and a loose talker, Miss Dorrit." With that he rubbed his hands as if the interview had been very satisfactory to him, panted away to the door, and urbanely nodded himself out again.

If Little Dorrit were beyond measure perplexed by this curious conduct on the part of her new acquaintance, and by finding herself involved in this singular treaty, her perplexity was not diminished by ensuing circumstances. Besides that Mr. Pancks took every opportunity afforded him in Mr. Casby's house of significantly glancing at her and snorting at her—which was not much, after what he had done already—he began to pervade her daily life. She saw him in the street, constantly. When she went to Mr. Casby's, he was always there. When she went to Mrs. Clennam's, he came there on any pretence, as if to keep her in his sight. A week had not gone by, when she found him, to her astonishment, in the Lodge one night, conversing with the turnkey on duty, and to all appearance one of his familiar companions. Her next surprise was to find him equally at his ease within the prison; to hear of his presenting himself among the visitors at her father's Sunday levee; to see him arm in arm with a Collegiate friend about the yard; to learn, from Fame, that he had greatly distinguished himself one evening at the social club that held its meetings in the Snuggery, by addressing a speech to the members of that institution, singing a song, and treating the company to five gallons of ale—report madly added a bushel of shrimps. The effect on Mr. Plornish of such of these phenomena as he became an eye-witness of, in his faithful visits, made an impression on Little Dorrit only second to that produced by the phenomena themselves. They seemed to gag and bind him. He could only stare, and sometimes weakly mutter that it wouldn't be believed down Bleeding Heart Yard that this was Pancks; but he never said a word more, or made a sign more, even to Little Dorrit. Mr. Pancks crowned his mysteries by making himself acquainted with Tip in some unknown manner, and taking a Sunday saunter into the College on that gentleman's arm. Throughout he never took any notice of Little Dorrit, save once or twice when he happened to come close to her, and there was no one very near; on which occasions, he said in passing, with a friendly look and a puff of encouragement, "Pancks the gipsy—fortune-telling."

Little Dorrit worked and strove as usual, wondering at all this, but keeping her wonder, as she had from her earliest years kept many heavier loads, in her own breast. A change had stolen, and was stealing yet, over the patient heart. Every day found her something more retiring than the day before. To pass in and out of the prison unnoticed, and elsewhere to be overlooked and forgotten, were, for herself, her chief desires.

To her own room too, strangely assorted room for her delicate youth and character, she was glad to retreat as often as she could without desertion of any duty. There were afternoon times when she was unemployed, when visitors dropped in to play a hand at cards with her father, when she could be spared and was better away. Then she would flit along the yard, climb the scores of stairs that led to her room, and take her seat at the window. Many combinations did those spikes upon the wall assume, many light shapes did the strong iron weave itself into, many golden touches fell upon the rust, while Little Dorrit sat there musing. New zig-zags sprung into the cruel pattern sometimes, when she saw it through a burst of tears; but beautified or hardened still, always over it and under it and through it, she was fain to look in her solitude, seeing everything with that ineffaceable brand.

A garret, and a Marshalsea garret without compromise, was Little Dorrit's room. Beautifully kept, it was ugly in itself, and had little but cleanliness and air to set it off; for what embellishment she had ever been able to buy, had gone to her father's room. Howbeit, for this poor place she showed an increasing love; and to sit in it alone became her favorite rest.

Insomuch, that on a certain afternoon, during the Pancks mysteries, when she was seated at her window, and heard Maggy's well-known step coming up the stairs, she was very much disturbed by the apprehension of being summoned away. As Maggy's step came higher up and nearer, she trembled and faltered; and it was as much as she could do to speak, when Maggy at length appeared.

"Please, Little Mother," said Maggy, panting for breath, "you must come down and see him. He's here."

"Who, Maggy?"

"Why, o'course Mr. Clennam. He's in your father's room, and he says to me, Maggy, will you be so kind as go and say it's only me."

"I am not very well, Maggy. I had better not go. I am going to lie down. See! I lie down now, to ease my head. Say, with my grateful regard, that you left me so, or I would have come."

"Well, it an't very polite though, Little Mother," said the staring Maggy, "to turn your face away, neither!"

Maggy was very susceptible to personal slights, and very ingenious in inventing them. "Putting both your hands afore your face too!" she went on. "If you can't bear the looks of a poor thing, it would be better to tell her so at once, and not go and shut her out like that, hurting her feelings and breaking her heart at ten year old, poor thing!"

"It's to ease my head, Maggy."

"Well, and if you cry to ease your head, Little Mother, let me cry too. Don't go and have all the crying to yourself," expostulated Maggy, "that an't not being greedy." And immediately began to blubber.

It was with some difficulty that she could be induced to go back with the excuse; but the promise of being told a story—of old her great delight—on condition that she concentrated her faculties upon the errand and left her little mistress to herself for an hour longer, combined with a misgiving on Maggy's part that she had left her good temper at the bottom of the staircase, prevailed. So away she went, muttering her message all the way to keep it in her mind, and, at the appointed time, came back.

"He was very sorry, I can tell you," she announced, "and wanted to send a doctor. And he's coming again to-morrow he is, and I don't think he'll have a good sleep to-night along o' hearing about your head, Little Mother. Oh my! Ain't you been a-crying!"

"I think I have, a little, Maggy."

"A little! Oh!"

"But it's all over now —all over for good, Maggy. And my head is much better and cooler, and I am quite comfortable. I am very glad I did not go down."

Her great staring child tenderly embraced her; and having smoothed her hair, and bathed her forehead and eyes with cold water (offices in which her awkward hands became skilful), hugged her again, exulted in her brighter looks, and stationed her in her chair by the window. Over against this chair, Maggy, with apoplectic exertions that were not at all required, dragged the box which was her seat on story-telling occasions, sat down upon it, hugged her own knees, and said, with a voracious appetite for stories, and with widely-opened eyes:

"Now, Little Mother, let's have a good 'un!"

"What shall it be about, Maggy?"

"Oh, let's have a Princess," said Maggy, "and let her be a reg'lar one. Beyond all belief, you know!"

Little Dorrit considered for a moment; and with a rather sad smile passing over her face, which was flushed by the sunset, began:

"Maggy, there was once upon a time a fine King, and he had everything he could wish for, and a great deal more. He had gold and silver, diamonds and rubies, riches of every kind. He had palaces, and he had——"

"Hospitals," interposed Maggy, still nursing her knees. "Let him have hospitals, because they're so comfortable. Hospitals with lots of Chicking."

"Yes, he had plenty of them, and he had plenty of everything."

"Plenty of baked potatoes, for instance?" said Maggy.

"Plenty of everything."

"Lor!" chuckled Maggy, giving her knees a hug. "Wasn't it prime!"

"This King had a daughter, who was the wisest and most beautiful Princess that ever was seen. When she was a child, she understood all her lessons before her masters taught them to her; and when she was grown up, she was the wonder of the world. Now, near the Palace where this Princess lived, there was a cottage in which there was a poor little tiny woman, who lived all alone by herself."

"A old woman," said Maggy, with an unctuous smack of her lips.

"No, not an old woman. Quite a young one."

"I wonder she warn't afraid," said Maggy. "Go on, please."

"The Princess passed the cottage nearly every day, and whenever she went by in her beautiful carriage, she saw the poor tiny woman spinning at her wheel, and she looked at the tiny woman, and the tiny woman looked at her. So, one day she stopped the coachman a little way from the cottage, and got out and walked on and peeped in at the door, and there, as usual, was the tiny woman spinning at her wheel, and she looked at the Princess, and the Princess looked at her."

"Like trying to stare one another out," said Maggy. "Please go on, Little Mother."

"The Princess was such a wonderful Princess that she had the power of knowing secrets, and she said to the tiny woman, Why do you keep it there? This showed her directly that the Princess knew why she lived all alone by herself, spinning at her wheel, and she kneeled down to the Princess, and asked her never to betray her. So, the Princess said, I never will betray you. Let me see it. So, the tiny woman closed the shutter of the cottage window and fastened the door, and, trembling from head to foot for fear that any one should suspect her, opened a very secret place, and showed the Princess a shadow."

"Lor!" said Maggy.

"It was the shadow of Some one who had gone by long before: of Some one who had gone on far away quite out of reach, never, never to come back. It was bright to look at; and when the tiny woman showed it to the Princess, she was proud of it with all her heart, as a great, great, treasure. When the Princess had considered it a little while, she said to the tiny woman, And you keep watch over this, every day? And she cast down her eyes, and whispered, Yes. Then the Princess said, Remind me why. To which the other replied, that no one so good and kind had ever passed that way, and that was why in the beginning. She said, too, that nobody missed it, that nobody was the worse for it, that Some one had gone on to those who were expecting him——"

"Some one was a man then?" interposed Maggy.

Little Dorrit timidly said yes, she believed so; and resumed:

"—Had gone on to those who were expecting him, and that this remembrance was stolen or kept back from nobody. The Princess made answer, Ah! But when the cottager died it would be discovered there. The tiny woman told her No; when that time came, it would sink quietly into her own grave, and would never be found."

"Well, to be sure!" said Maggy. "Go on, please."

"The Princess was very much astonished to hear this, as you may suppose, Maggy."

"(And well she might be," said Maggy.)

"So she resolved to watch the tiny woman, and see what came of it. Every day, she drove in her beautiful carriage by the cottage-door, and there she saw the tiny woman always alone by herself spinning at her wheel, and she looked at the tiny woman, and the tiny woman looked at her. At last one day the wheel was still, and the tiny woman was not to be seen. When the Princess made enquiries why the wheel had stopped, and where the tiny woman was, she was informed that the wheel had stopped because there was nobody to turn it, the tiny woman being dead."

("They ought to have took her to the Hospital," said Maggy, "and then she'd have got over it.")

"The Princess, after crying a very little for the loss of the tiny woman, dried her eyes and got out of her carriage at the place where she had stopped it before, and went to the cottage and peeped in at the door. There was nobody to look at her now, and nobody for her to look at, so she went in at once to search for the treasured shadow. But there was no sign of it to be found anywhere; and then she knew that the tiny woman had told her the truth, and that it would never give any body any trouble, and that it had sunk quietly into her own grave, and that she and it were at rest together.

"That's all, Maggy."

The sunset flush was so bright on Little Dorrit's face when she came thus to the end of her story, that she interposed her hand to shade it.

"Had she got to be old?" Maggy asked.

"The tiny woman?"

"Ah!"

"I don't know," said Little Dorrit. "But it would have been just the same, if she had been ever and ever so old."

"Would it raly!" said Maggy. "Well I suppose it would though." And sat staring and ruminating.

She sat so long with her eyes wide open, that at length Little Dorrit, to entice her from her box, rose and looked out of window. As she glanced down into the yard, she saw Pancks come in, and leer up with the corner of his eye as he went by.

"Who's he, Little Mother?" said Maggy. She had joined her at the window and was leaning on her shoulder. "I see him come in and out often."

"I have heard him called a fortune-teller," said Little Dorrit. "But I doubt if he could tell many people, even their past or present fortunes."

"Couldn't have told the Princess hers?" said Maggy.

Little Dorrit, looking musingly down into the dark valley of the prison, shook her head.

"Nor the tiny woman hers?" said Maggy.

"No," said Little Dorrit, with the sunset very bright upon her. "But let us come away from the window."

The Story of the Princess

CHAPTER XXV

CONSPIRATORS AND OTHERS

THE private residence of Mr. Pancks was in Pentonville, where he lodged on the second floor of a professional gentleman in an extremely small way, who had an inner-door within the street-door, poised on a spring and start-ing open with a click like a trap; and who wrote up in the fan-light, RUGG, GENERAL AGENT, ACCOUNTANT, DEBTS RECOVERED.

This scroll, majestic in its severe simplicity, illuminated a little slip of front garden abutting on the thirsty high road, where a few of the dustiest of leaves hung their dismal heads and led a life of choking. A professor of writing occupied the first-floor, and enlivened the garden railings with glass-cases containing choice examples of what his pupils had been before six lessons and while the whole of his young family shook the table, and what they had become after six lessons when the young family was under restraint. The tenancy of Mr. Pancks was limited to one airy bedroom; he covenanting and agreeing with Mr. Rugg his landlord, that in consideration of a certain scale of payments accurately defined, and on certain verbal notice duly given, he should be at liberty to elect to share the Sunday break-fast, dinner, tea, or supper, or each or any or all of those repasts or meals, of Mr. and Miss Rugg (his daughter) in the back parlor.

Miss Rugg was a lady of a little property, which she had acquired, together with much distinction in the neighbourhood, by having her heart severely lacerated and her feelings mangled by a middle-aged baker, resident in the vicinity, against whom she had, by the agency of Mr. Rugg, found it neces-sary to proceed at law to recover damages for a breach of promise of mar-riage. The baker, having been, by the counsel for Miss Rugg, witheringly denounced on that occasion up to the full amount of twenty guineas, at the rate of about eighteenpence an epithet, and having been cast in correspond-ing damages, still suffered occasional persecution from the youth of Penton-ville. But Miss Rugg, environed by the majesty of the law, and having her damages invested in the public securities, was regarded with consideration.

In the society of Mr. Rugg, who had a round white visage, as if all his blushes had been drawn out of him long ago, and who had a ragged yellow head like a worn-out hearth-broom; and in the society of Miss Rugg, who had little nankeen spots, like shirt buttons, all over her face, and whose own yellow tresses were rather scrubby than luxuriant; Mr. Pancks had usually dined on Sundays for some few years, and had twice a week, or so, enjoyed an evening collation of bread, Dutch cheese, and porter. Mr. Pancks was one of the very few marriageable men for whom Miss Rugg had no terrors, the argument with which he re-assured himself being twofold; that is to say, firstly, "that it wouldn't do twice," and secondly "that he wasn't worth it." Fortified within this double armour, Mr. Pancks snorted at Miss Rugg on easy terms.

Up to this time, Mr. Pancks had transacted little or no business at his quarters in Pentonville, except in the sleeping line; but, now that he had become a fortune-teller, he was often closeted after midnight with Mr. Rugg in his little front-parlor office, and, even after those untimely hours, burnt tallow in his bedroom. Though his duties as his proprietor's grubber were in no wise lessened; and though that service bore no greater resemblance to a bed of roses than was to be discovered in its many thorns; some new branch of industry made a constant demand upon him. When he cast off the Patriarch at night, it was only to take an anonymous craft in tow, and labor away afresh in other waters.

The advance from a personal acquaintance with the elder Mr. Chivery, to an introduction to his amiable wife and disconsolate son, may have been easy; but easy or not, Mr. Pancks soon made it. He nestled in the bosom of the tobacco business within a week or two after his first appearance in the College, and particularly addressed himself to the cultivation of a good understanding with Young John. In this endeavour he so prospered as to lure that pining shepherd forth from the groves, and tempt him to undertake mysterious missions; on which he began to disappear at uncertain intervals for as long a space as two or three days together. The prudent Mrs. Chivery, who wondered greatly at this change, would have protested against it as detrimental to the Highland typification on the doorpost, but for two forcible reasons; one, that her John was roused to take strong interest in the business which these starts were supposed to advance—and this she held to be good for his drooping spirits; the other, that Mr. Pancks confidentially agreed to pay her, for the occupation of her son's time, at the handsome rate of seven and sixpence per day. The proposal originated with himself, and was couched in the pithy terms, "If your John is weak enough, ma'am, not to take it, that is no reason why you should be, don't you see? So, quite between ourselves, ma'am, business being business, here it is!"

What Mr. Chivery thought of these things, or how much or how little he knew about them, was never gathered from himself. It has been already remarked that he was a man of few words; and it may be here observed, that he had imbibed a professional habit of locking everything up. He locked himself up as carefully as he locked up the Marshalsea debtors. Even his custom of bolting his meals may have been a part of an uniform whole; but there is no question, that, as to all other purposes, he kept his mouth as he kept the Marshalsea door. He never opened it without occasion. When it was necessary to let anything out, he opened it a little way, held it open just as long as sufficed for the purpose, and locked it again. Even as he would be sparing of his trouble at the Marshalsea door, and would keep a visitor who wanted to go out, waiting for a few moments if he saw another visitor coming down the yard, so that one turn of the key should suffice for both, similarly he would often reserve a remark if he perceived another on its way to his lips, and would deliver himself of the two together. As to any key to his inner knowledge being to be found in his face, the Marshalsea key was as legible an index to the individual characters and histories upon which it was turned.

That Mr. Pancks should be moved to invite any one to dinner at Pentonville, was an unprecedented fact in his calendar. But he invited Young John to dinner, and even brought him within range of the dangerous (because expensive) fascinations of Miss Rugg. The banquet was appointed for a Sunday, and Miss Rugg with her own hands stuffed a leg of mutton with oysters on the occasion, and sent it to the baker's—not *the* baker's, but an opposition establishment. Provision of oranges, apples, and nuts was also made. And rum was brought home by Mr. Pancks on Saturday night, to gladden the visitor's heart.

The store of creature comforts was not the chief part of the visitor's reception. Its special feature was a foregone family confidence and sympathy. When Young John appeared at half-past one, without the ivory hand and waistcoat of golden sprigs, the sun shorn of his beams by disastrous clouds, Mr. Pancks presented him to the yellow-haired Ruggs as the young man he had so often mentioned who loved Miss Dorrit.

"I am glad," said Mr. Rugg, challenging him specially in that character, "to have the distinguished gratification of making your acquaintance, sir. Your feelings do you honor. You are young; may you never outlive your feelings! If I was to outlive my own feelings, sir," said Mr. Rugg, who was a man of many words, and was considered to possess a remarkably good address; "If I was to outlive my own feelings, I'd leave fifty pound in my will to the man who would put me out of existence."

Miss Rugg heaved a sigh.

"My daughter, sir," said Mr. Rugg. "Anastatia, you are no stranger to the state of this young man's affections. My daughter has had her trials, sir," Mr. Rugg might have used the word more pointedly in the singular number, "and she can feel for you."

Young John, almost overwhelmed by the touching nature of this greeting, professed himself to that effect.

"What I envy you, sir, is," said Mr. Rugg, "allow me to take your hat —we are rather short of pegs—I'll put it in the corner, nobody will tread in it there—What I envy you, sir, is the luxury of your own feelings. I belong to a profession in which that luxury is sometimes denied us."

Young John replied, with acknowledgments, that he only hoped he did what was right, and what showed how entirely he was devoted to Miss Dorrit. He wished to be unselfish; and he hoped he was. He wished to do anything as laid in his power to serve Miss Dorrit, altogether putting himself out of sight; and he hoped he did. It was but little that he could do, but he hoped he did it.

"Sir," said Mr. Rugg, taking him by the hand, "you are a young man

that it does one good to come across. You are a young man that I should like
to put in the witness-box, to humanise the minds of the legal profession.
I hope you have brought your appetite with you, and intend to play a good
knife and fork?"

"Thank you, sir," returned Young John, "I don't eat much at present."

Mr. Rugg drew him a little apart. "My daughter's case, sir," said he, "at
the time when, in vindication of her outraged feelings and her sex, she
became the plaintiff in Rugg and Bawkins. I suppose I could have put it
in evidence, Mr. Chivery, if I had thought it worth my while, that the
amount of solid sustenance my daughter consumed at that period did not
exceed ten ounces per week."

"I think I go a little beyond that, sir," returned the other, hesitating, as
if he confessed it with some shame.

"But in your case there's no fiend in human form," said Mr. Rugg, with
argumentative smile and action of hand. "Observe, Mr. Chivery! No fiend
in human form!"

"No, sir, certainly," Young John added with simplicity, "I should be
very sorry if there was."

"The sentiment," said Mr. Rugg, "is what I should have expected from
your known principles. It would affect my daughter greatly, sir, if she heard
it. As I perceive the mutton, I am glad she didn't hear it. Mr. Pancks, on
this occasion, pray face me. My dear, face Mr. Chivery. For what we are
going to receive, may we (and Miss Dorrit) be truly thankful!"

But for a grave waggishness in Mr. Rugg's manner of delivering this
introduction to the feast, it might have appeared that Miss Dorrit was
expected to be one of the company. Pancks recognised the sally in his usual
way, and took in his provender in his usual way. Miss Rugg, perhaps making
up some of her arrears, likewise took very kindly to the mutton, and it
rapidly diminished to the bone. A bread-and-butter pudding entirely disappeared, and a considerable amount of cheese and radishes vanished by
the same means. Then came the dessert.

Then also, and before the broaching of the rum and water, came Mr.
Pancks's note-book. The ensuing business proceedings were brief but
curious, and rather in the nature of a conspiracy. Mr. Pancks looked over
his note-book which was now getting full, studiously; and picked out little
extracts, which he wrote on separate slips of paper on the table; Mr. Rugg,
in the meanwhile, looking at him with close attention, and Young John
losing his uncollected eye in mists of meditation. When Mr. Pancks, who
supported the character of chief conspirator, had completed his extracts,
he looked them over, corrected them, put up his note-book, and held them
like a hand at cards.

"Now, there's a churchyard in Bedfordshire," said Pancks. "Who
takes it?"

"I'll take it sir," returned Mr. Rugg, "if no one bids."

Mr. Pancks dealt him his card, and looked at his hand again.

"Now, there's an Enquiry in York," said Pancks. "Who takes it?"

"I am not good for York," said Mr. Rugg.

"Then perhaps," pursued Pancks, "you'll be so obliging, John Chivery?"

Young John assenting, Pancks dealt him his card, and consulted his hand again.

"There's a Church in London; I may as well take that. And a Family Bible; I may as well take that, too. That's two to me. Two to me," repeated Pancks, breathing hard over his cards. "Here's a Clerk at Durham for you, John, and an old seafaring gentleman at Dunstable for you, Mr. Rugg. Two to me, was it? Yes, two to me. Here's a Stone; three to me. And a Still-born Baby; four to me. And all, for the present, told."

When he had thus disposed of his cards, all being done very quietly and in a suppressed tone, Mr. Pancks puffed his way into his own breast-pocket and tugged out a canvas bag: from which, with a sparing hand, he told forth money for travelling expenses in two little portions. "Cash goes out fast," he said anxiously, as he pushed a portion to each of his male companions, "very fast."

"I can only assure you, Mr. Pancks," said Young John, "that I deeply regret my circumstances being such that I can't afford to pay my own charges, or that it's not advisable to allow me the time necessary for my doing the distances on foot. Because nothing could give me greater satisfaction than to walk myself off my legs without fee or reward."

This young man's disinterestedness appeared so very ludicrous in the eyes of Miss Rugg, that she was obliged to effect a precipitate retirement from the company, and to sit upon the stairs until she had had her laugh out. Meanwhile Mr. Pancks, looking, not without some pity, at Young John, slowly and thoughtfully twisted up his canvas bag as if he were wringing its neck. The lady returning as he restored it to his pocket, mixed rum and water for the party, not forgetting her fair self, and handed to every one his glass. When all were supplied, Mr. Rugg rose, and silently holding out his glass at arm's length above the centre of the table, by that gesture invited the other three to add theirs, and to unite in a general conspiratorial clink. The ceremony was effective up to a certain point, and would have been wholly so throughout, if Miss Rugg, as she raised her glass to her lips in completion of it, had not happened to look at Young John; when she was again so overcome by the contemptible comicality of his disinterestedness, as to splutter some ambrosial drops of rum and water around, and withdraw in confusion.

Such was the dinner without precedent, given by Pancks at Pentonville; and such was the busy and strange life Pancks led. The only waking moments at which he appeared to relax from his cares, and to recreate himself by going anywhere or saying anything without a pervading object, were when he showed a dawning interest in the lame foreigner with the stick, down Bleeding Heart Yard.

The foreigner, by name John Baptist Cavalletto—they called him Mr.

Baptist in the Yard—was such a chirping, easy, hopeful little fellow, that his attraction for Pancks was probably in the force of contrast. Solitary, weak, and scantily acquainted with the most necessary words of the only language in which he could communicate with the people about him, he went with the stream of his fortunes, in a brisk way that was new in those parts. With little to eat, and less to drink, and nothing to wear but what he wore upon him, or had brought there in one of the smallest bundles that ever were seen, he put as bright a face upon it as if he were in the most flourishing circumstances, when he first hobbled up and down the Yard, humbly propitiating the general good-will with his white teeth.

It was up-hill work for a foreigner, lame or sound, to make his way with the Bleeding Hearts. In the first place, they were vaguely persuaded that every foreigner had a knife about him; in the second, they held it to be a sound constitutional national axiom that he ought to go home to his own country. They never thought of enquiring how many of their own country-men would be returned upon their hands from divers parts of the world, if the principle were generally recognised; they considered it particularly and peculiarly British. In the third place, they had a notion that it was a sort of Divine visitation upon a foreigner that he was not an Englishman, and that all kinds of calamities happened to his country because it did things that England did not, and did not do things that England did. In this belief, to be sure, they had long been carefully trained by the Barnacles and Stiltstalkings, who were always proclaiming to them, officially and unoffi-cially, that no country which failed to submit itself to those two large fami-lies could possibly hope to be under the protection of Providence; and who, when they believed it, disparaged them in private as the most preju-diced people under the sun.

This, therefore, might be called a political position of the Bleeding Hearts; but they entertained other objections to having foreigners in the Yard. They believed that foreigners were always badly off; and though they were as ill off themselves as they could desire to be, that did not diminish the force of the objection. They believed that foreigners were dragooned and bayonetted; and though they certainly got their own skulls promptly fractured if they ˆhowed any ill humour, still it was with a blunt instrument, and that didn't count. They believed that foreigners were always immoral; and though they had an occasional assize at home, and now and then a divorce case or so, that had nothing to do with it. They believed that foreigners had no independent spirit, as never being escorted to the poll in droves by Lord Decimus Tite Barnacle, with colors flying and the tune of Rule Britannia playing. Not to be tedious, they had many other beliefs of a similar kind.

Against these obstacles, the lame foreigner with the stick had to make head as well as he could; not absolutely single-handed, because Mr. Arthur Clennam had recommended him to the Plornishes (he lived at the top of the same house), but still at heavy odds. However, the Bleeding Hearts were kind hearts; and when they saw the little fellow cheerily limping about with a good-humoured face, doing no harm, drawing no knives, committing no outrageous immoralities, living chiefly on farinaceous and milk diet, and playing with Mrs. Plornish's children of an evening, they began to think that although he could never hope to be an Englishman, still it would be hard to visit that affliction on his head. They began to accommodate themselves to his level, calling him "Mr. Baptist," but treating him like a baby, and laughing immoderately at his lively gestures and his childish English— more, because he didn't mind it, and laughed too. They spoke to him in very loud voices as if he were stone deaf. They constructed sentences, by way of teaching him the language in its purity, such as were addressed by the savages to Captain Cook, or by Friday to Robinson Crusoe. Mrs. Plornish was particularly ingenious in this art; and attained so much celebrity for saying "Me ope you leg well soon," that it was considered in the Yard but a very short remove indeed from speaking Italian. Even Mrs. Plornish herself began to think that she had a natural call towards that language. As he became more popular, household objects were brought into requisition for his instruction in a copious vocabulary; and whenever he appeared in the Yard, ladies would fly out at their doors crying, "Mr. Baptist—teapot!" "Mr. Baptist—dust-pan!" "Mr. Baptist—flour-dredger!" "Mr. Baptist— coffee-biggin!" At the same time exhibiting those articles, and penetrating him with a sense of the appalling difficulties of the Anglo-Saxon tongue.

It was in this stage of his progress, and in about the third week of his occupation, that Mr. Pancks's fancy became attracted by the little man. Mounting to his attic, attended by Mrs. Plornish as interpreter, he found Mr. Baptist with no furniture but his bed on the ground, a table, and a chair, carving with the aid of a few simple tools, in the blithest way possible.

"Now, old chap," said Mr. Pancks, "pay up!"

He had his money ready, folded in a scrap of paper, and laughingly handed it in; then with a free action, threw out as many fingers of his right hand as there were shillings, and made a cut crosswise in the air for an odd sixpence.

"Oh!" said Mr. Pancks, watching him, wonderingly. "That's it, is it? You're a quick customer. It's all right. I didn't expect to receive it, though."

Mrs. Plornish here interposed with great condescension, and explained to Mr. Baptist. "E please. E glad get money."

The little man smiled and nodded. His bright face seemed uncommonly attractive to Mr. Pancks. "How's he getting on in his limb?" he asked Mrs. Plornish.

"Oh, he's a deal better, sir," said Mrs. Plornish. "We expect next week he'll be able to leave off his stick entirely." (The opportunity being too favorable to be lost, Mrs. Plornish displayed her great accomplishment, by explaining, with pardonable pride, to Mr. Baptist, "E ope you leg well soon.")

"He's a merry fellow, too," said Mr. Pancks, admiring him as if he were a mechanical toy. "How does he live?"

"Why, sir," rejoined Mrs. Plornish, "he turns out to have quite a power of carving them flowers that you see him at now." (Mr. Baptist, watching their faces as they spoke, held up his work. Mrs. Plornish interpreted in her Italian manner, on behalf of Mr. Pancks, "E please. Double good!")

"Can he live by that?" asked Mr. Pancks.

"He can live on very little, sir, and it is expected as he will be able, in time, to make a very good living. Mr. Clennam got it him to do, and gives him odd jobs besides, in at the Works next door—makes 'em for him, in short, when he knows he wants 'em."

"And what does he do with himself, now, when he ain't hard at it?" said Mr. Pancks.

"Why, not much as yet, sir, on accounts I suppose of not being able to walk much; but he goes about the Yard, and he chats without particular understanding or being understood, and he plays with the children, and he¹¹ sits in the sun—he'll sit down anywhere, as if it was a arm-chair—and he'll sing, and he'll laugh!"

"Laugh!" echoed Mr. Pancks. "He looks to me as if every tooth in his head was always laughing."

"But whenever he gets to the top of the steps at t'other end of the Yard," said Mrs. Plornish, "he'll peep out in the curiousest way! So that some of us thinks he's peeping out towards where his own country is, and some of us thinks he's looking for somebody he don't want to see, and some of us don't know what to think."

Mr. Baptist seemed to have a general understanding of what she said; or perhaps his quickness caught and applied her slight action of peeping. In any case, he closed his eyes and tossed his head with the air of a man who had his sufficient reasons for what he did, and said in his own tongue, it didn't matter. Altro!

"What's Altro?" said Pancks.

"Hem! It's a sort of a general kind of a expression, sir," said Mrs. Plornish.

"Is it?" said Pancks. "Why, then Altro to you, old chap. Good afternoon. Altro!"

Mr. Baptist in his vivacious way repeating the word several times, Mr. Pancks in his duller way gave it him back once. From that time it became a frequent custom with Pancks the gipsy, as he went home jaded at night, to pass round by Bleeding Heart Yard, go quietly up the stairs, look in at Mr. Baptist's door, and, finding him in his room, to say "Hallo, old chap! Altro!" To which Mr. Baptist would reply, with innumerable bright nods and smiles, "Altro, signore, altro, altro, altro!" After this highly condensed conversation, Mr. Pancks would go his way; with an appearance of being lightened and refreshed.

END OF No. VII

CHAPTER XXVI

NOBODY'S STATE OF MIND

IF Arthur Clennam had not arrived at that wise decision firmly to restrain himself from loving Pet, he would have lived on in a state of much perplexity, involving difficult struggles with his own heart. Not the least of these would have been a contention, always waging within it, between a tendency to dislike Mr. Henry Gowan, if not to regard him with positive repugnance, and a whisper that the inclination was unworthy. A generous nature is not prone to strong aversions, and is slow to admit them even dispassionately; but when it finds ill-will gaining upon it, and can discern between-whiles that its origin is not dispassionate, such a nature becomes distressed.

Therefore Mr. Henry Gowan would have clouded Clennam's mind, and would have been far oftener present to it than more agreeable persons and subjects, but for the great prudence of his decision aforesaid. As it was, Mr. Gowan seemed transferred to Daniel Doyce's mind; at all events, it so happened that it usually fell to Mr. Doyce's turn, rather than to Clennam's, to speak of him in the friendly conversations they held together. These were of frequent occurrence now; as the two partners shared a portion of a roomy house in one of the grave old-fashioned City streets, lying not far from the Bank of England, by London Wall.

Mr. Doyce had been to Twickenham to pass the day. Clennam had excused himself. Mr. Doyce was just come home. He put in his head at the door of Clennam's sitting-room to say Good night.

"Come in, come in!" said Clennam.

"I saw you were reading," returned Doyce, as he entered, "and thought you might not care to be disturbed."

But for the notable resolution he had made, Clennam really might not have known what he had been reading; really might not have had his eyes upon the book for an hour past, though it lay open before him. He shut it up, rather quickly.

"Are they well?" he asked.

"Yes," said Doyce; "they are well. They are all well."

Daniel had an old workmanlike habit of carrying his pocket-handkerchief in his hat. He took it out and wiped his forehead with it, slowly repeating "they are all well. Miss Minnie looking particularly well, I thought."

"Any company at the cottage?"

"No, no company."

"And how did you get on, you four?" asked Clennam, gaily.

"There were five of us," returned his partner. "There was What's-his-name. He was there."

"Who is he?" said Clennam.

"Mr. Henry Gowan."

"Ah, to be sure!" cried Clennam, with unusual vivacity. "Yes!—I forgot him."

"As I mentioned, you may remember," said Daniel Doyce, "he is always there, on Sunday."

"Yes, yes," returned Clennam; "I remember now."

Daniel Doyce, still wiping his forehead, ploddingly repeated, "Yes. He was there, he was there. Oh yes, he was there. And his dog. *He* was there too."

"Miss Meagles is quite attached to—the—dog," observed Clennam.

"Quite so," assented his partner. "More attached to the dog than I am to the man."

"You mean Mr. ——?"

"I mean Mr. Gowan, most decidedly," said Daniel Doyce.

There was a gap in the conversation, which Clennam devoted to winding up his watch.

"Perhaps you are a little hasty in your judgment," he said. "Our judgments—I am supposing a general case——"

"Of course," said Doyce.

"Are so liable to be influenced by many considerations, which, almost without our knowing it, are unfair, that it is necessary to keep a guard upon them. For instance, Mr. ——"

"Gowan," quietly said Doyce, upon whom the utterance of the name almost always devolved.

"Is young and handsome, easy and quick, has talent, and has seen a good deal of various kinds of life. It might be difficult to give an unselfish reason for being prepossessed against him."

"Not difficult for me, I think, Clennam," returned his partner. "I see him bringing present anxiety, and, I fear, future sorrow, into my old friend's house. I see him wearing deeper lines into my old friend's face, the nearer he draws to, and the oftener he looks at, the face of his daughter. In short, I see him with a net about the pretty and affectionate creature whom he will never make happy."

"We don't know," said Clennam, almost in the tone of a man in pain, "that he will not make her happy."

"We don't know," returned his partner, "that the earth will last another hundred years, but we think it highly probable."

"Well, well!" said Clennam, "we must be hopeful, and we must at least try to be, if not generous (which, in this case, we have no opportunity of being), just. We will not disparage this gentleman, because he is successful in his addresses to the beautiful object of his ambition; and we will not question her natural right to bestow her love on one whom she finds worthy of it."

"May be, my friend," said Doyce. "May be also, that she is too young and petted, too confiding and inexperienced, to discriminate well."

"That," said Clennam, "would be far beyond our power of correction."

Daniel Doyce shook his head gravely, and rejoined, "I fear so."

"Therefore, in a word," said Clennam, "we should make up our minds that it is not worthy of us to say any ill of Mr. Gowan. It would be a poor thing to gratify a prejudice against him. And I resolve, for my part, not to depreciate him."

"I am not quite so sure of myself, and therefore I reserve my privilege of objecting to him," returned the other. "But, if I am not sure of myself, I am sure of you, Clennam, and I know what an upright man you are, and how much to be respected. Good night, my friend and partner!" He shook his hand in saying this, as if there had been something serious at the bottom of their conversation; and they separated.

By this time, they had visited the family on several occasions, and had always observed that even a passing allusion to Mr. Henry Gowan when he was not among them, brought back the cloud which had obscured Mr. Meagles's sunshine on the morning of the chance encounter at the Ferry. If Clennam had ever admitted the forbidden passion into his breast, this period might have been a period of real trial; under the actual circumstances, doubtless it was nothing—nothing.

Equally, if his heart had given entertainment to that prohibited guest, his silent fighting of his way through the mental condition of this period might have been a little meritorious. In the constant effort not to be betrayed into a new phase of the besetting sin of his experience, the pursuit of selfish objects by low and small means, and to hold instead to some high principle of honor and generosity, there might have been a little merit. In the resolution not even to avoid Mr. Meagles's house, lest, in the selfish sparing of himself, he should bring any slight distress upon the daughter through making her the cause of an estrangement which he believed the father would regret, there might have been a little merit. In the modest truthfulness of always keeping in view the greater equality of Mr. Gowan's years, and the greater attractions of his person and manner, there might have been a little merit. In doing all this and much more, in a perfectly unaffected way and with a manful and composed constancy, while the pain within him (peculiar as his life and history) was very sharp, there might have been some quiet strength of character. But, after the resolution he had made, of course he could have no such merits as these; and such a state of mind was nobody's—nobody's.

Mr. Gowan made it no concern of his whether it was nobody's or some-body's. He preserved his perfect serenity of manner on all occasions, as if the possibility of Clennam's presuming to have debated the great question were too distant and ridiculous to be imagined. He had always an affability to bestow on Clennam and an ease to treat him with, which might of itself (in the supposititious case of his not having taken that sagacious course) have been a very uncomfortable element in his state of mind.

"I quite regret you were not with us yesterday," said Mr. Henry Gowan, calling on Clennam next morning. "We had an agreeable day up the river there."

So he had heard, Arthur said.

"From your partner?" returned Henry Gowan. "What a dear old fellow he is!"

"I have a great regard for him."

"By Jove he is the finest creature!" said Gowan. "So fresh, so green, trusts in such wonderful things!"

Here was one of the many little rough points that had a tendency to grate on Clennam's hearing. He put it aside by merely repeating that he had a high regard for Mr. Doyce.

"He is charming! To see him mooning along to that time of life, laying down nothing by the way and picking up nothing by the way, is delightful. It warms a man. So unspoilt, so simple, such a good soul! Upon my life, Mr. Clennam, one feels desperately worldly and wicked, in comparison with such an innocent creature. I speak for myself, let me add, without including you. You are genuine, also."

"Thank you for the compliment," said Clennam, ill at ease; "you are too, I hope?"

"So so," rejoined the other. "To be candid with you, tolerably. I am not a great impostor. Buy one of my pictures, and I assure you, in confidence, it will not be worth the money. Buy one of another man's—any great professor who beats me hollow—and the chances are that the more you give him, the more he'll impose upon you. They all do it."

"All painters?"

"Painters, writers, patriots, all the rest who have stands in the market. Give almost any man I know, ten pounds, and he will impose upon you to a corresponding extent; a thousand pounds—to a corresponding extent; ten thousand pounds—to a corresponding extent. So great the success, so great the imposition. But what a capital world it is!" cried Gowan with warm enthusiasm. "What a jolly, excellent loveable world it is!"

"I had rather thought," said Clennam, "that the principle you mention was chiefly acted on by——"

"By the Barnacles?" interrupted Gowan, laughing.

"By the political gentlemen who condescend to keep the Circumlocution Office."

"Ah! Don't be hard upon the Barnacles," said Gowan, laughing afresh, "they are darling fellows! Even poor little Clarence, the born idiot of the family, is the most agreeable and most endearing blockhead! And by Jupiter, with a kind of cleverness in him too, that would astonish you!"

"It would. Very much," said Clennam, drily.

"And after all," cried Gowan, with that characteristic balancing of his which reduced everything in the wide world to the same light weight, "though I can't deny that the Circumlocution Office may ultimately shipwreck everybody and everything, still, that will probably not be in our time—and it's a school for gentlemen."

"It's a very dangerous, unsatisfactory, and expensive school to the people who pay to keep the pupils there, I am afraid," said Clennam, shaking his head.

"Ah! You are a terrible fellow," returned Gowan, airily. "I can understand how you have frightened that little donkey, Clarence, the most estimable of mooncalves (I really love him), nearly out of his wits. But enough of him, and of all the rest of them. I want to present you to my mother, Mr. Clennam. Pray do me the favor to give me the opportunity."

In nobody's state of mind, there was nothing Clennam would have desired less, or would have been more at a loss how to avoid.

"My mother lives in the most primitive manner down in that dreary red-brick dungeon at Hampton Court," said Gowan. "If you would make your own appointment, suggest your own day for permitting me to take you there to dinner, you would be bored and she would be charmed. Really that's the state of the case."

What could Clennam say after this? His retiring character included a great deal that was simple in the best sense, because unpractised and unused; and, in his simplicity and modesty, he could only say that he was happy to place himself at Mr. Gowan's disposal. Accordingly he said it, and the day was fixed. And a dreaded day it was on his part, and a very unwelcome day when it came, and they went down to Hampton Court together.

The venerable inhabitants of that venerable pile seemed, in those times, to be encamped there like a sort of civilised gipsies. There was a temporary air about their establishments, as if they were going away the moment they could get anything better; there was also a dissatisfied air about themselves, as if they took it very ill that they had not already got something much better. Genteel blinds and make-shifts were more or less observable as soon as their doors were opened; screens not half high enough, which made dining-rooms out of arched passages, and warded off obscure corners where footboys slept at night with their heads among the knives and forks; curtains which called upon you to believe that they didn't hide anything; panes of glass which requested you not to see them; many objects of various forms, feigning to have no connexion with their guilty secret, a bed; disguised traps in walls, which were clearly coal-cellars; affectations of no thoroughfares, which were evidently doors to little kitchens. Mental reservations and artful mysteries grew out of these things. Callers, looking steadily into the eyes of their receivers, pretended not to smell cooking three feet off; people, confronting closets accidentally left open, pretended not to see bottles; visitors, with their heads against a partition of thin canvas and a page and a young female at high words on the other side, made believe to be sitting in a primeval silence. There was no end to the small social accommodation-bills of this nature which the gipsies of gentility were constantly drawing upon, and accepting for, one another.

Some of these Bohemians were of an irritable temperament, as constantly soured and vexed by two mental trials: the first, the consciousness that they had never got enough out of the public; the second, the consciousness that the public were admitted into the building. Under the latter great wrong, a few suffered dreadfully—particularly on Sundays, when they had for some time expected the earth to open and swallow the public up; but which desirable event had not yet occurred, in consequence of some reprehensible laxity in the arrangements of the Universe.

Mrs. Gowan's door was attended by a family servant of several years' standing, who had his own crow to pluck with the public, concerning a situation in the Post Office which he had been for some time expecting, and to which he was not yet appointed. He perfectly knew that the public could never have got him in, but he grimly gratified himself with the idea that the public kept him out. Under the influence of this injury (and perhaps of some little straitness and irregularity in the matter of wages), he had grown neglectful of his person and morose in mind; and now beholding in Clennam one of the degraded body of his oppressors, received him with ignominy.

Mrs. Gowan, however, received him with condescension. He found her a courtly old lady, formerly a Beauty, and still sufficiently well-favored to have dispensed with the powder on her nose, and a certain impossible bloom under each eye. She was a little lofty with him: so was another old lady, dark-browed and high-nosed, and who must have had something real about her or she couldn't have existed, but it was certainly not her hair or her teeth or her figure or her complexion; so was a grey old gentleman of dignified and sullen appearance; both of whom had come to dinner. But, as they had all been in the British Embassy way in sundry parts of the earth, and as a British Embassy cannot better establish a character with the Circumlocution Office than by treating its compatriots with illimitable contempt (else it would become like the Embassies of other countries), Clennam felt that on the whole they let him off lightly.

The dignified old gentleman turned out to be Lord Lancaster Stilt-stalking, who had been maintained by the Circumlocution Office for

many years as a representative of the Britannic Majesty abroad. This
noble Refrigerator had iced several European courts in his time, and had
done it with such complete success that the very name of Englishman yet
struck cold to the stomachs of foreigners who had the distinguished honor
of remembering him, at a distance of a quarter of a century.

He was now in retirement, and hence (in a ponderous white cravat, like
a stiff snow-drift) was so obliging as to shade the dinner. There was a
whisper of the pervading Bohemian character in the nomadic nature of
the service, and its curious races of plates and dishes; but the noble Refrigerator, infinitely better than plate or porcelain, made it superb. He
shaded the dinner, cooled the wines, chilled the gravy, and blighted the
vegetables.

There was only one other person in the room: a microscopically small
footboy, who waited on the malevolent man who hadn't got into the Post
Office. Even this youth, if his jacket could have been unbuttoned and his
heart laid bare, would have been seen, as a distant adherent of the Barnacle
family, already to aspire to a situation under Government.

Mrs. Gowan with a gentle melancholy upon her, occasioned by her son's
being reduced to court the swinish public as a follower of the low Arts,
instead of asserting his birthright and putting a ring through its nose as
an acknowledged Barnacle, headed the conversation at dinner on the evil
days. It was then that Clennam learned for the first time what little pivots
this great world goes round upon.

"If John Barnacle," said Mrs. Gowan, after the degeneracy of the times
had been fully ascertained, "if John Barnacle had but abandoned his most
unfortunate idea of conciliating the mob, all would have been well, and
I think the country would have been preserved."

The old lady with the high nose assented, but added that if Augustus
Stiltstalking had in a general way ordered the cavalry out with instructions to charge, she thought the country would have been preserved.

The noble Refrigerator assented; but added that if William Barnacle and
Tudor Stiltstalking, when they came over to one another and formed their
ever memorable coalition, had boldly muzzled the newspapers, and
rendered it penal for any Editor-person to presume to discuss the conduct
of any appointed authority abroad or at home, he thought the country
would have been preserved.

It was agreed that the country (another word for the Barnacles and
Stiltstalkings) wanted preserving, but how it came to want preserving
was not so clear. It was only clear that the question was all about John
Barnacle, Augustus Stiltstalking, William Barnacle and Tudor Stiltstalking, Tom, Dick, or Harry Barnacle or Stiltstalking, because there
was nobody else but mob. And this was the feature of the conversation which impressed Clennam, as a man not used to it, very disagreeably: making him doubt if it were quite right to sit there, silently

hearing a great nation narrowed to such little bounds. Remembering, however, that in the Parliamentary debates, whether on the life of that nation's body or the life of its soul, the question was usually all about and between John Barnacle, Augustus Stiltstalking, William Barnacle and Tudor Stiltstalking, Tom, Dick, or Harry Barnacle or Stiltstalking, and nobody else; he said nothing on the part of mob, bethinking himself that mob was used to it.

Mr. Henry Gowan seemed to have a malicious pleasure in playing off the three talkers against each other, and in seeing Clennam startled by what they said. Having as supreme a contempt for the class that had thrown him off, as for the class that had not taken him on, he had no personal disquiet in anything that passed. His healthy state of mind appeared even to derive a gratification from Clennam's position of embarrassment and isolation among the good company; and if Clennam had been in that condition with which Nobody was incessantly contending, he would have suspected it, and would have struggled with the suspicion as a meanness, even while he sat at the table.

In the course of a couple of hours the noble Refrigerator, at no time less than a hundred years behind the period, got about five centuries in arrear, and delivered solemn political oracles appropriate to that epoch. He finished by freezing a cup of tea for his own drinking, and retiring at his lowest temperature.

Then Mrs. Gowan, who had been accustomed in her days of state to retain a vacant arm-chair beside her to which to summon her devoted slaves, one by one, for short audiences as marks of her especial favor, invited Clennam with a turn of her fan to approach the presence. He obeyed, and took the tripod recently vacated by Lord Lancaster Stiltstalking.

"Mr. Clennam," said Mrs. Gowan, "apart from the happiness I have in becoming known to you, though in this odiously inconvenient place—a mere barrack—there is a subject on which I am dying to speak to you. It is the subject in connexion with which my son first had, I believe, the pleasure of cultivating your acquaintance."

Clennam inclined his head, as a generally suitable reply to what he did not yet quite understand.

"First," said Mrs. Gowan, "now is she really pretty?"

In nobody's difficulties, he would have found it very difficult to answer; very difficult indeed to smile, and say "Who?"

"Oh! You know!" she returned. "This flame of Henry's. This unfortunate fancy. There! If it is a point of honor that I should originate the name—Miss Mickles—Miggles."

"Miss Meagles," said Clennam, "is very beautiful."

"Men are so often mistaken on those points," returned Mrs. Gowan, shaking her head, "that I candidly confess to you I feel anything but

sure of it, even now; though it is something to have Henry corroborated
with so much gravity and emphasis. He picked the people up at Rome,
I think?"

The phrase would have given nobody mortal offence. Clennam replied
"Excuse me, I doubt if I understand your expression."

"Picked the people up," said Mrs. Gowan, tapping the sticks of her
closed fan (a large green one, which she used as a hand-screen) upon her
little table. "Came upon them. Found them out. Stumbled against them."

"The people?"

"Yes. The Miggles people."

"I really cannot say," said Clennam, "where my friend Mr. Meagles
first presented Mr. Henry Gowan to his daughter."

"I am pretty sure he picked her up at Rome; but never mind where
—somewhere. Now (this is entirely between ourselves), is she very
plebeian?"

"Really, ma'am," returned Clennam, "I am so undoubtedly plebeian
myself, that I do not feel qualified to judge."

"Very neat!" said Mrs. Gowan, coolly unfurling her screen. "Very
happy! From which I infer that you secretly think her manner equal to
her looks?"

Clennam, after a moment's stiffness, bowed.

"That's comforting, and I hope you may be right. Did Henry tell me
you had travelled with them?"

"I travelled with my friend Mr. Meagles, and his wife and daughter,
during some months." (Nobody's heart might have been wrung by the
remembrance.)

"Really comforting, because you must have had a large experience of
them. You see, Mr. Clennam, this thing has been going on for a long time,
and I find no improvement in it. Therefore to have the opportunity of
speaking to one so well informed about it as yourself, is an immense relief
to me. Quite a boon. Quite a blessing, I am sure."

"Pardon me," returned Clennam, "but I am not in Mr. Henry Gowan's
confidence. I am far from being so well informed as you suppose me to be.
Your mistake makes my position a very delicate one. No word on this topic
has ever passed between Mr. Henry Gowan and myself."

Mrs. Gowan glanced at the other end of the room, where her son was
playing écarté on a sofa, with the old lady who was for a charge of cavalry.

"Not in his confidence? No," said Mrs. Gowan. "No word has passed
between you? No. That I can imagine. But there are unexpressed confidences, Mr. Clennam; and as you have been together intimately among
these people, I cannot doubt that a confidence of that sort exists in the
present case. Perhaps you have heard that I have suffered the keenest
distress of mind from Henry's having taken to a pursuit which—well!"
shrugging her shoulders, "a very respectable pursuit, I dare say, and some

artists are, as artists, quite superior persons; still, we never yet in our family have gone beyond an Amateur, and it is a pardonable weakness to feel a little——"

As Mrs. Gowan broke off to heave a sigh, Clennam, however resolute to be magnanimous, could not keep down the thought that there was mighty little danger of the family's ever going beyond an Amateur, even as it was.

"Henry," the mother resumed, "is self-willed and resolute; and as these people naturally strain every nerve to catch him, I can entertain very little hope, Mr. Clennam, that the thing will be broken off. I apprehend the girl's fortune will be very small; Henry might have done much better; there is scarcely anything to compensate for the connexion: still, he acts for himself; and if I find no improvement within a short time, I see no other course than to resign myself, and make the best of these people. I am infinitely obliged to you for what you have told me."

As she shrugged her shoulders, Clennam stiffly bowed again. With an uneasy flush upon his face, and hesitation in his manner, he then said, in a still lower tone than he had adopted yet:

"Mrs. Gowan, I scarcely know how to acquit myself of what I feel to be a duty, and yet I must ask you for your kind consideration in attempting to discharge it. A misconception on your part, a very great misconception if I may venture to call it so; seems to require setting right. You have supposed Mr. Meagles and his family to strain every nerve, I think you said——"

"Every nerve," repeated Mrs. Gowan, looking at him in calm obstinacy, with her green fan between her face and the fire.

"To secure Mr. Henry Gowan?"

The lady placidly assented.

"Now that is so far," said Arthur, "from being the case, that I know Mr. Meagles to be unhappy in this matter; and to have interposed all reasonable obstacles, with the hope of putting an end to it."

Mrs. Gowan shut up her great green fan, tapped him on the arm with it, and tapped her smiling lips. "Why, of course," said she. "Just what I mean."

Arthur watched her face for some explanation of what she did mean.

"Are you really serious, Mr. Clennam? Don't you see?"

Arthur did not see; and said so.

"Why, don't I know my son, and don't I know that this is exactly the way to hold him?" said Mrs. Gowan, contemptuously; "and do not these Miggles people know it, at least as well as I? Oh, shrewd people, Mr. Clennam: evidently people of business! I believe Miggles belonged to a Bank. It ought to have been a very profitable Bank, if he had much to do with its management. This is very well done, indeed."

"I beg and entreat you, ma'am——" Arthur interposed.

"Oh Mr. Clennam, can you really be so credulous!"

It made such a painful impression upon him to hear her talking in this haughty tone, and to see her patting her contemptuous lips with her fan, that he said very earnestly, "Believe me, ma'am, this is unjust, a perfectly groundless suspicion."

"Suspicion?" repeated Mrs. Gowan. "Not suspicion, Mr. Clennam, Certainty. It is very knowingly done indeed, and seems to have taken *you* in completely." She laughed; and again sat tapping her lips with her fan, and tossing her head, as if she added, "Don't tell me. I know such people will do anything for the honor of such an alliance."

At this opportune moment, the cards were thrown up, and Mr. Henry Gowan came across the room saying, "Mother, if you can spare Mr. Clennam for this time, we have a long way to go, and it's getting late." Mr. Clennam thereupon rose, as he had no choice but to do; and Mrs. Gowan showed him, to the last, the same look and the same tapped contemptuous lips.

"You have had a portentously long audience of my mother," said Gowan, as the door closed upon them. "I fervently hope she has not bored you?"

"Not at all," said Clennam.

They had a little open phaeton for the journey, and were soon in it on the road home. Gowan, driving, lighted a cigar; Clennam declined one. Do what he would, he fell into such a mood of abstraction, that Gowan said again, "I am very much afraid my mother has bored you?" To which he roused himself to answer, "Not at all;" and soon relapsed again.

In that state of mind which rendered nobody uneasy, his thoughtfulness would have turned principally on the man at his side. He would have thought of the morning when he first saw him rooting out the stones with his heel, and would have asked himself "Does he jerk me out of the path in the same careless, cruel way?" He would have thought, had this introduction to his mother been brought about by him because he knew what she would say, and that he could thus place his position before a rival and loftily warn him off, without himself reposing a word of confidence in him? He would have thought, even if there were no such design as that, had he brought him there to play with his repressed emotions, and torment him? The current of these meditations would have been stayed sometimes by a rush of shame, bearing a remonstrance to himself from his own open nature, representing that to shelter such suspicions, even for the passing moment, was not to hold the high, unenvious course he had resolved to keep. At those times, the striving within him would have been hardest; and looking up and catching Gowan's eyes, he would have started as if he had done him an injury.

Then, looking at the dark road and its uncertain objects, he would have gradually trailed off again into thinking, "Where are we driving, he and I, I wonder, on the darker road of life? How will it be with us, and with her, in the obscure distance?" Thinking of her, he would have been troubled

anew with a reproachful misgiving that it was not even loyal to her to
dislike him, and that in being so easily prejudiced against him he was less
deserving of her than at first.

"You are evidently out of spirits," said Gowan; "I am very much afraid
my mother must have bored you dreadfully."

"Believe me, not at all," said Clennam. "It's nothing—nothing!"

CHAPTER XXVII

FIVE-AND-TWENTY

A FREQUENTLY recurring doubt, whether Mr. Pancks's desire to collect
information relative to the Dorrit family could have any possible bearing
on the misgivings he had imparted to his mother on his return from his long
exile, caused Arthur Clennam much uneasiness at this period. What Mr.
Pancks already knew about the Dorrit family, what more he really wanted to
find out, and why he should trouble his busy head about them at all, were
questions that often perplexed him. Mr. Pancks was not a man to waste his
time and trouble in researches prompted by idle curiosity. That he had
a specific object Clennam could not doubt. And whether the attainment
of that object by Mr. Pancks's industry might bring to light, in some untimely way, secret reasons which had induced his mother to take Little
Dorrit by the hand, was a serious speculation.

Not that he ever wavered, either in his desire or his determination to
repair a wrong that had been done in his father's time, should a wrong
come to light, and be reparable. The shadow of a supposed act of injustice,
which had hung over him since his father's death, was so vague and form-
less that it might be the result of a reality widely remote from his idea of it.
But, if his apprehensions should prove to be well founded, he was ready at
any moment to lay down all he had, and begin the world anew. As the
fierce dark teaching of his childhood had never sunk into his heart, so the
first article in his code of morals was, that he must begin, in practical
humility, with looking well to his feet on Earth, and that he could never
mount on wings of words to Heaven. Duty on earth, restitution on earth,
action on earth: these first, as the first steep steps upward. Strait was the
gate and narrow was the way; far straiter and narrower than the broad
high road paved with vain professions and vain repetitions, motes from
other men's eyes and liberal delivery of others to the judgment—all cheap
materials, costing absolutely nothing.

No. It was not a selfish fear or hesitation that rendered him uneasy, but
a mistrust lest Pancks might not observe his part of the understanding
between them, and, making any discovery, might take some course upon

it without imparting it to him. On the other hand, when he recalled his conversation with Pancks, and the little reason he had to suppose that there was any likelihood of that strange personage being on that track at all, there were times when he wondered that he made so much of it. Laboring in this sea, as all barks labor in cross seas, he tossed about, and came to no haven.

The removal of Little Dorrit herself from their customary association, did not mend the matter. She was so much out, and so much in her own room, that he began to miss her and to find a blank in her place. He had written to her to enquire if she were better, and she had written back, very gratefully and earnestly, telling him not to be uneasy on her behalf, for she was quite well; but he had not seen her, for what, in their intercourse, was a long time.

He returned home one evening from an interview with her father, who had mentioned that she was out visiting—which was what he always said, when she was hard at work to buy his supper—and found Mr. Meagles in an excited state walking up and down his room. On his opening the door, Mr. Meagles stopped, faced round, and said,

"Clennam!—Tattycoram!"

"What's the matter?"

"Lost!"

"Why, bless my heart alive!" cried Clennam, in amazement. "What do you mean?"

"Wouldn't count five-and-twenty, sir; couldn't be got to do it; stopped at eight, and took herself off."

"Left your house?"

"Never to come back," said Mr. Meagles, shaking his head. "You don't know that girl's passionate and proud character. A team of horses couldn't draw her back now; the bolts and bars of the old Bastille couldn't keep her."

"How did it happen? Pray sit down and tell me."

"As to how it happened, it's not so easy to relate; because you must have the unfortunate temperament of the poor impetuous girl herself, before you can fully understand it. But it came about in this way. Pet and Mother and I have been having a good deal of talk together, of late. I'll not disguise from you, Clennam, that those conversations have not been of as bright a kind as I could wish; they have referred to our going away again. In proposing to do which, I have had, in fact, an object."

Nobody's heart beat quickly.

"An object," said Mr. Meagles, after a moment's pause, "that I will not disguise from you, either, Clennam. There's an inclination on the part of my dear child which I am sorry for. Perhaps you guess the person. Henry Gowan."

"I was not unprepared to hear it."

"Well!" said Mr. Meagles, with a heavy sigh, "I wish to God you had never had to hear it. However, so it is. Mother and I have done all we could to get the better of it, Clennam. We have tried tender advice, we have tried time, we have tried absence. As yet, of no use. Our late conversations have been upon the subject of going away for another year at least, in order that there might be an entire separation and breaking off for that term. Upon that question, Pet has been unhappy, and therefore Mother and I have been unhappy."

Clennam said that he could easily believe it.

"Well!" continued Mr. Meagles in an apologetic way, "I admit as a practical man, and I am sure Mother would admit as a practical woman, that we do, in families, magnify our troubles and make mountains of our molehills, in a way that is calculated to be rather trying to people who look on—to mere outsiders you know, Clennam. Still, Pet's happiness or unhappiness is quite a life or death question with us; and we may be excused, I hope, for making much of it. At all events, it might have been borne by Tattycoram. Now, don't you think so?"

"I do indeed think so," returned Clennam, in most emphatic recognition of this very moderate expectation.

"No, sir," said Mr. Meagles, shaking his head ruefully. "She couldn't stand it. The chafing and firing of that girl, the wearing and tearing of that girl within her own breast, has been such that I have softly said to her again and again in passing her, 'Five-and-twenty, Tattycoram, five-and-twenty!' I heartily wish she could have gone on counting five-and-twenty day and night, and then it wouldn't have happened."

Mr. Meagles, with a despondent countenance in which the goodness of his heart was even more expressed than in his times of cheerfulness and gaiety, stroked his face down from his forehead to his chin, and shook his head again.

"I said to Mother (not that it was necessary, for she would have thought it all for herself), we are practical people, my dear, and we know her story; we see, in this unhappy girl, some reflection of what was raging in her mother's heart before ever such a creature as this poor thing was, in the world; we'll gloss her temper over, Mother, we won't notice it at present, my dear, we'll take advantage of some better disposition in her, another time. So we said nothing. But, do what we would, it seems as if it was to be; she broke out violently one night."

"How, and why?"

"If you ask me Why," said Mr. Meagles, a little disturbed by the question, for he was far more intent on softening her case than the family's, "I can only refer you to what I have just repeated as having been pretty near my words to Mother. As to How, we had said Good night to Pet in her presence (very affectionately, I must allow), and she had attended Pet up-stairs—you remember she was her maid. Perhaps Pet, having been out of sorts, may have been a little more inconsiderate than usual in requiring services of her: but I don't know that I have any right to say so; she was always thoughtful and gentle."

"The gentlest mistress in the world."

"Thank you, Clennam," said Mr. Meagles, shaking him by the hand; "you have often seen them together. Well! We presently heard this unfortunate Tattycoram loud and angry, and before we could ask what was the matter, Pet came back in a tremble, saying she was frightened of her. Close after her came Tattycoram, in a flaming rage. 'I hate you all three,' says she, stamping her foot at us. 'I am bursting with hate of the whole house.'"

"Upon which you——?"

"I?" said Mr. Meagles, with a plain good faith, that might have commanded the belief of Mrs. Gowan herself: "I said, count five-and-twenty, Tattycoram."

Mr. Meagles again stroked his face and shook his head, with an air of profound regret.

"She was so used to do it, Clennam, that even then, such a picture of passion as you never saw, she stopped short, looked me full in the face, and counted (as I made out) to eight. But she couldn't control herself to go any further. There she broke down, poor thing, and gave the other seventeen to the four winds. Then it all burst out. She detested us, she was miserable with us, she couldn't bear it, she wouldn't bear it, she was determined to go away. She was younger than her young mistress, and would she remain to see *her* always held up as the only creature who was young and interesting, and to be cherished and loved? No. She wouldn't, she wouldn't, she wouldn't! What did we think she, Tattycoram, might have been if she had been caressed and cared for in her childhood, like her young mistress? As good as her? Ah! Perhaps fifty times as good. When we pretended to be so fond of one another, we exulted over her; that was what we did; we exulted over her, and shamed her. And all in the house did the same. They talked about their fathers and mothers, and brothers and sisters; they liked to drag them up, before her face. There was Mrs. Tickit, only yesterday, when her little grandchild was with her, had been amused by the child's trying to call her (Tattycoram) by the wretched name we gave her; and had laughed at the name. Why, who didn't; and who were we that we should have a right to name her like a dog or a cat? But, she didn't care. She would take no more benefits from us; she would fling us her name back again, and she would go. She would leave us that minute, nobody should stop her, and we should never hear of her again."

Mr. Meagles had recited all this with such a vivid remembrance of his original, that he was almost as flushed and hot by this time as he described her to have been.

"Ah, well!" he said, wiping his face. "It was of no use trying reason then, with that vehement panting creature (Heaven knows what her mother's story must have been); so I quietly told her that she should not go at that late hour of night, and I gave her my hand and took her to her room, and locked the house-doors. But she was gone this morning."

"And you know no more of her?"

"No more," returned Mr. Meagles. "I have been hunting about all day. She must have gone very early and very silently. I have found no trace of her, down about us."

"Stay!" said Clennam, after a moment's reflection. "I assume that you want to see her?"

"Yes, assuredly; I want to give her another chance; Mother and Pet want to give her another chance; come! You yourself," said Mr. Meagles, persuasively, as if the provocation to be angry were not his own at all, "want to give the poor passionate girl another chance, I know, Clennam."

"It would be strange and hard indeed if I did not," said Clennam, "when you are all so forgiving. What I was going to ask you was, have you thought of that Miss Wade?"

"I have. I did not think of her until I had pervaded the whole of our neighbourhood, and I don't know that I should have done so then, but for finding Mother and Pet, when I went home, full of the idea that Tattycoram must have gone to her. Then, of course, I recalled what she said that day at dinner when you were first with us."

"Have you any idea where Miss Wade is to be found?"

"To tell you the truth," returned Mr. Meagles, "it's because I have an addled jumble of a notion on that subject, that you found me waiting here. There is one of those odd impressions in my house which do mysteriously get into houses sometimes, which nobody seems to have picked up in a distinct form from anybody, and yet which everybody seems to have got hold of loosely from somebody and let go again, that she lives, or was living, thereabouts." Mr. Meagles handed him a slip of paper, on which was written the name of one of the dull bye-streets in the Grosvenor region, near Park Lane.

"Here is no number," said Arthur, looking over it.

"No number, my dear Clennam?" returned his friend. "No anything! The very name of the street may have been floating in the air, for, as I tell you, none of my people can say where they got it from. However, it's worth an enquiry; and as I would rather make it in company than alone, and as you too were a fellow-traveller of that immovable woman's, I thought perhaps——" Clennam finished the sentence for him by taking up his hat again, and saying he was ready.

It was now summer-time; a grey, hot, dusty evening. They rode to the top of Oxford Street, and, there alighting, dived in among the great streets of melancholy stateliness, and the little streets that try to be as stately and succeed in being more melancholy, of which there is a labyrinth near Park

Lane. Wildernesses of corner-houses, with barbarous old porticoes and appurtenances; horrors that came into existence under some wrong-headed person in some wrong-headed time, still demanding the blind admiration of all ensuing generations and determined to do so until they tumbled down; frowned upon the twilight. Parasite little tenements with the cramp in their whole frame, from the dwarf hall-door on the giant model of His Grace's in the Square, to the squeezed window of the boudoir commanding the dunghills in the Mews, made the evening doleful. Ricketty dwellings of undoubted fashion, but of a capacity to hold nothing comfortably except a dismal smell, looked like the last result of the great mansions' breeding in-and-in; and, where their little supplementary bows and balconies were supported on thin iron columns, seemed to be scrofulously resting upon crutches. Here and there a Hatchment, with the whole science of Heraldry in it, loomed down upon the street, like an Archbishop discoursing on Vanity. The shops, few in number, made no show; for popular opinion was as nothing to them. The pastry-cook knew who was on his books, and in that knowledge could be calm, with a few glass cylinders of dowager peppermint-drops in his window, and half-a-dozen ancient specimens of currant jelly. A few oranges formed the greengrocer's whole concession to the vulgar mind. A single basket made of moss, once containing plovers' eggs, held all that the poulterer had to say to the rabble. Everybody in those streets seemed (which is always the case at that hour and season) to be gone out to dinner, and nobody seemed to be giving the dinners they had gone to. On the door-steps there were lounging, footmen with bright parti-colored plumage and white polls, like an extinct race of monstrous birds; and butlers, solitary men of recluse demeanour, each of whom appeared distrustful of all other butlers. The roll of carriages in the Park was done for the day; the street lamps were lighting; and wicked little grooms in the tightest fitting garments, with twists in their legs answering to the twists in their minds, hung about in pairs, chewing straw and exchanging fraudulent secrets. The spotted dogs who went out with the carriages, and who were so associated with splendid equipages, that it looked like a condescension in those animals to come out without them, accompanied helpers to and fro on messages. Here and there was a retiring public-house which did not require to be supported on the shoulders of the people, and where gentlemen out of livery were not much wanted.

This last discovery was made by the two friends in pursuing their enquiries. Nothing was there, or anywhere, known of such a person as Miss Wade, in connexion with the street they sought. It was one of the parasite streets; long, regular, narrow, dull, and gloomy; like a brick and mortar funeral. They enquired at several little area gates, where a dejected youth stood spiking his chin on the summit of a precipitous little shoot of wooden steps, but could gain no information. They walked up the street on one side of the way, and down it on the other, what time two vociferous news-sellers, announcing an extraordinary event that had never happened and never would happen, pitched their hoarse voices into the secret chambers; but nothing came of it. At length they stood at the corner from which they had begun, and it had fallen quite dark, and they were no wiser.

It happened that in the street they had several times passed a dingy house, apparently empty, with bills in the windows, announcing that it was to let. The bills, as a variety in the funeral procession, almost amounted to a decoration. Perhaps because they kept the house separate in his mind, or perhaps because Mr. Meagles and himself had twice agreed in passing, "It is clear she don't live there," Clennam now proposed that they should go back and try that house before finally going away. Mr. Meagles agreed, and back they went.

They knocked once, and they rang once, without any response. "Empty," said Mr. Meagles, listening. "Once more," said Clennam, and knocked again. After that knock they heard a movement below, and somebody shuffling up towards the door.

The confined entrance was so dark, that it was impossible to make out distinctly what kind of person opened the door; but it appeared to be an old woman. "Excuse our troubling you," said Clennam. "Pray can you tell us where Miss Wade lives?" The voice in the darkness unexpectedly replied, "Lives here."

"Is she at home?"

No answer coming, Mr. Meagles asked again, "Pray, is she at home?" After another delay, "I suppose she is," said the voice abruptly; "you had better come in, and I'll ask."

They were summarily shut into the close black house; and the figure rustling away, and speaking from a higher level, said, "Come up if you please; you can't tumble over anything." They groped their way up-stairs towards a faint light, which proved to be the light of the street shining through a window; and the figure left them shut up in an airless room.

"This is odd, Clennam," said Mr. Meagles, softly.

"Odd enough," assented Clennam, in the same tone, "but we have succeeded; that's the main point. Here's a light coming!"

The light was a lamp, and the bearer was an old woman: very dirty, very wrinkled and dry. "She's at home," she said (and the voice was the same that had spoken before); "she'll come directly." Having set the lamp down on the table, the old woman dusted her hands on her apron, which she might have done for ever without cleaning them, looked at the visitors with a dim pair of eyes, and backed out.

The lady whom they had come to see, if she were the present occupant of the house, appeared to have taken up her quarters there, as she might have established herself in an Eastern caravanserai. A small square of carpet in the middle of the room, a few articles of furniture that evidently did not belong to the room, and a disorder of trunks and travelling articles,

formed the whole of her surroundings. Under some former regular inhabitant, the stifling little apartment had broken out into a pier-glass and
a gilt table; but the gilding was as faded as last year's flowers, and the glass
was so clouded that it seemed to hold in magic preservation all the fogs and
bad weather it had ever reflected. The visitors had had a minute or two to
look about them, when the door opened and Miss Wade came in.

She was exactly the same as when they had parted. Just as handsome,
just as scornful, just as repressed. She manifested no surprise in seeing
them, nor any other emotion. She requested them to be seated; and
declining to take a seat herself, at once anticipated any introduction of their
business.

"I apprehend," she said, "that I know the cause of your favoring me
with this visit. We may come to it at once."

"The cause then, ma'am," said Mr. Meagles, "is Tattycoram."

"So I supposed."

"Miss Wade," said Mr. Meagles, "will you be so kind as to say whether
you know anything of her?"

"Surely. I know she is here with me."

"Then, ma'am," said Mr. Meagles, "allow me to make known to you
that I shall be happy to have her back, and that my wife and daughter will
be happy to have her back. She has been with us a long time, we don't
forget her claims upon us, and I hope we know how to make allowances."

"You hope you know how to make allowances?" she returned, in a level,
measured voice. "For what?"

"I think my friend would say, Miss Wade," Arthur Clennam interposed,
seeing Mr. Meagles rather at a loss, "for the passionate sense that sometimes comes upon the poor girl, of being at a disadvantage. Which occasionally gets the better of better remembrances."

The lady broke into a smile, as she turned her eyes upon him. "Indeed?"
was all she answered.

She stood by the table so perfectly composed and still after this acknowledgment of his remark, that Mr. Meagles stared at her under a sort of
fascination, and could not even look to Clennam to make another move.
After waiting, awkwardly enough, for some moments, Arthur said:

"Perhaps it would be well if Mr. Meagles could see her, Miss Wade?"

"That is easily done," said she. "Come here, child." She had opened
a door while saying this, and now led the girl in by the hand. It was very
curious to see them standing together: the girl with her disengaged fingers
plaiting the bosom of her dress, half irresolutely, half passionately; Miss
Wade with her composed face attentively regarding her, and suggesting
to an observer with extraordinary force, in her composure itself (as a veil
will suggest the form it covers), the unquenchable passion of her own
nature.

"See here," she said, in the same level way as before, "Here is your patron, your master. He is willing to take you back, my dear, if you are sensible of the favor and choose to go. You can be, again, a foil to his pretty daughter, a slave to her pleasant wilfulness, and a toy in the house showing the goodness of the family. You can have your droll name again, playfully pointing you out and setting you apart, as it is right that you should be pointed out and set apart. (Your birth, you know; you must not forget your birth.) You can again be shown to this gentleman's daughter, Harriet, and kept before her, as a living reminder of her own superiority and her gracious condescension. You can recover all these advantages, and many more of the same kind which I dare say start up in your memory while I speak, and which you lose in taking refuge with me—you can recover them all, by telling these gentlemen how humbled and penitent you are, and by going back with them to be forgiven. What do you say, Harriet? Will you go?"

The girl who, under the influence of these words, had gradually risen in anger and heightened in color, answered, raising her lustrous black eyes for the moment, and clenching her hand upon the folds it had been puckering up, "I'll die sooner!"

Miss Wade, still standing at her side holding her hand, looked quietly round and said with a smile, "Gentlemen! What do you do upon that?"

Poor Mr. Meagles's inexpressible consternation in hearing his motives and actions so perverted, had prevented him from interposing any word until now; but now he regained the power of speech.

"Tattycoram," said he, "for I'll call you by that name still, my good girl, conscious that I meant nothing but kindness when I gave it to you, and conscious that you know it——"

"I don't!" said she, looking up again, and almost rending herself with the same busy hand.

"No, not now, perhaps," said Mr. Meagles, "not with that lady's eyes so intent upon you, Tattycoram," she glanced at them for a moment, "and that power over you which we see she exercises; not now, perhaps, but at another time. Tattycoram, I'll not ask that lady whether she believes what she has said, even in the anger and ill blood in which I and my friend here equally know she has spoken, though she subdues herself with a determination that any one who has once seen her is not likely to forget. I'll not ask you, with your remembrance of my house and all belonging to it, whether you believe it. I'll only say that you have no profession to make to me or mine, and no forgiveness to entreat; and that all in the world that I ask you to do, is to count five-and-twenty, Tattycoram."

She looked at him for an instant, and then said frowningly, "I won't. Miss Wade, take me away, please."

The contention that raged within her had no softening in it now; it was wholly between passionate defiance and stubborn defiance. Her rich color, her quick blood, her rapid breath, were all setting themselves against the opportunity of retracing her steps. "I won't. I won't. I won't!" she repeated in a low, thick voice. "I'd be torn to pieces first. I'd tear myself to pieces first!"

Miss Wade, who had released her hold, laid her hand protectingly on the girl's neck for a moment, and then said, looking round with her former smile, and speaking exactly in her former tone, "Gentlemen! What do you do upon that?"

"Oh, Tattycoram, Tattycoram!" cried Mr. Meagles, adjuring her besides with an earnest hand. "Hear that lady's voice, look at that lady's face, consider what is in that lady's heart, and think what a future lies before you. My child, whatever you may think, that lady's influence over you—astonishing to us, and I should hardly go too far in saying terrible to us, to see—is founded in passion fiercer than yours and temper more violent than yours. What can you two be together? What can come of it?"

"I am alone here, gentlemen," observed Miss Wade, with no change of voice or manner. "Say anything you will."

"Politeness must yield to this misguided girl, ma'am," said Mr. Meagles, "at her present pass; though I hope not altogether to dismiss it, even with the injury you do her so strongly before me. Excuse me for reminding you in her hearing—I must say it—that you were a mystery to all of us, and had nothing in common with any of us, when she unfortunately fell in your way. I don't know what you are, but you don't hide, can't hide, what a dark spirit you have within you. If it should happen that you are a woman, who, from whatever cause, has a perverted delight in making a sister-woman as wretched as she is (I am old enough to have heard of such), I warn her against you, and I warn you against yourself."

"Gentlemen!" said Miss Wade, calmly. "When you have concluded— Mr. Clennam, perhaps you will induce your friend——"

"Not without another effort," said Mr. Meagles, stoutly. "Tattycoram, my poor dear girl, count five-and-twenty."

"Do not reject the hope, the certainty, this kind man offers you," said Clennam, in a low emphatic voice. "Turn to the friends you have not forgotten. Think once more!"

"I won't! Miss Wade," said the girl, with her bosom swelling high, and speaking with her hand held to her throat, "take me away!"

"Tattycoram," said Mr. Meagles. "Once more yet! The only thing I ask of you in the world, my child! Count five-and-twenty!"

She put her hands tightly over her ears, confusedly tumbling down her bright black hair in the vehemence of the action, and turned her face resolutely to the wall. Miss Wade, who had watched her under this final appeal with that strange attentive smile, and that repressing hand upon her own bosom, with which she had watched her in her struggle at Marseilles, then put her arm about her waist as if she took possession of her for ever-more.

And there was a visible triumph in her face when she turned it to dismiss the visitors.

"As it is the last time I shall have this honor," she said, "and as you have spoken of not knowing what I am, and also of the foundation of my influence here, you may now   know that it is founded in a common cause. What your broken plaything is as to birth, I am. She has no name, I have no name. Her wrong is my wrong. I have nothing more to say to you."

This was addressed to Mr. Meagles, who sorrowfully went out. As Clennam followed, she said to him, with the same external composure and in the same level voice, but with a smile that is only seen on cruel faces: a very faint smile, lifting the nostril, scarcely touching the lips, and not breaking away gradually, but instantly dismissed when done with:

"I hope the wife of your dear friend, Mr. Gowan, may be happy in the contrast of her extraction to this girl's and mine, and in the high good fortune that awaits her."

CHAPTER XXVIII

NOBODY'S DISAPPEARANCE

NOT resting satisfied with the endeavours he had made to recover his lost charge, Mr. Meagles addressed a letter of remonstrance, breathing nothing but goodwill, not only to her, but to Miss Wade too. No answer coming to these epistles, or to another written to the stubborn girl by the hand of her late young mistress, which might have melted her if anything could (all three letters were returned weeks afterwards, as having been refused at the house-door), he deputed Mrs. Meagles to make the experiment of a personal interview. That worthy lady being unable to obtain one, and being stedfastly denied admission, Mr. Meagles besought Arthur to essay once more what he could do. All that came of his compliance was, his discovery that the empty house was left in charge of the old woman, that Miss Wade was gone, that the waifs and strays of furniture were gone, and that the old woman would accept any number of half-crowns and thank the donor kindly, but had no information whatever to exchange for those coins, beyond constantly offering for perusal a memor-
-andum relative to fixtures, which the house-agent's young man had left in the hall.

Unwilling, even under this discomfiture, to resign the ingrate and leave her hopeless, in case of her better dispositions obtaining the mastery over the darker side of her character, Mr. Meagles, for six successive days, published a discreetly covert advertisement in the morning papers, to the effect that if a certain young person who had lately left home without

reflection, would at any time apply at his address at Twickenham, everything would be as it had been before, and no reproaches need be appre-
hended. The unexpected consequences of this notification, suggested to
the dismayed Mr. Meagles for the first time that some hundreds of young
persons must be leaving their homes without reflection, every day; for,
shoals of wrong young people came down to Twickenham, who, not finding
themselves received with enthusiasm, generally demanded compensation
by way of damages, in addition to coach-hire there and back. Nor were
these the only uninvited clients whom the advertisement produced. The
swarm of begging-letter writers who would seem to be always watching
eagerly for any hook, however small, to hang a letter upon, wrote to say that
having seen the advertisement, they were induced to apply with confidence
for various sums, ranging from ten shillings to fifty pounds: not because
they knew anything about the young person, but because they felt that to
part with those donations would greatly relieve the advertiser's mind.
Several projectors, likewise, availed themselves of the same opportunity
to correspond with Mr. Meagles; as, for example, to apprise him that their
attention having been called to the advertisement by a friend, they begged
to state that if they should ever hear anything of the young person, they
would not fail to make it known to him immediately, and that in the meantime if he would oblige them with the funds necessary for bringing to
perfection a certain entirely novel description of Pump, the happiest
results would ensue to mankind.

Mr. Meagles and his family, under these combined discouragements,
had begun reluctantly to give up Tattycoram as irrecoverable, when the
new and active firm of Doyce and Clennam, in their private capacities,
went down on a Saturday to stay at the cottage until Monday. The senior
partner took the coach, and the junior partner took his walking-stick.

A tranquil summer sunset shone upon him as he approached the end of
his walk, and passed through the meadows by the river-side. He had that
sense of peace, and of being lightened of a weight of care, which country
quiet awakens in the breasts of dwellers in towns. Everything within his
view was lovely and placid. The rich foliage of the trees, the luxuriant
grass diversified with wild flowers, the little green islands in the river, the
beds of rushes, the water-lilies floating on the surface of the stream, the
distant voices in boats borne musically towards him on the ripple of the
water and the evening air, were all expressive of rest. In the occasional
leap of a fish, or dip of an oar, or twittering of a bird not yet at roost, or
distant barking of a dog, or lowing of a cow—in all such sounds, there was
the prevailing breath of rest, which seemed to encompass him in every
scent that sweetened the fragrant air. The long lines of red and gold in the
sky, and the glorious track of the descending sun, were all divinely calm.
Upon the purple tree-tops far away, and on the green height near at hand
up which the shades were slowly creeping, there was an equal hush.

Between the real landscape and its shadow in the water, there was no
division; both were so untroubled and clear, and, while so fraught with
solemn mystery of life and death, so hopefully reassuring to the gazer's
soothed heart, because so tenderly and mercifully beautiful.

Clennam had stopped, not for the first time by many times, to look
about him and suffer what he saw to sink into his soul, as the shadows,
looked at, seemed to sink deeper and deeper into the water. He was slowly
resuming his way, when he saw a figure in the path before him which he
had, perhaps, already associated with the evening and its impressions.

Minnie was there, alone. She had some roses in her hand, and seemed to
have stood still on seeing him, waiting for him. Her face was towards him,
and she appeared to have been coming from the opposite direction. There
was a flutter in her manner, which Clennam had never seen in it before;
and as he came near her, it entered his mind all at once that she was there
of a set purpose to speak to him.

She gave him her hand, and said, "You wonder to see me here by
myself? But the evening is so lovely, I have strolled further than I meant
at first. I thought it likely I might meet you, and that made me more confident. You always come this way, do you not?"

As Clennam said that it was his favorite way, he felt her hand falter on
his arm, and saw the roses shake.

"Will you let me give you one, Mr. Clennam? I gathered them as I
came out of the garden. Indeed, I almost gathered them for you, thinking
it so likely I might meet you. Mr. Doyce arrived more than an hour ago,
and told us you were walking down."

His own hand shook, as he accepted a rose or two from hers, and thanked
her. They were now by an avenue of trees. Whether they turned into it on
his movement or on hers, matters little. He never knew how that was.

"It is very grave here," said Clennam, "but very pleasant at this hour.
Passing along this deep shade, and out at that arch of light at the other
end, we come upon the ferry and the cottage by the best approach, I
think."

In her simple garden-hat and her light summer dress, with her rich
brown hair naturally clustering about her, and her wonderful eyes raised
to his for a moment, with a look in which regard for him and trustfulness
in him were strikingly blended with a kind of timid sorrow for him, she
was so beautiful, that it was well for his peace—or ill for his peace, he did
not quite know which—that he had made that vigorous resolution he had
so often thought about.

She broke a momentary silence by enquiring if he knew that papa had
been thinking of another tour abroad? He said he had heard it mentioned.
She broke another momentary silence by adding, with some hesitation,
that papa had abandoned the idea.

At this, he thought directly, "they are to be married."

"Mr. Clennam," she said, hesitating more timidly yet, and speaking so low that he bent his head to hear her. "I should very much like to give you my confidence, if you would not mind having the goodness to receive it. I should have very much liked to have given it to you long ago, because —I felt that you were becoming so much our friend."

"How can I be otherwise than proud of it at any time! Pray give it to me. Pray trust me."

"I could never have been afraid of trusting you," she returned, raising her eyes frankly to his face. "I think I would have done so some time ago, if I had known how. But I scarcely know how, even now."

"Mr. Gowan," said Arthur Clennam, "has reason to be very happy. God bless his wife and him!"

She wept, as she tried to thank him. He reassured her, took her hand as it lay with the trembling roses in it on his arm, took the remaining roses from it, and put it to his lips. At that time, it seemed to him, he first finally resigned the dying hope that had flickered in nobody's heart, so much to its pain and trouble; and from that time he became in his own eyes, as to any similar hope or prospect, a very much older man who had done with that part of life.

He put the roses in his breast and they walked on for a little while, slowly and silently, under the umbrageous trees. Then he asked her, in a voice of cheerful kindness, was there anything else that she would say to him as her friend and her father's friend, many years older than herself; was there any trust she would repose in him, any service she would ask of him, any little aid to her happiness that she could give him the lasting gratification of believing it was in his power to render?

She was going to answer, when she was so touched by some little hidden sorrow or sympathy—what could it have been?—that she said, bursting into tears, again: "O, Mr. Clennam! Good, generous, Mr. Clennam, pray tell me you do not blame me."

"I blame you?" said Clennam. "My dearest girl! I blame you? No!"

After clasping both her hands upon his arm, and looking confidentially up into his face, with some hurried words to the effect that she thanked him from her heart (as indeed she did, if it be the source of earnestness), she gradually composed herself, with now and then a word of encouragement from him, as they walked on slowly and almost silently under the darkening trees.

"And, now, Minnie Gowan," at length, said Clennam, smiling; "will you ask me nothing?"

"Oh! I have very much to ask of you."

"That's well! I hoped so; I am not disappointed."

"You know how I am loved at home, and how I love home. You can hardly think it perhaps, dear Mr. Clennam," she spoke with great agitation, "seeing me going from it of my own free will and choice, but I do so dearly love it!"

"I am sure of that," said Clennam. "Can you suppose I doubt it!"

"No, no. But it is strange, even to me, that loving it so much and being so much beloved in it, I can bear to cast it away. It seems so neglectful of it, so unthankful."

"My dear girl," said Clennam, "it is in the natural progress and change of time. All homes are left so."

"Yes, I know; but all homes are not left with such a blank in them as there will be in mine when I am gone. Not that there is any scarcity of far better and more endearing and more accomplished girls than I am; not that I am much; but that they have made so much of me!"

Pet's affectionate heart was overcharged, and she sobbed while she pictured what would happen.

"I know what a change papa will feel at first, and I know that at first I cannot be to him anything like what I have been these many years. And it is then, Mr. Clennam, then more than at any time, that I beg and entreat you to remember him, and sometimes to keep him company when you can spare a little while; and to tell him that you know I was fonder of him, when I left him, than I ever was in all my life. For there is nobody—he told me so himself when he talked to me this very day—there is nobody he likes so well as you, or trusts so much."

A clue to what had passed between the father and daughter dropped like a heavy stone into the well of Clennam's heart, and swelled the water to his eyes. He said, cheerily, but not quite so cheerily as he tried to say, that it should be done: that he gave her his faithful promise.

"If I do not speak of mamma," said Pet, more moved by, and more pretty in, her innocent grief, than Clennam could trust himself even now to consider—for which reason he counted the trees between them, and the fading light as they slowly diminished in number—"it is because mamma will understand me better in this action, and will feel my loss in a different way, and will look forward in a different manner. But you know what a dear, devoted mother she is, and you will remember her, too; will you not?"

Let Minnie trust him, Clennam said, let Minnie trust him to do all she wished.

"And, dear Mr. Clennam," said Minnie, "because papa and one whom I need not name, do not fully appreciate and understand one another yet, as they will by-and-bye; and because it will be the duty, and the pride, and pleasure of my new life, to draw them to a better knowledge of one another, and to be a happiness to one another, and to be proud of one another, and to love one another, both loving me so dearly; O, as you are a kind, true man! when I am first separated from home (I am going a long distance away), try to reconcile papa to him a little more, and use your great influence to keep him before papa's mind, free from prejudice and in his real form. Will you do this for me, as you are a noble-hearted friend?"

Poor Pet! Self-deceived, mistaken child! When were such changes ever made in men's natural relations to one another: when was such reconcilement of ingrain differences ever effected! It has been tried many times by other daughters, Minnie; it has never succeeded; nothing has ever come of it but failure.

So Clennam thought. So he did not say; it was too late. He bound himself to do all she asked, and she knew full well that he would do it.

They were now at the last tree in the avenue. She stopped, and withdrew her arm. Speaking to him with her eyes lifted up to his, and with the hand that had lately rested on his sleeve tremblingly touching one of the roses in his breast as an additional appeal to him, she said:

"Dear Mr. Clennam, in my happiness—for I am happy, though you have seen me crying—I cannot bear to leave any cloud between us. If you have anything to forgive me (not anything that I have wilfully done, but any trouble I may have caused you without meaning it, or having it in my power to help it), forgive me to-night out of your noble heart!"

He stooped to meet the guileless face that met his without shrinking. He kissed it, and answered, Heaven knew that he had nothing to forgive. As he stooped to meet the innocent face once again, she whispered "Good bye!" and he repeated it. It was taking leave of all his old hopes—all nobody's old restless doubts. They came out of the avenue next moment, arm-in-arm as they had entered it; and the trees seemed to close up behind them in the darkness, like their own perspective of the past.

The voices of Mr. and Mrs. Meagles, and Doyce, were audible directly, speaking near the garden gate. Hearing Pet's name among them, Clennam called out "She is here, with me." There was some little wondering and laughing until they came up; but as soon as they had all come together, it ceased, and Pet glided away.

Mr. Meagles, Doyce, and Clennam, without speaking, walked up and down on the brink of the river, in the light of the rising moon, for a few minutes; and then Doyce lingered behind, and went into the house. Mr. Meagles and Clennam walked up and down together for a few minutes more without speaking, until at length the former broke silence.

"Arthur," said he, using that familiar address for the first time in their communication, "do you remember my telling you, as we walked up and down one hot morning, looking over the harbor at Marseilles, that Pet's baby sister who was dead seemed to Mother and me to have grown as she had grown, and changed as she had changed?"

"Very well."

"You remember my saying that our thoughts had never been able to separate those twin sisters, and that in our fancy whatever Pet was, the other was?"

"Yes, very well."

"Arthur," said Mr. Meagles, much subdued, "I carry that fancy further to-night. I feel to-night, my dear fellow, as if you had loved my dead child very tenderly, and had lost her when she was like what Pet is now."

"Thank you," murmured Clennam, "thank you!" And pressed his hand.

"Will you come in?" said Mr. Meagles, presently.

"In a little while."

Mr. Meagles fell away, and he was left alone. When he had walked on the river's brink in the peaceful moonlight, for some half-an-hour, he put his hand in his breast and tenderly took out the handful of roses. Perhaps he put them to his heart, perhaps he put them to his lips, but certainly he bent down on the shore, and gently launched them on the flowing river. Pale and unreal in the moonlight, the river floated them away.

The lights were bright within doors when he entered, and the faces on which they shone, his own face not excepted, were soon quietly cheerful. They talked of many subjects (his partner never had had such a ready store to draw upon for the beguiling of the time), and so to bed, and to sleep. While the flowers, pale and unreal in the moonlight, floated away upon the river; and thus do greater things that once were in our breasts, and near our hearts, flow from us to the eternal seas.

CHAPTER XXIX

MRS. FLINTWINCH GOES ON DREAMING

THE house in the city preserved its heavy dullness through all these transactions, and the invalid within it turned the same unvarying round of life. Morning, noon, and night, morning, noon, and night, each recurring with its accompanying monotony, always the same reluctant return of the same sequences of machinery, like a dragging piece of clockwork.

The wheeled chair had its associated remembrances and reveries, one may suppose, as every place that is made the station of a human being has. Pictures of demolished streets and altered houses, as they formerly were when the occupant of the chair was familiar with them; images of people as they too used to be, with little or no allowance made for the lapse of time since they were seen; of these, there must have been many in the long routine of gloomy days. To stop the clock of busy existence, at the hour when we were personally sequestered from it; to suppose mankind stricken motionless, when we were brought to a stand-still; to be unable to measure the changes beyond our view, by any larger standard than the shrunken one of our own uniform and contracted existence; is the infirmity of many invalids, and the mental unhealthiness of almost all recluses.

What scenes and actors the stern woman most reviewed, as she sat from season to season in her one dark room, none knew but herself. Mr. Flint-winch, with his wry presence brought to bear upon her daily like some eccentric mechanical force, would perhaps have screwed it out of her, if there had been less resistance in her; but she was too strong for him. So far as Mistress Affery was concerned, to regard her liege-lord and her disabled mistress with a face of blank wonder, to go about the house after dark with her apron over her head, always to listen for the strange noises and sometimes to hear them, and never to emerge from her ghostly, dreamy, sleep-waking state, was occupation enough for her.

There was a fair stroke of business doing, as Mistress Affery made out, for her husband had abundant occupation in his little office, and saw more people than had been used to come there for some years. This might easily be, the house having been long deserted; but he did receive letters, and comers, and keep books, and correspond. Moreover, he went about to other counting-houses, and to wharves, and docks, and to the Custom House, and to Garraway's Coffee House, and the Jerusalem Coffee House, and on 'Change; so that he was much in and out. He began, too, sometimes of an evening, when Mrs. Clennam expressed no particular wish for his society, to resort to a tavern in the neighbourhood to look at the shipping news and closing prices in the evening paper, and even to exchange small socialities with mercantile Sea Captains who frequented that establishment. At some period of every day, he and Mrs. Clennam held a council on matters of business; and it appeared to Affery, who was always groping about, listening and watching, that the two clever ones were making money.

The state of mind into which Mr. Flintwinch's dazed lady had fallen, had now begun to be so expressed in all her looks and actions, that she was held in very low account by the two clever ones, as a person, never of strong intellect, who was becoming foolish. Perhaps because her appearance was not of a commercial cast, or perhaps because it occurred to him that his having taken her to wife might expose his judgment to doubt in the minds of customers, Mr. Flintwinch laid his commands upon her that she should hold her peace on the subject of their conjugal relations, and should no longer call him Jeremiah out of the domestic trio. Her frequent forgetful-ness of this admonition intensified her startled manner, since Mr. Flint-winch's habit of avenging himself on her remissness by making springs after her on the staircase, and shaking her, occasioned her to be always nervously uncertain when she might be thus waylaid next.

Little Dorrit had finished a long day's work in Mrs. Clennam's room, and was neatly gathering up her shreds and odds and ends before going home. Mr. Pancks, whom Affery had just shown in, was addressing an enquiry to Mrs. Clennam on the subject of her health, coupled with the remark that, "happening to find himself in that direction," he had looked in to enquire, on behalf of his proprietor, how she found herself. Mrs. Clennam, with a deep contraction of her brows, was looking at him.

"Mr. Casby knows," said she, "that I am not subject to changes. The change that I await here is the great change."

"Indeed, ma'am?" returned Mr. Pancks, with a wandering eye towards the figure of the little seamstress on her knee picking threads and frayings of her work from the carpet. "You look nicely, ma'am."

"I bear what I have to bear," she answered. "Do you what you have to do."

"Thank you, ma'am," said Mr. Pancks; "such is my endeavour."

"You are often in this direction, are you not?" asked Mrs. Clennam.

"Why yes, ma'am," said Pancks, "rather so lately; I have lately been round this way a good deal, owing to one thing and another."

"Beg Mr. Casby and his daughter not to trouble themselves, by deputy, about me. When they wish to see me, they know I am here to see them. They have no need to trouble themselves to send. You have no need to trouble yourself to come."

"Not the least trouble, ma'am," said Mr. Pancks. "You really are looking uncommonly nicely, ma'am."

"Thank you. Good evening."

The dismissal, and its accompanying finger pointed straight at the door, was so curt and direct that Mr. Pancks did not see his way to prolonging his visit. He stirred up his hair with his sprightliest expression, glanced at the little figure again, said "Good evening, ma'am; don't come down, Mrs. Affery; I know the road to the door," and steamed out. Mrs. Clennam, her chin resting on her hand, followed him with attentive and darkly distrustful eyes; and Affery stood looking at her, as if she were spell-bound.

Slowly and thoughtfully, Mrs. Clennam's eyes turned from the door by which Pancks had gone out, to Little Dorrit, rising from the carpet. With her chin drooping more heavily on her hand, and her eyes vigilant and lowering, the sick woman sat looking at her until she attracted her attention. Little Dorrit colored under such a gaze, and looked down. Mrs. Clennam still sat intent.

"Little Dorrit," she said when she at last broke silence, "what do you know of that man?"

"I don't know anything of him, ma'am, except that I have seen him about, and that he has spoken to me."

"What has he said to you?"

"I don't understand what he has said, he is so strange. But nothing rough or disagreeable."

"Why does he come here to see you?"

"I don't know, ma'am," said Little Dorrit, with perfect frankness.

"You know that he does come here to see you?"

"I have fancied so," said Little Dorrit. "But why he should come here or anywhere, for that, ma'am, I can't think."

Mrs. Clennam cast her eyes towards the ground, and with her strong, set face, as intent upon a subject in her mind as it had lately been upon the form that seemed to pass out of her view, sat absorbed. Some minutes elapsed before she came out of this thoughtfulness, and resumed her hard composure.

Little Dorrit in the meanwhile had been waiting to go, but afraid to disturb her by moving. She now ventured to leave the spot where she had been standing since she had risen, and to pass gently round by the wheeled chair. She stopped at its side to say "Good night, ma'am."

Mrs. Clennam put out her hand, and laid it on her arm. Little Dorrit, confused under the touch, stood faltering. Perhaps some momentary recollection of the story of the Princess may have been in her mind.

"Tell me, Little Dorrit," said Mrs. Clennam. "Have you many friends now?"

"Very few, ma'am. Besides you, only Miss Flora and—one more."

"Meaning," said Mrs. Clennam, with her unbent finger again pointing to the door, "that man?"

"Oh no, ma'am!"

"Some friend of his, perhaps?"

"No, ma'am." Little Dorrit earnestly shook her head. "Oh no! No one at all like him, or belonging to him."

"Well!" said Mrs. Clennam, almost smiling. "It is no affair of mine. I ask, because I take an interest in you; and because I believe I was your friend, when you had no other who could serve you. Is that so?"

"Yes, ma'am; indeed it is. I have been here many a time when, but for you and the work you gave me, we should have wanted everything."

"We," repeated Mrs. Clennam, looking towards the watch, once her dead husband's, which always lay upon her table. "Are there many of you?"

"Only father and I, now. I mean, only father and I to keep regularly out of what we get."

"Have you undergone many privations? You and your father, and who else there may be of you?" asked Mrs. Clennam, speaking deliberately and meditatively turning the watch over and over.

"Sometimes it has been rather hard to live," said Little Dorrit, in her soft voice, and timid uncomplaining way; "but I think not harder—as to that—than many people find it."

"That's well said!" Mrs. Clennam quickly returned. "That's the truth! You are a good, thoughtful girl. You are a grateful girl too, or I much mistake you."

"It is only natural to be that. There is no merit in being that," said Little Dorrit. "I am indeed."

Mrs. Clennam, with a gentleness of which the dreaming Affery had never dreamed her to be capable, drew down the face of her little seamstress, and kissed her on the forehead.

"Now go, Little Dorrit," said she, "or you will be late, poor child!"

In all the dreams Mistress Affery had been piling up since she first became devoted to the pursuit, she had dreamed nothing more astonishing than this. Her head ached with the idea that she would find the other clever one kissing Little Dorrit next, and then the two clever ones embracing each other and dissolving into tears of tenderness for all mankind. The idea quite stunned her, as she attended the light footsteps down the stairs, that the house-door might be safely shut.

On opening it to let Little Dorrit out, she found Mr. Pancks, instead of having gone his way, as in any less wonderful place and among less wonderful phenomena he might have been reasonably expected to do, fluttering up and down the court outside the house. The moment he saw Little Dorrit, he passed her briskly, said with his finger to his nose (as Mistress Affery distinctly heard), "Pancks the gipsy, fortune-telling," and went away. "Lord save us, here's a gipsy and a fortune-teller in it now!" cried Mistress Affery. "What next!"

She stood at the open door, staggering herself with this enigma, on a rainy, thundery evening. The clouds were flying fast, the wind was coming up in gusts, banging some neighbouring shutters that had broken loose, twirling the rusty chimney-cowls and weathercocks, and rushing round and round a confined adjacent churchyard as if it had a mind to blow the dead citizens out of their graves. The low thunder, muttering in all quarters of the sky at once, seemed to threaten vengeance for this attempted desecration, and to mutter, "Let them rest! Let them rest!"

Mistress Affery, whose fear of thunder and lightning was only to be equalled by her dread of the haunted house with a premature and preternatural darkness in it, stood undecided whether to go in or not, until the question was settled for her by the door blowing upon her in a violent gust of wind and shutting her out. "What's to be done now, what's to be done now!" cried Mistress Affery, wringing her hands in this last uneasy dream of all; "when she's all alone by herself inside, and can no more come down to open it than the churchyard dead themselves!"

In this dilemma, Mistress Affery, with her apron as a hood to keep the rain off, ran crying up and down the solitary paved enclosure several times. Why she should then stoop down and look in at the keyhole of the door, as if an eye would open it, it would be difficult to say; but it is none the less what most people would have done in the same situation, and it is what she did.

From this posture she started up suddenly, with a half scream, feeling something on her shoulder. It was the touch of a hand; of a man's hand.

The man was dressed like a traveller, in a foraging cap with fur about it, and a heap of cloak. He looked like a foreigner. He had a quantity of hair and moustache—jet black, except at the shaggy ends, where it had a tinge of red—and a high hook nose. He laughed at Mistress Affery's start and cry; and, as he laughed, his moustache went up under his nose, and his nose came down over his moustache.

"What's the matter?" he asked in plain English. "What are you frightened at?"

"At you," panted Affery.

"Me, madame?"

"And the dismal evening, and—and everything," said Affery. "And here! The wind has been and blown the door to, and I can't get in."

"Hah!" said the gentleman, who took that very coolly. "Indeed! Do you know such a name as Clennam about here?"

"Lord bless us, I should think I did, I should think I did!" cried Affery, exasperated into a new wringing of hands by the enquiry.

"Where about here?"

"Where!" cried Affery, goaded into another inspection of the keyhole. "Where but here in this house? And she's all alone in her room, and lost the use of her limbs and can't stir to help herself or me, and the t'other clever one's out, and Lord forgive me!" cried Affery, driven into a frantic dance by these accumulated considerations, "if I ain't a going headlong out of my mind!"

Taking a warmer view of the matter now that it concerned himself, the gentleman stepped back to glance at the house, and his eyes soon rested on the long narrow window of the little room near the hall-door.

"Where may the lady be who has lost the use of her limbs, madame?" he enquired, with that particular smile which Mistress Affery could not choose but keep her eyes upon.

"Up there!" said Affery. "Them two windows."

"Hah! I am of a fair size, but could not have the honor of presenting myself in that room without a ladder. Now, madame, frankly—frankness is a part of my character—shall I open the door for you?"

"Yes, bless you, sir, for a dear creetur, and do it at once," cried Affery, "for she may be a calling to me at this very present minute, or may be setting herself a-fire and burning herself to death, or there's no knowing what may be happening to her, and me a going out of my mind at thinking of it!"

"Stay, my good madame!" He restrained her impatience with a smooth white hand. "Business-hours, I apprehend, are over for the day?"

"Yes, yes, yes," cried Affery. "Long ago."

"Let me make, then, a fair proposal. Fairness is a part of my character. I am just landed from the packet-boat, as you may see." He showed her that his cloak was very wet, and that his boots were saturated with water; she had previously observed that he was dishevelled and sallow, as if from a rough voyage, and so chilled that he could not keep his teeth from chattering. "I am just landed from the packet-boat, madame, and have been delayed by the weather; the infernal weather! In consequence of this, madame, some necessary business that I should otherwise have transacted here within the regular hours (necessary business because money-business), still remains to be done. Now, if you will fetch any authorised neighbouring somebody to do it, in return for my opening the door, I'll open the door. If this arrangement should be objectionable, I'll——" and with the same smile he made significant feint of backing away.

Mistress Affery, heartily glad to effect the proposed compromise, gave in her willing adhesion to it. The gentleman at once requested her to do him the favor of holding his cloak, took a short run at the narrow window, made a leap at the sill, clung his way up the bricks, and in a moment had his hand at the sash, raising it. His eyes looked so very sinister, as he put his leg into the room and glanced round at Mistress Affery, that she thought, with a sudden coldness, if he were to go straight up-stairs to murder the invalid, what could she do to prevent him?

Happily he had no such purpose; for he re-appeared, in a moment, at the house-door. "Now, my dear madame," he said, as he took back his cloak and threw it on, "if you'll have the goodness to ——what the Devil's that!"

The strangest of sounds. Evidently close at hand from the peculiar shock it communicated to the air, yet subdued as if it were far off. A tremble, a rumble, and a fall of some light dry matter.

"What the Devil is it?"

"I don't know what it is, but I've heard the like of it over and over again," said Affery, who had caught his arm.

He could hardly be a very brave man, even she thought in her dreamy start and fright, for his trembling lips had turned colorless. After listening a few moments, he made light of it.

"Bah! Nothing! Now, my dear madame, I think you spoke of some clever personage. Will you be so good as to confront me with that genius?" He held the door in his hand, as though he were quite ready to shut her out again if she failed.

"Don't you say anything about the door and me, then," whispered Affery.

"Not a word."

"And don't you stir from here, or speak if she calls, while I run round the corner."

"Madame, I am a statue."

Affery had so vivid a fear of his going stealthily up-stairs the moment her back was turned, that, after hurrying out of sight, she returned to the gateway to peep at him. Seeing him still on the threshold, more out of the house than in it, as if he had no love for darkness and no desire to probe its mysteries, she flew into the next street, and sent a message into the tavern to Mr. Flintwinch who came out directly. The two returning together—the lady in advance, and Mr. Flintwinch coming up briskly behind, animated with the hope of shaking her before she could get housed —saw the gentleman standing in the same place in the dark, and heard the strong voice of Mrs. Clennam calling from her room, "Who is it? What is it? Why does no one answer? Who *is* that, down there?"

END OF No. VIII

CHAPTER XXX

THE WORD OF A GENTLEMAN

WHEN Mr. and Mrs. Flintwinch panted up to the door of the old house in the twilight, Jeremiah within a second of Affery, the stranger started back. "Death of my soul!" he exclaimed. "Why, how did you get here?"

Mr. Flintwinch, to whom these words were spoken, repaid the stranger's wonder in full. He gazed at him with blank astonishment; he looked over his own shoulder, as expecting to see some one he had not been aware of standing behind him; he gazed at the stranger again, speechlessly at a loss to know what he meant; he looked to his wife for explanation; receiving none, he pounced upon her, and shook her with such heartiness that he shook her cap off her head, saying between his teeth, with grim raillery, as he did it, "Affery, my woman, you must have a dose, my woman! This is some of your tricks! You have been dreaming again, mistress. What's it about? Who is it? What does it mean? Speak out or be choked! It's the only choice I'll give you."

Supposing Mistress Affery to have any power of election at the moment, her choice was decidedly to be choked; for she answered not a syllable to this adjuration, but, with her bare head wagging violently backwards and forwards, resigned herself to her punishment. The stranger, however, picking up her cap with an air of gallantry, interposed.

"Permit me," said he, laying his hand on the shoulder of Jeremiah, who stopped, and released his victim. "Thank you. Excuse me. Husband and wife I know, from this playfulness. Haha! Always agreeable to see that relation playfully maintained. Listen! May I suggest that somebody up-stairs, in the dark, is becoming energetically curious to know what is going on here?"

This reference to Mrs. Clennam's voice reminded Mr. Flintwinch to step into the hall and call up the staircase. "It's all right, I am here, Affery is coming with your light." Then he said to the latter flustered woman, who was putting her cap on, "Get out with you, and get up-stairs!" and then turned to the stranger, and said to him, "Now sir, what might you please to want?"

"I am afraid," said the stranger, "I must be so troublesome as to propose a candle."

"True," assented Jeremiah. "I was going to do so. Please to stand where you are, while I get one."

The visitor was standing in the doorway, but turned a little into the gloom of the house as Mr. Flintwinch turned, and pursued him with his eyes into the little room, where he groped about for a phosphorus box. When he found it, it was damp, or otherwise out of order; and match after match that he struck into it lighted sufficiently to throw a dull glare about his groping face, and to sprinkle his hands with pale little spots of fire, but not sufficiently to light the candle. The stranger, taking advantage of this fitful illumination of his visage, looked intently and wonderingly at him. Jeremiah, when he at last lighted the candle, knew he had been doing this, by seeing the last shade of a lowering watchfulness clear away from his face, as it broke into the doubtful smile that was a large ingredient in its expression.

"Be so good," said Jeremiah, closing the house-door, and taking a pretty sharp survey of the smiling visitor in his turn, "as to step into my counting-house.—It's all right, I tell you!" petulantly breaking off to answer the voice up-stairs, still unsatisfied, though Affery was there, speaking in persuasive tones. "Don't I tell you it's all right? Preserve the woman, has she no reason at all in her!"

"Timorous," remarked the stranger.

"Timorous?" said Mr. Flintwinch, turning his head to retort, as he went before with the candle. "More courageous than ninety men in a hundred, sir, let me tell you."

"Though an invalid?"

"Many years an invalid. Mrs. Clennam. The only one of that name left in the House now. My partner."

Saying something apologetically as he crossed the hall, to the effect that at that time of night they were not in the habit of receiving any one, and were always shut up, Mr. Flintwinch led the way into his own office, which presented a sufficiently business-like appearance. Here he put the light on his desk, and said to the stranger, with his wryest twist upon him, "Your commands."

"My name is Blandois."

"Blandois. I don't know it," said Jeremiah.

"I thought it possible," resumed the other, "that you might have been advised from Paris——"

"We have had no advice from Paris, respecting anybody of the name of Blandois," said Jeremiah.

"No?"

"No."

Jeremiah stood in his favorite attitude. The smiling Mr. Blandois, opening his cloak to get his hand to a breast pocket, paused to say, with a laugh in his glittering eyes, which it occurred to Mr. Flintwinch were too near together:

"You are so like a friend of mine! Not so identically the same as I supposed when I really did for the moment take you to be the same in the dusk —for which I ought to apologise; permit me to do so; a readiness to confess my errors is, I hope, a part of the frankness of my character—still, however, uncommonly like."

"Indeed?" said Jeremiah, perversely. "But I have not received any letter of advice from anywhere, respecting anybody of the name of Blandois."

"Just so," said the stranger.

"*Just* so," said Jeremiah.

Mr. Blandois, not at all put out by this omission on the part of the correspondents of the house of Clennam and Co., took his pocket-book from his breast pocket, selected a letter from that receptacle, and handed it to Mr. Flintwinch. "No doubt you are well acquainted with the writing. Perhaps the letter speaks for itself, and requires no advice. You are a far more competent judge of such affairs than I am. It is my misfortune to be, not so much a man of business, as what the world calls (arbitrarily) a gentleman."

Mr. Flintwinch took the letter, and read, under date of Paris, "We have to present to you, on behalf of a highly-esteemed correspondent of our Firm, M. Blandois, of this city," &c. &c. "Such facilities as he may require and such attentions as may lie in your power," &c. &c. "Also have to add that if you will honor M. Blandois' drafts at sight to the extent of, say Fifty Pounds sterling (£50)," &c. &c.

"Very good, sir," said Mr. Flintwinch. "Take a chair. To the extent of anything that our house can do—we are in a retired, old-fashioned, steady way of business, sir—we shall be happy to render you our best assistance. I observe, from the date of this, that we could not yet be advised of it. Probably you came over with the delayed mail that brings the advice."

"That I came over with the delayed mail, sir," returned Mr. Blandois, passing his white hand down his high-hooked nose, "I know to the cost of my head and stomach: the detestable and intolerable weather having racked them both. You see me in the plight in which I came out of the Packet within this half-hour. I ought to have been here hours ago, and then I should not have to apologise—permit me *to* apologise—for presenting myself so unseasonably, and frightening—no, by-the-bye, you said not frightening; permit me to apologise again—the esteemed lady, Mrs. Clennam, in her invalid chamber above stairs."

Swagger, and an air of authorised condescension, do so much, that Mr. Flintwinch had already begun to think this a highly gentlemanly personage. Not the less unyielding with him on that account, he scraped his chin and said, what could he have the honor of doing for Mr. Blandois to-night, out of business hours?

"Faith!" returned that gentleman, shrugging his cloaked shoulders, "I must change, and eat and drink, and be lodged somewhere. Have the kindness to advise me, a total stranger, where, and money is a matter of perfect indifference, until to-morrow. The nearer the place, the better. Next door, if that's all."

Mr. Flintwinch was slowly beginning, "For a gentleman of your habits, there is not in this immediate neighbourhood any hotel—" when Mr. Blandois took him up.

"So much for my habits! my dear sir," snapping his fingers. "A citizen of the world has no habits. That I am, in my poor way, a gentleman, by Heaven! I will not deny, but I have no unaccommodating prejudiced habits. A clean room, a hot dish for dinner, and a bottle of not absolutely poisonous wine, are all I want to-night. But I want that much, without the trouble of going one unnecessary inch to get it."

"There is," said Mr. Flintwinch, with more than his usual deliberation, as he met, for a moment, Mr. Blandois' shining eyes, which were restless; "there is a coffee-house and tavern close here, which, so far, I can recommend; but there's no style about it."

"I dispense with style!" said Mr. Blandois, waving his hand. "Do me the honor to show me the house, and introduce me there (if I am not too troublesome), and I shall be infinitely obliged."

Mr. Flintwinch, upon this, looked up his hat, and lighted Mr. Blandois across the hall again. As he put the candle on a bracket, where the dark old panelling almost served as an extinguisher for it, he bethought himself of going up to tell the invalid that he would not be absent five minutes.

"Oblige me," said the visitor, on his saying so, "by presenting my card of visit. Do me the favor to add, that I shall be happy to wait on Mrs. Clennam, to offer my personal compliments, and to apologise for having occasioned any agitation in this tranquil corner, if it should suit her convenience to endure the presence of a stranger for a few minutes, after he shall have changed his wet clothes and fortified himself with something to eat and drink."

Jeremiah made all dispatch, and said, on his return, "She'll be glad to see you, sir; but, being conscious that her sick room has no attractions, wishes me to say that she won't hold you to your offer, in case you should think better of it."

"To think better of it," returned the gallant Blandois, "would be to slight a lady; to slight a lady would be to be deficient in chivalry towards the sex; and chivalry towards the sex is a part of my character!" Thus expressing himself, he threw the draggled skirt of his cloak over this shoulder, and accompanied Mr. Flintwinch to the tavern; taking up on the road a porter, who was waiting with his portmanteau on the outer side of the gateway.

The house was kept in a homely manner, and the condescension of Mr. Blandois was infinite. It seemed to fill to inconvenience the little bar, in which the widow landlady and her two daughters received him; it was much too big for the narrow wainscoated room with a bagatelle-board in it, that was first proposed for his reception; it perfectly swamped the little private holiday sitting-room of the family, which was finally given up to him. Here, in dry clothes and scented linen, with sleeked hair, a great ring on each forefinger, and a massive show of watch-chain, Mr. Blandois waiting for his dinner, lolling on a window-seat with his knees drawn up, looked (for all the difference in the setting of the jewel) fearfully and wonderfully like a certain Monsieur Rigaud who had once so waited for his breakfast, lying on the stone ledge of the iron grating of a cell in a villanous dungeon at Marseilles.

His greed at dinner, too, was closely in keeping with the greed of Monsieur Rigaud at breakfast. His avaricious manner of collecting all the eatables about him, and devouring some with his eyes, while devouring others with his jaws, was the same manner. His utter disregard of other people, as shown in his way of tossing the little womanly toys of furniture about, flinging favorite cushions under his boots for a softer rest, and crushing delicate coverings with his big body and his great black head, had the same brute selfishness at the bottom of it. The softly moving hands that were so busy among the dishes had the old wicked facility of the hands that had clung to the bars. And when he could eat no more, and sat sucking his delicate fingers one by one and wiping them on a cloth, there wanted nothing but the substitution of vine-leaves to finish the picture.

On this man, with his moustache going up and his nose coming down in that most evil of smiles, and with his surface eyes looking as if they belonged to his dyed hair, and had had their natural power of reflecting light stopped by some similar process, Nature, always true, and never working in vain, had set the mark, Beware! It was not her fault, if the warning were fruitless. She is never to blame in any such instance.

Mr. Blandois, having finished his repast and cleaned his fingers, took a cigar from his pocket, and, lying on the window-seat again, smoked it out at his leisure, occasionally apostrophising the smoke as it parted from his thin lips in a thin stream:

"Blandois, you shall turn the tables on society, my little child. Haha! Holy blue, you have begun well, Blandois! At a pinch, an excellent master in English or French; a man for the bosom of families! You have a quick perception, you have humour, you have ease, you have insinuating manners, you have a good appearance; in effect, you are a gentleman! A gentleman you shall live, my small boy, and a gentleman you shall die. You shall win, however the game goes. They shall all confess your merit, Blandois. You shall subdue the society which has grievously wronged you, to your own high spirit. Death of my soul. You are high-spirited by right and by nature, my Blandois!"

To such soothing murmurs did this gentleman smoke out his cigar and drink out his bottle of wine. Both being finished, he shook himself into a sitting attitude; and with the concluding serious apostrophe, "Hold, then! Blandois, you ingenious one, have all your wits about you!" arose and went back to the house of Clennam and Co.

He was received at the door by Mistress Affery, who, under instructions from her lord, had lighted up two candles in the hall and a third on the staircase, and who conducted him to Mrs. Clennam's room. Tea was prepared there, and such little company arrangements had been made as usually attended the reception of expected visitors. They were slight on the greatest occasion, never extending beyond the production of the China tea-service, and the covering of the bed with a sober and sad drapery. For the rest, there was the bier-like sofa with the block upon it, and the figure in the widow's dress, as if attired for execution; the fire topped by the mound of damped ashes; the grate with its second little mound of ashes; the kettle, and the smell of black dye; all as they had been for fifteen years.

Mr. Flintwinch presented the gentleman commended to the consideration of Clennam and Co. Mrs. Clennam, who had the letter lying before her, bent her head and requested him to sit. They looked very closely at one another. That was but natural curiosity.

"I thank you, sir, for thinking of a disabled woman like me. Few who come here on business have any remembrance to bestow on one so removed from observation. It would be idle to expect that they should have. Out of sight, out of mind. When I am grateful for the exception, I don't complain of the rule."

Mr. Blandois, in his most gentlemanly manner, was afraid he had disturbed her by unhappily presenting himself at such an unconscionable time. For which he had already offered his best apologies to Mr. —— he begged pardon—but by name had not the distinguished honor—

"Mr. Flintwinch has been connected with the House many years."

Mr. Blandois was Mr. Flintwinch's most obedient humble servant. He entreated Mr. Flintwinch to receive the assurance of his profoundest consideration.

"My husband being dead," said Mrs. Clennam, "and my son preferring another pursuit, our old House has no other representative in these days than Mr. Flintwinch."

"What do you call yourself?" was the surly demand of that gentleman. "You have the head of two men."

"My sex disqualifies me," she proceeded with merely a slight turn of her eyes in Jeremiah's direction, "from taking a responsible part in the business, even if I had the ability; and therefore Mr. Flintwinch combines my interests with his own, and conducts it. It is not what it used to be; but some of our old friends (principally the writers of this letter) have the kindness not to forget us, and we retain the power of doing what they entrust to us as efficiently as we ever did. This however is not interesting to you. You are English, sir?"

"Faith, madame, no; I am neither born nor bred in England. In effect, I am of no country," said Mr. Blandois, stretching out his leg and smiting it: "I descend from half a dozen countries."

"You have been much about the world?"

"It is true. By Heaven, madame, I have been here and there and everywhere!"

"You have no ties, probably. Are not married?"

"Madame," said Mr. Blandois, with an ugly fall of his eyebrows, "I adore your sex, but I am not married—never was."

Mistress Affery, who stood at the table near him, pouring out the tea, happened in her dreamy state to look at him as he said these words, and to fancy that she caught an expression in his eyes which attracted her own eyes so that she could not get them away. The effect of this fancy was, to keep her staring at him with the teapot in her hand, not only to her own great uneasiness, but manifestly to his, too; and, through them both, to Mr. Clennam's and Mr. Flintwinch's. Thus a few ghostly moments supervened, when they were all confusedly staring without knowing why.

"Affery," her mistress was the first to say, "what is the matter with you?"

"I don't know," said Mistress Affery, with her disengaged left hand extended towards the visitor. "It ain't me. It's him!"

"What does this good woman mean?" cried Mr. Blandois, turning white, hot, and slowly rising with a look of such deadly wrath that it contrasted surprisingly with the slight force of his words. "How is it possible to understand this good creature!"

"It's *not* possible," said Mr. Flintwinch, screwing himself rapidly in that direction. "She don't know what she means. She's an idiot, a wanderer in her mind. She shall have a dose, she shall have such a dose! Get along with you, my woman," he added in her ear, "get along with you, while you know you're Affery, and before you're shaken to yeast."

Mistress Affery, sensible of the danger in which her identity stood, relinquished the teapot as her husband seized it, put her apron over her head, and in a twinkling vanished. The visitor gradually broke into a smile, and sat down again.

"You'll excuse her, Mr. Blandois," said Jeremiah, pouring out the tea himself; "she's failing and breaking up; that's what she's about. Do you take sugar, sir?"

"Thank you; no tea for me.—Pardon my observing it, but that's a very remarkable watch!"

The tea-table was drawn up near the sofa, with a small interval between

it and Mrs. Clennam's own particular table. Mr. Blandois in his gallantry
had risen to hand that lady her tea (her dish of toast was already there),
and it was in placing the cup conveniently within her reach that the watch,
lying before her as it always did, attracted his attention. Mrs. Clennam
looked suddenly up at him.

"May I be permitted? Thank you. A fine old-fashioned watch," he
said, taking it in his hand. "Heavy for use, but massive and genuine. I
have a partiality for everything genuine. Such as I am, I am genuine
myself. Hah! A gentleman's watch with two cases in the old fashion. May
I remove it from the outer case? Thank you. Aye? An old silk watch-lining,
worked with beads! I have often seen these among old Dutch people and
Belgians. Quaint things!"

"They are old-fashioned too," said Mrs. Clennam.

"Very. But this is not as old as the watch, I think?"

"I think not."

"Extraordinary how they used to complicate these cyphers!" remarked
Mr. Blandois, glancing up with his own smile again. "Now, is this D. N.
F.? It might be almost anything."

"Those are the letters."

Mr. Flintwinch who had been observantly pausing all this time with a
cup of tea in his hand, and his mouth open ready to swallow the contents,
began to do so: always entirely filling his mouth before he emptied it at a
gulp; and always deliberating again before he refilled it.

"D. N. F. was some tender lovely fascinating fair-creature, I make no
doubt," observed Mr. Blandois, as he snapped on the case again. "I
adore her memory on the assumption. Unfortunately for my peace of
mind, I adore but too readily. It may be a vice, it may be a virtue, but
adoration of female beauty and merit constitutes three parts of my character, madame."

Mr. Flintwinch had by this time poured himself out another cup of tea,
which he was swallowing in gulps as before, with his eyes directed to the
invalid.

"You may be heart-free here, sir," she returned to Mr. Blandois.
"Those letters are not intended, I believe, for the initials of any name."

"Of a motto perhaps," said Mr. Blandois, casually.

"Of a sentence. They have always stood, I believe, for Do Not
Forget!"

"And naturally," said Mr. Blandois, replacing the watch, and stepping
backward to his former chair, "you do *not* forget."

Mr. Flintwinch, finishing his tea, not only took a longer gulp than he
had taken yet, but made his succeeding pause under new circumstances:
that is to say, with his head thrown back and his cup still held at his lips,
while his eyes were still directed at the invalid. She had that force of face,
and that concentrated air of collecting her firmness or obstinacy, which

represented in her case what would have been gesture and action in another, as she replied with her deliberate strength of speech:

"No, sir, I do not forget. To lead a life as monotonous as mine has been during many years, is not the way to forget. To lead a life of self-correction, is not the way to forget. To be sensible of having (as we all have, every one of us, all the children of Adam!) offences to expiate and peace to make, does not justify the desire to forget. Therefore I have long dismissed it, and I neither forget nor wish to forget."

Mr. Flintwinch, who had latterly been shaking the sediment at the bottom of his tea-cup, round and round, here gulped it down, and putting the cup in the tea-tray, as done with, turned his eyes upon Mr. Blandois, as if to ask him what he thought of that?

"All expressed, madame," said Mr. Blandois, with his smoothest bow and his white hand on his breast, "by the word 'naturally,' which I am proud to have had sufficient apprehension and appreciation (but without appreciation I could not be Blandois) to employ."

"Pardon me, sir," she returned, "if I doubt the likelihood of a gentleman of pleasure, and change, and politeness, accustomed to court and to be courted—"

"Oh madame! By Heaven!"

"—If I doubt the likelihood of such a character, quite comprehending what belongs to mine in my circumstances. Not to obtrude doctrine upon you," she looked at the rigid pile of hard pale books before her, "(for you go your own way, and the consequences are on your own head), I will say this much: that I shape my course by pilots, strictly by proved and tried pilots, under whom I cannot be shipwrecked—can not be—and that if I were unmindful of the admonition conveyed in those three letters, I should not be half as chastened as I am."

It was curious how she seized the occasion to argue with some invisible opponent. Perhaps, with her own better sense, always turning upon herself and her own deception.

"If I forgot my ignorances in my life of health and freedom, I might complain of the life to which I am now condemned. I never do; I never have done. If I forgot that this scene, the Earth, is expressly meant to be a scene of gloom, and hardship, and dark trial, for the creatures who are made out of its dust, I might have some tenderness for its vanities. But I have no such tenderness. If I did not know that we are, every one, the subject (most justly the subject) of a wrath that must be satisfied, and against which mere actions are nothing, I might repine at the difference between me, imprisoned here, and the people who pass that gateway yonder. But I take it as a grace and favor to be elected to make the satisfaction I am making here, to know what I know for certain here, and to work out what I have worked out here. My affliction might otherwise have had no meaning to me. Hence I would forget, and I do forget, nothing. Hence I am contented, and say it is better with me than with millions."

As she spoke these words, she put her hand upon the watch, and restored it to the precise spot on her little table which it always occupied. With her touch lingering upon it, she sat for some moments afterwards, looking at it steadily and half-defiantly.

Mr. Blandois, during this exposition, had been strictly attentive, keeping his eyes fastened on the lady, and thoughtfully stroking his moustache with his two hands. Mr. Flintwinch had been a little fidgetty, and now struck in.

"There, there, there!" said he. "That is quite understood, Mrs. Clennam, and you have spoken piously and well. Mr. Blandois, I suspect, is not of a pious cast."

"On the contrary, sir!" that gentleman protested, snapping his fingers. "Your pardon! It's a part of my character. I am sensitive, ardent, conscientious, and imaginative. A sensitive, ardent, conscientious, and imaginative man, Mr. Flintwinch, must be that, or nothing!"

There was an inkling of suspicion in Mr. Flintwinch's face that he might be nothing, as he swaggered out of his chair (it was characteristic of this man, as it is of all men similarly marked, that whatever he did, he overdid, though it were sometimes by only a hair's-breadth), and approached to take his leave of Mrs. Clennam.

"With what will appear to you the egotism of a sick old woman, sir," she then said, "though really through your accidental allusion, I have been led away into the subject of myself and my infirmities. Being so considerate as to visit me, I hope you will be likewise so considerate as to overlook that. Don't compliment me, if you please." For he was evidently going to do it. "Mr. Flintwinch will be happy to render you any service, and I hope your stay in this city may prove agreeable."

Mr. Blandois thanked her, and kissed his hand several times. "This is an old room," he remarked, with a sudden sprightliness of manner, looking round when he got near the door. "I have been so interested that I have not observed it. But it's a genuine old room."

"It is a genuine old house," said Mrs. Clennam, with her frozen smile. "A place of no pretensions, but a piece of antiquity."

"Faith!" cried the visitor. "If Mr. Flintwinch would do me the favor to take me through the rooms on my way out, he could hardly oblige me more. An old house is a weakness with me. I have many weaknesses, but none greater. I love and study the picturesque, in all its varieties. I have been called picturesque myself. It is no merit to be picturesque—I have greater merits, perhaps—but I may be, by an accident. Sympathy, sympathy!"

"I tell you beforehand, Mr. Blandois, that you'll find it very dingy, and very bare," said Jeremiah, taking up the candle. "It's not worth your looking at." But Mr. Blandois, smiting him in a friendly manner on the back, only laughed; so the said Blandois kissed his hand again to Mrs. Clennam, and they went out of the room together.

"You don't care to go up-stairs?" said Jeremiah, on the landing.

"On the contrary, Mr. Flintwinch; if not tiresome to you, I shall be ravished!"

Mr. Flintwinch, therefore, wormed himself up the staircase, and Mr. Blandois followed close. They ascended to the great garret bedroom, which Arthur had occupied on the night of his return. "There, Mr. Blandois!" said Jeremiah, showing it, "I hope you may think that worth coming so high, to see. I confess I don't."

Mr. Blandois being enraptured, they walked through other garrets and passages, and came down the staircase again. By this time, Mr. Flintwinch had remarked that he never found the visitor looking at any room, after throwing one quick glance around, but always found the visitor looking at him, Mr. Flintwinch. With this discovery in his thoughts, he turned about on the staircase for another experiment. He met his eyes directly; and on the instant of their fixing one another, the visitor, with that ugly play of nose and moustache, laughed (as he had done at every similar moment since they left Mrs. Clennam's chamber) a diabolically silent laugh.

As a much shorter man than the visitor, Mr. Flintwinch was at the physical disadvantage of being thus disagreeably leered at from a height; and as he went first down the staircase, and was usually a step or two lower than the other, this disadvantage was at the time increased. He postponed looking at Mr. Blandois again until this accidental inequality was removed by their having entered the late Mr. Clennam's room. But, then twisting himself suddenly round upon him, he found his look unchanged.

"A most admirable old house," smiled Mr. Blandois. "So mysterious. Do you never hear any haunted noises here?"

"Noises?" returned Mr. Flintwinch. "No."

"Nor see any devils?"

"Not," said Mr. Flintwinch, grimly screwing himself at his questioner, "not any that introduce themselves under that name and in that capacity."

"Haha! A portrait here, I see."

(Still looking at Mr. Flintwinch, as if he were the portrait.)

"It's a portrait, sir, as you observe."

"May I ask the subject, Mr. Flintwinch?"

"Mr. Clennam, deceased. Her husband."

"Former owner of the remarkable watch, perhaps?" said the visitor.

Mr. Flintwinch, who had cast his eyes towards the portrait, twisted himself about again, and again found himself the subject of the same look and smile. "Yes, Mr. Blandois," he replied tartly. "It was his, and his uncle's before him, and Lord knows whose before him; and that's all I can tell you of its pedigree."

"That's a strongly marked character, Mr. Flintwinch, our friend up-stairs."

"Yes, sir," said Jeremiah, twisting himself at the visitor again, as he did during the whole of this dialogue, like some screw-machine that fell short of its grip; for the other never changed, and he always felt obliged to retreat a little. "She is a remarkable woman. Great fortitude—great strength of mind."

"They must have been very happy," said Blandois.

"Who?" demanded Mr. Flintwinch, with another screw at him.

Mr. Blandois shook his right forefinger towards the sick-room, and his left forefinger towards the portrait, and then putting his arms a-kimbo, and striding his legs wide apart, stood smiling down at Mr. Flintwinch with the advancing nose and the retreating moustache.

"As happy as most other married people, I suppose," returned Mr. Flintwinch. "I can't say. I don't know. There are secrets in all families."

"Secrets!" cried Mr. Blandois, quickly. "Say it again, my son."

"I say," replied Mr. Flintwinch, upon whom he had swelled himself so suddenly that Mr. Flintwinch found his face almost brushed by the dilated chest. "I say there are secrets in all families."

"So there are," cried the other, clapping him on both shoulders, and rolling him backwards and forwards. "Haha! you are right. So there are! Secrets? Holy blue! There are the devil's own secrets in some families, Mr. Flintwinch!" With that, after clapping Mr. Flintwinch on both shoulders several times, as if, in a friendly and humorous way, he were rallying him on a joke he had made, he threw up his arms, threw back his head, hooked his hands together behind it, and burst into a roar of laughter. It was in vain for Mr. Flintwinch to try another screw at him. He had his laugh out.

"But, favor me with the candle a moment," he said, when he had done. "Let us have a look at the husband of the remarkable lady. Hah!" holding up the light at arm's length. "A decided expression of face here too, though not of the same character. Looks as if he were saying—what is it—Do Not Forget—does he not, Mr. Flintwinch? By Heaven, sir, he does!"

As he returned him the candle, he looked at him once more; and then, leisurely strolling out with him into the hall, declared it to be a charming old house indeed, and one which had so greatly pleased him, that he would not have missed inspecting it for a hundred pounds.

Throughout these singular freedoms on the part of Mr. Blandois, which involved a general alteration in his demeanour, making it much coarser and rougher, much more violent and audacious, than before, Mr. Flintwinch, whose leathern face was not liable to many changes, preserved

its immobility intact. Beyond now appearing, perhaps, to have been left
hanging a trifle too long before that friendly operation of cutting down, he
outwardly maintained an equable composure. They had brought their
survey to a close in the little room at the side of the hall, and he stood there,
eyeing Mr. Blandois.

"I am glad you are so well satisfied, sir," was his calm remark. "I didn't
expect it. You seem to be quite in good spirits."

"In admirable spirits," returned Blandois. "Word of honor! never
more refreshed in spirits. Do you ever have presentiments, Mr.
Flintwinch?"

"I am not sure that I know what you mean by the term, sir," replied that
gentleman.

"Say in this case, Mr. Flintwinch, undefined anticipations of pleasure
to come."

"I can't say I am sensible of such a sensation at present," returned Mr.
Flintwinch, with the utmost gravity. "If I should find it coming on, I'll
mention it."

"Now I," said Blandois, "I, my son, have a presentiment to-night that
we shall be well acquainted. Do you find it coming on?"

"N—no," returned Mr. Flintwinch, deliberately enquiring of himself.
"I can't say I do."

"I have a strong presentiment that we shall become intimately acquainted.—You have no feeling of that sort yet?"

"Not yet," said Mr. Flintwinch.

Mr. Blandois, taking him by both shoulders again, rolled him about a
little in his former merry way, then drew his arm through his own, and
invited him to come off and drink a bottle of wine like a dear deep old dog
as he was.

Without a moment's indecision, Mr. Flintwinch accepted the invitation,
and they went out to the quarters where the traveller was lodged, through
a heavy rain which had rattled on the windows, roofs, and pavements, ever
since nightfall. The thunder and lightning had long ago passed over, but
the rain was furious. On their arrival in Mr. Blandois' room, a bottle of port
wine was ordered by that gallant gentleman; who (crushing every pretty
thing he could collect, in the soft disposition of his dainty figure) coiled
himself upon the window-seat, while Mr. Flintwinch took a chair opposite
to him, with the table between them. Mr. Blandois proposed having the
largest glasses in the house, to which Mr. Flintwinch assented. The
bumpers filled, Mr. Blandois, with a roystering gaiety, clinked the top of
his glass against the bottom of Mr. Flintwinch's, and the bottom of his
glass against the top of Mr. Flintwinch's, and drank to the intimate
acquaintance he foresaw. Mr. Flintwinch gravely pledged him, and drank
all the wine he could get, and said nothing. As often as Mr. Blandois clinked
glasses (which was at every replenishment), Mr. Flintwinch stolidly did his

part of the clinking, and would have stolidly done his companion's part of the
wine as well as his own: being, except in the article of palate, a mere cask.

In short, Mr. Blandois found that to pour port wine into the reticent
Flintwinch was, not to open him but to shut him up. Moreover, he had the
appearance of a perfect ability to go on all night; or, if occasion were, all
next day, and all next night; whereas Mr. Blandois soon grew indistinctly
conscious of swaggering too fiercely and boastfully. He therefore terminated the entertainment at the end of the third bottle.

"You will draw upon us to-morrow, sir?" said Mr. Flintwinch, with a
business-like face at parting.

"My Cabbage," returned the other, taking him by the collar with both
hands. "I'll draw upon you; have no fear. Adieu, my Flintwinch. Receive
at parting;" here he gave a southern embrace, and kissed him soundingly
on both cheeks; "the word of a gentleman! By a thousand Thunders, you
shall see me again!"

He did not present himself next day, though the letter of advice came
duly to hand. Enquiring after him at night, Mr. Flintwinch found, with
surprise, that he had paid his bill and gone back to the Continent by way of
Calais. Nevertheless, Jeremiah scraped out of his cogitating face a lively
conviction that Mr. Blandois would keep his word on this occasion, and
would be seen again.

CHAPTER XXXI

SPIRIT

ANYBODY may pass, any day, in the thronged thoroughfares of the
metropolis, some meagre, wrinkled, yellow old man (who might be supposed to have dropped from the stars, if there were any star in the Heavens
dull enough to be suspected of casting off so feeble a spark), creeping along
with a scared air, as though bewildered and a little frightened by the noise
and bustle. This old man is always a little old man. If he were ever a big old
man, he has shrunk into a little old man; if he were always a little old man,
he has dwindled into a less old man. His coat is of a color, and cut, that
never was the mode anywhere, at any period. Clearly, it was not made for
him, or for any individual mortal. Some wholesale contractor measured
Fate for five thousand coats of such quality, and Fate has lent this old coat
to this old man, as one of a long unfinished line of many old men. It has
always large dull metal buttons, similar to no other buttons. This old man
wears a hat, a thumbed and napless and yet an obdurate hat, which has
never adapted itself to the shape of his poor head. His coarse shirt and his

coarse neckcloth have no more individuality than his coat and hat; they have the same character of not being his—of not being anybody's. Yet this old man wears these clothes with a certain unaccustomed air of being dressed and elaborated for the public ways; as though he passed the greater part of his time in a nightcap and gown. And so, like the country mouse in the second year of a famine, come to see the town-mouse, and timidly threading his way to the town-mouse's lodging through a city of cats, this old man passes in the streets.

Sometimes, on holidays towards evening, he will be seen to walk with a slightly increased infirmity, and his old eyes will glimmer with a moist and marshy light. Then the little old man is drunk. A very small measure will overset him; he may be bowled off his unsteady legs with a half-pint pot. Some pitying acquaintance—chance acquaintance very often—has warmed up his weakness with a treat of beer, and the consequence will be the lapse of a longer time than usual before he shall pass again. For, the little old man is going home to the Workhouse; and on his good behaviour they do not let him out often (though methinks they might, considering the few years he has before him to go out in, under the sun); and on his bad behaviour they shut him up closer than ever, in a grove of two score and nineteen more old men, every one of whom smells of all the others.

Mrs. Plornish's father,—a poor little reedy piping old gentleman, like a worn-out bird; who had been in what he called the music-binding business, and met with great misfortunes, and who had seldom been able to make his way, or to see it or to pay it, or to do anything at all with it but find it no thoroughfare,—had retired of his own accord to the Workhouse which was appointed by law to be the Good Samaritan of his district (without the two pence, which was bad political economy), on the settlement of that execution which had carried Mr. Plornish to the Marshalsea College. Previous to his son-in-law's difficulties coming to that head, Old Nandy (he was always so called in his legal Retreat, but he was Old Mr. Nandy among the Bleeding Hearts) had sat in a corner of the Plornish fireside, and taken his bite and sup out of the Plornish cupboard. He still hoped to resume that domestic position, when Fortune should smile upon his son-in-law; in the meantime, while she preserved an immoveable countenance, he was, and resolved to remain, one of these little old men in a grove of little old men with a community of flavor.

But, no poverty in him, and no coat on him that never was the mode, and no Old Men's Ward for his dwelling-place, could quench his daughter's admiration. Mrs. Plornish was as proud of her father's talents as she could possibly have been if they had made him Lord Chancellor. She had as firm a belief in the sweetness and propriety of his manners as she could possibly have had if he had been Lord Chamberlain. The poor little old man knew some pale and vapid little songs, long out of date, about Chloe, and Phyllis,

and Strephon being wounded by the son of Venus; and for Mrs. Plornish
there was no such music at the Opera, as the small internal flutterings and
chirpings wherein he would discharge himself of these ditties, like a weak,
little, broken barrel-organ, ground by a baby. On his "days out," those
flecks of light in his flat vista of pollard old men, it was at once Mrs. Plornish's delight and sorrow, when he was strong with meat, and had taken
his full halfpenny-worth of porter, to say, "Sing us a song, Father." Then
would he give them Chloe, and, if he were in pretty good spirits, Phyllis
also—Strephon he had hardly been up to, since he went into retirement—
and then would Mrs. Plornish declare she did believe there never was such
a singer as Father, and wipe her eyes.

If he had come from Court on these occasions, nay, if he had been the
noble Refrigerator come home triumphantly from a foreign court to be
presented and promoted on his last tremendous failure, Mrs. Plornish
could not have handed him with greater elevation about Bleeding Heart
Yard. "Here's Father," she would say, presenting him to a neighbour.
"Father will soon be home with us for good, now. Ain't Father looking
well? Father's a sweeter singer than ever; you'd never have forgotten it, if
you had aheard him just now." As to Mr. Plornish, he had married these
articles of belief in marrying Mr. Nandy's daughter, and only wondered
how it was that so gifted an old gentleman had not made a fortune. This he
attributed, after much reflection, to his musical genius not having been
scientifically developed in his youth. "For why," argued Mr. Plornish,
"why go a binding music when you've got it in yourself? That's where it is,
I consider."

Old Nandy had a patron: one patron. He had a patron who, in a certain
sumptuous way—an apologetic way, as if he constantly took an admiring
audience to witness that he really could not help being more free with this
old fellow than they might have expected, on account of his simplicity and
poverty—was mightily good to him. Old Nandy had been several times to
the Marshalsea College, communicating with his son-in-law during his
short durance there; and had happily acquired to himself, and had by
degrees and in course of time much improved, the patronage of the Father
of that national institution.

Mr. Dorrit was in the habit of receiving this old man, as if the old man
held of him in vassalage under some feudal tenure. He made little treats
and teas for him, as if he came in with his homage from some outlying
district where the tenantry were in a primitive state. It seemed as if there
were moments when he could by no means have sworn but that the old
man was an ancient retainer of his, who had been meritoriously faithful.
When he mentioned him, he spoke of him casually as his old pensioner. He
had a wonderful satisfaction in seeing him, and in commenting on his
decayed condition after he was gone. It appeared to him amazing that he
could hold up his head at all, poor creature. "In the Workhouse, sir, the

Union: no privacy, no visitors, no station, no respect, no speciality. Most deplorable!"

It was old Nandy's birthday, and they let him out. He said nothing about its being his birthday, or they might have kept him in; for such old men should not be born. He passed along the streets as usual to Bleeding Heart Yard, and had his dinner with his daughter and son-in-law, and gave them Phyllis. He had hardly concluded, when Little Dorrit looked in to see how they all were.

"Miss Dorrit," said Mrs. Plornish. "Here's Father! Ain't he looking nice? And such voice he's in!"

Little Dorrit gave him her hand, and smilingly said she had not seen him this long time.

"No, they're rather hard on poor Father," said Mrs. Plornish, with a lengthening face, "and don't let him have half as much change and fresh air as would benefit him. But he'll soon be home for good, now. Won't you, Father?"

"Yes, my dear, I hope so. In good time, please God."

Here Mr. Plornish delivered himself of an oration which he invariably made, word for word the same, on all such opportunities. It was couched in the following terms:

"John Edward Nandy. Sir. While there's a ounce of wittles or drink of any sort in this present roof, you're fully welcome to your share on it. While there's a handful of fire or a mouthful of bed in this present roof, you're fully welcome to your share on it. If so be as there should be nothing in this present roof, you should be as welcome to your share on it as if it was something much or little. And this is what I mean and so I don't deceive you, and consequently which is to stand out is to entreat of you, and therefore why not do it?"

To this lucid address, which Mr. Plornish always delivered as if he had composed it (as no doubt he had) with enormous labor, Mrs. Plornish's father pipingly replied:

"I thank you kindly, Thomas, and I know your intentions well, which is the same I thank you kindly for. But no, Thomas. Until such times as it's not to take it out of your children's mouths, which take it is, and call it by what name you will it do remain and equally deprive though may they come and too soon they can not come, no Thomas, no!"

Mrs. Plornish, who had been turning her face a little away with a corner of her apron in her hand, brought herself back to the conversation again, by telling Miss Dorrit that Father was going over the water to pay his respects, unless she knew of any reason why it might not be agreeable.

Her answer was, "I am going straight home, and if he will come with me I shall be so glad to take care of him—so glad," said Little Dorrit, always thoughtful of the feelings of the weak, "of his company."

"There, Father!" cried Mrs. Plornish. "Ain't you a gay young man to be going for a walk along with Miss Dorrit! Let me tie your neck-handkerchief into a regular good bow, for you're a regular beau yourself, Father, if ever there was one."

With this filial joke his daughter smartened him up, and gave him a loving hug, and stood at the door with her weak child in her arms and her strong child tumbling down the steps, looking after her little old father as he toddled away with his arm under Little Dorrit's.

They walked at a slow pace, and Little Dorrit took him by the Iron Bridge and sat him down there for a rest, and they looked over at the water and talked about the shipping, and the old man mentioned what he would do if he had a ship full of gold coming home to him (his plan was to take a noble lodging for the Plornishes and himself at a Tea Gardens, and live there all the rest of their lives, attended on by the waiter), and it was a special birthday for the old man. They were within five minutes of their destination, when, at the corner of her own street, they came upon Fanny in her new bonnet bound for the same port.

"Why, good gracious me, Amy!" cried that young lady starting. "You never mean it!"

"Mean what, Fanny dear?"

"Well! I could have believed a great deal of you," returned the young lady with burning indignation, "but I don't think even I could have believed this, of even you!"

"Fanny!" cried Little Dorrit, wounded and astonished.

"Oh! Don't Fanny me, you mean little thing, don't! The idea of coming along the open streets, in the broad light of day, with a Pauper!" (firing off the last word as if it were a ball from an air-gun.)

"O Fanny!"

"I tell you not to Fanny me, for I'll not submit to it! I never knew such a thing. The way in which you are resolved and determined to disgrace us, on all occasions, is really infamous. You bad little thing!"

"Does it disgrace anybody," said Little Dorrit, very gently, "to take care of this poor old man?"

"Yes, miss," returned her sister, "and you ought to know it does. And you do know it does. And you do it because you know it does. The principal pleasure of your life is to remind your family of their misfortunes. And the next great pleasure of your existence is to keep low company. But, however, if you have no sense of decency, I have. You'll please to allow me to go on the other side of the way, unmolested."

With this, she bounced across to the opposite pavement. The old disgrace, who had been deferentially bowing a pace or two off (for Little Dorrit had let his arm go in her wonder, when Fanny began), and who had been hustled and cursed by impatient passengers for stopping the way, rejoined his companion, rather giddy, and said, "I hope nothing's wrong with your honored father, Miss? I hope there's nothing the matter in the honored family?"

"No, no," returned Little Dorrit. "No, thank you. Give me your arm again, Mr. Nandy. We shall soon be there now."

So, she talked to him as she had talked before, and they came to the Lodge and found Mr. Chivery on the lock, and went in. Now, it happened that the Father of the Marshalsea was sauntering towards the Lodge at the moment when they were coming out of it, entering the prison arm in arm. As the spectacle of their approach met his view, he displayed the utmost agitation and despondency of mind; and—altogether regardless of old Nandy, who, making his reverence, stood with his hat in his hand, as he always did in that gracious presence—turned about, and hurried in at his own doorway and up the staircase.

Leaving the old unfortunate, whom in an evil hour she had taken under her protection, with a hurried promise to return to him directly, Little Dorrit hastened after her father, and, on the staircase, found Fanny following her, and flouncing up with offended dignity. The three came into the room almost together; and the Father sat down in his chair, buried his face in his hands, and uttered a groan.

"Of course," said Fanny. "Very proper. Poor, afflicted Pa! Now, I hope you believe me, Miss!"

"What is it, father?" cried Little Dorrit, bending over him. "Have I made you unhappy, father? Not I, I hope!"

"You hope, indeed! I dare say! Oh, you"—Fanny paused for a sufficiently strong expression—"you Common-minded little Amy! You complete prison-child!"

He stopped these angry reproaches with a wave of his hand, and sobbed out, raising his face, and shaking his melancholy head at his younger daughter, "Amy, I know that you are innocent in intention. But you have cut me to the soul."

"Innocent in intention!" the implacable Fanny struck in. "Stuff in intention! Low in intention! Lowering of the family in intention!"

"Father!" cried Little Dorrit, pale and trembling, "I am very sorry. Pray forgive me. Tell me how it is, that I may not do it again!"

"How it is, you prevaricating little piece of goods!" cried Fanny. "You know how it is. I have told you already, so don't fly in the face of Providence by attempting to deny it!"

"Hush! Amy," said the father, passing his pocket-handkerchief several times across his face, and then grasping it convulsively in the hand that dropped across his knee, "I have done what I could to keep you select here; I have done what I could to retain you a position here. I may have succeeded; I may not. You may know it; you may not. I give no opinion. I have endured everything here but humiliation. That I have happily been spared—until this day."

Here his convulsive grasp unclosed itself, and he put his pocket-handkerchief to his eyes again. Little Dorrit, on the ground beside him, with her imploring hand upon his arm, watched him remorsefully.

Coming out of his fit of grief, he clenched his pocket-handkerchief once more.

"Humiliation I have happily been spared until this day. Through all my troubles there has been that—Spirit in myself, and that—that submission to it, if I may use the term, in those about me, which has spared me—ha—humiliation. But this day, this minute, I have keenly felt it."

"Of course! How could it be otherwise!" exclaimed the irrepressible Fanny. "Careering and prancing about with a Pauper!" (air-gun again).

"But, dear father," cried Little Dorrit, "I don't justify myself for having wounded your dear heart—no! Heaven knows I don't!" She clasped her hands in quite an agony of distress. "I do nothing but beg and pray you to be comforted, and overlook it. But if I had not known that you were kind to the old man yourself, and took much notice of him, and were always glad to see him, I would not have come here with him, father, I would not indeed. What I have been so unhappy as to do, I have done in mistake. I would not wilfully bring a tear to your eyes, dear love!" said Little Dorrit, her heart well nigh broken, "for anything the world could give me, or anything it could take away."

Fanny, with a partly angry and partly repentant sob, began to cry herself, and to say—as this young lady always said when she was half in a passion and half out of it, half-spiteful with herself and half-spiteful with everybody else—that she wished she was dead.

The Father of the Marshalsea in the meantime took his younger daughter to his breast, and patted her head.

"There, there! Say no more, Amy, say no more, my child. I will forget it as soon as I can. I," with hysterical cheerfulness, "I—shall soon be able to dismiss it. It is perfectly true, my dear, that I *am* always glad to see my old pensioner—as such, as such—and that I do—ha—extend as much protection and kindness to the—hum—the bruised reed—I trust I may so call him without impropriety—as in my circumstances, I can. It is quite true that this is the case, my dear child. At the same time, I preserve in doing this, if I may—ha—if I may use the expression —Spirit. Becoming Spirit. And there are some things which are," he stopped to sob, "irreconcileable with that, and wound that—wound it deeply. It is not that I have seen my good Amy attentive, and—ha—condescending to my old pensioner—it is not that that hurts me. It is, if I am to close the painful subject by being explicit, that I have seen my child, my own child, my own daughter, coming into this College out of the public streets—smiling! smiling!—arm in arm with—O my God, a livery!"

This reference to the coat of no cut and no time, the unfortunate gentleman gasped forth, in a scarcely audible voice, and with his clenched pocket-handkerchief raised in the air. His excited feelings might have found some further painful utterance, but for a knock at the door, which had been already twice repeated, and to which Fanny (still wishing herself dead, and indeed now going so far as to add, buried) cried "Come in!"

"Ah, Young John!" said the Father, in an altered and calmed voice. "What is it, Young John?"

"A letter for you, sir, being left in the Lodge just this minute, and a message with it, I thought, happening to be there myself, sir, I would bring it to your room." The speaker's attention was much distracted by the piteous spectacle of Little Dorrit at her father's feet, with her head turned away.

"Indeed, John? Thank you."

"The letter is from Mr. Clennam, sir—it's the answer—and the message was, sir, that Mr. Clennam also sent his compliments, and word that he would do himself the pleasure of calling this afternoon, hoping to see you, and likewise" attention more distracted than before "Miss Amy."

"Oh!" As the Father glanced into the letter (there was a bank-note in it), he reddened a little, and patted Amy on the head afresh. "Thank you, Young John. Quite right. Much obliged to you for your attention. No one waiting?"

"No, sir, no one waiting."

"Thank you, John. How is your mother, Young John?"

"Thank you, sir, she's not quite as well as we could wish—in fact, we none of us are, except father—but she's pretty well, sir."

"Say we sent our remembrances, will you? Say, kind remembrances, if you please, Young John."

"Thank you, sir, I will." And Mr. Chivery, junior, went his way, having spontaneously composed on the spot an entirely new epitaph for himself, to the effect that Here lay the body of John Chivery, Who, Having at such a date, Beheld the idol of his life, In grief and tears, And feeling unable to bear the harrowing spectacle, Immediately repaired to the abode of his inconsolable parents, And terminated his existence, By his own rash act.

"There, there, Amy!" said the Father, when Young John had closed the door, "let us say no more about it." The last few minutes had improved his spirits remarkably, and he was quite lightsome. "Where is my old pensioner all this while? We must not leave him by himself any longer, or he will begin to suppose he is not welcome, and that would pain me. Will you fetch him, my child, or shall I?"

"If you wouldn't mind, father," said Little Dorrit, trying to bring her sobbing to a close.

"Certainly I will go, my dear. I forgot; your eyes are rather red. There! Cheer up, Amy. Don't be uneasy about me. I am quite myself again, my love, quite myself. Go to your room, Amy, and make your face look comfortable and pleasant to receive Mr. Clennam."

"I would rather stay in my room, Father," returned Little Dorrit, finding it more difficult than before to regain her composure. "I would far rather not see Mr. Clennam."

"Oh, fie, fie, my dear, that's folly. Mr. Clennam is a very gentlemanly man—very gentlemanly. A little reserved at times; but I will say extremely gentlemanly. I couldn't think of your not being here to receive Mr. Clennam, my dear, especially this afternoon. So go and freshen yourself up, Amy; go and freshen yourself up, like a good girl."

Thus directed, Little Dorrit dutifully rose and obeyed: only pausing for a moment as she went out of the room, to give her sister a kiss of reconciliation. Upon which, that young lady, feeling much harassed in her mind, and having for the time worn out the wish with which she generally relieved it, conceived and executed the brilliant idea of wishing old Nandy dead, rather than that he should come bothering there like a disgusting, tiresome, wicked wretch, and making mischief between two sisters.

The Father of the Marshalsea, even humming a tune, and wearing his black velvet cap a little on one side, so much improved were his spirits, went down into the yard, and found his old pensioner standing hat in hand just within the gate, as he had stood all this time. "Come, Nandy!" said he, with great suavity. "Come up-stairs, Nandy; you know the way; why don't you come up-stairs?" He went the length, on this occasion, of giving him his hand, and saying, "How are you, Nandy? Are you pretty well?" To which that vocalist returned, "I thank you, honored sir, I am all the better for seeing your honor." As they went along the Yard, the Father of the Marshalsea presented him to a Collegian of recent date. "An old acquaintance of mine, sir, an old pensioner." And then said, "Be covered, my good Nandy; put your hat on," with great consideration.

His patronage did not stop here; for he charged Maggy to get the tea ready, and instructed her to buy certain tea cakes, fresh butter, eggs, cold ham, and shrimps: to purchase which collation, he gave her a bank-note for ten pounds, laying strict injunctions on her to be careful of the change. These preparations were in an advanced stage of progress, and his daughter Amy had come back with her work, when Clennam presented himself. Whom he most graciously received, and besought to join their meal.

"Amy, my love, you know Mr. Clennam even better than I have the happiness of doing. Fanny, my dear, you are acquainted with Mr. Clennam." Fanny acknowledged him haughtily; the position she tacitly took up in all such cases being that there was a vast conspiracy to insult the family by not understanding it, or sufficiently deferring to it, and here was one of the conspirators. "This, Mr. Clennam, you must know, is an old pensioner of mine, old Nandy, a very faithful old man." (He always spoke of him as an object of great antiquity, but he was two or three years younger than himself.) "Let me see. You know Plornish, I think? I think

The Pensioner-Entertainment

my daughter Amy has mentioned to me that you know poor Plornish?"

"Oh yes!" said Arthur Clennam.

"Well, sir, this is Mrs. Plornish's father."

"Indeed? I am glad to see him."

"You would be more glad if you knew his many good qualities, Mr. Clennam."

"I hope I shall come to know them, through knowing him," said Arthur, secretly pitying the bowed and submissive figure.

"It is a holiday with him, and he comes to see his old friends who are always glad to see him," observed the Father of the Marshalsea. Then he added behind his hand, "Union, poor old fellow. Out for the day."

By this time Maggy, quietly assisted by her Little Mother, had spread the board, and the repast was ready. It being hot weather and the prison very close, the window was as wide open as it could be pushed. "If Maggy will spread that newspaper on the window-sill, my dear," remarked the Father complacently and in a half whisper to Little Dorrit, "my old pensioner can have his tea there, while we are having ours."

So, with a gulf between him and the good company of about a foot in width, standard measure, Mrs. Plornish's father was handsomely regaled. Clennam had never seen anything like his magnanimous protection by that other Father, he of the Marshalsea; and was lost in the contemplation of its many wonders.

The most striking of these was perhaps the relishing manner in which he remarked on the pensioner's infirmities and failings. As if he were a gracious Keeper, making a running commentary on the decline of the harmless animal he exhibited.

"Not ready for more ham yet, Nandy? Why, how slow you are! (His last teeth," he explained to the company, "are going, poor old boy.")

At another time, he said, "No shrimps, Nandy?" and on his not instantly replying, observed, ("His hearing is becoming very defective. He'll be deaf directly.")

At another time, he asked him, "Do you walk much, Nandy, about the yard within the walls of that place of yours?"

"No, sir; no. I haven't any great liking for that."

"No, to be sure," he assented. "Very natural." Then he privately informed the circle ("Legs going.")

Once, he asked the pensioner, in that general clemency which asked him anything to keep him afloat, how old his younger grandchild was?

"John Edward," said the pensioner, slowly laying down his knife and fork to consider. "How old, sir? Let me think now."

The Father of the Marshalsea tapped his forehead. ("Memory weak.")

"John Edward, sir? Well, I really forget. I couldn't say, at this minute, sir, whether it's two and two months, or whether it's two and five months. It's one or the other."

"Don't distress yourself by worrying your mind about it," he returned, with infinite forbearance. ("Faculties evidently decaying—old man rusts in the life he leads!")

The more of these discoveries that he persuaded himself he made in the pensioner, the better he appeared to like him; and when he got out of his chair after tea, to bid the pensioner good bye, on his intimating that he feared, honored sir, his time was running out, he made himself look as erect and strong as possible.

"We don't call this a shilling, Nandy, you know," he said, putting one in his hand. "We call it tobacco."

"Honored sir, I thank you. It shall buy tobacco. My thanks and duty to Miss Amy and Miss Fanny. I wish you good night, Mr. Clennam."

"And mind you don't forget us, you know, Nandy," said the Father. "You must come again, mind, whenever you have an afternoon. You must not come out without seeing us, or we shall be jealous. Good night, Nandy. Be very careful how you descend the stairs, Nandy; they are rather uneven and worn." With that he stood on the landing, watching the old man down; and when he came into the room again, said, with a solemn satisfaction on him, "A melancholy sight that, Mr. Clennam, though one has the consolation of knowing that he doesn't feel it himself. The poor old fellow is a dismal wreck. Spirit broken and gone—pulverised—crushed out of him, sir, completely!"

As Clennam had a purpose in remaining, he said what he could responsive to these sentiments, and stood at the window with their enunciator, while Maggy and her Little Mother washed the tea-service and cleared it away. He noticed that his companion stood at the window with the air of an affable and accessible Sovereign, and that, when any of his people in the yard below looked up, his recognition of their salutes just stopped short of a blessing.

When Little Dorrit had her work on the table, and Maggy hers on the bedstead, Fanny fell to tying her bonnet as a preliminary to her departure. Arthur, still having his purpose, still remained. At this time the door opened, without any notice, and Mr. Tip came in. He kissed Amy as she started up to meet him, nodded to Fanny, nodded to his father, gloomed on the visitor without further recognition, and sat down.

"Tip, dear," said Little Dorrit mildly, shocked by this, "don't you see—"

"Yes, I see, Amy. If you refer to the presence of any visitor you have here—I say, if you refer to that," answered Tip, jerking his head with emphasis towards his shoulder nearest Clennam, "I see!"

"Is that all you say?"

"That's all I say. And I suppose," added the lofty young man, after a moment's pause, "the visitor will understand me, when I say that's all I say. In short, I suppose the visitor will understand, that he hasn't used me like a gentleman."

"I do not understand that," observed the obnoxious personage referred to, with tranquillity.

"No? Why, then, to make it clearer to you, sir, I beg to let you know, that when I address what I call a properly-worded appeal, and an urgent appeal, and a delicate appeal, to an individual, for a small temporary accommodation, easily within his power—easily within his power, mind!—and when that individual writes back word to me that he begs to be excused, I consider that he doesn't treat me like a gentleman."

The Father of the Marshalsea, who had surveyed his son in silence, no sooner heard this sentiment, than he began, in an angry voice:

"How dare you—" But his son stopped him.

"Now, don't ask me how I dare, father, because that's bosh. As to the fact of the line of conduct I choose to adopt towards the individual present, you ought to be proud of my showing a proper spirit."

"I should think so!" cried Fanny.

"A proper spirit?" said the father. "Yes, a proper spirit; a becoming spirit. Is it come to this, that my son teaches me—*me*—spirit!"

"Now, don't let us bother about it, father, or have any row on the subject. I have fully made up my mind that the individual present has not treated me like a gentleman. And there's an end of it."

"But there is not an end of it, sir," returned the father. "But there shall not be an end of it. You have made up your mind? You have made up your mind?"

"Yes, *I* have. What's the good of keeping on like that?"

"Because," returned the Father, in a great heat, "you had no right to make up your mind to what is monstrous, to what is—ha—immoral, to what is—hum—parricidal. No, Mr. Clennam, I beg, sir. Don't ask me to desist; there is a—hum—a general principle involved here, which rises even above considerations of—ha—hospitality. I object to the assertion made by my son. I—ha—I personally repel it."

"Why, what is it to you, father?" returned the son, over his shoulder.

"What is it to me, sir? I have a—hum—a spirit, sir, that will not endure it. I," he took out his pocket-handkerchief again and dabbed his face, "I am outraged and insulted by it. Let me suppose the case that I myself may at a certain time—ha—or times, have made a—hum—an appeal, and a properly-worded appeal, and a delicate appeal, and an urgent appeal, to some individual for a small temporary accommodation. Let me suppose that that accommodation could have been easily extended, and was not extended, and that that individual informed me that he begged to be excused. Am I to be told by my own son, that I therefore received treatment not due to a gentleman, and that I—ha—I submitted to it?"

His daughter Amy gently tried to calm him, but he would not on any account be calmed. He said his spirit was up, and wouldn't endure this.

Was he to be told that, he wished to know again, by his own son, on his own hearth, to his own face? Was that humiliation to be put upon him by his own blood?

"You are putting it on yourself, father, and getting into all this injury of your own accord," said the young gentleman morosely. "What I have made up my mind about, has nothing to do with you. What I said, had nothing to do with you. Why need you go trying on other people's hats?"

"I reply it has everything to do with me," returned the Father. "I point out to you, sir, with indignation, that—hum—the—ha—delicacy and peculiarity of your father's position should strike you dumb, sir, if nothing else should, in laying down such—ha—such unnatural principles. Besides; if you are not filial, sir, if you discard that duty, are you at least— hum—not a Christian? Are you—ha—an Atheist? And is it Christian, let me ask you, to stigmatise and denounce an individual for begging to be excused this time, when the same individual may—ha—respond with the required accommodation next time? Is it the part of a Christian not to— hum—not to try him again?" He had worked himself into quite a religious glow and fervor.

"I see precious well," said Mr. Tip, rising, "that I shall get no sensible or fair argument here to-night, and so the best thing I can do is to cut. Good night, Amy. Don't be vexed. I am very sorry it happens here, and you here, upon my soul I am; but I can't altogether part with my spirit, even for your sake, old girl."

With those words he put on his hat and went out, accompanied by Miss Fanny; who did not consider it spirited on her part to take leave of Clennam with any less opposing demonstration than a stare, importing that she had always known him for one of the large body of conspirators.

When they were gone, the Father of the Marshalsea was at first inclined to sink into despondency again, and would have done so, but that a gentle-man opportunely came up within a minute or two to attend him to the Snuggery. It was the gentleman Clennam had seen on the night of his own accidental detention there, who had that impalpable grievance about the misappropriated Fund on which the Marshal was supposed to batten. He presented himself as a deputation to escort the Father to the Chair; it being an occasion on which he had promised to preside over the assembled Collegians, in the enjoyment of a little Harmony.

"Such, you see, Mr. Clennam," said the Father, "are the incongruities of my position here. But a public duty! No man, I am sure, would more readily recognise a public duty than yourself."

Clennam besought him not to delay a moment.

"Amy, my dear, if you can persuade Mr. Clennam to stay longer, I can leave the honors of our poor apology for an establishment, with confidence in your hands, and perhaps you may do something towards erasing from Mr. Clennam's mind the—ha—untoward and unpleasant circumstance which has occurred since tea-time."

Clennam assured him that it had made no impression on his mind, and therefore required no erasure.

"My dear sir," said the Father, with a removal of his black cap and a grasp of Clennam's hand, combining to express the safe receipt of his note and enclosure that afternoon, "Heaven ever bless you!"

So, at last, Clennam's purpose in remaining was attained, and he could speak to Little Dorrit with nobody by. Maggy counted as nobody, and she was by.

CHAPTER XXXII

MORE FORTUNE-TELLING

MAGGY sat at her work in her great white cap, with its quantity of opaque frilling hiding what profile she had (she had none to spare), and her serviceable eye brought to bear upon her occupation, on the window side of the room. What with her flapping cap, and what with her unserviceable eye, she was quite partitioned off from her Little Mother, whose seat was opposite the window. The tread and shuffle of feet on the pavement of the yard had much diminished since the taking of the Chair; the tide of Collegians having set strongly in the direction of Harmony. Some few who had no music in their souls, or no money in their pockets, dawdled about; and the old spectacle of the visitor-wife and the depressed unseasoned prisoner still lingered in corners, as broken cobwebs and such unsightly discomforts draggle in corners of other places. It was the quietest time the College knew, saving the night-hours when the Collegians took the benefit of the act of sleep. The occasional rattle of applause upon the tables of the Snuggery, denoted the successful termination of a morsel of Harmony; or the responsive acceptance, by the united children, of some toast or sentiment offered to them by their Father. Occasionally, a vocal strain more sonorous than the generality informed the listener that some boastful bass was in blue water, or in the hunting-field, or with the rein-deer, or on the mountain, or among the heather; but the Marshal of the Marshalsea knew better, and had got him hard and fast.

As Arthur Clennam moved to sit down by the side of Little Dorrit, she trembled so that she had much ado to hold her needle. Clennam gently put his hand upon her work, and said "Dear Little Dorrit, let me lay it down."

She yielded it to him, and he put it aside. Her hands were then nervously clasping together, but he took one of them.

"How seldom I have seen you lately, Little Dorrit!"

"I have been busy, sir."

"But I heard only to-day," said Clennam, "by mere accident, of your having been with those good people close by me. Why not come to me, then?"

"I—I don't know. Or rather, I thought you might be busy too. You generally are now, are you not?"

He saw her trembling little form and her downcast face, and the eyes that drooped the moment they were raised to his—he saw them almost with as much concern as tenderness.

"My child, your manner is so changed!"

The trembling was now quite beyond her control. Softly withdrawing her hand, and laying it in her other hand, she sat before him with her head bent and her whole form trembling.

"My own Little Dorrit," said Clennam, compassionately.

She burst into tears. Maggy looked round of a sudden, and stared for at least a minute; but did not interpose. Clennam waited some little while before he spoke again.

"I cannot bear," he said then, "to see you weep; but I hope this is a relief to an overcharged heart."

"Yes it is, sir. Nothing but that."

"Well, well! I feared you would think too much of what passed here just now. It is of no moment; not the least. I am only unfortunate to have come in the way. Let it go by with these tears. It is not worth one of them. One of them? Such an idle thing should be repeated, with my glad consent, fifty times a day, to save you a moment's heart-ache, Little Dorrit."

She had taken courage now, and answered, far more in her usual manner, "You are so good! But even if there was nothing else in it to be sorry for and ashamed of, it is such a bad return to you——"

"Hush!" said Clennam, smiling and touching her lips with his hand. "Forgetfulness in you, who remember so many and so much, would be new indeed. Shall I remind you that I am not, and that I never was, anything but the friend whom you agreed to trust? No. You remember it, don't you?"

"I try to do so, or I should have broken the promise just now, when my mistaken brother was here. You will consider his bringing-up in this place, and will not judge him hardly, poor fellow, I know!" In raising her eyes with these words, she observed his face more nearly than she had done yet, and said, with a quick change of tone, "You have not been ill, Mr. Clennam?"

"No."

"Nor tried? Nor hurt?" she asked him, anxiously.

It fell to Clennam, now, to be not quite certain how to answer. He said in reply:

"To speak the truth, I have been a little troubled, but it is over. Do I show it so plainly? I ought to have more fortitude and self-command than that. I thought I had. I must learn them of you. Who could teach me better!"

He never thought that she saw in him what no one else could see. He never thought that in the whole world there were no other eyes that looked upon him with the same light and strength as hers.

"But it brings me to something that I wish to say," he continued, "and therefore I will not quarrel even with my own face for telling tales and being unfaithful to me. Besides, it is a privilege and pleasure to confide in my Little Dorrit. Let me confess then, that, forgetting how grave I was, and how old I was, and how the time for such things had gone by me with the many years of sameness and little happiness that made up my long life far away, without marking it—that, forgetting all this, I fancied I loved some one."

"Do I know her, sir?" asked Little Dorrit.

"No, my child."

"Not the lady who has been kind to me for your sake?"

"Flora. No, no. Did you think——"

"I never quite thought so," said Little Dorrit, more to herself than him. "I did wonder at it a little."

"Well!" said Clennam, abiding by the feeling that had fallen on him in the avenue on the night of the roses, the feeling that he was an older man, who had done with that tender part of life, "I found out my mistake, and I thought about it a little—in short, a good deal—and got wiser. Being wiser, I counted up my years, and considered what I am, and looked back, and looked forward, and found that I should soon be grey. I found that I had climbed the hill, and passed the level ground upon the top, and was descending quickly."

If he had known the sharpness of the pain he caused the patient heart, in speaking thus! While doing it, too, with the purpose of easing and serving her.

"I found that the day when any such thing would have been graceful in me, or good in me, or hopeful or happy for me, or any one in connexion with me, was gone, and would never shine again."

O! If he had known, if he had known! If he could have seen the dagger in his hand, and the cruel wounds it struck in the faithful bleeding breast of his Little Dorrit!

"All that is over, and I have turned my face from it. Why do I speak of this to Little Dorrit? Why do I show you, my child, the space of years that there is between us, and recall to you that I have passed, by the amount of your whole life, the time that is present to you?"

"Because you trust me, I hope. Because you know that nothing can touch you, without touching me; that nothing can make you happy or unhappy, but it must make me, who am so grateful to you, the same."

He heard the thrill in her voice, he saw her earnest face, he saw her clear true eyes, he saw the quickened bosom that would have joyfully thrown itself before him to receive a mortal wound directed at his breast, with the dying cry, "I love him!" and the remotest suspicion of the truth never dawned upon his mind. No. He saw the devoted little creature with her worn shoes, in her common dress, in her jail-home; a slender child in body, a strong heroine in soul; and the light of her domestic story made all else dark to him.

"For those reasons assuredly, Little Dorrit, but for another too. So far removed, so different, and so much older, I am the better fitted for your friend and adviser. I mean, I am the more easily to be trusted; and any little constraint that you might feel with another, may vanish before me. Why have you kept so retired from me? Tell me."

"I am better here. My place and use are here. I am much better here," said Little Dorrit, faintly.

"So you said that day, upon the bridge. I thought of it much afterwards. Have you no secret you could entrust to me, with hope and comfort, if you would?"

"Secret? No, I have no secret," said Little Dorrit, in some trouble.

They had been speaking in low voices; more because it was natural to what they said, to adopt that tone, than with any care to reserve it from Maggy at her work. All of a sudden Maggy stared again, and this time spoke:

"I say! Little Mother!"

"Yes, Maggy."

"If you an't got no secret of your own to tell him, tell him that about the Princess. *She* had a secret, you know."

"The Princess had a secret?" said Clennam, in some surprise. "What Princess was that, Maggy?"

"Lor! How you do go and bother a gal of ten," said Maggy, "catching the poor thing up in that way. Whoever said the Princess had a secret? *I* never said so."

"I beg your pardon. I thought you did."

"No, I didn't. How could I, when it was her as wanted to find it out? It was the little woman as had the secret, and she was always a spinning at her wheel. And so she says to her, why do you keep it there? And so, the t'other one says to her, no I don't; and so, the t'other one says to her, yes, you do; and then they both goes to the cupboard, and there it is. And she wouldn't go into the Hospital, and so she died. *You* know, Little Mother; tell him that. For it was a reg'lar good secret, that was!" cried Maggy, hugging herself.

Arthur looked at Little Dorrit for help to comprehend this, and was struck by seeing her so timid and red. But, when she told him that it was only a Fairy Tale she had one day made up for Maggy, and that there was nothing in it which she wouldn't be ashamed to tell again to anybody else, even if she could remember it, he left the subject where it was.

However, he returned to his own subject, by first entreating her to see him oftener, and to remember that it was impossible to have a stronger interest in her welfare than he had, or to be more set upon promoting it than he was. When she answered fervently, she well knew that, she never forgot it, he touched upon his second and more delicate point—the suspicion he had formed.

"Little Dorrit," he said, taking her hand again, and speaking lower than he had spoken yet, so that even Maggy in the small room could not hear him, "another word. I have wanted very much to say this to you; I have tried for opportunities. Don't mind me, who, for the matter of years, might be your father or your uncle. Always think of me as quite an old man. I know that all your devotion centres in this room, and that nothing to the last will ever tempt you away from the duties you discharge here. If I were not sure of it, I should, before now, have implored you, and implored your father, to let me make some provision for you in a more suitable place. But, you may have an interest—I will not say, now, though even that might be—may have, at another time, an interest in some one else; an interest not incompatible with your affection here."

She was very, very pale, and silently shook her head.

"It may be, dear Little Dorrit."

"No. No. No." She shook her head, after each slow repetition of the word, with an air of quiet desolation that he remembered long afterwards. The time came when he remembered it well, long afterwards, within those prison walls; within that very room.

"But, if it ever should be, tell me so, my dear child. Entrust the truth to me, point out the object of such an interest to me, and I will try with all the zeal, and honor, and friendship and respect that I feel for you, good Little Dorrit, of my heart, to do you a lasting service."

"O thank you, thank you! But, O no, O no, O no!" She said this, looking at him with her work-worn hands folded together, and in the same resigned accents as before.

"I press for no confidence now. I only ask you to repose unhesitating trust in me."

"Can I do less than that, when you are so good!"

"Then you will trust me fully? Will have no secret unhappiness, or anxiety, concealed from me?"

"Almost none."

"And you have none now?"

She shook her head. But she was very pale.

"When I lie down to-night, and my thoughts come back—as they will, for they do every night, even when I have not seen you—to this sad place, I may believe that there is no grief beyond this room, now, and its usual occupants, which preys on Little Dorrit's mind?"

She seemed to catch at these words—that he remembered, too, long afterwards—and said, more brightly, "Yes, Mr. Clennam; yes, you may!"

The crazy staircase, usually not slow to give notice when any one was coming up or down, here creaked under a quick tread, and a further sound was heard upon it, as if a little steam-engine with more steam than it knew what to do with, were working towards the room. As it approached, which it did very rapidly, it labored with increased energy; and, after knocking at the door, it sounded as if it were stooping down and snorting in at the keyhole.

Before Maggy could open the door, Mr. Pancks, opening it from without, stood without a hat and with his bare head in the wildest condition, looking at Clennam and Little Dorrit, over her shoulder. He had a lighted cigar in his hand, and brought with him airs of ale and tobacco smoke.

"Pancks the gipsy," he observed, out of breath, "fortune-telling."

He stood dingily smiling, and breathing hard at them, with a most curious air. As if, instead of being his proprietor's grubber, he were the triumphant proprietor of the Marshalsea, the Marshal, all the turnkeys, and all the Collegians. In his great self-satisfaction he put his cigar to his lips (being evidently no smoker), and took such a pull at it, with his right eye shut up tight for the purpose, that he underwent a convulsion of shuddering and choking. But even in the midst of that paroxysm, he still essayed to repeat his favorite introduction of himself, "Pa-ancks the gi-ipsy, fortune-telling."

"I am spending the evening with the rest of 'em," said Pancks. "I've been singing. I've been taking a part in White sand and grey sand. *I* don't know anything about it. Never mind. I'll take any part in anything. It's all the same, if you're loud enough."

At first, Clennam supposed him to be intoxicated. But, he soon perceived that though he might be a little the worse (or better) for ale, the staple of his excitement was not brewed from malt, or distilled from any grain or berry.

"How d'ye do, Miss Dorrit?" said Pancks. "I thought you wouldn't mind my running round, and looking in for a moment. Mr. Clennam I heard was here, from Mr. Dorrit. How are you, sir?"

Clennam thanked him, and said he was glad to see him so gay.

"Gay!" said Pancks. "I'm in wonderful feather, sir. I can't stop a minute, or I shall be missed, and I don't want 'em to miss me.—Eh, Miss Dorrit?"

He seemed to have an insatiate delight in appealing to her, and looking at her; excitedly sticking his hair up at the same moment, like a dark species of cockatoo.

"I haven't been here half-an-hour. I knew Mr. Dorrit was in the chair, and I said, 'I'll go and support him!' I ought to be down in Bleeding Heart Yard by rights; but I can worry them to-morrow.—Eh, Miss Dorrit?"

His little black eyes sparkled electrically. His very hair seemed to sparkle, as he roughened it. He was in that highly-charged state that one might have expected to draw sparks and snaps from him by presenting a knuckle to any part of his figure.

"Capital company here," said Pancks.—"Eh, Miss Dorrit?"

She was half afraid of him, and irresolute what to say. He laughed, with a nod towards Clennam.

"Don't mind him, Miss Dorrit. He's one of us. We agreed that you shouldn't take on to mind me before people, but we didn't mean Mr. Clennam. He's one of us. He's in it. An't you, Mr. Clennam?—Eh, Miss Dorrit?"

The excitement of this strange creature was fast communicating itself to Clennam. Little Dorrit, with amazement, saw this, and observed that they exchanged quick looks.

"I was making a remark," said Pancks, "but I declare I forget what it was. Oh, I know! Capital company here. I've been treating 'em all round.—Eh, Miss Dorrit?"

"Very generous of you," she returned, noticing another of the quick looks between the two.

"Not at all," said Pancks. "Don't mention it. I'm coming into my property, that's the fact. I can afford to be liberal. I think I'll give 'em a treat here. Tables laid in the yard. Bread in stacks. Pipes in faggots. Tobacco in hayloads. Roast beef and plum pudding for every one. Quart of double stout a head. Pint of wine too, if they like it, and the authorities give permission.—Eh, Miss Dorrit?"

She was thrown into such a confusion by his manner, or rather by Clennam's growing understanding of his manner (for she looked to him after every fresh appeal and cockatoo demonstration on the part of Mr. Pancks), that she only moved her lips in answer, without forming any word.

"And oh, by-the-bye!" said Pancks. "You were to live to know what was behind us on that little hand of yours. And so you shall, you shall, my darling.—Eh, Miss Dorrit?"

He had suddenly checked himself. Where he got all the additional black prongs from, that now flew up all over his head, like the myriads of points that break out in the last change of a great firework, was a wonderful mystery.

"But I shall be missed;" he came back to that; "and I don't want 'em to miss me. Mr. Clennam, you and I made a bargain. I said you should find me stick to it. You shall find me stick to it now, sir, if you'll step out of the room a moment. Miss Dorrit, I wish you good night. Miss Dorrit, I wish you good fortune."

He rapidly shook her by both hands, and puffed down-stairs. Arthur followed him with such a hurried step, that he had very nearly tumbled over him on the last landing, and rolled him down into the yard.

"What is it, for Heaven's sake!" Arthur demanded, when they burst out there both together.

"Stop a moment, sir. Mr. Rugg. Let me introduce him."

With those words he presented another man without a hat, and also with a cigar, and also surrounded with a halo of ale and tobacco smoke, which man, though not so excited as himself, was in a state which would have been akin to lunacy but for its fading into sober method when compared with the rampancy of Mr. Pancks.

"Mr. Clennam, Mr. Rugg," said Pancks. "Stop a moment. Come to the pump."

They adjourned to the pump. Mr. Pancks, instantly putting his head under the spout, requested Mr. Rugg to take a good strong turn at the handle. Mr. Rugg complying to the letter, Mr. Pancks came forth snorting and blowing to some purpose, and dried himself on his handkerchief.

"I am the clearer for that," he gasped to Clennam standing astonished. "But, upon my soul, to hear her father making speeches in that chair, knowing what we know, and to see her up in that room in that dress, knowing what we know, is enough to—give me a back, Mr. Rugg—a little higher, sir—that'll do!"

Then and there, on that Marshalsea pavement, in the shades of evening, did Mr. Pancks, of all mankind, fly over the head and shoulders of Mr. Rugg of Pentonville, General Agent, Accountant, and Recoverer of Debts. Alighting on his feet, he took Clennam by the button-hole, led him behind the pump, and pantingly produced from his pocket a bundle of papers. Mr. Rugg also pantingly produced from his pocket a bundle of papers.

"Stay!" said Clennam in a whisper. "You have made a discovery."

Mr. Pancks answered, with an unction which there is no language to convey, "We rather think so."

"Does it implicate any one?"

"How implicate, sir?"

"In any suppression, or wrong dealing of any kind?"

"Not a bit of it."

"Thank God!" said Clennam to himself. "Now, show me."

"You are to understand"—snorted Pancks, feverishly unfolding papers, and speaking in short high-pressure blasts of sentences, "Where's the Pedigree? Where's Schedule number four, Mr. Rugg? Oh! all right! Here we are.—You are to understand that we are this very day virtually complete. We shan't be legally for a day or two. Call it, at the outside, a week. We've been at it, night and day, for I don't know how long. Mr. Rugg, you know how long? Never mind. Don't say. You'll only confuse me. You shall tell her, Mr. Clennam. Not till we give you leave. Where's that rough total, Mr. Rugg? Oh! Here we are! There, sir! That's what you'll have to break to her. That man's your Father of the Marshalsea!"

END OF No. IX

CHAPTER XXXIII

RESIGNING herself to inevitable fate, by making the best of those people the Miggleses, and submitting her philosophy to the draught upon it, of which she had foreseen the likelihood in her interview with Arthur, Mrs. Gowan handsomely resolved not to oppose her son's marriage. In her progress to, and happy arrival at, this resolution, she was possibly influenced, not only by her maternal affections, but by three politic considerations.

Of these, the first may have been, that her son had never signified the smallest intention to ask her consent, or any mistrust of his ability to dispense with it; the second, that the pension bestowed upon her by a grateful country (and a Barnacle) would be freed from any little filial inroads, when her Henry should be married to the darling only child of a man in very easy circumstances; the third, that Henry's debts must clearly be paid down upon the altar-railing by his father-in-law. When, to these threefold points of prudence, there is added the fact that Mrs. Gowan yielded her consent the moment she knew of Mr. Meagles having yielded his, and that Mr. Meagles's objection to the marriage had been the sole obstacle in its way all along, it becomes the height of probability that the relict of the deceased Commissioner of nothing particular, turned these ideas in her sagacious mind.

Among her connexions and acquaintances, however, she maintained her individual dignity, and the dignity of the blood of the Barnacles, by diligently nursing the pretence that it was a most unfortunate business; that she was sadly cut up by it; that this was a perfect fascination, under which Henry labored; that she had opposed it for a long time, but what could a mother do; and the like. She had already called Arthur Clennam to bear witness to this fable, as a friend of the Meagles family; and she followed up the move by now impounding the family itself for the same purpose. In the first interview she accorded to Mr. Meagles, she slided herself into the position of disconsolately but gracefully yielding to irresistible pressure. With the utmost politeness and good-breeding, she feigned that it was she—not he—who had made the difficulty, and who at length gave way; and that the sacrifice was hers—not his. The same feint, with the same polite dexterity, she foisted on Mrs. Meagles, as a conjurer might have forced a card on that innocent lady; and, when her future daughter-in-law was presented to her by her son, she said, on embracing her, "My dear, what have you done to Henry that has bewitched him so!" at the same time allowing a few tears to carry before them, in little pills, the cosmetic powder on her nose; as a delicate but touching signal that she

suffered much inwardly, for the show of composure with which she bore
her misfortune.

Among the friends of Mrs. Gowan (who piqued herself at once on being
Society, and on maintaining intimate and easy relations with that Power),
Mrs. Merdle occupied a front row. True, the Hampton Court Bohemians,
without exception, turned up their noses at Merdle as an upstart; but they
turned them down again, by falling flat on their faces to worship his wealth.
In which compensating adjustment of their noses, they were pretty much
like Treasury, Bar, and Bishop, and all the rest of them.

To Mrs. Merdle, Mrs. Gowan repaired on a visit of self-condolence,
after having given the gracious consent aforesaid. She drove into town
for the purpose, in a one-horse carriage, irreverently called at that period
of English history, a pill-box. It belonged to a job-master in a small way,
who drove it himself, and who jobbed it by the day, or hour, to most of the
old ladies, in Hampton Court Palace; but it was a point of ceremony, in
that encampment, that the whole equipage should be tacitly regarded as
the private property of the jobber for the time being, and that the job-
master should betray personal knowledge of nobody but the jobber in
possession. So, the Circumlocution Barnacles, who were the largest job-
masters in the universe, always pretended to know of no other job but the
job immediately in hand.

Mrs. Merdle was at home, and was in her nest of crimson and gold, with
the parrot on a neighbouring stem watching her with his head on one side,
as if he took her for another splendid parrot of a larger species. To whom
entered Mrs. Gowan, with her favorite green fan, which softened the light
on the spots of bloom.

"My dear soul," said Mrs. Gowan, tapping the back of her friend's
hand with this fan, after a little indifferent conversation, "you are my only
comfort. That affair of Henry's that I told you of, is to take place. Now, how
does it strike you? I am dying to know, because you represent and express
Society so well."

Mrs. Merdle reviewed the bosom which Society was accustomed to
review; and having ascertained that show-window of Mr. Merdle's and
the London jewellers to be in good order, replied:

"As to marriage on the part of a man, my dear, Society requires that he
should retrieve his fortunes by marriage. Society requires that he should
gain by marriage. Society requires that he should found a handsome
establishment by marriage. Society does not see, otherwise, what he has to
do with marriage. Bird, be quiet!"

For, the parrot on his cage above them, presiding over the conference
as if he were a Judge (and indeed he looked rather like one), had wound up
the exposition with a shriek.

"Cases there are," said Mrs. Merdle, delicately crooking the little finger
of her favorite hand, and making her remarks neater by that neat action;

"cases there are where a man is not young or elegant, and is rich, and has a handsome establishment already. Those are of a different kind. In such cases——"

Mrs. Merdle shrugged her snowy shoulders and put her hand upon the jewel-stand, checking a little cough, as though to add, "why a man looks out for this sort of thing, my dear." Then the parrot shrieked again, and she put up her glass to look at him, and said, "Bird! Do be quiet!"

"But, young men," resumed Mrs. Merdle, "and by young men you know what I mean, my love—I mean people's sons who have the world before them—they must place themselves in a better position towards Society by marriage, or Society really will not have any patience with their making fools of themselves. Dreadfully worldly all this sounds," said Mrs. Merdle, leaning back in her nest and putting up her glass again, "does it not?"

"But it is true," said Mrs. Gowan, with a highly moral air.

"My dear, it is not to be disputed for a moment," returned Mrs. Merdle; "because Society has made up its mind on the subject, and there is nothing more to be said. If we were in a more primitive state, if we lived under roofs of leaves, and kept cows and sheep and creatures, instead of banker's accounts (which would be delicious; my dear, I am pastoral to a degree, by nature), well and good. But we don't live under leaves, and keep cows and sheep and creatures. I perfectly exhaust myself sometimes, in pointing out the distinction to Edmund Sparkler."

Mrs. Gowan, looking over her green fan when this young gentleman's name was mentioned, replied as follows:

"My love, you know the wretched state of the country—those unfortunate concessions of John Barnacle's!—and you therefore know the reasons for my being as poor as Thingummy."

"A Church-mouse?" Mrs. Merdle suggested with a smile.

"I was thinking of the other proverbial Church person—Job," said Mrs. Gowan. "Either will do. It would be idle to disguise, consequently, that there is a wide difference between the position of your son and mine. I may add, too, that Henry has talent——"

"Which Edmund certainly has not," said Mrs. Merdle, with the greatest suavity.

—"and that his talent, combined with disappointment," Mrs. Gowan went on, "has led him into a pursuit which—ah dear me! *You* know, my dear. Such being Henry's different position, the question is what is the most inferior class of marriage to which I can reconcile myself."

Mrs. Merdle was so much engaged with the contemplation of her arms (beautiful formed arms, and the very thing for bracelets), that she omitted to reply for a while. Roused at length by the silence, she folded the arms, and with admirable presence of mind looked her friend full in the face, and said interrogatively "Ye-es? And then?"

"And then, my dear," said Mrs. Gowan not quite so sweetly as before, "I should be glad to hear what you have to say to it."

Here the parrot, who had been standing on one leg since he screamed last, burst into a fit of laughter, bobbed himself derisively up and down on both legs, and finished by standing on one leg again, and pausing for a reply, with his head as much awry as he could possibly twist it.

"Sounds mercenary, to ask what the gentleman is to get with the lady," said Mrs. Merdle; "but Society *is* perhaps a little mercenary you know, my dear."

"From what I can make out," said Mrs. Gowan, "I believe I may say that Henry will be relieved from debt——"

"Much in debt?" asked Mrs. Merdle through her eye-glass.

"Why tolerably, I should think," said Mrs. Gowan.

"Meaning the usual thing; I understand; just so," Mrs. Merdle observed in a comfortable sort of way.

"And that the father will make them an allowance of three hundred a-year, or perhaps altogether something more. Which, in Italy——"

"Oh! Going to Italy?" said Mrs. Merdle.

"For Henry to study. You need be at no loss to guess why, my dear. That dreadful Art—"

True. Mrs. Merdle hastened to spare the feelings of her afflicted friend. She understood. Say no more!

"And that," said Mrs. Gowan, shaking her despondent head, "that's all. That," repeated Mrs. Gowan, furling her green fan for the moment and tapping her chin with it (it was on the way to being a double chin; might be called a chin and a half at present), "that's all! On the death of the old people, I suppose there will be more to come; but how it may be restricted or locked up, I don't know. And as to that, they may live for ever. My dear, they are just the kind of people to do it."

Now, Mrs. Merdle, who really knew her friend Society pretty well, and who knew what Society's mothers were, and what Society's daughters were, and what Society's matrimonial market was, and how prices ruled in it, and what scheming and counter-scheming took place for the high buyers, and what bargaining and huckstering went on, thought in the depths of her capacious bosom that this was a sufficiently good catch. Knowing, however, what was expected of her, and perceiving the exact nature of the fiction to be nursed, she took it delicately in her arms, and put her required contribution of gloss upon it.

"And that is all, my dear?" said she, heaving a friendly sigh. "Well, well! The fault is not yours. You have nothing to reproach yourself with. You must exercise the strength of mind for which you are renowned, and make the best of it."

"The girl's family have made," said Mrs. Gowan, "of course, the most strenuous endeavours to—as the lawyers say—to have and to hold Henry."

"Of course they have, my dear," said Mrs. Merdle.

"I have persisted in every possible objection, and have worried myself morning, noon, and night, for means to detach Henry from the connexion."

"No doubt you have, my dear," said Mrs. Merdle.

"And all of no use. All has broken down beneath me. Now tell me, my love. Am I justified in at last yielding my most reluctant consent to Henry's marrying among people not in Society; or, have I acted with inexcusable weakness?"

In answer to this direct appeal, Mrs. Merdle assured Mrs. Gowan (speaking as a Priestess of Society) that she was highly to be commended, that she was much to be sympathised with, that she had taken the highest of parts, and had come out of the furnace refined. And Mrs. Gowan, who of course saw through her own threadbare blind perfectly, and who knew that Mrs. Merdle saw through it perfectly, and who knew that Society would see through it perfectly, came out of this form, notwithstanding, as she had gone into it, with immense complacency and gravity.

The conference was held at four or five o'clock in the afternoon, when all the region of Harley Street, Cavendish Square, was resonant of carriage-wheels and double-knocks. It had reached this point when Mr. Merdle came home, from his daily occupation of causing the British name to be more and more respected in all parts of the civilised globe, capable of the appreciation of world-wide commercial enterprise and gigantic combinations of skill and capital. For, though nobody knew with the least precision what Mr. Merdle's business was, except that it was to coin money, these were the terms in which everybody defined it on all ceremonious occasions, and which it was the last new polite reading of the parable of the camel and the needle's eye to accept without enquiry.

For a gentleman who had this splendid work cut out for him, Mr. Merdle looked a little common, and rather as if, in the course of his vast trans-actions, he had accidentally made an interchange of heads with some inferior spirit. He presented himself before the two ladies, in the course of a dismal stroll through his mansion, which had no apparent object but escape from the presence of the chief butler.

"I beg your pardon," he said, stopping short in confusion; "I didn't know there was anybody here but the parrot."

However, as Mrs. Merdle said "You can come in!" and as Mrs. Gowan said she was just going, and had already risen to take her leave, he came in, and stood looking out at a distant window, with his hands crossed under his uneasy coat-cuffs, clasping his wrists as if he were taking himself into custody. In this attitude he fell directly into a reverie, from which he was only aroused by his wife's calling to him from her ottoman, when they had been for some quarter-of-an-hour alone.

"Eh? Yes?" said Mr. Merdle, turning towards her. "What is it?"

"What is it?" repeated Mrs. Merdle. "It is, I suppose, that you have not heard a word of my complaint."

"Your complaint, Mrs. Merdle?" said Mr. Merdle. "I didn't know that you were suffering from a complaint. What complaint?"

"A complaint of you," said Mrs. Merdle.

"Oh! A complaint of me," said Mr. Merdle. "What is the—what have I—what may you have to complain of in me, Mrs. Merdle?"

In his withdrawing, abstracted, pondering way, it took him some time to shape this question. As a kind of faint attempt to convince himself that he was the master of the house, he concluded by presenting his forefinger to the parrot, who expressed his opinion on that subject by instantly driving his bill into it.

"You were saying, Mrs. Merdle," said Mr. Merdle, with his wounded finger in his mouth, "that you had a complaint against me?"

"A complaint which I could scarcely show the justice of more emphatically, than by having to repeat it," said Mrs. Merdle. "I might as well have stated it to the wall. I had far better have stated it to the bird. He would at least have screamed."

"You don't want me to scream, Mrs. Merdle, I suppose," said Mr. Merdle, taking a chair.

"Indeed I don't know," retorted Mrs. Merdle, "but that you had better do that, than be so moody and distraught. One would at least know that you were sensible of what was going on around you."

"A man might scream, and yet not be that, Mrs. Merdle," said Mr. Merdle, heavily.

"And might be dogged, as you are at present, without screaming," returned Mrs. Merdle. "That's very true. If you wish to know the complaint I make against you, it is, in so many plain words, that you really ought not to go into Society, unless you can accommodate yourself to Society."

Mr. Merdle, so twisting his hands into what hair he had upon his head that he seemed to lift himself up by it as he started out of his chair, cried:

"Why, in the name of all the infernal powers, Mrs. Merdle, who does more for Society than I do? Do you see these premises, Mrs. Merdle? Do you see this furniture, Mrs. Merdle? Do you look in the glass and see yourself, Mrs. Merdle? Do you know the cost of all this, and who it's all provided for? And yet will you tell me that I oughtn't to go into Society? I, who shower money upon it in this way? I, who might be almost said—to—to—to harness myself to a watering-cart of money, and go about, saturating Society, every day of my life?"

"Pray don't be violent, Mr. Merdle," said Mrs. Merdle.

"Violent?" said Mr. Merdle. "You are enough to make me desperate.

You don't know half of what I do to accommodate Society. You don't know anything of the sacrifices I make for it."

"I know," returned Mrs. Merdle, "that you receive the best in the land. I know that you move in the whole Society of the country. And I believe I know (indeed, not to make any ridiculous pretence about it, I know I know) who sustains you in it, Mr. Merdle."

"Mrs. Merdle," retorted that gentleman, wiping his dull red and yellow face. "I know that, as well as you do. If you were not an ornament to Society, and if I was not a benefactor to Society, you and I would never have come together. When I say a benefactor to it, I mean a person who provides it with all sorts of expensive things to eat and drink and look at. But, to tell me that I am not fit for it after all I have done for it—after all I have done for it," repeated Mr. Merdle, with a wild emphasis that made his wife lift up her eyelids, "after all—all!—to tell me I have no right to mix with it after all, is a pretty reward."

"I say," answered Mrs. Merdle composedly, "that you ought to make yourself fit for it by being more *dégagé*, and less pre-occupied. There is a positive vulgarity in carrying your business affairs about with you as you do."

"How do I carry them about, Mrs. Merdle?" asked Mr. Merdle.

"How do you carry them about?" said Mrs. Merdle. "Look at yourself in the glass."

Mr. Merdle involuntarily turned his eyes in the direction of the nearest mirror, and asked, with a slow determination of his turbid blood to his temples, whether a man was to be called to account for his digestion?

"You have a physician," said Mrs. Merdle.

"He does me no good," said Mr. Merdle.

Mrs. Merdle changed her ground.

"Besides," said she, "your digestion is nonsense. I don't speak of your digestion. I speak of your manner."

"Mrs. Merdle," returned her husband, "I look to you for that. You supply manner, and I supply money."

"I don't expect you," said Mrs. Merdle, reposing easily among her cushions, "to captivate people. I don't want you to take any trouble upon yourself, or to try to be fascinating. I simply request you to care about nothing—or to seem to care about nothing—as everybody else does."

"Do I ever say I care about anything?" asked Mr. Merdle.

"Say? No! Nobody would attend to you if you did. But you show it."

"Show what? What do I show?" demanded Mr. Merdle hurriedly.

"I have already told you. You show that you carry your business cares and projects about, instead of leaving them in the City, or wherever else they belong to," said Mrs. Merdle. "Or seeming to. Seeming would be quite enough: I ask no more. Whereas you couldn't be more occupied with your day's calculations and combinations than you habitually show yourself to be, if you were a carpenter."

"A carpenter!" repeated Mr. Merdle, checking something like a groan. "I shouldn't so much mind being a carpenter, Mrs. Merdle."

"And my complaint is," pursued the lady, disregarding the low remark, "that it is not the tone of Society, and that you ought to correct it, Mr. Merdle. If you have any doubt of my judgment, ask even Edmund Sparkler " The door of the room had opened, and Mrs. Merdle now surveyed the head of her son through her glass. "Edmund; we want you here."

Mr. Sparkler, who had merely put in his head and looked round the room without entering (as if he were searching the house for that young lady with no nonsense about her), upon this followed up his head with his body, and stood before them. To whom, in a few easy words adapted to his capacity, Mrs. Merdle stated the question at issue.

The young gentleman, after anxiously feeling his shirt-collar as if it were his pulse and he were hypochondriacal, observed "That he had heard it noticed by fellers."

"Edmund Sparkler has heard it noticed," said Mrs. Merdle, with languid triumph. "Why, no doubt everybody has heard it noticed!" Which in truth was no unreasonable inference; seeing that Mr. Sparkler would probably be the last person, in any assemblage of the human species, to receive an impression from anything that passed in his presence.

"And Edmund Sparkler will tell you, I dare say," said Mrs. Merdle, waving her favorite hand towards her husband, "how he has heard it noticed."

"I couldn't," said Mr. Sparkler, after feeling his pulse as before, "couldn't undertake to say what led to it—'cause memory desperate loose. But being in company with the brother of a doosed fine gal—well educated too—with no biggodd nonsense about her—at the period alluded to——"

"There! Never mind the sister," remarked Mrs. Merdle, a little impatiently. "What did the brother say?"

"Didn't say a word, ma'am," answered Mr. Sparkler. "As silent a feller as myself. Equally hard up for a remark."

"Somebody said something," returned Mrs. Merdle. "Never mind who it was."

("Assure you I don't in the least," said Mr. Sparkler.)

"But tell us what it was."

Mr. Sparkler referred to his pulse again, and put himself through some severe mental discipline before he replied:

"Fellers referring to my Governor—expression not my own—occasionally compliment my Governor in a very handsome way on being immensely rich and knowing—perfect phenomenon of Buyer and Banker and that—but say the Shop sits heavy on him. Say he carries the Shop about, on his back rather—like Jew clothesman with too much business."

"Which," said Mrs. Merdle, rising, with her floating drapery about her, "is exactly my complaint. Edmund, give me your arm up-stairs."

Mr. Merdle, left alone to meditate on a better conformation of himself to Society, looked out of nine windows in succession, and appeared to see nine wastes of space. When he had thus entertained himself, he went down-stairs, and looked intently at all the carpets on the ground-floor; and then came up-stairs again, and looked intently at all the carpets on the first floor; as if they were gloomy depths, in unison with his oppressed soul. Through all the rooms he wandered, as he always did, like the last person on earth who had any business to approach them. Let Mrs. Merdle announce, with all her might, that she was At Home ever so many nights in a season, she could not announce more widely and unmistakeably than Mr. Merdle did that he was never at home.

At last he met the chief butler, the sight of which splendid retainer always finished him. Extinguished by this great creature, he sneaked to his dressing-room, and there remained shut up until he rode out to dinner, with Mrs. Merdle, in her own handsome chariot. At dinner, he was envied and flattered as a being of might, was Treasuried, Barred, and Bish-oped, as much as he would; and an hour after midnight came home alone, and being instantly put out again in his own hall, like a rushlight, by the chief butler, went sighing to bed.

CHAPTER XXXIV

A SHOAL OF BARNACLES

MR. HENRY GOWAN and the dog were established frequenters of the cottage, and the day was fixed for the wedding. There was to be a convocation of Barnacles on the occasion; in order that that very high and very large family might shed as much lustre on the marriage, as so dim an event was capable of receiving.

To have got the whole Barnacle family together, would have been impossible for two reasons. Firstly, because no building could have held all the members and connexions of that illustrious house. Secondly, because wherever there was a square yard of ground in British occupation, under the sun or moon, with a public post upon it, sticking to that post was a Barnacle. No intrepid navigator could plant a flag-staff upon any spot of earth, and take possession of it in the British name, but to that spot of earth, so soon as the discovery was known, the Circumlocution Office sent out a Barnacle and a dispatch-box. Thus the Barnacles were all over the world, in every direction—dispatch-boxing the compass.

But, while the so-potent art of Prospero himself would have failed in summoning the Barnacles from every speck of ocean and dry land on which there was nothing (except mischief) to be done, and anything to be pocketed, it was perfectly feasible to assemble a good many Barnacles. This, Mrs. Gowan applied herself to do; calling on Mr. Meagles frequently, with new additions to the list, and holding conferences with that gentleman when he was not engaged (as he generally was at this period) in examining and paying the debts of his future son-in-law, in the apartment of the scales and scoop.

One marriage guest there was, in reference to whose presence Mr. Meagles felt a nearer interest and concern than in the attendance of the most elevated Barnacle expected: though he was far from insensible of the honor of having such company. This guest was Clennam. But, Clennam had made a promise he held sacred, among the trees that summer night, and, in the chivalry of his heart, regarded it as binding him to many implied obligations. In forgetfulness of himself, and delicate service to her on all occasions, he was never to fail; to begin it, he answered Mr. Meagles cheerfully, "I shall come, of course."

His partner, Daniel Doyce, was something of a stumbling-block in Mr. Meagles's way, the worthy gentleman being not at all clear in his own anxious mind but that the mingling of Daniel with official Barnacleism might produce some explosive combination, even at a marriage breakfast. The national offender, however, lightened him of his uneasiness by coming down to Twickenham to represent that he begged, with the freedom of an old friend, and as a favor to one, that he might not be invited. "For," said he, "as my business with this set of gentlemen was to do a public duty and a public service, and as their business with me was to prevent it by wearing my soul out, I think we had better not eat and drink together with a show of being of one mind." Mr. Meagles was much amused by his friend's oddity; and patronised him with a more protecting air of allowance than usual, when he rejoined: "Well, well, Dan, you shall have your own crotchetty way."

To Mr. Henry Gowan, as the time approached, Clennam tried to convey by all quiet and unpretending means, that he was frankly and disinterestedly desirous of tendering him any friendship he would accept. Mr. Gowan treated him in return with his usual ease, and with his usual show of confidence, which was no confidence at all.

"You see, Clennam," he happened to remark in the course of conversation one day, when they were walking near the Cottage within a week of the marriage. "I am a disappointed man. That, you know already."

"Upon my word," said Clennam, a little embarrassed, "I scarcely know how."

"Why," returned Gowan. "I belong to a clan, or a clique, or a family, or a connexion, or whatever you like to call it, that might have provided for me in any one of fifty ways, and that took it into its head not to do it at all.

So here I am, a poor devil of an artist."

Clennam was beginning, "But on the other hand—" when Gowan took him up.

"Yes, yes, I know. I have the good fortune of being beloved by a beautiful and charming girl whom I love with all my heart."

("Is there much of it?" Clennam thought. And as he thought it, felt ashamed of himself.)

"And of finding a father-in-law who is a capital fellow and a liberal good old boy. Still, I had other prospects washed and combed into my childish head when it was washed and combed for me, and I took them to a public school when I washed and combed it for myself, and I am here without them, and thus I am a disappointed man."

Clennam thought (and as he thought it, again felt ashamed of himself), was this notion of being disappointed in life, an assertion of station which the bridegroom brought into the family as his property, having already carried it detrimentally into his pursuit? And was it a hopeful or a promising thing anywhere?

"Not bitterly disappointed, I think," he said aloud.

"Hang it, no; not bitterly," laughed Gowan. "My people are not worth that—though they are charming fellows, and I have the greatest affection for them. Besides, it's pleasant to show them that I can do without them, and that they may all go to the Devil. And besides again, most men are disappointed in life, somehow or other, and influenced by their disappointment. But it's a dear good world, and I love it!"

"It lies fair before you now," said Arthur.

"Fair as this summer river," cried the other, with enthusiasm, "and by Jove I glow with admiration of it, and with ardor to run a race in it. It's the best of old worlds! And my calling! The best of old callings, isn't it?"

"Full of interest and ambition, I conceive," said Clennam.

"And imposition," added Gowan, laughing; "we won't leave out the imposition. I hope I may not break down in that; but there, my being a disappointed man may show itself. I may not be able to face it out gravely enough. Between you and me, I think there is some danger of my being just enough soured not to be able to do that."

"To do what?" asked Clennam.

"To keep it up. To help myself in my turn, as the man before me helps himself in his, and pass the bottle of smoke. To keep up the pretence as to labor, and study, and patience, and being devoted to my art, and giving up many solitary days to it, and abandoning many pleasures for it, and living in it, and all the rest of it—in short to pass the bottle of smoke, according to rule."

"But it is well for a man to respect his own vocation, whatever it is; and to think himself bound to uphold it, and to claim for it the respect it deserves; is it not?" Arthur reasoned. "And your vocation, Gowan, may really demand this suit and service. I confess I should have thought that all Art did."

"What a good fellow you are, Clennam!" exclaimed the other, stopping to look at him, as if with irrepressible admiration. "What a capital fellow! *You* have never been disappointed. That's easy to see."

It would have been so cruel if he had meant it, that Clennam firmly resolved to believe he did not mean it. Gowan, without pausing, laid his hand upon his shoulder, and laughingly and lightly went on:

"Clennam, I don't like to dispel your generous visions, and I would give any money (if I had any) to live in such a rose-colored mist. But what I do in my trade, I do to sell. What all we fellows do, we do to sell. If we didn't want to sell it, for the most we can get for it, we shouldn't do it. Being work, it has to be done; but it's easily enough done. All the rest is hocus-pocus. Now here's one of the advantages, or disadvantages, of knowing a disappointed man. You hear the truth."

Whatever he had heard, and whether it deserved that name or another, it sank into Clennam's mind. It so took root there, that he began to fear Henry Gowan would always be a trouble to him, and that so far he had gained little or nothing from the dismissal of Nobody, with all his inconsistencies, anxieties, and contradictions. He found a contest still always going on in his breast, between his promise to keep Gowan in none but good aspects before the mind of Mr. Meagles, and his enforced observation of Gowan in aspects that had no good in them. Nor could he quite support his own conscientious nature against misgivings that he distorted and discolored him, by reminding himself that he never sought these discoveries, and that he would have avoided them with willingness and great relief. For, he never could forget what had been; and he knew that he had once disliked Gowan, for no better reason than that he had come in his way.

Harassed by these thoughts, he now began to wish the marriage over, Gowan and his young wife gone, and himself left to fulfil his promise, and discharge the generous function he had accepted. This last week was, in truth, an uneasy interval for the whole house. Before Pet, or before Gowan, Mr. Meagles was radiant; but, Clennam had more than once found him alone, with his view of the scales and scoop much blurred, and had often seen him look after the lovers, in the garden or elsewhere when he was not seen by them, with the old clouded face on which Gowan had fallen like a shadow. In the arrangement of the house for the great occasion, many little reminders of the old travels of the father and mother and daughter had to be disturbed, and passed from hand to hand; and sometimes, in the midst of these mute witnesses to the life they had had together, even Pet herself would yield to lamenting and weeping. Mrs. Meagles, the blithest and busiest of mothers, went about singing and cheering everybody; but she, honest soul, had her flights into store-rooms, where she would cry until her eyes were red, and would then come out, attributing that appearance to pickled onions and pepper, and singing clearer than ever. Mrs. Tickit, finding no balsam for a wounded mind in Buchan's Domestic Medicine, suffered greatly from low spirits, and from moving recollections of Minnie's infancy. When the latter were powerful with her, she usually sent up secret messages importing that she was not in parlor condition as to her attire, and that she solicited a sight of "her child" in the kitchen; there, she would bless her child's face, and bless her child's heart, and hug her child, in a medley of tears and congratulations, chopping-boards, rolling-pins, and pie-crust, with the tenderness of an attached old servant, which is a very pretty tenderness indeed.

But, all days come that are to be; and the marriage-day was to be, and it came; and with it came all the Barnacles who were bidden to the feast.

There was Mr. Tite Barnacle, from the Circumlocution Office and Mews Street, Grosvenor Square, with the expensive Mrs. Tite Barnacle *née* Stiltstalking, who made the Quarter Days so long in coming, and the three expensive Miss Tite Barnacles, double-loaded with accomplishments and ready to go off, and yet not going off with the sharpness of flash and bang that might have been expected, but rather hanging fire. There was Barnacle Junior, also from the Circumlocution Office, leaving the Tonnage of the country, which he was somehow supposed to take under his protection, to look after itself, and, sooth to say, not at all impairing the efficiency of his protection by leaving it alone. There was the engaging Young Barnacle, deriving from the sprightly side of the family, also from the Circumlocution Office, gaily and agreeably helping the occasion along, and treating it, in his sparkling way, as one of the official forms and fees of the Church Department of How not to do it. There were three other Young Barnacles, from three other offices, insipid to all the senses, and terribly in want of seasoning, doing the marriage as they would have "done" the Nile, old Rome, the new singer, or Jerusalem.

But, there was greater game than this. There was Lord Decimus Tite Barnacle himself, in the odor of Circumlocution—with the very smell of Dispatch-Boxes upon him. Yes, there was Lord Decimus Tite Barnacle, who had risen to official heights on the wings of one indignant idea, and that was, My Lords, that I am yet to be told that it behoves a Minister of this free country to set bounds to the philanthropy, to cramp the charity, to fetter the public spirit, to contract the enterprise, to damp the independent self-reliance, of its people. That was, in other words, that this great statesman was always yet to be told that it behoved the Pilot of the ship to do anything but prosper in the private loaf and fish trade ashore, the crew being able, by dint of hard pumping, to keep the ship above water without him. On this sublime discovery, in the great art How not to do it, Lord

Decimus had long sustained the highest glory of the Barnacle family; and let any ill-advised member of either House but try How to do it, by bringing in a Bill to do it, that Bill was as good as dead and buried when Lord Decimus Tite Barnacle rose up in his place, and solemnly said, soaring into indignant majesty as the Circumlocution cheering soared around him, that he was yet to be told, My Lords, that it behoved him as the Minister of this free country, to set bounds to the philanthropy, to cramp the charity, to fetter the public spirit, to contract the enterprise, to damp the independent self-reliance, of its people. The discovery of this Behoving Machine was the discovery of the political perpetual motion. It never wore out, though it was always going round and round in all the State Departments.

And there, with his noble friend and relative Lord Decimus, was William Barnacle, who had made the ever-famous coalition with Tudor Stiltstalking, and who always kept ready his own particular recipe for How not to do it; sometimes tapping the Speaker, and drawing it fresh out of him, with a "First, I will beg you, sir, to inform the House what Precedent we have for the course into which the honorable gentleman would precipitate us;" sometimes asking the honorable gentleman to favor him with his own version of the Precedent; sometimes telling the honorable gentleman that he (William Barnacle) would search for a Precedent; and oftentimes crushing the honorable gentleman flat on the spot, by telling him there was no Precedent. But, Precedent and Precipitate were, under all circumstances, the well-matched pair of battle-horses of this able Circumlocutionist. No matter that the unhappy honorable gentleman had been trying in vain, for twenty-five years, to precipitate William Barnacle into this—William Barnacle still put it to the House, and (at second-hand or so) to the country, whether he was to be precipitated into this. No matter that it was utterly irreconcileable with the nature of things and course of events, that the wretched honorable gentleman could possibly produce a Precedent for this—William Barnacle would nevertheless thank the honorable gentleman for that ironical cheer, and would close with him upon that issue, and would tell him to his teeth that there was NO Precedent for this. It might perhaps have been objected that the William Barnacle wisdom was not high wisdom, or the earth it bamboozled would never have been made, or, if made in a rash mistake, would have remained blank mad. But, Precedent and Precipitate together frightened all objection out of most people.

And there, too, was another Barnacle, a lively one, who had leaped through twenty places in quick succession, and was always in two or three at once, and who was the much respected inventor of an art which he practised with great success and admiration in all Barnacle Governments. This was, when he was asked a Parliamentary question on any one topic, to return an answer on any other. It had done immense service, and brought him into high esteem with the Circumlocution Office.

And there too was a sprinkling of less distinguished Parliamentary Barnacles, who had not as yet got anything snug, and were going through their probation to prove their worthiness. These Barnacles perched upon staircases and hid in passages, waiting their orders to make houses or not to make houses; and they did all their hearing, and ohing, and cheering, and barking, under directions from the heads of the family; and they put dummy motions on the paper in the way of other men's motions, and they stalled disagreeable subjects off until late in the night and late in the session, and then with virtuous patriotism cried out that it was too late; and they went down into the country, whenever they were sent, and swore that Lord Decimus had revived trade from a swoon and commerce from a fit, and had doubled the harvest of corn, quadrupled the harvest of hay, and prevented no end of gold from flying out of the Bank. Also these Barnacles were dealt, by the heads of the family, like so many cards below the court cards, to public meetings and dinners; where they bore testimony to all sorts of services on the part of their noble and honorable relatives, and buttered the Barnacles on all sorts of toasts. And they stood, under similar orders, at all sorts of elections; and they turned out of their own seats, on the shortest notice and the most unreasonable terms, to let in other men; and they fetched and carried, and toadied and jobbed, and corrupted, and ate heaps of dirt, and were indefatigable in the public service. And there was not a list, in all the Circumlocution Office, of places that might fall vacant anywhere within half a century, from a lord of the Treasury to a Chinese consul, and up again to a governor-general of India, but, as applicants for such places, the names of some or of every one of these hungry and adhesive Barnacles were down.

It was necessarily but a sprinkling of any class of Barnacles that attended the marriage, for there were not two score in all, and what is that subtracted from Legion! But, the sprinkling was a swarm in the Twickenham cottage, and filled it. A Barnacle (assisted by a Barnacle) married the happy pair, and it behoved Lord Decimus Tite Barnacle himself to conduct Mrs. Meagles to breakfast.

The entertainment was not as agreeable and natural as it might have been. Mr. Meagles, hove down by his good company while he highly appreciated it, was not himself. Mrs. Gowan was herself, and that did not improve him. The fiction that it was not Mr. Meagles who had stood in the way, but that it was the Family greatness, and that the Family greatness had made a concession, and there was now a soothing unanimity, pervaded the affair, though it was never openly expressed. Then the Barnacles felt that they for their parts would have done with the Meagleses, when the present patronising occasion was over; and the Meagleses felt the same for their parts. Then Gowan, asserting his rights as a disappointed man who had his

grudge against the family, and who perhaps had allowed his mother to
have them there, as much in the hope that it might give them some annoy-
ance as with any other benevolent object, aired his pencil and his poverty
ostentatiously before them, and told them he hoped in time to settle a crust
of bread and cheese on his wife, and that he begged such of them as (more
fortunate than himself) came in for any good thing, and could buy a
picture, to please to remember the poor painter. Then Lord Decimus, who
was a wonder on his own Parliamentary pedestal, turned out to be the
windiest creature here: proposing happiness to the bride and bridegroom
in a series of platitudes, that would have made the hair of any sincere
disciple and believer stand on end: and trotting, with the complacency of an
idiotic elephant, among howling labyrinths of sentences which he seemed
to take for high roads, and never so much as wanted to get out of. Then Mr.
Tite Barnacle could not but feel that there was a person in company, who
would have disturbed his life-long sitting to Sir Thomas Lawrence in full
official character, if such disturbance had been possible: while Barnacle
Junior did, with indignation, communicate to two vapid young gentlemen
his relatives, that there was a feller here, look here, who had come to our
Department without an appointment and said he wanted to know, you
know; and that, look here, if he was to break out now, as he might you
know (for you never could tell what an ungentlemanly Radical of that sort
would be up to next), and was to say, look here, that he wanted to know this
moment, you know, that would be Jolly; wouldn't it?

The pleasantest part of the occasion, by far, to Clennam, was the painfullest. When Mr. and Mrs. Meagles at last hung about Pet, in the room
with the two pictures (where the company were not), before going with her
to the threshold which she could never re-cross to be the old Pet and the old
delight, nothing could be more natural and simple than the three were.
Gowan himself was touched, and answered Mr. Meagles's "O, Gowan,
take care of her, take care of her!" with an earnest "Don't be so broken-
hearted, sir. By Heaven I will!"

And so, with last sobs and last loving words, and a last look to Clennam
of confidence in his promise, Pet fell back in the carriage, and her husband
waved his hand, and they were away for Dover. Though not until the
faithful Mrs. Tickit, in her silk gown and jet black curls, had rushed out
from some hiding-place, and thrown both her shoes after the carriage; an
apparition which occasioned great surprise to the distinguished company
at the windows.

The said company being now relieved from further attendance, and
the chief Barnacles being rather hurried (for they had it in hand just then
to send a mail or two, which was in danger of going straight to its destination, beating about the seas like the Flying Dutchman, and to arrange with
complexity for the stoppage of a good deal of important business otherwise in peril of being done), went their several ways; with all affability

conveying to Mr. and Mrs. Meagles, that general assurance that what they had been doing there, they had been doing at a sacrifice for Mr. and Mrs. Meagles's good, which they always conveyed to Mr. John Bull in their official condescension to that most unfortunate creature.

A miserable blank remained in the house, and in the hearts of the father and mother and Clennam. Mr. Meagles called only one remembrance to his aid, that really did him good.

"It's very gratifying, Arthur," he said, "after all, to look back upon."

"The past?" said Clennam.

"Yes—but I mean the company."

It had made him much more low and unhappy at the time, but now it really did him good. "It's very gratifying," he said, often repeating the remark in the course of the evening. "Such high company!"

CHAPTER XXXV

WHAT WAS BEHIND MR. PANCKS ON LITTLE DORRIT'S HAND

I T was at this time, that Mr. Pancks, in discharge of his compact with Clennam, revealed to him the whole of his gipsy story, and told him Little Dorrit's fortune. Her father was heir-at-law to a great estate that had long lain unknown of, unclaimed, and accumulating. His right was now clear, nothing interposed in his way, the Marshalsea gates stood open, the Marshalsea walls were down, a few flourishes of his pen and he was extremely rich.

In his tracking out of the claim to its complete establishment, Mr. Pancks had shown a sagacity that nothing could baffle, and a patience and secrecy that nothing could tire. "I little thought, sir," said Pancks, "when you and I crossed Smithfield that night, and I told you what sort of a Collector I was, that this would come of it. I little thought, sir, when I told you you were not of the Clennams of Cornwall, that I was ever going to tell you who *were* of the Dorrits of Dorsetshire." He then went on to detail, How, having that name recorded in his note-book, he was first attracted by the name alone. How, having often found two exactly similar names, even belonging to the same place, to involve no traceable consanguinity, near or distant, he did not at first give much heed to this; except in the way of speculation as to what a surprising change would be made in the condition of a little seamstress, if she could be shown to have any interest in so large a property. How he rather supposed himself to have pursued the idea into its next degree, because there was something uncommon in the quiet little seamstress, which pleased him and provoked his curiosity. How he had felt his way inch by inch, and "Moled it out, sir" (that was Mr. Pancks's expression), grain by grain. How, in the beginning of the labor described by this new verb, and to render which the more expressive Mr. Pancks shut his eyes in pronouncing it and shook his hair over them, he had alternated from sudden lights and hopes to sudden darkness and no hopes, and back again, and back again. How he had made acquaintances in the prison, expressly that he might come and go there as all other comers and goers did; and how his first ray of light was unconsciously given him by Mr. Dorrit himself, and by his son: to both of whom he easily became known; with both of whom he talked much, casually ("but always Moleing you'll observe," said Mr. Pancks); and from whom he derived, without being at all suspected, two or three little points of family history which, as he began to hold clues of his own, suggested others. How it had at length become plain to Mr. Pancks, that he had made a real discovery of the heir-at-law to a great fortune, and that his discovery had but to be ripened to legal fulness and perfection. How he had, thereupon, sworn his landlord, Mr. Rugg, to secresy in a solemn manner, and taken him into Moleing partnership. How they had employed John Chivery as their sole clerk and agent, seeing to whom he was devoted. And how, until the present hour, when authorities mighty in the Bank and learned in the law declared their successful labors ended, they had confided in no other human being.

"So if the whole thing had broken down, sir," concluded Pancks, "at the very last, say the day before the other day when I showed you our papers in the prison yard, or say that very day, nobody but ourselves would have been cruelly disappointed, or a penny the worse."

Clennam, who had been almost incessantly shaking hands with him throughout the narrative, was reminded by this to say, in an amazement which even the preparation he had had for the main disclosure scarcely smoothed down, "My dear Mr. Pancks, this must have cost you a great sum of money."

"Pretty well, sir," said the triumphant Pancks. "No trifle, though we did it as cheap as it could be done. And the outlay was a difficulty, let me tell you."

"A difficulty!" repeated Clennam. "But the difficulties you have so wonderfully conquered in the whole business!" shaking his hand again.

"I'll tell you how I did it," said the delighted Pancks, putting his hair into a condition as elevated as himself. "First, I spent all I had of my own. That wasn't much."

"I am sorry for it," said Clennam; "not that it matters now, though. Then, what did you do?"

"Then," answered Pancks, "I borrowed a sum of my proprietor."

"Of Mr. Casby?" said Clennam. "He's a fine old fellow."

"Noble old boy; an't he?" said Mr. Pancks, entering on a series of the dryest of snorts. "Generous old buck. Confiding old boy. Philanthropic old buck. Benevolent old boy! Twenty per cent I engaged to pay him, sir. But we never do business for less, at our shop."

Arthur felt an awkward consciousness of having, in his exultant condition, been a little premature.

"I said to that—boiling-over old Christian," Mr. Pancks pursued, appearing greatly to relish this descriptive epithet, "that I had got a little project on hand; a hopeful one; I told him a hopeful one; which wanted a certain small capital. I proposed to him to lend me the money on my note. Which he did, at twenty: sticking the twenty on in a business-like way, and putting it into the note, to look like a part of the principal. If I had broken down after that, I should have been his grubber for the next seven years at half wages and double grind. But he's a perfect Patriarch; and it would do a man good to serve him on such terms—on any terms."

Arthur for his life could not have said with confidence whether Pancks really thought so or not.

"When that was gone, sir," resumed Pancks, "and it did go, though I dribbled it out like so much blood, I had taken Mr. Rugg into the secret. I proposed to borrow of Mr. Rugg (or of Miss Rugg; it's the same thing; she made a little money by a speculation in the Common Pleas once). He lent it at ten, and thought that pretty high. But Mr. Rugg's a red-haired man, sir, and gets his hair cut. And as to the crown of his hat, it's high. And as to the brim of his hat, it's narrow. And there's no more benevolence bubbling out of *him*, than out of a ninepin."

"Your own recompense for all this, Mr. Pancks," said Clennam, "ought to be a large one."

"I don't mistrust getting it, sir," said Pancks. "I have made no bargain. I owed you one on that score; now, I have paid it. Money out of pocket made good, time fairly allowed for, and Mr. Rugg's bill settled, a thousand pounds would be a fortune to me. That matter I place in your hands. I authorise you, now, to break all this to the family in any way you think best. Miss Amy Dorrit will be with Mrs. Finching this morning. The sooner done the better. Can't be done too soon."

This conversation took place in Clennam's bedroom, while he was yet in bed. For, Mr. Pancks had knocked up the house and made his way in, very early in the morning; and, without once sitting down or standing still, had delivered himself of the whole of his details (illustrated with a variety of documents) at the bedside. He now said he would "go and look up Mr. Rugg," from whom his excited state of mind appeared to require another back; and bundling up his papers, and exchanging one more hearty shake of the hand with Clennam, he went at full speed down-stairs, and steamed off.

Clennam, of course, resolved to go direct to Mr. Casby's. He dressed and got out so quickly, that he found himself at the corner of the patriarchal street nearly an hour before her time; but he was not sorry to have the opportunity of calming himself with a leisurely walk.

When he returned to the street, and had knocked at the bright brass knocker, he was informed that she had come, and was shown up-stairs to Flora's breakfast-room. Little Dorrit was not there herself, but Flora was, and testified the greatest amazement at seeing him.

"Good gracious, Arthur—Doyce and Clennam!" cried that lady, "who would have ever thought of such a sight as this and pray excuse a wrapper for upon my word I really never and a faded check too which is worse but our little friend is making me a, not that I need mind mentioning it to you for you must know that there are such things a skirt, and having arranged that a trying on should take place after breakfast is the reason though I wish not so badly starched."

"I ought to make an apology," said Arthur, "for so early and abrupt a visit; but you will excuse it when I tell you the cause."

"In times for ever fled Arthur," returned Mrs. Finching, "pray excuse me Doyce and Clennam infinitely more correct and though unquestionably distant still 'tis distance lends enchantment to the view, at least I don't mean that and if I did I suppose it would depend considerably on the nature of the view, but I'm running on again and you put it all out of my head."

She glanced at him tenderly, and resumed:

"In times for ever fled I was going to say it would have sounded strange indeed for Arthur Clennam—Doyce and Clennam naturally quite different—to make apologies for coming here at any time, but that is past and what is past can never be recalled except in his own case as poor Mr F said when he was in spirits Cucumber and therefore never ate it."

She was making the tea when Arthur came in, and now hastily finished that operation.

"Papa," she said, all mystery and whisper, as she shut down the tea-pot lid, "is sitting prosingly breaking his new-laid egg in the back parlor over the City article exactly like the Woodpecker Tapping and need never know that you are here, and our little friend you are well aware may be fully trusted when she comes down from cutting out on the large table overhead."

Arthur then told her, in the fewest words, that it was their little friend he came to see; and what he had to announce to their little friend. At which astounding intelligence, Flora clasped her hands, fell into a tremble, and shed tears of sympathy and pleasure, like the good-natured creature she really was.

"For gracious sake let me get out of the way first," said Flora, putting her hands to her ears, and moving towards the door, "or I know I shall go off dead and screaming and make everybody worse, and the dear little thing only this morning looking so nice and neat and good and yet so poor and now a fortune is she really and deserves it too! and might I mention it to

Mr. F's aunt Arthur not Doyce and Clennam for this once or if objectionable not on any account."

Arthur nodded his free permission, since Flora shut out all verbal
communication. Flora nodded in return to thank him, and hurried out of
the room.

Little Dorrit's step was already on the stairs, and in another moment
she was at the door. Do what he would to compose his face, he could not
convey so much of an ordinary expression into it, but that the moment
she saw it she dropped her work, and cried "Mr. Clennam! What's the
matter!"

"Nothing, nothing. That is, no misfortune has happened. I have come
to tell you something, but it is a piece of great good-fortune."

"Good-fortune?"

"Wonderful fortune!"

They stood in a window, and her eyes, full of light, were fixed upon his
face. He put an arm about her, seeing her likely to sink down. She put a
hand upon that arm, partly to rest upon it, and partly so to preserve their
relative positions as that her intent look at him should be shaken by no
change of attitude in either of them. Her lips seemed to repeat "Wonderful
fortune?" He repeated it again, aloud.

"Dear Little Dorrit! Your father."

The ice of the pale face broke at the word, and little lights and shoots of
expression passed all over it. They were all expressions of pain. Her breath
was faint and hurried. Her heart beat fast. He would have clasped the little
figure closer, but he saw that the eyes appealed to him not to be moved.

"Your father can be free within this week. He does not know it; we must
go to him, from here, to tell him of it. Your father will be free within a few
days. Your father will be free within a few hours. Remember we must go
to him, from here, to tell him of it!"

That brought her back. Her eyes were closing, but they opened again.

"This is not all the good-fortune. This is not all the wonderful good-
fortune, my dear Little Dorrit. Shall I tell you more?"

Her lips shaped "Yes."

"Your father will be no beggar when he is free. He will want for nothing.
Shall I tell you more? Remember! He knows nothing of it; we must go to
him, from here, to tell him of it!"

She seemed to entreat him for a little time. He held her in his arm, and,
after a pause, bent down his ear to listen.

"Did you ask me to go on?"

"Yes."

"He will be a rich man. He is a rich man. A great sum of money is
waiting to be paid over to him as his inheritance; you are all henceforth
very wealthy. Bravest and best of children, I thank Heaven that you are
rewarded!"

As he kissed her, she turned her head towards his shoulder, and raised her arm towards his neck; cried out "Father! Father! Father!" and swooned away.

Upon which, Flora returned to take care of her, and hovered about her on a sofa, intermingling kind offices and incoherent scraps of conversation in a manner so confounding, that whether she pressed the Marshalsea to take a spoonful of unclaimed dividends, for it would do her good; or whether she congratulated Little Dorrit's father on coming into possession of a hundred thousand smelling-bottles; or whether she explained that she put seventy-five thousand drops of spirits of lavender on fifty thousand pounds of lump sugar, and that she entreated Little Dorrit to take that gentle restorative; or whether she bathed the foreheads of Doyce and Clennam in vinegar, and gave the late Mr. F more air; no one with any sense of responsibility could have undertaken to decide. A tributary stream of confusion, moreover, poured in from an adjoining bedroom, where Mr. F's Aunt appeared, from the sound of her voice, to be in a horizontal posture, awaiting her breakfast; and from which bower that inexorable lady snapped off short taunts, whenever she could get a hearing, as, "Don't believe it's his doing!" and "He needn't take no credit to himself for it!" and "It'll be long enough, I expect, afore he'll give up any of his own money!" all designed to disparage Clennam's share in the discovery, and to relieve those inveterate feelings with which Mr. F's Aunt regarded him.

But, Little Dorrit's solicitude to get to her father, and to carry the joyful tidings to him, and not to leave him in his jail a moment with this happiness in store for him and still unknown to him, did more for her speedy restoration than all the skill and attention on earth could have done. "Come with me to my dear father. Pray come and tell my dear father!" were the first words she said. Her father, her father. She spoke of nothing but him, thought of nothing but him. Kneeling down and pouring out her thankfulness with uplifted hands, her thanks were for her father.

Flora's tenderness was quite overcome by this, and she launched out among the cups and saucers into a wonderful flow of tears and speech.

"I declare," she sobbed, "I never was so cut up since your mama and my papa not Doyce and Clennam for this once but give the precious little thing a cup of tea and make her put it to her lips at least pray Arthur do, not even Mr. F's last illness for that was of another kind and gout is not a child's affection though very painful for all parties and Mr. F a martyr with his leg upon a rest and the wine trade in itself inflammatory for they will do it more or less among themselves and who can wonder, it seems like a dream I am sure to think of nothing at all this morning and now Mines of money is it really, but you must you know my darling love because you never will be strong enough to tell him all about it upon teaspoons, mightn't it be even best to try the directions of my own medical man for though the flavor is anything but agreeable still I force myself to do it as a prescription and find the benefit, you'd rather not why no my dear I'd rather not but still I do it as a duty, everybody will congratulate you some in earnest and some not and many will congratulate you with all their hearts but none more so I do assure you than from the bottom of my own I do myself though sensible of blundering and being stupid, and will be judged by Arthur not Doyce and Clennam for this once so good bye darling and God bless you and may you be very happy and excuse the liberty, vowing that the dress shall never be finished by anybody else but shall be laid by for a keepsake just as it is and called Little Dorrit though why that strangest of denominations at any time I never did myself and now I never shall!"

Thus Flora, in taking leave of her favorite. Little Dorrit thanked her, and embraced her, over and over again; and finally came out of the house with Clennam, and took coach for the Marshalsea.

It was a strangely unreal ride through the old squalid streets, with a bewildering sensation of being raised out of them, into an airy world of wealth and grandeur. When Arthur told her that she would soon ride in her own carriage through very different scenes, when all these familiar experiences would have vanished away, she looked frightened. But, when he substituted her father for herself, and told her how he would ride in his carriage, and how great and grand he would be, her tears of joy and innocent pride fell fast. Seeing that the happiness her mind could realise was all shining upon him, Arthur kept that single figure before her; and so they rode brightly through the poor streets in the prison neighbourhood, to carry him the great news.

When Mr. Chivery, who was on duty, admitted them into the Lodge, he saw something in their faces which filled him with astonishment. He stood looking after them, when they hurried into the prison, as though he perceived that they had come back accompanied by a ghost a-piece. Two or three Collegians whom they passed, looked after them too, and presently joining Mr. Chivery, formed a little group on the lodge steps, in the midst of which there spontaneously originated a whisper that the Father was going to get his discharge. Within a few minutes, it was heard in the remotest room in the College.

Little Dorrit opened the door from without, and they both entered. He was sitting in his old grey gown, and his old black cap, in the sunlight by the window, reading his newspaper. His glasses were in his hand, and he had just looked round; surprised at first, no doubt, by her step upon the stairs, not expecting her until night; surprised again, by seeing Arthur Clennam in her company. As they came in, the same unwonted look in both of them which had already caught attention in the yard below, struck him. He did not rise or speak, but laid down his glasses and his newspaper on the table beside him, and looked at them with his mouth a little open, and his lips trembling. When Arthur put out his hand, he touched it, but not with his usual state; and then he turned to his daughter, who had sat down close beside him with her hands upon his shoulder, and looked attentively in her face.

"Father! I have been made so happy this morning!"

"You have been made so happy, my dear?"

"By Mr. Clennam, father. He brought me such joyful and wonderful intelligence about you! If he had not, with his great kindness and gentleness, prepared me for it, father—prepared me for it, father—I think I could not have borne it."

Her agitation was exceedingly great, and the tears rolled down her face. He put his hand suddenly to his heart, and looked at Clennam.

"Compose yourself, sir," said Clennam, "and take a little time to think. To think of the brightest and most fortunate accidents of life. We have all heard of great surprises of joy. They are not at an end, sir. They are rare, but not at an end."

"Mr. Clennam? Not at an end? Not at an end for——" He touched himself upon the breast, instead of saying "me."

"No," returned Clennam.

"What surprise," he asked, keeping his left hand over his heart, and there stopping in his speech, while with his right hand he put his glasses exactly level on the table: "what such surprise can be in store for me?"

"Let me answer with another question. Tell me, Mr. Dorrit, what surprise would be the most unlooked for and the most acceptable to you. Do not be afraid to imagine it, or to say what it would be."

He looked stedfastly at Clennam, and, so looking at him, seemed to change into a very old haggard man. The sun was bright upon the wall beyond the window, and on the spikes at top. He slowly stretched out the hand that had been upon his heart, and pointed at the wall.

"It is down," said Clennam. "Gone!"

He remained in the same attitude, looking stedfastly at him.

"And in its place," said Clennam, slowly and distinctly, "are the means to possess and enjoy the utmost that they have so long shut out. Mr. Dorrit, there is not the smallest doubt that within a few days you will be free, and highly prosperous. I congratulate you with all my soul on this change of fortune, and on the happy future into which you are soon to carry the treasure you have been blest with here—the best of all the riches you can have elsewhere—the treasure at your side."

With those words, he pressed his hand and released it; and his daughter, laying her face against his, encircled him in the hour of his prosperity with her arms, as she had in the long years of his adversity encircled him with her love and toil and truth; and poured out her full heart in gratitude, hope, joy, blissful ecstacy, and all for him.

"I shall see him, as I never saw him yet. I shall see my dear love, with the dark cloud cleared away. I shall see him, as my poor mother saw him long ago. O my dear, my dear! O father, father! O thank God, thank God!"

He yielded himself to her kisses and caresses, but did not return them, except that he put an arm about her. Neither did he say one word. His stedfast look was now divided between her and Clennam, and he began to shake as if he were very cold. Explaining to Little Dorrit that he would run to the coffee-house for a bottle of wine, Arthur fetched it with all the haste he could use. While it was being brought from the cellar to the bar, a number of excited people asked him what had happened; when he hurriedly informed them, that Mr. Dorrit had succeeded to a fortune.

On coming back with the wine in his hand, he found that she had placed her father in his easy chair, and had loosened his shirt and neckcloth. They filled a tumbler with wine, and held it to his lips. When he had swallowed a little, he took the glass himself and emptied it. Soon after that, he leaned back in his chair and cried, with his handkerchief before his face.

After this had lasted a while, Clennam thought it a good season for diverting his attention from the main surprise, by relating its details. Slowly, therefore, and in a quiet tone of voice, he explained them as he best could, and enlarged on the nature of Pancks's service.

"He shall be—ha—he shall be handsomely recompensed, sir," said the Father, starting up and moving hurriedly about the room. "Assure yourself, Mr. Clennam, that everybody concerned shall be—ha—shall be nobly rewarded. No one, my dear sir, shall say that he has an unsatisfied claim against me. I shall repay the—hum—the advances I have had from you, sir, with peculiar pleasure. I beg to be informed, at your early convenience, what advances you have made my son."

He had no purpose in going about the room, but he was not still a moment.

"Everybody," he said, "shall be remembered. I will not go away from here in anybody's debt. All the people who have been—ha—well behaved towards myself and my family, shall be rewarded. Chivery shall be rewarded. Young John shall be rewarded. I particularly wish, and intend, to act munificently, Mr. Clennam."

"Will you allow me," said Arthur, laying his purse on the table, "to supply any present contingencies, Mr. Dorrit? I thought it best to bring a sum of money for the purpose."

"Thank you, sir, thank you. I accept with readiness, at the present moment, what I could not an hour ago have conscientiously taken. I am obliged to you for the temporary accommodation. Exceedingly temporary, but well timed—well timed." His hand had closed upon the money, and he carried it about with him. "Be so kind, sir, as to add the amount to those former advances to which I have already referred; being careful, if you please, not to omit advances made to my son. A mere verbal statement of the gross amount is all I shall—ha—all I shall require."

His eye fell upon his daughter at this point, and he stopped for a moment to kiss her, and to pat her head.

"It will be necessary to find a milliner, my love, and to make a speedy and complete change in your very plain dress. Something must be done with Maggy too, who at present is—ha—barely respectable, barely respectable. And your sister, Amy, and your brother. And *my* brother, your uncle—poor soul, I trust this will rouse him—messengers must be dispatched to fetch them. They must be informed of this. We must break it to them cautiously, but they must be informed directly. We owe it as a duty to them, and to ourselves, from this moment, not to let them—hum —not to let them do anything."

This was the first intimation he had ever given, that he was privy to the fact that they did something for a livelihood.

He was still jogging about the room, with the purse clutched in his hand, when a great cheering arose in the yard. "The news has spread already," said Clennam, looking down from the window. "Will you show yourself to them, Mr. Dorrit? They are very earnest, and they evidently wish it."

"I—hum—ha—I confess I could have desired, Amy my dear," he said, jogging about in a more feverish flutter than before, "to have made some change in my dress first, and to have bought a—hum—a watch and chain. But if it must be done as it is, it—ha—it must be done. Fasten the collar of my shirt, my dear. Mr. Clennam, would you oblige me—hum—with a blue neckcloth you will find in that drawer at your elbow. Button my coat across at the chest, my love. It looks—ha—it looks broader, buttoned."

With his trembling hand he pushed his grey hair up, and then, taking Clennam and his daughter for supporters, appeared at the window leaning on an arm of each. The Collegians cheered him very heartily, and he kissed his hand to them with great urbanity and protection. When he withdrew into the room again, he said "Poor creatures!" in a tone of much pity for their miserable condition.

Little Dorrit was deeply anxious that he should lie down to compose himself. On Arthur's speaking to her of his going to inform Pancks that he might now appear as soon as he would, and pursue the joyful business to its close, she entreated him in a whisper to stay with her, until her father should be quite calm and at rest. He needed no second entreaty; and she prepared her father's bed, and begged him to lie down. For another half-hour or more he would be persuaded to do nothing but go about the room, discussing with himself the probabilities for and against the Marshal's allowing the whole of the prisoners to go to the windows of the official residence which commanded the street, to see himself and family depart for ever in a carriage —which, he said, he thought would be a Sight for them. But, gradually, he began to droop and tire, and at last stretched himself upon the bed.

She took her faithful place beside him, fanning him and cooling his forehead; and he seemed to be falling asleep (always with the money in his hand), when he unexpectedly sat up and said:

"Mr. Clennam, I beg your pardon. Am I to understand, my dear sir, that I could—ha—could· pass through the Lodge at this moment, and—hum—take a walk?"

"I think not, Mr. Dorrit," was the unwilling reply. "There are certain forms to be completed; and although your detention here is now in itself a form, I fear it is one that for a little longer has to be observed too."

At this he shed tears again.

"It is but a few hours, sir," Clennam cheerfully urged upon him.

"A few hours, sir," he returned in a sudden passion. "You talk very easily of hours, sir! How long do you suppose, sir, that an hour is to a man who is choking for want of air?"

It was his last demonstration for that time; as, after shedding some more tears and querulously complaining that he couldn't breathe, he slowly fell into a slumber. Clennam had abundant occupation for his thoughts, as he sat in the quiet room watching the father on his bed, and the daughter fanning his face.

Little Dorrit had been thinking too. After softly putting his grey hair aside, and touching his forehead with her lips, she looked towards Arthur, who came nearer to her, and pursued in a low whisper the subject of her thoughts.

"Mr. Clennam, will he pay all his debts before he leaves here?"

"No doubt. All."

"All the debts for which he has been imprisoned here, all my life and longer?"

"No doubt."

There was something of uncertainty and remonstrance in her look; something that was not all satisfaction. He wondered to detect it, and said:

"You are glad that he should do so?"

"Are you?" asked Little Dorrit, wistfully.

"Am I? Most heartily glad!"

"Then I know I ought to be."

"And are you not?"

"It seems to me hard," said Little Dorrit, "that he should have lost so many years and suffered so much, and at last pay all the debts as well. It seems to me hard that he should pay in life and money both."

"My dear child—" Clennam was beginning.

"Yes, I know I am wrong," she pleaded timidly, "don't think any worse of me; it has grown up with me here."

The prison, which could spoil so many things, had tainted Little Dorrit's mind no more than this. Engendered as the confusion was, in compassion for the poor prisoner, her father, it was the first speck Clennam had ever seen, it was the last speck Clennam ever saw, of the prison atmosphere upon her.

He thought this, and forbore to say another word. With the thought, her purity and goodness came before him in their brightest light. The little spot made them the more beautiful.

Worn out with her own emotions, and yielding to the silence of the room, her hand slowly slackened and failed in its fanning movement, and her head dropped down on the pillow at her father's side. Clennam rose softly, opened and closed the door without a sound, and passed from the prison, carrying the quiet with him into the turbulent streets.

CHAPTER XXXVI

THE MARSHALSEA BECOMES AN ORPHAN

AND now the day arrived, when Mr. Dorrit and his family were to leave the prison for ever, and the stones of its much-trodden pavement were to know them no more.

The interval had been short, but he had greatly complained of its length, and had been imperious with Mr. Rugg touching the delay. He had been high with Mr. Rugg, and had threatened to employ some one else. He had requested Mr. Rugg not to presume upon the place in which he found him, but to do his duty, sir, and to do it with promptitude. He had told Mr. Rugg that he knew what lawyers and agents were, and that he would not submit to imposition. On that gentleman's humbly representing that he exerted himself to the utmost, Miss Fanny was very short with him; desiring to know what less he could do, when he had been told a dozen times that money was no object, and expressing her suspicion that he forgot whom he talked to.

Towards the Marshal, who was a Marshal of many years' standing, and with whom he had never had any previous difference, Mr. Dorrit comported himself with severity. That officer, on personally tendering his congratulations, offered the free use of two rooms in his house for Mr. Dorrit's occupation until his departure. Mr. Dorrit thanked him at the moment, and replied that he would think of it; but the Marshal was no sooner gone than he sat down and wrote him a cutting note, in which he remarked that he had never on any former occasion had the honor of receiving his congratulations (which was true, though indeed there had not been anything particular to congratulate him upon), and that he begged, on behalf of himself and family, to repudiate the Marshal's offer, with all those thanks which its disinterested character and its perfect independence of all worldly considerations demanded.

Although his brother showed so dim a glimmering of interest in their altered fortunes, that it was very doubtful whether he understood them, Mr. Dorrit caused him to be measured for new raiment by the hosiers, tailors, hatters, and bootmakers whom he called in for himself; and ordered that his old clothes should be taken from him and burned. Miss Fanny and Mr. Tip required no direction in making an appearance of great fashion and elegance; and the three passed this interval together at the best hotel in the neighbourhood—though truly, as Miss Fanny said, the best was very indifferent. In connexion with that establishment, Mr. Tip hired a cabriolet, horse, and groom, a very neat turn-out, which was usually to be observed for two or three hours at a time, gracing the Borough High Street, outside the Marshalsea courtyard. A modest little hired chariot and pair was also frequently to be seen there; in alighting from and entering which vehicle, Miss Fanny fluttered the Marshal's daughters by the display of inaccessible bonnets.

A great deal of business was transacted in this short period. Among other items, Messrs. Peddle and Pool, solicitors, of Monument Yard, were instructed by their client Edward Dorrit, Esquire, to address a letter to Mr. Arthur Clennam, enclosing the sum of twenty-four pounds nine shillings and eightpence, being the amount of principal and interest computed at the rate of five per cent per annum, in which their client believed himself to be indebted to Mr. Clennam. In making this communication and remittance, Messrs. Peddle and Pool were further instructed by their client to remind Mr. Clennam, that the favor of the advance now repaid (including gate-fees) had not been asked of him, and to inform him that it would not have been accepted if it had been openly proffered in his name. With which they requested a stamped receipt, and remained his obedient servants. A great deal of business had likewise to be done, within the so-soon-to-be-orphaned Marshalsea, by Mr. Dorrit so long its Father, chiefly arising out of applications made to him by Collegians for small sums of money. To these he responded with the greatest liberality, and with no lack of formality; always first writing to appoint a time at which the applicant might wait upon him in his room, and then receiving him in the midst of a vast accumulation of documents, and accompanying his donation (for he said in every such case, "it is a donation, not a loan") with a great deal of good counsel: to the effect that he, the expiring Father of the Marshalsea, hoped to be long remembered, as an example that a man might preserve his own and the general respect even there.

The Collegians were not envious. Besides that they had a personal and traditional regard for a Collegian of so many years standing, the event was creditable to the College, and made it famous in the newspapers. Perhaps more of them thought, too, than were quite aware of it, that the thing might in the lottery of chances have happened to themselves, or that something of the sort might yet happen to themselves, some day or other. They took it very well. A few were low at the thought of being left behind, and being left poor; but even these did not grudge the family their brilliant reverse. There might have been much more envy in politer places. It seems probable that mediocrity of fortune would have been disposed to be less magnanimous than the Collegians, who lived from hand to mouth—from the pawnbroker's hand to the day's dinner.

They got up an address to him, which they presented in a neat frame and glass (though it was not afterwards displayed in the family mansion or preserved among the family papers); and to which he returned a gracious answer. In that document he assured them, in a Royal manner, that he received the profession of their attachment with a full conviction of its sincerity; and again generally exhorted them to follow his example— which, at least in so far as coming into a great property was concerned, there is no doubt they would have gladly imitated. He took the same occasion of inviting them to a comprehensive entertainment, to be given to the whole College in the yard, and at which he signified he would have the honor of taking a parting glass to the health and happiness of all those whom he was about to leave behind.

He did not in person dine at this public repast (it took place at two in the afternoon, and his dinners now came in from the hotel at six), but his son was so good as to take the head of the principal table, and to be very free and engaging. He himself went about among the company, and took notice of individuals, and saw that the viands were of the quality he had ordered, and that all were served. On the whole, he was like a baron of the olden time, in a rare good humour. At the conclusion of the repast, he pledged his guests in a bumper of old Madeira; and told them that he hoped they had enjoyed themselves, and what was more, that they would enjoy themselves for the rest of the evening; that he wished them well; and that he bade them welcome. His health being drunk with acclamations, he was not so baronial after all but that in trying to return thanks he broke down, in the manner of a mere serf with a heart in his breast, and wept before them all. After this great success, which he supposed to be a failure, he gave them "Mr. Chivery and his brother officers;" whom he had beforehand presented with ten pounds each, and who were all in attendance. Mr. Chivery spoke to the toast, saying, What you undertake to lock up, lock up; but remember that you are, in the words of the fettered African, a man and a brother ever. The list of toasts disposed of, Mr. Dorrit urbanely went through the motions of playing a game at skittles with the Collegian who was the next oldest inhabitant to himself; and left the tenantry to their diversions.

But, all these occurrences preceded the final day. And now the day arrived when he and his family were to leave the prison for ever, and when the stones of its much trodden pavement were to know them no more.

Noon was the hour appointed for the departure. As it approached, there was not a Collegian within doors, nor a turnkey absent. The latter class of gentlemen appeared in their Sunday clothes, and the greater part of the Collegians were brightened up as much as circumstances allowed. Two or three flags were even displayed, and the children put on odds and ends of ribbon. Mr. Dorrit himself, at this trying time, preserved a serious but graceful dignity. Much of his attention was given to his brother, as to whose bearing on the great occasion he felt anxious.   •

"My dear Frederick," said he, "if you will give me your arm, we will pass among our friends together. I think it is right that we should go out arm in arm, my dear Frederick."

"Hah!" said Frederick. "Yes, yes, yes, yes."

"And if, my dear Frederick,—if you could, without putting any great constraint upon yourself, throw a little (pray excuse me, Frederick), a little polish into your usual demeanour——"

"William, William," said the other, shaking his head, "it's for you to do all that. I don't know how. All forgotten, forgotten!"

"But, my dear fellow," returned William, "for that very reason, if for no other, you must positively try to rouse yourself. What you have forgotten you must now begin to recall, my dear Frederick. Your position——"

"Eh?" said Frederick.

"Your position, my dear Frederick."

"Mine?" He looked first at his own figure, and then at his brother's, and then, drawing a long breath, cried, "Hah, to be sure! Yes, yes, yes."

"Your position, my dear Frederick, is now a fine one. Your position as my brother is a very fine one. And I know that it belongs to your conscientious nature, to try to become worthy of it, my dear Frederick, and to try to adorn it. To be no discredit to it, but to adorn it."

"William," said the other weakly, and with a sigh, "I will do anything you wish, my brother, provided that it lies in my power. Pray be so kind as to recollect what a limited power mine is. What would you wish me to do to-day, brother? Say what it is, only say what it is."

"My dearest Frederick, nothing. It is not worth troubling so good a heart as yours with."

"Pray trouble it," returned the other. "It finds it no trouble, William, to do anything it can for you."

William passed his hand across his eyes, and murmured with august satisfaction, "Blessings on your attachment, my poor dear fellow!" Then he said aloud, "Well, my dear Frederick, if you will only try, as we walk out, to show that you are alive to the occasion—that you think about it——"

"What would you advise me to think about it?" returned his submissive brother.

"Oh! my dear Frederick, how can I answer you? I can only say what, in leaving these good people, I think myself."

"That's it!" cried his brother. "That will help me."

"I find that I think, my dear Frederick, and with mixed emotions in which a softened compassion predominates, What will they do without me!"

"True," returned his brother. "Yes, yes, yes, yes. I'll think that as we go. What will they do without my brother! Poor things! What will they do without him!"

Twelve o'clock having just struck, and the carriage being reported ready in the outer courtyard, the brothers proceeded down-stairs arm-in-arm. Edward Dorrit, Esquire (once Tip), and his sister Fanny followed, also arm-in-arm; Mr. Plornish and Maggy, to whom had been entrusted the removal of such of the family effects as were considered worth removing, followed, bearing bundles and burdens to be packed in a cart.

In the yard, were the Collegians and turnkeys. In the yard, were Mr. Pancks and Mr. Rugg, come to see the last touch given to their work. In the yard, was Young John making a new epitaph for himself, on the occasion of his dying of a broken heart. In the yard, was the Patriarchal Casby, looking so tremendously benevolent that many enthusiastic Collegians grasped him fervently by the hand, and the wives and female relatives of many more Collegians kissed his hand, nothing doubting that he had done it all. In the yard, was the usual chorus of people proper to such a place. In the yard, was the man with the shadowy grievance respecting the Fund which the Marshal embezzled, who had got up at five in the morning to complete the copying of a perfectly unintelligible history of that transaction, which he had committed to Mr. Dorrit's care as a document of the last importance, calculated to stun the Government and effect the Marshal's downfall. In the yard, was the insolvent whose utmost energies were always set on getting into debt, who broke into prison with as much pains as other men have broken out of it, and who was always being cleared and complimented; while the insolvent at his elbow—a mere little, snivelling, striving tradesman, half dead of anxious efforts to keep out of debt—found it a hard matter, indeed, to get a Commissioner to release him with much reproof and reproach. In the yard, was the man of many children and many burdens, whose failure astonished everybody; in the yard, was the man of no children and large resources, whose failure astonished nobody. There, were the people who were always going out to-morrow, and always putting it off; there, were the people who had come in yesterday, and who were much more jealous and resentful of this freak of fortune than the seasoned birds. There, were some who, in pure meanness of spirit, cringed and bowed before the enriched Collegian and his family; there, were others who did so really because their eyes, accustomed to the gloom of their imprisonment and poverty, could not support the light of such bright sunshine. There, were many whose shillings had gone into his pocket to buy him meat and drink; but none who were now obtrusively Hail fellow well met! with him, on the strength of that assistance. It was rather to be remarked of the caged birds, that they were a little shy of the bird about to be so grandly free, and that they had a tendency to withdraw themselves towards the bars, and seem a little fluttered as he passed.

Through these spectators, the little procession, headed by the two brothers, moved slowly to the gate. Mr. Dorrit, yielding to the vast speculation how the poor creatures were to get on without him, was great, and sad, but not absorbed. He patted children on the head like Sir Roger de Coverley going to church, he spoke to people in the background by their Christian names, he condescended to all present, and seemed for their consolation to walk encircled by the legend in golden characters, "Be comforted, my people! Bear it!"

At last three honest cheers announced that he had passed the gate, and that the Marshalsea was an orphan. Before they had ceased to ring in the echoes of the prison walls, the family had got into their carriage, and the attendant had the steps in his hand.

Then, and not before, "Good Gracious!" cried Miss Fanny all at once, "Where's Amy!"

Her father had thought she was with her sister. Her sister had thought she was "somewhere or other." They had all trusted to finding her, as they had always done, quietly in the right place at the right moment. This going away was perhaps the very first action of their joint lives that they had got through without her.

A minute might have been consumed in the ascertaining of these points, when Miss Fanny, who, from her seat in the carriage, commanded the long narrow passage leading to the Lodge, flushed indignantly.

"Now I do say, Pa," cried she, "that this is disgraceful!"

"What is disgraceful, Fanny?"

"I do say," she repeated, "this is perfectly infamous! Really almost enough, even at such a time as this, to make one wish one was dead! Here is that child Amy, in her ugly old shabby dress, which she was so obstinate about, Pa, which I over and over again begged and prayed her to change, and which she over and over again objected to, and promised to change to-day, saying she wished to wear it as long as ever she remained in there with you—which was absolute romantic nonsense of the lowest kind— here is that child Amy disgracing us, to the last moment and at the last moment, by being carried out in that dress after all. And by that Mr. Clennam too!"

The offence was proved, as she delivered the indictment. Clennam appeared at the carriage-door, bearing the little insensible figure in his arms.

"She has been forgotten," he said, in a tone of pity not free from reproach. "I ran up to her room (which Mr. Chivery showed me), and found the door open, and that she had fainted on the floor, dear child. She appeared to have gone to change her dress, and to have sunk down overpowered. It may have been the cheering, or it may have happened sooner.

Take care of this poor cold hand, Miss Dorrit. Don't let it fall."

"Thank you, sir," returned Miss Dorrit, bursting into tears. "I believe I know what to do, if you'll give me leave. Dear Amy, open your eyes, that's a love! Oh, Amy, Amy, I really am so vexed and ashamed! Do rouse yourself, darling! Oh, why are they not driving on! Pray, Pa, do drive on!"

The attendant, getting between Clennam and the carriage-door, with a sharp "By your leave, sir!" bundled up the steps, and they drove away.

THE END OF THE FIRST BOOK

END OF No. X

BOOK THE SECOND

RICHES

———

CHAPTER I

FELLOW TRAVELLERS

In the autumn of the year, Darkness and Night were creeping up to the highest ridges of the Alps.

It was vintage time in the valleys on the Swiss side of the Pass of the Great Saint Bernard, and along the banks of the Lake of Geneva. The air there was charged with the scent of gathered grapes. Baskets, troughs, and tubs of grapes, stood in the dim village doorways, stopped the steep and narrow village streets, and had been carrying all day along the roads and lanes. Grapes, spilt and crushed under foot, lay about everywhere. The child carried in a sling by the laden peasant-woman toiling home, was quieted with picked-up grapes; the idiot sunning his big goître under the eaves of the wooden chalet by the way to the waterfall, sat munching grapes; the breath of the cows and goats was redolent of leaves and stalks of grapes; the company in every little cabaret were eating, drinking, talking grapes. A pity that no ripe touch of this generous abundance could be given to the thin, hard, stoney wine, which after all was made from the grapes!

The air had been warm and transparent through the whole of the bright day. Shining metal spires and church-roofs, distant and rarely seen, had sparkled in the view; and the snowy mountain-tops had been so clear that unaccustomed eyes, cancelling the intervening country, and slighting their rugged height for something fabulous, would have measured them as within a few hours' easy reach. Mountain-peaks of great celebrity in the valleys, whence no trace of their existence was visible sometimes for months together, had been since morning plain and near in the blue sky. And now, when it was dark below, though they seemed solemnly to recede, like spectres who were going to vanish, as the red dye of the sunset faded out of them and left them coldly white, they were yet distinctly defined in their loneliness, above the mists and shadows.

Seen from those solitudes, and from the Pass of the Great Saint Bernard, which was one of them, the ascending Night came up the mountain like a rising water. When it at last rose to the walls of the convent of the Great Saint Bernard, it was as if that weather-beaten structure were another Ark, and floated away upon the shadowy waves.

Darkness, outstripping some visitors on mules, had risen thus to the rough convent walls, when those travellers were yet climbing the mountain. As the heat of the glowing day, when they had stopped to drink at the streams of melted ice and snow, was changed to the searching cold of the frosty rarefied night air at a great height, so the fresh beauty of the lower journey had yielded to barrenness and desolation. A craggy track, up which the mules, in single file, scrambled and turned from block to block, as though they were ascending the broken staircase of a gigantic ruin, was their way now. No trees were to be seen, nor any vegetable growth, save a poor brown scrubby moss, freezing in the chinks of rock. Blackened skeleton arms of wood by the wayside pointed upward to the convent, as if the ghosts of former travellers overwhelmed by the snow, haunted the scene of their distress. Icicle-hung caves and cellars built for refuges from sudden storms, were like so many whispers of the perils of the place; never-resting wreaths and mazes of mist wandered about, hunted by a moaning wind; and snow, the besetting danger of the mountain, against which all its defences were taken, drifted sharply down.

The file of mules, jaded by their day's work, turned and wound slowly up the steep ascent; the foremost led by a guide on foot, in his broad-brimmed hat and round jacket, carrying a mountain staff or two upon his shoulder, with whom another guide conversed. There was no speaking among the string of riders. The sharp cold, the fatigue of the journey, and a new sensation of a catching in the breath, partly as if they had just emerged from very clear crisp water, and partly as if they had been sobbing, kept them silent.

At length, a light on the summit of the rocky staircase gleamed through the snow and mist. The guides called to the mules, the mules pricked up their drooping heads, the travellers' tongues were loosened, and in a sudden burst of slipping, climbing, jingling, clinking, and talking, they arrived at the convent door.

Other mules had arrived not long before, some with peasant-riders and some with goods, and had trodden the snow about the door into a pool of mud. Riding saddles and bridles, pack-saddles and strings of bells, mules and men, lanterns, torches, sacks, provender, barrels, cheeses, kegs of honey and butter, straw bundles and packages of many shapes, were crowded confusedly together in this thawed quagmire, and about the steps. Up here in the clouds, everything was seen through cloud, and seemed dissolving into cloud. The breath of the men was cloud, the breath of the mules was cloud, the lights were encircled by cloud, speakers close at hand were not seen for cloud, though their voices and all other sounds were surprisingly clear. Of the cloudy line of mules hastily tied to rings in

the wall, one would bite another, or kick another, and then the whole mist
would be disturbed: with men diving into it, and cries of men and beasts
coming out of it, and no bystander discerning what was wrong. In the
midst of this, the great stable of the convent, occupying the basement
story, and entered by the basement door, outside which all the disorder
was, poured forth its contribution of cloud, as if the whole rugged edifice
were filled with nothing else, and would collapse as soon as it had emptied
itself, leaving the snow to fall upon the bare mountain summit.

While all this noise and hurry were rife among the living travellers,
there, too, silently assembled in a grated house, half a dozen paces removed,
with the same cloud enfolding them, and the same snow flakes drifting in
upon them, were the dead travellers found upon the mountain. The mother,
storm-belated many winters ago, still standing in the corner with her baby
at her breast; the man who had frozen with his arm raised to his mouth in
fear or hunger, still pressing it with his dry lips after years and years. An
awful company, mysteriously come together! A wild destiny for that
mother to have foreseen, "Surrounded by so many and such companions
upon whom I never looked, and never shall look, I and my child will dwell
together inseparable, on the Great Saint Bernard, outlasting generations
who will come to see us, and will never know our name, or one word of
our story but the end."

The living travellers thought little or nothing of the dead just then. They
thought much more of alighting at the convent door, and warming themselves at the convent fire. Disengaged from the turmoil, which was already
calming down as the crowd of mules began to be bestowed in the stable,
they hurried shivering up the steps and into the building. There was a
smell within, coming up from the floor of tethered beasts, like the smell of
a menagerie of wild animals. There were strong arched galleries within,
huge stone piers, great staircases, and thick walls pierced with small sunken
windows—fortifications against the mountain storms, as if they had been
human enemies. There were gloomy vaulted sleeping rooms within,
intensely cold, but clean and hospitably prepared for guests. Finally, there
was a parlor for guests to sit in and to sup in, where a table was already laid,
and where a blazing fire shone red and high.

In this room, after having had their quarters for the night allotted to
them by two young Fathers, the travellers presently drew round the
hearth. They were in three parties; of whom the first, as the most numerous
and important, was the slowest, and had been overtaken by one of the others
on the way up. It consisted of an elderly lady, two grey-haired gentlemen,
two young ladies, and their brother. These were attended (not to mention
four guides), by a courier, two footmen, and two waiting-maids: which
strong body of inconvenience was accommodated elsewhere under the
same roof. The party that had overtaken them, and followed in their train,
consisted of only three members: one lady and two gentlemen. The third

party, which had ascended from the valley on the Italian side of the Pass, and had arrrived first, were four in number: a plethoric, hungry, and silent German tutor in spectacles, on a tour with three young men, his pupils, all plethoric, hungry, and silent, and all in spectacles.

These three groups sat round the fire eyeing each other dryly, and waiting for supper. Only one among them, one of the gentlemen belonging to the party of three, made advances towards conversation. Throwing out his lines for the Chief of the important tribe, while addressing himself to his own companions, he remarked, in a tone of voice which included all the company if they chose to be included, that it had been a long day, and that he felt for the ladies. That he feared one of the young ladies was not a strong or accustomed traveller, and had been over fatigued two or three hours ago. That he had observed, from his station in the rear, that she sat her mule as if she were exhausted. That he had, twice or thrice afterwards, done himself the honor of enquiring of one of the guides, when he fell behind, how the young lady did. That he had been enchanted to learn that she had recovered her spirits, and that it had been but a passing discomfort. That he trusted (by this time he had secured the eyes of the Chief, and addressed him) he might be permitted to express his hope that she was now none the worse, and that she would not regret having made the journey.

"My daughter, I am obliged to you, sir," returned the Chief, "is quite restored, and has been greatly interested."

"New to mountains perhaps?" said the insinuating traveller.

"New to—ha—to mountains," said the Chief.

"But you are familiar with them, sir?" the insinuating traveller assumed.

"I am—hum—tolerably familiar. Not of late years. Not of late years," replied the Chief, with a flourish of his hand.

The insinuating traveller, acknowledging the flourish with an inclination of his head, passed from the Chief to the second young lady, who had not yet been referred to, otherwise than as one of the ladies in whose behalf he felt so sensitive an interest.

He hoped she was not incommoded by the fatigues of the day.

"Incommoded certainly," returned the young lady, "but not tired."

The insinuating traveller complimented her on the justice of the distinction. It was what he had meant to say. Every lady must doubtless be incommoded, by having to do with that proverbially unaccommodating animal, the mule.

"We have had, of course," said the young lady, who was rather reserved and haughty, "to leave the carriages and fourgon at Martigny. And the impossibility of bringing anything that one wants to this inaccessible place, and the necessity of leaving every comfort behind, is not convenient."

"A savage place, indeed," said the insinuating traveller.

The elderly lady, who was a model of accurate dressing, and whose manner was perfect, considered as a piece of machinery, here interposed a remark in a low soft voice.

"But, like other inconvenient places," she observed, "it must be seen. As a place much spoken of, it is necessary to see it."

"Oh! I have not the least objection to seeing it, I assure you, Mrs. General," returned the other, carelessly.

"You, madame," said the insinuating traveller, "have visited this spot before?"

"Yes," returned Mrs. General. "I have been here before. Let me recommend you, my dear," to the former young lady, "to shade your face from the hot wood, after exposure to the mountain air and snow. You too, my dear," to the other and younger lady, who immediately did so; while the former merely said, "Thank you, Mrs. General, I am perfectly comfortable, and prefer remaining as I am."

The brother, who had left his chair to open a piano that stood in the room, and who had whistled into it and shut it up again, now came strolling back to the fire with his glass in his eye. He was dressed in the very fullest and completest travelling trim. The world seemed hardly large enough to yield him an amount of travel proportionate to his equipment.

"These fellows are an immense time with supper," he drawled. "I wonder what they'll give us! Has anybody any idea?"

"Not roast man I believe," replied the voice of the second gentleman of the party of three.

"I suppose not. What d'ye mean?" he enquired.

"That, as you are not to be served for the general supper, perhaps you will do us the favor of not cooking yourself at the general fire," returned the other.

The young gentleman, who was standing in an easy attitude on the hearth, cocking his glass at the company, with his back to the blaze and his coat tucked under his arms, something as if he were of the poultry species and were trussed for roasting, lost countenance at this reply; he seemed about to demand further explanation, when it was discovered—through all eyes turning on the speaker—that the lady with him, who was young and beautiful, had not heard what had passed, through having fainted with her head upon his shoulder.

"I think," said the gentleman in a subdued tone, "I had best carry her straight to her room. Will you call to some one to bring a light?" addressing his companion, "and to show the way? In this strange rambling place I don't know that I could find it."

"Pray let me call my maid," cried the taller of the young ladies.

"Pray let me put this water to her lips," said the shorter, who had not spoken yet.

Each doing what she suggested, there was no want of assistance. Indeed, when the two maids came in (escorted by the courier, lest any one should strike them dumb by addressing a foreign language to them on the road), there was a prospect of too much assistance. Seeing this, and saying as much in a few words to the slighter and younger of the two ladies, the gentleman put his wife's arm over his shoulder, lifted her up, and carried her away.

His friend, being left alone with the other visitors, walked slowly up and down the room, without coming to the fire again, pulling his black moustache in a contemplative manner, as if he felt himself committed to the late retort. While the subject of it was breathing injury in a corner, the Chief loftily addressed this gentleman.

"Your friend, sir," said he, "is—ha—is a little impatient; and, in his impatience, is not perhaps fully sensible of what he owes to—hum —to—but we will waive that, we will waive that. Your friend is a little impatient, sir."

"It may be so, sir," returned the other. "But having had the honor of making that gentleman's acquaintance at the hotel at Geneva, where we and much good company met some time ago, and having had the honor of exchanging company and conversation with that gentleman on several subsequent excursions, I can hear nothing—no, not even from one of your appearance and station, sir—detrimental to that gentleman."

"You are in no danger, sir, of hearing any such thing from me. In remarking that your friend has shown impatience, I say no such thing. I make that remark, because it is not to be doubted that my son, being by birth and by—ha—by education a—hum—a gentleman, would have readily adapted himself to any obligingly-expressed wish on the subject of the fire being equally accessible to the whole of the present circle. Which, in principle, I—ha—for all are—hum—equal on these occasions—I consider right."

"Good!" was the reply. "And there it ends! I am your son's obedient servant. I beg your son to receive the assurance of my profound consideration. And now, sir, I may admit, freely admit, that my friend is sometimes of a sarcastic temper."

"The lady is your friend's wife, sir?"

"The lady is my friend's wife, sir."

"She is very handsome."

"Sir, she is peerless. They are still in the first year of their marriage. They are still partly on a marriage, and partly on an artistic tour."

"Your friend is an artist, sir?"

The gentleman replied by kissing the fingers of his right hand, and wafting the kiss the length of his arm towards Heaven. As who should say, I devote him to the celestial Powers as an immortal artist!

"But he is a man of family," he added. "His connexions are of the best. He is more than an artist: he is highly connected. He may, in effect, have repudiated his connexions, proudly, impatiently, sarcastically (I make the concession of both words); but he has them. Sparks that have been struck out during our intercourse have shown me this."

"Well! I hope," said the lofty gentleman, with the air of finally dispos-
ing of the subject, "that the lady's indisposition may be only temporary."

"Sir, I hope so."

"Mere fatigue, I dare say."

"Not altogether mere fatigue, sir, for her mule stumbled to-day, and she fell from the saddle. She fell lightly, and was up again without assistance, and rode from us laughing; but she complained towards evening of a slight bruise in the side. She spoke of it more than once, as we followed your party up the mountain."

The head of the large retinue, who was gracious but not familiar, ap-
peared by this time to think that he had condescended more than enough. He said no more, and there was silence for some quarter of an hour until supper appeared.

With the supper, came one of the young Fathers (there seemed to be no old Fathers) to take the head of the table. It was like the supper of an ordinary Swiss hotel, and good red wine grown by the convent in more genial air was not wanting. The artist traveller calmly came and took his place at table when the rest sat down, with no apparent sense upon him of his late skirmish with the completely-dressed traveller.

"Pray," he enquired of the host, over his soup, "has your convent many of its famous dogs now?"

"Monsieur, it has three."

"I saw three in the gallery below. Doubtless the three in question."

The host, a slender, bright-eyed, dark young man of polite manners, whose garment was a black gown with strips of white crossed over it like braces, and who no more resembled the conventional breed of Saint Bernard monks than he resembled the conventional breed of Saint Bernard dogs, replied, doubtless those were the three in question.

"And I think," said the artist traveller, "I have seen one of them before."

It was possible. He was a dog sufficiently well known. Monsieur might have easily seen him in the valley or somewhere on the lake, when he (the dog) had gone down with one of the order to solicit aid for the convent.

"Which is done in its regular season of the year, I think?"

Monsieur was right.

"And never without the dog. The dog is very important."

Again Monsieur was right. The dog was very important. People were justly interested in the dog. As one of the dogs celebrated everywhere, Ma'amselle would observe.

Ma'amselle was a little slow to observe it, as though she were not yet well accustomed to the French tongue. Mrs. General, however, observed it for her.

"Ask him if he has saved many lives?" said, in his native English, the young man who had been put out of countenance.

The host needed no translation of the question. He promptly replied in French, "No. Not this one."

"Why not?" the same gentleman asked.

"Pardon," returned the host, composedly, "give him the opportunity and he will do it without doubt. For example, I am well convinced," smiling sedately, as he cut up the dish of veal to be handed round, on the young man who had been put out of countenance, "that if you, Monsieur, would give him the opportunity, he would hasten with great ardor to fulfil his duty."

The artist traveller laughed. The insinuating traveller (who evinced a provident anxiety to get his full share of the supper), wiping some drops of wine from his moustache with a piece of bread, joined the conversation.

"It is becoming late in the year, my Father," said he, "for tourist-travellers, is it not?"

"Yes, it is late. Yet two or three weeks, at most, and we shall be left to the winter snows."

"And then," said the insinuating traveller, "for the scratching dogs and the buried children, according to the pictures!"

"Pardon," said the host, not quite understanding the allusion. "How, then the scratching dogs and the buried children according to the pictures?"

The artist traveller struck in again, before an answer could be given.

"Don't you know," he coldly enquired across the table of his companion, "that none but smugglers come this way in the winter or can have any possible business this way?"

"Holy blue! No; never heard of it."

"So it is, I believe. And as they know the signs of the weather tolerably well, they don't give much employment to the dogs—who have consequently died out rather—though this house of entertainment is conveniently situated for themselves. Their young families, I am told, they usually leave at home. But it's a grand idea!" cried the artist traveller, unexpectedly rising into a tone of enthusiasm. "It's a sublime idea. It's the finest idea in the world, and brings tears into a man's eyes, by Jupiter!" He then went on eating his veal with great composure.

There was enough of mocking inconsistency at the bottom of this speech to make it rather discordant, though the manner was refined and the person well-favored, and though the depreciatory part of it was so skilfully thrown off, as to be very difficult for one not perfectly acquainted with the English language to understand, or, even understanding, to take offence at: so simple and dispassionate was its tone. After finishing his veal in the midst of silence, the speaker again addressed his friend.

"Look," said he, in his former tone, "at this gentleman our host, not yet in the prime of life, who in so graceful a way and with such courtly

urbanity and modesty presides over us! Manners fit for a crown! Dine
with the Lord Mayor of London (if you can get an invitation) and
observe the contrast. This dear fellow, with the finest cut face I ever
saw, a face in perfect drawing, leaves some laborious life and comes up
here I don't know how many feet above the level of the sea, for no other
purpose on earth (except enjoying himself, I hope, in a capital refectory)
than to keep an hotel for idle poor devils like you and me, and leave the bill
to our consciences! Why, isn't it a beautiful sacrifice? What do we want
more to touch us? Because rescued people of interesting appearance are
not, for eight or nine months out of every twelve, holding on here round
the necks of the most sagacious of dogs carrying wooden bottles, shall we
disparage the place? No! Bless the place. It's a great place, a glorious
place!"

The chest of the grey-haired gentleman who was the Chief of the important party, had swelled as if with a protest against his being numbered
among poor devils. No sooner had the artist traveller ceased speaking than
he spoke himself with great dignity, as having it incumbent on him to take
the lead in most places, and having deserted that duty for a little while.

He weightily communicated his opinion to their host, that his life must
be a very dreary life here in the winter.

The host allowed to Monsieur that it was a little monotonous. The air
was difficult to breathe for a length of time consecutively. The cold was
very severe. One needed youth and strength to bear it. However, having
them and the blessing of Heaven——

Yes, that was very good. "But the confinement," said the grey-haired
gentleman.

There were many days, even in bad weather, when it was possible to walk
about outside. It was the custom to beat a little track, and take exercise there.

"But the space," urged the grey-haired gentleman. "So small. So—ha—
very limited."

Monsieur would recall to himself that there were the refuges to visit, and
that tracks had to be made to them also.

Monsieur still urged, on the other hand, that the space was so—ha—hum
—so very contracted. More than that. It was always the same, always the
same.

With a deprecating smile, the host gently raised and gently lowered his
shoulders. That was true, he remarked, but permit him to say that almost
all objects had their various points of view. Monsieur and he did not see
this poor life of his from the same point of view. Monsieur was not used to
confinement.

"I—ha—yes, very true," said the grey-haired gentleman. He seemed
to receive quite a shock from the force of the argument.

Monsieur, as an English traveller surrounded by all means of travelling
pleasantly; doubtless possessing fortune, carriages, servants——

"Perfectly, perfectly. Without doubt," said the gentleman.

Monsieur could not easily place himself in the position of a person who had not the power to choose, I will go here to-morrow, or there next day; I will pass these barriers, I will enlarge those bounds. Monsieur could not realise, perhaps, how the mind accommodated itself in such things to the force of necessity.

"It is true," said Monsieur. "We will—ha—not pursue the subject. You are —hum—quite accurate, I have no doubt. We will say no more."

The supper having come to a close, he drew his chair away as he spoke, and moved back to his former place by the fire. As it was very cold at the greater part of the table, the other guests also resumed their former seats by the fire, designing to toast themselves well before going to bed. The host, when they rose from table, bowed to all present, wished them good night, and withdrew. But first the insinuating traveller had asked him if they could have some wine made hot; and as he had answered Yes, and had presently afterwards sent it in, that traveller, seated in the centre of the group, and in the full heat of the fire, was soon engaged in serving it out to the rest.

At this time, the younger of the two young ladies, who had been silently attentive in her dark corner (the firelight was the chief light in the sombre room, the lamp being smoky and dull) to what had been said of the absent lady, glided out. She was at a loss which way to turn, when she had softly closed the door; but, after a little hesitation among the sounding passages and the many ways, came to a room in a corner of the main gallery, where the servants were at their supper. From these she obtained a lamp, and a direction to the lady's room.

It was up the great staircase on the story above. Here and there, the bare white walls were broken by an iron grate, and she thought as she went along that the place was something like a prison. The arched door of the lady's room, or cell, was not quite shut. After knocking at it two or three times without receiving an answer, she pushed it gently open, and looked in.

The lady lay with closed eyes on the outside of the bed, protected from the cold by the blankets and wrappers with which she had been covered when she revived from her fainting fit. A dull light placed in the deep recess of the window, made little impression on the arched room. The visitor timidly stepped to the bed, and said, in a soft whisper, "Are you better?"

The lady had fallen into a slumber, and the whisper was too low to awake her. Her visitor, standing quite still, looked at her attentively.

"She is very pretty," she said to herself. "I never saw so beautiful a face. O how unlike me!"

It was a curious thing to say, but it had some hidden meaning, for it filled her eyes with tears.

"I know I must be right. I know he spoke of her that evening. I could very easily be wrong on any other subject. But not on this, not on this!"

With a quiet and tender hand she put aside a straying fold of the sleeper's hair, and then touched the hand that lay outside the covering.

"I like to look at her," she breathed to herself. "I like to see what has affected him so much."

She had not withdrawn her hand, when the sleeper opened her eyes, and started.

"Pray don't be alarmed. I am only one of the travellers from downstairs. I came to ask if you were better, and if I could do anything for you."

"I think you have already been so kind as to send your servants to my assistance?"

"No, not I; that was my sister. Are you better?"

"Much better. It is only a slight bruise, and has been well looked to, and is almost easy now. It made me giddy and faint in a moment. It had hurt me before; but at last, it overpowered me all at once."

"May I stay with you until some one comes? Would you like it?"

"I should like it, for it is lonely here; but I am afraid you will feel the cold too much."

"I don't mind cold. I am not delicate, if I look so." She quickly moved one of the two rough chairs to the bedside, and sat down. The other as quickly moved a part of some travelling wrapper from herself, and drew it over her, so that her arm, in keeping it about her, rested on her shoulder.

"You have so much the air of a kind nurse," said the lady, smiling on her, "that you seem as if you had come to me from home."

"I am very glad of it."

"I was dreaming of home when I woke just now. Of my old home, I mean, before I was married."

"And before you were so far away from it."

"I have been much farther away from it than this; but then I took the best part of it with me, and missed nothing. I felt solitary as I dropped asleep here, and, missing it a little, wandered back to it."

There was a sorrowfully affectionate and regretful sound in her voice, which made her visitor refrain from looking at her for the moment.

"It is a curious chance which at last brings us together, under this covering in which you have wrapped me," said the visitor, after a pause; "for do you know, I think I have been looking for you, some time."

"Looking for me?"

"I believe I have a little note here, which I was to give to you whenever I found you. This is it. Unless I greatly mistake, it is addressed to you. Is it not?"

The lady took it, and said yes, and read it. Her visitor watched her as she did so. It was very short. She flushed a little as she put her lips to her visitor's cheek, and pressed her hand.

"The dear young friend to whom he presents me, may be a comfort to me at some time, he says. She is truly a comfort to me, the first time I see her."

"Perhaps, you don't," said the visitor, hesitating—"perhaps you don't know my story? Perhaps he never told you my story?"

"No."

"O, no, why should he! I have scarcely the right to tell it myself at present, because I have been entreated not to do so. There is not much in it, but it might account to you for my asking you not to say anything about the letter here. You saw my family with me, perhaps? Some of them—I only say this to you—are a little proud, a little prejudiced."

"You shall take it back again," said the other, "and then my husband is sure not to see it. He might see it and speak of it, otherwise, by some accident. Will you put it in your bosom again, to be certain?"

She did so with great care. Her small, slight hand was still upon the letter, when they heard some one in the gallery outside.

"I promised," said the visitor, rising, "that I would write to him after seeing you (I could hardly fail to see you, sooner or later), and tell him if you were well and happy. I had better say you were well and happy?"

"Yes, yes, yes! Say I was very well and very happy. And that I thanked him affectionately, and would never forget him."

"I shall see you in the morning. After that we are sure to meet again before very long. Good night!"

"Good night. Thank you, thank you. Good night, my dear!"

Both of them were hurried and fluttered as they exchanged this parting, and as the visitor came out at the door. She had expected to meet the lady's husband approaching it; but the person in the gallery was not he: it was the traveller who had wiped the wine-drops from his moustache with the piece of bread. When he heard the step behind him, he turned round—for he was walking away in the dark.

His politeness, which was extreme, would not allow of the young lady's lighting herself down-stairs, or going down alone. He took her lamp, held it so as to throw the best light on the stone steps, and followed her all the way to the supper-room. She went down, not easily hiding how much she was inclined to shrink and tremble; for the appearance of this traveller was particularly disagreeable to her. She had sat in her quiet corner before supper, imagining what he would have been in the scenes and places within her experience, until he inspired her with an aversion, that made him little less than terrific.

He followed her down with his smiling politeness, followed her in, and resumed his seat in the best place on the hearth. There, with the wood-fire, which was beginning to burn low, rising and falling upon him in the dark room, he sat with his legs thrust out to warm, drinking the hot wine down to the lees, with a monstrous shadow imitating him on the wall and ceiling.

The tired company had broken up, and all the rest were gone to bed except the young lady's father, who dozed in his chair by the fire. The traveller had been at the pains of going a long way up-stairs to his sleeping-room, to fetch his pocket-flask of brandy. He told them so, as he poured its contents into what was left of the wine, and drank with a new relish.

"May I ask, sir, if you are on your way to Italy?"

The grey-haired gentleman had roused himself, and was preparing to withdraw. He answered in the affirmative.

"I also!" said the traveller. "I shall hope to have the honor of offering my compliments in fairer scenes, and under softer circumstances, than on this dismal mountain."

The gentleman bowed, distantly enough, and said he was obliged to him.

"We poor gentlemen, sir," said the traveller, pulling his moustache dry with his hand, for he had dipped it in the wine and brandy; "we poor gentlemen do not travel like princes, but the courtesies and graces of life are precious to us. To your health, sir!"

"Sir, I thank you."

"To the health of your distinguished family—of the fair ladies, your daughters!"

"Sir, I thank you again. I wish you good night. My dear, are our—ha—our people in attendance?"

"They are close by, father."

"Permit me!" said the traveller, rising and holding the door open, as the gentleman crossed the room towards it with his arm drawn through his daughter's. "Good repose! To the pleasure of seeing you once more! To to-morrow!"

As he kissed his hand, with his best manner and his daintiest smile, the young lady drew a little nearer to her father, and passed him with a dread of touching him.

"Humph!" said the insinuating traveller, whose manner shrunk and whose voice dropped when he was left alone. "If they all go to bed, why I must go. They are in a devil of a hurry. One would think the night would be long enough, in this freezing silence and solitude, if one went to bed two hours hence!"

Throwing back his head in emptying his glass, he cast his eyes upon the travellers' book, which lay on the piano, open, with pens and ink beside it, as if the night's names had been registered while he was absent. Taking it in his hand, he read these entries.

William Dorrit, Esquire Frederick Dorrit, Esquire Edward Dorrit, Esquire Miss Dorrit Miss Amy Dorrit Mrs. General	And suite. From France to Italy.

Mr. and Mrs. Henry Gowan. From France to Italy.

To which he added, in a small, complicated hand, ending with a long lean flourish, not unlike a lasso thrown at all the rest of the names:

Blandois. Paris. From France to Italy.

And then, with his nose coming down over his moustache, and his moustache going up under his nose, repaired to his allotted cell.

CHAPTER II

MRS. GENERAL

I T is indispensable to present the accomplished lady, who was of sufficient importance in the suite of the Dorrit Family to have a line to herself in the Travellers' Book.

Mrs. General was the daughter of a clerical dignitary in a cathedral town,
where she had led the fashion until she was as near forty-five as a single
lady can be. A stiff commissariat officer of sixty, famous as a martinet,
had then become enamoured of the gravity with which she drove the
proprieties four-in-hand through the cathedral town society, and had
solicited to be taken beside her on the box of the cool coach of ceremony to
which that team was harnessed. His proposal of marriage being accepted
by the lady, the commissary took his seat behind the proprieties with great
decorum, and Mrs. General drove until the commissary died. In the course
of their united journey, they ran over several people who came in the way
of the proprieties; but always in a high style, and with composure.

The commissary having been buried with all the decorations suitable
to the service (the whole team of proprieties were harnessed to his hearse,
and they all had feathers and black velvet housings, with his coat-of-arms
in the corner), Mrs. General began to enquire what quantity of dust and
ashes was deposited at the bankers'. It then transpired that the commissary
had so far stolen a march on Mrs. General as to have bought himself an
annuity some years before his marriage, and to have reserved that circumstance, in mentioning, at the period of his proposal, that his income was
derived from the interest of his money. Mrs. General consequently found
her means so much diminished, that, but for the perfect regulation of her
mind, she might have felt disposed to question the accuracy of that portion
of the late service which had declared that the commissary could take
nothing away with him.

In this state of affairs it occurred to Mrs. General, that she might "form
the mind," and eke the manners, of some young lady of distinction. Or,
that she might harness the proprieties to the carriage of some rich young
heiress or widow, and become at once the driver and guard of such vehicle
through the social mazes. Mrs. General's communication of this idea to
her clerical and commissariat connexion was so warmly applauded that,

but for the lady's undoubted merit, it might have appeared as though they wanted to get rid of her. Testimonials representing Mrs. General as a prodigy of piety, learning, virtue, and gentility, were lavishly contributed from influential quarters; and one venerable archdeacon even shed tears in recording his testimony to her perfections (described to him by persons on whom he could rely), though he had never had the honor and moral gratification of setting eyes on Mrs. General in all his life.

Thus delegated on her mission, as it were by Church and State, Mrs. General, who had always occupied high ground, felt in a condition to keep it, and began by putting herself up at a very high figure. An interval of some duration elapsed, in which there was no bid for Mrs. General. At length a county-widower, with a daughter of fourteen, opened negociations with the lady; and as it was a part either of the native dignity or of the artificial policy of Mrs. General (but certainly one or the other), to comport herself as if she were much more sought than seeking, the widower pursued Mrs. General until he prevailed upon her to form his daughter's mind and manners.

The execution of this trust occupied Mrs. General about seven years, in the course of which time she made the tour of Europe, and saw most of that extensive miscellany of objects which it is essential that all persons of polite cultivation should see with other people's eyes, and never with their own. When her charge was at length formed, the marriage, not only of the young lady, but likewise of her father the widower, was resolved on. The widower then finding Mrs. General both inconvenient and expensive, became of a sudden almost as much affected by her merits as the archdeacon had been, and circulated such praises of her surpassing worth, in all quarters where he thought an opportunity might arise of transferring the blessing to somebody else, that Mrs. General was a name more honorable than ever.

The phœnix was to let, on this elevated perch, when Mr. Dorrit, who had lately succeeded to his property, mentioned to his bankers that he wished to discover a lady, well-bred, accomplished, well connected, well accustomed to good society, who was qualified at once to complete the education of his daughters, and to be their matron or chaperon. Mr. Dorrit's bankers, as the bankers of the county-widower, instantly said, "Mrs. General."

Pursuing the light so fortunately hit upon, and finding the concurrent testimony of the whole of Mrs. General's acquaintance to be of the pathetic nature already recorded, Mr. Dorrit took the trouble of going down to the county of the county-widower, to see Mrs. General. In whom he found a lady of a quality superior to his highest expectations.

"Might I be excused," said Mr. Dorrit, "if I enquired—ha—what remune——"

"Why, indeed," returned Mrs. General, stopping the word, "it is a subject on which I prefer to avoid entering. I have never entered on it with my friends here; and I cannot overcome the delicacy, Mr. Dorrit, with which I have always regarded it. I am not, as I hope you are aware, a governess——"

"O dear no!" said Mr. Dorrit. "Pray, madam, do not imagine for a moment that I think so." He really blushed to be suspected of it.

Mrs. General gravely inclined her head. "I cannot, therefore, put a price upon services which it is a pleasure to me to render if I can render them spontaneously, but which I could not render in mere return for any consideration. Neither do I know how, or where, to find a case parallel to my own. It is peculiar."

No doubt. But how then (Mr. Dorrit not unnaturally hinted) could the subject be approached?

"I cannot object" said Mrs. General—"though even that is disagreeable to me—to Mr. Dorrit's enquiring, in confidence, of my friends here, what amount they may have been accustomed, at quarterly intervals, to pay to my credit at my bankers'."

Mr. Dorrit bowed his acknowledgments.

"Permit me to add," said Mrs. General, "that beyond this, I can never resume the topic. Also that I can accept no second or inferior position. If the honor were proposed to me of becoming known to Mr. Dorrit's family—I think two daughters were mentioned?——"

"Two daughters."

"I could only accept it on terms of perfect equality, as a companion, protector, Mentor, and friend."

Mr. Dorrit, in spite of his sense of his importance, felt as if it would be quite a kindness in her to accept it on any conditions. He almost said as much.

"I think," repeated Mrs. General, "two daughters were mentioned?"

"Two daughters," said Mr. Dorrit again.

"It would therefore," said Mrs. General, "be necessary to add a third more to the payment (whatever its amount may prove to be), which my friends here have been accustomed to make to my bankers."

Mr. Dorrit lost no time in referring the delicate question to the county-widower, and, finding that he had been accustomed to pay three hundred pounds a-year to the credit of Mrs. General, arrived, without any severe strain on his arithmetic, at the conclusion that he himself must pay four. Mrs. General being an article of that lustrous surface which suggests that it is worth any money, he made a formal proposal to be allowed to have the honor and pleasure of regarding her as a member of his family. Mrs. General conceded that high privilege, and here she was.

In person, Mrs. General, including her skirts which had much to do with it, was of a dignified and imposing appearance; ample, rustling, gravely voluminous; always upright behind the proprieties. She might have been taken—had been taken —to the top of the Alps and the bottom of Hercu-laneum, without disarranging a fold in her dress, or displacing a pin. If her countenance and hair had rather a floury appearance, as though from living in some transcendently genteel Mill, it was rather because she was a chalky creation altogether, than because she mended her complexion with violet powder, or had turned grey. If her eyes had no expression, it was probably because they had nothing to express. If she had few wrinkles, it was be-cause her mind had never traced its name or any other inscription on her face. A cool, waxy, blown-out woman, who had never lighted well.

Mrs. General had no opinions. Her way of forming a mind was to prevent it from forming opinions. She had a little circular set of mental grooves or rails, on which she started little trains of other people's opinions, which never overtook one another, and never got anywhere. Even her propriety could not dispute that there was impropriety in the world; but Mrs. General's way of getting rid of it was to put it out of sight, and make believe that there was no such thing. This was another of her ways of forming a mind—to cram all articles of difficulty into cupboards, lock them up, and say they had no existence. It was the easiest way, and, beyond all comparison, the properest.

Mrs. General was not to be told of anything shocking. Accidents, miseries, and offences, were never to be mentioned before her. Passion was to go to sleep in the presence of Mrs. General, and blood was to change to milk and water. The little that was left in the world, when all these deductions were made, it was Mrs. General's province to varnish. In that formation process of hers, she dipped the smallest of brushes into the largest of pots, and varnished the surface of every object that came under consideration. The more cracked it was, the more Mrs. General varnished it.

There was varnish in Mrs. General's voice, varnish in Mrs. General's touch, an atmosphere of varnish round Mrs. General's figure. Mrs. General's dreams ought to have been varnished—if she had any—lying asleep in the arms of the good Saint Bernard, with the feathery snow falling on his house-top.

CHAPTER III

ON THE ROAD

THE bright morning sun dazzled the eyes, the snow had ceased, the mists had vanished, the mountain air was so clear and light that the new sensation of breathing it was like the having entered on a new existence. To help the delusion, the solid ground itself seemed gone, and the mountain, a shining waste of immense white heaps and masses, to be a region of cloud floating between the blue sky above and the earth far below.

Some dark specks in the snow, like knots upon a little thread, beginning at the convent door and winding away down the descent in broken lengths which were not yet pieced together, showed where the Brethren were at work in several places clearing the track. Already the snow had begun to be foot-thawed again about the door. Mules were busily brought out, tied to the rings in the wall, and laden; strings of bells were buckled on, burdens were adjusted, the voices of drivers and riders sounded musically. Some of the earliest had even already resumed their journey; and, both on the level summit by the dark water near the convent, and on the downward way of yesterday's ascent, little moving figures of men and mules, reduced to miniatures by the immensity around, went with a clear tinkling of bells and a pleasant harmony of tongues.

In the supper-room of last night, a new fire piled upon the feathery ashes of the old one, shone upon a homely breakfast of loaves, butter, and milk. It also shone on the courier of the Dorrit family, making tea for his party from a supply he had brought up with him, together with several other small stores which were chiefly laid in for the use of the strong body of inconvenience. Mr. Gowan, and Blandois of Paris, had already breakfasted, and were walking up and down by the lake, smoking their cigars.

"Gowan, eh?" muttered Tip, otherwise Edward Dorrit, Esquire, turning over the leaves of the book, when the courier had left them to breakfast. "Then Gowan is the name of a puppy, that's all I have got to say! If it was worth my while, I'd pull his nose. But it isn't worth my while —fortunately for him. How's his wife, Amy? I suppose you know. You generally know things of that sort."

"She is better, Edward. But they are not going to-day."

"Oh! They are not going to-day! Fortunately for that fellow too," said Tip, "or he and I might have come into collision."

"It is thought better here that she should lie quiet to-day, and not be fatigued and shaken by the ride down until to-morrow."

"With all my heart. But you talk as if you had been nursing her. You haven't been relapsing into (Mrs. General is not here) into old habits, have you, Amy?"

He asked her the question with a sly glance of observation at Miss Fanny, and at his father too.

"I have only been in to ask her if I could do anything for her, Tip," said Little Dorrit.

"You needn't call me Tip, Amy child," returned that young gentleman with a frown; "because that's an old habit, and one you may as well lay aside."

"I didn't mean to say so, Edward dear. I forgot. It was so natural once, that it seemed at the moment the right word."

"Oh yes!" Miss Fanny struck in. "Natural, and right word, and once, and all the rest of it! Nonsense, you little thing! I know perfectly well why you have been taking such an interest in this Mrs. Gowan. You can't blind *me*."

"I will not try to, Fanny. Don't be angry."

"Oh! angry!" returned that young lady with a flounce. "I have no patience" (which indeed was the truth).

"Pray, Fanny," said Mr. Dorrit, raising his eyebrows, "what do you mean? Explain yourself."

"Oh! Never mind, Pa," replied Miss Fanny, "it's no great matter. Amy will understand me. She knew, or knew of, this Mrs. Gowan before yesterday, and she may as well admit that she did."

"My child," said Mr. Dorrit, turning to his younger daughter, "has your sister—any—ha—authority for this curious statement?"

"However meek we are," Miss Fanny struck in before she could answer, "we don't go creeping into people's rooms on the tops of cold mountains, and sitting perishing in the frost with people, unless we know something about them beforehand. It's not very hard to divine whose friend Mrs. Gowan is."

"Whose friend?" enquired her father.

"Pa, I am sorry to say," returned Miss Fanny, who had by this time succeeded in goading herself into a state of much ill-usage and grievance, which she was often at great pains to do: "that I believe her to be a friend of that very objectionable and unpleasant person, who, with a total absence of all delicacy, which our experience might have led us to expect from him, insulted us and outraged our feelings in so public and wilful a manner, on an occasion to which it is understood among us, that we will not more pointedly allude."

"Amy, my child," said Mr. Dorrit, tempering a bland severity with a dignified affection, "is this the case?"

Little Dorrit mildly answered, yes it was.

"Yes it is!" cried Miss Fanny. "Of course! I said so! And now, Pa, I do declare once for all," this young lady was in the habit of declaring the same thing once for all, every day of her life, and even several times in a day, "that this is shameful! I do declare once for all that it ought to be put a stop to. Is it not enough that we have gone through what is only known to ourselves, but are we to have it thrown in our faces, perseveringly and systematically, by the very person who should spare our feelings most? Are we to be exposed to this unnatural conduct every moment of our lives? Are we never to be permitted to forget? I say again, it is absolutely infamous!"

"Well, Amy," observed her brother, shaking his head, "you know I stand by you whenever I can, and on most occasions. But I must say, that upon my soul I do consider it rather an unaccountable mode of showing your sisterly affection, that you should back up a man who treated me in the most ungentlemanly way in which one man can treat another. And who," he added convincingly, "must be a low-minded thief, you know, or he never could have conducted himself as he did."

"And see," said Miss Fanny, "see what is involved in this! Can we ever hope to be respected by our servants? Never. Here are our two women, and Pa's valet, and a footman, and a courier, and all sorts of dependents, and yet, in the midst of these, we are to have one of ourselves rushing about with tumblers of cold water, like a menial! Why, a policeman," said Miss Fanny, "if a beggar had a fit in the street, could but go plunging about with tumblers, as this very Amy did in this very room before our very eyes last night!"

"I don't so much mind that, once in a way," remarked Mr. Edward; "but your Clennam, as he thinks proper to call himself, is another thing."

"He is a part of the same thing," returned Miss Fanny, "and of a piece with all the rest. He obtruded himself upon us in the first instance. We never wanted him. I always showed him, for one, that I could have dispensed with his company with the greatest pleasure. He then commits that gross outrage upon our feelings, which he never could or would have committed but for the delight he took in exposing us; and then we are to be demeaned for the service of his friends! Why, I don't wonder at this Mr. Gowan's conduct towards you. What else was to be expected when he was enjoying our past misfortunes—gloating over them at the moment!"

"Father—Edward—no indeed!" pleaded Little Dorrit. "Neither Mr. nor Mrs. Gowan had ever heard our name. They were, and they are, quite ignorant of our history."

"So much the worse," retorted Fanny, determined not to admit anything in extenuation, "for then you have *no* excuse. If they had known about us, you might have felt yourself called upon to conciliate them. That would have been a weak and ridiculous mistake, but I can respect a mistake, whereas I can't respect a wilful and deliberate abasing of those who should be nearest and dearest to us. No. I can't respect that. I can do nothing but denounce that."

"I never offend you wilfully, Fanny," said Little Dorrit, "though you are so hard with me."

"Then you should be more careful, Amy," returned her sister. "If you do such things by accident, you should be more careful. If I happened to have been born in a peculiar place, and under peculiar circumstances that blunted my knowledge of propriety, I fancy I should think myself bound to consider at every step, 'Am I going, ignorantly, to compromise any near and dear relations?' That is what I fancy *I* should do, if it was *my* case."

Mr. Dorrit now interposed, at once to stop these painful subjects by his authority, and to point their moral by his wisdom.

"My dear," said he to his younger daughter, "I beg you to—ha—to say no more. Your sister Fanny expresses herself strongly, but not without considerable reason. You have now a—hum—a great position to support. That great position is not occupied by yourself alone, but by—ha—by me, and—ha hum—by us. Us. Now, it is incumbent upon all people in an exalted position, but it is particularly so on this family, for reasons which I—ha—will not dwell upon, to make themselves respected. To be vigilant in making themselves respected. Dependents, to respect us, must be—ha— kept at a distance and—hum—kept down. Down. Therefore, your not exposing yourself to the remarks of our attendants, by appearing to have at any time dispensed with their services and performed them for yourself, is—ha—highly important."

"Why, who can doubt it?" cried Miss Fanny. "It's the essence of everything!"

"Fanny," returned her father, grandiloquently, "give me leave, my dear. We then come to—ha—to Mr. Clennam. I am free to say that I do not, Amy, share your sister's sentiments—that is to say altogether—hum— altogether—in reference to Mr. Clennam. I am content to regard that individual in the light of—ha—generally—a well-behaved person. Hum. A well-behaved person. Nor will I enquire whether Mr. Clennam did, at any time, obtrude himself on—ha—my society. He knew my society to be—hum—sought, and his plea might be that he regarded me in the light of a public character. But there were circumstances attending my—ha— slight knowledge of Mr. Clennam (it was very slight), which," here Mr. Dorrit became extremely grave and impressive, "would render it highly indelicate in Mr. Clennam to—ha—to seek to renew communication with me or with any member of my family, under existing circumstances. If Mr. Clennam has sufficient delicacy to perceive the impropriety of any such attempt, I am bound as a responsible gentleman to—ha—defer to that delicacy on his part. If, on the other hand, Mr. Clennam has not that delicacy, I cannot for a moment—ha—hold any correspondence with so— hum—coarse a mind. In either case, it would appear that Mr. Clennam is put altogether out of the question, and that we have nothing to do with him or he with us. Ha—Mrs. General!"

The entrance of the lady whom he announced, to take her place at the breakfast-table, terminated the discussion. Shortly afterwards, the courier announced that the valet, and the footman, and the two maids, and the four guides, and the fourteen mules, were in readiness; so the breakfast party went out to the convent door to join the cavalcade.

Mr. Gowan kept aloof with his cigar and pencil, but Mr. Blandois was on the spot, to pay his respects to the ladies. When he gallantly pulled off his slouched hat to Little Dorrit, she thought he had even a more sinister look, standing swart and cloaked in the snow, than he had had in the fire-light over night. But, as both her father and her sister received his homage with some favor, she refrained from expressing any distrust of him, lest it should prove to be a new blemish derived from her prison-birth.

Nevertheless, as they wound down the rugged way while the convent was yet in sight, she more than once looked round, and descried Mr. Blandois, backed by the convent smoke which rose straight and high from the chimneys in a golden film, always standing on one jutting point looking down after them. Long after he was a mere black stick in the snow, she felt as though she could yet see that smile of his, that high nose, and those eyes that were too near it. And even after that, when the convent was gone and some light morning clouds veiled the pass below it, the ghastly skeleton arms by the wayside seemed to be all pointing up at him.

More treacherous than snow, perhaps, colder at heart, and harder to melt, Blandois of Paris by degrees passed out of her mind, as they came down into the softer regions. Again the sun was warm, again the streams descending from glaciers and snowy caverns were refreshing to drink at, again they came among the pine trees, the rocky rivulets, the verdant heights and dales, the wooden chalets and rough zigzag fences, of Swiss country. Sometimes, the way so widened that she and her father could ride abreast. And then to look at him, handsomely clothed in his furs and broadcloths, rich, free, numerously served and attended, his eyes roving far away among the glories of the landscape, no miserable screen before them to darken his sight and cast its shadow on him, was enough.

Her uncle was so far rescued from that shadow of old, that he wore the clothes they gave him, and performed some ablutions as a sacrifice to the family credit, and went where he was taken, with a certain patient animal enjoyment, which seemed to express that the air and change did him good. In all other respects, save one, he shone with no light but such as was reflected from his brother. His brother's greatness, wealth, freedom, and grandeur, pleased him without any reference to himself. Silent and retiring, he had no use for speech when he could hear his brother speak; no desire to be waited on, so that the servants devoted themselves to his brother. The only noticeable change he originated in himself, was an alteration in his manner to his younger niece. Every day it refined more and more into a marked respect, very rarely shown by age to youth, and still more rarely susceptible, one would have said, of the fitness with which he invested it. On those occasions when Miss Fanny did declare once for all, he would take the next opportunity of baring his grey head before his younger niece, and of helping her to alight, or handing her to the carriage, or showing her any other attention, with the profoundest deference. Yet it never appeared misplaced or forced, being always heartily simple, spontaneous, and genuine. Neither would he ever consent, even at his brother's request, to be helped to any place before her, or to take precedence of her in anything. So jealous was he of her being respected, that on this very journey down from the Great Saint Bernard, he took sudden and violent umbrage at the footman's being remiss to hold her stirrup, though standing near when she dismounted; and unspeakably astonished the whole retinue by charging at him on a hard-headed mule, riding him into a corner, and threatening to trample him to death.

They were a goodly company, and the Innkeepers all but worshipped them. Wherever they went, their importance preceded them in the person of the courier riding before, to see that the rooms of state were ready. He was the herald of the family procession. The great travelling-carriage came next: containing, inside, Mr. Dorrit, Miss Dorrit, Miss Amy Dorrit, and Mrs. General; outside, some of the retainers, and (in fine weather) Edward Dorrit, Esquire, for whom the box was reserved. Then came the chariot containing Frederick Dorrit, Esquire, and an empty place occupied by Edward Dorrit, Esquire, in wet weather. Then came the fourgon with the rest of the retainers, the heavy baggage, and as much as it could carry of the mud and dust which the other vehicles left behind.

These equipages adorned the yard of the hotel at Martigny, on the return of the family from their mountain excursion. Other vehicles were there, much company being on the road, from the patched Italian Vettura —like the body of a swing from an English fair put upon a wooden tray on wheels, and having another wooden tray without wheels put atop of it— to the trim English carriage. But there was another adornment of the hotel which Mr. Dorrit had not bargained for. Two strange travellers embellished one of his rooms.

The Innkeeper, hat in hand in the yard, swore to the courier that he was blighted, that he was desolated, that he was profoundly afflicted, that he was the most miserable and unfortunate of beasts, that he had the head of a wooden pig. He ought never to have made the concession, he said, but the very genteel lady had so passionately prayed him for the accommodation of that room to dine in, only for a little half-hour, that he had been vanquished. The little half-hour was expired, the lady and gentleman were taking their little dessert and half-cup of coffee, the note was paid, the horses were ordered, they would depart immediately; but, owing to an unhappy destiny and the curse of Heaven, they were not yet gone.

Nothing could exceed Mr. Dorrit's indignation, as he turned at the foot of the staircase on hearing these apologies. He felt that the family dignity was struck at, by an assassin's hand. He had a sense of his dignity, which was of the most exquisite nature. He could detect a design upon it when nobody else had any perception of the fact. His life was made an agony by the number of fine scalpels that he felt to be incessantly engaged in dissecting his dignity.

"Is it possible, sir," said Mr. Dorrit, reddening excessively, "that you have—ha—had the audacity to place one of my rooms at the disposition of any other person?"

Thousands of pardons! It was the host's profound misfortune to have been overcome by that too genteel lady. He besought Monseigneur not to enrage himself. He threw himself on Monseigneur for clemency. If Monseigneur would have the distinguished goodness to occupy the other salon especially reserved for him, for but five minutes, all would go well.

"No, sir," said Mr. Dorrit. "I will not occupy any salon. I will leave your house without eating or drinking, or setting foot in it. How do you dare to act like this? Who am I that you—ha—separate me from other gentlemen?"

Alas! The host called all the universe to witness that Monseigneur was the most amiable of the whole body of nobility, the most important, the most estimable, the most honored. If he separated Monseigneur from others, it was only because he was more distinguished, more cherished, more generous, more renowned.

"Don't tell me so, sir," returned Mr. Dorrit, in a mighty heat. "You have affronted me. You have heaped insults upon me. How dare you? Explain yourself."

Ah, just Heaven, then, how could the host explain himself when he had nothing more to explain; when he had only to apologise, and confide himself to the so well-known magnanimity of Monseigneur!

"I tell you, sir," said Mr. Dorrit, panting with anger, "that you separate me—ha—from other gentlemen; that you make distinctions between me, and other gentlemen of fortune and station. I demand of you, why? I wish to know on—ha—what authority, on whose authority. Reply, sir. Explain. Answer why."

Permit the landlord humbly to submit to Monsieur the Courier then, that Monseigneur, ordinarily so gracious, enraged himself without cause. There was no why. Monsieur the Courier would represent to Monseigneur, that he deceived himself in suspecting that there was any why, but the why his devoted servant had already had the honor to present to him. The very genteel lady——

"Silence!" cried Mr. Dorrit. "Hold your tongue! I will hear no more of the very genteel lady; I will hear no more of you. Look at this family—my family—a family more genteel than any lady. You have treated this family with disrespect; you have been insolent to this family. I'll ruin you. Ha—send for the horses, pack the carriages, I'll not set foot in this man's house again!"

No one had interfered in the dispute, which was beyond the French colloquial powers of Edward Dorrit, Esquire, and scarcely within the province of the ladies. Miss Fanny, however, now supported her father with great bitterness; declaring, in her native tongue, that it was quite clear there was something special in this man's impertinence; and that she considered it important that he should be, by some means, forced to give up his authority for making distinctions between that family and other wealthy families. What the reasons of his presumption could be, she was at a loss to imagine; but reasons he must have, and they ought to be torn from him.

All the guides, mule-drivers, and idlers in the yard, had made themselves parties to the angry conference, and were much impressed by the courier's now bestirring himself to get the carriages out. With the aid of some dozen people to each wheel, this was done at a great cost of noise; and then the loading was proceeded with, pending the arrival of the horses from the post-house.

But, the very genteel lady's English chariot being already horsed and at the inn-door, the landlord had slipped up-stairs to represent his hard case. This was notified to the yard by his now coming down the staircase in attendance on the gentleman and the lady, and by his pointing out the offended majesty of Mr. Dorrit to them with a significant motion of his hand.

"Beg your pardon," said the gentleman, detaching himself from the lady, and coming forward. "I am a man of few words and a bad hand at an explanation—but lady here is extremely anxious that there should be no Row. Lady—a mother of mine, in point of fact—wishes me to say that she hopes no Row."

Mr. Dorrit, still panting under his injury, saluted the gentleman, and saluted the lady, in a distant, final, and invincible manner.

"No, but really—here, old feller; you!" This was the gentleman's way of appealing to Edward Dorrit, Esquire, on whom he pounced as a great and providential relief. "Let you and I try to make this all right. Lady so very much wishes no Row."

Edward Dorrit, Esquire, led a little apart by the button, assumed a diplomatic expression of countenance in replying, "Why you must confess, that when you bespeak a lot of rooms beforehand and they belong to you, it's not pleasant to find other people in 'em."

"No," said the other, "I know it isn't. I admit it. Still, let you and I try to make it all right, and avoid Row. The fault is not this chap's at all, but my mother's. Being a remarkably fine woman with no bigodd nonsense about her—well educated, too—she was too many for this chap. Regularly pocketed him."

"If that's the case——" Edward Dorrit, Esquire, began.

"Assure you 'pon my soul 'tis the case. Consequently," said the other gentleman, retiring on his main position, "why Row?"

"Edmund," said the lady from the doorway, "I hope you have explained, or are explaining, to the satisfaction of this gentleman and his family, that the civil landlord is not to blame?"

"Assure you, ma'am," returned Edmund, "perfectly paralyzing myself with trying it on." He then looked stedfastly at Edward Dorrit, Esquire, for some moments, and suddenly added, in a burst of confidence, "Old feller! *Is* it all right?"

"I don't know, after all," said the lady, gracefully advancing a step or two towards Mr. Dorrit, "but that I had better say myself, at once, that I assured this good man I took all the consequences on myself of occupying one of a stranger's suite of rooms during his absence, for just as much (or as little) time as I could dine in. I had no idea the rightful owner would come back so soon, nor had I any idea :hat he had come back, or I should have hastened to make restoration of my ill-gotten chamber, and to have offered my explanation and apology. I trust, in saying this——"

For a moment the lady, with a glass at her eye, stood transfixed and speechless before the two Miss Dorrits. At the same moment Miss Fanny, in the foreground of a grand pictorial composition formed by the family, the family equipages, and the family servants, held her sister tight under one arm to detain her on the spot, and with the other arm fanned herself with a distinguished air, and negligently surveyed the lady from head to foot.

The lady, recovering herself quickly—for it was Mrs. Merdle and she was not easily dashed—went on to add that she trusted, in saying this, she apologised for her boldness, and restored this well-behaved landlord to the favor that was so very valuable to him. Mr. Dorrit, on the altar of whose dignity all this was incense, made a gracious reply; and said that his people should—ha—countermand his horses, and he would—hum—overlook what he had at first supposed to be an affront, but now regarded as an honor. Upon this, the bosom bent to him; and its owner, with a wonderful command of feature, addressed a winning smile of adieu to the two sisters, as young ladies of fortune in whose favor she was much prepossessed, and whom she had never had the gratification of seeing before.

Not so, however, Mr. Sparkler. This gentleman, becoming transfixed at the same moment as his lady-mother, could not by any means unfix himself again, but stood stiffly staring at the whole composition with Miss Fanny in the foreground. On his mother's saying, "Edmund, we are quite ready; will you give me your arm?" he seemed, by the motion of his lips, to reply with some remark comprehending the form of words in which his shining talents found the most frequent utterance, but he relaxed no muscle. So fixed was his figure, that it would have been matter of some difficulty to bend him sufficiently to get him in at the carriage-door, if he had not received the timely assistance of a maternal pull from within. He was no sooner within, than the pad of the little window in the back of the chariot disappeared, and his eye usurped its place. There it remained as long as so small an object was discernible, and probably much longer, staring (as though something inexpressibly surprising should happen to a cod-fish) like an ill-executed eye in a large locket.

This encounter was so highly agreeable to Miss Fanny, and gave her so much to think of with triumph afterwards, that it softened her asperities exceedingly. When the procession was again in motion next day, she occupied her place in it with a new gaiety; and showed such a flow of spirits indeed, that Mrs. General looked rather surprised.

Little Dorrit was glad to be found no fault with, and to see that Fanny was pleased; but her part in the procession was a musing part, and a quiet one. Sitting opposite her father in the travelling-carriage, and recalling the old Marshalsea room, her present existence was a dream. All that she saw was new and wonderful, but it was not real; it seemed to her as if those visions of mountains and picturesque countries might melt away at any moment, and the carriage, turning some abrupt corner, bring up with a jolt at the old Marshalsea gate.

To have no work to do was strange, but not half so strange as having glided into a corner where she had no one to think for, nothing to plan and contrive, no cares of others to load herself with. Stranger as that was, it was far stranger yet to find a space between herself and her father, where others occupied themselves in taking care of him, and where she was never expected to be. At first, this was so much more unlike her old experience than even the mountains themselves, that she had been unable to resign herself to it, and had tried to retain her old place about him. But he had spoken to her alone, and had said that people—ha—people in an exalted position, my dear, must scrupulously exact respect from their dependants; and that for her, his daughter, Miss Amy Dorrit, of the sole remaining branch of the Dorrits of Dorsetshire, to be known to—hum—to occupy herself in fulfilling the functions of—ha hum—a valet, would be incompatible with that respect. Therefore, my dear, he—ha—he laid his parental injunctions upon her, to remember that she was a lady, who had now to conduct herself with—hum—a proper pride, and to preserve the rank of a lady; and consequently he requested her to abstain from doing what would occasion—ha—unpleasant and derogatory remarks. She had obeyed without a murmur. Thus it had been brought about that she now sat in her corner of the luxurious carriage with her little patient hands folded before her, quite displaced even from the last point of the old standing-ground in life on which her feet had lingered.

It was from this position that all she saw appeared unreal; the more surprising the scenes, the more they resembled the unreality of her own inner life as she went through its vacant places all day long. The gorges of the Simplon, its enormous depths and thundering waterfalls, the wonderful road, the points of danger where a loose wheel or a faltering horse would have been destruction, the descent into Italy, the opening of that beautiful land, as the rugged mountain-chasm widened and let them out from a gloomy and dark imprisonment—all a dream—only the old Marshalsea a reality. Nay, even the old mean Marshalsea was shaken to its foundations, when she pictured it without her father. She could scarcely believe that the prisoners were still lingering in the close yard, that the mean rooms were still every one tenanted, and that the turnkey still stood in the Lodge letting people in and out, all just as she well knew it to be.

With a remembrance of her father's old life in prison hanging about her like the burden of a sorrowful tune, Little Dorrit would wake from a dream of her birth-place into a whole day's dream. The painted room in which she awoke, often a humbled state-chamber in a dilapidated palace, would begin it; with its wild red autumnal vine-leaves overhanging the glass, its orange trees on the cracked white terrace outside the window, a group of monks and peasants in the little street below, misery and magnificence wrestling with each other upon every rood of ground in the prospect, no matter how widely diversified, and misery throwing magnificence with the strength of fate. To this would succeed a labyrinth of bare passages and pillared galleries, with the family procession already preparing in the quadrangle below, through the carriages and luggage being brought together by the servants for the day's journey. Then, breakfast in another painted chamber, damp-stained and of desolate proportions; and then the departure, which, to her timidity and sense of not being grand enough for her place in the ceremonies, was always an uneasy thing. For, then the courier (who himself would have been a foreign gentleman of high mark in the Marshalsea) would present himself to report that all was ready; and then her father's valet would pompously induct him into his travelling cloak; and then Fanny's maid, and her own maid (who was a weight on Little Dorrit's mind—absolutely made her cry at first, she knew so little what to do with her), would be in attendance; and then her brother's man would complete his master's equipment; and then her father would give his arm to Mrs. General, and her uncle would give his to her, and, escorted by the landlord and Inn servants, they would swoop down-stairs. There, a crowd would be collected to see them enter their carriages, which, amidst much bowing, and begging, and prancing, and lashing, and clattering, they would do; and so they would be driven madly through the narrow unsavoury streets, and jerked out at the town gate.

Among the day's unrealities would be, roads where the bright red vines were looped and garlanded together on trees for many miles; woods of olives; white villages and towns on hill-sides, lovely without, but frightful in their dirt and poverty within; crosses by the way; deep blue lakes with fairy islands, and clustering boats with awnings of bright colors and sails of beautiful forms; vast piles of building mouldering to dust; hanging-gardens where the weeds had grown so strong that their stems, like wedges driven home, had split the arch and rent the wall; stone-terraced lanes, with the lizards running into and out of every chink; beggars of all sorts everywhere: pitiful, picturesque, hungry, merry: children beggars and aged beggars. Often at posting-houses, and other halting places, these miserable creatures would appear to her the only realities of the day; and many a time, when the money she had brought to give them was all given away, she would sit with her folded hands, thoughtfully looking after some diminutive girl leading her grey father, as if the sight reminded her of something in the days that were gone.

Again, there would be places where they stayed the week together, in splendid rooms, had banquets every day, rode out among heaps of wonders, walked through miles of palaces, and rested in dark corners of great churches; where there were winking lamps of gold and silver among pillars and arches, kneeling figures dotted about at confessionals and on the pavements; where there was the mist and scent of incense; where there were pictures, fantastic images, gaudy altars, great heights and distances, all softly lighted through stained glass, and the massive curtains that hung in the doorways. From these cities, they would go on again, by the roads of vines and olives, through squalid villages where there was not a hovel without a gap in its filthy walls, not a window with a whole inch of glass or paper; where there seemed to be nothing to support life, nothing to eat, nothing to make, nothing to grow, nothing to hope, nothing to do but die.

Again they would come to whole towns of palaces, whose proper inmates were all banished, and which were all changed into barracks: troops of idle soldiers leaning out of the state-windows, where their accoutrements hung drying on the marble architecture, and showing to the mind like hosts of rats who were (happily) eating away the props of the edifices that supported them, and must soon, with them, be smashed on the heads of the other swarms of soldiers, and the swarms of priests, and the swarms of spies, who were all the ill-looking population left to be ruined, in the streets below.

Through such scenes, the family procession moved on to Venice. And here it dispersed for a time, as they were to live in Venice some few months, in a palace (itself six times as big as the whole Marshalsea) on the Grand Canal.

In this crowning unreality, where all the streets were paved with water, and where the deathlike stillness of the days and nights was broken by no sound but the softened ringing of church bells, the rippling of the current, and the cry of the gondoliers turning the corners of the flowing streets, Little Dorrit, quite lost by her task being done, sat down to muse. The family began a gay life, went here and there, and turned night into day; but, she was timid of joining in their gaieties, and only asked leave to be left alone.

Sometimes she would step into one of the gondolas that were always kept in waiting, moored to painted posts at the door—when she could escape from the attendance of that oppressive maid, who was her mistress, and a very hard one —and would be taken all over the strange city. Social people in other gondolas began to ask each other who the little solitary girl was whom they passed, sitting in her boat with folded hands, looking so pensively and wonderingly about her. Never thinking that it would be worth anybody's while to notice her or her doings, Little Dorrit, in her quiet, scared, lost manner, went about the city none the less.

But, her favorite station was the balcony of her own room, overhanging the canal, with other balconies below, and none above. It was of massive stone darkened by ages, built in a wild fancy which came from the East to that collection of wild fancies; and Little Dorrit was little indeed, leaning on the broad-cushioned ledge, and looking over. As she liked no place of an evening half so well, she soon began to be watched for, and many eyes in passing gondolas were raised, and many people said, There was the little figure of the English girl who was always alone.

Such people were not realities to the little figure of the English girl; such people were all unknown to her. She would watch the sunset, in its long low lines of purple and red, and its burning flush high up into the sky: so glowing on the buildings, and so lightening their structure, that it made them look as if their strong walls were transparent, and they shone from within. She would watch those glories expire; and then, after looking at the black gondolas underneath, taking guests to music and dancing, would raise her eyes to the shining stars. Was there no party of her own, in other times, on which the stars had shone? To think of that old gate now!

She would think of that old gate, and of herself sitting at it in the dead of the night, pillowing Maggy's head; and of other places and of other scenes associated with those different times. And then she would lean upon her balcony, and look over at the water, as though they all lay underneath it. When she got to that, she would musingly watch its running, as if, in the general vision, it might run dry, and show her the prison again, and herself, and the old room, and the old inmates, and the old visitors: all lasting realities that had never changed.

CHAPTER IV

A LETTER FROM LITTLE DORRIT

DEAR MR. CLENNAM.

I write to you from my own room at Venice, thinking you will be glad to hear from me. But I know you cannot be so glad to hear from me, as I am to write to you; for everything about you is as you have been accustomed to see it, and you miss nothing—unless it should be me, which can only be for a very little while together and very seldom—while everything in my life is so strange, and I miss so much.

When we were in Switzerland, which appears to have been years ago, though it was only weeks, I met young Mrs. Gowan, who was on a mountain excursion like ourselves. She told me she was very well and very happy. She sent you the message, by me, that she thanked you affectionately and would never forget you. She was quite confiding with me, and I loved her almost as soon as I spoke to her. But there is nothing singular in that; who could help loving so beautiful and winning a creature! I could not wonder at any one loving her. No, indeed.

It will not make you uneasy on Mrs. Gowan's account, I hope—for I remember that you said you had the interest of a true friend in her—if I tell you that I wish she could have married some one better suited to her. Mr. Gowan seems fond of her, and of course she is very fond of him, but I thought he was not earnest enough—I don't mean in that respect—I mean in anything. I could not keep it out of my mind that if I was Mrs. Gowan (what a change that would be, and how I must alter to become like her!) I should feel that I was rather lonely and lost, for the want of some one who was stedfast and firm in purpose. I even thought she felt this want a little, almost without knowing it. But mind you are not made uneasy by this, for she was "very well and very happy." And she looked most beautiful.

I expect to meet her again before long, and indeed have been expecting for some days past to see her here. I will ever be as good a friend to her as I can for your sake. Dear Mr. Clennam, I dare say you think little of having been a friend to me when I had no other (not that I have any other now, for I have made no new friends), but I think much of it, and I never can forget it.

I wish I knew but it is best for no one to write to me- how Mr. and Mrs. Plornish prosper in the business which my dear father bought for them, and that old Mr Nandy lives happily with them and his two grandchildren, and sings all his songs over and over again. I cannot quite keep back the tears from my eyes when I think of my poor Maggy, and of the blank she must have felt at first, however kind they all are to her, without her Little Mother Will you go and tell her, as a strict secret, with my love, that she never can have regretted our separation more than I have regretted it? And will you tell them all that I have thought of them every day, and that my heart is faithful to them everywhere? O, if you could know how faithful, you would almost pity me for being so far away and being so grand!

You will be glad, I am sure, to know that my dear father is very well in health, and that all these changes are highly beneficial to him, and that he is very different indeed from what he used to be when you used to see him. There is an improvement in my uncle too, I think, though he never complained of old, and never exults now. Fanny is very graceful, quick, and clever. It is natural to her to be a lady; she has adapted herself to our new fortunes, with wonderful ease.

This reminds me that I have not been able to do so, and that I sometimes almost despair of ever being able to do so. I find that I cannot learn. Mrs.

General is always with us, and we speak French and speak Italian, and she takes pains to form us in many ways. When I say we speak French and Italian, I mean they do. As for me, I am so slow that I scarcely get on at all. As soon as I begin to plan, and think, and try, all my planning, thinking, and trying go in old directions, and I begin to feel careful again about the expenses of the day, and about my dear father, and about my work, and then I remember with a start that there are no such cares left, and that in itself is so new and improbable that it sets me wandering again. I should not have the courage to mention this to any one but you.

It is the same with all these new countries and wonderful sights. They are very beautiful, and they astonish me, but I am not collected enough—not familiar enough with myself, if you can quite understand what I mean—to have all the pleasure in them that I might have. What I knew before them, blends with them, too, so curiously. For instance, when we were among the mountains, I often felt (I hesitate to tell such an idle thing, dear Mr. Clennam, even to you), as if the Marshalsea must be behind that great rock; or as if Mrs. Clennam's room where I have worked so many days, and where I first saw you, must be just beyond that snow. Do you remember one night when I came with Maggy to your lodging in Covent Garden? That room I have often and often fancied I have seen before me, travelling along for miles by the side of our carriage, when I have looked out of the carriage window after dark. We were shut out that night, and sat at the iron gate, and walked about till morning. I often look up at the stars, even from the balcony of this room, and believe that I am in the street again, shut out with Maggy. It is the same with people that I left in England. When I go about here in a gondola, I surprise myself looking into other gondolas as if I hoped to see them. It would overcome me with joy to see them, but I don't think it would surprise me much, at first. In my fanciful times, I fancy that they might be anywhere; and I almost expect to see their dear faces on the bridges or the quays.

Another difficulty that I have will seem very strange to you. It must seem very strange to any one but me, and does even to me: I often feel the old sad pity for—I need not write the word—for him. Changed as he is, and inexpressibly blest and thankful as I always am to know it, the old sorrowful feeling of compassion comes upon me sometimes with such strength, that I want to put my arms round his neck, tell him how I love him, and cry a little on his breast. I should be glad after that, and proud and happy. But I know that I must not do this; that he would not like it, that Fanny would be angry, that Mrs. General would be amazed; and so I quiet myself. Yet in doing so, I struggle with the feeling that I have come to be at a distance from him; and that even in the midst of all the servants and attendants, he is deserted, and in want of me.

Dear Mr. Clennam, I have written a great deal about myself, but I must write a little more still, or what I wanted most of all to say in this weak letter would be left out of it. In all these foolish thoughts of mine, which I have been so hardy as to confess to you because I know you will understand me if anybody can, and will make more allowance for me than anybody else would if you cannot—in all these thoughts, there is one thought scarcely ever—never—out of my memory, and that is that I hope you sometimes, in a quiet moment, have a thought for me. I must tell you that as to this, I have felt, ever since I have been away, an anxiety which I am very very anxious to relieve. I have been afraid that you may think of me in a new light, or a new character. Don't do that, I could not bear that— it would make me more unhappy than you can suppose. It would break my heart to believe that you thought of me in any way that would make me stranger to you, than I was when you were so good to me. What I have to pray and entreat of you is, that you will never think of me as the daughter of a rich person; that you will never think of me as dressing any better, or living any better, than when you first knew me. That you will remember me only as the little shabby girl you protected with so much tenderness, from whose threadbare dress you have kept away the rain, and whose wet feet you have dried at your fire. That you will think of me (when you think of me at all), and of my true affection and devoted gratitude, always, without change, as of

Your poor child,

LITTLE DORRIT.

P.S.—Particularly remember that you are not to be uneasy about Mrs. Gowan. Her words were, "Very well and very happy." And she looked most beautiful.

END OF No. XI

CHAPTER V

SOMETHING WRONG SOMEWHERE

THE family had been a month or two at Venice, when Mr. Dorrit, who was much among Counts and Marquises, and had but scant leisure, set an hour of one day apart, beforehand, for the purpose of holding some conference with Mrs. General.

The time he had reserved in his mind arriving, he sent Mr. Tinkler, his valet, to Mrs. General's apartment (which would have absorbed about a third of the area of the Marshalsea), to present his compliments to that lady, and represent him as desiring the favor of an interview. It being that period of the forenoon when the various members of the family had coffee in their own chambers, some couple of hours before assembling at breakfast in a faded hall which had once been sumptuous but was now the prey of watery vapours and a settled melancholy, Mrs. General was accessible to the valet. That envoy found her on a little square of carpet, so extremely diminutive in reference to the size of her stone and marble floor, that she looked as if she might have had it spread for the trying on of a ready-made pair of shoes; or as if she had come into possession of the enchanted piece of carpet, bought for forty purses by one of the three princes in the Arabian Nights, and had that moment been transported on it, at a wish, into a palatial saloon with which it had no connexion.

Mrs. General, replying to the envoy, as she set down her empty coffee-cup, that she was willing at once to proceed to Mr. Dorrit's apartment, and spare him the trouble of coming to her (which, in his gallantry, he had proposed), the envoy threw open the door, and escorted Mrs. General to the presence. It was quite a walk, by mysterious staircases and corridors, from Mrs. General's apartment,—hoodwinked by a narrow side street with a low gloomy bridge in it, and dungeon-like opposite tenements, their walls besmeared with a thousand downward stains and streaks, as if every crazy aperture in them had been weeping tears of rust into the Adriatic for centuries,—to Mr. Dorrit's apartment: with a whole English house-front of window, a prospect of beautiful church-domes rising into the blue sky sheer out of the water which reflected them, and a hushed murmur of the Grand Canal laving the doorways below, where his gondolas and gondoliers attended his pleasure, drowsily swinging in a little forest of piles.

Mr. Dorrit, in a resplendent dressing-gown and cap—the dormant grub that had so long bided its time among the Collegians had burst into a rare butterfly—rose to receive Mrs. General. A chair to Mrs. General. An easier chair, sir; what are you doing, what are you about, what do you mean? Now, leave us!

"Mrs. General," said Mr. Dorrit, "I took the liberty——"

"By no means," Mrs. General interposed. "I was quite at your disposition. I had had my coffee."

"I took the liberty," said Mr. Dorrit again, with the magnificent placidity of one who was above correction, "to solicit the favor of a little private conversation with you, because I feel rather worried respecting my—ha—my younger daughter. You will have observed a great difference of temperament, madam, between my two daughters?"

Said Mrs. General in response, crossing her gloved hands (she was never without gloves, and they never creased and always fitted), "There is a great difference."

"May I ask to be favored with your view of it?" said Mr. Dorrit, with a deference not incompatible with majestic serenity.

"Fanny," returned Mrs. General, "has force of character and self-reliance. Amy, none."

None? O Mrs. General, ask the Marshalsea stones and bars. O Mrs.

General, ask the milliner who taught her to work, and the dancing-master who taught her sister to dance. O Mrs. General, Mrs. General, ask me, her father, what I owe to her; and hear my testimony touching the life of this slighted little creature, from her childhood up!

No such adjuration entered Mr. Dorrit's head. He looked at Mrs. General, seated in her usual erect attitude on her coachbox behind the proprieties, and he said in a thoughtful manner, "True, madam."

"I would not," said Mrs. General, "be understood to say, observe, that there is nothing to improve in Fanny. But there is material there—perhaps, indeed, a little too much."

"Will you be kind enough, madam," said Mr. Dorrit, "to be—ha—more explicit? I do not quite understand my elder daughter's having—hum—too much material. What material?"

"Fanny," returned Mrs. General, "at present forms too many opinions. Perfect breeding forms none, and is never demonstrative."

Lest he himself should be found deficient in perfect breeding, Mr. Dorrit hastened to reply, "Unquestionably, madam, you are right." Mrs. General returned, in her emotionless and expressionless manner, "I believe so."

"But you are aware, my dear madam," said Mr. Dorrit, "that my daughters had the misfortune to lose their lamented mother when they were very young; and that, in consequence of my not having been until lately the recognised heir to my property, they have lived with me as a comparatively poor, though always proud, gentleman, in—ha hum—retirement!"

"I do not," said Mrs. General, "lose sight of the circumstance."

"Madam," pursued Mr. Dorrit, "of my daughter Fanny, under her present guidance and with such an example constantly before her——"

(Mrs. General shut her eyes.)

"—I have no misgivings. There is adaptability of character in Fanny. But my younger daughter, Mrs. General, rather worries and vexes my thoughts. I must inform you that she has always been my favorite."

"There is no accounting," said Mrs. General, "for these partialities."

"Ha—no," assented Mr. Dorrit. "No. Now, madam, I am troubled by noticing that Amy is not, so to speak, one of ourselves. She does not care to go about with us; she is lost in the society we have here; our tastes are evidently not her tastes. Which," said Mr. Dorrit, summing up with judicial gravity, "is to say, in other words, that there is something wrong in—ha—Amy."

"May we incline to the supposition," said Mrs. General, with a little touch of varnish, "that something is referable to the novelty of the position?"

"Excuse me, madam," observed Mr. Dorrit, rather quickly. "The daughter of a gentleman, though—ha—himself at one time comparatively far from affluent—comparatively—and herself reared in—hum—retirement, need not of necessity find this position so very novel."

"True," said Mrs. General, "true."

"Therefore, madam," said Mr. Dorrit, "I took the liberty" (he laid an emphasis on the phrase and repeated it, as though he stipulated, with urbane firmness, that he must not be contradicted again), "I took the liberty of requesting this interview, in order that I might mention the topic to you, and enquire how you would advise me?"

"Mr. Dorrit," returned Mrs. General, "I have conversed with Amy several times since we have been residing here, on the general subject of the formation of a demeanour. She has expressed herself to me as wondering exceedingly at Venice. I have mentioned to her that it is better not to wonder. I have pointed out to her that the celebrated Mr. Eustace, the classical tourist, did not think much of it; and that he compared the Rialto, greatly to its disadvantage, with Westminster and Blackfriars Bridges. I need not add, after what you have said, that I have not yet found my arguments successful. You do me the honor to ask me what I advise. It always appears to me (if this should prove to be a baseless assumption, I shall be pardoned), that Mr. Dorrit has been accustomed to exercise influence over the minds of others."

"Hum—madam," said Mr. Dorrit, "I have been at the head of—ha—of a considerable community. You are right in supposing that I am not unaccustomed to—an influential position."

"I am happy," returned Mrs. General, "to be so corroborated. I would therefore the more confidently recommend, that Mr. Dorrit should speak to Amy himself, and make his observations and wishes known to her. Being his favorite besides, and no doubt attached to him, she is all the more likely to yield to his influence."

"I had anticipated your suggestion, madam," said Mr. Dorrit, "but —ha—was not sure that I might—hum—not encroach on——"

"On my province, Mr. Dorrit?" said Mrs. General, graciously. "Do not mention it."

"Then, with your leave, madam," resumed Mr. Dorrit, ringing his little bell to summon his valet, "I will send for her at once."

"Does Mr. Dorrit wish me to remain?"

"Perhaps, if you have no other engagement, you would not object for a minute or two——"

"Not at all."

So, Tinkler the valet was instructed to find Miss Amy's maid, and to request that subordinate to inform Miss Amy that Mr. Dorrit wished to see her in his own room. In delivering this charge to Tinkler, Mr. Dorrit looked severely at him, and also kept a jealous eye upon him until he went out at the door, mistrusting that he might have something in his mind prejudicial to the family dignity; that he might have even got wind of some

Collegiate joke before he came into the service, and might be derisively reviving its remembrance at the present moment. If Tinkler had happened to smile, however faintly and innocently, nothing would have persuaded Mr. Dorrit, to the hour of his death, but that this was the case. As Tinkler happened, however, very fortunately for himself, to be of a serious and composed countenance, he escaped the secret danger that threatened him. And as on his return—when Mr. Dorrit eyed him again—he announced Miss Amy as if she had come to a funeral, he left a vague impression on Mr. Dorrit's mind that he was a well-conducted young fellow, who had been brought up in the study of his Catechism, by a widowed mother.

"Amy," said Mr. Dorrit, "you have just now been the subject of some conversation between myself and Mrs. General. We agree that you scarcely seem at home here. Ha—how is this?"

A pause.

"I think, father, I require a little time."

"Papa is a preferable mode of address," observed Mrs. General. "Father is rather vulgar, my dear. The word Papa, besides, gives a pretty form to the lips. Papa, potatoes, poultry, prunes, and prism, are all very good words for the lips: especially prunes and prism. You will find it serviceable, in the formation of a demeanour, if you sometimes say to yourself in company—on entering a room, for instance—Papa, potatoes, poultry, prunes and prism, prunes and prism."

"Pray, my child," said Mr. Dorrit, "attend to the—hum—precepts of Mrs. General."

Poor Little Dorrit, with a rather forlorn glance at that eminent varnisher, promised to try.

"You say, Amy," pursued Mr. Dorrit, "that you think you require time. Time for what?"

Another pause.

"To become accustomed to the novelty of my life, was all I meant," said Little Dorrit, with her loving eyes upon her father; whom she had very nearly addressed as poultry, if not prunes and prism too, in her desire to submit herself to Mrs. General and please him.

Mr. Dorrit frowned, and looked anything but pleased. "Amy," he returned, "it appears to me, I must say, that you have had abundance of time for that. Ha—you surprise me. You disappoint me. Fanny has conquered any such little difficulties, and—hum —why not you?"

"I hope I shall do better soon," said Little Dorrit.

"I hope so," returned her father. "I—ha—I most devoutly hope so, Amy. I sent for you, in order that I might say—hum—impressively say, in the presence of Mrs. General, to whom we are all so much indebted for obligingly being present among us, on—ha—on this or any other occasion," Mrs. General shut her eyes, "that I—ha hum—am not pleased with you.

You make Mrs. General's a thankless task. You—ha—embarrass me very much. You have always (as I have informed Mrs. General) been my favorite child; I have always made you a—hum—a friend and companion; in return, I beg—I—ha—I *do* beg, that you accommodate yourself better to—hum—circumstances, and dutifully do what becomes your—your station."

Mr. Dorrit was even a little more fragmentary than usual; being excited on the subject, and anxious to make himself particularly emphatic.

"I do beg," he repeated, "that this may be attended to, and that you will seriously take pains and try to conduct yourself in a manner both becoming your position as—ha—Miss Amy Dorrit, and satisfactory to myself and Mrs. General."

That lady shut her eyes again, on being again referred to; then, slowly opening them and rising, added these words:

"If Miss Amy Dorrit will direct her own attention to, and will accept of my poor assistance in, the formation of a surface, Mr. Dorrit will have no further cause of anxiety. May I take this opportunity of remarking, as an instance in point, that it is scarcely delicate to look at vagrants with the attention which I have seen bestowed upon them, by a very dear young friend of mine? They should not be looked at. Nothing disagreeable should ever be looked at. Apart from such a habit standing in the way of that graceful equanimity of surface which is so expressive of good breeding, it hardly seems compatible with refinement of mind. A truly refined mind will seem to be ignorant of the existence of anything that is not perfectly proper, placid, and pleasant." Having delivered this exalted sentiment, Mrs. General made a sweeping obeisance, and retired with an expression of mouth indicative of Prunes and Prism.

Little Dorrit, whether speaking or silent, had preserved her quiet earnestness and her loving look. It had not been clouded, except for a passing moment, until now. But now that she was left alone with him, the fingers of her lightly-folded hands were agitated, and there was repressed emotion in her face.

Not for herself. She might feel a little wounded, but her care was not for herself. Her thoughts still turned, as they always had turned, to him. A faint misgiving, which had hung about her since their accession to fortune, that even now she could never see him as he used to be before the prison days, had gradually begun to assume form in her mind. She felt, that, in what he had just now said to her, and in his whole bearing towards her, there was the well-known shadow of the Marshalsea wall. It took a new shape, but it was the old sad shadow. She began with sorrowful unwillingness to acknowledge to herself, that she was not strong enough to keep off the fear that no space in the life of man could overcome that quarter of a century behind the prison bars. She had no blame to bestow upon him, therefore: nothing to reproach him with, no emotions in her faithful heart but great compassion and unbounded tenderness.

This is why it was, that, even as he sat before her on his sofa, in the brilliant light of a bright Italian day, the wonderful city without and the splendors of an old palace within, she saw him at the moment in the long-familiar gloom of his Marshalsea lodging, and wished to take her seat beside him, and comfort him, and be again full of confidence with him, and of usefulness to him. If he divined what was in her thoughts, his own were not in tune with it. After some uneasy moving in his seat, he got up, and walked about, looking very much dissatisfied.

"Is there anything else you wish to say to me, dear father?"

"No, no. Nothing else."

"I am sorry you have not been pleased with me, dear. I hope you will not think of me with displeasure now. I am going to try, more than ever, to adapt myself as you wish to what surrounds me—for indeed I have tried all along, though I have failed, I know."

"Amy," he returned, turning short upon her. "You—ha—habitually hurt me."

"Hurt you, father! I!"

"There is a—hum—a topic," said Mr. Dorrit, looking all about the ceiling of the room, and never at the attentive, uncomplainingly shocked face, "a painful topic, a series of events which I wish—ha—altogether to obliterate. This is understood by your sister, who has already remonstrated with you in my presence; it is understood by your brother; it is understood by—ha hum—by every one of delicacy and sensitiveness, except yourself—ha—I am sorry to say, except yourself. You, Amy—hum—you alone and only you—constantly revive the topic, though not in words."

She laid her hand on his arm. She did nothing more. She gently touched him. The trembling hand may have said, with some expression, "Think of me, think how I have worked, think of my many cares!" But, she said not a syllable herself.

There was a reproach in the touch so addressed to him that she had not foreseen, or she would have withheld her hand. He began to justify himself; in a heated, stumbling, angry manner, which made nothing of it.

"I was there all those years. I was—ha—universally acknowledged as the head of the place. I—hum—I caused you to be respected there, Amy. I—ha hum—I gave my family a position there. I deserve a return. I claim a return. I say, sweep it off the face of the earth and begin afresh. Is that much? I ask, is *that* much?"

He did not once look at her, as he rambled on in this way; but gesticulated at, and appealed to, the empty air.

"I have suffered. Probably I know how much I have suffered, better than any one—ha—I say than any one! If *I* can put that aside, if *I* can eradicate the marks of what I have endured, and can emerge before the world a—ha—gentleman unspoiled, unspotted—is it a great deal to expect

—I say again, is it a great deal to expect—that my children should—hum—
do the same, and sweep that accursed experience off the face of the earth!"

In spite of his flustered state, he made all these exclamations in a carefully
suppressed voice, lest the valet should overhear anything.

"Accordingly, they do it. Your sister does it. Your brother does it. You
alone, my favorite child, whom I made the friend and companion of my
life when you were a mere—hum—Baby, do not do it. You alone say you
can't do it. I provide you with valuable assistance to do it. I attach an
accomplished and highly-bred lady—ha—Mrs. General, to you, for the
purpose of doing it. Is it surprising that I should be displeased? Is it
necessary that I should defend myself for expressing my displeasure? No!"

Notwithstanding which, he continued to defend himself, without any
abatement of his flushed mood.

"I am careful to appeal to that lady for confirmation, before I express any
displeasure at all. I—hum—I necessarily make that appeal within limited
bounds, or I—ha—should render legible, by that lady, what I desire to be
blotted out. Am I selfish? Do I complain for my own sake? No. No.
Principally for—ha hum—your sake, Amy."

This last consideration plainly appeared, from his manner of pursuing
it, to have just that instant come into his head.

"I said I was hurt. So I am. So I—ha—am determined to be, whatever
is advanced to the contrary. I am hurt, that my daughter, seated in the—
hum—lap of fortune, should mope and retire, and proclaim herself
unequal to her destiny. I am hurt that she should—ha—systematically
reproduce what the rest of us blot out; and seem—hum—I had almost
said positively anxious—to announce to wealthy and distinguished society,
that she was born and bred in—ha hum—a place that I, myself, decline to
name. But there is no inconsistency—ha—not the least, in my feeling hurt,
and yet complaining principally for your sake, Amy. I do; I say again, I do.
It is for your sake, that I wish you, under the auspices of Mrs. General,
to form a—hum—a surface. It is for your sake, that I wish you to have a—
ha—truly refined mind, and (in the striking words of Mrs. General) to be
ignorant of everything that is not perfectly proper, placid, and pleasant."

He had been running down by jerks, during his last speech, like a sort
of ill-adjusted alarum. The touch was still upon his arm. He fell silent;
and after looking about the ceiling again, for a little while, looked down at
her. Her head drooped, and he could not see her face; but her touch was
tender and quiet, and in the expression of her dejected figure there was
no blame—nothing but love. He began to whimper, just as he had done
that night in the prison when she afterwards sat at his bedside till morning;
exclaimed that he was a poor ruin and a poor wretch in the midst of his
wealth; and clasped her in his arms. "Hush, hush, my own dear! Kiss
me!" was all she said to him. His tears were soon dried, much sooner than
on the former occasion; and he was presently afterwards very high with

his valet, as a way of righting himself for having shed any.

With one remarkable exception, to be recorded in its place, this was the only time, in his life of freedom and fortune, when he spoke to his daughter Amy of the old days.

But, now, the breakfast hour arrived; and with it Miss Fanny from her apartment, and Mr. Edward from his apartment. Both these young persons of distinction were something the worse for late hours. As to Miss Fanny, she had become the victim of an insatiate mania for what she called "going into society;" and would have gone into it head-foremost fifty times between sunset and sunrise, if so many opportunities had been at her disposal. As to Mr. Edward, he, too, had a large acquaintance, and was generally engaged (for the most part, in diceing circles, or others of a kindred nature), during the greater part of every night. For, this gentleman, when his fortunes changed, had stood at the great advantage of being already prepared for the highest associates, and having little to learn: so much was he indebted to the happy accidents which had made him acquainted with horse-dealing and billiard-marking.

At breakfast, Mr. Frederick Dorrit likewise appeared. As the old gentleman inhabited the highest story of the palace, where he might have practised pistol-shooting without much chance of discovery by the other inmates, his younger niece had taken courage to propose the restoration to him of his clarionet: which Mr. Dorrit had ordered to be confiscated, but which she had ventured to preserve. Notwithstanding some objections from Miss Fanny, that it was a low instrument, and that she detested the sound of it, the concession had been made. But, it was then discovered that he had had enough of it, and never played it, now that it was no longer his means of getting bread. He had insensibly acquired a new habit of shuffling into the picture-galleries, always with his twisted paper of snuff in his hand (much to the indignation of Miss Fanny, who had proposed the purchase of a gold box for him that the family might not be discredited, which he had absolutely refused to carry when it was bought); and of passing hours and hours before the portraits of renowned Venetians. It was never made out what his dazed eyes saw in them: whether he had an interest in them merely as pictures, or whether he confusedly identified them with a glory that was departed, like the strength of his own mind. But he paid his court to them with great exactness, and clearly derived pleasure from the pursuit. After the first few days, Little Dorrit happened one morning to assist at these attentions. It so evidently heightened his gratification that she often accompanied him afterwards, and the greatest delight of which the old man had shown himself susceptible since his ruin, arose out of these excursions, when he would carry a chair about for her from picture to picture, and stand behind it, in spite of all her remonstrances, silently presenting her to the noble Venetians.

It fell out that at this family breakfast, he referred to their having seen in a gallery, on the previous day, the lady and gentleman whom they had encountered on the Great Saint Bernard. "I forget the name," said he. "I dare say you remember them, William? I dare say you do, Edward?"

"*I* remember 'em well enough," said the latter.

"I should think so," observed Miss Fanny, with a toss of her head, and a glance at her sister. "But they would not have been recalled to our remembrance, I suspect, if Uncle hadn't tumbled over the subject."

"My dear, what a curious phrase," said Mrs. General. "Would not inadvertently lighted upon, or accidentally referred to, be better?"

"Thank you very much, Mrs. General," returned the young lady, "no, I think not. On the whole, I prefer my own expression."

This was always Miss Fanny's way of receiving a suggestion from Mrs. General. But, she always stored it up in her mind, and adopted it at another time.

"I should have mentioned our having met Mr. and Mrs. Gowan, Fanny," said Little Dorrit, "even if Uncle had not. I have scarcely seen you since, you know. I meant to have spoken of it at breakfast; because I should like to pay a visit to Mrs. Gowan, and to become better acquainted with her, if Papa and Mrs. General do not object."

"Well, Amy," said Fanny, "I am sure I am glad to find you, at last, expressing a wish to become better acquainted with anybody in Venice. Though whether Mr. and Mrs. Gowan are desirable acquaintances, remains to be determined."

"Mrs. Gowan I spoke of, dear."

"No doubt," said Fanny. "But you can't separate her from her husband, I believe, without an Act of Parliament."

"Do you think, Papa," enquired Little Dorrit, with diffidence and hesitation, "there is any objection to my making this visit?"

"Really," he replied, "I—ha—what is Mrs. General's view?"

Mrs. General's view was, that not having the honor of any acquaintance with the lady and gentleman referred to, she was not in a position to varnish the present article. She could only remark, as a general principle observed in the varnishing trade, that much depended on the quarter from which the lady under consideration was accredited, to a family so conspicuously niched in the social temple as the family of Dorrit.

At this remark the face of Mr. Dorrit gloomed considerably. He was about (connecting the accrediting with an obtrusive person of the name of Clennam, whom he imperfectly remembered in some former state of existence) to blackball the name of Gowan finally, when Edward Dorrit, Esquire, came into the conversation, with his glass in his eye, and the preliminary remark of "I say—you there! Go out, will you!" Which was addressed to a couple of men who were handing the dishes round, as a courteous intimation that their services could be temporarily dispensed with.

Those menials having obeyed the mandate, Edward Dorrit, Esquire, proceeded.

"Perhaps it's a matter of policy to let you all know that these Gowans— in whose favor, or at least the gentleman's, I can't be supposed to be much prepossessed myself—are known to people of importance, if that makes any difference."

"That, I would say," observed the fair varnisher, "makes the greatest difference. The connexion in question, being really people of importance and consideration——"

"As to that," said Edward Dorrit, Esquire, "I'll give you the means of judging for yourself. You are acquainted, perhaps, with the famous name of Merdle?"

"The great Merdle!" exclaimed Mrs. General.

"*The* Merdle," said Edward Dorrit, Esquire. "They are known to him. Mrs. Gowan—I mean the dowager, my polite friend's mother—is intimate with Mrs. Merdle, and I know these two to be on their visiting-list."

"If so, a more undeniable guarantee could not be given," said Mrs. General to Mr. Dorrit, raising her gloves and bowing her head, as if she were doing homage to some visible graven image.

"I beg to ask my son, from motives of—ha—curiosity," Mr. Dorrit observed, with a decided change in his manner, "how he becomes possessed of this—hum—timely information?"

"It's not a long story, sir," returned Edward Dorrit, Esquire, "and you shall have it out of hand. To begin with, Mrs. Merdle is the lady you had the parley with, at what's-his-name place."

"Martigny," interposed Miss Fanny, with an air of infinite languor.

"Martigny," assented her brother, with a slight nod and a slight wink; in acknowledgment of which, Miss Fanny looked surprised, and laughed and reddened.

"How can that be, Edward?" said Mr. Dorrit. "You informed me that the name of the gentleman with whom you conferred was—ha—Sparkler. Indeed, you showed me his card. Hum. Sparkler."

"No doubt of it, father; but it doesn't follow that his mother's name must be the same. Mrs. Merdle was married before, and he is her son. She is in Rome now; where probably we shall know more of her, as you decide to winter there. Sparkler is just come here. I passed last evening in company with Sparkler. Sparkler is a very good fellow on the whole, though rather a bore on one subject, in consequence of being tremendously smitten with a certain young lady." Here Edward Dorrit, Esquire, eyed Miss Fanny through his glass across the table. "We happened last night to compare notes about our travels, and I had the information I have given you from Sparkler himself." Here he ceased; continuing to eye Miss Fanny through his glass, with a face much twisted, and not ornamentally so, in part by the action of keeping his glass in his eye, and in part by the great subtlety of his smile.

"Under these circumstances," said Mr. Dorrit, "I believe I express the sentiments of—ha—Mrs. General, no less than my own, when I say that there is no objection, but—ha hum—quite the contrary—to your gratifying your desire, Amy. I trust I may—ha—hail this desire," said Mr. Dorrit, in an encouraging and forgiving manner, "as an auspicious omen. It is quite right to know these people. It is a very proper thing. Mr. Merdle's is a name of—ha—world-wide repute. Mr. Merdle's undertakings are immense. They bring him in such vast sums of money, that they are regarded as—hum—national benefits. Mr. Merdle is the man of this time. The name of Merdle is the name of the age. Pray do everything on my behalf that is civil to Mr. and Mrs. Gowan, for we will—ha—we will certainly notice them."

This magnificent accordance of Mr. Dorrit's recognition settled the matter. It was not observed that Uncle had pushed away his plate, and forgotten his breakfast; but he was not much observed at any time, except by Little Dorrit. The servants were recalled, and the meal proceeded to its conclusion. Mrs. General rose and left the table. Little Dorrit rose and left the table. When Edward and Fanny remained whispering together across it, and when Mr. Dorrit remained eating figs and reading a French newspaper, Uncle suddenly fixed the attention of all three, by rising out of his chair, striking his hand upon the table, and saying, "Brother! I protest against it!"

If he had made a proclamation in an unknown tongue, and given up the ghost immediately afterwards, he could not have astounded his audience more. The paper fell from Mr. Dorrit's hand, and he sat petrified, with a fig half way to his mouth.

"Brother," said the old man, conveying a surprising energy into his trembling voice, "I protest against it! I love you; you know I love you dearly. In these many years, I have never been untrue to you in a single thought. Weak as I am, I would at any time have struck any man who spoke ill of you. But, brother, brother, brother, I protest against it!"

It was extraordinary to see of what a burst of earnestness such a decrepit man was capable. His eyes became bright, his grey hair rose on his head, markings of purpose on his brow and face which had faded from them for five-and-twenty years, started out again, and there was an energy in his hand that made its action nervous once more.

"My dear Frederick!" exclaimed Mr. Dorrit, faintly. "What is wrong? What is the matter?"

"How dare you," said the old man, turning round on Fanny, "how dare you do it? Have you no memory? Have you no heart?"

"Uncle!" cried Fanny, affrighted and bursting into tears, "why do you attack me in this cruel manner? What have I done?"

"Done?" returned the old man, pointing to her sister's place, "where's your affectionate, invaluable friend? Where's your devoted guardian? Where's your more than mother? How dare you set up superiorities against all these characters combined in your sister? For shame, you false girl, for shame!"

"I love Amy," cried Miss Fanny, sobbing and weeping, "as well as I love my life—better than I love my life. I don't deserve to be so treated. I am as grateful to Amy, and as fond of Amy, as it's possible for any human being to be. I wish I was dead. I never was so wickedly wronged. And only because I am anxious for the family credit."

"To the winds with the family credit!" cried the old man, with great scorn and indignation. "Brother, I protest against pride. I protest against ingratitude. I protest against any one of us here who have known what we have known, and have seen what we have seen, setting up any pretension that puts Amy at a moment's disadvantage, or to the cost of a moment's pain. We may know that it's a base pretension by its having that effect. It ought to bring a judgment on us. Brother, I protest against it, in the sight of God!"

As his hand went up above his head and came down on the table, it might have been a blacksmith's. After a few moments' silence, it had relaxed into its usual weak condition. He went round to his brother with his ordinary shuffling step, put the hand on his shoulder, and said, in a softened voice, "William, my dear, I felt obliged to say it; forgive me, for I felt obliged to say it!" and then went, in his bowed way, out of the palace hall, just as he might have gone out of the Marshalsea room.

All this time Fanny had been sobbing and crying, and still continued to do so. Edward, beyond opening his mouth in amazement, had not opened his lips, and had done nothing but stare. Mr. Dorrit also had been utterly discomfited, and quite unable to assert himself in any way. Fanny was now the first to speak.

"I never, never, never was so used!" she sobbed. "There never was anything so harsh and unjustifiable, so disgracefully violent and cruel! Dear, kind, quiet little Amy, too, what would she feel if she could know that she had been innocently the means of exposing me to such treatment! But I'll never tell her! No, good darling, I'll never tell her!"

This helped Mr. Dorrit to break his silence.

"My dear," said he, "I—ha—approve of your resolution. It will be— ha hum—much better not to speak of this to Amy. It might—hum—it might distress her. Ha. No doubt it would distress her greatly. It is considerate and right to avoid doing so. We will—ha—keep this to ourselves."

"But the cruelty of Uncle!" cried Miss Fanny. "O, I never can forgive the wanton cruelty of Uncle!"

"My dear," said Mr. Dorrit, recovering his tone, though he remained unusually pale, "I must request you not to say so. You must remember that your uncle is—ha—not what he formerly was. You must remember that your uncle's state requires—hum—great forbearance from us, great forbearance."

"I am sure," cried Fanny, piteously, "it is only charitable to suppose that there must be something wrong in him somewhere, or he never could have so attacked Me, of all the people in the world."

"Fanny," returned Mr. Dorrit, in a deeply fraternal tone, "you know, with his innumerable good points, what a—hum—Wreck your uncle is; and I entreat you, by the fondness that I have for him, and by the fidelity that you know I have always shown him, to—ha—to draw your own conclusions, and to spare my brotherly feelings."

This ended the scene; Edward Dorrit, Esquire, saying nothing throughout, but looking, to the last, perplexed and doubtful. Miss Fanny awakened much affectionate uneasiness in her sister's mind that day, by passing the greater part of it in violent fits of embracing her, and in alternately giving her brooches, and wishing herself dead.

CHAPTER VI

SOMETHING RIGHT SOMEWHERE

To be in the halting state of Mr. Henry Gowan; to have left one of two Powers in disgust, to want the necessary qualifications for finding promotion with another, and to be loitering moodily about on neutral ground, cursing both; is to be in a situation unwholesome for the mind, which time is not likely to improve. The worst class of sum worked in the every-day world, is cyphered by the diseased arithmeticians who are always in the rule of Subtraction as to the merits and successes of others, and never in Addition as to their own.

The habit, too, of seeking some sort of recompense in the discontented boast of being disappointed, is a habit fraught with degeneracy. A certain idle carelessness and recklessness of consistency soon comes of it. To bring deserving things down by setting undeserving things up, is one of its perverted delights; and there is no playing fast and loose with the truth, in any game, without growing the worse for it.

In his expressed opinions of all performances in the Art of painting that were completely destitute of merit, Gowan was the most liberal fellow on earth. He would declare such a man to have more power in his little finger (provided he had none), than such another had (provided he had much) in his whole mind and body. If the objection were taken that the thing commended was trash, he would reply, on behalf of his art, "My good fellow, what do we all turn out but trash? *I* turn out nothing else, and I make you a present of the confession."

To make a vaunt of being poor was another of the incidents of his splenetic state, though this may have had the design in it of showing that he ought to be rich; just as he would publicly laud and decry the Barnacles, lest it should be forgotten that he belonged to the family. Howbeit, these two subjects were very often on his lips; and he managed them so well, that he might have praised himself by the month together, and not have made himself out half so important a man as he did by his light disparagement of his claims on anybody's consideration.

Out of this same airy talk of his, it always soon came to be understood, wherever he and his wife went, that he had married against the wishes of his exalted relations, and had had much ado to prevail on them to countenance her. He never made the representation, on the contrary seemed to laugh the idea to scorn; but it did happen that, with all his pains to depreciate himself, he was always in the superior position. From the days of their honeymoon, Minnie Gowan felt sensible of being usually regarded as the wife of a man who had made a descent in marrying her, but whose chivalrous love for her had cancelled that inequality.

To Venice they had been accompanied by Monsieur Blandois of Paris, and at Venice Monsieur Blandois of Paris was very much in the society of Gowan. When they had first met this gallant gentleman at Geneva, Gowan had been undecided whether to kick him or encourage him; and had remained, for about four-and-twenty hours, so troubled to settle the point to his satisfaction, that he had thought of tossing up a five-franc piece on the terms "Tails, kick; heads, encourage," and abiding by the voice of the oracle. It chanced, however, that his wife expressed a dislike to the engaging Blandois, and that the balance of feeling in the hotel was against him. Upon that, Gowan resolved to encourage him.

Why this perversity, if it were not in a generous fit?—which it was not. Why should Gowan, very much the superior of Blandois of Paris, and very well able to pull that prepossessing gentleman to pieces, and find out the stuff he was made of, take up with such a man? In the first place, he opposed the first separate wish he observed in his wife, because her father had paid his debts, and it was desirable to take an early opportunity of asserting his independence. In the second place, he opposed the prevalent feeling, because, with many capacities of being otherwise, he was an ill-conditioned man. He found a pleasure in declaring that a courtier with the refined manners of Blandois ought to rise to the greatest distinction in any polished country. He found a pleasure in setting up Blandois as the type of elegance, and making him a satire upon others who piqued themselves on personal graces. He seriously protested that the bow of Blandois was perfect, that the address of Blandois was irresistible, and that the picturesque ease of Blandois would be cheaply purchased (if it were not a gift, and unpurchaseable) for a hundred thousand francs. That exaggeration in the manner of the man, which has been noticed as appertaining to him and to every such man, whatever his original breeding, as certainly as the sun belongs to this system, was acceptable to Gowan as a caricature, which he found it a humorous resource to have at hand for the ridiculing of numbers of people who necessarily did more or less of what Blandois over-did. Thus he had taken up with him; and thus, negligently strengthening these inclinations with habit, and idly deriving some amusement from his talk, he had glided into a way of having him for a companion. This, though he supposed him to live by his wits at play-tables and the like; though he suspected him to be a coward, while he himself was daring and courageous; though he thoroughly knew him to be disliked by Minnie; and though he cared so little for him, after all, that if he had given her any tangible personal cause to regard him with aversion, he would have had no compunction whatever in flinging him out of the highest window in Venice, into the deepest water of the city.

Little Dorrit would have been glad to make her visit to Mrs. Gowan, alone; but, as Fanny, who had not yet recovered from her Uncle's protest, though it was four-and-twenty hours of age, pressingly offered her company, the two sisters stepped together into one of the gondolas under Mr. Dorrit's window, and, with the courier in attendance, were taken in high state to Mrs. Gowan's lodging. In truth, their state was rather too high for the lodging, which was, as Fanny complained, "fearfully out of the way," and which took them through a complexity of narrow streets of water, which the same lady disparaged as "mere ditches."

The house, on a little desert island, looked as if it had broken away from somewhere else, and had floated by chance into its present anchorage, in company with a vine almost as much in want of training as the poor wretches who were lying under its leaves. The features of the surrounding picture were, a church with hoarding and scaffolding about it, which had been under supposititious repair so long that the means of repair looked a hundred years old, and had themselves fallen into decay; a quantity of washed linen, spread to dry in the sun; a number of houses at odds with one another and grotesquely out of the perpendicular, like rotten pre-Adamite cheeses cut into fantastic shapes and full of mites; and a feverish bewilderment of windows, with their lattice-blinds all hanging askew, and something draggled and dirty dangling out of most of them.

On the first floor of the house was a Bank—a surprising experience for any gentleman of commercial pursuits bringing laws for all mankind from a British city— where two spare clerks, like dried dragoons, in green velvet caps adorned with golden tassels, stood, bearded, behind a small counter in a small room, containing no other visible objects than an empty iron-safe with the door open, a jug of water, and a papering of garlands of roses; but who, on lawful requisition, by merely dipping their hands out of sight, could produce exhaustless mounds of five-franc pieces. Below the Bank, was a suite of three or four rooms with barred windows, which had the appearance of a jail for criminal rats. Above the Bank was Mrs. Gowan's residence.

Notwithstanding that its walls were blotched, as if missionary maps were bursting out of them to impart geographical knowledge; notwithstanding that its weird furniture was forlornly faded and musty, and that the prevailing Venetian odor of bilge water and an ebb-tide on a weedy shore was very strong; the place was better within, than it promised. The door was opened by a smiling man like a reformed assassin—a temporary servant—who ushered them into the room where Mrs. Gowan sat: with' the announcement that two beautiful English ladies were come to see the mistress.

Mrs. Gowan, who was engaged in needlework, put her work aside in a covered basket, and rose, a little hurriedly. Miss Fanny was excessively courteous to her, and said the usual nothings with the skill of a veteran.

"Papa was extremely sorry," proceeded Fanny, "to be engaged to-day (he is so much engaged here, our acquaintance being so wretchedly large!); and particularly requested me to bring his card for Mr. Gowan. That I may be sure to acquit myself of a commission which he impressed upon me at least a dozen times, allow me to relieve my conscience by placing it on the table at once."

Which she did, with veteran ease.

"We have been," said Fanny, "charmed to understand that you know the Merdles. We hope it may be another means of bringing us together."

"They are friends," said Mrs. Gowan, "of Mr. Gowan's family. I have not yet had the pleasure of a personal introduction to Mrs. Merdle, but I suppose I shall be presented to her at Rome."

"Indeed?" returned Fanny, with an appearance of amiably quenching her own superiority. "I think you'll like her."

"You know her very well?"

"Why, you see," said Fanny, with a frank action of her pretty shoulders, "in London one knows every one. We met her on our way here, and, to say the truth, papa was at first rather cross with her for taking one of the rooms that our people had ordered for us. However, of course that soon blew over, and we were all good friends again."

Although the visit had, as yet, given Little Dorrit no opportunity of conversing with Mrs. Gowan, there was a silent understanding between them, which did as well. She looked at Mrs. Gowan with keen and unabated interest; the sound of her voice was thrilling to her; nothing that was near her, or about her, or at all concerned her, escaped Little Dorrit. She was quicker to perceive the slightest matter here, than in any other case—but one.

"You have been quite well," she now said, "since that night?"

"Quite, my dear. And you?"

"Oh! I am always well," said Little Dorrit, timidly. "I—yes, thank yo·

There was no reason for her faltering and breaking off, other than that Mrs. Gowan had touched her hand in speaking to her, and their looks had met. Something thoughtfully apprehensive in the large, soft eyes, had checked Little Dorrit in an instant.

"You don't know that you are a favorite of my husband's, and that I am almost bound to be jealous of you?" said Mrs. Gowan.

Little Dorrit, blushing, shook her head.

"He will tell you, if he tells you what he tells me, that you are quieter, and quicker of resource, than any one he ever saw."

"He speaks far too well of me," said Little Dorrit.

"I doubt that; but I don't at all doubt that I must tell him you are here. I should never be forgiven, if I were to let you—and Miss Dorrit—go, without doing so. May I? You can excuse the disorder and discomfort of a painter's studio?"

The enquiries were addressed to Miss Fanny, who graciously replied that she would be beyond anything interested and enchanted. Mrs. Gowan went to a door, looked in beyond it, and came back. "Do Henry the favor to come in," said she. "I knew he would be pleased!"

The first object that confronted Little Dorrit, entering first, was Blandois of Paris in a great cloak and a furtive slouched hat, standing on a throne-platform in a corner, as he had stood on the Great Saint Bernard, when the warning arms seemed to be all pointing up at him. She recoiled from this figure, as it smiled at her.

"Don't be alarmed," said Gowan, coming from his easel behind the door. "It's only Blandois. He is doing duty as a model to-day. I am making a study of him. It saves me money to turn him to some use. We poor painters have none to spare."

Blandois of Paris pulled off his slouched hat, and saluted the ladies without coming out of his corner.

"A thousand pardons!" said he. "But the Professore here, is so inexorable with me, that I am afraid to stir."

"Don't stir, then," said Gowan, coolly, as the sisters approached the easel. "Let the ladies at least see the original of the daub, that they may know what it's meant for. There he stands, you see. A bravo waiting for his prey, a distinguished noble waiting to save his country, the common enemy waiting to do somebody a bad turn, an angelic messenger waiting to do somebody a good turn —whatever you think he looks most like!"

"Say, Professore Mio, a poor gentleman waiting to do homage to elegance and beauty," remarked Blandois.

"Or say, Cattivo Soggetto Mio," returned Gowan, touching the painted face with his brush in the part where the real face had moved, "a murderer

Instinct stronger than training

after the fact. Show that white hand of yours, Blandois. Put it outside the cloak. Keep it still."

Blandois' hand was unsteady; but he laughed, and that would naturally shake it.

"He was formerly in some scuffle with another murderer, or with a victim, you observe," said Gowan, putting in the markings of the hand with a quick, impatient, unskilful touch, "and these are the tokens of it. Outside the cloak, man!—Corpo di San Marco, what are you thinking of!"

Blandois of Paris shook with a laugh again, so that his hand shook more; now he raised it to twist his moustache, which had a damp appearance; and now he stood in the required position, with a little new swagger.

His face was so directed in reference to the spot where Little Dorrit stood by the easel, that throughout he looked at her. Once attracted by his peculiar eyes, she could not remove her own, and they had looked at each other all the time. She trembled now; Gowan, feeling it, and supposing her to be alarmed by the large dog beside him, whose head she caressed in her hand, and who had just uttered a low growl, glanced at her to say, "He won't hurt you, Miss Dorrit."

"I am not afraid of him," she returned, in the same breath; "but will you look at him?"

In a moment Gowan had thrown down his brush, and seized the dog with both hands by the collar.

"Blandois! How can you be such a fool as to provoke him! By Heaven, and the other place too, he'll tear you to bits! Lie down! Lion! Do you hear my voice, you rebel!"

The great dog, regardless of being half-choked by his collar, was obdurately pulling with his dead weight against his master, resolved to get across the room. He had been crouching for a spring, at the moment when his master caught him.

"Lion! Lion!" He was up on his hind legs, and it was a wrestle between master and dog. "Get back! Down, Lion! Get out of his sight, Blandois! What devil have you conjured into the dog?"

"I have done nothing to him."

"Get out of his sight, or I can't hold the wild beast! Get out of the room! By my soul, he'll kill you!"

The dog, with a ferocious bark, made one other struggle, as Blandois vanished; then, in the moment of the dog's submission, the master, little less angry than the dog, felled him with a blow on the head, and standing over him, struck him many times severely with the heel of his boot, so that his mouth was presently bloody.

"Now get you into that corner and lie down," said Gowan, "or I'll take you out and shoot you!"

Lion did as he was ordered, and lay down licking his mouth and chest. Lion's master stopped for a moment to take breath, and then, recovering his usual coolness of manner, turned to speak to his frightened wife and her visitors. Probably the whole occurrence had not occupied two minutes.

"Come, come, Minnie! You know he is always good-humoured and tractable. Blandois must have irritated him,—made faces at him. The dog has his likings and dislikings, and Blandois is no great favorite of his; but I am sure you'll give him a character, Minnie, for never having been like this before."

Minnie was too much disturbed to say anything connected in reply; Little Dorrit was already occupied in soothing her; Fanny, who had cried out twice or thrice, held Gowan's arm for protection; Lion, deeply ashamed of having caused them this alarm, came trailing himself along the ground, to the feet of his mistress.

"You furious brute," said Gowan, striking him with his foot again. "You shall do penance for this." And he struck him again, and yet again.

"O, pray don't punish him any more," cried Little Dorrit. "Don't hurt him. See how gentle he is!" At her entreaty, Gowan spared him; and he deserved her intercession, for truly he was as submissive, and as sorry, and as wretched as a dog could be.

It was not easy to recover this shock and make the visit unrestrained, even though Fanny had not been, under the best of circumstances, the least trifle in the way. In such further communication as passed among them before the sisters took their departure, Little Dorrit fancied it was revealed to her that Mr. Gowan treated his wife, even in his very fondness, too much like a beautiful child. He seemed so unsuspicious of the depths of feeling which she knew must lie below that surface, that she doubted if there could be any such depths in himself. She wondered whether his want of earnestness might be the natural result of his want of such qualities, and whether it was with people as with ships, that, in too shallow and rocky waters, their anchors had no hold, and they drifted anywhere.

He attended them down the staircase, jocosely apologising for the poor quarters to which such poor fellows as himself were limited, and remarking that when the high and mighty Barnacles, his relatives, who would be dreadfully ashamed of them, presented him with better, he would live in better, to oblige them. At the water's edge they were saluted by Blandois, who looked white enough after his late adventure, but who made very light of it, notwithstanding,—laughing at the mention of Lion.

Leaving the two together, under the scrap of vine upon the causeway, Gowan idly scattering the leaves from it into the water, and Blandois lighting a cigarette, the sisters were paddled away in state as they had come. They had not glided on for many minutes, when Little Dorrit became aware that Fanny was more showy in manner than the occasion appeared to require, and, looking about for the cause, through the window and through the open door, saw another gondola evidently in waiting on them.

As this gondola attended their progress in various artful ways; sometimes shooting on ahead, and stopping to let them pass; sometimes, when the way was broad enough, skimming along side by side with them; and sometimes following close astern; and as Fanny gradually made no disguise that she was playing off graces upon somebody within it, of whom she at the same time feigned to be unconscious; Little Dorrit at length asked who it was?

To which Fanny made the short answer, "That gaby."

"Who?" said Little Dorrit.

"My dear child," returned Fanny (in a tone suggesting that before her uncle's protest she might have said, You little fool, instead), "how slow you are! Young Sparkler."

She lowered the window on her side, and, leaning back and resting her elbow on it negligently, fanned herself with a rich Spanish fan of black and gold. The attendant gondola, having skimmed forward again, with some swift trace of an eye in the window, Fanny laughed coquettishly, and said, "Did you ever see such a fool, my love?"

"Do you think he means to follow you all the way?" asked Little Dorrit.

"My precious child," returned Fanny, "I can't possibly answer for what an idiot in a state of desperation may do, but I should think it highly probable. It's not such an enormous distance. All Venice would scarcely be that, I imagine, if he's dying for a glimpse of me."

"And is he?" asked Little Dorrit, in perfect simplicity.

"Well, my love, that really is an awkward question for *me* to answer," said her sister. "I believe he is. You had better ask Edward. He tells Edward he is, I believe. I understand he makes a perfect spectacle of himself at the Casino, and that sort of places, by going on about me. But you had better ask Edward, if you want to know."

"I wonder he doesn't call," said Little Dorrit, after thinking a moment.

"My dear Amy, your wonder will soon cease, if I am rightly informed. I should not be at all surprised if he called to-day. The creature has only been waiting to get his courage up, I suspect."

"Will you see him?"

"Indeed, my darling," said Fanny, "that's just as it may happen. Here he is again. Look at him. O, you simpleton!"

Mr. Sparkler had, undeniably, a weak appearance; with his eye in the window like a knot in the glass, and no reason on earth for stopping his bark suddenly, except the real reason.

"When you ask me if I will see him, my dear," said Fanny, almost as well composed in the graceful indifference of her attitude as Mrs. Merdle herself, "what do you mean?"

"I mean," said Little Dorrit "—I think I rather mean what do you mean, dear Fanny?"

Fanny laughed again, in a manner at once condescending, arch, and

affable; and said, putting her arm round her sister in a playfully affectionate
way:

"Now tell me, my little pet. When we saw that woman at Martigny,
how did you think she carried it off? Did you see what she decided on in
a moment?"

"No, Fanny."

"Then I'll tell you, Amy. She settled with herself, Now I'll never refer
to that meeting under such different circumstances, and I'll never pretend
to have any idea that these are the same girls. That's *her* way out of a
difficulty. What did I tell you, when we came away from Harley Street
that time? She is as insolent and false as any woman in the world. But in
the first capacity, my love, she may find people who can match her."

A significant turn of the Spanish fan towards Fanny's bosom, indicated
with great expression where one of these people was to be found.

"Not only that," pursued Fanny, "but she gives the same charge to
Young Sparkler; and doesn't let him come after me until she has got it
thoroughly into his most ridiculous of all ridiculous noddles (for one really
can't call it a head), that he is to pretend to have been first struck with me in
that Inn Yard."

"Why?" asked Little Dorrit.

"Why? Good gracious, my love!" (again very much in the tone of You
stupid little creature) "how can you ask? Don't you see that I may have
become a rather desirable match for a noodle? And don't you see that she
puts the deception upon us, and makes a pretence, while she shifts it from
her own shoulders (very good shoulders they are too, I must say),"
observed Miss Fanny, glancing complacently at herself, "of considering
our feelings?"

"But we can always go back to the plain truth."

"Yes, but if you please we won't," retorted Fanny. "No; I am not
going to have that done, Amy. The pretext is none of mine; it's hers, and
she shall have enough of it."

In the triumphant exaltation of her feelings, Miss Fanny, using her
Spanish fan with one hand, squeezed her sister's waist with the other, as
if she were crushing Mrs. Merdle.

"No," repeated Fanny. "She shall find me go her way. She took it, and
I'll follow it. And, with the blessing of fate and fortune, I'll go on improving
that woman's acquaintance until I have given her maid, before her eyes,
things from my dressmaker's ten times as handsome and expensive as she
once gave me from hers!"

Little Dorrit was silent: sensible that she was not to be heard on any
question affecting the family dignity; and unwilling to lose to no purpose
her sister's newly and unexpectedly restored favor. She could not concur,
but she was silent. Fanny well knew what she was thinking of; so well, that
she soon asked her.

Her reply was, "Do you mean to encourage Mr. Sparkler, Fanny?"

"Encourage him, my dear?" said her sister, smiling contemptuously, "that depends upon what you call encourage. No, I don't mean to encourage him. But I'll make a slave of him."

Little Dorrit glanced seriously and doubtfully in her face, but Fanny was not to be so brought to a check. She furled her fan of black and gold, and used it to tap her sister's nose; with the air of a proud beauty and a great spirit, who toyed with and playfully instructed a homely companion.

"I shall make him fetch and carry, my dear, and I shall make him subject to me. And if I don't make his mother subject to me, too, it shall not be my fault."

"Do you think—dear Fanny, don't be offended, we are so comfortable together now—that you can quite see the end of that course?"

"I can't say I have so much as looked for it yet, my dear," answered Fanny, with supreme indifference; "all in good time. Such are my intentions. And really they have taken me so long to develop, that here we are at home. And Young Sparkler at the door, enquiring who is within. By the merest accident, of course!"

In effect, the swain was standing up in his gondola, card-case in hand, affecting to put the question to a servant. This conjunction of circumstances led to his immediately afterwards presenting himself before the young ladies in a posture, which in ancient times would not have been considered one of favorable augury for his suit; since the gondoliers of the young ladies, having been put to some inconvenience by the chase, so neatly brought their own boat into the gentlest collision with the bark of Mr. Sparkler, as to tip that gentleman over like a large species of ninepin, and cause him to exhibit the soles of his shoes to the object of his dearest wishes: while the nobler portions of his anatomy struggled at the bottom of his boat, in the arms of one of his men.

However, as Miss Fanny called out with much concern, Was the gentleman hurt, Mr. Sparkler rose more restored than might have been expected, and stammered for himself with blushes, "Not at all so." Miss Fanny had no recollection of having ever seen him before, and was passing on, with a distant inclination of her head, when he announced himself by name. Even then, she was in a difficulty from being unable to call it to mind, until he explained that he had had the honor of seeing her at Martigny. Then she remembered him, and hoped his lady-mother was well.

"Thank you," stammered Mr. Sparkler, "she's uncommonly well—at least, poorly."

"In Venice?" said Miss Fanny.

"In Rome," Mr. Sparkler answered. "I am here by myself, myself. I came to call upon Mr. Edward Dorrit myself. Indeed, upon Mr. Dorrit likewise. In fact, upon the family."

Turning graciously to the attendants, Miss Fanny enquired whether

her papa or brother was within? The reply being that they were both within, Mr. Sparkler humbly offered his arm. Miss Fanny accepting it, was squired up the great staircase by Mr. Sparkler, who, if he still believed (which there is not any reason to doubt) that she had no nonsense about her, rather deceived himself.

Arrived in a mouldering reception-room, where the faded hangings, of a sad sea-green, had worn and withered until they looked as if they might have claimed kindred with the waifs of sea-weed drifting under the windows, or clinging to the walls and weeping for their imprisoned relations, Miss Fanny dispatched emissaries for her father and brother. Pending whose appearance, she showed to great advantage on a sofa completing Mr. Sparkler's conquest with some remarks upon Dante—known to that gentleman as an eccentric man in the nature of an Old File, who used to put leaves round his head, and sit upon a stool for some unaccountable purpose, outside the cathedral at Florence.

Mr. Dorrit welcomed the visitor with his highest urbanity, and most courtly manners. He enquired particularly after Mrs. Merdle. He enquired particularly after Mr. Merdle. Mr. Sparkler said, or rather twitched out of himself in small pieces by the shirt-collar, that Mrs. Merdle, having completely used up her place in the country, and also her house at Brighton, and being, of course, unable, don't you see, to remain in London when there wasn't a soul there, and not feeling herself this year quite up to visiting about at people's places, had resolved to have a touch at Rome, where a woman like herself, with a proverbially fine appearance and with no nonsense about her, couldn't fail to be a great acquisition. As to Mr. Merdle, he was so much wanted by the men in the City and the rest of those places, and was such a doosed extraordinary phenomenon in Buying and Banking and that, that Mr. Sparkler doubted if the monetary system of the country would be able to spare him: though that his work was occasionally one too many for him, and that he would be all the better for a temporary shy at an entirely new scene and climate, Mr. Sparkler did not conceal. As to himself, Mr. Sparkler conveyed to the Dorrit family that he was going, on rather particular business, wherever they were going.

This immense conversational achievement required time, but was effected. Being effected, Mr. Dorrit expressed his hope that Mr. Sparkler would shortly dine with them. Mr. Sparkler received the idea so kindly, that Mr. Dorrit asked what he was going to do that day, for instance? As he was going to do nothing that day (his usual occupation, and one for which he was particularly qualified), he was secured without postponement; being further bound over to accompany the ladies to the Opera in the evening.

At dinner-time Mr. Sparkler rose out of the sea, like Venus's son taking after his mother, and made a splendid appearance ascending the great staircase. If Fanny had been charming in the morning, she was now thrice charming, very becomingly dressed in her most suitable colors, and with an air of negligence upon her that doubled Mr. Sparkler's fetters, and rivetted them.

"I hear you are acquainted, Mr. Sparkler," said his host, at dinner, "with—ha—Mr. Gowan. Mr. Henry Gowan?"

"Perfectly, sir," returned Mr. Sparkler. "His mother and my mother are cronies, in fact."

"If I had thought of it, Amy," said Mr. Dorrit, with a patronage as magnificent as that of Lord Decimus himself, "you should have dispatched a note to them, asking them to dine to-day. Some of our people could have—ha—fetched them, and taken them home. We could have spared a—hum—gondola for that purpose. I am sorry to have forgotten this. Pray remind me of them to-morrow."

Little Dorrit was not without doubts how Mr. Henry Gowan might take their patronage; but, she promised not to fail in the reminder.

"Pray, does Mr. Henry Gowan paint—ha—Portraits?" enquired Mr. Dorrit.

Mr. Sparkler opined that he painted anything, if he could get the job.

"He has no particular walk?" said Mr. Dorrit.

Mr. Sparkler, stimulated by Love to brilliancy, replied that for a particular walk, a man ought to have a particular pair of shoes: as, for example, shooting, shooting-shoes; cricket, cricket-shoes. Whereas, he believed that Henry Gowan had no particular pair of shoes.

"No speciality?" said Mr. Dorrit.

This being a very long word for Mr. Sparkler, and his mind being exhausted by his late effort, he replied, "No, thank you. I seldom take it."

"Well!" said Mr. Dorrit. "It would be very agreeable to me, to present a gentleman so connected, with some—ha—Testimonial of my desire to further his interests, and develop the—hum—germs of his genius. I think I must engage Mr. Gowan to paint my picture. If the result should be—ha—mutually satisfactory, I might afterwards engage him to try his hand upon my family."

The exquisitely bold and original thought presented itself to Mr. Sparkler, that there was an opening here for saying there were some of the family (emphasising "some" in a marked manner) to whom no painter could render justice. But, for want of a form of words in which to express the idea, it returned to the skies.

This was the more to be regretted as Miss Fanny greatly applauded the notion of the portrait, and urged her Papa to act upon it. She surmised, she said, that Mr. Gowan had lost better and higher opportunities by marrying his pretty wife; and Love in a cottage, painting pictures for dinner, was so delightfully interesting, that she begged her Papa to give him the commission, whether he could paint a likeness or not: though indeed both she and Amy knew he could, from having seen a speaking likeness on his easel that day, and having had the opportunity of comparing it with the original. These remarks made Mr. Sparkler (as perhaps they were intended to do) nearly distracted; for while on the one hand they expressed Miss Fanny's susceptibility to the tender passion, she herself showed such an innocent unconsciousness of his admiration, that his eyes goggled in his head with jealousy of an unknown rival.

Descending into the sea again after dinner, and ascending out of it at the Opera staircase, preceded by one of their gondoliers, like an attendant Merman, with a great linen lantern, they entered their box, and Mr. Sparkler entered on an evening of agony. The theatre being dark, and the box light, several visitors lounged in during the representation; in whom Fanny was so interested, and in conversation with whom she fell into such charming attitudes, as she had little confidences with them, and little disputes concerning the identity of people in distant boxes, that the wretched Sparkler hated all mankind. But he had two consolations at the close of the performance. She gave him her fan to hold while she adjusted her cloak, and it was his blessed privilege to give her his arm down-stairs again. These crumbs of encouragement, Mr. Sparkler thought, would just keep him going; and it is not impossible that Miss Dorrit thought so too.

The Merman with his light was ready at the box-door, and other Mermen with other lights were ready at many of the doors. The Dorrit Merman held his lantern low, to show the steps, and Mr. Sparkler put on another heavy set of fetters over his former set, as he watched her radiant feet twinkling down the stairs beside him. Among the loiterers here, was Blandois of Paris. He spoke, and moved forward beside Fanny.

Little Dorrit was in front, with her brother and Mrs. General (Mr. Dorrit had remained at home); but, on the brink of the quay they all came together. She started again to find Blandois close to her, handing Fanny into the boat.

"Gowan has had a loss," he said, "since he was made happy to-day by a visit from fair ladies."

"A loss?" repeated Fanny, relinquished by the bereaved Sparkler, and taking her seat.

"A loss," said Blandois. "His dog, Lion."

Little Dorrit's hand was in his, as he spoke.

"He is dead," said Blandois.

"Dead?" echoed Little Dorrit. "That noble dog?"

"Faith, dear ladies!" said Blandois, smiling and shrugging his shoulders, "somebody has poisoned that noble dog. He is as dead as the Doges!"

CHAPTER VII

MOSTLY, PRUNES AND PRISM

MRS. GENERAL, always on her coach-box keeping the proprieties well together, took pains to form a surface on her very dear young friend, and Mrs. General's very dear young friend tried hard to receive it. Hard as she had tried in her laborious life to attain many ends, she had never tried harder, than she did now, to be varnished by Mrs. General. It made her anxious and ill at ease to be operated upon by that smoothing hand, it is true; but she submitted herself to the family want in its greatness as she had submitted herself to the family want in its littleness, and yielded to her own inclinations in this thing no more than she had yielded to her hunger itself, in the days when she had saved her dinner that her father might have his supper.

One comfort that she had under the Ordeal by General was more sustaining to her, and made her more grateful, than to a less devoted and affectionate spirit, not habituated to her struggles and sacrifices, might appear quite reasonable; and, indeed, it may often be observed in life, that spirits like Little Dorrit do not appear to reason half as carefully as the folks who get the better of them. The continued kindness of her sister was this comfort to Little Dorrit. It was nothing to her that the kindness took the form of tolerant patronage; she was used to that. It was nothing to her that it kept her in a tributary position, and showed her in attendance on the flaming car in which Miss Fanny sat on an elevated seat, exacting homage; she sought no better place. Always admiring Fanny's beauty, and grace, and readiness, and not now asking herself how much of her disposition to be strongly attached to Fanny was due to her own heart, and how much to Fanny's, she gave her all the sisterly fondness her great heart contained.

The wholesale amount of Prunes and Prism which Mrs. General infused into the family life, combined with the perpetual plunges made by Fanny into society, left but a very small residue of any natural deposit at the bottom of the mixture. This rendered confidences with Fanny doubly precious to Little Dorrit, and heightened the relief they afforded her.

"Amy," said Fanny to her, one night when they were alone, after a day so tiring that Little Dorrit was quite worn out, though Fanny would have taken another dip into society with the greatest pleasure in life, "I am going to put something into your little head. You won't guess what it is, I suspect."

"I don't think that's likely, dear," said Little Dorrit.

"Come, I'll give you a clue, child," said Fanny. "Mrs. General."

Prunes and Prism, in a thousand combinations, having been wearily in the ascendant all day—everything having been surface and varnish, and show without substance—Little Dorrit looked as if she had hoped that Mrs. General was safely tucked up in bed for some hours.

"*Now*, can you guess, Amy?" said Fanny.

"No, dear. Unless I have done anything," said Little Dorrit, rather alarmed, and meaning anything calculated to crack varnish and ruffle surface.

Fanny was so very much amused by the misgiving, that she took up her favorite fan (being then seated at her dressing-table with her armory of cruel instruments about her, most of them reeking from the heart of Sparkler), and tapped her sister frequently on the nose with it, laughing all the time.

"Oh, our Amy, our Amy!" said Fanny. "What a timid little goose our Amy is! But this is nothing to laugh at. On the contrary, I am very cross, my dear."

"As it is not with me, Fanny, I don't mind," returned her sister, smiling.

"Ah! But I do mind," said Fanny, "and so will you, Pet, when I enlighten you. Amy, has it never struck you that somebody is monstrously polite to Mrs. General?"

"Everybody is polite to Mrs. General," said Little Dorrit. "Because——"

"Because she freezes them into it?" interrupted Fanny, "I don't mean that; quite different from that. Come! Has it never struck you, Amy, that Pa is monstrously polite to Mrs. General?"

Amy, murmuring "No," looked quite confounded.

"No; I dare say not. But he is," said Fanny. "He is, Amy. And remember my words. Mrs. General has designs on Pa!"

"Dear Fanny, do you think it possible that Mrs. General has designs on any one?"

"Do I think it possible?" retorted Fanny. "My love, I know it. I tell you she has designs on Pa. And more than that, I tell you, Pa considers her such a wonder, such a paragon of accomplishment, and such an acquisition to our family, that he is ready to get himself into a state of perfect infatuation with her at any moment. And that opens a pretty picture of things, I hope! Think of me with Mrs. General for a Mama!"

Little Dorrit did not reply, "Think of me with Mrs. General for a Mama;" but she looked anxious, and seriously enquired what had led Fanny to these conclusions.

"Lard, my darling," said Fanny, tartly. "You might as well ask me how I know when a man is struck with myself! But, of course I do know. It happens pretty often; but I always know it. I know this, in much the same way, I suppose. At all events, I know it."

"You never heard Papa say anything?"

"Say anything?" repeated Fanny. "My dearest, darling child, what necessity has he had, yet awhile, to say anything!"

"And you have never heard Mrs. General say anything?"

"My goodness me, Amy," returned Fanny, "is she the sort of woman to say anything? Isn't it perfectly plain and clear that she has nothing to do, at present, but to hold herself upright, keep her aggravating gloves on, and go sweeping about? Say anything! If she had the ace of trumps in her hand, at whist, she wouldn't say anything, child. It would come out when she played it."

"At least, you may be mistaken, Fanny. Now may you not?"

"O yes, I *may* be," said Fanny, "but I am not. However, I am glad you can contemplate such an escape, my dear, and I am glad that you can take this for the present with sufficient coolness to think of such a chance. It makes me hope that you may be able to bear the connexion. I should not be able to bear it, and I should not try. I'd marry young Sparkler first."

"O, you would never marry him, Fanny, under any circumstances."

"Upon my word, my dear," rejoined that young lady, with exceeding indifference, "I wouldn't positively answer even for that. There's no knowing what might happen. Especially as I should have many opportunities, afterwards, of treating that woman, his mother, in her own style. Which I most decidedly should not be slow to avail myself of, Amy."

No more passed between the sisters then; but what had passed gave the two subjects of Mrs. General and Mr. Sparkler great prominence in Little Dorrit's mind, and thenceforth she thought very much of both.

Mrs. General, having long ago formed her own surface to such perfection that it hid whatever was below it (if anything), no observation was to be made in that quarter. Mr. Dorrit was undeniably very polite to her, and had a high opinion of her; but, Fanny, impetuous at most times, might easily be wrong for all that. Whereas, the Sparkler question was on the different footing that any one could see what was going on there, and Little Dorrit saw it, and pondered on it, with many doubts and wonderings.

The devotion of Mr. Sparkler was only to be equalled by the caprice and cruelty of his enslaver. Sometimes she would prefer him to such distinction of notice, that he would chuckle aloud with joy; next day, or next hour, she would overlook him so completely, and drop him into such an abyss of obscurity, that he would groan under a weak pretence of coughing. The constancy of his attendance never touched Fanny: though he was so inseparable from Edward, that when that gentleman wished for a change of society he was under the irksome necessity of gliding out like a conspirator, in disguised boats and by secret doors and back ways; though he was so solicitous to know how Mr. Dorrit was, that he called every other day to enquire, as if Mr. Dorrit were the prey of an intermittent fever; though he was so constantly being paddled up and down before the principal windows, that he might have been supposed to have made a wager for a large stake to be paddled a thousand miles in a thousand hours; though whenever the gondola of his mistress left the gate, the gondola of Mr.

Sparkler shot out from some watery ambush and gave chase, as if she were a fair smuggler and he a custom-house officer. It was probably owing to this fortification of the natural strength of his constitution with so much exposure to the air, and the salt sea, that Mr. Sparkler did not pine outwardly; but, whatever the cause, he was so far from having any prospect of moving his mistress by a languishing state of health, that he grew bluffer every day, and that peculiarity in his appearance of seeming rather a swelled boy than a young man became developed to an extraordinary degree of ruddy puffiness.

Blandois calling to pay his respects, Mr. Dorrit received him with affability as the friend of Mr. Gowan, and mentioned to him his idea of commissioning Mr. Gowan to transmit him to posterity. Blandois highly extolling it, it occurred to Mr. Dorrit that it might be agreeable to Blandois to communicate to his friend the great opportunity reserved for him. Blandois accepted the commission with his own free elegance of manner, and swore he would discharge it before he was an hour older. On his imparting the news to Gowan, that Master gave Mr. Dorrit to the Devil with great liberality some round dozen of times (for he resented patronage almost as much as he resented the want of it), and was inclined to quarrel with his friend for bringing him the message.

"It may be a defect in my mental vision, Blandois," said he, "but may I die if I see what you have to do with this."

"Death of my life," replied Blandois, "nor I neither, except that I thought I was serving my friend."

"By putting an upstart's hire in his pocket?" said Gowan, frowning. "Do you mean that? Tell your other friend to get his head painted for the sign of some public-house, and to get it done by a sign-painter. Who am I, and who is he?"

"Professore," returned the ambassador, "and who is Blandois?"

Without appearing at all interested in the latter question, Gowan angrily whistled Mr. Dorrit away. But, next day, he resumed the subject by saying in his off-hand manner, and with a slighting laugh, "Well, Blandois, when shall we go to this Mæcenas of yours? We journeymen must take jobs when we can get them. When shall we go and look after this job?"

"When you will," said the injured Blandois, "as you please. What have I to do with it? What is it to me?"

"I can tell you what it is to me," said Gowan. "Bread and cheese. One must eat! So come along, my Blandois."

Mr. Dorrit received them in the presence of his daughters and of Mr. Sparkler, who happened, by some surprising accident, to be calling there. "How are you, Sparkler?" said Gowan, carelessly. "When you have to live by your mother wit, old boy, I hope you may get on better than I do."

Mr. Dorrit then mentioned his proposal. "Sir," said Gowan, laughing, after receiving it gracefully enough, "I am new to the trade, and not expert at its mysteries. I believe I ought to look at you in various lights, tell you you are a capital subject, and consider when I shall be sufficiently disengaged to devote myself with the necessary enthusiasm to the fine picture I mean to make of you. I assure you," and he laughed again, "I feel quite a traitor in the camp of those dear, gifted, good, noble fellows, my brother artists, by not doing the hocus-pocus better. But I have not been brought up to it, and it's too late to learn it. Now, the fact is, I am a very bad painter, but not much worse than the generality. If you are going to throw away a hundred guineas or so, I am as poor as a poor relation of great people usually is, and I shall be very much obliged to you, if you'll throw them away upon me. I'll do the best I can for the money; and if the best should be bad, why even then, you may probably have a bad picture with a small name to it, instead of a bad picture with a large name to it."

This tone, though not what he had expected, on the whole suited Mr. Dorrit remarkably well. It showed that the gentleman, highly connected and not a mere workman, would be under an obligation to him. He expressed his satisfaction in placing himself in Mr. Gowan's hands, and trusted that he would have the pleasure, in their characters as private gentlemen, of improving his acquaintance.

"You are very good," said Gowan. "I have not forsworn society since I joined the brotherhood of the brush (the most delightful fellows on the face of the earth), and am glad enough to smell the old fine gunpowder now and then, though it did blow me into mid-air and my present calling. You'll not think, Mr. Dorrit," and here he laughed again, in the easiest way, "that I am lapsing into the freemasonry of the craft—for it's not so; upon my life I can't help betraying it wherever I go, though, by Jupiter, I love and honor the craft with all my might—if I propose a stipulation as to time and place?"

Ha! Mr. Dorrit could erect no—hum—suspicion of that kind, on Mr. Gowan's frankness.

"Again, you are very good," said Gowan. "Mr. Dorrit, I hear you are going to Rome. I am going to Rome, having friends there. Let me begin to do you the injustice I have conspired to do you, there—not here. We shall all be hurried during the rest of our stay here; and though there's not a poorer man with whole elbows, in Venice, than myself, I have not quite got all the Amateur out of me yet—compromising the trade again, you see!—and can't fall on to order, in a hurry, for the mere sake of the sixpences."

These remarks were not less favorably received by Mr. Dorrit than their predecessors. They were the prelude to the first reception of Mr. and Mrs. Gowan at dinner, and they skilfully placed Gowan on his usual ground in the new family.

His wife, too, they placed on her usual ground. Miss Fanny understood,

with particular distinctness, that Mrs. Gowan's good looks had cost her
husband very dear; that there had been a great disturbance about her in
the Barnacle family; and that the Dowager Mrs. Gowan, nearly heartbroken, had resolutely set her face against the marriage, until overpowered
by her maternal feelings. Mrs. General likewise clearly understood that
the attachment had occasioned much family grief and dissension. Of
honest Mr. Meagles no mention was made; except that it was natural
enough that a person of that sort should wish to raise his daughter out of
his own obscurity, and that nobody could blame him for trying his best
to do so.

Little Dorrit's interest in the fair subject of this easily accepted belief,
was too earnest and watchful to fail in accurate observation. She could see
that it had its part in throwing upon Mrs. Gowan the touch of shadow
under which she lived, and she even had an instinctive knowledge that
there was not the least truth in it. But, it had an influence in placing
obstacles in the way of her association with Mrs. Gowan, by making the
Prunes and Prism school excessively polite to her, but not very intimate
with her; and Little Dorrit, as an enforced sizar of that college, was obliged
to submit herself humbly to its ordinances.

Nevertheless, there was a sympathetic understanding already established
between the two, which would have carried them over greater difficulties,
and made a friendship out of a more restricted intercourse. As though
accidents were determined to be favorable to it, they had a new assurance
of congeniality in the aversion which each perceived that the other felt
towards Blandois of Paris; an aversion amounting to the repugnance and
horror of a natural antipathy towards an odious creature of the reptile kind.

And there was a passive congeniality between them, besides this active
one. To both of them, Blandois behaved in exactly the same manner; and
to both of them his manner had uniformly something in it, which they both
knew to be different from his bearing towards others. The difference was
too minute in its expression to be perceived by others, but they knew it to
be there. A mere trick of his evil eyes, a mere turn of his smooth white
hand, a mere hair's-breadth of addition to the fall of his nose and the rise
of his moustache in the most frequent movement of his face, conveyed to
both of them equally a swagger personal to themselves. It was as if he had
said, "I have a secret power in this quarter. I know what I know."

This had never been felt by them both in so great a degree, and never by
each so perfectly to the knowledge of the other, as on a day when he came to
Mr. Dorrit's to take his leave before quitting Venice. Mrs. Gowan was
herself there for the same purpose, and he came upon the two together;
the rest of the family being out. The two had not been together five
minutes, and the peculiar manner seemed to convey to them, "You were
going to talk about me. Hah! Behold me here to prevent it!"

"Gowan is coming here?" said Blandois, with his smile.

Mrs. Gowan replied he was not coming.

"Not coming!" said Blandois. "Permit your devoted servant, when you leave here, to escort you home."

"Thank you; I am not going home."

"Not going home!" said Blandois. "Then I am forlorn."

That he might be; but he was not so forlorn as to roam away and leave them together. He sat entertaining them with his finest compliments, and his choicest conversation; but, he conveyed to them, all the time, "No, no, no, dear ladies. Behold me here expressly to prevent it!"

He conveyed it to them with so much meaning, and he had such a diabolical persistency in him, that at length Mrs. Gowan rose to depart. On his offering his hand to Mrs. Gowan to lead her down the staircase, she retained Little Dorrit's hand in hers with a cautious pressure, and said, "No, thank you. But, if you will please to see if my boatman is there, I shall be obliged to you."

It left him no choice but to go down before them. As he did so, hat in hand, Mrs Gowan whispered:

"He killed the dog."

"Does Mr. Gowan know it?" Little Dorrit whispered.

"No one knows it. Don't look towards me; look towards him. He will turn his face in a moment. No one knows it, but I am sure he did. You are?"

"I—I think so," Little Dorrit answered.

"Henry likes him, and will not think ill of him; he is so generous and open himself. But you and I feel sure that we think of him as he deserves. He argued with Henry that the dog had been already poisoned when he changed so, and sprung at him. Henry believes it, but we do not. I see he is listening, but can't hear. Good bye, my love! Good bye!"

The last words were spoken aloud, as the vigilant Blandois stopped, turned his head, and looked at them from the bottom of the staircase. Assuredly he did look then, though he looked his politest, as if any real philanthropist could have desired no better employment than to lash a great stone to his neck, and drop him into the water flowing beyond the dark arched gateway in which he stood. No such benefactor to mankind being on the spot, he handed Mrs. Gowan to her boat, and stood there until it had shot out of the narrow view; when he handed himself into his own boat and followed.

Little Dorrit had sometimes thought, and now thought again as she retraced her steps up the staircase, that he had made his way too easily into her father's house. But, so many and such varieties of people did the same, through Mr. Dorrit's participation in his elder daughter's society mania, that it was hardly an exceptional case. A perfect fury for making acquaintances on whom to impress their riches and importance, had seized the House of Dorrit.

It appeared on the whole, to Little Dorrit herself, that this same society in which they lived, greatly resembled a superior sort of Marshalsea. Numbers of people seemed to come abroad, pretty much as people had come into the prison; through debt, through idleness, relationship, curiosity, and general unfitness for getting on at home. They were brought into these foreign towns in the custody of couriers and local followers, just as the debtors had been brought into the prison. They prowled about the churches and picture-galleries, much in the old, dreary, prison-yard manner. They were usually going away again to-morrow or next week, and rarely knew their own minds, and seldom did what they said they would do, or went where they said they would go: in all this again, very like the prison debtors. They paid high for poor accommodation, and disparaged a place while they pretended to like it: which was exactly the Marshalsea custom. They were envied when they went away, by people left behind feigning not to want to go: and that again was the Marshalsea habit invariably. A certain set of words and phrases, as much belonging to tourists as the College and the Snuggery belonged to the jail, was always in their mouths. They had precisely the same incapacity for settling down to anything, as the prisoners used to have; they rather deteriorated one another, as the prisoners used to do; and they wore untidy dresses, and fell into a slouching way of life: still, always like the people in the Marshalsea.

The period of the family's stay at Venice came, in its course, to an end, and they moved, with their retinue, to Rome. Through a repetition of the former Italian scenes, growing more dirty and more haggard as they went on, and bringing them at length to where the very air was diseased, they passed to their destination. A fine residence had been taken for them on the Corso, and there they took up their abode, in a city where everything seemed to be trying to stand still for ever on the ruins of something else—except the water, which, following eternal laws, tumbled and rolled from its glorious multitude of fountains.

Here, it seemed to Little Dorrit that a change came over the Marshalsea spirit of their society, and that Prunes and Prism got the upper hand. Everybody was walking about St. Peter's and the Vatican on somebody else's cork legs, and straining every visible object through somebody else's sieve. Nobody said what anything was, but everybody said what the Mrs. Generals, Mr. Eustace, or somebody else said it was. The whole body of travellers seemed to be a collection of voluntary human sacrifices, bound hand and foot, and delivered over to Mr. Eustace and his attendants, to have the entrails of their intellects arranged according to the taste of that sacred priesthood. Through the rugged remains of temples and tombs and palaces and senate halls and theatres and amphitheatres of ancient days, hosts of tongue-tied and blindfolded moderns were carefully feeling their way, incessantly repeating Prunes and Prism, in the endeavour to set their lips according to the received form. Mrs. General was in her pure element. Nobody had an opinion. There was a formation of surface going on around her on an amazing scale, and it had not a flaw of courage or honest free speech in it.

Another modification of Prunes and Prism insinuated itself on Little Dorrit's notice, very shortly after their arrival. They received an early visit from Mrs. Merdle, who led that extensive department of life in the Eternal City that winter; and the skilful manner in which she and Fanny fenced with one another on the occasion, almost made her quiet sister wink, like the glittering of small-swords.

"So delighted," said Mrs. Merdle, "to resume an acquaintance so inauspiciously begun at Martigny."

"At Martigny, of course," said Fanny. "Charmed, I am sure!"

"I understand," said Mrs. Merdle, "from my son Edmund Sparkler, that he has already improved that chance-occasion. He has returned quite transported with Venice."

"Indeed?" returned the careless Fanny. "Was he there long?"

"I might refer that question to Mr. Dorrit," said Mrs. Merdle, turning the bosom towards that gentleman; "Edmund having been so much indebted to him for rendering his stay agreeable."

"Oh, pray don't speak of it," returned Fanny. "I believe Papa had the pleasure of inviting Mr. Sparkler twice or thrice,—but it was nothing. We had so many people about us, and kept such open house, that if he had that pleasure, it was less than nothing."

"Except, my dear," said Mr. Dorrit, "except—ha—as it afforded me unusual gratification to—hum—show by any means, however slight and worthless, the—ha, hum—high estimation in which, in—ha—common with the rest of the world, I hold so distinguished and princely a character as Mr. Merdle's."

The Bosom received this tribute in its most engaging manner. "Mr. Merdle," observed Fanny, as a means of dismissing Mr. Sparkler into the background, "is quite a theme of Papa's, you must know, Mrs. Merdle."

"I have been—ha—disappointed, madam," said Mr. Dorrit, "to understand from Mr. Sparkler that there is no great—hum—probability of Mr. Merdle's coming abroad."

"Why, indeed," said Mrs. Merdle, "he is so much engaged, and in such request, that I fear not. He has not been able to get abroad for years. You, Miss Dorrit, I believe, have been almost continually abroad for a long time."

"Oh dear yes," drawled Fanny, with the greatest hardihood. "An immense number of years."

"So I should have inferred," said Mrs. Merdle.

"Exactly," said Fanny.

"I trust, however," resumed Mr. Dorrit, "that if I have not the—hum —great advantage of becoming known to Mr. Merdle on this side of the Alps or Mediterranean, I shall have that honor on returning to England. It is an honor I particularly desire and shall particularly esteem."

"Mr. Merdle," said Mrs. Merdle, who had been looking admiringly at Fanny through her eye-glass, "will esteem it, I am sure, no less."

Little Dorrit, still habitually thoughtful and solitary, though no longer alone, at first supposed this to be mere Prunes and Prism. But, as her father when they had been to a brilliant reception at Mrs. Merdle's, harped, at their own family breakfast-table, on his wish to know Mr. Merdle, with the contingent view of benefiting by the advice of that wonderful man in the disposal of his fortune, she began to think it had a real meaning, and to entertain a curiosity on her own part, to see the shining light of the time.

END OF No. XII

CHAPTER VIII

THE DOWAGER MRS. GOWAN IS REMINDED
THAT IT NEVER DOES

While the waters of Venice and the ruins of Rome were sunning themselves for the pleasure of the Dorrit family, and were daily being sketched out of all earthly proportion, lineament, and likeness, by travelling pencils innumerable, the firm of Doyce and Clennam hammered away in Bleeding Heart Yard, and the vigorous clink of iron upon iron was heard there through the working hours.

The younger partner had, by this time, brought the business into sound trim; and the elder, left free to follow his own ingenious devices, had done much to enhance the character of the factory. As an ingenious man, he had necessarily to encounter every discouragement that the ruling powers for a length of time had been able by any means to put in the way of his class of culprits; but that was only reasonable self-defence in the powers, since How to do it must obviously be regarded as the natural and mortal enemy of How not to do it. In this was to be found the basis of the wise system, by tooth and nail upheld by the Circumlocution Office, of warning every ingenious British subject to be ingenious at his peril: of harassing him, obstructing him, inviting robbers (by making his remedy uncertain, difficult, and expensive) to plunder him, and at the best of confiscating his property after a short term of enjoyment, as though invention were on a par with felony. The system had uniformly found great favor with the Barnacles, and that was only reasonable, too; for one who worthily invents must be in earnest, and the Barnacles abhorred and dreaded nothing half so much. That again was very reasonable; since in a country suffering under the affliction of a great amount of earnestness, there might, in an exceeding short space of time, be not a single Barnacle left sticking to a post.

Daniel Doyce faced his condition with its pains and penalties attached to it, and soberly worked on for the work's sake. Clennam, cheering him with a hearty co-operation, was a moral support to him, besides doing good service in his business relation. The concern prospered, and the partners were fast friends.

But Daniel could not forget the old design of so many years. It was not in reason to be expected that he should; if he could have lightly forgotten it, he could never have conceived it, or had the patience and perseverance to work it out. So Clennam thought, when he sometimes observed him of an evening looking over the models and drawings, and consoling himself by muttering with a sigh as he put them away again, that the thing was as true as it ever was.

To show no sympathy with so much endeavour, and so much disappointment, would have been to fail in what Clennam regarded as among the implied obligations of his partnership. A revival of the passing interest in the subject which had been by chance awakened at the door of the Circumlocution Office, originated in this feeling. He asked his partner to explain the invention to him; "having a lenient consideration," he stipulated, "for my being no workman, Doyce."

"No workman?" said Doyce. "You would have been a thorough workman if you had given yourself to it. You have as good a head for understanding such things as I have met with."

"A totally uneducated one, I am sorry to add," said Clennam.

"I don't know that," returned Doyce, "and I wouldn't have you say that. No man of sense who has been generally improved, and has improved himself, can be called quite uneducated as to anything. I don't particularly favor mysteries. I would as soon, on a fair and clear explanation, be judged by one class of man as another, provided he had the qualification I have named."

"At all events," said Clennam "—this sounds as if we were exchanging compliments, but we know we are not —I shall have the advantage of as plain an explanation as can be given."

"Well!" said Daniel, in his steady, even way, "I'll try to make it so."

He had the power, often to be found in union with such a character, of explaining what he himself perceived, and meant, with the direct force and distinctness with which it struck his own mind. His manner of demonstration was so orderly and neat and simple, that it was not easy to mistake him. There was something almost ludicrous in the complete irreconcileability of a vague conventional notion that he must be a visionary man, with the precise, sagacious travelling of his eye and thumb over the plans, their patient stoppages at particular points, their careful returns to other points whence little channels of explanation had to be traced up, and his steady manner of making everything good and everything sound, at each important stage, before taking his hearer on a line's-breadth further. His dismissal of himself from his description, was hardly less remarkable. He never said, I discovered this adaptation or invented that combination; but showed the whole thing as if the Divine artificer had made it, and he had happened to find it. So modest he was about it, such a pleasant touch of respect was mingled with his quiet admiration of it, and so calmly convinced he was that it was established on irrefragable laws.

Not only that evening, but for several succeeding evenings, Clennam was quite charmed by this investigation. The more he pursued it, and the oftener he glanced at the grey head bending over it, and the shrewd eye kindling with pleasure in it and love of it—instrument for probing his heart though it had been made through twelve long years—the less he could reconcile it to his younger energy to let it go without one effort more. At length he said:

"Doyce, it came to this at last—that the business was to be sunk with Heaven knows how many more wrecks, or begun all over again?"

"Yes," returned Doyce, "that's what the noblemen and gentlemen made of it after a dozen years."

"And pretty fellows too!" said Clennam, bitterly.

"The usual thing!" observed Doyce. "I must not make a martyr of myself, when I am one of so large a company."

"Relinquish it, or begin it all over again?" mused Clennam.

"That was exactly the long and the short of it," said Doyce.

"Then, my friend," cried Clennam, starting up, and taking his work-roughened hand, "it shall be begun all over again!"

Doyce looked alarmed, and replied, in a hurry—for him, "No, no. Better put it by. Far better put it by. It will be heard of, one day. I can put it by. You forget, my good Clennam; I *have* put it by. It's all at an end."

"Yes, Doyce," returned Clennam, "at an end as far as your efforts and rebuffs are concerned, I admit, but not as far as mine are. I am younger than you; I have only once set foot in that precious office, and I am fresh game for them. Come! I'll try them. You shall do exactly as you have been doing since we have been together. I will add (as I easily can) to what I have been doing, the attempt to get public justice done to you; and, unless I have some success to report, you shall hear no more of it."

Daniel Doyce was still reluctant to consent, and again and again urged that they had better put it by. But it was natural that he should gradually allow himself to be over-persuaded by Clennam, and should yield. Yield he did. So Arthur resumed the long and hopeless labor of striving to make way with the Circumlocution Office.

The waiting-rooms of that Department soon began to be familiar with his presence, and he was generally ushered into them by its janitors much as a pickpocket might be shown into a police-office; the principal difference being that the object of the latter class of public business is to keep the pickpocket, while the Circumlocution object was to get rid of Clennam. However, he was resolved to stick to the great Department; and so the work of form-filling, corresponding, minuting, memorandum-making, signing, counter-signing, counter-counter-signing, referring backwards and forwards, and referring sideways, crosswise, and zig-zag, recommenced.

Here arises a feature of the Circumlocution Office, not previously mentioned in the present record. When that admirable Department got into trouble, and was, by some infuriated member of Parliament, whom the smaller Barnacles almost suspected of laboring under diabolic possession, attacked, on the merits of no individual case, but as an Institution wholly abominable and Bedlamite; then the noble or right honorable Barnacle who represented it in the House, would smite that member and cleave him asunder, with a statement of the quantity of business (for the prevention of business) done by the Circumlocution Office. Then would that noble or right honorable Barnacle hold in his hand a paper containing a few figures, to which, with the permission of the House, he would entreat its attention. Then would the inferior Barnacles exclaim, (obeying orders), "Hear, Hear, Hear!" and "Read!" Then would the noble or right honorable Barnacle perceive, sir, from this little document, which he thought might carry conviction even to the perversest mind (Derisive laughter and cheering from the Barnacle fry), that within the short compass of the last financial half-year, this much-maligned Department (Cheers) had written and received fifteen thousand letters (Loud cheers), twenty-four thousand minutes (Louder cheers), and thirty-two thousand five hundred and seventeen memoranda (Vehement cheering). Nay, an ingenious gentleman connected with the Department, and himself a valuable public servant, had done him the favor to make a curious calculation of the amount of stationery consumed in it during the same period. It formed a part of this same short document; and he derived from it the remarkable fact, that the sheets of foolscap paper it had devoted to the public service would pave the footways on both sides of Oxford Street from end to end, and leave nearly a quarter of a mile to spare for the park (Immense cheering and laughter); while of tape—red tape—it had used enough to stretch, in graceful festoons, from Hyde Park Corner to the General Post Office. Then, amidst a burst of sacred exultation, would the noble or right honorable Barnacle sit down, leaving the mutilated fragments of the Member on the field. No one, after that exemplary demolition of him, would have the hardihood to hint that the more the Circumlocution Office did, the less was done, and that the greatest blessing it could confer on an unhappy public would be to do nothing.

With sufficient occupation on his hands, now that he had this additional task—such a task had many and many a serviceable man died of before his day—Arthur Clennam led a life of slight variety. Regular visits to his mother's dull sick room, and visits scarcely less regular to Mr. Meagles at Twickenham, were its only changes during many months.

He sadly and sorely missed Little Dorrit. He had been prepared to miss her very much, but not so much. He knew to the full extent only through experience, what a large place in his life was left blank when her familiar little figure went out of it. He felt, too, that he must relinquish the hope of its return, understanding the family character sufficiently well to be assured that he and she were divided by a broad ground of separation. The old interest he had had in her, and her old trusting reliance on him, were tinged with melancholy in his mind: so soon had change stolen over them, and so soon had they glided into the past with other secret tendernesses.

When he received her letter he was greatly moved, but did not the less sensibly feel that she was far divided from him by more than distance. It helped him to a clearer and keener perception of the place assigned him by the family. He saw that he was cherished in her grateful remembrance secretly, and that they resented him with the jail and the rest of its belongings.

Through all these meditations which every day of his life crowded about her, he thought of her otherwise in the old way. She was his innocent friend, his delicate child, his dear Little Dorrit. This very change of circumstances fitted curiously in with the habit, begun on the night when the roses floated away, of considering himself as a much older man than his years really made him. He regarded her from a point of view which in its remoteness, tender as it was, he little thought would have been unspeakable agony to her. He speculated about her future destiny, and about the husband she might have, with an affection for her which would have drained her heart of its dearest drop of hope, and broken it.

Everything about him tended to confirm him in the custom of looking on himself as an elderly man, from whom such aspirations as he had combated in the case of Minnie Gowan (though that was not so long ago either, reckoning by months and seasons), were finally departed. His relations with her father and mother were like those on which a widower son-in-law might have stood. If the twin sister, who was dead, had lived to pass away in the bloom of womanhood, and he had been her husband, the nature of his intercourse with Mr. and Mrs. Meagles would probably have been just what it was. This imperceptibly helped to render habitual the impression within him, that he had done with, and dismissed, that part of life.

He invariably heard of Minnie from them, as telling them in her letters how happy she was, and how she loved her husband; but inseparable from that subject, he invariably saw the old cloud on Mr. Meagles's face. Mr.

Meagles had never been quite so radiant since the marriage as before. He had never quite recovered the separation from Pet. He was the same good-humoured, open creature; but as if his face, from being much turned towards the pictures of his two children which could show him only one look, unconsciously adopted a characteristic from them, it always had now, through all its changes of expression, a look of loss in it.

One wintry Saturday when Clennam was at the cottage, the Dowager Mrs. Gowan drove up, in the Hampton Court equipage which pretended to be the exclusive equipage of so many individual proprietors. She descended, in her shady ambuscade of green fan, to favor Mr. and Mrs. Meagles with a call.

"And how do you both do, Papa and Mama Meagles?" said she, encouraging her humble connexions. "And when did you last hear from or about my poor fellow?"

My poor fellow was her son; and this mode of speaking of him politely kept alive, without any offence in the world, the pretence that he had fallen a victim to the Meagles wiles.

"And the dear pretty one," said Mrs. Gowan. "Have you later news of her than I have?"

Which also delicately implied that her son had been captured by mere beauty, and under its fascination had foregone all sorts of worldly advantages.

"I am sure," said Mrs. Gowan, without straining her attention on the answers she received, "it's an unspeakable comfort to know they continue happy. My poor fellow is of such a restless disposition, and has been so used to roving about, and to being inconstant and popular among all manner of people, that it's the greatest comfort in life. I suppose they're as poor as mice, Papa Meagles?"

Mr. Meagles, fidgetty under the question, replied, "I hope not, ma'am. I hope they will manage their little income."

"Oh! my dearest Meagles!" returned that lady, tapping him on the arm with the green fan and then adroitly interposing it between a yawn and the company, "how can you, as a man of the world and one of the most business-like of human beings—for you know you are business-like, and a great deal too much for us who are not——"

(Which went to the former purpose, by making Mr. Meagles out to be an artful schemer.)

"—How can you talk about their managing their little means? My poor dear fellow! The idea of his managing hundreds! And the sweet pretty creature too. The notion of her managing! Papa Meagles! Don't!"

"Well, ma'am," said Mr. Meagles, gravely, "I am sorry to admit, then, that Henry certainly does anticipate his means."

"My dear good man—I use no ceremony with you, because we are a kind of relations;—positively, Mama Meagles," exclaimed Mrs. Gowan cheerfully, as if the absurd coincidence then flashed upon her for the first time "a kind of relations! My dear good man, in this world none of us can have *everything* our own way."

This again went to the former point, and showed Mr. Meagles with all good breeding that, so far, he had been brilliantly successful in his deep designs. Mrs. Gowan thought the hit so good a one that she dwelt upon it; repeating "Not *everything*. No, no; in this world we must not expect *everything*, Papa Meagles."

"And may I ask, ma'am," retorted Mr. Meagles, a little heightened in color, "who does expect everything?"

"Oh, nobody, nobody!" said Mrs. Gowan. "I was going to say—but you put me out. You interrupting Papa, what was I going to say!"

Drooping her large green fan, she looked musingly at Mr. Meagles while she thought about it; a performance not tending to the cooling of that gentleman's rather heated spirits.

"Ah! Yes, to be sure!" said Mrs. Gowan. "You must remember that my poor fellow has always been accustomed to expectations. They may have been realised, or they may not have been realised——"

"Let us say, then, may not have been realised," observed Mr. Meagles.

The Dowager for a moment gave him an angry look; but tossed it off with her head and her fan, and pursued the tenor of her way in her former manner.

"It makes no difference. My poor fellow has been accustomed to that sort of thing, and of course you knew it, and were prepared for the consequences. I myself always clearly foresaw the consequences, and am not surprised. And you must not be surprised. In fact, can't be surprised. Must have been prepared for it."

Mr. Meagles looked at his wife, and at Clennam; bit his lip; and coughed.

"And now here's my poor fellow," Mrs. Gowan pursued, "receiving notice that he is to hold himself in expectation of a baby, and all the expenses attendant on such an addition to his family! Poor Henry! But it can't be helped now: it's too late to help it now. Only don't talk of anticipating means, Papa Meagles, as a discovery; because that would be too much."

"Too much, ma'am?" said Mr. Meagles, as seeking an explanation.

"There, there!" said Mrs. Gowan, putting him in his inferior place with an expressive action of her hand. "Too much for my poor fellow's mother to bear at this time of day. They are fast married, and can't be unmarried. There, there! I know that! You needn't tell me that, Papa Meagles. I know it very well. What was it I said just now? That it was a great comfort they continued happy. It is to be hoped they will still continue happy. It is to be hoped Pretty One will do everything she can to make my poor fellow happy, and keep him contented. Papa and Mama Meagles, we had better say no more about it. We never did look at this subject from the same side, and we never shall. There, there! Now I am good."

Truly, having by this time said everything she could say in maintenance of her wonderfully mythical position, and in admonition to Mr. Meagles that he must not expect to bear his honors of alliance too cheaply, Mrs. Gowan was disposed to forego the rest. If Mr. Meagles had submitted to a glance of entreaty from Mrs. Meagles, and an expressive gesture from Clennam, he would have left her in the undisturbed enjoyment of this state of mind. But Pet was the darling and pride of his heart; and if he could ever have championed her more devotedly, or loved her better, than in the days when she was the sunlight of his house, it would have been now, when, in its daily grace and delight, she was lost to it.

"Mrs. Gowan, ma'am," said Mr. Meagles, "I have been a plain man all my life. If I was to try—no matter whether on myself, or somebody else, or both—any genteel mystifications, I should probably not succeed in them."

"Papa Meagles," returned the Dowager, with an affable smile, but with the bloom on her cheeks standing out a little more vividly than usual, as the neighbouring surface became paler, "probably not."

"Therefore, my good madam," said Mr. Meagles, at great pains to restrain himself, "I hope I may, without offence, ask to have no such mystifications played off upon me."

"Mama Meagles," observed Mrs. Gowan, "your good man is incomprehensible."

Her turning to that worthy lady was an artifice to bring her into the discussion, quarrel with her, and vanquish her. Mr. Meagles interposed to prevent that consummation.

"Mother," said he, "you are inexpert, my dear, and it's not a fair match. Let me beg of you to remain quiet. Come, Mrs. Gowan, come! Let us try to be sensible; let us try to be good-natured; let us try to be fair. Don't you pity Henry, and I won't pity Pet. And don't be one-sided, my dear madam; it's not considerate, it's not kind. Don't let us say that we hope Pet will make Henry happy, or even that we hope Henry will make Pet happy," (Mr. Meagles himself did not look happy as he spoke the words) "but that we hope they will make each other happy."

"Yes sure, and there leave it, father," said Mrs. Meagles the kindhearted and comfortable.

"Why mother, no," returned Mr. Meagles, "not exactly there. I can't quite leave it there; I must say just half-a-dozen words more. Mrs. Gowan, I hope I am not over sensitive. I believe I don't look it."

"Indeed you do not," said Mrs. Gowan, shaking her head and the great green fan together, for emphasis.

"Thank you, ma'am; that's well. Notwithstanding which, I feel a little—

I don't want to use a strong word—now shall I say hurt?" asked Mr. Meagles at once with frankness and moderation, and with a conciliatory appeal in his tone.

"Say what you like," answered Mrs. Gowan. "It is perfectly indifferent to me."

"No, no, don't say that," urged Mr. Meagles, "because that's not responding amiably. I feel a little hurt, when I hear references made to consequences having been foreseen, and to its being too late now, and so forth."

"*Do* you, Papa Meagles?" said Mrs. Gowan. "I am not surprised."

"Well, ma'am," reasoned Mr. Meagles, "I was in hopes you would have been at least surprised, because to hurt me wilfully on so tender a subject is surely not generous."

"I am not responsible," said Mrs. Gowan, "for your conscience, you know."

Poor Mr. Meagles looked aghast with astonishment.

"If I am unluckily obliged to carry a cap about with me which is yours and fits you," pursued Mrs. Gowan, "don't blame *me* for its pattern, Papa Meagles, I beg!"

"Why, good Lord, ma'am!" Mr. Meagles broke out, "that's as much as to state——"

"Now, Papa Meagles, Papa Meagles," said Mrs. Gowan, who became extremely deliberate and prepossessing in manner whenever that gentleman became at all warm, "perhaps, to prevent confusion, I had better speak for myself than trouble your kindness to speak for me. It's as much as to state, you begin. If you please, I will finish the sentence. It is as much as to state—not that I wish to press it, or even recall it, for it is of no use now, and my only wish is to make the best of existing circumstances—that from the first to the last I always objected to this match of yours, and at a very late period yielded a most unwilling consent to it."

"Mother!" cried Mr. Meagles. "Do you hear this! Arthur! Do you hear this!"

"The room being of a convenient size," said Mrs. Gowan, looking about as she fanned herself, "and quite charmingly adapted in all respects to conversation, I should imagine that I am audible in any part of it."

Some moments passed in silence, before Mr. Meagles could hold himself in his chair with sufficient security to prevent his breaking out of it at the next word he spoke. At last he said: "Ma'am, I am very unwilling to revive them, but I must remind you what my opinions and my course were, all along, on that unfortunate subject."

"O, my dear sir!" said Mrs. Gowan, smiling and shaking her head with accusatory intelligence, "they were well understood by me, I assure you."

"I never, ma'am," said Mr. Meagles, "knew unhappiness before that time, I never knew anxiety before that time. It was a time of such distress to me, that——." That Mr. Meagles really could say no more about it, in short, but passed his handkerchief before his face.

"I understood the whole affair," said Mrs. Gowan, composedly looking over her fan. "As you have appealed to Mr. Clennam, I may appeal to Mr. Clennam, too. He knows whether I did or not."

"I am very unwilling," said Clennam, looked to by all parties, "to take any share in this discussion, more especially because I wish to preserve the best understanding and the clearest relations with Mr. Henry Gowan. I have very strong reasons indeed, for entertaining that wish. Mrs. Gowan attributed certain views of furthering the marriage to my friend here, in conversation with me before it took place; and I endeavoured to undeceive her. I represented that I knew him (as I did and do), to be strenuously opposed to it, both in opinion and action."

"You see?" said Mrs. Gowan, turning the palms of her hands towards Mr. Meagles, as if she were Justice herself, representing to him that he had better confess, for he had not a leg to stand on. "You see? Very good! Now, Papa and Mama Meagles both!" here she rose; "allow me to take the liberty of putting an end to this rather formidable controversy. I will not say another word upon its merits. I will only say that it is an additional proof of what one knows from all experience; that this kind of thing never answers—as my poor fellow himself would say, that it never pays—in one word, that it never does."

Mr. Meagles asked, What kind of thing?

"It is in vain," said Mrs. Gowan, "for people to attempt to get on together who have such extremely different antecedents; who are jumbled against each other in this accidental, matrimonial sort of way; and who cannot look at the untoward circumstance which has shaken them together, in the same light. It never does."

Mr. Meagles was beginning, "Permit me to say, ma'am——."

"No, don't!" returned Mrs. Gowan. "Why should you! It is an ascertained fact. It never does. I will therefore, if you please, go my way, leaving you to yours. I shall at all times be happy to receive my poor fellow's pretty wife, and I shall always make a point of being on the most affectionate terms with her. But as to these terms, semi-family and semi-stranger, semi-goring and semi-boring, they form a state of things quite amusing in its impracticability. I assure you it never does."

The Dowager here made a smiling obeisance, rather to the room than to any one in it, and therewith took a final farewell of Papa and Mama Meagles. Clennam stepped forward to hand her to the Pill-Box, which was at the service of all the Pills in Hampton Court Palace; and she got into that vehicle with distinguished serenity, and was driven away.

Thenceforth the Dowager, with a light and careless humour, often recounted to her particular acquaintance how, after a hard trial, she had found it impossible to know those people who belonged to Henry's wife, and who had made that desperate set to catch him. Whether she had come to the conclusion beforehand, that to get rid of them would give her favorite pretence a better air, might save her some occasional inconvenience, and could risk no loss (the pretty creature being fast married, and her father devoted to her), was best known to herself. Though this history has its opinion on that point too, and decidedly in the affirmative.

CHAPTER IX

APPEARANCE AND DISAPPEARANCE

"Arthur, my dear boy," said Mr. Meagles, on the evening of the following day, "Mother and I have been talking this over, and we don't feel comfortable in remaining as we are. That elegant connexion of ours—that dear lady who was here yesterday——"

"I understand," said Arthur.

"Even that affable and condescending ornament of society," pursued Mr. Meagles, "may misrepresent us, we are afraid. We could bear a great deal, Arthur, for her sake; but we think we would rather not bear that, if it was all the same to her."

"Good," said Arthur. "Go on."

"You see," proceeded Mr. Meagles, "it might put us wrong with our son-in-law, it might even put us wrong with our daughter, and it might lead to a great deal of domestic trouble. You see, don't you?"

"Yes indeed," returned Arthur, "there is much reason in what you say." He had glanced at Mrs. Meagles, who was always on the good and sensible side; and a petition had shone out of her honest face that he would support Mr. Meagles in his present inclinings.

"So we are very much disposed, are Mother and I," said Mr. Meagles, "to pack up bag and baggage and go among the Allongers and Marshongers once more. I mean, we are very much disposed to be off, strike right through France into Italy, and see our Pet."

"And I don't think," replied Arthur, touched by the motherly anticipation in the bright face of Mrs. Meagles (she must have been very like her daughter, once), "that you could do better. And if you ask me for my advice, it is that you set off to-morrow."

"Is it really, though?" said Mr. Meagles. "Mother, this is being backed in an idea?"

Mother, with a look which thanked Clennam in a manner very agreeable to him, answered that it was indeed.

"The fact is, besides, Arthur," said Mr. Meagles, the old cloud coming over his face, "that my son-in-law is already in debt again, and that I suppose I must clear him again. It may be as well, even on this account, that I should step over there, and look him up in a friendly way. Then again, here's Mother foolishly anxious (and yet naturally too) about Pet's state of health, and that she should not be left to feel lonesome at the present time. It's undeniably a long way off, Arthur, and a strange place for the poor love under all the circumstances. Let her be as well cared for as any lady in that land, still it is a long way off. Just as Home is Home though it's never so Homely, why you see," said Mr. Meagles, adding a new version to the proverb, "Rome is Rome though it's never so Romely."

"All perfectly true," observed Arthur, "and all sufficient reasons for going."

"I am glad you think so; it decides me. Mother, my dear, you may get ready. We have lost our pleasant interpreter (she spoke three foreign languages beautifully, Arthur; you have heard her many a time), and you must pull me through it, Mother, as well as you can. I require a deal of pulling through, Arthur," said Mr. Meagles, shaking his head, "a deal of pulling through. I stick at everything beyond a noun-substantive,—and I stick at him, if he's at all a tight one."

"Now I think of it," returned Clennam, "there's Cavalletto. He shall go with you if you like. I could not afford to lose him, but you will bring him safe back."

"Well! I am much obliged to you, my boy," said Mr. Meagles, turning it over, "but I think not. No, I think I'll be pulled through by Mother. Caval-looro (I stick at his very name to start with, and it sounds like the chorus to a comic song), is so necessary to you, that I don't like the thought of taking him away. More than that, there's no saying when we may come home again; and it would never do to take him away for an indefinite time. The cottage is not what it was. It only holds two little people less than it ever did, Pet, and her poor unfortunate maid Tattycoram; but it seems empty now. Once out of it, there's no knowing when we may come back to it. No, Arthur, I'll be pulled through by Mother."

They would do best by themselves perhaps, after all, Clennam thought; therefore did not press his proposal.

"If you would come down and stay here for a change, when it wouldn't trouble you," Mr. Meagles resumed, "I should be glad to think—and so would Mother too, I know—that you were brightening up the old place with a bit of life it was used to when it was full, and that the Babies on the wall there, had a kind eye upon them sometimes. You so belong to the spot, and to them, Arthur, and we should every one of us have been so happy if it had fallen out—but, let us see—how's the weather for travelling, now?" Mr. Meagles broke off, cleared his throat, and got up to look out of window.

They agreed that the weather was of high promise; and Clennam kept the talk in that safe direction until it had become easy again, when he gently diverted it to Henry Gowan, and his quick sense and agreeable qualities when he was delicately dealt with; he likewise dwelt on the indisputable affection he entertained for his wife. Clennam did not fail of his effect upon good Mr. Meagles, whom these commendations greatly cheered; and who took Mother to witness that the single and cordial desire of his heart in reference to their daughter's husband, was harmoniously to exchange friendship for friendship, and confidence for confidence. Within a few hours the cottage furniture began to be wrapped up for preservation in the family absence—or, as Mr. Meagles expressed it, the house began to put its hair in papers—and within a few days Father and Mother were gone, Mrs. Tickit and Dr. Buchan were posted, as of yore, behind the parlor blind, and Arthur's solitary feet were rustling among the dry fallen leaves in the garden walks.

As he had a liking for the spot, he seldom let a week pass without paying it a visit. Sometimes, he went down alone from Saturday to Monday; sometimes, his partner accompanied him; sometimes, he merely strolled for an hour or two about the house and garden, saw that all was right, and returned to London again. At all times and under all circumstances Mrs. Tickit, with her dark row of curls and Doctor Buchan, sat in the parlor window, looking out for the family return.

On one of his visits Mrs. Tickit received him with the words, "I have something to tell you, Mr. Clennam, that will surprise you." So surprising was the something in question, that it actually brought Mrs. Tickit out of the parlor window and produced her in the garden walk, when Clennam went in at the gate on its being opened for him.

"What is it, Mrs. Tickit?" said he.

"Sir," returned that faithful housekeeper, having taken him into the parlor and closed the door; "if ever I saw the led away and deluded child in my life, I saw her identically in the dusk of yesterday evening."

"You don't mean Tatty——"

"Coram yes I uo!" quoth Mrs. Tickit, clearing the disclosure at a leap.

"Where?"

"Mr. Clennam," returned Mrs. Tickit, "I was a little heavy in my eyes, being that I was waiting longer than customary for my cup of tea which was then preparing by Mary Jane. I was not sleeping, nor what a person would term correctly, dozing. I was more what a person would strictly call watching with my eyes closed."

Without entering upon an enquiry into this curious abnormal condition, Clennam said, "Exactly. Well?"

"Well, sir," proceeded Mrs. Tickit, "I was thinking of one thing and thinking of another. Just as you yourself might. Just as anybody might."

"Precisely so," said Clennam. "Well?"

"And when I do think of one thing and do think of another," pursued Mrs. Tickit, "I hardly need to tell you, Mr. Clennam, that I think of the family. Because, dear me! a person's thoughts," Mrs. Tickit said this with an argumentative and philosophic air, "however they may stray, will go more or less on what is uppermost in their minds. They *will* do it, sir, and a person can't prevent them."

Arthur subscribed to this discovery with a nod.

"You find it so yourself, sir, I'll be bold to say," said Mrs. Tickit, "and we all find it so. It an't our stations in life that changes us, Mr. Clennam; thoughts is free!—As I was saying, I was thinking of one thing and thinking of another, and thinking very much of the family. Not of the family in the present times only, but in the past times too. For when a person does begin thinking of one thing and thinking of another, in that manner as it's getting dark, what I say is that all times seem to be present, and a person must get out of that state and consider before they can say which is which."

He nodded again; afraid to utter a word, lest it should present any new opening to Mrs. Tickit's conversational powers.

"In consequence of which," said Mrs. Tickit, "when I quivered my eyes and saw her actual form and figure looking in at the gate, I let them close again without so much as starting; for that actual form and figure came so pat to the time when it belonged to the house as much as mine or your own, that I never thought at the moment of its having gone away. But, sir, when I quivered my eyes again and saw that it wasn't there, then it all flooded upon me with a fright, and I jumped up."

"You ran out directly?" said Clennam.

"I ran out," assented Mrs. Tickit, "as fast as ever my feet would carry me; and if you'll credit it, Mr. Clennam, there wasn't in the whole shining Heavens, no not so much as a finger of that young woman."

Passing over the absence from the firmament of this novel constellation, Arthur enquired of Mrs. Tickit if she herself went beyond the gate?

"Went to and fro, and high and low," said Mrs. Tickit, "and saw no sign of her!"

He then asked Mrs. Tickit how long a space of time she supposed there might have been between the two sets of ocular quiverings she had experienced? Mrs. Tickit, though minutely circumstantial in her reply, had no settled opinion between five seconds and ten minutes. She was so plainly at sea on this part of the case, and had so clearly been startled out of slumber, that Clennam was much disposed to regard the appearance as a dream. Without hurting Mrs. Tickit's feelings with that infidel solution of her mystery, he took it away from the cottage with him; and probably would have retained it ever afterwards, if a circumstance had not soon happened to change his opinion.

He was passing at nightfall along the Strand, and the lamplighter was going on before him, under whose hand the street-lamps, blurred by the foggy air, burst out one after another, like so many blazing sunflowers coming into full-blow all at once,—when a stoppage on the pavement, caused by a train of coal-waggons toiling up from the wharves at the river-side, brought him to a stand-still. He had been walking quickly, and going with some current of thought, and the sudden check given to both operations caused him to look freshly about him, as people under such circumstances usually do.

Immediately, he saw in advance—a few people intervening, but still so near to him that he could have touched them by stretching out his arm— Tattycoram and a strange man of a remarkable appearance: a swaggering man, with a high nose, and a black moustache as false in its color as his eyes were false in their expression, who wore his heavy cloak with the air of a foreigner. His dress and general appearance were those of a man on travel, and he seemed to have very recently joined the girl. In bending down (being much taller than she was), listening to whatever she said to him, he looked over his shoulder with the suspicious glance of one who was not unused to be mistrustful that his footsteps might be dogged. It was then that Clennam saw his face; as his eyes lowered on the people behind him in the aggregate, without particularly resting upon Clennam's face or any other.

He had scarcely turned his head about again, and it was still bent down, listening to the girl, when the stoppage ceased, and the obstructed stream of people flowed on. Still bending his head and listening to the girl, he went on at her side, and Clennam followed them, resolved to play this unexpected play out, and see where they went.

He had hardly made the determination (though he was not long about it), when he was again as suddenly brought up as he had been by the stoppage. They turned short into the Adelphi,—the girl evidently leading, —and went straight on, as if they were going to the Terrace which over-hangs the river.

There is always, to this day, a sudden pause in that place to the roar of the great thoroughfare. The many sounds become so deadened that the change is like putting cotton in the ears, or having the head thickly muffled. At that time the contrast was far greater; there being no small steam-boats on the river, no landing-places but slippery narrow stairs and foot-causeways, no railroad on the opposite bank, no hanging bridge or fish-market near at hand, no traffic on the nearest bridge of stone, nothing moving on the stream but watermen's wherries and coal-lighters. Long and broad black tiers of the latter, moored fast in the mud as if they were never to move again, made the shore funereal and silent after dark; and kept what little water-movement there was, far out towards mid-stream. At any hour later than sunset, and not least at that hour when most of the people who have anything to eat at home are going home to eat it, and when most of those who have nothing have hardly yet slunk out to beg or steal, it was a deserted place and looked on a deserted scene.

Such was the hour when Clennam stopped at the corner, observing the girl and the strange man as they went down the street. The man's footsteps were so noisy on the echoing stones that he was unwilling to add the sound of his own. But, when they had passed the turning and were in the darkness of the dark corner leading to the terrace, he made after them with such indifferent appearance of being a casual passenger on his way, as he could assume.

When he rounded the dark corner, they were walking along the terrace, towards a figure which was coming towards them. If he had seen it by itself, under such conditions of gas-lamp, mist, and distance, he might not have known it at first sight; but with the figure of the girl to prompt him, he at once recognised Miss Wade.

He stopped at the corner, seeming to look back expectantly up the street, as if he had made an appointment with some one to meet him there; but he kept a careful eye on the three. When they came together, the man took off his hat, and made Miss Wade a bow. The girl appeared to say a few words as though she presented him, or accounted for his being late, or early, or what not; and then fell a pace or so behind, by herself. Miss Wade and the man then began to walk up and down; the man having the appearance of being extremely courteous and complimentary in manner; Miss Wade having the appearance of being extremely haughty.

When they came down to the corner and turned, she was saying, "If I pinch myself for it, sir, that is my business. Confine yourself to yours, and ask me no question."

"By Heaven, ma'am!" he replied, making her another bow. "It was my profound respect for the strength of your character, and my admiration of your beauty."

"I want neither the one nor the other from any one," said she, "and certainly not from you of all creatures. Go on with your report."

"Am I pardoned?" he asked, with an air of half-abashed gallantry.

"You are paid," she said, "and that is all you want."

Whether the girl hung behind because she was not to hear the business, or as already knowing enough about it, Clennam could not determine. They turned and she turned. She looked away at the River, as she walked with her hands folded before her; and that was all he could make of her without showing his face. There happened, by good fortune, to be a lounger really waiting for some one; and he sometimes looked over the railing at the water, and sometimes came to the dark corner and looked up the street, rendering Arthur less conspicuous.

When Miss Wade and the man came back again, she was saying, "You must wait until to-morrow."

"A thousand pardons!" he returned. "My faith! Then it's not convenient to-night?"

"No. I tell you I must get it before I can give it to you."

She stopped in the roadway, as if to put an end to the conference. He of course stopped too. And the girl stopped.

"It's a little inconvenient," said the man. "A little. But, Holy blue! that's nothing, in such a service. I am without money to-night by chance. I *have* a good banker in this city, but I would not wish to draw upon the house until the time when I shall draw for a round sum."

"Harriet," said Miss Wade, "arrange with him—this gentleman here— for sending him some money to-morrow." She said it with a slur of the word gentleman which was more contemptuous than any emphasis, and walked slowly on.

The man bent his head again, and the girl spoke to him as they both followed her. Clennam ventured to look at the girl as they moved away. He could note that her rich black eyes were fastened upon the man with a scrutinising expression, and that she kept at a little distance from him, as they walked side by side to the further end of the terrace.

A loud and altered clank upon the pavement warned him, before he could discern what was passing there, that the man was coming back alone. Clennam lounged into the road, towards the railing; and the man passed at a quick swing, with the end of his cloak thrown over his shoulder, singing a scrap of a French song.

The whole vista had no one in it now but himself. The lounger had lounged out of view, and Miss Wade and Tattycoram were gone. More than ever bent on seeing what became of them, and on having some information to give his good friend Mr. Meagles, he went out at the further end of the terrace, looking cautiously about him. He rightly judged that, at first at all events, they would go in a contrary direction from their late companion. He soon saw them in a neighbouring bye-street, which was not a thorough-fare, evidently allowing time for the man to get well out of their way. They walked leisurely arm-in-arm down one side of the street, and returned on the opposite side. When they came back to the street-corner, they changed their pace for the pace of people with an object and a distance before them, and walked steadily away. Clennam, no less steadily, kept them in sight.

They crossed the Strand, and passed through Covent Garden (under the windows of his old lodging where dear Little Dorrit had come that night), and slanted away north-east, until they passed the great building whence Tattycoram derived her name, and turned into the Gray's Inn Road. Clennam was quite at home here, in right of Flora, not to mention the Patriarch and Pancks, and kept them in view with ease. He was beginning to wonder where they might be going next, when that wonder was lost in the greater wonder with which he saw them turn into the Patriarchal street. That wonder was in its turn swallowed up in the greater wonder with which he saw them stop at the Patriarchal door. A low double knock at the bright brass knocker, a gleam of light into the road from the opened door, a brief pause for enquiry and answer, and the door was shut, and they were housed.

After looking at the surrounding objects for assurance that he was not in an odd dream, and after pacing a little while before the house, Arthur knocked at the door. It was opened by the usual maid-servant, and she showed him up at once, with her usual alacrity, to Flora's sitting-room.

There was no one with Flora but Mr. F's Aunt, which respectable gentlewoman, basking in a balmy atmosphere of tea and toast, was ensconced in an easy chair by the fireside, with a little table at her elbow, and a clean white handkerchief spread over her lap, on which two pieces of toast at that moment awaited consumption. Bending over a steaming vessel of tea, and looking through the steam, and breathing forth the steam, like a malignant Chinese enchantress engaged in the performance of unholy rites, Mr. F's Aunt put down her great teacup, and exclaimed, "Drat him, if he an't come back again!"

It would seem from the foregoing exclamation that this uncompromising relative of the lamented Mr. F, measuring time by the acuteness of her sensations and not by the clock, supposed Clennam to have lately gone away; whereas at least a quarter of a year had elapsed since he had had the temerity to present himself before her.

"My goodness Arthur!" cried Flora, rising to give him a cordial reception, "Doyce and Clennam what a start and a surprise for though not far from the machinery and foundry business and surely might be taken sometimes if at no other time about mid-day when a glass of sherry and a humble sandwich of whatever cold meat in the larder might not come amiss nor taste the worse for being friendly for you know you buy it somewhere and wherever bought a profit must be made or they would never keep the place it stands to reason without a motive still never seen and learnt now not to be expected, for as Mr. F himself said if seeing is believing not seeing is believing too and when you don't see you may fully believe you're not remembered not that I expect you Arthur Doyce and Clennam to remember me why should I for the days are gone but bring another teacup here directly and tell her fresh toast and pray sit near the fire."

Arthur was in the greatest anxiety to explain the object of his visit; but was put off for the moment, in spite of himself, by what he understood of the reproachful purport of these words, and by the genuine pleasure she testified in seeing him.

"And now pray tell me something all you know," said Flora, drawing her chair near to his, "about the good dear quiet little thing and all the changes of her fortunes carriage people now no doubt and horses without number most romantic, a coat-of-arms of course and wild beasts on their hind legs showing it as if it was a copy they had done with mouths from ear to ear good gracious, and has she her health which is the first consideration after all for what is wealth without it Mr. F himself so often saying when his twinges came that sixpence a-day and find yourself and no gout so much preferable, not that he could have lived on anything like it being the last man or that the precious little thing though far too familiar an expression now had any tendency of that sort much too slight and small but looked so fragile bless her!"

Mr. F's Aunt, who had eaten a piece of toast down to the crust, here solemnly handed the crust to Flora, who ate it for her as a matter of business. Mr. F's Aunt then moistened her ten fingers in slow succession at her lips, and wiped them in exactly the same order on the white handkerchief; then took the other piece of toast, and fell to work upon it. While pursuing this routine, she looked at Clennam with an expression of such intense severity that he felt obliged to look at her in return, against his personal inclinations.

"She is in Italy, with all her family, Flora," he said, when the dread lady was occupied again.

"In Italy is she really?" said Flora, "with the grapes and figs growing everywhere and lava necklaces and bracelets too that land of poetry with burning mountains picturesque beyond belief though if the organ-boys come away from the neighbourhood not to be scorched nobody can wonder being so young and bringing their white mice with them most humane, and is she really in that favored land with nothing but blue about her and dying gladiators and Belvederas though Mr. F himself did not believe for his objection when in spirits was that the images could not be true there being no medium between expensive quantities of linen badly got up and all in creases and none whatever, which certainly does not seem probable though perhaps in consequence of the extremes of rich and poor which may account for it."

Arthur tried to edge a word in, but Flora hurried on again.

"Venice Preserved too," said she, "I think you have been there is it well or ill preserved for people differ so and Maccaroni if they really eat it like the conjurors why not cut it shorter, you are acquainted Arthur— dear Doyce and Clennam at least not dear and most assuredly not Doyce for I have not the pleasure but pray excuse me—acquainted I believe with Mantua what *has* it got to do with Mantua-making for I never have been able to conceive?"

"I believe there is no connexion, Flora, between the two"—Arthur was beginning, when she caught him up again.

"Upon your word no isn't there I never did but that's like me I run away with an idea and having none to spare I keep it, alas there was a time dear Arthur that is to say decidedly not dear nor Arthur neither but you understand me when one bright idea gilded the what's-his-name horizon of et cetera but it is darkly clouded now and all is over."

Arthur's increasing wish to speak of something very different was by this time so plainly written on his face, that Flora stopped in a tender look, and asked him what it was?

"I have the greatest desire, Flora, to speak to some one who is now in this house—with Mr. Casby no doubt. Some one whom I saw come in, and who, in a misguided and deplorable way, has deserted the house of a friend of mine."

"Papa sees so many and such odd people," said Flora rising, "that I shouldn't venture to go down for any one but you Arthur but for you I would willingly go down in a diving-bell much more a dining-room and will come back directly if you'll mind and at the same time *not* mind Mr. F's Aunt while I'm gone."

With those words and a parting glance, Flora bustled out, leaving Clennam under dreadful apprehensions of his terrible charge.

The first variation which manifested itself in Mr. F's Aunt's demeanour when she had finished her piece of toast, was a loud and prolonged sniff. Finding it impossible to avoid construing this demonstration into a defiance of himself, its gloomy significance being unmistakeable, Clennam looked plaintively at the excellent though prejudiced lady from whom it emanated, in the hope that she might be disarmed by a meek submission.

"None of your eyes at me," said Mr. F's Aunt, shivering with hostility. "Take that."

"That" was the crust of the piece of toast. Clennam accepted the boon with a look of gratitude, and held it in his hand under the pressure of a little embarrassment, which was not relieved when Mr. F's Aunt, elevating her voice into a cry of considerable power, exclaimed "He has a proud stomach, this chap! He's too proud a chap to eat it!" and, coming out of her chair, shook her venerable fist so very close to his nose as to tickle the surface. But for the timely return of Flora, to find him in this difficult situation, further consequences might have ensued. Flora, without the least discomposure or surprise, but congratulating the old lady in an approving manner on being "very lively to-night," handed her back to her chair.

"He has a proud stomach, this chap," said Mr. F's relation, on being reseated. "Give him a meal of chaff!"

"Oh! I don't think he would like that, aunt," returned Flora.

"Give him a meal of chaff, I tell you," said Mr. F's Aunt, glaring round Flora on her enemy. "It's the only thing for a proud stomach. Let him eat it up every morsel. Drat him, give him a meal of chaff!"

Under a general pretence of helping him to this refreshment, Flora got him out on the staircase; Mr. F's Aunt even then constantly reiterating, with inexpressible bitterness, that he was "a chap," and had "a proud stomach," and over and over again insisting on that equine provision being made for him which she had already so strongly prescribed.

"Such an inconvenient staircase and so many corner-stairs Arthur," whispered Flora, "would you object to putting your arm round me under my pelerine?"

With a sense of going down-stairs in a highly ridiculous manner, Clennam descended in the required attitude, and only released his fair burden at the dining-room door; indeed, even there she was rather difficult to get rid of, remaining in his embrace to murmur, "Arthur for mercy's sake don't breathe it to papa!"

She accompanied Arthur into the room, where the Patriarch sat alone, with his list shoes on the fender, twirling his thumbs as if he had never left off. The youthful Patriarch, aged ten, looked out of his picture-frame above him, with no calmer air than he. Both smooth heads were alike beaming, blundering, and bumpy.

"Mr. Clennam, I am glad to see you. I hope you are well, sir, I hope you are well. Please to sit down, please to sit down."

"I had hoped, sir," said Clennam, doing so, and looking round with a face of blank disappointment, "not to find you alone."

"Ah, indeed?" said the Patriarch, sweetly. "Ah, indeed?"

"I told you so you know papa," cried Flora.

"Ah, to be sure!" returned the Patriarch. "Yes, just so. Ah, to be sure!"

"Pray, sir," demanded Clennam anxiously, "is Miss Wade gone?"

"Miss ——? Oh, you call her Wade," returned Mr. Casby. "Highly proper."

Arthur quickly returned, "What do you call her?"

"Wade," said Mr. Casby. "Oh, always Wade."

After looking at the philanthropic visage, and the long silky white hair for a few seconds, during which Mr. Casby twirled his thumbs, and smiled at the fire as if he were benevolently wishing it to burn him that he might forgive it, Arthur began:

"I beg your pardon, Mr. Casby——"

"Not so, not so," said the Patriarch, "not so."

"——But, Miss Wade had an attendant with her—a young woman brought up by friends of mine, over whom her influence is not considered very salutary, and to whom I should be glad to have the opportunity of giving the assurance that she has not yet forfeited the interest of those protectors."

"Really, really?" returned the Patriarch.

"Will you therefore be so good as to give me the address of Miss Wade?"

"Dear, dear, dear!" said the Patriarch, "how very unfortunate! If you had only sent in to me when they were here! I observed the young woman, Mr. Clennam. A fine full-colored young woman, Mr. Clennam, with very dark hair and very dark eyes. If I mistake not, if I mistake not?"

Arthur assented, and said once more with new expression, "If you will be so good as to give me the address."

"Dear, dear, dear!" exclaimed the Patriarch in sweet regret. "Tut, tut, tut! What a pity, what a pity! I have no address, sir. Miss Wade mostly lives abroad, Mr. Clennam. She has done so for some years, and she is (if I may say so of a fellow creature and a lady) fitful and uncertain to a fault, Mr. Clennam. I may not see her again for a long, long time. I may never see her again. What a pity, what a pity!"

Clennam saw, now, that he had as much hope of getting assistance out of the Portrait as out of the Patriarch; but he said nevertheless:

"Mr. Casby, could you, for the satisfaction of the friends I have mentioned, and under any obligation of secrecy that you may consider it your duty to impose, give me any information at all touching Miss Wade? I have seen her abroad, and I have seen her at home, but I know nothing of her. Could you give me any account of her whatever?"

"None," returned the Patriarch, shaking his big head with his utmost benevolence. "None at all. Dear, dear, dear! What a real pity that she stayed so short a time, and you delayed! As confidential agency business, agency business, I have occasionally paid this lady money; but what satisfaction is it to you, sir, to know that?"

"Truly none at all," said Clennam.

"Truly," assented the Patriarch, with a shining face as he philanthropically smiled at the fire, "none at all, sir. You hit the wise answer, Mr. Clennam. Truly, none at all, sir."

His turning of his smooth thumbs over one another as he sat there, was so typical to Clennam of the way in which he would make the subject revolve if it were pursued, never showing any new part of it nor allowing it to make the smallest advance, that it did much to help to convince him of his labor having been in vain. He might have taken any time to think about it, for Mr. Casby, well accustomed to get on anywhere by leaving everything to his bumps and his white hair, knew his strength to lie in silence. So there Casby sate, twirling and twirling, and making his polished head and forehead look largely benevolent in every knob.

With this spectacle before him, Arthur had risen to go, when from the inner Dock where the good ship Pancks was hove down when out in no cruising ground, the noise was heard of that steamer laboring towards them. It struck Arthur that the noise began demonstratively far off, as though Mr. Pancks sought to impress on any one who might happen to think about it, that he was working on from out of hearing.

Mr. Pancks and he shook hands, and the former brought his employer a letter or two to sign. Mr. Pancks in shaking hands merely scratched his eyebrow with his left forefinger and snorted once, but Clennam, who understood him better now than of old, comprehended that he had almost done for the evening and wished to say a word to him outside. Therefore, when he had taken his leave of Mr. Casby, and (which was a more difficult process) of Flora, he sauntered in the neighbourhood on Mr. Pancks's line of road.

He had waited but a short time when Mr. Pancks appeared. Mr. Pancks shaking hands again with another expressive snort, and taking off his hat to put his hair up, Arthur thought he received his cue to speak to him as one who knew pretty well what had just now passed. Therefore he said, without any preface:

"I suppose they were really gone, Pancks?"

"Yes," replied Pancks. "They were really gone."

"Does he know where to find that lady?"

"Can't say. I should think so."

Mr. Pancks did not? No, Mr. Pancks did not. Did Mr. Pancks know anything about her?

"I expect," rejoined that worthy, "I know as much about her, as she knows about herself. She is somebody's child—anybody's—nobody's. Put her in a room in London here with any six people old enough to be her parents, and her parents may be there for anything she knows. They may be in any house she sees, they may be in any churchyard she passes, she may run against 'em in any street, she may make chance acquaintances of 'em at any time; and never know it. She knows nothing about 'em. She knows nothing about any relative whatever. Never did. Never will."

"Mr. Casby could enlighten her, perhaps?"

"May be," said Pancks. "I expect so, but don't know. He has long had money (not overmuch as I make out) in trust to dole out to her when she can't do without it. Sometimes she's proud and won't touch it for a length of time; sometimes she's so poor that she must have it. She writhes under her life. A woman more angry, passionate, reckless, and revengeful never lived. She came for money to-night. Said she had peculiar occasion for it."

"I think," observed Clennam musing, "I by chance know what occasion —I mean into whose pocket the money is to go."

"Indeed?" said Pancks. "If it's a compact, I'd recommend that party to be exact in it. I wouldn't trust myself to that woman, young and handsome as she is, if I had wronged her; no, not for twice my proprietor's money! Unless," Pancks added as a saving clause, "I had a lingering illness on me, and wanted to get it over."

Arthur, hurriedly reviewing his own observation of her, found it to tally pretty nearly with Mr. Pancks's view.

"The wonder is to me," pursued Pancks, "that she has never done for my proprietor, as the only person connected with her story she can lay hold of. Mentioning that, I may tell you, between ourselves, that I am sometimes tempted to do for him myself."

Arthur started and said, "Dear me, Pancks, don't say that!"

"Understand me," said Pancks, extending five cropped coaly finger-nails on Arthur's arm; "I don't mean, cut his throat. But, by all that's precious, if he goes too far, I'll cut his hair!"

Having exhibited himself in the new light of enunciating this tremendous threat, Mr. Pancks, with a countenance of grave import, snorted several times and steamed away.

CHAPTER X

THE DREAMS OF MRS. FLINTWINCH THICKEN

The shady waiting-rooms of the Circumlocution Office, where he passed a good deal of time in company with various troublesome Convicts who were under sentence to be broken alive on that wheel, had afforded Arthur Clennam ample leisure, in three or four successive days, to exhaust the subject of his late glimpse of Miss Wade and Tattycoram. He had been able to make no more of it and no less of it, and in this unsatisfactory condition he was fain to leave it.

During this space he had not been to his mother's dismal old house. One of his customary evenings for repairing thither now coming round, he left his dwelling and his partner at nearly nine o'clock, and slowly walked in the direction of that grim home of his youth.

It always affected his imagination as wrathful, mysterious, and sad; and his imagination was sufficiently impressible to see the whole neighbourhood under some tinge of its dark shadow. As he went along, upon a dreary night, the dim streets by which he went seemed all depositories of oppressive secrets. The deserted counting-houses, with their secrets of books and papers locked up in chests and safes; the banking-houses, with their secrets of strong rooms and wells, the keys of which were in a very few secret pockets and a very few secret breasts; the secrets of all the dispersed grinders in the vast mill, among whom there were doubtless plunderers, forgers, and trust-betrayers of many sorts, whom the light of any day that dawned might reveal; he could have fancied that these things, in hiding, imparted a heaviness to the air. The shadow thickening and thickening as he approached its source, he thought of the secrets of the lonely church-vaults, where the people who had hoarded and secreted in iron coffers were in their turn similarly hoarded, not yet at rest from doing harm; and then of the secrets of the river, as it rolled its turbid tide between two frowning wildernesses of secrets, extending, thick and dense, for many miles, and warding off the free air and the free country swept by winds and wings of birds.

The shadow still darkening as he drew near the house, the melancholy room which his father had once occupied, haunted by the appealing face he had himself seen fade away with him when there was no other watcher by the bed, arose before his mind. Its close air was secret. The gloom, and must, and dust of the whole tenement, were secret. At the heart of it his mother presided, inflexible of face, indomitable of will, firmly holding all the secrets of her own and his father's life, and austerely opposing herself, front to front, to the great final secret of all life.

He had turned into the narrow and steep street from which the court or enclosure wherein the house stood opened, when another footstep turned into it behind him, and so close upon his own that he was jostled to the wall. As his mind was teeming with these thoughts, the encounter took him altogether unprepared, so that the other passenger had had time to say, boisterously, "Pardon! Not my fault!" and to pass on before the instant had elapsed which was requisite to his recovery of the realities about him.

When that moment had flashed away, he saw that the man striding on before him, was the man who had been so much in his mind during the last few days. It was no casual resemblance, helped out by the force of the impression the man had made upon him. It was the man; the man he had followed in company with the girl, and whom he had overheard talking to Miss Wade.

The street was a sharp descent and was crooked too, and the man (who although not drunk had the air of being flushed with some strong drink) went down it so fast that Clennam lost him as he looked at him. With no defined intention of following him, but with an impulse to keep the figure in view a little longer, Clennam quickened his pace to pass the twist in the street which hid him from his sight. On turning it, he saw the man no more.

Standing now, close to the gateway of his mother's house, he looked down the street: but it was empty. There was no projecting shadow large enough to obscure the man; there was no turning near that he could have taken; nor had there been any audible sound of the opening and closing of a door. Nevertheless, he concluded that the man must have had a key in his hand, and must have opened one of the many house-doors and gone in.

Ruminating on this strange chance and strange glimpse, he turned into the courtyard. As he looked, by mere habit, towards the feebly-lighted windows of his mother's room, his eyes encountered the figure he had just lost, standing against the iron railings of the little waste enclosure looking up at those windows, and laughing to himself. Some of the many vagrant cats who were always prowling about there by night, and who had taken fright at him, appeared to have stopped when he had stopped, and were looking at him with eyes by no means unlike his own from tops of walls and porches, and other safe points of pause. He had only halted for a moment to entertain himself thus; he immediately went forward, throwing the end of his cloak off his shoulder as he went, ascended the unevenly-sunken steps, and knocked a sounding knock at the door.

Clennam's surprise was not so absorbing but that he took his resolution without any incertitude. He went up to the door too, and ascended the steps too. His friend looked at him with a braggart air, and sang to himself:

"Who passes by this road so late?
          Compagnon de la Majolaine;
Who passes by this road so late?
          Always gay!"

After which he knocked again.

"You are impatient, sir," said Arthur.

"I am, sir. Death of my life, sir," returned the stranger, "it's my character to be impatient!"

The sound of Mistress Affery cautiously chaining the door before she opened it, caused them both to look that way. Affery opened it a very little, with a flaring candle in her hands, and asked who was that, at that time of night with that knock? "Why, Arthur!" she added with astonishment, seeing him first. "Not you, sure? Ah, Lord save us! No," she cried out, seeing the other. "Him again!"

"It's true! Him again, dear Mrs. Flintwinch," cried the stranger. "Open the door, and let me take my dear friend Jeremiah to my arms! Open the door, and let me hasten myself to embrace my Flintwinch!"

"He's not at home," said Affery.

"Fetch him!" cried the stranger. "Fetch my Flintwinch! Tell him that it is his old Blandois, who comes from arriving in England; tell him that it is his little boy who is here, his cabbage, his well-beloved! Open the door, beautiful Mrs. Flintwinch, and in the meantime let me to pass up-stairs, to present my compliments—homage of Blandois—to my lady! My lady lives always? It is well. Open then!"

To Arthur's increased surprise, Mistress Affery, stretching her eyes wide at himself, as if in warning that this was not a gentleman for him to interfere with, drew back the chain, and opened the door. The stranger, without any ceremony, walked into the hall, leaving Arthur to follow him.

"Dispatch then! Achieve then! Bring my Flintwinch! Announce me to my lady!" cried the stranger, clanking about the stone floor.

"Pray tell me, Affery," said Arthur, aloud and sternly, as he surveyed him from head to foot with indignation; "who is this gentleman?"

"Pray tell me, Affery," the stranger repeated in his turn, "who—ha, ha, ha!—who is this gentleman?"

The voice of Mrs. Clennam opportunely called from her chamber above, "Affery, let them both come up. Arthur, come straight to me!"

"Arthur?" exclaimed Blandois, taking off his hat at arm's length, and bringing his heels together from a great stride in making him a flourishing bow. "The son of my lady? I am the all-devoted of the son of my lady!"

Arthur looked at him again in no more flattering manner than before, and, turning on his heel without acknowledgment, went up-stairs. The visitor followed him up-stairs. Mistress Affery took the key from behind the door, and deftly slipped out to fetch her lord.

A bystander, informed of the previous appearance of Monsieur Blandois in that room, would have observed a difference in Mrs. Clennam's present reception of him. Her face was not one to betray it; and her suppressed manner, and her set voice, were equally under her control. It wholly consisted in her never taking her eyes off his face from the moment of his entrance, and in her twice or thrice, when he was becoming noisy, swaying herself a very little forward in the chair in which she sat upright, with her hands immovable upon its elbows; as if she gave him the assurance that he should be presently heard at any length he would. Arthur did not fail to observe this; though the difference between the present occasion and the former was not within his power of observation.

"Madame," said Blandois, "do me the honor to present me to Monsieur, your son. It appears to me, madame, that Monsieur, your son, is disposed to complain of me. He is not polite."

"Sir," said Arthur, striking in expeditiously, "whoever you are, and however you come to be here, if I were the master of this house I would lose no time in placing you on the outside of it."

"But you are not," said his mother, without looking at him. "Unfortunately for the gratification of your unreasonable temper, you are not the master, Arthur."

"I make no claim to be, mother. If I object to this person's manner of conducting himself here, and object to it so much, that if I had any authority here I certainly would not suffer him to remain a minute, I object on your account."

"In the case of objection being necessary," she returned, "I could object for myself. And of course I should."

The subject of their dispute, who had seated himself, laughed loud, and rapped his leg with his hand.

"You have no right," said Mrs. Clennam, always intent on Blandois, however directly she addressed her son, "to speak to the prejudice of any gentleman (least of all a gentleman from another country), because he does not conform to your standard, or square his behaviour by your rules. It is possible that the gentleman may, on similar grounds, object to you."

"I hope so," returned Arthur.

"The gentleman," pursued Mrs. Clennam, "on a former occasion brought a letter of recommendation to us from highly esteemed and responsible correspondents. I am perfectly unacquainted with the gentleman's object in coming here at present. I am entirely ignorant of it, and cannot be supposed likely to be able to form the remotest guess at its nature;" her habitual frown became stronger, as she very slowly and weightily emphasised those words; "but, when the gentleman proceeds to explain his object, as I shall beg him to have the goodness to do to myself and Flintwinch, when Flintwinch returns, it will prove, no doubt, to be one more or less in the usual way of our business, which it will be both our business and our pleasure to advance. It can be nothing else."

"We shall see, madame!" said the man of business.

"We shall see," she assented. "The gentleman is acquainted with Flintwinch; and when the gentleman was in London last, I remember to have heard that he and Flintwinch had some entertainment or good-fellowship together. I am not in the way of knowing much that passes outside this room, and the jingle of little worldly things beyond it does not much interest me; but I remember to have heard that."

"Right, madame. It is true." He laughed again, and whistled the burden of the tune he had sung at the door.

"Therefore, Arthur," said his mother, "the gentleman comes here as an acquaintance, and no stranger; and it is much to be regretted that your unreasonable temper should have found offence in him. I regret it. I say so to the gentleman. You will not say so, I know; therefore I say it for myself and Flintwinch, since with us two the gentleman's business lies."

The key of the door below was now heard in the lock, and the door was heard to open and close. In due sequence Mr. Flintwinch appeared; on whose entrance the visitor rose from his chair laughing loud, and folded him in a close embrace.

"How goes it, my cherished friend!" said he. "How goes the world, my Flintwinch? Rose-colored? So much the better, so much the better! Ah, but you look charming! Ah, but you look young and fresh as the flowers of Spring! Ah, good little boy! Brave child, brave child!"

While heaping these compliments on Mr. Flintwinch, he rolled him about with a hand on each of his shoulders, until the staggerings of that gentleman, who under the circumstances was dryer and more twisted than ever, were like those of a teetotum nearly spent.

"I had a presentiment, last time, that we should be better and more intimately acquainted. Is it coming on you, Flintwinch? Is it yet coming on?"

"Why, no, sir," retorted Mr. Flintwinch. "Not unusually. Hadn't you better be seated? You have been calling for some more of that port, sir, I guess?"

"Ah! Little joker! Little pig!" cried the visitor. "Ha ha ha ha!" And throwing Mr. Flintwinch away, as a closing piece of raillery, he sat down again.

The amazement, suspicion, resentment, and shame, with which Arthur looked on at all this, struck him dumb. Mr. Flintwinch, who had spun backward some two or three yards under the impetus last given to him, brought himself up with a face completely unchanged in its stolidity except as it was affected by shortness of breath, and looked hard at Arthur. Not a whit less reticent and wooden was Mr. Flintwinch outwardly, than in the usual course of things: the only perceptible difference in him being that the knot of cravat which was generally under his ear, had worked round to the back of his head: where it formed an ornamental appendage, not unlike a bag-wig, and gave him something of a courtly appearance.

As Mrs. Clennam never removed her eyes from Blandois (on whom they had some effect, as a steady look has on a lower sort of dog), so Jeremiah never removed his from Arthur. It was as if they had tacitly agreed to take their different provinces. Thus, in the ensuing silence, Jeremiah stood scraping his chin and looking at Arthur, as though he were trying to screw his thoughts out of him with an instrument.

After a little, the visitor, as if he felt the silence irksome, rose, and impatiently put himself with his back to the sacred fire which had burned through so many years. Thereupon Mrs. Clennam said, moving one of her hands for the first time, and moving it very slightly with an action of dismissal:

"Please to leave us to our business, Arthur."

"Mother, I do so with reluctance."

"Never mind with what," she returned, "or with what not. Please to leave us. Come back at any other time when you may consider it a duty to bury half an hour wearily here. Good night."

She held up her muffled fingers that he might touch them with his, according to their usual custom, and he stooped over her wheeled chair to touch her face with his lips. He thought, then, that her cheek was more strained than usual, and that it was colder. As he followed the direction of her eyes, in rising again, towards Mr. Flintwinch's good friend, Mr. Blandois, Mr. Blandois snapped his finger and thumb with one loud contemptuous snap.

"I leave your—your business acquaintance in my mother's room, Mr. Flintwinch," said Clennam, "with a great deal of surprise and a great deal of unwillingness."

The person referred to snapped his finger and thumb again.

"Good night, mother."

"Good night."

"I had a friend once, my good comrade Flintwinch," said Blandois, standing astride before the fire, and so evidently saying it to arrest Clennam's retreating steps, that he lingered near the door; "I had a friend once, who had heard so much of the dark side of this city and its ways, that he wouldn't have confided himself alone by night with two people who had an interest in getting him under the ground—my faith! not even in a respectable house like this—unless he was bodily too strong for them. Bah! What a poltroon, my Flintwinch! Eh?"

"A cur, sir."

"Agreed! A cur. But he wouldn't have done it, my Flintwinch, unless he had known them to have the will to silence him, without the power. He wouldn't have drunk from a glass of water, under such circumstances—not even in a respectable house like this, my Flintwinch—unless he had seen one of them drink first, and swallow too!"

Disdaining to speak, and indeed not very well able, for he was half-choking, Clennam only glanced at the visitor as he passed out. The visitor saluted him with another parting snap, and his nose came down over his moustache and his moustache went up under his nose, in an ominous and ugly smile.

"For Heaven's sake, Affery," whispered Clennam, as she opened the door for him in the dark hall, and he groped his way to the sight of the night-sky, "what is going on here?"

Her own appearance was sufficiently ghastly, standing in the dark with her apron thrown over her head, and speaking behind it in a low, deadened voice.

"Don't ask me anything, Arthur. I've been in a dream for ever so long. Go away!"

He went out, and she shut the door upon him. He looked up at the windows of his mother's room, and the dim light, deadened by the yellow blinds, seemed to say a response after Affery, and to mutter, "Don't ask me anything. Go away!"

CHAPTER XI

A LETTER FROM LITTLE DORRIT

DEAR MR. CLENNAM.

As I said in my last that it was best for nobody to write to me, and as my sending you another little letter can therefore give you no other trouble than the trouble of reading it (perhaps you may not find leisure for even that, though I hope you will some day), I am now going to devote an hour to writing to you again. This time, I write from Rome.

We left Venice before Mr. and Mrs. Gowan did, but they were not so long upon the road as we were, and did not travel by the same way, and so when we arrived we found them in a lodging here, in a place called the Via Gregoriana. I dare say you know it.

Now, I am going to tell you all I can about them, because I know that is what you most want to hear. Theirs is not a very comfortable lodging, but perhaps I thought it less so when I first saw it than you would have done, because you have been in many countries and have seen many different customs. Of course it is a far, far better place—millions of times—than any I have ever been used to until lately; and I fancy I don't look at it with my own eyes, but with hers. For it would be easy to see that she has always been brought up in a tender and happy home, even if she had not told me so with great love for it.

Well, it is a rather bare lodging up a rather dark common staircase, and it is nearly all a large dull room, where Mr. Gowan paints. The windows are blocked up where any one could look out, and the walls have been all drawn over with chalk and charcoal by others who have lived there before—oh, I should think, for years! There is a curtain more dust-colored than red, which divides it, and the part behind the curtain makes the private sitting-room. When I first saw her there she was alone, and her work had fallen out of her hand, and she was looking up at the sky shining through the tops of the windows. Pray do not be uneasy when I tell you, but it was not quite so airy, nor so bright, nor so cheerful, nor so happy and youthful altogether as I should have liked it to be.

On account of Mr. Gowan painting Papa's picture (which I am not quite convinced I should have known from the likeness if I had not seen him doing it), I have had more opportunities of being with her since then, than I might have had without this fortunate chance. She is very much alone. Very much alone indeed.

Shall I tell you about the second time I saw her? I went one day, when it happened that I could run round by myself, at four or five o'clock in the afternoon. She was then dining alone, and her solitary dinner had been brought in from somewhere, over a kind of brazier with a fire in it, and she had no company or prospect of company, that I could see, but the old man who had brought it. He was telling her a long story (of robbers outside the walls, being taken up by a stone statue of a Saint), to entertain her—as he said to me when I came out, "because he had a daughter of his own, though she was not so pretty."

I ought now to mention Mr. Gowan, before I say what little more I have to say about her. He must admire her beauty, and he must be proud of her, for everybody praises it, and he must be fond of her, and I do not doubt that he is—but in his way. You know his way, and if it appears as careless and discontented in your eyes as it does in mine, I am not wrong in thinking that it might be better suited to her. If it does not seem so to you, I am quite sure I am wholly mistaken; for your unchanged poor child confides in your knowledge and goodness more than she could ever tell you, if she was to try. But don't be frightened, I am not going to try.

Owing (as I think, if you think so, too) to Mr. Gowan's unsettled and dissatisfied way, he applies himself to his profession very little. He does nothing steadily or patiently; but equally takes things up and throws them down, and does them, or leaves them undone, without caring about them. When I have heard him talking to Papa during the sittings for the picture, I have sat wondering whether it could be that he has no belief in anybody else, because he has no belief in himself. Is it so? I wonder what you will say when you come to this! I know how you will look, and I can almost hear the voice in which you would tell me on the Iron Bridge.

Mr. Gowan goes out a good deal among what is considered the best company here—though he does not look as if he enjoyed it or liked it when he is with it—and she sometimes accompanies him, but lately she has gone out very little. I think I have noticed that they have an inconsistent way of

speaking about her, as if she had made some great self-interested success
in marrying Mr. Gowan, though, at the same time, the very same people
would not have dreamed of taking him for themselves or their daughters.
Then he goes into the country besides, to think about making sketches;
and in all places where there are visitors, he has a large acquaintance and
is very well known. Besides all this, he has a friend who is much in his
society both at home and away from home, though he treats this friend
very coolly and is very uncertain in his behaviour to him. I am quite sure
(because she has told me so), that she does not like this friend. He is so
revolting to me, too, that his being away from here, at present, is quite
a relief to my mind. How much more to hers!

But what I particularly want you to know, and why I have resolved to
tell you so much even while I am afraid it may make you a little uncomfortable without occasion, is this. She is so true and so devoted, and knows
so completely that all her love and duty are his for ever, that you may be
certain she will love him, admire him, praise him, and conceal all his faults,
until she dies. I believe she conceals them, and always will conceal them,
even from herself. She has given him a heart that can never be taken back;
and however much he may try it, he will never wear out its affection. You
know the truth of this, as you know everything, far far better than I; but
I cannot help telling you what a nature she shows, and that you can never
think too well of her.

I have not yet called her by her name in this letter, but we are such
friends now that I do so when we are quietly together, and she speaks to
me by my name—I mean, not my Christian name, but the name you gave
me. When she began to call me Amy, I told her my short story, and that
you had always called me Little Dorrit. I told her that the name was much
dearer to me than any other, and so she calls me Little Dorrit too.

Perhaps you have not heard from her father or mother yet, and may not
know that she has a baby son. He was born only two days ago, and just
a week after they came. It has made them very happy. However, I must tell
you, as I am to tell you all, that I fancy they are under a constraint with
Mr. Gowan, and that they feel as if his mocking way with them was sometimes a slight given to their love for her. It was but yesterday when I was
there, that I saw Mr. Meagles change color, and get up and go out, as if he
was afraid that he might say so, unless he prevented himself by that means.
Yet I am sure they are both so considerate, good-humoured, and reasonable,
that he might spare them. It is hard in him not to think of them a
little more.

I stopped at the last full-stop to read all this over. It looked at first as
if I was taking on myself to understand and explain so much, that I was
half inclined not to send it. But when I had thought it over a little, I felt
more hopeful of your knowing at once that I had only been watchful for
you, and had only noticed what I think I have noticed because I was

quickened by your interest in it. Indeed, you may be sure that is the truth.

And now I have done with this subject in the present letter, and have little left to say.

We are all quite well, and Fanny improves every day. You can hardly think how kind she is to me, and what pains she takes with me. She has a lover, who has followed her, first all the way from Switzerland, and then all the way from Venice, and who has just confided to me that he means to follow her everywhere. I was much confused by his speaking to me about it, but he would. I did not know what to say, but at last I told him that I thought he had better not. For Fanny (but I did not tell him this) is much too spirited and clever to suit him. Still, he said he would, all the same. I have no lover, of course.

If you should ever get so far as this in this long letter, you will perhaps say, Surely Little Dorrit will not leave off without telling me something about her travels, and surely it is time she did. I think it is indeed, but I don't know what to tell you. Since we left Venice we have been in a great many wonderful places, Genoa and Florence among them, and have seen so many wonderful sights, that I am almost giddy when I think what a crowd they make. But you could tell me so much more about them than I can tell you, that why should I tire you with my accounts and descriptions?

Dear Mr. Clennam, as I had the courage to tell you what the familiar difficulties in my travelling mind were before, I will not be a coward now. One of my frequent thoughts is this:—Old as these cities are, their age itself is hardly so curious, to my reflections, as that they should have been in their places all through those days when I did not even know of the existence of more than two or three of them, and when I scarcely knew of anything outside our old walls. There is something melancholy in it, and I don't know why. When we went to see the famous leaning tower at Pisa, it was a bright sunny day, and it and the buildings near it looked so old, and the earth and sky looked so young, and its shadow on the ground was so soft and retired! I could not at first think how beautiful it was, or how curious, but I thought, "O how many times when the shadow of the wall was falling on our room, and when that weary tread of feet was going up and down the yard—O how many times this place was just as quiet and lovely as it is to-day!" It quite overpowered me. My heart was so full, that tears burst out of my eyes, though I did what I could to restrain them. And I have the same feeling often—often.

Do you know that since the change in our fortunes, though I appear to myself to have dreamed more than before, I have always dreamed of myself as very young indeed? I am not very old, you may say. No, but that is not what I mean. I have always dreamed of myself as a child learning to do needlework. I have often dreamed of myself as back there, seeing faces in the yard little known, and which I should have thought I had quite forgotten; but, as often as not, I have been abroad here—in Switzerland, or France, or Italy—somewhere where we have been—yet always as that little child. I have dreamed of going down to Mrs. General, with the patches on my clothes in which I can first remember myself. I have over and over again dreamed of taking my place at dinner at Venice when we have had a large company, in the mourning for my poor mother which I wore when I was eight years old, and wore long after it was threadbare and would mend no more. It has been a great distress to me to think how irreconcileable the company would consider it with my father's wealth, and how I should displease and disgrace him and Fanny and Edward by so plainly disclosing what they wished to keep secret. But I have not grown out of the little child in thinking of it; and at the self-same moment I have dreamed that I have sat with the heart-ache at table, calculating the expenses of the dinner, and quite distracting myself with thinking how they were ever to be made good. I have never dreamed of the change in our fortunes itself; I have never dreamed of your coming back with me that memorable morning to break it; I have never even dreamed of you.

Dear Mr. Clennam, it is possible that I have thought of you—and others—so much by day, that I have had no thoughts left to wander round you by night. For I must now confess to you that I suffer from home-sickness—that I long so ardently and earnestly for home, as sometimes, when no one sees me, to pine for it. I cannot bear to turn my face further away from it. My heart is a little lightened when we turn towards it, even for a few miles, and with the knowledge that we are soon to turn away again. So dearly do I love the scene of my poverty and your kindness. O so dearly, O so dearly!

Heaven knows when your poor child will see England again. We are all fond of the life here (except me), and there are no plans for our return. My dear father talks of a visit to London late in this next spring, on some affairs connected with the property, but I have no hope that he will bring me with him.

I have tried to get on a little better under Mrs. General's instruction, and I hope I am not quite so dull as I used to be. I have begun to speak and understand, almost easily, the hard languages I told you about. I did not remember, at the moment when I wrote last, that you know them both; but I remembered it afterwards, and it helped me on. God bless you, dear Mr. Clennam. Do not forget

Your ever grateful and affectionate

LITTLE DORRIT.

P.S. Particularly remember that Minnie Gowan deserves the best remembrance in which you can hold her. You cannot think too generously or too highly of her. I forgot Mr. Pancks last time. Please, if you should see him, give him your Little Dorrit's kind regard. He was very good to Little D.

END OF No. XIII

CHAPTER XII

IN WHICH A GREAT PATRIOTIC CONFERENCE IS HOLDEN

THE famous name of Merdle became, every day, more famous in the land. Nobody knew that the Merdle of such high renown had ever done any good to any one, alive or dead, or to any earthly thing; nobody knew that he had any capacity or utterance of any sort in him, which had ever thrown, for any creature, the feeblest farthing-candle ray of light on any path of duty or diversion, pain or pleasure, toil or rest, fact or fancy, among the multiplicity of paths in the labyrinth trodden by the sons of Adam; nobody had the smallest reason for supposing the clay of which this object of worship was made, to be other than the commonest clay, with as clogged a wick smouldering inside of it as ever kept an image of humanity from tumbling to pieces. All people knew (or thought they knew) that he had made himself immensely rich; and, for that reason alone, prostrated themselves before him, more degradedly and less excusably than the darkest savage creeps out of his hole in the ground to propitiate, in some log or reptile, the Deity of his benighted soul.

Nay, the high priests of this worship had the man before them as a protest against their meanness. The multitude worshipped on trust—though always distinctly knowing why—but the officiators at the altar had the man habitually in their view. They sat at his feasts, and he sat at theirs. There was a spectre always attendant on him, saying to these high priests, "Are such the signs you trust, and love to honor; this head, these eyes, this mode of speech, the tone and manner of this man? You are the levers of the Circumlocution Office, and the rulers of men. When half a dozen of you fall out by the ears, it seems that mother earth can give birth to no other rulers. Does your qualification lie in the superior knowledge of men, which accepts, courts, and puffs this man? Or, if you are competent to judge aright the signs I never fail to show you when he appears among you, is your superior honesty your qualification?" Two rather ugly questions these, always going about town with Mr. Merdle; and there was a tacit agreement that they must be stifled.

In Mrs. Merdle's absence abroad, Mr. Merdle still kept the great house open, for the passage through it of a stream of visitors. A few of these took affable possession of the establishment. Three or four ladies of distinction and liveliness used to say to one another, "Let us dine at our dear Merdle's next Thursday. Whom shall we have?" Our dear Merdle would then receive his instructions; and would sit heavily among the company at table and wander lumpishly about his drawing-rooms afterwards, only remarkable for appearing to have nothing to do with the entertainment beyond being in its way.

The Chief Butler, the Avenging-Spirit of this great man's life, relaxed nothing of his severity. He looked on at these dinners when the bosom was not there, as he looked on at other dinners when the bosom was there; and his eye was a basilisk to Mr. Merdle. He was a hard man, and would never bate an ounce of plate or a bottle of wine. He would not allow a dinner to be given, unless it was up to his mark. He set forth the table for his own dignity. If the guests chose to partake of what was served, he saw no objection; but it was served for the maintenance of his rank. As he stood by the sideboard he seemed to announce, "I have accepted office to look at this which is now before me, and to look at nothing less than this." If he missed the presiding bosom, it was as a part of his own state of which he was, from unavoidable circumstances, temporarily deprived. Just as he might have missed a centre-piece, or a choice wine-cooler, which had been sent to the Banker's.

Mr. Merdle issued invitations for a Barnacle dinner. Lord Decimus was to be there, Mr. Tite Barnacle was to be there, the pleasant young Barnacle was to be there; and the Chorus of Parliamentary Barnacles who went about the provinces when the House was up, warbling the praises of their Chief, were to be represented there. It was understood to be a great occasion. Mr. Merdle was going to take up the Barnacles. Some delicate little negociations had occurred between him and the noble Decimus—the young Barnacle of engaging manners acting as negociator—and Mr. Merdle had decided to cast the weight of his great probity and great riches into the Barnacle scale. Jobbery was suspected by the malicious; perhaps because it was indisputable that if the adherence of the immortal Enemy of Mankind could have been secured by a job, the Barnacles would have jobbed him—for the good of the country, for the good of the country.

Mrs. Merdle had written to this magnificent spouse of hers, whom it was heresy to regard as anything less than all the British Merchants since the days of Whittington rolled into one, and gilded three feet deep all over—had written to this spouse of hers, several letters from Rome, in quick succession, urging upon him with importunity that now or never was the time to provide for Edmund Sparkler. Mrs. Merdle had shown him that the case of Edmund was urgent, and that infinite advantages might result from his having some good thing directly. In the grammar of Mrs. Merdle's verbs on this momentous subject, there was only one Mood, the Imperative; and that Mood has only one Tense, the Present. Mrs. Merdle's verbs were so pressingly presented to Mr. Merdle to conjugate, that his sluggish blood and his long coat-cuffs became quite agitated.

In which state of agitation, Mr. Merdle, evasively rolling his eyes round the Chief Butler's shoes without raising them to the index of that stupendous creature's thoughts, had signified to him his intention of giving a special dinner: not a very large dinner, but a very special dinner. The Chief Butler had signified, in return, that he had no objection to look on at the most expensive thing in that way that could be done: and the day of the dinner was now come.

Mr. Merdle stood in one of his drawing-rooms, with his back to the fire, waiting for the arrival of his important guests. He seldom or never took the liberty of standing with his back to his fire, unless he was quite alone. In the presence of the Chief Butler, he could not have done such a deed. He would have clasped himself by the wrists in that constabulary manner of his, and have paced up and down the hearthrug, or gone creeping about among the rich objects of furniture, if his oppressive retainer had appeared in the room at that very moment. The sly shadows which seemed to dart out of hiding when the fire rose, and to dart back into it when the fire fell, were sufficient witnesses of his making himself so easy. They were even more than sufficient, if his uncomfortable glances at them might be taken to mean anything.

Mr. Merdle's right hand was filled with the evening paper, and the evening paper was full of Mr. Merdle. His wonderful enterprise, his wonderful wealth, his wonderful Bank, were the fattening food of the evening paper that night. The wonderful Bank, of which he was the chief projector, establisher, and manager, was the latest of the many Merdle wonders. So modest was Mr. Merdle withal, in the midst of these splendid achievements, that he looked far more like a man in possession of his house under a distraint, than a commercial Colossus bestriding his own hearthrug, while the little ships were sailing in to dinner.

Behold the vessels coming into port! The engaging young Barnacle was the first arrival; but Bar overtook him on the staircase. Bar, strengthened as usual with his double eye-glass and his little jury droop, was overjoyed to see the engaging young Barnacle; and opined that we were going to sit *in Banco*, as we lawyers called it, to take a special argument?

"Indeed," said the sprightly young Barnacle, whose name was Ferdinand: "how so?"

"Nay," smiled Bar. "If *you* don't know, how can *I* know? *You* are in the innermost sanctuary of the temple; *I* am one of the admiring concourse on the plain without."

Bar could be light in hand, or heavy in hand, according to the customer he had to deal with. With Ferdinand Barnacle he was gossamer. Bar was likewise always modest and self-depreciatory—in his way. Bar was a man of great variety; but one leading thread ran through the woof of all his patterns. Every man with whom he had to do was, in his eyes, a juryman; and he must get that juryman over, if he could.

"Our illustrious host and friend," said Bar; "our shining mercantile star; —going into politics?"

"Going? He has been in Parliament some time, you know," returned the engaging young Barnacle.

"True," said Bar, with his light-comedy laugh for special jurymen: which was a very different thing from his low-comedy laugh for comic tradesmen on common juries: "he has been in Parliament for some time. Yet hitherto our star has been a vacillating and wavering star? Humph?"

An average witness would have been seduced by the Humph? into an affirmative answer. But Ferdinand Barnacle looked knowingly at Bar as they strolled up-stairs, and gave him no answer at all.

"Just so, just so," said Bar, nodding his head, for he was not to be put off in that way, "and therefore I spoke of our sitting *in Banco* to take a special argument—meaning this to be a high and solemn occasion, when, as Captain Macheath says, 'the Judges are met: a terrible show!' We lawyers are sufficiently liberal, you see, to quote the Captain, though the Captain is severe upon us. Nevertheless, I think I could put in evidence an admission of the Captain's," said Bar, with a little jocose roll of his head; for, in his legal current of speech, he always assumed the air of rallying himself with the best grace in the world; "an admission of the Captain's that Law, in the gross, is at least intended to be impartial. For, what says the Captain, if I quote him correctly—and if not," with a light-comedy touch of his double eye-glass on his companion's shoulder, "my learned friend will set me right:

> 'Since laws were made for every degree,
> To curb vice in others as well as in me,
> I wonder we ha'n't better company
> Upon Tyburn Tree!'"

These words brought them to the drawing-room, where Mr. Merdle stood before the fire. So immensely astounded was Mr. Merdle by the entrance of Bar with such a reference in his mouth, that Bar explained himself to have been quoting Gay. "Assuredly not one of our Westminster Hall authorities," said he, "but still no despicable one to a man possessing the largely-practical Mr. Merdle's knowledge of the world."

Mr. Merdle looked as if he thought he would say something, but subsequently looked as if he thought he wouldn't. The interval afforded time for Bishop to be announced.

Bishop came in with meekness, and yet with a strong and rapid step, as if he wanted to get his seven-league dress-shoes on, and go round the world to see that everybody was in a satisfactory state. Bishop had no idea that there was anything significant in the occasion. That was the most remarkable trait in his demeanour. He was crisp, fresh, cheerful, affable, bland; but so surprisingly innocent!

Bar slided up to prefer his politest enquiries in reference to the health of Mrs. Bishop. Mrs. Bishop had been a little unfortunate in the article of taking cold at a Confirmation, but otherwise was well. Young Mr. Bishop was also well. He was down, with his young wife and little family, at his Cure of Souls.

The representatives of the Barnacle Chorus dropped in next, and Mr.

Merdle's physician dropped in next. Bar, who had a bit of one eye and a bit of his double eye-glass for every one who came in at the door, no matter with whom he was conversing or what he was talking about, got among them all by some skilful means, without being seen to get at them, and touched each individual gentleman of the jury on his own individual favorite spot. With some of the Chorus, he laughed about the sleepy member who had gone out into the lobby the other night, and voted the wrong way : with others, he deplored that innovating spirit in the time which could not even be prevented from taking an unnatural interest in the public service and the public money : with the physician he had a word to say about the general health ; he had also a little information to ask him for, concerning a professional man, of unquestioned erudition and polished manners—but those credentials in their highest development he believed were the possession of other professors of the healing art (jury droop)—whom he had happened to have in the witness-box the day before yesterday, and from whom he had elicited in cross-examination that he claimed to be one of the exponents of this new mode of treatment which appeared to Bar to—eh ?—well, Bar thought so ; Bar had thought, and hoped, Physician would tell him so. Without presuming to decide where doctors disagreed, it did appear to Bar, viewing it as a question of common sense and not of so-called legal penetration, that this new system was—might he, in the presence of so great an authority—say, Humbug ? Ah ! Fortified by such encouragement, he could venture to say Humbug ; and now Bar's mind was relieved.

Mr. Tite Barnacle, who, like Dr. Johnson's celebrated acquaintance, had only one idea in his head, and that was a wrong one, had appeared by this time. This eminent gentleman and Mr. Merdle, seated diverse ways and with ruminating aspects, on a yellow ottoman in the light of the fire, holding no verbal communication with each other, bore a strong general resemblance to the two cows in the Cuyp picture over against them.

But, now, Lord Decimus arrived. The Chief Butler, who up to this time had limited himself to a branch of his usual function by looking at the company as they entered (and that, with more of defiance than favor), put himself so far out of his way as to come up-stairs with him and announce him. Lord Decimus being an overpowering peer, a bashful young member of the Lower House, who was the last fish but one caught by the Barnacles and who had been invited on this occasion to commemorate his capture, shut his eyes when his Lordship came in.

Lord Decimus nevertheless was glad to see the Member. He was also glad to see Mr. Merdle, glad to see Bishop, glad to see Bar, glad to see Physician, glad to see Tite Barnacle, glad to see Chorus, glad to see Ferdinand his private secretary. Lord Decimus, though one of the greatest of the earth, was not remarkable for ingratiatory manners, and Ferdinand had coached him up to the point of noticing all the fellows he might find there, and saying he was glad to see them. When he had achieved this rush of vivacity and condescension, his Lordship composed himself into the picture after Cuyp, and made a third cow in the group.

Bar, who felt that he had got all the rest of the jury and must now lay hold of the Foreman, soon came sliding up, double eye-glass in hand. Bar tendered the weather, as a subject neatly aloof from official reserve, for the Foreman's consideration. Bar said that he was told (as everybody always is told, though who tells them, and why, will for ever remain a mystery), that there was to be no wall-fruit this year. Lord Decimus had not heard anything amiss of his peaches, but rather believed, if his people were correct, he was to have no apples. No apples? Bar was lost in astonishment and concern. It would have been all one to him, in reality, if there had not been a pippin on the surface of the earth, but his show of interest in this apple question was positively painful. Now, to what, Lord Decimus—for we troublesome lawyers loved to gather information, and could never tell how useful it might prove to us—to what, Lord Decimus, was this to be attributed? Lord Decimus could not undertake to propound any theory about it. This might have stopped another man; but, Bar sticking to him fresh as ever, said, "As to pears, now?"

Long after Bar got made Attorney-General, this was told of him as a master-stroke. Lord Decimus had a reminiscence about a pear-tree, formerly growing in a garden near the back of his dame's house at Eton, upon which pear-tree the only joke of his life perennially bloomed. It was a joke of a compact and portable nature, turning on the difference between Eton pears and Parliamentary pairs; but, it was a joke, a refined relish of which would seem to have appeared to Lord Decimus impossible to be had, without a thorough and intimate acquaintance with the tree. Therefore, the story at first had no idea of such a tree, sir, then gradually found it in winter, carried it through the changing seasons, saw it bud, saw it blossom, saw it bear fruit, saw the fruit ripen, in short cultivated the tree in that diligent and minute manner before it got out of the bed-room window to steal the fruit, that many thanks had been offered up by belated listeners for the tree's having been planted and grafted prior to Lord Decimus's time. Bar's interest in apples was so over-topped by the rapt suspense with which he pursued the changes of these pears, from the moment when Lord Decimus solemnly opened with "Your mentioning pears recalls to my remembrance a pear-tree," down to the rich conclusion, "And so we pass, through the various changes of life, from Eton pears to Parliamentary pairs," that he had to go down-stairs with Lord Decimus, and even then to be seated next to him at table, in order that he might hear the anecdote out. By that time, Bar felt that he had secured the Foreman, and might go to dinner with a good appetite.

It was a dinner to provoke an appetite, though he had not had one. The rarest dishes, sumptuously cooked and sumptuously served; the choicest fruits; the most exquisite wines; marvels of workmanship in gold and silver, china and glass; innumerable things delicious to the senses of taste, smell, and sight, were insinuated into its composition. O, what a wonderful man this Merdle, what a great man, what a master man, how blessedly and enviably endowed—in one word, what a rich man!

He took his usual poor eighteenpennyworth of food, in his usual indigestive way, and had as little to say for himself as ever a wonderful man had. Fortunately Lord Decimus was one of those sublimities who have no occasion to be talked to, for they can be at any time sufficiently occupied with the contemplation of their own greatness. This enabled the bashful young member to keep his eyes open long enough at a time to see his dinner. But, whenever Lord Decimus spoke, he shut them again.

The agreeable young Barnacle, and Bar, were the talkers of the party. Bishop would have been exceedingly agreeable also, but that his innocence stood in his way. He was so soon left behind. When there was any little hint of anything being in the wind, he got lost directly. Worldly affairs were too much for him; he couldn't make them out at all.

This was observable when Bar said, incidentally, that he was happy to have heard that we were soon to have the advantage of enlisting on the good side, the sound and plain sagacity—not demonstrative or ostentatious, but thoroughly sound and practical—of our friend Mr. Sparkler.

Ferdinand Barnacle laughed, and said oh yes, he believed so. A vote was a vote, and always acceptable.

Bar was sorry to miss our good friend Mr. Sparkler to-day, Mr. Merdle.

"He is away with Mrs. Merdle," returned that gentleman, slowly coming out of a long abstraction, in the course of which he had been fitting a table-spoon up his sleeve. "It is not indispensable for him to be on the spot."

"The magic name of Merdle," said Bar, with the jury droop, "no doubt will suffice for all."

"Why—yes—I believe so," assented Mr. Merdle, putting the spoon aside, and clumsily hiding each of his hands in the coat-cuff of the other hand. "I believe the people in my interest down there, will not make any difficulty."

"Model people!" said Bar.

"I am glad you approve of them," said Mr. Merdle.

"And the people of those other two places, now," pursued Bar, with a bright twinkle in his keen eye, as it slightly turned in the direction of his magnificent neighbour; "we lawyers are always curious, always inquisitive, always picking up odds and ends for our patchwork minds, since there is no knowing when and where they may fit into some corner;—the people of those other two places, now? Do they yield so laudably to the vast and cumulative influence of such enterprise and such renown; do those little rills become absorbed so quietly and easily, and, as it were by the influence of natural laws, so beautifully, in the swoop of the majestic stream as it flows upon its wondrous way enriching the surrounding lands; that their course is perfectly to be calculated, and distinctly to be predicated?"

Mr. Merdle, a little troubled by Bar's eloquence, looked fitfully about the nearest salt-cellar for some moments, and then said, hesitating:

"They are perfectly aware, sir, of their duty to Society. They will return anybody I send to them for that purpose."

"Cheering to know," said Bar. "Cheering to know."

The three places in question were three little rotten holes in this Island, containing three little ignorant, drunken, guzzling, dirty, out of the way constituencies, that had reeled into Mr. Merdle's pocket. Ferdinand Barnacle laughed in his easy way, and airily said they were a nice set of fellows. Bishop, mentally perambulating among paths of peace, was altogether swallowed up in absence of mind.

"Pray," asked Lord Decimus, casting his eyes around the table, "what is this story I have heard of a gentleman long confined in a debtors' prison, proving to be of a wealthy family, and having come into the inheritance of a large sum of money? I have met with a variety of allusions to it. Do you know anything of it, Ferdinand?"

"I only know this much," said Ferdinand, "that he has given the Department with which I have the honor to be associated;" this sparkling young Barnacle threw off the phrase sportively, as who should say, We know all about these forms of speech, but we must keep it up, we must keep the game alive; "no end of trouble, and has put us into innumerable fixes."

"Fixes?" repeated Lord Decimus, with a majestic pausing and pondering on the word that made the bashful member shut his eyes quite tight. "Fixes?"

"A very perplexing business indeed," observed Mr. Tite Barnacle, with an air of grave resentment.

"What," said Lord Decimus, "was the character of his business; what was the nature of these—a—fixes, Ferdinand?"

"Oh, it's a good story, as a story," returned that gentleman; "as good a thing of its kind, as need be. This Mr. Dorrit (his name is Dorrit) had incurred a responsibility to us, ages before the fairy came out of the Bank and gave him his fortune, under a bond he had signed for the performance of a contract which was not at all performed. He was partner in a house in some large way—spirits, or buttons, or wine, or blacking, or oatmeal, or woollen, or pork, or hooks and eyes, or iron, or treacle, or shoes, or something or other that was wanted for troops, or seamen, or somebody—and the house burst, and we being among the creditors, detainers were lodged on the part of the Crown in a scientific manner, and all the rest of it. When the fairy had appeared and he wanted to pay us off, Egad we had got into such an exemplary state of checking and counter-checking, signing and counter-signing, that it was six months before we knew how to take the money, or how to give a receipt for it. It was a triumph of public business," said this handsome young Barnacle, laughing heartily. "You never saw such a lot of forms in your life. 'Why,' the attorney said to me one day, 'if I wanted this office to give me two or three thousand pounds instead of take it, I couldn't have more trouble about it.' 'You are right, old fellow,' I told him, 'and in future you'll know that we have something to do here.'" The pleasant young Barnacle finished by once more laughing heartily. He was a very easy, pleasant fellow indeed, and his manners were exceedingly winning.

Mr. Tite Barnacle's view of the business was of a less airy character. He took it ill that Mr. Dorrit had troubled the Department by wanting to pay the money, and considered it a grossly informal thing to do after so many years. But, Mr. Tite Barnacle was a buttoned-up man, and consequently a weighty one. All buttoned-up men are weighty. All buttoned-up men are believed in. Whether or no the reserved and never-exercised power of unbuttoning, fascinates mankind; whether or no wisdom is supposed to condense and augment when buttoned up, and to evaporate when unbuttoned; it is certain that the man to whom importance is accorded is the buttoned-up man. Mr. Tite Barnacle never would have passed for half his current value, unless his coat had been always buttoned-up to his white cravat.

"May I ask," said Lord Decimus, "if Mr. Darrit—or Dorrit—has any family?"

Nobody else replying, the host said, "He has two daughters, my lord."

"Oh! You are acquainted with him?" asked Lord Decimus.

"Mrs. Merdle is. Mr. Sparkler is, too. In fact," said Mr. Merdle, "I rather believe that one of the young ladies has made an impression on Edmund Sparkler. He is susceptible, and—I—think—the conquest——" Here Mr. Merdle stopped, and looked at the table-cloth: as he usually did when he found himself observed or listened to.

Bar was uncommonly pleased to find that the Merdle family, and this family, had already been brought into contact. He submitted, in a low voice across the table to Bishop, that it was a kind of analogical illustration of those physical laws, in virtue of which Like flies to Like. He regarded this power of attraction in wealth to draw wealth to it, as something remarkably interesting and curious—something indefinably allied to the loadstone and gravitation. Bishop, who had ambled back to earth again when the present theme was broached, acquiesced. He said it was indeed highly important to Society that one in the trying situation of unexpectedly finding himself invested with a power for good or for evil in Society, should become, as it were, merged in the superior power of a more legitimate and more gigantic growth, the influence of which (as in the case of our friend, at whose board we sat) was habitually exercised in harmony with the best interests of Society. Thus, instead of two rival and contending flames, a larger and a lesser, each burning with a lurid and uncertain glare, we had a blended and a softened light whose genial ray diffused an equable warmth throughout the land. Bishop seemed to like his own way of putting the case very much, and rather dwelt upon it; Bar, meanwhile (not to throw away a juryman), making a show of sitting at his feet and feeding on his precepts.

The dinner and dessert being three hours long, the bashful member cooled in the shadow of Lord Decimus faster than he warmed with food and drink, and had but a chilly time of it. Lord Decimus, like a tall tower in a flat country, seemed to project himself across the table-cloth, hide the light from the honorable member, cool the honorable member's marrow, and give him a woeful idea of distance. When he asked this unfortunate traveller to take wine, he encompassed his faltering steps with the gloomiest of shades; and when he said, "Your health, sir!" all around him was barrenness and desolation.

At length Lord Decimus, with a coffee-cup in his hand, began to hover about among the pictures, and to cause an interesting speculation to arise in all minds as to the probabilities of his ceasing to hover, and enabling the smaller birds to flutter up-stairs; which could not be done until he had urged his noble pinions in that direction. After some delay, and several stretches of his wings which came to nothing, he soared to the drawing-rooms.

And here a difficulty arose, which always does arise, when two people are specially brought together at a dinner to confer with one another. Everybody (except Bishop, who had no suspicion of it) knew perfectly well that this dinner had been eaten and drunk, specifically to the end that Lord Decimus and Mr. Merdle should have five minutes' conversation together. The opportunity so elaborately prepared was now arrived, and it seemed from that moment that no merely human ingenuity could so much as get the two chieftains into the same room. Mr. Merdle and his noble guest persisted in prowling about at opposite ends of the perspective. It was in vain for the engaging Ferdinand to bring Lord Decimus to look at the bronze horses near Mr. Merdle. Then Mr. Merdle evaded, and wandered away. It was in vain for him to bring Mr. Merdle to Lord Decimus to tell him the history of the unique Dresden vases. Then, Lord Decimus evaded and wandered away, while he was getting his man up to the mark.

"Did you ever see such a thing as this?" said Ferdinand to Bar, when he had been baffled twenty times.

"Often," returned Bar.

"Unless I butt one of them into an appointed corner, and you butt the other," said Ferdinand, "it will not come off after all."

"Very good," said Bar. "I'll butt Merdle, if you like; but, not my lord."

Ferdinand laughed, in the midst of his vexation. "Confound them both!"

said he, looking at his watch. "I want to get away. Why the deuce can't they come together! They both know what they want and mean to do. Look at them!"

They were still looming at opposite ends of the perspective, each with an absurd pretence of not having the other on his mind, which could not have been more transparently ridiculous though his real mind had been chalked on his back. Bishop, who had just now made a third with Bar and Ferdinand, but whose innocence had again cut him out of the subject and washed him in sweet oil, was seen to approach Lord Decimus and glide into conversation.

"I must get Merdle's doctor to catch and secure him, I suppose," said Ferdinand; "and then I must lay hold of my illustrious kinsman, and decoy him if I can—drag him if I can't—to the conference."

"Since you do me the honor," said Bar, with his slyest smile, "to ask for my poor aid, it shall be yours with the greatest pleasure. I don't think this is to be done by one man. But, if you will undertake to pen my lord into that furthest drawing-room where he is now so profoundly engaged, I will undertake to bring our dear Merdle into the presence, without the possibility of getting away."

"Done!" said Ferdinand. "Done!" said Bar.

Bar was a sight wondrous to behold, and full of matter, when, jauntily waving his double eye-glass by its ribbon, and jauntily drooping to an Universe of Jurymen, he, in the most accidental manner ever seen, found himself at Mr. Merdle's shoulder, and embraced that opportunity of mentioning a little point to him, on which he particularly wished to be guided by the light of his practical knowledge. (Here he took Mr. Merdle's arm and walked him gently away.) A banker whom we would call A. B. advanced a considerable sum of money, which we would call fifteen thousand pounds, to a client or customer of his, whom he would call P. Q. (Here, as they were getting towards Lord Decimus, he held Mr. Merdle tight.) As a security for the repayment of this advance to P. Q. whom we would call a widow lady, there were placed in A. B.'s hands the title deeds of a freehold estate, which we would call Blinkiter Doddles. Now, the point was this. A limited right of felling and lopping in the woods of Blinkiter Doddles, lay in the son of P. Q. then past his majority, and whom we would call X. Y.——but really this was too bad! In the presence of Lord Decimus, to detain the host with chopping our dry chaff of law, was really too bad! Another time! Bar was truly repentant, and would not say another syllable. Would Bishop favor him with half a dozen words? (He had now set Mr. Merdle down on a couch, side by side with Lord Decimus, and to it they must go now, or never.)

And now the rest of the company, highly excited and interested, always excepting Bishop who had not the slightest idea that anything was going on, formed in one group round the fire in the next drawing-room, and pretended to be chatting easily on an infinite variety of small topics, while everybody's thoughts and eyes were secretly straying towards the secluded pair. The Chorus were excessively nervous, perhaps as laboring under the dreadful apprehension that some good thing was going to be diverted from them. Bishop alone talked steadily and evenly. He conversed with the great Physician on that relaxation of the throat with which young curates were too frequently afflicted, and on the means of lessening the great prevalence of that disorder in the church. Physician, as a general rule, was of opinion that the best way to avoid it was to know how to read, before you made a profession of reading. Bishop said dubiously, did he really think so? And Physician said, decidedly, yes he did.

Ferdinand, meanwhile, was the only one of the party who skirmished on the outside of the circle; he kept about midway between it and the two, as if some sort of surgical operation were being performed by Lord Decimus on Mr. Merdle, or by Mr. Merdle on Lord Decimus, and his services might at any moment be required as Dresser. In fact, within a quarter of an hour, Lord Decimus called to him "Ferdinand!" and he went, and took his place in the conference for some five minutes more. Then a half-suppressed gasp broke out among the Chorus; for, Lord Decimus rose to take his leave. Again coached up by Ferdinand to the point of making himself popular, he shook hands in the most brilliant manner with the whole company, and even said to Bar "I hope you were not bored by my pears?" To which Bar retorted "Eton, my lord, or Parliamentary?" neatly showing that he had mastered the joke, and delicately insinuating that he could never forget it, while life remained.

All the grave importance that was buttoned up in Mr. Tite Barnacle, took itself away next; and Ferdinand took himself away next, to the opera. Some of the rest lingered a little, marrying golden liqueur glasses to Buhl tables with sticky rings; on the desperate chance of Mr. Merdle's saying something. But, Mr. Merdle, as usual, oozed sluggishly and muddily about his drawing-room, saying never a word.

In a day or two it was announced to all the town, that Edmund Sparkler, Esquire, son-in-law of the eminent Mr. Merdle of world-wide renown, was made one of the Lords of the Circumlocution Office; and proclamation was issued, to all true believers, that this admirable appointment was to be hailed as a graceful and gracious mark of homage, rendered by the graceful and gracious Decimus, to that commercial interest which must ever in a great commercial country—and all the rest of it, with blast of trumpet. So, bolstered by this mark of Government homage, the wonderful Bank and all the other wonderful undertakings went on and went up; and gapers came to Harley Street, Cavendish Square, only to look at the house where the golden wonder lived.

And when they saw the Chief Butler looking out at the hall-door in his moments of condescension, the gapers said how rich he looked, and wondered how much money he had in the wonderful Bank. But, if they had known that respectable Nemesis better, they would not have wondered about it, and might have stated the amount with the utmost precision.

CHAPTER XIII

THE PROGRESS OF AN EPIDEMIC

THAT it is at least as difficult to stay a moral infection as a physical one; that such a disease will spread with the malignity and rapidity of the Plague; that the contagion, when it has once made head, will spare no pursuit or condition, but will lay hold on people in the soundest health, and become developed in the most unlikely constitutions; is a fact as firmly established by experience as that we human creatures breathe an atmosphere. A blessing beyond appreciation would be conferred upon mankind, if the tainted, in whose weakness or wickedness these virulent disorders are bred, could be instantly seized and placed in close confinement (not to say summarily smothered) before the poison is communicable.

As a vast fire will fill the air to a great distance with its roar, so the sacred flame which the mighty Barnacles had fanned caused the air to resound more and more, with the name of Merdle. It was deposited on every lip, and carried into every ear. There never was, there never had been, there never again should be, such a man as Mr. Merdle. Nobody, as aforesaid, knew what he had done; but everybody knew him to be the greatest that had appeared.

Down in Bleeding Heart Yard, where there was not one unappropriated halfpenny, as lively an interest was taken in this paragon of men as on the Stock Exchange. Mrs. Plornish, now established in the small grocery and general trade in a snug little shop at the crack end of the Yard, at the top of the steps, with her little old father and Maggy acting as assistants, habitually held forth about him over the counter, in conversation with her customers. Mr. Plornish, who had a small share in a small builder's business in the neighbourhood, said, trowel in hand, on the tops of scaffolds and on the tiles of houses, that people did tell him as Mr. Merdle was *the* one, mind you, to put us all to rights in respects of that which all on us looked to, and to bring us all safe home as much we needed, mind you, fur toe be brought. Mr. Baptist, sole lodger of Mr. and Mrs. Plornish, was reputed in whispers to lay by the savings which were the result of his simple and moderate life, for investment in one of Mr. Merdle's certain enterprises. The female Bleeding Hearts, when they came for ounces of tea and hundredweights of talk, gave Mrs. Plornish to understand, That how, ma'am, they had heard from their cousin Mary Anne, which worked in the line, that his lady's dresses would fill three waggons. That how she was as handsome a lady, ma'am, as lived, no matter wheres, and a busk like marble itself. That how, according to what they was told, ma'am, it was her son by a former husband as was took into the Government; and a General he had been, and armies he had marched again and victory crowned, if all you heard was to be believed. That how it was reported that Mr. Merdle's words had been, that if they could have made it worth his while to take the whole government he would have took it without a profit, but that take it he could not and stand a loss. That how it was not to be expected, ma'am, that he should lose by it, his ways being, as you might say and utter no falsehood, paved with gold; but that how it was much to be regretted that something handsome hadn't been got up to make it worth his while; for it was such and only such that knowed the heighth to which the bread and butchers' meat had rose, and it was such and only such that both could and would bring that heighth down.

So rife and potent was the fever in Bleeding Heart Yard, that even Mr. Pancks's rent-days caused no interval in the patients. The disease took the singular form, on those occasions, of causing the infected to find an unfathomable excuse and consolation in allusions to the magic name.

"Now, then!" Mr. Pancks would say, to a defaulting lodger, "Pay up! Come on!"

"I haven't got it, Mr. Pancks," Defaulter would reply. "I tell you the truth, sir, when I say I haven't got so much as a single sixpence of it to bless myself with."

"This won't do, you know," Mr. Pancks would retort. "You don't expect it *will* do; do you?"

Defaulter would admit, with a low-spirited "No, sir," having no such expectation.

"My proprietor isn't going to stand this, you know," Mr. Pancks would proceed. "He don't send me here for this. Pay up! Come!"

The Defaulter would make answer, "Ah, Mr. Pancks. If I was the rich gentleman whose name is in everybody's mouth—if my name was Merdle, sir—I'd soon pay up, and be glad to do it."

Dialogues on the rent-question usually took place at the house-doors or in the entries, and in the presence of several deeply-interested Bleeding Hearts. They always received a reference of this kind with a low murmur of response, as if it were convincing; and the Defaulter, however blank and discomfited before, always cheered up a little in making it.

"If I was Mr. Merdle, sir, you wouldn't have cause to complain of me then. No, believe me!" the Defaulter would proceed with a shake of the head. "I'd pay up so quick then, Mr. Pancks, that you shouldn't have to ask me."

The response would be heard again here, implying that it was impossible to say anything fairer, and that this was the next thing to paying the money down.

Mr. Pancks would be now reduced to saying as he booked the case, "Well! You'll have the broker in, and be turned out; that's what'll happen to you. It's no use talking to me about Mr. Merdle. You are not Mr. Merdle, any more than I am."

"No, sir," the Defaulter would reply. "I only wish you *were* him, sir."

The response would take this up quickly: replying with great feeling, "Only wish you *were* him, sir."

"You'd be easier with us if you were Mr. Merdle, sir," the Defaulter would go on, with rising spirits, "and it would be better for all parties. Better for our sakes, and better for yours, too. You wouldn't have to worry no one then, sir. You wouldn't have to worry us, and you wouldn't have to worry yourself. You'd be easier in your own mind, sir, and you'd leave others easier, too, you would, if you were Mr. Merdle."

Mr. Pancks, in whom these impersonal compliments produced an irresistible sheepishness, never rallied after such a charge. He could only bite his nails and puff away to the next Defaulter. The responsive Bleeding Hearts would then gather round the Defaulter whom he had just abandoned, and the most extravagant rumours would circulate among them, to their great comfort, touching the amount of Mr. Merdle's ready money.

From one of the many such defeats of one of many rent-days, Mr. Pancks, having finished his day's collection, repaired with his note-book under his arm, to Mrs. Plornish's corner. Mr. Pancks's object was not professional, but social. He had had a trying day, and wanted a little brightening. By this time he was on friendly terms with the Plornish family, having often looked in upon them, at similar seasons, and borne his part in recollections of Miss Dorrit.

Mrs. Plornish's shop-parlor had been decorated under her own eye, and presented, on the side towards the shop, a little fiction in which Mrs. Plornish unspeakably rejoiced. This poetical heightening of the parlor consisted in the wall being painted to represent the exterior of a thatched cottage; the artist having introduced (in as effective a manner as he found compatible with their highly disproportionate dimensions) the real door and window. The modest sun-flower and holly-hock were depicted as flourishing with great luxuriance on this rustic dwelling, while a quantity of dense smoke issuing from the chimney indicated good cheer within, and also, perhaps, that it had not been lately swept. A faithful dog was represented as flying at the legs of the friendly visitor, from the threshold; and a circular pigeon-house, enveloped in a cloud of pigeons, arose from behind the garden-paling. On the door (when it was shut), appeared the semblance of a brass plate, presenting the inscription, Happy Cottage, T. and M. Plornish; the partnership expressing man and wife. No Poetry and no Art ever charmed the imagination more than the union of the two in this counterfeit cottage charmed Mrs. Plornish. It was nothing to her that Plornish had a habit of leaning against it as he smoked his pipe after work, when his hat blotted out the pigeon-house and all the pigeons, when his back swallowed up the dwelling, when his hands in his pockets uprooted the blooming garden and laid waste the adjacent country. To Mrs. Plornish, it was still a most beautiful cottage, a most wonderful deception; and it made no difference that Mr. Plornish's eye was some inches above the level of the gable bedroom in the thatch. To come out into the shop after it was shut, and hear her father sing a song inside this cottage, was a perfect Pastoral to Mrs. Plornish, the Golden Age revived. And truly if that famous period had been revived, or had ever been at all, it may be doubted whether it would have produced many more heartily admiring daughters than the poor woman.

Warned of a visitor by the tinkling bell at the shop-door, Mrs. Plornish came out of Happy Cottage to see who it might be. "I guessed it was you, Mr. Pancks," said she, "for it's quite your regular night; ain't it? Here's father, you see, come out to serve at the sound of the bell, like a brisk young shopman. Ain't he looking well? Father's more pleased to see you than if you was a customer, for he dearly loves a gossip; and when it turns upon Miss Dorrit, he loves it all the more. You never heard father in such voice as he's in at present," said Mrs. Plornish, her own voice quavering, she was so proud and pleased. "He gave us Strephon last night, to that degree that Plornish gets up and makes him this speech across the table. 'John Edward Nandy,' says Plornish to father, 'I never heard you come the warbles as I have heard you come the warbles this night.' An't it gratifying, Mr. Pancks, though; really?"

Mr. Pancks, who had snorted at the old man in his friendliest manner, replied in the affirmative, and casually asked whether that lively Altro chap had come in yet? Mrs. Plornish answered no, not yet, though he had gone to the West-End with some work, and had said he should be back by tea-time. Mr. Pancks was then hospitably pressed into Happy Cottage, where he encountered the elder Master Plornish just come home from school. Examining that young student, lightly, on the educational proceedings of the day, he found that the more advanced pupils who were in large text and the letter M, had been set the copy, "Merdle, Millions."

"And how are *you* getting on, Mrs. Plornish," said Pancks, "since we're mentioning millions?"

"Very steady indeed, sir," returned Mrs. Plornish. "Father dear, would you go into the shop and tidy the window a little bit before tea, your taste being so beautiful?"

John Edward Nandy trotted away, much gratified, to comply with his daughter's request. Mrs. Plornish, who was always in mortal terror of mentioning pecuniary affairs before the old gentleman, lest any disclosure she made might rouse his spirit and induce him to run away to the workhouse, was thus left free to be confidential with Mr. Pancks.

"It's quite true that the business is very steady indeed," said Mrs. Plornish, lowering her voice; "and has a excellent connexion. The only thing that stands in its way, sir, is the Credit."

This drawback, rather severely felt by most people who engaged in commercial transactions with the inhabitants of Bleeding Heart Yard, was a large stumbling-block in Mrs. Plornish's trade. When Mr. Dorrit had established her in the business, the Bleeding Hearts had shown an amount of emotion and a determination to support her in it, that did honor to human nature. Recognising her claim upon their generous feelings as one who had long been a member of their community, they pledged themselves, with great feeling, to deal with Mrs. Plornish, come what would, and bestow their patronage on no other establishment. Influenced by these noble sentiments, they had even gone out of their way to purchase little luxuries in the grocery and butter line to which they were unaccustomed; saying to one another, that if they did stretch a point, was it not for a neighbour and a friend, and for whom ought a point to be stretched if not for such? So stimulated, the business was extremely brisk, and the articles in stock went off with the greatest celerity. In short, if the Bleeding Hearts had but paid, the undertaking would have been a complete success; whereas, by reason of their exclusively confining themselves to owing, the profits actually realised had not yet begun to appear in the books.

Mr. Pancks was making a very porcupine of himself by sticking his hair up, in the contemplation of this state of accounts, when old Mr. Nandy, re-entering the cottage with an air of mystery, entreated them to come and look at the strange behaviour of Mr. Baptist, who seemed to have met with something that had scared him. All three going into the shop, and watching through the window, then saw Mr. Baptist, pale and agitated, go through the following extraordinary performances. First, he was observed hiding at the top of the steps leading down into the Yard, and peeping up and down the street, with his head cautiously thrust out close to the side of the shop-door. After very anxious scrutiny, he came out of his retreat, and went briskly down the street as if he were going away altogether; then, suddenly turned about, and went, at the same pace and with the same feint, up the street. He had gone no further up the street than he had gone down, when he crossed the road and disappeared. The object of this last manœuvre was only apparent, when his entering the shop with a sudden twist, from the steps again, explained that he had made a wide and obscure circuit round to the other, or Doyce and Clennam, end of the Yard, and had come through the Yard and bolted in. He was out of breath by that time, as he might well be; and his heart seemed to jerk faster than the little shop-bell, as it quivered and jingled behind him with his hasty shutting of the door.

"Hallo, old chap!" said Mr. Pancks. "Altro, old boy! What's the matter?"

Mr. Baptist, or Signor Cavalletto, understood English now almost as well

Mr. Baptist is supposed to have seen something

as Mr. Pancks himself, and could speak it very well too. Nevertheless, Mrs. Plornish, with a pardonable vanity in that accomplishment of hers which made her all but Italian, stepped in as interpreter.

"E ask know," said Mrs. Plornish, "what go wrong?"

"Come into the happy little cottage, Padrona," returned Mr. Baptist, imparting great stealthiness to his flurried back-handed shake of his right forefinger. "Come there!"

Mrs. Plornish was proud of the title Padrona, which she regarded as signifying: not so much Mistress of the house, as Mistress of the Italian tongue. She immediately complied with Mr. Baptist's request, and they all went into the cottage.

"E ope you no fright," said Mrs. Plornish then, interpreting Mr. Pancks in a new way, with her usual fertility of resource. "What appen? Peaka Padrona!"

"I have seen some one," returned Baptist. "I have rincontrato him."

"Im? Oo im?" asked Mrs. Plornish.

"A bad man. A baddest man. I have hoped that I should never see him again."

"Ow you know im bad?" asked Mrs. Plornish.

"It does not matter, Padrona. I know it too well."

"E see you?" asked Mrs. Plornish.

"No. I hope not. I believe not."

"He says," Mrs. Plornish then interpreted, addressing her father and Pancks with mild condescension, "that he has met a bad man, but he hopes the bad man didn't see him.—Why," enquired Mrs. Plornish, reverting to the Italian language, "why ope bad man no see?"

"Padrona, dearest," returned the little foreigner whom she so considerately protected, "do not ask, I pray. Once again, I say it matters not. I have fear of this man. I do not wish to see him, I do not wish to be known of him—never again! Enough, most beautiful. Leave it!"

The topic was so disagreeable to him, and so put his usual liveliness to the rout, that Mrs. Plornish forbore to press him further: the rather as the tea had been drawing for some time on the hob. But she was not the less surprised and curious for asking no more questions; neither was Mr. Pancks, whose expressive breathing had been laboring hard, since the entrance of the little man, like a locomotive engine with a great load getting up a steep incline. Maggy, now better dressed than of yore, though still faithful to the monstrous character of her cap, had been in the back-ground from the first with open mouth and eyes, which staring and gaping features were not diminished in breadth by the untimely suppression of the subject. However, no more was said about it, though much appeared to be thought on all sides: by no means excepting the two young Plornishes, who partook of the evening meal as if their eating the bread and butter were rendered almost superfluous by the painful probability of the worst of men shortly presenting himself for the purpose of eating them. Mr. Baptist, by degrees, began to chirp a little; but never stirred from the seat he had taken behind the door and close to the window, though it was not his usual place. As often as the little bell rang, he started and peeped out secretly, with the end of the little curtain in his hand, and the rest before his face; evidently not at all satisfied but that the man he dreaded had tracked him through all his doublings and turnings, with the certainty of a terrible bloodhound.

The entrance, at various times, of two or three customers and of Mr. Plornish, gave Mr. Baptist just enough of this employment to keep the attention of the company fixed upon him. Tea was over, and the children were abed, and Mrs. Plornish was feeling her way to the dutiful proposal that her father should favor them with Chloe, when the bell again rang, and Mr. Clennam came in.

Clennam had been poring late over his books and letters; for, the waiting-rooms of the Circumlocution Office ravaged his time sorely. Over and above that, he was depressed and made uneasy by the late occurrence at his mother's. He looked worn and solitary. He felt so, too; but, nevertheless, was returning home from his counting-house by that end of the Yard, to give them the intelligence that he had received another letter from Miss Dorrit.

The news made a sensation in the cottage which drew off the general attention from Mr. Baptist. Maggy, who pushed her way into the fore-ground immediately, would have seemed to draw in the tidings of her Little Mother, equally at her ears, nose, mouth, and eyes, but that the last were obstructed by tears. She was particularly delighted when Clennam assured her that there were hospitals, and very kindly conducted hospitals, in Rome. Mr. Pancks rose into new distinction in virtue of being specially remembered in the letter. Everybody was pleased and interested, and Clennam was well repaid for his trouble.

"But you are tired, sir. Let me make you a cup of tea," said Mrs. Plornish, "if you'd condescend to take such a thing in the cottage; and many thanks to you, too, I am sure, for bearing us in mind so kindly."

Mr. Plornish deeming it incumbent on him, as host, to add his personal acknowledgments, tendered them in the form which always expressed his highest ideal of a combination of ceremony with sincerity.

"John Edward Nandy," said Mr. Plornish, addressing the old gentleman. "Sir. It's not too often that you see unpretending actions without a spark of pride, and therefore when you see them give grateful honor unto the same, being that if you don't and live to want 'em it follows serve you right."

To which Mr. Nandy replied:

"I am heartily of your opinion, Thomas, and which your opinion is the same as mine, and therefore no more words and not being backwards with that opinion, which opinion giving it as yes, Thomas, yes, is the opinion in which yourself and me must ever be unanimously jined by all, and where there is not difference of opinion there can be none but one opinion, which fully no, Thomas, Thomas, no!"

Arthur, with less formality, expressed himself gratified by their high appreciation of so very slight an attention on his part; and explained as to the tea that he had not yet dined, and was going straight home to refresh after a long day's labor, or he would have readily accepted the hospitable offer. As Mr. Pancks was somewhat noisily getting his steam up for departure, he concluded by asking that gentleman if he would walk with him? Mr. Pancks said he desired no better engagement, and the two took leave of Happy Cottage.

"If you will come home with me, Pancks," said Arthur, when they got into the street, "and will share what dinner or supper there is, it will be next door to an act of charity; for, I am weary and out of sorts to-night."

"Ask me to do a greater thing than that," said Pancks, "when you want it done, and I'll do it."

Between this eccentric personage and Clennam, a tacit understanding and accord had been always improving since Mr. Pancks flew over Mr. Rugg's back in the Marshalsea Yard. When the carriage drove away on the memorable day of the family's departure, these two had looked after it together, and had walked slowly away together. When the first letter came from Little Dorrit, nobody was more interested in hearing of her than Mr. Pancks. The second letter, at that moment in Clennam's breast-pocket, particularly remembered him by name. Though he had never before made any profession or protestation to Clennam, and though what he had just said was little enough as to the words in which it was expressed, Clennam had long had a growing belief that Mr. Pancks, in his own odd way, was becoming attached to him. All these strings intertwining, made Pancks a very cable of anchorage that night.

"I am quite alone," Arthur explained as they walked on. "My partner is away, busily engaged at a distance on his branch of our business, and you shall do just as you like."

"Thank you. You didn't take particular notice of little Altro just now; did you?" said Pancks.

"No. Why?"

"He's a bright fellow, and I like him," said Pancks. "Something has gone amiss with him to-day. Have you any idea of any cause that can have overset him?"

"You surprise me! None whatever."

Mr. Pancks gave his reasons for the enquiry. Arthur was quite unprepared for them, and quite unable to suggest an explanation of them.

"Perhaps you'll ask him," said Pancks, "as he's a stranger?"

"Ask him what?" returned Clennam.

"What he has on his mind."

"I ought first to see for myself that he has something on his mind, I think," said Clennam. "I have found him in every way so diligent, so grateful (for little enough), and so trustworthy, that it might look like suspecting him. And that would be very unjust."

"True," said Pancks. "But, I say! You oughtn't to be anybody's proprietor, Mr. Clennam. You're much too delicate."

"For the matter of that," returned Clennam laughing, "I have not a large proprietary share in Cavalletto. His carving is his livelihood. He keeps the keys of the Factory, watches it every alternate night, and acts as a sort of housekeeper to it generally; but, we have little work in the way of his ingenuity, though we give him what we have. No! I am rather his adviser than his proprietor. To call me his standing counsel and his banker would be nearer the fact. Speaking of being his banker, is it not curious, Pancks, that the ventures which run just now in so many people's heads, should run even in little Cavalletto's?"

"Ventures?" retorted Pancks, with a snort. "What ventures?"

"These Merdle enterprises."

"Oh! Investments," said Pancks. "Aye, aye! I didn't know you were speaking of investments."

His quick way of replying caused Clennam to look at him, with a doubt whether he meant more than he said. As it was accompanied, however, with a quickening of his pace and a corresponding increase in the laboring of his machinery, Arthur did not pursue the matter, and they soon arrived at his house.

A dinner of soup and a pigeon-pie, served on a little round table before the fire, and flavored with a bottle of good wine, oiled Mr. Pancks's works in a highly effective manner. So that when Clennam produced his Eastern pipe, and handed Mr. Pancks another Eastern pipe, the latter gentleman was perfectly comfortable.

They puffed for a while in silence, Mr. Pancks like a steam-vessel with wind, tide, calm water, and all other sea-going conditions, in her favor. He was the first to speak, and he spoke thus:

"Yes. Investments is the word."

Clennam, with his former look, said "Ah!"

"I am going back to it, you see," said Pancks.

"Yes. I see you are going back to it," returned Clennam, wondering why.

"Wasn't it a curious thing that they should run in little Altro's head? Eh?" said Pancks as he smoked. "Wasn't that how you put it?"

"That was what I said."

"Aye! But, think of the whole Yard having got it. Think of their all meeting me with it, on my collecting days, here and there and everywhere. Whether they pay, or whether they don't pay. Merdle, Merdle, Merdle. Always Merdle."

"Very strange how these runs on an infatuation prevail," said Arthur.

"An't it?" returned Pancks. After smoking for a minute or so, more dryly than comported with his recent oiling, he added: "Because you see these people don't understand the subject."

"Not a bit," assented Clennam.

"Not a bit," cried Pancks. "Know nothing of figures. Know nothing of money questions. Never made a calculation. Never worked it, sir!"

"If they had——" Clennam was going on to say; when Mr. Pancks, without change of countenance, produced a sound so far surpassing all his usual efforts, nasal or bronchial, that he stopped.

"If they had?" repeated Pancks in an enquiring tone.

"I thought you—spoke," said Arthur, hesitating what name to give the interruption.

"Not at all," said Pancks. "Not yet. I may in a minute. If they had?"

"If they had," observed Clennam, who was a little at a loss how to take his friend, "why, I suppose they would have known better."

"How so, Mr. Clennam?" Pancks asked, quickly, and with an odd effect of having been from the commencement of the conversation loaded with the heavy charge he now fired off. "They're right, you know. They don't mean to be, but they're right."

"Right in sharing Cavalletto's inclination to speculate with Mr. Merdle?"

"Per-fectly, sir," said Pancks. "I've gone into it. I've made the calculations. I've worked it. They're safe and genuine." Relieved by having got to this, Mr. Pancks took as long a pull as his lungs would permit at his Eastern pipe, and looked sagaciously and steadily at Clennam while inhaling and exhaling too.

In those moments, Mr. Pancks began to give out the dangerous infection with which he was laden. It is the manner of communicating these diseases; it is the subtle way in which they go about.

"Do you mean, my good Pancks," asked Clennam, emphatically, "that you would put that thousand pounds of yours, let us say, for instance, out at this kind of interest?"

"Certainly," said Pancks. "Already done it, sir."

Mr. Pancks took another long inhalation, another long exhalation, another long sagacious look at Clennam.

"I tell you, Mr. Clennam, I've gone into it," said Pancks. "He's a man of immense resources—enormous capital—government influence. They're the best schemes afloat. They're safe. They're certain."

"Well!" returned Clennam, looking first at him gravely, and then at the fire gravely. "You surprise me!"

"Bah!" Pancks retorted. "Don't say that, sir. It's what you ought to do yourself. Why don't you do as I do?"

Of whom Mr. Pancks had taken the prevalent disease, he could no more have told than if he had unconsciously taken a fever. Bred at first, as many physical diseases are, in the wickedness of men, and then disseminated in their ignorance, these epidemics, after a period, get communicated to many sufferers who are neither ignorant nor wicked. Mr. Pancks might, or might not, have caught the illness himself from a subject of this class; but, in this category he appeared before Clennam, and the infection he threw off was all the more virulent.

"And you have really invested," Clennam had already passed to that word, "your thousand pounds, Pancks?"

"To be sure, sir!" replied Pancks, boldly, with a puff of smoke. "And only wish it was ten!"

Now, Clennam had two subjects lying heavy on his lonely mind that night; the one, his partner's long-deferred hope; the other, what he had seen and heard at his mother's. In the relief of having this companion, and of feeling that he could trust him, he passed on to both, and both brought him round again, with an increase and acceleration of force, to his point of departure.

It came about in the simplest manner. Quitting the investment subject, after an interval of silent looking at the fire through the smoke of his pipe, he told Pancks how and why he was occupied with the great National Department. "A hard case it has been, and a hard case it is, on Doyce," he finished by saying, with all the honest feeling the topic roused in him.

"Hard indeed," Pancks acquiesced. "But you manage for him, Mr. Clennam?"

"How do you mean?"

"Manage the money part of the business?"

"Yes. As well as I can."

"Manage it better, sir," said Pancks. "Recompense him for his toils and disappointments. Give him the chances of the time. He'll never benefit himself in that way, patient and pre-occupied workman. He looks to you, sir."

"I do my best, Pancks," returned Clennam, uneasily. "As to duly weighing and considering these new enterprises, of which I have had no experience, I doubt if I am fit for it. I am growing old."

"Growing old?" cried Pancks. "Ha, ha!"

There was something so indubitably genuine in the wonderful laugh, and series of snorts and puffs, engendered in Mr. Pancks's astonishment at, and utter rejection of, the idea, that his being quite in earnest could not be questioned.

"Growing old?" cried Pancks. "Hear, hear, hear! Old? Hear him, hear him!"

The positive refusal expressed in Mr. Pancks's continued snorts, no less than in these exclamations, to entertain the sentiment for a single instant, drove Arthur away from it. Indeed, he was fearful of something happening to Mr. Pancks, in the violent conflict that took place between the breath he jerked out of himself and the smoke he jerked into himself. This abandonment of the second topic threw him on the third.

"Young, old, or middle-aged, Pancks," he said, when there was a favorable pause, "I am in a very anxious and uncertain state; a state that even leads me to doubt whether anything now seeming to belong to me, may be really mine. Shall I tell you how this is? Shall I put a great trust in you?"

"You shall, sir," said Pancks, "if you believe me worthy of it."

"I do."

"You may!" Mr. Pancks's short and sharp rejoinder, confirmed by the sudden outstretching of his coaly hand, was most expressive and convincing. Arthur shook the hand warmly.

He then, softening the nature of his old apprehensions as much as was possible, consistently with their being made intelligible, and never alluding to his mother by name, but speaking vaguely of a relation of his, confided to Mr. Pancks a broad outline of the misgivings he entertained, and of the interview he had witnessed. Mr. Pancks listened with such interest that, regardless of the charms of the Eastern pipe, he put it in the grate among the fire-irons, and occupied his hands during the whole recital in so erecting the loops and hooks of hair all over his head, that he looked, when it came to a conclusion, like a journeyman Hamlet in conversation with his father's spirit.

"Brings me back, sir," was his exclamation then, with a startling touch on Clennam's knee, "brings me back, sir, to the Investments! I don't say anything of your making yourself poor, to repair a wrong you never committed. That's you. A man must be himself. But, I say this. Fearing you may want money to save your own blood from exposure and disgrace— make as much as you can!"

Arthur shook his head, but looked at him thoughtfully too.

"Be as rich as you can, sir," Pancks adjured him with a powerful concentration of all his energies on the advice. "Be as rich as you honestly can. It's your duty. Not for your sake, but for the sake of others. Take time by the forelock. Poor Mr. Doyce (who really *is* growing old) depends upon you. Your relative depends upon you. You don't know what depends upon you."

"Well, well, well!" returned Arthur. "Enough for to-night."

"One word more, Mr. Clennam," retorted Pancks, "and then enough for to-night. Why should you leave all the gains to the gluttons, knaves, and impostors? Why should you leave all the gains that are to be got, to my proprietor and the like of him? Yet you're always doing it. When I say you, I mean such men as you. You know you are. Why, I see it every day of my life. I see nothing else. It's my business to see it. Therefore I say," urged Pancks, "Go in and win!"

"But what of Go in and lose?" said Arthur.

"Can't be done, sir," returned Pancks. "I have looked into it. Name up, everywhere—immense resources—enormous capital—great position—high connexion—government influence. Can't be done!"

Gradually, after this closing exposition, Mr. Pancks subsided; allowed his hair to droop as much as it ever would droop on the utmost persuasion; reclaimed the pipe from the fire-irons, filled it anew, and smoked it out. They said little more; but were company to one another in silently pursuing the same subjects, and did not part until midnight. On taking his leave, Mr. Pancks, when he had shaken hands with Clennam, worked completely round him before he steamed out at the door. This, Arthur received as an assurance that he might implicitly rely on Pancks, if he should ever come to need assistance; either in any of the matters of which they had spoken that night, or on any other subject that could in any way affect himself.

At intervals all next day, and even while his attention was fixed on other things, he thought of Mr. Pancks's investment of his thousand pounds, and of his having "looked into it." He thought of Mr. Pancks's being so sanguine in this matter, and of his not being usually of a sanguine character. He thought of the great National Department, and of the delight it would be to him to see Doyce better off. He thought of the darkly threatening place that went by the name of Home in his remembrance, and of the gathering shadows which made it yet more darkly threatening than of old. He observed anew that wherever he went, he saw, or heard, or touched, the celebrated name of Merdle; he found it difficult even to remain at his desk a couple of hours, without having it presented to one of his bodily senses through some agency or other. He began to think it was curious too that it should be everywhere, and that nobody but he should seem to have any mistrust of it. Though indeed he began to remember, when he got to this, even *he* did not mistrust it; he had only happened to keep aloof from it.

Such symptoms, when a disease of the kind is rife, are usually the signs of sickening.

CHAPTER XIV

TAKING ADVICE

WHEN it became known to the Britons on the shore of the yellow Tiber, that their intelligent compatriot Mr. Sparkler was made one of the Lords of their Circumlocution Office, they took it as a piece of news with which they had no nearer concern than with any other piece of news—any other Accident or Offence—in the English papers. Some laughed; some said, by way of complete excuse, that the post was virtually a sinecure, and any fool who could spell his name was good enough for it; some, and these were the more solemn political oracles, said that Decimus did wisely to strengthen himself, and that the sole constitutional purpose of all places within the gift of Decimus, was, that Decimus should strengthen himself. A few bilious Britons there were who would not subscribe to this article of faith; but their objection was purely theoretical. In a practical point of view, they listlessly abandoned the matter, as being the business of some other Britons unknown, somewhere, or nowhere. In like manner, at home, great numbers of Britons maintained, for as long as four and twenty consecutive hours, that those invisible and anonymous Britons "ought to take it up;" and that if they quietly acquiesced in it, they deserved it. But of what class the remiss Britons were composed, and where the unlucky creatures hid themselves, and why they hid themselves, and how it constantly happened that they neglected their interests, when so many other Britons were quite at a loss to account for their not looking after those interests, was not, either upon the shore of the yellow Tiber or the shore of the black Thames, made apparent to men.

Mrs. Merdle circulated the news, as she received congratulations on it, with a careless grace that displayed it to advantage, as the setting displays the jewel. Yes, she said, Edmund had taken the place. Mr. Merdle wished him to take it, and he had taken it. She hoped Edmund might like it, but really she didn't know. It would keep him in town a good deal, and he preferred the country. Still, it was not a disagreeable position—and it was a position. There was no denying that the thing was a compliment to Mr. Merdle, and was not a bad thing for Edmund if he liked it. It was just as well that he should have something to do, and it was just as well that he should have something for doing it. Whether it would be more agreeable to Edmund than the army, remained to be seen.

Thus the Bosom; accomplished in the art of seeming to make things of small account, and really enhancing them in the process. While Henry Gowan, whom Decimus had thrown away, went through the whole round of his acquaintance between the Gate of the People and the town of Albano, vowing, almost (but not quite) with tears in his eyes, that Sparkler was the sweetest-tempered, simplest-hearted, altogether most loveable jackass that ever grazed on the public common; and that only one circumstance could have delighted him (Gowan) more, than his (the beloved jackass's) getting this post, and that would have been his (Gowan's) getting it himself. He said, it was the very thing for Sparkler. There was nothing to do, and he would do it charmingly; there was a handsome salary to draw, and he would draw it charmingly; it was a delightful, appropriate, capital appointment; and he almost forgave the donor his slight of himself, in his joy that the dear donkey for whom he had so great an affection was so admirably stabled. Nor did his benevolence stop here. He took pains, on all social occasions, to draw Mr. Sparkler out, and make him conspicuous before the company; and, although the considerate action always resulted in that young gentleman's making a dreary and forlorn mental spectacle of himself, the friendly intention was not to be doubted.

Unless, indeed, it chanced to be doubted by the object of Mr. Sparkler's affections. Miss Fanny was now in the difficult situation of being universally known in that light, and of not having dismissed Mr. Sparkler, however capriciously she used him. Hence, she was sufficiently identified with the gentleman to feel compromised by his being more than usually ridiculous; and hence, being by no means deficient in quickness, she sometimes came to his rescue against Gowan and did him very good service. But, while doing this, she was ashamed of him, undetermined whether to get rid of him or more decidedly encourage him, distracted with apprehensions that she was every day becoming more and more immeshed in her uncertainties, and tortured by misgivings that Mrs. Merdle triumphed in her distress. With this tumult in her mind, it is no subject for surprise that Miss Fanny came home one night in a state of agitation from a concert and ball at Mrs. Merdle's house, and, on her sister affectionately trying to soothe her, pushed that sister away from the toilette-table at which she sat angrily trying to cry, and declared with a heaving bosom that she detested everybody, and she wished she was dead.

"Dear Fanny, what is the matter? Tell me."

"Matter, you little Mole," said Fanny. "If you were not the blindest of the blind, you would have no occasion to ask me. The idea of daring to pretend to assert that you have eyes in your head, and yet ask me what's the matter!"

"Is it Mr. Sparkler, dear?"

"Mis-ter Spar-kler!" repeated Fanny, with unbounded scorn, as if he were the last subject in the Solar system that could possibly be near her mind. "No, Miss Bat, it is not."

Immediately afterwards, she became remorseful for having called her sister names; declaring with sobs that she knew she made herself hateful, but that everybody drove her to it.

"I don't think you are well to-night, dear Fanny."

"Stuff and nonsense!" replied the young lady, turning angry again; "I am as well as you are. Perhaps I might say, better, and yet make no boast of it."

Poor Little Dorrit, not seeing her way to the offering of any soothing words that would escape repudiation, deemed it best to remain quiet. At first, Fanny took this ill, too; protesting to her looking-glass, that of all the trying sisters a girl could have, she did think the most trying sister was a flat sister. That she knew she was at times a wretched temper; that she knew she made herself hateful; that when she made herself hateful, nothing would do her half the good of being told so; but that, being afflicted with a flat sister, she never *was* told so, and the consequence resulted that she was absolutely tempted and goaded into making herself disagreeable. Besides (she angrily told her looking-glass), she didn't want to be forgiven. It was not a right example, that she should be constantly stooping to be forgiven by a younger sister. And this was the Art of it—that she was always being placed in the position of being forgiven, whether she liked it or not. Finally she burst into violent weeping, and, when her sister came and sat down at her side to comfort her, said, "Amy, you're an Angel!"

"But, I tell you what, my pet," said Fanny, when her sister's gentleness had calmed her, " it now comes to this; that things cannot and shall not go on as they are at present going on, and that there must be an end of this, one way or other."

As the announcement was vague, though very peremptory, Little Dorrit returned, "Let us talk about it."

"Quite so, my dear," assented Fanny, as she dried her eyes. "Let us talk about it. I am rational again now, and you shall advise me. *Will* you advise me, my sweet child?"

Even Amy smiled at the notion, but she said, "I will, Fanny, as well as I can."

"Thank you, dearest Amy," returned Fanny, kissing her. "You are my Anchor."

Having embraced her Anchor with great affection, Fanny took a bottle of sweet toilette water from the table, and called to her maid for a fine handkerchief. She then dismissed that attendant for the night, and went on to be advised; dabbing her eyes and forehead from time to time, to cool them.

"My love," Fanny began, "our characters and points of view are sufficiently different (kiss me again, my darling), to make it very probable that I shall surprise you by what I am going to say. What I am going to say, my dear, is, that notwithstanding our property, we labor, socially speaking, under disadvantages. You don't quite understand what I mean, Amy?"

"I have no doubt I shall," said Amy, mildly, "after a few words more."

"Well, my dear, what I mean, is, that we are, after all, new comers into fashionable life."

"I am sure, Fanny," Little Dorrit interposed in her zealous admiration, "no one need find that out in you."

"Well, my dear child, perhaps not," said Fanny, "though it's most kind and most affectionate in you, you precious girl, to say so." Here she dabbed her sister's forehead, and blew upon it a little. "But, you are," resumed Fanny, "as is well known, the dearest little thing that ever was! To resume, my child. Pa is extremely gentlemanly and extremely well informed, but he is, in some trifling respects, a little different from other gentlemen of his fortune: partly on account of what he has gone through, poor dear: partly, I fancy, on account of its often running in his mind that other people are thinking about that, while he is talking to them. Uncle, my love, is altogether unpresentable. Though a dear creature to whom I am tenderly attached, he is, socially speaking, shocking. Edward is frightfully expensive and dissipated. I don't mean that there is anything ungenteel in that itself—far from it—but I do mean that he doesn't do it well, and that he doesn't, if I may so express myself, get the money's-worth in the sort of dissipated reputation that attaches to him."

"Poor Edward!" sighed Little Dorrit, with the whole family history in the sigh.

"Yes. And poor you and me too," returned Fanny, rather sharply. "Very true! Then, my dear, we have no mother, and we have a Mrs. General. And I tell you again, darling, that Mrs. General, if I may reverse a common proverb and adapt it to her, is a cat in gloves who *will* catch mice. That woman, I am quite sure and confident, will be our mother-in-law."

"I can hardly think, Fanny——" Fanny stopped her.

"Now, don't argue with me about it, Amy," said she, "because I know better." Feeling that she had been sharp again, she dabbed her sister's forehead again, and blew upon it again. "To resume once more, my dear. It then becomes a question with me (I am proud and spirited, Amy, as you very well know: too much so, I daresay) whether I shall make up my mind to take it upon myself to carry the family through."

"How ?" asked her sister, anxiously.

"I will not," said Fanny, without answering the question, "submit to be mother-in-lawed by Mrs. General; and I will not submit to be, in any respect whatever, either patronised or tormented by Mrs. Merdle."

Little Dorrit laid her hand upon the hand that held the bottle of sweet water, with a still more anxious look. Fanny, quite punishing her own forehead with the vehement dabs she now began to give it, fitfully went on.

"That he has, somehow or other, and how is of no consequence, attained a very good position, no one can deny. That it is a very good connexion, no one can deny. And as to the question of clever or not clever, I doubt very much whether a clever husband would be suitable to me. I cannot submit. I should not be able to defer to him enough."

"O, my dear, dear Fanny!" expostulated Little Dorrit, upon whom a kind of terror had been stealing as she perceived what her sister meant. "If you loved any one, all this feeling would change. If you loved any one, you would no more be yourself, but you would quite lose and forget yourself in your devotion to him. If you loved him, Fanny——" Fanny stopped the dabbing hand, and was looking at her fixedly.

"O, indeed!" cried Fanny. "Really ? Bless me, how much some people know of some subjects! They say every one has a subject, and I certainly seem to have hit upon yours, Amy. There, you little thing, I was only in fun," dabbing her sister's forehead; "but, don't you be a silly puss, and don't you think flightily and eloquently about degenerate impossibilities. There! Now, I'll go back to myself."

"Dear Fanny, let me say first, that I would far rather we worked for a scanty living again, than I would see you rich and married to Mr. Sparkler."

"*Let* you say, my dear?" retorted Fanny. "Why, of course, I will *let* you say anything. There is no constraint upon you, I hope. We are together to talk it over. And as to marrying Mr. Sparkler, I have not the least intention of doing so to-night, my dear, or to-morrow morning either."

"But at some time?"

"At no time, for anything I know at present," answered Fanny, with indifference. Then, suddenly changing her indifference into a burning restlessness, she added, "You talk about the clever men, you little thing! It's all very fine and easy to talk about the clever men; but where are they? *I* don't see them anywhere near *me!*"

"My dear Fanny, so short a time——"

"Short time or long time," interrupted Fanny, "I am impatient of our situation, I don't like our situation, and very little would induce me to change it. Other girls, differently reared and differently circumstanced altogether, might wonder at what I say or may do. Let them. They are driven by their lives and characters; I am driven by mine."

"Fanny, my dear Fanny, you know that you have qualities to make you the wife of one very superior to Mr. Sparkler."

"Amy, my dear Amy," retorted Fanny, parodying her words, "I know that I wish to have a more defined and distinct position, in which I can assert myself with greater effect against that insolent woman."

"Would you therefore—forgive my asking, Fanny—therefore marry her son?"

"Why, perhaps," said Fanny, with a triumphant smile. "There may be many less promising ways of arriving at an end than that, my dear. That piece of insolence may think, now, that it would be a great success to get her son off upon me, and shelve me. But, perhaps she little thinks how I would retort upon her if I married her son. I would oppose her in everything, and compete with her. I would make it the business of my life."

Fanny set down the bottle when she came to this, and walked about the room; always stopping and standing still while she spoke.

"One thing I could certainly do, my child: I could make her older. And I would!"

This was followed by another walk.

"I would talk of her as an old woman. I would pretend to know—if I didn't, but I should from her son—all about her age. And she should hear me say, Amy: affectionately, quite dutifully and affectionately: how well she looked, considering her time of life. I could make her seem older, at once, by being myself so much younger. I may not be as handsome as she is; I am not a fair judge of that question, I suppose; but, I know I am handsome enough to be a thorn in her side. And I would be!"

"My dear sister, would you condemn yourself to an unhappy life for this?"

"It wouldn't be an unhappy life, Amy. It would be the life I am fitted for. Whether by disposition, or whether by circumstances, is no matter; I am better fitted for such a life than for almost any other."

There was something of a desolate tone in those words; but, with a short proud laugh she took another walk, and after passing a great looking-glass came to another stop.

"Figure! Figure, Amy! Well. The woman has a good figure. I will give her her due, and not deny it. But, is it so far beyond all others that it is altogether unapproachable? Upon my word, I am not so sure of it. Give some much younger women the latitude as to dress that she has, being married; and we would see about that, my dear!"

Something in the thought that was agreeable and flattering, brought her back to her seat in a gayer temper. She took her sister's hands in hers, and clapped all four hands above her head as she looked in her sister's face laughing:

"And the dancer, Amy, that she has quite forgotten—the dancer who bore no sort of resemblance to me, and of whom I never remind her, oh dear no!—should dance through her life, and dance in her way, to such a tune as would disturb her insolent placidity a little. Just a little, my dear Amy, just a little!"

Meeting an earnest and imploring look in Amy's face, she brought the four hands down, and laid only one on Amy's lips.

"Now, don't argue with me, child," she said in a sterner way, "because it is of no use. I understand these subjects much better than you do. I have not nearly made up my mind, but it may be. Now we have talked this over comfortably, and may go to bed. You best and dearest little mouse, Good Night!" With those[1] words Fanny weighed her Anchor, and—having taken so much advice—left off being advised for that occasion.

Thenceforward, Amy observed Mr. Sparkler's treatment by his enslaver, with new reasons for attaching importance to all that passed between them. There were times when Fanny appeared quite unable to endure his mental feebleness, and when she became so sharply impatient of it that she would all but dismiss him for good. There were other times when she got on much better with him; when he amused her, and when her sense of superiority seemed to counterbalance that opposite side of the scale. If Mr. Sparkler had been other than the faithfullest and most submissive of swains, he was sufficiently hard pressed to have fled from the scene of his trials, and have set at least the whole distance from Rome to London between himself and his enchantress. But, he had no greater will of his own than a boat has when it is towed by a steam-ship; and he followed his cruel mistress through rough and smooth, on equally strong compulsion.

Mrs. Merdle, during these passages, said little to Fanny, but said more about her. She was, as it were, forced to look at her, through her eye-glass, and in general conversation to allow commendations of her beauty to be wrung from her by its irresistible demands. The defiant character it assumed when Fanny heard these extollings (as it generally happened that she did), was not expressive of concessions to the impartial bosom; but, the utmost revenge the bosom took was, to say audibly, "a spoilt beauty— but with that face and shape, who could wonder?"

It might have been about a month or six weeks after the night of the advice, when Little Dorrit began to think she detected some new understanding between Mr. Sparkler and Fanny. Mr. Sparkler, as if in adherence to some compact, scarcely ever spoke without first looking towards Fanny, for leave. That young lady was too discreet ever to look back again: but, if Mr. Sparkler had permission to speak, she remained silent; if he had not, she herself spoke. Moreover, it became plain whenever Henry Gowan attempted to perform the friendly office of drawing him out, that he was not to be drawn. And not only that, but Fanny would presently, without any pointed application in the world, chance to say something with such a sting in it, that Gowan would draw back as if he had put his hand into a bee-hive.

There was yet another circumstance which went a long way to confirm Little Dorrit in her fears, though it was not a great circumstance in itself. Mr. Sparkler's demeanour towards herself, changed. It became fraternal. Sometimes, when she was in the outer circle of assemblies—at their own residence, at Mrs. Merdle's, or elsewhere—she would find herself stealthily supported round the waist by Mr. Sparkler's arm. Mr. Sparkler never offered the slightest explanation of this attention; but merely smiled with an air of blundering, contented, good-natured proprietorship, which, in so heavy a gentleman, was ominously expressive.

Little Dorrit was at home one day, thinking about Fanny with a heavy heart. They had a room at one end of their drawing-room suite, nearly all irregular bay-window, projecting over the street, and commanding all the picturesque life and variety of the Corso, both up and down. At three or four o'clock in the afternoon, English time, the view from this window was very bright and peculiar; and Little Dorrit used to sit and muse here, much as she had been used to wile away the time in her balcony at Venice. Seated thus one day, she was softly touched on the shoulder, and Fanny said, "Well, Amy dear," and took her seat at her side. Their seat was a part of the window; when there was anything in the way of a procession going on, they used to have bright draperies hung out at the window, and used to kneel or sit on this seat and look out at it, leaning on the brilliant color. But there was no procession that day, and Little Dorrit was rather surprised by Fanny's being at home at that hour, as she was generally out on horseback then.

"Well, Amy," said Fanny, "what are you thinking of, little one?"

"I was thinking of you, Fanny."

"No? What a coincidence! I declare here's some one else. You were not thinking of this some one else too; were you, Amy?"

Amy *had* been thinking of this some one else too; for, it was Mr. Sparkler. She did not say so, however, as she gave him her hand. Mr. Sparkler came and sat down on the other side of her, and she felt the fraternal railing come behind her, and apparently stretch on to include Fanny.

"Well, my little sister," said Fanny, with a sigh, "I suppose you know what this means?"

"She's as beautiful as she's doated on," stammered Mr. Sparkler— "and there's no nonsense about her—it's arranged——"

"You needn't explain, Edmund," said Fanny.

"No, my love," said Mr. Sparkler.

"In short, pet," proceeded Fanny, "on the whole, we are engaged. We must tell papa about it, either to-night or to-morrow, according to the opportunities. Then it's done, and very little more need be said."

"My dear Fanny," said Mr. Sparkler, with deference, "I should like to say a word to Amy."

"Well, well! Say it, for goodness sake," returned the young lady.

"I am convinced, my dear Amy," said Mr. Sparkler, "that if ever there was a girl, next to your highly-endowed and beautiful sister, who had no nonsense about her——"

"We know all about that, Edmund," interposed Miss Fanny. "Never mind that. Pray go on to something else besides our having no nonsense about us."

"Yes, my love," said Mr. Sparkler. "And I assure you, Amy, that nothing can be a greater happiness to myself, myself—next to the happiness of being so highly honored with the choice of a glorious girl who hasn't an atom of——"

"Pray, Edmund, pray!" interrupted Fanny, with a slight pat of her pretty foot upon the floor.

"My love, you're quite right," said Mr. Sparkler, "and I know I have a habit of it. What I wished to declare was, that nothing can be a greater happiness to myself, myself—next to the happiness of being united to pre-eminently the most glorious of girls—than to have the happiness of cultivating the affectionate acquaintance of Amy. I may not myself," said Mr. Sparkler manfully, "be up to the mark on some other subjects at a short notice, and I am aware that if you were to poll Society the general opinion might be that I am not; but on the subject of Amy, I AM up to the mark!"

Mr. Sparkler kissed her, in witness thereof.

"A knife and fork and an apartment," proceeded Mr. Sparkler, growing, in comparison with his oratorical antecedents, quite diffuse, "will ever be at Amy's disposal. My Governor, I am sure, will always be proud to enter-tain one whom I so much esteem. And regarding my mother," said Mr. Sparkler, "who is a remarkably fine woman, with——"

"Edmund, Edmund!" cried Miss Fanny, as before.

"With submission, my soul," pleaded Mr. Sparkler. "I know I have a habit of it, and I thank you very much, my adorable girl, for taking the trouble to correct it; but my mother is admitted on all sides to be a remarkably fine woman, and she really hasn't any."

"That may be, or may not be," returned Fanny, "but pray don't mention it any more."

"I will not, my love," said Mr. Sparkler.

"Then in fact you have nothing more to say, Edmund; have you?" enquired Fanny.

"So far from it, my adorable girl," answered Mr. Sparkler, "I apologise for having said so much."

Mr. Sparkler perceived, by a kind of inspiration, that the question implied had he not better go? He therefore withdrew the fraternal railing, and neatly said that he thought he would, with submission, take his leave. He did not go without being congratulated by Amy, as well as she could discharge that office in the flutter and distress of her spirits.

When he was gone, she said, "O, Fanny, Fanny!" and turned to her sister in the bright window, and fell upon her bosom and cried there. Fanny laughed at first; but soon laid her face against her sister's and cried too—a little. It was the last time Fanny ever showed that there was any hidden, suppressed, or conquered feeling in her on that matter. From that hour, the way she had chosen lay before her, and she trod it with her own imperious self-willed step.

END OF No. XIV

CHAPTER XV

NO JUST CAUSE OR IMPEDIMENT WHY THESE TWO PERSONS SHOULD NOT BE JOINED TOGETHER

MR. DORRIT, on being informed by his elder daughter that she had accepted matrimonial overtures from Mr. Sparkler, to whom she had plighted her troth, received the communication, at once with great dignity and with a large display of parental pride; his dignity dilating with the widened prospect of advantageous ground from which to make acquaintances, and his parental pride being developed by Miss Fanny's ready sympathy with that great object of his existence. He gave her to understand that her noble ambition found harmonious echoes in his heart; and bestowed his blessing on her, as a child brimful of duty and good principle, self-devoted to the aggrandisement of the family name.

To Mr. Sparkler, when Miss Fanny permitted him to appear, Mr.

Dorrit said, he would not disguise that the alliance Mr. Sparkler did him the honor to propose was highly congenial to his feelings; both as being in unison with the spontaneous affections of his daughter Fanny, and as opening a family connexion of a gratifying nature with Mr. Merdle, the master spirit of the age. Mrs. Merdle also, as a leading lady rich in distinction, elegance, grace, and beauty, he mentioned in very laudatory terms. He felt it his duty to remark (he was sure a gentleman of Mr. Sparkler's fine sense would interpret him with all delicacy), that he could not consider this proposal definitively determined on, until he should have had the privilege of holding some correspondence with Mr. Merdle; and of ascertaining it to be so far accordant with the views of that eminent gentleman as that his (Mr. Dorrit's) daughter would be received on that footing, which her station in life and her dowry and expectations warranted him in requiring that she should maintain in what he trusted he might be allowed, without the appearance of being mercenary, to call the Eye of the Great World. While saying this, which his character as a gentleman of some little station, and his character as a father, equally demanded of him, he would not be so diplomatic as to conceal that the proposal remained in hopeful abeyance and under conditional acceptance, and that he thanked Mr. Sparkler for the compliment rendered to himself and to his family. He concluded with some further and more general observations on the—ha—character of an independent gentleman, and the—hum—character of a possibly too partial and admiring parent. To sum the whole up shortly, he received Mr. Sparkler's offer very much as he would have received three or four half-crowns from him in the days that were gone.

Mr. Sparkler, finding himself stunned by the words thus heaped upon his inoffensive head, made a brief though pertinent rejoinder; the same being neither more nor less than that he had long perceived Miss Fanny to have no nonsense about her, and that he had no doubt of its being all right with his Governor. At that point, the object of his affections shut him up like a box with a spring lid, and sent him away.

Proceeding shortly afterwards to pay his respects to the Bosom, Mr. Dorrit was received by it with great consideration. Mrs. Merdle had heard of this affair from Edmund. She had been surprised at first, because she had not thought Edmund a marrying man. Society had not thought Edmund a marrying man. Still, of course she had seen, as a woman (we women did instinctively see these things, Mr. Dorrit!), that Edmund had been immensely captivated by Miss Dorrit, and she had openly said that Mr. Dorrit had much to answer for in bringing so charming a girl abroad to turn the heads of his countrymen.

"Have I the honor to conclude, madam," said Mr. Dorrit, "that the direction which Mr. Sparkler's affections have taken, is—ha—approved of by you?"

"I assure you, Mr. Dorrit," returned the lady, "that, personally, I am charmed."

That was very gratifying to Mr. Dorrit.

"Personally," repeated Mrs. Merdle, "charmed."

This casual repetition of the word personally, moved Mr. Dorrit to express his hope that Mr. Merdle's approval, too, would not be wanting?

"I cannot," said Mrs. Merdle, "take upon myself to answer positively for Mr. Merdle; gentlemen, especially gentlemen who are what Society calls capitalists, having their own ideas of these matters. But I should think—merely giving an opinion, Mr. Dorrit—I should think Mr. Merdle would be upon the whole," here she held a review of herself before adding at her leisure, "quite charmed."

At the mention of gentlemen whom Society called capitalists, Mr. Dorrit had coughed, as if some internal demur were breaking out of him. Mrs. Merdle had observed it, and went on to take up the cue.

"Though indeed, Mr. Dorrit, it is scarcely necessary for me to make that remark, except in the mere openness of saying what is uppermost to one whom I so highly regard, and with whom I hope I may have the pleasure of being brought into still more agreeable relations. For, one cannot but see the great probability of your considering such things from Mr. Merdle's own point of view, except indeed that circumstances have made it Mr. Merdle's accidental fortune, or misfortune, to be engaged in business transactions, and that they, however vast, may a little cramp his horizon. I am a very child as to having any notion of business," said Mrs. Merdle; "but, I am afraid, Mr. Dorrit, it may have that tendency."

This skilful see-saw of Mr. Dorrit and Mr. Merdle, so that each of them sent the other up, and each of them sent the other down, and neither had the advantage, acted as a sedative on Mr. Dorrit's cough. He remarked, with his utmost politeness, that he must beg to protest against its being supposed, even by Mrs. Merdle, the accomplished and graceful (to which compliment she bent herself), that such enterprises as Mr. Merdle's, apart as they were from the puny undertakings of the rest of men, had any lower tendency than to enlarge and expand the genius in which they were conceived. "You are generosity itself," said Mrs. Merdle in return, smiling her best smile; "let us hope so. But I confess I am almost superstitious in my ideas about business."

Mr. Dorrit threw in another compliment here, to the effect that business, like the time which was precious in it, was made for slaves; and that it was not for Mrs. Merdle, who ruled all hearts at her supreme pleasure, to have anything to do with it. Mrs. Merdle laughed, and conveyed to Mr. Dorrit an idea that the bosom flushed—which was one of her best effects.

"I say so much," she then explained, "merely because Mr. Merdle has always taken the greatest interest in Edmund, and has always expressed

the strongest desire to advance his prospects. Edmund's public position
I think you know. His private position rests wholly with Mr. Merdle. In
my foolish incapacity for business, I assure you I know no more."

Mr. Dorrit again expressed, in his own way, the sentiment that business
was below the ken of enslavers and enchantresses. He then mentioned his
intention, as a gentleman and a parent, of writing to Mr. Merdle. Mrs.
Merdle concurred with all her heart—or with all her art, which was exactly
the same thing—and herself dispatched a preparatory letter by the next
post, to the eighth wonder of the world.

In his epistolary communication, as in his dialogues and discourses on
the great question to which it related, Mr. Dorrit surrounded the subject
with flourishes, as writing-masters embellish copy-books and cyphering-
books: where the titles of the elementary rules of arithmetic diverge into
swans, eagles, griffins, and other caligraphic recreations, and where the
capital letters go out of their minds and bodies into ecstasies of pen and
ink. Nevertheless, he did render the purport of his letter sufficiently clear,
to enable Mr. Merdle to make a decent pretence of having learnt it from
that source. Mr. Merdle replied to it, accordingly. Mr. Dorrit replied to
Mr. Merdle; Mr. Merdle replied to Mr. Dorrit; and it was soon announced
that the corresponding powers had come to a satisfactory understanding.

Now, and not before, Miss Fanny burst upon the scene, completely
arrayed for her new part. Now, and not before, she wholly absorbed Mr.
Sparkler in her light, and shone for both and twenty more. No longer
feeling that want of a defined place and character which had caused her
so much trouble, this fair ship began to steer steadily on a shaped course,
and to swim with a weight and balance that developed her sailing qualities.

"The preliminaries being so satisfactorily arranged, I think I will
now, my dear," said Mr. Dorrit, "announce—ha—formally, to Mrs.
General——"

"Papa," returned Fanny, taking him up short, upon that name, "I
don't see what Mrs. General has got to do with it."

"My dear," said Mr. Dorrit, "it will be an act of courtesy to—hum—
a lady, well bred and refined——"

"Oh! I am sick of Mrs. General's good breeding and refinement, papa,"
said Fanny. "I am tired of Mrs. General."

"Tired," repeated Mr. Dorrit, in reproachful astonishment, "of—ha—
Mrs. General!"

"Quite disgusted with her, papa," said Fanny. "I really don't see that
she has anything to do with my marriage. Let her keep to her own matrimonial projects—if she has any."

"Fanny," returned Mr. Dorrit, with a grave and weighty slowness upon
him, contrasting strongly with his daughter's levity: "I beg the favor of
your explaining—ha—what it is you mean."

"I mean, papa," said Fanny, "that if Mrs. General should happen to have any matrimonial projects of her own, I dare say they are quite enough to occupy her spare time. And that if she has not, so much the better; but still I don't wish to have the honor of making announcements to her."

"Permit me to ask you, Fanny," said Mr. Dorrit, "why not?"

"Because she can find my engagement out for herself, papa," retorted Fanny. "She is watchful enough, I dare say. I think I have seen her so. Let her find it out for herself. If she should not find it out for herself, she will know it when I am married. And I hope you will not consider me wanting in affection for you, papa, if I say it strikes me that will be quite time enough for Mrs. General."

"Fanny," returned Mr. Dorrit, "I am amazed, I am displeased, by this— hum—this capricious and unintelligible display of animosity towards— ha—Mrs. General."

"Do not, if you please, papa," urged Fanny, "call it animosity, because I assure you I do not consider Mrs. General worth my animosity."

At this, Mr. Dorrit rose from his chair with a fixed look of severe reproof, and remained standing in his dignity before his daughter. His daughter, turning the bracelet on her arm, and now looking at him, and now looking from him, said, "Very well, papa. I am truly sorry if you don't like it; but I can't help it. I am not a child, and I am not Amy, and I must speak."

"Fanny," gasped Mr. Dorrit, after a majestic silence, "if I request you to remain here, while I formally announce to Mrs. General, as an exemplary lady who is—hum—a trusted member of this family, the—ha—the change that is contemplated among us; if I—ha—not only request it, but— hum—insist upon it——"

"Oh, papa," Fanny broke in with pointed significance, "if you make so much of it as that, I have in duty nothing to do but comply. I hope I may have my thoughts upon the subject, however, for I really cannot help it under the circumstances." So, Fanny sat down with a meekness which, in the junction of extremes, became defiance; and her father, either not deigning to answer, or not knowing what to answer, summoned Mr. Tinkler into his presence.

"Mrs. General."

Mr. Tinkler, unused to receive such short orders in connexion with the fair varnisher, paused. Mr. Dorrit, seeing the whole Marshalsea and all its Testimonials in the pause, instantly flew at him with, "How dare you, sir? What do you mean?"

"I beg your pardon, sir," pleaded Mr. Tinkler, "I was wishful to know——"

"You wished to know nothing, sir," cried Mr. Dorrit, highly flushed. "Don't tell me you did. Ha. You didn't. You were guilty of mockery, sir."

"I assure you, sir——" Mr. Tinkler began.

"Don't assure me!" said Mr. Dorrit. "I will not be assured by a domestic.

You were guilty of mockery. You shall leave me—hum—the whole establishment shall leave me. What are you waiting for?"

"Only for my orders, sir."

"It's false," said Mr. Dorrit, "you have your orders. Ha—hum. My compliments to Mrs. General, and I beg the favor of her coming to me, if quite convenient, for a few minutes. Those are your orders."

In his execution of this mission, Mr. Tinkler perhaps expressed that Mr. Dorrit was in a raging fume. However that was, Mrs. General's skirts were very speedily heard outside, coming along—one might almost have said bouncing along—with unusual expedition. Albeit, they settled down at the door and swept into the room with their customary coolness.

"Mrs. General," said Mr. Dorrit, "take a chair."

Mrs. General, with a graceful curve of acknowledgment, descended into the chair which Mr. Dorrit offered.

"Madam," pursued that gentleman, "as you have had the kindness to undertake the—hum—formation of my daughters, and as I am persuaded that nothing nearly affecting them can—ha—be indifferent to you——"

"Wholly impossible," said Mrs. General in the calmest of ways.

"—I therefore wish to announce to you, madam, that my daughter now present——"

Mrs. General made a slight inclination of her head to Fanny. Who made a very low inclination of her head to Mrs. General, and came loftily upright again.

"—That my daughter Fanny is—ha—contracted to be married to Mr. Sparkler, with whom you are acquainted. Hence, madam, you will be relieved of half your difficult charge—ha—difficult charge." Mr. Dorrit repeated it with his angry eye on Fanny. "But not, I hope, to the—hum—diminution of any other portion, direct or indirect, of the footing you have at present the kindness to occupy in my family."

"Mr. Dorrit," returned Mrs. General, with her gloved hands resting on one another in exemplary repose, "is ever considerate, and ever but too appreciative of my friendly services."

(Miss Fanny coughed, as much as to say, "You are right.")

"Miss Dorrit has no doubt exercised the soundest discretion of which the circumstances admitted, and I trust will allow me to offer her my sincere congratulations. When free from the trammels of passion," Mrs. General closed her eyes at the word, as if she could not utter it, and see anybody; "when occurring with the approbation of near relatives; and when cementing the proud structure of a family edifice; these are usually auspicious events. I trust Miss Dorrit will allow me to offer her my best congratulations."

Here Mrs. General stopped, and added internally, for the setting of her face, "Papa, potatoes, poultry, prunes, and prism."

"Mr. Dorrit," she superadded aloud, "is ever most obliging; and for the attention, and I will add distinction, of having this confidence imparted to me by himself and Miss Dorrit at this early time, I beg to offer the tribute of my thanks. My thanks, and my congratulations, are equally the meed of Mr. Dorrit and of Miss Dorrit."

"To me," observed Miss Fanny, "they are excessively gratifying—inexpressibly so. The relief of finding that you have no objection to make, Mrs. General, quite takes a load off my mind, I am sure. I hardly know what I should have done," said Fanny, "if you had interposed any objection, Mrs. General."

Mrs. General changed her gloves, as to the right glove being uppermost and the left undermost, with a Prunes and Prism smile.

"To preserve your approbation, Mrs. General," said Fanny, returning the smile with one in which there was no trace of those ingredients, "will of course be the highest object of my married life; to lose it, would of course be perfect wretchedness. I am sure your great kindness will not object, and I hope papa will not object, to my correcting a small mistake you have made, however. The best of us are so liable to mistakes, that even you, Mrs. General, have fallen into a little error. The attention and distinction you have so impressively mentioned, Mrs. General, as attaching to this confidence, are, I have no doubt, of the most complimentary and gratifying description; but they don't at all proceed from me. The merit of having consulted you on the subject would have been so great in me, that I feel I must not lay claim to it when it really is not mine. It is wholly papa's. I am deeply obliged to you for your encouragement and patronage, but it was papa who asked for it. I have to thank you, Mrs. General, for relieving my breast of a great weight by so handsomely giving your consent to my engagement, but you have really nothing to thank me for. I hope you will always approve of my proceedings after I have left home, and that my sister also may long remain the favored object of your condescension, Mrs. General."

With this address, which was delivered in her politest manner, Fanny left the room with an elegant and cheerful air—to tear up-stairs with a flushed face as soon as she was out of hearing, pounce in upon her sister, call her a little Dormouse, shake her for the better opening of her eyes, tell her what had passed below, and ask her what she thought about Pa now?

Towards Mrs. Merdle, the young lady comported herself with great independence and self-possession; but not as yet with any more decided opening of hostilities. Occasionally they had a slight skirmish, as when Fanny considered herself patted on the back by that lady, or as when Mrs. Merdle looked particularly young and well; but Mrs. Merdle always soon terminated those passages of arms by sinking among her cushions with the gracefullest indifference, and finding her attention otherwise engaged. Society (for that mysterious creature sat upon the Seven Hills too) found

Miss Fanny vastly improved by her engagement. She was much more accessible, much more free and engaging, much less exacting; insomuch that she now entertained a host of followers and admirers, to the bitter indignation of ladies with daughters to marry, who were to be regarded as having revolted from Society on the Miss Dorrit grievance, and erected a rebellious standard. Enjoying the flutter she caused, Miss Dorrit not only haughtily moved through it in her own proper person, but haughtily, even ostentatiously, led Mr. Sparkler through it too: seeming to say to them all, "If I think proper to march among you in triumphal procession attended by this weak captive in bonds, rather than a stronger one, that is my business. Enough that I choose to do it!" Mr. Sparkler, for his part, questioned nothing; but went wherever he was taken, did whatever he was told, felt that for his bride-elect to be distinguished was for him to be distinguished on the easiest terms, and was truly grateful for being so openly acknowledged.

The winter passing on towards the spring while this condition of affairs prevailed, it became necessary for Mr. Sparkler to repair to England, and take his appointed part in the expression and direction of its genius, learning, commerce, spirit, and sense. The land of Shakespeare, Milton, Bacon, Newton, Watt, the land of a host of past and present abstract philosophers, natural philosophers, and subduers of Nature and Art in their myriad forms, called to Mr. Sparkler to come and take care of it, lest it should perish. Mr. Sparkler, unable to resist the agonised cry from the depths of his country's soul, declared that he must go.

It followed that the question was rendered pressing when, where, and how, Mr. Sparkler should be married to the foremost girl in all this world with no nonsense about her. Its solution, after some little mystery and secresy, Miss Fanny herself announced to her sister.

"Now, my child," said she, seeking her out one day, "I am going to tell you something. It is only this moment broached; and naturally I hurry to you the moment it *is* broached."

"Your marriage, Fanny ?"

"My precious child," said Fanny, "don't anticipate me. Let me impart my confidence to you, you flurried little thing, in my own way. As to your guess, if I answered it literally, I should answer no. For really it is not my marriage that is in question, half as much as it is Edmund's."

Little Dorrit looked, and perhaps not altogether without cause, somewhat at a loss to understand this fine distinction.

"I am in no difficulty," exclaimed Fanny, "and in no hurry. I am not wanted at any public office, or to give any vote anywhere else. But Edmund is. And Edmund is deeply dejected at the idea of going away by himself, and, indeed, I don't like that he should be trusted by himself. For, if it's possible—and it generally is—to do a foolish thing, he is sure to do it."

As she concluded this impartial summary of the reliance that might be safely placed upon her future husband, she took off, with an air of business, the bonnet she wore, and dangled it by its strings upon the ground.

"It is far more Edmund's question, therefore, than mine. However we need say no more about that. That is self-evident on the face of it. Well, my dearest Amy! The point arising, is he to go by himself, or is he not to go by himself, this other point arises, are we to be married here and shortly, or are we to be married at home months hence?"

"I see I am going to lose you, Fanny."

"What a little thing you are," cried Fanny, half tolerant and half impatient, "for anticipating one! Pray, my darling, hear me out. That woman," she spoke of Mrs. Merdle, of course, "remains here until after Easter; so, in the case of my being married here and going to London with Edmund, I should have the start of her. That is something. Further, Amy. That woman being out of the way, I don't know that I greatly object to Mr. Merdle's proposal to Pa that Edmund and I should take up our abode in that house—*you* know—where you once went with a dancer, my dear—until our own house can be chosen and fitted up. Further still, Amy. Papa having always intended to go to town himself, in the spring,—you see, if Edmund and I were married here, we might go off to Florence, where papa might join us, and we might all three travel home together. Mr. Merdle has entreated Pa to stay with him in that same mansion I have mentioned, and I suppose he will. But he is master of his own actions; and upon that point (which is not at all material), I can't speak positively."

The difference between papa's being master of his own actions and Mr. Sparkler's being nothing of the sort, was forcibly expressed by Fanny in her manner of stating the case. Not that her sister noticed it; for she was divided between regret at the coming separation, and a lingering wish that she had been included in the plans for visiting England.

"And these are the arrangements, Fanny dear?"

"Arrangements!" repeated Fanny. "Now, really, child, you are a little trying. You know I particularly guarded myself against laying my words open to any such construction. What I said was, that certain questions present themselves; and these are the questions."

Little Dorrit's thoughtful eyes met hers, tenderly and quietly.

"Now, my own sweet girl," said Fanny, weighing her bonnet by the strings with considerable impatience, "it's no use staring. A little owl could stare. I look to you for advice, Amy. What do you advise me to do?"

"Do you think," asked Little Dorrit persuasively, after a short hesitation, "do you think, Fanny, that if you were to put it off for a few months, it might be, considering all things, best?"

"No, little Tortoise," retorted Fanny, with exceeding sharpness. "I don't think anything of the kind."

Here, she threw her bonnet from her altogether, and flounced into a chair. But, becoming affectionate almost immediately, she flounced out of it again, and kneeled down on the floor to take her sister, chair and all, in her arms.

"Don't suppose I am hasty or unkind, darling, because I really am not. But you are such a little oddity! You make one bite your head off, when one wants to be soothing beyond everything. Didn't I tell you, you dearest baby, that Edmund can't be trusted by himself? And don't you know that he can't?"

"Yes, yes, Fanny. You said so, I know."

"And you know it, I know," retorted Fanny. "Well, my precious child! If he is not to be trusted by himself, it follows, I suppose, that I should go with him?"

"It—seems so, love," said Little Dorrit.

"Therefore, having heard the arrangements that are feasible to carry out that object, am I to understand, dearest Amy, that on the whole you advise me to make them?"

"It—seems so, love," said Little Dorrit again.

"Very well!" cried Fanny with an air of resignation, "then I suppose it must be done! I came to you, my sweet, the moment I saw the doubt, and the necessity of deciding. I have now decided. So let it be!"

After yielding herself up, in this pattern manner, to sisterly advice and the force of circumstances, Fanny became quite benignant: as one who had laid her own inclinations at the feet of her dearest friend, and felt a glow of conscience in having made the sacrifice. "After all, my Amy," she said to her sister, "you are the best of small creatures, and full of good sense; and I don't know what I shall ever do without you!"

With which words she folded her in a closer embrace, and a really fond one.

"Not that I contemplate doing without you, Amy, by any means, for I hope we shall ever be next to inseparable. And now, my pet, I am going to give you a word of advice. When you are left alone here with Mrs. General——"

"I am to be left alone here, with Mrs. General?" said Little Dorrit, quietly.

"Why, of course, my precious, till papa comes back! Unless you call Edward company, which he certainly is not, even when he is here, and still more certainly is not when he is away at Naples or in Sicily. I was going to say—but you are such a beloved little Marplot for putting one out—when you are left alone here with Mrs. General, Amy, don't you let her slide into any sort of artful understanding with you that she is looking

after Pa, or that Pa is looking after her. She will, if she can. *I* know her sly
manner of feeling her way with those gloves of hers. But, don't you comprehend her on any account. And if Pa should tell you when he comes
back, that he has it in contemplation to make Mrs. General your mama
(which is not the less likely because I am going away), my advice to you is,
that you say at once 'Papa, I beg to object most strongly. Fanny cautioned
me about this, and she objected, and I object.' I don't mean to say that
any objection from you, Amy, is likely to be of the smallest effect, or that
I think you likely to make it with any degree of firmness. But there is
a principle involved—a filial principle—and I implore you not to submit to
be mother-in-lawed by Mrs. General, without asserting it in making every
one about you as uncomfortable as possible. I don't expect you to stand
by it—indeed, I know you won't, Pa being concerned—but I wish to
rouse you to a sense of duty. As to any help from me, or as to any opposition
that I can offer to such a match, you shall not be left in the lurch, my love.
Whatever weight I may derive from my position as a married girl not
wholly devoid of attractions —used, as that position always shall be, to
oppose that woman—I will bring to bear, you may depend upon it, on the
head and false hair (for I am confident it's not all real, ugly as it is, and
unlikely as it appears that any one in their senses would go to the expense
of buying it), of Mrs. General!"

Little Dorrit received this counsel without venturing to oppose it,
but without giving Fanny any reason to believe that she intended to act
upon it. Having now, as it were, formally wound up her single life and
arranged her worldly affairs, Fanny proceeded with characteristic ardor
to prepare for the serious change in her condition.

The preparation consisted in the dispatch of her maid to Paris under
the protection of the Courier, for the purchase of that outfit for a bride on
which it would be extremely low, in the present narrative, to bestow an
English name, but to which (on a vulgar principle it observes of adhering to
the language in which it professes to be written) it declines to give a French
one. The rich and beautiful wardrobe purchased by these agents, in the
course of a few weeks made its way through the intervening country,
bristling with custom-houses, garrisoned by an immense army of shabby
mendicants in uniform, who incessantly repeated the Beggar's Petition
over it, as if every individual warrior among them were the ancient
Belisarius: and of whom there were so many Legions, that unless the
Courier had expended just one bushel and a half of silver money in relieving their distresses, they would have worn the wardrobe out before
it got to Rome, by turning it over and over. Through all such dangers,
however, it was triumphantly brought, inch by inch, and arrived at its
journey's end in fine condition.

There it was exhibited to select companies of female viewers, in whose
gentle bosoms it awakened implacable feelings. Concurrently, active

preparations were made for the day on which some of its treasures were to
be publicly displayed. Cards of breakfast-invitation were sent out to half
the English in the city of Romulus; the other half made arrangements to
be under arms, as criticising volunteers, at various outer points of the
solemnity. The most high and illustrious English Signor Edgardo Dorrit,
came post through the deep mud and ruts (from forming a surface under
the improving Neapolitan nobility), to grace the occasion. The best hotel,
and all its culinary myrmidons, were set to work to prepare the feast. The
drafts of Mr. Dorrit almost constituted a run on the Torlonia Bank. The
British Consul hadn't had such a marriage in the whole of his Consularity.

The day came, and the She-Wolf in the Capitol might have snarled
with envy to see how the Island Savages contrived these things now-a-
days. The murderous-headed statues of the wicked Emperors of the
Soldiery, whom sculptors had not been able to flatter out of their villanous
hideousness, might have come off their pedestals to run away with the
Bride. The choked old fountain, where erst the Gladiators washed, might
have leaped into life again to honor the ceremony. The Temple of Vesta
might have sprung up anew from its ruins, expressly to lend its countenance to the occasion. Might have done; but did not. Like sentient
things—even like the lords and ladies of creation sometimes—might have
done much, but did nothing. The celebration went off with admirable
pomp: monks in black robes, white robes, and russet robes stopped to
look after the carriages; wandering peasants in fleeces of sheep, begged and
piped under the house-windows; the English volunteers defiled; the day
wore on to the hour of vespers: the festival wore away; the thousand
churches rang their bells without any reference to it; and Saint Peter
denied that he had anything to do with it.

But, by that time the Bride was near the end of the first day's journey
towards Florence. It was the peculiarity of these nuptials that they were
all Bride. Nobody noticed the Bridegroom. Nobody noticed the first
Bridesmaid. Few could have seen Little Dorrit (who held that post) for
the glare, even supposing many to have sought her. So, the Bride had
mounted into her handsome chariot, incidentally accompanied by the
Bridegroom; and after rolling for a few minutes smoothly over a fair
pavement, had begun to jolt through a Slough of Despond, and through
a long, long avenue of wrack and ruin. Other nuptial carriages are said to
have gone the same road, before and since.

If Little Dorrit found herself left a little lonely and a little low that
night, nothing would have done so much against her feeling of depression
as the being able to sit at work by her father as in the old time, and help him
to his supper and his rest. But that was not to be thought of now, when they
sat in the state-equipage with Mrs. General on the coach-box. And as to
supper! If Mr. Dorrit had wanted supper, there was an Italian cook and
there was a Swiss confectioner, who must have put on caps as high as the

Pope's Mitre, and have performed the mysteries of Alchemists in a copper-saucepaned laboratory below, before he could have got it.

He was sententious and didactic that night. If he had been simply loving, he would have done Little Dorrit more good; but she accepted him as he was—when had she not accepted him as he was!—and made the most and best of him. Mrs. General at length retired. Her retirement for the night was always her frostiest ceremony; as if she felt it necessary that the human imagination should be chilled into stone, to prevent its following her. When she had gone through her rigid preliminaries, amounting to a sort of genteel platoon-exercise, she withdrew. Little Dorrit then put her arm round her father's neck, to bid him good night.

"Amy, my dear," said Mr. Dorrit, taking her by the hand, "this is the close of a day, that has—ha—greatly impressed and gratified me."

"A little tired you, dear, too?"

"No," said Mr. Dorrit, "no: I am not sensible of fatigue when it arises from an occasion so—hum—replete with gratification of the purest kind."

Little Dorrit was glad to find him in such heart, and smiled from her own heart.

"My dear," he continued. "This is an occasion—ha—teeming with a good example. With a good example, my favorite and attached child—hum—to you."

Little Dorrit, fluttered by his words, did not know what to say, though he stopped, as if he expected her to say something.

"Amy," he resumed; "your dear sister, our Fanny, has contracted—ha hum—a marriage, eminently calculated to extend the basis of our—ha—connexion, and to—hum—consolidate our social relations. My love, I trust that the time is not far distant when some—ha—eligible partner may be found for you."

"Oh no! Let me stay with you. I beg and pray that I may stay with you! I want nothing but to stay and take care of you!"

She said it like one in sudden alarm.

"Nay, Amy, Amy," said Mr. Dorrit. "This is weak and foolish, weak and foolish. You have a—ha—responsibility imposed upon you by your position. It is, to develop that position, and be—hum—worthy that position. As to taking care of me; I can—ha—take care of myself. Or," he added after a moment, "if I should need to be taken care of, I—hum—can, with the—ha—blessing of Providence, *be* taken care of. I—ha hum—I cannot, my dear child, think of engrossing, and—ha—as it were, sacrificing you."

O what a time of day at which to begin that profession of self-denial; at which to make it, with an air of taking credit for it; at which to believe it, if such a thing could be!

"Don't speak, Amy. I positively say I cannot do it. I—ha—must not do it. My—hum—conscience would not allow it. I therefore, my love, take the opportunity afforded by this gratifying and impressive occasion of—ha—solemnly remarking, that it is now a cherished wish and purpose of mine to see you—ha—eligibly (I repeat eligibly) married."

"Oh no, dear! Pray!"

"Amy," said Mr. Dorrit, "I am well persuaded that if the topic were referred to any person of superior social knowledge, of superior delicacy, and sense—let us say, for instance, to—ha—Mrs. General—that there would not be two opinions as to the—hum—affectionate character and propriety of my sentiments. But, as I know your loving and dutiful nature from—hum—from experience, I am quite satisfied that it is necessary to say no more. I have—hum—no husband to propose at present, my dear; I have not even one in view. I merely wish that we should—ha—understand each other. Hum. Good night, my dear and sole remaining daughter. Good night. God bless you!"

If the thought ever entered Little Dorrit's head, that night, that he could give her up lightly now, in his prosperity, and when he had it in his mind to replace her with a second wife, she drove it away. Faithful to him still, as in the worst times through which she had borne him single-handed, she drove the thought away; and entertained no harder reflection, in her tearful unrest, than that he now saw everything through their wealth, and through the care he always had upon him that they should continue rich, and grow richer.

They sat in their equipage of state, with Mrs. General on the box, for three weeks longer, and then he started for Florence to join Fanny. Little Dorrit would have been glad to bear him company so far, only for the sake of her own love, and then to have turned back alone, thinking of dear England. But, though the Courier had gone on with the Bride, the Valet was next in the line; and the succession would not have come to her, as long as any one was to be got for money.

Mrs. General took life easily—as easily, that is, as she could take anything—when the Roman establishment remained in their sole occupation; and Little Dorrit would often ride out in a hired carriage that was left them, and alight alone and wander among the ruins of old Rome. The ruins of the vast old Amphitheatre, of the old Temples, of the old commemorative Arches, of the old trodden highways, of the old tombs, besides being what they were, to her, were ruins of the old Marshalsea—ruins of her own old life—ruins of the faces and forms that of old peopled it—ruins of its loves, hopes, cares, and joys. Two ruined spheres of action and suffering were before the solitary girl often sitting on some broken fragment; and in the lonely places, under the blue sky, she saw them both together.

Up, then, would come Mrs. General: taking all the color out of everything, as Nature and Art had taken it out of herself; writing Prunes and Prism, in Mr. Eustace's text, wherever she could lay a hand; looking everywhere for Mr. Eustace and company, and seeing nothing else; scratching up the dryest little bones of antiquity, and bolting them whole without any human visitings—like a Ghoule in gloves.

CHAPTER XVI

GETTING ON

THE newly-married pair, on their arrival in Harley Street, Cavendish Square, London, were received by the Chief Butler. That great man was not interested in them, but on the whole endured them. People must continue to be married and given in marriage, or Chief Butlers would not be wanted. As nations are made to be taxed, so families are made to be butlered. The Chief Butler, no doubt, reflected that the course of nature required the wealthy population to be kept up, on his account.

He therefore condescended to look at the carriage from the Hall-door without frowning at it, and said, in a very handsome way, to one of his men, "Thomas, help with the luggage." He even escorted the Bride up-stairs into Mr. Merdle's presence; but, this must be considered as an act of homage to the sex (of which he was an admirer, being notoriously captivated by the charms of a certain Duchess), and not as a committal of himself with the family.

Mr. Merdle was slinking about the hearthrug, waiting to welcome Mrs. Sparkler. His hand seemed to retreat up his sleeve as he advanced to do so, and he gave her such a superfluity of coat-cuff that it was like being received by the popular conception of Guy Fawkes. When he put his lips to hers, besides, he took himself into custody by the wrists, and backed himself among the ottomans, and chairs and tables, as if he were his own Police officer, saying to himself "Now, none of that! Come! I've got you, you know, and you go quietly along with me!"

Mrs. Sparkler, installed in the rooms of state—the innermost sanctuary of down, silk, chintz, and fine linen—felt that so far her triumph was good, and her way made, step by step. On the day before her marriage, she had bestowed on Mrs. Merdle's maid with an air of gracious indifference, in Mrs. Merdle's presence, a trifling little keepsake (bracelet, bonnet, and two dresses, all new) about four times as valuable as the present formerly made by Mrs. Merdle to her. She was now established in Mrs. Merdle's own rooms, to which some extra touches had been given to render them more worthy of her occupation. In her mind's eye, as she lounged there, surrounded by every luxurious accessory that wealth could obtain or invention devise, she saw the fair bosom that beat in unison with the exultation of her thoughts, competing with the bosom that had been famous so long, outshining it, and deposing it. Happy? Fanny must have been happy. No more wishing one's self dead now.

The Courier had not approved of Mr. Dorrit's staying in the house of a friend, and had preferred to take him to an hotel in Brook Street, Grosvenor Square. Mr. Merdle ordered his carriage to be ready early in the morning, that he might wait upon Mr. Dorrit immediately after breakfast.

Bright the carriage looked, sleek the horses looked, gleaming the harness looked, luscious and lasting the liveries looked. A rich, responsible turn-out. An equipage for a Merdle. Early people looked after it as it rattled along the streets, and said, with awe in their breath, "There he goes!"

There he went, until Brook Street stopped him. Then, forth from its magnificent case came the jewel; not lustrous in itself, but quite the contrary.

Commotion in the office of the hotel. Merdle! The landlord, though a gentleman of a haughty spirit who had just driven a pair of thorough-bred horses into town, turned out to show him up-stairs. The clerks and servants cut him off by back-passages, and were found accidentally hovering in doorways and angles, that they might look upon him. Merdle! O ye sun, moon, and stars, the great man! The rich man, who had in a manner revised the New Testament, and already entered into the kingdom of Heaven. The man who could have any one he chose to dine with him, and who had made the money! As he went up the stairs, people were already posted on the lower stairs, that his shadow might fall upon them when he came down. So were the sick brought out and laid in the track of the Apostle—who had *not* got into the good society, and had *not* made the money.

Mr. Dorrit, dressing-gowned and newspapered, was at his breakfast. The Courier, with agitation in his voice, announced "Miss' Mairdale!" Mr. Dorrit's over-wrought heart bounded as he leaped up.

"Mr. Merdle, this is—ha—indeed an honor. Permit me to express the—hum—sense, the high sense, I entertain of this—ha hum—highly grati-fying act of attention. I am well aware, sir, of the many demands upon your time, and its—ha—enormous value." Mr. Dorrit could not say enormous roundly enough for his own satisfaction. "That you should—ha—at this early hour, bestow any of your priceless time upon me, is—ha—a compliment that I acknowledge with the greatest esteem." Mr. Dorrit positively trembled in addressing the great man.

Mr. Merdle uttered, in his subdued, inward, hesitating voice, a few sounds that were to no purpose whatever; and finally said, "I am glad to see you, sir."

"You are very kind," said Mr. Dorrit. "Truly kind." By this time the visitor was seated, and was passing his great hand over his exhausted forehead. "You are well, I hope, Mr. Merdle?"

"I am as well as I—yes, I am as well as I usually am," said Mr. Merdle. "Your occupations must be immense."

"Tolerably so. But—Oh dear no, there's not much the matter with *me*," said Mr. Merdle, looking round the room.

"A little dyspeptic?" Mr. Dorrit hinted.

"Very likely. But I—Oh, I am well enough," said Mr. Merdle.

There were black traces on his lips where they met, as if a little train of gunpowder had been fired there; and he looked like a man who, if his natural temperament had been quicker, would have been very feverish that morning. This, and his heavy way of passing his hand over his forehead, had prompted Mr. Dorrit's solicitous enquiries.

"Mrs. Merdle," Mr. Dorrit insinuatingly pursued, "I left, as you will be prepared to hear, the—ha—observed of all observers, the—hum— admired of all admirers, the leading fascination and charm of Society in Rome. She was looking wonderfully well when I quitted it."

"Mrs. Merdle," said Mr. Merdle, "is generally considered a very attractive woman. And she is, no doubt. I am sensible of her being so."

"Who can be otherwise?" responded Mr. Dorrit.

Mr. Merdle turned his tongue in his closed mouth—it seemed rather a stiff and unmanageable tongue —moistened his lips, passed his hand over his forehead again, and looked all round the room again, principally under the chairs.

"But," he said, looking Mr. Dorrit in the face for the first time, and immediately afterwards dropping his eyes to the buttons of Mr. Dorrit's waistcoat; "if we speak of attractions, your daughter ought to be the subject of our conversation. She is extremely beautiful. Both in face and figure, she is quite uncommon. When the young people arrived last night, I was really surprised to see such charms."

Mr. Dorrit's gratification was such that he said—ha—he could not refrain from telling Mr. Merdle verbally, as he had already done by letter, what honor and happiness he felt in this union of their families. And he offered his hand. Mr. Merdle looked at the hand for a little while, took it on his for a moment as if his were a yellow salver or fish-slice, and then returned it to Mr. Dorrit.

"I thought I would drive round the first thing," said Mr. Merdle, "to offer my services, in case I can do anything for you; and to say that I hope you will at least do me the honor of dining with me to-day, and every day when you are not better engaged, during your stay in town."

Mr. Dorrit was enraptured by these attentions.

"Do you stay long, sir?"

"I have not at present the intention," said Mr. Dorrit, "of—ha— exceeding a fortnight."

"That's a very short stay, after so long a journey," returned Mr. Merdle.

"Hum. Yes," said Mr. Dorrit. "But the truth is—ha—my dear Mr.

Merdle, that I find a foreign life so well suited to my health and taste, that I—hum—have but two objects in my present visit to London. First, the—ha—the distinguished happiness and—ha—privilege which I now enjoy and appreciate; secondly, the arrangement—hum—the laying out, that is to say, in the best way of—ha hum—my money."

"Well, sir," said Mr. Merdle, after turning his tongue again, "if I can be of any use to you in that respect, you may command me."

Mr. Dorrit's speech had had more hesitation in it than usual, as he approached the ticklish topic, for he was not perfectly clear how so exalted a potentate might take it. He had doubts whether reference to any individual capital, or fortune, might not seem a wretchedly retail affair to so wholesale a dealer. Greatly relieved by Mr. Merdle's affable offer of assistance, he caught at it directly, and heaped acknowledgments upon him.

"I scarcely—ha—dared," said Mr. Dorrit, "I assure you, to hope for so—hum—vast an advantage as your direct advice and assistance. Though of course I should, under any circumstances, like the—ha hum—rest of the civilised world, have followed in Mr. Merdle's train."

"You know we may almost say we are related, sir," said Mr. Merdle, curiously interested in the pattern of the carpet, "and, therefore, you may consider me at your service."

"Ha. Very handsome, indeed!" cried Mr. Dorrit. "Ha. Most handsome!"

"It would not," said Mr. Merdle, "be at the present moment easy for what I may call a mere outsider to come into any of the good things—of course I speak of my own good things——"

"Of course, of course!" cried Mr. Dorrit, in a tone implying that there were no other good things.

"—Unless at a high price. At what we are accustomed to term a very long figure."

Mr. Dorrit laughed in the buoyancy of his spirit. Ha, ha, ha! Long figure. Good. Ha. Very expressive, to be sure!

"However," said Mr. Merdle, "I do generally retain in my own hands the power of exercising some preference—people in general would be pleased to call it favor—as a sort of compliment for my care and trouble."

"And public spirit and genius," Mr. Dorrit suggested.

Mr. Merdle, with a dry, swallowing action, seemed to dispose of those qualities like a bolus; then added, "As a sort of return for it. I will see, if you please, how I can exert this limited power (for people are jealous and it is limited), to your advantage."

"You are very good," replied Mr. Dorrit. "You are *very* good."

"Of course," said Mr. Merdle, "there must be the strictest integrity and uprightness in these transactions; there must be the purest faith between man and man; there must be unimpeached and unimpeachable confidence; or business could not be carried on."

Mr. Dorrit hailed these generous sentiments with fervor.

"Therefore," said Mr. Merdle, "I can only give you a preference to a certain extent."

"I perceive. To a defined extent," observed Mr. Dorrit.

"Defined extent. And perfectly above-board. As to my advice, however," said Mr. Merdle, "that is another matter. That, such as it is——"

Oh! Such as it was! (Mr. Dorrit could not bear the faintest appearance of its being depreciated, even by Mr. Merdle himself.)

"—That, there is nothing in the bonds of spotless honor between myself and my fellow-man to prevent my parting with, if I choose. And that," said Mr. Merdle, now deeply intent upon a dust-cart that was passing the windows, "shall be at your command whenever you think proper."

New acknowledgment from Mr. Dorrit. New passages of Mr. Merdle's hand over his forehead. Calm and silence. Contemplation of Mr. Dorrit's waistcoat-buttons, by Mr. Merdle.

"My time being rather precious," said Mr. Merdle, suddenly getting up, as if he had been waiting in the interval for his legs, and they had just come, "I must be moving towards the City. Can I take you anywhere, sir? I shall be happy to set you down, or send you on. My carriage is at your disposal."

Mr. Dorrit bethought himself that he had business at his banker's. His banker's was in the City. That was fortunate; Mr. Merdle would take him into the City. But, surely he might not detain Mr. Merdle while he assumed his coat? Yes, he might, and must; Mr. Merdle insisted on it. So, Mr. Dorrit, retiring into the next room, put himself under the hands of his valet, and in five minutes came back, glorious.

Then, said Mr. Merdle, "Allow me, sir. Take my arm!" Then, leaning on Mr. Merdle's arm, did Mr. Dorrit descend the staircase, seeing the worshippers on the steps, and feeling that the light of Mr. Merdle shone by reflection in himself. Then, the carriage, and the ride into the City; and the people who looked at them; and the hats that flew off grey heads; and the general bowing and crouching before this wonderful mortal, the like of which prostration of spirit was not to be seen—no, by high Heaven, no! (it may be worth thinking of by Fawners of all denominations) —in Westminster Abbey and Saint Paul's Cathedral put together, on any Sunday in the year. It was a rapturous dream to Mr. Dorrit, to find himself set aloft in this public car of triumph, making a magnificent progress to that befitting destination, the golden Street of the Lombards.

There, Mr. Merdle insisted on alighting and going his way a-foot, and leaving his poor equipage at Mr. Dorrit's disposition. So, the dream increased in rapture when Mr. Dorrit came out of the bank alone, and people looked at *him* in default of Mr. Merdle, and when, with the ears of his mind, he heard the frequent exclamation as he rolled glibly along, "A wonderful man to be Mr. Merdle's friend!"

At dinner that day, although the occasion was not foreseen and provided for, a brilliant company of such as are not made of the dust of the earth, but of some superior article for the present unknown, shed their lustrous benediction upon Mr. Dorrit's daughter's marriage. And Mr. Dorrit's daughter that day began, in earnest, her competition with that woman not present; and began it so well, that Mr. Dorrit could all but have taken his affidavit, if required, that Mrs. Sparkler had all her life been lying at full length in the lap of luxury, and had never heard of such a rough word in the English tongue as Marshalsea.

Next day, and the day after, and every day, all graced by more dinner company, cards descended on Mr. Dorrit like theatrical snow. As the friend and relative by marriage of the illustrious Merdle, Bar, Bishop, Treasury, Chorus, Everybody, wanted to make or improve Mr. Dorrit's acquaintance. In Mr. Merdle's heaps of offices in the City, when Mr. Dorrit appeared at any of them on his business taking him Eastward (which it frequently did, for it throve amazingly), the name of Dorrit was always a passport to the great presence of Merdle. So the dream increased in rapture every hour, as Mr. Dorrit felt increasingly sensible that this connexion had brought him forward indeed.

Only one thing sat otherwise than auriferously, and at the same time lightly, on Mr. Dorrit's mind. It was the Chief Butler. That stupendous character looked at him, in the course of his official looking at the dinners, in a manner that Mr. Dorrit considered questionable. He looked at him, as he passed through the hall and up the staircase, going to dinner, with a glazed fixedness that Mr. Dorrit did not like. Seated at table in the act of drinking, Mr. Dorrit still saw him through his wine-glass, regarding him with a cold and ghostly eye. It misgave him that the Chief Butler must have known a Collegian, and must have seen him in the College—perhaps had been presented to him. He looked as closely at the Chief Butler as such a man could be looked at, and yet he did not recall that he had ever seen him elsewhere. Ultimately he was inclined to think that there was no reverence in the man, no sentiment in the great creature. But, he was not relieved by that; for, let him think what he would, the Chief Butler had him in his supercilious eye, even when that eye was on the plate and other table-garniture; and he never let him out of it. To hint to him that this confinement in his eye was disagreeable, or to ask him what he meant, was an act too daring to venture upon; his severity with his employers and their visitors being terrific, and he never permitting himself to be approached with the slightest liberty.

CHAPTER XVII

MISSING

The term of Mr. Dorrit's visit was within two days of being out, and he was about to dress for another inspection by the Chief Butler (whose victims were always dressed expressly for him), when one of the servants of the hotel presented himself bearing a card. Mr. Dorrit, taking it, read:
"Mrs. Finching."

The servant waited in speechless deference.

"Man, man," said Mr. Dorrit, turning upon him with grievous indignation, "explain your motive in bringing me this ridiculous name. I am wholly unacquainted with it. Finching, sir?" said Mr. Dorrit, perhaps avenging himself on the Chief Butler by Substitute. "Ha! What do you mean by Finching?"

The man, man, seemed to mean Flinching as much as anything else, for he backed away from Mr. Dorrit's severe regard, as he replied, "A lady, sir."

"I know no such lady, sir," said Mr. Dorrit. "Take this card away. I know no Finching, of either sex."

"Ask your pardon, sir. The lady said she was aware she might be unknown by name. But, she begged me to say, sir, that she had formerly the honor of being acquainted with Miss Dorrit. The lady said, sir, the youngest Miss Dorrit."

Mr. Dorrit knitted his brows, and rejoined, after a moment or two, "Inform Mrs. Finching, sir," emphasising the name as if the innocent man were solely responsible for it, "that she can come up."

He had reflected, in his momentary pause, that unless she were admitted she might leave some message, or might say something below, having a disgraceful reference to that former state of existence. Hence the concession, and hence the appearance of Flora, piloted in by the man, man.

"I have not the pleasure," said Mr. Dorrit, standing, with the card in his hand, and with an air which imported that it would scarcely have been a first-class pleasure if he had had it, "of knowing either this name, or yourself, madam. Place a chair, sir."

The responsible man, with a start, obeyed, and went out on tiptoe. Flora, putting aside her veil with a bashful tremor upon her, proceeded to introduce herself. At the same time a singular combination of perfumes was diffused through the room, as if some brandy had been put by mistake in a lavender-water bottle, or as if some lavender-water had been put by mistake in a brandy bottle.

"I beg Mr. Dorrit to offer a thousand apologies and indeed they would be far too few for such an intrusion which I know must appear extremely bold in a lady and alone too but I thought it best upon the whole however difficult and even apparently improper though Mr. F's aunt would have willingly accompanied me and as a character of great force and spirit would probably have struck one possessed of such a knowledge of life as no doubt with so many changes must have been acquired, for Mr. F himself said frequently that although well educated in the neighbourhood of Black-heath at as high as eighty guineas which is a good deal for parents and the plate kept back too on going away but that is more a meanness than its value that he had learnt more in his first year as a commercial traveller with a large commission on the sale of an article that nobody would hear of much less buy which preceded the wine trade a long time than in the whole six years in that academy conducted by a college Bachelor, though why a Bachelor more clever than a married man I do not see and never did but pray excuse me that is not the point."

Mr. Dorrit stood rooted to the carpet, a statue of mystification.

"I must openly admit that I have no pretensions," said Flora, "but having known the dear little thing which under altered circumstances appears a liberty but is not so intended and Goodness knows there was no favor in half-a-crown a-day to such a needle as herself but quite the other way and as to anything lowering in it far from it the laborer is worthy of his hire and I am sure I only wish he got it oftener and more animal food and less rheumatism in the back and legs poor soul."

"Madam," said Mr. Dorrit, recovering his breath by a great effort, as the relict of the late Mr. Finching stopped to take hers; "madam," said Mr. Dorrit, very red in the face, "if I understand you to refer to—ha—to anything in the antecedents of—hum—a daughter of mine, involving—ha hum—daily compensation, madam, I beg to observe that the—ha—fact, assuming it—ha—to *be* fact, never was within my knowledge. Hum. I should not have permitted it. Ha. Never! Never!"

"Unnecessary to pursue the subject," returned Flora, "and would not have mentioned it on any account except as supposing it a favorable and only letter of introduction but as to being fact no doubt whatever and you may set your mind at rest for the very dress I have on now can prove it and sweetly made though there is no denying that it would tell better on a better figure for my own is much too fat though how to bring it down I know not, pray excuse me I am roving off again."

Mr. Dorrit backed to his chair in a stony way, and seated himself, as Flora gave him a softening look and played with her parasol.

"The dear little thing," said Flora, "having gone off perfectly limp and white and cold in my house or at least papa's for though not a freehold still a long lease at a peppercorn on the morning when Arthur—foolish habit of our youthful days and Mr. Clennam far more adapted to existing circumstances particularly addressing a stranger and that stranger a gentleman in an elevated station—communicated the glad tidings imparted by a person of the name of Pancks emboldens me."

At the mention of these two names, Mr. Dorrit frowned, stared, frowned again, hesitated with his fingers at his lips, as he had hesitated long ago, and said, "Do me the favor to—ha—state your pleasure, madam."

"Mr. Dorrit," said Flora, "you are very kind in giving me permission and highly natural it seems to me that you should be kind for though more stately I perceive a likeness filled out of course but a likeness still, the object of my intruding is my own without the slightest consultation with any human being and most decidedly not with Arthur—pray excuse me Doyce and Clennam I don't know what I am saying Mr. Clennam solus—for to put that individual linked by a golden chain to a purple time when all was ethereal out of any anxiety would be worth to me the ransom of a monarch not that I have the least idea how much that would come to but using it as the total of all I have in the world and more."

Mr. Dorrit, without greatly regarding the earnestness of these latter words, repeated, "State your pleasure, madam."

"It's not likely I well know," said Flora, "but it's possible and being possible when I had the gratification of reading in the papers that you had arrived from Italy and were going back I made up my mind to try it for you might come across him or hear something of him and if so what a blessing and relief to all!"

"Allow me to ask, madam," said Mr. Dorrit, with his ideas in wild confusion, "to whom—ha—TO WHOM," he repeated it with a raised voice in mere desperation, "you at present allude?"

"To the foreigner from Italy who disappeared in the City as no doubt you have read in the papers equally with myself," said Flora, "not referring to private sources by the name of Pancks from which one gathers what dreadfully ill-natured things some people are wicked enough to whisper most likely judging others by themselves and what the uneasiness and indignation of Arthur—quite unable to overcome it Doyce and Clennam—cannot fail to be."

It happened, fortunately for the elucidation of any intelligible result, that Mr. Dorrit had heard or read nothing about the matter. This caused Mrs. Finching, with many apologies for being in great practical difficulties as to finding the way to her pocket among the stripes of her dress, at length to produce a police handbill, setting forth that a foreign gentleman of the name of Blandois, last from Venice, had unaccountably disappeared on such a night in such a part of the city of London; that he was known to have entered such a house, at such an hour; that he was stated by the inmates of that house to have left it, at about so many minutes before midnight; and that he had never been beheld since. This, with exact particulars of time and locality, and with a good detailed description of the foreign gentleman who had so mysteriously vanished, Mr. Dorrit read at large.

"Blandois!" said Mr. Dorrit. "Venice! And this description! I know this gentleman. He has been in my house. He is intimately acquainted with a gentleman of good family (but in indifferent circumstances), of whom I am a—hum—patron."

"Then my humble and pressing entreaty is the more," said Flora, "that in travelling back you will have the kindness to look for this foreign gentleman along all the roads and up and down all the turnings and to make enquiries for him at all the hotels and orange trees and vineyards and volcanoes and places for he must be somewhere and why doesn't he come forward and say he's there and clear all parties up?"

"Pray, madam," said Mr. Dorrit, referring to the handbill again, "who is Clennam and Co.? Ha. I see the name mentioned here, in connexion with the occupation of the house which Monsieur Blandois was seen to enter: who is Clennam and Co.? Is it the individual of whom I had formerly —hum—some—ha—slight transitory knowledge, and to whom I believe you have referred? Is it—ha—that person?"

"It's a very different person indeed," replied Flora, "with no limbs and wheels instead and the grimmest of women though his mother."

"Clennam and Co. a—hum—a mother!" exclaimed Mr. Dorrit.

"And an old man besides," said Flora.

Mr. Dorrit looked as if he must immediately be driven out of his mind by this account. Neither was it rendered more favorable to sanity by Flora's dashing into a rapid analysis of Mr. Flintwinch's cravat, and describing him, without the lightest boundary line of separation between his identity and Mrs. Clennam's, as a rusty screw in gaiters. Which compound of man and woman, no limbs, wheels, rusty screw, grimness, and gaiters, so completely stupefied Mr. Dorrit, that he was a spectacle to be pitied.

"But I would not detain you one moment longer," said Flora, upon whom his condition wrought its effect, though she was quite unconscious of having produced it, "if you would have the goodness to give me your promise as a gentleman that both in going back to Italy and in Italy too you would look for this Mr. Blandois high and low and if you found or heard of him make him come forward for the clearing of all parties."

By that time Mr. Dorrit had so far recovered from his bewilderment, as to be able to say, in a tolerably connected manner, that he should consider that his duty. Flora was delighted with her success, and rose to take her leave.

"With a million thanks," said she, "and my address upon my card in case of anything to be communicated personally, I will not send my love to the dear little thing for it might not be acceptable and indeed there is no dear little thing left in the transformation so why do it but both myself and Mr. F's Aunt ever wish her well and lay no claim to any favor on our side you may be sure of that but quite the other way for what she undertook to do she did and that is more than a great many of us do, not to say anything of her doing it as well as it could be done and I myself am one of them for I have said ever since I began to recover the blow of Mr. F's death that I would learn the Organ of which I am extremely fond but of which I am ashamed to say I do not yet know a note, good evening!"

When Mr. Dorrit, who attended her to the room-door, had had a little time to collect his senses, he found that the interview had summoned back discarded reminiscences which jarred with the Merdle dinner-table. He wrote and sent off a brief note excusing himself for that day, and ordered dinner presently in his own rooms at the hotel. He had another reason for this. His time in London was very nearly out, and was anticipated by engagements; his plans were made for returning; and he thought it behoved his importance to pursue some direct enquiry into the Blandois disappearance, and be in a condition to carry back to Mr. Henry Gowan the result of his own personal investigation. He therefore resolved that he would take advantage of that evening's freedom to go to Clennam and Co.'s, easily to be found by the direction set forth in the handbill; and see the place, and ask a question or two there, himself.

Having dined as plainly as the establishment and the Courier would let him, and having taken a short sleep by the fire for his better recovery from Mrs. Finching, he set out in a hackney cabriolet alone. The deep bell of Saint Paul's was striking nine as he passed under the shadow of Temple Bar, headless and forlorn in these degenerate days.

As he approached his destination through the bye-streets and waterside ways, that part of London seemed to him an uglier spot at such an hour than he had ever supposed it to be. Many long years had passed since he had seen it; he had never known much of it; and it wore a mysterious and dismal aspect in his eyes. So powerfully was his imagination impressed by it, that when his driver stopped, after having asked the way more than once, and said to the best of his belief this was the gateway they wanted, Mr. Dorrit stood hesitating, with the coach-door in his hand, half afraid of the dark look of the place.

Truly, it looked as gloomy that night, as even it had ever looked. Two of the handbills were posted on the entrance wall, one on either side, and as the lamp flickered in the night air, shadows passed over them, not unlike the shadows of fingers following the lines. A watch was evidently kept upon the place. As Mr. Dorrit paused, a man passed in from over the way, and another man passed out from some dark corner within; and both looked at him in passing, and both remained standing about.

As there was only one house in the enclosure, there was no room for uncertainty, so he went up the steps of that house and knocked. There was a dim light in two windows on the first floor. The door gave back a dreary, vacant sound, as though the house were empty; but, it was not, for a light was visible, and a step was audible, almost directly. They both came to the door, and a chain grated, and a woman with her apron thrown over her face and head stood in the aperture.

"Who is it?" said the woman.

Mr. Dorrit, much amazed by this appearance, replied that he was from Italy, and that he wished to ask a question relative to the missing person, whom he knew.

"Hi!" cried the woman, raising a cracked voice. "Jeremiah!"

Upon this, a dry old man appeared, whom Mr. Dorrit thought he identified by his gaiters, as the rusty screw. The woman was under apprehensions of the dry old man, for she whisked her apron away as he approached, and disclosed a pale affrighted face. "Open the door, you fool," said the old man; "and let the gentleman in."

Mr. Dorrit, not without a glance over his shoulder towards his driver and the cabriolet, walked into the dim hall. "Now, sir," said Mr. Flintwinch, "you can ask anything here, you think proper; there are no secrets here, sir."

Before a reply could be made, a strong stern voice, though a woman's, called from above, "Who is it?"

"Who is it?" returned Jeremiah. "More enquiries. A gentleman from Italy."

"Bring him up here!"

Mr. Flintwinch muttered, as if he deemed that unnecessary; but, turning to Mr. Dorrit, said, "Mrs. Clennam. She *will* do as she likes. I'll show you the way." He then preceded Mr. Dorrit up the blackened staircase; that gentleman, not unnaturally looking behind him on the road, saw the woman following, with her apron thrown over her head again in her former ghastly manner.

Mrs. Clennam had her books open on her little table. "Oh!" said she abruptly, as she eyed her visitor with a steady look. "You are from Italy, sir, are you. Well?"

Mr. Dorrit was at a loss for any more distinct rejoinder at the moment than "Ha—well?"

"Where is this missing man? Have you come to give us information where he is? I hope you have?"

"So far from it, I—hum—have come to seek information."

"Unfortunately for us, there is none to be got here. Flintwinch, show the gentleman the handbill. Give him several to take away. Hold the light for him to read it."

Mr. Flintwinch did as he was directed, and Mr. Dorrit read it through, as if he had not previously seen it; glad enough of the opportunity of collecting his presence of mind, which the air of the house and of the people in it had a little disturbed. While his eyes were on the paper, he felt that the eyes of Mr. Flintwinch and of Mrs. Clennam were on him. He found, when he looked up, that this sensation was not a fanciful one.

"Now, you know as much," said Mrs. Clennam, "as we know, sir. Is Mr. Blandois a friend of yours?"

"No—a—hum—an acquaintance," answered Mr. Dorrit.

"You have no commission from him, perhaps?"

"I? Ha. Certainly not."

The searching look turned gradually to the floor, after taking Mr. Flintwinch's face in its way. Mr. Dorrit, discomfited by finding that he was the questioned instead of the questioner, applied himself to the reversal of that unexpected order of things.

"I am—ha—a gentleman of property, at present residing in Italy with my family, my servants, and—hum—my rather large establishment. Being in London for a short time on affairs connected with—ha—my estate, and hearing of this strange disappearance, I wished to make myself acquainted with the circumstances at first-hand, because there is—ha hum—an English gentleman in Italy whom I shall no doubt see on my return, who has been in habits of close and daily intimacy with Monsieur Blandois. Mr. Henry Gowan. You may know the name."

"Never heard of it."

Mrs. Clennam said it, and Mr. Flintwinch echoed it.

"Wishing to—ha—make the narrative coherent and consecutive to him," said Mr. Dorrit, "may I ask—say three questions?"

"Thirty, if you choose."

"Have you known Monsieur Blandois long?"

"Not a twelvemonth. Mr. Flintwinch here, will refer to the books and tell you when, and by whom at Paris, he was introduced to us. If that," Mrs. Clennam added, "should be any satisfaction to you. It is poor satisfaction to us."

"Have you seen him often?"

"No. Twice. Once before, and——"

"That once," suggested Mr. Flintwinch.

"And that once."

"Pray, madam," said Mr. Dorrit, with a growing fancy upon him, as he recovered his importance, that he was in some superior way in the Commission of the Peace; "pray, madam, may I enquire, for the greater satisfaction of the gentleman whom I have the honor to—ha—retain, or protect, or let me say to—hum—know—to know—— Was Monsieur Blandois here on business, on the night indicated in this printed sheet?"

"On what he called business," returned Mrs. Clennam.

"Is—ha—excuse me— is its nature to be communicated?"

"No."

It was evidently impracticable to pass the barrier of that reply.

"The question has been asked before," said Mrs. Clennam, "and the answer has been, No. We don't choose to publish our transactions, however unimportant, to all the town. We say, No."

"I mean, he took away no money with him, for example?" said Mr. Dorrit.

"He took away none of ours, sir, and got none here."

"I suppose," observed Mr. Dorrit, glancing from Mrs. Clennam to Mr. Flintwinch, and from Mr. Flintwinch to Mrs. Clennam, "you have no way of accounting to yourself for this mystery?"

"Why do you suppose so?" rejoined Mrs. Clennam.

Disconcerted by the cold and hard enquiry, Mr. Dorrit was unable to assign any reason for his supposing so.

"I account for it, sir," she pursued after an awkward silence on Mr. Dorrit's part, "by having no doubt that he is travelling somewhere, or hiding somewhere."

"Do you know—ha—why he should hide anywhere?"

"No."

It was exactly the same No as before, and put another barrier up.

"You asked me if I accounted for the disappearance to myself," Mrs. Clennam sternly reminded him, "not if I accounted for it to you. I do not pretend to account for it to you, sir. I understand it to be no more my business to do that, than it is yours to require that."

Mr. Dorrit answered with an apologetic bend of his head. As he stepped back, preparatory to saying he had no more to ask, he could not but observe how gloomily and fixedly she sat with her eyes fastened on the ground, and a certain air upon her of resolute waiting; also, how exactly the self-same expression was reflected in Mr. Flintwinch, standing at a little distance from her chair, with his eyes also on the ground, and his right hand softly rubbing his chin.

At that moment, Mistress Affery (of course, the woman with the apron) dropped the candlestick she held, and cried out, "There! O good Lord! there it is again. Hark, Jeremiah! Now!"

If there were any sound at all, it was so slight that she must have fallen into a confirmed habit of listening for sounds; but, Mr. Dorrit believed he did hear a something, like the falling of dry leaves. The woman's terror, for a very short space, seemed to touch the three; and they all listened.

Mr. Flintwinch was the first to stir. "Affery, my woman," said he, sidling at her with his fists clenched, and his elbows quivering with impatience to shake her, "you are at your old tricks. You'll be walking in your sleep next, my woman, and playing the whole round of your distempered antics. You must have some physic. When I have shown this gentleman out, I'll make you up such a comfortable dose, my woman; such a comfortable dose!"

It did not appear altogether comfortable in expectation to Mistress Affery; but Jeremiah, without further reference to his healing medicine, took another candle from Mrs. Clennam's table, and said, "Now, sir; shall I light you down?"

Mr. Dorrit professed himself obliged, and went down. Mr. Flintwinch shut him out and chained him out, without a moment's loss of time. He was again passed by the two men, one going out and the other coming in; got into the vehicle he had left waiting, and was driven away.

Before he had gone far, the driver stopped to let him know that he had given his name, number, and address to the two men, on their joint requisition; and also the address at which he had taken Mr. Dorrit up, the hour at which he had been called from his stand, and the way by which he had come. This did not make the night's adventure run the less hotly in Mr. Dorrit's mind, either when he sat down by his fire again, or when he went to bed. All night he haunted the dismal house, saw the two people resolutely waiting, heard the woman with her apron over her face cry out about the noise, and found the body of the missing Blandois, now buried in a cellar and now bricked up in a wall.

CHAPTER XVIII

A CASTLE IN THE AIR

MANIFOLD are the cares of wealth and state. Mr. Dorrit's satisfaction in remembering that it had not been necessary for him to announce himself to Clennam and Co. or to make an allusion to his having ever had any knowledge of the intrusive person of that name, had been damped overnight, while it was still fresh, by a debate that arose within him whether or no he should take the Marshalsea in his way back, and look at the old gate. He had decided not to do so; and had astonished the coachman by being very fierce with him for proposing to go over London Bridge and recross the river by Waterloo Bridge—a course which would have taken him almost within sight of his old quarters. Still, for all that, the question had raised a conflict in his breast; and, for some odd reason or no reason, he was vaguely dissatisfied. Even at the Merdle dinner-table next day, he was so out of sorts about it, that he continued at intervals to turn it over and over, in a manner frightfully inconsistent with the good society surrounding him. It made him hot to think what the Chief Butler's opinion of him would have been, if that illustrious personage could have plumbed with that heavy eye of his the stream of his meditations.

The farewell banquet was of a gorgeous nature, and wound up his visit in a most brilliant manner. Fanny combined with the attractions of her youth and beauty, a certain weight of self-sustainment as if she had been married twenty years. He felt that he could leave her with a quiet mind to tread the paths of distinction, and wished—but without abatement of patronage, and without prejudice to the retiring virtues of his favorite child—that he had such another daughter.

"My dear," he told her at parting, "our family looks to you to—ha—assert its dignity and—hum—maintain its importance. I know you will never disappoint it."

"No, papa," said Fanny, "you may rely upon that, I think. My best love to dearest Amy, and I will write to her very soon."

"Shall I convey any message to—ha—anybody else?" asked Mr. Dorrit, in an insinuating manner.

"Papa," said Fanny, before whom Mrs. General instantly loomed, "no, I thank you. You are very kind, Pa, but I must beg to be excused. I have no other message to send, I thank you, dear papa, that it would be at all agreeable to you to take."

They parted in an outer drawing-room, where only Mr. Sparkler waited on his lady, and dutifully bided his time for shaking hands. When Mr. Sparkler was admitted to this closing audience, Mr. Merdle came creeping in with much more appearance of arms in his sleeves than if he had been the twin brother of Miss Biffin, and insisted on escorting Mr. Dorrit down-stairs. All Mr. Dorrit's protestations being in vain, he enjoyed the honor of being accompanied to the hall-door by this distinguished man, who (as Mr. Dorrit told him in shaking hands on the step) had really over-whelmed him with attentions and services, during his memorable visit. Thus they parted; Mr. Dorrit entering his carriage with a swelling breast, not at all sorry that his Courier, who had come to take leave in the lower regions, should have an opportunity of beholding the grandeur of his departure.

The aforesaid grandeur was yet full upon Mr. Dorrit when he alighted at his hotel. Helped out by the Courier and some half dozen of the hotel servants, he was passing through the hall with a serene magnificence, when lo! a sight presented itself that struck him dumb and motionless. John Chivery, in his best clothes, with his tall hat under his arm, his ivory-handled cane genteelly embarrassing his deportment, and a bundle of cigars in his hand!

"Now, young man," said the porter. "This is the gentleman. This young man has persisted in waiting, sir, saying you would be glad to see him."

Mr. Dorrit glared on the young man, choked, and said, in the mildest of tones, "Ah! Young John! It is Young John, I think; is it not?"

"Yes, sir," returned Young John.

"I—ha—thought it was Young John!" said Mr. Dorrit. "The young man may come up," turning to the attendants, as he passed on: "oh yes, he may come up. Let Young John follow. I will speak to him above."

Young John followed, smiling and much gratified. Mr. Dorrit's rooms were reached. Candles were lighted. The attendants withdrew.

"Now, sir," said Mr. Dorrit, turning round upon him and seizing him by the collar when they were safely alone. "What do you mean by this?"

The amazement and horror depicted in the unfortunate John's face—
for he had rather expected to be embraced next—were of that powerfully
expressive nature, that Mr. Dorrit withdrew his hand and merely glared
at him.

"How dare you do this?" said Mr. Dorrit. "How do you presume to
come here? How dare you insult me?"

"I insult you, sir?" cried Young John. "Oh!"

"Yes, sir," returned Mr. Dorrit. "Insult me. Your coming here is an
affront, an impertinence, an audacity. You are not wanted here. Who sent
you here? What—ha—the Devil do you do here?"

"I thought, sir," said Young John, with as pale and shocked a face as
ever had been turned to Mr. Dorrit's in his life—even in his College life:
"I thought, sir, you mightn't object to have the goodness to accept a
bundle——"

"Damn your bundle, sir!" cried Mr. Dorrit in irrepressible rage. "I—
hum—don't smoke."

"I humbly beg your pardon, sir. You used to."

"Tell me that again," cried Mr. Dorrit, quite beside himself, "and I'll
take the poker to you!"

John Chivery backed to the door.

"Stop, sir!" cried Mr. Dorrit. "Stop! Sit down. Confound you, sit
down!"

John Chivery dropped into the chair nearest the door, and Mr. Dorrit
walked up and down the room; rapidly at first; then, more slowly. Once, he
went to the window, and stood there with his forehead against the glass.
All of a sudden, he turned and said:

"What else did you come for, sir?"

"Nothing else in the world, sir. Oh dear me! Only to say, sir, that I
hoped you was well, and only to ask if Miss Amy was well?"

"What's that to you, sir?" retorted Mr. Dorrit.

"It's nothing to me, sir, by rights. I never thought of lessening the
distance betwixt us, I am sure. I know it's a liberty, sir, but I never thought
you'd have taken it ill. Upon my word and honor, sir," said Young John,
with emotion, "in my poor way, I am too proud to have come, I assure you,
if I had thought so."

Mr. Dorrit was ashamed. He went back to the window, and leaned his
forehead against the glass for some time. When he turned, he had his
handkerchief in his hand, and he had been wiping his eyes with it, and he
looked tired and ill.

"Young John, I am very sorry to have been hasty with you, but—ha—
some remembrances are not happy remembrances, and—hum—you
shouldn't have come."

"I feel that now, sir," returned John Chivery; "but I didn't before, and
Heaven knows I meant no harm, sir."

"No. No," said Mr. Dorrit. "I am—hum—sure of that. Ha. Give me your hand, Young John, give me your hand."

Young John gave it; but Mr. Dorrit had driven his heart out of it, and nothing could change his face now, from its white, shocked look.

"There!" said Mr. Dorrit, slowly shaking hands with him. "Sit down again, Young John."

"Thank you, sir—but I'd rather stand."

Mr. Dorrit sat down instead. After painfully holding his head a little while, he turned it to his visitor, and said, with an effort to be easy:

"And how is your father, Young John? How—ha—how are they all, Young John?"

"Thank you, sir. They're all pretty well, sir. They're not any ways complaining."

"Hum. You are in your—ha—old business I see, John?" said Mr. Dorrit, with a glance at the offending bundle he had anathematized.

"Partly, sir. I am in my," John hesitated a little, "—father's business likewise."

"Oh indeed!" said Mr. Dorrit. "Do you—ha hum—go upon the—ha ——"

"Lock, sir? Yes, sir."

"Much to do, John?"

"Yes, sir; we're pretty heavy at present. I don't know how it is, but we generally *are* pretty heavy."

"At this time of the year, Young John?"

"Mostly at all times of the year, sir. I don't know the time that makes much difference to us. I wish you good night, sir."

"Stay a moment, John—ha—stay a moment. Hum. Leave me the cigars, John, I—ha—beg."

"Certainly, sir." John put them, with a trembling hand, on the table.

"Stay a moment, Young John; stay another moment. It would be a—ha —a gratification to me to send a little—hum—Testimonial, by such a trusty messenger, to be divided among—ha hum—them—*them*—according to their wants. Would you object to take it, John?"

"Not in any ways, sir. There's many of them, I'm sure, that would be the better for it."

"Thank you, John. I—ha—I'll write it, John."

His hand shook so that he was a long time writing it, and wrote it in a tremulous scrawl at last. It was a cheque for one hundred pounds. He folded it up, put it in Young John's hand, and pressed the hand in his.

"I hope you'll—ha—overlook—hum—what has passed, John."

"Don't speak of it, sir, on any accounts. I don't in any ways bear malice, I'm sure."

But, nothing while John was there could change John's face to its natural color and expression, or restore John's natural manner.

"And John," said Mr. Dorrit, giving his hand a final pressure, and releasing it, "I hope we—ha—agree that we have spoken together in confidence; and that you will abstain, in going out, from saying anything to any one that might—hum—suggest that—ha—once I——"

"Oh! I assure you, sir," returned John Chivery, "in my poor humble way, sir, I'm too proud and honorable to do it, sir."

Mr. Dorrit was not too proud and honorable to listen at the door, that he might ascertain for himself whether John really went straight out, or lingered to have any talk with any one. There was no doubt that he went direct out at the door, and away down the street with a quick step. After remaining alone for an hour, Mr. Dorrit rang for the Courier, who found him with his chair on the hearth-rug, sitting with his back towards him and his face to the fire. "You can take that bundle of cigars to smoke on the journey, if you like," said Mr. Dorrit, with a careless wave of his hand. "Ha—brought by—hum—little offering from—ha—son of old tenant of mine."

Next morning's sun saw Mr. Dorrit's equipage upon the Dover road, where every red-jacketed postilion was the sign of a cruel house, established for the unmerciful plundering of travellers. The whole business of the human race, between London and Dover, being spoliation, Mr. Dorrit was way-laid at Dartford, pillaged at Gravesend, rifled at Rochester, fleeced at Sittingbourne, and sacked at Canterbury. However, it being the Courier's business to get him out of the hands of the banditti, the Courier bought him off at every stage; and so the red-jackets went gleaming merrily along the spring landscape, rising and falling to a regular measure, between Mr. Dorrit in his snug corner, and the next chalky rise in the dusty highway.

Another day's sun saw him at Calais. And having now got the Channel between himself and John Chivery, he began to feel safe, and to find that the foreign air was lighter to breathe than the air of England.

On again by the heavy French roads for Paris. Having now quite recovered his equanimity, Mr. Dorrit, in his snug corner, fell to castle-building as he rode along. It was evident that he had a very large castle in hand. All day long he was running towers up, taking towers down, adding a wing here, putting on a battlement there, looking to the walls, streng-thening the defences, giving ornamental touches to the interior, making in all respects a superb castle of it. His preoccupied face so clearly denoted the pursuit in which he was engaged, that every cripple at the post-houses, not blind, who shoved his little battered tin-box in at the carriage window for Charity in the name of Heaven, Charity in the name of our Lady, Charity in the name of all the Saints, knew as well what work he was at, as their countryman Le Brun could have known it himself, though he had made that English traveller the subject of a special physiognomical treatise.

Arrived at Paris, and resting there three days, Mr. Dorrit strolled much about the streets alone, looking in at the shop-windows, and particularly the jewellers' windows. Ultimately, he went into the most famous jeweller's, and said he wanted to buy a little gift for a lady.

It was a charming little woman to whom he said it—a sprightly little woman, dressed in perfect taste, who came out of a green velvet bower to attend upon him, from posting up some dainty little books of account which one could hardly suppose to be ruled for the entry of any articles more commercial than kisses, at a dainty little shining desk which looked in itself like a sweetmeat.

For example, then, said the little woman, what species of gift did Monsieur desire? A love-gift?

Mr. Dorrit smiled, and said, Eh, well! Perhaps. What did he know? It was always possible; the sex being so charming. Would she show him some?

Most willingly, said the little woman. Flattered and enchanted to show him many. But pardon! To begin with, he would have the great goodness to observe that there were love-gifts, and there were nuptial gifts. For example, these ravishing ear-rings and this necklace so superb to correspond, were what one called a love-gift. These brooches and these rings, of a beauty so gracious and celestial, were what one called, with the permission of Monsieur, nuptial gifts.

Perhaps it would be a good arrangement, Mr. Dorrit hinted, smiling, to purchase both, and to present the love-gift first, and to finish with the nuptial offering?

Ah Heaven! said the little woman, laying the tips of the fingers of her two little hands against each other, that would be generous indeed, that would be a special gallantry! And without doubt the lady so crushed with gifts would find them irresistible.

Mr. Dorrit was not sure of that. But, for example, the sprightly little woman was very sure of it, she said. So Mr. Dorrit bought a gift of each sort, and paid handsomely for it. As he strolled back to his hotel afterwards, he carried his head high: having plainly got up his castle, now, to a much loftier altitude than the two square towers of Notre Dame.

Building away with all his might, but reserving the plans of his castle exclusively for his own eye, Mr. Dorrit posted away for Marseilles. Building on, building on, busily, busily, from morning to night. Falling asleep, and leaving great blocks of building material dangling in the air; waking again, to resume work and get them into their places. What time the Courier in the rumble, smoking Young John's best cigars, left a little thread of thin light smoke behind—perhaps as *he* built a castle or two, with stray pieces of Mr. Dorrit's money.

Not a fortified town that they passed in all their journey was as strong, not a Cathedral summit was as high, as Mr. Dorrit's castle. Neither the Saone nor the Rhone sped with the swiftness of that peerless building; nor was the Mediterranean deeper than its foundations; nor were the

distant landscapes on the Cornice road, nor the hills and bay of Genoa the
Superb, more beautiful. Mr. Dorrit and his matchless castle were disem-
barked among the dirty white houses and dirtier felons of Civita Vecchia,
and thence scrambled on to Rome as they could, through the filth that
festered on the way.

END OF No. XV

CHAPTER XIX

THE STORMING OF THE CASTLE IN THE AIR

THE sun had gone down full four hours, and it was later than most
travellers would like it to be for finding themselves outside the walls of
Rome, when Mr. Dorrit's carriage, still on its last wearisome stage, rattled
over the solitary Campagna. The savage herdsmen and the fierce-looking
peasants, who had chequered the way while the light lasted, had all gone
down with the sun, and left the wilderness blank. At some turns of the road,
a pale flare on the horizon, like an exhalation from the ruin-sown land,
showed that the city was yet far off; but, this poor relief was rare and short-
lived. The carriage dipped down again into a hollow of the black dry sea,
and for a long time there was nothing visible save its petrified swell and
the gloomy sky.

Mr. Dorrit, though he had his castle-building to engage his mind,
could not be quite easy in that desolate place. He was far more curious, in
every swerve of the carriage and every cry of the postilions, than he had
been since he quitted London. The valet on the box evidently quaked.
The Courier in the rumble was not altogether comfortable in his mind.
As often as Mr. Dorrit let down the glass, and looked back at him (which
was very often), he saw him smoking John Chivery out, it is true, but still
generally standing up the while and looking about him, like a man who had
his suspicions, and kept upon his guard. Then would Mr. Dorrit, pulling
up the glass again, reflect that those postilions were cut-throat looking
fellows, and that he would have done better to have slept at Civita Vecchia,
and have started betimes in the morning. But, for all this, he worked at
his castle in the intervals.

And now, fragments of ruinous enclosure, yawning window-gap and
crazy wall, deserted houses, leaking wells, broken water-tanks, spectral
cypress-trees, patches of tangled vine, and the changing of the track to a
long, irregular, disordered lane, where everything was crumbling away,
from the unsightly buildings to the jolting road—now, these objects showed
that they were nearing Rome. And now, a sudden twist and stoppage of

the carriage inspired Mr. Dorrit with the mistrust that the brigand moment was come for twisting him into a ditch and robbing him; until, letting down the glass again and looking out, he perceived himself assailed by nothing worse than a funeral procession, which came mechanically chaunting by, with an indistinct show of dirty vestments, lurid torches, swinging censers, and a great cross borne before a priest. He was an ugly priest by torchlight; of a lowering aspect, with an overhanging brow; and as his eyes met those of Mr. Dorrit, looking bareheaded out of the carriage, his lips, moving as they chaunted, seemed to threaten that important traveller; likewise the action of his hand, which was in fact his manner of returning the traveller's salutation, seemed to come in aid of that menace. So thought Mr. Dorrit, made fanciful by the weariness of building and travelling, as the priest drifted past him, and the procession straggled away, taking its dead along with it. Upon their so-different way went Mr. Dorrit's company too; and soon, with their coach-load of luxuries from the two great capitals of Europe, they were (like the Goths reversed) beating at the gates of Rome.

Mr. Dorrit was not expected by his own people that night. He had been; but, they had given him up until to-morrow, not doubting that it was later than he would care, in those parts, to be out. Thus, when his equipage stopped at his own gate, no one but the porter appeared to receive him. Was Miss Dorrit from home? he asked. No. She was within. Good, said Mr. Dorrit to the assembling servants; let them keep where they were; let them help to unload the carriage; he would find Miss Dorrit for himself.

So, he went up his grand staircase, slowly, and tired, and looked into various chambers which were empty, until he saw a light in a small anteroom. It was a curtained nook, like a tent, within two other rooms; and it looked warm, and bright in color, as he approached it through the dark avenue they made.

There was a draped doorway, but no door; and as he stopped here, looking in unseen, he felt a pang. Surely not like jealousy? For why like jealousy? There were only his daughter and his brother there: he, with his chair drawn to the hearth, enjoying the warmth of the evening wood fire; she, seated at a little table, busied with some embroidery-work. Allowing for the great difference in the still-life of the picture, the figures were much the same as of old; his brother being sufficiently like himself to represent himself, for a moment, in the composition. So had he sat many a night, over a coal fire far away; so had she sat, devoted to him. Yet surely there was nothing to be jealous of in the old miserable poverty. Whence, then, the pang in his heart?

"Do you know, uncle, I think you are growing young again?"

Her uncle shook his head, and said, "Since when, my dear; since when?"

"I think," returned Little Dorrit, plying her needle, "that you have been growing younger for weeks past. So cheerful, uncle, and so ready, and so interested!"

"My dear child—all you."

"All me, uncle!"

"Yes, yes. You have done me a world of good. You have been so considerate of me, and so tender with me, and so delicate in trying to hide your attentions from me, that I —well, well, well! It's treasured up, my darling, treasured up."

"There is nothing in it but your own fresh fancy, uncle," said Little Dorrit, cheerfully.

"Well, well, well!" murmured the old man. "Thank God!"

She paused for an instant in her work to look at him, and her look revived that former pain in her father's breast; in his poor weak breast, so full of contradictions, vacillations, inconsistencies, the little peevish perplexities of this ignorant life, mists which the morning without a night only can clear away.

"I have been freer with you, you see, my dove," said the old man, "since we have been alone. I say, alone, for I don't count Mrs. General; I don't care for her; she has nothing to do with me. But I know Fanny was impatient of me. And I don't wonder at it, or complain of it, for I am sensible that I must be in the way, though I try to keep out of it as well as I can. I know I am not fit company for our company. My brother William," said the old man admiringly, "is fit company for monarchs; but not so your uncle, my dear. Frederick Dorrit is no credit to William Dorrit, and he knows it quite well. Ah! Why, here's your father, Amy! My dear William, welcome back! My beloved brother, I am rejoiced to see you!"

(Turning his head in speaking, he had caught sight of him as he stood in the doorway.)

Little Dorrit with a cry of pleasure put her arms about her father's neck, and kissed him again and again. Her father was a little impatient, and a little querulous. "I am glad to find you at last, Amy," he said. "Ha. Really I am glad to find—hum—any one to receive me at last. I appear to have been—ha—so little expected, that upon my word I began—ha hum—to think it might be right to offer an apology for—ha—taking the liberty of coming back at all."

"It was so late, my dear William," said his brother, "that we had given you up for to-night."

"I am stronger than you, dear Frederick," returned his brother, with an elaboration of fraternity in which there was severity; "and I hope I can travel without detriment at—ha—any hour I choose."

"Surely, surely," returned the other, with a misgiving that he had given offence. "Surely, William."

"Thank you, Amy," pursued Mr. Dorrit, as she helped him to put off his wrappers, "I can do it without assistance. I—ha—need not trouble you, Amy. Could I have a morsel of bread and a glass of wine, or—hum—would it cause too much inconvenience?"

"Dear father, you shall have supper in a very few minutes."

"Thank you, my love," said Mr. Dorrit, with a reproachful frost upon him; "I—ha—am afraid I am causing inconvenience. Hum. Mrs. General pretty well?"

"Mrs. General complained of a headache, and of being fatigued; and so, when we gave you up, she went to bed, dear."

Perhaps Mr. Dorrit thought that Mrs. General had done well in being overcome by the disappointment of his not arriving. At any rate, his face relaxed, and he said with obvious satisfaction, "Extremely sorry to hear that Mrs. General is not well."

During this short dialogue, his daughter had been observant of him, with something more than her usual interest. It would seem as though he had a changed or worn appearance in her eyes, and he perceived and resented it; for, he said, with renewed peevishness, when he had divested himself of his travelling cloak, and had come to the fire:

"Amy, what are you looking at? What do you see in me that causes you to—ha—concentrate your solicitude on me in that—hum—very particular manner?"

"I did not know it, father; I beg your pardon. It gladdens my eyes to see you again; that's all."

"Don't say that's all, because—ha—that's not all. You—hum—you think," said Mr. Dorrit, with an accusatory emphasis, "that I am not looking well."

"I thought you looked a little tired, love."

"Then you are mistaken," said Mr. Dorrit. "Ha, I am *not* tired. Ha, hum. I am very much fresher than I was, when I went away."

He was so inclined to be angry, that she said nothing more in her justification, but remained quietly beside him embracing his arm. As he stood thus, with his brother on the other side, he fell into a heavy doze of not a minute's duration, and awoke with a start.

"Frederick," he said, turning on his brother: "I recommend you to go to bed immediately."

"No, William. I'll wait and see you sup."

"Frederick," he retorted, "I beg you to go to bed. I—ha—make it a personal request that you go to bed. You ought to have been in bed long ago. You are very feeble."

"Hah!" said the old man, who had no wish but to please him. "Well, well, well! I dare say I am."

"My dear Frederick," returned Mr. Dorrit, with an astonishing superiority to his brother's failing powers, "there can be no doubt of it. It is painful to me to see you so weak. Ha. It distresses me. Hum. I don't find you looking at all well. You are not fit for this sort of thing. You should be more careful, you should be very careful."

"Shall I go to bed?" asked Frederick.

"Dear Frederick," said Mr. Dorrit, "do, I adjure you! Good night, brother. I hope you will be stronger to-morrow. I am not at all pleased with your looks. Good night, dear fellow." After dismissing his brother in this gracious way, he fell into a doze again, before the old man was well out of the room: and he would have stumbled forward upon the logs, but for his daughter's restraining hold.

"Your uncle wanders very much, Amy," he said, when he was thus roused. "He is less—ha—coherent, and his conversation is more—hum—broken, than I have—ha hum—ever known. Has he had any illness since I have been gone?"

"No, father."

"You—ha—see a great change in him, Amy?"

"I had not observed it, dear."

"Greatly broken," said Mr. Dorrit. "Greatly broken. My poor, affectionate, failing Frederick! Ha. Even taking into account what he was before, he is—hum—sadly broken!"

His supper, which was brought to him there, and spread upon the little table where he had seen her working, diverted his attention. She sat at his side as in the days that were gone, for the first time since those days ended. They were alone, and she helped him to his meat and poured out his drink for him, as she had been used to do in the prison. All this happened now, for the first time since their accession to wealth. She was afraid to look at him much, after the offence he had taken; but she noticed two occasions in the course of his meal when he all of a sudden looked at her, and looked about him, as if the association were so strong that he needed assurance from his sense of sight that they were not in the old prison-room. Both times, he put his hand to his head as if he missed his old black cap—though it had been ignominiously given away in the Marshalsea, and had never got free to that hour, but still hovered about the yards on the head of his successor.

He took very little supper, but was a long time over it, and often reverted to his brother's declining state. Though he expressed the greatest pity for him, he was almost bitter upon him. He said that poor Frederick—ha hum —drivelled. There was no other word to express it; drivelled. Poor fellow! It was melancholy to reflect what Amy must have undergone from the excessive tediousness of his society—wandering and babbling on, poor dear estimable creature, wandering and babbling on—if it had not been for the relief she had had in Mrs. General. Extremely sorry, he then repeated with his former satisfaction, that that—ha—superior woman was poorly.

Little Dorrit, in her watchful love, would have remembered the lightest thing he said or did that night, though she had had no subsequent reason to recall that night. She always remembered, that when he looked about him under the strong influence of the old association, he tried to keep it out of her mind, and perhaps out of his own too, by immediately expatiating on the great riches and great company that had encompassed him in his absence, and on the lofty position he and his family had to sustain. Nor did she fail to recall that there were two under-currents, side by side, pervading all his discourse and all his manner; one, showing her how well he had got on without her, and how independent he was of her; the other, in a fitful and unintelligible way almost complaining of her, as if it had been possible that she had neglected him while he was away.

His telling her of the glorious state that Mr. Merdle kept, and of the Court that bowed before him, naturally brought him to Mrs. Merdle. So naturally indeed, that although there was an unusual want of sequence in the greater part of his remarks, he passed to her at once, and asked how she was.

"She is very well. She is going away next week."

"Home?" asked Mr. Dorrit.

"After a few weeks' stay upon the road."

"She will be a vast loss here," said Mr. Dorrit. "A vast—ha—acquisition at home. To Fanny, and to—hum—the rest of the—ha—great world."

Little Dorrit thought of the competition that was to be entered upon, and assented very softly.

"Mrs. Merdle is going to have a great farewell Assembly, dear, and a dinner before it. She has been expressing her anxiety that you should return in time. She has invited both you and me to her dinner."

"She is—ha—very kind. When is the day?"

"The day after to-morrow."

"Write round in the morning, and say that I have returned, and shall—hum—be delighted."

"May I walk with you up the stairs to your room, dear?"

"No!" he answered, looking angrily round; for he was moving away, as if forgetful of leave-taking. "You may not, Amy. I want no help. I am your father, not your infirm uncle!" He checked himself, as abruptly as he had broken into this reply, and said, "You have not kissed me, Amy. Good night, my dear! We must marry—ha—we must marry you, now." With that he went, more slowly and more tired, up the staircase to his rooms, and, almost as soon as he got there, dismissed his valet. His next care was to look about him for his Paris purchases, and, after opening their cases and carefully surveying them, to put them away under lock and key. After that, what with dozing and what with castle-building, he lost himself for a long time, so that there was a touch of morning on the eastward rim of the desolate Campagna when he crept to bed.

Mrs. General sent up her compliments in good time next day, and hoped he had rested well after his fatiguing journey. He sent down his compliments, and begged to inform Mrs. General that he had rested very well indeed, and was in high condition. Nevertheless, he did not come forth from his own rooms until late in the afternoon; and, although he had then caused himself to be magnificently arrayed for a drive with Mrs. General and his daughter, his appearance was scarcely up to his description of himself.

As the family had no visitors that day, its four members dined alone together. He conducted Mrs. General to the seat at his right hand, with immense ceremony; and Little Dorrit could not but notice, as she followed with her uncle, both that he was again elaborately dressed, and that his manner towards Mrs. General was very particular. The perfect formation of that accomplished lady's surface rendered it difficult to displace an atom of its genteel glaze, but Little Dorrit thought she descried a slight thaw of triumph in a corner of her frosty eye.

Notwithstanding what may be called in these pages the Pruney and Prismatic nature of the family banquet, Mr. Dorrit several times fell asleep while it was in progress. His fits of dozing were as sudden as they had been over-night, and were as short and profound. When the first of these slumberings seized him, Mrs. General looked almost amazed: but, on each recurrence of the symptoms, she told her polite beads, Papa, Potatoes, Poultry, Prunes, and Prism; and, by dint of going through that infallible performance very slowly, appeared to finish her rosary at about the same time as Mr. Dorrit started from his sleep.

He was again painfully aware of a somnolent tendency in Frederick (which had no existence out of his own imagination), and after dinner, when Frederick had withdrawn, privately apologised to Mrs. General for the poor man. "The most estimable and affectionate of brothers," he said, "but—ha hum—broken up altogether. Unhappily, declining fast."

"Mr. Frederick, sir," quoth Mrs. General, "is habitually absent and drooping, but let us hope it is not so bad as that."

Mr. Dorrit, however, was determined not to let him off. "Fast declining, madam. A wreck. A ruin. Mouldering away, before our eyes. Hum. Good Frederick!"

"You left Mrs. Sparkler quite well and happy, I trust?" said Mrs. General, after heaving a cool sigh for Frederick.

"Surrounded," replied Mr. Dorrit, "by—ha—all that can charm the taste, and—hum—elevate the mind. Happy, my dear madam, in a—hum—husband."

Mrs. General was a little fluttered; seeming delicately to put the word away with her gloves, as if there were no knowing what it might lead to.

"Fanny," Mr. Dorrit continued, "Fanny, Mrs. General, has high qualities. Ha. Ambition—hum—purpose, consciousness of—ha—position, determination to support that position—ha hum—grace, beauty, and native nobility."

"No doubt," said Mrs. General (with a little extra stiffness).

"Combined with these qualities, madam," said Mr. Dorrit, "Fanny has —ha—manifested one blemish which has made me—hum—made me uneasy, and—ha—I must add angry; but which I trust may now be considered at an end, even as to herself, and which is undoubtedly at an end as to—ha—others."

"To what, Mr. Dorrit," returned Mrs. General, with her gloves again somewhat excited, "can you allude? I am at a loss to——"

"Do not say that, my dear madam," interrupted Mr. Dorrit.

Mrs. General's voice, as it died away, pronounced the words, "at a loss to imagine."

After which, Mr. Dorrit was seized with a doze for about a minute, out of which he sprang with spasmodic nimbleness.

"I refer, Mrs. General, to that—ha—strong spirit of opposition, or— hum—I might say—ha—jealousy in Fanny, which has occasionally risen against the—ha—sense I entertain of—hum—the claims of—ha—the lady with whom I have now the honor of communing."

"Mr. Dorrit," returned Mrs. General, "is ever but too obliging, ever but too appreciative. If there have been moments when I have imagined that Miss Dorrit has indeed resented the favorable opinion Mr. Dorrit has formed of my services, I have found, in that only too high opinion, my consolation and recompense."

"Opinion of your services, madam?" said Mr. Dorrit.

"Of," Mrs. General repeated, in an elegantly impressive manner, "my services."

"Of your services alone, dear madam?" said Mr. Dorrit.

"I presume," retorted Mrs. General, in her former impressive manner, "of my services alone. For, to what else," said Mrs. General, with a slightly interrogative action of her gloves, "could I impute——?"

"To—ha—yourself, Mrs. General. Ha hum. To yourself and your merits," was Mr. Dorrit's rejoinder.

"Mr. Dorrit will pardon me," said Mrs. General, "if I remark that this is not a time or place for the pursuit of the present conversation. Mr. Dorrit will excuse me if I remind him that Miss Dorrit is in the adjoining room, and is visible to myself while I utter her name. Mr. Dorrit will forgive me if I observe that I am agitated, and that I find there are moments when weaknesses I supposed myself to have subdued, return with redoubled power. Mr. Dorrit will allow me to withdraw."

"Hum. Perhaps we may resume this—ha—interesting conversation," said Mr. Dorrit, "at another time; unless it should be, what I hope it is not—hum—in any way disagreeable to—ha—Mrs. General."

"Mr. Dorrit," said Mrs. General, casting down her eyes as she rose with a bend, "must ever claim my homage and obedience."

Mrs. General then took herself off in a stately way, and not with that amount of trepidation upon her which might have been expected in a less remarkable woman. Mr. Dorrit, who had conducted his part of the dialogue with a certain majestic and admiring condescension—much as some people may be seen to conduct themselves in Church, and to perform their part in the Service—appeared, on the whole, very well satisfied with himself and with Mrs. General too. On the return of that lady to tea, she had touched herself up with a little powder and pomatum, and was not without moral enhancement likewise; the latter showing itself in much sweet patronage of manner towards Miss Dorrit, and in an air of as tender interest in Mr. Dorrit as was consistent with rigid propriety. At the close of the evening, when she rose to retire, Mr. Dorrit took her by the hand, as if he were going to lead her out into the Piazza of the People to walk a minuet by moonlight, and with great solemnity conducted her to the room door, where he raised her knuckles to his lips. Having parted from her with what may be conjectured to have been a rather bony kiss, of a cosmetic flavor, he gave his daughter his blessing, graciously. And having thus hinted that there was something remarkable in the wind, he again went to bed.

He remained in the seclusion of his own chamber next morning; but, early in the afternoon, sent down his best compliments to Mrs. General, by Mr. Tinkler, and begged she would accompany Miss Dorrit on an airing without him. His daughter was dressed for Mrs. Merdle's dinner before he appeared. He then presented himself, in a refulgent condition as to his attire, but looking indefinably shrunken and old. However, as he was plainly determined to be angry with her if she so much as asked him how he was, she only ventured to kiss his cheek, before accompanying him to Mrs. Merdle's with an anxious heart.

The distance that they had to go was very short, but he was at his building work again before the carriage had half traversed it. Mrs. Merdle received him with great distinction; the bosom was in admirable preservation, and on the best terms with itself; the dinner was very choice; and the company was very select.

It was principally English; saving that it comprised the usual French Count and the usual Italian Marchese—decorative social milestones, always to be found in certain places, and varying very little in appearance. The table was long, and the dinner was long; and Little Dorrit, overshadowed by a large pair of black whiskers and a large white cravat, lost sight of her father altogether, until a servant put a scrap of paper in her hand, with a whispered request from Mrs. Merdle that she would read it directly. Mrs. Merdle had written on it in pencil, "Pray come and speak to Mr. Dorrit. I doubt if he is well."

She was hurrying to him, unobserved, when he got up out of his chair, and leaning over the table called to her, supposing her to be still in her place:

"Amy, Amy, my child!"

The action was so unusual, to say nothing of his strange eager appearance and strange eager voice, that it instantaneously caused a profound silence.

"Amy, my dear," he repeated. "Will you go and see if Bob is on the lock!"

She was at his side, and touching him, but he still perversely supposed her to be in her seat, and called out, still leaning over the table, "Amy, Amy. I don't feel quite myself. Ha. I don't know what's the matter with me. I particularly wish to see Bob. Ha. Of all the turnkeys, he's as much my friend as yours. See if Bob is in the Lodge, and beg him to come to me."

All the guests were now in consternation, and everybody rose.

"Dear father, I am not there; I am here, by you."

"Oh! You are here, Amy! Good. Hum. Good. Ha. Call Bob. If he has been relieved, and is not on the lock, tell Mrs. Bangham to go and fetch him."

She was gently trying to get him away; but he resisted, and would not go.

"I tell you, child," he said petulantly, "I can't be got up the narrow stairs without Bob. Ha. Send for Bob. Hum. Send for Bob—best of all the turn-keys—send for Bob!"

He looked confusedly about him, and, becoming conscious of the number of faces by which he was surrounded, addressed them:

"Ladies and gentlemen, the duty—ha—devolves upon me of—hum—welcoming you to the Marshalsea. Welcome to the Marshalsea! The space is—ha—limited—limited—the parade might be wider; but you will find it apparently grow larger after a time—a time, ladies and gentlemen—and the air is, all things considered, very good. It blows over the—ha—Surrey hills. Blows over the Surrey hills. This is the Snuggery. Hum. Supported by a small subscription of the—ha—Collegiate body. In return for which—hot water —general kitchen—and little domestic advantages. Those who are habituated to the—ha—Marshalsea, are pleased to call me its Father. I am accustomed to be complimented by strangers as the—ha—Father of the Marshalsea. Certainly, if years of residence may establish a claim to so —ha—honorable a title, I may accept the—hum—conferred distinction. My child, ladies and gentlemen. My daughter. Born here!"

She was not ashamed of it, or ashamed of him. She was pale and frightened; but she had no other care than to soothe him and get him away, for his own dear sake. She was between him and the wondering faces, turned round upon his breast with her own face raised to his. He held her clasped in his left arm, and between whiles her low voice was heard tenderly imploring him to go away with her.

"Born here," he repeated, shedding tears. "Bred here. Ladies and gentlemen, my daughter. Child of an unfortunate father, but—ha—always a gentleman. Poor, no doubt, but—hum—proud. Always proud. It has become a—hum—not infrequent custom for my—ha—personal admirers —personal admirers solely—to be pleased to express their desire to acknowledge my semi-official position here, by offering—ha—little tributes, which usually take the form of—ha—Testimonials—pecuniary Testimonials. In the acceptance of those—ha—voluntary recognitions of my humble endeavours to—hum—to uphold a Tone here—a Tone—I beg it to be understood that I do not consider myself compromised. Ha. Not compromised. Ha. Not a beggar. No; I repudiate the title! At the same time far be it from me to—hum—to put upon the fine feelings by which my partial friends are actuated, the slight of scrupling to admit that those offerings are—hum—highly acceptable. On the contrary, they are most acceptable. In my child's name, if not in my own, I make that admission in the fullest manner, at the same time reserving—ha—shall I say my personal dignity? Ladies and gentlemen, God bless you all!"

By this time, the exceeding mortification undergone by the Bosom had occasioned the withdrawal of the greater part of the company into other rooms. The few who had lingered thus long followed the rest, and Little Dorrit and her father were left to the servants and themselves. Dearest and most precious to her, he would come with her now, would he not? He replied to her fervid entreaties, that he would never be able to get up the narrow stairs without Bob, where was Bob, would nobody fetch Bob! Under pretence of looking for Bob, she got him out against the stream of gay company now pouring in for the evening assembly, and got him into a coach that had just set down its load, and got him home.

The broad stairs of his Roman palace were contracted in his failing sight to the narrow stairs of his London prison; and he would suffer no one but her to touch him, his brother excepted. They got him up to his room without help, and laid him down on his bed. And from that hour his poor maimed spirit, only remembering the place where it had broken its wings, cancelled the dream through which it had since groped, and knew of nothing beyond the Marshalsea. When he heard footsteps in the street, he took them for the old weary tread in the yards. When the hour came for locking up, he supposed all strangers to be excluded for the night. When the time for opening came again, he was so anxious to see Bob that they were fain to patch up a narrative how that Bob—many a year dead then, gentle turnkey—had taken cold, but hoped to be out to-morrow, or the next day, or the next at furthest.

He fell away into a weakness so extreme that he could not raise his hand. But, he still protected his brother according to his long usage; and would say with some complacency, fifty times a day, when he saw him standing by his bed, "My good Frederick, sit down. You are very feeble indeed."

They tried him with Mrs. General, but he had not the faintest knowledge of her. Some injurious suspicion lodged itself in his brain, that she wanted to supplant Mrs. Bangham, and that she was given to drinking. He charged her with it in no measured terms; and was so urgent with his daughter to go round to the Marshal and entreat him to turn her out, that she was never reproduced after the first failure.

Saving that he once asked "if Tip had gone outside?" the remembrance of his two children not present, seemed to have departed from him. But, the child who had done so much for him and had been so poorly repaid, was never out of his mind. Not that he spared her, or was fearful of her being spent by watching and fatigue; he was not more troubled on that score than he had usually been. No; he loved her in his old way. They were in the jail again, and she tended him, and he had constant need of her, and could not turn without her; and he even told her, sometimes, that he was content to have undergone a great deal for her sake. As to her, she bent over his bed with her quiet face against his, and would have laid down her own life to restore him.

When he had been sinking in this painless way for two or three days, she observed him to be troubled by the ticking of his watch—a pompous gold watch that made as great a to-do about its going, as if nothing else went but itself and Time. She suffered it to run down; but he was still uneasy, and showed that was not what he wanted. At length he roused himself to explain that he wanted money to be raised on this watch. He was quite pleased when she pretended to take it away for the purpose, and afterwards had a relish for his little tastes of wine and jelly, that he had not had before.

He soon made it plain that this was so; for, in another day or two he sent off his sleeve-buttons and finger-rings. He had an amazing satisfaction in entrusting her with these errands, and appeared to consider it equivalent to making the most methodical and provident arrangements. After his trinkets, or such of them as he had been able to see about him, were gone, his clothes engaged his attention; and it is as likely as not that he was kept alive for some days by the satisfaction of sending them, piece by piece, to an imaginary pawnbroker's.

Thus for ten days Little Dorrit bent over his pillow, laying her cheek against his. Sometimes she was so worn out that for a few minutes they would slumber together. Then she would awake; to recollect with fast-flowing silent tears what it was that touched her face, and to see, stealing over the cherished face upon the pillow, a deeper shadow than the shadow of the Marshalsea Wall.

Quietly, quietly, all the lines of the plan of the great Castle melted, one after another. Quietly, quietly, the ruled and cross-ruled countenance on which they were traced, became fair and blank. Quietly, quietly, the re-flected marks of the prison bars and of the zig-zag iron on the wall-top, faded away. Quietly, quietly, the face subsided into a far younger likeness of her own than she had ever seen under the grey hair, and sank to rest.

At first her uncle was stark distracted. "O my brother! O William, William! You to go before me; you to go alone; you to go, and I to remain!

You, so far superior, so distinguished, so noble; I, a poor useless creature fit for nothing, and whom no one would have missed!"

It did her, for the time, the good of having him to think of, and to succour. "Uncle, dear Uncle, spare yourself, spare me!"

The old man was not deaf to the last words. When he did begin to restrain himself, it was that he might spare her. He had no care for himself; but, with all the remaining power of the honest heart, stunned so long and now awaking to be broken, he honored and blessed her.

"O God," he cried, before they left the room, with his wrinkled hands clasped over her. "Thou seest this daughter of my dear dead brother! All that I have looked upon, with my half-blind and sinful eyes, Thou hast discerned clearly, brightly. Not a hair of her head shall be harmed before Thee. Thou wilt uphold her here, to her last hour. And I know Thou wilt reward her hereafter!"

They remained in a dim room near, until it was almost midnight, quiet and sad together. At times his grief would seek relief, in a burst like that in which it had found its earliest expression; but, besides that his little strength would soon have been unequal to such strains, he never failed to recall her words, and to reproach himself and calm himself. The only utterance with which he indulged his sorrow, was the frequent exclamation that his brother was gone, alone; that they had been together in the outset of their lives, that they had fallen into misfortune together, that they had kept together through their many years of poverty, that they had remained together to that day; and that his brother was gone alone, alone!

They parted, heavy, and sorrowful. She would not consent to leave him anywhere but in his own room, and she saw him lie down in his clothes upon his bed, and covered him with her own hands. Then she sank upon her own bed, and fell into a deep sleep: the sleep of exhaustion and rest, though not of complete release from a pervading consciousness of affliction. Sleep, good Little Dorrit. Sleep through the night!

It was a moonlight night; but, the moon rose late, being long past the full. When it was high in the peaceful firmament, it shone through half-closed lattice blinds into the solemn room where the stumblings and wanderings of a life had so lately ended. Two quiet figures were within the room; two figures, equally still and impassive, equally removed by an untraversable distance from the teeming earth and all that it contains, though soon to lie in it.

One figure reposed upon the bed. The other, kneeling on the floor, drooped over it; the arms easily and peacefully resting on the coverlet; the face bowed down, so that the lips touched the hand over which with its last breath it had bent. The two brothers were before their Father; far beyond the twilight judgments of this world; high above its mists and obscurities.

CHAPTER XX

INTRODUCES THE NEXT

THE passengers were landing from the packet on the pier at Calais. A low-lying place and a low-spirited place Calais was, with the tide ebbing out towards low water-mark. There had been no more water on the bar than had sufficed to float the packet in; and now the bar itself, with a shallow break of sea over it, looked like a lazy marine monster just risen to the surface, whose form was indistinctly shown as it lay asleep. The meagre lighthouse all in white, haunting the sea-board, as if it were the ghost of an edifice that had once had color and rotundity, dripped melancholy tears after its late buffeting by the waves. The long rows of gaunt black piles, slimy and wet and weather-worn, with funeral garlands of sea-weed twisted about them by the late tide, might have represented an unsightly marine cemetery. Every wave-dashed, storm-beaten object, was so low and so little, under the broad grey sky, in the noise of the wind and sea, and before the curling lines of surf, making at it ferociously, that the wonder was there was any Calais left, and that its low gates and low wall and low roofs and low ditches and low sand-hills and low ramparts and flat streets, had not yielded long ago to the undermining and besieging sea, like the fortifications children make on the sea-shore.

After slipping among oozy piles and planks, stumbling up wet steps, and encountering many salt difficulties, the passengers entered on their comfortless peregrination along the pier; where all the French vagabonds and English outlaws in the town (half the population) attended to prevent their recovery from bewilderment. After being minutely inspected by all the English, and claimed and reclaimed and counter-claimed as prizes by all the French, in a hand-to-hand scuffle three quarters of a mile long, they were at last free to enter the streets, and to make off in their various directions, hotly pursued.

Clennam, harassed by more anxieties than one, was among this devoted band. Having rescued the most defenceless of his compatriots from situations of great extremity, he now went his way alone; or as nearly alone as he could be, with a native gentleman in a suit of grease and a cap of the same material, giving chase at a distance of some fifty yards, and continually calling after him "Hi! Ice-say! You! Seer! Ice-say! Nice Oatel!"

Even this hospitable person, however, was left behind at last, and Clennam pursued his way, unmolested. There was a tranquil air in the town after the turbulence of the Channel and the beach, and its dulness in that comparison was agreeable. He met new groups of his countrymen, who had all a straggling air of having at one time over-blown themselves, like certain uncomfortable kinds of flowers, and of being, now, mere weeds.

They had all an air, too, of lounging out a limited round, day after day, which strongly reminded him of the Marshalsea. But, taking no further note of them than was sufficient to give birth to the reflection, he sought out a certain street and number, which he kept in his mind.

"So Pancks said," he murmured to himself, as he stopped before a dull house answering to the address. "I suppose his information to be correct and his discovery, among Mr. Casby's loose papers, indisputable; but, without it, I should hardly have supposed this to be a likely place."

A dead sort of house, with a dead wall over the way and a dead gateway at the side, where a pendant bell-handle produced two dead tinkles, and a knocker produced a dead flat surface-tapping that seemed not to have depth enough in it to penetrate even the cracked door. However, the door jarred open on a dead sort of spring; and he closed it behind him as he entered a dull yard, soon brought to a close at the back by another dead wall, where an attempt had been made to train some creeping shrubs, which were dead; and to make a little fountain in a grotto, which was dry; and to decorate that with a little statue, which was gone.

The entry to the house was on the left, and it was garnished, as the outer gateway was, with two printed bills in French and English, announcing Furnished Apartments to let, with immediate possession. A strong cheerful peasant woman, all stocking, petticoat, white cap, and ear-ring, stood here in a dark doorway, and said with a pleasant show of teeth, "Ice-say! Seer! Who?"

Clennam, replying in French, said the English lady; he wished to see the English lady. "Enter then and ascend, if you please," returned the peasant woman, in French likewise. He did both, and followed her up a dark bare staircase to a back room on the first floor. Hence, there was a gloomy view of the yard that was dull, and of the shrubs that were dead, and of the fountain that was dry, and of the pedestal of the statue that was gone.

"Monsieur Blandois," said Clennam.

"With pleasure, Monsieur."

Thereupon the woman withdrew, and left him to look at the room. It was the pattern of room always to be found in such a house. Cool, dull, and dark. Waxed floor, very slippery. A room not large enough to skait in; not adapted to the easy pursuit of any other occupation. Red and white curtained windows, little straw mat, little round table with a tumultuous assemblage of legs underneath, clumsy rush-bottomed chairs, two great red velvet armchairs affording plenty of space to be uncomfortable in, bureau, chimney-glass in several pieces pretending to be in one piece, pair of gaudy vases of very artificial flowers; between them a Greek warrior with his helmet off, sacrificing a clock to the Genius of France.

After some pause, a door of communication with another room was opened, and a lady entered. She manifested great surprise on seeing

Clennam, and her glance went round the room in search of some one else.

"Pardon me, Miss Wade. I am alone."

"It was not your name that was brought to me."

"No; I know that. Excuse me. I have already had experience that my name does not predispose you to an interview; and I ventured to mention the name of one I am in search of."

"Pray," she returned, motioning him to a chair so coldly, that he remained standing, "what name was it that you gave?"

"I mentioned the name of Blandois."

"Blandois?"

"A name you are acquainted with."

"It is strange," she said, frowning, "that you should still press an undesired interest in me and my acquaintances, in me and my affairs, Mr. Clennam. I don't know what you mean."

"Pardon me. You know the name?"

"What can you have to do with the name? What can I have to do with the name? What can you have to do with my knowing or not knowing any name? I know many names and I have forgotten many more. This may be in the one class, or it may be in the other, or I may never have heard it. I am acquainted with no reason for examining myself, or for being examined, about it."

"If you will allow me," said Clennam, "I will tell you my reason for pressing the subject. I admit that I do press it, and I must beg you to forgive me if I do so, very earnestly. The reason is all mine. I do not insinuate that it is in any way yours."

"Well, sir," she returned, repeating, a little less haughtily than before, her former invitation to him to be seated: to which he now deferred, as she seated herself. "I am at least glad to know that this is not another bondswoman of some friend of yours, who is bereft of free choice, and whom I have spirited away. I will hear your reason, if you please."

"First, to identify the person of whom we speak," said Clennam, "let me observe that it is the person you met in London some time back. You will remember meeting him near the river—in the Adelphi?"

"You mix yourself most unaccountably with my business," she replied, looking full at him with stern displeasure. "How do you know that?"

"I entreat you not to take it ill. By mere accident."

"What accident?"

"Solely, the accident of coming upon you in the street and seeing the meeting."

"Do you speak of yourself, or of some one else?"

"Of myself. I saw it."

"To be sure it was in the open street," she observed, after a few moments of less and less angry reflection. "Fifty people might have seen it. It would have signified nothing if they had."

"Nor do I make my having seen it of any moment, nor (otherwise than as an explanation of my coming here) do I connect my visit with it, or the favor that I have to ask."

"Oh! You have to ask a favor! It occurred to me," and the handsome face looked bitterly at him, "that your manner was softened, Mr. Clennam."

He was content to protest against this by a slight action without contesting it in words. He then referred to Blandois' disappearance, of which it was probable she had heard? No. However probable it was to him, she had heard of no such thing. Let him look round him (she said), and judge for himself what general intelligence was likely to reach the ears of a woman who had been shut up there while it was rife, devouring her own heart. When she had uttered this denial, which he believed to be true, she asked him what he meant by disappearance? That led to his narrating the circumstances in detail, and expressing something of his anxiety to discover what had really become of the man, and to repel the dark suspicions that clouded about his mother's house. She heard him with evident surprise, and with more marks of suppressed interest than he had before seen in her; still they did not overcome her distant, proud, and self-secluded manner. When he had finished, she said nothing but these words:

"You have not yet told me, sir, what I have to do with it, or what the favor is. Will you be so good as come to that?"

"I assume," said Arthur, persevering in his endeavour to soften her scornful demeanour, "that being in communication—may I say, confidential communication?—with this person——"

"You may say, of course, whatever you like," she remarked; "but I do not subscribe to your assumptions, Mr. Clennam, or to any one's."

"—that being, at least, in personal communication with him," said Clennam, changing the form of his position, in the hope of making it unobjectionable, "you can tell me something of his antecedents, pursuits, habits, usual place of residence. Can give me some little clue by which to seek him out in the likeliest manner, and either produce him, or establish what has become of him. This is the favor I ask, and I ask it in a distress of mind for which I hope you will feel some consideration. If you should have any reason for imposing conditions upon me, I will respect it without asking what it is."

"You chanced to see me in the street with the man," she observed, after being, to his mortification, evidently more occupied with her own reflections on the matter than with his appeal. "Then you knew the man before?"

"Not before; afterwards. I never saw him before, but I saw him again on this very night of his disappearance. In my mother's room, in fact. I left him there. You will read in this paper all that is known of him."

He handed her one of the printed bills, which she read with a steady and attentive face.

"This is more than *I* knew of him," she said, giving it back.

Clennam's looks expressed his heavy disappointment, perhaps his incredulity; for, she added in the same unsympathetic tone: "You don't believe it. Still, it is so. As to personal communication; it seems that there was personal communication between him and your mother. And yet you say you believe *her* declaration that she knows no more of him!"

A sufficiently expressive hint of suspicion was conveyed in these words, and in the smile by which they were accompanied, to bring the blood into Clennam's cheeks.

"Come, sir," she said, with a cruel pleasure in repeating the stab, "I will be as open with you as you can desire. I will confess that if I cared for my credit (which I do not), or had a good name to preserve (which I have not, for I am utterly indifferent to its being considered good or bad), I should regard myself as heavily compromised by having had anything to do with this fellow. Yet he never passed in at *my* door—never sat in colloquy wiɫn *me* until midnight."

She took her revenge for her old grudge in thus turning his subject against him. Hers was not the nature to spare him, and she had no compunction.

"That he is a low, mercenary wretch; that I first saw him prowling about Italy (where I was, not long ago), and that I hired him there, as the suitable instrument of a purpose I happened to have; I have no objection to tell you. In short, it was worth my while, for my own pleasure—the gratification of a strong feeling—to pay a spy who would fetch and carry for money. I paid this creature. And I dare say that if I had wanted to make such a bargain, and if I could have paid him enough, and if he could have done it in the dark, free from all risk, he would have taken any life with as little scruple as he took my money. That, at least, is my opinion of him; and I see it is not very far removed from yours. Your mother's opinion of him, I am to assume (following your example of assuming this and that), was vastly different."

"My mother, let me remind you," said Clennam, "was first brought into communication with him in the unlucky course of business."

"It appears to have been an unlucky course of business that last brought her into communication with him," returned Miss Wade; "and business hours on that occasion were late."

"You imply," said Arthur, smarting under these cool-handed thrusts, of which he had deeply felt the force already, "that there was something——"

"Mr. Clennam," she composedly interrupted, "recollect that I do not speak by implication about the man. He is, I say again without disguise, a low mercenary wretch. I suppose such a creature goes where there is occasion for him. If I had not had occasion for him, you would not have seen him and me together."

Wrung by her persistence in keeping that dark side of the case before him, of which there was a half-hidden shadow in his own breast, Clennam was silent.

"I have spoken of him as still living," she added, "but he may have been put out of the way for anything I know. For anything I care, also. I have no further occasion for him."

With a heavy sigh and a despondent air, Arthur Clennam slowly rose. She did not rise also, but said, having looked at him in the meanwhile with a fixed look of suspicion, and lips angrily compressed:

"He was the chosen associate of your dear friend, Mr. Gowan, was he not? Why don't you ask your dear friend to help you?"

The denial that he was a dear friend rose to Arthur's lips; but, he repressed it, remembering his old struggles and resolutions, and said:

"Further than that he has never seen Blandois since Blandois set out for England, Mr. Gowan knows nothing additional about him. He was a chance acquaintance, made abroad."

"A chance acquaintance, made abroad!" she repeated. "Yes. Your dear friend has need to divert himself with all the acquaintances he can make, seeing what a wife he has. I hate his wife, sir."

The anger with which she said it, the more remarkable for being so much under her restraint, fixed Clennam's attention, and kept him on the spot. It flashed out of her dark eyes as they regarded him, quivered in her nostrils, and fired the very breath she exhaled; but her face was otherwise composed into a disdainful serenity, and her attitude was as calmly and haughtily graceful as if she had been in a mood of complete indifference.

"All I will say is, Miss Wade," he remarked, "that you can have received no provocation to a feeling in which I believe you have no sharer."

"You may ask your dear friend, if you choose," she returned, "for his opinion upon that subject."

"I am scarcely on those intimate terms with my dear friend," said Arthur, in spite of his resolutions, "that would render my approaching the subject very probable, Miss Wade."

"I hate him," she returned. "Worse than his wife, because I was once dupe enough, and false enough to myself, almost to love him. You have seen me, sir, only on common-place occasions, when I dare say you have thought me a common-place woman, a little more self-willed than the generality. You don't know what I mean by hating, if you know me no better than that; you can't know, without knowing with what care I have studied myself, and people about me. For this reason I have for some time inclined to tell you what my life has been—not to propitiate your opinion, for I set no value on it; but, that you may comprehend, when you think of your dear friend and his dear wife, what I mean by hating. Shall I give you something I have written and put by for your perusal, or shall I hold my hand?"

Arthur begged her to give it to him. She went to the bureau, unlocked it, and took from an inner drawer a few folded sheets of paper. Without any conciliation of him, scarcely addressing him, rather speaking as if she were speaking to her own looking-glass for the justification of her own stubbornness, she said, as she gave them to him:

"Now you may know what I mean by hating! No more of that. Sir, whether you find me temporarily and cheaply lodging in an empty London house or in a Calais apartment, you find Harriet with me. You may like to see her before you leave. Harriet, come in!" She called Harriet again. The second call produced Harriet, once Tattycoram.

"Here is Mr. Clennam," said Miss Wade; "not come for you; he has given you up.—I suppose you have, by this time?"

"Having no authority or influence—yes," assented Clennam.

"Not come in search of you, you see; but still seeking some one. He wants that Blandois man."

"With whom I saw you in the Strand in London," hinted Arthur.

"If you know anything of him, Harriet, except that he came from Venice—which we all know—tell it to Mr. Clennam freely."

"I know nothing more about him," said the girl.

"Are you satisfied?" Miss Wade enquired of Arthur.

He had no reason to disbelieve them; the girl's manner being so natural as to be almost convincing, if he had had any previous doubts. He replied, "I must seek for intelligence elsewhere."

He was not going in the same breath; but, he had risen before the girl entered, and she evidently thought he was. She looked quickly at him, and said:

"Are they well, sir?"

"Who?"

She stopped herself in saying what would have been "all of them;" glanced at Miss Wade; and said "Mr. and Mrs. Meagles."

"They were, when I last heard of them. They are not at home. By the way, let me ask you. Is it true that you were seen there?"

"Where? Where does any one say I was seen?" returned the girl, sullenly casting down her eyes.

"Looking in at the garden gate of the cottage?"

"No," said Miss Wade. "She has never been near it."

"You are wrong, then," said the girl. "I went down there, the last time we were in London. I went one afternoon when you left me alone. And I did look in."

"You poor-spirited girl," returned Miss Wade with infinite contempt; "does all our companionship, do all our conversations, do all your old complainings, tell for so little as that?"

"There was no harm in looking in at the gate for an instant," said the girl. "I saw by the windows that the family were not there."

"Why should you go near the place?"

"Because I wanted to see it. Because I felt that I should like to look at it again."

As each of the two handsome faces looked at the other, Clennam felt how each of the two natures must be constantly tearing the other to pieces.

"Oh!" said Miss Wade, coldly subduing and removing her glance; "if you had any desire to see the place where you led the life from which I rescued you because you had found out what it was, that is another thing. But, is that your truth to me? Is that your fidelity to me? Is that the common cause I make with you? You are not worth the confidence I have placed in you. You are not worth the favor I have shown you. You are no higher than a spaniel, and had better go back to the people who did worse than whip you."

"If you speak so of them with any one else by to hear, you'll provoke me to take their part," said the girl.

"Go back to them," Miss Wade retorted. "Go back to them."

"You know very well," retorted Harriet in her turn, "that I won't go back to them. You know very well that I have thrown them off, and never can, never shall, never will, go back to them. Let them alone, then, Miss Wade."

"You prefer their plenty to your less fat living here," she rejoined. "You exalt them and slight me. What else should I have expected? I ought to have known it."

"It's not so," said the girl, flushing high, "and you don't say what you mean. I know what you mean. You are reproaching me, under-handed, with having nobody but you to look to. And because I have nobody but you to look to, you think you are to make me do, or not do, everything you please, and are to put any affront upon me. You are as bad as they were, every bit. But I will not be quite tamed and made submissive. I will say again that I went to look at the house, because I had often thought that I should like to see it once more. I will ask again how they are, because I once liked them, and at times thought they were kind to me."

Hereupon Clennam said that he was sure they would still receive her kindly, if she should ever desire to return.

"Never!" said the girl passionately. "I shall never do that. Nobody knows that better than Miss Wade, though she taunts me because she has made me her dependant. And I know I am so; and I know she is overjoyed when she can bring it to my mind."

"A good pretence!" said Miss Wade, with no less anger, haughtiness, and bitterness; "but too threadbare to cover what I plainly see in this. My poverty will not bear competition with their money. Better go back at once, better go back at once, and have done with it!"

Arthur Clennam looked at them, standing a little distance asunder in the dull confined room, each proudly cherishing her own anger; each, with a fixed determination, torturing her own breast, and torturing the other's. He said a word or two of leave-taking; but, Miss Wade barely inclined her head, and Harriet, with the assumed humiliation of an abject dependant and serf (but not without defiance for all that), made as if she were too low to notice or to be noticed.

He came down the dark winding stairs into the yard, with an increased sense upon him of the gloom of the wall that was dead, and of the shrubs that were dead, and of the fountain that was dry, and of the statue that was gone. Pondering much on what he had seen and heard in that house, as well as on the failure of all his efforts to trace the suspicious character who was lost, he returned to London and to England by the packet that had taken him over. On the way, he unfolded the sheets of paper, and read in them what is reproduced in the next chapter.

CHAPTER XXI

THE HISTORY OF A SELF TORMENTOR

I HAVE the misfortune of not being a fool. From a very early age I have detected what those about me thought they hid from me. If I could have been habitually imposed upon, instead of habitually discerning the truth, I might have lived as smoothly as most fools do.

My childhood was passed with a grandmother; that is to say, with a lady who represented that relative to me, and who took that title on herself. She had no claim to it, but I—being to that extent a little fool—had no suspicion of her. She had some children of her own family in her house, and some children of other people. All girls; ten in number, including me. We all lived together, and were educated together.

I must have been about twelve years old when I began to see how determinedly those girls patronised me. I was told I was an orphan. There was no other orphan among us; and I perceived (here was the first disadvantage of not being a fool), that they conciliated me in an insolent pity, and in a sense of superiority. I did not set this down as a discovery, rashly. I tried them often. I could hardly make them quarrel with me. When I succeeded with any of them, they were sure to come, after an hour or two, and begin a reconciliation. I tried them over and over again, and I never knew them wait for me to begin. They were always forgiving me, in their vanity and condescension. Little images of grown people!

One of them was my chosen friend. I loved that stupid mite in a passionate way that she could no more deserve, than I can remember without feeling ashamed of, though I was but a child. She had what they called an amiable temper, an affectionate temper. She could distribute, and did distribute, pretty looks and smiles to every one among them. I believe there was not a soul in the place, except myself, who knew that she did it purposely to wound and gall me!

Nevertheless, I so loved that unworthy girl, that my life was made stormy by my fondness for her. I was constantly lectured and disgraced for what was called "trying her;" in other words, charging her with her little perfidy and throwing her into tears by showing her that I read her heart. However, I loved her, faithfully; and one time I went home with her for the holidays.

She was worse at home than she had been at school. She had a crowd of cousins and acquaintances, and we had dances at her house, and went out to dances at other houses, and, both at home and out, she tormented my love beyond endurance. Her plan was, to make them all fond of her—and so drive me wild with jealousy. To be familiar and endearing with them all —and so make me mad with envying them. When we were left alone in our bedroom at night, I would reproach her with my perfect knowledge of her baseness; and then she would cry and cry and say I was cruel, and then I would hold her in my arms till morning: loving her as much as ever, and often feeling as if, rather than suffer so, I could so hold her in my arms and plunge to the bottom of a river—where I would still hold her, after we were both dead.

It came to an end, and I was relieved. In the family, there was an aunt, who was not fond of me. I doubt if any of the family liked me much; but, I never wanted them to like me, being altogether bound up in the one girl. The aunt was a young woman, and she had a serious way with her eyes of watching me. She was an audacious woman, and openly looked compassionately at me. After one of the nights that I have spoken of, I came down into a greenhouse before breakfast. Charlotte (the name of my false young friend) had gone down before me, and I heard this aunt speaking to her about me as I entered. I stopped where I was, among the leaves, and listened.

The aunt said, "Charlotte, Miss Wade is wearing you to death, and this must not continue." I repeat the very words I heard.

Now, what did she answer? Did she say, "It is I who am wearing her to death, I who am keeping her on a rack and am the executioner, yet she tells me every night that she loves me devotedly, though she knows what I make her undergo"? No; my first memorable experience was true to what I knew her to be, and to all my experience. She began sobbing and weeping (to secure the aunt's sympathy to herself), and said "Dear aunt, she has an unhappy temper; other girls at school, besides I, try hard to make it better; we all try hard."

Upon that, the aunt fondled her, as if she had said something noble instead of despicable and false, and kept up the infamous pretence by replying, "But there are reasonable limits, my dear love, to everything, and I see that this poor miserable girl causes you more constant and useless distress than even so good an effort justifies."

The poor miserable girl came out of her concealment, as you may be prepared to hear, and said, "Send me home." I never said another word to either of them, or to any of them, but "Send me home, or I will walk home alone, night and day!" When I got home, I told my supposed grandmother that, unless I was sent away to finish my education somewhere else, before that girl came back, or before any one of them came back, I would burn my sight away by throwing myself into the fire, rather than I would endure to look at their plotting faces.

I went among young women next, and I found them no better. Fair words and fair pretences; but, I penetrated below those assertions of themselves and depreciations of me, and they were no better. Before I left them, I learned that I had no grandmother and no recognised relation. I carried the light of that information both into my past and into my future. It showed me many new occasions on which people triumphed over me, when they made a pretence of treating me with consideration, or doing me a service.

A man of business had a small property in trust for me. I was to be a governess. I became a governess; and went into the family of a poor noble-man, where there were two daughters—little children, but the parents, wished them to grow up, if possible, under one instructress. The mother was young and pretty. From the first, she made a show of behaving to me with great delicacy. I kept my resentment to myself; but, I knew very well that it was her way of petting the knowledge that she was my Mistress, and might have behaved differently to her servant if it had been her fancy.

I say I did not resent it, nor did I; but I showed her, by not gratifying her, that I understood her. When she pressed me to take wine, I took water. If there happened to be anything choice at table, she always sent it to me: but, I always declined it, and ate of the rejected dishes. These disappoint-ments of her patronage were a sharp retort, and made me feel independent.

I liked the children. They were timid, but on the whole disposed to attach themselves to me. There was a nurse, however, in the house, a rosy-faced woman always making an obtrusive pretence of being gay and good-humoured, who had nursed them both, and who had secured their affections before I saw them. I could almost have settled down to my fate but for this woman. Her artful devices for keeping herself before the children in constant competition with me, might have blinded many in my place; but, I saw through them from the first. On the pretext of arranging my rooms and waiting on me and taking care of my wardrobe (all of which she did, busily), she was never absent. The most crafty of her many subtleties was her feint of seeking to make the children fonder of me. She would lead them to me, and coax them to me. "Come to good Miss Wade, come to dear Miss Wade, come to pretty Miss Wade. She loves you very much. Miss Wade is a clever lady, who has read heaps of books, and can tell you far better and more interesting stories than I know. Come and hear Miss

Wade!" How could I engage their attention, when my heart was burning against these ignorant designs? How could I wonder, when I saw their innocent faces shrinking away, and their arms twining round her neck, instead of mine? Then she would look up at me, shaking their curls from her face as she did it, and say, "They'll come round soon, Miss Wade; they're very simple and loving, ma'am; don't be at all cast down about it, ma'am"—exulting over me!

There was another thing the woman did. At times, when she saw that she had safely plunged me into a black despondent brooding, by these means, she would call the attention of the children to it, and would show them the difference between herself and me. "Hush! Poor Miss Wade is not well. Don't make a noise, my dears, her head aches. Come and comfort her. Come and ask her if she is better; come and ask her to lie down. I hope you have nothing on your mind, ma'am. Don't take on, ma'am, and be sorry!"

It became intolerable. Her ladyship my Mistress coming in one day when I was alone, and at the height of feeling that I could support it no longer, I told her I must go. I could not bear the presence of that woman Dawes.

"Miss Wade! Poor Dawes is devoted to you; would do anything for you!"

I knew beforehand she would say so; I was quite prepared for it; I only answered, it was not for me to contradict my Mistress; I must go.

"I hope, Miss Wade," she returned, instantly assuming the tone of superiority she had always so thinly concealed, "that nothing I have ever said or done since we have been together, has justified your use of that disagreeable word, Mistress. It must have been wholly inadvertent on my part. Pray tell me what it is."

I replied that I had no complaint to make, either of my Mistress or to my Mistress; but, I must go.

She hesitated a moment, and then sat down beside me, and laid her hand on mine. As if that honor would obliterate any remembrance!

"Miss Wade, I fear you are unhappy, through causes over which I have no influence."

I smiled, thinking of the experience the word awakened, and said, "I have an unhappy temper, I suppose."

"I did not say that."

"It is an easy way of accounting for anything," said I.

"It may be; but I did not say so. What I wish to approach, is something very different. My husband and I have exchanged some remarks upon the subject, when we have observed with pain that you have not been easy with us."

"Easy? Oh! You are such great people, my lady," said I.

"I am unfortunate in using a word which may convey a meaning—and evidently does—quite opposite to my intention." (She had not expected my reply, and it shamed her.) "I only mean, not happy with us. It is a difficult topic to enter on; but, from one young woman to another, perhaps —in short, we have been apprehensive that you may allow some family circumstances of which no one can be more innocent than yourself, to prey upon your spirits. If so, let us entreat you not to make them a cause of grief. My husband himself, as is well known, formerly had a very dear sister who was not in law his sister, but who was universally beloved and respected——"

I saw directly, that they had taken me in, for the sake of the dead woman, whoever she was, and to have that boast of me and advantage of me; I saw, in the nurse's knowledge of it, an encouragement to goad me as she had done; and I saw, in the children's shrinking away, a vague impression that I was not like other people. I left that house that night.

After one or two short and very similar experiences, which are not to the present purpose, I entered another family where I had but one pupil: a girl of fifteen, who was the only daughter. The parents here were elderly people: people of station and rich. A nephew whom they had brought up, was a frequent visitor at the house, among many other visitors; and he began to pay me attention. I was resolute in repulsing him; for, I had determined when I went there, that no one should pity me or condescend to me. But, he wrote me a letter. It led to our being engaged to be married.

He was a year younger than I, and young-looking even when that allowance was made. He was on absence from India, where he had a post that was soon to grow into a very good one. In six months we were to be married, and were to go to India. I was to stay in the house, and was to be married from the house. Nobody objected to any part of the plan.

I cannot avoid saying, he admired me; but, if I could, I would. Vanity has nothing to do with the declaration, for, his admiration worried me. He took no pains to hide it; and caused me to feel among the rich people as if he had bought me for my looks, and made a show of his purchase to justify himself. They appraised me in their own minds, I saw, and were curious to ascertain what my full value was. I resolved that they should not know. I was immovable and silent before them; and would have suffered any one of them to kill me, sooner than I would have laid myself out to bespeak their approval.

He told me I did not do myself justice. I told him I did, and it was because I did and meant to do so to the last, that I would not stoop to propitiate any of them. He was concerned and even shocked, when I added that I wished he would not parade his attachment before them; but, he said he would sacrifice even the honest impulses of his affection to my peace.

Under that pretence, he began to retort upon me. By the hour together, he would keep at a distance from me, talking to any one rather than to me.

I have sat alone and unnoticed, half an evening, while he conversed with his young cousin, my pupil. I have seen all the while, in people's eyes, that they thought the two looked nearer on an equality than he and I. I have sat, divining their thoughts, until I have felt that his young appearance made me ridiculous, and have raged against myself for ever loving him.

For, I did love him once. Undeserving as he was, and little as he thought of all these agonies that it cost me—agonies which should have made him wholly and gratefully mine to his life's end—I loved him. I bore with his cousin's praising him to my face, and with her pretending to think that it pleased me, but full well knowing that it rankled in my breast; for his sake. While I have sat in his presence recalling all my slights and wrongs, and deliberating whether I should not fly from the house at once and never see him again—I have loved him.

His aunt (my Mistress you will please to remember) deliberately, wilfully, added to my trials and vexations. It was her delight to expatiate on the style in which we were to live in India, and on the establishment we should keep, and the company we should entertain, when he got his advancement. My pride rose against this barefaced way of pointing out the contrast my married life was to present to my then dependent and inferior position. I suppressed my indignation; but, I showed her that her intention was not lost upon me, and I repaid her annoyances by affecting humility. What she described, would surely be a great deal too much honor for me, I would tell her. I was afraid I might not be able to support so great a change. Think of a mere governess, her daughter's governess, coming to that high distinction! It made her uneasy and made them all uneasy, when I answered in this way. They knew that I fully understood her.

It was at the time when my troubles were at their highest, and when I was most incensed against my lover for his ingratitude in caring as little as he did for the innumerable distresses and mortifications I underwent on his account, that your dear friend, Mr. Gowan, appeared at the house. He had been intimate there for a long time, but had been abroad. He understood the state of things at a glance, and he understood me.

He was the first person I had ever seen in my life who had understood me. He was not in the house three times before I knew that he accompanied every movement of my mind. In his coldly easy way with all of them, and with me, and with the whole subject, I saw it clearly. In his light protestations of admiration of my future husband, in his enthusiasm regarding our engagement and our prospects, in his hopeful congratulations on our future wealth and his despondent references to his own poverty—all equally hollow, and jesting, and full of mockery—I saw it clearly. He made me feel more and more resentful, and more and more contemptible, by always presenting to me everything that surrounded me, with some new hateful light upon it, while he pretended to exhibit it in its best aspect for my admiration and his own. He was like the dressed-up Death in the Dutch series; whatever figure he took upon his arm, whether it was youth or age, beauty or ugliness, whether he danced with it, sang with it, played with it, or prayed with it, he made it ghastly.

You will understand, then, that when your dear friend complimented me, he really condoled with me; that when he soothed me under my vexations, he laid bare every smarting wound I had; that when he declared my "faithful swain" to be "the most loving young fellow in the world, with the tenderest heart that ever beat," he touched my old misgiving that I was made ridiculous. These were not great services, you may say. They were acceptable to me, because they echoed my own mind, and confirmed my own knowledge. I soon began to like the society of your dear friend, better than any other.

When I perceived (which I did, almost as soon) that jealousy was growing out of this, I liked this society still better. Had I not been subjected to jealousy, and were the endurances to be all mine? No. Let him know what it was! I was delighted that he should know it; I was delighted that he should feel keenly, and I hoped he did. More than that. He was tame in comparison with Mr. Gowan, who knew how to address me on equal terms, and how to anatomise the wretched people around us.

This went on, until the aunt, my Mistress, took it upon herself to speak to me. It was scarcely worth alluding to; she knew I meant nothing; but, she suggested from herself, knowing it was only necessary to suggest, that it might be better, if I were a little less companionable with Mr. Gowan.

I asked her how she could answer for what I meant? She could always answer, she replied, for my meaning nothing wrong. I thanked her, but said I would prefer to answer for myself, and to myself. Her other servants would probably be grateful for good characters, but I wanted none.

Other conversation followed, and induced me to ask her how she knew that it was only necessary for her to make a suggestion to me, to have it obeyed? Did she presume on my birth, or on my hire? I was not bought, body and soul. She seemed to think that her distinguished nephew had gone into a slave-market and purchased a wife.

It would probably have come, sooner or later, to the end to which it did come, but she brought it to its issue at once. She told me, with assumed commiseration, that I had an unhappy temper. On this repetition of the old wicked injury, I withheld no longer, but exposed to her all I had known of her and seen in her, and all I had undergone within myself since I had occupied the despicable position of being engaged to her nephew. I told her that Mr. Gowan was the only relief I had had in my degradation; that I had borne it too long, and that I shook it off too late; but, that I would see none of them more. And I never did.

Your dear friend followed me to my retreat, and was very droll on the severance of the connexion; though he was sorry, too, for the excellent people (in their way the best he had ever met), and deplored the necessity of breaking mere house-flies on the wheel. He protested before long, and far more truly than I then supposed, that he was not worth acceptance by a woman of such endowments, and such power of character; but—well, well!——

Your dear friend amused me and amused himself as long as it suited his inclinations; and then reminded me that we were both people of the world, that we both understood mankind, that we both knew there was no such thing as romance, that we were both prepared for going different ways to seek our fortunes like people of sense, and that we both foresaw that whenever we encountered one another again we should meet as the best friends on earth. So he said, and I did not contradict him.

It was not very long before I found that he was courting his present wife, and that she had been taken away to be out of his reach. I hated her then, quite as much as I hate her now; and naturally, therefore, could desire nothing better than that she should marry him. But, I was restlessly curious to look at her—so curious that I felt it to be one of the few sources of entertainment left to me. I travelled a little: travelled until I found myself in her society, and in yours. Your dear friend, I think, was not known to you then, and had not given you any of those signal marks of his friendship which he has bestowed upon you.

In that company I found a girl, in various circumstances of whose position there was a singular likeness to my own, and in whose character I was interested and pleased to see much of the rising against swollen patronage and selfishness, calling themselves kindness, protection, benevolence, and other fine names, which I have described as inherent in my nature. I often heard it said, too, that she had "an unhappy temper." Well understanding what was meant by the convenient phrase, and wanting a companion with a knowledge of what I knew, I thought I would try to release the girl from her bondage and sense of injustice. I have no occasion to relate that I succeeded.

We have been together ever since, sharing my small means.

CHAPTER XXII

WHO PASSES BY THIS ROAD SO LATE?

ARTHUR CLENNAM had made his unavailing expedition to Calais, in the midst of a great pressure of business. A certain barbaric Power with valuable possessions on the map of the world, had occasion for the services of one or two engineers, quick in invention and determined in execution: practical men, who could make the men and means their ingenuity perceived to be wanted, out of the best materials they could find at hand; and who were as bold and fertile in the adaptation of such materials to their purpose, as in the conception of their purpose itself. This Power, being a barbaric one, had no idea of stowing away a great national object in a Circumlocution Office, as strong wine is hidden from the light in a cellar, until its fire and youth are gone, and the laborers who worked in the vine-yard and pressed the grapes are dust. With characteristic ignorance, it acted on the most decided and energetic notions of How to do it; and never showed the least respect for, or gave any quarter to, the great political science How not to do it. Indeed it had a barbarous way of striking the latter art and mystery dead, in the person of any enlightened subject who practised it.

Accordingly, the men who were wanted, were sought out and found: which was in itself a most uncivilised and irregular way of proceeding. Being found, they were treated with great confidence and honor (which again showed dense political ignorance), and were invited to come at once and do what they had to do. In short, they were regarded as men who meant to do it, engaging with other men who meant it to be done.

Daniel Doyce was one of the chosen. There was no foreseeing at that time whether he would be absent months, or years. The preparations for his departure, and the conscientious arrangement for him of all the details and results of their joint business, had necessitated labor within a short compass of time, which had occupied Clennam day and night. He had slipped across the water in his first leisure, and had slipped as quickly back again for his farewell interview with Doyce.

Him Arthur now showed, with pains and care, the state of their gains and losses, responsibilities and prospects. Daniel went through it all in his patient manner, and admired it all exceedingly. He audited the accounts, as if they were a far more ingenious piece of mechanism than he had ever constructed, and afterwards stood looking at them, weighing his hat over his head by the brims, as if he were absorbed in the contemplation of some wonderful engine.

"It's all beautiful, Clennam, in its regularity and order. Nothing can be plainer. Nothing can be better."

"I am glad you approve, Doyce. Now, as to the management of our capital while you are away, and as to the conversion of so much of it as the business may need from time to time——" His partner stopped him.

"As to that, and as to everything else of that kind, all rests with you. You will continue in all such matters to act for both of us, as you have done hitherto, and to lighten my mind of a load it is much relieved from."

"Though, as I often tell you," returned Clennam, "you unreasonably depreciate your business qualities."

"Perhaps so," said Doyce, smiling. "And perhaps not. Anyhow, I have a calling that I have studied more than such matters, and that I am better fitted for. I have perfect confidence in my partner, and I am satisfied that he will do what is best. If I have a prejudice connected with money and money-figures," continued Doyce, laying that plastic workman's thumb of his on the lappel of his partner's coat, "it is against speculating. I don't think I have any other. I dare say I entertain that prejudice, only because I have never given my mind fully to the subject."

"But you shouldn't call it a prejudice," said Clennam. "My dear Doyce, it is the soundest sense."

"I am glad you think so," returned Doyce, with his grey eye looking kind and bright.

"It so happens," said Clennam, "that just now, not half an hour before you came down, I was saying the same thing to Pancks, who looked in here. We both agreed that, to travel out of safe investments, is one of the most dangerous, as it is one of the most common, of those follies which often deserve the name of vices."

"Pancks?" said Doyce, tilting up his hat at the back, and nodding with an air of confidence. "Aye, aye, aye! That's a cautious fellow."

"He is a very cautious fellow indeed," returned Arthur. "Quite a specimen of caution."

They both appeared to derive a larger amount of satisfaction from the cautious character of Mr. Pancks than was quite intelligible, judged by the surface of their conversation.

"And now," said Daniel, looking at his watch, "as time and tide wait for no one, my trusty partner, and as I am ready for starting, bag and baggage, at the gate below, let me say a last word. I want you to grant a request of mine."

"Any request you can make.—Except," Clennam was quick with his exception, for his partner's face was quick in suggesting it, "except that I will abandon your invention."

"That's the request, and you know it is," said Doyce.

"I say, No, then. I say positively, No. Now that I have begun, I will have some definite reason, some responsible statement, something in the nature of a real answer, from those people."

"You will not," returned Doyce, shaking his head. "Take my word for it, you never will."

"At least, I'll try," said Clennam. "It will do me no harm to try."

"I am not certain of that," rejoined Doyce, laying his hand persuasively on his shoulder. "It has done me harm, my friend. It has aged me, tired me, vexed me, disappointed me. It does no man any good to have his patience worn out, and to think himself ill-used. I fancy, even already, that unavailing attendance on delays and evasions has made you something less elastic than you used to be."

"Private anxieties may have done that for the moment," said Clennam, "but not official harrying. Not yet. I am not hurt yet."

"Then you won't grant my request?"

"Decidedly, No," said Clennam. "I should be ashamed if I submitted to be so soon driven out of the field, where a much older and a much more sensitively interested man contended with fortitude so long."

As there was no moving him, Daniel Doyce returned the grasp of his hand, and, casting a farewell look round the counting-house, went downstairs with him. Doyce was to go to Southampton to join the small staff of his fellow-travellers; and a coach was at the gate, well furnished and packed, and ready to take him there. The workmen were at the gate to see him off, and were mightily proud of him. "Good luck to you, Mr. Doyce!" said one of the number. "Wherever you go, they'll find as they've got a man among 'em, a man as knows his tools and as his tools knows, a man as is willing and a man as is able, and if that's not a man where is a man!" This oration from a gruff volunteer in the back-ground, not previously suspected of any powers in that way, was received with three loud cheers; and the speaker became a distinguished character for ever afterwards. In the midst of the three loud cheers, Daniel gave them all a hearty "Good Bye, Men!" and the coach disappeared from sight, as if the concussion of the air had blown it out of Bleeding Heart Yard.

Mr. Baptist, as a grateful little fellow in a position of trust, was among the workmen, and had done as much towards the cheering as a mere foreigner could. In truth, no men on earth can cheer like Englishmen, who do so rally one another's blood and spirit when they cheer in earnest, that the stir is like the rush of their whole history, with all its standards waving at once, from Saxon Alfred's downward. Mr. Baptist had been in a manner whirled away before the onset, and was taking his breath in quite a scared condition when Clennam beckoned him to follow up-stairs, and return the books and papers to their places.

In the lull consequent on the departure—in that first vacuity which ensues on every separation, foreshadowing the great separation that is always overhanging all mankind—Arthur stood at his desk, looking dreamily out at a gleam of sun. But, his liberated attention soon reverted to the theme that was foremost in his thoughts, and began, for the hundredth time, to dwell upon every circumstance that had impressed itself upon his mind, on the mysterious night when he had seen the man at his mother's. Again the man jostled him in the crooked street, again he followed the man and lost him, again he came upon the man in the courtyard looking at the house, again he followed the man and stood beside him on the door-steps.

> "Who passes by this road so late?
>   Compagnon de la Majolaine;
> Who passes by this road so late?
>   Always gay!"

It was not the first time, by many, that he recalled the song of the child's game, of which the fellow had hummed this verse while they stood side by side; but, he was so unconscious of having repeated it audibly, that he started to hear the next verse,

> "Of all the king's knights 'tis the flower,
> Compagnon de la Majolaine;
> Of all the king's knights 'tis the flower,
> Always gay!"

Cavalletto had deferentially suggested the words and tune; supposing him to have stopped short for want of more.

"Ah! You know the song, Cavalletto?"

"By Bacchus, yes, sir! They all know it in France. I have heard it many times, sung by the little children. The last time when it I have heard," said Mr. Baptist, formerly Cavalletto, who usually went back to his native construction of sentences when his memory went near home, "is from a sweet little voice. A little voice, very pretty, very innocent. Altro!"

"The last time I heard it," returned Arthur, "was in a voice quite the reverse of pretty, and quite the reverse of innocent." He said it more to himself than to his companion, and added to himself, repeating the man's next words, "Death of my life, sir, it's my character to be impatient!"

"EH!" cried Cavalletto, astounded, and with all his color gone in a moment.

"What is the matter?"

"Sir! You know where I have heard that song the last time?"

With his rapid native action, his hands made the outline of a high hook nose, pushed his eyes near together, dishevelled his hair, puffed out his upper lip to represent a thick moustache, and threw the heavy end of an ideal cloak over his shoulder. While doing this, with a swiftness incredible to one who has not watched an Italian peasant, he indicated a very remarkable and sinister smile. The whole change passed over him like a flash of light, and he stood in the same instant, pale and astonished, before his patron.

"In the name of Fate and wonder," said Clennam, "what do you mean? Do you know a man of the name of Blandois?"

"No!" said Mr. Baptist, shaking his head.

"You have just now described a man who was by, when you heard that song; have you not?"

"Yes!" said Mr. Baptist, nodding fifty times.

"And was he not called Blandois?"

"No!" said Mr. Baptist. "Altro, Altro, Altro, Altro!" He could not reject the name sufficiently, with his head and his right forefinger going at once.

"Stay!" cried Clennam, spreading out the handbill on his desk. "Was this the man? You can understand what I read aloud?"

"Altogether. Perfectly."

"But look at it, too. Come here and look over me, while I read."

Mr. Baptist approached, followed every word with his quick eyes, saw and heard it all out with the greatest impatience, then clapped his two hands flat upon the bill as if he had fiercely caught some noxious creature, and cried, looking eagerly at Clennam, "It is the man! Behold him!"

"This is of far greater moment to me," said Clennam, in great   agitation, "than you can imagine. Tell   me where you knew the man."

Mr. Baptist, releasing the paper very slowly and with much discomfiture, and drawing himself back two or three paces, and making as though he dusted his hands, returned, very much against his will:

"At Marsiglia—Marseilles."

"What was he?"

"A prisoner, and—Altro! I believe yes!—an," Mr. Baptist crept closer again to whisper it, "Assassin!"

Clennam fell back as if the word had struck him a blow: so terrible did it make his mother's communication with the man appear. Cavalletto dropped on one knee, and implored him, with a redundancy of gesticulation, to hear what had brought himself into such foul company.

He told with perfect truth how it had come of a little contraband trading, and how he had in time been released from prison, and how he had gone away from those antecedents. How, at the house of entertainment called the Break of Day at Chalons on the Saone, he had been awakened in his bed at night, by the same assassin, then assuming the name of Lagnier, though his name had formerly been Rigaud; how the assassin had proposed that they should join their fortunes together; how he held the assassin in such dread and aversion that he had fled from him at daylight, and how he had ever since been haunted by the fear of seeing the assassin again and being claimed by him as an acquaintance. When he had related this, with an emphasis and poise on the word, assassin, peculiarly belonging to his own language, and which did not serve to render it less terrible to Clennam, he suddenly sprang to his feet, pounced upon the bill again, and with a vehemence that would have been absolute madness in any man of Northern origin, cried "Behold the same assassin! Here he is!"

In his passionate raptures, he at first forgot the fact that he had lately seen the assassin in London. On his remembering it, it suggested hope to Clennam that the recognition might be of later date than the night of the visit at his mother's; but, Cavalletto was too exact and clear about time and place, to leave any opening for doubt that it had preceded that occasion.

"Listen,"   said Arthur, very seriously. "This man, as we have read here, has wholly disappeared."

"Of it I am well content!" said Cavalletto, raising his eyes piously. "A thousand thanks to Heaven! Accursed assassin!"

"Not so," returned Clennam; "for, until something more is heard of him, I can never know an hour's peace."

"Enough, Benefactor; that is quite another thing. A million of excuses!"

"Now, Cavalletto," said Clennam, gently turning him by the arm, so that they looked into each other's eyes. "I am certain that for the little I have been able to do for you, you are the most sincerely grateful of men."

"I swear it!" cried the other.

"I know it. If you could find this man, or discover what has become of him, or gain any later intelligence whatever of him, you would render me a service above any other service I could receive in the world, and would make me (with far greater reason) as grateful to you as you are to me."

"I know not where to look," cried the little man, kissing Arthur's hand in a transport. "I know not where to begin. I know not where to go. But, courage! Enough! It matters not! I go, in this instant of time!"

"Not a word to any one but me, Cavalletto."

"Al-tro!" cried Cavalletto. And was gone with great speed.

END OF No. XVI

CHAPTER XXIII

MISTRESS AFFERY MAKES A CONDITIONAL PROMISE RESPECTING HER DREAMS

LEFT alone, with the expressive looks and gestures of Mr. Baptist, otherwise Giovanni Baptista Cavalletto, vividly before him, Clennam entered on a weary day. It was in vain that he tried to control his attention, by directing it to any business occupation or train of thought; it rode at anchor by the haunting topic, and would hold to no other idea. As though a criminal should be chained in a stationary boat on a deep clear river, condemned, whatever countless leagues of water flowed past him, always to see the body of the fellow creature he had drowned lying at the bottom, immovable, and unchangeable, except as the eddies made it broad or long, now expanding, now contracting its terrible lineaments; so Arthur, below the shifting current of transparent thoughts and fancies which were gone and succeeded by others as soon as come, saw, steady and dark, and not to be stirred from its place, the one subject that he endeavoured with all his might to rid himself of, and that he could not fly from.

The assurance he now had, that Blandois, whatever his right name, was one of the worst of characters, greatly augmented the burden of his anxieties. Though the disappearance should be accounted for to-morrow, the fact that his mother had been in communication with such a man, would remain unalterable. That the communication had been of a secret kind, and that she had been submissive to him and afraid of him, he hoped might be known to no one beyond himself; yet, knowing it, how could he separate it from his old vague fears, and how believe that there was nothing evil in such relations?

Her resolution not to enter on the question with him, and his knowledge of her indomitable character, enhanced his sense of helplessness. It was like the oppression of a dream, to believe that shame and exposure were impending over her and his father's memory, and to be shut out, as by a brazen wall, from the possibility of coming to their aid. The purpose he had brought home to his native country, and had ever since kept in view, was, with her greatest determination, defeated by his mother herself, at the time of all others when he feared that it pressed most. His advice, energy, activity, money, credit, all his resources whatsoever, were all made useless. If she had been possessed of the old fabled influence, and had turned those who looked upon her into stone, she could not have rendered him more completely powerless (so it seemed to him in his distress of mind) than she did, when she turned her unyielding face to his, in her gloomy room.

But, the light of that day's discovery, shining on these considerations, roused him to take a more decided course of action. Confident in the rectitude of his purpose, and impelled by a sense of overhanging danger closing in around, he resolved, if his mother would still admit of no approach, to make a desperate appeal to Affery. If she could be brought to become communicative, and to do what lay in her to break the spell of secrecy that enshrouded the house, he might shake off the paralysis of which every hour that passed over his head made him more acutely sensible. This was the result of his day's anxiety, and this was the decision he put in practice when the day closed in.

His first disappointment, on arriving at the house, was to find the door open, and Mr. Flintwinch smoking a pipe on the steps. If circumstances had been commonly favorable, Mistress Affery would have opened the door to his knock. Circumstances being uncommonly unfavorable, the door stood open, and Mr. Flintwinch was smoking his pipe on the steps.

"Good evening," said Arthur.

"Good evening," said Mr. Flintwinch.

The smoke came crookedly out of Mr. Flintwinch's mouth, as if it circulated through the whole of his wry figure and came back by his wry throat, before coming forth to mingle with the smoke from the crooked chimneys and the mists from the crooked river.

"Have you any news?" said Arthur.

"We have no news," said Jeremiah.

"I mean of the foreign man," Arthur explained.

"*I* mean of the foreign man," said Jeremiah.

He looked so grim, as he stood askew, with the knot of his cravat under his ear, that the thought passed into Clennam's mind, and not for the first time by many, could Flintwinch for a purpose of his own have got rid of Blandois? Could it have been his secret, and his safety, that were at issue? He was small and bent, and perhaps not actively strong; yet he was as tough as an old yew tree, and as crafty as an old jackdaw. Such a man, coming behind a much younger and more vigorous man, and having the will to put an end to him and no relenting, might do it pretty surely in that solitary place at a late hour.

While, in the morbid condition of his thoughts, these thoughts drifted over the main one that was always in Clennam's mind, Mr. Flintwinch, regarding the opposite house over the gateway with his neck twisted and one eye shut up, stood smoking with a vicious expression upon him; more as if he were trying to bite off the stem of his pipe, than as if he were enjoying it. Yet he was enjoying it, in his own way.

"You'll be able to take my likeness, the next time you call, Arthur, I should think," said Mr. Flintwinch, drily, as he stooped to knock the ashes out.

Rather conscious and confused, Arthur asked his pardon, if he had stared at him unpolitely. "But my mind runs so much upon this matter," he said, "that I lose myself."

"Hah! Yet I don't see," returned Mr. Flintwinch, quite at his leisure, "why it should trouble *you*, Arthur."

"No?"

"No," said Mr. Flintwinch, very shortly and decidedly: much as if he were of the canine race, and snapped at Arthur's hand.

"Is it nothing to me to see those placards about? Is it nothing to me to see my mother's name and residence hawked up and down, in such an association?"

"I don't see," returned Mr. Flintwinch, scraping his horny cheek, "that it need signify much to you. But I'll tell you what I do see, Arthur," glancing up at the windows; "I see the light of fire and candle in your mother's room!"

"And what has that to do with it?"

"Why sir, I read by it," said Mr. Flintwinch, screwing himself at him, "that if it's advisable (as the proverb says it is) to let sleeping dogs lie, it's just as advisable, perhaps, to let missing dogs lie. Let 'em be. They generally turn up soon enough."

Mr. Flintwinch turned short round when he had made this remark, and went into the dark hall. Clennam stood there, following him with his eyes, as he dipped for a light in the phosphorus-box in the little room at the side, got one after three or four dips, and lighted the dim lamp against the wall. All the while, Clennam was pursuing the probabilities—rather as if they were being shown to him by an invisible hand than as if he himself were conjuring them up—of Mr. Flintwinch's ways and means of doing that darker deed, and removing its traces by any of the black avenues of shadow that lay around them.

"Now, sir," said the testy Jeremiah; "will it be agreeable to walk up-stairs?"

"My mother is alone, I suppose?"

"Not alone," said Mr. Flintwinch. "Mr. Casby and his daughter are with her. They came in while I was smoking, and I stayed behind to have my smoke out."

This was the second disappointment. Arthur made no remark upon it, and repaired to his mother's room, where Mr. Casby and Flora had been taking tea, anchovy paste, and hot buttered toast. The relics of those delicacies were not yet removed, either from the table, or from the scorched countenance of Affery, who, with the kitchen toasting-fork still in her hand, looked like a sort of allegorical personage; except that she had a consider-able advantage over the general run of such personages, in point of signifi-cant emblematical purpose.

Flora had spread her bonnet and shawl upon the bed, with a care indica-tive of an intention to stay some time. Mr. Casby too, was beaming near the hob, with his benevolent knobs shining as if the warm butter of the toast were exuding through the patriarchal skull, and with his face as ruddy as if the coloring matter of the anchovy paste were mantling in the patriarchal visage. Seeing this, as he exchanged the usual salutations, Clennam decided to speak to his mother without postponement.

It had long been customary, as she never changed her room, for those who had anything to say to her apart, to wheel her to her desk; where she sat, usually with the back of her chair turned towards the rest of the room, and the person who talked with her seated in a corner, on a stool which was always set in that place for that purpose. Except that it was long since the mother and son had spoken together without the intervention of a third person, it was an ordinary matter of course within the experience of visitors for Mrs. Clennam to be asked, with a word of apology for the interruption, if she could be spoken with on a matter of business, and, on her replying in the affirmative, to be wheeled into the position described.

Therefore, when Arthur now made such an apology, and such a request, and moved her to her desk and seated himself on the stool, Mrs. Finching merely began to talk louder and faster, as a delicate hint that she could overhear nothing, and Mr. Casby stroked his long white locks with sleepy calmness.

"Mother, I have heard something to-day which I feel persuaded you don't know, and which I think you should know, of the antecedents of that man I saw here."

"I know nothing of the antecedents of the man you saw here, Arthur."

She spoke aloud. He had lowered his own voice; but, she rejected that advance towards confidence as she rejected every other, and spoke in her usual key and in her usual stern voice.

"I have received it on no circuitous information; it has come to me direct."

She asked him, exactly as before, if he were there to tell her what it was?

"I thought it right that you should know it."

"And what is it?"

"He has been a prisoner in a French jail."

She answered with composure "I should think that very likely."

"But, in a jail for criminals, mother. On an accusation of murder."

She started at the word, and her looks expressed her natural horror. Yet she still spoke aloud, when she demanded:

"Who told you so?"

"A man who was his fellow-prisoner."

"That man's antecedents, I suppose, were not known to you, before he told you?"

"No."

"Though the man himself was?"

"Yes."

"My case, and Flintwinch's, in respect of this other man! I dare say the resemblance is not so exact, though, as that your informant became known to you through a letter from a correspondent, with whom he had deposited money? How does that part of the parallel stand?"

Arthur had no choice but to say that his informant had not become known to him through the agency of any such credentials, or indeed of any credentials at all. Mrs. Clennam's attentive frown expanded by degrees into a severe look of triumph, and she retorted with emphasis, "Take care how you judge others, then. I say to you, Arthur, for your good, take care how you judge!"

Her emphasis had been derived from her eyes quite as much as from the stress she laid upon her words. She continued to look at him; and if, when he entered the house, he had had any latent hope of prevailing in the least with her, she now looked it out of his heart.

"Mother, shall I do nothing to assist you?"

"Nothing."

"Will you entrust me with no confidence, no charge, no explanation? Will you take no counsel with me? Will you not let me come near you?"

"How can you ask me? You separated yourself from my affairs. It was not my act; it was yours. How can you consistently ask me such a question? You know that you left me to Flintwinch, and that he occupies your place."

Glancing at Jeremiah, Clennam saw in his very gaiters that his attention was closely directed to them, though he stood leaning against the wall scraping his jaw, and pretending to listen to Flora as she held forth in a most distracting manner on a chaos of subjects, in which mackerel, and Mr. F's Aunt in a swing, had become entangled with cockchafers and the wine trade.

"A prisoner, in a French jail, on an accusation of murder," repeated Mrs. Clennam, steadily going over what her son had said. "That is all you know of him from the fellow-prisoner?"

"In substance, all."

"And was the fellow-prisoner his accomplice and a murderer, too? But, of course, he gives a better account of himself than of his friend; it is needless to ask. This will supply the rest of them here with something new to talk about. Casby, Arthur tells me——"

"Stay, mother! Stay, stay!" He interrupted her, hastily, for it had not entered his imagination that she would openly proclaim what he had told her.

"What now?" she said, with displeasure. "What more?"

"I beg you to excuse me, Mr. Casby—and you, too, Mrs. Finching—for one other moment, with my mother——"

He had laid his hand upon her chair, or she would otherwise have wheeled it round with the touch of her foot upon the ground. They were still face to face. She looked at him, as he ran over the possibilities of some result he had not intended, and could not foresee, being influenced by Cavalletto's disclosure becoming a matter of notoriety, and hurriedly arrived at the conclusion that it had best not be talked about; though perhaps he was guided by no more distinct reason than that he had taken it for granted that his mother would reserve it to herself and her partner.

"What now?" she said again, impatiently. "What is it?"

"I did not mean, mother, that you should repeat what I have communicated. I think you had better not repeat it."

"Do you make that a condition with me?"

"Well! Yes."

"Observe, then! It is you who make this a secret," said she, holding up her hand, "and not I. It is you, Arthur, who bring here doubts and suspicions and entreaties for explanations, and it is you, Arthur, who bring secrets here. What is it to me, do you think, where the man has been, or what he has been? What can it be to me? The whole world may know it, if they care to know it; it is nothing to me. Now, let me go."

He yielded to her imperious but elated look, and turned her chair back to the place from which he had wheeled it. In doing so he saw elation in the face of Mr. Flintwinch, which most assuredly was not inspired by Flora. This turning of his intelligence, and of his whole attempt and design against himself, did even more than his mother's fixedness and firmness to convince him that his efforts with her were idle. Nothing remained but the appeal to his old friend Affery.

But, even to get to the very doubtful and preliminary stage of making the appeal, seemed one of the least promising of human undertakings. She was so completely under the thrall of the two clever ones, was so systematically kept in sight by one or other of them, and was so afraid to go about the house besides, that every opportunity of speaking to her alone appeared to be forestalled. Over and above that, Mistress Affery, by some means (it was not very difficult to guess, through the sharp arguments of her liege lord), had acquired such a lively conviction of the hazard of saying anything under any circumstances, that she had remained all this time in a corner guarding herself from approach with that symbolical instrument of hers; so that, when a word or two had been addressed to her by Flora, or even by the bottle-green patriarch himself, she had warded off conversation with the toasting-fork, like a dumb woman.

After several abortive attempts to get Affery to look at him while she cleared the table and washed the tea-service, Arthur thought of an expedient which Flora might originate. To whom he therefore whispered, "Could you say you would like to go through the house?"

Now, poor Flora, being always in fluctuating expectation of the time when Clennam would renew his boyhood, and be madly in love with her again, received this whisper with the utmost delight; not only as rendered precious by its mysterious character, but as preparing the way for a tender interview in which he would declare the state of his affections. She immediately began to work out the hint.

"Ah dear me the poor old room," said Flora, glancing round, "looks just as ever Mrs. Clennam I am touched to see except for being smokier which was to be expected with time and which we must all expect and reconcile ourselves to being whether we like it or not as I am sure I have had to do myself if not exactly smokier dreadfully stouter which is the same or worse, to think of the days when papa used to bring me here the least of girls a perfect mass of chilblains to be stuck upon a chair with my feet on the rails and stare at Arthur—pray excuse me—Mr. Clennam—the least of boys in the frightfullest of frills and jackets ere yet Mr. F appeared a misty shadow on the horizon paying attentions like the well-known spectre of some place in Germany beginning with a B is a moral lesson inculcating that all the paths in life are similar to the paths down in the North of England where they get the coals and make the iron and things gravelled with ashes!"

Having paid the tribute of a sigh to the instability of human existence, Flora hurried on with her purpose.

"Not that at any time," she proceeded, "its worst enemy could have said it was a cheerful house for that it was never made to be but always highly impressive, fond memory recalls an occasion in youth ere yet the judgment was mature when Arthur—confirmed habit—Mr. Clennam—took me down into an unused kitchen eminent for mouldiness and proposed to secrete me there for life and feed me on what he could hide from his

meals when he was at home for the holidays and on dry bread in disgrace
which at that halcyon period too frequently occurred, would it be inconvenient or asking too much to beg to be permitted to revive those scenes
and walk through the house?"

Mrs. Clennam, who responded with a constrained grace to Mrs. Finching's good nature in being there at all, though her visit (before Arthur's
unexpected arrival) was undoubtedly an act of pure good nature and no
self-gratification, intimated that all the house was open to her. Flora rose
and looked to Arthur for his escort. "Certainly," said he, aloud; "and Affery
will light us, I dare say."

Affery was excusing herself with "Don't ask nothing of me, Arthur!"
when Mr. Flintwinch stopped her with "Why not? Affery, what's the
matter with you, woman? Why not, jade!" Thus expostulated with, she
came unwillingly out of her corner, resigned the toasting-fork into one of
her husband's hands, and took the candlestick he offered from the other.

"Go before, you fool!" said Jeremiah. "Are you going up, or down, Mrs.
Finching?"

Flora answered, "Down."

"Then go before, and down, you Affery," said Jeremiah. "And do it
properly, or I'll come rolling down the bannisters, and tumbling over
you!"

Affery headed the exploring party; Jeremiah closed it. He had no
intention of leaving them. Clennam looking back, and seeing him following, three stairs behind, in the coolest and most methodical manner,
exclaimed in a low voice, "Is there no getting rid of him!" Flora re-assured
his mind, by replying promptly, "Why though not exactly proper Arthur
and a thing I couldn't think of before a younger man or a stranger still I
don't mind him if you so particularly wish it and provided you'll have the
goodness not to take me too tight."

Wanting the heart to explain that this was not at all what he meant,
Arthur extended his supporting arm round Flora's figure. "Oh my goodness me," said she, "you are very obedient indeed really and it's extremely
honorable and gentlemanly in you I am sure but still at the same time if you
would like to be a little tighter than that I shouldn't consider it intruding."

In this preposterous attitude, unspeakably at variance with his anxious
mind, Clennam descended to the basement of the house; finding that wherever it became darker than elsewhere, Flora became heavier, and that when
the house was lightest she was too. Returning from the dismal kitchen-
regions, which were as dreary as they could be, Mistress Affery passed
with the light into his father's old room, and then into the old dining-room;
always passing on before like a phantom that was not to be overtaken, and
neither turning nor answering when he whispered, "Affery! Affery! I
want to speak to you!"

In the dining-room, a sentimental desire came over Flora to look into the dragon closet which had so often swallowed Arthur in the days of his boyhood—not improbably because, as a very dark closet, it was a likely place to be heavy in. Arthur, fast subsiding into despair, had opened it, when a knock was heard at the outer door.

Mistress Affery, with a suppressed cry, threw her apron over her head.

"What? You want another dose!" said Mr. Flintwinch. "You shall have it, my woman, you shall have a good one! Oh! You shall have a sneezer, you shall have a teaser!"

"In the meantime is anybody going to the door?" said Arthur.

"In the meantime, *I* am going to the door, sir," returned the old man: so savagely, as to render it clear that in a choice of difficulties he felt he must go, though he would have preferred not to go. "Stay here the while, all! Affery, my woman, move an inch, or speak a word in your foolishness, and I'll treble your dose!"

The moment he was gone, Arthur released Mrs. Finching: with some difficulty, by reason of that lady's misunderstanding his intentions, and making her arrangements with a view to tightening instead of slackening.

"Affery, speak to me now!"

"Don't touch me, Arthur!" she cried, shrinking from him. "Don't come near me. He'll see you. Jeremiah will. Don't!"

"He can't see me," returned Arthur, suiting the action to the word, "if I blow the candle out."

"He'll hear you," cried Affery.

"He can't hear me," returned Arthur, suiting the action to the word again, "if I draw you into this black closet, and speak here. Why do you hide your face?"

"Because I am afraid of seeing something."

"You can't be afraid of seeing anything in this darkness, Affery."

"Yes, I am. Much more than if it was light."

"Why are you afraid?"

"Because the house is full of mysteries and secrets; because it's full of whisperings and counsellings; because it's full of noises. There never was such a house for noises. I shall die of 'em, if Jeremiah don't strangle me first. As I expect he will."

"I have never heard any noises here, worth speaking of."

"Ah! But you would, though, if you lived in the house, and was obliged to go about it as I am," said Affery; "and you'd feel that they was so well worth speaking of, that you'd feel you was nigh bursting, through not being allowed to speak of 'em. Here's Jeremiah! You'll get me killed."

"My good Affery, I solemnly declare to you that I can see the light of the open door on the pavement of the hall, and so could you if you would uncover your face and look."

"I durstn't do it," said Affery, "I durstn't never, Arthur. I'm always blindfolded when Jeremiah an't a looking, and sometimes even when he is."

"He cannot shut the door without my seeing him," said Arthur. "You are as safe with me as if he was fifty miles away."

("I wish he was!" cried Affery.)

"Affery, I want to know what is amiss here; I want some light thrown on the secrets of this house."

"I tell you, Arthur," she interrupted, "noises is the secrets, rustlings and stealings about, tremblings, treads overhead and treads underneath."

"But those are not all the secrets."

"I don't know," said Affery. "Don't ask me no more. Your old sweetheart an't far off, and she's a blabber."

His old sweetheart, being in fact so near at hand that she was then reclining against him in a flutter, a very substantial angle of forty-five degrees, here interposed to assure Mistress Affery with greater earnestness than directness of asseveration, that whatever she heard should go no further, but should be kept inviolate, "if on no other account on Arthur's —sensible of intruding in being too familiar Doyce and Clennam's."

"I make an imploring appeal to you, Affery, to you, one of the few agreeable early remembrances I have, for my mother's sake, for your husband's sake, for my own, for all our sakes. I am sure you can tell me something connected with the coming here of this man, if you will."

"Why, then I'll tell you, Arthur," returned Affery——"Jeremiah's a coming!"

"No, indeed he is not. The door is open, and he is standing outside, talking."

"I'll tell you then," said Affery, after listening, "that the first time he ever come he heard the noises his own self. 'What's that?' he said to me. 'I don't know what it is,' I says to him, catching hold of him, 'but I have heard it over and over again.' While I says it, he stands a looking at me, all of a shake, he do."

"Has he been here often?"

"Only that night, and the last night."

"What did you see of him on the last night, after I was gone?"

"Them two clever ones had him all alone to themselves. Jeremiah come a dancing at me sideways, after I had let you out (he always comes a dancing at me sideways when he's going to hurt me), and he said to me, 'Now, Affery,' he said, 'I am a coming behind you, my woman, and a going to run you up.' So he took and squeezed the back of my neck in his hand, till it made me open my mouth, and then he pushed me before him to bed, squeezing all the way. That's what he calls running me up, he do. Oh, he's a wicked one!"

"And did you hear or see no more, Affery!"

"Don't I tell you I was sent to bed, Arthur! Here he is!"

"I assure you he is still at the door. Those whisperings and counsellings,

Affery, that you have spoken of. What are they?"

"How should I know! Don't ask me nothing about 'em, Arthur. Get away!"

"But, my dear Affery; unless I can gain some insight into these hidden things, in spite of your husband and in spite of my mother, ruin will come of it."

"Don't ask me nothing," repeated Affery. "I have been in a dream for ever so long. Go away, go away!"

"You said that, before," returned Arthur. "You used the same expression that night, at the door, when I asked you what was going on here. What do you mean by being in a dream?"

"I an't a going to tell you. Get away! I shouldn't tell you, if you was by yourself; much less with your old sweetheart here."

It was equally vain for Arthur to entreat, and for Flora to protest. Affery, who had been trembling and struggling the whole time, turned a deaf ear to all adjuration, and was bent on forcing herself out of the closet.

"I'd sooner scream to Jeremiah than say another word! I'll call out to him, Arthur, if you don't give over speaking to me. Now here's the very last word I'll say afore I call to him.—If ever you begin to get the better of them two clever ones your own self (you ought to it, as I told you when you first come home, for you haven't been a living here long years, to be made afeard of your life as I have), then do you get the better of 'em afore my face; and then do you say to me, Affery tell your dreams! Maybe, then I'll tell 'em!"

The shutting of the door stopped Arthur from replying. They glided into the places where Jeremiah had left them; and Clennam, stepping forward as that old gentleman returned, informed him that he had accidentally extinguished the candle. Mr. Flintwinch looked on as he re-lighted it at the lamp in the hall, and preserved a profound taciturnity respecting the person who had been holding him in conversation. Perhaps his irascibility demanded compensation for some tediousness that the visitor had expended on him; however that was, he took such umbrage at seeing his wife with her apron over her head, that he charged at her, and taking her veiled nose between his thumb and finger, appeared to throw the whole screw-power of his person into the wring he gave it.

Flora, now permanently heavy, did not release Arthur from the survey of the house, until it had extended even to his old garret bedchamber. His thoughts were otherwise occupied than with the tour of inspection: yet he took particular notice at the time, as he afterwards had occasion to remember, of the airlessness and closeness of the house; that they left the track of their footsteps in the dust on the upper floors; and that there was a resistance to the opening of one room door, which occasioned Affery to cry out that somebody was hiding inside, and to continue to believe so, though somebody was sought and not discovered. When they at last returned to his mother's room, they found her, shading her face with her muffled hand, and talking in a low voice to the Patriarch as he stood before the fire. Whose blue eyes, polished head, and silken locks, turning towards them as they came in, imparted an inestimable value and inexhaustible love of his species to his remark:

"So you have been seeing the premises, seeing the premises—premises— seeing the premises!"

It was not in itself a jewel of benevolence or wisdom, yet he made it an exemplar of both that one would have liked to have a copy of.

CHAPTER XXIV

THE EVENING OF A LONG DAY

THAT illustrious man, and great national ornament, Mr. Merdle, continued his shining course. It began to be widely understood that one who had done society the admirable service of making so much money out of it, could not be suffered to remain a commoner. A baronetcy was spoken of with confidence; a peerage was frequently mentioned. Rumour had it that Mr. Merdle had set his golden face against a baronetcy; that he had plainly intimated to Lord Decimus that a baronetcy was not enough for him; that he had said, "No: a Peerage, or plain Merdle." This was reported to have plunged Lord Decimus as nigh to his noble chin in a slough of doubts as so lofty a personage could be sunk. For, the Barnacles, as a group of themselves in creation, had an idea that such distinctions belonged to them; and that when a soldier, sailor, or lawyer, became ennobled, they let him in, as it were, by an act of condescension, at the family door, and immediately shut it again. Not only (said Rumour) had the troubled Decimus his own hereditary part in this impression, but he also knew of several Barnacle claims already on the file, which came into collision with that of the master spirit. Right or wrong, Rumour was very busy; and Lord Decimus, while he was, or was supposed to be, in stately excogitation of the difficulty, lent her some countenance, by taking, on several public occasions, one of those elephantine trots of his through a jungle of over- grown sentences, waving Mr. Merdle about on his trunk as Gigantic Enterprise, The Wealth of England, Elasticity, Credit, Capital, Prosperity, and all manner of blessings.

So quietly did the mowing of the old scythe go on, that fully three months had passed unnoticed since the two English brothers had been laid in one tomb in the strangers' cemetery at Rome. Mr. and Mrs. Sparkler were established in their own house: a little mansion, rather of the Tite Barnacle class, quite a triumph of inconvenience, with a perpetual smell in it of the day before yesterday's soup and coach-horses, but extremely dear, as being exactly in the centre of the habitable globe. In this enviable abode (and envied it really was by many people), Mrs. Sparkler had intended to proceed at once to the demolition of the Bosom, when active hostilities had been suspended by the arrival of the Courier with his tidings of death. Mrs. Sparkler, who was not unfeeling, had received them with a violent burst of grief, which had lasted twelve hours; after which she had arisen to see about her mourning, and to take every precaution that could ensure its being as becoming as Mrs. Merdle's. A gloom was then cast over more than one distinguished family (according to the politest sources of intelligence), and the Courier went back again.

Mr. and Mrs. Sparkler had been dining alone, with their gloom cast over them, and Mrs. Sparkler reclined on a drawing-room sofa. It was a hot summer Sunday evening. The residence in the centre of the habitable globe, at all times stuffed and close as if it had an incurable cold in its head, was that evening particularly stifling. The bells of the churches had done their worst in the way of clanging among the unmelodious echoes of the streets, and the lighted windows of the churches had ceased to be yellow in the grey dusk, and had died out opaque black. Mrs. Sparkler, lying on her sofa looking through an open window at the opposite side of the narrow street, over boxes of mignonette and flowers, was tired of the view. Mrs. Sparkler, looking at another window where her husband stood in the balcony, was tired of that view. Mrs. Sparkler, looking at herself in her mourning, was even tired of that view: though, naturally, not so tired of that as of the other two.

"It's like lying in a well," said Mrs. Sparkler, changing her position fretfully. "Dear me, Edmund, if you have anything to say, why don't you say it?"

Mr. Sparkler might have replied with ingenuousness, "My life, I have nothing to say." But, as the repartee did not occur to him, he contented himself with coming in from the balcony and standing at the side of his wife's couch.

"Good gracious, Edmund!" said Mrs. Sparkler, more fretfully still, "you are absolutely putting mignonette up your nose! Pray don't!"

Mr. Sparkler, in absence of mind—perhaps in a more literal absence of mind than is usually understood by the phrase—had smelt so hard at a sprig in his hand as to be on the verge of the offence in question. He smiled, said, "I ask your pardon, my dear," and threw it out of window.

"You make my head ache by remaining in that position, Edmund," said Mrs. Sparkler, raising her eyes to him, after another minute; "you look so aggravatingly large by this light. Do sit down."

"Certainly, my dear," said Mr. Sparkler. And took a chair on the same spot.

"If I didn't know that the longest day was past," said Fanny, yawning in a dreary manner, "I should have felt certain this was the longest day. I never did experience such a day."

"Is this your fan, my love?" asked Mr. Sparkler, picking up one, and presenting it.

"Edmund," returned his wife more wearily yet, "don't ask weak questions, I entreat you not. Whose can it be but mine?"

"Yes, I thought it was yours," said Mr. Sparkler.

"Then you shouldn't ask," retorted Fanny. After a little while, she turned on her sofa and exclaimed, "Dear me, dear me, there never was such a long day as this!" After another little while, she got up slowly, walked about, and came back again.

"My dear," said Mr. Sparkler, flashing with an original conception, "I think you must have got the fidgets."

"Oh! Fidgets!" repeated Mrs. Sparkler. "Don't!"

"My adorable girl," urged Mr. Sparkler, "try your aromatic vinegar. I have often seen my mother try it, and it seemingly refreshed her. And she is, as I believe you are aware, a remarkably fine woman with no non——"

"Good Gracious!" exclaimed Fanny, starting up again, "it's beyond all patience! This is the most wearisome day that ever did dawn upon the world, I am certain!"

Mr. Sparkler looked meekly after her as she lounged about the room, and he appeared to be a little frightened. When she had tossed a few trifles about, and had looked down into the darkening street out of all the three windows, she returned to her sofa, and threw herself among its pillows.

"Now, Edmund, come here! Come a little nearer, because I want to be able to touch you with my fan, that I may impress you very much with what I am going to say. That will do. Quite close enough. Oh, you *do* look so big!"

Mr. Sparkler apologised for the circumstance, pleaded that he couldn't help it, and said that "our fellows," without more particularly indicating whose fellows, used to call him by the name of Quinbus Flestrin, Junior, or the Young Man Mountain.

"You ought to have told me so, before," Fanny complained.

"My dear," returned Mr. Sparkler, rather gratified, "I didn't know it would interest you, or I would have made a point of telling you."

"There! For goodness sake, don't talk," said Fanny; "I want to talk, myself. Edmund, we must not be alone any more. I must take such precautions as will prevent my being ever again reduced to the state of dreadful depression in which I am this evening."

"My dear," answered Mr. Sparkler; "being, as you are well known to be, a remarkably fine woman, with no——"

"Oh, good GRACIOUS!" cried Fanny.

Mr. Sparkler was so discomposed by the energy of this exclamation, accompanied with a flouncing up from the sofa and a flouncing down again, that a minute or two elapsed before he felt himself equal to saying, in explanation:

"I mean, my dear, that everybody knows you are calculated to shine in society."

"Calculated to shine in society," retorted Fanny, with great irritability; "yes, indeed! And then what happens? I no sooner recover, in a visiting point of view, the shock of poor dear papa's death, and my poor uncle's—though I do not disguise from myself that the last was a happy release, for, if you are not presentable, you had much better die——"

"You are not referring to me, my love, I hope?" Mr. Sparkler humbly interrupted.

"Edmund, Edmund, you would wear out a Saint. Am I not expressly speaking of my poor uncle?"

"You looked with so much expression at myself, my dear girl," said Mr. Sparkler, "that I felt a little uncomfortable. Thank you, my love."

"Now you have put me out," observed Fanny, with a resigned toss of her fan, "and I had better go to bed."

"Don't do that, my love," urged Mr. Sparkler. "Take time."

Fanny took a good deal of time: lying back with her eyes shut, and her eyebrows raised with a hopeless expression, as if she had utterly given up all terrestrial affairs. At length, without the slightest notice, she opened her eyes again, and recommenced in a short, sharp manner.

"What happens then, I ask? What happens? Why, I find myself at the very period when I might shine most in society, and should most like for very momentous reasons to shine in society—I find myself in a situation which to a certain extent disqualifies me for going into society. It's too bad, really!"

"My dear," said Mr. Sparkler, "I don't think it need keep you at home."

"Edmund, you ridiculous creature," returned Fanny, with great indignation; "do you suppose that a woman in the bloom of youth, and not wholly devoid of personal attractions, can put herself, at such a time, in competition as to figure with a woman in every other way her inferior? If you do suppose such a thing, your folly is boundless."

Mr. Sparkler submitted that he had thought "it might be got over."

"Got over!" repeated Fanny, with immeasurable scorn.

"For a time," Mr. Sparkler submitted.

Honoring the last feeble suggestion with no notice, Mrs. Sparkler declared with bitterness that it really was too bad, and that positively it was enough to make one wish one was dead!

"However," she said, when she had in some measure recovered from her sense of personal ill-usage; "provoking as it is, and cruel as it seems, I suppose it must be submitted to."

"Especially as it was to be expected," said Mr. Sparkler.

"Edmund," returned his wife, "if you have nothing more becoming to do than to attempt to insult the woman who has honored you with her hand, when she finds herself in adversity, I think *you* had better go to bed!"

Mr. Sparkler was much afflicted by the charge, and offered a most tender and earnest apology. His apology was accepted; but Mrs. Sparkler requested him to go round to the other side of the sofa and sit in the window-curtain, to tone himself down.

"Now, Edmund," she said, stretching out her fan, and touching him with it at arm's length, "what I was going to say to you when you began as usual to prose and worry, is, that I shall guard against our being alone any more, and that when circumstances prevent my going out to my own satisfaction, I must arrange to have some people or other always here; for, I really cannot, and will not, have another such day as this has been."

Mr. Sparkler's sentiments as to the plan were, in brief, that it had no nonsense about it. He added, "And besides, you know it's likely that you'll soon have your sister——"

"Dearest Amy, yes!" cried Mrs. Sparkler, with a sigh of affection. "Darling little thing! Not, however, that Amy would do here alone."

Mr. Sparkler was going to say "No?" interrogatively. But, he saw his danger and said it assentingly. "No. Oh dear no; she wouldn't do here alone."

"No, Edmund. For, not only are the virtues of the precious child of that still character that they require a contrast—require life and movement around them, to bring them out in their right colors and make one love them of all things; but, she will require to be roused, on more accounts than one."

"That's it," said Mr. Sparkler. "Roused."

"Pray don't, Edmund! Your habit of interrupting without having the least thing in the world to say, distracts one. You must be broken of it. Speaking of Amy;—my poor little pet was devotedly attached to poor papa, and no doubt will have lamented his loss exceedingly, and grieved very much. I have done so myself. I have felt it dreadfully. But Amy will no doubt have felt it even more, from having been on the spot the whole time, and having been with poor dear papa at the last: which I unhappily was not."

Here Fanny stopped to weep, and to say, Dear, dear, beloved papa! How truly gentlemanly he was! What a contrast to poor uncle!

"From the effects of that trying time," she pursued, "my good little Mouse will have to be roused. Also, from the effects of this long attendance upon Edward in his illness: an attendance which is not yet over, which may even go on for some time longer, and which in the meanwhile unsettles us all, by keeping poor dear papa's affairs from being wound up. Fortunately, however, the papers with his agents here being all sealed up and locked up, as he left them when he providentially came to England, the affairs are in that state of order that they can wait until my brother Edward recovers his health in Sicily, sufficiently to come over, and administer, or execute, or whatever it may be that will have to be done."

"He couldn't have a better nurse to bring him round," Mr. Sparkler made bold to opine.

"For a wonder, I can agree with you," returned his wife, languidly turning her eyelids a little in his direction (she held forth, in general, as if to the drawing-room furniture), "and can adopt your words. He couldn't have a better nurse to bring him round. There are times when my dear child is a little wearing, to an active mind; but, as a nurse, she is Perfection. Best of Amys!"

Mr. Sparkler, growing rash on his late success, observed that Edward had had, biggodd, a long bout of it, my dear girl.

"If Bout, Edmund," returned Mrs. Sparkler, "is the slang term for indisposition, he has. If it is not, I am unable to give an opinion on the barbarous language you address to Edward's sister. That he contracted Malaria Fever somewhere—either by travelling day and night to Rome, where, after all, he arrived too late to see poor dear papa before his death— or under some other unwholesome circumstances—is indubitable, if that is what you mean. Likewise, that his extremely careless life has made him a very bad subject for it indeed."

Mr. Sparkler considered it a parallel case to that of some of our fellows in the West Indies with Yellow Jack. Mrs. Sparkler closed her eyes again, and refused to have any consciousness of our fellows, of the West Indies, or of Yellow Jack.

"So, Amy," she pursued when she re-opened her eyelids, "will require to be roused from the effects of many tedious and anxious weeks. And lastly, she will require to be roused from a low tendency which I know very well to be at the bottom of her heart. Don't ask me what it is, Edmund, because I must decline to tell you."

"I am not going to, my dear," said Mr. Sparkler.

"I shall thus have much improvement to effect in my sweet child," Mrs. Sparkler continued, "and cannot have her near me too soon. Amiable and dear little Twoshoes! As to the settlement of poor papa's affairs, my interest in that is not very selfish. Papa behaved very generously to me when I was married, and I have little or nothing to expect. Provided he has made no will that can come into force, leaving a legacy to Mrs. General, I am contented. Dear papa, dear papa!"

She wept again, but Mrs. General was the best of restoratives. The name soon stimulated her to dry her eyes and say:

"It is a highly encouraging circumstance in Edward's illness, I am thankful to think, and gives one the greatest confidence in his sense not being impaired, or his proper spirit weakened—down to the time of poor dear papa's death at all events —that he paid off Mrs. General instantly,

and sent her out of the house. I applaud him for it. I could forgive him a
great deal, for doing, with such promptitude, so exactly what I would have
done myself!"

Mrs. Sparkler was in the full glow of her gratification, when a double
knock was heard at the door. A very odd knock. Low, as if to avoid making
a noise and attracting attention. Long, as if the person knocking were pre-
occupied in mind, and forgot to leave off.

"Halloa!" said Mr. Sparkler. "Who's this!"

"Not Amy and Edward, without notice and without a carriage!" said
Mrs. Sparkler. "Look out."

The room was dark, but the street was lighter, because of its lamps.
Mr. Sparkler's head peeping over the balcony looked so very bulky and
heavy, that it seemed on the point of overbalancing him and flattening the
unknown below.

"It's one fellow," said Mr. Sparkler. "I can't see who—stop though!"

On this second thought, he went out into the balcony again and had
another look. He came back as the door was opened, and announced that
he believed he had identified "his governor's tile." He was not mistaken,
for his governor, with his tile in his hand, was introduced immediately
afterwards.

"Candles!" said Mrs. Sparkler, with a word of excuse for the darkness.

"It's light enough for me," said Mr. Merdle.

When the candles were brought in, Mr. Merdle was discovered standing behind the door, picking his lips. "I thought I'd give you a call," he
said. "I am rather particularly occupied just now; and, as I happened to
be out for a stroll, I thought I'd give you a call."

As he was in dinner dress, Fanny asked him where he had been
dining?

"Well," said Mr. Merdle, "I haven't been dining anywhere, particularly."

"Of course you have dined?" said Fanny.

"Why—no I haven't exactly dined," said Mr. Merdle.

He had passed his hand over his yellow forehead, and considered, as if
he were not sure about it. Something to eat, was proposed. "No, thank
you," said Mr. Merdle, "I don't feel inclined for it. I was to have dined out
along with Mrs. Merdle. But as I didn't feel inclined for dinner, I let Mrs.
Merdle go by herself just as we were getting into the carriage, and thought
I'd take a stroll instead."

Would he have tea, or coffee? "No, thank you," said Mr. Merdle. "I
looked in at the Club, and got a bottle of wine."

At this period of his visit, Mr. Merdle took the chair which Edmund
Sparkler had offered him, and which he had hitherto been pushing slowly
about before him, like a dull man with a pair of skates on for the first time,
who could not make up his mind to start. He now put his hat upon another

chair beside him, and, looking down into it as if it were some twenty feet deep, said again: "You see I thought I'd give you a call."

"Flattering to us," said Fanny, "for you are not a calling man."

"N—no," returned Mr. Merdle, who was by this time taking himself into custody under both coat-sleeves. "No, I am not a calling man."

"You have too much to do, for that," said Fanny. "Having so much to do, Mr. Merdle, loss of appetite is a serious thing with you, and you must have it seen to. You must not be ill."

"Oh! I am very well," replied Mr. Merdle, after deliberating about it. "I am as well as I usually am. I am well enough. I am as well as I want to be."

The master-mind of the age, true to its characteristic of being at all times a mind that had as little as possible to say for itself and great difficulty in saying it, became mute again. Mrs. Sparkler began to wonder how long the master-mind meant to stay.

"I was speaking of poor papa when you came in, sir."

"Aye? Quite a coincidence," said Mr. Merdle.

Fanny did not see that; but, felt it incumbent on her to continue talking. "I was saying," she pursued, "that my brother's illness has occasioned a delay in examining and arranging papa's property."

"Yes," said Mr. Merdle; "yes. There has been a delay."

"Not that it is of consequence," said Fanny.

"Not," assented Mr. Merdle, after having examined the cornice of all that part of the room which was within his range: "not that it is of any consequence."

"My only anxiety is," said Fanny, "that Mrs. General should not get anything."

"*She* won't get anything," said Mr. Merdle.

Fanny was delighted to hear him express the opinion. Mr. Merdle, after taking another gaze into the depths of his hat, as if he thought he saw something at the bottom, rubbed his hair and slowly appended to his last remark the confirmatory words, "Oh dear no. No. Not she. Not likely."

As the topic seemed exhausted, and Mr. Merdle, too, Fanny enquired if he were going to take up Mrs. Merdle and the carriage, in his way home?

"No," he answered; "I shall go by the shortest way, and leave Mrs. Merdle to—" here he looked all over the palms of both his hands as if he were telling his own fortune—"to take care of herself. I dare say she'll manage to do it."

"Probably," said Fanny.

There was then a long silence; during which, Mrs. Sparkler, lying back on her sofa again, shut her eyes and raised her eyebrows in her former retirement from mundane affairs.

"But, however," said Mr. Merdle, "I am equally detaining you and myself. I thought I'd give you a call you know."

"Charmed, I am sure," said Fanny.

"So I am off," added Mr. Merdle, getting up. "Could you lend me a penknife?"

It was an odd thing, Fanny smilingly observed, for her who could seldom prevail upon herself even to write a letter, to lend to a man of such vast business as Mr. Merdle. "Isn't it?" Mr. Merdle acquiesced; "but I want one; and I know you have got several little wedding keepsakes about, with scissors and tweezers and such things in them. You shall have it back to-morrow."

"Edmund," said Mrs. Sparkler, "open (now, very carefully I beg and beseech, for you are so very awkward) the mother of pearl box on my little table there, and give Mr. Merdle the mother of pearl penknife."

"Thank you," said Mr. Merdle; "but if you have got one with a darker handle, I think I should prefer one with a darker handle."

"Tortoise-shell?"

"Thank you," said Mr. Merdle; "yes. I think I should prefer tortoise-shell."

Edmund accordingly received instructions to open the tortoise-shell box, and give Mr. Merdle the tortoise-shell knife. On his doing so, his wife said to the master-spirit graciously:

"I will forgive you, if you ink it."

"I'll undertake not to ink it," said Mr. Merdle.

The illustrious visitor then put out his coat-cuff, and for a moment entombed Mrs. Sparkler's hand: wrist, bracelet, and all. Where his own hand shrunk to, was not made manifest, but it was as remote from Mrs. Sparkler's sense of touch as if he had been a highly meritorious Chelsea Veteran or Greenwich Pensioner.

Thoroughly convinced, as he went out of the room, that it was the longest day that ever did come to an end at last, and that there never was a woman, not wholly devoid of personal attractions, so worn out by idiotic and lump-ish people, Fanny passed into the balcony for a breath of air. Waters of vexation filled her eyes; and they had the effect of making the famous Mr. Merdle, in going down the street, appear to leap, and waltz, and gyrate, as if he were possessed by several Devils.

CHAPTER XXV

THE CHIEF BUTLER RESIGNS THE SEALS OF OFFICE

THE dinner-party was at the great Physician's. Bar was there, and in full force. Ferdinand Barnacle was there, and in his most engaging state. Few ways of life were hidden from Physician, and he was oftener in its darkest

places than even Bishop. There were brilliant ladies about London who
perfectly doted on him, my dear, as the most charming creature and the
most delightful person, who would have been shocked to find themselves
so close to him if they could have known on what sights those thoughtful
eyes of his had rested within an hour or two, and near to whose beds, and
under what roofs, his composed figure had stood. But, Physician was a
composed man, who performed neither on his own trumpet, nor on the
trumpets of other people. Many wonderful things did he see and hear, and
much irreconcileable moral contradiction did he pass his life among; yet
his equality of compassion was no more disturbed than the Divine Master's
of all healing was. He went, like the rain, among the just and unjust, doing
all the good he could, and neither proclaiming it in the synagogues nor at
the corners of streets.

As no man of large experience of humanity, however quietly carried it
may be, can fail to be invested with an interest peculiar to the possession
of such knowledge, Physician was an attractive man. Even the daintier
gentlemen and ladies who had no idea of his secret, and who would have
been startled out of more wits than they had, by the monstrous impropriety of his proposing to them "Come and see what I see!" confessed his
attraction. Where he was, something real was. And half a grain of reality,
like the smallest portion of some other scarce natural productions, will
flavor an enormous quantity of diluent.

It came to pass, therefore, that Physician's little dinners always presented
people in their least conventional lights. The guests said to themselves,
whether they were conscious of it or no, "Here is a man who really has an
acquaintance with us as we are, who is admitted to some of us every day
with our wigs and paint off, who hears the wanderings of our minds, and
sees the undisguised expression of our faces, when both are past our control; we may as well make an approach to reality with him, for the man has
got the better of us and is too strong for us." Therefore Physician's guests
came out so surprisingly at his round table that they were almost natural.

Bar's knowledge of that agglomeration of Jurymen which is called
humanity was as sharp as a razor, yet a razor is not a generally convenient
instrument, and Physician's plain bright scalpel, though far less keen,
was adaptable to far wider purposes. Bar knew all about the gullibility
and knavery of people; but, Physician could have given him a better insight
into their tenderness and affections, in one week of his rounds, than
Westminster Hall and all the circuits put together, in threescore years and
ten. Bar always had a suspicion of this, and perhaps was glad to encourage
it (for, if the world were really a great Law Court one would think that the
last day of Term could not too soon arrive); and so he liked and respected
Physician quite as much as any other kind of man did.

Mr. Merdle's default left a Banquo's chair at the table; but, if he had
been there, he would have merely made the difference of Banquo in it, and

consequently he was no loss. Bar, who picked up all sorts of odds and ends
about Westminster Hall, much as a raven would have done if he had passed
as much of his time there, had been picking up a good many straws lately
and tossing them about to try which way the Merdle wind blew. He now
had a little talk on the subject with Mrs. Merdle herself; sliding up to that
lady, of course, with his double eye-glass and his Jury droop.

"A certain bird," said Bar; and he looked as if it could have been no
other bird than a magpie; "has been whispering among us lawyers lately,
that there is to be an addition to the titled personages of this realm."

"Really?" said Mrs. Merdle.

"Yes," said Bar. "Has not the bird been whispering in very different
ears from ours—in lovely ears?" He looked expressively at Mrs. Merdle's
nearest ear-ring.

"Do you mean mine?" asked Mrs. Merdle.

"When I say, lovely," said Bar, "I always mean you."

"You never mean anything, I think," returned Mrs. Merdle (not displeased.)

"Oh, cruelly unjust!" said Bar. "But, the bird."

"I am the last person in the world to hear news," observed Mrs. Merdle,
carelessly arranging her stronghold. "Who is it?"

"What an admirable witness you would make!" said Bar. "No jury
(unless we could impannel one of blind men) could resist you, if you were
ever so bad a one; but, you would be such a good one!"

"Why, you ridiculous man?" asked Mrs. Merdle, laughing.

Bar waved his double eye-glass three or four times between himself and
the Bosom, as a rallying answer, and enquired in his most insinuating
accents:

"What am I to call the most elegant, accomplished, and charming of
women, a few weeks, or it may be a few days, hence?"

"Didn't your bird tell you what to call her?" answered Mrs. Merdle.
"Do ask it to-morrow, and tell me the next time you see me, what it
says!"

This led to further passages of similar pleasantry between the two;
but, Bar, with all his sharpness, got nothing out of them. Physician, on
the other hand, taking Mrs. Merdle down to her carriage and attending on
her as she put on her cloak, enquired into the symptoms with his usual
calm directness.

"May I ask," he said, "is this true about Merdle?"

"My dear doctor," she returned, "you ask me the very question that I
was half disposed to ask you."

"To ask me! Why me?"

"Upon my honor, I think Mr. Merdle reposes greater confidence in you
than in any one."

"On the contrary, he tells me absolutely nothing, even professionally.

You have heard the talk, of course?"

"Of course I have. But, you know what Mr. Merdle is; you know how taciturn and reserved he is. I assure you I have no idea what foundation for it there may be. I should like it to be true; why should I deny that to you! You would know better, if I did!"

"Just so," said Physician.

"But whether it is all true, or partly true, or entirely false, I am wholly unable to say. It is a most provoking situation, a most absurd situation; but, you know Mr. Merdle, and are not surprised."

Physician was not at all surprised, handed her into her carriage, and bade her Good Night. He stood for a moment at his own hall-door, looking sedately at the elegant equipage as it rattled away. On his return up-stairs, the rest of the guests soon dispersed, and he was left alone. Being a great reader of all kinds of literature (and never at all apologetic for that weakness), he sat down comfortably to read.

The clock upon his study table pointed to a few minutes short of twelve, when his attention was called to it by a ringing at the door bell. A man of plain habits, he had sent his servants to bed and must needs go down to open the door. He went down, and there found a man without hat or coat, whose shirt sleeves were rolled up tight to his shoulders. For a moment, he thought the man had been fighting: the rather, as he was much agitated and out of breath. A second look, however, showed him that the man was particularly clean, and not otherwise discomposed as to his dress than as it answered this description.

"I come from the warm-baths, sir, round in the neighbouring street."

"And what is the matter at the warm-baths?"

"Would you please to come directly, sir. We found that, lying on the table."

He put into the physician's hand a scrap of paper. Physician looked at it, and read his own name and address written in pencil; nothing more. He looked closer at the writing, looked at the man, took his hat from its peg, put the key of his door in his pocket, and they hurried away together.

When they came to the warm-baths, all the other people belonging to that establishment were looking out for them at the door, and running up and down the passages. "Request everybody else to keep back, if you please," said the physician aloud to the master; "and do you take me straight to the place, my friend," to the messenger.

The messenger hurried before him, along a grove of little rooms, and turning into one at the end of the grove, looked round the door. Physician was close upon him, and looked round the door too.

There was a bath in that corner, from which the water had been hastily drained off. Lying in it, as in a grave or sarcophagus, with a hurried drapery of sheet and blanket thrown across it, was the body of a heavily-made man, with an obtuse head, and coarse, mean, common features. A skylight had been opened, to release the steam with which the room had been filled; but, it hung, condensed into water-drops, heavily upon the walls, and heavily upon the face and figure in the bath. The room was still hot, and the marble of the bath still warm; but, the face and figure were clammy to the touch. The white marble at the bottom of the bath was veined with a dreadful red. On the ledge at the side were an empty laudanum-bottle and a tortoise-shell handled penknife—soiled, but not with ink.

"Separation of jugular vein—death rapid—been dead at least half an hour." This echo of the physician's words ran through the passages and little rooms, and through the house, while he was yet straightening himself from having bent down to reach to the bottom of the bath, and while he was yet dabbling his hands in water; redly veining it as the marble was veined, before it mingled into one tint.

He turned his eyes to the dress upon the sofa, and to the watch, money, and pocket-book on the table. A folded note half buckled up in the pocket-book, and half protruding from it, caught his observant glance. He looked at it, touched it, pulled it a little further out from among the leaves, said quietly, "This is addressed to me," and opened and read it.

There were no directions for him to give. The people of the house knew what to do; the proper authorities were soon brought; and they took an equable business-like possession of the deceased and of what had been his property, with no greater disturbance of manner or countenance than usually attends the winding-up of a clock. Physician was glad to walk out into the night air—was even glad, in spite of his great experience, to sit upon a door-step for a little while: feeling sick and faint.

Bar was a near neighbour of his, and, when he came to the house, he saw a light in the room where he knew his friend often sat late, getting up his work. As the light was never there when Bar was not, it gave him assurance that Bar was not yet in bed. In fact, this busy bee had a verdict to get to-morrow, against evidence, and was improving the shining hours in setting snares for the gentlemen of the jury.

Physician's knock astonished Bar; but, as he immediately suspected that somebody had come to tell him that somebody else was robbing him, or otherwise trying to get the better of him, he came down promptly and softly. He had been clearing his head with a lotion of cold water, as a good preparative to providing hot water for the heads of the jury, and had been reading with the neck of his shirt thrown wide open, that he might the more freely choke the opposite witnesses. In consequence, he came down looking rather wild. Seeing Physician, the least expected of men, he looked wilder and said, "What's the matter?"

"You asked me once what Merdle's complaint was."

"Extraordinary answer! I know I did."

"I told you I had not found it out."

"Yes. I know you did."

"I have found it out."

"My God!" said Bar, starting back, and clapping his hand upon the other's breast. "And so have I! I see it in your face."

They went into the nearest room, where Physician gave him the letter to read. He read it through, half a dozen times. There was not much in it as to quantity; but, it made a great demand on his close and continuous attention. He could not sufficiently give utterance to his regret that he had not himself found a clue to this. The smallest clue, he said, would have made him master of the case, and what a case it would have been to have got to the bottom of!

Physician had engaged to break the intelligence in Harley Street. Bar could not at once return to his inveiglements of the most enlightened and remarkable jury he had ever seen in that box, with whom, he could tell his learned friend, no shallow sophistry would go down, and no unhappily abused professional tact and skill prevail (this was the way he meant to begin with them); so he said he would go too, and would loiter to and fro near the house while his friend was inside. They walked there, the better to recover self-possession in the air; and the wings of day were fluttering the night when Physician knocked at the door.

A footman of rainbow hues, in the public eye, was sitting up for his master—that is to say, was fast asleep in the kitchen, over a couple of candles and a newspaper, demonstrating the great accumulation of mathematical odds against the probabilities of a house being set on fire by accident. When this serving-man was roused, Physician had still to await the rousing of the Chief Butler. At last that noble creature came into the dining-room in a flannel gown and list shoes; but with his cravat on, and a Chief Butler all over. It was morning now. Physician had opened the shutters of one window while waiting, that he might see the light.

"Mrs. Merdle's maid must be called, and told to get Mrs. Merdle up, and prepare her as gently as she can, to see me. I have dreadful news to break to her."

Thus Physician to the Chief Butler. The latter, who had a candle in his hand, called his man to take it away. Then he approached the window with dignity; looking on at Physician's news exactly as he had looked on at the dinners in that very room.

"Mr. Merdle is dead."

"I should wish," said the Chief Butler, "to give a month's notice."

"Mr. Merdle has destroyed himself."

"Sir," said the Chief Butler, "that is very unpleasant to the feelings of one in my position, as calculated to awaken prejudice; and I should wish to leave immediate."

"If you are not shocked, are you not surprised, man?" demanded the Physician, warmly.

The Chief Butler, erect and calm, replied in these memorable words.

"Sir, Mr. Merdle never was the gentleman, and no ungentlemanly act on Mr. Merdle's part would surprise me. Is there anybody else I can send to you, or any other directions I can give before I leave, respecting what you would wish to be done?"

When Physician, after discharging himself of his trust up-stairs, rejoined Bar in the street, he said no more of his interview with Mrs. Merdle than that he had not yet told her all, but that what he had told her, she had borne pretty well. Bar had devoted his leisure in the street to the construction of a most ingenious man-trap for catching the whole of his jury at a blow; having got that matter settled in his mind, it was lucid on the late catastrophe, and they walked home slowly, discussing it in every bearing. Before parting, at Physician's door, they both looked up at the sunny morning sky, into which the smoke of a few early fires and the breath and voices of a few early stirrers were peacefully rising, and then looked round upon the immense city, and said, If all those hundreds and thousands of beggared people who were yet asleep, could only know, as they two spoke, the ruin that impended over them, what a fearful cry against one miserable soul would go up to Heaven!

The report that the great man was dead, got about with astonishing rapidity. At first, he was dead of all the diseases that ever were known, and of several bran-new maladies invented with the speed of Light to meet the demand of the occasion. He had concealed a dropsy from infancy, he had inherited a large estate of water on the chest from his grandfather, he had had an operation performed upon him every morning of his life for eighteen years, he had been subject to the explosion of important veins in his body after the manner of fireworks, he had had something the matter with his lungs, he had had something the matter with his heart, he had had something the matter with his brain. Five hundred people who sat down to breakfast entirely uninformed on the whole subject, believed before they had done breakfast, that they privately and personally knew Physician to have said to Mr. Merdle, "You must expect to go out, some day, like the snuff of a candle," and that they knew Mr. Merdle to have said to Physician, "A man can die but once." By about eleven o'clock in the forenoon, something the matter with the brain, became the favorite theory against the field; and by twelve the something had been distinctly ascertained to be "Pressure."

Pressure was so entirely satisfactory to the public mind, and seemed to make everybody so comfortable, that it might have lasted all day but for Bar's having taken the real state of the case into Court at half-past nine. This led to its beginning to be currently whispered all over London by about one, that Mr. Merdle had killed himself. Pressure, however, so far from being overthrown by the discovery, became a greater favorite than ever. There was a general moralising upon Pressure, in every street. All the people who had tried to make money and had not been able to do it, said, There you were! You no sooner began to devote yourself to the pursuit of wealth, than you got Pressure. The idle people improved the occasion in a similar manner. See, said they, what you brought yourself to by work, work, work! You persisted in working, you overdid it, Pressure ensued, and you were done for! This consideration was very potent in many quarters, but nowhere more so than among the young clerks and partners who had never been in the slightest danger of overdoing it. These one and all declared, quite piously, that they hoped they would never forget the warning as long as they lived, and that their conduct might be so regulated as to keep off Pressure, and preserve them, a comfort to their friends, for many years.

But, at about the time of High 'Change, Pressure began to wane, and appalling whispers to circulate, east, west, north, and south. At first they were faint, and went no further than a doubt whether Mr. Merdle's wealth would be found to be as vast as had been supposed; whether there might not be a temporary difficulty in "realising" it; whether there might not even be a temporary suspension (say a month or so), on the part of the wonderful Bank. As the whispers became louder, which they did from that time every minute, they became more threatening. He had sprung from nothing, by no natural growth or process that any one could account for; he had been, after all, a low, ignorant fellow; he had been a down-looking man, and no one had ever been able to catch his eye; he had been taken up by all sorts of people, in quite an unaccountable manner; he had never had any money of his own, his ventures had been utterly reckless, and his expenditure had been most enormous. In steady progression, as the day declined, the talk rose in sound and purpose. He had left a letter at the Baths addressed to his physician, and his physician had got the letter, and the letter would be produced at the Inquest on the morrow, and it would fall like a thunderbolt upon the multitude he had deluded. Numbers of men in every profession and trade would be blighted by his insolvency; old people who had been in easy circumstances all their lives would have no place of repentance for their trust in him but the workhouse; legions of women and children would have their whole future desolated by the hand of this mighty scoundrel. Every partaker of his magnificent feasts would be seen to have been a sharer in the plunder of innumerable homes; every servile worshipper of riches who had helped to set him on his pedestal, would have done better to worship the Devil point-blank. So, the talk, lashed louder and higher by confirmation on confirmation, and by edition after edition of the evening papers, swelled into such a roar when night came, as might have brought one to believe that a solitary watcher on the gallery above the Dome of Saint Paul's would have perceived the night air to be laden with a heavy muttering of the name of Merdle, coupled with every form of execration.

For, by that time it was known that the late Mr. Merdle's complaint had been, simply, Forgery and Robbery. He, the uncouth object of such wide-spread adulation, the sitter at great men's feasts, the roc's egg of great ladies' assemblies, the subduer of exclusiveness, the leveller of pride, the patron of patrons, the bargain-driver with a Minister for Lordships of the Circumlocution Office, the recipient of more acknowledgment within some ten or fifteen years, at most, than had been bestowed in England upon all peaceful public benefactors, and upon all the leaders of all the Arts and Sciences, with all their works to testify for them, during two centuries at least—he, the shining wonder, the new constellation to be followed by the wise men bringing gifts, until it stopped over certain carrion at the bottom of a bath and disappeared—was simply the greatest Forger and the greatest Thief that ever cheated the gallows.

CHAPTER XXVI

REAPING THE WHIRLWIND

WITH a precursory sound of hurried breath and hurried feet, Mr. Pancks rushed into Arthur Clennam's Counting-house. The Inquest was over, the letter was public, the Bank was broken, the other model structures of straw had taken fire and were turned to smoke. The admired piratical ship had blown up, in the midst of a vast fleet of ships of all rates, and boats of all sizes; and on the deep was nothing but ruin: nothing but burning hulls, bursting magazines, great guns self-exploded tearing friends and neighbours to pieces, drowning men clinging to unseaworthy spars and going down every minute, spent swimmers, floating dead, and sharks.

The usual diligence and order of the Counting-house at the Works were overthrown. Unopened letters and unsorted papers lay strewn about the desk. In the midst of these tokens of prostrated energy and dismissed hope, the master of the Counting-house stood idle in his usual place, with his arms crossed on the desk, and his head bowed down upon them.

Mr. Pancks rushed in and saw him, and stood still. In another minute, Mr. Pancks's arms were on the desk, and Mr. Pancks's head was bowed down upon them; and for some time they remained in these attitudes, idle and silent, with the width of the little room between them.

Mr. Pancks was the first to lift up his head and speak.

"I persuaded you to it, Mr. Clennam. I know it. Say what you will. You can't say more to me than I say to myself. You can't say more than I deserve."

"O, Pancks, Pancks!" returned Clennam, "don't speak of deserving. What do I, myself, deserve!"

"Better luck," said Pancks.

"I," pursued Clennam, without attending to him, "who have ruined my partner! Pancks, Pancks, I have ruined Doyce! The honest, self-helpful, indefatigable old man, who has worked his way all through his life; the man who has contended against so much disappointment, and who has brought out of it such a good and hopeful nature; the man I have felt so much for, and meant to be so true and useful to; I have ruined him—brought him to shame and disgrace—ruined him, ruined him!"

The agony into which the reflection wrought his mind was so distressing to see, that Mr. Pancks took hold of himself by the hair of his head, and tore it in desperation at the spectacle.

"Reproach me!" cried Pancks. "Reproach me, sir, or I'll do myself an injury. Say, You fool, you villain. Say, Ass, how could you do it; Beast, what did you mean by it! Catch hold of me somewhere. Say something abusive to me!" All the time, Mr. Pancks was tearing at his tough hair in a most pitiless and cruel manner.

"If you had never yielded to this fatal mania, Pancks," said Clennam, more in commiseration than retaliation, "it would have been how much better for you, and how much better for me!"

"At me again, sir!" cried Pancks, grinding his teeth in remorse. "At me again!"

"If you had never gone into those accursed calculations, and brought out your results with such abominable clearness," groaned Clennam, "it would have been how much better for you, Pancks, and how much better for me!"

"At me again, sir!" exclaimed Pancks, loosening his hold of his hair; "at me again, and again!"

Clennam, however, finding him already beginning to be pacified, had said all he wanted to say, and more. He wrung his hand, only adding, "Blind leaders of the blind, Pancks! Blind leaders of the blind! But Doyce, Doyce, Doyce; my injured partner!" That brought his head down on the desk once more.

Their former attitudes and their former silence were once more first encroached upon by Pancks.

"Not been to bed, sir, since it began to get about. Been high and low, on the chance of finding some hope of saving any cinders from the fire. All in vain. All gone. All vanished."

"I know it," returned Clennam, "too well."

Mr. Pancks filled up a pause with a groan that came out of the very depths of his soul.

"Only yesterday, Pancks," said Arthur; "only yesterday, Monday, I had the fixed intention of selling, realising, and making an end of it."

"I can't say as much for myself, sir," returned Pancks. "Though it's wonderful how many people I've heard of, who *were* going to realise yesterday, of all days in the three hundred and sixty-five, if it hadn't been too late!"

His steam-like breathings, usually droll in their effect, were more tragic than so many groans; while, from head to foot, he was in that begrimed, besmeared, neglected state, that he might have been an authentic portrait of Misfortune which could scarcely be discerned through its want of cleaning.

"Mr. Clennam, had you laid out—everything?" He got over the break before the last word, and also brought out the last word itself with great difficulty.

"Everything."

Mr. Pancks took hold of his tough hair again, and gave it such a wrench that he pulled out several prongs of it. After looking at these with an eye of wild hatred, he put them in his pocket.

"My course," said Clennam, brushing away some tears that had been silently dropping down his face, "must be taken at once. What wretched amends I can make must be made. I must clear my unfortunate partner's reputation. I must retain nothing for myself. I must resign to our creditors the power of management I have so much abused, and I must work out as much of my fault—or crime—as is susceptible of being worked out, in the rest of my days."

"Is it impossible, sir, to tide over the present?"

"Out of the question. Nothing can be tided over now, Pancks. The sooner the business can pass out of my hands, the better for it. There are engagements to be met, this week, which would bring the catastrophe before many days were over, even if I would postpone it for a single day, by going on for that space, secretly knowing what I know. All last night I thought of what I would do; what remains is to do it."

"Not entirely of yourself?" said Pancks, whose face was as damp as if his steam were turning into water as fast as he dismally blew it off. "Have some legal help."

"Perhaps I had better."

"Have Rugg."

"There is not much to do. He will do it as well as another."

"Shall I fetch Rugg, Mr. Clennam?"

"If you could spare the time. I should be much obliged to you."

Mr. Pancks put on his hat that moment, and steamed away to Pentonville. While he was gone, Arthur never raised his head from the desk, but remained in that one position.

Mr. Pancks brought his friend and professional adviser Mr. Rugg back with him. Mr. Rugg had had such ample experience, on the road, of Mr. Pancks's being at that present in an irrational state of mind, that he opened his professional mediation by requesting that gentleman to take himself out of the way. Mr. Pancks, crushed and submissive, obeyed.

"He is not unlike what my daughter was, sir, when we began the Breach of Promise action of Rugg and Bawkins, in which she was Plaintiff," said

Mr. Rugg. "He takes too strong and direct an interest in the case. His feelings are worked upon. There is no getting on, in our profession, with feelings worked upon, sir."

As he pulled off his gloves and put them in his hat, he saw, in a side glance or two, that a great change had come over his client.

"I am sorry to perceive, sir," said Mr. Rugg, "that you have been allowing your own feelings to be worked upon. Now, pray don't, pray don't. These losses are much to be deplored, sir, but we must look 'em in the face."

"If the money I have sacrificed had been all my own, Mr. Rugg," sighed Clennam, "I should have cared far less."

"Indeed, sir?" said Mr. Rugg, rubbing his hands with a cheerful air. "You surprise me. That's singular, sir. I have generally found, in my experience, that it's their own money people are most particular about. I have seen people get rid of a good deal of other people's money, and bear it very well; very well indeed."

With these comforting remarks, Mr. Rugg seated himself on an office-stool at the desk, and proceeded to business.

"Now, Mr. Clennam, by your leave, let us go into the matter. Let us see the state of the case. The question is simple. The question is the usual plain, straightforward, common-sense question. What can we do for ourself? What can we do for ourself?"

"That is not the question with me, Mr. Rugg," said Arthur. "You mistake it in the beginning. It is, what can I do for my partner, how can I best make reparation to him?"

"I am afraid, sir, do you know," argued Mr. Rugg persuasively, "that you are still allowing your feelings to be worked upon? I *don't* like the term 'reparation,' sir, except as a lever in the hands of counsel. Will you excuse my saying that I feel it my duty to offer you the caution, that you really must not allow your feelings to be worked upon?"

"Mr. Rugg," said Clennam, nerving himself to go through with what he had resolved upon, and surprising that gentleman by appearing, in his despondency, to have a settled determination of purpose; "you give me the impression that you will not be much disposed to adopt the course I have made up my mind to take. If your disapproval of it should render you unwilling to discharge such business as it necessitates, I am sorry for it, and must seek other aid. But, I will represent to you at once, that to argue against it with me is useless."

"Good, sir," answered Mr. Rugg, shrugging his shoulders. "Good, sir. Since the business is to be done by some hands, let it be done by mine. Such was my principle in the case of Rugg and Bawkins. Such is my principle in most cases."

Clennam then proceeded to state to Mr. Rugg his fixed resolution. He told Mr. Rugg that his partner was a man of great simplicity and integrity, and that in all he meant to do, he was guided above all things by a knowledge of his partner's character, and a respect for his feelings. He explained that his partner was then absent on an enterprise of importance, and that it particularly behoved himself publicly to accept the blame of what he had rashly done, and publicly to exonerate his partner from all participation in the responsibility of it, lest the successful conduct of that enterprise should be endangered by the slightest suspicion wrongfully attaching to his partner's honor and credit in another country. He told Mr. Rugg that to clear his partner morally, to the fullest extent, and publicly and unreservedly to declare that he, Arthur Clennam, of that Firm, had of his own sole act, and even expressly against his partner's caution, embarked its resources in the swindles that had lately perished, was the only real atonement within his power; was a better atonement to the particular man than it would be to many men; and was therefore the atonement he had first to make. With this view, his intention was to print a declaration to the foregoing effect, which he had already drawn up; and, besides circulating it among all who had dealings with the House, to advertise it in the public papers. Concurrently with this measure (the description of which cost Mr. Rugg innumerable wry faces and great uneasiness in his limbs), he would address a letter to all the creditors, exonerating his partner in a solemn manner, informing them of the stoppage of the House until their pleasure could be known and his partner communicated with, and humbly submitting himself to their direction. If, through their consideration for his partner's innocence, the affairs could ever be got into such train as that the business could be profitably resumed, and its present downfall overcome, then his own share in it should revert to his partner, as the only reparation he could make to him in money value for the distress and loss he had unhappily brought upon him, and he himself, at as small a salary as he could live upon, would ask to be allowed to serve the business as a faithful clerk.

Though Mr. Rugg saw plainly that there was no preventing this from being done, still the wryness of his face and the uneasiness of his limbs so sorely required the propitiation of a Protest, that he made one. "I offer no objection, sir," said he, "I argue no point with you. I will carry out your views, sir; but, under protest." Mr. Rugg then stated, not without prolixity, the heads of his protest. These were, in effect, Because the whole town, or he might say the whole country, was in the first madness of the late discovery, and the resentment against the victims would be very strong: those who had not been deluded being certain to wax exceedingly wroth with them for not having been as wise as they were; and those who had been deluded, being certain to find excuses and reasons for themselves, of which they were equally certain to see that other sufferers were wholly devoid; not to mention the great probability of every individual sufferer persuading himself, to his violent indignation, that but for the example of all the other sufferers he never would have put himself in the way of suffering. Because such a declaration as Clennam's, made at such a time, would certainly draw down upon him a storm of animosity, rendering it impossible to calculate on forbearance in the creditors, or on unanimity among them; and exposing him a solitary target to a straggling cross-fire, which might bring him down from half a dozen quarters at once.

To all this Clennam merely replied that, granting the whole protest, nothing in it lessened the force, or could lessen the force, of the voluntary and public exoneration of his partner. He therefore, once for all, requested Mr. Rugg's immediate aid in getting the business dispatched. Upon that, Mr. Rugg fell to work; and Arthur, retaining no property to himself but his clothes and books, and a little loose money, placed his small private banker's-account with the papers of the business.

The disclosure was made, and the storm raged fearfully. Thousands of people were wildly staring about for somebody alive to heap reproaches on; and this notable case, courting publicity, set the living somebody so much wanted, on a scaffold. When people who had nothing to do with the case were so sensible of its flagrancy, people who lost money by it could scarcely be expected to deal mildly with it. Letters of reproach and invective showered in from the creditors; and Mr. Rugg, who sat upon the high stool every day and read them all, informed his client within a week that he feared there were writs out.

"I must take the consequences of what I have done," said Clennam. "The writs will find me here."

On the very next morning, as he was turning into Bleeding-Heart Yard by Mrs. Plornish's corner, Mrs. Plornish stood at the door waiting for him, and mysteriously besought him to step into Happy Cottage. There he found Mr. Rugg.

"I thought I'd wait for you here. I wouldn't go on to the Counting-house this morning if I was you, sir."

"Why not, Mr. Rugg?"

"There are as many as five out, to my knowledge."

"It cannot be too soon over," said Clennam. "Let them take me, at once."

"Yes, but," said Mr. Rugg, getting between him and the door, "hear reason, hear reason. They'll take you soon enough, Mr. Clennam, I don't doubt; but, hear reason. It almost always happens, in these cases, that some insignificant matter pushes itself in front and makes much of itself. Now, I find there's a little one out—a mere Palace Court jurisdiction —and I have reason to believe that a caption may be made upon that. I wouldn't be taken upon that."

"Why not?" asked Clennam.

"I'd be taken on a full-grown one, sir," said Mr. Rugg. "It's as well to keep up appearances. As your professional advisor, I should prefer your

being taken on a writ from one of the Superior Courts, if you have no
objection to do me that favor. It looks better."

"Mr. Rugg," said Arthur in his dejection, "my only wish is, that it
should be over. I will go on, and take my chance."

"Another word of reason, sir!" cried Mr. Rugg. "Now, this *is* reason.
The other may be taste; but this is reason. If you should be taken on the
little one, sir, you would go to the Marshalsea. Now, you know what the
Marshalsea is. Very close. Excessively confined. Whereas in the King's
Bench——" Mr. Rugg waved his right hand freely, as expressing abun-
dance of space.

"I would rather," said Clennam, "be taken to the Marshalsea than to
any other prison."

"Do you say so indeed, sir?" returned Mr. Rugg. "Then this is taste,
too, and we may be walking."

He was a little offended at first, but he soon overlooked it. They walked
through the Yard to the other end. The Bleeding Hearts were more interested in Arthur since his reverses than formerly: now regarding him as one
who was true to the place and had taken up his freedom. Many of them came
out to look after him, and to observe to one another, with great unctuous-
ness, that he was "pulled down by it." Mrs. Plornish and her father stood
at the top of the steps at their own end, much depressed and shaking
their heads.

There was nobody visibly in waiting when Arthur and Mr. Rugg arrived
at the Counting-house. But, an elderly member of the Jewish persuasion,
preserved in rum, followed them close, and looked in at the glass before
Mr. Rugg had opened one of the day's letters. "Oh!" said Mr. Rugg,
looking up. "How do you do? Step in.—Mr. Clennam, I think this is the
gentleman I was mentioning."

The gentleman explained the object of his visit to be "a tyfling madder
ob bithznithz," and executed his legal function.

"Shall I accompany you, Mr. Clennam?" asked Mr. Rugg politely,
rubbing his hands.

"I would rather go alone, thank you. Be so good as send me my clothes."
Mr. Rugg in a light airy way replied in the affirmative, and shook hands
with him. He and his attendant then went down-stairs, got into the first
conveyance they found, and drove to the old gates.

"Where I little thought, Heaven forgive me," said Clennam to himself,
"that I should ever enter thus!"

Mr. Chivery was on the lock, and Young John was in the Lodge: either
newly released from it, or waiting to take his own spell of duty. Both were
more astonished on seeing who the new prisoner was, than one might
have thought turnkeys would have been. The elder Mr. Chivery shook
hands with him in a shame-faced kind of way, and said, "I don't call to
mind, sir, as I was ever less glad to see you." The younger Mr. Chivery,

more distant, did not shake hands with him at all; he stood looking at him in a state of indecision so observable, that it even came within the observation of Clennam with his heavy eyes and heavy heart. Presently afterwards, Young John disappeared into the jail.

As Clennam knew enough of the place to know that he was required to remain in the Lodge a certain time, he took a seat in a corner, and feigned to be occupied with the perusal of letters from his pocket. They did not so engross his attention, but that he saw, with gratitude, how the elder Mr. Chivery kept the Lodge clear of prisoners; how he signed to some, with his keys, not to come in, how he nudged others with his elbow to go out, and how he made his misery as easy to him as he could.

Arthur was sitting with his eyes fixed on the floor, recalling the past, brooding over the present, and not attending to either, when he felt himself touched upon the shoulder. It was by Young John; and he said, "You can come now."

He got up and followed Young John. When they had gone a step or two within the inner iron-gate, Young John turned and said to him:

"You want a room. I have got you one."

"I thank you heartily."

Young John turned again, and took him in at the old doorway, up the old staircase, into the old room. Arthur stretched out his hand. Young John looked at it, looked at him—sternly —swelled, choked, and said:

"I don't know as I can. No, I find I can't. But I thought you'd like the room, and here it is for you."

Surprise at this inconsistent behaviour yielded when he was gone (he went away directly), to the feelings which the empty room awakened in Clennam's wounded breast, and to its crowding associations with the one good and gentle creature who had sanctified it. Her absence in his altered fortunes made it, and him in it, so very desolate and so much in need of such a face of love and truth, that he turned against the wall to weep, sobbing out, as his heart relieved itself, "O my Little Dorrit!"

END OF No. XVII

CHAPTER XXVII

THE PUPIL OF THE MARSHALSEA

THE day was sunny, and the Marshalsea, with the hot noon striking upon it, was unwontedly quiet. Arthur Clennam dropped into a solitary arm-chair, itself as faded as any debtor in the jail, and yielded himself to his thoughts.

In the unnatural peace of having gone through the dreaded arrest, and got there, —the first change of feeling which the prison most commonly induced, and from which dangerous resting-place so many men had slipped down to the depths of degradation and disgrace, by so many ways,—he could think of some passages in his life, almost as if he were removed from them into another state of existence. Taking into account where he was, the interest that had first brought him there when he had been free to keep away, and the gentle presence that was equally inseparable from the walls and bars about him and from the impalpable remembrances of his later life which no walls nor bars could imprison, it was not remarkable that everything his memory turned upon should bring him round again to Little Dorrit. Yet it was remarkable to him; not because of the fact itself; but because of the reminder it brought with it, how much the dear little creature had influenced his better resolutions.

None of us clearly know to whom or to what we are indebted in this wise, until some marked stop in the whirling wheel of life brings the right perception with it. It comes with sickness, it comes with sorrow, it comes with the loss of the dearly loved, it is one of the most frequent uses of adversity. It came to Clennam in his adversity, strongly and tenderly. "When I first gathered myself together," he thought, "and set something like purpose before my jaded eyes, whom had I before me, toiling on, for a good object's sake, without encouragement, without notice, against ignoble obstacles that would have turned an army of received heroes and heroines? One weak girl! When I tried to conquer my misplaced love, and to be generous to the man who was more fortunate than I, though he should never know it or repay me with a gracious word, in whom had I watched patience, self-denial, self-subdual, charitable construction, the noblest generosity of the affections? In the same pure girl! If I, a man, with a man's advantages and means and energies, had slighted the whisper in my heart, that if my father had erred, it was my first duty to conceal the fault and to repair it, what youthful figure with tender feet going almost bare on the damp ground, with spare hands ever working, with its slight shape but half protected from the sharp weather, would have stood before me to put me to shame? Little Dorrit's." So always, as he sat alone in the faded chair, thinking. Always, Little Dorrit. Until it seemed to him as if he met with the reward of having wandered away from her, and suffered anything to pass between him and his remembrance of her virtues.

His door was opened, and the head of the elder Chivery was put in a very little way, without being turned towards him.

"I am off the lock, Mr. Clennam, and going out. Can I do anything for you?"

"Many thanks. Nothing."

"You'll excuse me opening the door," said Mr. Chivery; "but I couldn't make you hear."

"Did you knock?"

"Half a dozen times."

Rousing himself, Clennam observed that the prison had awakened from its noontide doze, that the inmates were loitering about the shady yard, and that it was late in the afternoon. He had been thinking for hours.

"Your things is come," said Mr. Chivery, "and my son is going to carry 'em up. I should have sent 'em up, but for his wishing to carry 'em himself. Indeed he would have 'em himself, and so I couldn't send 'em up. Mr. Clennam, could I say a word to you?"

"Pray come in," said Arthur; for Mr. Chivery's head was still put in at the door a very little way, and Mr. Chivery had but one ear upon him, instead of both eyes. This was native delicacy in Mr. Chivery—true politeness; though his exterior had very much of a turnkey about it, and not the least of a gentleman.

"Thank you, sir," said Mr. Chivery, without advancing; "it's no odds me coming in. Mr. Clennam, don't you take no notice of my son (if you'll be so good), in case you find him cut up anyways difficult. My son has a art, and my son's art is in the right place. Me and his mother knows where to find it, and we find it sitiwated correct."

With this mysterious speech, Mr. Chivery took his ear away and shut the door. He might have been gone ten minutes, when his son succeeded him.

"Here's your portmanteau," he said to Arthur, putting it carefully down.

"It's very kind of you. I am ashamed that you should have the trouble."

He was gone, before it came to that; but soon returned, saying exactly as before, "here's your black box;" which he also put down with care.

"I am very sensible of this attention. I hope we may shake hands now, Mr. John."

Young John, however, drew back, turning his right wrist in a socket made of his left thumb and middle-finger, and said, as he had said at first, "I don't know as I can. No; I find I can't!" He then stood regarding the prisoner sternly, though with a swelling humour in his eyes that looked like pity.

"Why are you angry with me," said Clennam, "and yet so ready to do me these kind services? There must be some mistake between us. If I have done anything to occasion it, I am sorry."

"No mistake, sir," returned John, turning the wrist backwards and forwards in the socket, for which it was rather tight. "No mistake, sir, in the feelings with which my eyes behold you at the present moment! If I was at all fairly equal to your weight, Mr. Clennam—which I am not; and if you weren't under a cloud—which you are; and if it wasn't against all rules of the Marshalsea—which it is; those feelings are such, that they would stimulate me, more to having it out with you in a Round on the present spot, than to anything else I could name."

Arthur looked at him for a moment in some wonder, and some little anger. "Well, well!" he said. "A mistake, a mistake!" Turning away, he sat down, with a heavy sigh, in the faded chair again.

Young John followed him with his eyes, and, after a short pause, cried out, "I beg your pardon!"

"Freely granted," said Clennam, waving his hand, without raising his sunken head. "Say no more. I am not worth it."

"This furniture, sir," said Young John in a voice of mild and soft explanation, "belongs to me. I am in the habit of letting it out to parties without furniture, that have the room. It an't much, but it's at your service. Free, I mean. I could not think of letting you have it on any other terms. You're welcome to it for nothing."

Arthur raised his head again, to thank him, and to say he could not accept the favor. John was still turning his wrist, and still contending with himself in his former divided manner.

"What is the matter between us?" said Arthur.

"I decline to name it, sir," returned Young John, suddenly turning loud and sharp. "Nothing's the matter."

Arthur looked at him again, in vain, for any explanation of his behaviour.[3] After a while, Arthur turned away his head again. Young John said, presently afterwards, with the utmost mildness:

"The little round table, sir, that's nigh your elbow, was—you know whose—I needn't mention him—he died, a great gentleman. I bought it of an individual that he gave it to, and that lived here after him. But the individual wasn't any ways equal to him. Most individuals would find it hard to come up to his level."

Arthur drew the little table nearer, rested his arm upon it, and kept it there.

"Perhaps you may not be aware, sir," said Young John, "that I intruded upon him when he was over here in London. On the whole he was of opinion that it *was* an intrusion, though he was so good as to ask me to sit down and to enquire after father and all other old friends. Leastways humblest acquaintances. He looked, to me, a good deal changed, and I said so when I came back. I asked him if Miss Amy was well——"

"And she was?" said Arthur.

"I should have thought you would have known without putting the question to such as me," returned Young John, after appearing to take a large invisible pill. "Since you do put the question, I am sorry I can't answer it. But the truth is, he looked upon the enquiry as a liberty, and said, 'What was that to me?' It was then I became quite aware I was intruding: of which I had been fearful before. However, he spoke very handsome afterwards; very handsome."

They were both silent for several minutes: except that Young John remarked, at about the middle of the pause, "He both spoke and acted very handsome."

It was again Young John who broke the silence, by enquiring:

"If it's not a liberty, how long may it be your intentions, sir, to go without eating and drinking?"

"I have not felt the want of anything yet," returned Clennam. "I have no appetite just now."

"The more reason why you should take some support, sir," urged Young John. "If you find yourself going on sitting here for hours and hours partaking of no refreshment because you have no appetite, why then you should and must partake of refreshment without an appetite. I'm going to have tea in my own apartment. If it's not a liberty, please to come and take a cup. Or I can bring a tray here, in two minutes."

Feeling that Young John would impose that trouble on himself if he refused, and also feeling anxious to show that he bore in mind both the elder Mr. Chivery's entreaty, and the younger Mr. Chivery's apology, Arthur rose and expressed his willingness to take a cup of tea in Mr. John's apartment. Young John locked his door for him as they went out, slided the key into his pocket with great dexterity, and led the way to his own residence.

It was at the top of the house nearest to the gateway. It was the room to which Clennam had hurried, on the day when the enriched family had left the prison for ever, and where he had lifted her insensible from the floor. He foresaw where they were going, as soon as their feet touched the stair-case. The room was so far changed that it was papered now, and had been repainted, and was far more comfortably furnished; but, he could recall it just as he had seen it in that single glance, when he raised her from the ground and carried her down to the carriage.

Young John looked hard at him, biting his fingers.

"I see you recollect the room, Mr. Clennam?"

"I recollect it well, Heaven bless her!"

Oblivious of the tea, Young John continued to bite his fingers and to look at his visitor, as long as his visitor continued to glance about the room. Finally, he made a start at the teapot, gustily rattled a quantity of tea into it from a cannister, and set off for the common kitchen to fill it with hot water.

The room was so eloquent to Clennam, in the changed circumstances of his return to the miserable Marshalsea; it spoke to him so mournfully of her, and of his loss of her; that it would have gone hard with him to resist it, even though he had not been alone. Alone, he did not try. He laid his hand on the insensible wall, as tenderly as if it had been herself that he touched, and pronounced her name in a low voice. He stood at the window, looking over the prison-parapet with its grim spiked border, and breathed a benediction through the summer haze towards the distant land where she was rich and prosperous.

Young John was some time absent, and, when he came back, showed that he had been outside, by bringing with him fresh butter in a cabbage leaf, some thin slices of boiled ham in another cabbage leaf, and a little basket of water-cresses and salad herbs. When these were arranged upon the table to his satisfaction, they sat down to tea.

Clennam tried to do honor to the meal, but unavailingly. The ham sickened him, the bread seemed to turn to sand in his mouth. He could force nothing upon himself but a cup of tea.

"Try a little something green," said Young John, handing him the basket.

He took a sprig or so of water-cress, and tried again; but, the bread turned to a heavier sand than before, and the ham (though it was good enough of itself) seemed to blow a faint simoom of ham through the whole Marshalsea.

"Try a little more something green, sir," said Young John; and again handed the basket.

It was so like handing green meat into the cage of a dull imprisoned bird, and John had so evidently bought the little basket as a handful of fresh relief from the stale hot paving-stones and bricks of the jail, that Clennam said, with a smile, "It was very kind of you to think of putting this between the wires; but, I cannot even get this down to-day."

As if the difficulty were contagious, Young John soon pushed away his own plate, and fell to folding the cabbage leaf that had contained the ham. When he had folded it into a number of layers, one over another, so that it was small in the palm of his hand, he began to flatten it between both his hands, and to eye Clennam attentively.

"I wonder," he at length said, compressing his green packet with some force, "that if it's not worth your while to take care of yourself for your own sake, it's not worth doing for some one else's."

"Truly," returned Arthur, with a sigh and a smile, "I don't know for whose."

"Mr. Clennam," said John, warmly, "I'm surprised that a gentleman who is capable of the straightforwardness that you are capable of, should be capable of the mean action of making me such an answer. Mr. Clennam, I am surprised that a gentleman who is capable of having a heart of his own, should be capable of the heartlessness of treating mine in that way. I am astonished at it, sir. Really and truly I am astonished!"

Having got upon his feet to emphasise his concluding words, Young John sat down again, and fell to rolling his green packet on his right leg; never taking his eyes off Clennam, but surveying him with a fixed look of indignant reproach

"I had got over it, sir," said John. "I had conquered it, knowing that it *must* be conquered, and had come to the resolution to think no more about it. I shouldn't have given my mind to it again, I hope, if to this prison you had not been brought, and in an hour unfortunate for me, this day!" (In his agitation Young John adopted his mother's powerful construction of sentences.) "When you first came upon me, sir, in the Lodge, this day, more as if a Upas tree had been made a capture of than a private defendant, such mingled streams of feelings broke loose again within me that everything was for the first few minutes swept away before them, and I was going round and round in a vortex. I got out of it. I struggled, and got out of it. If it was the last word I had to speak, against that vortex with my utmost powers I strove, and out of it I came. I argued that if I had been rude, apologies was due, and those apologies without a question of demeaning, I did make. And now, when I've been so wishful to show that one thought is next to being a holy one with me and goes before all others—now, after all, you dodge me when I ever so gently hint at it, and throw me back upon myself. For, do not, sir," said Young John, "do not be so base as to deny that dodge you do, and thrown me back upon myself you have!"

All amazement, Arthur gazed at him, like one lost, only saying "What is it? What do you mean, John?" But, John, being in that state of mind in which nothing would seem to be more impossible to a certain class of people than the giving of an answer, went ahead blindly.

"I hadn't," John declared, "no, I hadn't and I never had, the audaciousness to think, I am sure, that all was anything but lost. I hadn't, no, why should I say I hadn't if I ever had, any hope that it was possible to be so blest, not after the words that passed, not even if barriers insurmountable had not been raised! But, is that a reason why I am to have no memory, why I am to have no thoughts, why I am to have no sacred spots, nor anything?"

"What can you mean?" cried Arthur.

"It's all very well to trample on it, sir," John went on, scouring a very prairie of wild words, "if a person can make up his mind to be guilty of the action. It's all very well to trample on it, but it's there. It may be that it couldn't be trampled upon if it wasn't there. But, that doesn't make it gentlemanly, that doesn't make it honorable, that doesn't justify throwing a person back upon himself after he has struggled and strived out of himself, like a butterfly. The world may sneer at a turnkey, but he's a man—when he isn't a woman, which among female criminals he's expected to be."

Ridiculous as the incoherence of his talk was, there was yet a truthfulness in Young John's simple, sentimental character, and a sense of being wounded in some very tender respect, expressed in his burning face and in the agitation of his voice and manner, which Arthur must have been cruel to disregard. He turned his thoughts back to the starting-point of this unknown injury; and in the meantime Young John, having rolled his green packet pretty round, cut it carefully into three pieces, and laid it on a plate as if it were some particular delicacy.

"It seems to me just possible," said Arthur, when he had retraced the conversation to the water-cresses and back again, "that you have made some reference to Miss Dorrit?"

"It is just possible, sir," returned John Chivery.

"I don't understand it. I hope I may not be so unlucky as to make you think I mean to offend you again, for I never have meant to offend you yet, when I say I don't understand it."

"Sir," said Young John, "will you have the perfidy to deny that you know and long have known that I felt towards Miss Dorrit, call it not the presumption of love, but adoration and sacrifice?"

"Indeed, John, I will not have any perfidy if I know it; why you should suspect me of it, I am at a loss to think. Did you ever hear from Mrs. Chivery, your mother, that I went to see her once?"

"No, sir," returned John, shortly. "Never heard of such a thing."

"But, I did. Can you imagine why?"

"No, sir," returned John, shortly. "I can't imagine why."

"I will tell you. I was solicitous to promote Miss Dorrit's happiness; and if I could have supposed that Miss Dorrit returned your affection——"

Poor John Chivery turned crimson to the tips of his ears. "Miss Dorrit never did, sir. I wish to be honorable and true, so far as in my humble way I can, and I would scorn to pretend for a moment that she ever did, or that she ever led me to believe she did; no, nor even that it was ever to be expected in any cool reason that she would or could. She was far above me in all respects at all times. As likewise," added John, "similarly was her gen-teel family."

His chivalrous feeling towards all that belonged to her, made him so very respectable, in spite of his small stature and his rather weak legs, and his very weak hair, and his poetical temperament, that a Goliath might have sat in his place demanding less consideration at Arthur's hands.

"You speak, John," he said with cordial admiration, "like a Man."

"Well, sir," returned John, brushing his hand across his eyes, "then I wish you'd do the same."

He was quick with this unexpected retort, and it again made Arthur regard him with a wondering expression of face.

"Leastways," said John, stretching his hand across the tea-tray, "if too strong a remark, withdrawn! But, why not, why not? When I say to you, Mr. Clennam, take care of yourself for some one else's sake, why not be open though a turnkey? Why did I get you the room which I knew you'd like best? Why did I carry up your things? Not that I found 'em heavy; I don't mention 'em on that accounts; far from it. Why have I culti-vated you in the manner I have done, since the morning? On the ground of your own merits? No. They're very great, I've no doubt at all; but not on the ground of them. Another's merits have had their weight, and have had far more weight with Me. Then why not speak free!"

"Unaffectedly, John," said Clennam, "you are so good a fellow, and I have so true a respect for your character, that if I have appeared to be less sensible than I really am, of the fact that the kind services you have rendered me to-day are attributable to my having been trusted by Miss Dorrit as her friend,—I confess it to be a fault, and I ask your forgiveness."

"Oh! why not," John repeated with returning scorn, "why not speak free!"

"I declare to you," returned Arthur, "that I do not understand you. Look at me. Consider the trouble I have been in. Is it likely that I would wilfully add to my other self-reproaches, that of being ungrateful or treacherous to you? I do *not* understand you."

John's incredulous face slowly softened into a face of doubt. He rose, backed into the garret-window of the room, beckoned Arthur to come there, and stood looking at him thoughtfully.

"Mr. Clennam, do you mean to say that you don't know?"

"What, John?"

"Lord," said Young John, appealing with a gasp to the spikes on the wall. "He says, What!"

Clennam looked at the spikes, and looked at John; and looked at the spikes, and looked at John.

"He says What! And what is more," exclaimed Young John, surveying him in a doleful maze, "he appears to mean it! Do you see this window, sir?"

"Of course, I see this window."

"See this room?"

"Why, of course I see this room."

"That wall opposite, and that yard down below? They have all been witnesses of it, from day to day, from night to night, from week to week, from month to month. For, how often have I seen Miss Dorrit here, when she has not seen me!"

"Witnesses of what?" said Clennam.

"Of Miss Dorrit's love."

"For whom?"

"You!" said John. And touched him with the back of his hand upon the breast, and backed to his chair, and sat down in it with a pale face, holding the arms, and shaking his head at him.

If he had dealt Clennam a heavy blow, instead of laying that light touch upon him, its effect could not have been to shake him more. He stood amazed; his eyes looking at John; his lips parted, and seeming now and then to form the word "Me!" without uttering it; his hands dropped at his sides: his whole appearance that of a man who has been awakened from sleep, and stupefied by intelligence beyond his full comprehension.

"Me!" he at length said aloud.

"Ah!" groaned Young John. "You!"

He did what he could to muster a smile, and returned, "Your fancy. You are completely mistaken."

"I mistaken, sir!" said Young John. "*I* completely mistaken on that subject! No, Mr. Clennam, don't tell me so. On any other, if you like, for I don't set up to be a penetrating character, and am well aware of my own deficiencies. But, *I* mistaken on a point that has caused me more smart in my breast than a flight of savages' arrows could have done! *I* mistaken on a point that almost sent me into my grave, as I sometimes wished it would, if the grave could only have been made compatible with the tobacco-business and father and mother's feelings! I mistaken on a point that, even at the present moment, makes me take out my pocket handkercher like a great girl, as people say: though I am sure I don't know why a great girl should be a term of reproach, for every rightly constituted male mind loves 'em great and small! Don't tell me so, don't tell me so!"

Still highly respectable at bottom, though absurd enough upon the surface, Young John took out his pocket handkerchief, with a genuine absence both of display and concealment, which is only to be seen in a man with a great deal of good in him, when he takes out his pocket handkerchief for the purpose of wiping his eyes. Having dried them, and indulged in the harmless luxury of a sob and a sniff, he put it up again.

The touch was still in its influence so like a blow, that Arthur could not get many words together to close the subject with. He assured John Chivery when he had returned his handkerchief to his pocket, that he did all honor to his disinterestedness and to the fidelity of his remembrance of Miss Dorrit. As to the impression on his mind, of which he had just relieved it—— here John interposed, and said, "No impression! Certainty!" —as to that they might perhaps speak of it at another time, but would say no more now. Feeling low-spirited and weary, he would go back to his room, with John's leave, and come out no more that night. John assented, and he crept back in the shadow of the wall to his own lodging.

The feeling of the blow was still so strong upon him, that when the dirty old woman was gone whom he found sitting on the stairs outside his door, waiting to make his bed, and who gave him to understand while doing it, that she had received her instructions from Mr. Chivery, "not the old 'un but the young 'un," he sat down in the faded arm-chair, pressing his head between his hands, as if he had been stunned. Little Dorrit love him! More bewildering to him than his misery, far.

Consider the improbability. He had been accustomed to call her his child, and his dear child, and to invite her confidence by dwelling upon the difference in their respective ages, and to speak of himself as one who was turning old. Yet she might not have thought him old. Something reminded him that he had not thought himself so, until the roses had floated away upon the river.

He had her two letters among other papers in his box, and he took them out and read them. There seemed to be a sound in them like the sound of her sweet voice. It fell upon his ear with many tones of tenderness, that were not insusceptible of the new meaning. Now, it was that the quiet desolation of her answer, "No, No, No," made to him that night in that very room—that night, when he had been shown the dawn of her altered fortune, and when other words had passed between them which he had been destined to remember, in humiliation and a prisoner—rushed into his mind.

Consider the improbability.

But, it had a preponderating tendency, when considered, to become fainter. There was another and a curious enquiry of his own heart's that concurrently became stronger. In the reluctance he had felt to believe that she loved any one; in his desire to set that question at rest; in a half-formed consciousness he had had, that there would be a kind of nobleness in his helping her love for any one; was there no suppressed something on his own side that he had hushed as it arose? Had he ever whispered to himself that he must not think of such a thing as her loving him, that he must not take advantage of her gratitude, that he must keep his experience in remembrance as a warning and reproof; that he must regard such youthful hopes as having passed away, as his friend's dead daughter had passed away; that he must be steady in saying to himself that the time had gone by him, and he was too saddened and old?

He had kissed her when he raised her from the ground, on the day when she had been so consistently and expressively forgotten. Quite as he might have kissed her, if she had been conscious? No difference?

The darkness found him occupied with these thoughts. The darkness also found Mr. and Mrs. Plornish knocking at his door. They brought with them a basket, filled with choice selections from that stock in trade which met with such a quick sale and produced such a slow return. Mrs. Plornish was affected to tears. Mr. Plornish amiably growled, in his philosophical but not lucid manner, that there was ups, you see, and there was downs. It was in wain to ask why ups, why downs; there they was, you know. He had heerd it given for a truth that accordin' as the world went round, which round it did rewolve undoubted, even the best of gentlemen must take his turn of standing with his ed upside down and all his air a flying the wrong way into what you might call Space. Wery well then. What Mr. Plornish said was, wery well then. That gentleman's ed would come up'ards when his turn come, that gentleman's air would be a pleasure to look upon being all smooth again, and wery well then!

It has been already stated that Mrs. Plornish, not being philosophical, wept. It further happened that Mrs. Plornish, not being philosophical, was intelligible. It may have arisen out of her softened state of mind, out of her sex's wit, out of a woman's quick association of ideas, or out of a woman's no association of ideas, but it further happened somehow that Mrs. Plornish's intelligibility displayed itself upon the very subject of Arthur's meditations.

"The way father has been talking about you, Mr. Clennam," said Mrs. Plornish, "you couldn't hardly believe. It's made him quite poorly. As to his voice, this misfortune has took it away. You know what a sweet singer father is; but he couldn't get a note out for the children at tea, if you'll credit what I tell you."

While speaking, Mrs. Plornish shook her head, and wiped her eyes, and looked retrospectively about the room.

"As to Mr. Baptist," pursued Mrs. Plornish, "whatever he'll do when he comes to know of it, I can't conceive nor yet imagine. He'd have been here before now, you may be sure, but that he's away on confidential business of your own. The persevering manner in which he follows up that business, and gives himself no rest from it—it really do," said Mrs. Plornish, winding up in the Italian manner, "as I say to him, Mooshatto-nisha padrona."

Though not conceited, Mrs. Plornish felt that she had turned this Tuscan sentence with peculiar elegance. Mr. Plornish could not conceal his exultation in her accomplishments as a linguist.

"But what I say is, Mr. Clennam," the good woman went on, "there's always something to be thankful for, as I'm sure you will yourself admit. Speaking in this room, it's not hard to think what the present something is. It's a thing to be thankful for, indeed, that Miss Dorrit is not here to know it."

Arthur thought she looked at him with particular expression.

"It's a thing," reiterated Mrs. Plornish, "to be thankful for, indeed, that Miss Dorrit is far away. It's to be hoped she is not likely to hear of it. If she had been here to see it, sir, it's not to be doubted that the sight of you," Mrs. Plornish repeated those words—"not to be doubted, that the sight of *you*—in misfortune and trouble, would have been almost too much for her affectionate heart. There's nothing I can think of, that would have touched Miss Dorrit so bad as that."

Of a certainty, Mrs. Plornish did look at him now, with a sort of quivering defiance in her friendly emotion.

"Yes!" said she. "And it shows what notice father takes, though at his time of life, that he says to me, this afternoon, which Happy Cottage knows I neither make it up nor anyways enlarge, 'Mary, it's much to be rejoiced in that Miss Dorrit is not on the spot to behold it.' Those were father's words. Father's own words was, 'Much to be rejoiced in, Mary, that Miss Dorrit is not on the spot to behold it.' I says to father then, I says to him,

'Father, you are right!' That," Mrs. Plornish concluded with the air of a very precise legal witness, "is what passed betwixt father and me. And I tell you nothing but what did pass betwixt me and father."

Mr. Plornish, as being of a more laconic temperament, embraced this opportunity of interposing with the suggestion that she should now leave Mr. Clennam to himself. "For, you see," said Mr. Plornish, gravely, "I know what it is, old gal." He repeated that valuable remark several times, as if it appeared to him to include some great moral secret. Finally, the worthy couple went away arm in arm.

Little Dorrit, Little Dorrit. Again, for hours. Always Little Dorrit!

Happily, if it ever had been so, it was over, and better over. Granted, that she had loved him, and he had known it and had suffered himself to love her, what a road to have led her away upon—the road that would have brought her back to this miserable place! He ought to be much comforted by the reflection that she was quit of it for ever; that she was, or would soon be, married (vague rumours of her father's projects in that direction had reached Bleeding Heart Yard, with the news of her sister's marriage); and that the Marshalsea gate had shut for ever on all those perplexed possibilities, of a time that was gone.

Dear Little Dorrit!

Looking back upon his own poor story, she was its vanishing-point. Everything in its perspective led to her innocent figure. He had travelled thousands of miles towards it; previous unquiet hopes and doubts had worked themselves out before it; it was the centre of the interest of his life; it was the termination of everything that was good and pleasant in it; beyond there was nothing but mere waste, and darkened sky.

As ill at ease as on the first night of his lying down to sleep within those dreary walls, he wore the night out with such thoughts. What time, Young John lay wrapt in peaceful slumber, after composing and arranging the following monumental inscription on his pillow.

STRANGER!

RESPECT THE TOMB OF

JOHN CHIVERY, JUNIOR,

WHO DIED AT AN ADVANCED AGE

NOT NECESSARY TO MENTION.

HE ENCOUNTERED HIS RIVAL, IN A DISTRESSED STATE,

AND FELT INCLINED

TO HAVE A ROUND WITH HIM;

BUT, FOR THE SAKE OF THE LOVED ONE,

CONQUERED THOSE FEELINGS OF BITTERNESS,

AND BECAME

MAGNANIMOUS.

CHAPTER XXVIII

AN APPEARANCE IN THE MARSHALSEA

THE opinion of the community outside the prison gates bore hard on Clennam as time went on, and he made no friends among the community within. Too depressed to associate with the herd in the yard, who got together to forget their cares; too retiring and too unhappy to join in the poor socialities of the tavern; he kept his own room, and was held in distrust. Some said he was proud; some objected that he was sullen and reserved; some were contemptuous of him, for that he was a poor-spirited dog who pined under his debts. The whole population were shy of him on these various counts of indictment, but especially the last, which involved a species of domestic treason; and he soon became so confirmed in his seclusion, that his only time for walking up and down was when the evening Club were assembled at their songs and toasts and sentiments, and when the yard was nearly left to the women and children.

Imprisonment began to tell upon him. He knew that he idled and moped. After what he had known of the influences of imprisonment within the four small walls of the very room he occupied, this consciousness made him afraid of himself. Shrinking from the observation of other men, and shrinking from his own, he began to change very sensibly. Anybody might see that the shadow of the wall was dark upon him.

One day when he might have been some ten or twelve weeks in jail, and when he had been trying to read, and had not been able to release even the imaginary people of the book from the Marshalsea, a footstep stopped at his door, and a hand tapped at it. He arose and opened it, and an agreeable voice accosted him with "How do you do, Mr. Clennam ? I hope I am not unwelcome in calling to see you."

It was the sprightly young Barnacle, Ferdinand. He looked very good-natured and prepossessing, though overpoweringly gay and free, in contrast with the squalid prison.

"You are surprised to see me, Mr. Clennam," he said, taking the seat which Clennam offered him.

"I must confess to being much surprised."

"Not disagreeably, I hope ?"

"By no means."

"Thank you. Frankly," said the engaging young Barnacle, "I have been excessively sorry to hear that you were under the necessity of a temporary retirement here, and I hope (of course as between two private gentlemen) that our place has had nothing to do with it ?"

"Your office ?"

"Our Circumlocution place."

"I cannot charge any part of my reverses upon that remarkable establishment."

"Upon my life," said the vivacious young Barnacle, "I am heartily glad to know it. It is quite a relief to me to hear you say it. I should have so exceedingly regretted our place having had anything to do with your difficulties."

Clennam again assured him that he absolved it of the responsibility.

"That's right," said Ferdinand. "I am very happy to hear it. I was rather afraid in my own mind that we might have helped to floor you, because there is no doubt that it is our misfortune to do that kind of thing now and then. We don't want to do it; but if men will be gravelled, why— we can't help it."

"Without giving an unqualified assent to what you say," returned Arthur, gloomily, "I am much obliged to you for your interest in me."

"No, but really! Our place is," said the easy Young Barnacle, "the most inoffensive place possible. You'll say we are a Humbug. I won't say we are not; but all that sort of thing is intended to be, and must be. Don't you see?"

"I do not," said Clennam.

"You don't regard it from the right point of view. It is the point of view that is the essential thing. Regard our place from the point of view that we only ask you to leave us alone, and we are as capital a Department as you'll find anywhere."

"Is your place there to be left alone?" asked Clennam.

"You exactly hit it," returned Ferdinand. "It is there with the express intention that everything shall be left alone. That is what it means. That is what it's for. No doubt there's a certain form to be kept up that it's for something else, but it's only a form. Why, good Heaven, we are nothing but forms! Think what a lot of our forms you have gone through. And you have never got any nearer to an end?"

"Never!" said Clennam.

"Look at it from the right point of view, and there you have us— official and effectual. It's like a limited game of cricket. A field of outsiders are always going in to bowl at the Public Service, and we block the balls."

Clennam asked what became of the bowlers? The airy Young Barnacle replied that they grew tired, got dead beat, got lamed, got their backs broken, died off, gave it up, went in for other games.

"And this occasions me to congratulate myself again," he pursued, "on the circumstance that our place has had nothing to do with your temporary retirement. It very easily might have had a hand in it; because it is undeniable that we are sometimes a most unlucky place, in our effects upon people who will not leave us alone. Mr. Clennam, I am quite unreserved with you. As between yourself and myself, I know I may be. I was so, when I first saw you making the mistake of not leaving us alone; because I perceived that you were inexperienced and sanguine, and had—I hope you'll not object to my saying—some simplicity?"

"Not at all."

"Some simplicity. Therefore I felt what a pity it was, and I went out of my way to hint to you (which really was not official, but I never am official when I can help it), something to the effect that if I were you, I wouldn't bother myself. However, you did bother yourself, and you have since bothered yourself. Now, don't do it any more."

"I am not likely to have the opportunity," said Clennam.

"Oh yes, you are! You'll leave here. Everybody leaves here. There are no ends of ways of leaving here. Now, don't come back to us. That entreaty is the second object of my call. Pray, don't come back to us. Upon my honor," said Ferdinand in a very friendly and confiding way, "I shall be greatly vexed if you don't take warning by the past and keep away from us."

"And the invention?" said Clennam.

"My good fellow," returned Ferdinand, "if you'll excuse the freedom of that form of address, nobody wants to know of the invention, and nobody cares twopence-halfpenny about it."

"Nobody in the Office, that is to say?"

"Nor out of it. Everybody is ready to dislike and ridicule any invention. You have no idea how many people want to be left alone. You have no idea how the Genius of the country (overlook the Parliamentary nature of the phrase, and don't be bored by it) tends to being left alone. Believe me, Mr. Clennam," said the sprightly young Barnacle, in his pleasantest manner, "our place is not a wicked Giant to be charged at full tilt; but, only a wind-mill showing you, as it grinds immense quantities of chaff, which way the country wind blows."

"If I could believe that," said Clennam, "it would be a dismal prospect for all of us."

"Oh! Don't say so!" returned Ferdinand. "It's all right. We must have humbug, we all like humbug, we couldn't get on without humbug. A little humbug, and a groove, and everything goes on admirably, if you leave it alone."

With this hopeful confession of his faith as the head of the rising Barnacles who were born of woman, to be followed under a variety of watchwords which they utterly repudiated and disbelieved, Ferdinand rose. Nothing could be more agreeable than his frank and courteous bearing, or adapted with a more gentlemanly instinct to the circumstances of his visit.

"Is it fair to ask," he said, as Clennam gave him his hand with a real feeling of thankfulness for his candor and good humour, "whether it is true that our late lamented Merdle is the cause of this passing inconvenience?"

"I am one of the many he has ruined. Yes."

"He must have been an exceedingly clever fellow," said Ferdinand Barnacle.

Arthur, not being in a mood to extol the memory of the deceased, was silent.

"A consummate rascal of course," said Ferdinand, "but remarkably clever! One cannot help admiring the fellow. Must have been such a master of humbug. Knew people so well—got over them so completely—did so much with them!"

In his easy way, he was really moved to genuine admiration.

"I hope," said Arthur, "that he and his dupes may be a warning to people not to have so much done with them again."

"My dear Mr. Clennam," returned Ferdinand, laughing, "have you really such a verdant hope? The next man who has as large a capacity and as genuine a taste for swindling, will succeed as well. Pardon me, but I think you really have no idea how the human bees will swarm to the beating of any old tin kettle; in that fact lies the complete manual of governing them. When they can be got to believe that the kettle is made of the precious metals, in that fact lies the whole power of men like our late lamented. No doubt there are here and there," said Ferdinand politely, "exceptional cases, where people have been taken in for what appeared to them to be much better reasons; and I need not go far to find such a case; but, they don't invalidate the rule. Good day! I hope that when I have the pleasure of seeing you next, this passing cloud will have given place to sunshine. Don't come a step beyond the door. I know the way out perfectly. Good day!"

With those words, the best and brightest of the Barnacles went downstairs, hummed his way through the Lodge, mounted his horse in the front courtyard, and rode off to keep an appointment with his noble kinsman: who wanted a little coaching before he could triumphantly answer certain infidel Snobs, who were going to question the Nobs about their statesmanship.

He must have passed Mr. Rugg on his way out, for, a minute or two afterwards, that ruddy-headed gentleman shone in at the door, like an elderly Phœbus.

"How do you do to-day, sir?" said Mr. Rugg. "Is there any little thing I can do for you to-day, sir?"

"No, I thank you."

Mr. Rugg's enjoyment of embarrassed affairs was like a housekeeper's enjoyment in pickling and preserving, or a washerwoman's enjoyment of a heavy wash, or a dustman's enjoyment of an overflowing dust binn, or any other professional enjoyment of a mess in the way of business.

"I still look round, from time to time, sir," said Mr. Rugg, cheerfully, "to see whether any lingering Detainers are accumulating at the gate. They have fallen in pretty thick, sir; as thick as we could have expected."

He remarked upon the circumstance as if it were matter of congratulation: rubbing his hands briskly, and rolling his head a little.

"As thick," repeated Mr. Rugg, "as we could reasonably have expected. Quite a shower-bath of 'em. I don't often intrude upon you, now, when I look round, because I know you are not inclined for company, and that if you wished to see me, you would leave word in the Lodge. But I am here pretty well every day, sir. Would this be an unseasonable time, sir," asked Mr. Rugg, coaxingly, "for me to offer an observation?"

"As seasonable a time as any other."

"Hum! Public opinion, sir," said Mr. Rugg, "has been busy with you."

"I don't doubt it."

"Might it not be advisable, sir," said Mr. Rugg, more coaxingly yet, "now to make, at last and after all, a trifling concession to public opinion? We all do it in one way or another. The fact is, we must do it."

"I cannot set myself right with it, Mr. Rugg, and have no business to expect that I ever shall."

"Don't say that, sir, don't say that. The cost of being moved to the Bench is almost insignificant, and if the general feeling is strong that you ought to be there, why—really——"

"I thought you had settled, Mr. Rugg," said Arthur, "that my determination to remain here was a matter of taste."

"Well, sir, well! But is it good taste, is it good taste? That's the question." Mr. Rugg was so soothingly persuasive as to be quite pathetic. "I was almost going to say, is it good feeling? This is an extensive affair of yours; and your remaining here where a man can come for a pound or two, is remarked upon, as not in keeping. It is *not* in keeping. I can't tell you, sir, in how many quarters I hear it mentioned. I heard comments made upon it last night, in a Parlor frequented by what I should call, if I did not look in there now and then myself, the best legal company—I heard, there, comments on it that I was sorry to hear. They hurt me, on your account. Again, only this morning at breakfast. My daughter (but a woman, you'll say: yet still with a feeling for these things, and even with some little personal experience, as the plaintiff in Rugg and Bawkins) was expressing her great surprise; her great surprise. Now, under these circumstances, and considering that none of us can quite set ourselves above public opinion, wouldn't a trifling concession to the opinion be—Come, sir!" said Mr. Rugg, "I will put it on the lowest ground of argument, and say, Amiable?"

Arthur's thoughts had once more wandered away to Little Dorrit, and the question remained unanswered.

"As to myself, sir," said Mr. Rugg, hoping that his eloquence had reduced him to a state of indecision, "it is a principle of mine not to consider myself when a client's inclinations are in the scale. But, knowing your considerate character and general wish to oblige, I will repeat that I should prefer your being in the Bench. Your case has made a noise; it is a creditable case to be professionally concerned in; I should feel on a better standing with my connexion, if you went to the Bench. Don't let that influence you, sir. I merely state the fact."

So errant had the prisoner's attention already grown in solitude and dejection, and so accustomed had it become to commune with only one silent figure within the ever-frowning walls, that Clennam had to shake off a kind of stupor before he could look at Mr. Rugg, recall the thread of his talk, and hurriedly say, "I am unchanged, and unchangeable, in my decision. Pray, let it be; let it be!" Mr. Rugg, without concealing that he was nettled and mortified, replied:

"Oh! Beyond a doubt, sir! I have travelled out of the record, sir, I am aware, in putting the point to you. But really, when I hear it remarked in several companies and in very good company, that however worthy of a foreigner, it is not worthy of the spirit of an Englishman to remain in the Marshalsea when the glorious liberties of his island home admit of his removal to the Bench, I thought I would depart from the narrow professional line marked out to me, and mention it. Personally," said Mr. Rugg, "I have no opinion on the topic."

"That's well," returned Arthur.

"Oh! None at all, sir!" said Mr. Rugg. "If I had, I should have been unwilling, some minutes ago, to see a client of mine visited in this place by a gentleman of high family riding a saddle-horse. But it was not my business. If I had, I might have wished to be now empowered to mention to another gentleman, a gentleman of military exterior at present waiting in the Lodge, that my client had never intended to remain here, and was on the eve of removal to a superior abode. But my course as a professional machine is clear; I have nothing to do with it. Is it your good pleasure to see the gentleman, sir?"

"Who is waiting to see me, did you say?"

"I did take that unprofessional liberty, sir. Hearing that I was your professional adviser, he declined to interpose before my very limited function was performed. Happily," said Mr. Rugg, with sarcasm, "I did not so far travel out of the record as to ask the gentleman for his name."

"I suppose I have no resource but to see him," sighed Clennam, wearily.

"Then it *is* your good pleasure, sir?" retorted Rugg. "Am I honored by your instructions to mention as much to the gentleman, as I pass out? I am? Thank you, sir. I take my leave." His leave he took accordingly, in dudgeon.

The gentleman of military exterior had so imperfectly awakened

Clennam's curiosity, in the existing state of his mind, that a half forgetful-
ness of such a visitor's having been referred to, was already creeping over
it as a part of the sombre veil which almost always dimmed it now, when
a heavy footstep on the stairs aroused him. It appeared to ascend them,
not very promptly or spontaneously, yet with a display of stride and clatter
meant to be insulting. As it paused for a moment on the landing outside
his door, he could not recall his association with the peculiarity of its
sound, though he thought he had one. Only a moment was given him for
consideration. His door was immediately swung open by a thump, and
in the doorway stood the missing Blandois, the cause of many anxieties.

"Salve, fellow jail-bird!" said he. "You want me, it seems. Here I am!"

Before Arthur could speak to him in his indignant wonder, Cavalletto
followed him into the room. Mr. Pancks followed Cavalletto. Neither of
the two had been there, since its present occupant had had possession of it.
Mr. Pancks, breathing hard, sidled near the window, put his hat on the
ground, stirred his hair up with both hands, and folded his arms, like
a man who had come to a pause in a hard day's work. Mr. Baptist, never
taking his eyes from his dreaded chum of old, softly sat down on the floor
with his back against the door and one of his ankles in each hand: resuming
the attitude (except that it was now expressive of unwinking watchfulness),
in which he had sat before the same man in the deeper shade of another
prison, one hot morning at Marseilles.

"I have it on the witnessing of these two madmen," said Monsieur
Blandois, otherwise Lagnier, otherwise Rigaud, "that you want me,
brother-bird. Here I am!"

Glancing round contemptuously at the bedstead, which was turned up
by day, he leaned his back against it as a resting-place, without removing his
hat from his head, and stood defiantly lounging with his hands in his pockets.

"You villain of ill-omen!" said Arthur. "You have purposely cast
a dreadful suspicion upon my mother's house. Why have you done it?
What prompted you to the devilish invention?"

Monsieur Rigaud, after frowning at him for a moment, laughed. "Hear
this noble gentleman! Listen, all the world, to this creature of Virtue!
But, take care, take care. It is possible, my friend, that your ardor is a little
compromising. Holy blue! It is possible."

"Signore!" interposed Cavalletto, also addressing Arthur: "for to
commence, hear me! I received your instructions to find him, Rigaud; is it
not?"

"It is the truth."

"I go, consequentementally," it would have given Mrs. Plornish great
concern if she could have been persuaded that his occasional lengthening of
an adverb in this way, was the chief fault of his English, "first, among my
countrymen. I ask them what news in Londra, of foreigners arrived. Then,
I go among the French. Then, I go among the Germans. They all tell me.

The great part of us know well the other, and they all tell me. But!—no person can tell me nothing of him, Rigaud. Fifteen times," said Cavalletto, thrice throwing out his left hand with all its fingers spread, and doing it so rapidly that the sense of sight could hardly follow the action, "I ask of him in every place where go the foreigners; and fifteen times," repeating the same swift performance, "they know nothing. But!——"

At his significant Italian rest on the word "But," his back-handed shake of his right forefinger came into play; a very little, and very cautiously.

"But!—After long time when I have not been able to find that he is here in Londra, some one tells me of a soldier with white hair—hey?—not hair like this that he carries—white—who lives retired secretementally, in a certain place. But!—" with another rest upon the word, "who sometimes in the after-dinner, walks, and smokes. It is necessary, as they say in Italy (and as they know, poor people), to have patience. I have patience. I ask where is this certain place. One believes it is here, one believes it is there. Eh well! It is not here, it is not there. I wait, patientissamentally. At last I find it. Then I watch; then I hide, until he walks and smokes. He is a soldier with grey hair—But!—" a very decided rest indeed, and a very vigorous play from side to side of the back-handed forefinger—"he is also this man that you see."

It was noticeable, that, in his old habit of submission to one who had been at the trouble of asserting superiority over him, he even then bestowed upon Rigaud a confused bend of his head, after thus pointing him out.

"Eh well, Signore!" he cried in conclusion, addressing Arthur again. "I waited for a good opportunity. I writed some words to Signor Panco" an air of novelty came over Mr. Pancks with this designation, "to come and help. I showed him, Rigaud, at his window to Signor Panco, who was often the spy in the day. I slept at night near the door of the house. At last we entered, only this to-day, and now you see him! As he would not come up in presence of the illustrious Advocate," such was Mr. Baptist's honorable mention of Mr. Rugg, "we waited down below there, together, and Signor Panco guarded the street."

At the close of this recital, Arthur turned his eyes upon the impudent and wicked face. As it met his, the nose came down over the moustache, and the moustache went up under the nose. When nose and moustache had settled into their places again, Monsieur Rigaud loudly snapped his fingers half a dozen times; bending forward to jerk the snaps at Arthur, as if they were palpable missiles which he jerked into his face.

"Now, Philosopher!" said Rigaud. "What do you want with me?"

"I want to know," returned Arthur, without disguising his abhorrence, "how you dare direct a suspicion of murder against my mother's house?"

"Dare!" cried Rigaud. "Ho ho! Hear him! Dare? Is it dare? By Heaven, my small boy, but you are a little imprudent!"

"I want that suspicion to be cleared away," said Arthur. "You shall be taken there, and be publicly seen. I want to know, moreover, what business you had there, when I had a burning desire to fling you down-stairs. Don't frown at me, man! I have seen enough of you to know that you are a bully, and coward. I need no revival of my spirits from the effects of this wretched place, to tell you so plain a fact, and one that you know so well."

White to the lips, Rigaud stroked his moustache, muttering "By Heaven, my small boy, but you are a little compromising of my lady your respectable mother"—and seemed for a minute undecided how to act. His indecision was soon gone. He sat himself down with a threatening swagger, and said:

"Give me a bottle of wine. You can buy wine here. Send one of your madmen to get me a bottle of wine. I won't talk to you without wine. Come! Yes or no?"

"Fetch him what he wants, Cavalletto," said Arthur scornfully, producing the money.

"Contraband beast," added Rigaud, "bring Port wine! I'll drink nothing but Porto-Porto."

The contraband beast, however, assuring all present, with his significant finger, that he peremptorily declined to leave his post at the door, Signor Panco offered his services. He soon returned, with the bottle of wine: which, according to the custom of the place, originating in a scarcity of corkscrews among the Collegians (in common with a scarcity of much else), was already opened for use.

"Madman! A large glass," said Rigaud.

Signor Panco put a tumbler before him; not without a visible conflict of feeling on the question of throwing it at his head.

"Haha!" boasted Rigaud. "Once a gentleman, and always a gentleman. A gentleman from the beginning, and a gentleman to the end. What the Devil! A gentleman must be waited on, I hope? It's a part of my character to be waited on!"

He half filled the tumbler as he said it, and drank off the contents when he had done saying it.

"Hah!" smacking his lips. "Not a very old prisoner *that!* I judge by your looks, brave sir, that imprisonment will subdue your blood much sooner than it softens this hot wine. You are mellowing—losing body and color, already. I salute you!"

He tossed off another half glass: holding it up both before and afterwards, so as to display his small, white hand.

"To business," he then continued. "To conversation. You have shown yourself more free of speech than body, sir."

"I have used the freedom of telling you, what you know yourself to be. You know yourself, as we all know you, to be far worse than that."

"Add, always, a gentleman, and it's no matter. Except in that regard, we are all alike. For example; you couldn't for your life be a gentleman;

I couldn't for my life be otherwise. How great the difference! Let us go on. Words, sir, never influenced the course of the cards, or the course of the dice. Do you know that? You do? I also play a game, and words are without power over it."

Now that he was confronted with Cavalletto, and knew that his story was known—whatever thin disguise he had worn, he dropped; and faced it out, with a bare face, as the infamous wretch he was.

"No, my son," he resumed, with a snap of his fingers. "I play my game to the end in spite of words; and Death of my Body and Death of my Soul! I'll win it. You want to know why I played this little trick that you have interrupted? Know then that I had, and that I have—do you understand me? have—a commodity to sell to my lady your respectable mother. I described my precious commodity, and fixed my price. Touching the bargain, your admirable mother was a little too calm, too stolid, too immovable and statue-like. In fine, your admirable mother vexed me. To make variety in my position, and to amuse myself—what! a gentleman must be amused at somebody's expense!—I conceived the happy idea of disappearing. An idea, see you, that your characteristic mother and my Flintwinch would have been well enough pleased to execute. Ah! Bah, bah, bah, don't look as from high to low at me! I repeat it. Well enough pleased, excessively enchanted, with all their hearts ravished. How strongly will you have it?"

He threw out the lees of his glass on the ground, so that they nearly spattered Cavalletto. This seemed to draw his attention to him anew. He set down his glass and said:

"I'll not fill it. What! I am born to be served. Come then, you Cavalletto, and fill!"

The little man looked at Clennam, whose eyes were occupied with Rigaud, and, seeing no prohibition, got up from the ground, and poured out from the bottle into the glass. The blending, as he did so, of his old submission with a sense of something humorous; the striving of that with a certain smouldering ferocity, which might have flashed fire in an instant (as the born gentleman seemed to think, for he had a wary eye upon him); and the easy yielding of all, to a good-natured, careless, predominant propensity to sit down on the ground again; formed a very remarkable combination of character.

"This happy idea, brave sir," Rigaud resumed after drinking, "was a happy idea for several reasons. It amused me, it worried your dear mama and my Flintwinch, it caused you agonies (my terms for a lesson in politeness towards a gentleman), and it suggested to all the amiable persons interested that your entirely devoted is a man to fear. By Heaven, he is a man to fear! Beyond this; it might have restored her wit to my lady your mother—might, under the pressing little suspicion your wisdom has recognised, have persuaded her at last to announce, covertly, in the journals

that the difficulties of a certain contract would be removed by the appearance of a certain important party to it. Perhaps yes, perhaps no. But, that
you have interrupted. Now, what is it you say? What is it you want?"

Never had Clennam felt more acutely that he was a prisoner in bonds,
than when he saw this man before him, and could not accompany him to
his mother's house. All the undiscernible difficulties and dangers he had
ever feared, were closing in, when he could not stir hand or foot.

"Perhaps, my friend, Philosopher, man of virtue, Imbecile, what you
will; perhaps," said Rigaud, pausing in his drink to look out of his glass
with his horrible smile, "you would have done better to leave me alone?"

"No! At least," said Clennam, "you are known to be alive and unharmed.
At least you cannot escape from these two witnesses; and they can produce
you before any public authorities, or before hundreds of people."

"But will not produce me before one," said Rigaud, snapping his
fingers again with an air of triumphant menace. "To the Devil with your
witnesses! To the Devil with your produced! To the Devil with yourself!
What? Do I know what I know, for that? Have I my commodity on sale,
for that? Bah, poor debtor! You have interrupted my little project. Let it
pass. How then? What remains? To you, nothing; to me, all. Produce *me*?
Is that what you want? I will produce myself, only too quickly. Contrabandist! Give me pen, ink, and paper."

Cavalletto got up again as before, and laid them before him in his former
manner. Rigaud, after some villanous thinking and smiling, wrote and
read aloud as follows:

"To Mrs. Clennam.
"Wait answer.

"Prison of the Marshalsea.
"At the apartment of your son.

"Dear Madame,
    "I am in despair to be informed to-day by our prisoner here (who
has had the goodness to employ spies to seek me, living for politic reasons
in retirement), that you have had fears for my safety.

"Re-assure yourself, dear madame. I am well, I am strong and constant.

"With the greatest impatience I should fly to your house, but that I
foresee it to be possible, under the circumstances, that you will not yet
have quite definitively arranged the little proposition I have had the
honor to submit to you. I name one week from this day, for a last final
visit on my part; when you will unconditionally accept it or reject it, with
its train of consequences.

"I suppress my ardor to embrace you and achieve this interesting
business, in order that you may have leisure to adjust its details to our
perfect mutual satisfaction.

"In the meanwhile, it is not too much to propose (our prisoner having deranged my housekeeping), that my expenses of lodging and nourishment at an hotel shall be paid by you.

"Receive, dear madame, the assurance of my highest and most distinguished consideration,

"RIGAUD BLANDOIS.

"A thousand friendships to that dear Flintwinch.

"I kiss the hands of Madame F."

When he had finished this epistle, Rigaud folded it, and tossed it with a flourish at Clennam's feet. "Hola you! Apropos of producing, let somebody produce that at its address, and produce the answer here."

"Cavalletto," said Arthur. "Will you take this fellow's letter?"

But, Cavalletto's significant finger again expressing that his post was at the door to keep watch over Rigaud, now he had found him with so much trouble, and that the duty of his post was to sit on the floor backed up by the door, looking at Rigaud and holding his own ankles,—Signor Panco once more volunteered. His services being accepted, Cavalletto suffered the door to open barely wide enough to admit of his squeezing himself out, and immediately shut it on him.

"Touch me with a finger, touch me with an epithet, question my superiority as I sit here drinking my wine at my pleasure," said Rigaud, "and I'll follow the letter and cancel my week's grace. *You* wanted me? You have got me! How do you like me?"

"You know," returned Clennam, with a bitter sense of his helplessness, "that when I sought you, I was not a prisoner."

"To the Devil with you and your prison," retorted Rigaud, leisurely, as he took from his pocket a case containing the materials for making cigarettes, and employed his facile hands in folding a few for present use; "I care for neither of you. Contrabandist! A light."

Again Cavalletto got up, and gave him what he wanted. There had been something dreadful in the noiseless skill of his cold, white hands, with the fingers lithely twisting about and twining over one another like serpents. Clennam could not prevent himself from shuddering inwardly, as if he had been looking on at a nest of those creatures.

"Hola, Pig!" cried Rigaud, with a noisy, stimulating cry, as if Cavalletto were an Italian horse or mule. "What! The infernal old jail was a respectable one to this. There was dignity in the bars and stones of that place. It was a prison for men. But this? Bah! A hospital for imbeciles!"

He smoked his cigarette out, with his ugly smile so fixed upon his face, that he looked as though he were smoking with his drooping beak of a nose, rather than his mouth; like a fancy in a weird picture. When he had lighted a second cigarette at the still-burning end of the first, he said to Clennam:

"One must pass the time in the madman's absence. One must talk. One can't drink strong wine all day long, or I would have another bottle. She's handsome, sir. Though not exactly to my taste, still, by the Thunder and the Lightning! handsome. I felicitate you on your admiration."

"I neither know nor ask," said Clennam, "of whom you speak."

"Della bella Gowana, sir, as they say in Italy. Of the Gowan, the fair Gowan."

"Of whose husband you were the—follower, I think?"

"Sir? Follower? You are insolent. The friend."

"Do you sell all your friends?"

Rigaud took his cigarette from his mouth, and eyed him with a momentary revelation of surprise. But, he put it between his lips again, as he answered with coolness:

"I sell anything that commands a price. How do your lawyers live, your politicians, your intriguers, your men of the Exchange? How do you live? How do you come here? Have you sold no friend? Lady of mine! I rather think, yes!"

Clennam turned away from him towards the window, and sat looking out at the wall.

"Effectively, sir," said Rigaud, "Society sells itself and sells me: and I sell Society. I perceive you have acquaintance with another lady. Also handsome. A strong spirit. Let us see. How do they call her? Wade."

He received no answer, but could easily discern that he had hit the mark.

"Yes!" he went on, "that handsome lady and strong spirit addresses me in the street, and I am not insensible. I respond. That handsome lady and strong spirit does me the favor to remark, in full confidence, 'I have my curiosity, and I have my chagrins. You are not more than ordinarily honorable, perhaps?' I announce myself, 'Madame, a gentleman from the birth, and a gentleman to the death; but *not* more than ordinarily honorable. I despise such a weak fantasy.' Thereupon she is pleased to compliment. 'The difference between you and the rest is,' she answers, 'that you say so.' For, she knows Society. I accept her congratulations with gallantry and politeness. Politeness and little gallantries are inseparable from my character. She then makes a proposition, which is, in effect, that she has seen us much together; that it appears to her that I am for the passing time the cat of the house, the friend of the family; that her curiosity and her chagrins awaken the fancy to be acquainted with their movements, to know the manner of their life, how the fair Gowana is beloved, how the fair Gowana is cherished, and so on. She is not rich, but offers such and such little recompenses for the little cares and derangements of such services; and I graciously—to do everything graciously is a part of my character—consent to accept them. O yes! So goes the world. It is the mode."

Though Clennam's back was turned while he spoke, and thenceforth to the end of the interview, he kept those glittering eyes of his that were too near together, upon him, and evidently saw in the very carriage of the head, as he passed, with his braggart recklessness, from clause to clause of what he said, that he was saying nothing which Clennam did not already know.

"Whoof! The Fair Gowana!" he said, lighting a third cigarette with a sound as if his lightest breath could blow her away. "Charming, but imprudent! For it was not well of the fair Gowana to make mysteries of letters from old lovers, in her bedchamber on the mountain, that her husband might not see them. No, no. That was not well. Whoof! The Gowana was mistaken there."

"I earnestly hope," cried Arthur aloud, "that Pancks may not be long gone, for this man's presence pollutes the room."

"Aye! But he'll flourish here, and everywhere," said Rigaud, with an exulting look and snap of his fingers. "He always has; he always will!" Stretching his body out on the only three chairs in the room besides that on which Clennam sat, he sang, smiting himself on the breast as the gallant personage of the song:

> "Who passes by this road so late?
> Compagnon de la Majolaine;
> Who passes by this road so late?
> Always gay!

Sing the Refrain, pig! You could sing it once, in another jail. Sing it! Or, by every Saint who was stoned to death, I'll be affronted and compromising; and then some people who are not dead yet, had better have been stoned along with them!

> Of all the king's knights 'tis the flower,
> Compagnon de la Majolaine;
> Of all the king's knights 'tis the flower,
> Always gay!"

Partly in his old habit of submission, partly because his not doing it might injure his benefactor, and partly because he would as soon do it as anything else, Cavalletto took up the Refrain this time. Rigaud laughed, and fell to smoking with his eyes shut.

Possibly another quarter of an hour elapsed before Mr. Pancks's step was heard upon the stairs, but the interval seemed to Clennam insupportably long. His step was attended by another step; and, when Cavalletto opened the door, he admitted Mr. Pancks and Mr. Flintwinch. The latter was no sooner visible, than Rigaud rushed at him and embraced him boisterously.

"How do you find yourself, sir?" said Mr. Flintwinch, as soon as he could disengage himself, which he struggled to do with very little ceremony. "Thank you, no; I don't want any more." This was in reference to another menace of affection from his recovered friend. "Well, Arthur. You remember what I said to you about sleeping dogs and missing ones. It's come true, you see."

He was as imperturbable as ever, to all appearance, and nodded his head in a moralising way as he looked round the room.

"And this is the Marshalsea prison for debt!" said Mr. Flintwinch. "Hah! You have brought your pigs to a very indifferent market, Arthur."

If Arthur had patience, Rigaud had not. He took his little Flintwinch, with fierce playfulness, by the two lappels of his coat, and cried:

"To the Devil with the Market, to the Devil with the Pigs, and to the Devil with the Pig-Driver! Now! Give me the answer to my letter."

"If you can make it convenient to let go a moment, sir," returned Mr. Flintwinch, "I'll first hand Mr. Arthur a little note that I have for him."

He did so. It was in his mother's maimed writing, on a slip of paper, and contained only these words:

"I hope it is enough that you have ruined yourself. Rest contented without more ruin. Jeremiah Flintwinch is my messenger and representative. Your affectionate M. C."

Clennam read this twice, in silence, and then tore it to pieces. Rigaud in the meanwhile stepped into a chair, and sat himself on the back, with his feet upon the seat.

"Now, Beau Flintwinch," he said, when he had closely watched the note to its destruction, "the answer to my letter?"

"Mrs. Clennam did not write it, Mr. Blandois, her hands being cramped, and she thinking it as well to send it verbally by me." Mr. Flintwinch screwed this out of himself, unwillingly and rustily. "She sends her compliments, and says she doesn't on the whole wish to term you unreasonable, and that she agrees. But without prejudicing the appointment that stands for this day week."

Monsieur Rigaud, after indulging in a fit of laughter, descended from his throne, saying "Good! I go to seek an hotel!" But, there his eyes encountered Cavalletto, who was still at his post.

"Come, Pig," he added. "I have had you for a follower against my will; now, I'll have you against yours. I tell you, my little reptiles, I am born to be served. I demand the service of this contrabandist as my domestic, until this day week."

In answer to Cavalletto's look of enquiry, Clennam made him a sign to go; but he added aloud, "unless you are afraid of him." Cavalletto replied with a very emphatic finger-negative. "No, master, I am not afraid of him, when I no more keep it secretementally that he was once my comrade." Rigaud took no notice of either remark, until he had lighted his last cigarette and was quite ready for walking.

"Afraid of him," he said then, looking round upon them all. "Whoof! My children, my babies, my little dolls, you are all afraid of him. You give

him his bottle of wine here; you give him meat, drink, and lodging, there;
you dare not touch him with a finger or an epithet. No. It is his character
to triumph! Whoof!

> Of all the king's knights he's the flower,
> And he's always gay!"

With this adaptation of the Refrain to himself, he stalked out of the
room, closely followed by Cavalletto, whom perhaps he had pressed into
his service because he tolerably well knew it would not be easy to get rid
of him. Mr. Flintwinch, after scraping his chin and looking about with
caustic disparagement of the Pig-Market, nodded to Arthur, and followed.
Mr. Pancks, still penitent and depressed, followed too; after receiving
with great attention a secret word or two of instructions from Arthur, and
whispering back that he would see this affair out, and stand by it to the
end. The prisoner, with the feeling that he was more despised, more
scorned and repudiated, more helpless, altogether more miserable and
fallen, than before, was left alone again.

CHAPTER XXIX

A PLEA IN THE MARSHALSEA

HAGGARD anxiety and remorse are bad companions to be barred up
with. Brooding all day, and resting very little indeed at night, will not
arm a man against misery. Next morning, Clennam felt that his health was
sinking, as his spirits had already sunk, and that the weight under which
he bent was bearing him down.

Night after night, he had arisen from his bed of wretchedness at
twelve or one o'clock, and had sat at his window watching the sickly lamps
in the yard, and looking upward for the first wan trace of day, hours before
it was possible that the sky could show it to him. Now, when the night
came, he could not even persuade himself to undress.

For, a burning restlessness set in, an agonised impatience of the prison,
and a conviction that he was going to break his heart and die there, which
caused him indescribable suffering. His dread and hatred of the place
became so intense that he felt it a labor to draw his breath in it. The sensation of being stifled, sometimes so overpowered him, that he would stand
at the window holding his throat and gasping. At the same time, a longing
for other air, and a yearning to be beyond the blind blank wall, made him
feel as if he must go mad with the ardor of the desire.

Many other prisoners had had experience of this condition before
him, and its violence and continuity had worn themselves out in their

cases, as they did in his. Two nights and a day exhausted it. It came back by fits, but those grew fainter and returned at lengthening intervals. A desolate calm succeeded; and the middle of the week found him settled down in the despondency of low, slow fever.

With Cavalletto and Pancks away, he had no visitors to fear but Mr. and Mrs. Plornish. His anxiety, in reference to that worthy pair, was that they should not come near him; for, in the morbid state of his nerves, he sought to be left alone, and spared the being seen so subdued and weak. He wrote a note to Mrs. Plornish representing himself as occupied with his affairs, and bound by the necessity of devoting himself to them, to remain for a time even without the pleasant interruption of a sight of her kind face. As to Young John, who looked in daily at a certain hour, when the turnkeys were relieved, to ask if he could do anything for him; he always made a pretence of being engaged in writing, and to answer cheerfully in the negative. The subject of their only long conversation had never been revived between them. Through all these changes of unhappiness, however, it had never lost its hold on Clennam's mind.

The sixth day of the appointed week was a moist, hot, misty day. It seemed as though the prison's poverty, and shabbiness, and dirt, were growing, in the sultry atmosphere. With an aching head and a weary heart, Clennam had watched the miserable night out, listening to the fall of rain on the yard pavement, thinking of its softer fall upon the country earth. A blurred circle of yellow haze had risen up in the sky in lieu of sun, and he had watched the patch it put upon his wall, like a bit of the prison's raggedness. He had heard the gates open; and the badly shod feet that waited outside shuffle in; and the sweeping, and pumping, and moving about, begin, which commenced the prison morning. So ill and faint, that he was obliged to rest many times in the process of getting himself washed, he had at length crept to his chair by the open window. In it he sat dozing, while the old woman who arranged his room went through her morning's work.

Light of head with want of sleep and want of food (his appetite, and even his sense of taste, having forsaken him), he had been two or three times conscious, in the night, of going astray. He had heard fragments of tunes and songs, in the warm wind, which he knew had no existence. Now that he began to doze in exhaustion, he heard them again; and voices seemed to address him, and he answered, and started.

Dozing and dreaming, without the power of reckoning time, so that a minute might have been an hour and an hour a minute, some abiding impression of a garden stole over him—a garden of flowers, with a damp warm wind gently stirring their scents. It required such a painful effort to lift his head for the purpose of enquiring into this, or enquiring into anything, that the impression appeared to have become quite an old and importunate one when he looked round. Beside the tea-cup on his table he saw, then, a blooming nosegay: a wonderful handful of the choicest and most lovely flowers.

Nothing had ever appeared so beautiful in his sight. He took them up and inhaled their fragrance, and he lifted them to his hot head, and he put them down and opened his parched hands to them, as cold hands are opened to receive the cheering of a fire. It was not until he had delighted in them for some time, that he wondered who had sent them; and opened his door to ask the woman who must have put them there, how they had come into her hands. But, she was gone, and seemed to have been long gone; for the tea she had left for him on the table was cold. He tried to drink some, but could not bear the odor of it; so he crept back to his chair by the open window, and put the flowers on the little round table of old.

When the first faintness consequent on having moved about had left him, he subsided into his former state. One of the night-tunes was playing in the wind, when the door of his room seemed to open to a light touch, and, after a moment's pause, a quiet figure seemed to stand there, with a black mantle on it. It seemed to draw the mantle off and drop it on the ground, and then it seemed to be his Little Dorrit in her old, worn dress. It seemed to tremble, and to clasp its hands, and to smile, and to burst into tears.

He roused himself, and cried out. And then he saw, in the loving, pitying, sorrowing, dear face, as in a mirror, how changed he was; and she came towards him; and with her hands laid on his breast to keep him in his chair, and with her knees upon the floor at his feet, and with her lips raised up to kiss him, and with her tears dropping on him as the rain from Heaven had dropped upon the flowers, Little Dorrit, a living presence, called him by his name.

"O, my best friend! Dear Mr. Clennam, don't let me see you weep! Unless you weep with pleasure to see me. I hope you do. Your own poor child come back!"

So faithful, tender, and unspoiled by Fortune. In the sound of her voice, in the light of her eyes, in the touch of her hands, so Angelically comforting and true!

As he embraced her, she said to him, "They never told me you were ill," and drawing an arm softly round his neck, laid his head upon her bosom, put a hand upon his head, and resting her cheek upon that hand, nursed him as lovingly, and GOD knows as innocently, as she had nursed her father in that room when she had been but a baby, needing all the care from others that she took of them.

When he could speak, he said, "Is it possible that you have come to me? And in this dress?"

"I hoped you would like me better in this dress than any other. I have always kept it by me, to remind me: though I wanted no reminding. I am not alone, you see. I have brought an old friend with me."

Looking round, he saw Maggy in her big cap which had been long abandoned, with a basket on her arm as in the bygone days, chuckling rapturously.

"It was only yesterday evening that I came to London with my brother. I sent round to Mrs. Plornish almost as soon as we arrived, that I might hear of you and let you know I had come. Then I heard that you were here. Did you happen to think of me in the night? I almost believe you must have thought of me a little. I thought of you so anxiously, and it appeared so long to morning."

"I have thought of you——" he hesitated what to call her. She perceived it in an instant.

"You have not spoken to me by my right name yet. You know what my right name always is with you."

"I have thought of you, Little Dorrit, every day, every hour, every minute, since I have been here."

"Have you? Have you?"

He saw the bright delight of her face, and the flush that kindled in it, with a feeling of shame. He, a broken, bankrupt, sick, dishonored, prisoner.

"I was here, before the gates were opened, but I was afraid to come straight to you. I should have done you more harm than good, at first; for the prison was so familiar and yet so strange, and it brought back so many remembrances of my poor father, and of you too, that at first it overpowered me. But, we went to Mr. Chivery before we came to the gate, and he brought us in, and got John's room for us—my poor old room, you know—and we waited there a little. I brought the flowers to the door, but you didn't hear me."

She looked something more womanly than when she had gone away, and the ripening touch of the Italian sun was visible upon her face. But, otherwise she was quite unchanged. The same deep, timid earnestness that he had always seen in her, and never without emotion, he saw still. If it had a new meaning that smote him to the heart, the change was in his perception, not in her.

She took off her old bonnet, hung it in the old place, and noiselessly began, with Maggy's help, to make his room as fresh and neat as it could be made, and to sprinkle it with a pleasant smelling water. When that was done, the basket which was filled with grapes and other fruit, was unpacked, and all its contents were quietly put away. When that was done, a moment's whisper dispatched Maggy to dispatch somebody else to fill the basket again; which soon came back replenished with new stores, from which a present provision of cooling drink and jelly, and a prospective supply of roast chicken and wine and water, were the first extracts. These various arrangements completed, she took out her old needlecase to make him a curtain for his window; and thus, with a quiet reigning in the room, that seemed to diffuse itself through the else noisy prison, he found himself composed in his chair with Little Dorrit working at his side.

To see the modest head again bent down over its task, and the nimble fingers busy at their old work—though she was not so absorbed in it but that her compassionate eyes were often raised to his face, and, when they drooped again, had tears in them—to be so consoled and comforted, and to believe that all the devotion of this great nature was turned to him in his adversity, to pour out its inexhaustible wealth of goodness upon him, did not steady Clennam's trembling voice or hand, or strengthen him in his weakness. Yet, it inspired him with an inward fortitude, that rose with his love. And how dearly he loved her, now, what words can tell!

As they sat side by side, in the shadow of the wall, the shadow fell like light upon him. She would not let him speak much, and he lay back in his chair, looking at her. Now and again, she would rise and give him the glass that he might drink, or would smooth the resting-place of his head; then she would gently resume her seat by him, and bend over her work again.

The shadow moved with the sun, but she never moved from his side, except to wait upon him. The sun went down, and she was still there. She had done her work now, and her hand, faltering on the arm of his chair since its last tending of him, was hesitating there yet. He laid his hand upon it, and it clasped him with a trembling supplication.

"Dear Mr. Clennam, I must say something to you before I go. I have put it off from hour to hour, but I must say it."

"I too, dear Little Dorrit. I have put off what I must say."

She nervously moved her hand towards his lips as if to stop him; then it dropped, trembling, into its former place.

"I am not going abroad again. My brother is, but I am not. He was always attached to me, and he is so grateful to me now—so much too grateful, for it is only because I happened to be with him in his illness—that he says I shall be free to stay where I like best, and to do what I like best. He only wishes me to be happy, he says."

There was one bright star shining in the sky. She looked up at it while she spoke, as if it were the fervent purpose of her own heart shining above her.

"You will understand, I dare say, without my telling you, that my brother has come home to find my dear father's will, and to take possession of his property. He says, if there is a will, he is sure I shall be left rich; and if there is none, that he will make me so."

He would have spoken; but she put up her trembling hand again, and he stopped.

"I have no use for money, I have no wish for it. It would be of no value at all to me, but for your sake. I could not be rich, and you here. I must always be much worse than poor, with you distressed. Will you let me lend you all I have? Will you let me give it to you? Will you let me show you that I never have forgotten, that I never can forget, your protection of me when this was my home? Dear Mr. Clennam, make me of all the world the happiest, by saying Yes! Make me as happy as I can be in leaving you here, by saying nothing to-night, and letting me go away with the hope that you will think of it kindly; and that for my sake—not for yours, for mine, for nobody's but mine!—you will give me the greatest joy I can experience on earth, the joy of knowing that I have been serviceable to you, and that I have paid some little of the great debt of my affection and gratitude. I can't say what I wish to say. I can't visit you here where I have lived so long, I can't think of you here where I have seen so much, and be as calm and comforting as I ought. My tears will make their way. I cannot keep them back. But pray, pray, pray, do not turn from your Little Dorrit, now, in your affliction! Pray, pray, pray, I beg you and implore you with all my grieving heart, my friend—my dear!—take all I have, and make it a Blessing to me!"

The star had shone on her face until now, when her face sank upon his hand and her own.

It had grown darker when he raised her in his encircling arm, and softly answered her.

"No, darling Little Dorrit. No, my child. I must not hear of such a sacrifice. Liberty and hope would be so dear, bought at such a price, that I could never support their weight, never bear the reproach of possessing them. But, with what ardent thankfulness and love I say this, I may call Heaven to witness!"

"And yet you will not let me be faithful to you in your affliction?"

"Say, dearest Little Dorrit, and yet I will try to be faithful to you. If, in the bygone days when this was your home and when this was your dress, I had understood myself (I speak only of myself) better, and had read the secrets of my own breast more distinctly; if, through my reserve and self-mistrust, I had discerned a light that I see brightly now when it has passed far away, and my weak footsteps can never overtake it; if I had then known, and told you that I loved and honored you, not as the poor child I used to call you, but as a woman whose true hand would raise me high above myself, and make me a far happier and better man; if I had so used the opportunity there is no recalling—as I wish I had, O I wish I had!—and if something had kept us apart then, when I was moderately thriving, and when you were poor; I might have met your noble offer of your fortune, dearest girl, with other words than these, and still have blushed to touch it. But, as it is, I must never touch it, never!"

She besought him, more pathetically and earnestly, with her little supplicatory hand, than she could have done in any words.

"I am disgraced enough, my Little Dorrit. I must not descend so low as that, and carry you—so dear, so generous, so good—down with me. GOD bless you, GOD reward you! It is past."

He took her in his arms, as if she had been his daughter.

"Always so much older, so much rougher, and so much less worthy, even what I was must be dismissed by both of us, and you must see me only as I am. I put this parting kiss upon your cheek, my child—who might have been more near to me, who never could have been more dear— a ruined man far removed from you, for ever separated from you, whose course is run, while yours is but beginning. I have not the courage to ask to be forgotten by you in my humiliation; but I ask to be remembered only as I am."

The bell began to ring, warning visitors to depart. He took her mantle from the wall, and tenderly wrapped it round her.

"One other word, my Little Dorrit. A hard one to me, but it is a necessary one. The time when you and this prison had anything in common, has long gone by. Do you understand?"

"O! you will never say to me," she cried, weeping bitterly, and holding up her clasped hands in entreaty, "that I am not to come back any more! You will surely not desert me so!"

"I would say it, if I could; but I have not the courage quite to shut out this dear face, and abandon all hope of its return. But do not come soon, do not come often! This is now a tainted place, and I well know that the taint of it clings to me. You belong to much brighter and better scenes. You are not to look back here, my Little Dorrit; you are to look away to very different and much happier paths. Again, GOD bless you in them! GOD reward you!"

Maggy, who had fallen into very low spirits, here cried, "Oh get him into a hospital; do get him into a hospital, Mother! He'll never look like his self again, if he an't got into a hospital. And then the little woman as was always a spinning at her wheel, she can go to the cupboard with the Princess and say, what do you keep the Chicking there for? and then they can take it out and give it to him, and then all be happy!"

The interruption was seasonable, for the bell had nearly rung itself out. Again tenderly wrapping her mantle about her, and taking her on his arm (though, but for her visit, he was almost too weak to walk), Arthur led Little Dorrit down-stairs. She was the last visitor to pass out at the Lodge, and the gate jarred heavily and hopelessly upon her.

With the funeral clang that it sounded into Arthur's heart, his sense of weakness returned. It was a toilsome journey up-stairs to his room, and he re-entered its dark solitary precincts, in unutterable misery.

When it was almost midnight, and the prison had long been quiet, a cautious creak came up the stairs, and a cautious tap of a key was given at his door. It was Young John. He glided in, in his stockings, and held the door closed, while he spoke in a whisper.

"It's against all rules, but I don't mind. I was determined to come through, and come to you."

"What is the matter?"

"Nothing's the matter, sir. I was waiting in the courtyard for Miss Dorrit when she came out. I thought you'd like some one to see that she was safe."

"Thank you, thank you! You took her home, John?"

"I saw her to her hotel. The same that Mr. Dorrit was at. Miss Dorrit walked all the way, and talked to me so kind, it quite knocked me over. Why do you think she walked instead of riding?"

"I don't know, John."

"To talk about you. She said to me, 'John, you was always honorable, and if you'll promise me that you will take care of him, and never let him want for help and comfort when I am not there, my mind will be at rest so far.' I promised her. And I'll stand by you," said John Chivery, "for ever!"

Clennam, much affected, stretched out his hand to this honest spirit.

"Before I take it," said John, looking at it, without coming from the door, "guess what message Miss Dorrit gave me."

Clennam shook his head.

"'Tell him,'" repeated John, in a distinct, though quavering voice, "'that his Little Dorrit sent him her undying love.' Now it's delivered. Have I been honorable, sir?"

"Very, very!"

"Will you tell Miss Dorrit I've been honorable, sir?"

"I will indeed."

"There's my hand, sir," said John, "and I'll stand by you for ever!"

After a hearty squeeze, he disappeared with the same cautious creak upon the stair, crept shoeless over the pavement of the yard, and, locking the gates behind him, passed out into the front where he had left his shoes. If the same way had been paved with burning ploughshares, it is not at all improbable that John would have traversed it with the same devotion, for the same purpose.

END OF No. XVIII

CHAPTER XXX

CLOSING IN

THE last day of the appointed week touched the bars of the Marshalsea gate. Black, all night, since the gate had clashed upon Little Dorrit, its iron stripes were turned by the early-glowing sun into stripes of gold. Far aslant across the city, over its jumbled roofs, and through the open tracery of its church towers, struck the long bright rays, bars of the prison of this lower world.

Throughout the day, the old house within the gateway remained untroubled by any visitors. But, when the sun was low, three men turned in at the gateway and made for the dilapidated house.

Rigaud was the first, and walked by himself, smoking. Mr. Baptist was the second, and jogged close after him, looking at no other object. Mr. Pancks was the third, and carried his hat under his arm for the liberation of his restive hair; the weather being extremely hot. They all came together at the door-steps.

"You pair of madmen!" said Rigaud, facing about. "Don't go yet!"

"We don't mean to," said Mr. Pancks.

Giving him a dark glance in acknowledgement of his answer, Rigaud knocked loudly. He had charged himself with drink for the playing out of his game, and was impatient to begin. He had hardly finished one long resounding knock, when he turned to the knocker again and began another. That was not yet finished, when Jeremiah Flintwinch opened the door, and they all clanked into the stone hall. Rigaud, thrusting Mr. Flintwinch aside, proceeded straight up-stairs. His two attendants followed him, Mr. Flintwinch followed them, and they all came trooping into Mrs. Clennam's quiet room. It was in its usual state; except that one of the windows was wide open, and Affery sat on its old-fashioned window-seat, mending a stocking. The usual articles were on the little table; the usual deadened fire was in the grate; the bed had its usual pall upon it; and the mistress of all sat on her black bier-like sofa, propped up by her black angular bolster that was like the head'sman's block.

Yet there was a nameless air of preparation in the room, as if it were strung up for an occasion. From what the room derived it—every one of its small variety of objects being in the fixed spot it had occupied for years—no one could have said without looking attentively at its mistress, and that, too, with a previous knowledge of her face. Although her unchanging black dress was in every plait precisely as of old, and her unchanging attitude was rigidly preserved, a very slight additional setting of her features and contraction of her gloomy forehead was so powerfully marked, that it marked everything about her.

"Who are these!" she said, wonderingly, as the two attendants entered. "What do these people want here?"

"Who are these, dear madame, is it?" returned Rigaud. "Faith, they are friends of your son the prisoner. And what do they want here, is it? Death, madame, I don't know. You will do well to ask them."

"You know you told us, at the door, not to go yet," said Pancks.

"And you know you told me, at the door, you didn't mean to go," retorted Rigaud. "In a word, madame, permit me to present two spies of the prisoner's—madmen, but spies. If you wish them to remain here during our little conversation, say the word. It is nothing to me."

"Why should I wish them to remain here?" said Mrs. Clennam. "What have I to do with them?"

"Then, dearest madame," said Rigaud, throwing himself into an arm-chair so heavily that the old room trembled, "you will do well to dismiss them. It is your affair. They are not *my* spies, not *my* rascals."

"Hark! You Pancks," said Mrs. Clennam, bending her brows upon him angrily, "you Casby's clerk! Attend to your employer's business and your own. Go. And take that other man with you."

"Thank you, ma'am," returned Mr. Pancks, "I am glad to say I see no objection to our both retiring. We have done all we undertook to do for Mr. Clennam. His constant anxiety has been (and it grew worse upon him when he became a prisoner), that this agreeable gentleman should be brought back here, to the place from which he slipped away. Here he is—brought back. And I will say," added Mr. Pancks, "to his ill-looking face, that in my opinion the world would be no worse for his slipping out of it altogether."

"Your opinion is not asked," answered Mrs. Clennam. "Go."

"I am sorry not to leave you in better company, ma'am," said Pancks; "and sorry, too, that Mr. Clennam can't be present. It's my fault, that is."

"You mean his own," she returned.

"No, I mean mine, ma'am," said Pancks, "for it was my misfortune to lead him into a ruinous investment." (Mr. Pancks still clung to that word, and never said speculation.) "Though I can prove by figures," added Mr. Pancks with an anxious countenance, "that it ought to have been a good investment. I have gone over it since it failed, every day of my life, and it comes out—regarded as a question of figures—triumphant. The present is not a time or place," Mr. Pancks pursued, with a longing glance into his hat, where he kept his calculations, "for entering upon the figures; but the figures are not to be disputed. Mr. Clennam ought to have been at this moment in his carriage-and-pair, and I ought to have been worth from three to five thousand pound."

Mr. Pancks put his hair erect with a general aspect of confidence, that could hardly have been surpassed if he had had the amount in his pocket. These incontrovertible figures had been the occupation of every moment of his leisure since he had lost his money, and were destined to afford him consolation to the end of his days.

"However," said Mr. Pancks, "enough of that. Altro, old boy, you have seen the figures, and you know how they come out." Mr. Baptist, who had not the slightest arithmetical power of compensating himself in this way, nodded, with a fine display of bright teeth.

At whom Mr. Flintwinch had been looking, and to whom he then said: "Oh! It's you, is it? I thought I remembered your face, but I wasn't certain till I saw your teeth. Ah! yes, to be sure. It was this officious refugee," said Jeremiah to Mrs. Clennam, "who came knocking at the door, on the night when Arthur and Chatterbox were here, and who asked me a whole Catechism of questions about Mr. Blandois."

"It is true," Mr. Baptist cheerfully admitted. "And behold him, padrone! I have found him, consequentementally."

"I shouldn't have objected," returned Mr. Flintwinch, "to your having broken your neck consequentementally."

"And now," said Mr. Pancks, whose eye had often stealthily wandered to the window-seat, and the stocking that was being mended there, "I've only one other word to say before I go. If Mr. Clennam was here—but unfortunately, though he has so far got the better of this fine gentleman as to return him to this place against his will, he is ill and in prison—ill and in prison, poor fellow—if he was here," said Mr. Pancks, taking one step aside towards the window-seat, and laying his right hand upon the stocking; "he would say, 'Affery, tell your dreams!' "

Mr. Pancks held up his right forefinger between his nose and the stocking, with a ghostly air of warning, turned, steamed out, and towed Mr. Baptist after him. The house-door was heard to close upon them, their steps were heard passing over the dull pavement of the echoing courtyard, and still nobody had added a word. Mrs. Clennam and Jeremiah had exchanged a look; and had then looked, and looked still, at Affery; who sat mending the stocking with great assiduity.

"Come!" said Mr. Flintwinch at length, screwing himself a curve or two in the direction of the window-seat, and rubbing the palms of his hands on his coat-tail as if he were preparing them to do something: "Whatever has to be said among us, had better be begun to be said, without more loss of time.—So, Affery, my woman, take yourself away!"

In a moment, Affery had thrown the stocking down, started up, caught hold of the window-sill with her right hand, lodged herself upon the window-seat with her right knee, and was flourishing her left hand, beating expected assailants off.

"No, I won't, Jeremiah—no I won't—no I won't! I won't go, I'll stay here. I'll hear all I don't know, and say all I know. I will, at last, if I die for it. I will, I will, I will, I will!"

Mr. Flintwinch, stiffening with indignation and amazement, moistened the fingers of one hand at his lips, softly described a circle with them in the palm of the other hand, and continued with a menacing grin to screw himself in the direction of his wife: gasping some remark as he advanced, of which, in his choking anger, only the words "Such a dose!" were audible.

"Not a bit nearer, Jeremiah!" cried Affery, never ceasing to beat the air. "Don't come a bit nearer to me, or I'll rouse the neighbourhood! I'll throw myself out of window! I'll scream Fire and Murder! I'll wake the dead! Stop where you are, or I'll make shrieks enough to wake the dead!"

The determined voice of Mrs. Clennam echoed "Stop!" Jeremiah had stopped already.

"It is closing in, Flintwinch. Let her alone. Affery, do you turn against me after these many years?"

"I do, if it's turning against you to hear what I don't know, and say what I know. I have broke out now, and I can't go back. I am determined to do it. I will do it, I will, I will, I will! If that's turning against you, yes, I turn against both of you two clever ones. I told Arthur when he first come home, to stand up against you. I told him it was no reason, because I was afeard of my life of you, that he should be. All manner of things have been a going on since then, and I won't be run up by Jeremiah, nor yet I won't be dazed, and scared, nor made a party to I don't know what, no more. I won't, I won't, I won't! I'll up for Arthur when he has nothing left, and is ill, and in prison, and can't up for himself. I will, I will, I will, I will!"

"How do you know, you heap of confusion," asked Mrs. Clennam sternly, "that in doing what you are doing now, you are even serving Arthur?"

"I don't know nothing rightly about anything," said Affery; "and if ever you said a true word in your life, it's when you call me a heap of confusion, for you two clever ones have done your most to make me such. You married me whether I liked it or not, and you've led me, pretty well ever since, such a life of dreaming and frightening as never was known, and what do you expect me to be but a heap of confusion? You wanted to make me such, and I am such; but I won't submit no longer; no, I won't, I won't, I won't, I wont!" She was still beating the air against all comers.

After gazing at her in silence, Mrs. Clennam turned to Rigaud. "You see and hear this foolish creature. Do you object to such a piece of distraction remaining where she is?"

"I, madame?" he replied, "do I? That's a question for you."

"I do not," she said, gloomily. "There is little left to choose now. Flintwinch, it is closing in."

Mr. Flintwinch replied by directing a look of red vengeance at his wife, and then, as if to pinion himself from falling upon her, screwed his crossed arms into the breast of his waistcoat, and with his chin very near one of his elbows stood in a corner, watching Rigaud in the oddest attitude. Rigaud for his part arose from his chair, and seated himself on the table, with his legs dangling. In this easy attitude, he met Mrs. Clennam's set face, with his moustache going up and his nose coming down.

"Madame, I am a gentleman——"

"Of whom," she interrupted in her steady tones, "I have heard disparagement, in connexion with a French jail and an accusation of murder."

He kissed his hand to her, with his exaggerated gallantry. "Perfectly. Exactly. Of a lady too! What absurdity! How incredible! I had the honor of making a great success then; I hope to have the honor of making a great success now. I kiss your hands. Madame, I am a gentleman (I was going to observe), who when he says, 'I will definitely finish this or that affair at this present sitting,' does definitely finish it. I announce to you, that we are arrived at our last sitting, on our little business. You do me the favor to follow, and to comprehend?"

She kept her eyes fixed upon him with a frown. "Yes."

"Further, I am a gentleman to whom mere mercenary trade-bargains are unknown, but to whom money is always acceptable as the means of pursuing his pleasures. You do me the favor to follow, and to comprehend?"

"Scarcely necessary to ask, one would say. Yes."

"Further, I am a gentleman of the softest and sweetest disposition, but who, if trifled with, becomes enraged. Noble natures under such circumstances become enraged. I possess a noble nature. When the lion is awakened—that is to say, when I enrage—the satisfaction of my animosity is as acceptable to me as money. You always do me the favor to follow, and to comprehend?"

"Yes," she answered, somewhat louder than before.

"Do not let me derange you; pray be tranquil. I have said we are now arrived at our last sitting. Allow me to recall the two sittings we have held."

"It is not necessary."

"Death, madame," he burst out, "it's my fancy! Besides, it clears the way. The first sitting was limited. I had the honor of making your acquaintance—of presenting my letter; I am a Knight of Industry, at your service, madame, but my polished manners had won me so much of success, as a master of languages, among your compatriots who are as stiff as their own starch is to one another, but are ever ready to relax to a foreign gentleman of polished manners—and of observing one or two little things," he glanced around the room and smiled, "about this honorable house, to know which was necessary to assure me, and to convince me that I had the distinguished pleasure of making the acquaintance of the lady I sought. I achieved this. I gave my word of honor, to our dear Flintwinch, that I would return. I gracefully departed."

Her face neither acquiesced nor demurred. The same when he paused and when he spoke, it as yet showed him always the one attentive frown, and the dark revelation before mentioned of her being nerved for the occasion.

"I say, gracefully departed, because it was graceful to retire without alarming a lady. To be morally graceful, not less than physically, is a part of the character of Rigaud Blandois. It was also politic, as leaving you, with something overhanging you, to expect me again with a little anxiety, on a day not named. But your slave is politic. By Heaven, madame, politic! Let us return. On the day not named, I have again the honor to render myself at your house. I intimate that I have something to sell, which, if not bought, will compromise madame whom I highly esteem. I explain myself generally. I demand—I think it was a thousand pounds. Will you correct me?"

Thus forced to speak, she replied, with constraint, "You demanded as much as a thousand pounds."

"I demand at present, Two. Such are the evils of delay. But to return once more. We are not accordant; we differ on that occasion. I am playful; playfulness is a part of my amiable character. Playfully, I become as one slain and hidden. For, it may alone be worth half the sum, to madame, to be freed from the suspicions that my droll idea awakens. Accident and spies intermix themselves against my playfulness, and spoil the fruit, perhaps—who knows? only you and Flintwinch—when it is just ripe. Thus, madame, I am here for the last time. Listen! Definitely the last."

As he struck his straggling boot-heels against the flap of the table, meeting her frown with an insolent gaze, he began to change his tone for a fiercer one.

"Bah! Stop an instant! Let us advance by steps. Here is my Hotel-note to be paid, according to contract. Five minutes hence we may be at daggers' points. I'll not leave it till then, or you'll cheat me. Pay it! Count me the money!"

"Take it from his hand and pay it, Flintwinch," said Mrs. Clennam.

He spirted it into Mr. Flintwinch's face, when the old man advanced to take it; and held forth his hand, repeating noisily, "Pay it! Count it out! Good money!" Jeremiah picked the bill up, looked at the total with a bloodshot eye, took a small canvass bag from his pocket, and told the amount into his hand.

Rigaud chinked the money, weighed it in his hand, threw it up a little way and caught it, chinked it again.

"The sound of it, to the bold Rigaud Blandois, is like the taste of fresh meat to the tiger. Say, then, madame. How much?"

He turned upon her suddenly, with a menacing gesture of the weighted hand that clenched the money, as if he were going to strike her with it.

"I tell you again, as I told you before, that we are not rich here, as you suppose us to be, and that your demand is excessive. I have not the present means of complying with such a demand, if I had ever so great an inclination."

"If!" cried Blandois. "Hear this lady with her If! Will you say that you have not the inclination?"

"I will say what presents itself to me, and not what presents itself to you."

"Say it then. As to the inclination. Quick! Come to the inclination, and I know what to do."

She was no quicker, and no slower, in her reply. "It would seem that you have obtained possession of a paper—or of papers—which I assuredly have the inclination to recover."

Rigaud, with a loud laugh, drummed his heels against the table, and chinked his money. "I think so! I believe you there!"

"The paper might be worth, to me, a sum of money. I cannot say how much, or how little."

"What the Devil!" he asked savagely. "Not after a week's grace to consider?"

"No! I will not, out of my scanty means—for I tell you again, we are poor here, and not rich—I will not offer any price for a power that I do not know the worst and the fullest extent of. This is the third time of your hinting and threatening. You must speak explicitly, or you may go where you will and do what you will. It is better to be torn to pieces at a spring, than to be a mouse at the caprice of such a cat."

He looked at her so hard with those eyes too near together, that the sinister sight of each, crossing that of the other, seemed to make the bridge of his hooked nose crooked. After a long survey, he said, with the further setting-off of his infernal smile:

"You are a bold woman!"

"I am a resolved woman."

"You always were. What? She always was; is it not so, my little Flintwinch?"

"Flintwinch, say nothing to him. It is for him to say here, and now, all he can; or to go hence, and do all he can. You know this to be our determination. Leave him to his action on it."

She did not shrink under his evil leer, or avoid it. He turned it upon her again, but she remained steady at the point to which she had fixed herself. He got off the table, placed a chair near the sofa, sat down in it, and leaned an arm upon the sofa close to her own, which he touched with his hand. Her face was ever frowning, attentive, and settled.

"It is your pleasure then, madame, that I shall relate a morsel of family history in this little family society," said Rigaud, with a warning play of his lithe fingers on her arm. "I am something of a doctor. Let me touch your pulse."

She suffered him to take her wrist in his hand. Holding it, he proceeded to say:

"A history of a strange marriage, and a strange mother, and a revenge, and a suppression.——Aye, aye, aye? This pulse is beating curiously! It appears to me that it doubles while I touch it. Are these the usual changes of your malady, madame?"

There was a struggle in her maimed arm as she twisted it away, but there was none in her face. On his face there was his own smile.

"I have lived an adventurous life. I am an adventurous character. I have known many adventurers; interesting spirits—amiable society! To one of them I owe my knowledge, and my proofs—I repeat it, estimable lady—proofs—of the ravishing little family history I go to commence. You will be charmed with it. But, bah! I forget. One should name a history. Shall I name it the history of a house? But, bah, again. There are so many houses. Shall I name it the history of this house?"

Leaning over the sofa, poised on two legs of his chair and his left elbow; that hand often tapping her arm, to beat his words home; his legs crossed; his right hand sometimes arranging his hair, sometimes smoothing his moustache, sometimes striking his nose, always threatening her whatever it did; coarse, insolent, rapacious, cruel, and powerful; he pursued his narrative at his ease.

"In fine, then, I name it the history of this house. I commence it. There live here, let us suppose, an uncle and nephew. The uncle, a rigid old gentleman of strong force of character; the nephew, habitually timid, repressed, and under constraint."

Mistress Affery, fixedly attentive in the window-seat, biting the rolled up end of her apron, and trembling from head to foot, here cried out, "Jeremiah, keep off from me! I've heerd in my dreams, of Arthur's father and his uncle. He's a talking of them. It was before my time here; but I've heerd in my dreams that Arthur's father was a poor, irresolute, frightened chap, who had had everything but his orphan life scared out of him when he was young, and that he had no voice in the choice of his wife even, but his uncle chose her. There she sits! I heerd it in my dreams, and you said it to her own self."

As Mr. Flintwinch shook his fist at her, and as Mrs. Clennam gazed upon her, Rigaud kissed his hand to her.

"Perfectly right, dear Madame Flintwinch. You have a genius for dreaming."

"I don't want none of your praises," returned Affery. "I don't want to have nothing at all to say to you. But Jeremiah said they was dreams, and I'll tell 'em as such!" Here she put her apron in her mouth again, as if she were stopping somebody else's mouth—perhaps Jeremiah's, which was chattering with threats as if he were grimly cold.

"Our beloved Madame Flintwinch," said Rigaud, "developing all of a sudden a fine susceptibility and spirituality, is right to a marvel. Yes. So runs the history. Monsieur, the uncle, commands the nephew to marry. Monsieur says to him in effect, 'My nephew, I introduce to you a lady of strong force of character, like myself: a resolved lady, a stern lady, a lady who has a will that can break the weak to powder: a lady without pity, without love, implacable, revengeful, cold as the stone, but raging as the fire.' Ah! what fortitude! Ah, what superiority of intellectual strength! Truly, a proud and noble character that I describe in the supposed words of Monsieur, the uncle. Ha, ha, ha! Death of my soul, I love the sweet lady!"

Mrs. Clennam's face had changed. There was a remarkable darkness of color on it and the brow was more contracted. "Madame, madame," said Rigaud, tapping her on the arm, as if his cruel hand were sounding a musical instrument, "I perceive I interest you. I perceive I awaken your sympathy. Let us go on!"

The drooping nose and the ascending moustache had, however, to be hidden for a moment with the white hand, before he could go on; he enjoyed the effect he made, so much.

"The nephew, being, as the lucid Madame Flintwinch has remarked, a poor devil who has had everything but his orphan life frightened and famished out of him —the nephew abases his head, and makes response; 'My uncle, it is to you to command. Do as you will!' Monsieur, the uncle, does as he will. It is what he always does. The auspicious nuptials take place; the newly married come home to this charming mansion; the lady is received, let us suppose, by Flintwinch. Hey, old intriguer?"

Jeremiah, with his eyes upon his mistress, made no reply. Rigaud looked from one to the other, struck his ugly nose, and made a clucking with his tongue.

"Soon, the lady makes a singular and exciting discovery. Thereupon, full of anger, full of jealousy, full of vengeance, she forms—see you, madame!—a scheme of retribution, the weight of which she ingeniously forces her crushed husband to bear himself, as well as execute upon her enemy. What superior intelligence!"

"Keep off, Jeremiah!" cried the palpitating Affery, taking her apron from her mouth again. "But it was one of my dreams that you told her, when you quarrelled with her one winter evening, at dusk—there she sits and you looking at her—that she oughtn't to have let Arthur, when he come home, suspect his father, only; that she had always had the strength and the power; and that she ought to have stood up more, to Arthur, for his father. It was in the same dream where you said to her that she was not—not something, but I don't know what, for she burst out tremendous and stopped you. You know the dream as well as I do. When you come down-stairs into the kitchen with the candle in your hand, and hitched my apron off my head. When you told me I had been dreaming. When you wouldn't believe the noises." After this explosion Affery put her apron into her mouth again; always keeping her hand on the window-sill, and her knee on the window-seat, ready to cry out or jump out, if her lord and master approached.

Rigaud had not lost a word of this.

"Haha!" he cried, lifting his eyebrows, folding his arms, and leaning back in his chair. "Assuredly, Madame Flintwinch is an oracle! How shall we interpret the oracle, you and I, and the old intriguer? He said that you were not, —— ? And you burst out and stopped him! What was it you were not? What is it you are not? Say then, madame!"

Under this ferocious banter, she sat breathing harder, and her mouth was troubled. Her lips quivered and opened, in spite of her utmost efforts to keep them still.

"Come then, madame! Speak, then! Our old intriguer said that you were not—— and you stopped him. He was going to say that you were not—what? I know already, but I want a little confidence from you. How, then? You are not what?"

She tried again to repress herself, but broke out vehemently, "Not Arthur's mother!"

"Good," said Rigaud. "You are amenable."

With the set expression of her face all torn away by the explosion of her passion, and with a bursting from every rent feature of the smouldering fire so long pent up, she cried out, "I will tell it myself! I will not hear it from your lips, and with the taint of your wickedness upon it. Since it must be seen, I will have it seen by the light I stood in. Not another word. Hear me!"

"Unless you are a more obstinate and more persisting woman, than even I know you to be," Mr. Flintwinch interposed, "you had better leave Mr. Rigaud, Mr. Blandois, Mr. Beelzebub, to tell it in his own way. What does it signify when he knows all about it?"

"He does not know all about it."

"He knows all he cares about it," Mr. Flintwinch testily urged.

"He does not know *me*."

"What do you suppose he cares for you, you conceited woman?" said Mr. Flintwinch.

"I tell you, Flintwinch, I will speak. I tell you, when it has come to this, I will tell it with my own lips, and will express myself throughout it. What! Have I suffered nothing in this room, no deprivation, no imprisonment, that I should condescend at last to contemplate myself in such a glass as *that!* Can you see him? Can you hear him? If your wife were a hundred times the ingrate that she is, and if I were a thousand times more hopeless than I am of inducing her to be silent if this man is silenced, I would tell it myself, before I would bear the torment of hearing it from him."

Rigaud pushed his chair a little back; pushed his legs out straight before him; and sat with his arms folded, over against her.

"You do not know what it is," she went on, addressing him, "to be brought up strictly, and straitly. I was so brought up. Mine was no light youth of sinful gaiety and pleasure. Mine were days of wholesome repression, punishment, and fear. The corruption of our hearts, the evil of our ways, the curse that is upon us, the terrors that surround us—these were the themes of my childhood. They formed my character, and filled me with an abhorrence of evil-doers. When old Mr. Gilbert Clennam proposed his orphan nephew to my father for my husband, my father impressed upon me that his bringing-up had been, like mine, one of severe restraint. He told me, that besides the discipline his spirit had undergone, he had lived in a starved house, where rioting and gaiety were unknown, and where every day was a day of toil and trial like the last. He told me that he had been a man in years, long before his uncle had acknowledged him as one; and that from his schooldays to that hour, his uncle's roof had been a sanctuary to him from the contagion of the irreligious and dissolute. When, within a twelvemonth of our marriage, I found my husband, at that time when my father spoke of him, to have sinned against the Lord and outraged me by holding a guilty creature in my place, was I to doubt that it had been appointed to me to make the discovery, and that it was appointed to me to lay the hand of punishment upon that creature of perdition? Was I to dismiss in a moment—not my own wrongs—what was I! but all the rejection of sin, and all the war against it, in which I had been bred?"

She laid her wrathful hand upon the watch on the table.

"No! 'Do not forget.' The initials of those words are within here now, and were within here then. I was appointed to find the old letter that referred to them, and that told me what they meant, and whose work they were, and why they were worked, lying with this watch in his secret drawer. But for that appointment, there would have been no discovery. 'Do not forget.' It spoke to me like a voice from an angry cloud. Do not forget the deadly sin, do not forget the appointed discovery, do not forget the appointed suffering. I did not forget. Was it my own wrong I remembered? Mine! I was but a servant and a minister. What power could I have had over them, but that they were bound in the bonds of their sin, and delivered to me!"

More than forty years had passed over the grey head of this determined woman, since the time she recalled. More than forty years of strife and struggle with the whisper that, by whatever name she called her vindictive pride and rage, nothing through all eternity could change their nature. Yet, gone those more than forty years, and come this Nemesis now looking her in the face, she still abided by her old impiety—still reversed the order of Creation, and breathed her own breath into a clay image of her Creator. Verily, verily, travellers have seen many monstrous idols in many countries; but, no human eyes have ever seen more daring, gross, and shocking images of the Divine nature, than we creatures of the dust make in our own likenesses, of our own bad passions.

"When I forced him to give her up to me, by her name and place of abode," she went on in her torrent of indignation and defence; "when I accused her, and she fell hiding her face at my feet, was it my injury that I asserted, were they my reproaches that I poured upon her? Those who were appointed of old to go to wicked kings and accuse them—were they not ministers and servants? And had not I, unworthy, and far-removed from them, sin to denounce? When she pleaded to me her youth, and his wretched and hard life (that was her phrase for the virtuous training he had belied), and the desecrated ceremony of marriage there had secretly been between them, and the terrors of want and shame that had overwhelmed

them both, when I was first appointed to be the instrument of their punishment, and the love (for she said the word to me, down at my feet) in which
she had abandoned him and left him to me, was it *my* enemy that became
my footstool, were they the words of *my* wrath that made her shrink and
quiver! Not unto me the strength be ascribed; not unto me the wringing of
the expiation!"

Many years had come, and gone, since she had had the free use even of
her fingers; but, it was noticeable that she had already more than once
struck her clenched hand vigorously upon the table, and that when she
said these words she raised her whole arm in the air, as though it had been
a common action with her.

"And what was the repentance that was extorted from the hardness of
her heart and the blackness of her depravity? I, vindictive and implacable?
It may seem so, to such as you who know no righteousness, and no appointment except Satan's. Laugh; but I will be known as I know myself, and as
Flintwinch knows me, though it is only to you and this half-witted woman."

"Add, to yourself, madame," said Rigaud. "I have my little suspicions,
that madame is rather solicitous to be justified to herself."

"It is false. It is not so. I have no need to be," she said, with great energy
and anger.

"Truly?" retorted Rigaud. "Hah!"

"I ask, what was the penitence, in works, that was demanded of her?
'You have a child; I have none. You love that child. Give him to me.
He shall believe himself to be my son, and he shall be believed by every
one to be my son. To save you from exposure, his father shall swear never
to see or communicate with you more; equally to save him from being
stripped by his uncle, and to save your child from being a beggar, you shall
swear never to see or communicate with either of them more. That done,
and your present means, derived from my husband, renounced, I charge
myself with your support. You may, with your place of retreat unknown,
then leave, if you please, uncontradicted by me, the lie that when you
passed out of all knowledge but mine, you merited a good name.' That was
all. She had to sacrifice her sinful and shameful affections; no more. She
was then free to bear her load of guilt in secret, and to break her heart in
secret; and through such present misery (light enough for her, I think!) to
purchase her redemption from endless misery, if she could. If, in this, I
punished her here, did I not open to her a way hereafter? If she knew herself
to be surrounded by insatiable vengeance and unquenchable fires, were
they mine? If I threatened her, then and afterwards, with the terrors that
encompassed her, did I hold them in my right hand?"

She turned the watch upon the table, and opened it, and, with an un-
softening face, looked at the worked letters within.

"They did *not* forget. It is appointed against such offences that the
offenders shall not be able to forget. If the presence of Arthur was a daily

reproach to his father, and if the absence of Arthur was a daily agony to his mother, that was the just dispensation of Jehovah. As well might it be charged upon me, that the stings of an awakened conscience drove her mad, and that it was the will of the disposer of all things that she should live so, many years. I devoted myself to reclaim the otherwise predestined and lost boy; to give him the reputation of an honest origin; to bring him up in fear and trembling, and in a life of practical contrition for the sins that were heavy on his head before his entrance into this condemned world. Was that a cruelty? Was I too, not visited with consequences of the original offence, in which I had no complicity? Arthur's father and I lived no further apart, with half the globe between us, than when we were together in this house. He died, and sent this watch back to me, with its Do not forget. I do NOT forget, though I do not read it as he did. I read, in it, that I was appointed to do these things. I have so read these three letters since I have had them lying on this table, and I did so read them, with equal distinctness, when they were thousands of miles away."

As she took the watch-case in her hand, with that new freedom in the use of her hand of which she showed no consciousness whatever, bending her eyes upon it as if she were defying it to move her, Rigaud cried with a loud and contemptuous snapping of his fingers, "Come, madame! Time runs out. Come, lady of piety, it must be! You can tell nothing I don't know. Come to the money stolen, or I will! Death of my soul, I have had enough of your other jargon. Come straight to the stolen money!"

"Wretch, that you are," she answered, and now her hands clasped her head; "through what fatal error of Flintwinch's, through what incompleteness on his part, who was the only other person helping in these things and trusted with them, through whose and what bringing together of the ashes of a burnt paper, you have become possessed of that codicil, I know no more than how you acquired the rest of your power here——"

"And yet," interrupted Rigaud, "it is my odd fortune to have by me, in a convenient place that I know of, that same short little addition to the will of Monsieur Gilbert Clennam, written by a lady and witnessed by the same lady, and our old intriguer! Ah, bah, old intriguer, crooked little puppet! Madame, let us go on. Time presses. You or I to finish?"

"I!" she answered, with increased determination, if it were possible. "I, because I will not endure to be shown myself, and have myself shown to any one, with your horrible distortion of me. You, with your practices of infamous foreign prisons and galleys, would make it the money that impelled me. It was not the money."

"Bah, bah, bah! I repudiate, for the moment, my politeness, and say, Lies, lies, lies. You know you suppressed the deed, and kept the money."

"Not for the money's sake, wretch!" She made a struggle as if she were starting up; even as if, in her vehemence, she had almost risen on her disabled feet. "If Gilbert Clennam, reduced to imbecility, at the point of death, and laboring under the delusion of some imaginary relenting towards a girl, of whom he had heard that his nephew had once had a fancy for her, which he had crushed out of him, and that she afterwards drooped away into melancholy and withdrawal from all who knew her—if, in that state of weakness, he dictated to me, whose life she had darkened with her sin, and who had been appointed to know her wickedness from her own hand and her own lips, a bequest meant as a recompense to her for supposed unmerited suffering; was there no difference between my spurning that injustice, and coveting mere money—a thing which you, and your comrades in the prisons, may steal from any one?"

"Time presses, madame. Take care!"

"If this house was blazing from the roof to the ground," she returned, "I would stay in it to justify myself, against my righteous motives being classed with those of stabbers and thieves."

Rigaud snapped his fingers tauntingly in her face. "One thousand guineas to the little beauty you slowly hunted to death. One thousand guineas to the youngest daughter her patron might have at fifty, or (if he had none) brother's youngest daughter, on her coming of age, 'as the remembrance his disinterestedness may like best, of his protection of a friendless young orphan girl.' Two thousand guineas. What! You will never come to the money?"

"That patron," she was vehemently proceeding, when he checked her.

"Names! Call him Mr. Frederick Dorrit. No more evasions!"

"That Frederick Dorrit was the beginning of it all. If he had not been a player of music, and had not kept, in those days of his youth and prosperity, an idle house where singers, and players, and such-like children of Evil, turned their backs on the Light and their faces to the Darkness, she might have remained in her lowly station, and might not have been raised out of it to be cast down. But, no. Satan entered into that Frederick Dorrit, and counselled him that he was a man of innocent and laudable tastes who did kind actions, and that here was a poor girl with a voice for singing music with. Then he is to have her taught. Then Arthur's father, who has all along been secretly pining in the ways of virtuous ruggedness, for those accursed snares which are called the Arts, becomes acquainted with her. And so, a graceless orphan, training to be a singing girl, carries it, by that Frederick Dorrit's agency, against me, and I am humbled and deceived!— Not I, that is to say," she added quickly, as color flushed into her face; "a greater than I. What am I?"

Jeremiah Flintwinch, who had been gradually screwing himself towards her, and who was now very near her elbow without her knowing it, made a specially wry face of objection when she said these words, and moreover twitched his gaiters, as if such pretensions were equivalent to little barbs in his legs.

"Lastly," she continued, "for I am at the end of these things, and I will say no more of them, and you shall say no more of them, and all that remains will be to determine whether the knowledge of them can be kept among us who are here present; lastly, when I suppressed the paper, with the knowledge of Arthur's father—"

"But not with his consent, you know," said Mr. Flintwinch.

"Who said with his consent?" She started to find Jeremiah so near her, and drew back her head, looking at him with some rising distrust. "You were often enough between us, when he would have had me produce it and I would not, to have contradicted me if I had said, with his consent. I say, when I suppressed that paper, I made no effort to destroy it, but kept it by me, here in this house, many years. The rest of the Gilbert property being left to Arthur's father, I could at any time, without un-settling more than the two sums, have made a pretence of finding it. But, besides that I must have supported such pretence by a direct falsehood, (a great responsibility,) I have seen no new reason, in all the time I have been tried here, to bring it to light. It was a rewarding of sin; the wrong result of a delusion. I did what I was appointed to do, and I have undergone, within these four walls, what I was appointed to undergo. When the paper was at last destroyed—as I thought—in my presence, she had long been dead, and her patron, Frederick Dorrit, had long been deservedly ruined and imbecile. He had no daughter. I had found the niece before then; and what I did for her was better for her, far, than the money of which she would have had no good." She added, after a moment, as though she addressed the watch: "She herself was innocent, and I might not have forgotten to relinquish it to her, at my death;" and sat looking at it.

"Shall I recall something to you, worthy madame?" said Rigaud. "The little paper was in this house, on the night when our friend the prisoner—jail-comrade of my soul—came home from foreign countries. Shall I recall yet something more to you? The little singing-bird that never was fledged, was long kept in a cage, by a guardian of your appointing, well-enough known to our old intriguer here. Shall we coax our old intriguer to tell us when he saw him last?"

"I'll tell you!" cried Affery, unstopping her mouth. "I dreamed it, first of all my dreams. Jeremiah, if you come a-nigh me now, I'll scream to be heard at Saint Paul's! The person as this man has spoken of, was Jeremiah's own twin brother; and he was here in the dead of the night, on the night when Arthur come home, and Jeremiah with his own hands give him this paper, along with I don't know what more, and he took it away in an iron box.—Help! Murder! Save me from Jere-*mi*-ah!"

Mr. Flintwinch had made a run at her, but Rigaud had caught him in his arms midway. After a moment's wrestle with him, Flintwinch gave up, and put his hands in his pockets.

"What!" cried Rigaud, rallying him as he poked and jerked him back with his elbows. "Assault a lady with such a genius for dreaming? Ha, ha, ha! Why, she'll be a fortune to you as an exhibition. All that she dreams comes true. Ha, ha, ha! You're so like him, Little Flintwinch. So like him, as I knew him (when I first spoke English for him to the host) in the Cabaret of the Three Billiard Tables, in the little street of the high roofs, by the wharf at Antwerp! Ah, but he was a brave boy to drink. Ah, but he was a brave boy to smoke! Ah, but he lived in a sweet bachelor-apartment—furnished, on the fifth floor, above the wood and charcoal merchant's, and the dress-makers, and the chair-makers, and the maker of tubs—where I knew him too, and where, with his cognac and tobacco, he had twelve sleeps a day and one fit, until he had a fit too much, and ascended to the skies. Ha, ha, ha! What does it matter how I took possession of the papers in his iron box? Perhaps he confided it to my hands for you, perhaps it was locked and my curiosity was piqued, perhaps I suppressed it. Ha, ha, ha! What does it matter, so that I have it safe? We are not particular here; hey, Flintwinch? We are not particular here; is it not so, madame?"

Retiring before him with vicious counter-jerks of his own elbows, Mr. Flintwinch had got back into his corner, where he now stood with his hands in his pockets, taking breath, and returning Mrs. Clennam's stare.

"Ha, ha, ha! But what's this?" cried Rigaud. "It appears as if you don't know, one the other. Permit me, Madame Clennam who suppresses, to present Monsieur Flintwinch who intrigues."

Mr. Flintwinch, unpocketing one of his hands to scrape his jaw, advanced a step or so in that attitude, still returning Mrs. Clennam's look, and thus addressed her:

"Now, I know what you mean by opening your eyes so wide at me, but you needn't take the trouble, because I don't care for it. I've been telling you for how many years, that you're one of the most opiniated and obstinate of women. That's what *you* are. You call yourself humble and sinful, but you are the most Bumptious of your sex. That's what *you* are. I have told you, over and over again when we have had a tiff, that you wanted to make everything go down before you, but I wouldn't go down before you—that you wanted to swallow up everybody alive, but I wouldn't be swallowed up alive. Why didn't you destroy the paper when you first laid hands upon it? I advised you to; but no, it's not your way to take advice. You must keep it, forsooth. Perhaps you may carry it out at some other time, forsooth. As if I didn't know better than that! I think I see your pride carrying it out, with a chance of being suspected of having kept it by you. But that's the way you cheat yourself. Just as you cheat yourself into making out, that you didn't do all this business because you were a rigorous woman, all slight, and spite, and power, and unforgivingness, but because you were a servant and a minister, and were appointed to do it. Who are you, that you should be appointed to do it? That may be your religion, but it's my gammon. And, to tell you all the truth while I am about it," said Mr. Flintwinch, crossing his arms, and becoming the express image of irascible doggedness, "I have been rasped—rasped these forty years—by your taking such high ground even with me, who knows better; the effect of it being coolly to put me on low ground. I admire you very much; you are a woman of strong head and great talent; but the strongest head, and the greatest talent, can't rasp a man for forty years without making him sore. So I don't care for your present eyes. Now, I am coming to the paper, and mark what I say. You put it away somewhere, and you keep your own counsel where. You're an active woman at that time, and if you want to get that paper, you can get it. But, mark! There comes a time when you are struck into what you are now, and then if you want to get that paper, you can't get it. So it lies, long years, in its hiding-place. At last, when we are expecting Arthur home every day, and when any day may bring him home, and it's impossible to say what rummaging he may make about the house, I recommend you five thousand times, if you can't get at it, to let me get at it, that it may be put in the fire. But no—no one but you knows where it is, and that's power; and, call yourself whatever humble names you will, I call you a female Lucifer in appetite for power! On a Sunday night, Arthur comes home. He has not been in this room ten minutes, when he speaks of his father's watch. You know very well that the Do Not Forget, at the time when his father sent that watch to you, could only mean, the rest of the story being then all dead and over, Do Not Forget the suppression. Make restitution! Arthur's ways have frightened you a bit, and the paper shall be burnt after all. So, before that jumping jade and Jezabel," Mr. Flintwinch grinned at his wife, "has got you into bed, you at last tell me where you have put the paper, among the old ledgers in the cellars, where Arthur himself went prowling the very next morning. But, it's not to be burnt on a Sunday night. No; you are strict, you are; we must wait over twelve o'clock, and get into Monday. Now, all this is a swallowing of me up alive, that rasps me; so, feeling a little out of temper, and not being as strict as yourself, I take a look at the document before twelve o'clock, to refresh my memory as to its appearance—fold up one of the many yellow old papers in the cellars like it—and afterwards, when we have got into Monday morning, and I have, by the light of your lamp, to walk from you, lying on that bed, to this grate, make a little exchange like the conjuror, and burn accordingly. My brother Ephraim, the lunatic keeper (I wish he had had himself to keep in a strait-waistcoat), had had many jobs since the close of the long job he got from you, but had not done well. His wife died (not that that was much; mine might have died instead, and welcome), he speculated unsuccessfully in lunatics, he got into difficulty about over-roasting a patient to bring him to reason, and he got into debt. He was going out of the way, on what he had been able to scrape up, and a trifle from me. He was here that early Monday morning, waiting for the tide; in short, he was going to Antwerp, where (I am afraid you'll be shocked at my saying, And be damned to him!) he made the acquaintance of this gentleman. He had come a long way, and, I thought then, was only sleepy; but, I suppose now, was drunk. When Arthur's mother had been under the care of him and his wife, she had been always writing, incessantly writing,—mostly letters of confession to you, and Prayers for forgiveness. My brother had handed, from time to time, lots of these sheets to me. I thought I might as well keep them to myself, as have them swallowed up alive too; so I kept them in a box, looking them over when I felt in the humour. Convinced that it was advisable to get the paper out of the place, with Arthur coming about it, I put it into this same box, and I locked the whole up with two locks, and I trusted it to my brother to take away and keep, till I should write about it. I did write about it, and never got an answer. I didn't know what to make of it, till this gentleman favored us with his first visit. Of course, I began to suspect how it was, then; and I don't want his word for it now to understand, how he gets his knowledge from my papers, and your paper, and my brother's cognac and tobacco talk (I wish he'd had to gag himself). Now, I have only one thing more to say, you hammer-headed woman, and that is, that I haven't altogether made up my mind whether I might, or might not, have ever given you any trouble about the codicil. I think not; and that I should have been quite satisfied with knowing I had got the better of you, and that I held the power over you. In the present state of circumstances, I have no more explanation to give you till this time tomorrow-night. So you may as well," said Mr. Flintwinch, terminating his oration with a screw, "keep your eyes open at somebody else, for it's no use keeping 'em open at me."

She slowly withdrew them when he had ceased, and dropped her forehead on her hand. Her other hand pressed hard upon the table, and again the curious stir was observable in her, as if she were going to rise.

"This box can never bring, elsewhere, the price it will bring here. This knowledge can never be of the same profit to you, sold to any other person, as sold to me. But, I have not the present means of raising the sum you have demanded. I have not prospered. What will you take now, and what at another time, and how am I to be assured of your silence?"

"My angel," replied Rigaud, "I have said what I will take, and time presses. Before coming here, I placed copies of the most important of these papers in another hand. Put off the time till the Marshalsea gate shall be shut for the night, and it will be too late to treat. The prisoner will have read them."

She put her two hands to her head again, uttered a loud exclamation, and started to her feet. She staggered for a moment, as if she would have fallen; then stood firm.

"Say what you mean. Say what you mean, man!"

Before her ghostly figure, so long unused to its erect attitude, and, so stiffened in it, Rigaud fell back and dropped his voice. It was, to all the three, almost as if a dead woman had risen.

"Miss Dorrit," answered Rigaud, "the little niece of Monsieur Frederick, whom I have known across the water, is attached to the prisoner. Miss Dorrit, little niece of Monsieur Frederick, watches at this moment over the prisoner, who lies ill. For her, I with my own hands left a packet at the prison, on my way here, with a letter of instructions, '*for his sake*'—she will do anything for his sake—to keep it without breaking the seal, in case of its being reclaimed before the hour of shutting up to-night—if it should not be reclaimed before the ringing of the prison bell, to give it to him; and it encloses a second copy for herself, which he must give to her. What! I don't trust myself among you, now we have got so far, without giving my secret a second life. And as to its not bringing me, elsewhere, the price it will bring here, say then, madame, have you limited and settled the price the little niece will give—for his sake—to hush it up? Once more I say, time presses. The packet not reclaimed before the ringing of the bell to-night, you cannot buy. I sell, then, to the little girl!"

Once more the stir and struggle in her, and she ran to a closet, tore the door open, took down a hood or shawl, and wrapped it over her head. Affery, who had watched her in terror, darted to her in the middle of the room, caught hold of her dress, and went on her knees to her.

"Don't, don't, don't! What are you doing? Where are you going? You're a fearful woman, but I don't bear you no ill-will. I can do poor Arthur no good now, that I see; and you needn't be afraid of me. I'll keep your secret. Don't go out, you'll fall dead in the street. Only promise me, that, if it's the poor thing that's kept here, secretly, you'll let me take charge of her and be her nurse. Only promise me that, and never be afraid of me."

Mrs. Clennam stood still for an instant, at the height of her rapid haste, saying in stern amazement:

"Kept here? She has been dead a score of years and more. Ask Flintwinch—ask *him*. They can both tell you that she died, when Arthur went abroad."

"So much the worse," said Affery, with a shiver, "for she haunts the house, then. Who else rustles about it, making signals by dropping dust so softly? Who else comes and goes, and marks the walls with long crooked touches, when we are all a-bed? Who else holds the doors sometimes? But don't go out—don't go out! Mistress, you'll die in the street!"

Her mistress only disengaged her dress from the beseeching hands, said to Rigaud, "Wait here till I come back!" and ran out of the room. They saw her, from the window, run wildly through the courtyard and out at the gateway.

For a few moments they stood motionless. Affery was the first to move, and she, wringing her hands, pursued her mistress. Next, Jeremiah Flintwinch, slowly backing to the door, with one hand in a pocket and the other rubbing his chin, twisted himself out in his reticent way. Lastly

Rigaud, left alone, composed himself upon the window-seat of the open window, in the old Marseilles-Jail attitude. He laid his cigarettes and fire-box ready to his hand, and fell to smoking.

"Whoof! Almost as dull as the infernal old jail. Warmer, but almost as dismal. Wait till she comes back? Yes, certainly; but where is she gone, and how long will she be gone? No matter! Rigaud Lagnier Blandois, my amiable subject, you will get your money. You will enrich yourself. You have lived a gentleman; you will die a gentleman. You triumph, my little boy; but it is your character to triumph. Whoof!"

In the hour of his triumph, his moustache went up and his nose came down, as he ogled a great beam over his head with particular satisfaction.

CHAPTER XXXI

CLOSED

THE sun had set, and the streets were dim in the dusty twilight, when the figure so long unused to them hurried on its way. In the immediate neighbourhood of the old house, it attracted little attention, for there were only a few straggling people to notice it; but, ascending from the river, by the crooked ways that led to London Bridge, and passing into the great main road, it became surrounded by astonishment.

Resolute and wild of look, rapid of foot, and yet weak and uncertain, conspicuously dressed in its black garments and with its hurried head-covering, gaunt and of an unearthly paleness, it pressed forward, taking no more heed of the throng than a sleep-walker. More remarkable by being so removed from the crowd it was among, than if it had been lifted on a pedestal to be seen, the figure attracted all eyes. Saunterers pricked up their attention to observe it; busy people, crossing it, slackened their pace and turned their heads; companions pausing and standing aside, whispered one another to look at this spectral woman who was coming by; and the sweep of the figure as it passed seemed to create a vortex, drawing the most idle and most curious after it.

Made giddy by the turbulent irruption of this multitude of staring faces into her cell of years, by the confusing sensation of being in the air and the yet more confusing sensation of being a-foot, by the unexpected changes in half-remembered objects, and the want of likeness between the controllable pictures her imagination had often drawn of the life from which she was secluded, and the overwhelming rush of the reality, she held her way as if she were environed by distracting thoughts, rather than by external humanity and observation. But, having crossed the bridge, and gone some distance straight onward, she remembered that she must ask for a direction; and it was only then, when she stopped and turned to look about her for a promising place of enquiry, that she found herself surrounded by an eager glare of faces.

"Why are you encircling me ?" she asked, trembling.

None of those who were nearest answered; but, from the outer ring, there arose a shrill cry of " 'Cause you're mad!"

"I am as sane as any one here. I want to find the Marshalsea prison."

The shrill outer circle again retorted, "Then that 'ud show you was mad if nothing else did, 'cause it's right opposite!"

A short, mild, quiet-looking young man, made his way through to her, as a whooping ensued on this reply, and said: "Was it the Marshalsea you wanted ? I'm going on duty there. Come across with me."

She laid her hand upon his arm, and he took her over the way; the crowd, rather injured by the near prospect of losing her, pressing before and behind and on either side, and recommending an adjournment to Bedlam. After a momentary whirl in the outer courtyard, the prison-door opened, and shut upon them. In the Lodge, which seemed by contrast with the outer noise a place of refuge and peace, a yellow lamp was already striving with the prison shadows.

"Why, John!" said the turnkey who had admitted them. "What is it ?"

"Nothing, father; only this lady not knowing her way, and being badgered by the boys. Who did you want, ma'am ?"

"Miss Dorrit. Is she here ?"

The young man became more interested. "Yes, she is here. What might your name be ?"

"Mrs. Clennam."

"Mr. Clennam's mother ?" asked the young man.

She pressed her lips together, and hesitated. "Yes. She had better be told it is his mother."

"You see," said the young man, "the Marshal's family living in the country at present, the Marshal has given Miss Dorrit one of the rooms in his house, to use when she likes. Don't you think you had better come up there, and let me bring Miss Dorrit ?"

She signified her assent, and he unlocked a door, and conducted her up a side staircase into a dwelling-house above. He showed her into a darkening room, and left her. The room looked down into the darkening prison-yard, with its inmates strolling here and there, leaning out of windows, communing as much apart as they could with friends who were going away, and generally wearing out their imprisonment as they best might, that summer evening. The air was heavy and hot; the closeness of the place, oppressive; and from without there arose a rush of free sounds, like the jarring memory of such things in a headache and heartache. She

stood at the window, bewildered, looking down into this prison as it were
out of her own different prison, when a soft word or two of surprise made
her start, and Little Dorrit stood before her.

"Is it possible, Mrs. Clennam, that you are so happily recovered as——"

Little Dorrit stopped, for there was neither happiness nor health in the
face that turned to her.

"This is not recovery; it is not strength; I don't know what it is."
With an agitated wave of her hand, she put all that aside. "You have
had a packet left with you, which you were to give to Arthur if it was not
reclaimed before this place closed to-night."

"Yes."

"I reclaim it."

Little Dorrit took it from her bosom, and gave it into her hand, which
remained stretched out, after receiving it.

"Have you any idea of its contents?"

Frightened by her being there, with that new power of movement in
her, which, as she had said herself, was not strength, and which was unreal
to look upon, as though a picture or a statue had been animated, Little
Dorrit answered, "No."

"Read them."

Little Dorrit took the packet from the still outstretched hand, and broke
the seal. Mrs. Clennam then gave her the inner packet that was addressed
to herself, and held the other. The shadow of the wall and of the prison-
buildings, which made the room sombre at noon, made it too dark to read
there, with the dusk deepening apace, save in the window. In the window,
where a little of the bright summer evening sky could shine upon her,
Little Dorrit stood, and read. After a broken exclamation or so of wonder
and of terror, she read in silence. When she had finished, she looked
round, and her old mistress bowed herself before her.

"You know, now, what I have done."

"I think so. I am afraid so; though my mind is so hurried, and so sorry,
and has so much to pity, that it has not been able to follow all I have read,"
said Little Dorrit, tremulously.

"I will restore to you what I have withheld from you. Forgive me. Can
you forgive me?"

"I can, and Heaven knows I do! Do not kiss my dress and kneel to me;
you are too old to kneel to me; I forgive you freely, without that."

"I have more to ask yet."

"Not in that posture," said Little Dorrit. "It is unnatural to see your
grey hair lower than mine. Pray rise; let me help you." With that she
raised her up, and stood rather shrinking from her, but looking at her
earnestly.

"The great petition that I make to you (there is another which grows
out of it), the great supplication that I address to your merciful and gentle

heart, is, that you will not disclose this to Arthur until I am dead. If you think, when you have had time for consideration, that it can do him any good to know it while I am yet alive, then tell him. But, you will not think that; and in such case, will you promise me to spare me until I am dead?"

"I am so sorry, and what I have read has so confused my thoughts," returned Little Dorrit, "that I can scarcely give you a steady answer. If I should be quite sure that to be acquainted with it will do Mr. Clennam no good——"

"I know you are attached to him, and will make him the first consideration. It is right that he should be the first consideration; I ask that. But, having regarded him, and still finding that you may spare me for the little time I shall remain on earth, will you do it?"

"I will."

"GOD bless you!"

She stood in the shadow so that she was only a veiled form to Little Dorrit in the light; but, the sound of her voice, in saying those three grateful words, was at once fervent and broken. Broken by emotion as unfamiliar to her frozen eyes as action to her frozen limbs.

"You will wonder, perhaps," she said in a stronger tone, "that I can better bear to be known to you whom I have wronged, than to the son of my enemy who wronged me.—For, she did wrong me! She not only sinned grievously against the Lord, but she wronged me. What Arthur's father was to me, she made him. From our marriage day I was his dread, and that she made me. I was the scourge of both, and that is referable to her. You love Arthur (I can see the blush upon your face; may it be the dawn of happier days to both of you!), and you will have thought already that he is as merciful and kind as you, and why do I not trust myself to him as soon as to you. Have you not thought so?"

"No thought," said Little Dorrit, "can be quite a stranger to my heart, that springs out of the knowledge that Mr. Clennam is always to be relied upon for being kind and generous and good."

"I do not doubt it. Yet Arthur is, of the whole world, the one person from whom I would conceal this, while I am in it. I kept over him as a child, in the days of his first remembrance, my restraining and correcting hand. I was stern with him, knowing that the transgressions of the parents are visited on their offspring, and that there was an angry mark upon him at his birth. I have sat with him and his father, seeing the weakness of his father yearning to unbend to him; and forcing it back, that the child might work out his release in bondage and hardship. I have seen him, with his mother's face, looking up at me in awe from his little books, and trying to soften me with his mother's ways that hardened me."

The shrinking of her auditress stopped her for a moment in her flow of words, delivered in a retrospective gloomy voice.

"For his good. Not for the satisfaction of my injury. What was I, and what was the worth of that, before the curse of Heaven! I have seen that child grow up; not to be pious in a chosen way (his mother's offence lay too heavy on him for that), but still to be just and upright, and to be submissive to me. He never loved me, as I once half-hoped he might—so frail we are, and so do the corrupt affections of the flesh war with our trusts and tasks; but, he always respected me, and ordered himself dutifully to me. He does to this hour. With an empty place in his heart that he has never known the meaning of, he has turned away from me, and gone his separate road; but, even that he has done considerately and with deference. These have been his relations towards me. Yours have been of a much slighter kind, spread over a much shorter time. When you have sat at your needle in my room, you have been in fear of me, but you have supposed me to have been doing you a kindness; you are better informed now, and know me to have done you an injury. Your misconstruction and misunderstanding of the cause in which, and the motives with which, I have worked out this work, is lighter to endure than his would be. I would not, for any worldly recompense I can imagine, have him in a moment, however blindly, throw me down from the station I have held before him all his life, and change me altogether, into something he would cast out of his respect, and think detected and exposed. Let him do it, if it must be done, when I am not here to see it. Let me never feel, while I am still alive, that I die before his face, and utterly perish away from him, like one consumed by lightning and swallowed by an earthquake."

Her pride was very strong in her, the pain of it and of her old passions was very sharp with her, when she thus expressed herself. Not less so, when she added:

"Even now, I see *you* shrink from me, as if I had been cruel."

Little Dorrit could not gainsay it. She tried not to show it, but she recoiled with dread from the state of mind that had burnt so fiercely and lasted so long. It presented itself to her with no sophistry upon it, in its own plain nature.

"I have done," said Mrs. Clennam, "what it was given to me to do. I have set myself against evil; not against good. I have been an instrument of severity against sin. Have not mere sinners like myself been commissioned to lay it low in all time?"

"In all time?" repeated Little Dorrit.

"Even if my own wrong had prevailed with me, and my own vengeance had moved me, could I have found no justification? None in the old days when the innocent perished with the guilty, a thousand to one? When the wrath of the hater of the unrighteous was not slaked even in blood, and yet found favor?"

"O, Mrs. Clennam, Mrs. Clennam," said Little Dorrit, "angry feelings and unforgiving deeds are no comfort and no guide to you and me. My life has been passed in this poor prison, and my teaching has been very defective; but, let me implore you to remember later and better days. Be guided, only by the healer of the sick, the raiser of the dead, the friend of all who were afflicted and forlorn, the patient Master who shed tears of compassion for our infirmities. We cannot but be right if we put all the rest away, and do everything in remembrance of Him. There is no vengeance and no infliction of suffering in His life, I am sure. There can be no confusion in following Him, and seeking for no other footsteps, I am certain!"

In the softened light of the window, looking from the scene of her early trials to the shining sky, she was not in stronger opposition to the black figure in the shade, than the life and doctrine on which she rested were to that figure's history. It bent its head low again, and said not a word. It remained thus, until the first warning bell began to ring.

"Hark!" cried Mrs. Clennam, starting. "I said I had another petition. It is one that does not admit of delay. The man who brought you this packet and possesses these proofs, is now waiting at my house, to be bought off. I can keep this from Arthur, only by buying him off. He asks a large sum; more than I can get together to pay him, without having time. He refuses to make any abatement, because his threat is, that if he fails with me he will come to you. Will you return with me, and show him that you already know it? Will you return with me and try to prevail with him? Will you come and help me with him? Do not refuse what I ask in Arthur's name, though I dare not ask it for Arthur's sake!"

Little Dorrit yielded willingly. She glided away into the prison for a few moments, returned, and said she was ready to go. They went out by another staircase, avoiding the Lodge; and, coming into the front court-yard, now all quiet and deserted, gained the street.

It was one of those summer evenings when there is no greater darkness than a long twilight. The vista of street and bridge was plain to see, and the sky was serene and beautiful. People stood and sat at their doors, playing with children and enjoying the evening; numbers were walking for air; the worry of the day had almost worried itself out, and few but themselves were hurried. As they crossed the bridge, the clear steeples of the many churches looked as if they had advanced out of the murk that usually enshrouded them and come much nearer. The smoke that rose into the sky had lost its dingy hue and taken a brightness upon it. The beauties of the sunset had not faded from the long light films of cloud that lay at peace in the horizon. From a radiant centre, over the whole length and breadth of the tranquil firmament, great shoots of light streamed among the early stars, like signs of the blessed later covenant of peace and hope that changed the crown of thorns into a glory.

Less remarkable, now that she was not alone and it was darker, Mrs. Clennam hurried on at Little Dorrit's side, unmolested. They left the great thoroughfare at the turning by which she had entered it, and wound their way down among the silent, empty, cross-streets. Their feet were at the gateway, when there was a sudden noise like thunder.

"What was that! Let us make haste in," cried Mrs. Clennam.

They were in the gateway. Little Dorrit, with a piercing cry, held her back.

In one swift instant, the old house was before them, with the man lying smoking in the window; another thundering sound, and it heaved, surged outward, trembled asunder in fifty places, collapsed, and fell. Deafened by the noise, stifled, choked, and blinded by the dust, they hid their faces and stood rooted to the spot. The dust storm, driving between them and the placid sky, parted for a moment and showed them the stars. As they looked up, wildly crying for help, the great pile of chimneys which was then alone left standing, like a tower in a whirlwind, rocked, broke, and hailed itself down upon the heap of ruin, as if every tumbling fragment were intent on burying the crushed wretch deeper.

So blackened by the flying particles of rubbish as to be unrecognisable, they ran back from the gateway into the street crying, and shrieking. There, Mrs. Clennam dropped upon the stones; and she never from that hour moved so much as a finger again, or had the power to speak one word. For upwards of three years she reclined in her wheeled chair, looking attentively at those about her, and appearing to understand what they said; but, the rigid silence she had so long held was evermore enforced upon her, and, except that she could move her eyes and faintly express a negative and affirmative with her head, she lived and died a statue.

Affery had been looking for them at the prison, and had caught sight of them at a distance on the bridge. She came up to receive her old mistress in her arms, to help to carry her into a neighbouring house, and to be faithful to her. The mystery of the noises was out now; Affery, like greater people, had always been right in her facts, and always wrong in the theories she deduced from them.

When the storm of dust had cleared away and the summer night was calm again, numbers of people choked up every avenue of access, and parties of diggers were formed to relieve one another in digging among the ruins. There had been a hundred people in the house at the time of its fall, there had been fifty, there had been fifteen, there had been two. Rumour finally settled the number at two: the foreigner and Mr. Flintwinch.

The diggers dug all through the short night by flaring pipes of gas, and on a level with the early sun, and deeper and deeper below it as it rose into its zenith, and aslant of it as it declined, and on a level with it again as it departed. Sturdy digging, and shovelling, and carrying away, in carts, barrows, and baskets, went on without intermission, by night and by day; but, it was night for the second time when they found the dirty heap of rubbish that had been the foreigner, before his head had been shivered to atoms, like so much glass, by the great beam that lay upon him, crushing him.

Still, they had not come upon Flintwinch yet; so, the sturdy digging and shovelling and carrying away went on without intermission by night and by day. It got about that the old house had had famous cellarage (which indeed was true), and that Flintwinch had been in a cellar at the moment, or had had time to escape into one, and that he was safe under its strong arch, and even that he had been heard to cry, in hollow, subterranean, suffocated notes, "Here I am!" At the opposite extremity of the town it was even known that the excavators had been able to open a communication with him through a pipe, and that he had received both soup and brandy by that channel, and that he had said with admirable fortitude that he was All right, my lads, with the exception of his collar-bone. But, the digging and shovelling and carrying away went on without intermission, until the ruins were all dug out, and the cellars laid open to the light; and still no Flintwinch, living or dead, all right or all wrong, had been turned up by pick or spade.

It began, then, to be perceived that Flintwinch had not been there at the time of the fall; and it began then to be perceived that he had been rather busy elsewhere, converting securities into as much money as could be got for them on the shortest notice, and turning to his own exclusive account, his authority to act for the Firm. Affery, remembering that the clever one had said he would explain himself further in four-and-twenty hours' time, determined for her part that his taking himself off within that period with all he could get, was the final satisfactory sum and substance of his promised explanation; but, she held her peace, devoutly thankful to be quit of him. As it seemed reasonable to conclude that a man who had never been buried could not be unburied, the diggers gave him up when their task was done, and did not dig down for him into the depths of the earth.

This was taken in ill part by a great many people, who persisted in believing that Flintwinch was lying somewhere among the London geological formations. Nor was their belief much shaken by repeated intelligence which came over in course of time, that an old man, who wore the tie of his neckcloth under one ear, and who was very well known to be an Englishman, consorted with the Dutchmen on the quaint banks of the canals at the Hague, and in the drinking-shops of Amsterdam, under the style and designation of Mynheer von Flyntevynge.

CHAPTER XXXII

GOING

ARTHUR continuing to lie very ill in the Marshalsea, and Mr. Rugg descrying no break in the legal sky affording a hope of his enlargement, Mr. Pancks suffered desperately from self-reproaches. If it had not been for those infallible figures which proved that Arthur, instead of pining in imprisonment, ought to be promenading in a carriage and pair, and that Mr. Pancks, instead of being restricted to his clerkly wages, ought to have from three to five thousand pounds of his own, at his immediate disposal, that unhappy arithmetician would probably have taken to his bed, and there have made one of the many obscure persons who turned their faces to the wall and died, as a last sacrifice to the late Mr. Merdle's greatness. Solely supported by his unimpugnable calculations, Mr. Pancks led an unhappy and restless life; constantly carrying his figures about with him in his hat, and not only going over them himself on every possible occasion, but entreating every human being he could lay hold of to go over them with him, and observe what a clear case it was. Down in Bleeding Heart Yard, there was scarcely an inhabitant of any note to whom Mr. Pancks had not imparted his demonstration, and, as figures are catching, a kind of cyphering measles broke out in that locality, under the influence of which the whole Yard was light-headed.

The more restless Mr. Pancks grew in his mind, the more impatient he became of the Patriarch. In their later conferences, his snorting had assumed an irritable sound which boded the Patriarch no good; likewise, Mr. Pancks had on several occasions looked harder at the Patriarchal bumps than was quite reconcileable with the fact of his not being a painter, or a peruke-maker, in search of the living model.

However, he had steamed in and out of his little back Dock, according as he was wanted or not wanted in the Patriarchal presence, and business had gone on in its customary course. Bleeding Heart Yard had been harrowed by Mr. Pancks, and cropped by Mr. Casby, at the regular seasons; Mr. Pancks had taken all the drudgery and all the dirt of the business as his share; Mr. Casby had taken all the profits, all the ethereal vapor, and all the moonshine, as *his* share; and, in the form of words which that benevolent beamer generally employed on Saturday evenings, when he twirled his fat thumbs after striking the week's balance, "everything had been satisfactory to all parties—all parties—satisfactory, sir, to all parties."

The Dock of the Steam-Tug, Pancks, had a leaden roof, which, frying in the very hot sunshine, may have heated the vessel. Be that as it may, one glowing Saturday evening, on being hailed by the lumbering bottle-green ship, the Tug instantly came working out of the Dock in a highly heated condition.

"Mr. Pancks," was the Patriarchal remark, "you have been remiss, you have been remiss, sir."

"What do you mean by that?" was the short rejoinder.

The Patriarchal state, always a state of calmness and composure, was so particularly serene that evening as to be provoking. Everybody else within the bills of mortality was hot; but, the Patriarch was perfectly cool. Everybody was thirsty, and the Patriarch was drinking. There was a fragrance of limes or lemons about him; and he had made a drink of golden sherry, which shone in a large tumbler, as if he were drinking the evening sunshine. This was bad, but not the worst. The worst was, that with his big blue eyes, and his polished head, and his long white hair, and his bottle-green legs stretched out before him, terminating in his easy shoes easily crossed at the instep, he had a radiant appearance of having in his extensive benevolence made the drink for the human species, while he himself wanted nothing but his own milk of human kindness.

Wherefore, Mr. Pancks said, "What do you mean by that?" and put his hair up with both hands, in a highly portentous manner.

"I mean, Mr. Pancks, that you must be sharper with the people, sharper with the people, much sharper with the people, sir. You don't squeeze them. You don't squeeze them. Your receipts are not up to the mark. You must squeeze them, sir, or our connexion will not continue to be as satisfactory as I could wish it to be, to all parties. All parties."

"*Don't* I squeeze 'em?" retorted Mr. Pancks. "What else am I made for?"

"You are made for nothing else, Mr. Pancks. You are made to do your duty, but you don't do your duty. You are paid to squeeze, and you must squeeze to pay." The Patriarch so much surprised himself by this brilliant turn, after Doctor Johnson, which he had not in the least expected or intended, that he laughed aloud; and repeated with great satisfaction, as he twirled his thumbs and nodded at his youthful portrait, "Paid to squeeze, sir, and must squeeze to pay."

"Oh!" said Pancks. "Anything more?"

"Yes, sir, yes, sir. Something more. You will please, Mr. Pancks, to squeeze the Yard again, the first thing on Monday morning."

"Oh!" said Pancks. "An't that too soon? I squeezed it dry to-day."

"Nonsense, sir. Not near the mark, not near the mark."

"Oh!" said Pancks, watching him as he benevolently gulped down a good draught of his mixture. "Anything more?"

"Yes, sir, yes, sir, something more. I am not at all pleased, Mr. Pancks, with my daughter; not at all pleased. Besides calling much too often to enquire for Mrs. Clennam, Mrs. Clennam, who is not just now in circumstances that are by any means calculated to—to be satisfactory to all parties, she goes, Mr. Pancks, unless I am much deceived, to enquire for Mr. Clennam in jail. In jail."

"He's laid up, you know," said Pancks. "Perhaps it's kind."

"Pooh, pooh, Mr. Pancks. She has nothing to do with that, nothing to do with that. I can't allow it. Let him pay his debts and come out, come out; pay his debts, and come out."

Although Mr. Pancks's hair was standing up like strong wire, he gave it another double-handed impulse in the perpendicular direction, and smiled at his proprietor in a most hideous manner.

"You will please to mention to my daughter, Mr. Pancks, that I can't allow it, can't allow it," said the Patriarch, blandly.

"Oh!" said Pancks. "You couldn't mention it yourself?"

"No sir, no; you are paid to mention it," the blundering old booby could not resist the temptation of trying it again, "and you must mention it to pay, mention it to pay."

"Oh!" said Pancks. "Anything more?"

"Yes, sir. It appears to me, Mr. Pancks, that you yourself are too often and too much in that direction, that direction. I recommend you, Mr. Pancks, to dismiss from your attention both your own losses and other people's losses, and to mind your business, mind your business."

Mr. Pancks acknowledged this recommendation with such an extra-ordinarily abrupt, short, and loud utterance of the monosyllable "Oh!" that even the unwieldy Patriarch moved his blue eyes in something of a hurry, to look at him. Mr. Pancks, with a sniff of corresponding intensity, then added, "Anything more?"

"Not at present, sir, not at present. I am going," said the Patriarch, finishing his mixture, and rising with an amiable air, "to take a little stroll, little stroll. Perhaps I shall find you here when I come back. If not sir, duty, duty; squeeze, squeeze, squeeze, on Monday; squeeze on Monday!"

Mr. Pancks, after another stiffening of his hair, looked on at the Patriarchal assumption of the broad-brimmed hat, with a momentary appearance of indecision contending with a sense of injury. He was also hotter than at first, and breathed harder. But, he suffered Mr. Casby to go out, without offering any further remark, and then took a peep at him over the little green window-blinds. "I thought so," he observed. "I knew where you were bound to. Good!" He then steamed back to his Dock, put it carefully in order, took down his hat, looked round the Dock, said "Good bye!" and puffed away on his own account. He steered straight for Mrs. Plornish's end of Bleeding Heart Yard, and arrived there, at the top of the steps, hotter than ever.

At the top of the steps, resisting Mrs. Plornish's invitations to come and sit along with father in Happy Cottage—which to his relief were not so numerous as they would have been on any other night than Saturday, when the connexion who so gallantly supported the business with everything but money gave their orders freely—at the top of the steps, Mr. Pancks remained until he beheld the Patriarch, who always entered the Yard at the other end, slowly advancing, beaming, and surrounded by suitors. Then Mr. Pancks descended and bore down upon him, with his utmost pressure of steam on.

The Patriarch, approaching with his usual benignity, was surprised to see Mr. Pancks, but supposed him to have been stimulated to an immediate

squeeze instead of postponing that operation until Monday. The population of the Yard were astonished at the meeting, for the two powers had
never been seen there together, within the memory of the oldest Bleeding
Heart. But, they were overcome by unutterable amazement, when Mr.
Pancks, going close up to the most venerable of men, and halting in front
of the bottle-green waistcoat, made a trigger of his right thumb and forefinger, applied the same to the brim of the broad-brimmed hat, and, with
singular smartness and precision, shot it off the polished head as if it had
been a large marble.

Having taken this little liberty with the Patriarchal person, Mr. Pancks
further astounded and attracted the Bleeding Hearts by saying in an
audible voice, "Now, you sugary swindler, I mean to have it out with
you!"

Mr. Pancks and the Patriarch were instantly the centre of a press, all
eyes and ears; windows were thrown open, and doorsteps were thronged.

"What do you pretend to be," said Mr. Pancks. "What's your moral
game? What do you go in for? Benevolence, an't it? YOU benevolent!"
Here Mr. Pancks, apparently without the intention of hitting him, but
merely to relieve his mind and expend his superfluous power in wholesome
exercise, aimed a blow at the bumpy head, which the bumpy head ducked
to avoid. This singular performance was repeated, to the ever increasing
admiration of the spectators, at the end of every succeeding article of Mr.
Pancks's oration.

"I have discharged myself from your service," said Pancks, "that I may
tell you what you are. You're one of a lot of impostors that are the worst lot
of all the lots to be met with. Speaking as a sufferer by both, I don't know
that I wouldn't as soon have the Merdle lot as your lot. You're a driver in
disguise, a screwer by deputy, a wringer, and squeezer, and shaver by
substitute. You're a philanthropic sneak. You're a shabby deceiver!"

(The repetition of the performance at this point was received with a
burst of laughter.)

"Ask these good people who's the hard man here. They'll tell you
Pancks, I believe."

This was confirmed with cries of "Certainly," and "Hear!"

"But I tell you, good people—Casby! This mound of meekness, this
lump of love, this bottle-green smiler, this is your driver!" said Pancks.
"If you want to see the man who would flay you alive—here he is! Don't
look for him in me, at thirty shillings a-week, but look for him in Casby, at
I don't know how much a-year!"

"Good!" cried several voices. "Hear Mr. Pancks!"

"Hear Mr. Pancks?" cried that gentleman (after repeating the popular
performance), "Yes, I should think so! It's almost time to hear Mr.
Pancks. Mr. Pancks has come down into the Yard to-night, on purpose that

you should hear him. Pancks is only the Works; but here's the Winder!"

The audience would have gone over to Mr. Pancks, as one man, woman, and child, but for the long, grey, silken locks, and the broad-brimmed hat.

"Here's the Stop," said Pancks, "that sets the tune to be ground. And there is but one tune, and its name is Grind, Grind, Grind! Here's the Proprietor, and here's his Grubber. Why, good people, when he comes smoothly spinning through the Yard to-night, like a slow-going benevolent Humming-Top, and when you come about him with your complaints of the Grubber, you don't know what a cheat the Proprietor is! What do you think of his showing himself to-night, that I may have all the blame on Monday? What do you think of his having had me over the coals this very evening, because I don't squeeze you enough? What do you think of my being, at the present moment, under special orders to squeeze you dry on Monday?"

The reply was given in a murmur of "Shame!" and "Shabby!"

"Shabby?" snorted Pancks. "Yes, I should think so! The lot that your Casby belongs to, is the shabbiest of all the lots. Setting their Grubbers on, at a wretched pittance, to do what they're ashamed and afraid to do and pretend not to do, but what they will have done, or give a man no rest! Imposing on you to give their Grubbers nothing but blame, and to give them nothing but credit! Why, the worst-looking cheat in all this town who gets the value of eighteenpence under false pretences, an't half such a cheat as this sign-post of The Casby's Head here!"

Cries of "That's true!" and "No more he an't!"

"And see what you get of these fellows, besides," said Pancks. "See what more you get of these precious Humming-Tops, revolving among you with such smoothness that you've no idea of the pattern painted on 'em, or the little window in 'em! I wish to call your attention to myself for a moment. I an't an agreeable style of chap, I know that very well."

The auditory were divided on this point; its more uncompromising members crying, "No you are not," and its politer materials, "Yes, you are."

"I am, in general," said Mr. Pancks, "a dreary Plodder, and a dry, uncomfortable Grubber. That's your humble servant. There's his full-length portrait, painted by himself and presented to you, warranted a likeness! But what's a man to be, with such a man as this for his Proprietor? What can be expected of him? Did anybody ever find boiled mutton and caper-sauce growing in a cocoa-nut?"

None of the Bleeding Hearts ever had, it was clear from the alacrity of their response.

"Well," said Mr. Pancks, "and neither will you find in Grubbers like myself, under Proprietors like this, pleasant qualities. I've been a Grubber from a boy. What has my life been? Fag and grind, fag and grind, turn the wheel, turn the wheel! I haven't been agreeable to myself, and I haven't been likely to be agreeable to anybody else. If I was a shilling a week less useful in ten years' time, this impostor would give me a shilling a week less; if as useful a man could be got at sixpence cheaper, he would be taken in my place at sixpence cheaper. Bargain and sale, bless you! Fixed principles! Oh! it is a mighty fine sign-post, is The Casby's Head," said Mr. Pancks, surveying it with anything rather than admiration; "but the real name of the House is The Sham's Arms. Its motto is, Keep the Grubber always at it. Is any gentleman present," said Mr. Pancks, breaking off and looking round, "acquainted with the English Grammar?"

Bleeding Heart Yard was shy of claiming that acquaintance.

"It's no matter," said Mr. Pancks. "I merely wish to remark that the task this Proprietor has set me, has been, never to leave off conjugating the Imperative Mood Present Tense of the verb To keep always at it. Keep thou always at it. Let him keep always at it. Keep we or do we keep always at it. Keep ye or do ye or you keep always at it. Let them keep always at it. Here is your benevolent Patriarch of a Casby, and there is his golden rule. He is uncommonly improving to look at, and I am not at all so. He is as sweet as honey, and I am as dull as ditch-water. He provides the pitch, and I handle it, and it sticks to me. Now," said Mr. Pancks, closing upon his late Proprietor again, from whom he had withdrawn a little for the better display of him to the Yard; "as I am not accustomed to speak in public, and as I have made a rather lengthy speech, all circumstances considered, I shall bring my observations to a close by requesting you to get out of this."

The Last of the Patriarchs had been so seized by assault, and required so much room to catch an idea in, and so much more room to turn it in, that he had not a word to offer in reply. He appeared to be meditating some Patriarchal way out of his delicate position, when Mr. Pancks, once more suddenly applying the trigger to his hat, shot it off again with his former dexterity. On the preceding occasion, one or two of the Bleeding Heart Yarders had obsequiously picked it up and handed it to its owner; but, Mr. Pancks had now so far impressed his audience, that the Patriarch had to turn and stoop for it himself.

Quick as lightning, Mr. Pancks, who, for some moments, had had his right hand in his coat pocket, whipped out a pair of shears, swooped upon the Patriarch behind, and snipped off short, the sacred locks that flowed upon his shoulders. In a paroxysm of animosity and rapidity, Mr. Pancks then caught the broad-brimmed hat out of the astounded Patriarch's hand, cut it down into a mere stewpan, and fixed it on the Patriarch's head.

Before the frightful results of this desperate action, Mr. Pancks himself recoiled in consternation. A bare-polled, goggle-eyed, big-headed, lumbering personage stood staring at him, not in the least impressive, not in the least venerable, who seemed to have started out of the earth to ask what was become of Casby. After staring at this phantom in return, in silent awe, Mr. Pancks threw down his shears, and fled for a place of hiding, where he might lie sheltered from the consequences of his crime. Mr. Pancks deemed it prudent to use all possible dispatch in making off, though he was pursued by nothing but the sound of laughter in Bleeding Heart Yard, rippling through the air, and making it ring again.

CHAPTER XXXIII

GOING!

THE changes of a fevered room are slow and fluctuating; but, the changes of the fevered world are rapid and irrevocable.

It was Little Dorrit's lot to wait upon both kinds of change. The Marshalsea walls, during a portion of every day, again embraced her in their shadows as their child while she thought for Clennam, worked for him, watched him, and only left him still to devote her utmost love and care to him. Her part in the life outside the gate urged its pressing claims upon her, too, and her patience untiringly responded to them. Here was Fanny, proud, fitful, whimsical, further advanced in that disqualified state for going into society which had so much fretted her on the evening of the tortoise-shell knife, resolved always to want comfort, resolved not to be comforted, resolved to be deeply wronged, and resolved that nobody should have the audacity to think her so. Here was her brother, a weak, proud, tipsy, young old man, shaking from head to foot, talking as indistinctly as if some of the money he plumed himself upon had got into his mouth and couldn't be got out, unable to walk alone in any act of his life, and patronising the sister whom he selfishly loved (he always had that negative merit, ill-starred and ill-launched Tip!), because he suffered her to lead him. Here was Mrs. Merdle in gauzy mourning—the original cap whereof had possibly been rent to pieces in a fit of grief, but had certainly yielded to a highly becoming article from the Parisian market—warring with Fanny foot to foot, and breasting her with her desolate bosom every hour in the day. Here was poor Mr. Sparkler, not knowing how to keep the peace between them, but humbly inclining to the opinion that they could do no better than agree that they were both remarkably fine women, and that there was no nonsense about either of them—for which gentle recommendation they united in falling upon him frightfully. Then, too, here was Mrs. General, got home from foreign parts, sending a Prune and a Prism by post every other day, demanding a new Testimonial by way of recommendation to some vacant appointment or other. Of which remarkable gentlewoman it may be finally observed, that there surely never was a gentlewoman of whose transcendent fitness for any vacant appointment on the face of this earth, so many people were (as the warmth of her Testimonials evinced) so perfectly satisfied—or who was so very unfortunate in having a large circle of ardent and distinguished admirers, who never themselves happened to want her, in any capacity.

On the first crash of the eminent Mr. Merdle's decease, many important persons had been unable to determine whether they should cut Mrs. Merdle, or comfort her. As it seemed, however, essential to the strength of their own case that they should admit her to have been cruelly deceived, they graciously made the admission and continued to know her. It followed that Mrs. Merdle, as a woman of fashion and good breeding, who had been sacrificed to the wiles of a vulgar barbarian (for, Mr. Merdle was found out, from the crown of his head to the sole of his foot, the moment he was found out in his pocket), must be actively championed by her order, for her order's sake. She returned this fealty, by causing it to be understood that she was even more incensed against the felonious shade of the deceased than anybody else was; thus on the whole she came out of her furnace like a wise woman, and did exceedingly well.

Mr. Sparkler's Lordship was fortunately one of those soft shelves on which a gentleman is considered to be put away for life, unless there should be reasons for hoisting him up with the Barnacle crane to a more lucrative height. That patriotic servant accordingly stuck to his colors (the Standard of four Quarterings), and was a perfect Nelson in respect of nailing them to the mast. On the profits of his intrepidity, Mrs. Sparkler and Mrs. Merdle, inhabiting different floors of the genteel little temple of inconvenience to which the smell of the day before yesterday's soup and coach-horses was as constant as Death to man, arrayed themselves to fight it out in the lists of Society, sworn rivals. And Little Dorrit, seeing all these things as they developed themselves, could not but wonder, anxiously, into what back corner of the genteel establishment Fanny's children would be poked by-and-bye, and who would take care of those unborn little victims.

Arthur being far too ill to be spoken with on subjects of emotion or anxiety, and his recovery greatly depending on the repose into which his weakness could be hushed, Little Dorrit's sole reliance during this heavy period was on Mr. Meagles. He was still abroad; but, she had written to him, through his daughter, immediately after first seeing Arthur in the Marshalsea, and since, confiding her uneasiness to him on the points on which she was most anxious, but especially on one. To that one, the continued absence of Mr. Meagles abroad, instead of his comforting presence in the Marshalsea, was referable.

Without disclosing the precise nature of the documents that had fallen into Rigaud's hands, Little Dorrit had confided the general outline of that story to Mr. Meagles, to whom she had also recounted his fate. The old cautious habits of the scales and scoop at once showed Mr. Meagles the importance of recovering the original papers; wherefore, he wrote back to Little Dorrit, strongly confirming her in the solicitude she expressed on that head, and adding that he would not come over to England "without making some attempt to trace them out."

By this time, Mr. Henry Gowan had made up his mind that it would be agreeable to him not to know the Meagleses. He was so considerate as to lay no injunctions on his wife in that particular; but, he mentioned to Mr. Meagles that personally they did not appear to him to get on together, and that he thought it would be a good thing if—politely, and without any scene, or anything of that sort—they agreed that they were the best fellows in the world, but were best apart. Poor Mr. Meagles, who was already sensible that he did not advance his daughter's happiness by being constantly slighted in her presence, said "Good, Henry! You are my Pet's husband; you have displaced me, in the course of nature; if you wish it, good!" This arrangement involved the contingent advantage, which perhaps Henry Gowan had not foreseen, that both Mr. and Mrs. Meagles were more liberal than before to their daughter, when their communication was only with her and her young child; and that his high spirit found itself better provided with money, without being under the degrading necessity of knowing whence it came.

Mr. Meagles, at such a period, naturally seized an occupation with great ardor. He knew from his daughter the various towns which Rigaud had been haunting, and the various hotels at which he had been living for some time back. The occupation he set himself was, to visit these with all discretion and speed, and, in the event of finding anywhere that he had left a bill unpaid, and a box or parcel behind, to pay such bill, and bring away such box or parcel.

With no other attendant than Mother, Mr. Meagles went upon this pilgrimage, and encountered a number of adventures. Not the least of his difficulties was, that he never knew what was said to him, and that he pursued his enquiries among people who never knew what he said to them. Still, with an unshaken confidence that the English tongue was somehow the mother tongue of the whole world, only the people were too stupid to know it, Mr. Meagles harangued inn-keepers in the most voluble manner, entered into loud explanations of the most complicated sort, and utterly renounced replies in the native language of the respondents, on the ground that they were "all bosh." Sometimes interpreters were called in; whom Mr. Meagles addressed in such idiomatic terms of speech, as instantly to extinguish and shut up—which made the matter worse. On a balance of the account, however, it may be doubted whether he lost much; for, although he found no property, he found so many debts and various associations of discredit with the proper name which was the only word he made intelligible, that he was almost everywhere overwhelmed with injurious accusations. On no fewer than four occasions, the police were called in to receive denunciations of Mr. Meagles as a Knight of Industry, a good-for-nothing, and a thief; all of which opprobrious language he bore with the best temper (having no idea what it meant), and was in the most ignominious manner escorted to steamboats and public carriages, to be got rid of, talking all the while, like a cheerful and fluent Briton as he was, with Mother under his arm.

But, in his own tongue, and in his own head, Mr. Meagles was a clear, shrewd, persevering man. When he had "worked round," as he called it, to Paris in his pilgrimage, and had wholly failed in it so far, he was not disheartened. "The nearer to England I follow him, you see, Mother," argued Mr. Meagles, "the nearer I am likely to come to the papers, whether they turn up or no. Because it is only reasonable to conclude, that he would deposit them somewhere where they would be safe from people over in England, and where they would yet be accessible to himself, don't you see."

At Paris, Mr. Meagles found a letter from Little Dorrit, lying waiting for him; in which she mentioned that she had been able to talk for a minute or two with Mr. Clennam, about this man who was no more; and that when she told Mr. Clennam that his friend Mr. Meagles who was on his way to see him had an interest in ascertaining something about the man if he could, he had asked her to tell Mr. Meagles that he had been known to Miss Wade, then living in such a street at Calais. "Oho!" said Mr. Meagles.

As soon afterwards as might be, in those Diligence days, Mr. Meagles rang the cracked bell at the cracked gate, and it jarred open, and the peasant-woman stood in the dark doorway, saying, "Ice-say! Seer! Who?" In acknowledgment of whose address, Mr. Meagles murmured to himself that there was some sense about these Calais people, who really did know something of what you and themselves were up to; and returned, "Miss Wade, my dear." He was then shown into the presence of Miss Wade.

"It's some time since we met," said Mr. Meagles, clearing his throat; "I hope you have been pretty well, Miss Wade?"

Without hoping that he or anybody else had been pretty well, Miss Wade asked him to what she was indebted for the honor of seeing him again? Mr. Meagles, in the meanwhile, glanced all round the room, without observing anything in the shape of a box.

"Why, the truth is, Miss Wade," said Mr. Meagles, in a comfortable, managing, not to say coaxing, voice, "it is possible that you may be able to throw a light upon a little something that is at present dark. Any unpleasant bygones between us, are bygones, I hope. Can't be helped now. You recollect my daughter? Times change so! A mother!"

In his innocence, Mr. Meagles could not have struck a worse key-note.

He paused for any expression of interest, but paused in vain.

"That is not the subject you wished to enter on?" she said, after a cold silence.

"No, no," returned Mr. Meagles, "No. I thought your good nature might——"

"I thought you knew," she interrupted, with a smile, "that my good nature is not cursorily awakened."

"Don't say so," said Mr. Meagles; "you do yourself an injustice. However, to come to the point." For he was sensible of having gained nothing by approaching it in a roundabout way. "I have heard from my friend Clennam, who, you will be sorry to hear, has been and still is very ill——"

He paused again, and again she was silent.

"——that you had some knowledge of one Blandois, lately killed in London by a violent accident. Now, don't mistake me! I know it was a slight knowledge," said Mr. Meagles, dexterously forestalling an angry interruption which he saw about to break. "I am fully aware of that. It was a slight knowledge, I know. But, the question is," Mr. Meagles's voice here became comfortable again, "did he, on his way to England last time, leave a box of papers, or a bundle of papers, or some papers or other in some receptacle or other—any papers—with you: begging you to allow him to leave them here for a short time, until he wanted them?"

"The question is?" she repeated. "Whose question is?"

"Mine," said Mr. Meagles. "And not only mine, but Clennam's question, and other people's question. Now, I am sure," continued Mr. Meagles, whose heart was overflowing with Pet, "that you can't have any unkind feeling towards my daughter; it's impossible. Well! It's her question, too; being one in which a particular friend of hers is nearly interested. So here I am, frankly to say that *is* the question, and to ask, Now, did he?"

"Upon my word," she returned, "I seem to be a mark for everybody who knew anything of a man I once in my life hired, and paid, and dismissed, to aim their questions at!"

"Now don't," remonstrated Mr. Meagles, "don't! Don't take offence, because it's the plainest question in the world, and might be asked of any one. The documents I refer to were not his own, were wrongfully obtained, might at some time or other be troublesome to an innocent person to have in keeping, and are sought by the people to whom they really belong. He passed through Calais going to London, and there were reasons why he should not take them with him then, why he should wish to be able to put his hand upon them readily, and why he should distrust leaving them with people of his own sort. Did he leave them here? I declare, if I knew how to avoid giving you offence, I would take any pains to do it. I put the question personally, but there's nothing personal in it. I might put it to any one; I have put it already to many people. Did he leave them here? Did he leave anything here?"

"No."

"Then unfortunately, Miss Wade, you know nothing about them?"

"I know nothing about them. I have now answered your unaccountable question. He did not leave them here, and I know nothing about them."

"There!" said Mr. Meagles, rising. "I am sorry for it; that's over; and I hope there is not much harm done.—Tattycoram well, Miss Wade?"

"Harriet well? Oh yes!"

"I have put my foot in it again," said Mr. Meagles, thus corrected. "I can't keep my foot out of it, here, it seems. Perhaps, if I had thought twice about it, I might never have given her the jingling name. But, when one means to be good-natured and sportive with young people, one doesn't think twice. Her old friend leaves a kind word for her, Miss Wade, if you should think proper to deliver it."

She said nothing as to that; and Mr. Meagles; taking his honest face out of the dull room, where it shone like a sun, took it to the Hotel where he had left Mrs. Meagles, and where he made the Report: "Beaten, Mother; no effects!" He took it next to the London Steam Packet, which sailed in the night; and next to the Marshalsea.

The faithful John was on duty, when Father and Mother Meagles presented themselves at the wicket towards nightfall. Miss Dorrit was not there then, he said; but, she had been there in the morning, and invariably came in the evening. Mr. Clennam was slowly mending; and Maggy and Mrs. Plornish and Mr. Baptist took care of him by turns. Miss Dorrit was sure to come back that evening before the bell rang. There was the room the Marshal had lent her, up-stairs, in which they could wait for her, if they pleased. Mistrustful that it might be hazardous to Arthur to see him without preparation, Mr. Meagles accepted the offer; and they were left shut up in the room, looking down through its barred window into the jail.

The cramped area of the prison had such an effect on Mrs. Meagles that she began to weep, and such an effect on Mr. Meagles that he began to gasp for air. He was walking up and down the room, panting, and making himself worse by laboriously fanning himself with his handkerchief, when he turned towards the opening door.

"Eh? Good Gracious!" said Mr. Meagles, "this is not Miss Dorrit! Why, Mother, look! Tattycoram!"

No other. And in Tattycoram's arms was an iron box some two feet square. Such a box had Affery Flintwinch seen in the first of her dreams, going out of the old house in the dead of the night, under Double's arm. This, Tattycoram put on the ground at her old master's feet; this, Tattycoram fell on her knees by, and beat her hands upon, crying half in exultation and half in despair, half in laughter and half in tears, "Pardon, dear Master, take me back dear Mistress, here it is!"

"Tatty!" exclaimed Mr. Meagles.

"What you wanted!" said Tattycoram. "Here it is! I was put in the next room not to see you. I heard you ask her about it, I heard her say she hadn't got it, I was there when he left it, and I took it at bedtime and brought it away. Here it is!"

"Why, my girl," cried Mr. Meagles, more breathless than before, "how did you come over?"

"I came in the boat with you. I was sitting wrapped up at the other end. When you took a coach at the wharf, I took another coach, and followed you here. She never would have given it up, after what you had said to her about its being wanted; she would sooner have sunk it in the sea, or burnt it. But, here it is!"

The glow and rapture that the girl was in, with her "Here it is!"

"She never wanted it to be left, I must say that for her; but he left it, and I know well that after what you said, and after her denying it, she never would have given it up. But here it is! Dear kind Master, dear kind Mistress, take me back again, and give me back the dear old name! Let this intercede for me. Here it is!"

Father and Mother Meagles never deserved their names better, than when they took the headstrong foundling-girl into their protection again.

"Oh! I have been so wretched," cried Tattycoram, weeping much more, after that, than before; "always so unhappy, and so repentant! I was afraid of her, from the first time I ever saw her. I knew she had got a power over me, through understanding what was bad in me, so well. It was a madness in me, and she could raise it whenever she liked. I used to think, when I got into that state, that people were all against me because of my first beginning; and the kinder they were to me, the worse fault I found in them. I made it out that they triumphed above me, and that they wanted to make me envy them, when I know—when I even knew then, if I would—that they never thought of such a thing. And my beautiful young mistress not so happy as she ought to have been, and I gone away from her! Such a brute and wretch as she must think me! But you'll say a word to her for me, and ask her to be as forgiving as you two are? For, I am not so bad as I was," pleaded Tattycoram; "I am bad enough, but not so bad as I was, indeed. I have had Miss Wade before me all this time, as if it was my own self grown ripe—turning everything the wrong way, and twisting all good into evil. I have had her before me all this time, finding no pleasure in anything but in keeping me as miserable, suspicious, and tormenting as herself. Not that she had much to do, to do that," cried Tattycoram, in a closing great burst of distress, "for I was as bad as bad could be. I only mean to say, that, after what I have gone through, I hope I shall never be quite so bad again, and that I shall get better by very slow degrees. I'll try very hard. I won't stop at five-and-twenty, sir. I'll count five-and-twenty hundred, five-and-twenty thousand!"

Another opening of the door, and Tattycoram subsided, and Little

Dorrit came in, and Mr. Meagles with pride and joy produced the box, and her gentle face was lighted up with grateful happiness and joy. The secret was safe now! She could keep her own part of it from him; he should never know of her loss; in time to come, he should know all that was of import to himself; but, he should never know what concerned her, only. That was all past, all forgiven, all forgotten.

"Now, my dear Miss Dorrit," said Mr. Meagles; "I am a man of business—or at least I was —and I am going to take my measures, promptly, in that character. Had I better see Arthur to-night?"

"I think not to-night. I will go to his room and ascertain how he is. But I think it will be better not to see him to-night."

"I am much of your opinion, my dear," said Mr. Meagles, "and therefore I have not been any nearer to him than this dismal room. Then I shall probably not see him for some little time to come. But I'll explain what I mean when you come back."

She left the room. Mr. Meagles, looking through the bars of the window, saw her pass out of the Lodge below him into the prison-yard. He said gently, "Tattycoram, come to me a moment, my good girl."

She went up to the window.

"You see that young lady who was here just now—that little, quiet, fragile figure passing along there, Tatty? Look. The people stand out of the way to let her go by. The men—see the poor, shabby fellows—pull off their hats to her quite politely, and now she glides in at that doorway. See her, Tattycoram?"

"Yes, sir."

"I have heard tell, Tatty, that she was once regularly called the child of this place. She was born here, and lived here many years. I can't breathe here. A doleful place, to be born and bred in, Tattycoram?"

"Yes indeed, sir!"

"If she had constantly thought of herself, and settled with herself that everybody visited this place upon her, turned it against her, and cast it at her, she would have led an irritable and probably an useless existence. Yet I have heard tell, Tattycoram, that her young life has been one of active resignation, goodness, and noble service. Shall I tell you what I consider those eyes of hers that were here just now, to have always looked at, to get that expression?"

"Yes, if you please, sir."

"Duty, Tattycoram. Begin it early, and do it well; and there is no antecedent to it, in any origin or station, that will tell against us with the Almighty, or with ourselves."

They remained at the window, Mother joining them and pitying the prisoners, until she was seen coming back. She was soon in the room, and recommended that Arthur, whom she had left calm and composed, should not be visited that night.

"Good!" said Mr. Meagles, cheerily. "I have not a doubt that's best.

I shall trust my remembrances then, my sweet nurse, in your hands, and I well know they couldn't be in better. I am off again to-morrow morning."

Little Dorrit, surprised, asked him where?

"My dear," said Mr. Meagles, "I can't live without breathing. This place has taken my breath away, and I shall never get it back again until Arthur is out of this place."

"How is that a reason for going off again to-morrow morning?"

"You shall understand," said Mr. Meagles. "To-night we three will put up at a City Hotel. To-morrow morning, Mother and Tattycoram will go down to Twickenham, where Mrs. Tickit, sitting attended by Dr. Buchan in the parlor-window, will think them a couple of ghosts; and I shall go abroad again for Doyce. We must have Dan here. Now, I tell you my love, it's of no use writing and planning and conditionally speculating, upon this and that and the other, at uncertain intervals and distances; we must have Doyce here. I devote myself, at daybreak to-morrow morning, to bringing Doyce here. It's nothing to me to go and find him. I'm an old traveller, and all foreign languages and customs are alike to me—I never understand anything about any of 'em. Therefore I can't be put to any inconvenience. Go at once I must, it stands to reason; because I can't live, without breathing freely; and I can't breathe freely, until Arthur is out of this Marshalsea. I am stifled at the present moment, and have scarcely breath enough to say this much, and to carry this precious box down-stairs for you."

They got into the street as the bell began to ring, Mr. Meagles carrying the box. Little Dorrit had no conveyance there: which rather surprised him. He called a coach for her, and she got into it, and he placed the box beside her when she was seated. In her joy and gratitude she kissed his hand.

"I don't like that, my dear," said Mr. Meagles. "It goes against my feeling of what's right, that *you* should do homage to *me*—at the Marshalsea Gate."

She bent forward, and kissed his cheek.

"You remind me of the days," said Mr. Meagles, suddenly drooping—"but she's very fond of him, and hides his faults, and thinks that no one sees them—and he certainly is well connected, and of a very good family!"

It was the only comfort he had in the loss of his daughter, and if he made the most of it, who would blame him?

CHAPTER XXXIV

GONE

On a healthy autumn day, the Marshalsea prisoner, weak but otherwise restored, sat listening to a voice that read to him. On a healthy autumn day; when the golden fields had been reaped and ploughed again, when the summer fruits had ripened and waned, when the green perspectives of hops had been laid low by the busy pickers, when the apples clustering in the orchards were russet, and the berries of the mountain ash were crimson among the yellowing foliage. Already in the woods, glimpses of the hardy winter that was coming, were to be caught through unaccustomed openings among the boughs where the prospect shone defined and clear, free from the bloom of the drowsy summer weather, which had rested on it as the bloom lies on the plum. So, from the sea-shore the ocean was no longer to be seen lying asleep in the heat, but its thousand sparkling eyes were open, and its whole breadth was in joyful animation, from the cool sand on the beach to the little sails on the horizon, drifting away like autumn-tinted leaves that had drifted from the trees.

Changeless and barren, looking ignorantly at all the seasons with its fixed, pinched face of poverty and care, the prison had not a touch of any of these beauties on it. Blossom what would, its bricks and bars bore uniformly the same dead crop. Yet Clennam, listening to the voice as it read to him, heard in it all that great Nature was doing, heard in it all the soothing songs she sings to man. At no Mother's knee but hers, had he ever dwelt in his youth on hopeful promises, on playful fancies, on the harvests of tenderness and humility that lie hidden in the early-fostered seeds of the imagination; on the oaks of retreat from blighting winds, that have the germs of their strong roots in nursery acorns. But, in the tones of the voice that read to him, there were memories of an old feeling of such things, and echoes of every merciful and loving whisper that had ever stolen to him in his life.

When the voice stopped, he put his hand over his eyes, murmuring that the light was strong upon them.

Little Dorrit put the book by, and presently arose quietly to shade the window. Maggy sat at her needlework in her old place. The light softened, Little Dorrit brought her chair closer to his side.

"This will soon be over now, dear Mr. Clennam. Not only are Mr. Doyce's letters to you so full of friendship and encouragement, but Mr. Rugg says his letters to him are so full of help, and that everybody (now a little anger is past) is so considerate, and speaks so well of you, that it will soon be over now."

"Dear girl. Dear heart. Good angel!"

"You praise me far too much. And yet it is such an exquisite pleasure to me to hear you speak so feelingly, and to—and to see," said Little Dorrit, raising her eyes to his, "how deeply you mean it, that I cannot say Don't."

He lifted her hand to his lips.

"You have been here many, many times, when I have not seen you, Little Dorrit?"

"Yes, I have been here sometimes when I have not come into the room."

"Very often?"

"Rather often," said Little Dorrit, timidly.

"Every day?"

"I think," said Little Dorrit, after hesitating, "that I have been here at least twice, every day."

He might have released the little light hand, after fervently kissing it again; but that, with a very gentle lingering where it was, it seemed to court being retained. He took it in both of his, and it lay softly on his breast.

"Dear Little Dorrit, it is not my imprisonment only that will soon be over. This sacrifice of you must be ended. We must learn to part again, and to take our different ways so wide asunder. You have not forgotten what we said together, when you came back?"

"O no, I have not forgotten it. But something has been—You feel quite strong to–day, don't you?"

"Quite strong."

The hand he held, crept up a little nearer to his face.

"Do you feel quite strong enough to know what a great fortune I have got?"

"I shall be very glad to be told. No fortune can be too great or good for Little Dorrit."

"I have been anxiously waiting to tell you. I have been longing and longing to tell you. You are sure you will not take it?"

"Never!"

"You are quite sure you will not take half of it?"

"Never, dear Little Dorrit!"

As she looked at him silently, there was something in her affectionate face that he did not quite comprehend; something that could have broken into tears in a moment, and yet that was happy and proud.

"You will be sorry to hear what I have to tell you about Fanny. Poor Fanny has lost everything. She has nothing left but her husband's income. All that papa gave her when she married, was lost as your money was lost. It was in the same hands, and it is all gone."

Arthur was more shocked than surprised to hear it. "I had hoped it might not be so bad," he said: "but I had feared a heavy loss there, knowing the connexion between her husband and the defaulter."

"Yes. It is all gone. I am very sorry for Fanny; very, very, very sorry for poor Fanny. My poor brother, too!"

"Had *he* property in the same hands?"

"Yes! And it is all gone.—How much do you think my own great fortune is?"

As Arthur looked at her enquiringly, with a new apprehension on him, she withdrew her hand, and laid her face down on the spot where it had rested.

"I have nothing in the world. I am as poor as when I lived here. When papa came over to England, he confided everything he had to the same hands, and it is all swept away. O my dearest and best, are you quite sure you will not share my fortune with me now?"

Locked in his arms, held to his heart, with his manly tears upon her own cheek, she drew the slight hand round his neck, and clasped it in its fellow-hand.

"Never to part, my dearest Arthur; never any more until the last! I never was rich before, I never was proud before, I never was happy before. I am rich in being taken by you, I am proud in having been resigned by you, I am happy in being with you in this prison, as I should be happy in coming back to it with you, if it should be the will of GOD, and comforting and serving you with all my love and truth. I am yours anywhere, everywhere! I love you dearly! I would rather pass my life here with you, and go out daily, working for our bread, than I would have the greatest fortune that ever was told, and be the greatest lady that ever was honored. O, if poor papa may only know how blest at last my heart is, in this room where he suffered for so many years!"

Maggy had of course been staring from the first, and had of course been crying her eyes out, long before this. Maggy was now so overjoyed that, after hugging her little mother with all her might, she went down-stairs like a clog-hornpipe to find somebody or other to whom to impart her gladness. Whom should Maggy meet but Flora and Mr. F's Aunt opportunely coming in? And whom else, as a consequence of that meeting, should Little Dorrit find waiting for herself, when, a good two or three hours afterwards, she went out?

Flora's eyes were a little red, and she seemed rather out of spirits. Mr. F's Aunt was so stiffened that she had the appearance of being past bending, by any means short of powerful mechanical pressure. Her bonnet was cocked up behind in a terrific manner; and her stony reticule was as rigid as if it had been petrified by the Gorgon's head, and had got it at that moment inside. With these imposing attributes, Mr. F's Aunt, publicly seated on the steps of the Marshal's official residence, had been for the two or three hours in question a great boon to the younger inhabitants of the Borough, whose sallies of humour she had considerably flushed herself by resenting, at the point of her umbrella, from time to time.

"Painfully aware, Miss Dorrit, I am sure," said Flora, "that to propose an adjournment to any place to one so far removed by fortune and so courted and caressed by the best society must ever appear intruding even if not a pie-shop far below your present sphere and a back-parlor though a civil man but if for the sake of Arthur—cannot overcome it more improper now than ever late Doyce and Clennam—one last remark I might wish to make one last explanation I might wish to offer perhaps your good nature might excuse under pretence of three kidney ones the humble place of conversation."

Rightly interpreting this rather obscure speech, Little Dorrit returned that she was quite at Flora's disposition. Flora accordingly led the way across the road to the pie-shop in question; Mr. F's Aunt stalking across in the rear, and putting herself in the way of being run over, with a perseverance worthy of a better cause.

When the "three kidney ones," which were to be a blind to the conversation, were set before them on three little tin platters, each kidney one ornamented with a hole at the top, into which the civil man poured hot gravy out of a spouted can as if he were feeding three lamps, Flora took out her pocket-handkerchief.

"If Fancy's fair dreams," she began, "have ever pictured that when Arthur—cannot overcome it pray excuse me—was restored to freedom even a pie as far from flaky as the present and so deficient in kidney as to be in that respect like a minced nutmeg might not prove unacceptable if offered by the hand of true regard such visions have for ever fled and all is cancelled but being aware that tenderer relations are in contemplation beg to state that I heartily wish well to both and find no fault with either not the least, it may be withering to know that ere the hand of Time had made me much less slim than formerly and dreadfully red on the slightest exertion particularly after eating I well know when it takes the form of a rash it might have been and was not through the interruption of parents and mental torpor succeeded until the mysterious clue was held by Mr. F still I would not be ungenerous to either and I heartily wish well to both."

Little Dorrit took her hand, and thanked her for all her old kindness.

"Call it not kindness," returned Flora, giving her an honest kiss, "for you always were the best and dearest little thing that ever was if I may take the liberty and even in a money point of view a saving being Conscience itself though I must add much more agreeable than mine ever was to me for though not I hope more burdened than other people's yet I have always found it far readier to make one uncomfortable than comfortable and evidently taking a greater pleasure in doing it but I am wandering, one hope I wish to express ere yet the closing scene draws in and it is that I do trust for the sake of old times and old sincerity that Arthur will know that I didn't desert him in his misfortunes but that I came backwards and forwards constantly to ask if I could do anything for him and that I sat in the pie-shop where they very civilly fetched something warm in a tumbler from the hotel and really very nice hours after hours to keep him company over the way without his knowing it."

Flora really had tears in her eyes now, and they showed her to great advantage.

"Over and above which," said Flora, "I earnestly beg you as the dearest thing that ever was if you'll still excuse the familiarity from one who moves in very different circles to let Arthur understand that I don't know after all whether it wasn't all nonsense between us though pleasant at the time and trying too and certainly Mr. F did work a change and the spell being broken nothing could be expected to take place without weaving it afresh which various circumstances have combined to prevent of which perhaps not the least powerful was that it was not to be, I am not prepared to say that if it had been agreeable to Arthur and had brought itself about naturally in the first instance I should not have been very glad being of a lively disposition and moped at home where papa undoubtedly is the most aggravating of his sex and not improved since having been cut down by the hand of the Incendiary into something of which I never saw the counterpart in all my life but jealousy is not my character nor ill-will though many faults."

Without having been able closely to follow Mrs. Finching through this labyrinth, Little Dorrit understood its purpose, and cordially accepted the trust.

"The withered chaplet my dear," said Flora, with great enjoyment, "is then perished the column is crumbled and the pyramid is standing upside down upon its what's-his-name call it not giddiness call it not weakness call it not folly I must now retire into privacy and look upon the ashes of departed joys no more but taking the further liberty of paying for the pastry which has formed the humble pretext of our interview will for ever say Adieu!"

Mr. F's Aunt, who had eaten her pie with great solemnity, and who had been elaborating some grievous scheme of injury in her mind, since her first assumption of that public position on the Marshal's steps, took the present opportunity of addressing the following Sibyllic apostrophe to the relict of her late nephew.

"Bring him for'ard, and I'll chuck him out o' winder!"

Flora tried in vain to soothe the excellent woman, by explaining that they were going home to dinner. Mr. F's Aunt persisted in replying, "Bring him for'ard, and I'll chuck him out o' winder!" Having reiterated this demand an immense number of times, with a sustained glare of defiance at Little Dorrit, Mr. F's Aunt folded her arms, and sat down in a corner of the pie-shop parlor; stedfastly refusing to budge until such time as "he" should have been "brought for'ard," and the chucking portion of his destiny accomplished.

In this condition of things, Flora confided to Little Dorrit that she had not seen Mr. F's Aunt so full of life and character for weeks; that she would find it necessary to remain there "hours perhaps," until the inexorable old lady could be softened; and that she could manage her best alone. They parted, therefore, in the friendliest manner, and with the kindest feeling on both sides.

Mr. F's Aunt holding out like a grim fortress, and Flora becoming in need of refreshment, a messenger was dispatched to the hotel for the tumbler already glanced at, which was afterwards replenished. With the aid of its contents, a newspaper, and some skimming of the cream of the pie-stock, Flora got through the remainder of the day in perfect good humour; though occasionally embarrassed by the consequences of an idle rumour which circulated among the credulous infants of the neighbourhood, to the effect that an old lady had sold herself to the pie-shop, to be made up, and was then sitting in the pie-shop parlor, declining to complete her contract. This attracted so many young persons of both sexes, and, when the shades of evening began to fall, occasioned so much interruption to the business, that the merchant became very pressing in his proposals that Mr. F's Aunt should be removed. A conveyance was accordingly brought to the door, which, by the joint efforts of the merchant and Flora, this remarkable woman was at last induced to enter; though not without even then putting her head out at the window, and demanding to have him "brought for'ard" for the purpose originally mentioned. As she was observed at this time to direct baleful glances towards the Marshalsea, it has been supposed that this admirably consistent female intended by "him," Arthur Clennam. This, however, is mere speculation; who the person was, who, for the satisfaction of Mr. F's Aunt's mind, ought to have been brought forward, and never was brought forward, will never be positively known.

The autumn days went on, and Little Dorrit never came to the Marshalsea now, and went away without seeing him. No, no, no.

One morning, as Arthur listened for the light feet, that every morning ascended winged to his heart, bringing the heavenly brightness of a new love into the room where the old love had wrought so hard and been so true; one morning, as he listened, he heard her coming, not alone.

"Dear Arthur," said her delighted voice outside the door, "I have someone here. May I bring some one in?"

He had thought from the tread there were two with her. He answered "Yes," and she came in with Mr. Meagles. Sunbrowned and jolly Mr. Meagles looked, and he opened his arms and folded Arthur in them, like a sunbrowned and jolly father.

"Now, I am all right," said Mr. Meagles, after a minute or so. "Now, it's over. Arthur, my dear fellow, confess at once that you expected me before."

"I did," said Arthur; "but Amy told me——"

"Little Dorrit. Never any other name." (It was she who whispered it).

"—But my Little Dorrit told me that, without asking for any further explanation, I was not to expect you until I saw you."

"And now you see me, my boy," said Mr. Meagles, shaking him by the hand stoutly; "and now you shall have any explanation and every explanation. The fact is, I *was* here,—came straight to you from the Allongers and Marshongers, or I should be ashamed to look you in the face this day, — but you were not in company trim at the moment, and I had to start off again to catch Doyce."

"Poor Doyce!" sighed Arthur.

"Don't call him names that he don't deserve," said Mr. Meagles. "*He's* not poor; *he's* doing well enough. Doyce is a wonderful fellow over there. I assure you, he is making out his case like a house a-fire. He has fallen on his legs, has Dan. Where they don't want things done and find a man to do 'em, that man's off his legs; but where they do want things done and find a man to do 'em, that man's on his legs. You won't have occasion to trouble the Circumlocution Office any more. Let me tell you, Dan has done without 'em!"

"What a load you take from my mind!" cried Arthur. "What happiness you give me!"

"Happiness?" retorted Mr. Meagles. "Don't talk about happiness till you see Dan. I assure you, Dan is directing works and executing labors over yonder, that it would make your hair stand on end to look at. He's no public offender, bless you, now! He's medalled and ribboned, and starred and crossed, and I don't-know-what all'd, like a born nobleman. But we mustn't talk about that over here."

"Why not?"

"Oh, egad!" said Mr. Meagles, shaking his head very seriously, "he must hide all those things under lock and key when he comes over here. They won't do, over here. In that particular, Britannia is a Britannia in the Manger—won't give her children such distinctions herself, and won't allow them to be seen, when they're given by other countries. No, no, Dan!" said Mr. Meagles, shaking his head again. "That won't do here!"

"If you had brought me (except for Doyce's sake) twice what I have lost," cried Arthur, "you would not have given me the pleasure that you give me in this news."

"Why, of course, of course," assented Mr. Meagles. "Of course I know that, my good fellow, and therefore I come out with it in the first burst. Now, to go back, about catching Doyce. I caught Doyce. Ran against him, among a lot of those dirty brown dogs in women's nightcaps a great deal too big for 'em, calling themselves Arabs and all sorts of incoherent races. *You* know 'em! Well! He was coming straight to me, and I was going straight to him, and so we came back together."

"Doyce in England?" exclaimed Arthur.

"There!" said Mr. Meagles, throwing open his arms. "I am the worst man in the world to manage a thing of this sort. I don't know what I should have done if I had been in the diplomatic line—right, perhaps! The long and the short of it is, Arthur, we have both been in England this fortnight. And if you go on to ask where Doyce is at the present moment, why, my plain answer is—here he is! And now I can breathe again, at last!"

Doyce darted in from behind the door, caught Arthur by both hands, and said the rest for himself.

"There are only three branches of my subject, my dear Clennam," said Doyce, proceeding to mould them severally, with his plastic thumb on the palm of his hand, "and they're soon disposed of. First, not a word more from you about the past. There was an error in your calculations. I know what that is. It affects the whole machine, and failure is the consequence. You will profit by the failure, and will avoid it another time. I have done a similar thing myself, in construction, often. Every failure teaches a man something, if he will learn; and you are too sensible a man not to learn from this failure. So much for firstly. Secondly. I was sorry you should have taken it so heavily to heart, and reproached yourself so severely; I was travelling home night and day to put matters right, with the assistance of our friend, when I fell in with our friend as he has informed you. Thirdly. We two agreed, that, after what you had undergone, after your distress of mind, and after your illness, it would be a pleasant surprise if we could so far keep quiet as to get things perfectly arranged without your knowledge, and then come and say that all the affairs were smooth, that everything was right, that the business stood in greater want of you than it ever did, and that a new and prosperous career was opened before you and me as partners. That's thirdly. But you know we always make an allowance for friction, and so I have reserved space to close in. My dear Clennam, I thoroughly confide in you; you have it in your power to be quite as useful to me, as I have, or have had, it in my power to be useful to you; your old place awaits you, and wants you very much; there is nothing to detain you here, one half-hour longer."

There was a silence, which was not broken until Arthur had stood for some time at the window with his back towards them, and until his little wife that was to be, had gone to him and stayed by him.

"I made a remark a little while ago," said Daniel Doyce then, "which I am inclined to think was an incorrect one. I said there was nothing to detain you here, Clennam, half an hour longer. Am I mistaken in supposing that you would rather not leave here till to-morrow morning? Do I know, without being very wise, where you would like to go, direct, from these walls and from this room?"

"You do," returned Arthur. "It has been our cherished purpose."

"Very well!" said Doyce. "Then, if this young lady will do me the honor of regarding me for four-and-twenty hours in the light of a father, and will take a ride with me now towards Saint Paul's Churchyard, I dare say I know what we want to get there."

Little Dorrit and he went out together soon afterwards, and Mr. Meagles lingered behind to say a word to his friend.

"I think, Arthur, you will not want Mother and me in the morning, and we will keep away. It might set Mother thinking about Pet; she's a soft-hearted woman. She's best at the cottage, and I'll stay there and keep her company."

With that they parted for the time. And the day ended, and the night ended, and the morning came, and Little Dorrit, simply dressed as usual, and having no one with her but Maggy, came into the prison with the sunshine. The poor room was a happy room that morning. Where in the world was there a room so full of quiet joy!

"My dear love," said Arthur. "Why does Maggy light the fire? We shall be gone directly."

"I asked her to do it. I have taken such an odd fancy. I want you to burn something for me."

"What?"

"Only this folded paper. If you will put it in the fire with your own hand, just as it is, my fancy will be gratified."

"Superstitious, darling Little Dorrit? Is it a charm?"

"It is anything you like best, my own," she answered, laughing with glistening eyes and standing on tiptoe to kiss him, "if you will only humour me when the fire burns up."

So they stood before the fire, waiting: Clennam with his arm about her waist, and the fire shining, as fire in that same place had often shone, in Little Dorrit's eyes. "Is it bright enough now?" said Arthur. "Quite bright enough now," said Little Dorrit. "Does the charm want any words to be said?" asked Arthur, as he held the paper over the flame. "You can say (if you don't mind) 'I love you!' " answered Little Dorrit. So he said it, and the paper burned away.

They passed very quietly along the yard; for, no one was there, though many heads were stealthily peeping from the windows. Only one face, familiar of old, was in the Lodge. When they had both accosted it, and spoken many kind words, Little Dorrit turned back one last time with her hand stretched out, saying, "Good bye, good John! I hope you will live very happy, dear!"

Then they went up the steps of the neighbouring Saint George's Church, and went up to the altar, where Daniel Doyce was waiting in his paternal character. And there, was Little Dorrit's old friend who had given her the Burial Register for a pillow: full of admiration that she should come back to them to be married, after all.

And they were married, with the sun shining on them through the painted figure of Our Saviour on the window. And they went into the very room where Little Dorrit had slumbered after her party, to sign the Marriage Register. And there, Mr. Pancks (destined to be chief clerk to Doyce and Clennam, and afterwards partner in the house), sinking the Incendiary in the peaceful friend, looked in at the door to see it done, with Flora gallantly supported on one arm and Maggy on the other, and a back-ground of John Chivery and father, and other turnkeys, who had run round for the moment, deserting the parent Marshalsea for its happy child. Nor had Flora the least signs of seclusion upon her, notwithstanding her recent declaration; but on the contrary was wonderfully smart, and enjoyed the ceremonies mightily, though in a fluttered way.

Little Dorrit's old friend held the inkstand as she signed her name, and the clerk paused in taking off the good clergyman's surplice, and all the witnesses looked on with special interest. "For, you see," said Little Dorrit's old friend, "this young lady is one of our curiosities, and has come now to the third volume of our Registers. Her birth is in what I call the first volume; she lay asleep on this very floor, with her pretty head on what I call the second volume; and she's now a-writing her little name as a bride, in what I call the third volume."

They all gave place when the signing was done, and Little Dorrit and her husband walked out of the church alone. They paused for a moment on the steps of the portico, looking at the fresh perspective of the street in the autumn morning sun's bright rays, and then went down.

Went down into a modest life of usefulness and happiness. Went down to give a mother's care, in the fulness of time, to Fanny's neglected children no less than to their own, and to leave that lady going into Society for ever and a day. Went down to give a tender nurse and friend to Tip for some few years, who was never vexed by the great exactions he made of her, in return for the riches he might have given her if he had ever had them, and who lovingly closed his eyes upon the Marshalsea and all its blighted fruits. They went quietly down into the roaring streets, inseparable and blessed; and as they passed along in sunshine and in shade, the noisy and the eager, and the arrogant and the froward and the vain, fretted, and chafed, and made their usual uproar.

THE END

The Third Volume of the Registers

THE NUMBER PLANS

THESE are Dickens's working notes, originally on foolscap sheets, each folded at right angles to its longer side. The left-hand half-sheet contains, as a rule, suggestions for the number; the right-hand half-sheet is used for a list of chapters, the contents often noted after the writing of the number, as reminders.

This transcript follows the underlining of the original, and as far as possible the order in which entries were made; their actual position and spacing can often be only approximate. Diagonal bars dividing entries are omitted, but interpreted by separation. Deleted words are given or indicated except where the identical word was substituted. Full stops are omitted in headings of numbers, books, and chapters.

(⟨Nobody's Fault⟩ Little Dorrit—Nº I)

Waiting Room? No

Office? No

French Town? Yes

Man from China? Yes

Prison? Yes

Quarantine? Yes

Family and two daughters? No

Working jeweller and his daughters? No

People to meet and part as travellers do, and the future connexion between them in the story, not to be now shewn to the reader but to be worked out as in life. Try this uncertainty and this not-putting of them together, as a new means of interest. Indicate and carry through this intention.

New sort of practical People ⎫
⎬ Meagles
Father   Mother — Baby ⎭

Tattycoram

Reserved Woman. Introduce Miss—Wade?

Chapter I
Sun and Shadow

Marseilles- -Hot dusty picture Cold, shaded prison—Two men

Little Genoese- -or Neopolitan?- Picture of an Italian—-Monsieur Rigaud, with his nose going up & his moustache coming down Signor John Baptist Cavalletto Cavalletti

Jailer's child

Qui est-ce-qui passe ici si tard compagnon de la Majolaine

Chapter II

⟨Baby ⟨Practical People⟩ Quarantine

Bring in Father Mother Baby Meagles.

Arthur Clennam. From China. Indicates his story.

"Practical people" New and better aspect thereof than usual: shewing how to be practical, not politico-economically.

Miss Wade Tattycoram

Travellers disperse—thus all travellers through life

Chapter III
Home

Dismal London Sunday. Summer evening.
Coming on wet.

Arthur Clennam's home. His mother.
Father's Watch

Matthew Crag Casby Casbeach Flintwich
Flintwinch and his wife Jessie Affery

Old Sweetheart available

Dreary days of childhood

Add

Chapter IV

Mrs. Flintwinch has a dream

Arthur and his mother?—Yes

His old sweetheart? Not yet.

The man who comfortably charges everything on Providence? Not yet.

Dorrit?—Yes.

The Father of the Marshalsea	Turnkey
	Ruined brother (the clarionet-player I saw at the Ambigu in Paris.)
The Child of the Marshalsea	Son & Daughter— she, a dancer
	Dorrit.

Chapter IV
Family Affairs

Scene with Arthur and his mother

Flintwinch

Lead through to Dorrit—Can she have anything to do with it? Watch her

Chapter V
The Father of the Marshalsea

Dorrit's father
Turnkey.
Father's wife—Dorrit born in the Prison
Mrs. ⟨?Fl rx⟩ Flinx Dr. Haggage

20 years—The father of the Marshalsea—Proud of it   The Plasterer—friend

Chapter VI
The Child of the Marshalsea

Dorrit's Progress—Doll gets like the prison people

Turnkey perplexed how to "tie it up"—Never does tie it up, but dies.

Clara? Amy? Fanny? Ella?
She becomes the prop and stay of the rest
This was the life and this the history of Dorrit

Chapter VII
The Lock

Arthur in the room—The Family picture—The Brother. Tip

"Testimonial"

Gets locked in and has to sleep there. Parallel Imprisonments—his mother's and the Father's of the Marshalsea

Arthur and Dorrit? Yes

Public office?
    and
"Aristocratic" Quarter? Yes

M. Rigaud? Yes.

Baby and the Meagleses? Mr.—Slightly

Miss Wade in the prison? Not yet

Her father? Not yet

The Theatre? Not yet.

Chapter IX
Little Mother

Uncle's lodging

Interview between Clennam and Dorrit On
    the Iron bridge

Make way for The Stiltstalkings—Stilt-
    stalkers—Barnacles

Her protegée. Maggy—Bangham? Maggy

My Little Mother

Chapter X
Containing the whole Science of Government

How not to do it.

Mr. Tite Barnacle and his family Mews
    Street   Grosvenor Square

House like a bottle of smell. When the foot-
    man opens the door he seems to take the
    stopper out.

"Look here. You know"—Young Barnacle.

Inventor. Daniel Doyce
    Bleeding Heart Yard

Chapter XI
Let Loose

Rigaud out

Comes on foot to Chalons and there en-
    counters Cavalletto. At the Daybreak?—
    Break of Day? Describe small Auberge of
    that sort.

Little Italian runs away from him

Sunrise picture—Cavalletto making off in the
    red light down the long road

Charging everything on Providence? No

Miss Wade. Her surroundings and antecedents? No

The Meagleses? No

Bleeding Heart Yard and the Plasterer? | Yes.

Clennam's old sweetheart? Yes. Flora. Flora Casby

More of his character? Yes.
How he stands towards Dorrit? Hardly.
Faint indications

Lagnier? No

The Theatre? No.

(Little Dorrit.—N⁰ IV)

Chapter XII
Bleeding Heart Yard

Description "Bleeding Heart, Bleeding Heart, Bleeding away."

Plornish and Family.

Get Tip out. Captain Maroon   Horse Chaunting.

Chapter XIII
Patriarchal

Old Christopher Casby, the Patriarch. Wooden-headed old Booby

Unwieldy ship and Steam Tug—Panx—Pancks.

Flora.

"Mr. F's Aunt"

Accident to Little Cavalletto.

⟨Chapter XIV⟩

Lead up, through the state of Arthur Clennam's mind to "Little Dorrit"

Late at Night. Nowhere to go to. Maggy

Chapter ⟨XV.⟩ XIV
Little Dorrit's ⟨Eyes⟩ Party

"Spare my father, the giving him anything. Can't bear him to be seen by you in his moments of degradation.

Out all night—Woman in the street.

"If it really was a party now!"—
Burial Register for a pillow.

This was Little Dorrit's party ⟨? after⟩ The vice desertion, wretchedness of the great Capital. This was the party from which she went home.

Rigaud? No

Miss Wade? Carry on

The Meagles family? Practical

Mr.
Mrs.   } Yes
Pet
Tattycoram

Fanny Dorrit and the Theatre? } No
Her Uncle?

Mrs. Clennam, Mrs. Flintwinch Jeremiah?
Yes

Arthur and Doyce in Partnership? Pave the
way

Mrs. Flintwinch dreams again? Yes.

Chapter XV
Mrs. Flintwinch has another Dream

Carry on the idea indicated in last Chapter
of Nᵒ I.

Begin (with a view to Rigaud catastrophe)
    the mysterious sounds in the old house.
Mr. Flintwinch "giving it to" Mrs. Clennam.
Affery falls into a haunted state of mind

Chapter XVI
Nobody's Weakness

Mr. Meagles's house   Curiosities Pictures
    Sticky old Saints—mere Fly Traps
    Daniel Doyce   Tattycoram   Miss Wade
Clennam falls in love with Pet. Decides
    not to—Quite clear not to.
So flows the quiet river—so many miles an
    hour the set of the current, here the lilies,
    there the rushes—nothing distracted—
    nothing put out—on, on, to the Eternal
    Seas

Chapter XVII
Nobody's Rival

Clennam's Rival. Gowan—Henry Gowan
Languid Artist career. You may put a man
    in a govt. but you can't make anything else
    of him that he is not fit for.
Ferryboat Scene
Young Barnacle. Doyce sees how it is—Rain

Chapter XVIII
Little Dorrit's Lover

First suggestion of her being in love with
    Clennam
Through Turnkey's son—Young George?
    Young John (Sentimental) Chivery
Iron bridge again
Tobacco business
The family gentility—always the gentility
Tombstone idea

(Little Dorrit—Nº VI)

Chapter XIX

The Father of the Marshalsea in two or three relations

Fanny Dorrit?	Yes
The Theatre?	Yes
Her Uncle?	

Start from the Marshalsea, carrying on from last Nº? Yes

Miss Wade? No

Lagnier? No.

Flora Casby?   No.   Hold over.
Pancks?

The two brothers

Condense, if possible, the whole fatherly character

Scene with the father and daughter

You have never seen me "No no, I have never seen him in my life!"

Chapter XX

Moving in Society

Family Pride   The Theatre

Indistinctly seen, as Little Dorrit saw it

Now Ladies—Now Darlings Uncle in the Orchestra. Sunk from the upper sky.

Mrs. Merdle—Bosom—Society, Society, Society.

The Shadow of the Marshalsea on whom?

Chapter XXI

Mr. Merdle's Complaint

People like the houses they Inhabit—Suppose a dinner party of houses

Still Society—always Society—Everything for Society

Dinner and reception—Society there—Treasury, Admiralty, Church, Bar, Physic

The Physician and Mr. Merdle's mysterious complaint (to wit: ⟨Forgery⟩ Fraud & Forgery bye & bye

Young Sparkler

Shadow continued

Chapter XXII

⟨Conferences⟩ A puzzle

Mrs. Chivery—"Since in this house I have been," construction

Our John sits among the linen disconsolate—says its like Groves.

Dawn of Little Dorrit's love for Arthur—Maggy—

The Shadow of the Marshalsea Wall

(Little Dorrit.—Nº VII)

Casby? Yes.

Flora, Mr. F's Aunt? Yes

Pancks? Yes.

Miss Wade? No

Lagnier? No

Cavalletto? Carry through

The Meagleses? No
    Pet and Gowran? No. (Next Nº)

Daniel Doyce? Slightly

Plornish Family? No.

Chapter XXIII
Machinery in motion

Clennam in partnership with Doyce.

The Factory—Picture

Visit from Flora, Mr. F's Aunt, & the patriarch—Prepare for bringing Flora & Little Dorrit together.

Pancks—Pave the way for his discovery, and the end of book 1st. Indicate Pancks's relations with the Patriarch

Chapter XXIV
Fortune-Telling

Flora and Little Dorrit together.
    Little Dorrit understands Flora to be dear to Clennam

Pancks again

Little Dorrit tells Maggy a story.
    Her Prison Window

Chapter XXV
Conspirators and others

Carry on Pancks His lodgings—Mr. Bugg Rugg of Pentonville Miss Rugg (and her breach of promise)

Work in Chivery

Work in John Baptist Cavaletto Bleeding Heart Yard & foreigners

Mrs. Plornish as Interpreter "Altro old chap!" "Al-tro Signore! Altro, Altro Altro!

Clennam and Pet? Yes.

Gow⟨r⟩an? Yes.

Sprightly Young Barnacle? No.

Tattycoram? Yes.

Miss Wade? Yes.

Merdle?

Chapter XXVI
Nobody's state of mind

Dissection of Clennam's feelings in respect of Gowan. He is ashamed of them in his own eyes- thinking it ungenerous to enter-tain them- -always contending with them. Resolves never to disparage him.

Hampton Court Palace and Mrs. Gowan
A Noble Refrigerator in company —British Embassy
Nothing but Barnacles, Stiltstalkings, and Mob.
Mrs. Gowan and Clennam

The Ride home.

Chapter XXVII
Five and Twenty

Work out Tattycoram's spiriting away.
Park Lane Picture. Evening

Empty house—Interview with Miss Wade & Tattycoram
A common cause between them.

Chapter XXVIII
Nobody's disappearance

Mr. Clennam's Advertisement.

Clennam on the Summer Evening Scene with Pet, delicately shewing that the father and mother have been for him, and that they all know of his affection. Very Delicate.

The dead twin daughter
And the roses, floating away.

Chapter XXIX
Mrs. Flintwinch goes on dreaming

The old house in the City—Carry through.

Glimpse of Little Dorrit and Pancks, to carry through.

Arrival of Rigaud to close the chapter Mysterious sounds again, as he enters.

Rigaud.   Yes.
═══

The Merdles?   No- Next time
══════════════   ══

Chivery?   Slightly

Tip?   ⎫ Carry through, except
              ⎪ the   Uncle- Family
Fanny?   ⎬ Spirit Working up, to
              ⎪ what they are likely to
Father and Uncle? ⎭ be in a higher station

Little Dorrit   Yes· With Clennam
═══   ═══   ═══════════

And Flora? ⎫
  Pancks?   ⎬ No.
  Casby?   ⎭

Chapter XXX
The Word of a Gentleman

Pursue Rigaud, and the beginning of his
influence over Mr. Flintwinch and Mrs.
Clennam

Suspend it all. Hanging Sword.

Scene in Mrs. Clennam's room
"You shall see me again, Flintwinch!"—
⟨That⟩ The word of a gentleman—he will
certainly keep it

Chapter XXXI
Spirit

Mrs. Plornish's father, Old Nandy. Shew
what he is to the father of the Marshalsea
(a poor old foil), and what the Father of the
Marshalsea is to him.

┌─────────┐
│ Fanny   │
└─────────┘

Patron.   Magnanimous patron
Open with old Pauper out for the day—

Picture

Groves of old men in Marylebone Workhouse)
"My old Pensioner"—Failing Sir—failing
fast—no spirit—
And Tips Spirit, and his father's Christian
spirit.

Chapter XXXII
More Fortune-Telling

In the Marshalsea. From End of Last
Chapter.
Little Dorrit and Clennam—He putting
before her his condition as that "much
older man who has done with that part of
life," and unconsciously stabbing her to
the heart.

┌─────────┐
│ Maggy   │
└─────────┘

Oh! If he had but known, if he had but
known!—Prepare for the time to come—

in that room, long afterwards
Pancks, immensely excited—Strong pre-

paration for the end of the book

"There Sir; thats what you'll have to
break to her!" "That's ⟨man's⟩ your
Father of the Marshalsea.

(Little Dorrit.—Nº X)

Chapter XXXIII
Mrs. Merdle's Complaint

Society?	
and	
Barnacles?	
Merdles?	Yes.
Flora?	
Casby?	
Pet's Marriage.	

Release of the Father of the Marshalsea, and enrichment of the whole family.

Mrs. Gowan's reception of Pet, and submission to her son's marriage- -in other words, to his having his debts paid

Mr. and Mrs. Meagles, and their loss.

Society's idea of a Marriage.

Clennam has already pledged himself to ⟨Minn⟩ Pet, to use his influence with her father, towards elevating her husband in his good opinion. Observe this always

As opposed to Mr. Merdle's complaint – His heavy and careworn manner, is not fit for Society.

Mrs. Gowan's pretext, dandled about between herself & Mrs. Merdle. Open with this

Edmund Sparkler—Pave the way for a change in Mr. Merdle's manner.

Chapter XXXIV
⟨A disappointed Man⟩ A Shoal of Barnacles

Pet's Wedding.

A "disappointed man," Gowan.

The Shoal of Barnacles and Lord Decimus. And yet the company does Mr. Meagles good "Such high company!"

Chapter XXXV
What was behind Mr. Pancks on Little Dorrit's hand

Pancks authorizes Clennam to "break it" to the Family—
Summing up of the Conspiracy

Clennam with Little Dorrit at Flora's (Flora) Both with Mr. Dorrit at the Marshalsea.

Contrast of father and daughter.

Chapter XXXVI
The Marshalsea becomes an Orphan

The Departure from the Prison—Feast etc
Two Brothers—"What will they do without me.

All particulars and   ⟨Casb⟩   Casby
family procession

But no mention of Little Dorrit until the end. Quite forgotten. And brought out insensible by Clennam.

End of The First Book

(Little Dorrit.—N° XI)

Book The Second
Riches

Rigaud to meet Gowan and his wife
And the Dorrits?   Yes.

And Pet and Little Dorrit to become
   acquainted?   Yes

The Great St. Bernard?   Yes

Venice?   Yes.

Foreign picture and foreign atmosphere?
   Yes, generally.

Mrs. General?   Yes

Little Dorrits Letter to Clennam?   Yes

On the road abroad—with a reference to
   "Little Dorrit's party?   Yes

Chapter I
Fellow Travellers

Ascending the Great St. | Gowan's
Bernard on Mules | character

Convent Parlor—hint of Mrs. General

All the Dorrits, the Gowans, and Rigaud
—Pet and Little Dorrit—interview

Travellers' Book.   All the names at last.   Not
told before   And "Blandois of Paris.
From France to Italy."

Chapter II
On the Road

| Transpose
| this and the
| following
| chapter

To Martigny.

Bring out Little Dorrit's new position—
removed from her old cares about her
father—quite displaced.

Family gentility.   Fanny and Tip.

Meeting with Mrs. Merdle and Mr. Sparkler.
"No Row."

Musing.   Little Dorrit taken on to Venice—
Watching the water evening picture.

Chapter III
Mrs. General

| Transpose
| this, and the
| preceding
| chapter

Her character—history—and varnishing pro-
perties

Chapter IV
A Letter from Little Dorrit

Always think of your poor child Little D.

(Little Dorrit.—N° XII)

Pursue the Dorrit Family

and
Mrs. General.
And the Gowans?   Yes.

And Merdles?

Pave the way—with the first stone—to Mr.
Merdle's ruining everybody?   Yes.

The Uncle, and his new trait?   Yes.

Blandois.   Carry him on?   Yes.

To shew why, and how, by degrees, Gowan
takes to him? How it is a part of Gowan's
character to do so?   Yes.

Bring the family to Rome for the winter?
Yes.

And work through Fanny, suspicion of
Mrs. General's having a design on Mr.
Dorrit. Also the Sparkler affair. ⟨Also⟩
Lead, very carefully, on.

Chapter V
Something wrong somewhere

Pursue the objections to Amy

Mr. Dorrit and Mrs. General—"Papa—
potatoes, poultry, prunes, and prism.

Varnishing | Pave the Merdle way |

A companion scene between the father &
daughter, to the old scene in the Marshalsea

Uncle's Protest—Effect on ⟨fanny⟩ Fanny
—alternately giving Amy brooches, and
wishing herself dead

Chapter VI
Something right somewhere

Anatomize Gowan, and see what breeds
about his heart

His wife's position too.

Visit of ⟨Amy⟩ Little Dorrit and Fanny.
(Remember the Bank at Venice)

Blandois and the dog

Pave on the Merdle way, with Sparkler.
Fanny   Opera

Dog poisoned (by Blandois) already — —
Dead as the Doges, Maam.

Chapter VII
Mostly, Prunes and Prism

Fanny
(Society like the Marshalsea)

Rome and Mr. Eustace. Still Prunes and
Prism.

Mrs. Merdle. Work distantly up to Mr.
Merdle.

(Little Dorrit.—Nº XIII)

Back to Clennam. Yes

Clennam and Doyce? Yes.

Flora? Yes

Casby? Yes

Pancks? Yes

The Plornishes? | Next time
    Old Nandy? |
    Maggy? | "They settled that
                | the weather"—

Mr. Merdle? Next time

Mrs. Clennam? |
    The Flintwinches? | Yes. Carry on
    And Blandois? |

Miss Wade and Tattycoram? |
                          | Yes. Carry
                          | on.
Meagleses? |

Another Letter from Little Dorrit? Yes

Letter from Mrs. Gowan to her daughter in law? No

Chapter VIII

The Dowager Mrs. Gowan is reminded that "it never does"

Clennam resolves to besiege the Circumlocution Office for Doyce.

New feature of the Circumlocution

Mrs. Gowans calls. And politely cuts and finally disposes of the Meagleses.

Chapter IX

Appearance and disappearance

Tattycoram and Miss Wade, in union with Blandois

Adelphi Terrace, after Dark.

Clennam follows them to the Patriarchs

Flora on Italy—Mr. F's Aunt "Drat him if he an't come back!"

Patriarch evades, and he loses them

Close with Pancks.

Chapter X

The Dreams of Mrs. Flintwinch thicken

The Secret City after dark

Clennam going to his mother's, is run against by Blandois

Blandois in the old house in the City.
Swagger, swagger

Chapter XI

A Letter from Little Dorrit

Pursue former letter.

Then the state of the Gowans—Minnie has a little boy.

Little Dorrit's dreams

The Bleeding Heart Yard people? <u>Yes</u>

Mr. Merdle   Yes.

Begin Clennam's course downward? <u>Yes</u>

Engage Fanny to Edmund Sparkler.

Chapter XII

In which a great patriotic conference is holden

Mr. Merdle's Barnacle dinner, for the great patriotic purpose of making Young Spark-ler a Lord of the Treasury

Bar, Bishop, and Physician there. Bishop's innocence

Tite Barnacle buttoned up.	Cuyp Cows on an ottoman
Parliamentary Chorus	
The Wonderful Bank	

Chapter XIII

The Progress of an Epidemic

Bleeding Heart Yard and the name of Merdle—the enchanted name

Mrs. Plornish's Cottage— Happy Cottage	Mr. Plornish and John Edward Nandy

Cavalletto has seen Rigaud.

Foreshadow Clennam's loss, through Pancks's persuasion.

Infection and sickening

Chapter XIV

Taking Advice

Delicately trace out the process of Fanny's engagement to Sparkler; shewing how it came about, and how such a mind in such a person naturally worked that way

"My sweet child, you are my Anchor! <u>Will</u> you advise me?

Mr. Dorrit to come to London.
  Invest his property with Mr. Merdle
  And return full of plans, never to be
  accomplished.
  Tone on to his dying in next Nº

Fanny to marry Edmund Sparkler?   Yes

Miss Wade and Tattycoram?
                                    No.
Meagleses?
  And Gowans?

Blandois? Yes. Missing.
  And Mrs. Clennam and the Flintwinches?
  Yes.

Chapter XV

No just cause or impediment why these two persons should not be joined together

Fanny and Mrs. General

Fanny and Amy

She acts upon advice.

The Marriage and marriage plans for England

The Pair go first; Mr. Dorrit follows and joins them

Little Dorrit in Old Rome. Ruins, Ruins, all

Chapter XVI
Getting on

Open at the Chief Butler's

Mr. Dorrit and Mr. Merdle come together

If Mr. Merdle can help in the disposition of the property—O most kind! Most considerate.

Done

Chapter XVII
Missing

Flora to Mr. Dorrit, to lead up to Clennam and Co.

Mr. Dorrit goes to the old house   Handbill

Scene there—Strengthening mystery

Chapter XVIII
A Castle in the Air

John Chivey and Mr. Dorrit.

So Mr. Dorrit returns to Rome, building, building, building the castle, that is to come down Crash! in the next Chapter

After the death of the brothers:
   Take Clennam and his fortunes? Carry through
   His mother and the Flintwinches? No
   Rigaud's disappearance? Carry through
   Miss Wade and Tattycoram? Yes
   Gowan and his wife? No. Except through Miss Wade

The History of a Self Tormentor

From her own point of view. Dissect it.

Change this to two Chapters, getting the Self-Tormentor Narrative by itself

XX
Clennam's visit

XXI
Narrative

(Little Dorrit.—N⁰ XVI)

Chapter XIX
The Storming of the Castle in the Air

Open on the Compagna, going home by night.

Little Dorrit and her Uncle. Father ⟨j⟩ sensitive and jealous at the sight

Pave on to Mrs. Merdle's great dinner

> —First,
> Mrs. General

"My dear, will you go and see if Bob is on the Lock. Ladies and gentlemen ⟨I am the Father of th⟩ Welcome to the Marshalsea. I am the Father of the Marshalsea. This is my child—Born here"

> His watch And clothes
> Imaginary Pawnbroker's

Dies. Uncle stealing down to him in the night and dies kissing his hand

Chapter XX
Containing the history of a Self-Tormentor

Calais at Low Water.

Clennam lands from the Packet, to seek information of Rigaud from Miss Wade Blandois

(Pancks supposed to have found her address by diving among the Patriarch's papers)

Calais Lodging

Miss Wade's Story. Unconsciously laying bare all her character.

Then shew Tattycoram like her, and the two torturing each other.

No information. Clennam goes back

Chapter XXII
Who passes by this road so late?

Barbaric Power wants engineers

Get Doyce away on his expedition

Arthur Clennam and Cavalletto.

"Compagnon de la Majolaine"

Cavalletto off in search. Throw the interest back to the first chapter. Run the two ends of the book together

(Little Dorrit.—N⁰ XVII

The Gowans?
And Meagleses? | No

Fanny and spouse? Yes.
Merdles? Yes. His suicide and demolition

Affery Flintwinch? | Yes
Mrs. Clennam? | ‾‾‾‾‾
Flintwinch? | Altogether

Clennam going downward? Yes. Gone

Casby? | Carry through at Mrs.
And Flora too? | Clennams

Pancks?

Close with a Letter from Little Dorrit?
No—Not to weaken her next appearance

Chapter XXIII
Mistress Affery makes a conditional promise respecting her dreams

Pave the way.
Both with the noises—to impress them again,
for their connexion from the first with the
Catastrophe there: and with Affery—for
the telling of her dreams.

> Flora & Casby

Chapter XXIV
The Evening of a long Day

Hot summer night—Domesticity of Fanny
and her husband
Such a long, long, Day.—Oh you do look so
big, Edmund—Good gracious!

Take up Amy, through them.
To them, enter Merdle—Thought I'd give
you a call. Could you lend me a pen-knife?
Tortoise shell
Not to be inked

Chapter XXV
The Chief Butler resigns the Seals of Office

Dinner-party at Physician's—Bar there, &
Mrs. Merdle. Merdle going to be a
Baronet at least.
Midnight—"I come from the Warm Baths
Sir, in the neighbouring Street
Merdle dead by his own hand Bar—Chief
Butler Gradually work it up—His com-
plaint—Forgery and Fraud. He, greatest
robber and greatest Thief Ever known.
He this adored man

Chapter XXVI
Reaping The Whirlwind

General Smash abroad—Clennam, ruined
himself and ruined his partner
Penitent Pancks—Rugg—No Staving it off—
Marshalsea—"O my little Dorrit!"

(Little Dorrit.—N⁰ XVIII)

Clennam in the Marshalsea, and lodged in
the old room.
Little Dorrit comes to him in the old dress,
and attended by Maggy in the old way.

The Merdle Image smashed? (Done last N⁰)

Cavalletto with news?   Yes

John Chivery   Yes

Ferdinand Barnacle.   Yes   (Final)

Chapter XXVII
The Pupil of the Marshalsea

Clennam learns in his prison—imperfectly
and vaguely—that he has loved Little
Dorrit—
When John Chivery completes the lesson, and
tells him that she loved him. Scene between
them—"Take a bit of something green"—
Then the Plornishes—And brooding reflections—Little Dorrit, always Little Dorrit!

Chapter XXVIII
An Appearance in the Marshalsea

Drooping Downward

Scene with Ferdinand Barnacle, who delivers
a kind of confession of his political faith
—or want of any faith

Mr. Rugg, and "deferring to the opinion of
Society"

Cavalletto and Pancks, with Rigaud

Italian character

Letter to Mrs. Clennam—One week from
this day

Compagnon de la Majolaine
And he's always Gay!

| Prepare finally, for the last
scene at the old house |
|---|

Chapter XXIX
A Plea in the Marshalsea

Ever downward, always downward
Clennam Ill

Little Dorrit's return, and her offer.

Scene between her and Arthur | Star |

Arthur's refusal of Little D's offer

Close with John Chivery stealing in at night,
to bring her "undying love" to him

1

Mems: for working the Story round.—
Retrospective

Mr. Flintwinch has a brother just like him —or a twin brother—who appeared in the beginning of the book, and took away with him a box (31 and 32) Affery saw him.

Arthur Clennam in his interview with his mother, and on his first opportunity after coming home, asked her if it had ever occurred to her to suspect that his father had unhappily wronged any one and made no reparation? Also reminded her with what earnestness his father, dying, had given him his watch for her, containing the watchpaper "Do not forget," and had tried to write some word. Also, how that "I knew that your ascendancy over him was the cause of his going to China to take care of the business there, while you took care of it here"; and that "it was your will that I should remain with you until I was twenty, and then go to him as I did." (35) He said all this at forty. When he connected his suspicions with Little Dorrit, and asked her ⟨if⟩ (in the Marshalsea, on his first visit there) whether she had known his mother long?—She replied, "I think, two years"— "She does not even know that I live here. We have a friend, father and I—a poor laboring man, but the best of friends—and I wrote out that I wished to do needlework, and gave his address. And he got what I wrote out, displayed at a few places where it cost nothing, and Mrs. Clennam found me that way, and sent for me (62).

Mr. Flintwinch once being alone with Mrs. Clennam reproached her for "not having cleared Arthur's father to him and for "leaning against the dead." (131) Affery overheard.

⟨Mrs. Clennam once being alone with Little Dorrit asked her, softening and with interest, if she⟩

Mems: for working the Story round.—
Prospective ⟨   ⟩
(To work out in N°s XIX and XX)

2

How connected with the Dorrits?

⟨F   ⟩ Arthur's father's Uncle, who had no other relation, left a will, ⟨whi⟩ by which he made him his sole heir, except a legacy of ⟨a th⟩ two thousand guineas (?) to the girl, under the charge of Frederick Dorrit, or in default of her being alive to his youngest ⟨Niece⟩ ⟨nearest⟩ ⟨Daughter⟩ ⟨   ⟩ female relative, daughter or Niece. Mrs. Clennam withheld this will—"I will make restitution when I see fit—I will find it one day.—He was not in his right mind when he made it. It was weakness—imbecility."

2

Mems: continued

Retrospective

On the same occasion Jeremiah said (of Arthur's father) "he was an undecided, irresolute chap, who had had everything but his orphan life scared out of him when he was young. And when he brought you home here, the wife his uncle had named for him" —&c. (131) Affery overheard.

Mrs. Clennam once being alone with Little Dorrit, asked her, softening and with interest, if she had undergone many privations &c. (253.). Affery overheard.

Prospective

(⟨The⟩ ⟨These⟩ To work out in Nᵒˢ XIX and XX)

I

When Arthur's father (weak and irresolute) married Mrs. Clennam, in accordance with his Uncle's directions, he was already married, in a false name:—or as good as married

⟨His wife was⟩ ⟨She was⟩ The girl was An orphan. Training in music, under the patronage of Frederick of the Clarionet—

To ⟨his wife⟩ her, Mrs. Clennam (the Uncle being still alive) went ⟨   ⟩ vindictive and with her heart full of ⟨hatred⟩ raging hatred—⟨and⟩ I have discovered it. If you love him, give him up. Submit yourself to me—Live under my custody. Live under my ⟨m   le⟩ eye. Never see him more. Give me that child of yours to be my child. I will breed him severely and religiously; ⟨to be a Servant of the Lord⟩ ⟨he shall be⟩ to be rescued from ⟨the   ⟩ the ignominy of his birth, and to be a Servant of the Lord. ⟨You shall do penance⟩ As for you, do penance and die   As for you, the father. Suffer for your child's sake—made your heir and your lawful son

They ⟨consented⟩ yielded and consented. She ⟨died⟩ was placed under the care of Flintwinch's brother. She died. She had written numerous appeals to Mrs. Clennam. She had implored to see her son. She had left her story. They were in the box. The D.N.F. watchpaper was her working He died abroad, and Rigaud got the box.

What was the appeal to Mrs. Clennam. Do Not Forget? Do not forget the restitution

Mems: To be done

(Little Dorrit.—Nos XIX and XX)

Rigaud's Secret out—Afferys Dreams—Rigaud's death.

The Meagleses, Gowan and wife?—Generally

Casby. Flora? <u>Yes</u>

The Plornishes and Old Nandy?—No

Cavalletto? No

Doyce. Yes

Miss Wade and Tattycoram. Yes

Mrs. General. Enthusiastic recommendations on the part of her connexion—⟨Yes⟩ Nobody recommending, wants her though!

Fanny and her husband

Mrs. Merdle Generally

Chapters.

Opening Chapter

Discovery Dᵒ

Flight of Mrs. Clennam, & return with Little D

Chapter XXX
Closing In

Take Rigaud to the old house—Rigaud, Mrs. Flintwinch, Flintwinch, Affery

Tell the whole story, <u>working it out as much as possible through Mrs. Clennam herself,</u> so as to present her character very strongly.

Affery's dreams. Pancks has been deputed by Arthur to call for them

Mrs. Clennam's immobility gradually & frightfully thawing Up and out

Finish Flintwinch.

Leave Rigaud Smoking in the window

Chapter XXXI
Closed

The packet tonight

Mrs. Clennam rushes to Little Dorrit

Room looking into the jail

"Know the packet yourself, but for God's sake keep it from Arthur. Come back with me to the man!"

Set the darkness and vengeance against the New Testament.

Back—House falls at last. Rigaud Smashed.

Chapter XXXII
Going

Take up characters to be disposed of

Mr. Pancks's figures

Shew what a Humbug the Patriarch is.

Pancks does it, and crops him close

Chapter XXXIII
Going

Take up characters again

Mr. Meagles

Original papers ⟨got by⟩ produced by penitent Tattycoram

Mr. Meagles off for Doyce

Chapter XXXIV
Gone

On an Autumn morning

Scene (reserve carefully till now) between Little Dorrit and Arthur

⟨Chapter XXXV⟩

Shall I tell you what my fortune is? And are you sure you will not share it?

Flora
   Mr. F's Aunt

Meagles and Doyce

They will go out of the Marshalsea to be married—straight to be married—Very quiet conclusion.

EXPLANATORY NOTES

xxi *Court of Enquiry at Chelsea.* The Roebuck Committee. See Introduction, p. viii.

xxi *Merdle . . . British Bank.* See Introduction, p. viii.

xxi *Marshalsea Prison are yet standing.* Not used as a prison after 1849, though much of the outer walls and shell, converted to other uses, survived into the early 1970s. Only part of an outer wall, facing St. George's burial-ground (now a small park), remains.

1 *THIRTY years ago, Marseilles.* Dickens was at Marseilles in 1844 and 1845 and described his impressions in *Pictures from Italy*, 1846.

4 *strachino cheese.* Very soft cheese made in northern Italy.

5 *Who passes . . . gay.* The words of an old French children's singing game, literally translated by Dickens. 'Majolaine' should be 'Marjolaine'.

8 *theatrical air.* Characteristic of Pierre-François Lacenaire (1800–36). See Introduction, p. viii.

15 *Coram.* Thomas Coram (1668–1751) who founded the Hospital in 1739.

23 *ten young men . . . night.* The third Calender's story, *The Arabian Nights Entertainments*, ed. J. Scott, 1811, i. 275, which Dickens possessed.

23 *my lord, their county member.* Lord Robert Grosvenor (1801–63), M.P. for Middlesex, whose bill to prevent Sunday trading caused riots in Hyde Park on 24 June, 1 and 8 July 1855.

23 *butcher's meat.* Live animals destined for slaughter. Grosvenor was interested in sanitation.

23 *congregation would be scanty.* A census report of 1851–3 on religious worship revealed that many people were not church-goers.

24 *Sundays . . . of bitterness and mortification.* For a factual parallel to Arthur's upbringing, see Introduction, pp. vii–viii.

25 *Belzoni.* Giovanni Battista Belzoni (1778–1823), Italian explorer of Egyptian antiquities, whose story may have suggested Doyce's foreign enterprise.

28 *watch-paper.* Inserted as lining in watch's outer case.

35 *all friends round Saint Paul's.* Cf. 'all friends round the Wrekin'.

45 *consideration money.* Wages.

48 the *Marshalsea Prison . . . is gone now.* The new Marshalsea (1813–49) in Borough High Street where Dickens's father was confined for debt in 1824. Improvement in the position of debtors by 1844 led to its closure. The Church of St. George the Martyr is still there.

48 *right little, tight little island.* Quoted sarcastically from Charles Dibdin's patriotic song, 'The Island', *Songs, Naval and National*, 1841.

49 *corner pin.* Front pin in a game of skittles.

50–1 *all-fours . . . sea-jacket.* A game of cards; reefing jacket.

51 *paunch trade.* Tripe.

54 *ninepence short.* Three tots of gin cost 9*d*.

60 *kit.* A small fiddle used by dancing-masters.

61 *playing a clarionet . . . Orchestra.* See Dickens's note (p. 694).

62 *Palace Court.* Marshalsea Court. Evolving from the Earl Marshal's Court in Edward III's reign, originally had the Marshalsea Prison (on a different site) attached to it.

63 *Clifford's Inn.* In Fleet Street until demolished in 1934.

75 *Rag Fair.* Centre of London's second-hand clothes trade, the district around Cutler Street according to Henry Mayhew, *London Labour and the London Poor*, 1861–2.

79 *Iron Bridge.* Old Southwark Bridge, built 1815–19. A toll-bridge (see below, p. 182) until 1864.

81 *Mr. Tite Barnacle.* First named 'Mr. Stiltingstalk of Grosvenor Square' in MS, and believed by James Fitzjames Stephen to be a caricature of his father, Under-Secretary of State for the Colonies.

87 *CONTAINING THE WHOLE SCIENCE OF GOVERNMENT.* Written Sept. 1855; see Introduction, p. viii.

88 *HOW NOT TO DO IT.* Cf. Thomas Carlyle's terms, 'Donothingism' (*Past and Present*, 1843, III. iii), and 'No-Government' ('The New Downing Street', *Latter-Day Pamphlets*, 1850).

88 *every new premier . . . dismiss you.* Parliament had reduced Dickens to despair. In a letter (4 Oct. 1855), he writes: 'We appear to me to have proved the failure of representative institutions without an educated and advanced people to support them.'

88 *jobbing people, jobbed people.* Persons misusing public office for private or party advantage and persons thus victimized.

89 *parliamentary motions.* See Introduction, p. viii.

91 *in the way.* At hand.

96 *hocussed.* Stupefied with drugged liquor.

98 *nobs . . . snobs.* Superior and inferior persons.

101 *Brazen Head.* Roger Bacon's legendary fabrication which was able to prophesy.

101 *to begin it all over again.* This account would be true up to 1851. The Patent Law Amendment Act (1852) improved the situation.

112 *BLEEDING HEART YARD.* The name survives off Greville (then Charles) Street, Hatton Garden.

112 *old rustic road towards a suburb.* Theobald's Road; Theobalds, Herts., where James I had a hunting lodge.

117 *'Chaunter' . . . shot.* Fraudulent dealers made a weak-winded horse seem sound by dosing him with shot.

121 *list shoes.* Slippers made from cloth's selvage or border.

127 *fish.* Small, flat, fish-shaped pieces of bone or ivory used as counters in games.

128 *Paul and Virginia.* Bernardin de Saint-Pierre, *Paul et Virginie*, 1787, a romance.

128 *third place.* The MS shows that Flora means Canton.

129 *Scotland.* That is, Gretna Green, where runaway couples could marry at a blacksmith's smithy.

136 *Whole Duty of Man.* Ironically echoes Eccles. 12:13.

151 *woolsack.* Lord Chancellorship.

158 *Twickenham*. Twelve miles S.W. of St. Paul's.

160 *time being out*. Apprenticeship concluded.

167 *Domestic Medicine*. William Buchan, *Domestic Medicine; or, The Family Physician*, 1769.

172 *Kingston*. On Thames, three miles south of Twickenham.

174 *Pall-Mall pace*. Dickens may possibly have Thackeray, a great clubman, in mind.

175 *hung midway*. Mohammed's coffin was believed to float in the air in his tomb at Medina; Richard Francis Burton's visit to Medina and Mecca (1853) and his account (1855) were a recent sensation.

176 *became a full fountain*. 'Story of the Sisters who envied their younger Sister', *Arabian Nights*, v. 360.

180 *Horsemonger Lane . . . Jail*. Now Union Street, S.E.1; the Surrey county jail (1798–1879), now demolished.

180 *life-size Highlander*. Sign for tobacconist's.

181 *marshalling . . . go*. From *Macbeth*, II. i. 42.

182 *Middlesex side*. North bank of Thames.

185 *slop-work*. Ready-made cheap clothing.

192 *as her mother had ministered to her*. Euphrasia fed her imprisoned father, Evander, King of Syracuse, on her own milk.

192 *moral Lord Chesterfield*. Ironic. Lord Chesterfield (1694–1773) gave worldly-wise advice in his *Letters to his Son*, 1774.

195 *Newmarket coat*. Long, close-fitting, and originally worn for riding.

198 *mugged*. Made a face (theatrical slang).

203 *whose something mind*. Pope, *Essay on Man*, i. 99–100 ('untutored mind').

206 *MR. MERDLE'S COMPLAINT*. This ironic device was derived from Samuel Warren, 'The Forger' [1830], *Passages from the Diary of a Late Physician*, 1830–7.

207 *Storr and Mortimer*. Celebrated New Bond Street jewellers.

209 *Jack in the Green*. Figure in May-Day festival, enclosed in wooden or wicker pyramidal framework covered with leaves. Here, refers not to the cage-crinoline, which came in only in late 1856, but to fashionable skirts that were still very wide.

209 *Judith*. In the Apocrypha, Judith decapitates Holofernes.

210 *Bar*. Based on Sir Fitzroy Kelly (1796–1880); 'K.F.' in Forster's biography of Dickens.

212 *Achilles*. Physician is unwittingly ironic, since Merdle, like Achilles, has a vulnerable heel.

218 *George*. Old galleried inn (part of which survives), in Borough High Street.

219 *You are not afflicted . . . like yourself*. Deleted by mistake in proof by printer of first edition, Dickens then deleting the opening of next paragraph, 'O, not . . . from me!' to make sense. The missing section was restored only in the Clarendon edition (1979).

219 *stay at home! . . . Don't*. Between 'home!' and 'Don't', the printer of first edition failed to delete the following paragraph which Dickens marked for deletion and which has appeared in all editions up to the Clarendon: 'The agonised way in which she poured this out as if it burst of itself from her

suppressed heart, made it difficult for Clennam to keep the tears from his eyes as he saw and heard her.'

223 *Abel's murder.* Gen. 4: 1–5.

225 *of other days around people.* Echoes Thomas Moore's 'Oft, in the Stilly Night', *National Airs*, 1818.

225 *the golden bowl.* Cf. Eccles. 12: 6.

232 *Great Mogul.* Title assumed by Mogul emperors of Delhi in India; one was still ruling, under British protection, in 1856.

237 *man in the iron mask.* Alexandre Dumas popularized the legend of this famous prisoner in *Dix ans plus tard, ou le vicomte de Bragelonne*, 1848–50.

237 *Spartan boy with the fox biting him.* The boy did not reveal the stolen fox under his cloak even when it gnawed at his entrails.

237 *started off at score.* Broke into impetuous speech.

239 *laid up in ordinary.* Put away in dock out of commission (nautical).

241 *grubber.* Money-grubber (sordidly amassing wealth).

255 *coffee-biggin.* Coffee-pot with strainer for infusion of coffee.

263 *Refrigerator.* At this time, a vessel filled with cold water, used in industry for condensing alcoholic and other vapours.

263 *abroad or at home.* John Delane, editor of *The Times* (1841–77), who exposed many scandals, and his war-correspondent William Henry Russell's despatches from the Crimea alarmed conservatives.

268 *Strait . . . judgment.* See Matt. 7: 13–15.

273 *spotted dogs.* Dalmatians, trained to run behind carriages.

285 *Custom . . . 'Change'.* The Custom House (built 1813–17; modified 1826–8) is in Lower Thames Street. Garraway's, where business was transacted, stood until 1866 in Change Alley, next to the original home of the Stock Exchange. The Jerusalem, originally in Change Alley had moved to Cowper's Court by 1856. To 'go on 'Change' means to frequent places where commercial business is transacted.

299–300 *the Earth . . . millions.* Expresses the Calvinist doctrine that salvation is predestined and extended through grace to the elect only.

305 *Workhouse . . . economy.* The Good Samaritan gave two pence to the inn-keeper to care for the man who fell among thieves (Luke 10: 35). Here Dickens refers to the harsh new Poor Law of 1834.

307 *such old men should not be born.* Reflects, with bitter irony, the Malthusian objection to excessive breeding among the poor.

310 *bruised reed.* Isa. 42: 3.

324 *White sand and grey sand.* Traditional three-part round.

328 *It belonged . . . in hand.* Playing throughout on two senses deriving from 'job': to hire out for a period; to use a public office for private advantage.

331 *the needle's eye.* Matt. 19: 24.

335 *Prospero. The Tempest*, v. i. 33–50.

337 *bottle of smoke.* Indulge in fiction of social co-operation; the hookah draws tobacco smoke through a cooling bottle of water and its mouthpiece is passed around.

339 *odor of Circumlocution.* Suggests Lord Palmerston (1784–1865), ironically implying physical, mental, and moral decay and reflecting a contemporary view of Palmerston's senile state.

339 *private loaf and fish trade ashore.* Spoils of jobbery.

346 *'tis distance lends enchantment to the view.* Thomas Campbell, *Pleasures of Hope*, 1799, Pt. 1, 1.7.

346 *Woodpecker Tapping.* From the popular song by Thomas Moore.

355 *Monument Yard.* Paved yard near the Monument just north of London Bridge; not identified but described in *Martin Chuzzlewit*, 1843–4, chs. viii, xxxvii.

356 *a man and a brother ever.* The inscription 'Am I not a man and a brother?' on a Wedgwood medallion depicting a negro in chains (1768) was adopted by the Anti-Slavery Society in 1823.

359 *Sir Roger de Coverley going to church.* Addison, *Spectator*, No. 112.

362–3 *Darkness outstripping . . . and high.* Drawn from Dickens's visit in 1846.

364 *fourgon.* Baggage-waggon.

387 *Simplon.* Pass over the Alps, visited by Dickens in 1844 and 1853.

389 *in the streets below.* Refers to Austrian occupation of northern Italy as observed by Dickens in 1853.

390 *realities that never changed.* Dickens had already sketched an unreal, dream-like view of Venice in *Pictures*.

394 *princes in the Arabian Nights.* 'The Story of Prince Ahmed and the Fairy Perie Banou', *Arabian Nights*, v. 260–3.

394 *hoodwinked.* Covered up from sight.

394 *low gloomy bridge.* Though the Dorrits are staying at a palace on the Grand Canal, Dickens has in mind the Bridge of Sighs.

396 *Mr. Eustace, the classical tourist.* Dickens had a copy of John Chetwode Eustace, *Classical Tour through Italy*, 1841.

402 *Act of Parliament.* An absolute divorce could be obtained only through a private Act of Parliament until the Matrimonial Causes Act (1857).

420 *dead as the Doges.* Napoleon destroyed the office of Venice's chief magistrate along with the Republic in 1797.

430 *light of the time.* In MS, Dickens substituted 'time' for 'world', deleting a blasphemously ironic reference to Holman Hunt's painting, *The Light of the World* (1854).

444 *overhangs the river.* The area, near Charing Cross, now much altered, was laid out by the Adam brothers in 1768–74.

444 *nearest bridge of stone.* The earlier Waterloo Bridge (1817–1939).

448 *lava necklaces and bracelets.* Articles found in the volcanic debris burying Herculaneum and Pompeii.

448 *dying gladiators and Belvederas.* Refers to two classical sculptures, the dying gladiator (Capitoline Museum, Rome) and the Apollo Belvedere (Vatican), but Flora hurries on to 'Venice Preserved' because Belvidera was the heroine of Thomas Otway's play (1682).

448 *Mantua-making.* Dressmaking, 'Mantua' being a corruption of 'manteau'.

451 *benevolent in every knob.* Followed in MS and early proof by 'as if he had got baptismal water on the brain', a blasphemous joke which backfired on Dickens when it was removed only after much difficulty. See Clarendon *Little Dorrit*, p. xxxiv.

466 *Colossus bestriding his own hearthrug. Julius Caesar*, 1. ii. 133–6.

467 *Tyburn Tree.* From John Gay, *The Beggar's Opera*, 1728. The hero, Mac-

heath, is a highwayman, the ironic point being that Merdle was liable to hanging for forgery in the 1820s.

469 *dame's house.* A dame or matron at Eton College kept a boarding-house; a housemaster who did not teach classics was also called a dame.

471 *Mr. Merdle's pocket.* The Reform Bill (1832) removed only the worst 'rotten' and 'pocket' constituencies and, without a secret ballot, corruption was still rife in 1856.

475 *Buhl.* Wood inlaid with brass or silver.

487 *diseases.* Recalls the cholera epidemics of 1849 and 1854.

489 *journeyman Hamlet.* Suggested by *Hamlet*, III. ii. 34–42.

491 *Albano.* Between the northern gate (Porta del Popolo) of Rome and Albano, 12 miles to the south.

494 *who* will *catch mice.* From proverb, 'A cat in gloves catches no mice'.

508 *Marplot.* One who frustrates a design by officious interference; character in Susannah Centlivre's *The Busy Body*, 1709.

509 *Beggar's Petition . . . Belisarius.* Well known from a poem (1769) by Revd. Thomas Moss in the spelling book; Justinian's great general, reputed to have ended as a blind beggar.

510 *Emperors of the Soldiery.* Dissolute Roman emperors, raised to the purple by the Praetorian Guard.

510 *avenue of wrack and ruin.* The wording suggests Dickens is fusing memories of a journey south over the Pontine Marshes to Fondi in 1845 with his account of Fanny's progress northwards over the Campagna; Dickens himself journeyed south before returning to Rome and proceeding to Florence.

514 *kingdom of Heaven.* Matt. 19:16–24.

517 *golden Street of the Lombards.* Lombard Street, celebrated banking thoroughfare.

523 *headless.* Traitors' heads were displayed as late as 1772 on Temple Bar, a gateway then separating the Strand and Fleet Street.

527 *buried in a cellar.* An echo of the sensational Manning murder case (1849) which haunted Dickens.

528 *Miss Biffin.* Dickens had an old show-bill relating to her. A fairground entertainer, she was born without legs or arms in 1784.

531 *physiognomical treatise.* Charles le Brun (1619–90), French painter, published two such treatises. Later scientific authorities on the physiognomy of the emotions confirm Dickens's criticism of Le Brun.

534 *its dead along with it.* Dickens drew on an incident during 1845 described in *Pictures*.

534 *gates of Rome.* Whereas Alaric's Goths had plundered Rome (AD 410), Mr. Dorrit's party had arrived with treasures from London and Paris.

560 *he made it ghastly.* Hans Holbein the Younger's *The Dance of Death* [1523–4].

568 *brazen wall.* Jer. 15:20.

568 *into stone.* Like Medusa, the Gorgon of Greek fable.

573 *spectre . . . B.* The Spectre of the Brocken (Hartz Mountains), a huge human shadow cast by the sun on a bank of cloud or mist.

575 *suiting the action to the word. Hamlet*, III. ii. 20–1.

580 *Man Mountain.* From Swift's *Gulliver's Travels*, I. ii.

583 *Yellow Jack.* Yellow Fever.

583 *Twoshoes.* Heroine of *Goody Two-Shoes*, 1765, a nursery tale.

586 *the longest day.* Ironically sinister echo of *Macbeth*, IV. iii. 241.

587 *Westminster Hall . . . circuits . . . Term.* Seat of chief courts of England until 1825; districts toured by Assize courts judges, and the journeys thus made; period during which the courts sit.

587 *a Banquo's chair.* Cf. *Macbeth*, III. iv.

590 *dabbling . . . tint.* Echoes *Macbeth*, II. ii. 59–62.

593 *time of High 'Change.* Period of greatest business activity on 'Change in the City of London.

593 *roc's egg.* Huge egg which would hatch out the hostile bird-like monster of Sinbad's second voyage in the *Arabian Nights*, ii. 18.

594 *self-helpful.* The Victorian sense was current as early as 1831; Samuel Smiles, *Self-Help*, 1859, was delivered as lectures in 1845.

607 *Upas tree.* Fabulous Javanese tree so poisonous as to destroy all life for miles around.

615 *gravelled.* Run aground, like a ship, on gravel, beach, or mud, and thus on the way to being wrecked.

616 *only a windmill.* Cervantes, *Don Quixote*, I. viii.

641 *Knight of Industry.* 'Chevalier d'industrie', 'a gentleman who lives by his wits'.

657 *Bedlam.* Then situated in St. George's Fields, Lambeth.

660 *a thousand to one.* Refers to Sodom and Gomorrah's destruction (Gen. 18:23–5).

662 *collapsed and fell.* Dickens refuted the *Edinburgh Review*'s charge that he borrowed this catastrophe from a recent and convenient fall of houses in Tottenham Court Road.

665 *milk of human kindness. Macbeth*, I. v. 17.

665 *after Doctor Johnson.* Adapted from Samuel Johnson's *Prologue at the Opening of the Theatre in Drury Lane*, 1747, l. 54.

671 *Quarterings.* Heraldic term, but also refers humorously to Sparkler's salary which, as a contemporary civil servant, he would receive quarterly.

683 *Sibyllic.* Sibylline; a Sibyl was a prophetess.

684 *to be made up.* Like one of Sweeney Todd's victims in the popular contemporary story (1846–7).

687 *Saint Paul's Churchyard.* Where Doctor's Commons, which issued special marriage licences, stood until 1867.

FURTHER READING

Editions

Charles Dickens, *Little Dorrit*, ed. Harvey Peter Sucksmith, The Clarendon Dickens (1979).
—— *Miscellaneous Papers*, ed. B. W. Matz (1908).
—— *The Letters of Charles Dickens*, ed. Madeline House, Graham Storey, Kathleen Tillotson, *et al.* (Pilgrim edn.; 1965– (in progress)).
—— *The Speeches of Charles Dickens*, ed. K. J. Fielding (1960).

Bibliography

Thomas Hatton and Arthur H. Cleaver (eds.), *A Bibliography of the Periodical Works of Charles Dickens* (1933).
Philip Collins (ed.), *A Dickens Bibliography* (1970).
R. C. Churchill (ed.), *A Bibliography of Dickensian Criticism 1836–1975* (1975).
Alan M. Cohn and K. K. Collins (eds.), *The Cumulated Dickens Checklist 1970–79* (1982).
Lionel Stevenson (ed.), *Victorian Fiction: A Guide to Research* (1964).
George H. Ford (ed.), *A Second Guide to Research* (1978).

Biographies

John Forster, *The Life of Charles Dickens* (1872–4); ed. J. W. T. Ley (1928); ed. A. J. Hoppé (Everyman, 1966).
Edgar Johnson, *Charles Dickens: His Tragedy and Triumph* (1953; abridged reprint, 1978).
Peter Ackroyd, *Dickens* (1990).

Background

Humphry House, *The Dickens World* (1941).
Asa Briggs, *Victorian People* (1955; rev. edn. 1970, 1972).
—— *The Age of Improvement* (1959).
Walter E. Houghton, *The Victorian Frame of Mind* (1957).
Robert L. Patten, *Dickens and his Publishers* (1978).
Michael Steig, *Dickens and Phiz* (1978).

Criticism

George H. Ford, *Dickens and his Readers* (1955).

—— and Lauriat Lane, Jr. (eds.), *The Dickens Critics* (1961) (includes Lionel Trilling's introduction to *Little Dorrit*).

K. J. Fielding, *Charles Dickens: A Critical Introduction* (1958; rev. edn. 1965).

John Butt and Kathleen Tillotson, *Dickens at Work* (1957).

J. H. Miller, *Charles Dickens: The World of his Novels* (1958).

M. Engel, *The Maturity of Dickens* (1959).

Robert Garis, *The Dickens Theatre* (1965).

J. C. Reid, *Dickens: Little Dorrit* (1967).

H. M. Daleski, *Dickens and the Art of Analogy* (1970).

F. R. and Q. D. Leavis, *Dickens the Novelist* (1970).

Harvey Peter Sucksmith, *The Narrative Art of Charles Dickens* (1970).

—— 'The Melodramatic Villain in *Little Dorrit*', *Dickensian*, 71 (1975), 76–83.

—— 'Dickens among the Pre-Raphaelites: Mr. Merdle and Holman Hunt's "The Light of the World"', *Dickensian*, 72 (1976), 158–63.

Philip Collins (ed.), *Dickens: The Critical Heritage* (1971).

John Carey, *The Violent Effigy: A Study in Dickens's Imagination* (1973).

Edward Heatley, 'The Redeemed Feminine of *Little Dorrit*', *Dickens Studies Annual*, 4 (1975), 153–64.

F. S. Schwarzbach, *Dickens and the City* (1979).

Dennis Walder, *Dickens and Religion* (1981).

Michael Slater, *Dickens and Women* (1983).

Don Richard Cox (ed.), *Sexuality in Victorian Literature* (1984).

Fred Kaplan, *Sacred Tears: Sentimentality in Victorian Literature* (1987).

Iain Crawford, '"Machinery in Motion": Time in *Little Dorrit*', *Dickensian*, 84 (1988), 30–41.

Charlotte Rotkin, *Deception in Dickens' "Little Dorrit"* (1989).

Trey Philpotts, 'The Real Marshalsea', *Dickensian*, 87 (1991), 133–45.

Patricia Ingham, *Dickens, Women and Language* (1992).

Yael Halevi-Wise, 'Little Dorrit's Story: A Window into the Novel', *Dickensian*, 94 (1998), 184–94.

The Oxford World's Classics Website

www.worldsclassics.co.uk

- Information about new titles
- Explore the full range of Oxford World's Classics
- Links to other literary sites and the main OUP webpage
- Imaginative competitions, with bookish prizes
- Peruse the Oxford World's Classics Magazine
- Articles by editors
- Extracts from Introductions
- A forum for discussion and feedback on the series
- Special information for teachers and lecturers

www.worldsclassics.co.uk

American Literature

British and Irish Literature

Children's Literature

Classics and Ancient Literature

Colonial Literature

Eastern Literature

European Literature

History

Medieval Literature

Oxford English Drama

Poetry

Philosophy

Politics

Religion

The Oxford Shakespeare

Westward

"Solid writing and superb storytelling."
—American Cowboy magazine

"*Westward* is a treasure for all western enthusiasts."
—True West

"Fans of history in any form will find *Westward* especially delightful." *—El Paso Times*

"A marvelous collection that can only help make reading westerns respectable once again."
—Kirkus Reviews

"Commendable . . . Enthusiasts of the Old West should enjoy the variety and the new twists given familiar tales." *—Denver Post*

"Cotton Smith tells the story of Leander H. McNelly, a compelling and tragic hero who served in the famed Texas Rangers." *—Wichita Eagle*

"The modern western writer has a keener fidelity to history than any of his predecessors."
—Dallas Morning News

RIDE AWAY

A CORRIGAN BROTHERS WESTERN

COTTON SMITH

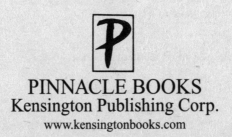

PINNACLE BOOKS
Kensington Publishing Corp.
www.kensingtonbooks.com

ISBN-13: 978-0-7860-3709-4
ISBN-10: 0-7860-3709-1

First printing: January 2016

10 9 8 7 6 5 4 3 2 1

Printed in the United States of America

First electronic edition: January 2016

ISBN-13: 978-0-7860-3710-0
ISBN-10: 0-7860-3710-5

To Katie, Bobby, Gus, Maggie, and Jesse

CHAPTER ONE

The Texas midmorning sky looked like God hadn't decided what to make of the day as Tade Balkins drove the stagecoach toward the Wilkon relay station. No driver got more out of his horses, taking great pride in always being on time. He was well respected on the Southern Overland Mail line that ran from Hays City to El Paso, then on to Santa Fe, Tucson, San Diego, and finally Los Angeles. Even with railroad construction heating up again after the war, it was still an important route.

As far as the eye could see was empty desert plain, marked with rock, catclaw, dry brush, mesquite, and a creek bed with only the memory of water. To the north were dark crests promising better land and water. Tade was holding the six-horse team to a steady trot, talking to them as usual. He would bring them into a controlled run when the stage got closer to the station. A full gallop was really for appearance. It looked impressive to pull the charging horses to a hard stop in front of a destination. Sitting beside him,

Hank Johnson rode shotgun and was having difficulty staying awake. Last night had been a drunken one.

"Doin' good, boys. Doin' good. Ah, that's just a tumbleweed. Nothin' to worry about," Tade assured the horses, then glanced over at the dozing guard and nudged him awake. "Better stay alert, Hank. Bad country along here."

"Yeah, I know. Jes' got a nasty headache."

"Atlee Forsyth, she'll have some good hot coffee. That'll help."

"Wish she had some whiskey."

Tade frowned and returned to talking to his horses.

Inside the coach, seven passengers were dulled by the never-ending bouncing and the ever-swirling dust.

"Is your ranch near here, Mr. Corrigan?"

The question to Deed Corrigan came from Rebecca Tuttle, the younger of the two women sitting across from him. Clearly she wanted to talk and had been doing so almost nonstop since the stage rolled out in the morning.

Dressed like a woman ready to stroll down the main street of El Paso, her green dress shimmered with its overskirts caught up and accented with black ribbons. Her flat-crowned straw hat held one large bow in the center of her forehead, matching the smaller ones on her dress. A jacket bodice, with a neckline close to her neck and black cuffs, completed the outfit. Brown ringlets framed her round face; light rouge highlighted her ample cheeks. To those in the coach, she looked like a woman of high social standing. Nothing could have been further from the truth. Her last cent had been spent on this stagecoach ticket.

Without waiting for Deed to answer, Rebecca explained that she was on the way to El Paso to meet her intended, a farmer she had met two years before in Ohio. Indeed, it was her only hope. That wasn't expressed—just a sweet smile when she stated her intention.

Politely, Deed Corrigan touched the brim of his ill-shaped hat and explained that his ranch was about three hours' ride from the station and he was returning home from a cattle drive to Kansas. It was more than he had said on the trip so far. His face, accented by a thick mustache, was deeply tanned from countless days on horseback. Long brown hair brushed against his shoulders. The bullet belt around Deed's waist held a heavy Remington .44 revolver with its long barrel extending past the holster's open end. Tan leather cuffs covered the frayed ends of his faded red shirt. A once-blue neckerchief hung loosely around his neck. Spurs were Mexican in styling and his worn Levi's were shoved into knee-high boots.

Around Deed's neck hung a small, Oriental-looking brass circle on a rawhide thong. Engraved on the circle was the Japanese word, *Bushido*. No one asked what it meant. Hanging unseen down the back of his shirt was a sheathed throwing knife, attached to the thong.

Next to him sat a fat drummer, Persam Torce, representing several companies making fine linens and other cloth goods. He had declared often of their quality, whether anyone asked or not. Stuffed into a store-bought suit that didn't fit, he said he, too, was headed to El Paso and wondered if it was much farther, or if a railroad went there.

"It's a ways, mister. No railroad yet either," Deed said, grinning. "Better get used to this."

Frowning, Persam Torce looked at Deed. "Is it really necessary to be armed as you are, sir?"

"Only if you want to stay alive . . . *sir*." Deed's answer carried an edge.

Torce pulled on his collar. "Surely, there are law officers with the responsibility to protect us."

On the far side of the same bench, sitting next to the drummer, a well-dressed passenger with long sideburns, thick spectacles, and black bowler leaned forward, laughed, and said, "Tell that to the next bunch of highwaymen, or war party, we see."

Returning to his reading, the gentleman's Victorian black suitcoat flared open to reveal the butt of a silver-plated revolver in a shoulder holster. He also carried a sleeve gun, probably a derringer, Deed figured by the way he favored his right wrist. On the man's lap was an opened book of Tennyson he had been enjoying since the coach left Hays. This was the first time he had said anything to anyone, except to introduce himself earlier to Deed as James Hannah. A name known to many in the region; the name of a man of the gun—a gun for hire. The singular introduction was an indication Hannah was aware of Deed Corrigan's reputation as a fighting man as well.

In the middle bench sat another drummer who sold Swedish furniture and held tightly to one of the straps hanging from the coach roof for use by middle-bench passengers to balance themselves. Wearing a dust-covered top hat, he acted as if he hadn't heard the conversation or cared about it. He hadn't said where he was headed.

The far bench seat held Rebecca Tuttle and a German couple. Neither Hermann Beinrigt, a skinny farmer in worn overalls, nor his wife, Olivia, had talked to anyone so far, only whispered to each other in German. Tade Balkins told Deed earlier the couple hoped to lease land for farming near El Paso, where relatives lived. Their farm in Kansas had been lost to drought and grasshoppers.

As the coach rattled and banged across the uneven prairie, Rebecca glanced at James Hannah, eager for a new target for her thoughts, and asked, "Are you going on to El Paso?" Her smile was warm, very warm.

Hannah looked up from his book.

But the question went unanswered as Torce glanced out the window and yelled, "Oh my God, it's Indians!"

Rebecca turned to the window and screamed.

Eighteen painted Comanches on horseback had appeared over a shallow ridge and were swarming toward the coach, like bees near a disturbed nest. All carried painted war shields. Half were waving rifles or revolvers and the rest, bows and arrows or short lances. Without a word, Deed and Hannah yanked free their revolvers and turned to their respective windows.

"Giddyap, boys! Earn your pay. Come on!" Tade yelled and snapped his nine-foot bullwhip over the horses' heads to get their full attention. They were running full out in five strides and surprised the war party with their sudden swiftness.

CHAPTER TWO

Quickly, the menacing war party reacted to the now-racing coach. Riding as if they were part of their horses, the warriors had long black hair decorated with feathers, glass beads, silver conchos, and pieces of fur. A streak of color lined the central part of each warrior's head, from forehead back along the crown. Eagle feathers were attached to their side locks. A beaver-fur-wrapped braid on each side of their heads was highlighted with bright cloth, and a special braided scalp lock, accented with a smaller feather, bounced on top of their heads.

Several wore antelope skins as breech clouts or war shirts, a sign they were of the Antelope band, the fiercest of Comanches and the terror of the entire region. Deed, Hannah, and the stagecoach guard began firing at them, but without success. The bouncing of the heavy vehicle made accuracy nearly impossible.

Hurdling across the land, the stage slammed across a shallow creek that fed into the bigger stream near the station, spraying water and launching its passengers against each other, then cut through a crusted band of dried alkali, sending up a snow of white powder.

Four warriors outraced the rest of the war party and closed in on the hard-running stage. Two went on one side of the coach; two, on the other. The guard fired at the closest warrior and managed to kill his horse, sending its rider stumbling onto the prairie. Hank Johnson scrambled to find the sack of shotgun slugs at his feet. Hannah leveled his Smith & Wesson .44 Russian revolver, holding it with both hands, and fired at the second warrior, whose face, chest, and leggings were striped in black. Hannah's bullets cut across the Comanche's stomach and slammed into his right arm. Yelping in pain, the Indian swung away from the coach.

On the left side of the coach, the other two warriors were spread out; one was nearing the hard-running team and the other, just out of Deed's line of sight, was near the back of the coach. The front warrior, with his lower face painted red, drew an arrow from the handful he held next to his bow. Stretching out behind Tade Balkins to shoot, the guard fired too quickly and missed, barely catching the Comanche with a few stray buckshot. Deed leaned out of the coach window and fired, missing twice. His third and fourth shots slammed into the warrior's back just as he unleashed an arrow. The shaft struck the front edge of the driver's box. Deed emptied his Remington into the Indian's flailing body. Tade yelled his thanks as Deed ducked back inside.

The fourth warrior swooped near the same window. He swung low on his pony to thrust his lance inside, but Deed saw him coming. As the Comanche shoved it through the opened coach window, Deed Corrigan dropped his empty gun, grabbed and yanked hard on the spear. He pulled the surprised warrior, still holding the lance, from his horse and slammed him against the coach. For an instant, the warrior's face was pinned against the coach window. Deed's open left hand drove into the Comanche's exposed Adam's apple as if his hand were an axe.

The blow was so swift and fierce that only James Hannah and the farming couple realized what had happened.

A soft gurgle followed the Indian as his limp body slid down the outside of the coach. Deed Corrigan let go of the lance and retrieved his Remington revolver, pushed his hat brim against its crown, and began reloading. The lance bounced off the top-hatted drummer's knees and fell harmlessly on the coach floor.

"Will they go away now?" Rebecca blurted.

Deed finished reloading and looked up. "Doubt it."

The coach banged over a small ridge and slammed through a cluster of stunted cedar trees. Their stout branches scraped along the coach and forced Deed to duck back inside, but the trees gave the stagecoach a moment of reprieve from the war party as they were forced to ride around the trees or slow down to ride through them.

Leaning out the window, Deed yelled at the driver to hand down a rifle, then fired his revolver twice at the rest of the Indians racing to catch them and missed both times.

"Ain't got one, mister," Tade Balkins yelled back. "Unless you can get yurn in your gear. In the back boot." He licked his lips and added, "Pull down them leather curtains. It'll keep some of them arrows out."

He cracked his whip again and yelled at the horses. "Won't do much about them bullets though."

Hannah looked over at Deed and said, "Don't even think about going up there to get your rifle, Corrigan. You'd be a pincushion in seconds."

"If I could get to my Spencer, it'd make them think twice."

"Yeah, well, the only word that counts there is *if*," Hannah growled and fired again. "We're doing all right. Could use another shooter though."

"I've got to go now. Once they get around the coach, we won't be able to handle them." Deed said, "An old Japanese warrior friend says to always find a way to attack."

"Wonder if he ever fought red devils like these?"

"Count on it."

Both men pulled down the leather curtains at the same time. Quickly, Deed replaced the two spent cartridges in his handgun and unbuckled his heavy gunbelt. Beside him, Persam Torce was whimpering and praying loudly.

In the middle bench, the top-hatted drummer looked like he couldn't believe what was happening as he heard the war party's yells become louder again. He held a handkerchief close to his mouth to avoid any unexpected vomiting. His eyes went from Deed Corrigan to James Hannah to the lance at his feet.

Rebecca Tuttle sobbed and slid to the floor, as if it would keep her safe. She held her hands over her head and squeezed her eyes shut. An arrow burst through the closed curtains and slammed into where she had been. She glanced at it and shrieked.

"God could use a little help here, partner. Can you shoot?" Deed said to the praying Persam Torce, holding out his holstered revolver and gunbelt. "N-No, sir. I am a m-man of G-God."

"You can pray *and* shoot, you know. Lots of folks do. My big brother does. Real good at it, too."

For a moment, Deed considered giving his gun to Torce anyway, but decided against it. He swung back to the coach window, aimed at an Indian's exposed leg over the back of his running horse, fired and missed. The coach itself flew in the air, then banged back to the ground, jarring everyone inside. The drummer on the middle bench grunted and grabbed his chest. A crimson circle appeared on his boiled shirt. He looked down and collapsed in front of the praying Persam Torce.

"Get down there and see if you can help him. Stop the bleeding. Do something. Anything," Deed said and returned to the coach window, touching the brass circle at his neck and mumbling some ritual-sounding phrase to himself.

The stage station was in sight, barely, but the young rancher didn't expect much help there. It was a relay station, not a fort. He must go now, before the entire war party encircled the coach. He must. He jammed a new cartridge into the Remington and was ready to go.

James Hannah looked at the terrified Torce and growled, "At least you can pray for him, dumb ass." He pushed aside the leather curtain and fired at a warrior galloping past, barely visible by swinging to the outside of his horse.

Persam Torce's hands trembled as he fumbled for a handkerchief.

"*Guten tag, Herr Corrigan.* If *du* vould, *Ich* vould . . .

borrow *der* gun," the thin-faced German farmer said. "I vould . . . do *der* covering *für du.*"

Deed stared at him, nodded, and handed over the gun and gunbelt.

"This has a hair trigger. Better point it out the window before you cock. There's six beans in the wheel. Uh, six bullets. Usually I leave the chamber under the hammer empty. Not now though."

Taking the handgun as if it were hot, the farmer pushed aside the curtain, pointed the weapon out the coach window, aimed, and fired. Missing.

"*Ja.* God bless *du, Herr Corrigan,*" the farmer's wife, Olivia Beinrigt, whispered.

Opening the door, he swung out on it. The hinges creaked with his weight. He shoved his boot into the window where he had been shooting and tried to balance himself as the coach rocked and bounced. A misstep here would be fatal. A blue-faced warrior swung his lathered horse closer to the coach. As the warrior shrieked his war cry and swung his tomahawk, Deed let go of the coach rail with his right hand and grabbed the warrior's forearm as it came at him. His powerful move stopped the downward motion, but the Comanche grinned at him and reached for the knife carried at his waist.

Deed thought about gambling and letting go of the Indian's forearm and reaching for his own knife. The chances of doing that and staying on the coach weren't likely. As he shifted his boots, he heard the German farmer fire three times and the warrior groaned and fell away.

"Thanks, you saved my bacon," Deed yelled and released the limp Indian's arm.

"*Ja. Bitte sehr.*"

Guessing that meant "you're welcome," Deed Corrigan pushed the body away and clambered onto the coach roof. Scurrying across the roof to the back boot, he found his gear and yanked free the Spencer carbine and a box with reloading tubes. Each tube held seven cartridges for quick reloading. The 52-caliber breechloader held one bullet in the chamber and seven in the magazine. After loading the big gun, he yanked two suitcases free of the boot and arranged them on either side of him. The thick luggage would provide some protection from bullets and arrows. Stretching out, he balanced the carbine against the railing, cocked and aimed the big gun. Bullets sang past his head and an arrow thudded into the coach roof inches from his thigh.

One warrior with his mouth painted with a yellow handprint got close enough to the coach to grab the canvas covering the back boot. A shot from Deed drove the warrior from his horse, but his grip tore open the canvas. Three suitcases and a mailbag flew into the air and banged on the ground. Three warriors jumped from their horses and ripped open the luggage and waved colorful pieces of clothing as each treasure was uncovered. A thick-waisted Comanche, with his face and body painted half white and half blue, yanked a tweed suitcoat over his breastplate and painted arms; another tried putting on a dress; a hand mirror became a prized find for the third. Their stay was short as Deed's Spencer tore into the warrior staring at himself in the mirror. He staggered and fell. The other two quickly returned to their mounts, wearing their new garments.

Steadily, the war party gained on the weary coach horses. The coach banged along the well-defined road with Comanches on both sides, but wary due to the shooting of Hannah, Beinrigt, Johnson, and especially Deed. In the driver's box, the shotgun guard straightened and tumbled over the driver's box with two arrows protruding from his throat and chest. Tade Balkins tried to grab the dead guard's shotgun, but couldn't reach it as the weapon fell against the corner of the driver's box. He returned his attention to the horses, snapping his nine-foot-long whip over the lathered horses and urging them on as they bounded closer to the line of cottonwoods that edged the open yard of the relay station.

The fat Persam Torce sat cross-legged on the coach floor, praying beside the dead man in the top hat. He looked at the others as if this couldn't be happening and began to laugh weirdly and then to sob. Olivia Beinrigt patted the hysterical Rebecca's shoulder and told her it would all soon pass.

Deed's accuracy took down a warrior in a white-woman's dress. James Hannah yelled that he was hit and dropped his fancy gun. It thudded on the coach floor. Rebecca Tuttle wailed hysterically. The German woman told her to be quiet. The stagecoach thumped over some rocks and everyone was jolted again; Deed thought he was going to be thrown and grabbed the railing.

"I'm all right. I'm all right. It just burned my damn elbow," Hannah said gruffly and picked up the weapon and straightened his eyeglasses. His right coat sleeve showed a trace of blood, but he continued to focus on the war party outside.

"*Sehr gut*," Olivia Beinrigt said, watching her husband carefully aim and fire. From his silence, she assumed he hadn't hit a Comanche. She hid her concern from the distraught younger woman; expressing her fear would do nothing. Above, she heard the loud roar of Deed Corrigan's Spencer and said a silent prayer for his safety. Her husband looked down at the gun to reload it and an arrow slammed through his shoulder with the bloody point extruding from his back. Hermann Beinrigt looked at his wife and collapsed. The gun thudded onto the coach floor. His wife sobbed, bit her lip, then leaned forward to stroke her wounded husband's pale face.

Chapter Three

Unaware of the incoming stage's peril, Wilkon Station Manager Caleb Forsyth led a fresh team of horses out of the corral in preparation for the expected coach to the relay post. Morning sounds were strangely missing and he thought it was too quiet, but shoved the concern out of his mind. Not even the leaves of the cottonwoods, guarding the northwest edge of the stage station area, were fluttering.

A lone dirt devil spun its way across the open ground and disappeared over the hill as if hurrying to the nearby town of Wilkon. The well pump groaned about the day and the two lead horses were nervous, their ears on full alert. Off to the side of the yard was the separate adobe home where his family lived and a small cooling house for meat, milk, and butter. A barn, corral, blacksmith shed, the relay station building itself, and its accompanying outhouses, were the only other structures.

The coach wasn't in sight, but would be soon; Tade Balkins was never late.

"Easy, boys. It's all just fine an' dandy. Tade'll treat you right," he said and patted the closest bay's neck.

As always, Caleb's twelve-year-old son, Benjamin, was at his father's side. He was a good helper with a knack for handling horses. The boy patted the nose of the other lead horse and called him by a name no one else used. Beside the boy was a black-and-white dog named Cooper. The happy animal was rarely away from Benjamin and today was no exception.

Behind them, the one-eyed Mexican, Billy Lee Montez, was closing the corral gate next to the weathered barn with one hand and swatting at a horsefly who wanted to make his acquaintance with his other. He had been with the Forsyths since they took over the station two years ago. Billy Lee was good with horses and a better-than-average blacksmith. The Forsyths had developed the swing relay station into one of the best-run operations on the route, a station with a reputation for excellent food, fast service, and cleanliness. All of those attributes were due to Caleb's wife, Atlee.

All three heard the gunfire before the coach was in sight. It was Billy Lee who first realized what the sounds meant.

"Oh Lord me God! It ees Comanche!" the Mexican yelled.

"Go to the station, Benjamin! Stay there. Take Cooper with you," Caleb commanded, pushing his son toward the main building where his wife was preparing a meal for the passengers. The frightened boy hesitated, then ran to the building with Cooper at his heels.

His face taut with the knowledge of what was coming,

Caleb turned the team toward the corral. "Billy Lee, let's get these horses back in the corral."

"*Sí. Pronto.*" The Mexican had already reopened the gate "Gonna get *mi* shotgun. It is in de barn," he yelled over his shoulder.

Caleb Forsyth hurried the anxious horses into the corral and closed the gate. He stepped away, saw his son and dog disappear into the relay station, and returned his focus to the as yet empty horizon. Turning, he ran to the house and grabbed the offered Henry from his son, ignored his wife's plea to come inside, knelt on the planked porch, and waited. It was his duty to protect the stage.

Without further discussion, Atlee Forsyth grabbed the seven-shot Spencer carbine from the rack of rifles on the wall and went to a gun port in the wall. A heavy weapon, she had mastered its kick. Frowning, Benjamin aimed a Burnside carbine from another gun port. His father had taught him how to shoot with the weapon. The rack still held an English Whitworth musket, another Burnside carbine, and a double-barreled shotgun. Several pistols lay at the base of the rack.

A few minutes later, the coach roared into view with warriors snapping at it like mad dogs. Inside the coach, only Hannah was shooting now. Deed's firing had kept them farther away than they wanted. From a safe distance, the war leader studied Deed Corrigan. To quit now would mean his disgrace; no warrior would follow him again into battle. Across the leader's shoulders was draped an antelope skin decorated with silver conchos and bits of colored cloth. In the leader's scalp lock was a black feather with a red circle near the top.

His striking appearance was reinforced by the glistening sorrel horse he rode, painted for war and wearing feathers streaming in the powerful mount's mane and tail. Seeing Deed reload, he commanded two warriors to kill the lead coach horses. He raised his shield to the sky, then leaned over and touched the ground with his shield, both movements made to reinforce his war medicine. A hundred yards from the relay station's barn, two warriors raced forward to comply with his command; one on each side of the coach.

Deed whirled from his position on top and missed twice. Inside the coach, Hannah cursed and also missed. The Comanches fired their rifles at close range and the two lead Morgan horses grunted and tumbled forward, sending the coach in a furious, sideways skid. Deed brought down one of the Comanches. But it was too late; the damage was done. The other warrior spun away, yelling his war medicine. The coach was uncontrollable as Tade fought to stop the other horses and keep the wobbling vehicle upright. Inside, Hannah cursed and was unable to fire. Both women cried. Deed grabbed for the railing and hung on.

"Whoa, boys! Whoa! Stay up. Stay up, damn you, stay up!"

As the one-ton Concord stage lurched and skidded to a stop, Tade Balkins dropped the reins and jumped down from the driver's box. Whinnying, the remaining horses stumbled against each other. The two carriage-suspension thoroughbraces, three-inch-thick strips of leather, groaned but held. The middle horses went down in a snarl of harness and flailing legs. The two rear horses stutter-stepped fearfully, but remained upright, coming to a complete halt. Tade staggered toward the barn and was helped inside by Billy Lee Montez.

"I'm getting out. God will protect me," Persam Torce yelled, then pushed open the door and tumbled out of the coach before Hannah could stop him. A few feet from the coach, Torce knelt and began to pray, holding a cross in his hands.

A warrior, wearing a sleeveless military jacket reined up next to him and raised his tomahawk. Hannah fired twice and the savage shuddered, slid off his horse backward, and thudded on the prairie, face-down. Torce stood and began walking to the station as if it were a nice day in the park, but two other warriors rode past the coach yipping, and the first clubbed him to the ground and leaped off his snorting horse to scalp him. A third warrior was close behind. Caleb Forsyth's shots from the station's porch snapped into the warrior as he grabbed the dead man's hair. The Comanche jerked, tried to step away and collapsed, dropping his knife.

"Get inside, Caleb! You can't help him," Atlee declared from the window and returned to the gun port a few feet away.

Caleb Forsyth swung around to go inside as two bullets tore into his body. He stumbled and reached for the door. An arrow drove through his back and the bloody steel point came out his stomach. He took a step and fell. Opening the door, Atlee threw her gun inside, then grabbed her prone husband and, with Benjamin helping, dragged him inside, leaving a trail of blood. Cooper barked and ran around the mortally wounded man. With Caleb inside, she slammed shut the door and shoved the heavy support beam in place as bullets and another arrow hammered against it.

"God, hold him here with us . . . please," she gasped.

Cooper laid down next to Caleb, resting his head on the man's unmoving shoulder.

With only a momentary glance at her husband, Atlee returned to her post and aimed the Spencer through the gun port—this time at two warriors, now dismounted and coming toward the porch.

"Reload Pa's gun," Atlee commanded, not taking her eyes from the Indians.

One of her shots ripped through the right leg of the tallest and he staggered. A second bullet hit him in the chest and he fell against the porch. The other brandished his bow, but ran for his horse. Her shots missed him. Benjamin fired the reloaded Henry, but also missed. The second warrior grabbed his horse's mane, swung onto its back, and galloped away, yelling.

"Ma, I've only got eight bullets after this." Benjamin finished reloading the Henry. His voice was drained of emotion and he dared not look at the unmoving face of his father.

"All right, son. The Burnside is loaded. So is the Whitworth. The shotgun's ready, too."

"They only shoot once."

"We can reload. Get them down. There's ball and powder in the cabinet. Shotgun shells, too."

"Ma? Are we going to die? Is Pa . . . dead?"

Atlee glared in her son's direction and declared, "No, we are not. We are going to fight. Your father would want that. He's in God's hands now." She turned back to her shooting post. "Benjamin, two men in the coach. One's on top. They're shooting at the Comanches! I can see them. They're good, Benjamin."

"As good as Pa . . . was?"

"Nobody's that good, son."

Her face was flushed and her brown hair was halfway out of its regular tight bun. Even under stress, she was an attractive woman. Her light blue dress was torn at the right sleeve and her bosom was heaving, but she had never wavered or whimpered, only grabbed a gun when she saw the war party. It wasn't the first time Comanches had attempted to stop a stagecoach coming to their station and they had managed to successfully drive them off without any loss. But this was different. She knew her husband was dead.

The other Forsyth child, Elizabeth, was six and sat near the fireplace, ablaze with flame. She was playing with a cloth doll; her round cheeks were flushed from the heat, but seemingly, she had no sense of what was happening.

"Our horses! They're after our horses!" she muttered, took careful aim, and fired through the rifle hole, winging a yellow-painted warrior.

Leaving the wounded brave, three other warriors headed for the corral and the agitated coach horses there. Deed resumed shooting from the top of the coach, making them retreat. One staggered and fell a few feet from the corral gate. The two remaining Indians headed for the barn that held two additional teams of coach horses and the family's three personal mounts and a milk cow. Billy Lee Montez emptied both barrels of his shotgun at them. One warrior fell in the doorway. The last warrior hurried to his horse as Deed's big gun slammed against a

spent shell. A new cartridge tube was shoved in place
and he looked for other targets as the warrior galloped away.

From the other side of the coach, James Hannah
fired at a fleeing warrior and missed. He yelled, "Deed,
I thought they'd come at us hard now that we've
stopped, but they're gathering behind us. Near those
trees. Are they quitting?"

"We've stung 'em. Maybe we can help them with
that thought."

Meanwhile, the remaining war party had pulled
back fifty yards with the war leader waving toward the
coach. Deed figured they were puzzled by their lack
of success. Half the warriors were down. Dead or
wounded. They hadn't expected to lose men in battle,
not like this anyway. Some of the warriors were openly
questioning their leader's war medicine. They were
used to hitting outlying farmers or ranches, or attacking a lone stage coach, all easy prey for red raiders
who struck like lightning. Not so today. It must mean
their war leader's *puhahante*, his war medicine, was
broken.

Stretching out, Deed balanced his carbine against
the railing, cocked and aimed the big gun. The war
leader's war cry jerked to a stop and he folded from
his horse; his head a bloody mess with a huge bullet
hole between his eyes. His fellow warriors stared at
their dead leader in disbelief. They must flee or be destroyed by the angry spirits now turning on them.
Deed fired again and another warrior's chest became
a crimson ball as he fell from his horse. The remaining
warriors kicked their ponies into a frightened retreat.
He emptied the Spencer at their retreat, taking another Comanche from his horse.

Triumphant cheers exploded from the coach. The German woman said something to her husband that no one understood. Leaving his book in the coach, Hannah popped open the coach door and stepped out, holding his revolver. He told Rebecca it was safe to come out. She glanced at Deed as she left and hurried to the station. The gunman looked up at Deed.

"Looks like we got it done, Corrigan."

"Yeah. How's it inside?"

"Ah, the German took an arrow. In his shoulder. He's hurt bad, I think."

"Damn."

"Yeah."

With that, Hannah began walking among the closest downed Comanches, shooting each one again. Deed swung down and saw the wounded farmer in his wife's lap. He was conscious, but in considerable pain.

Opening the coach door, Deed said, "That arrow needs to come out. The sooner, the better."

Olivia Beinrigt blinked and told him what had happened.

"Let me get the arrow out, then we can get him to the station. All right?"

"*Ja, danke.*"

Acrid gunsmoke laid heavily inside the coach as Deed entered and grabbed his sheathed throwing knife from behind his collar. He knelt beside the struggling farmer and cut off the arrowhead with his blade. A fly found the oozing wound and he swiped at it with his open hand.

"I'm going to pull this out now. It's going to hurt. You ready?" he said to the white-faced Beinrigt.

"J-Ja."

Putting his left hand against the man's bloody shoulder, Deed Corrigan took hold of the arrow shaft with his right and pulled it free. The farmer grimaced and fainted. Removing his neckerchief, Deed wadded and pressed the cloth against the bleeding.

"We can clean that wound when we get to the station." He looked up at the German woman. "You take care of your man till then. Keep this pressed tight. Let up in a few minutes, then do it again. Need to stop the bleeding. I'll get Mr. Hannah to help carry him."

Spiderwebs of crow's feet jumped around Olivia's pale blue eyes. Her plain gray dress was splattered with her husband's blood.

"Danke," she said and patted his arm. *"Du* are most brave."

He smiled and buckled on his gunbelt and yelled to James Hannah.

The bespectacled gunman returned to the coach to help Deed carry the wounded farmer, leaving the dead top-hatted man in the coach. Olivia walked proudly beside them, holding her husband's hand.

"How bad they get you?" Deed asked, glancing at the gunman's bloody coat sleeve as they walked.

"It's nothing. Just a scratch," Hannah said. "How's the German?"

Deed glanced at Olivia. "Going to be all right, I think. Lost a lot of blood. He'll need some time." He adjusted his hold on the wounded man's shoulders. "He saved my life, you know. Cut down one of those bastards when I was in a bad spot getting on top."

"Yeah, you're a lucky man, Corrigan. I'll have to remember that." Hannah's laugh was warm.

"You'd better." Deed chuckled.

CHAPTER FOUR

At the relay station, young Benjamin Forsyth opened the door for the incoming passengers. Cooper barked for attention. Rebecca Tuttle was talking loudly to no one in particular.

"Thanks, son," Deed Corrigan started to say something else, but saw the unmoving man stretched out on the planked floor.

The look in the boy's eyes was the only answer he needed. At the fireplace, Benjamin's younger sister continued to play with her doll, unaware of what had happened to her father or the violence that had occurred outside.

"I'm mighty sorry," he said and looked at James Hannah. "Let's put Mr. Beinrigt over there. On that bunk." Bunks were set up in the back of the station for drivers and guards, but not for passengers. If necessary to stop overnight, passengers would have to sleep on the floor.

The boy turned away so no one could see him crying as the two gunfighters laid the wounded

German on the bunk. Olivia Beinrigt asked for water to clean the wound and a tearstained Atlee Forsyth brought her a bucket filled from their inside water barrel. Cooper moved to be next to Benjamin and the boy scratched his floppy ears as unstoppable tears ran down his freckled face.

With her straw hat in her hand, the agitated Rebecca Tuttle hurried over to Deed and Hannah and asked, between sobs, "Are they gone? Will they come back?"

"Guess nobody knows about Indians for sure," Deed said. "But I reckon we're safe. For now. They'll head back to their camp. Take a vote on a new leader. That won't come fast. Or they might just head south. Look for an easier target. We cut them up pretty bad. They aren't used to that."

She smiled and said, "Thank you. You were so brave. So were you, Mr. Hannah."

"Just trying to stay alive, Miss Tuttle," Hannah said, adjusting his glasses.

"Mr. Beinrigt did his part and more," Deed added.

Atlee stepped beside them. "I'm Mrs. Forsyth. My husband and I run this station. I want to thank you for stopping the Comanches. That's the worst it's ever been."

Her youngest, Elizabeth, wandered over and hugged her mother's leg, receiving a warm pat on the head. Atlee glanced at her husband's body. "T-They k-killed my Caleb."

The younger woman frowned at Atlee's interruption, slammed her hat back on her head, and walked away with its ribbons flopping in her face.

"I'm so sorry we couldn't save your husband." Deed took off his hat. "Ma'am? Would you like us to . . .

carry Mr. Forsyth . . . somewhere? Till we can bury him proper?" His voice was gentle and his eyes met hers.

"Thank you, Mr.—"

"It's Deed Corrigan, ma'am. Deed, if you please."

"Thank you, Deed. Please call me Atlee."

"Yes, ma . . . Atlee."

"My son and I will be serving supper soon. I'm sure all of you would find some food and coffee refreshing, after this awful time." Her face looked like it was going to crack.

"Atlee . . . let us take care of that. You and your son, why don't you go to your home. Be by yourselves," Deed said.

"No. This is our station. Our job. Caleb would want us here."

Deed Corrigan shook his head, stepped away, and asked James Hannah to help him move the body. The bespectacled gunman nodded and the two of them left carrying the body. After whispering some instructions to Deed, Atlee Forsyth watched them leave, swallowed hard, and went to the station's kitchen. Benjamin and Cooper followed.

Elizabeth studied the men carrying her father out of the house, turned toward her mother, and asked, "What's the matter with Pa? Is he sick? He's so quiet."

Atlee swallowed. "Your father is with God. Please come and help me."

Elizabeth's next question went unheard.

As they carried the dead man to his house, Hannah observed, "Never liked looking at a dead man. Even one I killed. One minute, he's full of life. The next, he's dirt."

"Yeah. Especially when he's a good man." Deed

eased around a large clump of grass, holding Caleb Forsyth's shoulders. "Watch that bunch of grass."

"Got it. The man's heavy, isn't he? Think those red bastards'll be back?"

"Don't think so, but we'll have to keep an eye out."

Not far away was a small stream that also provided a spring-fed well, assisted by an energetic windmill. Just over the hill was the small town of Wilkon, named after the man who built the first general store to assist travelers. They passed a chicken coop surrounded by a fence, housing a dozen chickens and a rooster. Next to it was a well-tilled garden, yielding potatoes, carrots, onions, cabbage, and corn. Deed was certain the two far trees were apple trees. Ten feet from the house was the stone cooling shed.

"Looks like they're pretty near self-sufficient here," Hannah observed as he shifted the dead man's weight in his arms.

"Yeah. Bet we'd find a milk cow in the barn," Deed answered.

Deed balanced the body with one hand and opened the door to the house with the other. "We were lucky those Comanches didn't get the horses earlier."

"Yeah. Interesting way to live," Hannah said, keeping the door open with his elbow as they stepped inside. "You know, all they do is fight." He grinned. "The two of us would've fit right in."

"Could be. Wouldn't care much about slapping paint all over me though."

Hannah chuckled.

"That's quite a good-looking pistol you're carrying, James," Deed said, nodding in the direction of Hannah's opened coat.

"Oh, yeah. Really like this gun. Smith & Wesson made them for the Russian army. Most accurate handgun I've ever found," Hannah said. "Got this one, well, let's just say I found it."

"That's good enough for me."

The Forsyth's adobe-and-timber home was clean, tidy, and felt of a woman's presence. Following Atlee's directions, they laid Caleb Forsyth on the bed in the front bedroom; Hannah straightened his coat, now smeared with dried blood. Deed covered the dead man's still face and body with a blanket that had been folded in the corner of the room. A second bedroom, built on for Benjamin and Elizabeth, stuck out from the core of the house.

A stone fireplace with an open hearth held a gray bank of coals in need of stirring to keep them producing warmth. In the main room, a large brown sofa was pushed against the south wall. A torn spot on the side of the sofa had been sewn together. A large table with four unmatched wooden chairs held a small vase of prairie flowers, now days past their prime. In another corner of the main room was an ornate desk, accented with Spanish-style carving. Above the desk was a framed photograph of Caleb and Atlee on their wedding day. A small kitchen held a cast-iron stove and a row of cabinets.

"That's one tough lady," Hannah said as they walked back to the front door. "Didn't fall apart when her man went down."

"Got a feeling she will . . . when everybody's gone," Deed said.

"Going to be rough on these folks. Wonder what she and the kids'll do?"

Deed didn't want to think of their options and merely shook his head.

Hannah studied him a moment and said, "Holt Corrigan is your brother, I take it."

"Yeah. Haven't seen him for a long time."

"Heard he was in a gunfight in Amarillo. Got himself killed."

"Heard that, too. Possible, but I doubt it. Not Holt."

Hannah grinned. "Me too. No offense, but there's another story. About you. Two years ago in Austin the way I heard it. Three fellas were leaving the bank after robbing it and ran into you." He cocked his head and pushed back his glasses. "You took down the first gunman with only your hands—while he was pointing a six-gun at your belly. In a split second, you grabbed the gun, killed the second outlaw, and wounded the third. Heard that story all over Texas." He paused and added, "Thought it was crazy talk . . . until I saw you in action today. Now I've got a hunch it was true."

"Didn't have much choice."

"Sure. It's good to be lucky, too."

As they left the small house, two shadowed figures rode up to the far edge of the station area, beside the cottonwoods, leading a third saddled horse. The closest rider swung his Winchester to his shoulder from its position across his saddle and studied the now-quiet attack scene. The second rider, an older Japanese man, carried a long, curved sword on a sheath across his back and a long knife was belted at his waist. From the station, Cooper barked but made no attempt to leave the safety of the station.

Shielding his eyes with his hand, Hannah declared, "Two men are out there. Just rode up. Don't think I know them. One's an Oriental. The other's white. I think he's only got one arm."

Deed smiled. "Sounds like my brother. And my best friend, Silka."

"What?"

"My brother. Blue Corrigan. Lost his left arm in the war. I'm the youngest of the three of us." Deed shook his long hair, brushing against his shoulders. "We planned to meet here. I'm on the way back from our cattle drive to Abilene. Looks like they've got a horse for me.

"And that's Silka with Blue. Silka's our partner. Nakashima Silka is his full name. Silka's easier to say and he doesn't mind. He used to be a samurai warrior back in Japan. Kinda think of him as our uncle. Long story." Deed smiled "Come on, I'll introduce you."

"You go on. I'll head back to the station and see how things are going there," Hannah said, waving his hand in dismissal. "I'll meet 'em later."

"Sure."

CHAPTER FIVE

Blue Corrigan watched the bespectacled man head for the station while his younger brother strode across the open yard.

Without warning, a wounded warrior Hannah had overlooked, jumped up and ran at Deed waving a tomahawk and yelling. In one smooth motion, Deed pivoted to his left, grabbed the Indian's right wrist with his left hand, and smashed his right elbow into the charging Comanche's face. Deed yanked away the tomahawk, then drove his fist into the attacker's chest. The Comanche gasped and fell.

A shot from one of the riders ended any further attempt. Smoke trailed from the barrel of Blue's rifle. He had fired it like a pistol, one-handed, pushing the stock against his leg. Licking his lower lip, he returned it to his saddle scabbard and swung down. The Oriental nodded and dismounted, too.

As if nothing had happened, Deed strolled over to the two riders. Of medium height and build, the two brothers looked a lot alike, resembling their late father, even down to their once-broken noses, courtesy of their brother, Holt. Deed was eight years younger than Blue, an inch taller, fifteen pounds heavier, and definitely wilder. Blue was as intense as Deed, but directed it toward building a great ranch.

Deed's reputation for fighting grew as well; Holt's reputation was more like that of a ghost. Neither Blue nor Deed had seen him since the war ended. Two years younger than Blue, Holt had been riding the outlaw trail, still fighting the war that had ended so long ago. Distinctly, the three brothers had elements of their mother's approach to life within them. Deed cared about all things of nature, from snakes to birds to deer, much like that of an Indian; his fighting instincts, however, came from their father.

Holt had picked up their mother's fascination with superstition and reincarnation, believing he had once been a Roman soldier, a knight in King Arthur's Round Table, even a jaguar in South America, in different lifetimes. He carried a panther's claw in his pocket and had since he was twelve. His first experience in believing he had lived before had occurred during the war. An enlightening experience, he said. His superstitious ways increased then as well. No one laughed when he told the stories, not even Deed. Like his younger brother, Holt's fierce fighting abilities had come from their father.

Blue's beliefs, however, were more traditional. In fact, he served the Wilkon church as a part-time minister, along with a townsman, whenever the circuit rider wasn't available. Their mother had loved reading, especially the Bible, and so did Blue; their father believed in the need for righteous behavior, but also in never backing down.

Blue's coat and chaps showed signs of trail dust. The sleeve of his left arm was pinned against his coat. Yankee artillery fire had blown it off; he was lucky to have survived. One of his pockets was jammed with extra cartridges. In the other was a small Bible his mother had given him. He always carried it, even during the war, and credited the scripture with saving his life. At his hip was a holstered Walch Navy 12-shot revolver with two triggers and two hammers. Weighing two pounds, it was twelve inches long. Rarely seen in this part of Texas, Blue had taken the gun from a dead Union officer during the war and decided he liked it, especially since reloading a standard six-shooter wasn't easy one-handed.

"Glad you could make it." Deed gave his brother a warm hug, then turned to Silka and hugged him, saying, "*Nana korobi, ya oki.*"

The old samurai smiled, recognizing the Japanese saying: fall down seven times, get up eight. "Velly good. A warrior must do so."

The short, stocky Japanese man was many years older than the Corrigan brothers, had a graying mustache, and wore his hair pulled back tight to a tail in back. Carried in a sheath across his back was a classic samurai sword. Nakashima Silka's clothes were nondescript, but definitely those of a cowboy; a broad-brimmed hat was weathered and flopping. Around his neck was a small engraved brass circle just like Deed wore. It, too, carried a hidden knife behind the Oriental's back.

He had left Japan when the samurai were forced out and made his way to Texas, learning English as he traveled. In many ways, he was like a stepfather to all three Corrigan brothers and had taught Deed, in particular, how to fight—and fight well—with any weapon and with one's hands and feet. Silka taught the classic samurai way of the warrior, *Bushido*, the importance of inner strength and determination, with moments of concentrated energy. At its core were honor and freedom from the fear of death. His swords were the only physical remains of his previous way of life. Under his careful training, Deed had become a fierce warrior even though he didn't want the reputation.

Deed, Holt, and Blue, with Silka's considerable help, had built up their family's ranch southeast of the stage station and a few miles outside of Wilkon. Theirs was one of five ranches doing well in the region; two were quite large, the Bar 3 and the Lazy S. Their mother and sister had died of pneumonia when Blue was eighteen; Holt, sixteen; and Deed, ten. Their father had died six months before their mother from a broken neck after a horse threw him. Three years later, Blue and Holt left to fight for the Confederacy while the much-younger brother, Deed, stayed with Silka to keep the ranch afloat. While the older brothers were gone, Silka had honed Deed's fighting skills.

"It'll be good to get home," Deed said, patting the nose of the extra horse, a steady buckskin that he favored. "Seems like I've been gone a long time."

"Well, you have, Deed," Blue said and glanced at the station, "but one of us needs to go on to El Paso. Just bought a fine stallion . . . from August Magnuson. Figured we'd breed him with some of our best mustang mares."

"Magnuson? He's got some mighty good horse-flesh. Usually wants a lot for 'em, too."

Blue smiled. "He's in a bind for cash. Made us a mighty good offer. Couldn't pass it up. Silka agreed." His smile got wider and he glanced at the former samurai who nodded agreement. "At least, I hope you've got money from the trail drive."

"In my gear." Deed motioned toward the coach. "I can go on. I'll take what we need to pay Magnuson and give the rest to you two. We did well."

Blue looked around and said, "Good. Sorry we didn't get here sooner. That must've been a bad bunch." He closed his eyes briefly and said a silent prayer for the dead souls.

"Came out of the earth, it seemed like," Deed said.

The Oriental asked, "How many hurt?"

"Two passengers as well as the shotgun guard are dead. So is the station manager. Another passenger, a German farmer, got hit hard in the shoulder," Deed said. "He's inside being cared for by his wife." He shook his head.

"What happened to your driver?" Blue asked.

"Last time I saw him, he was running for that barn. I think the stock tender's in there, too. Haven't had time to look. Or cared to." Deed motioned toward the barn, then turned toward three painted Indian horses standing with their heads down, adorned with paint and feathers tied to their manes and tails. He gathered their simple reins and led the ponies to the water trough, then let them loose in the corral. Blue and Silka tied their own horses to the trees and headed for the coach's downed horses.

As they walked, Deed asked, "Ever hear of a gunman named James Hannah?"

Blue nodded. "Most have, I reckon."

"Yeah. Doesn't look like a gunman though."

"*Hai*, what does gunman look like?" Silka asked, a slight smile working its way onto his flat face.

"Some would say Holt, I guess. Or me." Deed bit his lower lip.

Silka waved his arms in disagreement. "No. You are *fighter*. Warrior. Big difference."

Deed rubbed his mouth with his thumb. "Anyway, Hannah was a big part of our making it. He and I just took the station manager's body to his house. We'll bury him later. Wherever Mrs. Forsyth wants."

"Where's he headed? James Hannah," Blue said, glancing at the station again.

"Going to El Paso, I think. Why?"

Blue said, "Well, it's one more gun."

"Yeah, a good one."

Finally Tade Balkins and Billy Lee Montez emerged from the barn; the one-eyed Mexican holding his shotgun and looking both ways with each step. Tade's face was taut and his rapid-fire speech made it obvious he was coiled and nervous. Silka's presence seemed to make him even more on edge.

"Any more of those red devils left?" He glanced at Silka without meaning to do so, then looked away.

"They're gone—or dead. We killed their leader and that sent the rest running," Deed said, motioning to the bodies lying across the yard.

"Thank God for that," Tade shook his head.

"Yes, thank God," Blue repeated.

"Never had 'em come at me like that before. Holy damn!" Tade shook his head again. "They got Hank early on. My guard, ya know. Was. Then the bastards cut down my two lead horses. Damn them to blazes. They were great Morgans. Two of the line's best."

"*O soroshi*," Silka said solemnly.

Tade stared at him as if the old samurai had just given a war cry. Both Corrigan brothers recognized the Japanese word for "awful," but added no comments of their own. It seemed to Deed that the driver was more upset about his two horses dying than losing his guard. He introduced Tade to Blue and Silka, and asked to be introduced to Billy Lee. After mumbling an introduction, Tade walked over to the coach while the others exchanged greetings.

"Hard to believe. Those red bastards didn't even try for the gold." The stagecoach driver shook his head and motioned toward the heavy box under his seat. It was filled with gold coins, certificates, and bars for the El Paso Bank.

Deed glanced at Blue, then Silka, then back to the high-strung driver. "They got the station manager, too, while you were hiding out in the barn."

"Caleb Forsyth? They killed Caleb? My God, that's awful!" For an instant, it looked like Tade was going to kick the closest Indian's body. Either he didn't get the bite of Deed's remark or chose to ignore it.

"Yeah. You lost two passengers, too. Another, Mr. Beinrigt, is hurt bad. We carried him into the station."

Silka walked over to the coach and muttered something in Japanese. Tade licked his lips and stared at the dead drummer still wearing his top hat, as if seeing the body for the first time, then gazed at the expressionless Silka. "Where are the womenfolk?"

"They're inside. They're all right."

"Oh. Well, that's good." Tade walked over to the two dead horses. "I've got to get going again. Mail's gotta get through, ya know."

It was Blue who spoke first and his words were practical. "Well, we can't leave these dead horses here to rot. Maybe we can pull them out of the way. We're going to need to hook up some of the team in the barn to haul the dead ones away."

"Sure. Sure." Tade was already gathering strewn-about clothing from the broken-open luggage and laying the garments and suitcases in the coach. One mail bag was ripped apart so he gathered the loose envelopes and boxes and placed them inside the coach as well.

"We're going to need your help *here*," Deed said.

Tade looked up. "Oh, sure. I wasn't thinking. Wasn't thinking."

Billy Lee Montez laid the shotgun against the coach and helped untangle the harness. The two rear horses were eager to get away from the nightmare of snarled leather. The left rear horse reared and snorted. Billy calmed the frightened horse into standing again. Unharnessing the animals was slow work, but gradually they freed one of the downed middle Morgans and the animal stood, shook itself, and was ready to be led away with the other two. The remaining middle horse had a badly broken leg and couldn't stand. Mercifully, Deed shot the animal, then knelt, touched the dead animal's head, and said a silent prayer. Blue and Silka watched without comment.

Billy said, "I bring grease for de axles."

"Let's get these horses out of here first," Blue affirmed. "We'll need some horses to pull them."

"*Sí.* I bring two hosses. Enough?"

Silka nodded. "Velly good. Bring rope also."

Billy hurried away and Blue and Silka walked the three unhurt coach horses to the holding corral. Returning to their own horses, they led them to the water trough and then retied them to the outside of the corral gate. Billy brought a set of harnessed horses and they finally got the three dead horses dragged away into a long ravine, surrounded by brush. Tade urged them on while leaning against the coach and watching the old samurai walk among the downed Comanches, using his long sword to assure himself that they were all dead since James Hannah had obviously missed one.

"What do you want to do about these dead Indians? The ones close in here?" Deed asked. "They'll bring coyotes and buzzards—and smell like hell."

Tade shook his head. "Well, I've got to get this coach going. Hate to leave you with that mess, but I gotta."

Blue shook his head. "You're full of all kinds of good news. We need to drag these Indians off someplace out of sight and smell."

"I guess I'll help," Deed said.

"Well, those Comanches will come back to get them. Count on it." Blue motioned toward the horizon with his good hand.

Silka agreed. "Hai. They will come. It is their way."

"*Sí,*" Billy added.

Blue recommended they wait until the coach left, then haul the dead Indians beyond the stage yard and out of sight. The stage could be moved up closer to the station so the passengers wouldn't have to walk among the dead to get on. The dead passengers and the shotgun guard would require separate graves. How and where the dead station manager would be laid to rest would be Atlee Forsyth's decision. Deed reminded Tade that two suitcases on top would need reloading and the removal of some arrows. There were a few bullet holes too; but not much could be done about them.

The anxious driver said he would take care of the suitcases. After greasing the axles, Billy Lee helped Tade lead out the fresh team and harness them to the coach. Tade was obviously eager to get moving again. He headed to the station to get something to eat and tell the passengers that the coach was ready. The Mexican disappeared into the barn again.

After lifting the dead drummer from the stage and laying him on the ground, Deed, Silka, and Blue headed for the house, talking to each other.

CHAPTER SIX

"So the drive went well? Your wire said so," Blue asked his brother, patting him on the back, as they walked toward the station.

"Real good, big brother. Got top price. Those boys were eager to get beef headed east."

"*Hontou*?" Silka asked.

"Yeah, really."

All three laughed. Deed said again that the cattle-drive money was hidden away in his gear. He added, "Lost three steers crossing a river. Another five were trampled during a stampede. But we picked up twenty stray head along the way. Willy found most of them. Unbranded stuff."

"What started the stampede? A storm?"

"Yes and no. One night the herd was tense, wouldn't settle because a storm was coming. You know how Willy can start burping when he's nervous," Deed explained. "Well, he belched so damn loud after eating, it took us half the night getting the herd back together," Deed said, chuckling. "Some of the men took to calling him Boom."

"Is he worth keeping? That could've been bad."

"Willy works harder than three men," Deed said. "Belches louder than three men, too."

"Sure. Your call."

"He'll stand."

Blue glanced at his younger brother and started walking again. "While you were gone, we had some terrible tragedies around here." He paused and frowned. "The Regan family was murdered in their home. Looked like Comanches hit the Bar 3."

"My God! Jason and Martha . . . their kids? That's awful, Blue."

"Yeah, it was; Isaiah Tuscott came to our ranch just after dawn to tell us," Blue said. "He was going there to help Jason with an addition to their main house. We rode there as fast as we could. Little Jeremy had hidden. We found him and brought him home to stay with us. But he was the only one that made it."

"How'd you know it was Comanches?"

Shifting his shoulders as if to remove an unseen burden, Blue explained about finding arrows, a tomahawk, unshod horse tracks, and that the adults had been scalped.

Deed grimaced. "I'm surprised the war party attacked at night. Thought they were afraid a warrior killed would never find his way to heaven. Did they burn the ranch house?"

"No."

"That's strange too."

"Yeah. You know, usually a ranch is pretty empty during roundup and trail-drive time, but Jason doesn't go on the drives anymore. That busted leg of his won't hold up. So it was he and his family except for their six-year-old son, Jeremy. All dead. And scalped." Blue looked away. "You remember Ol' Joel, don't you? They got him, too. Bless his soul. Looked like he fought them for a long time."

"Damn. How long did he work for the Regans?"

"Must've been thirty years, at least."

Blue straightened his back. "It gets worse. The Wilkon Bank foreclosed on the Bar 3. Had a big loan, according to the bank president."

"So who owns the Bar 3 now?"

"Same fellow who bought the bank. Lives in El Paso. It all happened not long after you left for Abilene," Blue said. "He bought the H-5 and the Roof-M, too."

"That's convenient," Deed snorted. "So only three ranches around here now. His combined spread, the Lazy S, and us."

"Hai. It is so," Silka agreed. The former samurai studied the brothers without saying more, then examined the station area, and looked at the Corrigan boys again.

"I take it you don't think it was Comanches," Deed said, cocking his head.

"Not sure. Once I got him to talk about it, Jeremy said some things about white men attacking the place," Blue said, a little above a whisper. "And the whole thing with the bank loan. Don't know why they would have borrowed money. Not them anyway. Must have been a cash-flow problem." He rubbed his chin. "I can understand the H-5 and Roof-M selling out. They're both small. Probably tired of it all. You know, they've been putting their trail herds with the Bar 3 the last couple of years."

"Well, I saw the Bar 3 herd on the trail when I was

coming back. A big one. At least three thousand head," Deed said. "Didn't recognize any of their hands on the trail. Or their trail boss. Thought it was strange. Now it makes sense. So, what happened to the money from their drive?"

"Bank has no record of any deposit like that."

Silka's face hardened. "Hai. Blue, you know it was not Comanche. You know it was this Agon Bordner."

"Who's Agon Bordner?" Deed asked.

"The guy who bought the bank—and the Bar 3 and the other two."

Deed glanced at Silka. "That's a mighty big spread. Biggest around here. Even bigger when you add in the H-5 and the Roof-M."

"It is so," Silka declared and studied Deed's face.

Blue explained he hadn't met Agon Bordner, only heard that he lived in a big house in El Paso, adding that he thought a man had a right to take advantage of a situation if he could. It was like him to view everyone in a positive light. Almost as much as their late mother had.

Silka looked at him and grinned. "He is velly fat, they say."

Blue quickly added Bordner had a fine reputation in El Paso—that he was active in the Baptist church there, even sang in the choir.

"What happened to the Merefords and the Hansons? Are they still around?"

"No. Both families left right away, right after they sold," Blue said. "And that's even worse. Comanches hit their wagons somewhere north of here. Killed them all."

"That's awful. Awful."

"Yeah, they were good folks," Blue said.

All three men were quiet.

Deed was the first to speak, "Well, who's running the Bar 3 now?"

"A fellow named Dixie Murphy's the new foreman. Met him once in town. A hard man to like. But I'm sure he's a good cowman." Blue licked his lips and changed the subject. "How many of our boys are coming back?"

"Just the regulars. Willy, Harmon, Chico, Little Jake and Too Tall are bringing back the chuck wagon and the remuda—and Judas."

Judas was the name they called a large, black long-horn steer that led their herds to market. The rest of the drovers had hooked on to a drive headed for Wyoming. Too Tall was what everyone called their cook, a short, stocky man with a temper to match. Deed said Taol Sanchez hit town with a big herd of over two thousand, two days after they got in. Oldest son of Felix Sanchez, the owner of the huge Lazy S, he was also happy with the prices received for his beef.

Blue stopped walking and turned to Deed. "How are those folks doing, the ones inside?"

"About like you'd expect, I guess. Mrs. Forsyth's trying to go on," Deed said, glancing at the station as they resumed walking. "The Forsyths had turned this into a damn good relay operation, you know."

Looking around at the readied coach, Deed added, "Guess Mrs. Forsyth and her kids will need to go in the stage. To somewhere safe. El Paso's the next big town. Unless they want to go into Wilkon. Don't think they have much money. Won't be easy for her."

A black snake slid across their path. Blue reached for his holstered gun as it stopped and hissed.

"Let it go. He's not disturbing us," Deed said and

knelt beside the snake. Behind him, Silka drew his long sword.

"It's all right. No one will hurt you," Deed spoke to the agitated reptile.

Neither Blue nor Silka moved, but watched the snake. Slowly, it uncoiled and resumed its journey. Silka said something in Japanese. Deed stood and the three men began walking again with no further mention of the reptile. Blue knew his younger brother had a sense for nature that few could match. It reminded him of their mother.

Silka thought he should remain outside and let them bring him something to eat, instead of going into the station. Not everyone liked to have Orientals near, he indicated. Both Corrigan brothers rejected the idea.

"If they don't want you, they don't want us," Deed said and slapped Silka on the back.

The old samurai faked being hurt by the affectionate display and smiled.

Stepping inside, Cooper growled as they entered, then hurried to greet them with his tail wagging. Deed bent over to return the greeting. They were surprised to see Atlee Forsyth serving Hannah, Rebecca, and Tade around the long table as if nothing had occurred. Large bowls of beef stew, baskets of biscuits, and fresh coffee were being enjoyed. Hermann Beinrigt was lying down on the couch, and Olivia was putting a wet rag on his forehead. Little Elizabeth stood next to her, holding a bowl of water. Deed walked over to them and put his hand on the farmer's good shoulder.

"How's he doing, Mrs. Beinrigt?"

"He *ist* fair, I think. Much *blut ist* lost. *Du* save his life." Olivia held out a slightly shaking hand.

Taking hers with both hands, Deed leaned toward her and smiled. "He saved mine." Releasing the handshake, he stood and introduced his brother and Silka who removed their hats.

Olivia looked up and greeted both.

Stepping next to Deed, Elizabeth declared, "My papa is dead, you know. He is in heaven."

Deed blurted, "I'm so sorry."

The little girl lifted the bowl so it could be fully seen. "I'm helping Mrs. Beinrigt."

"I'm sure you are. I'm sure you are." Deed realized the little girl had no concept of death. Why should she?

Her next statement made him wince. "Papa is with Washington now. He was our cat, till he died last year."

Deed knelt beside her and brushed away the long strands of hair that had stuck to her warm cheek. "Uh, I'm sure they will be very happy together."

She turned to him and declared, "I think Papa will be back in a week or so. Like when he went to El Paso."

Deed swallowed and couldn't think of anything to say.

From behind them came Atlee Forsyth's, with what seemed to be an overly bright salutation. "Deed, I'm glad you're here. Mr. Hannah said you'd be coming inside. There's plenty of stew and biscuits. Coffee's hot and fresh." She wiped her right hand on her apron. "Who are your friends?"

Deed turned toward her. "This is my brother, Blue Corrigan. We own a ranch not far from Wilkon." He pointed at Blue, then at Silka. "And this is our best friend and partner. Most folks call him Silka."

Silka bowed formally.

"How nice to meet you," she said. "Please have a seat. You are most welcome."

Blue touched the brim of his hat with his hand. "Glad to meet you, ma'am. Awful sorry about your husband."

Her eyes took in his sewn-up sleeve, then went to his face. "Thank you. He was a very good man. But we'll make do. We have to." Her eyes brightened. "Caleb would have wanted that."

Tade rose from his chair and waved his arm. "Told her she should go with us to El Paso. She won't go. Maybe you can talk her into going into Wilkon."

Still holding the bowl of water, Elizabeth walked over to her mother. "Is that like going to Heaven?"

"I'll tell you later, sweetheart. Please be quiet now."

Folding her arms, Atlee stared at the three men. "Please sit down. Mr. Balkins informs us the stage will be leaving soon."

Mrs. Beinrigt came over and guided Elizabeth back to the couch, asking for her help. Deed sat down at the table with Silka and Blue on either side of him. With separate trips, Atlee placed bowls of stew in front of them, along with ironware, cups, and a basket of biscuits. Blue murmured a prayer of grace before beginning to eat. Hannah watched him without saying anything.

"Ma'am, I know Willard Epson, your district agent. A good man," Blue said, looking up and watching her move along the table, refreshing coffee cups.

"Yes, I have met Mr. Epson several times." Her voice was rigid.

"Of course"—Blue licked his lips—"he will need to know—"

Atlee Forsyth stiffened, holding the coffeepot near her bosom. "Because he will want a *man* running this station?"

Blue looked at Deed, then Silka, and said, "Most likely . . . ma'am."

"So don't tell him. I just told you that we will do just fine."

Blue stared at her, wishing he hadn't started this line of conversation.

"I can run this station. I'll hire someone to help Mr. Montez—and we'll keep serving passengers well as we have always done." Her eyelids blinked back tears that were trying to get attention.

"Yes, ma'am. I'm sure you can."

The room was silent while Atlee resumed pouring coffee for everyone. The others were finishing their dessert, fat slices of gooseberry pie. Pushing away from the table, Tade Balkins headed for the door and announced the stage would be leaving in five minutes.

Wiping his mouth with his sleeve, Tade said, "I have to report what happened, Mrs. Forsyth. Part of my job." His eyes didn't meet hers as he opened the door.

It was Deed who spoke first, "Tade, if you have to say anything, tell your boss the station is operating well, and that Mrs. Forsyth has hired additional help." He looked at Atlee. "If you'll let me, I'll stay on and help Billy till you can find somebody regular."

Blue tried not to look surprised, but this was so like his younger brother to step into a fight. Any fight.

Deed glared at the stunned driver. "You don't have to report that last part."

For a moment, Deed thought she was going to rush

over and hug him. Instead, she swallowed, bit her lip, and said, "That would be most helpful. W-We appreciate your generosity."

Rebecca Tuttle put down her coffee cup hard, almost spilling the remaining contents. "You mean you're not going on with us? What will we do for protection? Mr. Hannah can't do it all." Her eyes were wild and her hands trembled.

Deed glanced at Blue. "My brother will be riding guard, Miss Tuttle. You will be quite protected. We've got business in El Paso."

A hint of a smile tugged at Blue's mouth. He should have known Deed would pull him into the situation. He always did.

"But he's, he's . . . injured."

"Blue can shoot better with one arm than most with two," Deed said. "He'll keep you safe."

With a deep sigh, Rebecca nodded and stared into her coffee cup as if just realizing it was there.

Blue glanced at his brother. "Yes, I intend to ride as the guard to El Paso."

Blue recalled Deed carrying a hurt fawn two miles to their home when he was ten. He had found it when out hunting. The little deer had healed under his care and been returned to the wild, but it always stayed close to the Corrigan house. Blue and Holt teased Deed that the animal thought he was its mother. One day the deer didn't come back. Deed and his brothers searched for the deer all day before deciding it had found a deer family of its own. Much of the rest of their childhood was deeply marred by their parents' deaths.

Tade rubbed his hands and feigned more satisfaction than he felt that a one-armed man would be riding guard. "Mighty good. Finish up folks. We need to get going." He turned and left the station, slamming the door behind him.

The Corrigan brothers talked quietly for a few moments, with Deed thanking Blue for understanding his sudden change of heart. Silka said he would return to the ranch, taking Blue's horse with him. The extra mount brought for Deed would remain at the station for their later return. Blue would throw his saddle, saddle bags, and bridle onto the coach for the ride back from El Paso on the new stallion or he would buy an extra mount there. Silka was to tell his wife what had happened. Bina wouldn't like it, but she would understand. The former samurai would take the trail-drive money with him, too, after Blue took what he needed for the new stallion and expenses in El Paso.

Her shoulders rising and falling with relief, Atlee came forward and said, "I should be able to hire someone in a few days."

"Sure."

Benjamin burst in from the kitchen, his eyes reddened and his face flushed. "We don't need anybody's help, mister. I'm the head of the family now. It's my job to take over for Pa. Nobody else." Cooper was at his side.

Setting his fork on his plate, Deed hesitating before answering, "I know how you feel, son. Blue and I lost both of our parents when we were about your age. It's rough. Nobody's taking the place of your pa. I'm just helping Billy with the horses. You and your ma will run the place."

"That's enough, Benjamin. Mr. Corrigan is being most generous." Atlee's face was hard and her eyes sought her son's.

The boy started to say something else, then spun around and went back into the kitchen. Cooper trotted alongside. Elizabeth noticed his performance and headed toward the kitchen, almost spilling the bowl with its remaining water.

Blue, Deed, and Silka returned to eating without more comment. Atlee left the table and went over to the Beinrigts at the couch.

"If you want to stay here until your husband is better able to travel, you are most welcome," she said, putting her hand on Olivia's shoulder. "There are two beds here. For drivers and guards when they need them. Nobody will be needing them."

Olivia patted her hand and said, "*Danke.* Dat vould be most *gut. Mein* Hermann *ist* . . . veak. I could also vork for *du.* To help."

At the table, Blue introduced himself to the bespectacled gunfighter, "James Hannah, I believe." He stood and leaned across the table, extending his hand.

Pushing his glasses back with his left hand, Hannah rose to shake Blue's hand. "Glad to meet you."

"My brother tells me you made the difference today."

"Glad I could help." Hannah returned to his seat. "Say, do any of you know anything about a fella named Agon Bordner?"

"Well, he just bought the bank in Wilkon . . . and a big ranch near here, the Bar 3, and two others. Biggest rancher in this neck of the woods now," Blue said. "Likes to sing in his church choir, I hear." A frown gathered above his eyes. "Why do you ask?"

"He wants to hire me. Sent gold for my expenses. I'm supposed to meet him in El Paso. To discuss a job."

CHAPTER SEVEN

In El Paso's finest restaurant, the Lone Star, Agon Bordner was enjoying a noon meal of an enormous rare steak, six fried eggs, three baked potatoes, sliced beets, a basket of fresh biscuits, and a bottle of red wine. As usual, he ate alone in a back room reserved for parties and meetings. A waiter stood quietly next to the closed door to accommodate any need he might have.

Bordner was a huge man with bulging eyes that rarely seemed to blink; his hair was thinning and long over his ears, curling around his white paper collar. He wore a custom-tailored, navy blue suit, accented by a huge, gold watch chain stretched across his mountainous stomach and vest. Like his voracious appetite, his business desire was to join the handful of great ranchers—Charles Goodnight, Richard King, John Chisum, and Henry Miller—with, like them, hundreds of thousands of acres under his control. They had overcome drought, fluctuating cattle prices, and Eastern financial panics. All he had to do was take control of the five ranches around Wilkon, and he already had three—one of them, the largest in the region. He smiled at the thought, took another bite of steak, and washed it down with half of his wineglass. The waiter rushed over to refill it.

His strategy to achieve this goal was simple, brutal—and, so far, effective. First, he had purchased the Wilkon Bank. Well, the price was basically a steal with several of his gunmen convincing the president-owner that it was time for him to leave. His men had gotten a big laugh out of actually stealing a bank, not robbing it. One of his men, Willard Hixon, had taken over as president. From there, Bordner would take control of one ranch at a time. The initial ranch acquisition was the Bar 3, the largest ranch in the region. The former owner and his family were murdered in the night. Comanches were blamed. He took over after a large Bar 3 loan from the Wilkon Bank surfaced.

The two small ranches abutting the Bar 3 were then coerced into selling. When the two families left for a more peaceful life, Bordner's men followed and killed them, taking back the money used in the purchases. Again, Comanches were blamed. Keeping his operation flush with actual cash was a secondary, but essential, strategy.

Taking another mouthful of potato and gravy, he let his mind wander over the details of the Bar 3 massacre, as his right hand man Rhey Selmon had related. His fascination with such gory details had no bounds. Of course, he wasn't personally involved in the night's savagery. Such endeavors had ended years ago when he murdered his stepfather, cut up the body, and fed the pieces to the family's hogs. Since then, he had mostly hired his killings done. But not always.

Smiling, he hummed part of a hymn that his church choir was practicing, then began singing,

> "*Rock of ages, cleft for me,*
> *Let me hide myself in thee;*
> *Let the water and the blood,*
> *From thy wounded side which flowed,*
> *Be of sin the double cure,*
> *Save from wrath and make me pure.*"

He stopped singing and gulped a drink of wine. Singing made him thirsty. He loved singing and had bought robes for the choir so there would be one big enough for him. It didn't hurt his image either, he knew. On several occasions, he had even sung a solo, but only when requested. People would have a difficult time believing such an upstanding churchgoing man could be behind the largest land grab in Texas history. That was the idea.

He hummed more of the hymn and motioned to the waiter, told him to bring more gravy and another bottle of wine. The anxious man hurried away to handle the request. Agon Bordner had come from New Mexico Territory with his gang under Rhey's direction. Together they had built a gang of thieves, gunmen, bank robbers, and rustlers, as well as specialists. Specialists like Willard Hixon, a wizard with numbers and an artist at forging signatures. They could have stayed in New Mexico, enjoying the fruits of their well-planned stagecoach and bank robberies. But Bordner wanted more; he wanted a cattle empire. And Texas was the place to take it. His men were happy to follow him—especially now that they were settled into the Bar 3, glad to leave their camp in the hills. The money earned from the Bar 3 trail drive gave him the kind of cash he needed to keep them happy.

Snorting and laughing, Bordner yelled, "Texas! Look out, here comes Agon Bordner!"

The fourth ranch on his list of acquisitions was the Lazy S, almost as big as the Bar 3 and owned by a Mexican family with deep roots in the region. The attack would take place within the month with the same strategy and Comanches would be blamed again. That would leave only the Corrigan spread with its excellent, year-round water.

However, the first step in that acquisition, a crucial one, would be to eliminate Deed Corrigan. Even Rhey Selmon, his right-hand man and excellent with a gun, wanted no part of him. Neither did Macy Shields, his next best gunman. Nor did Sear Georgian, the brute with a lust for beating up men and women, who had especially enjoyed the Bar 3 massacre.

After Deed was killed, that would leave Blue Corrigan and the crazy Japanese fighter who rode with them. The two would still be a significant force, but without Deed, Rhey was certain he and his men could handle them. Once they were dead, a bill of sale would surface. Bordner had sent for the well-known gunman, James Hannah, to join in this phase of elimination and expected his arrival any day now. Rhey Selmon had mentioned the possibility that the third brother, Holt Corrigan, might get involved, but just in passing. Holt was a known outlaw and not part of the LC ranch operation. Rhey wasn't certain if he was even alive. There had been talk of a gunfight in an Amarillo saloon that had ended his life, though Sear Georgian told them it wasn't true. Just a saloon tale that actually involved another man named Holt.

Bordner grinned and steak juice ran down his chin. The waiter returned with a bowl of hot gravy and a bottle of wine. The large man accepted them without comment and the waiter returned to his post by the door. After pouring gravy over his remaining potatoes, beets, and eggs, he started eating again.

Since coming to Texas, his wealth had grown greater by a series of stagecoach and bank robberies all done with care. Owning the Wilkon Bank gave him access to the timing of shipments of gold and gold certificates. Rhey Selmon took it from there, sending teams of gunmen wherever they were needed. Whenever possible, they made sure Holt Corrigan was blamed. It kept the Texas Rangers and Pinkertons looking for him.

Utterly without scruples, Rhey was the driving force in Bordner's scheme to become the dominant rancher in the region. Another member of the gang, Dixie Murphy, took care of the cattle operations; he was a mean man, well suited to Bordner's task. Two days ago, Dixie wired Bordner about catching up with the Bar 3 cattle herd en route to Kansas, successfully selling the beef in Abilene, and now returning. Left unstated in the wire was what had happened to the original Bar 3 drovers.

A knock on the door startled both Bordner and the waiter.

"Boss, I need to talk with you." The voice was Rhey Selmon's.

Bordner motioned for the waiter to let in his associate. How unlike Rhey to interrupt his lunch. Surely this had to be more than a report of moving the gang to the Bar 3 as planned. Bordner planned to move there himself in the next week or two.

Tall and skinny, Rhey Selmon entered. He was loyal to one man, Agon Bordner, and one cause, helping Bordner become a cattle baron. The two were alike in their love of greed and power. Physically, they were as different as night and day. Although hollow cheeked and thin, Rhey was quite strong and never seemed to sleep much. Regardless of the weather or the season, he wore a long bearskin coat. His clothes were of the range and nondescript. His eyes were ice blue and slightly crossed. Black hair strung from a narrow-brimmed hat. At his waist were two crossed gunbelts holding twin silver-plated revolvers with pearl handles, the only things of distinction that he wore or owned.

"What is it, Rhey? Can't you see I'm dining?" Bordner said angrily. "Surely your news could have waited."

"One of the Regan kids is alive," the tall gunman blurted.

Bordner stared at his lieutenant without speaking, then motioned for the waiter to leave the room. Gulping his words, Rhey told him one of his men had overheard Blue Corrigan's wife buying canned milk and candy at the general store and telling why the purchase was necessary. For a moment, the fat man thought he was going to vomit. How could this be?

"I thought you were better than that, Rhey," he growled and slammed a fat fist against the top of the table. The filled glass jumped and spilled red wine down the side. "You've got to find that little brat—and kill him before he starts telling the world what really happened."

"Right," Rhey took a deep breath.

Bordner crossed his fat arms. "Wait. Nothing's been

damaged. Not really. Nobody's going to believe that kid. What is he, five or six? Give me some time by myself and I'll figure out our next move."

"Do you still want us to get the kid?"

"No. If you shoot him now, it'll only look suspicious. We'll wait until James Hannah gets here. I'll give him that job." Bordner speared another slice of steak with his fork. "Say, three of Rose's best doves are coming to my place tonight. Want to join in?"

Both men laughed.

"Are the boys outside?"

"Yeah, except the men I sent to hold up the stage."

"Send 'em in. I need to talk to Sear. Tell the waiter, we're going to need more food. Lots of it."

CHAPTER EIGHT

Although nervous at first, Rebecca Tuttle began to relax as the stagecoach rumbled across the Chihuahuan Desert. James Hannah had been nice enough, but he was inclined toward reading and sleeping and she was left to her thoughts most of the time. She found herself thinking about Deed Corrigan. She wished he had continued with them and felt a little jealous that he had stayed to help Atlee Forsyth.

She told herself Deed had stayed because the new widow was frightened about being attacked again, but Rebecca wasn't certain that was the reason. She tried to concentrate on the farmer waiting for her, the man she was going to marry. His face wouldn't come to her mind. Only the face of Deed Corrigan. Her unstoppable conversation focused on Hannah, even though he wasn't particularly responsive.

At last the Franklin Mountains came into view, indicating the coach was nearing El Paso. Tade Balkins was visibly weary and Blue Corrigan was having trouble staying alert as well. The edgy driver had mentioned missing his regular guard at least six times and each time Blue had acknowledged how hard it must be. Tade had followed each statement with a concern about a one-armed man being tough enough if they had any more trouble. The rest of their conversation had been strained. Tade was upset about losing time in delivery of the mail and Blue's words of comfort did little to help his stress. Nor did Blue tell him that he had been a sharpshooter for the Confederacy during the war.

Ahead, the road took a jog to the left, disappearing behind a cluster of huge yellow and gray boulders that looked like God had placed them there for no other reason than that he could. As the tiring team of Morgans neared the large rocks, four masked horsemen swung into view, firing their revolvers in the air and demanding that the stage stop.

"Halt! This is Holt Corrigan," one masked holdup man yelled.

"No. You're not." Blue's reaction was an instant assault. Sliding forward to kneel in the driver's box, he placed his Winchester against the front edge and fired the gun six times—as fast as he could aim, pull the trigger, and lever a new cartridge with his one hand. Two outlaws spun from their saddles and hit the ground, groaning. Their pistols spun by themselves, as if frozen in the moment, before thudding near the wounded men.

"Keep 'em going, Tade!" Blue yelled.

Smoking shells popped around Blue as he focused on the remaining two outlaws who were firing at them. The jerking coach made it difficult to aim, but Blue kept leveling the rifle to maintain a steady field of fire, now shooting with the gun against his hip for balance.

One of the outlaw's bullets clipped Blue's hat; two others drove into the front of the driver's box and sent a wood sliver into Blue's right hand and the sudden pain forced him to stop firing for a moment, then he resumed as if nothing had happened. The coach thundered toward the outlaws with Tade yelling and snapping his whip to keep the horses in an out-right run. The outlaws' mounts became difficult to control. Stutter-stepping. Rearing. Shaking their heads wildly.

An outlaw in a tan vest and dark blue shirt backed his horse off the road, far enough to settle the mount. He wrapped the reins around the saddle horn, drew a second handgun and began firing again with both weapons. The other outlaw, blond hair streaming from his hat, spurred his horse wide of the road and into a hard lope with the intention of getting Blue in a crossfire.

"I've got this one, Blue!" Hannah yelled and fired three times from the coach's window.

The blond outlaw grunted and slumped against his horse's neck. Hannah aimed his Smith & Wesson with both hands and fired again, popping a black hole in the man's exposed check, in spite of the coach's uneven movement. The gunfighter smoothly shoved new cartridges into his gun and told the once-again screaming Rebecca that it would soon be over.

In front, the remaining outlaw held up his hands with his guns still in them.

"Keep going, Tade. He's had enough."

As the coach rumbled past the stunned stagecoach robber, Hannah fired three times and the remaining outlaw crumpled from his saddle.

"Hey! He was finished," Blue yelled back at the bespectacled gunman.

"Any man holding two guns isn't finished in my book," Hannah answered. "But you're welcome." He reloaded his gun and shoved it back into his shoulder holster. "Miss Tuttle, it is over. There is nothing more to be afraid of."

"Oh thank you, sir. Thank you."

"A hug would be nice."

She stared at him for a moment, then leaned over and gave him a warm embrace.

Above, Tade Balkins looked over at Blue reloading his rifle, shoving new cartridges into the gun with it laying on his lap. "Be all right if I ease 'em down a mite? They've been pushed hard. Too hard, maybe."

"You bet. Bring them to a walk. They did well."

Wiping his brow with his hand, Tade pulled on the horse team to bring them out of their run. "Well, I sure had you figured wrong. Never thought you'd come out shootin' like that. Lordy!" He grinned. "That was somethin' to see."

"I understand," Blue said, laying the reloaded rifle on his lap. "The good Lord expects us to defend ourselves against evil, whether we've got one arm or two." He smiled. "Besides, there wasn't much time to turn the other cheek."

"Easy now, boys. Easy." Tade pulled on the reins and watched the tired animals slowly slip into a trot and finally, a walk. "I can sure see how you and Deed are brothers. That's for sure. No offense."

"None taken. We *are* alike in many ways. But Deed is a far better fighter." Blue could hear Rebecca jabbering inside the couch. Hannah would have his hands full calming her down, he thought.

"Man said he were Holt Corrigan. Any kin?" Tade asked.

"Holt's our brother and that wasn't him. Haven't seen him much since the war. He would've been involved in every bank and stage holdup in three states, if you believed everything you hear."

"Prob'ly best," Tade said and decided to mention a story he'd recently heard about Holt Corrigan. "Speaking o' that, heard your brother . . . Holt . . . was in a gunfight over near the border. Last year, it was. Said he died."

"Yeah, heard that, too. Like I said, I don't put much stock in gossip."

Tade waited for more, but none was coming and he said, "Heard he was one of the heroes who stopped all those Yankees at Sabine Pass. Just forty-three Confederates with rifles and six small cannon stopped a Federal fleet of fifteen thousand men tryin' to land."

"That's true. Holt was there and part of that victory," Blue said. "Lieutenant Richard Dowling led them. Sank a gunboat, captured a couple more, and turned away the rest of that whole fleet. Took four hundred prisoners. Best of all, they didn't lose a man."

Tade nodded. "Yeah, that must've been something. Heard every one of them boys got a silver medal from Jeff Davis, only command that got that. Really something."

Tade wanted to ask why Holt was an outlaw, but decided he shouldn't and the talking ended for a while. "Ya see that mountain? That's Franklin. Got a red clay shape in it. Real odd-like. Indians think it's a thunderbird." Tade was actually smiling. "Supposed to be a holy place for 'em."

"I'm sure it is," Blue said. "Doesn't have to be a

cathedral to talk to God. Or listen. My dear mother, bless her soul, used to say a man's own church is within his heart."

Tade looked over at Blue. "Hey, you're bleeding. They hit ya?"

"Naw, just a piece of wood caught me." Blue studied his bloody hand.

"Better have a look at that," Tade said, talking warmly now.

"No. I'm all right. Just a nick. The bleeding will stop soon enough."

"Want me to stop an' he'p ya?"

"No thanks. I'm all right, really."

Tade nodded and returned to studying the passing arid land.

Blue had never been to El Paso before, or for that matter, seen the Rio Grande defining the border between El Paso and Mexico. The business with Magnuson's horse had been done by telegraph. So he enjoyed the scenery and the driver's change in attitude. Tade pointed out a volcanic peak to the west, rising from within the Rio Grande Rift and actually on the New Mexico side of the big river. He said there were a number of ancient volcanic craters a couple of days' ride west. The town itself had responded well after the war and was a distinctive mixture of domed Spanish mansions, adobe tenements, and new structures of wood and brick, more northern in style and texture. Blue listened without comment, enjoying the driver's sudden interest in talking.

Ahead of the coach, on the outskirts of town stood a three-story, Victorian-styled home, surrounded by a white picket fence. Elaborately trimmed in shades of brown and light blue paint, the wooden building featured a wraparound porch with a matching deck on the second floor. It would have been a distinctive house in any Eastern city, but in El Paso it was absolutely dominant.

"That's Agon Bordner's place. He's kinda new to town," Tade drawled and motioned with his head. "Bought the Bar 3 north o' here, you know. An' a couple o' small places, too." He waved his hand toward the house.

"Heard that. Bought the Wilkon Bank, too."

Tade continued talking as if Blue hadn't spoken. He said Bordner had come from New Mexico and liked to live elegantly.

"Yeah, there's all kinds of stories about his one-man banquets," Tade laughed and massaged the sets of reins in his right hand. "Biggest man I ever seed."

"Interesting he lives here and hasn't moved to his new ranch," Blue said, studying the advancing signs of town.

"Hear tell he leaves all that to a hard-assed cowman name of Murphy. Dixie Murphy. Got a finger missing from his left hand," Tade held up his left hand. "Roping problem." He shook his head. "Also heard he's got a reputation for having some cows with an awful lot of calves. Too many calves."

"I don't put much stock in gossip."

As they passed the big Victorian mansion, Blue couldn't help wondering what kind of man this Agon Bordner was.

"Over there's the ol' Peterson place," Tade interrupted Blue's thoughts, pointing toward the gray skeleton of a house. "Nobody knows what happened to him. One day he was gone. Just gone. Nobody lives there now."

They passed a small adobe cottage where a middle-aged woman was outside, separating cream from milk, pouring the white liquid through a hand-crank separator. Six chickens clucked across the sandy earth in front of her. Tade waved and she waved back.

At Blue's suggestion, Tade didn't make his tired horses run again to have a showy entrance at the stage station and reined them easily to a stop. A major point in the route, from here the stagecoach headed toward Santa Fe with a new driver as well as a new team of horses.

Commercial activity in town was strong with four-story hotels, general stores, saloons, grocery stores offering East Coast delicacies, and theaters crowded against distinctive Roman Catholic cathedrals and old missions. Newcomers included businessmen, priests, prostitutes, and gunfighters. After the Civil War's conclusion, the town's population began to grow and talk of the railroad coming to El Paso fueled even more interest in the town.

Everywhere Blue looked, there seemed to be aristocratic ranchers and rich merchants mixed with cotton farmers and copper-mine workers. In the distance, he saw a church and two Catholic cathedrals. The town was full and loud. He felt very tired and glad to have arrived. His mind darted to his wife, Bina. He missed her and their son and daughter very much. He always did when away. And now there was Jeremy. He couldn't wait to get home.

A tall man in a rumpled suit and an ill-fitting bowler bolted from the station. His long-jawed face was red and his right hand kept making and unmaking fists at his side. In his left hand was a heavy bag of new mail and express.

"Balkins, you're late!" Willard Epson, the stage-line district agent, snapped.

"Well, you oughta be damn glad we made it at all. Had serious Comanche trouble outside of Forsyth's station," Tade blurted, waving his arms. "An' four masked owlhoots tried to hold us up just outside of town. Blue, here, cut 'em down hard. He an' Mr. Hannah, one of my passengers."

"What? Comanches? Holdup men?" Epson stopped and put his hand over his mouth in surprise. He was all set to give his driver a dressing-down for being late and realized they had been lucky to get through at all.

"Was the gold—?"

"Safe as a baby's behind." Tade Balkins swung down and explained what had happened, complimenting Deed and Hannah—and Blue—for their help in getting the mail and gold through safely.

Tade took the mail bag from Epson and handed him the El Paso–bound mail bag. Meanwhile, Blue grabbed his saddlebags and bedroll from the rear boot and threw them down. He would wait to get his saddle until the driver unloaded the boot itself. Cradling his Winchester between what remained of his left arm and his good right arm, he climbed down, grasping the coach rails with his lone hand. He made a fist to drive away the lingering pain from the slight wound.

Epson listened intently as Tade began unloading the luggage that belonged to Rebecca and Hannah. He told his boss about the two passengers being killed and wondered what to do about their luggage, about losing Hank Johnson, his guard, about the German couple staying at the Forsyth station, and finally, that Caleb Forsyth had been killed. For the first time, Epson noticed Blue only had one arm. His eyes asked the question.

"Lost it in the war, Mr. Epson," Blue responded to the unstated concern. "Been shooting one-handed since then. Pretty good at it. The Lord decided I needed to show others that two hands aren't necessary to be successful."

"Guess so."

Forcing himself into a state of control, Epson thanked Hannah and Blue, and asked Rebecca if she needed assistance to the hotel. She glanced at Hannah and said that she did not. From across the street came a strutting bank president puffing on a large cigar and eager to retrieve the gold box.

Blue studied the oncoming man for a moment, a tall man in a tailored suit with a trim mustache and receding hairline. Two men carrying shotguns and wearing sidearms were a few steps behind him.

"Say, aren't you Dave Copate? Fought with my brother at Sabine Pass?" Blue asked.

"Well, howdy, Blue. You bet I am. It's good to see you again," Copate held out his hand and Blue laid down his rifle and shook it. "What brings you to our fair town?"

Blue told him and Copate asked, "How's Holt doing? Really doing, I mean. I hear all these awful stories and I don't believe them. He saved my life, you know."

"Wish I knew. Haven't seen Holt for years, I'm sorry to say. I don't believe the stories either, but I'm his brother."

"Well, when you do, tell him Dave Copate asked about him and sent good wishes."

"Sure will."

"Excuse me, Blue, but I'd better get this to the bank," Copate said.

"Of course. Need some help?"

"No. That's what these two are for." He chuckled, waved, and motioned to the two armed men. Shifting their shotguns to their left hands, each man took one of the straps on the heavy box and followed him away.

Epson paled and started to shake. "Holt Corrigan your brother?"

"Yes. Why?"

"N-No reason, I guess. Just—"

"You were wondering if I was going to rob your stage, is that it, Mr. Epson?" Blue growled. "I'm here to buy a stallion from Mr. Magnuson for our ranch. My brother Deed and I own a spread near Wilkon." He cocked his head. "Haven't seen Holt in years. Not since the war. You'd know more about him than I would." He paused and added, "If I were you, I wouldn't believe every story that came along about my brother. As far as I know, he hasn't broken any laws. He didn't like losing the war, but a lot other men felt the same way. He also didn't think he had to beg for amnesty. I'm proud of him for that."

"Oh, of course. Of course. Well, welcome to El Paso," Epson smiled. "If I can do anything to make your stay better, please ask."

With his saddlebags and bedroll draped over his shoulder and his Winchester in his right hand, Blue explained that he had ridden the coach to assure the red-faced district agent that the station was in good hands. Tade added his support, saying Mrs. Forsyth had already hired Deed Corrigan to help her; the driver glanced at Blue, who shook his head, and Tade said nothing more. Behind them four new passengers waited for their luggage to be taken and to board.

"Deed Corrigan? Didn't you just say he was your brother?" Epson asked.

"Yes. I met up with him at Forsyth's station," Blue said, leaning his Winchester against his leg. "He was returning from a trail drive to Abilene." He called it the *Forsyth's station* deliberately.

Folding his arms, Epson said, "He's mighty good with a gun and his fists, I hear."

Blue's smile didn't reach his eyes. "He's a very good man—and this coach wouldn't be here if it weren't for him and Mr. Hannah."

Epson rubbed his mouth and looked away. "Yes. Yes. But I still have to replace Mrs. Forsyth. We can't have a *woman* running our relay station. Surely you understand."

Blue put his lone hand on the other man's shoulder. "I surely don't, Mr. Epson. And if I were you, I'd rethink that idea. From what I hear, that's one of your best stations. And it isn't because the horses are harnessed correctly or your barn is always clean. Or hadn't you noticed the way your passengers talk about Mrs. Forsyth's food." He took his hand away and picked up his rifle. "Now I'm going to get something to eat, a little sleep, and go buy a horse tomorrow. All right if I put my gear in your station until then?"

Apologetically, Epson said it was fine to leave his things there, added that he owed Blue for riding guard, and offered him a regular guard job. Blue thanked him and declined without an explanation, adjusting the saddlebags and bedroll on his shoulder. He walked over to the boardwalk and laid them down.

Epson turned away and told Tade to take the luggage of the deceased into the station and he would attempt to find any relatives to inform them of the sad loss. Behind them, the tired team of horses was led away by a black man and a new team brought out. A passenger asked Tade a question and he said a new driver would be taking them west. Blue returned to the stagecoach, gathered his saddle and placed it on the boardwalk next to his saddlebags and bedroll, keeping his rifle. Tade insisted that he take Blue's gear inside for him.

After retrieving his handsome valise and talking quietly with Rebecca, Hannah joined the two men.

"Blue, I'm headed to the Lone Star across the street for a steak and some whiskey before I meet with that Bordner fella. Care to join me?"

"Sounds good." Blue grinned.

"How's your hand? Should we have a doc take a look at it? You need to take care of that one, you know," Hannah said, motioning toward Blue's blood-stained hand.

"Oh, no thanks. It's nothing. You probably got hit worse at the station." Blue pointed at the dried bloodstains on Hannah's coat sleeve.

"Guess we're both lucky. Like your brother."

"Yeah."

"Gentlemen, let me buy your dinners," Epson said eagerly. "Our stage-line owes you a debt of gratitude."

Hannah pushed on his glasses. "That's true. Instead of two dinners, let's make it two hundred apiece. We saved your ass outside of town—and his brother and I did it earlier against those red bastards. In fact, make it another two hundred for Deed. And we'll call it even. I don't care much for debts of gratitude."

Epson swallowed and looked like he had been slapped, but managed to find his voice. "Well, of course. Of course. Let me just do that. I'll go get the money. I'll bring it to the Lone Star." He spun and left.

"Think we'll see him again?" Hannah chuckled.

"Good question. He looked scared enough."

CHAPTER NINE

James Hannah and Blue Corrigan walked into the crowded Lone Star restaurant and looked for an empty table. Blue noticed that several men saw them and whispered something. He guessed they recognized the infamous gunman. It made him smile.

The smoky room was filled with tables of ranchers, copper-mine workers, and a few hungry cowboys. The walls themselves flickered with the presence of oil lamps attempting to drive away the grayness. Blue's gaze didn't latch on to any person he recognized, but he didn't expect to see anyone. Hannah said he planned to meet Agon Bordner here. Someone like the fat businessman would be easy to spot anywhere, Blue thought. There was a back room. Maybe Agon Bordner was already there.

They found an empty table in the middle of the restaurant. After laying his valise on the floor next to his chair, Hannah drew his handgun as they sat and laid the weapon in his lap. An old habit. Blue laid his rifle on the floor under his feet. The table wobbled on an uneven leg. Frowning, Hannah took one of the forks on the table and pushed it under the short leg.

"There. That's better," he said and tried the table's steadiness with both hands and was satisfied.

"Nice work. You remind me of Deed."

"I take that as a high compliment."

"It was so intended."

A round-faced waiter with a patchy beard took their order and quickly retreated to the kitchen. A few minutes later, a well-made-up woman of uncertain age brought a tray holding a bottle of whiskey and two glasses. Her fringed crimson dress swayed rhythmically as she approached their table, enjoying the attention she created.

She glanced at Blue and turned to Hannah. "Your steaks will be coming real soon. If there is anything else I can do for you, gentlemen. Anything at all. I'm Cheyenne."

"Thank you, Cheyenne. Maybe later." Hannah winked.

She smiled and the corners of her mouth crinkled. After pouring whiskey into both glasses, she flitted her eyelashes and looked again at Blue. "I've never taken care of a one-armed man before." She curtsied and left, swishing her red dress as she left.

Hannah chuckled and reached for the drinks, handing one to Blue. "Must be nice to be liked."

"She wanted some spiritual guidance."

"Well, I'm sure she'd be happy to be on her knees. In front of you."

"Bless her." Blue smiled.

They toasted each other and downed the fiery liquid. Hannah poured both another drink. "Not to be nosey, Blue, but when are you headed back?"

"Tomorrow, I hope. Plan on a good night's sleep at

the hotel, then get a horse at the livery tomorrow morning and head out to Magnuson's ranch. We're buying one of his stallions for breeding. Then I'll start back. Take both horses with me. Might buy a third for a packhorse."

"Not taking the stage?"

"Had enough of those for a while."

Hannah sipped his drink. "Yeah. Me too."

Blue nursed his as well. He didn't drink much. Never had. Not because of any religious dedication; Silka had warned them years ago of whiskey's power to rob a man of the ability to react smartly. All three brothers had taken his advice to heart, even Holt. At least, he wasn't drinking the last time Blue saw him.

Their conversation slid easily over a range of topics: Comanches and their ways; the holdup and whether the posse would be successful in finding any of the bandits; guns; El Paso; cattle; books; railroads; and women. Blue shared that his brother Holt was superstitious, but didn't say anything about his belief in reincarnation. That led to a discussion about religion. Finally they talked of horses and Blue repeated about the Magnuson horses and how good they were, and that the Corrigan brothers planned to do some breeding with some strong mustangs they owned. Blue told him about his wife, Bina, and their daughter, Mary Jo. He mentioned a young boy was staying with them because of a recent tragedy to the boy's family and indicated it was a Comanche raid.

Before Hannah could ask more, the waiter brought their steaks, sizzling and steaming on white plates, along with large helpings of chili beans, sliced beets, and warm tortillas. The one-armed cattleman asked for coffee and the waiter hurried to bring it; his responses had increased considerably since someone told him that he was serving the infamous gunman, James Hannah.

Hannah watched Blue bow his head and move his lips.

"You do that at every meal, Blue?" Hannah asked.

"Yes, but I didn't mean to embarrass you. Forgive me."

Hannah shook his head. "I think that's what religion's all about isn't it? Forgiveness."

"Good point."

Hannah asked if he needed help with cutting the steak. Blue declined, saying that he had learned to cut meat with one hand. Without more talking, both men began to eat with gusto. After they were finished, Blue enjoyed a second cup of coffee and Hannah savored another whiskey.

"Do you like to read, Blue?"

"Yes, I do. Our sweet mother got me hooked," Blue said. "Other than the Bible, I favor Tennyson. Anything Tennyson."

"'My strength is as the strength of ten.'"

"'Because my heart is pure.'"

Hannah grinned. "And you thought I was going to say 'All in the valley of death rode the six hundred.'"

It was Blue's turn to smile. "Read anything besides Tennyson?"

"Well, not the Bible. But I've got a book in my gear that's about a clergyman who's accused of stealing, *The Last Chronicle of Barset*," Hannah said. "It's the second part of *The Small House of Allington*."

"A preacher accused of stealing, huh? *The Last Chronicle of Barset*. I'll have to check that out."

"You'd like it."

Hannah rolled his head to relieve some stiffness

and asked about Silka. Blue told him that Silka had come riding up a few months after the loss of their family. All three boys were exhausted and depressed; cash money was nonexistent. The Oriental became sort of a second father to the boys, guiding their development of the ranch itself.

Blue smiled. "The first time we met him, he said, 'I am Nakashima Silka. I am Samurai.' Put his right fist against his heart and added, 'Warrior. In Japan. I lived Bushido . . . way of the warrior. None dare to challenge me. Silka always win. Kill all enemy.'" Blue took a sip of the hot coffee, lost in yesterday.

Looking away for a moment, he continued the story. Silka had brought his wife and two children to California to protect them from the revolution that was tearing at his homeland, but they had died.

"Silka kept telling us 'Soon, samurai will be no more.' The old man is a fascinating fellow. Told us stories that were wild and hard to believe, but I'm sure to this day they were all true." He cocked his head to the side and grinned.

"Seems like he spoke pretty good American. How'd that happen?" Hannah twirled his forefinger in his drink.

Blue explained Silka had learned English while traveling across the country, worked hard at it, and was proud of the way he now talked. His accent was only visible on certain words, usually ones with an *r*. Or an occasional Japanese phrase when he was excited.

"He didn't want to work on the railroad like so many from his land. So he rode to Texas . . . found us. Glad he did. Don't think we would've made it without him." Blue took another sip of coffee and studied the room again as he did.

He said Deed, in particular, followed the old man's instructions eagerly. Most of the training was in the evenings after chores were finished for the day. Each night turned into a lesson on fighting strategy, or defending oneself with "empty hands"—without weapons—and handling a sword and a knife.

"I can see his training in both of you," Hannah said and told about Deed's take-charge actions during the Comanche attack.

"Sounds like Deed. Over and over, Silka would say, you must train your muscles to do what you want. Without thinking about it. You cannot expect any move to be right, if you do not practice it."

"Makes good sense. Wish I'd had somebody to teach me like that."

Blue nodded. "He's one special man, that's for sure. Always positive. Always stressed the importance of quick moves. 'When you are attacked, time is vital. Practice each move a hundred times. A thousand times. Until you are comfortable with a move. Every move. Speed comes with such practice. The trick is to unbalance the opponent. You must be calm. Confident,' he would say and, if we did it right, 'Ah so . . . good.'"

Blue continued, "Right after the war, Deed, Silka, and I kept Northern carpetbaggers from taking over our ranch. The Union-controlled government left us alone as well. We had no back taxes or bank debt, thanks to Silka's careful management during the war."

Both men smiled. Hannah finished his drink and poured himself another; Blue declined any more whiskey, but waved at the waiter for more coffee. The waiter hurried over to fill Blue's cup and paused to ask Hannah if he needed anything. The gunman waved him away.

"What did you do in the war?" Hannah asked without looking up.

"Sharpshooter. Part of Ewell's outfit. Holt was with Dowling at Sabine Pass. Lucky we both made it."

"Heard about Sabine Pass. Holt's a hero in a lot of Texans' eyes." Straightening his tie, Hannah volunteered, "I was a sharpshooter, too. Only, for the boys in blue. With Sherman when he cut Georgia apart."

"Terrible time, that war."

"Yeah. Terrible."

After another drink, Hannah said he grew up in Indiana; his father was a minister, but his mother was the churchy one. He was the middle of three sons; the oldest died in the Civil War. The youngest was a farmer in Ohio. Early on, Hannah had taught school. He came home early one day and found his wife in bed with their neighbor, killed both, and rode away. The only thing he was good at was killing people and he found out there was money in it. He didn't say more and Blue nodded his head.

Sipping his coffee, Blue asked if he expected Agon Bordner to come to the restaurant. Smiling, Hannah said he was certain the man was in the back room already. Blue started to ask if he was going to take the job when a distraught Rebecca Tuttle burst into the restaurant and stood in the doorway, looking around the room.

"Something must be wrong with Rebecca . . . ah, Miss Tuttle," Hannah said and stood.

Blue turned in his seat to watch her advance and got out of his chair to greet her. He was annoyed that her sudden presence had kept him from asking about Hannah taking a job with Bordner.

"Afternoon, ma'am," Hannah said warmly. "Would you care to join us?"

"Yes, we'd be honored," Blue added.

"Oh, James, I don't know what to do," she desperately wanted to hug the gunman but didn't. "Elmer Risner isn't in town . . . and no one seems to have even heard of him."

Hannah stepped close to her. "There, there. Sit down. Tell us about it."

The distraught young woman almost fell into the offered chair. Hannah waved at the waiter.

"Have you eaten, Miss Tuttle?"

She tried to say no, but couldn't and began to cry. Hannah poured whiskey into Blue's empty glass and handed it to her.

"Sip on this. It'll make you feel better."

After tasting the offered drink, wincing, and eventually swallowing the hot liquid, Rebecca explained her situation. She had used all her money to pay for the trip to El Paso and didn't know what she was going to do. Both Hannah and Blue listened silently. Finally, she stopped talking and a lone tear dribbled down her right cheek.

Hannah leaned forward, laying his arms on the table. "Life deals bad hands. To all of us." He paused and motioned toward Blue. "Blue, here, lost both his parents when he was a kid. His arm in the war." He licked his lips and swallowed. "I lost my wife, the only woman I ever loved."

He straightened and a cold appearance returned to his face. "So, you can wait to see if this Elmer Risner fellow shows up—or make new plans."

Rebecca put her hand over her mouth to curb her rising emotions. Hannah reached into his coat pocket, retrieved a small sack of gold coins and laid it on the table in front of her.

"Here," he said. "This'll take care of you for a while. Till you figure out what's next."

Her eyes took in the sack in disbelief, then she gushed, "Oh! Oh! Thank you. Thank you. How can I repay you?" She looked at Blue, then back at the amused gunman. "You can have me any time you want, I promise."

"That's not necessary, my dear. We all need a little help from time to time." Hannah glanced at Blue and grinned.

Her hands rose to cup her breasts to demonstrate her sincerity when Willard Epson made a surprise appearance and with a dramatic presentation gave both men an envelope, then another one for Blue to give to Deed. Blue thanked him; Hannah began checking the contents of his envelope. Epson said he needed to get back to the station and left.

"How about that, Blue. I thought we'd have to go over there and scare him to get this," Hannah said and chuckled. "Mine's right. How about yours . . . and Deed's?"

"Haven't looked."

As Blue reviewed the gold certificates in the envelope, a stocky man in a bowler hat and an ill-fitting suit strolled over to the table. His sneer looked permanent and thick eyebrows mingled in the middle of his forehead.

"You James Hannah?" he asked.

"Who wants to know?" Hannah said, looking at Rebecca.

"I do."

The response came with a slight jerk at the corner of

his sneer. The man wore a Mexican-tooled cartridge belt holding a holstered Colt. Blue noticed a slight bulge under his coat, indicating a second gun in a shoulder holster.

"Funny name. *I do*," Hannah growled without looking at the man.

Blue smiled. "Wonder if he has a brother named *I don't*."

Hannah laughed and pushed his eyeglasses into place with his left hand. His right dropped to his lap and curled around his gun. Unaware of the growing tension, the waiter stepped around the standing gunman and placed a filled plate in front of Rebecca. Blue was fascinated to see her begin eating as if she hadn't had food in days. How quickly a few coins changes one's perspective on life, he thought.

The stocky man's eyes darted from Hannah to Blue to Rebecca and back again to Hannah. Through gritted teeth, he said, "Mr. Bordner wants to see you. In the back room."

"He knows where I am . . . Mr. *I-do*."

The man moved both hands to his gunbelt and locked his thumbs into place. It was a slow, deliberate move, so he wouldn't be mistaken, but still an attempt to threaten. Blue's hand eased off the table toward his own holstered Walch revolver and flipped off the thong holding its hammers. This wasn't his fight, but he had no intention of staying out of it. Hannah downed the rest of his whiskey, holding the glass in his left hand. He put it down on the table and winked at Blue.

Cocking his head toward the waiting Bordner henchman, he growled, "You still here? You're starting to bother me. Go away."

"I'm supposed to bring you to his room. In back.

Now. Those are my orders," the henchman said. "Oh, Mr. Bordner said this meal was on him. All of it."

"Nice to have a generous boss," Hannah growled.

Blue thought there was a softening in the man's voice as if wishing someone else had been given this task.

Blue spoke first, "James, I need to check out the livery. I'll see that Miss Tuttle gets to the hotel. You go ahead and visit with Bordner. From what I hear, he's a fine Christian gentleman. No reason to get this poor fella into trouble."

"Will I see you later?" Hannah asked, ignoring the waiting henchman, whose face showed signs of relief.

"Probably not. I'll be headed out early."

Hannah turned toward the flushed henchman. "Tell your boss I'll be over in a few minutes. Wouldn't want to get you into trouble."

The man's face blinked with relief and he spun and left. After saying good-bye, Hannah stood, reholstered his gun, and walked to the back room and slowly opened the door.

Around the table sat five men. It was easy to tell which one was Agon Bordner. He looked like a huge bullfrog in expensive clothes. As far as Hannah could tell, the fat man wasn't armed. Bordner was finishing a second meal of fried chicken and mashed potatoes with a large glass of dark red wine. Already seated at the table with him was the henchman from a few minutes ago and two other hard-looking men, all armed. Another skinny man with greasy hair and a worn suit looked out of place. Their plates were empty and their glasses held whiskey, not wine.

Only a handful of minutes before, Bordner had just learned that three of his men were dead after the ill-fated stage holdup. Only Curly Matthews got away. From the excited outlaw's description, it was that one-armed cowboy—and James Hannah—doing the shooting. Bordner had told Curly to stay out of sight, ride for the Bar 3, and stay there until he was called.

"Mr. Bordner, how are you?" Hannah said, easing into the room.

"Fine, sir. Absolutely fine." Bordner raised his hand in a warm gesture. "I understand you've been a little busy, getting rid of vermin on the road."

"News travels fast in El Paso. Yeah, we did have a little activity coming in. Four amateurs. One got away."

"Too bad. We need law and order around here. It wasn't Holt Corrigan and his bunch, I take it."

"No. it wasn't."

As if on cue, three of the four men rose and left, headed for the bar. The remaining gunman wore a bearskin coat like Hannah had never seen before. At his waist were two crossed gunbelts holding twin revolvers. One gun lay in his lap. Nothing in his eyes indicated he liked Hannah. Rhey Selmon was known for three things: being fast with a gun, being loyal to Bordner, and owning big horses. Currently he was riding a bay over sixteen hands high and weighing well over eleven hundred pounds. The animal was far and away the fastest horse in the region. Selmon had been in two cattle wars, served a prison term, and killed three men in standup fights before he met up with Bordner.

"James Hannah, meet Rhey Selmon. You two will have a lot in common."

CHAPTER TEN

Blue Corrigan walked with Rebecca Tuttle to the hotel; his rifle was at his side. She wanted to talk about James Hannah, or rather ask questions about him. He was eager to be rid of her, but tried to hide his impatience.

"Is James, uh, Mr. Hannah, married?" she asked, straightening her collar, and tried to act casual as they navigated the rutted street.

"His wife died a few years ago," Blue said, watching a freighter rumble past.

"Oh, that's too bad." She couldn't hide a smile. "Is he coming . . . to the hotel?"

"Don't know about that, Miss Tuttle," he answered. "He was talking business, I believe."

A fancy carriage, pulled by two handsome bays, bounced in front of them. An older gentleman with curly white hair drove; a trim lady, wearing a tilted blue hat with matching feathers, sat at his side. She glanced at Blue and smiled. He nodded.

Blue was glad Rebecca was silent as they completed

crossing the street. Stepping onto the boardwalk, he opened the hotel door for her. She bobbed her head and entered. The lobby was lined with big leather chairs and a matching sofa. In the far corner, a large Regulator wall clock proudly told the time. Adjacent to it was an elk's head with antlers. Musty-smelling, full-length curtains flanked the main window. A drummer sat in the corner, smoking a cigar and reading a newspaper. In an adjoining room, the hotel restaurant was quiet.

Rebecca had checked in earlier and Blue wondered how she had intended to pay, but said nothing. She thanked him and asked if he would tell Hannah that she was in room 211. He reminded her that he wasn't likely to see him. With barely a pause, she turned to the desk clerk and told him that a Mr. Hannah should be informed of her room number. The round-faced, bald man with wispy brown hair edging around large ears said he would do so and smiled slightly.

Blue almost felt sorry for Hannah.

As she hurried upstairs, Blue told the manager that he, too, wanted a room. The chubby clerk asked if he wanted one next to Miss Tuttle's. The one-armed Corrigan brother grunted negatively.

The manager turned toward the maze of cubbyholes for keys and mail behind him. "One-fourteen's open."

"Fine."

"Two bits. In advance."

Blue shoved coins across the desktop, wondered if Rebecca had been required to pay in advance, then took the key and left, heading for the stage station.

Epson was sitting behind a desk and nodded as he entered. Blue tied his saddlebags and bedroll to the saddle, then shoved his rifle in its saddle sleeve. Putting everything together made it easier to handle it with his lone hand. He swung the saddle over his shoulder and headed for the livery. Epson muttered a half-hearted good-bye.

As Blue Corrigan stepped off the boardwalk to cross the alley, a familiar voice called out, "Blue."

Even before he turned, he knew it was his brother Holt. Grinning, Blue turned into the shadowed alley. His pinned-up shirtsleeve fluttered as he spun.

"How are you, Holt?"

"Sixes and sevens. No fires turning hollow. Haven't come across any knives on the ground either."

"Better than aces and eights." Blue laid down his saddle and held out his hand. Holt took off his right-hand glove and grabbed Blue's hand. They shook hands and then hugged each other. He knew Holt's references to fires turning hollow and finding knives were superstitions that indicated bad things were coming.

In a low-crowned black hat and full beard, Holt was two inches shorter than Blue. In his hatband was a red cardinal's feather, something he considered especially lucky. Under his coat, he wore two shoulder-holstered Russian Smith & Wesson .44 revolvers. An ivory panther silhouette was inlaid in each black grip. He looked older, much older, than the last time Blue had seen him two years ago. His face was drawn and his eyes, dark and tired. Over the past several years, Holt Corrigan and other ex-Confederates were charged with plundering their way across the region, robbing banks, military payrolls, and stages.

North of them, the James-Younger gang had discovered trains were easier to rob than banks. Sympathetic Southerners had taken to calling Holt Corrigan "el Jaguar." Blue wondered if they had heard about Holt's belief in having been the animal once, or if it was simply a tribute to his cunning and bravery.

"Saw you in the Lone Star, having dinner with James Hannah," Holt said, holding his one glove in his gloved left hand. "I was there. In the corner. Most folks don't know me by sight. Just reputation."

Blue told him what had happened and asked why Holt hadn't come over to join them. Holt smiled, but didn't answer.

"Deed in town, too?" Holt asked, taking a cigar from his coat pocket.

"No, he's helping at the Wilkon coach station."

"Doing what?"

Blue explained the situation.

"She pretty? This widow?" Holt cocked his head to the side and snapped a match into flame off his pants.

"Yeah, but—"

"Never mind. Say, I heard a wild tale about him taking down some bank robbers. In Austin, I think it was. One had a gun on him and Deed took him with his bare hands. That right?"

"Well, that's what happened."

"Is he nuts?" Holt held the flame to the cigar.

"No. Just good. Very good."

"Silka worked his magic I guess, while we were fightin' Yankees."

Blue smiled. "Well, I heard you were in a gunfight in Amarillo . . . and were killed. Anything to that?"

Holt chuckled. "Guess not. Don't think I'm dead. Yet. An' I haven't been in Amarillo in a long time." He turned his head slightly again and exhaled the smoke. A stray string of sunlight caught the long scar on his right cheek, a reminder of a cavalry battle. "You still preachin'?"

"I help with services in town from time to time. Me an' another man fill in when the circuit rider can't be there."

"Good for you. How's Bina and the kids?"

"Doing well. Thanks for asking." Blue said, "Didn't know you were in El Paso."

"Yeah, got an apartment not far from here. Nice an' quiet." Holt pulled on the cigar again.

"Nobody looking for you?" Blue was aware that, at the mention of the apartment, his brother hadn't invited him to stay, but also realized it was Holt's way of keeping Blue from appearing to be involved if something should happen and his cover was blown.

"Nobody's looking for Samuel Holton." Holt watched a circle of smoke wander away. "That's what I go by in town."

"Oh, okay. Samuel Holton. I'll have to remember that," Blue said.

A quick look at the alley entrance was followed by Holt changing the subject and telling Blue that the attempted stage holdup men were part of Agon Bordner's gang. Blue was surprised and told him about the Bar 3 ranch now being in Bordner's hands.

A pulsing vein dancing down his forehead, Holt said, "That fat sonuvabitch wants to own everything around there. Those were his men that hit the Bar 3, you know. And killed the folks who owned the H-5 and Roof-M, after they sold out. Got Bordner's money back that way."

"I didn't know. You sure of that?"

"Yeah. He'll be coming after you boys soon. That boy's got plans as big as he is."

"Well, there's only the Lazy S and us left."

A couple passed along the alley entrance, talking loudly. Holt retreated into the shadows until they were gone.

Blue started to say his brother was too jumpy, but decided against it. Instead, he put his hand on Holt's shoulder. "Come home, Holt. We've got a place for you. We need you. The ranch is growing. War's been over a long time."

"That's all you need," Holt said, removing Blue's hand from his shoulder. "There'd be lawmen all over your place. It'd give that fat bastard just the opportunity he wants. Believe me, Blue, he's going to come after the ranch hard, like a raccoon after bread crumbs."

Blue rubbed his unshaved chin. "Holt, you're our brother, pure and simple. We stand together. Always have. Always will." He paused and said, "Give yourself up. All of us got amnesty. No Texas jury is going to convict you. You can start over with us. We could sure use the help and your bedroom is waiting for you."

Smiling, the third Corrigan brother shifted his weight from his right to his left side. "That's mighty nice talk, Blue. Like something from one of your pretty sermons. But the time is long past for that . . . and you know it as well as I do. Every bank robbery and stagecoach holdup in Texas is supposed to have been done by me."

Blue glanced back at the alley opening, but no one

was crossing. He looked again at his brother. Holt had changed, no longer the cocky kid who loved to fight and loved to win even more. More than the war had changed him though. Holt's longtime sweetheart had married another man while Holt and Blue were at war. That heartbreak had sent Holt riding, looking for a war that was no more, except in the minds of some bitter Southerners. He had never returned.

"Did you know Allison Johnson's a widow?" Blue said, mentioning Holt's former sweetheart. "Her husband died of pneumonia last year."

"Who?"

"Come on, Holt."

Taking a long pull of his cigar, Holt exhaled and watched the smoke ring dance in front of his face again. "Deed needs to be careful," he finally said. "Going to be some crazy young guns wanting to try him. Get a reputation quick." The statement was an indication Holt didn't want to hear any more about coming home or his former sweetheart.

"He knows. You didn't answer my question about how you knew it was Bordner's men who attacked the Bar 3."

Holt frowned. "I wasn't with them, if that's what you're wondering. A couple of Bordner's men told me. They were drinking heavy and happy to be moving to the Bar 3. Their hideout was none too comfortable, I reckon. You know Bordner's got that no-good Rhey Selmon with him."

"Rhey Selmon? Heard of him. Thought he was in New Mexico."

"He was. They all were. Rhey is Bordner's right-hand man. Likes to kill."

"Sorry to hear that."

"Yeah. Sear Georgian's with him, too. A nasty bull of a man. Huge. Likes beating up men and women, I hear. Awful good with a gun though," Holt said, "Macy Shields, too. He rode with Bloody Bill Anderson. Remember?"

"I remember."

They talked a few more minutes about cattle and horses before Holt asked him if the family had any money in the El Paso Bank. Blue said they didn't and asked why.

"Well, it's a Yankee bank. Figured we might relieve it of some those Yankee dollars."

"No, Holt, it isn't a Yankee bank," Blue said. "That bank is owned by three ex-Confederates. One of them is Dave Copate. You rode with him, remember? At Sabine Pass." He licked his lips. "I ran into Dave at the stage station. He asked about you and said to greet you. Said he didn't believe the stories he'd heard . . . about you robbing banks."

Holt looked surprised, then caught himself and drew the revolver from his left shoulder holster with his right hand, opened the loading clip, half-cocked the gun, and spun its cylinder to check the loads. His right-hand glove remained in his left hand. "We'll see. You know my spirit demands that I fight. That's what I am, what I've always been."

Blue shook his head negatively. "Building a ranch is a fight. A tough one. So's raising a family or helping a town grow. Lots of ways to fight. Lots of ways better than robbing banks. Or pretending to fight a war that was lost a long time ago."

Holt's only response was to toss the cigar on the ground and crush it with his boot. He named the four former Rebels riding with him. Blue knew two of them; they had been childhood friends. They were camped north of El Paso in an old cabin while Holt stayed at the apartment as Samuel Holton.

Behind them came the swish of a dress, then a sweet call to Blue. He turned to see Rebecca Tuttle standing between the two boardwalks. Her hat was slanted a bit sideways but her smile was warm. Holt stepped back quickly; his right-hand glove dropped to the ground.

"I thought that was you, Mr. Corrigan. Are you talking to Mr. Hannah? It's hard to see in that alley," Rebecca proclaimed.

Blue stepped in front of Holt and heard his revolver cock. "No, Miss Tuttle, I'm not. Just met an old friend from the war."

"You haven't seen him, have you?"

"No, ma'am, not since you and I left the Lone Star."

She tossed her long curls and they danced along her shoulders. "Oh. Of course. I think I'll walk over there and see if he's still there."

"Sure. You do that. Be careful crossing the street."

She turned with a flirty bounce and was gone.

"What the hell was that all about?" Holt said, easing the hammer down on the weapon and returning it to his shoulder holster.

Blue chuckled. "She was on the stage with us. Supposed to be meeting some Ohio farmer to get married. Only he hasn't showed." He motioned in the direction of the restaurant. "Afraid that means Hannah was elected. Only he doesn't know it yet."

"Poor bastard."

"I can introduce you. She's real pretty."

Holt laughed, then looked down at his dropped glove. "No thanks, but would you mind picking that up for me, big brother?"

"Sure, Holt." Blue bent over and retrieved the glove. He recalled Holt saying it was bad luck for a man to pick up his dropped glove, or any dropped glove. He smiled and handed the glove to his brother. "Does this mean I'll have bad luck?"

"Oh no, Blue. Returning a glove brings good luck. I'm sure of it."

"Good."

They shook hands again and Holt went out the back of the alley, reminding his brother that Agon Bordner would be coming with a lot of gunmen and every intention of taking control of Wilkon and everything around it. Blue stood, watching him disappear, wishing he could do something to bring his brother home—wondering if he should go after him and try again. Maybe Holt was right; maybe it was too late. He retrieved his saddle and headed for the livery. A prayer for Holt's safety came from his lips.

The livery smelled of grain, manure, hay, and leather as Blue walked through the opened doors. A bear of a man with crossed eyes and an old derby perched on his head approached from a back stall, holding a pitchfork.

"Good day to ya. Stranger in town, I reckon," he said, leaning on the fork handle.

"Yeah. The name's Blue Corrigan. From up around Wilkon."

The livery operator glanced at Blue's pinned-up sleeve and said, "Reckon ya bin in the war, mister. That ri't?"

"Yes. I fought for the Confederacy. We lost."

"Yeah, I know'd. Fought fer the Stars 'n Bars myself. Rode with Pickett till we got all cut up at Gettysburg." The man's face saddened.

"I was with Ewell."

The liveryman started to hold out his hand to shake Blue's, realized his mistake, and hurriedly put his hand to his side. Blue grinned, swung the saddle to the ground, and held out his own. The man shook Blue's hand warmly. The man's name was Abe Jennings and he had worked at the livery for two years.

"Always glad to meet a fella Rebel," Jennings said, pulling on the straps of his overalls.

"Me too," Blue said. "I came to buy a horse. If you've got a good one for sale. Riding back to Wilkon. A gelding."

"You betcha. Got a couple ya'd like. That buckskin ri't back thar. Fourth stall. You kin have 'im fer . . . say twenty." He pointed toward the stall. "Or I've got this bay. Ov'r hyar. I let ya have 'im fer the same price. I'll throw in the head leather. Unless ya got some elsewhar. Got a few more out in the corral out back. These are my bestest though."

"Got a bridle. I'll take a sackful of oats instead."

"Sure nuff. Say, ya ain't related to that outlaw fella, Holt Corrigan, are ya?"

"He's my brother."

Abe's face tightened and he bit his lower lip. "Whaddya say I let ya have either one o' them . . . fer ten dollars?"

"Abe, that's kind of you, but twenty each is fair."

"No sah. We gonna make it ten . . . an' two sacks o' grain. Iffen I were ten years younger I'd join 'em. By Gawd, I would."

Blue said, "Mind if I look them over."

Abe smiled and his face glowed with relief. "Ya go ri't ahead, Mistah Corrigan. Take all the time ya need, yes sah."

Blue went to the bay first and talked with the horse, running his hands along the animal's legs. The gelding stood quietly, but its ears were on alert. Thick chested, the bay looked like it could run all day. He decided on the horse without looking at the buckskin. He paused and decided to take both horses; the buckskin would carry his supplies.

"That buckskin work as a packhorse?" he asked, patting the bay on the neck.

"Sure nuff. Broke to most anythin'."

"I'll take both, Abe."

"Fine choice, Mistah Corrigan. Fine choice." The huge man licked his chapped lips and added, "Iffen ya sees yer brother, tell him Abe Jennings tolt him to ride well."

"Sure."

CHAPTER ELEVEN

As soon as he left his brother, Holt Corrigan rode
to the most southern part of town, keeping mainly to
the back streets, more out of habit than necessity. Few
really knew what he looked like. He reined in outside
a small cantina bursting with music. He'd been here
several times before, but not lately. They knew he was
Holt Corrigan and went by the name Sam Holton, but
left him alone. Friendly, but not too friendly. He wres-
tled with his thoughts; Blue's words wouldn't leave
him no matter how hard he tried to laugh them away.

Pulling his coat over his holstered guns, he pushed
through the door. It took a moment for his eyes to
adjust. The room was small and a fire in the fireplace
brought warmth to the entire saloon. Holt noticed the
fire was even, then saw flames dart up and disappear.
That meant strangers were coming. That was logical,
in a saloon. Darting shadows played with each other
along the walls as gas lamps did their best to chase
them away. In the far corner, an old Mexican was

singing and playing the guitar. His voice was smooth and clear.

A bar dominated the room. Behind it was another Mexican named Emilio who owned the cantina. He wore a multicolored shirt, was broad-shouldered, and looked tough, but his smile was warm as he recognized Holt. The rest of the cantina was filled with tables and chairs. At the bar, four vaqueros glanced Holt's way, nodded, and returned to their conversation. Holt moved to an empty table and sat down, making sure the doorway was in his direct sight.

He slid one of his revolvers from a shoulder holster onto his lap, along with the glove from his right hand. He wouldn't drop it again. A young woman with long black hair came to the table. He wanted tequila.

With a toothy smile, she returned with a bottle and a glass. He thanked her, poured himself a drink from the bottle, and dipped the glass against his coat sleeve, letting some of the tequila spread onto the cloth. Only then did he savor the smoky taste of the liquor. Having a drink poured on someone was good luck. His mind was racing. Blue's words stung even more. Was he kidding himself to think he was fighting the war? Blue had moved on and the ranch was prospering. Had he been fooling himself with his belief that he only robbed Yankee banks? Blue had jerked him hard with the news that the town bank was owned by former Confederates—one of them, a soldier he had been with at Sabine Pass.

He sipped the tequila slowly. Was Blue right? Could he give himself up and get a fair trial? What if he did and they whisked him away to some military tribunal? They'd hang him quickly, he knew.

Holt forced himself to look around the cantina.

The music was lively now and smiling men at the table closest to the old man were clapping in rhythm. He started to pour himself another drink, but decided against it. What had the old samurai told him and his brothers? He chuckled to himself; Deed had listened well and learned much from Silka. More than he and Blue had.

Could he really become a rancher as Blue had said? Was his brother right about no Texas jury convicting him? He was aware that many robberies had been attributed to him, and many gunfights, when he had never been close. What if he gave himself up to the lawman in Wilkon? Blue and Deed would be close by to help him with his defense. He had never killed anyone robbing a Union bank, but had wounded Union soldiers who pursued him and had definitely robbed stages and banks that held Yankee money.

Who was he fooling? He was an outlaw, a wanted man. He missed his chance when the war was over. Why hadn't he been smart enough to rejoin his brothers and the others when he could have done it. That answer he already knew; he couldn't come to grips with the idea that the Confederacy had been beaten.

Beaten!

He had never been beaten before. Oh, he'd lost fist fights growing up, but not many, and not for long. If an older boy or boys had whipped him, he thought of nothing else until he could return the favor. He told himself, even then, that they were from a previous life and that he had been victorious over them in that earlier time. He recalled several campfires turning hollow before the news of Lee's surrender to Grant.

A fire turning hollow in its middle was a sure omen of death, death to the Confederacy.

He shook his head to clear it. The young girl who had waited on him was dancing beside the old man and every man in the cantina was clapping and yelling. Everyone was happy. His mind jumped to a happy time when he was walking with Allison Johnson, holding her hand.

Three men burst through the door and Holt's hand dropped to the gun in his lap. The music continued, but the woman quit dancing. At a nod from the bartender, she hurried toward the bar. Holt knew the man in the bearskin coat. Rhey Selmon. A known gunman who worked for Agon Bordner. He guessed the other two were Bordner henchmen as well. They were looking for someone, that was obvious. The three gunmen sauntered toward the bar. The second gunman, a blond-haired man with strange eyes and a weak chin, shoved the waitress out of the way as they moved. She stumbled against the closest table and fell down. Selmon was talking quietly to the bartender.

Holt drew his second gun as he grabbed his first. "Help the little lady up. And apologize."

The music stopped and the room was silent.

Turning toward Holt, the strange-eyed gunman said, "What did you say?"

"You heard me. You were rude to that woman. Help her up. Say you're sorry."

"Or what?"

Holt smiled. "Guess. It involves lead."

The woman stood, brushed herself off, and said something in Spanish. The bartender said, "It is all right. She no hurt." He started to add "Señor Corrigan," but quickly changed it to "Holton."

Selmon turned slowly toward Holt as did the other two gunmen. "There are three of us, mister. That doesn't add up well for you."

Holt held his right-hand gun on the strange-eyed gunman and his second on Selmon. "You don't count real well, friend. Look around."

Angry, Selmon and the others glanced around the room. Every Mexican in the cantina was holding a gun on them, even the old man with the guitar.

"There'll be another time, *Mr. Holton*," Selmon said.

"Any time you want to die."

Selmon's mouth was a snarl and he motioned for the others to follow him out. Holt watched them go, then kept his attention on the door in case they burst in again. The thought hit him that they could be looking for Blue. He decided to go after them. Grabbing the glove on his lap, he stood and tossed coins on the table. Before he could shove the chair out of the way, the bartender came over.

"Señor, they look for a James Hannah. I do not know him," the bartender said. "Do you?"

Holt remembered Blue telling him about Hannah and the attempted stage robbery.

"No, can't say that I do. Heard he's good with a gun," Holt said, returning his guns to his shoulder holsters. "But I know that fellow in the bearskin coat. Rhey Selmon. He's one mean bastard. Works for that fat man, you know, Agon Bordner."

"*Sí*. He is *mucho* bad *hombre*."

"Yeah, he's that. An' more."

Looking around to make sure no one was listening, the bartender said in a hoarse whisper, "My friend, Pedro . . . he tell me the fat one hires more guns."

"Scary."

"*Sí.*"

"Thanks, amigo, I'll be back one of these days." Holt took the tequila bottle in his left hand.

"Thank you for helping Regina. That was good. You are always welcome here, Señor Holton. *Vaya con Dios.*"

They shook hands and Holt left, carrying the bottle and his one glove. He didn't see Selmon or his men anywhere. He slipped the bottle into his saddlebags and mounted. Riding back through town, he thought about stopping at the bank to see if Blue was right about Dave Copate being there. Just to say hi. Chuckling, he pulled up in front of the adobe building with the big BANK sign. A week ago, he was thinking about robbing it with some other ex-Confederates and returning to his apartment to hide. No one thought Samuel Holton was the notorious Holt Corrigan. He even gave some consideration to finding Blue and riding with him.

For the first time in years, Holt felt good, as if a huge weight had been lifted. Was this sensation related to a previous life? He believed that many such incidents had their birth in another time. He shook his head to eliminate the thought. What did it matter? He was here and this was now. He was a wanted man, but his face wasn't well known. Somewhere he had read that the authorities in Missouri didn't know what Jesse and Frank James looked like either.

He swung down, flipped the reins around the hitchrail, shoved the tequila bottle into his saddlebags, then removed both gloves and put them in as well. He pulled his coat to fully cover his guns. Maybe he should leave them with his horse. Finally, he decided to leave one gun in his saddlebags beside the bottle, but he hesitated about being unarmed. Sliding the second gun into his back waistband, Holt adjusted his hat, touched the cardinal feather for luck, and went into the bank.

The lobby was busy with lines in front of three tellers. A young man in a too-large business suit greeted him, asking how he could be helped. His manner was condescending and Holt figured it wasn't personal, that he was so with all customers. Holt smiled and figured the arrogant young man would pee in his pants at the first sign of a holdup, or if he knew he was talking to Holt Corrigan.

"I'd like to see Mr. Copate, if he's in."

"I see. Do you have an appointment?"

Holt tried to keep smiling. "No. I'm just an old friend from the war. If he's too busy, I'll come back."

"Your name, sir?" The young man licked his lips. "I'll check with Mr. Copate. He is a very busy man, you know."

"I'm sure he is. Tell him . . . Samuel Holton is here. We fought together at Sabine Pass."

The young man's eyes widened at hearing Sabine Pass and he spun and disappeared into an office just off the lobby.

Holt touched his hat brim as an older couple passed him on the way out. He was uneasy; he couldn't recall being in a bank for any reason other than to rob it. He rubbed his chin. This was silly. Why would a successful businessman come out to see a man whose name he didn't know?

He turned toward the door and a familiar voice called out, "Mr. Holton, how good to see you! It's been too long."

Spinning around, Holt saw a tall man in a tailored

suit smiling. They shook hands and the banker's voice dropped to a whisper, "I was sure it was you, Holt. Please don't tell me you're going to hold up my bank. I've heard all the stories." Copate said, "Never believed them for a minute."

Holt tried to smile. "You're good to see me, Dave. Don't have any reason to be here. Headed for my brothers' ranch. Up near Wilkon." He was amazed the words came out of his mouth. He glanced at a stocky businessman passing. "Going to start . . . over. Going to try anyway." Now he was really surprising himself. "Yeah, the newspapers have me in every holdup in the Southwest. I must have some damn fast horses."

Copate chuckled. "Glad to hear you're headed for your ranch, Holt. Let me know if I can help," he said, putting a hand on Holt's shoulder. "You saved my life, you know."

"You'd have done the same for me."

Copate bit his lip. "I don't know, man. You cut down six Yankees with your rifle and handguns and took out four more with the butt of your empty rifle." He smiled. "Come into my office. We need to catch up. Got some good whiskey there." He winked.

"Uh, sure. Never been in the office of a bank president before."

Copate laughed.

A half hour later, Holt left the bank and rode north toward his apartment.

Across town, Agon Bordner was perplexed; he had expected James Hannah to accept the job to get rid of Deed Corrigan for three hundred dollars, another two hundred for eliminating the Japanese warrior,

and two hundred more for the remaining Regan boy.
A bonus of another two hundred would be paid when
Bordner took actual control of their spread. That was
an attractive offer. Anywhere.

The delay was especially puzzling since the gunman
had made the trip all the way from Kansas just to talk
with him about the job.

"Wonder if I should've offered more money?"

Only a few hours ago, Hannah told him that he
would consider the offer and get back to him, then
left the Lone Star. None of Bordner's men had seen
him around town since then. He wasn't used to having
a hired gun ask for more time to consider his offer.
He decided that he would go as high as four hundred
for Deed, three hundred for the Oriental—and leave
the killing of the boy to Rhey Selmon.

Coatless with his vest unbuttoned, he stormed
about his mansion's second-story library, swearing
and waving his massive arms. A cold cigar lay forgotten on the edge of the walnut desk. Next to it was an
untouched cup of coffee and a plate of donuts. His
coat and hat lay on the desk chair. He thought better
with them off—and by himself.

"Maybe he's afraid of Deed Corrigan," Bordner
said to himself. "Or maybe he's made friends with
his brother. Willard said that was Blue Corrigan with
him . . . and a young woman." He didn't believe the
statement, but it was always smart to state the worst
possible scenario and work from there. It kept him
from being surprised.

On a hunch, he had sent Rhey Selmon to check on
the possibility of friendship between James Hannah
and Blue Corrigan with the stage-line district agent;
his top gunman had returned saying a friendship was

likely, that it was Hannah and Blue who stopped the holdup—and it was Hannah and Deed Corrigan who earlier stopped a real Comanche attack on the coach. Unasked, the district agent had also told him proudly that the stage-line had paid them bonuses for their efforts. Rhey said he would look for Hannah around town.

With Rhey's report whirling through his mind, the fat businessman walked over to the elongated window overlooking the street. He glanced back at the crumpled telegram on his desk from Willard Hixon, president of the Wilkon Bank and one of his New Mexico gang. The message informed him that two Texas Rangers were in town to investigate the Regan murders and the Bar 3 takeover. Hixon would handle the situation without any problem, Bordner was convinced of that. Neither the county sheriff nor the Wilkon marshal would be a factor. After all, the only witness was a six-year-old boy. But it reminded him that he needed to meet with the county sheriff and see if an understanding could be struck. His thoughts wandered to the idea of Macy Shields taking over as the town's marshal. Sear Georgian would assist him, but not wear a badge. That would be too great a stretch. He chuckled at the thought.

"What could that boy say?" Bordner rubbed his double chin. "The worst, that it was white men. Not Comanches. So what? That could describe Comancheros." He licked his rubbery lips. "There's absolutely nothing tied to me. I'm just a businessman who happened to be in position to profit from someone else's misfortune. Happens all the time." He chuckled, remembered his cigar, and returned to it, relighting the black cheroot with a match from his vest pocket.

Clenching his fists, he stepped away from the desk, puffing vigorously on the cigar, and acknowledged that he was worried that he hadn't heard from Hannah. A fleeting thought passed through his mind: what if Hannah had decided to go to work for the Corrigans?

"Couldn't be. Couldn't be. They don't have that kind of money in the first place." His heavy jowls jiggled as he paced. Sweat gathered on his shirt in places where it touched his skin. The only reason they were eating together was the coincidence of their traveling together. That's all. His mind wandered to the other Corrigan brother, the outlaw. Was there some way he was involved and Hannah didn't want to deal with him as well? The boys said Holt Corrigan was an outcast from the others and didn't have anything to do with them or the ranch. Still—

A knock on the closed library door brought a hard response from Bordner.

"Whaddya want?"

"I's be . . . sorry, suh," a gray-haired black butler stammered, bowing slightly. "Mistah Hannah, he be hyar. He say ya tolt him to come. Yessuh, that's what he say."

Bordner's eyes flashed, and for a moment, he looked like an attacking wolverine; then his face lightened. "Uh, sure. Sure, Adam. Send him in"—he looked over at the desk—"bring some fresh coffee. For both of us." He waved his arms. "No. Bring whiskey. My best. And two glasses."

"Yessuh."

Buttoning his vest, Bordner refocused his mind.

* * *

After leaving his buckskin horse at the livery, Holt walked to his apartment, unsure of what he should do next. His statement about returning to his brothers' ranch had come without any conscious decision. It sounded good at the time. But now it seemed like a silly idea. He was an outlaw.

His simple room seemed even smaller and lonelier than before. A bed and a scratched dresser with a washbasin and pitcher were the only items in the room, except for a tiny closest where he kept his extra clothes, ammunition, and several guns. In one pair of pants was a handkerchief that had belonged to their mother. And in another pocket was a piece of a Confederate flag. Usually he carried them. Probably the reason he saw Blue was the fact he hadn't been carrying either.

Holding the bottle of tequila in both hands, he stood in the center of the room and shook his head. What a crummy way to live. He knew most outlaws spent their lives in similar or worse conditions. Always running. Always hiding. After taking a long drink from the bottle, he sat down on the edge of the bed and began his daily exercise of cleaning his two hand-guns and the rifle from his saddle sleeve. The ritual was precise, ending with him touching each gun with the cardinal feather from his hat. The tequila bottle sat on the floor near his boots. His conversation with David Copate bubbled in his mind; Copate was enthusiastic and positive. Why couldn't he be that way? Holt returned the feather to his hat, reached down, retrieved the bottle, and drank.

Thoughts of all kinds spun through his head as he oiled the weapons. Images of the war . . . earlier times with his brothers and Silka. Sweet moments with Allison Johnson, once when they peeled an apple and threw the peelings over her head. The peelings were to land in the shape of the first letter of the name of their first child. It was sort of an *S*. The awful moment when he got her letter of good-bye and the madness afterward when he tried to get killed by rushing an entrenched Yankee patrol and ended up killing them all. The rush of reality afterward that he had lived before, perhaps many times. Then the completeness of defeat and the recollection of spiritual signs he had missed that the Confederacy was doomed. The one-man attacks he made on Union camps. How could anyone accept the fact that the South had lost? He drank some more and laid down on the bed with his clothes on. He rarely slept any other way, and he rarely slept well. To sleep well was to die.

Sleep came slowly and brought fierce nightmares of pumas, Roman gladiators and knights, fires and apple peelings . . . and Allison.

CHAPTER TWELVE

Time passed quickly for Deed Corrigan. Caleb Corrigan's body was buried under a small cherry tree at the north edge of the station area; the family had planted the slender tree three years earlier. The dead Comanches were dragged away, and that night warriors returned to take away the bodies. There had been no Indian problems since. Nor was there any sign of them.

The two dead passengers were buried on the north side of the cottonwoods and identified with simple wooden head markers. Before driving away, Tade Balkins had promised to have the district agent wire their relatives about the sad event, if any could be located. Atlee planned on preserving selected fruits and vegetables in jars for the winter. A nearby farmer was happy to sell them fresh corn, beans, cucumbers, and tomatoes.

Stages came and went regularly. Passengers of all sorts stopped at the station and enjoyed Atlee's food. Cattlemen and farmers, miners and hunters, drummers and peddlers, newspapermen and actors, gamblers and gunmen, prostitutes and soldiers, men and women from everywhere. The routine of the stagecoach operation was harder and more demanding than Deed had realized. Monday, Wednesday, and Friday departures from each end of the Hays City–Santa Fe run were operated with the same running time of four and a half days. The stage-line ran twenty-four hours a day, every day, regardless of weather. The Barlow and Sanderson Company was the line's owner, but they sublet contracts running from Santa Fe to El Paso and Tucson to Sand and Cook's Stage-Line, headquartered in El Paso.

All in all, the entire line covered 2,000 miles, using 1,200 animals and more than 300 regular employees. About every fifteen miles or so was a relay station waiting with fresh horses. Home stations were those with food and overnight lodging for the passengers. The Forsyths had hoped to become such a location. Of course, Wells Fargo controlled everything involving the mail, west and north. And mail delivery was always the primary objective; passengers were an afterthought.

No railroad existed west of Fort Worth, which is why the relay stations continued to be important, especially the Forsyth station since it had such a good name. Elsewhere in Texas, independent railroad companies were stretching their wings. The days of the stagecoach and relay stations as the king of transportation were ending, but feeder lines like this one continued to profit.

Billy Montez and Caleb Forsyth had done an excellent job of managing the horses, keeping them well fed and healthy, and maintaining the harnesses in top shape. Little things eventually made big differences. Deed's mentor, Silka, the former samurai, had taught him that, and the stage operation was clear testimony to that fact. Harnesses were checked each night and whatever horses were at the station were examined for leg problems, sore backs, or broken horseshoes. From the beginning, Caleb had insisted on having an extra team of horses on hand at all times, in addition to the team being readied for the next stage. Billy had gone to a neighbor and secured horses to replace the ones killed in the raid, with the promise that the neighbor would be paid as soon as the next stage came with the money.

Work with the horses was constant. Since a horse's stomach was small, it needed to eat a lot of small meals during each day, usually four. This was complicated by the daily arrival and departure of a team of horses. The order for feeding was important: water first, then hay, and lastly, grain. Always in small rations. And never any water after grain. Water expanded the grain and brought on colic. Billy was a stickler when it came to the quality of hay, using only good green, clean and bright. Usually timothy. Nothing dirty or dusty—and definitely not moldy. Mold was poisonous and could kill a horse. Mucking out the stalls was a daily task.

Feeding was just part of the work. All of the animals had their hooves picked daily—to remove packed manure, dirt, and small rocks—and checked for loose or cracked horseshoes, as well as stone bruises. Billy liked to say, "No foot. No mistah." All of the horses were brushed and combed. Deed told himself they would start implementing the same kind of procedures at the ranch.

Deed and Billy had become a good team handling

the horses, and Atlee worked long hours, making certain incoming passengers were well fed and the setting was bright and cheery. Olivia Beinrigt had become an excellent help inside as well; she and her husband slept in the bunks set up for employees, but rarely used. They had moved the beds into a corner and put up a bedsheet to provide privacy. Hermann Beinrigt was slowly recovering. Benjamin spent most of his time helping his mother and Olivia; Deed saw him only during meals and figured that was best. The boy was grieving and rarely spoke to him or anyone, except his mother.

Atlee never talked of losing her husband, but Deed heard her sobbing late one night when he was unable to sleep and was walking past the cabin to make certain she and her kids were okay. The next day, he asked if she needed to talk and her response was negative, swift, and brittle. He never asked again. Blue would be returning from El Paso soon with their new stallion, and they would ride to their ranch together. He wasn't sure how he felt about that.

Midday brought two hard-looking riders headed from the direction of Wilkon. Deed told Billy to get his shotgun and stay out of sight, but close by. The one-eyed Mexican laid the hammer beside his anvil and hurried the horse he was shoeing into the barn. Deed was positive he didn't know the men. Something about their easy lope in the open made him think these weren't outlaws, but he couldn't be certain in this wild land. A survey of the surrounding land convinced him they were alone.

He walked over to the corral and picked up the Spencer carbine resting there along with a box of reloading tubes. He had kept both handy since the Comanche attack. Cocking the big gun, he slid into the shadows. No sense in making a target of himself until he knew who they were.

"There are only two, Billy. No others behind," Deed whispered.

"*Sí.* That is 'nuff."

"Yeah."

Even at this distance, Deed was impressed with the appearance of their horses. Powerfully built and long legged, they were animals made for speed and endurance. Definitely not ranch horses; the kind outlaws rode—or lawmen. The advancing riders' hands were empty, except for the reins they held. He was now sure they were alone and not looking for trouble.

At the outskirts of the station area, the two men reined up near the cottonwoods. One of them reached into his coat pocket, produced a badge, and pinned it on his vest. The stouter of the two did the same. Rangers, Deed thought. Texas Rangers.

Deed stepped out of the shadows and hailed their arrival.

"Afternoon, men. How can we help you?"

His movement into the sunlight surprised them. Their first reactions were movements toward their holstered guns. Seeing the cocked Spencer in Deed's hands stopped that idea before it was too late. They walked their horses closer and stopped a few yards away.

"Howdy. We're Rangers," the lawman in front announced, moving his hands slowly to his saddle horn.

"I can see that by your badges. Welcome. Climb down and water your horses."

"Many thanks," he said, swinging easily from the saddle.

Both lawmen wore knee-length boots, heavy Mexican-roweled spurs, buttoned vests, and long black trail coats. Double-rowed cartridge belts carried a six-gun and a Bowie knife, holstered on the left side with the gun butt forward. Even their thick mustaches looked alike. The only differences between them were their heights and their hats. The man who had spoken was taller and wore a flat-brimmed hat that the wind had permanently pushed up in front. The shorter, stockier lawman wore a weathered hat with a tripointed crown and wide brims curled up on the sides and gathered in the front.

The taller Ranger took off his hat and swatted at the trail dust clinging to his coat and clothes.

"Just came from Wilkon." He squinted and crow's feet rushed into the corners of his gray eyes. "You look familiar, mister. Do we know you?"

Uncocking his carbine, Deed chuckled. "Now that's a question a fellow doesn't want to hear from a lawman. I'm Deed Corrigan."

The second Ranger, now dismounted as well, stomped his heavy boots making the spurs sing and said, "Thought so. Holt's your brother, right?"

"He is."

"Easy now, I wasn't pushing. My own brother rode owlhoot for three years."

"Sorry to hear it. Haven't seen Holt since the war."

"We talked with your wife. Bina, right?" He pulled the glove off his right hand and held it out.

"No, that's my brother's wife, Bina. Blue's in El Paso on business."

"Oh sure. She told us you were helping here till

things got settled from the Indian attack." He nodded toward the station. "I'm Hendel Rice. And this here long-legged galoot is Revel Williams. We're part of Captain Waters's company."

"Glad to meet both of you." Deed shook hands with the two Rangers and called out for Billy. The Mexican eased from the barn door, laid his shotgun against its weathered side, and walked over. Deed introduced him to the Rangers.

"You boys look like you were expecting trouble," Revel Williams said and motioned toward Billy's shotgun and Deed's Spencer.

"Better safe than sorry, the saying goes." Deed patted Billy on his shoulder. "Had a bad time with Comanches a week back. Killed the station manager and two passengers."

"You didn't think we were Indians, did you?" Revel asked with a hint of humor in his eyes.

"No, but men riding horses like these aren't cowhands or farmers." Deed rubbed the nose of the closest bay.

The Rangers explained they had come to the region because of the Bar 3 massacre, Agon Bordner taking control of the ranch because of the overdue loan, and the killings of the two other ranch families.

"All the killings Comanches?" Deed glanced at Billy.

"Appears so."

"You're sure?" Deed rubbed his chin with his left hand; his right held his carbine at his side.

"Now look. We don't like this either, but there's nothing illegal we can see. Nothing we can prove anyway. Agon Bordner wasn't even close by. Lives in El Paso, you know, living grand. We've seen his place."

Rice looked Deed in the eyes. "Has a good reputation there. Strong churchgoing fella. Hear he's generous to the church an' all."

Deed studied both men. They were typical Rangers. Hard but fair. Naturally inclined to be suspicious.

From the station doorway, Atlee appeared. "Deed? Do we have visitors?"

He turned toward her, smiling. "Yes, Mrs. Forsyth. Rangers. They were investigating trouble nearby." He hadn't told her about the Bar 3.

A frown slid across her face, but was followed by a warm smile. "Please tell them to come in for coffee and something to eat. You and Billy, too."

Cooper came to the door, wagging his tail.

"Yes, boss." He had deliberately not used her first name—and called her boss—wanting to reinforce the fact she was in charge. Turning back to the Rangers, he said, "I'd suggest you take her up on that. Best food anywhere around."

"Heard that. You don't have to ask me twice." Rice chuckled. "Neither one o' us are much for trail cookin'. We get by, but it's nothin' to crow about."

Deed pushed his hat back on his forehead. "We had heard that the bank was holding a big loan. How about their trail-drive money? That was a big herd they brought in. At least three thousand head. Saw it myself when we were headed back. I was a week or so ahead with our herd but was still in town."

"The bank has no record of any deposit," Williams responded. "No one's found any money at the ranch either."

"What about the money Bordner paid for those two small ranches?"

"Don't know if anybody's said anything about it,"

Williams said. "Guess they had it with them when the Indians hit 'em."

"Comanches don't take money."

"No, I reckon they don't."

Without speaking, Billy Montez took the reins of their horses and led them away while Deed walked with the Rangers towards the station door. Atlee and Cooper had already disappeared inside.

"Sometimes bad things happen to good folks," Rice observed, watching Billy take the horses to the big watering trough. "It's going to take a few years to get rid of the Comanches, but we'll get it done."

"I wasn't talking about Comanches."

Changing the subject, Williams asked Deed what had happened here a week ago. Deed told them about the Comanche attack, about Caleb Forsyth and two passengers being killed, and that Mrs. Forsyth had assumed the responsibilities of running the station. The Rangers were surprised to hear a woman was in charge, but Deed assured them that she was managing quite well and he was only helping out until she could hire someone permanent.

"You mentioned meeting my brother's wife," Deed said and pulled his hat back down on his forehead as he went ahead up the steps and opened the door. Cooper came out and waited in the doorway to greet everyone.

"Yeah, and the Regan kid," Williams added. "A hard-lookin' Chinese fella was there, too. She said he was a longtime family friend."

"Japanese. He is. The best. Nakashima Silka. He's also our partner." Deed leaned over to pet Cooper.

"We had heard about the kid's survival. In Wilkon,

folks are pretty upset about what's happened," Williams said, studying the station as they approached. "The boy told us it wasn't Indians. It was white men." He bit his upper lip beneath his mustache. "But he was real scared and didn't see much. Hid in a cooling shack. Gosh, he's only six, you know."

"Yeah, I know. My brother and some friends found him."

"As far as we can tell, this Bordner fella just happened to be in the right place at the right time to pick up the ranch. It adds to the other two he just bought," Rice added as stepped onto the front porch of the station.

"Again, there's nothing wrong with the deal. Just good business. Best we can tell he was only taking advantage of a bad situation, one that wasn't his doing." Williams waved his arms as they reached the porch. "County sheriff agrees. So did the Wilkon marshal."

Deed didn't respond, but watched Cooper waiting at the door.

Removing his second glove, Williams paused over a large bowl of water resting on the porch railing, and laid both gloves beside it. "Could've been Comancheros riding with the redskins, you know." He washed his hands and doused his face, then dried himself with the clean towel resting nearby.

After tying the Rangers' horses to the corral rail, Billy hurried and caught up with them as Rice took his turn washing up. Elizabeth came rushing through the door and held up her arms for Deed to hold her, which he was happy to do. Cooper changed his mind about going inside and spun around to be next to the two of them.

"I got flowers from our garden," she said, smiling into his face. "You'll see them when you come in."

"Well, I can hardly wait."

He introduced her to the Rangers and Elizabeth greeted them enthusiastically and asked if they had met Cooper. Both Rangers smiled and said they hadn't had the pleasure.

"This is Cooper. Cooper Forsyth," she said and motioned toward the dog.

"Glad to know you, Cooper," Rice responded and doffed his hat in an exaggerated motion.

Elizabeth giggled.

Williams also tipped his hat and knelt to scratch Cooper's head.

Inside Atlee greeted the Rangers warmly and directed them to the table, covered with a red-and-white checkered tablecloth. What remained of the flowers Elizabeth picked from the Forsyth garden had been gathered into a bright bouquet in the center. Behind the sheet, Hermann Beinrigt was sleeping soundly on the farthest cot. Even Deed was impressed with the appearance of the entire room. Cooper took a position near the fireplace, stretched out comfortably to watch everything. The planked floor had been swept clean and the station looked cheery.

To himself, Deed thought the coach line would be foolish not to let her run the station; Atlee Forsyth was the consummate host. He put Elizabeth in the chair beside him and sat down. She smiled at him and asked if all the horses were well. He assured her they were.

Smiling, Atlee brought in a plate piled high with thick beef sandwiches; Olivia brought bowls of pickles, baked beans, and scalloped corn. Both women quickly filled the men's coffee cups and returned to the kitchen. Minutes later, Atlee and Olivia joined them with plates of their own. Atlee was eager for conversation of happenings outside of her world. So was Olivia. Rangers Williams and Rice were happy to oblige with stories from their travels throughout Texas.

Benjamin wandered into the room, looking sad, but determined to find out if the Rangers were here to take them away from the station. Atlee introduced him and he became defensive.

"If you had been here a week ago, my pa wouldn't have been killed," he declared.

"That's enough, Benjamin. These men have many responsibilities. Not just this corner of Texas," Atlee snapped.

Benjamin folded his arms. Elizabeth began to cry, and Deed leaned over to whisper to her. She wiped her eyes and sat up straight. Williams responded that he was sorry about what had happened and added that a ranch west of the station had been raided two months ago and everyone on it had been killed; two other families had been killed leaving the area; and that they were sorry not to have been able to get to the station in time to save Benjamin's father.

"Sounds like you messed up some more," Benjamin said and marched out the door, slamming it hard.

Flushed with embarrassment, Atlee said, "I'm so sorry, gentlemen. My son has taken the loss of his father very hard. But that is no excuse for such rudeness."

Williams finished his coffee. "Think nothing of it, Mrs. Forsyth. We wish we'd been here, too. Now we need to get riding. Our captain is expecting us in Waco."

"Certainly, gentlemen. It was my honor to serve you."

CHAPTER THIRTEEN

Nightfall found Atlee Forsyth alone in her bedroom. Everything was readied for the stage tomorrow morning. Having Olivia was proving a special advantage. Every bone in the young woman's body ached from the hard days of work, labor that never seemed to end, only to begin again the next morning.

She whimpered and then chastised herself for feeling sorry for herself, but this was actually the hardest part of the day. Being alone at night. Alone with her memories. She and Caleb had planned to eventually start a hotel of their own, probably in Wilkon. Now that was gone, along with his warmth and love.

Beside her bed was a narrow walnut table Caleb had made. An opened Bible lay across its top. Next to the good book was a flickering gas lamp and a pad of paper and pencil. Every day since his death she had made a list of the things that needed to be done the next day. Tomorrow. That was what had kept her going. Tomorrow. She could hear her children sleeping in the other room. Just barely, but she could hear them.

Benjamin was struggling with the loss of his father; Elizabeth, however, seemed content, especially when Deed was around her. After the Rangers left, she asked Deed what he had said to Elizabeth to stop her crying and he said he told the little girl that her mother needed her to be strong and not cry. Atlee smiled. Elizabeth would miss Deed greatly when he returned to his ranch. At her questioning, he had also told her about the Bar 3 massacre, the curious ownership that followed, the purchase of two other small ranches, and the killing of the two families involved. She hadn't asked any follow-up questions and he hadn't elaborated.

Raindrops popped along the roof, the vanguard of the expected rain. Good, she thought, that will help knock down the dust. Atlee stared into the darkness toward her dresser and imagined a film of dust on its top, just as there was dust seemingly everywhere no matter how hard, and often, she and Olivia cleaned.

She needed to go into Wilkon for supplies and to hire a man to replace Deed. What would she have done without him? Her mind raced, thinking about his steadfastness, his courage—and his caring. His warm smile came to her mind and she shook her head to rid its appearance. She had heard the stories of his fighting skill. In the West, such tales traveled fast. There were stories about the third Corrigan brother, Holt, but they were darker and it didn't seem, to her, like the man could be related to Deed at all. Seeing him, hearing him, being around him had made her feel secure. She didn't want to admit that, even to herself.

"Forgive me, Caleb. I am so lonely. So lonely," she muttered and a single tear dribbled down her cheek.

Billy had told her about Deed—and James Hannah—fighting and destroying the will of the war party attacking the stage, as well as killing several warriors while she was also fighting and watching her husband die. That awful day was a dull ache to her. Billy said both were quick with a gun—dangerous men. He smiled when he said it.

Atlee and Caleb had come here from eastern Texas after two years of drought had forced them from their farm. Just as drought had brought the Beinrigts to the stage station. She had been mulling over the idea of asking them to stay; Hermann might be a good fit to work with Billy. Then she wouldn't need to hire someone she didn't know. Olivia had become an excellent help in the kitchen and with serving the passengers. It wouldn't be long before Hermann would be up and around. She decided to talk with them about it tomorrow. They could build a room onto the cottage or section off the station for them to live in.

Tomorrow.

There was no choice but to make the station the best on the route, to make it impossible to replace her. Elizabeth and Benjamin depended on her success, even though they didn't realize it.

"Caleb, I miss you so much." Her eyes crinkled and more tears came. She was powerless to stop them. For minutes, the sobbing consumed her, taking all of her energy, all of her will.

Finally, with a cough, she stopped crying. It was time to plan, not to feel sorry for herself. Her father had always told her that thinking was what separated man from animals. The ability to evaluate situations before acting. To look for the best option before one chose. She gathered her small pad of paper and pencil. Her list of needed supplies took only a few minutes to prepare. When in town, she would also explore a possible replacement for Deed. Surely there were good men looking for steady work, if her idea about the Beinrigts didn't pan out.

Deed Corrigan. What a mysterious man. In Western parlance, he would be considered a "bad man" she was certain. Not an outlaw, rather a bad man to mess with. But he had his own concerns; the Corrigan ranch needed him as much as she did. His face came again into her mind. Smiling. Always smiling. She shook her head to make the image leave. She had no business thinking of him in that way. Her husband was barely cold in the ground. She shook her head even more strongly and took a deep breath.

In thinking about the other killings, it was clear he didn't think Comanches were to blame for the ranch being attacked or the families wiped out. From his way of talking, it seemed he believed a rich man in El Paso was behind the atrocities. She shuddered at the thought. Surely Deed had to be wrong. How could anyone be so cold to want wealth that way?

Rain was coming harder now, bringing thunder and lightning. She heard footsteps and knew the noise had awakened her children and Cooper. Benjamin wouldn't want to admit it, but he would like to sleep in her bed as much as Elizabeth.

Slipping from the covers, she grabbed the gas lamp and met them in the doorway. "What do you say we all sleep together tonight? It's a good rainy night for that," she offered warmly.

Cooper barked joyfully and both children laughed.

Across the open yard, Deed listened to the pounding rain in the comfort of his blankets in the tack room. Billy Sanchez was asleep in the tiny room built for him at the south end of the barn. All of the horses were in the barn and safe. His mind wandered from the horses, to the Corrigan ranch, to Atlee. He had no business thinking of her; she was a grieving widow. Yet he couldn't get her face out of his thoughts. At least, not for long. Thoughts of her would sneak into his consciousness when he least expected it. Foolish, he told himself. And wrong.

As soon as Blue returned from El Paso, they would leave for their ranch. He wasn't worried about Agon Bordner coming for their land—not yet anyway—even with its fine valleys and excellent water. But it was wise to plan for that attempt. Acquiring the region's biggest ranch would take time to fully control. And another ranch attacked right now would draw serious attention from the Rangers. They were already suspicious. Besides, their ranch was small compared to either the Bar 3 or the Lazy S, although much bigger than the two small ranches Bordner had also acquired.

Caleb Forsyth, or someone, had built the relay station and the barn well; there were a few leaks here and there in the barn but they were tiny. The tack room held all of the harnesses on wooden pegs, better than nails because they didn't rust. Each horse's stall had a manger for feed and a rack built underneath for hay. The rack was built low to keep dust out of the horse's eyes. Smart, he thought.

As he settled into sleep again, a different sound

caught his ears. Slight. Muffled. Then a soft whinny. It was probably nothing. Just one of the horse's acting up.

No. His mind locked on to the issue.

Someone was trying to steal the horses!

He spun from his bed with his revolver in hand, ignoring his boots. Barefooted, he eased from the tack room with his cartridge belt slung over his shoulder and shoved the second Remington usually holstered there into his waistband. His eyes adapted quickly to the darkness and he saw definite movement at the stables. Four Comanches had returned to steal the stagecoach horses. It would be the ultimate show of bravery and daring to prove the strength of their war medicine by coming back to the station where so many of their war party had died. A rainy night was perfect they had decided; no white people would be awake or listening.

Like tanned ghosts, the warriors moved silently to open the stalls and lead out the horses. Capturing such fine animals would, indeed, bring worthy praise from their fellow tribesmen. A big bay was agitated by the Indians and reared.

Shooting now was too risky. Deed couldn't be certain where a horse's head ended and a Comanche began. He must get closer. One warrior swung bareback onto a big sorrel and directed the animal toward the opened barn door. Heavy rain glistened from the opening. If Deed waited any longer, the warrior would vanish into the wet night with the treasured horse. He guessed the remaining warriors intended to make the horses run from the barn and that this mounted warrior was the leader of the horse-stealing party.

In one motion, he cocked the Remington and fired.

Three times. The continuous roar was a bomb in the barn. The warrior tumbled from the horse and the animal reared, but someone slid in front of the frightened animal, blocking the door, then slamming it shut again. Deed heard whispered Spanish and the horse settled where it stood, stomping its hooves and snorting. From that silhouette came the unforgiving boom-boom of a shotgun and a second warrior collapsed as he ran toward the barn door. In the brief flash, Deed saw what he already knew; Billy was there, blocking the way.

From the closest stall, a painted warrior hurled himself at Deed, swinging his tomahawk. Deed fired and missed. The war club slammed against the top of his hand and drove the gun from him. Deed's right hand was numbed and bleeding from the glancing blow. Instead of reaching for the second revolver in his waistband, Deed jammed his open hand against the warrior's chin. A follow-up left-leg power kick drove into the Comanche's stomach and a third blow, again with his left hand, was a vicious open-handed chop against the Comanche's neck that stopped the warrior completely. Deed shook his right hand, trying to regain feeling.

Leaving the horse he was leading from a middle stall, a fourth warrior came at Deed, screaming a fierce war cry that filled the barn. Deed blocked the downward thrust of his tomahawk with his left hand raised against the warrior's arm. In one fluid motion, Deed delivered an open-handed smack into the Indian's throat with his injured right hand. As the warrior gasped for breath, Deed drew his second revolver from his waistband with his left hand. He rammed his gun into the warrior's stomach and fired.

In minutes, it was over.

Deed was drenched in nervous sweat and his right hand had no feeling and a cut along the back of his hand brought fingers of blood across it.

"Billy? You all right? That's the last of them, I think, but we'd better check."

"*Sí.* And you, amigo?"

"Yeah. Let's check the stalls and get these horses settled down. We were lucky."

"*Sí.* That is so."

Lights were on in the Forsyth cottage and the station itself. From the doorway of the cottage, Atlee peered into the rain and yelled, "Deed . . . Billy? Are you all right? What's happening?"

Olivia was at the doorway of the station, holding a lamp in her left hand and a pistol in the other. In a handful of yelled sentences, Deed explained the attempted raid and that all was well. Olivia invited everyone to come to the station while she put on coffee and warmed up some biscuits. Even in the rain, it sounded good to all of them.

"Put your hand in de water. Leave it there, amigo," Billy said. "I will get the hosses back into their places."

"Thanks. Good idea." Deed went to a water bucket near the tack room and put his right hand into the cooling liquid. The wound had stopped bleeding, but the numbness remained.

Soon a celebration of sorts took over the night, although nearly everyone was soaked. Deed and Billy, Atlee and her two children and Cooper gathered around the reenergized fireplace. Hermann was up and had stoked the fire into compliance. Atlee was shocked to see Deed was wounded as Billy recounted with some awe in his voice how the young gunfighter had bested three of the attackers. Olivia put on a pan of water to boil for cleaning the wound.

Deed insisted that the wound was not serious, but neither woman paid any attention to his protestations.

Chapter Fourteen

"Señor Deed, it is time to get de horses ready," Billy Montez announced, coming out of the barn. Last night's attempted horse stealing was forgotten for the moment. The four dead Comanches had been dragged out of sight, left for their fellow tribesmen to retrieve, if they dared.

Deed chuckled to himself. He didn't need reminding by the Mexican who felt it was his duty to tell him every time a stage was coming. This coach would be arriving from the north. They gathered a fresh team with Billy coaxing them in Spanish. Since the raid that killed his father, Benjamin hadn't helped with the horses, but Cooper had and was bouncing alongside Deed.

"Billy, that back bay's got something wrong with his leg." Deed pointed with his left hand; his right was painfully sore and badly bruised. "Back right." He had taken to carrying a revolver in his waistband for left-hand use.

"*Sí.* We must check it."

An examination showed the animal was nursing a strained leg muscle. It wasn't serious, but running with the team now could lead to something permanent. The limping horse was removed from the team and replaced with another. The injury might have occurred during the failed Comanche raid on the barn, but it was impossible to know for certain.

"Waco will not like being away from his friends. Bingo will not either. But it must be so," Billy said. Waco was the name he called the limping horse and Bingo was the name of the replacement. He had a pet name for every horse that came through the station. Deed did his best to remember them; although he was certain the names changed occasionally.

"Kinda like people, I guess," Deed said, leading the injured horse away.

"*Sí.* Liniment is inside."

"Good."

Soon, a bearded driver with a cocky attitude brought the coach into the station with a hard gallop as all drivers liked to do. A huge wad of tobacco in his mouth made it difficult for him to speak without shifting it to the side of his mouth.

"Whoa, you fleabags! Whoa!"

As if on cue, the glistening horses stutter-stepped to a stop. The coach's wheels groaned as he slammed on the brake and reined hard. Unlike Tade Balkins, Pip Mateau was a scruffy-looking teamster in a soiled leather jacket with long, matted fringe and a bowler hat.

Pip spat a thick, brown stream and hollered, "Ever'body out. Good chow. Hot coffee waitin'. Outhouses in the back. Will be a' goin' again in thirty minutes. Not thirty-five. Thirty."

He wrapped the reins around the brake and eased down, greeting Billy warmly. "Hey, Billy, you ol' Mex, this new team any good?" He waved his arms at the new horses and spat again. "I'm givin' ya a ri't smart, good bunch. You betcha. Don't let Balkins have em, ya hear."

Billy grinned and hollered back something in Spanish. Deed picked up several choice swearwords, all delivered in good-natured fun.

"Hey, who's this hombre packin' the six-gun— an' the busted-up hand?" Pip Mateau stopped his advance as passengers filed out, stretching their arms, behind him.

"*Sí*. This is Señor Deed Corrigan. He's helping. For a short time. *Bueno*," Billy said.

Yanking off his dirty gloves, Pip held out his right hand. Deed smiled and extended his left. "My right's a bit sore." The driver switched hands and shook Deed's left heartily.

"Ain't you the fella who took down a gunman with your hands—and him pointing a six-gun at your belly? Heard that last year, I'm thinkin'. Down in Austin, it was."

"Didn't have any choice." Deed leaned down to pat Cooper.

Pip eyed him carefully and changed the subject. "Got a load of express this trip. No gold. Big load o' mail," Pip declared. "And eleven passengers." He motioned toward the two men climbing down from the coach's roof and spat, admiring the thickness of it.

Deed didn't think either man was armed.

"Can ya believe it, I've even got one o' them spirit guys on board."

Deed watched the passengers head for the station. "A spiritualist?"

"Yeah. You know, hears ghosts and makes them write stuff on magic slates . . . ring bells an' sech," Pip spat again and nearly hit his own boot. "Scary pecker, if ya ask me."

"That him?" Deed nodded toward a well-dressed man in a black broadcloth suit with a scarlet scarf around his neck.

The man's handsome face was accented with a black goatee. His dark eyes seemed to take in everything and his smile looked like he had a secret worth laughing about. Beside the man was a woman of undeterminable age, wearing a veil attached to a triangular black hat. Her dress was also black and flowing and she carried a large purse as if it contained something sacred. The man glanced at Deed, Billy, and Pip as he strode toward the station. The woman only looked ahead.

"Yeah, that's him. Longstreet, I think. Like the Rebel general. No relation. I asked him," Pip said and rolled his neck to relieve the stiffness. "Heard him asking about Mrs. Forsyth here." He rolled the wad around in his mouth. "The word's out 'bout her dead husband, ya know. He wanted to know all 'bout it."

"Excuse me, Pip," Deed said. "Billy, can you handle the team? I'm going to make sure he doesn't bother her."

"*Sí.*"

Scratching his beard, Pip watched Deed hurry to the station. He turned to Billy. "Hear tell he's a heller with a gun—or his fists."

"*Sí.* He save many life when Comanche attack stage. He and a man name of Hannah. James Hannah." The

one-eyed Mexican glanced at the fast-walking Deed.
"Last night, Deed kill three Comanche who try to steal
our hosses. I kill one."

Pip shook his head in admiration. "What happened
to his right hand? Looks all black and blue."

"A Comanche hit him with tomahawk." Billy swallowed. "Señor Deed kill him with bare hands."

"Lordy." Pip watched Deed. "Did you say James
Hannah? Everybody knows that name. He's supposed
to be meaner than Hardin."

"*Sí*, it is so."

"Is this Deed feller that good, too?"

"*Sí.*"

"Damn." Pip spat a long, brown stream, admiring its
strength. "Say is he any relation to that Rebel outlaw,
Holt Corrigan? A bad one, I hear."

"Maybe so. He no talk of it. I no ask."

"Sure."

Deed hurried to the station, adjusting the gun in
his waistband. Cooper bounded ahead of him. He
wasn't particularly good with a gun left handed, but
he couldn't even grip one with his right. He stepped
inside, allowing the dog to enter first, and saw Longstreet talking to Atlee and Olivia as they served the
other passengers. Hermann Beinrigt had moved to
the sofa and was sitting up. The spiritualist's assistant
stood near Longstreet as if she were attached.

"Mrs. Forsyth, your late husband, Caleb, has been
trying to reach you," Longstreet declared in a silky
voice. "Have you heard any strange sounds at night?
Or felt a soft breeze that shouldn't be there? That was
your beloved . . . Caleb," he oozed. "I know because
he has come to me . . . for help. I am Eugene Longstreet, noted spiritualist and mesmerist. Many have

found spiritualism to be quite comforting in such an awful time of grief." He paused and motioned toward his assistant. "And this is Amenmeit, my assistant. She comes from Egypt and is schooled in the science of the otherworld."

Olivia appeared annoyed. Atlee's face was unreadable.

Deed stepped between the women and Longstreet. "Mister, please take a seat. Mrs. Forsyth is busy."

The look from the mesmerist was one of pure hatred. "I am sharing something personal and very important to Mrs. Forsyth. Please leave us alone."

"I can handle this, Mr. Corrigan. Is the new team ready?" Atlee's voice was stern.

Deed nodded and left, hearing Longstreet say, "Not everyone understands what it's like to lose a loved one. Or to learn that one can actually communicate with him again. I can arrange to stay over and conduct a special séance for you. My work in El Paso won't begin until next week."

Angry, Deed went outside where Pip and Billy were finishing with the harnessing of the new team. Cooper was inspecting something in the kitchen and didn't make the retreat in time to follow.

"Did that ghost hombre go at her?" Pip asked and spat.

"Said she could handle it."

Pip spat again. "Wanna bet that bastard stays over?"

"Mucho bad," Billy said.

"None of my business." Deed patted the lead horse's neck with his left hand. "You ready to go?"

"Whenever. I'd like to grab some of Mrs. Forsyth's good stew real quick," Pip said.

"Go on. I'll help Billy."

Pip nodded, spat, and headed for the station.

Inside, Longstreet continued, "Your husband wants me to tell you how proud he is of you—and of Benjamin. He misses you and—"

"Excuse me. Mr. Longstreet, isn't it? But we must take care of our guests," Atlee declared, moving past the mesmerist. "Olivia, will you begin pouring coffee please? Thank you." She turned toward Longstreet. "If you want to eat before the stage leaves, I would suggest you sit down."

Amenmeit's only response was a disgusted snort. She turned and walked out, leaving Longstreet alone with the two women.

"If it pleases you, Mrs. Forsyth, my assistant and I could sleep there." Longstreet's smile was waxen and his eyes sought hers as he pointed to the cots set aside for coach employees, now used by the Beinrigts.

Atlee stopped, holding a large bowl of biscuits. "Mr. Longstreet, I guess I need to be more clear. I have no interest whatsoever in your nonsense. You are a guest here as all passengers are. If you want to eat something, please sit down. If not, please leave."

Longstreet appeared stunned for a moment. Atlee thought he was going to burst into a rage, but he forced himself to calm.

"As you wish, I will tell your husband that you have no interest in talking to him." He made a dramatic turn toward the door, hesitating and expecting to be stopped.

"Do make sure *die Tür ist* shut ven you leave," Olivia Beinrigt growled.

Outside, Amenmeit walked up to the coach, looking for Deed. She walked over to him, standing close. "There are spirits around you. They speak of danger.

You are a dangerous man, they say. Your own spirit carries something of the Orient."

"Well, good day to you, too, ma'am," Deed responded and continued checking the harness.

"I will tell the Great Longstreet that you are not one to be bothered. There is much death around you."

"Tell *Great* anything you want"—Deed leaned his outstretched hand against the coach—"but if he messes anymore with Mrs. Forsyth and her children, he's going to have to answer to me." He glared at her. "He won't like that outcome."

She blinked and stepped closer, letting her bosom brush against his extended right arm. "I was hoping we could be together tonight." She batted her thick eyelashes. "Amenmeit will make you very happy."

"You aren't worried about all those ghosts around me?" Deed grinned.

"You mock Amenmeit."

"You catch on fast," he said and stepped past her. "Excuse me, but the ghosts and I have work to do."

Her eyes flashed hatred as he brushed past.

"Billy, have you double-checked the back boot?" Deed spun around and strode toward the rear of the coach.

"No. I have not, Señor Deed. I will."

With her hands on her hips, the dark-skinned woman snarled, "Deed Corrigan, you will die a horrible death. I can see it." A savage statement of foreign words followed.

Deed didn't respond as he double-checked the harness.

From the station, a disgruntled Longstreet appeared, walking toward the coach. Amenmeit went to him and spoke angrily, pointing and waving. The spiritualist glanced up at Deed several times. Finished with the new team and checking the coach, Deed and Billy walked toward the corral, paying no attention to either of them.

Puffing out his chest, Longstreet said something to her and headed toward Deed, now leaning against the corral. Deed watched him advance and decided he wasn't going to wait for the spiritualist to perform. He stood straight, waiting. A look of surprise popped into Longstreet's eyes as he realized this strange man was definitely not going to avoid him. He had counted on his fiery advance to make Deed go elsewhere to avoid contact.

Fifteen feet from Longstreet, Deed stepped closer and growled, "Ghost-man, this isn't one of your night shenanigans. If you want to face me, you're going to join your ghosts. Here and now. Your choice. Make it."

Longstreet shivered visibly, then turned around, shouting more loudly than necessary, "Let's get in the coach, Amenmeit. We need to get to El Paso as soon as possible."

"Good idea. More ghosts there. And gullible folks," Deed snapped, watching the mesmerist retreat.

Longstreet's strange assistant started to respond; her eyes blinked rapidly but she decided to enter the coach instead. Longstreet followed, mumbling under his breath. Behind them came the other passengers, talking among themselves about the good food.

As Deed stepped away from the corral, Blue rode into the open area on a tall bay and trailing a handsome sorrel stallion and a buckskin packhorse on lead-ropes. He was weary from his long ride from El Paso, but happy to see his brother.

"Hey, Blue, you're back," Deed yelled. "How'd it go?"

Reining up, Blue told him about the attempted holdup; Rebecca Tuttle being stood up; James Hannah's meeting with Agon Bordner; meeting briefly with Holt; and their outlaw brother's assessment of the fat man's intentions.

Deed glanced around, "So James Hannah is now working for Bordner. How about that."

"Probably, but I don't know that for a fact," Blue said, swinging slowly from his horse. His legs felt like they wouldn't support him. He stood beside the tired horse he'd been riding, leaning slightly against the animal. Beside it, the sorrel and buckskin were sweating lightly and the stallion looked ready to run. "Last time I saw Hannah, he was strolling across the restaurant to see Bordner—in a back room."

Blue patted the bay horse he had been riding and changed the subject. "How're things going here? What happened to your hand, Deed?"

In a few short sentences, Deed told his older brother how things were going at the relay station, complimenting Atlee on her attitude and determination. He briefly mentioned the raid on the horses and dismissed his hurt hand as not much.

Blue guided his three horses to the water trough with the reins and the lead-ropes in his right hand. Their conversation was interrupted by Pip Mateau, who came out of the relay station and yelled the stage was leaving. With only a nod to the two brothers, he climbed onto the driver's box, unwrapped the reins, and yelled again.

"Everyone's in, Pip," Deed assured him. "Including the ghost man . . . and his whatever."

Pip Mateau laughed, waved, and shouted a good-bye. With a vigorous spit toward his horses, the bearded driver snapped the reins and the horses began to gallop.

After the stage left, Deed walked over to the drinking sorrel and patted its back. "How is this big rascal? Did you ride him?"

"Oh yeah. Handles good. A little headstrong. Probably could run all day," Blue said, from the other side of the sorrel, "He'll be a hit with our mares."

"Reckon so. What's his name?"

"Magnuson called him Captain."

"Captain. I like it."

Blue told Deed that he had gold certificates for two hundred dollars for him from the stage-line, a reward for fighting off the Comanches. He told about Hannah's demands and his surprise that the manager had complied.

"Good, we can put that to good use at the ranch," Deed said, slapping his brother on the back. "You can buy something nice for Bina, too."

"Already did."

"All right, big brother." Deed smiled, took off his hat, and wiped his forehead with his single forearm, then returned the hat.

He suggested they take the horses to the barn for rubdowns and some oats while they talked. Billy passed them, holding a broken piece of harness and talking furiously in Spanish. Inside, Blue took off the heavy saddle and saddle blanket and began to rub the livery horse's back with his fist full of straw. The horses chewed on hay while the brothers groomed them. Deed loosened the pack on the buckskin's back and placed the canvas arrangement on the ground, using mostly his left hand, with his right only for balance. The weight was still painful. With a currycomb and brush, he started brushing the quiet horse.

"Man, that is one fine looking animal," Deed praised.

"Yeah, thought so, too. Magnuson said he's pretty gentle for a stallion," Blue said, turning away from rubbing the livery horse.

"Did you talk to the district manager . . . about here?" Deed asked as he worked.

"Yeah. Willard Epson didn't sound like a man who was comfortable with the idea of a woman station manager," Blue said, shaking his head. "I told him to keep his mind open. That this was his best station. And it wasn't because the horses were harnessed correctly. Or given good rubdowns."

"Couldn't have said it better, big brother."

"I'd expect him to make a surprise visit soon. To see for himself."

"Tell her that."

They finished cleaning the horses and left them enjoying buckets of oats. At the doorway to the station, Atlee Forsyth stepped onto the porch, hailed Blue's arrival, and invited him in.

"Had anything to eat today?" Deed asked. "This is when we usually do. After the coach leaves."

"Coffee and jerky this morning on the trail. You saw my pack, getting thin."

"Then you're ready for some good chow. Atlee's one fine cook."

"Atlee?" Blue cocked his head.

"Uh, Mrs. Forsyth. She asked to be called by her first name."

"Sure."

They took a few steps toward the house and Blue asked, "Are you going to be able to leave here now?"

Deed stared at the house for a moment before responding. "Got no choice. You and Silka are going to need help."

"Yeah. You're right," Blue said. "Does . . . Atlee know?"

"I'm sure she's guessed. It was just supposed to be until you got back from El Paso."

As they entered the station, Billy went directly to sit down. Deed and Blue went to the smiling young woman. "Atlee, you remember my older brother, Blue."

"Of course, I do," she said and smiled. "How did the trip to El Paso go? Well, I trust."

Blue was surprised to see how fresh and happy Atlee appeared. Olivia Beinrigt was in the kitchen, humming a tune only she and her husband knew. Even Hermann Beinrigt was looking definitely improved and stood, stoking the fireplace. Cooper watched the German farmer for a few moments, then trotted over to greet the Corrigan brothers. Blue noticed that Benjamin was not around and decided not to tell her about the attempted holdup. There was no need to burden her with such news.

"It went fine, ma'am. Thanks for asking." Blue removed his hat. "I did talk with Mr. Epson for a few minutes." He added, "After Tade Balkins told him about the Indian trouble here."

"I see." Her response was cool, but not quizzical.

Folding his arms, Blue told her about the exchange, making no attempt to whitewash the district manager's remarks, but added that he thought Epson would make a surprise visit soon—and before making any judgment.

She smiled. "We're ready. Anytime."

Motioning toward the table, she changed the subject. "Please sit down, Mr. Corrigan. I'm certain you're hungry."

"It does smell mighty good. And please call me Blue. I get real tense when I hear *Mister*." He looked over at Deed sitting down next to Billy. "Reckon I'm going to have a hard time getting my brother back to the ranch after all this good food."

"My name is Atlee. And Deed shot a deer several days ago. He and Billy skinned and dressed it. We're so lucky to have his help."

Blue glanced at Deed and winked.

Elizabeth hurried to get a chair next to Deed. As they gathered around the table, Atlee asked Deed if he would favor them by saying grace.

"Or course." He folded his hands and closed his eyes. "Dear Lord, thank you for this bountiful food set before us. Thank you for giving us one of your precious animals that we might be strengthened to serve you better. And bring your gentle hand upon all of us that we might have peace. In your name we ask this . . . Amen."

Blue glanced at his younger brother and smiled. It was the first time he could remember Deed saying grace since they were youngsters. Deed smiled back.

Dishes were quickly passed and the group began to eat. Little conversation passed among them. From the kitchen, the young boy appeared. Both Blue and Deed watched him from the corner of their eyes. It was Deed who spoke first.

"Benjamin, after we eat, I'd sure like to get your opinion on one of the coach horses if you've got the time. Leg problem." He paused and added, "And I'd like you to see the new stallion my brother just bought in El Paso. He's a fine one."

Without waiting for a response, Deed turned to his brother beside him. "This young man has a real eye for horses, Blue. Learned from his pa, I reckon."

Licking his lips, Benjamin responded, "I have chores." There was no emotion in his eyes or his words.

Atlee brought a cup of coffee to her mouth and paused. "Olivia and I will do just fine, Benjamin. You go on ahead and help . . . Deed." She sipped her coffee and returned the cup to the table.

Benjamin said nothing, but sat down at the empty chair next to his mother. Atlee filled his plate without asking what he wanted.

"I'm not hungry," Benjamin declared. "You know my pa used to shoot deer for us all the time."

"I'm sure he did," Blue said.

"It's no big deal like my ma is trying to make it."

Atlee's eyes flashed. "That's enough, son. Deed has been gracious enough to help us for a few days. Till we get everything settled again."

"We don't need no help."

Deed's eyes met Blue's, then he turned toward the boy. "I'm sure you don't. Anyway, I'll be leaving with my brother in the next day or so. We've got work to do on our ranch."

The look on Atlee's face was a mixture of sadness and anger. She wiped her mouth with a napkin to hide her emotions. She intended to ask the Beinrigts to stay, but hadn't done so yet, telling herself that Hermann needed to recover more. And, therefore, she needed Deed to continue helping she had told herself.

It was Olivia who spoke first, "Herr Corrigan, you vill be missed. Much, I think. You are needed here a little longer. *Ja.*"

Atlee coughed and regained her composure. "We all knew he couldn't stay long. We have been most fortunate to have . . . his help this long."

Elizabeth looked at Deed with a face that was close to tears. "Y-You c-can't go."

Placing his coffee cup back on the table, Blue studied Atlee's tortured face and knew what had to happen.

"Deed, I think you need to stay here another week or so. At least until Epson makes his inspection." He rubbed his chin. "I'll go on to the ranch."

CHAPTER FIFTEEN

Blue Corrigan rode away from the stage station, happy he had convinced his younger brother to stay. It hadn't been hard, but Deed needed a reason. A reason other than spending more time near Atlee Forsyth.

He swung the big bay past the line of cottonwoods, down a brush-guarded wash, past a whitened buffalo skull and headed toward their ranch. On a long lead-rope tied to his saddle horn, trotted the sorrel stallion and packhorse behind him. It would be good to get home to Bina and their children, five-year-old Mary Jo and three-year-old Matthew. He missed them sorely and wondered how Jeremy was adjusting.

Obviously, his brother had feelings for the young widow. And she for him. There was energy between them that they couldn't express. It was too soon, way too soon. He just hoped Deed wouldn't be hurt emotionally. Sometimes, though, that couldn't be helped with things of the heart. Maybe he should have told Deed that she needed time. A lot of it. No, Deed would have just gotten angry at the idea that he cared about her. Blue eased his horses out of the wash, across a long grassy draw, and past an undercut bank that protected the remains of an old campfire. A startled antelope bounded away, disappearing over the rolling hill.

The sky was cloudless with the beginnings of fall's crispness in the air. On patrol, an eagle flew crossing patterns high above. As Blue rode, his mind wandered to his small church and being glad to return to the pulpit. It felt right there. Not that he thought he was a gifted speaker, rather that he could offer words that would sometimes help and comfort. Words that came from God, he thought. He had been working on a return sermon based on the idea about how a person responds to receiving a few coins he or she didn't expect, as was the case with Rebecca Tuttle. How this simple blessing could be seen in many other forms of living. His mother had talked often about the need for happiness in a person's life and the ability to find it in everyday things. She thought the power of self-control was the way to true happiness. She believed that little miracles happened all the time but, for the most part, people didn't see or appreciate them. Of course, she also saw good and bad luck omens in all manner of occurrences. Holt reminded him of their mother in that respect.

Turning sharply out of the draw, he picked up the trail that led to Wilkon and, after a half mile, turned to the right, across flat grasslands toward their ranch. Passing a gentle slope that ended in a shelf of rock, his thoughts also took in the attack on the Bar 3 ranch and the murders of the Merefords and Hansons after they left. People would be on edge, worried about Comanches attacking again. From the pulpit, he should speak reassuringly about being prepared, about praying, about working together and that this awfulness would also pass. Yes, he must do that. Maybe he should tell his parishioners about the attack on the stagecoach so they would understand that he knew what he was talking about. It might sound like bragging, but Deed—and James Hannah—had saved lives.

He wasn't ready yet to pronounce that Agon Bordner was behind the tragedy. He struggled with that thought; Holt wasn't one to overstate issues, but he was the brother who saw evil everywhere, especially Yankee evil.

Craggy sandstone hills lay ahead and to his right, a lonely caprock that had marked this trail for centuries, he guessed. The slopes didn't look high enough to hide anything, but Blue knew they could keep an entire war party out of sight until they wanted to be seen. He eased his horses down a draw flanked by brush and mesquite on both sides. Not far was a muddy stream flanked by pecan, live oak, and cottonwood trees.

Blue's mind drifted back to Agon Bordner and what he had done. It was still hard to believe the man had made the killings and takeovers occur. Both Holt and Deed were positive he had, but they were always inclined to question and challenge. Holt had been quite firm about what he heard from some of Bordner's men. It didn't sound like one of Holt's pronouncements about Yankee maliciousness.

Riding out of the draw, he forced himself to pay attention to his surroundings. He had been riding for over two hours without actually being aware of where he was going. That was a good way to ride into serious trouble, especially with the possibility of Comanches around. Ahead, the muddy creek had gotten deeper and ran smoother, parallel to the trail. He pulled his horse toward the relief and the big sorrel and buckskin followed, balking initially at the tug of the leadropes. The stallion didn't like being led; it wanted to lead. A small hollow had once been a buffalo wallow.

Swinging down, he led the horses to the trickling water and let the animals nuzzle its coolness. After tying the reins to a low-hanging branch and the leadropes to another, he squatted against a large rock to rest for a few minutes. The ride from El Paso had been long and hard.

A twinge came to the stub of Blue's left arm, as if his limb was yet there and his arm was simply aching from overuse. His mind spun away to that awful day when his Confederate cavalry successfully attacked a larger, entrenched Union force. As he had swung his sweating horse toward retreating Federal troopers, a howitzer shell exploded near him, killing his horse and tearing up his arm.

He rarely allowed himself to think of that time. It served no purpose. Even in his shell-shocked memories, he recalled Holt coming to him and yelling for a medic. He recalled Holt cursing at himself for not picking up a black feather laying on the ground and sticking it upright. Not doing so was what had caused Blue's injury. His outlaw brother had remained with him at a field hospital, returning to duty only after the threat of court-martial. A month later, General Robert E. Lee surrendered. Blue saw Holt only briefly, trying to get him to return to their ranch with him. Soon stories of Holt Corrigan were popping up in

Texas, about bank and stagecoach robberies, even Union paymaster wagons.

He shuddered and returned to the present, but only momentarily as his thoughts spun to his younger brother. Silka had taught Deed how to deal with an enemy who puts a gun to his ribs, a different situation than when a gun is presented to one's back. In one split-second motion, Deed learned to pivot to his left, wrapping the enemy's right wrist with his left arm, and smashing his elbow into the man's face. Keeping control of the man's wrist, Deed would then grab the top of the gun barrel and push the gun away from his own body. Silka liked to end this movement with a grab of the man's throat or by driving one's fist into the attacker's chest. So did Deed.

Silka's teaching had been thorough. Deed could handle any kind of attack, from a headlock to an attempted hip throw, from a choke hold from behind to an overhead club attack. From a gun pointed at him to a bear hug. From a knife attack to a well-thrown haymaker. All moves and their responses were second nature to Deed. The former samurai's fighting techniques were difficult to master, but Deed had been driven to be as good as his teacher and friend.

Possibly, it was because he was the youngest of three brothers. Possibly it was another reason. Regardless, Deed Corrigan was becoming as well-known as Holt, but for different reasons.

"Sun, moon, mountain, river. All divine," he repeated one of Silka's favorite sayings. "Skills . . . and inspiration . . . necessary to develop self, also divine."

He drank from the stream and chewed on a piece of jerky. His thoughts wandered to James Hannah and his likely relationship with Agon Bordner. What would happen? Would Hannah accept Bordner's offer, whatever it was? If Bordner was planning on taking over all of this part of Texas, what would he want Hannah to do? If Bordner was behind the attack on the Bar 3, then he obviously had a gang of men hidden somewhere. Where? Blue didn't know. His thoughts went to his family and he shivered. Deed was an exceptional fighter whose natural instincts and skills had been honed by Silka's teaching. He and Holt had learned much as well, but it was Deed who had become special.

He spoke the answer to what Hannah would be hired to do, as if delivering a sermon. "James Hannah will be hired to kill Deed. Bordner will figure his own men can handle the rest of us."

For a moment, he didn't move. He couldn't. How could this be? Was Agon Bordner such an evil man? He wished Holt was back with them again, but that wasn't going to happen; Holt had made that clear. He had crossed the line from Confederate soldier to bitter guerrilla fighter to outlaw. He had decided it was best that he stay away. Wherever *away* was.

Bina's gentle face came to his mind. Her image was always close. She had been his wife for five years and theirs was love at first sight. A Mescalero Apache educated by missionaries, she was a compassionate woman, as well as a spiritual teacher in her own way. Being with her made him whole. She loved to sit on their porch at dusk and watch the birds flit around the land. A bird feeder had been one of her earliest requests. It was the only request he could recall. In some ways, she reminded him of his late mother. When he was little, he thought his mother could actually talk to the birds and hoped that one day he would be able to do that.

What would Bina say about Agon Bordner? Or James Hannah? She would tell him to wait, but to be ready. Yes, that's what she would say.

Blue shut his eyes and prayed.

His mother had believed in daily meditation, but never insisted that her sons do the same. She felt every person was his or her own master. No person should interfere with another person's search for identity of purpose. Bina said much the same thing.

No answer came from his prayer, except they must be prepared for this unthinkable action. Maybe that was the answer. Deed had told him about the Rangers coming to Wilkon, but it was unrealistic to think they would be able to stop a massive takeover . . . at least, until it was too late. A stray thought entered his mind: have a meeting with the Sanchezes, the family that owned the Lazy S.

Yes, that made good sense. Together, they could plan how to survive any further advance by Bordner.

Overhead, a hawk surveyed the land, moving across bundles of white clouds and dipping toward something unseen. Blue took another swig from the stream and thought again about Bina. Her English was quite good and he knew some Apache. Bina's faith was fascinating, believing that man was connected to all animals, all insects, all plants, all rocks and minerals. A oneness with the world. A giant circle of the spirit. That had been his mother's belief as well. Occasionally, he wondered if she had been an Indian or had such a bloodline. None of the brothers knew anything about their grandparents, only that they had lived in Ohio and died there.

His wife had actually taught him much about the power of the Great Spirit and the directing of its great force, the energy of the universe, to heal and guide. That every being had an identity and a purpose. To live up to this purpose required the power of self-control, which brought true happiness. He had used some of her beliefs in sermons, like "One cannot be taught until one tries to learn" or "Nothing is free; everything has a cost." And the thought he liked best was "Enjoy the world. Do not let the world enjoy you."

She had told him that often more than one spirit occupied a body, and when that happened, the person was torn between doing good and bad and would then be different personalities at different times. Only a special ceremony could drive out the bad spirit. It reminded him of the Bible stories about Jesus forcing demons out of a person.

Of course, Bina also believed if someone stepped on a black bug, it would rain. He chuckled at the thought. It was more like something Holt would say. But it was part of the Apache belief that humans were connected to the circle of all life, all animals, all plants, the sky, the earth, the winds. Not above it or in its center, just another part of the great circle.

Her name meant "musical instrument" in Apache and Blue thought it was a most appropriate name. She told Blue that he should answer to only one authority, the Great Spirit. To Blue, it seemed like Bina had come from some faraway place, and yet most of her thoughts were very practical. Their love was deep, in spite of the difference in race—and the anger it caused among some of both races. They had met on the

reservation, a planned Christian gathering, and that
had begun a serious courtship.

Most of his friends were aghast at the idea of his
being with an Indian; some townspeople couldn't believe he would possibly think of taking a savage into
his home. He didn't care; he wanted to be with her—
forever. Even now, there were people in Wilkon who
looked at her, at them, with disgust. He managed to
forgive their ignorance most of the time. Interestingly
enough, the Sanchezes had greeted her warmly.
Maybe it was because they, too, felt the sting of racial
prejudice.

There was one woman who came up to him after a
church service and told him that he was going to hell
for living with an Apache woman. Bina had laughed
when he related the incident to her and told him that
they both should pray for the woman.

"I miss you, Bina," he whispered.

The sorrel snorted and Blue immediately became
alert. This was not country in which to assume one
was safe. He stood and walked to the horses, lifting
his Winchester from its saddle scabbard and cocking
it one-handed into readiness by pushing the stock
against his upper leg for leverage. Nothing troubling
was in sight and the horses were grazing again. Gradually, his thoughts returned to Deed. Dedrick William
Corrigan was his full name but everyone called him
Deed, except their mother. Holt's birth name was
Holton Jefferson Corrigan, their mother's father's
name. His own birth name was Bluemont Wade Corrigan, a combination of their father's and their paternal
grandfather's names. *Bluemont* had brought more than

his share of fistfights in school, but his brothers had always been eager to step in and turn things around.

Uncocking the rifle, he returned it to the scabbard and lifted himself into his saddle. Grabbing the lead-ropes of the sorrel and the packhorse, he eased into a lope. Soon he was into broken country that became rolling plains. Cattle country. If Agon Bordner thought it would be easy taking control of the LC ranch by killing Deed, he was seriously underestimating Silka. And himself. And Bina.

Ahead were six grazing cattle. LC steers. He reined toward the animals and got them moving. This wasn't LC land; it was pasture filed on by the Lazy S and recognized as theirs. Certainly there was no need to cause problems with Felix Sanchez and his family. The Sanchezes had owned the ranch for three generations. Next to the Bar 3, it was the biggest ranch in the region.

The six steers trotted in front of him, eager to get away from his presence. Finally, they curled off into a wide spoon of land that was the beginning of LC pasture and he let them go. The sorrel snorted as if wanting to chase them.

"It's all right, Captain. They're home. So are you," he said.

Blue Corrigan rode into the LC ranch yard, happy to return. A number of sturdy buildings comprised the ranch. Two large barns held their best horses and three milk cows, as well as serving as the storage area for feed. The ranch yard also featured two corrals, a bunkhouse, and a small cooling house for meat and butter. Farther to the south was a well that provided water all year round and an empty bunkhouse. Outside the barns was a small toolshed. The main house had a separate wing built so that Silka and Deed could live separately from Blue and his family, giving them all their privacy. Another bedroom had been kept for Holt; Deed had insisted on it. The additions gave the house a strange, bulging appearance, but no one seemed to mind.

The ranch was a good one, thanks in large part to their parents' careful selection of the land. Three protected valleys were rich in grass and water. Springs dotted the area, coupled with a healthy stream that cut across two of their main grazing areas. Five thousand head of cattle and a string of mustangs were spread throughout their acres—acres that were owned by them, truly owned with all of the necessary ownership files. Their third valley had been bought from another ranch just after the war and it, along with the other two valleys, gave them a fine operation. The herds were shifted from one valley to another as needed. Blunt hills and long benches offered natural fencing to keep the animals from drifting.

The ranch itself lay in one of the valleys with a well-built two-story ranch house featuring a porch and a second-story balcony. Silka had directed the construction of this large house after the war; most of it was built by Blue and Deed. The one-armed rancher surveyed the ranch and took satisfaction in its appearance; they had painted all the buildings a year ago.

Three ranch dogs barked an alert and the stallion pawed the ground and flattened its ears. An Oriental man came to the door of the main house. His hand shielded the sun from his face. In his other hand was a rifle.

"Afternoon, Silka," Blue yelled as he walked his horses toward the house.

Silka's face lit up in recognition and he waved back. A smile cut across his flat face and he shouted, "*Konnichiwa!*"

Returning the Japanese greeting with gusto, Blue swung down and flipped the reins over the hitchrail in front of the wood-planked porch, then tied the lead-ropes to the rack. He left the pack alone except to retrieve a wrapped package.

"Where Deed?" Silka eased onto the porch.

"Stayed at the stage station. Be there another week or so. Needs to stay until they can get someone to replace him," Blue reported. "Got any coffee on?"

"Sure, that we have. You go ahead. Bina be most glad to see you," Silka said. "I want closer look at stallion first."

"Well, he's a handsome one," Blue said, stepping inside and laying his package on the table near the door.

Hurrying from the kitchen, Bina welcomed him with a long embrace. Kissing wasn't something Apaches did, but she took to it enthusiastically on occasion. She was a bright part of the Corrigan family, with an inviting smile and warm eyes. Their house matched her personality. Warm and definitely accented in blue, her favorite color. Even the sofa was blue. A wall cabinet held a collection of small items, also mainly blue. He liked to think her emphasis on blue was because his name was the same as the color.

Over coffee, he shared what had happened at the station and in El Paso. Bina offered no comment about Holt, or James Hannah, or Agon Bordner, but said Jeremy Regan was asleep, as were their two children, Matthew and Mary Jo. All three had spent the morning riding with Silka.

"How is Jeremy doing?" Blue asked, sipping the strong coffee.

"Well, as good as one could expect, I think. He misses his mom and dad something fierce," she said. "But he never grumbles. I think he really likes being with Matthew—and Matthew likes him around. So does Mary Jo."

"That's good. It'll take time."

She looked up at him and smiled. "I've been thinking we should adopt him. If he's willing. Make him a part of . . . us."

"That sounds wonderful, Bina. Knew you would think of somehow helping the boy, so I got you a present in El Paso. Hope you like it." He got up and handed the wrapped brown-paper package to her.

Smiling, she opened the gift and withdrew a straw hat decorated with fake wildflowers and blue ribbons to tie under her chin to hold it place.

She stood and put it on. "Oh, Blue it's beautiful. I love it; Blue. I love you." Her kiss was an invitation.

CHAPTER SIXTEEN

Morning's cooling breezes had disappeared around the Forsyth station. Hermann Beinrigt and Billy Lee Montez had a fresh team waiting for the expected stage coming from El Paso. The horses stood in the corral, ready to be hooked up and came with Billy's usual unneeded advice. Two days ago, Tade Balkins had brought in a stage from there and told them to expect a visit from Willard Epson on the next stage. Tade liked Atlee and the way she had run the station and wanted her to stay in charge.

Deed Corrigan watched the two men. He was glad Olivia was busy helping in the kitchen because he wanted to be alone. Lately, Benjamin had been spending time with him too, usually with the horses. This morning, however, the boy was doing schoolwork as mandated by his mother.

Deed's right hand was weak so he continued to carry his Remington revolver shoved into his pants for left-hand usage. Years ago, Silka had insisted he learn to handle all weapons with either hand, so it wasn't difficult, just slower.

The young gunfighter paused at the barn door and listened to the land. Shadows had lost control and the heat of the day was increasing. But his mind wasn't on the coming day, it was time for him to get back to the ranch. Fall roundup was getting close and this autumn's effort would be more important than ever. The Bar 3, under its new ownership, would bring tension. Hopefully nothing more than that, but it wasn't likely.

The Beinrigts had agreed to stay and help Atlee. Hermann was not yet at full strength, but getting better all the time and he was eager to help. Deed knew he wasn't needed here anymore. Not really. No one said so, but he knew. Of course, he had stayed to be around when the district agent came. With the Beinrigts in place even that wasn't necessary.

He walked past the barn, scuffing his boots against the dry dirt. His spurs tried to sing, but only sounded like tinny clatter. At the gray edge of the stage station yard, a coyote appeared.

"Not today, friend," he said. "The chickens are not out yet. Go find a rabbit."

The scrawny animal disappeared.

He couldn't remember feeling so sad since his parents and little sister died. He was being a fool staying here; others may not realize it, but the only reason he remained was to be near Atlee. Just seeing her was like finding a beautiful flower in the middle of winter. He had known other women. Sally Cummins in Wilkon was quite fond of him, but he didn't care that much for her. It was silly to think about Atlee. At all. The best thing for him to do was to ride away.

Ride away. Yes, that's what he must do. He would wait for the arrivals from El Paso. If Willard Epson didn't come, he would leave anyway. It had been early spring since he last had been at the ranch, taking a herd north as the grass was turning green. That was home . . . or was it? Oh, how he would miss Elizabeth, Benjamin, Cooper . . . and Atlee. Had they become home, his real home? He shook his head to dismiss the thought.

Billy's shout brought Deed from his reverie and he wondered if the district agent would be onboard as Tade had said. He hoped Willard Epson would be agreeable, but he still had an uneasy feeling he hadn't shared with anyone. He rubbed his right hand; the injury was healing nicely. Opening and closing his right fist repeatedly forced the end of stiffness.

Out of the corner of his eye, Deed saw Atlee Forsyth standing in the doorway of the station. He figured she was wondering the same thing. Surely, the district manager would recognize her value to the stage-line. Surely. He wanted to go over and kiss her good morning, but knew that was ridiculous to even think. He glanced her way again and she smiled as if reading his mind and he blushed.

The coach banged into the station yard and the team of proud horses strutted to a stop. Billy hurried up and opened the coach door with an enthusiastic greeting, more so than usual. Had he the same feeling about the district agent being onboard?

The first passenger sitting next to the door was, indeed, Willard Epson. He turned to the woman next to him, said something, and bounded out.

As, the stout driver swung down from his seat he yelled to Billy, "Hey, Billy, the El Paso Bank was robbed.

They're saying it was the Holt Corrigan gang. Got away with over ten thousand in gold and paper. Posses are combing this part of Texas."

"Ten thousand! That is mucho."

"You betcha. The bank was holding an army pay-roll, they said," the driver declared. "Not everybody's sayin' it was Holt Corrigan though. Hell, the bank president hisself claims there's no way it was. Ain't that somethin'."

Billy glanced at Deed. The young gunfighter shrugged. He wondered if Holt had held up the bank while Blue was in town. Surely Holt wouldn't do that to his brother if he knew Blue was there.

The shotgun guard followed the driver from the stage and both headed for the station. Halfway there, the driver stopped and turned around. "Say, Mr. Epson, you're going to want to have some of Mrs. Forsyth's eatin'. Best on the line. By far."

Even if he hadn't recognized Epson from Blue's earlier description, Deed would have realized the tall, long-jawed man coming toward him in the rumpled suit and bowler that didn't quite fit his head was the district manager. Epson waved his understanding to the retreating driver, then continued to Deed.

"Mr. Deed Corrigan, I believe." Willard Epson shifted the briefcase to his left hand and extended his right. "I met your brother in El Paso. Believe he was there on some horse-buying business. I trust he gave you our check and our thanks . . . for helping drive off the Comanches." He tugged on his bowler in a nervous movement. "Thanks, too, for stepping in here. That was an awful incident."

He saw Deed extending his left hand and switched

the briefcase back to his right. He wanted to ask about Deed's right hand, but decided against it.

"Sorry about the left hand, Mr. Epson, but I sprained it . . . on some harness a few days ago," Deed lied. He didn't want to make it sound like he was vital to the station's continued protection. "Got the money and no thanks needed for my helping here. I wasn't really needed. Mrs. Forsyth runs quite an operation," Deed responded. "I assume you're here to look things over. Best you've got, I'll bet."

"Well, perhaps so, but I started out thinking I needed to have a man in charge," Epson said, his face reddening as he avoided Deed's stare. "Just wouldn't be right, you know."

"No, I don't know." Deed took a step away from Epson.

"Wait, please," Epson said, tugging on his soiled paper shirt collar and keeping his eyes on Billy as the one-eyed Mexican began to unhitch the tired horses. "On the trip all I kept hearing from the passengers was that they were looking forward to Mrs. Forsyth's station and her cooking." He licked his lips and stared at Deed. "So I thought why not? At least I should give her the chance, you know. Nobody's talking about our other stations like that. In fact, I've been thinking about making it a home station. You know, with sleeping quarters for passengers." He tried to smile. "And you'll be here . . . to help."

"Actually, Hermann Beinrigt is taking my place. Olivia, his wife, has been an important addition as well," Deed said. "Hermann really knows his way around horses. Been doing a lot of work." Deed motioned toward the barn. "He's over there now. With the new team."

"Really? Where are they staying?"

Deed explained and hoped he hadn't made a mistake in telling Epson of the change.

"Well, good, I look forward to meeting them," Epson said. He wanted to add that he was relieved that a Corrigan wasn't going to be around the station—it made him uneasy with the reputation of the outlaw Holt Corrigan—but didn't dare express the thought. After all, *this* Deed Corrigan was a known gunfighter.

"Good. Both are helping serve now, I believe," Deed said. "That's very good news about making this a home station. Mrs. Forsyth will be pleased." He grinned. "Guess I won't need that buckboard after all."

"Buckboard? I don't understand."

"Well, if you decided the station needed a man running it," Deed said, "All of us would have been riding out of here within the hour, headed for my ranch."

Epson's jaw dropped and then he began to chuckle. "That's blackmail, Mr. Corrigan."

"No. That would have been justice."

"Good enough. I'd better go see Mrs. Forsyth," Epson said. "I'll be needing a place to sleep until the inbound stage comes tomorrow."

The rest of the day was a blur at the excitement of Epson's announcement. For Deed, it was bittersweet. It was time to leave.

Early the next morning, he was saddling his buckskin gelding when Benjamin walked into the stable.

"Where ya goin', Deed?" he asked with his hands in his pockets and a hard look on his face.

"Mornin', Benjamin. I'll be heading for my ranch, son," Deed said, knowing this was part of leaving he wasn't going to like.

"You're leavin' . . . us? Well, it figures. Never wanted you here anyway. No way you could replace my pa."

"Wasn't trying to replace your pa. Just wanted to help. Make sure the station stayed up and running. Now Hermann and Olivia will be helping your mother," Deed said, tightening the cinch. "And I've got work to do on my ranch. Roundup's coming."

"I-I thought you liked us. Especially Elizabeth, Ma, and Cooper. Maybe not me because of the way I acted but—" The boy's eyes were reddening.

Deed turned toward him. "I do like you, a lot, Benjamin. You. Your sister. Your mother. Cooper. All of you. But I can't stay."

"Well, like I said, I shoulda known you'd leave."

Deed took a step toward the boy. "Hey, wait a minute, fella. I didn't say I wouldn't be back." He paused and added, "I was going to ask your mother if you could join us for the roundup. You can stay with me at the ranch."

Benjamin looked at Deed suspiciously. "You mean it . . . or are you just saying that?"

"No, I mean it. Really. But your ma will have to say it's all right."

"Let's go ask her!"

Benjamin leaped forward and, for the first time since Deed arrived, hugged him. Deed caught and enveloped the boy in his arms.

Then stepping back and letting him down with his hands on Benjamin's shoulders, Deed said, "You'll be a good addition to our roundup. You're a smart, hard worker and you know horses."

"You won't be sorry. But I am sorry for the way I've been acting. I wanted to be Ma's man."

"You are and always will be. Nothing will change that. Now let's go talk with your mother before I ride."

They walked together toward the station, chatting easily. Atlee was standing in the doorway as they approached. Fifteen feet behind them came Billy and Hermann, having just fed the horses.

"I was just going to call you all in for breakfast," she said and smiled. "Should have plenty of time to eat before today's stage gets here."

Benjamin jumped onto the porch, barely able to contain his excitement. "Ma, Deed wants me to come to his ranch for the roundup. I can, can't I?"

Atlee tried not to look startled at the change in Benjamin and covered it with the question, "What about your schoolwork?"

The boy frowned momentarily, then said, "I'll get it done before I go, I promise."

Stepping up beside him, Deed put his arm on Benjamin's shoulder. "I should've said something to you first."

Her eyebrows raised. "Where are you going?"

He tried to smile, but couldn't. "Heading for the ranch. You don't need me here any longer. You got great news from Epson." He glanced toward Billy and Hermann walking toward them.

"I see."

"Ma, can I? Can I? Please!"

Her eyes left Deed's face and focused on her son. "Yes, you can. If you get all your schoolwork done and Mr. Corrigan wants you."

"He'll be a good help, I'm sure," Deed said, avoiding her returned gaze. "Be a good experience for him, too."

"Certainly. What about Elizabeth?" Atlee motioned

toward the kitchen. "She'll be heartbroken to hear you're leaving and coming back for Benjamin."

Deed grimaced. He hadn't thought of that.

Crossing her arms, Atlee told her son to wash his hands and face, then asked Deed if it would be possible that Elizabeth could go and play with Blue's children for the same days that Benjamin was on the roundup with him.

"Oh, that's a great idea!" Deed said. "We've got plenty of room and Blue's kids would like having Elizabeth to play with!" He was aware she had taken a step closer to him and had the feeling she was going to say something else, but didn't.

"It's settled then," she said finally and reached out to touch his arm. "Come and eat before you go. Mr. Epson's already at the table."

"I'm not surprised. He made a smart decision yesterday. Congratulations!"

Atlee smiled, withdrew her hand to push back a stray lock of hair that had escaped from her tight bun. "He told me you were going to take all of us away from here if he didn't give me the job."

"Well, I might've said something like that." Deed rubbed his chin and watched Benjamin hurry past them and into the station.

Atlee smiled. "That is so like you, Deed. Very kind." She looked into his face. "Would you really have done that?"

He could feel redness crawling up his neck. "Yes. I would have, if you'd have come." He looked back at her. "I'm sorry about not asking you about Benjamin earlier. He saw me saddling up and was upset. It just sorta came to me."

"Of course he was upset. Though he didn't show it,

I think he was starting to change his feelings about you. You mean a lot to him. To both children."

"Losing your pa is rough for a whole family, but for a boy it is especially so because he feels he has to become the man of the house. I was lucky. I had two older brothers and Silka to be the men of the house."

Glancing toward the washstand, Deed saw Billy and Hermann. Not looking at her, he said, "I'll wash up and be in. Be good to hit the trail with a full stomach."

Atlee's voice was crisp. "Did you plan on riding out without even saying good-bye?"

"Well, no. No. I wouldn't have done that."

"I would hope not." She touched his arm again. "You know you're an important part of . . . this family."

Billy and Hermann joined them on the porch and exchanged morning pleasantries, mostly about the weather. Neither man was aware Deed planned on leaving and both were upset by the news.

"*Ich bin nicht* zo strong yet," Hermann Beinrigt declared, waving his arms. "Ve be needing *du. Ja.*"

Billy blurted something that was mostly Spanish; the only word Deed caught was *Comanches.* Without waiting for Deed's response, Atlee spun and went inside.

Quietly, the young gunfighter said, "Now that Mrs. Forsyth has been given the manager's job, I need to get back to the ranch." He cocked his head. "But I'll be back. Benjamin's going to help with our roundup."

Both men thought that was a good idea as the threesome headed for the washstand. A tin basin awaited with a bucket of fresh water, a bar of soap with three bubbles bursting on its surface, and a roller towel. They washed up without talking, then entered the station. All three held their hats in their hands.

Benjamin, Elizabeth, and Willard Epson were already at the table. The fireplace was aglow with new wood and stirred ashes. Wonderful breakfast smells rushed to meet them. Even for Atlee, the breakfast was grand. Hotcakes, warm syrup, eggs, bacon, fresh biscuits, and apple-butter jam and hot coffee.

A bit of syrup stuck to his chin, Epson greeted Deed with a waving fork. "Morning, Deed. Better sit down before I eat up all the profits. I can see why everybody's raving about the food here." He stuffed a piece of pancake and egg into his mouth. "You know, even after the railroads are going again in Texas, this would be an excellent spot for a home station."

"Makes sense to me." Deed headed for the table as Billy and Hermann found chairs.

Benjamin wanted Deed to sit next to him. So did Elizabeth. He suggested the boy move over one chair so he could sit between them. Olivia came from the kitchen with a plate stacked with steaming hotcakes and a fresh pot of coffee. From the expression on her face, Deed guessed Atlee had told her that he was leaving. It aggravated him; why should he feel guilty about going to his own ranch? The only reason he had stayed this long was to be near Atlee and that was a silly reason, he told himself. The sooner he left, the better for all of them.

Olivia poured coffee into Deed's cup and leaned close to whisper in his ear, "She *ist* most upset. She cares . . . about you. You know this."

Deed forked two flapjacks, planted them on his plate, and muttered, "No, I don't know that."

Elizabeth leaned toward him and declared, "I helped make the batter for the hotcakes."

"I'll bet they're extra good," Deed said.

She beamed.

Quietly, Deed turned and told her he would be leaving for his ranch. Her face broke into sadness and tears festered in the corners of her eyes.

"Now don't cry," Deed whispered. "I'll be coming back. Benjamin's going to help with our roundup . . . and you will come with us, to play with my brother's children. It'll be lots of fun."

He took a sip of coffee and told her about Blue's children, Matthew and Mary Jo, and a visiting child, Jeremy. He didn't explain about Jeremy's reason for being there. Elizabeth's countenance brightened as he told her about the new adventure.

"We could go with you now and help," she said, wide-eyed.

Deed took another sip and told her there was much work to do before the roundup started.

"Isn't there stuff we could do?" she said.

Deed looked up and saw Atlee standing across the table, watching the exchange.

"That's enough, Elizabeth. Mr. Corrigan needs to go," she said.

The rest of the meal was mostly quiet with Billy and Hermann discussing a horse they thought should be taken out of rotation for a few days. Even Benjamin and Elizabeth were silent. Deed excused himself, thanked Atlee and Olivia and left.

He checked the cinch on his saddle, rechecked it, hoping against hope that Atlee might come to say good-bye. Finally, he swung into the saddle and nudged the bay into a smooth lope. He didn't intend to look back, but he did. Atlee was standing in the station's doorway with her hand shielding the sunlight from her face. She saw him glance in her direction and waved. He swallowed, waved back, then spurred his horse into a gallop.

The ride home was the longest and loneliest he could recall. Twice he stopped and almost turned around, but knew he couldn't. Blue and Silka needed him at the ranch; they had been most understanding to let him stay this long at the station. Atlee Forsythe was a widow, a new widow; he had no business thinking about her as he did.

CHAPTER SEVENTEEN

After a week of drunkenness and mental conflict, Holt Corrigan decided to ride for his brothers' ranch. If nothing else, he could go by Samuel Holton for the rest of his life. He told his landlord of his plan to look for work on a ranch up north and the quiet man had advised that jobs were scarce, but he had heard that Agon Bordner was hiring. Thanking him, Holt shook the man's hand and left.

First, though, he must tell his fellow ex-Confederates of his intentions. He owed them that. Purchasing a second horse from the livery, Holt bought supplies and left El Paso. The ride north was dusty, as a dry autumn settled around the land. He rode carefully, keeping away from ridges and places of possible ambush. It wasn't likely any soldiers would be out here, but the way to stay alive was to be careful all the time. At night, he kept his fires to a small hatful with no smoke and put them out as soon as his supper was finished. Once, he observed some tiny blue flames in the fire and knew it meant spirits were close. He assumed they were friendly and told them so.

Studying the barren region, he rode up to the deserted-looking cabin in the belly of a forgotten canyon well north of El Paso. Smoke twisting from the chimney told him his friends were there as planned. The nose of a rifle was evident from the corner of the lone window, then it disappeared.

"Yo, the cabin! Can I come in? Looking for some hot coffee," Holt yelled as he neared, keeping both hands in full view of the cabin's unseen occupants.

Like him, the men inside were considered outlaws. They had missed the window of amnesty by several years and by their own decisions. Now the United States Army and the Texas Rangers sought their capture.

A lanky, bearded silhouette stepped into the doorway with the heavy door creaking its objection to opening.

"Ya alone, Holt?" The silhouette hollered back. A rifle was cradled in his arms.

"Alone as always, Everett."

The silhouette was Everett Reindal, a former lieutenant in the Confederate army under Early's command. He and Holt hadn't met until after the war. Everett looked more haggard than the last time Holt had seen him, over a month ago.

Walking his bay to the cabin's hitchrail, Holt dismounted and flipped the reins around its pole and then led the packhorse to the rail and tied its leadrope to the crossbar.

"Put yer hosses in the corral out back," Everett said, motioning over his shoulder with his rifle. "That's whar ours be."

"No thanks, Everett. I'll be riding on in a bit."

"Somebody chasin' ya?"

"Not that I know of. I'm heading for my brothers' ranch."

Everett frowned. "What 'bout the El Paso Bank? Thought we was gonna hit thar next. Yeh were supposed to be checkin' it out."

Holt took off his hat and slapped it against his pants and coat to remove some of the trail dust and give him time to form an answer. There was no easy way around it, he was quitting their mad crusade, if that's what it was. When he thought about it, he realized most of them just liked stealing.

"Naw, not me. Some old Confederate friend of mine runs it," he answered and held out his hand. "Did you know Dave Copate. He was with me at Sabine Pass."

"Yer kiddin'," Everett Reindal shook Holt's hand, but his eyes sought more information.

"No. I talked to him about three weeks ago. In his bank office."

Everett looked doubtful. "Weren't he 'fraid ya'd rob him?"

"Didn't act like it. He was glad to see me." Holt returned his hat to his head and proceeded to tell that he had decided to return to ranching and get on with his life.

Everett turned toward the other unseen occupants of the cabin. "Y'all hear that? Holt's givin' up the fight."

"War's been over a long time," Holt said.

"Never thought I'd hear ya say that," Everett spat. "It ain't fer us. We're never givin' up. Nossir."

Rushing to the doorway, a grizzled man in torn Rebel pants and a misshapen hat demanded, "How do we know ya ain't got Federals trailin' ya? Go a long way to gettin' amnesty iffen they got us."

"Don't be a fool, Hoffman. You can start over today," Holt blurted. "Nobody knows what we look like. Hell, nobody even knows *your* name. The Federals only know *mine*." He folded his arms. "I came to tell you what I was going to do. You can do anything you want."

The grizzled man put his hand on the heavy gunbelt holding four revolvers. "Maybe we won't let ya go."

From the cabin, another voice called out, "Ya be a fraud, Holt Corrigan. Ya tolt us ya'd never surrender."

A fourth man in a filthy hat with the right side brim pinned to the crown limped to the doorway and waved his arms. "Come on, Holt. This hyar's only the start. France'll be comin' to he'p us real soon."

"France, Leap?" Both Everett and Holt asked at the same time.

"Yessirree. Once France gits in, we'll have the money we need for guns an' cannon . . . an' we kin drive them Yanks all the way to D.C.," the man called Leap proclaimed.

Holt looked at Everett and shook his head. Clearly Leap was insane. Everett knew it, too.

Holt took several steps off the porch and back to his bay; pulling free the lead-rope of the packhorse, he stopped and said, "My brothers need me more than you boys do. They're going up against Agon Bordner and his bunch." He pulled free the reins, stepped into the stirrup, and swung up. "You're always welcome at our table."

"Hate to see ya go, Holt," Everett Reindal said. "Ya know we might end up ridin' for Bordner. Hear tell he's payin' good money."

Leap continued outside, babbling about seeing French ships.

"If you do, don't come tellin' me about fighting for the South. You'll just be hired guns, doing bad things to good folks."

From the cabin came a loud Rebel yell and "Long live the Confederacy!"

Holt wrapped the lead-rope of his packhorse around his saddle horn and swung his horse away. He waved and kicked his horse into a gallop and the pack-horse reluctantly followed. He half expected them to shoot at him. But the only thing he heard was Everett's yell, "Ride careful, Holt Corrigan. Ride careful."

Telling his friends good-bye was the easy part, he knew. A trial, maybe several, would come next. What if he were put in prison? A shiver went through him. He trusted Blue to know what was best. He was through running and pretending to fight a war that didn't exist except in the minds of a few. Besides, he knew Agon Bordner and his gang would be going after the LC ranch. His brothers would need another gun, after that he would surrender.

Holt's mind raced into the past as he rode. Thoughts long kept locked into place came rushing out. He wondered what had happened to the silver medal he had received from Jefferson Davis for the Sabine Pass victory. There had been other battles, too many, but none so dramatic. He remembered the day the news came that Lee had surrendered to Grant. He had gone on a one-man rampage attacking Union camps, firing at anything that moved. It wasn't long before he and a handful of like-minded Rebels were holding up Union payroll wagons. That had evolved into holding up Union banks. All the time, he had told himself that they were fighting for the South. How foolish it all seemed now.

Just as foolish was the thought that the Federal army was going to let him get away with such actions. Foolish—

Nightfall came and he camped in a narrow hollow. Holt rested on a log and pushed sticks into his small fire. Behind him was a tall, crested bank that made up one side of the hollow. Not far away, his horses grazed contentedly. His small coffeepot bubbled with the heat and Holt sliced some bacon into a skillet. He was hungry and put in six slices, before rewrapping the bacon in an oilskin and returning it to his saddlebag. He grabbed a biscuit from another sack.

The bacon spat and gurgled and he took a slice, spearing it with his knife. It was too hot to eat, so he laid the meat on a flat rock and poured himself a cup of coffee. After eating the bacon and drinking down the coffee, he added a few stick to the coals and retreated once more to his saddlebags resting with his other gear. He pulled out the piece of Confederate flag, returned to the fire, and tossed the jagged cloth into the hungry flames. Standing erect, he saluted as the flag remnant turned black and gradually disappeared. Satisfied with his little ceremony ending his private war, he kicked dirt over the dying fire and doused it with the remains of his coffeepot. First, though, he put the grounds into a handkerchief. Wasting coffee grounds was something he had learned not to do.

Out of long habit, he cleaned and reloaded his revolvers and rifle, touching them with the feather from his hat. His mind flitted away, further and further. Was he seeing glimpses of another life? Were his brothers with him in another time? He was afraid of heights and believed that's how he had died in a previous life, falling from some high place or being pushed. There were times during the war when he had the strong feeling that he had been in this battle before, only with different weapons and against a different enemy.

He shook his head. At times there was great sorrow within him, a sadness that seemed to well up from somewhere else. During the war, he had heard that the actions in one life had a direct effect on the next. A person must be reborn endless times until he found the purpose God had for him. If so, what was his purpose?

Once, after a successful battle, he had run into a long-haired, wild-looking preacher who told him that the reason Mary didn't recognize Jesus at the tomb and that the disciples didn't know him on the road was that he didn't look the same because Jesus had been reincarnated. The thought had really stuck, although he never told the story to anyone.

Finally, his thoughts slid to a pretty summer day when he walked with Allison Johnson. They kissed behind the Johnson barn and she promised to wait. He rode out to enlist the next day.

He stretched out on his bedroll and tried to sleep. Maybe he should ride back and rejoin his comrades. He didn't remember going to sleep. Morning sun woke him. His resolve came with its growing warmth. His brothers, and Silka, needed his gun and his savvy.

When he walked to the dead fire, a tiny flame popped through the dirt, then another and another. He decided that was a sign he was headed in the right direction. Deciding he was hungry, he stoked the fire into full strength and grabbed the skillet and coffeepot.

A jay landed on a nearby branch and began to scold him. He decided the bird wasn't an omen, just hungry. He tossed pieces of a biscuit in the jay's direction. Immediately, it flew down and gobbled them up.

He laughed. "That's all you get, buddy." Then he tossed some more crumbs.

Satisfied, the jay returned to the branch and whistled softly.

"You're welcome."

He finished his breakfast, saddled up, and rode out, singing about goober peas. The jay followed for a few minutes before flying away.

"Well, I thought we were going to be friends," Holt muttered. "You remind me of Allison Johnson." He began to laugh. Spluttery at first, then a long bellow. It was the first time he had been able to even smile about her decision. This was going to be a good day, he decided.

CHAPTER EIGHTEEN

A lone quail fluttered from the thick brush and sought another place to hide. Seconds later, Deed Corrigan cleared the halfmoon hill rimming the southern lip of the Corrigan ranch yard. He reined up the bay and studied the busy scene below. A soft autumn breeze ran through his shoulder-length hair on its way to a row of cottonwood trees. Overhead, the sun was easing into afternoon.

Behind the house he could see the top of the old oak tree that shaded the graves of their father, mother, and sister. How long ago that seemed, almost like it was part of another life. He thought of Holt and what he would say about that, shook his head, and studied the activity. Neither of his parents' faces, nor that of his sister, came to his mind anymore. Only blurred images. Silka had become a father—guiding, teaching, caring. He touched the brass circle at his neck.

In the farthest corral, a cowboy rode a semibroke mustang, a regular fall task to turn all of their horses into good work mounts. He guessed it was Chico.

Standing next to the corral was Little Jake, waiting to take the next horse. All their horses would be needed for the fall roundup. The systematic search of the territory for cattle was hard, time-consuming, and involved the cooperation of all the ranches in the area. Or had in the past.

Not far from the corrals, another man was singeing the whiskers off a new rope over a small fire. Most likely it was Harmon. Tied to two trees was another new rope, pulled tight to get out the kinks. He smiled; ropes didn't last long around there, even when they had been waterproofed with beef tallow. Old ropes were cut up into shorter piggin' strings for tying calves' legs to quiet them for branding.

He felt guilty about not being here before. Breaking horses was something he usually was involved in and good at doing. But he shouldn't have had the guilt. His presence had given Atlee Forsyth the strength to go on, and the protection from Indians. It had been important to stay. Still, it hurt to see others hard at work.

Sitting on a bench beside the ranch house was Willy, repairing a saddle. A few feet away were two more saddles. It was a time when all gear must be in top shape; a bridle or cinch snapping at the wrong moment could bring serious injury or worse. At his feet was a long-eared brown dog napping; another was inspecting something just inside the barn door.

Silka was shoeing a roan; he had learned the skill moving across the country and took pride in his work. An anvil and bellows was kept very busy this time of year. Of course, like most ranches, there was a keg of good 'nuffs, or shoes of various sizes ready to put on a horse without heating them. As expected, Silka didn't like them.

The horse wrangler, Harmon Payne, was a well-built cowboy who liked to spout phrases from Sir Walter Scott and Tennyson. The Corrigans knew he had been a teacher in Ohio before coming to Texas. Something had happened there, but no one asked. He was loyal to a fault and tougher than his thin frame would indicate. Willy Court was average-sized, cocky, and always interested in a fight, and he, too, would stand for the ranch. Jacob Jason, or "Little Jake" as most called him, was a short, fiery hand, ready for anything and anyone. Chico was a hardy Mexican; he knew little English, but knew cattle and horses well. Deed wondered if Blue was planning on hiring any other short-term help for the roundup. He figured the three hands would be kept on during the winter months.

Not far from the southern corral was the chuck wagon they had brought back. It, too, would be needed for the autumnal gathering. All of the area ranches supplied their own. He figured their black cook, Too Tall, was back, too. The short man also did the cooking for the ranch. His real name was Oliver Gistale, but nobody called him that.

Chickens were pecking the ground on the west side of the house, oblivious to the rest of the world. Somewhere a rooster strutted, letting the world know who was in charge. He didn't see Blue or Bina, but saw the children playing on the east side. He nudged the bay into an easy lope and hallooed the ranch as he neared. The dog snapped from its nap, barked, and headed toward Deed. Silka looked up and waved. All three children stopped playing, then came running and laughing toward him, too.

"Uncle Deed! Uncle Deed!" the two Corrigan children clamored together. Jeremy lagged a few steps behind, unsure of who this stranger was in front of them.

Grinning, Deed swung from the saddle, knelt, and spread his arms. The two kids piled into him, talking at the same time. He gathered from their happy chatter that their parents, Blue and Bina, were both in the barn.

Standing a few feet away, Jeremy watched with his hands behind his back.

Deed smiled, patted both Corrigan children, and said, "And you must be Jeremy. I'm Deed."

"Yes, sir."

"I've heard a lot about you, Jeremy," Deed said. "You're a brave young man."

"If you say so, sir."

Deed laughed. "How about calling me Deed?"

"Yes, s— Deed." The boy smiled.

"Come and join our little gang," Deed motioned. Without hesitation this time, Jeremy took a half skip and rushed into them. They all laughed.

From the barn came Blue, joining Silka in his advance to welcome Deed. The children giggled and hurried to return to the game near the house. A hearty handshake from both men made him feel at home again.

"Good that you are home, Deed," Silka said, patting the young gunfighter's shoulders. "No one can break the horses like you do, son."

"Don't know about that, but I'm ready to take my turn."

"Well, we have a blind bucker. Set him aside, hoping

you'd give him a go," Silka said. "If you can't set him straight, we'll just let him go. Too dangerous."

Having dealt with a blind bucker before, Deed knew that this was a horse that went crazy with fear whenever it was ridden, bucking into anything. More dangerous to itself than its rider, the horse was likely to injure itself bucking over something or trying to.

Before he could respond, Blue told him that Taol Sanchez, oldest son of their neighbor, had ridden over yesterday to discuss the roundup. The Sanchezes felt the Bar 3 should be invited to the roundup gathering, in spite of the unfortunate circumstances. A two-week target date for the roundup to start had been set.

"How like Ol' Man Sanchez," Deed responded. "Thinks everybody is good if given a chance."

"Well, it's not as simple as that, Deed," Blue said. "But he does believe in the goodness of people. In this case, though, he knows the Bar 3 land is too great to ignore. Likely some of our cattle have drifted over there, too."

"You mean *theirs*."

Blue grinned. "Guess so."

"What about Ol' Joel? Who's gonna be the wagon boss?"

In previous years, the Bar 3's veteran cowhand had served in the important role as wagon boss, the man in charge of sending riders to cover the land. So a new person would have to be chosen. Blue thought someone from the Lazy S would be the likely replacement.

"What if the foreman of the Bar 3 wants one of his men to run the roundup?"

"We'll deal with that if it comes," Blue answered. "So far, I haven't heard if they even plan to join us."

"Not sure riding with them is a good idea, Blue," Deed said, leading his horse.

"You want the Sanchez boys to do that alone?"

Silka shook his head and they walked toward the barn without talking.

Breaking the silence, Blue asked about things at the station. Deed told them about the division agent approving Atlee as the station manager and that he was considering making it an overnight stop, expanding the station with sleeping quarters for passengers. He explained the German farming couple had agreed to stay on and help, so he felt it was a good time to leave.

Studying his brother for a moment, Blue asked, "How did it go? When you left."

"Went fine," Deed said, glancing at the children now back at their play. "Oh, I invited Benjamin, the Forsyth boy, to join us for the roundup. Be a good experience for him." He paused and added, "Uh, and Elizabeth, his sister, you know, to join your kids for a few days. Hope that's all right."

"Of course it is. And Atlee?"

"Uh, she said it was fine, as long as Benjamin promised to get his schoolwork done first."

Blue smiled. "Good, but that's not what I meant. I'm sure she was sorry to see you leave."

Glancing away, Deed tugged on his hat brim. "Uh, no, I don't think so. Well, I was good help, you know, but she's got it under control now."

Talk continued about the roundup and the idea of branding the newborn calves early, before Agon Bordner could make another move to control the region and rustle any cattle he could find and brand them with his Bar 3. Bordner's takeover of the Bar 3 reminded Silka of the perilous days of feudal Japan where nothing and no one were safe. Blue believed the man would abide by the unwritten rules of the roundup, that ranchers who went out to brand calves before the others were called "sooners" and were frowned upon. Blue didn't want the family breaking those rules. Deed and Silka didn't think that would deter Bordner or his foreman, Dixie Murphy.

Deed stopped and his bay nudged him from behind. "Have you seen any Bar 3 riders around?"

"No. It's been real quiet," Blue answered, pausing alongside his brother. "At least around our range."

"Are you worried about them?" Deed started walking again.

Silka studied the leaves of a maple tree as they passed. Its leaves were beginning to show the first signs of crimson. He smiled and commented on their beauty. Both the Corrigan brothers agreed, but weren't really paying attention.

"What do you want to do?" Blue asked, his voice barely hiding his agitation.

"I'm sorry, Blue. That wasn't right of me." Deed kicked a rock as they continued down the hill. "You think this Agon Bordner is going to be satisfied with the Bar 3 and the two little places?"

Blue took three steps before responding. "Wish I could say yes, but he does sound like a man who wants to be a king—"

"And we stand in his way . . . us and the Sanchezes," Deed finished the statement.

"That's about it." Blue stared off, as if he could see a rider. "We've been keeping a close eye on our range and our cattle. One or two of us ride a part of it every day."

Blue informed Deed about the herd's condition. Overall it was in good shape in spite of the dry summer. There hadn't been any signs of screw worm, usually identified by cattle twitching and giving off a rancid odor. As usual, they also worried about steers being bitten by rattlesnakes, displaying swollen jaws or low-slung heads. Only one steer had been put down because of such an encounter. Patches of locoweed, a boghole, or alkaline water were all noted and cattle kept from them. Because of the dryness, there was concern about quicksand where there had been a stream. The ground had to be worked until moisture came to the top.

Most of their herd was young and, largely, short-horn of English lineage. A few mossy-backed long-horns roamed the hills, continuing to make riding among the herd a dangerous proposition. At this time of the year, the Corrigans liked to keep their herd on a higher range, leaving the lower lands for winter. Cattle that had been raised on the prairie had a tendency to stay out of timber, even if the trees gave them respite from winter storms. So the lower lands were the best practical solution.

Blue told the story of Willy getting completely covered in mud while getting a calf out of a bog. The calf's mother thanked him by trying to butt the muddy cowboy after the small animal was successfully removed.

That brought a laugh from all three, then they walked in silence for a while, and Deed asked about Bina. Two dogs ran over, checked them out, then pranced away to more interesting adventures.

"Well, right now she's taking care of the new stallion and some of our best mares. They're in the barn."

Blue grinned. "About this time next year, we'll have some fine new colts."

"Don't know anybody who can handle horses any better," Deed said and smiled. "It's good to be home, boys. Seems like forever."

"Well, a lot has happened since spring," Blue said and patted his brother on the back.

"Seems so. Where's that bad horse, Silka?" Deed asked.

"He is over here. There. The paint."

"That's a good-looking animal. Goes crazy, huh?"

"Hai. It is pity we cannot ride such a fine horse," Silka said.

A spotted, black-and-white mustang stood quietly in the corner of the unused corral. It was saddled and bridled. A lead-rope held it close to the corral bar.

"When no one is on him, he is so quiet. *O soroshi* when a man gets on."

Deed recalled *o soroshi* meant "awful" and that it wasn't like Silka to overstate anything.

"Where'd you get him?" Deed asked.

"Just showed up this summer with a bunch of mustangs we rounded up," Blue said.

"Go and ask Bina to join me, will you?"

Slipping through the corral bars, Deed walked up to the paint horse. Its ears laid back on its head and the animal trembled.

"Hey, boy. I'm not going to hurt you. Can't we be friends?" He put his hand on the horse's chest, then worked his hand up to its nose. The horse jerked frantically to get away, but the lead-rope held it close to the corral.

Deed was patient. He guessed somewhere in the animal's life it had been harmed or threatened by a man. No one would, or should, ride such a dangerous horse. But sometimes, it just took a different approach to make it a worthwhile animal. Certainly, the paint was a handsome steed and worth the effort.

Bina slipped through the corral bars and walked over to him. Her eyes were a question.

"Hi, Bina, sorry to greet you like this, but I need your help," Deed said.

"Of course, what would you like me to do?"

"Have you ever been around this horse?" Deed asked, stepping back from the paint.

"No, I have not. It is good-looking horse."

"I think so, too. I am told he goes crazy when he's ridden. I want you to talk with him. Maybe we can calm him down," Deed said, running his hand over the horse's neck. The horse trembled even more and tried to jerk away. "Right now, he's dangerous and not worth keeping."

Bina walked up to the horse and spoke to him, rubbing its ears, nose, and all around its body. Deed didn't recognize any of what she was saying and assumed she was talking in Apache. The horse was calm, but indifferent. She stopped and began talking to the horse in a distinctly different language. Her words were careful as if she wasn't as sure of herself. He knew some of what she was saying and realized she was talking to the horse in Comanche. The horse's ears went up and it leaned against her to listen. In Comanche, she told the horse not to be afraid, that he was a warrior's horse, and that a real warrior would soon be riding him. This would be an honor. Deed smiled; he didn't catch every word, but enough to realize she was instructing the animal on how it should act.

Silka and Blue watched from outside the corral.

"I think we've just discovered something, boys," Deed called back. "This is an Indian horse. He doesn't like white men. Scared of them."

"Are you sure?" Blue asked.

Deed looked over at Bina. "Well, it looks that way, doesn't it, Bina?"

"He is not Apache horse. He is Comanche horse. A fine one. I know not if he will let you ride him. You are white man. I tell him you great warrior, that it is honor for him."

"But he's a gelding. How can that be? I didn't think Apaches or Comanches cut their horses." Deed stepped next to her and patted the horse. Its ears went back again.

"Apache and Comanche sometimes do this. Learn from white man. Not all things from white man bad." She smiled and looked at him.

"I know a little Comanche. Not like you, but some."

She smiled. "It is not words. It is smell. You smell like white man. He is afraid of white man." She cocked her head. "I do not quite smell like an Indian either, but enough."

Deed frowned. "What can we do about that?"

"You go live in Comanche lodge for a moon, a month." She smiled.

Deed laughed out loud. "Don't think we've got that long. Anything else I could do?"

She patted the paint horse again, talking to it in the Comanche language. She stepped away and looked at Deed. "You must fool him, Deed Corrigan. I go for some things in house. You wait."

"All right."

She walked through the corral and went to the

house. Deed went over to Silka and Blue, standing behind the corral fence, and told them what they were going to do.

"You really think you can make him think you're a Comanche?" Blue asked. "Even if you do, we can't do that with every rider."

"Well, maybe he ends up in my string. If it works."

"*Uma no mimi ni nembutsu,*" Silka blurted. He meant the project was a wasted effort.

"We'll see. I have to try. That's too much animal to go to waste," Deed responded.

"Maybe you should blindfold him," Silka said.

Blue pushed his hat back on his forehead. "Don't know what good that'll do. He already bucks and runs like he can't see."

Silka folded his arms. "It is to keep horse from knowing Deed is not Comanche."

Blue grinned. "Sometimes I think Deed is one, a wild one."

"You're lots of help," Deed chuckled.

Returning to the horse, he talked quietly, trying to remember any Comanche phrases that might help and thought the horse might be somewhat more calm than earlier, but it might be his imagination. Horses raised by Indians weren't always changeable to white riders. He remembered a fine horse raised by a woman that went absolutely nuts when a man tried to ride it. Nothing could change it. Around a woman, the horse was sweet and gentle; around a man, the horse was a killer.

Bina returned with a small bowl; two eagle feathers with the ends tied with rawhide strings, dancing in the air; and several long ribbons.

"What's all that?" Deed asked.

"Put your hands in this. It is cold ashes and grease. It cut down on your . . . smell. Maybe fool him into thinking you are Comanche warrior."

"You make it sound like I need a bath. Do I need to put a feather in my hair or something?"

She smiled. "No. This horse will not care. Really. After you rub your hands, act like you are painting it for war, I will show you. Maybe this works. Maybe it does not. He may be loco."

"I know, but I've got to try."

Deed submerged his hands in the gooey mixture of ashes and grease, then held them up. A few ash flakes fluttered away and a string of grease ran down his right hand.

"Streak his face and his chest with . . . paint."

Carefully, Deed smeared lines of grease onto the horse's face and chest and ended it with a handprint on the horse's shoulder. Approving, Bina handed him the two feathers and ribbons and took the bowl.

"Tie one feather onto his mane. Tie the other on his tail. Tie a ribbon to both."

Deed talked to the horse as he tied on the feathers and ribbons. "All right. I'm going to get on."

"Wait!" Silka yelled. "I have idea. Wait." Silka sprinted away and returned with a coiled rope and a small brass ring. "We do nose-and-leg tie."

"Sure."

"I will help."

Working quickly, Silka loosened the saddle cinch and slid the metal ring into place. He retightened the cinch, adjusting the ring so it was in the middle of the horse's belly. They tied the rope on the bridle, then ran it between the paint's front legs, through the

ring, and then tied the taut rope to the horse's right
hind ankle.

"If he rears or bucks, he'll pull his hind leg out
from under himself. Maybe that will calm him down.
He will know it not a good thing to do. You alert and
jump," Silka advised.

Deed talked to the horse, reassuring him, and
swung into the saddle, but kept his boots out of the
stirrups. The paint stood with its ears alert. He nudged
the horse forward with his knees, talking reassuringly
as he did, mostly in English.

As if suddenly aware of the weight on its back, the
paint horse tried to rear. The rope yanked its hind leg
forward as the animal raised its head. The horse
bounced on its rump and fell over. Deed kicked free
and jumped away. He stutter-stepped backward and
maintained his balance.

Walking over to the horse, he talked to it as the
startled animal stood and shook the saddle, rattling
the stirrups like they were playthings.

"Okay, bud. We're going to do this again. There's
nothing to be gained by acting up."

From the corral, Silka yelled for him to forget the
idea. Deed ignored the advice, grabbed the reins,
checked the cinch, and remounted.

The paint horse started to rear again but felt the
pressure of the rope pull on his back leg. He crow-
hopped sideways and Deed encouraged him to walk.
The paint hesitated, then began moving. Another attempt to rear reminded the horse of its limitations.
Gradually, its head dropped, indicating it was comfortable with the man on its back. Deed wanted to shout,
but knew this was only the beginning. It would take
several rides before the paint was ready to be used on

the roundup. He wondered if the horse was going to require painting, feathers, and ribbons each time it was ridden. He hoped not.

"What shall we call him, Bina?"

"Call him Warrior."

"Warrior. I like that. Warrior, it is," Deed said and patted the horse's neck. "I'm going to bring him over your way, Silka. Will you please take off the rope."

Reluctantly, Silka removed the rope. The paint horse took a few tentative strides and realized it was free of restraints. The bucking that followed jerked Deed's head back and his hat went flying. The young gunfighter shoved his boots forward and withstood the animal's attempt to throw him.

"Hang on, Deed!" Blue hollered. "If he starts running, jump off. He'll hurt both of you."

Quietly, Bina stood inside the corral, against the fencing, and said, "Deed, he will stop this. He has not been ridden for a long time . . . by any rider. He is full of life. He is not loco."

Silka stared at her, unconvinced.

After three more jumps, the paint horse settled down and began to walk again as if nothing had happened.

Deed caught his breath and yelled, "Open the gate and let's see what happens."

He directed the paint toward the opened gate. The paint horse saw the opening and burst into a gallop and, in three strides, was running all out across the yard. After circling the open space, horse and rider disappeared in a blur over the first ridge. Silka wanted to get a horse and go looking for them, worried about Deed.

Bina told him to wait and Blue tried to act more

confident than he felt. His younger brother could ride, really ride, but this was different. A horse like that could hurt its rider and itself, but Bina seemed quietly assured. Maybe his brother really *was* more Comanche than he thought.

Minutes passed.

"I go for Deed. He may be hurt," Silka declared and headed for the barn.

"Wait, Silka. I see him coming. Over there. See?" Blue pointed with his lone arm toward the south. A silhouette was apparent. Deed and the horse were loping easily toward the ranch yard. The eagle feathers and ribbons fluttered in the wind.

Bina laughed. "It is Deed . . . and Warrior."

CHAPTER NINETEEN

Two black, polished surreys pulled into the Bar 3 ranch yard. As if a king were arriving, Agon Bordner got out of the first carriage, said something to the black driver, and headed for the magnificent ranch house. He was more agile than his huge frame would suggest and his bearing would make any Eastern potentate jealous.

He looked upon the region as his kingdom, his right. No one else deserved to own and operate this land. No one. All of Texas would be awed by what he would achieve here. He had decided it was time to make the next move in controlling this territory and fully expected it to happen as planned. Being closer was vital to his strategy; he trusted Rhey Selmon, but no one else. Not even his Bar 3 foreman, Dixie Murphy.

From the other surrey, two cooks and a gray-haired butler emerged, giving orders to each other. Pulling into the ranch yard were two buckboards. One piled with foodstuffs and a second laden with cooking gear, a large bed, a rocking chair, and an oil painting of Bordner, looking like a prince. The fat man would leave the settling into the spacious main house to his staff; he wanted to talk with Selmon and Murphy.

"Good to see you, boss!"

The hearty greeting from Dixie Murphy came from the doorway. The cattleman's lean frame was dwarfed by the huge door. He had fought for the South during the conflict and fled to Mexico with Nathan Bedford Forrest's cavalry, returning when Bordner contacted him through a mutual friend.

"Have you eaten?" Dixie asked.

"Of course not."

"I'll have Terrell fix us some steaks." Dixie motioned toward an unseen kitchen.

"That won't be necessary, Dixie," Bordner responded. "My people know what I want. We've been over the menu several times. They'll handle the meals from now on."

"Uh, sure. How 'bout a whiskey till it's ready."

"That would be fine, if it's good whiskey. Is Rhey here?"

"Inside."

"Good."

The Bar 3 ranch house was big and attractively decorated with oil paintings of Texas scenes and mostly French furniture. Bordner liked the decor, but decided he would expand the kitchen and put in a wine cellar. His bed would be installed in the first bedroom and Dixie would move to another. His favorite rocking chair would be brought into the main room as well. It was the only chair he had found that could hold him. The large oil painting of himself would need to be displayed prominently as well.

Rhey Selmon was sitting in the main room drinking whiskey when Bordner and Dixie entered. As usual, the gunman wore his bearskin coat and twin crossed gunbelts. He made no attempt to stand.

"Glad you're here, Agon. I'm headed for Wilkon this afternoon as ordered."

Selmon was the only Bordner gunman who called him by his first name or dared to do so to his face. Bordner smiled, knowing that Selmon, with two men, was to kill the town marshal, then have Macy Shields take over as the Wilkon lawman. Bank president Willard Hixon would handle the town council. One of Bordner's men, Jephrum Virdin, had become the apparent owner of the Wilkon General Store in the past week, so there was another Bordner man to help with the voting. The previous owner had left town without notice.

Selmon swallowed the rest of his whiskey, slammed the empty glass on a nearby coffee table in front of him, and stood.

"I want it done clean. Just the way I told you. Exactly the way." Bordner accepted a glass and watched Dixie pour brown liquid into it. When the foreman paused, the fat man pushed the glass against the bottle to indicate more whiskey was needed.

"Waid and Peter are going with me. They'll get the lawman," Selmon said, adjusting his fur coat. "Then Macy Shields will arrest them. Citizen's arrest." He chuckled.

"How good are Waid and Peter?" Bordner asked.

"Good enough. Why?"

"Change of plans." Bordner studied the painting on the wall again.

"Oh?"

"You and Macy will kill Waid and Peter after they kill the marshal."

Selmon shook his head. "That's not going to sit well with the boys, Agon."

"So what? I don't want any loose ends." Bordner stared at him until Selmon looked away. "Oh yeah, almost forgot. We don't need to worry about the county law either. Had a nice chat with Sheriff Matthew R. Lucas. In fact, he's coming by for supper."

Licking his lips, Selmon smiled. How like his boss to take care of every detail. Obviously, Sheriff Lucas was now on the take.

Bordner tasted his drink, frowned, and told Dixie, "I'm thinking we should hit the Lazy S and the LC during roundup. Get it done all at once. We can blame it on the Comanches again."

"No, boss," Dixie gulped his own whiskey and continued, "Everybody will be spread out, looking for cattle. Tough to get everybody, or even find all of them." He poured another. "Besides that, I'm not interested in going against Deed Corrigan. You know that."

Selmon nodded. "Neither am I, Agon."

"Is Hannah gonna get rid of Deed Corrigan like you talked?" Dixie growled.

"Yes."

Bordner took three black cigars from his inside coat pocket and handed one each to his key men and bit off the end of one and spit it on the floor.

"When?" Selmon asked, his eyes flashing.

"That's up to him. He hadn't left El Paso when we did. Said he had some business to handle first."

"I'll believe it when I see it," Selmon growled.

Bordner stirred his drink with his finger and ignored the comment. "All right. We'll do this more slowly. I want the Lazy S before roundup, then we'll take over the Corrigan ranch after Deed's dead. Probably after the roundup." He swallowed most of the whiskey. "No mistakes this time."

No mistakes meant no one left alive.

"So you want the Lazy S before the roundup?" Dixie asked. "Could let them Mex boys do their gatherin' and brandin'. Save us the trouble."

"No. I want control of the two biggest ranches now," Bordner snapped. "Besides, I intend to rename the whole thing. Got a new brand already registered." He made a motion that looked like two *M*s pushed together forming a crown. He smiled, "This whole thing'll become the Crown Ranch."

"Give us a couple of days. We'll hit them and the house at the same time," Dixie growled.

"Good," Bordner said, waiting for Dixie to light his smoke, then the foreman's own.

"Check with Simpson. I'm getting hungry."

Selmon wanted to know how James Hannah was going to kill Deed Corrigan and get away from his brother and that damn Jap. It didn't matter to him if Hannah didn't get away. That was okay too.

Bordner looked annoyed; he wasn't used to being questioned, even by Selmon. He drank the glass of whiskey in one gulp, then responded, "I don't know, Rhey. Last I heard Deed was still at that stage station outside of Wilkon. I figure he'll go there. Get Corrigan while he's alone."

"No, he's not at the station. Some of the boys saw him and his one-armed brother talking with Old Man Sanchez two days ago," Rhey Selmon growled.

"Well, I guess that's Hannah's problem." Bordner looked surprised. "But if Hannah fails, I've got another way to get rid of both of them. Legal-like. And then we get rid of Hannah."

Selmon laughed out loud.

Sunday found Blue Corrigan taking his turn in the pulpit of the town's church. He really didn't have the time to prepare because of roundup preparations, but considered it his responsibility. The handmade pews were full as usual. Bina and their three children were in the front row to his left. She was always reluctant; many white people weren't comfortable around her, especially in the church. She told him the Great Spirit was not contained within a building and that he could be worshipped anywhere. He didn't disagree, but felt it was important for their children.

Townspeople were still coming in so he decided to wait before starting. The church door swung open and Agon Bordner entered, nearly blocking out the sunlight. Down the middle of the church he strolled, smiling broadly and greeting everyone as he entered. He glanced at Blue, nodded, and took a seat on the front row to his right. Only one other person sat there—an elderly woman who was hard of hearing. In the back row, several hard-looking men were taking seats and urging others to move.

"Welcome. What a good morning to gather together and worship our Lord," Blue announced. "Let us begin our service with a prayer and then we'll sing Hymn 37, 'A Mighty Fortress Is Our God.'"

The congregation thumbed through their hymnals,

a recent gift from the Corrigans and sent all the way from Cincinnati, Ohio.

He stepped away from the homemade pulpit and it swayed slightly. "Please bow your heads. O Lord, hear us this morning as we humbly seek your love. Grant us your forgiveness for our sins and touch us with your grace. Help us to love each other more and to help our community grow strong. We ask this in your holy name, amen."

He lifted his eyes and began to sing.

> *"A mighty fortress is our God,*
> *a bulwark never failing;*
> *our helper he amid the flood . . .*
> *of mortal ills prevailing.*
> *For still our ancient foe*
> *doth seek to work us woe;*
> *his craft and power are great . . .*
> *and armed with cruel hate,*
> *on earth is not his equal."*

The singing was uneven yet joyful. Bordner's voice boomed above the rest of the congregation and Blue tried to ignore its intensity. Few did, however. The rest of the service went without incident. Blue's sermon was short and based on Deed's thoughts—and Bina's.

"As we go about our daily tasks, it is important that we see God's hand everywhere we look. In things we don't really see, but should and savor for their special-ness. Like the richness of ripened corn or the glory of contented cattle . . . the beauty of a snowflake or the song of a gentle rain . . . the sweet song of a robin or the haunting call of an owl . . . the breathtaking wonder of dawn itself and the opportunity to serve

God another day." He looked at Bina. "The magic of
your wife's smile. Or your husband's." He turned
toward the silent audience. "Or the beauty of a stag
deer in tall grass, the wonder of a harnessed team of
horses working in unison . . . the comfort of a fire
on a cold evening . . . or the sheer magnificence of a
running horse or a happy child . . . and the love of our
families for each other. All are gifts from God. All are
miracles from him. All should be accepted with thankfulness. Amen. Let us together say the Lord's Prayer.
Our Father who art in Heaven, hallowed be thy
name—"

After the service, Blue stood at the back of the
church and talked with townspeople as they exited the
church. The last to leave was Agon Bordner. Bina and
the children waited in the front as usual.

He strolled up to Blue and said in a dry voice, "Very
good service, Corrigan. You definitely have a gift of
the tongue. May I suggest that you take this gift and
apply it elsewhere. I will buy your ranch. With cash."

"Our ranch isn't for sale, Bordner. Neither is the
Lazy S."

"That's too bad, Corrigan." Bordner put on his rumpled hat and headed for his carriage. Four mounted
men waited. A fifth helped him into the vehicle. It
wasn't easy.

Adjusting his great weight, Bordner looked back
at Blue, slightly out of breath. "I would hate to see
anything happen to your fine family."

Blue's granite face broke. "Touch my family, Bordner, and you will die a horrible death."

"My, my. Such words from a man of God." He
turned to his driver and ordered him to drive away.

Blue heard his shrill laughter as they left.

CHAPTER TWENTY

Dawn was an hour away, but Deed Corrigan was up and fully dressed, stoking the reluctant fire in the stone fireplace into rebirth. Silka was still sleeping in his room, which was part of the added wing of the ranch house. As far as Deed knew, so were Blue and his family. Their regular hands, Chico, Willy, Little Jake, and Harmon were in the bunkhouse. He figured Too Tall would be coming from there soon to start breakfast.

Coming back to the ranch three days ago held mixed emotions for him as his thoughts were rarely away from Atlee Forsyth. He missed her terribly. But he needed to be here and she didn't have any feelings for him. He kept telling himself that.

He had shared his feelings about Atlee with Silka and the old samurai told him that she needed time and that he should work hard to keep from thinking about her too much. So far he hadn't said anything to Blue; that would bring an uninvited warning from his older brother. Maybe he should talk with Bina; she was level-headed and compassionate. She would give him a woman's perspective.

The fire was well banked, as usual, last night. Among the ashes were nuggets of embers waiting to be coaxed to life once more. He added larger chunks of wood as soon as the fire decided to respond. Today he planned on readying more horses for the roundup; he liked working the half-wild mustangs because it kept his mind off Atlee. Some would need reshodding as well. Warrior was developing into a fine horse, but one Deed only trusted himself to ride. Roundup was scheduled to start next week.

As was his custom, he said a silent prayer as he worked the fire and watched the golden sparks pop up to greet him. It was a prayer of thanks and a wish for a good day; it was a Japanese prayer Silka had taught him long ago.

Two days ago, he and Blue had met with Felix Sanchez, the patriarch of the Lazy S family, and his oldest son, Taol. It was the Sanchezes' recommendation that Blue take over as wagon boss. They also reported that Dixie Murphy would be participating in the roundup and was looking forward to it. The news had pleased everyone, except Deed. He didn't trust Murphy, or his boss, Agon Bordner, and had said so. Blue and the others were willing to give them a chance. He had no doubt that working with Dixie Murphy and the rest of the new Bar 3 riders would be awkward at best, but Blue insisted that they, at least, try to act civilly.

He cocked his head to try to catch the faint sound over the now crackling wood. It wasn't a coyote or wind. No, someone was in pain. Great pain. He grabbed his

Winchester cradled against the doorframe, strapped
on his gunbelt, and shoved a second pistol into his belt.
Opening the door carefully, he stepped out on the
porch. The uneven gray light made it difficult to distin-
guish a tree from a rider. Then he saw a lone figure.

A man, barely in the saddle, was advancing toward
the ranch house. A sombrero bounced on the man's
back, held by a stampede string at his neck. The horse
was lathered and moving more out of fear than any
direction being given. The rider yelped again, an
agonizing cry for help, then slumped against the
horse's neck.

"Silka! Blue! Willy . . . Harmon! Chico! Little Jake!
We've got trouble!" Deed yelled and hurried toward
the horse and rider.

The horse stumbled, then came to stop. One rein
dragged on the ground. White with sweat, the animal
was heaving for breath that wouldn't come fast
enough. Even in the grayness, Deed recognized the
rider as Paul Sanchez, the youngest Sanchez son.

As Deed approached, he could see Paul's white
shirt was soaked in blood. The young Mexican's eyes
fluttered open.

"S-Señor Deed . . . our ranch it's . . . been a-ttacked."
He struggled to say more, but couldn't.

In their long johns, Willy and Harmon were only a
handful of steps behind Deed, both holding six-guns.
Chico was fully dressed and so was Little Jake. Silka
came dressed and carrying his long samurai sword
in one hand and its sheath in the other. Blue came
running from the main house, wearing only pants
and boots. In his right hand was the Walch 12-shot
navy revolver.

"Get him down," Deed said, then told Harmon to go for water and rags.

As they stretched the badly wounded Mexican vaquero on the ground, Bina arrived, also fully dressed and holding a shotgun. Laying the gun beside her, she knelt beside Paul and began pulling part his blood-soaked shirt. Harmon brought a bucket of water with a dipper and towels from the bunkhouse. They were the only cloths he could find. The young Mexican rose on his elbows and drank gratefully from the filled dipper offered by Blue. Too Tall, the short, fat-bellied black cook, came, panting for breath. Quietly, he told Blue that coffee was on. Chico led the worn-out Sanchez horse away, walking it to cool it down before letting the animal have any water.

After a few sips of water, Paul Sanchez sank back to the ground, muttering. In a halting mixture of English and Spanish, Paul explained that their riders had been shot from ambush. An ongoing gunfight had ensued, but he didn't know if all the vaqueros were killed. He remembered seeing their foreman, Cliente, alive and fighting. At the same time, another force of gunmen struck the grand ranch house itself.

"Is it Comanches?" Deed leaned over.

"No, Señor. It is Americanos from the Bar 3. My father t-told me to ride for . . . y-you. T-That you would . . . help us." Paul shut his eyes to absorb the pain enveloping his body.

"Of course, we will," Deed said with clenched teeth and stood. "Willy, Little Jake, saddle our horses. Get everybody ready to ride."

Paul Sanchez reopened his eyes and saw Bina. "T-Thank you, Señora. Y-You are most kind. My family—" He gave a long sigh and was unconscious.

Riding a black-tailed roan, Willy brought up two saddled horses, one was Deed's buckskin. He belched and it filled the morning with thunder. Silka laughed. Chico rode up, leading a third mount. He had turned the Sanchez horse over to Too Tall, who didn't like the idea but accepted the animal with the warning to continue to walk the horse and not to let it drink until it was completely cooled down.

Little Jake rode beside Chico, ready to join in the fight. Deed swung into the saddle, holding his Winchester. Silka took the reins of a stocky bay and mounted, returning his sword to its sheath and pulling his rifle free from its saddle scabbard.

"Bina, leave Paul here. There is nothing more we can do for him that rest and the good Lord can't handle. We'll move him to the house when we return. You need to get back inside, barricade the door and stay there. We don't know if they will come for us, too." He looked around at Blue climbing into the saddle. "No. Blue, stay with your family and make sure you are all safe. We must ride. Now. It might not be too late."

Bina nodded and stood, grabbing up the shotgun. Blue glanced at her and told Deed that he was not staying behind, but was coming, too.

Too Tall was frightened, holding the Sanchez horse. "But, what if they come here?"

"I don't think they will, but stay alert," Blue said. "If they do, we'll hear their shots and return."

"I no worry. You go. Hurry. Sanchez family good people," Bina declared.

Willy's expression was sour. "But, but, Deed, it sounds like there's thirty guns. You can't—"

"Willy, I know what's there. But we can't leave the

fight to our friends. Maybe we can drive them off before it's too late. Or maybe we can end this thing," Deed said and kicked his horse into a gallop. "Stay here if you want."

Red streaks were cutting swaths across the dull sky as they rode for the Lazy S. Harmon wondered what they would do, or could do, against a horde of gunmen. But he knew his employers; Deed was brave, but not foolhardy, and so was his brother. He wasn't sure of the former samurai; Silka might decide a glorious death would be to ride straight into the attackers. He shivered at the thought.

Harmon glanced at Silka who nodded and said something in Japanese. The cowboy admitted to himself that the Oriental was mysterious and hard to figure.

Blue looked over at Deed. "This would be a good time to have Holt with us, wouldn't it?"

"Any time, big brother. Any time."

Harmon was always fascinated by the way Blue rode one-handed, holding the reins and balancing his rifle against the saddle pommel. He made it look easy. Harmon had tried it once and the gun had slid away after only a few strides of his horse.

To avoid giving in to his doubts and fears, in a strong voice Harmon declared, "And this stern joy which warriors feel . . . in foemen worthy of their steel.'"

"I like that, Harmon. What's it from?" Blue asked.

"Sir Walter Scott's *The Lady of the Lake*, canto 5."

Willy raised and lowered his shoulders and Silka declared, "If they still there, we surprise them. Catch in crossfire. Velly good."

This time Harmon nodded. It sounded good to him.

All rode with their rifles readied over their saddles and waited for Deed's commands. Blue had no problem with Deed taking control. They rode without further words, until sounds of gunfire broke through the early morning.

"Well, that's a damn good sign. The Lazy S boys are still alive and fighting," Deed observed. "Maybe we *can* catch these bastards in a crossfire."

They reined up alongside a gathering of rocks and boulders. It looked like the stones had met long ago and never left. Deed studied the Sanchez ranch yard with his field glasses.

"Can't see how many for sure. Looks like they've got the ranch surrounded," Deed advised, lowering the glasses. "They're spread out around that old stone fence. You know, the one that goes all around the ranch yard."

"Well, we've still got time then," Blue responded.

"Not much. The Sanchezes won't be able to stop a full-out charge."

As they rode closer, he outlined what they were going to do. Blue, Willy, and Chico would head for a ridge west of the ranch house. It was a long hiccup of land, crowded with brush and timber, a good position from which to direct fire at the attackers on that side. Silka would ride with a reluctant Harmon to the north side. Their destination was a group of cottonwoods, twenty yards from the stone fence. Deed and Little Jake would swing to the east side and positions there. After neutralizing the other parts, the south side would then be in a crossfire.

"Start shooting when you get into position," Deed advised and patted the rifle lying across his saddle. "Maybe they'll get smart and give up."

"If they don't?" Harmon asked, shifting the rifle ahead of him.

"Then we're in for a long morning," Deed responded.

"*Ame futte ji katamaru,*" Silka said.

"What's that mean?"

Deed smiled. "It's a Japanese expression. Means rained-on ground hardens. Uh, adversity builds character."

"Oh sure."

"We gonna shoot 'em in the back?" Willy asked, wide-eyed.

"No. We'll give them a chance to surrender. Our first shot will be over their heads," Deed said. "Our second won't. Remember these bastards killed our friends at the Bar 3 and they're trying to do that at the Lazy S." He wasn't at all certain that Silka would give any Bar 3 men such a chance, but kept the thought to himself.

Blue started to say something about killing, but changed his mind and only said, "Keep us safe, Lord."

Nodding, Deed touched the small circle at his neck. Silka did the same and they split into three groups and rode toward the ranch.

A few minutes later, Blue and the others dismounted quietly on the back side of a long ridge west of the Sanchez ranch house. They tied their horses away from where they intended to fire. Spreading out, they crawled into positions behind rocks and earthen mounds. Twenty yards in front of them, silhouettes were shooting at the dark ranch house from behind the stone fence. In places, the rocks had crumbled into heaps. Scattered gunfire occasionally answered from the house. Here and there were dead raiders and a few bodies of vaqueros.

Gunfire opened on the north side.

"That'll be Silka," Blue said. "Guess it's time."

He laid his rife against a boulder and drew his Walch handgun. Ahead of them, Bar 3 gunmen turned toward the sounds of the increased gunfire, uncertain of its meaning. His first shot clipped the dirt to the right of a gunman with a long scar along his right cheek. He squinted toward the north and yelled, "What the hell? Nobody's supposed to charge till we get the order from Selmon."

Willy belched so loud it made all of the Bar 3 gunmen jump, even the scar-faced leader. Chico and Willy opened fire with their rifles, spitting lead in the direction of the spread-out attackers, completely surprised by the counterattack.

On the far side of the ranch, Deed turned to Little Jake. "We're late. There's no time to hide."

He tied the reins together, looped the connected leathers through his left arm, and pulled both pistols from his belt. Glancing at Jake, he kicked his horse into a run toward the eight Bar 3 gunmen strung out along the east barricade. The tough, short cowhand followed, levering his Winchester into action, and holding his reins with his left hand, wrapped around the rifle.

The east side Bar 3 attackers were concentrating on the surprise firing across the ranch yard. Galloping toward them, Deed's two pistols dropped the first Bar 3 gunman as he spun toward him. Deed's horse slammed into the second man as the young gunfighter fired at the remaining line of attackers.

One wounded gunman, whose hat flew off revealing a bald head, gulped, "Damn! That's Deed Corrigan!"

The taller gunman next to him stared at the two

horsemen thundering toward them. "Deed Corrigan? Hell!" He dropped his rifle and raised his hands. Nodding, the bald man lowered his rifle. Deed rode past, shooting at the other Bar 3 gunmen with both hands.

Less than a minute behind Deed and Jake came Silka, swinging his long sword from horseback. Harmon bit his lower lip and followed, his worst fear realized. The samurai had already dispatched the four Bar 3 gunmen on the north and hopped back on his horse to help Deed. The bald gunman raised his rifle to shoot at Deed's back. Silka's sword nearly decapitated the gunman. His rifle fired into the morning sky as he fell dead against the short wall.

From the west side, Blue's clear voice rang out. "Bar 3, you're surrounded. Throw down your guns and put up your hands. Or die behind that stone wall. Your choice. Make it now." So far, he had only wounded two men and hoped that would be the end of it. Chico and Willy had already moved to a new location where they could fire directly into the remaining Bar 3 raiders on the south.

All along the south barricade, some of the Bar 3 men dropped their guns and stood.

Swinging around the crumbling corner of the rock fence, Deed emptied both of his guns into a lanky gunman, standing three feet from the corner on the south side. Beside him, a fat-bellied outlaw hurried a rifle shot at the charging gunfighter. Deed's sweating horse jumped sideways as the bullet burned its neck.

As the fat gunman recocked his Henry, Deed threw both empty guns at him, which he was able to duck, and the man brought his rifle up to fire again. An instant behind the tossed guns, Deed's throwing knife followed. The razor-sharp blade, carried behind his neck, drove into the man's throat. His rifle exploded, its bullet singing into the air. The gunfighter leaped from his horse toward the staggering man, who was pulling at the embedded blade with both hands. Deed picked up the dropped rifle and slammed the butt into the gunman's stomach. As the gunman groaned in pain, Deed slammed his open hand into the man's throat. Then Deed's left hand came thundering against the man's neck and he collapsed.

Behind him, Jake caught a bullet and slumped against his horse.

Around the ranch yard, all was quiet. The shooting was over.

Silka thundered up, brandishing his bloody sword.

"Deed, you 'right?" Silka asked.

"Yeah, but Jake's been hit." He pulled the knife from the dead gunman's throat, wiped it on the man's shirt, and returned the blade to its scabbard behind his back.

They turned to the wounded cowhand, leaving Harmon to handle the remaining gunmen still standing. Jake gritted his teeth and mumbled something while Silka worked at cleaning the wound. Blue and Willy eased across the yard, directing the surrendered Bar 3 attackers. From the house came a brown-and-white dog, trotting among them. From the tree line, Chico appeared, leading six saddled horses. Deed picked up his revolvers and began reloading one.

"*Sí*, is Bar 3 hosses. More in de trees. All without shoes," he declared. In his other hand was a large sack filled with Indian weapons and feathers. He held up the sack. "Here is their leave-behinds to make it look like Comanche. *Sí*."

"Unshod horses and feathers. That figures," Blue responded, studying the wall for any stragglers. "Makes them appear to be Indians. Willy, go with Chico and bring up the rest of their horses."

"Will do, boss."

On the west side, a disgruntled Rhey Selmon, in his bearskin coat, stood quietly, his guns laying at his feet. He told the man next to him to surrender, that Agon Bordner would take care of them, and ordered the scar-faced man to do the same.

From the long adobe house came Felix Sanchez with a pistol in each hand. His shoulder was bloodied; his silver hair was matted with sweat. A sombrero bounced on his back, attached by a rawhide string.

"Gracias, amigos. Gracias," Felix shouted. "How is my Paul?"

Behind him came two small children, his grandchildren. His oldest son, Taol, stepped into the yard from another door, brandishing a rifle and looking for someone to shoot.

"He's hurt bad," Blue said, "but he's tough. My Bina is with him."

"God is with us."

"Let's hang these bastards by those trees," Deed growled.

Blue looked at him. "No, we're taking them to town. They'll stand trial . . . and then hang."

"What about Dixie Murphy? And what's his name, the fat man?" Deed growled, reloading his second handgun. "They're behind all this."

"I know. But we're going to need some of his men to testify to that. The sheriff can be the eyewitness, then he'll arrest them." Blue's manner indicated he didn't intend to argue about the matter.

"All right, but I want to be there when he does."

"Sure."

The closest Bar 3 gunman, holding his bleeding arm, looked at Deed. "A-Are you Deed Corrigan?"

"I am. Want to make something of it?" Deed's face was dark.

"Hell no. Dixie told us you were dead. Said that gunslick James Hannah did you in."

Snorting, Deed said, "James Hannah's a friend of mine."

"Should've known Dixie was full of it."

Chapter Twenty-one

"Dixie! We got ambushed!" The scared rider reined up his lathered horse at the Bar 3 ranch yard, jumped down, and ran inside.

Dixie Murphy was talking about cattle with Agon Bordner at a round table. The fat man was devouring a stack of hotcakes, smothered in butter and hot maple syrup, along with six fried eggs. A plate piled with bacon and slices of ham was to his left. They were awaiting word on the successful attack on the Lazy S. The necessary Lazy S loan papers lay on the table between them.

Dixie turned toward the shouting. His hand dropped to the holstered handgun at his waist.

"What the hell's goin' on, Wyman?" the crooked cowman yelled.

"It's the Corrigans. They hit us. Had us surrounded. We never saw them comin'." The scared cowboy swallowed and fought to gain control of his emotions.

"What? That can't be." Dixie looked at Bordner, wiping syrup from his chin. "There couldn't be more

than seven or eight of those bastards to begin with."
Dixie stood and slammed his fist on the table. The
impact turned over the syrup pitcher. Bordner
reached over and resettled it, ignoring the spilled
stickiness. It was his first reaction to anything so far.

Wyman explained what had happened at the
Sanchez ranch, then added, "I thought you said James
Hannah was going to take care of Deed Corrigan." He
swallowed to find courage. "They were all there, including that Oriental with the big sword."

Shaking his head in disbelief, Wyman continued,
"Rhey had us spread all around the Sanchez ranch
house. Behind that old stone fence of theirs. We
picked off all their riders first. Had 'em where we
wanted, holed up." He shook his head again. "Then,
all of a sudden . . . the Corrigans were around us,
tearing us apart."

"How'd you get away?" Dixie growled, crossing his
arms.

"Almost didn't. They got Pete. Me an' him were
holdin' all our hosses."

"I didn't tell you *when* Hannah was going to kill Corrigan, dammit, did I!" Dixie yelled and waved his arms.

Looking up, Bordner put a fried egg into his mouth
and let the yolk drip down his chin as he spoke. "I
assume the objective of eliminating the Sanchezes was
not achieved."

Wyman glanced at the furious Dixie, then at Bordner, then away. "I . . . uh, I don't know."

"Did they get Rhey?"

"Don't know. Guess so."

"Did you leave the sacks of Indian weapons behind?"
Bordner asked and shoved another egg into his mouth.

"Ah, they was on two of our hosses we was . . . watchin'."

"So, the attack was not only a failure, evidence of it being a staged Comanche attack is now in Deed Corrigan's hands." Bordner gulped coffee and waved at the cook to bring more.

"Ah, guess so."

A gunshot blistered the room and the cook dropped the coffeepot. Wyman stared wide-eyed at his reddening shirt around his shirt pocket. A second bullet hit him just below the nose and the cowboy crashed to the ground. A third went into the top of his head. His leg twitched and then was still.

Stunned, Dixie looked over at Bordner. A smoking revolver was in the big man's hand. A long-barreled, silver-plated Smith & Wesson, it looked almost like a derringer in his huge fist.

"Now, Dixie," Bordner said calmly, "Take this piece of garbage, put it on his horse, and ride for town. Halfway there, shoot the horse and leave both." He paused to drink the rest of his coffee and looked around, irritated that the cook had disappeared into the kitchen. "It'll look like he and his horse were wounded leaving the ambush and made it that far."

Dixie nodded without speaking, staring at the missing forefinger on his left hand.

"Ride hard for town. You need to be there before they do. Find Sheriff Lucas and tell him the Bar 3 was attacked and outlaws stole thirty head of horses," Bordner said, cutting into the remaining pancakes. "Tell him that the horses had been brought up to the big corral for shoeing for the roundup and they were all unshod."

Dixie nodded again and managed to ask what if the Corrigans came to town with some of his men.

"I would expect that. They may even come here first. That's another reason for you to be gone."

"Stay in town after you tell the sheriff. Tell Macy, ah, the new marshal, too," Bordner said and began buttering the sliced pancakes, then decided they were cold and yelled, "Simpson, bring in some fresh hotcakes. These aren't worth eating." He looked up at Murphy. "Tell Macy that I expect our men to . . . escape."

Late afternoon lay on their shoulders as Deed Corrigan, Felix Sanchez, and Chico rode into Wilkon with nine tied Bar 3 gunmen on their horses. One was Rhey Selmon. A buckboard, driven by Taol, the oldest Sanchez son, held the bodies of the dead gunmen. One was the body of Wyman, found on the way. Another five wounded attackers also rode their horses, flanked by three Sanchez vaqueros. Blue, Willy, Harmon, and Silka, carrying rifles across their saddles, rode alongside.

Up and down both sides of the main street, people stopped to gaze and whisper. County Sheriff Matthew R. Lucas exited his small office next to what passed for a courthouse, an old warehouse converted for the town's greater good. Lucas was a short, stocky man with a no-nonsense manner, not unlike that of a teacher. Not far behind the county lawman came Marshal Macy Shields and Dixie Murphy.

"Afternoon, Mr. Corrigan, what have you here?" Shields asked.

Deed glanced toward the senior Sanchez and let him speak first.

"We bring the gunmen who try to kill us . . . like they kill our *amigos* at the Bar 3 this spring," Felix Sanchez spoke slowly with his head held high.

Sheriff Lucas smiled. "Glad you weren't hurt, Señor Sanchez." His graying hair told of a strong man who had served the county for twenty years.

"They wound *muy mal* my youngest son, Paul," the gray-haired rancher said. "If not for our Corrigan *amigos*, we will have not made it, I fear."

"Sounds like the same bunch that hit the Bar 3 last night. Mr. Murphy, the foreman of the Bar 3, reported his ranch was attacked last night and thirty horses were stolen," Lucas reported, trying to look stern.

Deed's eyes shot toward the gray-haired county lawman. "What?"

Calmly, the sheriff motioned toward Murphy, standing next to the city marshal on the corner of the boardwalk. "I said Mr. Murphy reported his ranch was attacked last night and thirty of his horses were stolen."

Blue reined up next to Deed, who told him about Dixie Murphy's claim.

"Convenient," Blue declared loudly, staring at Murphy. "So what happened to the outlaws' other horses, the ones they would've been riding?"

Murphy shrugged.

"Bet we can get a few of these boys to say different," Deed said quietly to Blue.

"Not our job, Deed. It's the sheriff's." Blue turned toward the nervous lawman and expressed their concern that Murphy was lying.

"It's pretty obvious this is the same bunch that wiped out the Regan family," Blue said.

"Maybe," came the tight-lipped reply from Lucas. "I'll check into it, but the horse stealing sounds legit to me." He motioned toward the arrested gunmen. "Mr. Murphy said they had put twenty-eight head in the corral. They were to be shod before roundup." He shrugged his shoulders and looked over at Macy Shields who smiled.

"Marshal, all right if I put this bunch in your jail?"

The skinny town lawman folded his arms and smiled again. "Yeah. I'll need to release Jimmy Wedgeberry first. He was in overnight for being drunk and raising cain."

Macy Shields was dressed in his customary white suspenders, or they had been white once, and a faded blue bib shirt. His eyes were tiny and too close together. As usual, he wore a bandana tied over his head like a pirate, instead of a hat. He had figured in several pointless killings in Texas and Kansas. Nothing was ever proved, however.

Blue leaned forward in his saddle. "There are nine bodies in the wagon. We weren't about to bury them on good Lazy S land. Figured they're the county's problem." He straightened his back.

Tugging on the brim of his hat, Deed growled, "Or we can dump them on Bar 3 land. That's where they came from."

Sheriff Lucas frowned and stared at the wagon, unable to meet either brother's gaze. "Oh, all right. Can you drive 'em to the city's cemetery? I'll get some boys to bury 'em."

"Yes, but you'd best get some boys there to dig real quick. Won't be long before the smell'll be something awful," Blue answered. "If you want, I'll say words over them." He motioned toward the wounded gunmen in the wagon. "Better have Doc take a look at them, too."

"You're leaving me with quite a mess."

"Maybe so, but they left the Sanchezes with loyal hands killed. One of their sons is shot up, and our good hand, Jake, wounded," Deed said, nudging his horse forward to stop next to the sheriff. Deed's eyes were hot as he glared at the uncomfortable lawman. "An' I don't buy that crap about stolen horses for one minute, Lucas. And if you do, you're not the man I thought you were."

Blue reined his horse away. "Come on, Deed. Let's get this done. We've got work to do."

Deed nodded, then spun his horse toward the boardwalk where Dixie Murphy and Marshal Shields stood. "Murphy, tell that fat-ass boss of yours that this is not over. The Regans were friends of ours. So are the Sanchezes. We don't forget friends."

Murphy spat a brown stream of tobacco juice into the street and snorted, "Go to hell, Corrigan."

"Deed, *come on*," Blue yelled. "He isn't worth it."

Deed glanced at his brother as Murphy's hand dropped to his holstered gun. Deed looked back with his own Remington in his fist. No one saw him draw.

"I'm not as nice as my brother," Deed said between clenched teeth. "I don't think everybody is good. Or honest."

Sheriff Lucas waved his arms. "That's enough, Corrigan. Mr. Murphy is a law-abiding citizen in this county. You remember that."

"Sure, Sheriff. Sure. And I'm a buffalo." Deed spun his revolver in his hand, holstered it, and loped away to catch up with Blue and the others. The wagon rolled toward the cemetery at the far end of town.

Nightfall brought a sense of comfort to Wilkon after the day of excitement. The Corrigan brothers, Felix Sanchez, and their men rode out at dusk. Dixie Murphy decided to stay overnight, telling the livery operation to leave his horses outside and saddled in the corral. He would be taking them back to the ranch in the morning and would hire some men to help. The livery corral brimmed with milling horses, serving as the only visible reminder of the day's activity.

A hearing was scheduled for the morning in the justice of the peace's office. Quietly, Murphy met with the two lawmen to make certain they understood what was to happen. The three men stood behind the jail, smoking and talking. After a few minutes, they split up with Murphy heading for the Longhorn saloon; Sheriff Lucas heading for his home on Third Street; and Marshal Shields entering the jail.

Inside the jail, the Bar 3 gunmen were crowded into five small cells. Rhey Selman gripped the cell bars and said, "Macy, get us out of here. We're not going quietly."

"Shut up, Selman, and listen."

Macy Shields explained what was going to happen . . . that a deputy would be in charge for the night and would be given a jug of whiskey. As he spoke, Shields handed keys and three revolvers to Selmon.

"Keep 'em out of sight," Shields ordered. "This needs to go quiet-like. Your horses are at the livery corral—still saddled. Murphy wants you to take all of them so he's got an alibi. Go back to the Bar 3 but stay out of sight. Go to one of the outer shacks."

"All right. When do we do this?" Selmon asked, keeping one gun and passing on the other weapons.

"My deputy'll be here in an hour." Shields grinned. "Be patient. When he's snoring, you can open the cells."

"What about him?"

"Coldcock him. Don't shoot," Shields said. "And

don't run to the corral. Walk. Ride out the same way, real easy-like. Two or three at a time. If you do it right, nobody will know you're gone till morning, when I check in."

"What about the Corrigans?"

"Leave that to Bordner."

CHAPTER TWENTY-TWO

At midday, a grim Sheriff Lucas rode up to the LC ranch yard. With him were eight riders, all towns-men, all uneasy about their assignment as members of the sheriff's posse.

From the corral, Deed and Blue met them as they rode into the yard. Silka and Chico came from the barn. It was obvious something was wrong.

"The attackers broke out last night. Coldcocked the deputy. Got a night's lead on us," Lucas stated with little emotion.

With his hands on his hips, Deed snarled, "Been to the Bar 3? There's where they came from, Sheriff."

From the back of the posse came a gruff reply from Dixie Murphy. "I told you they were my horses, Corri-gan, but not my men. I intend to get them back. Whether you go or not."

"They're headed toward El Paso," Sheriff Lucas declared without looking at either man.

"Kinda headed the wrong direction, aren't you?" Deed said.

"Thought you'd want to ride with us," Sheriff Lucas said. "Some of these boys need to . . . get home. We'll go next to the Lazy S and see if they want to help."

Deed was silent and glanced at Silka, who nodded.

"All right. Send the husbands home to their wives," Deed finally said. He turned to Blue and suggested that he, Silka, and the others continue with roundup preparation. He asked Chico if he would go with him, but that he certainly didn't have to do so. The Mexican readily agreed and Blue thought it made sense. Silka thought it would be better if he went along, instead, but Deed told him it was more important for him to stay at the ranch. The former samurai's face was unreadable, but he didn't say anything more.

Soon, Deed and Chico were riding away with Sheriff Lucas and the posse. After picking up the middle son, Thomas Sanchez, and two vaqueros from the Lazy S, five men from the original group left for town and the rest continued on. The outlaws' trail was not hard to follow with so many horses involved. They were definitely more interested in gaining distance than in deceiving pursuit.

Thomas Sanchez took the point at Deed's request and his trail-reading skills were quickly apparent. The day was overcast with the likelihood of an autumn rain coming . . . and soon. After pausing at a feisty creek to water their mounts, the posse continued with little talking among themselves. Deed even refrained from chewing on Dixie Murphy, who was now bringing up the rear. For the first time, Deed realized the crooked cowman had put on a bright red scarf around this neck. Deed was certain he wasn't wearing it earlier, but said nothing.

The afternoon sun was easing toward the horizon and Deed suggested to Thomas Sanchez that they

should look for a place to camp for the night. Sheriff
Lucas insisted they keep going for another hour or so,
that they were cutting into the outlaws' lead. The logic
was hard to argue with and Deed and Thomas agreed.

Ahead was a towering mesa with its twin positioned
on the other side of the trail. The area was known as
Oak Tree Canyon. Through it lay more open country with occasional bursts of scrub pine. On either
side of the mesas were heavily forested areas, broken
by rock and a sometimes creek. A perfect place for an
ambush, Deed thought and drew his Spencer from its
saddle scabbard. He leaned forward and patted his
buckskin on the neck. Chico noticed Deed readying
his rifle and did the same. Deed saw Sheriff Lucas was
wearing his lawman's badge; the metal star danced a
little, even in the overcast afternoon.

"How come you're wearing a star?" Deed asked.
"Kinda gives us away, doesn't it?"

The gray-haired lawman glanced at his shirt and
shrugged his shoulders. "Thought it made sense for
people to know we're the law. You know, the law is
coming."

"Interesting," Deed said. "Most lawmen I know
don't wear their badges on the trail. It gives them
away. Where we're riding could easily be an ambush."

"It'll be fine, Corrigan. You take care of yourself."

"That's what I am trying to do." Shifting in his
saddle, Deed studied the nearing mesas. He yelled to
Thomas three horse lengths in front of him, "Thomas,
I don't like this. Ride careful."

The young Mexican nodded his agreement and
patted the rifle laying across his saddle in front of him.

Halfway up the hillside on the left, a flicker of light
came and disappeared in an instant.

"Thomas, ambush!" Deed yelled and kicked his horse, firing in the direction of the brief flash and wheeling toward the trees to his right.

Rifle fire from a dozen spots exploded from both mesas. Thomas Sanchez went down, then his two vaqueros under the heavy fire. Five bullets sought Deed at once and drove him from his frightened horse. One bullet creased his horse's chest. Another drilled a hole in his hat and one cut across the top of his left ear, barely missing his head. A fourth sliced across his upper left arm, ripping through his shirtsleeve. And a fifth clipped his left thigh. The buckskin ran on. The young gunfighter hit the ground. His carbine went flying into the woods. So did his hat. For a minute, he wasn't cognizant of what was going on. Around him, bullets tore into the posse, except for Sheriff Lucas and Dixie Murphy who were riding safely toward the mesas.

Deed saw Chico get hit in the face and crumble to the ground. One of the two townsmen with the posse flopped next to Deed. He stared at the young gunfighter through frightened eyes, tried to speak, and died.

Blinking away the shock, Deed reached up and touched his left ear; its top was bleeding and hurting. He had come close to being killed. Crawling on his hands and knees, he found his carbine, grabbed it, and moved on reaching a shallow ravine that once had been a creek. Sounds of gunfire gradually lessened as he forced himself to keep moving. He knew the outlaws would soon leave the mesas to see if any posse men remained alive.

He had to find a hiding place before he passed out. He must. His left arm was throbbing and his shirtsleeve was crimson. He was certain he'd also been hit near his left thigh. He didn't think any of the wounds were serious, but he was losing a considerable amount of blood and was growing weak from the shock.

Splatters of a cold rain drummed against the land.

At the end of the ravine sat a fat pool of water—stagnant water. To his right was a long rock shelf, running twenty yards. He forced himself up onto the shelf and crawled along its uneven frame, dragging his carbine with him. Maybe he could lay there and rest. Maybe. Fifteen yards along the way, he came to a crevice that looked like a possible hideaway. He stood, became dizzy, and dropped again to his knees. Patience was the key, Silka would remind him if he were here. Do not panic. Think.

Rain was coming hard now and that would wash away any signs of his movements. Standing slowly again, he saw the crevice opened into a cave that was at least twenty feet long and almost man-high. He slipped inside and slid to the ground. If they found him here, he would die, but he couldn't go any farther. He cocked the Spencer using both hands.

Crawling across the rocky floor was a black spider. Deed watched the tiny creature as it moved up onto his boot.

"Evening, little buddy," he said. "Got some Indian friends that think you're a pretty powerful fellow. Sorry to bother you, but I had to get out of the rain."

The spider crawled up across his boot, down, and wandered toward the back of the cave. Shortly afterward, he fell asleep.

On the trail, outlaws squished across the soaked land, swearing at being wet and making certain none of the downed posse lived, with additional shots to their heads. Wearing a yellow slicker over his bear-fur coat, Rhey Selmon looked up at the sheriff and Dixie Murphy.

"Ya did good, lawman. Agon will be pleased. Probably a bonus in it for ya," Selmon praised and wiped rain from his face.

Sheriff Lucas looked nauseous and said nothing.

"I don't see Corrigan's body, do you?" Murphy said, shifting in his saddle.

"No. Haven't found it yet. Washita said he hit him in the head. Knocked him off his horse," Selmon said. "I hit him, too. Arm or shoulder. Could've been hit four or five times. Ike was shooting at him, too."

Watching the rain soak the land, Murphy said, "Well, I want to see his body. I want to put a bullet between his eyes, for good measure. The bastard almost ruined things for us." He swung his horse toward the mesa. "Keep looking."

Less than two miles away, Holt Corrigan heard the gunshots before the rain came. He had seen the clouds, quickly gathered wood for a fire, and taken refuge under a cliff before the sky opened up. He knew he wasn't far from the largest ranch in the area, the Bar 3, but still a long way from his brothers' ranch. The intensity of gunfire told him that it wasn't a hunt; it was a gun battle. All that gunfire meant someone was surely dead. As soon as the word *dead* came to his mind, he tried to unthink it. He didn't want to pull death to him by thinking of it. Besides, there was nothing he could do about it, one way or the other. Probably a disagreement over cattle ownership, so he began assembling his gathered wood for a fire and soon got it started. He was surprised to see the fire turn hollow, and he jammed short branches into its middle to eliminate the bad sign. There wasn't anything he could do at the moment, except make certain his guns were cleaned and ready.

CHAPTER TWENTY-THREE

It was dark when Deed Corrigan awoke. The rain had stopped and the night was cold. He woke up shivering. At first, he didn't know where he was, but gradually his mind returned him to the situation. His left arm was stiff, so was his left thigh. His ear burned with pain. Gradually, he determined that neither his leg nor his arm wound held any lead. He was hungry and thirsty. The second desire should be easily handled. Outside the cave were puddles of rainwater collected in the rock shelf's pockets. He forced himself to make certain his Spencer and handgun were dry and ready. It took twice as long as it should.

Cradling his Spencer in his right arm, he half-crawled, half-dragged himself to the first rain puddle and drank it dry. He edged himself along the shelf to the second water and did his best to clean his wounds, even putting his ear into the cool water. He was weak, but he was alive. More than he could say for the rest of the posse, he feared.

Obviously, Sheriff Lucas was involved with Agon

Bordner's grand scheme. Probably on the take. How sad, Deed thought. At one time, Matthew R. Lucas had been a good man.

Using his right hand against the rock wall for balance, he stood and tried to put weight on his wounded left leg, but couldn't and almost fell down. The rock shelf itself was wet as he worked slowly toward the lower land. Halfway across, he slipped and fell. The pain in his left leg made him bite his lip to keep from crying out. Slowly, he stood and started again. He figured the outlaws would search the area for him and he wasn't going far without a horse.

There was a definite possibility that his buckskin would be near, unless they had taken it. After the initial fear, the animal would seek him out. Horses liked the comfort of being around people, and the buckskin was a favorite. Likely the animal would return to the trail to graze and wait. The repulsion of blood and dead bodies might change that, however. But Deed had to try and return to the trail. Some of the other posse horses might there as well. And, he reminded himself, so might be a bunch of outlaws.

But it was early. Dawn was least an hour away. Not too many outlaws liked getting up early, especially on a cold, wet morning. Still, he had to be wary of guards left behind to watch for him and any other posse member that made it.

Backtracking through the woods was slow. He couldn't put any weight on his wounded leg and it was bleeding again. A long, crooked branch was serving as a crutch. Deed couldn't remember feeling so weary. He even considered leaving his Spencer, but knew that wouldn't be wise. From the cover of brush, he studied the awful reminders of the ambush. White corpses lay in various poses of death, apparently untouched since the fighting. As expected, three horses were grazing nearby; one with its saddle upside-down. His buckskin was among them.

The smell of woodsmoke reached him before he saw its reason. Two men were crowded around a small, balky fire trying to keep warm. A blackened coffeepot sat on top of a half-burned log. A skillet of bacon slices was sizzling. Both bacon and coffee smelled delicious. On the ground nearby were tin cups and plates. Obviously, the guards were there to watch for Deed's return. Neither were paying attention as he worked his way along the edge of the trail to a position where he could cover both easily.

Dizziness tried to grab him, but he shook his head. Not now. Not now. He saw that his hat still lay within the trees near where he had fallen. Crawling, he managed to get to it and put it on, ignoring the hole through the crown and the fact that the edge rested on his injured ear.

Then, leaning on his crutch, he took a few steps forward.

"Mornin', boys," he said, aiming his carbine at them.

Both men jumped and reached for rifles lying beside them.

"Don't. Unless you want to start the morning . . . dead," Deed growled.

"You must be Deed Corrigan," the long-faced outlaw said. "Looks like our boys cut you up pretty bad."

"Looks can be deceiving," Deed said, shifting his

weight to his bad leg, then shifting it back. "You can tell Murphy and Lucas I'll be coming for them."

The taller outlaw with a long chin that held a long-ago scar straightened his back. "Tell them yourself, Corrigan. They'll be along. All of 'em. Real soon."

"You'd better hope not. The two of you won't see them arrive."

"I gotta move that bacon. It's gonna burn." Leaning over in front of the fire, the taller outlaw took hold of the skillet as if to shift it away from the flames.

Dropping his crutch, Deed realized the significance of the man using his left hand to control the skillet and stepped back and to the right as the outlaw flung the hot grease and bacon at him while reaching for his holstered gun.

Two quick shots from Deed hit the outlaw heart high as two pieces of bacon reached his waist and the grease splattered around his boots. The movement sent a dull ache through his left arm.

"Your turn." Deed swung his recocked Spencer in the direction of the second outlaw. The man took a half step forward, froze, and raised his hands.

After directing him to unbuckle his sidearm and drop a backup gun, Deed told him to take the two rifles and his pistols over to the wooded area and throw them into the forest. While that was being done, Deed picked up a slice of bacon, ate it, then retrieved the dead outlaw's revolver, shoving it into his belt. His gaze rarely left the submissive outlaw; then Deed ordered the man to lay down across the fire from him with his head pointed away and his arms and legs outstretched.

Satisfied the man couldn't or wouldn't do anything quickly, Deed ate another piece of bacon while he

searched the dead outlaw for any hidden weapons
and found a short-barreled Smith & Wesson Bulldog
revolver. He shoved the gun into his back waistband,
ate another piece of bacon from the ground, and
poured himself a cup of coffee. It was hot and strong,
but tasted good. He was weak and couldn't move
quickly, and the rest of the gang would not likely be
far away. The gunshots might have alerted them, but
he couldn't worry about it.

Drawing the outlaw's main gun, he began hobbling
toward his buckskin, leaving the crutch where he had
discarded it. As he walked past the terrified outlaw,
Deed slugged his head with the butt of his Spencer.
It didn't make sense to gamble on the man staying in
place for long and Deed needed time.

The buckskin's head came up and its ears pricked
as Deed neared. Would the animal shy away from
him? Deed's strength was draining fast; he wouldn't
be able to trail after the horse if it moved away. But
the buckskin nickered and rubbed its nose against
Deed's chest as he came close.

"Yeah, it's me, boy. We're going to ride out of here,
but you have to help me."

Deed took the downed reins, shoved the carbine
into its sleeve and led the horse to some boulders that
looked like God had been playing dice with them
before leaving. There was no way he would be able to
mount the horse with his wounded leg. He would get
on from the wrong side, and do so from an elevated
position. Finding the right rock, he led the horse
alongside, then eased his good leg into the stirrup
and tried to slide his left leg across the saddle.

The buckskin wanted to move out, but Deed
held the reins tightly with his right hand and forced

himself to complete mounting. His left leg screamed in pain. At least he was in place and he eased the reins. The buckskin took off with a familiar canter, then into a smooth lope. Deed hoped he would be able to stay conscious long enough to reach their ranch. He had to, to do otherwise was to die.

"Not today. Not going to die today."

The buckskin's ears twisted to catch the words.

"It's all right, boy, I'm just a little weak right now." He forced his left arm toward the pommel and wrapped the reins around his wrist and the pommel to help keep him upright if he passed out.

CHAPTER TWENTY-FOUR

Thirty minutes after Deed rode away, Dixie Murphy, Sheriff Lucas, Rhey Selmon, and the rest of the Bar 3 gunmen rode up to the ambush site, leading the rest of the unridden horses. They were surprised to see the lone outlaw drinking coffee by his campfire.

"What the hell happened?" Murphy screamed as he reined up next to the man, who stood and wiped off his pants.

"Ah, Deed Corrigan. That's what happened. He jumped us. Got away. About a half hour ago, I reckon," the outlaw said, scratching his boot heel on the ground and rubbing his sore head where Deed had hit him.

"Why didn't you go after him? That's why you boys were here," Murphy demanded.

"I didn't have no gun. Made me throw 'em in the woods. Yonder." He motioned toward the thick grove of trees. "Then he knocked me out. When I came around, I looked, but couldn't find them."

Rhey Selmon cursed and so did Dixie Murphy.

"If he gets away, there's no telling what kind of hell he'll create," Lucas said, shaking his head.

"Won't be too good for you, that's for sure," Selmon grunted and turned toward his men. "You three, grab an extra horse each and go after Corrigan. He's hurt . . . bad. Stop him."

The three men nudged their mounts forward, grabbing the reins of three other saddled horses.

"Push 'em hard and you'll catch him," Murphy declared, waving his arm in the direction of Deed's escape. "Just let 'em go when you switch. They'll head for the Bar 3 after a while." He bit off a chaw from a square of tobacco. "We'll take a roundabout way to the ranch. Don't want anybody tracking us there. Come as soon as he's dead."

Sheriff Lucas watched them gallop away with the extra horses beside them. "What should I do?"

Selmon spun toward him and fired. "Nothing, Sheriff. Nothing at all."

The county lawman's eyes widened, his hands extended as if to stop the bullets.

"No—"

Selmon fired three more times and Lucas fell face-down from his horse. Mud popped around him; his leg twitched and was still.

"What the hell was that all about?" Murphy screamed. "You just killed the county sheriff."

"Agon's orders."

Selmon turned toward the cattleman and fired again. Murphy grabbed his arm and screamed again. "Damn you, I'll—"

Holding up his left hand, Selmon explained, "Agon

thought it would look a little suspicious if you were
the only one in the posse not hurt."

"Oh, damn. Couldn't you have just grazed me?"

"I was trying."

"Damn."

CHAPTER TWENTY-FIVE

Dizzy and weak, Deed Corrigan weaved in the saddle. Ahead was a cluster of cottonwoods. He remembered there should be water, especially after the rain. His horse needed to rest as well.

Over the hill behind him came three riders, whipping their horses in a fierce gallop. They had to be Bar 3 gunmen coming to finish the job. He spurred the buckskin into a run it couldn't keep up long. Ahead was a small ridge. That would have to do. He was too far from the cottonwoods to make it. Nearing the ridge, he slowed his horse and untied the reins from his left hand. He pulled his carbine from its sleeve and tossed it on the ground. Trying to dismount while holding the gun could prove disastrous. The horse threw its head, wanting to run in spite of its weariness.

"Not now, boy. I need you to stop. Whoa."

Angling across the hills, Holt Corrigan saw three horsemen chasing after a lone rider, who was wounded. Deed! It was his brother!

Dismounting, Holt drew his rifle and knelt. He raised the gun to his shoulder and began firing. The lead rider grabbed his chest and tumbled from his horse. Holt's next shots missed, but the two remaining gunmen were now aware of his presence. From the ridge in front of them, Deed propped his rifle against a rock, laid his wounded arm across the barrel and shot one-handed. A second rider's face turned red and he fell off the back of his horse. The third rider tried to turn his horse around, but the animal wouldn't obey. Bullets from both Deed and Holt brought him down. The three empty horses ran past Deed as he slowly stood.

Who had helped him? Was it one of the Lazy S vaqueros? He wasn't far from the Sanchez ranch. He watched as the figure remounted and rode toward him, waving.

Holt!

How in the world? Deed wondered but was very happy, whatever the reason. He was weak and went to his knees.

"Hey, Deed, what the hell you doing out here?" Holt asked as he rode up. "Wait a minute. You're hurt. Really hurt." He swung his horse around toward the attackers. "Hold on, Deed. I gotta check on these bastards first, so they won't cause us more problems."

Holt walked his horse next to the closest outlaw and jumped down, holding his rifle in his right hand. The dead gunman's face was a red pumpkin. He yanked free the man's pistols and a knife and threw them in Deed's direction, then went to the second downed gunman. Stepping close, he kicked the prone man in the ribs. Hard. The grunt that followed was what Holt expected.

"When you turn over, peckerhead, you'd better have empty hands," Holt growled. "I'd like an excuse to put a bullet in your head."

"I-I'm hurt. R-Real bad."

"Tell somebody who gives a damn," Holt responded. "You bastards were trying to kill my little brother." He pointed his rifle at the slowly moving man. "I oughta put a bullet in your head just for good measure."

"P-Please . . . mister," the long-faced outlaw said, holding his side. His shirt was mostly crimson.

"Shut up."

"P-Please I was j-just followin' orders."

"Who sent you?"

"Uh, nobody."

Holt fired and the outlaw screamed and grabbed his right knee. "That's one knee gone. Want to try two?" Holt levered a new cartridge into his rifle.

"Oh God, no! No! Dixie Murphy and Rhey Selmon, they sent us."

"That's better. What's going on here?"

The outlaw jabbered about what had happened, the attack and arrest at the Lazy S, the escape from jail, the ambush of the posse, the involvement of the county sheriff. Holt stripped the man of his weapons and tossed them toward his brother, then walked on to the third outlaw. The man was dead; Holt disarmed him, shoving his guns into his waistband and heading for his brother.

"Hey, are you Holt Corrigan?" the long-faced outlaw asked. "I heard you was dead."

Holt smiled. "Heard that, too. I'm Sam Holton."

"Sam H-Holton? Do I know you?"

"No. I don't hang around with scum." Holt hurried to his wounded brother.

"I'm all right. Nothing serious. They caught us in an ambush yesterday."

"I heard." Holt looked up. "Think any more of those bastards will be coming?"

"Don't know. I doubt it. Getting too close to the Lazy S."

"You've got blood in your hair, on your ear."

"Yeah, they nicked my ear. Think a little piece is gone."

Holt examined Deed's ear. "Yeah. But no one will notice if you keep your hair long."

"I guess I was lucky."

"Are you carrying any lead?" Holt asked.

"No. Just been bleeding a lot."

"Your ear looks like somebody bit it."

"Yeah, a bullet."

"Can you ride?" Holt asked, shoving his rifle into its sleeve and pulling his canteen from his saddle and handing to Deed.

"I got here, didn't I?"

Deed took the canteen and drank deeply, holding it with his right hand. His left hand was at his side. He tried to put weight on his left leg but it wouldn't hold him and he fell.

"Careful, little brother. Go slow."

"Yeah, maybe so. Can you get my horse? The buckskin might let you. He's a good one," Deed said.

"Sure. Can you hold mine?"

"Got it."

After slipping the canteen sling over his saddle horn, Holt walked to Deed's grazing horse. The buckskin raised his head and his ears went up as Holt approached.

"Easy, buck. Easy now. I'm Deed's brother. Nothing

to get excited about. Right?" Holt held out his opened palm for the horse to sniff, then slid it along the animal's face to take hold of his halter, then the reins. "See, buck. Nothing to it. Going to be fine, you and me. Let's go over here where Deed is."

He led the horse back to Deed. The buckskin shook its head and snorted, smelling Deed's blood.

"You're all right, Buck. It's old blood," Holt helped Deed into the saddle, holding the reins of both horses, then retrieved Deed's Spencer and returned it to the saddle scabbard.

"Tie my hands . . . and my boots," Deed said. "There's piggin' strings in my saddlebags."

Holt looked over at the wounded outlaw, who was laying down, holding his bloody knee. Two of the outlaw horses were grazing nearby; the third was nowhere in sight.

After Holt had laced his brother into place, he jammed the collected outlaw guns, barrel first, into the muddy ground.

"Deed, think I'd better get rid of those rifles on their horses before we go. Don't want to give ol' one knee any ideas," Holt said.

"They might not let you get close."

"We'll see. If they don't, I'll send 'em running."

Mounting, Holt swung his horse toward the quiet horses. The closest bay tensed as he rode up, but didn't move. He eased alongside the animal and yanked the rifle clear and laid it across his saddle in front of him. The second rifle was lifted as easily and Holt pulled away, balancing both guns in front of him.

The wounded outlaw watched him and called out, "You better keep ridin', Corrigan. Bordner's gonna git all of you. You, too, Holton."

Holt's eyes were hot. For an instant, his fingers found the trigger of the top rifle, then he relaxed. "Tell that fat bastard *we'll* be coming after *him*. Tell him to get his fat ass out of here."

The outlaw muttered something the Corrigan brothers didn't understand as they rode away with Holt leading Deed's horse. After a few minutes, Holt threw the two outlaw rifles into the brush.

"Holt, I'm mighty glad to see you," Deed said through clenched teeth. "Blue said he talked with you in El Paso."

"Yeah, he told me to quit fighting a dead war and come home. So, here I am."

Deed smiled. "Blue makes a lot of sense sometimes. Kinda like Ma used to."

"Right."

"You didn't rob the El Paso bank?"

"No. Blue said it was owned by Confederates. So I went to see for myself. Ended up talking with Dave Copate. We fought together at Sabine Pass. Good man," Holt said. "He told me a lot of what Blue said."

"We got word at the Forsyth station that the bank had been robbed."

"Really. Well, it wasn't me."

Deed shook his head. "Yeah, the stage driver said that the bank president claimed it wasn't you. Was real strong about it."

Holt was silent, then changed the subject. "How far to the next . . . friendly ranch?"

"The Lazy S is about three hours from here. Due north."

They rode on, each with his own thoughts, into a wide and broken land. Ahead of them grazing cattle were mere dots on a light brown canvas. Overhead, the sky was a mass of jagged gray clouds, as if a long heavenly fire had turned ashen.

Holt was worried about more Bar 3 riders following them or coming up on them from some unseen draw. They were crossing Bar 3 land; he knew that. Deed was mumbling to himself, barely conscious.

They passed a cluster of stunted cedar, enclosing what had once been a buffalo wallow. Ahead he saw a large open tank holding water. As they approached, Deed woke up, shook his head, and told him to head toward a patch of brittlebush far to the left and to a gathering of trees just beyond. He grimaced that the tank was filled with scum and gestured that good water lay within the trees. Holt nodded and wheeled his horse in that direction, still leading Deed's horse. They passed a snow-white steer skeleton, cleared a fat ridge, entered a shallow wash, and rode into a magnificent meadow, unseen from just a handful of yards away. In front of them was a sparkling pond, fed by two occasional streams and offering solace to a small gathering of cottonwood, pecan, and oak trees. A half-dozen steers drank from its wetness.

"Told ya," Deed muttered.

"Lucky guess," Holt growled. "Want down?"

"No thanks. Better not. Might have trouble getting back on." Deed's face was white with shock.

"All right." Holt dismounted and led both horses to the pond. Several steers moved away as they advanced. All wore Bar 3 brands.

While the animals drank, Holt Corrigan studied their surroundings. It was fine cattle country. Far to their left was a long arroyo that appeared to be filled with cattle. To their right was a patch of sandstone bursting with heavy rock. The sandstone was still heavy with last

night's rain. In all directions, the land was empty of
riders. At least it would be difficult to surprise them in
this flat country. Somewhere a quail whispered an in-
quiring song. Holt wondered if it was a sign and what
kind. He decided it must be a good sign; how could a
bird singing be an indication of bad things coming?

After the horses had watered well, they took off
again. Holt knew the land, but not like Deed and Blue
did. It had been long years since his departure. Deed
was asleep in the saddle and Holt let him rest.

A late afternoon sun laid slanting rays across the
two Corrigan brothers as they rode closer to the Lazy S.
Ahead of them, two antelope were surprised from
their grazing and began to run. Deed was apparently
asleep, bobbing in the saddle. Holt watched four
riders appear in the horizon and advance from a
ridge to the northwest.

He knew at once it was Comanches.

Taking a knife from his belt, Holt turned to Deed.
"Little brother, wake up. Got four Indians coming.
Wake up." He leaned over and cut free Deed's hands
with his knife.

Deed blinked his eyes, trying to regain his senses,
then began rubbing his stiff hands.

"Got an idea, Deed. Make like you're crazy in the
head. You know, yelling crazy stuff. Wave your arms,"
Holt told him as the watched the warriors advance.

"You think it's worth it. I can shoot."

"We'll try that next."

Deed began to holler a mixture of Japanese phrases
and biblical verses, anything he could recall. "*Nakitsura
ni hachi! Ame futte ji katamaru!* There is a lion in the
way; a lion is in the streets. *Tonari no shibafu wa noi!*
The Lord bless thee and keep thee; the Lord make his

face shine upon thee, and be gracious unto thee; the Lord lift up his countenance upon thee, and give thee peace. *Fuku sui bon ni kaerazu!*" He waved his right arm wildly, looking up to the sky.

As they rode closer to the Indians, Holt said the Comanche words for medicine man while he made the signs. He put his fist at his forehead, extended two fingers skyward, then spiraled his fist upward. That was followed with holding up one finger. His left hand held his rifle in front of his saddle.

The Indians made signs of understanding and moved out of their way. After clearing a short ridge, Holt said, "Come on, let's ride before they change their minds."

They galloped hard across the broken plain and gradually brought their horses back to a trot, then a walk.

"Damn, that was wild," Holt said, shaking his head.

"Sure was. I was out of stuff to yell," Deed said and chuckled. "Never can tell about Indians."

"Yeah. Never. You sure must be feeling better to yell like that."

"Didn't have much choice."

They rode silently for another hour when three riders became visible from the northwest. They were largely silhouettes. As they came closer, Deed could make out their sombreros and a stray ray of sun found one of their large-roweled spurs.

"They're friends, Holt. Lazy S vaqueros. Wave at them."

"You're sure."

"Yes."

The Corrigan brothers rode easily forward as the three vaqueros slipped beside them, eager to hear what had happened. Deed's bloody shirt and pants told part of the story. Four brown and lean men with unrelenting dark eyes flashed ready smiles. Each was armed with a rifle and gunbelt; each had an extra cartridge belt across his shoulders. Large-roweled spurs seemed a part of their bodies.

The lead vaquero with steel-gray hair and piercing eyes groaned when told the news about Sanchez's son and the vaqueros with the posse. A cigarette dangled from his lips.

"Are you the one they call *El Punta*?" he asked.

"No, I'm Sam Holton," Holt held out his hand.

Taking it firmly, the man said, "I am Cliente, foreman of the Lazy S."

"Good to know you," Holt said. "I take it you've met my little brother." He smiled. "Guess that gave it away. Sorry. Too many folks trying to catch up with Holt Corrigan these days."

Straightening his back, Cliente said, "I understand. Señor Deed Corrigan is a most honored man in our *ranchero*. He save us. He and his brother, Blue. And Silka, the one with the long knives. You are most welcome . . . Sam Holton."

"Thanks. Agon Bordner behind all this?"

"*Sí*, the fat man and his guns. Many guns. They outnumber us two times. Maybe more," Cliente tossed his dead cigarette. "We are cowmen, not gunmen."

"All of us will have to get smarter and tougher," Holt drawled.

"*Sí*. Let us ride for our *ranchero*, amigos," Cliente said. "Your brother need rest. We will send out a wagon to bring home the bodies of Thomas Sanchez and our friends who rode with the posse."

Deed bit his lower lip and asked if they would also

bring Chico's body back for burying at their ranch. Cliente readily agreed, then said something in Spanish to two of his men. They wheeled their horses and galloped back. Deed guessed Cliente was being careful and didn't want to take a chance on Bar 3 riders coming up on them. A look at Holt told him that his brother was thinking the same thing.

Motioning for the Corrigan brothers to follow, Cliente rolled another cigarette and said, "So now we fight the law as well as the fat man." He snapped a match to flame on his pants, inhaled, and added, "Roundup will be a *buen' ocasión* to attack us, I fear. We will be spread out and worried about our beeves."

Deed nodded, too tired to respond. His wounds were bleeding again, bringing fresh pain. Sleep would be welcomed. Forcing himself to speak, he said, "Not having the roundup would play right into their hands. They'd brand everything that moved."

"*Sí.* It is a tough thing we are in."

"Well, it's a cinch they won't be joining us this year," Holt said, searching his coat pocket for a cigar.

Deed smiled at the use of *us.* It was good to have Holt back. They rode for a few minutes; then Holt turned to his brother, leaned towards him, and just above a whisper, said, "Earlier I told those boys I was Sam Holton. You should know that I am going by that name for now. At least to outsiders. I'll deal with the other later."

"Sure . . . Sam."

As soon as they reached the Lazy S hacienda, Cliente jumped down and went inside; he found Felix Sanchez and told him about Deed and Sam following. Felix met them at the hitchrail in front; reddened eyes told them that the news of his son's death had already reached the family. Cliente was beside him.

"Amigos. It is *bueno* that you make it, Señor Deed," Felix said in a voice thick with sadness.

"Felix, I'm so sorry about Thomas. We rode right into it," Deed said.

"Sheriff Lucas shall die by my hand," the big Mexican rancher said.

Holt leaned forward in his saddle. "You know something? Don't be surprised if Sheriff what's his name is already dead. With Deed getting away, his value to Bordner isn't much."

Deed looked at him with a question in his eyes. "What about Murphy?"

"Naw. He's too good a cattleman."

Felix Sanchez waved his arms. "*Por favor*, where are my manners? Come in and eat. Señor Deed, you must rest. You come as well, Señor Holton." The Sanchez family swarmed around Deed, insisting that he be treated for his wounds even as Deed insisted he was fine.

"Señor Deed, you have been bleeding *muy mal*," the gray-haired Maria Sanchez, Felix's wife, declared. "Come now and let us clean your wounds. Find some new clothes."

Sanchez's daughters, Tina and Lea, laughed and took him by the arm. Both were in their late teens and striking young women. Felix nodded agreement and his oldest son, Taol, shouted his support. Holt laughed and patted his brother on the back.

Maria turned to Holt. "You must eat too, Señor Holton. You have saved our Deed." It was obvious they realized he was Deed's older brother, but honored Holt's wish to be called Sam Holton.

"Sounds great."

Felix Sanchez told them that his youngest son, Paul, had been moved back home and was resting well and Felix's thanks for saving Paul and all at the ranch came again. Deed was so tired he wasn't sure he could stand. They entered the great house, taking in its quiet majesty. Adobe walls held the temperatures well and everywhere the Corrigans looked were paintings, Mexican artifacts, Indian pottery, and handwoven rugs. A large gun rack held a dozen rifles and three shotguns.

Heavy chairs, hand engraved, awaited them around the massive wooden table. Felix and Cliente were already seated and talking. Holt sat down, after washing his face and hands outside. A few minutes later, Deed joined them wearing a new shirt and pants, flared at the bottom. He looked pale, but acted like he was fine. His ear was bandaged and it smelled like his arm and thigh had been dressed as well. He was wearing his gunbelt, but had discarded the outlaw revolvers picked up at their camp.

"You look ready for church services, even Blue would be pleased," Holt said and added, "I'm going to ride with Cliente and his riders back to the ambush. Felix wants the bodies back here as soon as possible. You'll stay here, all right?"

"Uh, sure. Sure."

Felix's daughters brought in steaming plates of tortillas, beef, and beans, with plenty of fresh, hot coffee. After finishing, Deed asked if it would be all right for him to lie down for a few minutes. The two daughters led him to one of the extra bedrooms and he was asleep in minutes.

CHAPTER TWENTY-SIX

Rhey Selmon reported to Agon Bordner and was surprised at the oversized boss's reaction—or rather, the lack of it. Savoring a freshly baked apple pie, the huge man stopped eating as his top gunman reported that all of the posse had been killed except Deed Corrigan, but he was wounded and three men had gone after him to finish the job.

In the far corner, a man was playing the violin for Bordner's enjoyment as he ate. He hadn't shared with Selmon or Murphy that two Texas Rangers had made an appearance while they were gone. Bordner had fed them generously and given them a place to sleep, then they had ridden on. He was certain they believed his story about an unknown band of renegades attacking his ranch, stealing horses, and then attacking the Lazy S.

Bordner looked up, apple syrup dripping down his chin. "What about Lucas?"

"He's dead," Selmon said. "Murphy's wounded. Just skinned his arm. Like you ordered."

"Good. Good." Bordner took another bite of pie, enjoying the combination of crust and fruit. "Fine job on the pie, Simpson," he yelled to the unseen cook.

Outside of the ranch was a burst of noise and Selmon went to see what was happening. He came back, frowning.

"That's Benson. He's shot up some," Selmon said. "Some stranger gunned down the other two."

Bordner licked his fingers and called for more coffee. Without turning toward Selmon, he asked, "What stranger?"

Hitching his gunbelt as if to challenge someone, Selmon said that a stranger who called himself Sam Holton showed up as they were closing in on the wounded Deed Corrigan. He made the difference and they rode off together.

"This stranger was leading Deed's horse. Deed had his hands tied to the pommel and his boots to the stirrups, to keep him steady," Selmon said. "Like I said, he was carrying lead. Don't know how bad though. He's a tough sonuvabitch." He cocked his head to the side. "From what Benson says, this other guy was, too."

"Ever hear of a Sam Holton?"

"No."

"Well, well, that's not a good day's work, Rhey. You didn't kill them," Bordner said and pushed another quarter section of pie into his mouth and followed it with coffee.

Selmon looked at him, worried about what Bordner would do.

Bordner told him to keep the arrested and escaped Bar 3 men there on the ranch, except when on specific assignment. To make it easier for them, he had ordered extra whiskey and a wagonload of prostitutes to be brought in for their enjoyment. He planned to keep three for himself.

Rhey Selmon smiled and left to tell the men.

The fat man was pleased with several outcomes of the last few days. The men who had attacked the Lazy S and survived the Corrigan counterattack were back and no law would be looking for them. So were all of their horses. That brought his force to twenty-two men. Not as many as he wanted, but enough if he used them well, and more were available for hire in El Paso. The Lazy S had lost another three men; he was certain Felix Sanchez had no more than ten men left to operate and protect his ranch.

Murphy was ordered to go to town and report on the posse's demise. He was to say he didn't know if Deed Corrigan was alive or not, only that his body wasn't there when he rode away. He was to tell the town editor that he had been hit on the head and had been unconscious until after the ambush was over. Bordner wanted the town council to select an interim county sheriff until an election could be held and he wanted Macy Shields to hold both jobs, at least for now. It would make the final takeover of the region's cattle lands so much easier. He prided himself on thinking long-term. That was the key. None of his men knew all of his plans. Not Dixie Murphy. Not Rhey Selmon. Not Macy Shields. Not anyone.

He finished the pie with a flourish and lit up a black cigar. The women should arrive anytime this afternoon.

After returning from town, Murphy was to oversee the gathering of cows with calves for fall branding. There would be no cooperation with the Sanchezes or the Corrigans, of course. He had already merged the two small ranches into the Bar 3 and all of the new animals were being marked with his bar crown brand. He loved the look of it. Sheer power he thought. Murphy's men were to stay on their side of the boundary between the Bar 3 and the Lazy S spreads. Bordner wanted it to appear that he was a law-abiding citizen and any trouble that occurred was not his doing.

He didn't like hearing about a gun-savvy stranger helping Deed Corrigan. Things he couldn't control upset him. He planned on having Murphy drive some cattle to the railroad crew working around Houston to provide some immediate cash. Selmon would also be directed to rob the El Paso stage, at least once more. Bordner had kept his men away from robbing the trains; he didn't like the idea of Pinkertons back-tracking them . . . to him.

Bordner pulled on his cigar and waved at the violinist to leave. The house was quiet and he liked that. He took the cigar from his mouth, studied it, and called out for Selmon. The gunfighter was in the other room and responded quickly.

"Did you leave all the bodies where they fell?" Bordner asked.

"Yeah."

"Do you think the Sanchezes will send a wagon to bring back the bodies of their men?" Bordner ran his finger along the table.

Selmon rubbed his chin. "Hadn't thought about it. But, yeah, I reckon so."

"Yes. So do I. Here's what I want you to do." Bordner had decided he wanted to hit the Sanchez ranch again, right now when they wouldn't be expecting it.

"Take men with you and wait. Out of sight. When you see the wagon and their men leave the Lazy S, I want to you to hit the ranch again. They won't be expecting it." He returned the cigar to his mouth.

Controlling the county law would make it all go smoothly. Since the owning family was Mexican, he didn't expect much of an outcry from the rest of the community. Except for the Corrigans. They would be dealt with separately.

CHAPTER TWENTY-SEVEN

It was late afternoon and cool. Holt was checking his rifle as Cliente picked three men to go with him and the burial wagon.

Deed woke up suddenly and scrambled from the room. He was light-headed, but knew he was stronger than he felt. His voice was steady, even though he was not. He walked toward the front of the hacienda, using his right hand to balance his movements, touching anything that went in the direction he sought to go.

From the kitchen, Tina Sanchez heard him and came to see to what was happening.

"Wait, Holt! Wait. I think Bordner will use this time to strike here," Deed hollered.

"Señor Corrigan, you must get back in bed," Tina said and took his arm.

"No. I can't. Please, I must stop them." He brushed her hand from his arm and continued toward the doorway. She wasn't sure what to do and hurried after him.

Holt was the first to hear and stop what he was

doing, then Cliente did the same, holding up his hand for his men to wait.

"We're outside, Deed. Getting ready to leave," Holt called back.

"Wait. Hear me," Deed opened the door. "They will attack as soon as you leave. It makes too much sense. Felix and his wife are dealing with their sadness . . . and Cliente will have three or four men with him. That leaves only a handful to guard this place. It is perfect for them. If they come, it'll be with twenty guns. Maybe more," Deed said. "How many can you stand?"

Tina Sanchez stopped behind him, admiring his broad shoulders, but used the excuse of steadying him to put her hands around his waist and hold him upright. Both girls were smitten by the Corrigan brothers.

"Eight," Cliente said and grimaced. "They kill half our men before."

"Well, let's give them something to shoot at, first," Deed said, holding onto the porch railing.

"Have you lost more blood than I thought, little brother?" Holt looked at Deed as if he were crazy.

Tina touched Deed's arm; he looked at her, swiveled, and said, "Tina, I'm fine. Really. *Muchas gracias.*"

She flashed a wide smile, sought his eyes for an instant, and releasing him, stepped away.

Deed explained they could fix five or six dummies and put them in the yard as if they were talking. It would make the Bar 3 gunmen think they could get most of the Lazy S men in one quick attack. Likely, it would put the attackers in an exposed position, or at least bunched together.

"Think it'll work?" Holt asked, laying his rifle against the wagon.

Cliente grinned. "I like it."

"Well, the shadows will help," Deed said. "Even if it doesn't, it'll confuse them."

The Sanchez women, even Maria, eagerly joined the masquerade effort. Flour sacks were filled with straw and tied to become dummy heads. Wooden frames were nailed together to provide the body and hold shirts, pants, and the sacks. A sombrero topped each dummy and a serape was draped across what appeared to be a shoulder.

An hour later, six dummies were placed on the south side of the main ranch yard, grouped together as if they were talking. Even Holt was impressed. In the dusk, they looked almost real. Deed said people would see what they expected to see.

Satisfied, Cliente left with the burial wagon and three outriders, all were Sanchez women disguised as men. Cliente would ride for an hour, then stop and wait. He would turn back when he heard gunfire. In the dusk, sounds of gunfire would travel a long way. There was a risk that Bar 3 men would attack the wagon first, but they decided it wouldn't be worth it to Bordner since the ranch would be forewarned.

Holt stationed all of the vaqueros on the flat roof of the ranchero. They were spread out, covering the complete ranch yard from above, and were to remain out of sight until he gave the signal to fire. Holt and Deed took positions inside the house, each watching a different direction. The oldest son, Taol, settled into watching the north. Felix refused to stay out of the fight and joined his son with his pistols and a band of cartridges over his shoulder.

Now they must wait, letting late afternoon shadows creep across the yard. It would be dark in two hours. For the Corrigan brothers, waiting was easy; Silka had taught both the importance of waiting. It wasn't the opposite of attacking, just a matter of timing the attack. Although Holt was worried about Deed, his wounded brother assured him he was strong enough to help.

Outside, a light breeze whispered through a cluster of junipers near the front door and caught the sleeves of the dummies, making them dance in the fading twilight.

"Maybe it'll look like they're excited," Holt whispered and motioned toward the dummies.

"Yeah. From a distance, it'll probably help. Unless the sleeves really start whipping around," Deed said.

"Wait, I hear something. Down by the fence," Holt said and shifted his rifle into readiness. "Down there." With his right hand, he reached up and touched the cardinal feather in his hatband.

"Yeah, I see them. Must be ten or so right there," Deed said. He propped his Spencer carbine on the back of a second chair in front of him and aimed it out the opened window. The chair was turned away from him and the back made it easier to steady his gun. On the floor beside him was a box with reloading tubes. In his gunbelt, Deed had returned the two outlaw handguns taken earlier.

Felix had told them not to worry about shooting out window glass, but the Corrigan brothers knew the value of glass and thought it best to open the windows where they might be firing. Felix and his son were unseen, watching from another part of the house.

"Looks like they're planning on getting closer. I see a few climbing the fence," Deed said.

Holt looked over at him and grinned; turning a chair around was good luck. He wondered if his brother knew that. Then he saw Deed touch the small, Oriental brass circle hanging around his neck on a rawhide thong. Holt knew what Bushido meant and nodded.

"Yeah, I don't think the bastards in front of our dummies will try that. They'll stay behind the fence," Holt said and wiped the sweat from his forehead. "Figure it's too risky. Your idea is working." He moved next to the window. "But I got a few coming over the fence on this side, too. They're right next to that batch of sagebrush."

"When do you want to welcome them?"

"Let's wait. They closer they get, the bigger the surprise. For them," Holt said.

"Agreed. But not too close. If they get next to the house, our roof shooters won't be able to stop them."

"That's why we're here, little brother."

A long row of orange flame erupted in the semi-darkness, all from the Bar 3 rifles along the stone fence in front of the dummies. The roar tore into the silence. Sombreros flew from the dummies and the filled sacks split open. The clothes whirled in different directions and two shirts fell from their wooden frames.

"Now," Holt said and fired.

His first shot caught the closest raider crawling toward the house in the head. Levering his Winchester, he missed the second man but Holt's next shots slammed into him and the man collapsed and didn't move. Above, the roof was alive with vaquero rifle fire

at the targets along the fence, well defined by the gray
land behind them.

Deed fired at the lead attacker on his side of the
ranch yard, balancing the gun barrel on the chair in
front of him. The man was slammed backward by
the heavy shot and crumbled to the ground. Deed
laid his wounded left arm across the top of the gun
and levered a new round. Bullets crashed into the
window, but stopped as the vaqueros on the roof
poured lead into the small groups.

Firing again, Deed saw the attacker spin halfway
around. He gave up on the Spencer, yanked free his
revolver and moved to the side of the window. The
sudden movement made him dizzy for a moment and
he leaned against the wall to right his head. His left
arm was bleeding again. He wouldn't have the range
or impact, but he could shoot quicker with the handgun. Cocking and firing so fast it sounded like a long
round of thunder, the young gunfighter dropped two
attackers.

From somewhere, a cry went up to retreat, to run,
and the attackers inside and outside the fence broke
and ran. A gruff voice yelled at them to stand and
fight, but the words were ignored.

Holt shoved new cartridges into his rifle and fired
at the fleeing shadows. Two men stumbled and fell.
From the roof came cries of victory.

Deed heard firing from the front part of the house,
followed by Spanish yells of vengeance. His Remington empty, he drew a second handgun from his belt,
cocked and fired as a would-be attacker reached the
stone fence. Deed knew Blue would have let him go.
The man grabbed his side. Bullets from the roof
slammed him to the ground.

Almost as soon as it started, the battle was over. Racing across the land came Cliente with the buckboard and riders. They fired at the fleeing men as they grabbed their picketed horses. Holt was glad to see Cliente keep his riders moving toward the ranch, instead of following the escaping Bar 3 men. The attackers might be scared now, but they would soon realize their superior numbers. Holt and Deed watched as the attackers rode away into the night, and Cliente kept coming toward the ranch.

From the northern part of the house came Felix and Taol, both lighting cigarettes.

"Aiee, it was good," Felix declared. "Let us follow and end this."

"No." Holt's word was firm. "They still outnumber you. We could ride into an ambush ourselves."

Felix shook his head. "*Sí*, you are right, Señor Holt. It is that I want this over. I want this fat man and his devils stopped."

"I know. We all do. But we've got to be smart. Bordner is."

From the rooftop, the vaqueros were firing into the bodies strewn about the ranch yard.

Deed hobbled over to them. He was sweating heavily and his left sleeve had a circle of crimson.

"You all right, Deed?" Holt asked, watching his brother. "You're bleeding."

"Yeah. Just a little weak, that's all." He looked down at his sticky shirtsleeve. "Guess I popped it open. No big deal."

"When Cliente gets here, we shall put the dead men in his wagon and dump them on Bar 3 land," Taol said, watching Cliente bring the wagon into the yard.

Cheering went up from the roof and the women riders waved their rifles in triumph.

"Yeah. Take their guns and bullets, though. We may need them," Deed said.

"What if Bordner tries to claim his men were attacked on their own land?" Holt asked, shoving new cartridges into his rifle.

"That would be hard to prove," Deed responded.

"*Sí*, you are right, amigo," Taol said. There was a sadness in his eyes and his shoulders rose and fell.

Deed put his hand on the younger Mexican's shoulder. "In the morning, you and I will ride to town. We'll wire the Rangers and tell them what happened. That should put an end to it. At least for now."

"I'll go with Cliente to bring back . . . the bodies," Holt said, "then, when you come back from town, we can ride to our ranch. Together."

"Sounds good to me," Deed said. "It's been cool. Chico's body should be all right, I guess."

"Unless the coyotes have torn it up." Holt glanced at the Sanchezes talking quietly. "Maybe one of the Sanchez women could ride to the ranch and tell them you're all right. They'll be worried about the posse. Especially that old samurai."

"Makes good sense. I'm sure they'd be glad to," Deed answered. "I've been thinking to suggest they start stationing a few men on the roof. All the time, night and day."

"Good idea, little brother."

CHAPTER TWENTY-EIGHT

Wilkon was well into its morning routine when Deed Corrigan rode in with Taol Sanchez. The night's rest had strengthened the young gunfighter, but his left arm remained weak and numb and he carried it at his side. His leg was stiff, but definitely healing. He was wearing the same borrowed shirt, having refused the offer of another. If there was time, he would see the doctor; he had promised Holt.

The ride into town had been a quiet one with the two men lost in their thoughts. Deed liked Taol and felt sorry for the tragedies Agon Bordner had brought on his family. He knew, too, that Bordner wouldn't stop with the Lazy S, he would want the Corrigan spread as well.

What they found in town was a surprise. After wiring the Rangers at the telegraph office located within the lumberyard office, they went to the marshal to report what had happened, more of a courtesy than a necessity. The marshal was responsible for town matters only; the county sheriff was in charge of enforcing the law in the county, but Deed now knew Sheriff Lucas was crooked.

Macy Shields greeted them with a sneer and told them that Dixie Murphy had already reported on the posse's fate and he had sent a deputy with a burial team to the ambush site. As usual, he was wearing a bandana tied over his head instead of a hat, as well as once-white suspenders. Murphy, too, had been wounded in the ambush, he said.

"So the bunch that got away swung back and hit you Mexes again. Is that it?" Shields said without standing. He was seated behind the marshal's desk. A cup of coffee rested on the scratched desktop, along with stacks of paper.

Deed bristled. "Yeah, your boss tried again, Shields. But you boys still aren't good enough." He cocked his head. "I'd like it if you referred to my friend as *Mister* Sanchez."

"I don't give a damn what you'd like, Corrigan. I'm the acting county sheriff now, too. Lucas got it in the ambush." Shields reached for his coffee with his left hand as his right dropped to his lap. "Town council just voted. Smart of 'em."

"Let's see . . . Bordner owns the bank . . . and the local law. Anything else?"

Taol stared at Shields through slitted eyes. "We will have justice. It will come."

"Maybe so, Mex. Maybe so," Shields said. "If I was you, I'd see what Agon Bordner wants to give you for your place . . . and ride on while you still can."

"Come on, Taol," Deed said. "We'll deal with real lawmen when they get here."

Shields's right hand moved toward the holstered gun at his waist.

"I wouldn't try that, Shields," Deed said, his gun already in his hand.

The crooked lawman took a deep breath and moved both hands to the desktop. Deed holstered his gun and they turned to leave.

Shields found his courage. "Oh, by the way, I wouldn't try buying anything in the general store, Mex. Lazy S's credit's no good there. Neither's your money. The town only wants Americans around here." He chuckled. "For that matter, neither is yours, Corrigan. We don't like your brother's Injun wife." His eyes widened to match the sneer of his mouth. "Maybe Bordner'll be good enough to pay you for that piece of land you're sitting on, too."

Taol Sanchez's teeth clenched and his hand dropped to his handgun.

Deed took a step in front of him to stop his draw.

"Come on, Taol. Nothing good's going to come from staying here."

"*Sí*, but just one time, I—"

"Anytime you want to die, Mex. Anytime," Shields said and stared at Deed. "Hear you took some lead when the posse went down. I can see your ear's bandaged. That's a real shame, Corrigan."

"How would you know that?" Deed's eyes were cold as he turned back to Shields.

"Murphy said you and he were the only two that made it out."

"Interesting, since he wasn't around when the shooting started. Neither was Lucas. I'd like to have a chat with him about that," Deed growled.

"He done left for the Bar 3."

"Convenient."

They left and Taol suggested they check at the

general store. If Shields was right, they would need to make arrangements in another town, probably Amarillo, and that was a two-day trip one way. Taol yanked free the reins and mounted.

"Yes, we should," Deed said as he swung into the saddle, "but likely it's as Shields said. Bordner is trying to tighten the noose around us."

Taol's face tightened. "I think we ride to the Bar 3 and end this."

"It's not going to be that easy," Deed said. "Matter of fact, Bordner would like us to try that."

"*Sí*, but it feels *bueno* to think of it."

As they rode down the street, a store owner in shirt-sleeves ran from his drugstore toward them, waving.

"Mr. Corrigan . . . do you know what happened to the posse? My brother is with them," the bald man said, his eyes asking the rest of his question.

Reining up, Deed shook his head. "Taol's brother, two of his men, and I were with the posse. We were ambushed two days out of town. South of here, near Oak Tree Canyon. Evidently Dixie Murphy and I were the only ones to make it." He made no mention of his belief that both Murphy and Lucas were involved in the setting of the ambush. This wasn't the time or the man to share it with.

The man's face wilted.

"I think the marshal is putting together a burial committee to ride out there. The Sanchezes are headed there as well."

"How'd you and Mr. Murphy make it safe?" the businessman blurted.

"With me, it was God's plan. I was only wounded," Deed said. "With Murphy, it was Agon Bordner's plan."

He leaned forward and patted the distraught man on his shoulder.

"I-I don't understand," the man said.

Deed clicked his buckskin into a walk. "You'd better . . . or Bordner will own you, too."

He glanced over at Taol and said, "Let's check out the store."

Nodding to the man, they rode on, reined up at the store with the big sign reading WILKON GENERAL MERCHANDISE, swung down, and went inside.

At the marshal's office, a huge man came from the cell area, holding a broom. Sear Georgian glared at Shields. "Well, so Deed Corrigan is hurt. Maybe I hurt him some more."

"Good idea, Sear, but don't wear a gun," Shields said. "You don't want to give him an excuse to use his."

"I won't need it. I'll break his back. Tear him apart." He placed the broom against the wall and left.

Shields felt a shiver run down his back. Sear Georgian was a monster. He didn't know why Bordner kept him around. It had to be for moments like this. Georgian would beat Deed Corrigan senseless, especially with him being wounded.

Inside the general store, a man neither knew stepped from behind the counter. He was tall with combed-back, curly hair, a nose that looked like a turnip, and a mustache that needed trimming. He wore a crumpled suitcoat and wrinkled tie.

When he spoke, his voice was nasal and thin. "Mr. Sanchez . . . Mr. Corrigan, I believe. Correct? I am Jephrum Virdin, owner of this establishment. It is my duty, my responsibility, to inform both of you that your business is not welcome here." He glanced away at several customers. "I would ask you to leave."

Taol's face turned dark red and he mumbled a curse in Spanish.

"Virdin, this madness will end soon," Deed snarled. "And your fat boss won't make it. When that happens, you'd better not be in Wilkon when I ride in."

"Is that a threat, Mr. Corrigan?"

Deed's smile was hateful. "I don't make threats, Virdin. Just a helpful projection of what life holds for you."

A fury was growing within Deed, a fury that could be reckless and unstoppable, a fury he tried hard to contain most times, a fury that had gotten him into trouble before.

Taol spat that they should leave and Deed suggested he go out to the horses, that he wanted to buy something for the Sanchez women. Taol took a deep breath to release his own anger and left.

"I told you that your business wasn't welcome, Mr. Corrigan," Virdin said, crossing his arms and trying to look intimidating.

"Heard that." Deed walked over to a table displaying big silk scarves, neatly stacked and folded. He picked up three—one, crimson; one, pink; and one, turquoise. Setting them aside, he selected two more—one in pink; the other, green.

Turning to Virdin, Deed asked if he had any dolls. Stunned, the man pointed at a nearby shelf where three dolls were sitting. He examined them and took the middle one with blond hair and dressed in a blue gingham dress with a white apron.

"Get me six sacks, Virdin. Small sacks."

The surprised man went to the counter and returned with the requested brown sacks. Deed took them, placed the doll inside the first and then slid each scarf inside a separate sack. He dropped three gold coins at the man's feet.

"Keep the difference, Virdin."

Turning, he heard scuffling, followed by a fierce curse.

"Hold these for me, Virdin." Deed handed him back the filled sacks, pulled his holstered Remington, and ran to the store doorway. Virdin watched him go, then picked up the coins.

On the boardwalk, Sear Georgian stood laughing and kicking at an unconscious Taol. He was huge, more creature than man with ham-like fists and broad shoulders.

Cocking his gun, Deed growled, "Back away from my friend, mister."

The brute of a man stepped backward and grinned, showing a mouth of broken and missing teeth. His face was heavily pockmarked with earlier acne and his thinning hair was slicked back and long.

"Ah, Deed Corrigan. Ya gonna shoot me? I ain't carryin'." He raised his fists, then kicked Taol in the ribs again. "He 'tacked me, ya know. Jes' defendin' myse'f."

Watching them from ten feet away, an older, stoop-shouldered woman with a blue scarf tied around her head, revealing mostly white curls declared, "He did not, you brute. And you know it, mister. You hit him from the back. I saw it."

Georgian laughed and a string of phlegm wiggled from one nostril, then jumped back. "So what are you gonna do about it, Corrigan? I'm gonna kick this Mex to death."

Deed knew he had no business fighting anyone, much less a thug like Sear Georgian, who was three inches taller and forty pounds heavier. But if he didn't step in, the man was going to beat on Taol until he was broken. Georgian was unarmed, so any use of a gun by Deed would be tantamount to murder, no matter the circumstances. There was nothing left to do but try to stop him. The anger growing within him was actually welcoming the idea.

He looked back into the store, uncocked his gun, and said, "Virdin, take this gun for a few minutes. I won't need it until later. Got something to do."

The storekeeper hurried to the doorway and took the heavy gun, stunned by his desire to help and even more amazed by his own statement, "Be careful. He'll kill you, Mr. Corrigan."

Deed nodded.

"Now yer gonna die, Corrigan," Georgian growled and delivered a roundhouse swing at Deed's head as he turned back.

The old woman screamed her alarm.

Deed's left arm blocked the powerful blow, taking it full force on his wounded arm. It felt like a club had slammed against him. His arm went numb and the wound began to bleed. Georgian followed with a high right that Deed managed to duck and counter with an opened right hand to the big man's Adam's apple.

Georgian grabbed his throat with both hands, gasping for air. If Deed had hit him harder, it would have killed him. Still, the blow gave Deed time to set himself. He realized the man was a brawler used to winning by sheer strength and the fear of his opponent, but he was no fighter. But any one of Georgian's blows would be enough to knock him out. That would mean destruction of his body or death.

Moving in front of the unconscious Taol, Deed

balanced himself in a wide stance and drove his right leg into Georgian's midsection like an axe while the bigger man tried to clear his throat of the earlier blow. Deed's wounded left leg buckled and he nearly fell.

Georgian pushed Deed away and rattled him with a thundering right to his head that brought blood to his mouth. Deed countered with a right hook to Georgian's face that popped the skin with a stomach-turning sound, cracking a red line down his cheek. Screaming obscenities, Georgian swung fiercely, but missed.

Moving away from the blow, Deed tripped on Taol and fell. Grinning, the bloody-faced big man ran at him, but the young gunfighter spun to his right, extending his right arm to balance himself on his hand. Rotating his hips, he drove his aching left leg into the bigger man's stomach. As soon as his boot hit Georgian, Deed jumped to his feet. His spurs jingled as he stood and tried to ignore the pain in his leg and arm, and the roar in his head. Georgian was struggling with the pain in his stomach.

A small crowd had gathered beside the old woman to watch the brawl, but no one made any attempt to stop it.

Deed staggered the bigger man with a vicious back slap of his open right hand to Georgian's face. Georgian launched a wild swing that thundered against Deed's shoulder and made his knees wobble. Seeing his weakened position, Georgian made a vicious grab for Deed's face to gouge out his eyes. As the huge man's hands reached Deed's face, the young gunfighter's left elbow hit Georgian's nose like a sharp axe cutting into a log. Georgian staggered sideways. Deed moved in, missing with his right fist, but connecting with a left to the man's stomach.

Ignoring Deed's blow to his midsection, Georgian rushed and grabbed him, squeezing against his back. Deed gasped, felt an awful pain run down his spine, then bent his knees as best he could and rammed his head upward into Georgian's exposed chin. The big man staggered backwards, releasing Deed. The young gunfighter followed with another open-handed jab to his stomach and Georgian whimpered.

Swinging and missing, Georgian brought up his knee toward Deed's groin, but Deed spun to the side, letting the blow slam into his thigh. It still made him gasp. Deed's anger was total and his rage took over. It was time to end this. If the fight went longer, the man's sheer strength would wear him down.

Rebalancing himself, Deed drove his fist into the man's chest, right at Georgian's heart. He forced his left arm to raise and half-block Georgian's wicked swing. It was losing power; even so, the blow was hard enough to make Deed wince.

Deed managed to back off, then went into a half crouch, ignoring the pain in his leg and arm. Hate was making him fierce and powerful. His left arm swung at his side, too weak to raise again. Georgian's face was a mass of blood and skin and he was definitely moving slower. He lunged at Deed in a desperate attempt to grab him again.

Deed's opened right hand drove into Georgian's stomach, then quickly thudded against his neck. The big man stumbled and as he fell, Deed grabbed a handful of Georgian's hair and held him as his right elbow smashed into the man's face. Georgian thudded against the boardwalk and didn't move.

Deed weaved and caught himself against the store's support beam. Certain that Georgian wasn't going to move, he turned to Taol, now trying to stand. A cut above Deed's eye was bringing a string of salty blood into it; he wiped it away.

"Can you ride, Taol?"

"*Sí*. Did you kill him?"

"Don't think so, but he won't feel very good for a long while," Deed said. "Let's get out of here."

He helped the young Mexican to his saddle; Taol's grimace indicated cracked ribs. A white-faced Virdin walked from the store, holding the sacks, now carefully folded together and tied with the doll sack on the bottom, and Deed's revolver and ceremoniously handed them to Deed.

"Mr. Corrigan, that was impressive, sir," Jephrum Virdin said. "I didn't think anyone could stop him like that." He took a deep breath and added, "I never did like Sear Georgian."

Heaving for breath, Deed mouthed his thanks, taking the gun first in his right hand. His left arm was stiff, but he managed to take hold of the string holding the sacks together. He looked down at his hands; both were bloody and sore.

Running down the boardwalk came Sheriff Macy Shields. He stutter-stepped as he approached the prone body of Sear Georgian. "What the hell?"

Watching him from his saddle, Deed held his handgun against the pommel. The energy from battle was leaving him fast.

"You're under arrest, Corrigan, for assaulting a citizen of Wilkon," Shields bellowed.

Virdin waved his arms. "No, Macy, that cannot be.

I have to live in this town and Sear started it all. He just wasn't good enough to end it." He stared at Shields. "Go and get the doctor. Georgian is badly hurt." He couldn't resist looking at Deed. "Ride away, Mr. Corrigan, and your friend, Mr. Sanchez. You will not be bothered more this day."

"Maybe, but we're not turning our backs on dirt-bags like your so-called sheriff here." Deed raised his gun so Shields could see it. "Shields, throw your gun in that horse tank." He shifted the sacks to rest in front of him on the saddle.

Shields glared at him. "I won't do that."

Deed cocked his gun. It felt heavy and he added his left hand to its support, which didn't want to move quickly. "I won't ask again. I'm tired of what Bordner is doing. So killing you is just a start to making it right again."

Shields hesitated, then tossed the gun into the tank. The weapon splashed and sank.

"Now, that hideaway. In your back waistband. Bring it out with two fingers."

Shields grumbled and slowly complied. The second gun, a short-barreled Colt, splashed into the dirty water and sank.

Deed told Taol to pull away and the Mexican nodded and eased his horse away from the hitchrail. As Deed followed, a young woman ran toward him. It was Sally Cummins.

"Oh, Deed, are you all right?" she asked with widened eyes. She was wearing a light brown, fitted dress with a short waistcoat. The color of the cloth matched her hair, pulled back into a bun.

"Yes, Miss Cummins, I'm all right."

"Will you come to see me . . . soon? I miss you, Deed."

"Guess that'll be up to Agon Bordner and his gang." He blinked and saw Atlee Forsyth and wished she was here.

Putting her hand on his leg, she bit her lower lip. "Oh, this whole thing is awful. Just awful. I wish everyone could get along."

"That's a nice wish," Deed said, touched the brim of his hat with his right hand still holding his gun, and pulled his horse away from the hitchrail. "Take care of yourself, Miss Cummins."

CHAPTER TWENTY-NINE

At the Forsyth relay station, the morning El Paso stage rumbled into the yard right on time. Pervious Findel was the driver, a happy, red-haired man known for singing while he drove. Most said he sang well. A former Union artillery captain during the war, Pervious was dependable and always on time, or ahead of it. Just like today.

> "A tear was in her eye . . .
> I said, I've come from Dixie land . . .
> Susanna, don't you break down and cry . . .
> I said, Oh, Susanna . . .
> Now, don't you cry for me . . .
> 'Cause I come from Alabama
> with my banjo on my knee."

He timed the ending of his song as he reined up in the station yard.

Billy Lee Montez and Hermann Beinrigt hurried

out with a new team. Helping them was a determined Benjamin.

"All out, folks. Some good eatin's here. Hot coffee too," Pervious hollered as he slammed on the heavy brake. "We'll be rollin' again in fifteen minutes so don't you all dally."

Passengers emerged from both sides of the coach, stretched, and headed for the station. At the doorway, Atlee Forsyth waited to greet them. The last two passengers to emerge were familiar: James Hannah and Rebecca Tuttle.

The bespectacled gunman recognized Billy and Hermann and reintroduced himself. "Good day to you, men. I'm James Hannah. Came through here with Deed Corrigan a while back." He looked at the German farmer, smiled, and said, "Believe you caught a nasty arrow on that trip, sir. Good to see you up and around."

"*Danke.* It *ist gut* to see you, Herr Hannah."

Pushing his glasses back on his nose, Hannah continued, "You remember Miss Tuttle, I'm certain. She's my bride, Mrs. James Hannah."

Rebecca blushed and Hannah grinned.

"Where's Deed? I want to see him," the gunman asked, waving his hand toward the barn.

The German farmer tugged on the bridle of the lead horse and told him about Deed returning to his ranch.

"You folks better get somethin' to eat," Pervious yelled as he climbed down from the driver's box. "Gonna be a long spell before there's more grub. None like this, I reckon."

Hannah nodded. "Thanks. But we're getting off here."

"Thought you folks were going to Kansas."

"Yeah, we are. But I've got some business here first."

From the station doorway, Atlee Forsyth watched as the passengers came toward where she was standing. For an instant, she expected to see Deed Corrigan step out of the stage.

She missed Deed, thought of him often, and felt guilty about it. She should be missing her late husband and she did. But her heart was looking for something to heal the loss he left, and Deed was that answer. She knew it was wrong to feel this way, but she did.

"Oh, Deed—" she caught herself and looked back at Olivia Beinrigt in the main room setting the table. "Stage is here, Olivia."

"*Gut.* Ve *ist* ready."

The last couple to get out were familiar to Atlee: James Hannah and Rebecca Tuttle. The two of them walked slowly toward the station with the bespectacled gunman doing most of the talking.

At the doorway, Atlee greeted the all the passengers warmly and motioned them into the main room. Then turning to the couple, said, "Well, how good to see you again, Mr. Hannah . . . and you, too . . . Miss—"

"It's Mrs.—Mrs. Hannah," Rebecca said with a wide smile.

Hannah blushed and asked, "Is Deed around?"

It was Atlee's turn to blush. "Oh, I'm sorry. Uh, Mr. Corrigan went back to his ranch some time ago."

Frowning, Hannah asked if the ranch was far. Atlee

explained the location, then excused herself to help with the other guests. Hannah joined Rebecca inside the station. She was talking with Olivia.

"Would it be possible to rent a buckboard or a carriage?" Hannah interrupted. "My wife and I need to go into town."

Rebecca looked surprised. "I thought we were going on to Kansas, honey."

"We are, dear. But I need to see Deed Corrigan. It's important."

"Certainly, dear."

Atlee walked over from the table with a coffeepot in her hand. "Mr. Hannah, if you promise to return it soon, I can let you borrow one of our buckboards." She smiled. "Or you can wait here, Mr. Corrigan is expected back sometime this week. He's asked Benjamin to help with their roundup. And my Elizabeth is going along to play with his brother's children."

Hannah took off his glasses and cleaned them with a white handkerchief from his pocket.

"Where would we sleep?" he asked, returning the glasses to his nose.

Atlee said they could sleep on the employees' bed, the one not being used by the Beinrigts.

"That would be excellent. We'll wait."

CHAPTER THIRTY

Blue Corrigan saw the riders clearing the ridge as he walked out of the barn. Late morning sun was trying to warm the day. He knew in one glance it was Deed and Holt, leading a third horse with a blanket-wrapped body strapped over it. Two days ago, Tina Sanchez had ridden over to tell them what was happening. The news was most appreciated; both Blue and Silka were getting worried. Hearing that Holt was with Deed gave Blue a warm feeling that he couldn't quite describe. And seeing them now made him raise his eyes to the sky and thank the Lord.

He yelled at Silka who was shoeing the paint horse called Warrior. The animal had gradually settled into a solid working horse and could outrun any horse on the ranch, except the sorrel stallion, Captain.

Willy and Harmon had gone to inspect one of their line cabins and wouldn't be back until tomorrow afternoon. Little Jake was in the bunkhouse recovering from his gunshot wound.

"Silka, it's Deed!"

The older man hurried the horse to the closest corral and let it loose. "Aiee, we are blessed." He continued to where Blue was standing watching the riders.

"Is that Holt with him?" Silka said, putting a hand to his forehead to block out the autumn sun.

"Yes."

"It is a good truth then. They bring a body," Silka said.

"I'm afraid it's Chico."

"Aiee. I remember."

Blue and Silka waved and Deed and Holt returned the greeting. In minutes, the two brothers reined up alongside Blue and Silka. Happiness was evident even in Silka's usually stoic face. They dismounted and shook hands.

As they walked the horses to the barn, Deed and Holt took turns telling them about what had happened to the posse, to the outlaws chasing a wounded Deed, the second attack on the Lazy S, and the problems in town. Blue and Silka knew most of it already, but not the events in town. They had stayed for the Sanchez family's burial of their son and the two vaqueros.

Deed said, "We brought Chico's body home."

"That was the right thing to do," Blue responded.

Silka studied Deed. "How bad is your ear, son?"

Touching his bandaged ear, Deed said, "Oh, it's all right. I was lucky."

"Looks like it," Blue said and patted Deed's shoulder, then turned to Holt. "Mighty glad you came along when you did Holt. And mighty glad to have you with us."

Holt smiled and touched the feather in his hat. "Took some time for me to get smart."

Deed led his buckskin toward the barn, his limp

barely noticeable. The blood that had been on his pant leg and shirtsleeve were barely noticeable. The Sanchez women had done a good job of cleaning them. He was tired, but it felt good to be home.

Holt followed with the other horses. Silka and Blue stayed with them. Holt told them about Deed's fight in town with Sear Georgian as Taol had relayed it to him. Holt knew of the big man and thought it was an amazing fight.

Silka frowned. "You should not have done that. You were hurt. You could have been hurt bad."

"Oh, I think he thought I was wounded worse than I was," Deed said. "Only a couple of flesh wounds. They just bled a lot."

"Evidently he wasn't hurt too much," Holt laughed. "Taol told me that the big son of a bitch was cut down like a tree." He turned to Silka. "You taught him well, old man."

Chico's body was carefully taken from his horse and laid on the ground. After unsaddling and rubbing down the horses, they led them to the water tank, then to stalls where they were grained.

"I think we should bury Chico before we go inside," Deed said.

"Yes," Blue agreed.

Neither Holt nor Silka responded. Deed went to get a shovel and Holt followed. They would bury the cowhand's remains in the family cemetery. Blue went to the house to inform Bina of his brothers' return and made a stop at the bunkhouse to inform Jake. The short cowhand got up and joined them at the grave site. His arm was in a tight sling, prepared by Bina.

After Holt, Deed, and Silka took turns digging,

Chico was buried. Jake volunteered to help, but they wouldn't let him. Blue returned before they were finished and told them that Too Tall nearly had dinner ready. At Deed's urging, Blue stood at the head of the grave next to a temporary marker Silka had made. A running iron had burned CHICO into the main piece of the small, nailed-together, wooden cross. No one knew Chico's last name or when he was born or if he had any relatives to contact.

Blue removed his hat and so did the others. Holt picked up a small dirt clod and massaged it in his hand, letting the crumbles fall through his fingers. Touching a new grave was good luck, he told himself. Only Deed noticed.

With his eyes closed, Blue said, "Lord, we give to you this day the soul of our good friend, Chico. You know his full name, but we never did. He was a steady and loyal hand. Keep him close. Amen."

"Amen," the others muttered.

Their walk to the main house was subdued; Jake excused himself and went to the bunkhouse. No one wanted to think beyond the moment. Holt walked with his arm around Blue. Even in the sadness of the day, it was good to be back. He would tell Blue and Silka later that he planned to go by the name Sam Holton. A lot of men changed their names, maybe Chico had. His eyes took in the ranch buildings; it was like seeing them for the first time, and yet, it wasn't. More like seeing them as if they had been part of another life. He smiled. They were.

Finally, Blue started talking about their cattle. It had been an excellent summer and the fall crop of calves was plentiful. He shook his head and declared they would have their hands full finding and branding all of them.

At the porch railing were two pans of fresh water, soap, and new towels. The men took turns washing up as the talk continued about the roundup. Blue thought they should separate the herd for market next spring, putting the steers and older cows in a separate group in one of their valleys.

Deed dried his hands and asked, "Makes sense to me. How soon are we starting?"

"Everything's ready, but we'll be shorthanded without Chico. Little Jake shouldn't be in a saddle, but I know he'll try, no matter what we say."

"What am I going to do about the Forsyth kids? I promised Benjamin he could ride with us," Deed asked. "And Elizabeth would stay with Bina and your kids. But it may not be safe. We're likely to get hit by Bordner's men." He shook his head. "What am I saying? It won't be safe for your family to stay here either."

"You think he'll try something now, during the roundup?" Blue said, "I was counting on Benjamin becoming a welcome hand."

"What about me? Am I chopped liver?" Holt asked.

"Of course not," Blue chuckled. "We've needed you for a long time." He cocked his head. "I figured you'd take Chico's string. We'd set aside some gentle ones for Benjamin."

"That sounds better," Holt said.

Deed's concern went unanswered and they headed for the front door, continuing to talk of cattle.

Bina greeted them warmly when they entered. Holt was careful to step into the house with his right foot first, that would bring good luck to everyone within.

"Bina, you know my brother, Holt. It's been a long time though," Blue said.

"Oh, Holt, how good to see you again," she declared. "Blue talks often of you."

Holt smiled. "Now I know why he's done so well, Bina. He has you."

Deed agreed with his statement and slid past the two of them and into the main room where Blue had already gone.

Her smile was broad. "You are most kind." She said something in Apache that Holt didn't know, but assumed it was a welcome message. Realizing her statement was not understood, she quickly apologized, "Oh, I am sorry. I forget when I am excited. I said our lodge is yours. Of course, it is. This is your parents' home. Forgive me."

"Thank you. It's good to be here." Holt ignored the thought that the ranch was indeed his, or at least his parents'. The statement was caring.

From around the corner, Blue's children and Jeremy came running to their Uncle Deed. He grabbed each one with a big hug.

"Uncle Dee, you hurt," Matthew said, pointing at the dried blood on his clothes.

"Yeah, I uh, I fell down. Kinda clumsy of me."

Mary Jo put her hands on her hips and declared, "Uncle Deed, bad boy. You were fighting. I know." It was like being scolded by his mother.

He laughed and said, "Come and see your Uncle Holt. You probably don't remember him. He's your father's brother and mine."

He introduced them to the bearded stranger. "This is your Uncle Holt. Uncle Holt, this is Matthew . . . and Mary Jo . . . and Jeremy."

Forgetting his plan to go by Sam Holton for the moment, Holt squatted on his heels and drew the three children close. "My goodness, it is good to see you. Let's see, Matthew, I only heard about you." He smiled and touched Mary Jo's cheek. "And you were only a baby."

Jeremy tried to step away, but Holt took his arm gently and pulled him back. "And you, sir, I'm proud to meet for the first time. Jeremy, I hope we can become good friends."

The boy smiled. "I do, too."

Blue came over and suggested the children go help in the kitchen and let the men talk over some matters. All three children hugged Holt again and ran toward the kitchen.

Holt stood and shook his head. "Man, now that's something to come home to."

"Yes, I'm very lucky."

"Seems to me luck runs in the family," Holt said. "Maybe I can catch some of it."

"You already have." Blue patted him on the back. "Let's go in here while we wait."

The four men walked into a living room warmed by a huge stone fireplace that dominated the room. Right away, Holt was pleased to see the well-banked fire was burning evenly. An occasional blue flame told him spirits were close. He decided they were the spirits of their parents and sister.

A large blue sofa and rolltop desk made up the rest of the room, along with a small table holding a kerosene lamp. Blue headed to the rolltop desk that had belonged to their parents. Above it was a framed photograph of their parents on their wedding day. Next to it was another photograph of the three children with them. In the picture, a twelve-year-old Blue had his arm on the shoulder of four-year-old Deed who was looking at his oldest brother and ten-year-old Holt was looking at the camera and smiling stiffly.

Blue rolled up the front piece where a bottle of Tennessee whiskey and glasses sat. The bottle was nearly full. Holt was surprised there was liquor in the house, but said nothing. He guessed the bottle had been there for years.

"I keep this for Christmas Eve. And for special occasions, like the birth of my children," Blue said. "This is a special occasion."

He poured a finger full of the brown liquid into four glasses.

"Here's to Holt's return," he said, handing out the glasses and holding up his own.

Both Deed and Silka were amazed at Blue producing whiskey, but it did seem like an appropriate time. Silka nodded and held his glass next to Blue's.

"*Ame futte ji katamaru*," the old samurai declared.

Deed and Blue repeated the acclamation. Holt mumbled something no one understood, but grinned afterwards.

He clinked his glass against the others. "It's great to be home." He swallowed the fiery drink in one gulp and returned the glass to the desk. Blue added his.

"Reckon that's all the whiskey we'll drink. For a long time," he smiled at Silka. "Right, Silka?"

Without any expression, the Japanese warrior added his emptied glass to the desk. "Hai, it is so." Holt wished he could have another, but still felt uncomfortable asking.

"If you don't mind an old Rebel making a suggestion," Holt continued, "I think it's time we attacked that fat bastard. You've been on the defensive long enough."

"That's easy to say," Deed snapped, putting his emptied glass beside Holt's and Silka's. "They've got twice as many guns as the Lazy S and us combined. And they own the county law. Hell, they might even own a Ranger or two, for all we know."

"He's just a man."

"Right, and a fat one, but if we attack the Bar 3, Bordner'll have the Rangers all over us," Blue said. "I think that's what he wants. An attack from us or the Sanchezes so he can go to the Rangers and have us arrested."

"Blue's right," Deed added.

"I think we get with the Sanchezes and get on with our roundup," Blue said. "If we don't, all the calves around will be wearing Bordner's brand. Then it won't matter."

"How the roundup would go without involving the Bar 3 is a serious consideration," Blue said.

"We can't leave our beef along there," Deed said, referring to the border of their ranch and the Bar 3 land. "Murphy's men'll brand everything that moves."

"Well, riding on their land will mean shooting, you know that," Blue said. "Felix Sanchez is willing to stay on their own land to avoid more bloodshed."

"What if Holt and I take care of the stray cattle on the Bar 3 land? I know I'm not afraid to cross over and I'm pretty sure Holt isn't either," Deed said and added, "But first, I'm going to ride to the Forsyth station and tell Atlee that the kids can't come. It's too dangerous."

Holt said, "You're right, Deed. They will be very disappointed, I'm sure, but now's not the time. And when you come back, I will be with you when you ride onto Bar 3 land."

"Thanks, Holt. That helps, I guess. What about Bina and your family, Blue? Do we dare leave them during the roundup?" Deed responded.

From the other room came the call that dinner was ready.

"We can talk more after we eat," Blue said. "It's not a good idea to keep Too Tall waiting."

They laughed and it eased the tension.

Holt could see the kitchen as they walked to the dining room table. Mismatched chairs surrounded it. The table was set with a bouquet of dried autumn flowers and leaves as a centerpiece.

The kitchen itself was controlled by a cast-iron stove, the same one that had toiled in the house since it was just their parents. Too Tall, the black cook, filled it with his intensity. A large upright pantry contained white ironstone plates, heavy iron tableware, pots, pans, two buckets, a large copper double boiler, and a dozen empty canning jars. On the floor, a large box was filled with sacks of flour, beans, and salt. A large china water basin, a lamp—and their meal of roasted grouse with peas and mashed potatoes—covered most of the small kitchen counter. Blue had shot six grouse yesterday.

At the table, Blue said grace and Too Tall began serving filled plates. Bina followed with hot coffee. Holt sat between Matthew and Mary Jo, with Jeremy next to her. They bombarded him with questions, most of which brought chuckles. The talk stayed happy until after the meal was finished and the children left.

* * *

Meanwhile, at the Bar 3, Agon Bordner was furious. He had just learned from Macy Shields that Deed had whipped Sear Georgian in front of witnesses. Before that, Rhey Selmon had informed him that vaqueros were stationed on the roof of the Lazy S ranch house night and day. Attacking them again would be difficult and costly in men.

"What the hell!" Bordner yelled and slammed his fist on the dining room table. "I don't believe it. Deed was shot, Rhey and Dixie told me. Shot several times. Can nobody whip him!"

"Well, boss, he sure looked like it, but he tore up Sear something fierce. Be down for a long time," Shields said.

"Why didn't you arrest him?" Bordner screamed again.

Shields shrugged his shoulders. "He had a gun on me."

"Did Corrigan hold a gun on Sear?"

"No. He gave it to Virdin while they fought," Shields continued. "Leastwise, that's what folks told me. I wasn't there."

"Virdin? What the hell. Why was Virdin there?" Bordner growled and glared at his gunman.

Shields straightened his back. "Corrigan bought some scarves in Virdin's store before the fight."

"I told Virdin to shut Corrigan and Sanchez out."

"He said he told them."

Bordner rubbed his unshaved chin.

"Dammit, boss, he stood up for Corrigan. Virdin did. Told me I couldn't arrest him 'cuz he lived in town. Virdin said that."

"I thought you said Corrigan had a gun on you."

"He did. Virdin gave it to him . . . when the fight was done."

Bordner shook his head. "Damn! Simpson, I'm hungry. Bring me something to eat." He stared at Shields again. "Get out of my sight, Macy. I thought you were better than that." The enormous man waved his gunman and his protests away.

He was also angry with himself. In the past few days, he had been going over his last conversation with James Hannah. The famed gunman had come to his house after considering Bordner's offer and said, "I'll take your money, Bordner."

"*I'll take your money.*"

Bordner had been tossing that phrase around in his head. He replayed the conversation out loud. "Hannah hadn't said he would take the job or that he would kill Deed Corrigan. He had simply stated, 'I'll take your money' and I had been so damn glad Hannah had returned that I hadn't really listened.

"The only thing I asked the son of a bitch was 'when' and he said that he had some other business in the area. I said 'fine.' Then he downed his drink, took the money, and left, and I let it go at that."

He slammed his fist on the table and yelled again for Simpson.

"What a stupid fool," he muttered and forced himself to think of his next move. He prided himself on that ability. Whatever was done was done and the key was to move on. An idea was trying to break through and he must let it. What if they left the Lazy S alone for a while and attacked the LC ranch while the men were working the roundup. What if Rhey Selmon and some of his men slipped into the Corrigan compound. He didn't care what happened to the Indian wife of

Blue's; she deserved raping, living like a white person. Same with Blue's children.

Bordner licked his blubbery lips. Yes. Yes. That would break them, pure and simple.

Grinning, he yelled again, "Simpson, I want a steak. Medium rare. And eggs. Over easy."

CHAPTER THIRTY-ONE

Two days later, Deed Corrigan rode to the Forsyth station, leading a saddled bay horse. It was Blue's idea; the older mount was no longer useful for ranch work, yet it was a sturdy animal with years of light service left. Blue suggested he give Chester to Benjamin to ease his disappointment in not coming to the roundup.

He didn't like what he had to do. Even seeing Atlee again was going to be tough. The day was overcast and it matched his thoughts. He was also carrying scarves for Atlee and Olivia and a doll for little Elizabeth. Maria Sanchez and her daughters had been pleased with his earlier gifts, so he hoped the Forsyth women would be as well. Especially Atlee. Still, it wasn't the way he wanted to return.

Benjamin saw him coming and ran from the station to meet him. Elizabeth was only a few steps behind. Cooper bounded next to them, barking joyfully.

"You came back! Is it roundup time?" Benjamin asked as the gunfighter stopped in front of the station.

Deed dismounted slowly, feeling every ache in his

body more than he should. "Benjamin, we're going to have to wait on you helping with the roundup. We've got some bad people trying to take our land. It's going to be dangerous. I hate it, but you can't come now. Maybe later when all this is settled."

Benjamin looked like he had been hit in the face. Without saying a word, he spun around and went toward the station.

"Wait, Benjamin, please," Deed called. "This is Chester . . . and he's yours. He would've been in your roundup string. I thought you might like to have him anyway."

The boy stopped and turned around. "He's mine?"

"All yours," Deed responded. "Well, if it's all right with your mother."

"Can I ride him?"

"Hop on. He's a good horse."

Benjamin took the offered lead-rope. The reins were tied and resting over the saddle horn.

"That's your saddle, too."

Stepping forward, Elizabeth asked, "How about me?"

"Well, it's too dangerous for you, too, at the ranch," Deed said.

She dropped her hands to her sides, lowered her head, and began to sob. Long tears filled her little face.

He went over to her, knelt, and hugged her. "I brought something for you."

She stopped crying. "What is it?"

"I'll get it for you now." He went to his saddlebags and produced three folded sacks. He handed the largest to Elizabeth and her eyes brightened.

Looking up, he saw Atlee standing in the doorway.

"What do you say, Elizabeth," Atlee said.

"Oh, thank you . . . Deed. Thank you very much."
She opened the sack and pulled out the doll and her
mouth opened wide. "Oh . . . oh, it's beautiful. I love
it. Thank you. Thank you." She rushed over to Deed
and hugged him. "I'm going to name her Jessica.
Jessica Forsyth."

Dancing past her mother, Elizabeth disappeared
inside the house, singing a made-up song about Jessica
Forsyth.

"Well, good day, Mr. Corrigan," she said. "Is something wrong? We've been hoping you'd come. Every
day, I think." She chuckled. "Won't you come in?
Olivia just made some cookies and the coffee's hot."

"No thanks, I need to get going. The boys are waiting on me." He took off his hat and stood. "We've got
bad problems at the ranch. Agon Bordner and his
men are trying to take control of every ranch around.
Only two left." He grimaced. "I can't have Benjamin
and Elizabeth there right now. It isn't safe. I just can't.
I-I'm sorry."

"So am I, but I understand, Deed. I really do," Atlee
said. "Please come in for some coffee. You were very
nice to come all this way, even if it was bad news." She
studied his face. "You've had trouble already, haven't
you? What happened to your ear?"

Deed put his hand to his bandaged ear and told
her in several sentences about the posse's ambush and
his escape, and the attacks on the Lazy S. He didn't
mention the fight in town, but did say the county law
was now in the hands of a Bordner man.

"Oh that's awful! You're lucky to be alive, Deed."

"I am a lucky man, Mrs. Forsyth."

She frowned. "Atlee, remember? Or have your forgotten all about me?"

"There's no way I could forget you . . . Atlee." He looked into her eyes for a moment, then away. "Oh, I brought a horse for Benjamin. It's one of our older mounts. Real gentle. Thought it might help . . . some. If that's all right."

"That's very generous of you, Deed."

He cocked his head. "Oh I almost forgot. I brought something for . . . you and Mrs. Beinrigt, too."

He walked to the doorway and handed her the two sacks.

"I thought you'd like the pink one. The green one is for Mrs. Beinrigt."

Biting her lower lip, Atlee opened the top sack and withdrew the silk scarf. "Oh, it's beautiful, Deed. So beautiful. How very thoughtful of you." She folded it and tied it around her neck.

"Glad you like it."

Billy Lee Montez and Hermann Beinrigt came out of the barn just as he walked toward Atlee. They barely noticed Benjamin riding the bay around the yard.

"Señor Deed, you are back!" Billy Lee said.

"*Willkommen,*" Hermann added, in welcome.

Deed wanted to talk with Atlee, that's all he had thought about riding over, but she told him that they could talk later, not to worry about her children, and went inside. He walked over to the two men and they began telling him about the station and how smoothly it was running. Deed thought they were trying hard to convince him; he glanced over his shoulder. The doorway was empty. He felt something sink inside.

He turned back to force himself to listen to them as they explained changes they had made in handling the horses, reshoeing, and feeding. Hermann had introduced a checking system when a team of tired horses came in. Deed nodded, but didn't really hear them. Part of him wished he hadn't returned. It was silly to think of Atlee.

Inside the station, Olivia finally spoke up about Deed. She and Atlee had become good friends. "You must *nicht* let Deed Corrigan get avay, Atlee. Your husband vas *ein gut* man, but he *ist nicht* here. Deed *ist*. You haff mourned long enough," Olivia said, folding her arms. "Deed Corrigan *ist gut* man. He vants you . . . *und* you vant him. *Lasst* him go *nicht*, Atlee."

Outside, Deed was distracted by a sharp call, "Hey, Corrigan!"

He spun around. It was James Hannah. He was cleaning his glasses. Excusing himself, Deed walked over to the bespectacled gunman. Hermann and Billy Lee returned to the barn, still talking to each other about what more they wanted to do.

"Good to see you, James," Deed said, holding out his hand.

Hannah returned his glasses to his nose and shook Deed's hand enthusiastically.

"What brings you here?" Deed asked.

"You."

"Me?" Deed was wary. Blue told him that he might be working for Agon Bordner.

Hannah cocked his head. "Bordner wants you killed. Paid me five hundred dollars to do it."

Deed shifted his legs to balance himself. If this was going to turn into a gunfight, he must be ready. He glanced down at his gunbelt, then at Hannah "That's a lot of money."

Hannah watched Deed setting himself. "Yeah, it is. But you be easy now. You aren't going to need that gun with me. I thought you boys might be wanting another gun. This Bordner wants the whole region. All of it. But if you don't want my help, I'll ride on with my bride."

He laughed. "I just couldn't see letting that much money go to waste. So I told him that I would take his money." He shook his head. "I didn't say that I'd do anything for it, just that I'd take it. I guess he was too excited to really listen to what I was saying.

"It's going to pay for a nice honeymoon for my bride and a new start in Wichita. I've got relatives there. So, I thought Mrs. Hannah and I could go to town. What's the name, Wilkon, yeah, that's it," Hannah said flicking away imaginary dust from his vest. "Then I'd be real close if you needed me. We are friends, remember. Oh, and you remember Rebecca Tuttle, don't you?"

Deed frowned. "Yes, she was going to El Paso to marry some farmer."

"Uh, the farmer didn't ever show up and—"

"Well, congratulations, James."

Deed chuckled and Hannah joined in.

Deed told him what had happened at the Lazy S, with the posse, and in town and that Bordner's man was now county sheriff as well as town marshal. Hannah chuckled again when he heard about Deed downing Sear Georgian.

"Damn it, man. No wonder Bordner wants someone to kill you. None of his men are good enough."

"Are you?"

Hannah licked his lips. "Come on, Deed. I'm not

interested in that kind of talk. As I said, if you don't want me, we'll catch the next stage to Kansas."

"I'd like your help," Deed said. "A whole lot. Bordner's got twenty guns and a lot of ego."

Hannah pushed on his glasses. "I'll tell Rebecca that we're headed for Wilkon. Mrs. Forsyth said there was a buckboard we could borrow."

"Thank you. I'm glad you're here, James."

They shook hands again and Hannah went into the stage station. As Deed watched him, Atlee came to the doorway.

"Deed, would you mind going with me around back for a minute. I need some . . . help." Her face was creased with a frown. "Olivia likes her scarf. Green is her favorite color."

"That's great. Of course, glad to help."

She stepped off the porch and walked to the corner of the station. "Benjamin and Elizabeth will be fine. They were disappointed, but they'll be fine. I told them there would be other roundups when the danger was gone. Your gifts were very thoughtful . . . and very appreciated."

He followed her around to the back of the station, wondering what she wanted. Maybe it was a load of supplies, but he couldn't remember them ever being placed there before. She stopped at the back of the station and waited.

Pushing back his hat from his forehead, Deed stepped closer, still unsure of what she wanted. He didn't see anything that needed moving.

"It would have been fun having your kids at the ranch. And Benjamin would've been a good addition," he said awkwardly. "I'm so sorry about all this."

"You've been so wonderful. Don't know what we, I, would have done without you Deed."

Deed scuffed his right boot in the ground and watched the dirt turn up around it. "Wasn't much. You'd have been fine without me. You're quite a woman . . . Atlee." He looked up and she was staring into his face, only two feet away.

Reaching out, Atlee touched his arm and held it, then moved closer. "May I ask you something? Promise you won't laugh."

"Of course. You can tell me anything or ask me anything. I probably won't know the answer though." He forced a chuckle.

"I really think I can ask you anything, Deed," she whispered. "It's part of what makes you so special. To me."

Deed tried to think of something to say, but couldn't.

She took a half step closer to him, her hand remaining on his arm. Deed could smell the deliciousness of her. A little like violets, he thought, mixed with the fresh smell of soap. And woman. It was intoxicating.

"Will you wait for me?" she asked, looking into his eyes.

Deed swallowed. "I, uh, I don't understand."

Tears began to roll down her cheeks and he touched her face to remove them without thinking about it.

"I was married to a good man. We had plans together. And Caleb was taken from me."

"I-I know that. I am very sorry but—"

She touched two fingers to his lips to shush him and left them there. "I am in m-mourning . . . and must be," she stammered. "But you came along and turned everything upside down. I know my life should be with you . . . now. I know that." She blinked. "I'm in mourning and need to be. W-Will you wait for me, s-so I can become your wife, if you'll have me?"

Gently, he removed her fingers from his mouth and held her hand. "Atlee, nothing would make me happier than to have you beside me as my wife. I will wait forever if—"

She pushed against him and her mouth found his. They held each other and kissed, and kissed.

"I love you," she whispered.

"I've loved you since I first saw you."

Nothing else mattered.

CHAPTER THIRTY-TWO

Riding back to the ranch was a blur for Deed. All he could think of was Atlee's declaration of love for him. Her kisses were imprinted on his mind like fire. Hannah and Rebecca sat beside him on the buckboard seat while his horse was hitched behind. Rebecca did most of the talking. She seemed determined to comment on everything they passed.

Their destination had changed somewhat. Rebecca would stay in town at the Wilkon Hotel while Hannah went to the ranch to help guard it. Deed had shared the concern about Bordner's men attacking when they were gone and Hannah decided that he should stay there. Deed told him that his older brother Holt was with them and that he was going to stay at the ranch as well. Bina and her children were going to be with the roundup; it was safer they thought.

Rebecca didn't like being separated from her new husband, but gradually understood the seriousness of the situation. After letting her off at the hotel and getting her settled in the best room available, Deed and Hannah headed for the ranch. The town itself was quiet, something expected at roundup time. Hannah told her not to use his name and, if asked, to say her husband was coming in on the next stagecoach.

Clearing the last ridge, Deed pulled up so Hannah could see the entire ranch yard and get an idea of where Bordner's men might attack. He had already told the gunman that he didn't think Bordner knew about his brother returning, and that Holt was going by Sam Holton. Hannah asked a few questions, mostly about available rifles and ammunition. Clucking to the horses, Deed headed for the ranch. As they pulled up, Holt stepped from the house, cradling a Winchester in his arms.

"Well, well, I do believe it's James Hannah," he said cheerfully. "Good to have you with us."

"And to you . . . Sam Holton," Hannah said.

Deed said, "James has agreed to stay at the ranch and give you a hand while we're working the roundup."

"Sounds good to me. Got some fresh coffee on," Holt declared as they shook hands. "Bina . . . that's Blue's wife . . . she left us some good food. We sure won't starve."

"How about guns?"

They walked inside and Holt showed him their collected weapons and the boxes of cartridges.

"Got two barrels of water in the kitchen, too," Holt said. "All the comforts of home."

"Sounds good to me," Hannah said. "When do you expect them?"

"I'm guessing they'll wait a day or two. Keep an eye

on who's working the roundup," Deed said and poured coffee for the three of them.

"You don't think they'll get suspicious when they see Blue's wife and children at the roundup?"

Deed nodded. "We hope they don't. Bina's going to be dressed like a man. And the kids are going to stay inside the chuck wagon during the day. They won't like it, but they'll do it."

After drinking his coffee, Deed saddled and rode out on the paint horse, Warrior, heading out to the roundup camp. Hannah settled into reading Henry Wadsworth Longfellow's *Tales of a Wayside Inn* and Holt strolled around the ranch. They would take turns guarding when night came. The ranch dogs trailed Deed to the far edge of the ranch yard before turning back. The thought nettled him about leaving the ranch, but he pushed it away, confident that Holt and Hannah could do serious damage to any attackers. In fact, both men seemed to be looking forward to it.

At the roundup camp, he rode up to a wild symphony of sound of bawling calves and yelling men, mixed with heavy dust, wood smoke, and the smell of burning cowhide. Most of the valley was covered by grazing cattle gathered during the day. Herefords made up most of the herd, but there were longhorns mixed with them.

Short-term fences of brush and logs kept the gathered animals from straying. From dawn to dark, riders worked to bring in the cattle, separating them into one herd of cows with calves and a separate herd of steers and older cows. An occasional bull was in this group as well. Come spring this bunch would be moved to market in Kansas.

A sturdy pole corral had been built to hold calves while the youngsters were branded. Their mothers were allowed to stand around the corral as long as they weren't unruly. New calves were branded to match their mothers; unbranded strays were divided as to ownership. A long rope tied between two cottonwoods held the horses not being ridden at the moment.

Two Sanchez riders were overseeing a smaller herd of unbranded strays. They wouldn't allow these cattle to drift back to the main herd. Any cattle carrying brands other than the Lazy S or LC were eased out of the herd and made to return to their home ranges. As Deed rode up, four riders cleared the woods; each had a roped cow and a calf trailing behind them. He didn't recognize any of the men.

Blue rode toward his brother and waved with his lone hand, still holding the reins. It was his first time serving as the roundup wagon boss and he wanted everything to go well. He directed the combined team of LC and Lazy S riders so there would be no gaps in the ground covered. He had hired six men from town to help with the roundup and they were proving to be good hands. Deed eased the paint toward his brother. In spite of the turbulent time, the roundup was well organized and underway as planned. A lot of that was due to Blue's leadership.

Riding between them, Willy brought a terrified calf toward the branding fire. He was working as one of the cutting riders, or ketch hands. Their job was to separate unbranded calves from their mothers.

Willy yelled, "Got a Lazy S comin' in."

Blue looked at Deed and grinned.

Off to the side, Taol and two men were charged with removing scrotums from the young calves. Each removed bloody sack was tossed into a large pot, usually accompanied by a Mexican cheer. A supper of fried "mountain oysters" would be a traditional celebration when the roundup was over. Another group was also checking beeves that had been separated from the others for disease, sores, or open wounds. Any cow with thin flanks, or a swollen jaw, or a drooping head, was given special treatment. Likely the animal had been bitten by a rattlesnake. At their feet were medicine bottles, cutting tools, and large cans of ointment.

Sweating heavily, Harmon Payne coordinated the branding while other sweaty men worked diligently and fast over a hot fire. Behind them both, Cliente, the Lazy S foreman, was keeping tally in a leatherbound book. A thin cigar extended from his mouth.

Blue told Deed that Silka, Little Jake, and some vaqueros were working the heavy thickets for cows and their calves entrenched in the thick growth encircling the ravines. All riders had stayed on the combined land of the two ranches. Unspoken was the need at some point to cross into Bar 3 land. There were too many strays to ignore, especially Lazy S cattle.

Deed asked where Blue wanted him. Blue suggested he stick around and help with the gathered calves. It was too late to ride out to the heavy brush. Deed had the feeling that Blue was favoring him and told him that his wounds had healed, except for the top of his ear. Blue dismissed his suggestion as the reason and said he was welcome to ride out if he wanted to do so, but they were almost overrun with the calves gathered so far.

The remainder of the afternoon went fast. Several cowboys went to the creek to soak their feet; others began talking horse and boots. A boghole had been discovered to the north and that brought stories of other bogholes and quicksand. Later that night, as they gathered around the campfire and ate, Deed sat quietly with Silka. Blue was eating with Bina and their children, happy to be free of the chuck wagon.

"I'm going to ride back, Silka. If Bordner's men hit the ranch, it'll probably be with a lot of men," Deed declared.

Silka shook his head. "It is long ride there and back. Maybe for nothing. They may not come or it may be only a few. They will think only a woman stays."

"It's our ranch," Deed said. "I heard Cliente talking about sending men back to their ranch tonight. And he's got four vaqueros already standing guard on their roof."

"Tell Blue. I ride with you," Silka said and laid down his plate.

Blue understood and wanted to go with them, but knew he couldn't. His primary responsibility right now was to the roundup. After saddling his buckskin and Silka's favorite bay, they rode out. It was already dark, but they knew the trail well. Holt and Hannah were glad for the interruption; there had been no signs of trouble and both were bored. Holt insisted Deed and Silka sleep and would be awakened if necessary.

The night was uneventful and the two men rode back to the roundup camp early the next morning. They rode in and dismounted as far from the gathered herds as possible. A horse freed of its rider might shake the saddle and scare the cattle. Deed reported that all was well at the ranch and Blue was relieved.

Shortly after breakfast, a mossy-eared longhorn bull broke away from the second herd, angry at the rider working his cows, and charged the camp, looking for something to ram. Yells broke through the camp. Willy was loping his horse to the calf pen when he saw the bull coming at him. He swerved his horse but not enough and the bull slammed into the bay and sent Willy flying. The enraged bull spun around and headed back for Willy, stunned on the ground. Frightened, Willy's horse went running.

Cliente got a rope over the bull's head and Harmon added a second, but the animal snapped them like they were string. Taking his empty dish and cup to the chuck wagon, Deed ran for his Spencer on his horse. Cliente was closer to his rifle and fired into the charging animal. The bull staggered, but kept coming. Deed fired and then Cliente again. Stumbling forward, the bull fell on its horns five feet from the dazed Willy.

"That was too close," Blue said and walked over to the downed cowhand. "Willy, are you all right?"

"Huh?"

Blue helped him to his feet; Harmon rushed over to help. They half-carried, half-dragged him to the campfire. One of the vaqueros brought Willy's bedroll from the chuck wagon and spread it out. Bina came with water and towels.

"Willy, you rest here for a while." Blue and Harmon laid him down on his blankets.

"I'm fine. Jes' fine." He tried to stand and fell.

"Stay put, Willy," Blue commanded and eased the man to his sleeping blankets.

Cliente reported that Willy's bay only got a long scratch and should be just fine. They decided to have a couple of the men skin the bull; Too Tall would direct the effort.

"Some beef would be good," the Mexican foreman said with a grin. "He was one of ours. So dinner is on us."

The day was long and hard. Deed rode with Silka and two vaqueros and they each went through five horses working in the long draws and heavy brush where the cattle liked to hide. Several cows wearing old H-5 and Roof-M brands were found, along with a handful of Bar 3 animals. All were herded to Bar 3 land. When they couldn't see any longer, they rode in. Blue announced they would move the camp tomorrow, closer to Bar 3 range.

After rubbing down their horses, Silka headed for a nearby stream and placed his lariat in it for the night. He thought it gave the rope stiffness needed to lasso calves. A recovered Willy got to belching loudly around the campfire and one of his especially forceful presentations scared the horses and cattle. It took half an hour to calm the herd and the remuda. Willy apologized, but no one thought it was funny. Several hands thought it would have been better if the bull had knocked him out. Blue suggested he take a walk after eating from now on, away from the camp.

As soon as supper was over, Deed and Silka rode again for the ranch. Both were weary and sore, but felt it was important. Before they left, a full moon rose and showered the land with a silvery light as they rode, giving everything a strange glow.

Gunshots broke into the night as Deed and Silka neared their home. They reined their horses to a stop on the ridge that overlooked the ranch yard. Silhouettes were moving like ants on disturbed dirt.

"Looks like they weren't surprised," Deed said and yanked his Spencer free of its sleeve.

Drawing his Winchester from its sheath, Silka pointed at a small group of men riding away. "Look, they run."

"Let's encourage them to keep running."

"*Hai.*"

They fired almost simultaneously at the fleeing men. Silka levered his Winchester four times and Deed fired once more. They didn't expect to hit anything; it just felt good. The sound of horses galloping away filled the night and then there was silence.

From the house came a loud yell. "Deed. Silka. You missed all the fun. Come on in!"

Deed recognized the voice as his brother's.

A moment later, Hannah added his challenge. "Hey, that was fun. We dusted those boys real good."

"Hey, Deed! We got fresh coffee on," Holt yelled. "I think there were five of them. Think they thought only Bina was here."

Deed and Silka rode toward the house, watching the shadows for any possible movement. Halfway to the house, a body lay sprawled.

Appearing in the doorway, Holt appeared. "I knew it was going to be a good night. See that moon? Full as can be. That's good luck for sure."

CHAPTER THIRTY-THREE

Now that the roundup was over, Deed was going to ride over to the Forsyth station and see Atlee and her children. It was Blue's suggestion and he could hardly wait. His brother had told him to take Hannah to town in the borrowed buckboard, then go on to the station. Both Holt and Silka agreed with the idea.

Hannah had wanted to move to town to be with his bride now anyway, although the Corrigan brothers invited him to bring Rebecca to the ranch. Hannah winked, saying they had important matters to deal with. He was glad that Deed would take him and return the buckboard back to the Forsyth station.

Everything was gradually feeling normal around the ranch. Deed's mind danced with thoughts of Atlee. Everything in him wanted to ride out the Forsyth station and take her in his arms. But he knew the trouble with Bordner was far from over. It only meant that attacking the two remaining ranches wasn't efficient.

Bordner's men hadn't tried anything since their ill-fated attack on the LC ranch house. The gathering of strayed Lazy S and LC cattle on Bar 3 land had also gone without incident. With nothing from Bordner, Blue thought it meant the fat man was going to settle in as a rancher. Deed and Holt figured something bad was coming. Holt had pointed to a hollow fire last night as a sign of danger coming.

Deed promised to only be gone for the day. Blue decided to ride over to the Sanchez ranch and discuss any concerns they might have. Dropping Hannah off at the hotel in town, Deed turned the buckboard toward Atlee. Tugging on his hat and looking down at himself, Deed cleared the cottonwoods lining the back side of the station yard. His heart beat faster as he drew closer. His saddled buckskin was on a lead-rope behind the wagon. Maybe Atlee had changed her mind. Maybe she had just felt particularly lonely that day. Maybe—

Benjamin saw him and came running with Cooper at his side.

"Is the roundup over? Are the bad guys gone?" the boy asked almost before Deed pulled to a stop.

"Yes to the first. No to the second," Deed grinned. "Thought I'd bring back the buckboard Mr. Hannah borrowed and get a chance to see you. How is everyone?"

"Ma will be very happy you're here," Benjamin chirped. "She talks about you all the time."

Deed dismounted. "How's Chester?"

"Oh, he's great. I rode him this morning," Benjamin said. "He's in the barn right now. I take real good care of him." He glanced toward the barn. "You want to see him?"

"Sure. Later." Deed wrapped the reins around the brake handle and climbed down. He knelt to rub

Cooper's ears. "Think I'll go inside and see everyone first."

Benjamin said, "Sure. They're getting ready for the stage." He looked toward the north, placing his hand above his eyes to shield them from the sun. "It's the one from Kansas."

Deed patted the boy on the shoulder and walked to the opened station door. "Anybody around here know when the next stage comes in?"

Surprised whoops followed, then Atlee hurried toward him. An instant before reaching him, she stopped, catching her emotions.

Flustered, she smiled. "W-Well, Mr. Corrigan. H-How good to see you. I-Is your roundup over?"

From behind her came a happy German, then a warm "*Willkommen! Willkommen, Herr Corrigan.* Come in."

"Oh, yes . . . Deed, please," Atlee said, touching her hair.

"Thank you. I-It's good to see you again."

Squealing, Elizabeth came hurrying from the kitchen, holding the doll Deed had given her.

"Deed . . . Deed . . . you're back!"

It made him feel good that she had always called him by his given name, almost from the first.

He leaned over and held out his arms. She half-jumped into them and he hugged and spun her around. Her giggling filled the room. When he put her down again, she showed him her doll and asked him if he remembered her name.

"Let's see. Is it Jessica?" Deed's smile covered his face.

"Oh, you remembered!"

Atlee stepped to them and took his hand. Holding

it at her side, they walked to the table where Olivia waited. Both women were wearing their scarves.

"Herr Corrigan, now I can thank you for this beautiful scarf. *Danke*," Olivia said. "I think Hermann *ist* jealous. *Ja.*" She chuckled.

"Glad you like it. I hear the stage is coming soon," Deed said, aware that Atlee still held his hand. "Didn't see Hermann or Billy Lee when I came in."

"They must be in *der* barn getting *der* horses ready," Olivia said.

He turned to Atlee, hardly containing himself from hugging her. "Where do you want me to put the buckboard, the one the Hannahs borrowed?"

Atlee's face glowed. "Oh, I suppose around in the back of the barn. I'll show you."

Olivia winked as Deed excused himself and they went outside, still holding hands. As soon as they rounded the barn, Atlee leaned against him, bringing his face to hers with a hand. They kissed.

"Oh, Deed, I miss you so."

Deed touched her face. "Not as much as I miss you, Atlee. You are all I can think about."

Their embrace was interrupted by the thundering advance of the incoming stage. They heard Billy Lee and Hermann telling each other to get the new team.

She laughed. "I guess I've got to go to work. How long can you stay?"

Deed shrugged his shoulders. "I've got to go back later today. I promised to only be gone for the day. Troubles with Bordner are only going to get worse, I fear. At least we have our brother Holt with us. Blue talked to him in El Paso and he came back."

"Oh, that's wonderful about your brother, but not

about you leaving so soon!" She kissed him on the cheek and spun away to go back into the station.

The day went too fast and he reluctantly rode out on his buckskin, waving as he rode. They had had only one other quiet moment together, in the kitchen, but he told himself it would keep him happy for a little while. He wanted to ask her how long she needed to be in mourning, but couldn't bring himself to do so.

The evening went slowly with Deed's mind wrapped around being with Atlee. It was late morning when he saw riders coming as he walked from the barn. Retrieving his carbine propped against the barn wall, Deed stepped outside and into a morning shadow, cocking the gun with practiced ease.

Three riders.

He recognized them: the acting county sheriff, Macy Shields, and the two Rangers who had come to the Forsyth station. This wasn't going to be a social call.

"Aho, the ranch!" The call came from one of the Rangers.

"Morning, men," Deed called out. "What can we do for you? Are you finally getting around to investigating the trouble the Bar 3's been bringing?"

From around the corner came Blue and not far behind him was Silka. Holt stayed in the house.

"What's this all about?" Blue asked as he stepped beside his brother.

"Don't know, Blue. This here's Macy Shields, one of Bordner's men. Bordner set him up as acting sheriff. Acting is probably the right word for him," Deed said, not taking his eyes from Shields. "I met these two Rangers at the Forsyth station when I was helping there. This is Mr. Rice . . . and I think this is Mr. Williams. This is my brother, Blue, and our partner, Silka."

"You have a good memory," Ranger Rice said.

"Thanks. It comes in handy now and then."

Rice leaned forward in his saddle and pushed back his hat with its pushed-up brim. "Boys, this isn't a good day, I'm afraid. You two and your brother, Holt, are accused of robbing the Wilkon bank. We need to take you in for questioning."

The second Ranger looked around. "Is Holt here?"

Deed snorted. "No, he's not. You know that."

Blue said, "I don't know whether to laugh or cry about this silliness, Ranger. When did this supposedly happen?"

"Yesterday," Ranger Williams responded. "And it isn't silly to us. The bank president recognized you, Blue, and said you called your brothers, Holt and Deed, by name. He said you all wore masks." He hesitated. "Having just one arm stood out." The tall Ranger took a deep breath. "He said you were in the bank for a loan before that and were turned down. He guessed you needed the money. About two thousand in gold and certificates were taken."

"Yesterday? I was—"

Blue stepped forward, nudging Deed to the side and stopping him from continuing his statement. "Put the gun down, Deed. So you think we robbed the bank and came back here. Does that make any sense to you? Or am I missing something?"

The shorter Ranger growled. "That's not our problem. We need to search your place for Holt."

"I just told you he's not here," Deed snapped.

"Can't take your word for it. We've got to search." The shorter, stockier lawman with the misshapen hat declared. He brushed his long black trail coat as if that would remove the layers of dust.

"Look away then, but knock on the door before you go in," Blue said. "My wife is putting our children down for a nap."

"Come on, men," Marshal Shields said and eased his horse in the direction of the house.

Blue turned to the Rangers. "Gentlemen, we have no problem with you boys looking through our place. But we must insist that this man stay outside. He's more coyote than lawman and I don't want him in our house. If you weren't here, he wouldn't be allowed to stay on our land."

"Wait a minute, I'm the law in this county," Shields snarled. "It's my job to keep the peace."

"Then keep it by staying on your horse," Deed said, glaring at him.

Williams, the taller Ranger, tugged on his trail coat. "That'll be just fine."

Shields's hand dropped to his holstered handgun.

"You didn't have the guts to try that before, Shields," Deed's hard voice made even the Rangers wince.

Ranger Williams said, "That's enough, Shields. Ranger Rice and I will conduct the search. You wait here." He swung down. "And don't do anything . . . stupid."

Blue turned to his brother. "Deed, why don't you get our hands out of the bunkhouse so the Rangers can search more easily, all right?" He winked and only Deed caught it. "Tell Bina that the Rangers are going to search the house on the way, will you?"

"Sure." He spun around and headed for the house.

"Rangers, you're welcome to start in our house or the barn, whatever," Blue turned back to the mounted men. "Just leave your horses and we'll see that they're watered."

"I appreciate that, but you know we have to take you in for a hearing," Rice, the shorter, stocky Ranger, dismounted.

"Who's conducting this hearing?" Blue asked.

"It'll be Judge Pence. Oscar Pence. You know, the circuit court judge. He's in town."

"That's interesting timing." Blue held out his hand and took the offered reins of both horses.

The two Rangers walked to the house, talking quietly to each other. Bina met them at the door and welcomed them inside. Deed was already walking toward the bunkhouse.

Shields started to get down and Blue said, "Stay on your horse, Shields. When we take the horses to water, you can ride over. Wouldn't keep a good horse from that, even when it's being ridden by a crook."

The county lawman glared at him. "You're gonna be sorry, Corrigan. You and your damn brothers. All o' you are going to prison. You should've known you can't beat Agon Bordner. He's gonna be king of this whole region."

Blue laughed and led the Rangers' horses to the water tank. Shields followed without saying anything more. From the bunkhouse, Deed reappeared with Silka, Holt, Willy, Harmon, and Little Jake. None were armed. Holt had slipped out of the back door and gone to the bunkhouse after Deed had told him what was happening.

A few minutes later, the Rangers reappeared.

"Rangers, you're welcome to search the bunkhouse and the barn," Blue said, holding the reins of the drinking horses. Casually, he said, "These are our permanent hands . . . Willy, Sam, Harmon, and Jake. They'll stay out of your way."

The Rangers nodded and headed for the bunkhouse.

"Sam, Willy, will you saddle us some horses," Blue asked.

Holt smiled and he and Willy hurried toward the barn. The Rangers were coming out of the bunkhouse and headed for the back side of the barn. He was uneasy, but trusted his brother's instinct.

Deed moved over to where Blue was standing with the horses. "What are we going to do?" he whispered.

"We're going in. Clear this thing up," Blue responded.

"This is a setup, Blue. You know that," Deed snapped.

"Of course it is. But I don't see any other way," Blue muttered.

"How about using our guns."

"That's just what Bordner would like—us firing at Texas Rangers doing their duty."

Inside the barn, Willy and Holt began saddling mounts. The animals blew softly as they placed blankets on their backs. Most of the roundup horses had already had their shoes removed and been turned out for the winter. Only those needed for the next few months were in the barn and kept shod.

Holt saw a spider prance across the back of the stall. Good luck, he decided. Definitely good luck. As he swung the saddle into place, Ranger Williams stepped beside the opened stall.

"Sorry we have to do this," Williams said. "But we have to, you know."

Holt cocked his head and reached for the cinch

under the horse's belly. "Yeah, guess so. They didn't do it, you know."

"Don't think so either. Do I know you?"

"Don't know. Where you from?" Holt said. "I came from Kansas."

"Oh. You looked sorta familiar to me."

"Really? Some folks around say I look like I should be one of the Corrigan brothers." He grinned.

Williams smiled. "Not hardly."

From the next stall, Willy yelled, "You know, I had a guy say that about me. Last year it was."

Williams turned toward his partner. "See anything, Rice?"

"No. It's clear."

"All right, let's get moving to town."

The Rangers reappeared from the barn with Holt and Willy leading the saddled horses. "We'll take the two of you to town. Will you go peacefully?"

"Yes. But we're keeping our guns until we get there," Blue said. "I don't trust Bordner or his bunch."

Ranger Williams looked at his fellow lawman. "That'll work for us. No tricks now."

"No tricks. May I tell my wife good-bye?" Blue asked.

"I'll go with you," Ranger Rice declared.

"That won't be necessary," Ranger Williams responded. "He just gave us his word."

Ranger Rice mumbled something under his breath and remounted.

After a brief good-bye, Blue returned to the group carrying several towels and a newspaper. He said the towels were for washing themselves in the morning and the paper, for catching up on their reading. What no one knew was that Blue had a needle and a small circle of thread in his pocket to execute an idea Bina had suggested. He shoved the towels and newspaper into his saddlebags and mounted his horse. Deed noticed his brother had a glove shoved into his back pocket. Also unknown to anyone was a loaded derringer hidden in Blue's boot, again Bina's suggestion.

Coming up next to him, Holt said, "I won't let you guys take this fall."

"I know. Ride for the station. We're going to need Mrs. Forsyth to testify," Blue said quietly. "Same with Felix Sanchez. Tell Silka to bring the money from the drive. All of it. We're going to end this. One way or the other."

"I'll take care of it."

Blue looked at his brother and nudged his horse into a lope to catch up to Deed. The two brothers rode out with a Ranger on either side of them. At Deed's insistence, Shields rode in front.

A half hour later, Rhey Selmon in his bearskin coat and six riders cleared a ravine and rode up. The man with a long scar across the bottom of his face and the blond gunman with strange eyes and a weak chin rode on either side of him. They were surprised to see guns in the Corrigan brothers' hands. Both Rangers drew their six guns from their double-rowed cartridge belts and demanded to know what the riders wanted.

"Just thought you might want some protection riding to town," Rhey said. "Comanches are still out, you know."

Deed laughed. "So are you bastards."

Waving his gun, Ranger Williams said, "That's not needed. You boys head on back to where you came from. Do it now."

Rhey gave Shields a hard glare. Shields shrugged his shoulders and the gunman reined his horse around and kicked it into a gallop. His men followed without a word. The scar-faced man turned to look at them, then hurried to catch up.

CHAPTER THIRTY-FOUR

When they reached the jail, Blue and Deed surrendered their gunbelts and stepped into separate cells. Deed made no attempt to mention his throwing knife behind his back; Blue kept the derringer in his boot and the lawmen didn't search them. Ranger Williams promised either he or Rice would stand guard and both Corrigan brothers said they appreciated it.

An hour later, Judge Oscar Pence came to visit. Stoop shouldered and gray bearded, he looked like a man in charge of the world and had the reputation of being hard but fair. His voice carried a definite Missouri twang though and his manner was more woodsman than magistrate. In his cheek was a chaw of tobacco and his hand held a small tin can for spitting tobacco juice. He wore a shoulder holster carrying a long-barreled revolver. Deed guessed he would know how to use it.

"Deed Corrigan and Blue Corrigan. Heard about both of ya. And that brother, Holt, too. Hard men all o' ya. Especially Deed. Heard ya whupped a giant o' a man a few days back. Mostly to protect a Mexican friend. I like that."

Judge Pence paused and looked at Blue. "Hear ya preach some, Blue. That's good. Won't help ya none in my court, but it's good." He spat in the can. "I trust ya know what y'all are in here for. You're accused of robbin' the town bank. Serious stuff."

"We know the charges. They're false," Blue answered. "It's the latest trick by Agon Bordner to get control of all the ranches around here."

"Heard 'bout that, too. This hearin' is all about findin' the truth," Judge Pence declared, his graying eyebrows arching. "Whar's yer brother. He's accused o' this, too."

"Don't know, Judge. They came to the ranch and took us," Blue said and glanced at Deed.

"Heard he's been ridin' outlaw after the war."

Deed finally said, "He's a good man. Fought for the South. Was one of the heroes at Sabine Pass. But he's been blamed for every bank and stage robbery around."

"Heard that, too. He'd get a fair trial in my court."

Blue took hold of a cell bar with his one hand. "Judge, I assume a hearing is more informal than a trial. That right?"

"I'll give ya some leeway as long as it makes sense to me, if that's what you're askin'," Judge Pence said. "Are ya representin' yourselves?"

"Yes, we are."

"Kinda risky, ya know." The gray-haired man folded his arms. "Ya be up against Sylvestor Tritt. Been brought in by the bank from El Paso. Slick. Real slick. Been in my court a time or two representin' some real scum."

"How long ago did he get here?" Deed asked, stepping to the front of the cell.

"Don' know. Does it matter?" Judge Pence spat into his can.

"Well, it's a long way to El Paso and we were supposed to have robbed that bank just yesterday," Deed said. "I'd like to know when he got the word to come here."

Judge Pence blinked his eyes. "Hmm. So would I." He straightened his worn cravat. "The hearin' will start tomorrow mornin'. Nine o'clock. Sheriff Shields told me it was goin' to be held at McCollum's restaurant." He chuckled. "Evidently there's a lotta folks who want to sit in." He spat and looked at the accumulating brown juice.

"I'll bet," Blue said. "We'll be ready, Judge."

"Hope so, son. Hope so." He glanced over his shoulder. "Oh, there's a stranger outside. Asked to see you. A Mr. James Hannah. Do you want to see him?"

"Sure. He's an old friend."

"Well, I hear he's a professional shootist."

"Maybe so, but he's our friend and has our backs. Everything around here is owned by Agon Bordner. The sheriff. Bank. General store. We have our doubts about you," Blue said.

Pence's face hardened. "Wal, I ain't owned by nobody nowhere."

"We sure hope so, Judge." Blue smiled.

Judge Pence stomped away, alternating talking to himself and spitting into his can. After the Corrigan brothers had a brief conversation with Hannah, he left.

Most of the rest of the night was spent in preparation for the hearing. They didn't sleep much; Blue insisted that his brother join him in prayer. For once, Deed agreed.

Morning found them escorted to McCollum's restaurant by the two Rangers. It was a cold day, blustery and gray. They went first to the outhouse behind the jail so the brothers could relieve themselves. The walk was casual with the two lawmen more interested in the weather than the hearing. Neither noticed that Blue had hidden his good right arm inside his shirt and stuffed his empty left sleeve with towels to appear as if it were his good arm. A left-hand glove, stuffed with pages of the newspaper, had been sewn to his shirtsleeve, giving the appearance of a hand. The fake arm hung at his side.

Rearranged for the trial, the restaurant was already packed with townspeople when Blue and Deed entered, escorted by the two Rangers. Several greeted them with encouragement. More didn't look at them. Eight Bar 3 men had already cornered the best tables near the back of the restaurant where the trial would be held. The front of the restaurant was lined with additional interested people, standing and waiting. At the back near the kitchen, a table had been set aside for Pence to preside. One chair was placed for him; another at the table's edge for witnesses. Two other tables had been arranged a few feet away—one for the prosecution and one for the defense.

Shields was already sitting at the prosecution table, grinning like a cat. Next to him was a narrow-faced man with a carrot nose in a finely tailored black suit. His black eyebrows were thick, nearly becoming one.

A matching goatee gave his thin face an evil look. Blue and Deed decided this must be Sylvestor Tritt.

Agon Bordner sat at the table closest to Shields and Tritt. At his table were Dixie Murphy, Willard Hixon, Jephrum Virdin, the scar-faced gunman, and the blond gunman from the ride to town. All were talking and laughing. Deed noticed that Dixie and all the gunmen were armed. They should have expected as much with Shields as the sheriff. Someone was missing. Who? Oh yes, Deed thought to himself, it's that gunman in the bearskin coat, Rhey Selmon. He's too easily recognized to be here, even when the hearing is about us, he guessed.

As Deed and Blue moved to the defendants' table, Murphy snarled, "This is going to be a wonderful day. You Corrigans are going down."

Tritt glanced at them, then back to a paper he was studying.

Ignoring the threat, Deed looked around and saw Atlee enter the restaurant with Silka. He smiled at her and she mouthed, "I love you." Deed felt his heart bounce and returned the silent message. A few minutes later, Felix Sanchez walked in, accompanied by Cliente and Taol. They stood at the front area of the restaurant. Deed was glad to see they were armed with gunbelts. Felix's eyes sought both brothers in a silent affirmation of support.

Ranger Williams walked over to the Sanchez men to tell them they couldn't have weapons in the courtroom. Instead of complying, Felix pointed to the tables of Bar 3 gunmen.

"Take them first."

The Ranger pushed his hat back on his forehead and walked away. He wasn't about to try disarming

those tables. Not alone. And not with just Ranger Rice
helping. Everyone should have been disarmed when
they entered. That was the sheriff's job. He would talk
with the judge.

As Deed and Blue sat down at the table reserved for
the defendants, Judge Pence entered from the kitchen
and took his position behind the first table. In his
right hand was a gavel; in his left was the tin can. A
chaw was evident in his mouth. He wore a black robe
and Deed noticed a slight bulge near his upper left
arm. The magistrate was wearing his gun.

After banging the table for attention, Judge Pence
made a simple statement that the purpose of a preliminary hearing was to determine whether sufficient
evidence existed for the accused to be bound over for
actual trial. He declared that the trial would be conducted in such a way as he decided and that he, and
only he, would determine if such was needed. For emphasis, he spat a thick brown stream into his tin can.

The blond gunman yelled, "Hang the no-good
bastards. He tried to kill our friend, Sear."

Bordner's hearty chuckle punctuated the declaration and he withdrew a black cigar from his coat
pocket, bit off the end, and lit it. Smoke declared his
sense of control in the room.

Judge Pence slammed down his gavel. "This is my
hearing. I will not tolerate any kind of outburst from
those in this courtroom." He glared at the man who
had shouted.

Ranger Williams sidled next to the gray-haired
magistrate and told him of armed men in the room.
Judge Pence nodded, banged his gavel again, and
announced, "I have been informed by a trusted Ranger
that several men were allowed into this courtroom

carrying guns. I'll have none of that here. Sheriff, you and the Rangers move through the citizenry and take their guns. Put them in the back of the room where they can be obtained when this hearing has ended." He spat into his can. "Do it. Now."

Shields got slowly to his feet and looked at Bordner who nodded approval, then whispered, "Give them your visible weapons."

Rangers Williams and Rice and Sheriff Shields accepted the guns, shoving most of them into their waistbands. The Sanchez men and Silka complied with the command and Shields slunk back to his chair. The Rangers took a position beside the judge.

Looking around the room, Judge Pence said, "All right. Court is in session." He turned to Sylvestor Tritt. "Is the prosecution ready?"

"We are, Your Honor."

"Proceed."

Clearing his throat, Tritt stood, straightening his coat. "The prosecution will show without a doubt that the three Corrigan brothers did rob the bank of Wilkon and abscond with over two thousand dollars of this town's money. I call Willard Hixon as our first witness. He is president of the bank and a respected citizen of this town."

Looking nervous, Hixon rose from the table and took the witness chair.

From the table, Dixie Murphy growled, "Tear 'em up, Hixon."

After being sworn in by Shields, Tritt asked him to describe the events of yesterday. He told the story of the robbery, almost as if reciting something written for him. The three Corrigan brothers, wearing masks, had entered the bank around four o'clock with guns

drawn. He was alone in the bank at that time, except
for a single teller. The brothers had taken $2,300 in
gold and certificates. He finished, took a deep breath,
and was visibly relieved.

"Mr. Hixon, it is my understanding that one of the
brothers, Blue, I believe, had sought a loan from you
earlier in the day. Is that correct?" Tritt asked.

"Uh, yes, it is. Blue said they were desperate for
cash and needed the money to keep the ranch going
through the winter," Hixon said and licked his lips.
"I couldn't in good conscience give them such a loan.
The fine people of Wilkon deserved better."

"Thank you, Mr. Hixon. We appreciate your forth-
rightness in this unfortunate matter." Tritt glanced at
Bordner who smiled. "And we have a witness, the
teller who was also working in the bank at that time."

Judge Pence nodded and turned to Blue. "Do you
boys wish to question this witness?"

"Yes."

Hixon's look at Bordner was one of near panic.

Blue started to stand and the cuff of his left "arm"
caught on the edge of the desk. He looked down and
bit his lip, unsure of what to do. Deed leaned over and
grabbed a piece of paper on the desk in front of Blue,
hitting and clearing his shirtsleeve as he did. Blue resumed with his left "arm" resting against the table.

"Mr. Hixon, you, sir, are a liar and are doing so
under oath. That's perjury."

"What?"

The crowd burst into angry yells. Judge Pence
pounded his gavel for silence, then reprimanded Blue
for his statement.

"Sorry, Your Honor, our parents always taught us
to tell the truth. So I don't have much sympathy for

liars. But this is a court hearing, so we'll do this piece by piece, witness by witness," Blue said and turned to Hixon. "You said we came to you and needed a loan or we wouldn't get through the winter, is that correct?"

"Well, I—"

"Is that what you said, Hixon?"

"Uh, yes, I—"

"Your Honor, I'd like to call our ranch partner, Nakashima Silka to come forward. He is bringing with him the money left over from our cattle drive to Kansas this summer," Blue said and looked toward the front part of the restaurant. "If the judge would like to do so, he is welcome to count it. There is $4,012. As anyone in this place would agree, we don't need more money . . . and we certainly didn't ask Hixon, or anyone else, for a loan. You will also note we didn't trust Hixon enough to put the money in his bank."

Brushing against Bordner as he passed, Silka brought the money forward in a large satchel and opened it in front of the judge. Deed thought it looked strange for his friend not to be wearing a sword. Judge Pence studied the contents for a moment and said, "It's not necessary for me to count it. There is obviously a lot of money there. I accept the fact ya had no need to borrow."

From somewhere in the audience, a voice called out, "Go get 'em, Blue!"

Judge Pence stared, but didn't say anything.

"Thank you," Blue said. "Now, Hixon, your first lie is exposed. Let's look at the rest of this fairy tale you told. You said three Corrigan brothers came into your bank at four o'clock yesterday. Is that right?"

"Uh, yes." Hixon's forehead was glistening.

"You said the robbers were masked," Blue continued. "How did you decide it was Deed, Holt, and me?"

Hixon straightened his back. "You called out to your brothers by name, Deed and Holt. And, of course, you were one-armed. Uh, like now."

"I see," Blue looked down at the table. "You're certain you saw me like this? My right arm gone and my left hand all right."

"Absolutely. Come on, Blue. You had a gun in your left hand, pointing it right at me."

"Deed, help me, will you?"

Deed assisted his brother in taking off his shirt to reveal that his right arm was good and not his left. He rebuttoned his shirt, letting his right arm fill out the correct sleeve. The empty left sleeve dangled at his side. Gasps popped throughout the restaurant and Judge Pence put his hand over his mouth to hide a chuckle.

"So, you were wrong again, Hixon. I have no left arm. You have no truth."

"Well, I—"

Sylvestor Tritt jumped up. "Obviously, Your Honor, under the stress of being robbed at gunpoint, anyone could make such a mistake. The defendant was trying to fool the witness with a trick."

Blue looked at Tritt. "Tritt, perhaps you're right. It was an attempt to catch your witness in another lie . . . and it did. We were certain your client was lying and that changes everything, doesn't it."

"I warned ya," Judge Pence said, but with almost a gentleness.

"Your Honor, we have two witnesses to testify about our whereabouts two days ago, when this robbery was supposed to have been committed." Blue looked toward the front of the restaurant. "My brother, Deed, was visiting the Forsyth stage station yesterday. He has helped them during the fall. The station manager is here to so testify," Blue said. "And I was visiting our neighbors, the Sanchezes, to discuss how we might get rid of the awfulness of Agon Bordner and his gunmen. Mr. Felix Sanchez is here, along with his oldest son, Taol, and his foreman, Cliente. I can bring them forward now or later." He paused and added, "I don't know where our brother, Holt, is. For all I know he may be at our ranch. I do know he wasn't with us in the bank two days ago. *Nor were we.*" He glared at Hixon. "And so does Hixon."

A murmur ran through the crowd that Judge Pence ignored. He pointed at Tritt. "This is a hearing, not a trial. I have no problem with not keeping with procedure. If you agree, Mr. Tritt."

The prosecuting attorney was annoyed. This wasn't how the hearing was supposed to go. Bordner had told him this was going to be easy. Behind him, Dixie Murphy was making comments about shooting the two Corrigan brothers and leaving. He was beginning to think that made sense.

"Your Honor, I would prefer to stay with accepted procedure."

"As ya wish." He glared at Tritt, then at Bordner. "But I must advise ya that I am already inclined to dismiss this hearing for lack of evidence. And to charge yer first witness with perjury." He looked back at Tritt. "Are we clear . . . Tritt?"

"Of course, Your Honor, but I believe you will understand the seriousness of the matter if we are allowed to continue."

"I wasn't finished questioning your witness, Tritt," Blue declared, his fingers poised on the table.

This time Judge Pence chuckled out loud, spit into his can to help regain his composure, and said, "Please continue, Mr. Corrigan."

"Thank you. Before we go any further, Hixon," Blue said, staring at the nervous banker, "When did you hire slick stuff here?"

Hixon was startled and glanced at Bordner adjusting a gold ring on his pinky finger. His cigar was stuck in the corner of his mouth sending a curl of smoke around his massive head. He didn't appear to be listening.

Shrugging his shoulders, Hixon answered, "Uh, I hired him yesterday."

"The day after the bank was supposedly robbed. That right?"

"Yes, that's right."

Blue's smile didn't reach his eyes. "Tell me then, how that happens. Tritt is from El Paso. That's a long way from here."

Hixon hadn't expected that. The crowd blurted "Ahhh" in unison.

Tritt folded his arms. "If it pleases the court, I was in town on business this week. Other business."

Spinning around, Blue asked, "What other business would that be, Tritt?"

The prosecuting attorney ran his hand along the top of his head. He hated being called Tritt without the respect of *Mr. Tritt* and that the Corrigan brothers were not intimidated by his very presence. His eyelids blinked rapidly.

"My business is confidential and of no concern to this court."

Judge Pence leaned forward. "This court wants to know. It seems a bit contrived for ya to be hyar. Remember, Mr. Tritt, I know yer record and it mostly smells."

From his table, Bordner stood and yelled, "This is ridiculous. I hired Mr. Tritt to work on a railroad opportunity I am considering. He's been staying at my ranch the last week. Satisfied?"

After spitting into his can, Judge Pence snarled, "Sit down, Bordner. I didn't ask ya. But it is interestin' that nobody around here seems to know anything without checking with ya first."

"We're finished with this witness for now, Your Honor, but we reserve the right to call him back," Blue said.

Looking at his notes, Tritt told J. R. Peterson, the teller, to take the stand. A small man in a tight paper collar, he stood, holding his hat, in the middle of the room. He hesitated and said, "No. I'm not. This is stupid. No one tried to rob our bank and Hixon knows it. I'm leaving town." He turned and rushed for the door.

Shields was livid; he jumped up to go after the frightened man.

"Don't try it, Shields," Deed snapped. "You aren't that good."

For an instant, the sheriff considered going for his gun; Deed wasn't armed.

"What's the matter, Shields? I don't have a gun. This is a perfect chance for you." Deed stood with his arms outstretched.

Shields licked his lips and glanced around. Both Rangers were holding their guns on him. Without saying another word, he returned to the prosecution's table.

Judge Pence reinforced the command and asked Tritt if he had any more evidence to present. Tritt turned to Bordner, shrugged, and said he did not. Blue was asked to present his witnesses and he called Atlee Forsyth and then Felix Sanchez to the stand. Smiling at Deed through her testimony, Atlee declared that Deed was at the station and Felix declared that Blue was at their ranch when the robbery was supposed to have happened. She looked radiant, wearing Deed's pink scarf around her neck and a tailored tweed suitcoat and skirt.

Stunned, Tritt asked that the witnesses' testimony be dismissed because they were not worthy and because they were friends of the Corrigans.

Disgusted, Judge Pence said, "Their testimony is valid. Contrary to Mr. Hixon's."

Blue decided to press further. "Your Honor, it is clear we did not rob this bank. I want to take advantage of this courtroom situation and present evidence of a much more sinister nature. If it pleases the court."

Pence grinned. "I'm listening."

CHAPTER THIRTY-FIVE

Blue Corrigan pointed at the sulking attorney. "Let's take a good look at all this. Slick here was hired by Agon Bordner and brought to town last week for this hearing only. Bet on it. Bordner owns the bank, hired Hixon, and had him make up this tale about us robbing the bank.

"Bordner also owns the general store and tried to force the Sanchezes and us out by refusing our business. He took ownership of the biggest ranch around here in a shady way," Blue continued. "To continue with Bordner's attempt to own everything around here, I would like to call Mr. James Hannah to the stand." He motioned toward the front of the restaurant.

Bordner growled, "This isn't a hearing. It's a joke." He stood up and brushed the ashes off his suitcoat.

"Sit down. I'll decide that, Mr. Bordner," Judge Pence declared. "I'm sure y'all will have an opportunity to speak your piece."

James Hannah appeared from the crowd at the

front of the restaurant and ambled to the witness chair. After being sworn in, he straightened his glasses.

"Mr. Hannah, would you please tell the court of your involvement with Mr. Bordner?"

"Be happy to," Hannah shifted in the chair so he could see the fat man clearly and glared at him. Only Deed seemed to notice he was wearing a shoulder holster under his suitcoat.

"Bordner tried to hire me to kill Deed Corrigan," Hannah testified. "He was afraid of him and none of his men wanted to tangle with Deed. From firsthand knowledge, I can tell you they were smart not to try. The offer was five hundred in gold. I didn't take the job." He folded his arms for emphasis. "They tried attacking his ranch when the men were gone and that didn't work. I was there. This fake robbery was the only way they could figure out how to bring down Deed and his brothers. It isn't going to work either. The fat man underestimated them again."

The courtroom exploded in a fury of voices. Judge Pence banged his gavel and banged it more to try to bring the room to silence.

"Thank you, Mr. Hannah." Blue held up a sheet of paper. "This telegram is from the governor of New Mexico stating that Agon Bordner is wanted for murder and cattle rustling there. So are Bordner's henchmen, Macy Shields, Rhey Selmon, Sear Georgian, and Willard Hixon."

Waving his arms, Bordner shouted, "This is ridiculous! I am not on trial here. I have never met this man before. I am leaving. Come on, Dixie, let's get out of here. I'm hungry."

"Yes, you are, Bordner . . . and you aren't leaving." Deed snapped. "Neither are you, Dixie."

Bordner's mouth opened and his cigar fell on the floor. He couldn't bend over to get the smoke and asked Dixie Murphy to retrieve it for him. Snorting, the cattleman leaned over and retrieved it. Bordner looked at the cigar and threw it back to the floor. Dixie grunted.

Blue turned back to Hixon, sitting at the table. "You are still under oath, Hixon. Did you fake the loan that the Regans were supposed to have signed? Be careful what you say. This nightmare is all over, but you might save yourself from hanging—if you speak the truth."

Hixon looked down at his hands.

"I asked you a question, Hixon. I expect an *honest* answer."

Sitting up straight, Tritt growled. "You don't have to answer that."

"No, you don't. Slick here is right for a change. But if you're smart, you will. Look at me," Blue demanded. "You are involved in a scheme that killed innocent people. In a few minutes, I'm going to bring in a boy who survived the Bar 3 attack and he is going to identify who was involved. Another witness will nail Bordner himself and his men to that terrible crime. You can listen to slick or you can help yourself stay away from a rope."

Across the table, Bordner demanded that Hixon remain silent. Dixie reinforced it with a threat.

Blue laughed. "Isn't it interesting, Hixon. They don't sound so tough anymore, do they?"

In a small voice, Hixon cracked, "Y-Yes, I-I faked the loan. I-I didn't know anybody w-was going to be killed.

H-Honest." He looked up and his eyes were welling with tears. "Stay away from me, Shields."

"What about the Merefords and the Hansons?"

"R-Rhey and his bunch killed them. Made it look like Indians did it. Like they did at the Bar 3 and took back the money Bordner paid them for their places."

"Thank you, Hixon. May God have mercy on your soul," Blue said.

Judge Pence banged his gavel. "I rule Blue, Deed, and Holt Corrigan are innocent of robbing the bank. I question that it was ever robbed." He shuffled this robe and drew his long-barreled revolver, cocked, and aimed it at Bordner. "I also order the arrest of Agon Bordner, Rhey Selmon, Sear Georgian, Willard Hixon, and Macy Shields to be held for a hearing on charges of the murders of the Regan family and the families of the Merefords and the Hansons, and deceitful gain of the Bar 3, H-5, and the Roof-M." He looked toward the front of the restaurant. "Rangers, do your duty. I request the Sanchezes to get their guns and help with this task. You are hereby deputized."

Tritt waved his arms. "But . . . but—"

"Shut up, Tritt," Judge Pence shouted. "You're done here."

Felix, Taol, and Cliente went to the pile of guns; Silka followed to get his sword.

As the two Rangers stepped forward with their guns drawn, Bordner pulled a hidden gun from his coat pocket. Murphy and the Bar 3 men drew their concealed weapons.

"Drop your guns, Rangers, or you die. You, too, Judge," Bordner declared. "And you bastard Corrigans are going to die now. You've caused me too much trouble."

The Rangers dropped their guns and raised their hands.

Instead of complying, Judge Pence fired and clipped Murphy's shoulder. Murphy spun and fired back, blasting splinters from the judge's table as he turned it over and ducked behind the heavy surface. Judge Pence peeked over the table and fired again. Three other men fired at the gray-haired magistrate, missing.

A wild-eyed Tritt ran toward the kitchen but was stopped by the restaurant owner brandishing a shotgun. He held up his hands and began crying.

Bordner turned toward Deed, smiled, and cocked his revolver. "Good-bye, Deed Corrigan."

Deed's hand dropped behind his shirt and drew his throwing knife. The blade hit Bordner in the heart so quickly the fat man didn't react until it struck deep. Bordner's gun went off, slamming a bullet past Deed's head and into the restaurant wall. Bordner groaned and grabbed the knife to withdraw it as his shirt turned crimson. Deed rushed him and slammed his opened right hand down against Bordner's gun-holding wrist and grabbed the gun with his other hand, yanking it upward and free. A thunderous blow across Bordner's face with the gun in his fist followed. The fat man crumpled to the ground, knocking the table and his chair over as he fell.

At the same time, from the witness chair, Hannah pulled free his Smith & Wesson .44 Russian revolver and fired three times, hitting Shields and a tall Bar 3 gunman. He tried to move to the judge's table for protection. Gunshots from the other Bar 3 gunmen hammered Hannah and he collapsed.

Blue withdrew the derringer from his boot, fired, and missed as the wounded Murphy and the rest of the Bar 3 gunmen headed for the door, brandishing their six-guns. The courtroom was wild with fear. Townspeople dropped to the floor, hiding behind chairs. One woman stood and screamed. Three men ran out the restaurant door.

Deed stalked the fleeing gunmen firing Bordner's gun. From the other side of the restaurant Silka, Felix, Taol, and Cliente closed in with their retrieved weapons. Deed and Taol put four bullets into Murphy as the cattleman fired at Felix. The crooked cattleman stumbled to the floor. The blond-haired outlaw with the strange eyes stared at the dead Murphy, then spun toward Deed firing as he turned. Deed emptied his gun into the outlaw. The outlaw's gun fired into the ceiling and dropped from his hand as he fell.

The rest of the Bar 3 gunmen were stunned, except for the scar-faced cowboy. He swung his gun toward Deed. Silka flew in and drove his sword through the man.

Suddenly it was over. Felix Sanchez commanded, "Drop the guns."

Scared by Silka's deadly attack, the gunmen dropped their weapons and raised their hands. With the help of the Sanchezes, the two Rangers led them away to the jail. Blue walked over to the massive body lying on the floor. He felt for a pulse. There was none. He pulled Deed's knife free, wiped the blade on the fat man's suit and pushed it into his belt. Agon Bordner and his dream of the Crown Ranch were dead.

Throughout the room, people began to stand, talk, and leave.

Along the front of the restaurant, Deed saw Atlee and went over to her. She hugged him tightly. "Oh, Deed, I was so scared."

"It's all over now."

"I love you, Deed."

"I love you, Atlee."

From near the doorway, Silka started to go to Deed, then saw their embrace and stopped. He smiled, touched the brass circle worn around his neck and muttered a Japanese blessing of love.

Judge Pence walked from behind the table, returning his gun to his shoulder holster and shook hands with Blue. "Well done. I was hopin' ya'd git the job done. Jason Regan was my cousin. I knew it was dirty work that got their place. Been trying to find a way to bring down that big bastard ever since." He shook his head and explained that the Rangers also suspected Bordner's gang of robbing stagecoaches, using knowledge of money shipments from his bank ownership, but couldn't prove it.

"Wish we'd known that earlier." Blue rubbed the sleeved stub of his left arm.

"Like I said, we didn't have no proof," Judge Pence said. "Say, I'd sure like to see that telegram."

"Sure." Blue stepped to the defendants' table, retrieved the sheet of paper, and handed it to him as he walked to the slumped figure near the judge's table. "I've got to check on James."

Deed and Atlee hurried to Blue, who was holding Hannah's head and talking softly to the badly wounded gunman. Hannah stared at him with glazed eyes.

"Stay with us, James," Blue encouraged. "We'll get a doc in here." He looked up at Deed. "Get some water from the kitchen. And some towels."

"Sure." Deed went to the kitchen with Atlee following.

"I-I'd rather have some w-whiskey," Hannah stammered. "Tell R-Rebecca that I'm sorry we aren't going to get to K-Kansas."

"Don't be silly, James. You'll be up and around in no time."

Breathing heavily, Hannah took hold of Blue's arm. "You think because I've been hanging out with Deed some of his luck has come my way?"

Blue smiled and nodded.

Hannah shut his eyes, then blinked them open. "Just in case, the rest of Bordner's money is in the hotel room. In the dresser. Third drawer. F-For Rebecca."

"Okay. But you can get it yourself when you're up and about."

Returning from the kitchen, Deed had a bucket of water and Atlee was carrying towels.

Deed looked toward the front door and said, "Doc's here."

Dr. Sandor hurried toward Hannah, looked at all the people milling around, and grabbed the closest two men, saying, "Take him to my office immediately. I will save him."

Wide eyed, Rebecca came running into the restaurant just as the two men were carrying Hannah out. Sobbing, she asked the doctor if he was still alive. Reassured she grabbed her husband's hand and went with him to the doctor's office.

Meanwhile, the gray-haired magistrate walked over holding his tobacco spit can, almost giddy, and declared, "Thar's nothin' on this so-called telegram. It's blank." A grin was working its way onto the corner of his mouth until he saw Hannah being carried out.

"Is yer friend gonna make it?"

"He is a *good* friend and Doc said he's going to make it," Blue said and murmured a blessing. He stood and turned to Judge Pence. "You're right. Holt told us where Bordner came from and we took a chance."

Judge Pence laughed. "How about that thar witness who was going to incriminate Bordner?"

"That would've been Holt."

"Holt? Your brother?"

Blue explained the situation, including Holt going by the name Sam Holton.

"I see," Judge Pence said. "What about the kid?"

Blue answered, "That would've been Jeremy Regan."

"I thought the whole family was killed. The boy's alive?"

"Yes. He lives with us now," Blue said. "We're going to adopt him. Can you make it official?"

"Sure, we kin do it now. I'll write it up. Goin' back to what ya said, could Jeremy have identified any o' them?"

He grinned. "No, I don't think so. I was bluffing."

Pence rubbed his chin. "I'd sure like to see the boy. I remember that he favored his ma."

"He's a fine youngster. We're happy to have him as part of our family."

"Those were some mighty big bluffs ya ran, son," Pence remarked and spit into his can. "Wish I'd have known that earlier," he smiled, repeating Blue's earlier statement.

"Guess so," Blue said. "We didn't see another way. Didn't think you'd let us do it."

Pence nodded. "Wal, I'd a' bin real tempted to let

ya do it, but prob'ly not, bein' that bluffin' ain't truly legal."

Looking dazed, Sylvestor Tritt tiptoed from the kitchen, glanced at them, and hurried past.

Pence put out a hand to stop the lawyer. "Tritt, I don' wanna see ya in my court ever again." He spit into his can and stared at the disgraced attorney.

Tritt lowered his head and left. As he cleared the restaurant door, there was a commotion. Into the restaurant with only his right hand raised came Rhey Selmon in his bearskin coat. His shirt was bloody and he could only raise the one arm. His holsters were empty. Behind him with one of Selmon's silver-plated guns pointed at the wounded gunman was Holt Corrigan. The other was shoved into Holt's waistband.

"Where do you want this bear boy? Saw him hiding when I rode in. He wasn't as brave as he thought," Holt said. "Go on. Get in here."

"Oh, hi, *Sam*," Blue said.

Holt's gaze took in the room and stopped when it came to the massive body of Agon Bordner. "Came in to give my *brothers* a hand. Doesn't look like you needed it."

The emphasis on *brothers* was deliberate. He touched the cardinal feather in his hatband and motioned toward the street. "Saw another hombre in a coat and tie come busting out of the general store and hurry toward the livery. Anybody we should go after?"

Deed cocked his head. "Ah, Sam, that'll be Jephrum Virdin. Bordner hired him to run the store but he's a harmless fool. In a way he helped me."

Both brothers were trying to make Holt realize a judge was present. Holt was too proud of his brothers' finally stopping Agon Bordner's evil to pay attention, or care.

Judge Pence waved his arms. "Take Rhey Selmon over to the jail. That's where the rest of them are. Consider yourself deputized." He looked over at Blue and winked.

Blue realized Pence knew it was Holt.

Holt looked at his brothers. "Deputized?"

"Uh, Sam, this is Circuit Court Judge Oscar Pence," Blue declared, frowning at Holt.

Turning toward the infamous outlaw, Pence said, "I reckon one o' the heroes of Sabine Pass deserves that . . . and more, Holt Corrigan. Ya bin a' helpin' clear up this mess too. As kin to the Regans, I appreciate that more than ya know. So let's resolve this hyar outlaw issue ri't now."

Holt stood without moving. Selmon attempted to step away, but Holt jammed his gun in the gunman's back and he froze, cursing.

"David Copate, he's a banker in El Paso an' a friend o' mine. He tolt me yer name's bin attached to all sorts o' holdups . . . an' he thinks it's wrong. Jes' like this hyar so-called holdup an' the robbery o' his own bank. Ya weren't at neither. I agree with Copate." He cocked his head and grinned. "An' thar's no way a court's gonna prove ya did any other holdup, iffen ya did."

He spit into the can and looked at Deed and Blue. "Ya know you all got amnesty at the end o' that awful war, but it takes a while fer that nasty business to end fer some. An' some are too proud to ask."

Glancing at the dead Bordner, Pence folded his arms, being careful with the spit can. "Holt Corrigan, I also heard ya stopped ol' bear boy thar an' two o'

Bordner's gunslicks from hurtin' a lady at Emilio's."
Pence smiled and looked back at Holt. "Yeah, good stuff
kin git 'round, too, Holt. Emilio's another friend o'
mine." He ran his hand through his gray hair. "Ya know,
Texas needs good men like ya helpin' it grow, not
runnin' from past mistakes." He unfolded his arms and
spit again. "Ya should have amnesty, too, Holt Corrigan,
an' I'm gonna do it. I'll write this up. Holt, ya are now a
free man. But it's gonna cost ya."

Holt frowned. Was the judge asking for a bribe?
Blue looked at Deed who shrugged.

"I hereby appoint ya actin' county sheriff. Ya will
handle that job till the next county election. Deal?"

Holt nodded and couldn't stop grinning. "Deal."

The three brothers looked at each other and broke
into wide grins. Blue walked over to Macy Shields's
body and pulled the badge from his shirt. He brought
it to Pence.

"How about swearing him in right now, Judge?"

"Good idee." Pence spit into the can, took the
badge, and walked over to Holt.

"Ah, hold up . . . yer left hand, Holt. That's plenty
good nuff. Ya got business with the other."

Lifting his left hand, Holt repeated Pence's oath. "I
swear to uphold the laws of the county and of the
great state of Texas to the best of my ability, so help
me God."

Pence pinned the badge on Holt's shirt and patted
him on the shoulder. "Do good, boy."

"I will, sir."

"Got a feelin' that's so."

Deed and Blue cheered, so did Atlee.

Holt smiled and shoved his gun into Rhey Selmon's
back. "Come on, bear boy."

The gunman swore and they left with a grinning Holt pushing him to walk faster.

Smiling, Pence returned to the back of the restaurant and put his arms around Blue's and Deed's shoulders. He patted them both.

"Reckon the court'll have to decide what to do with the Bar 3 and them other two ranches. Come to think on it, thar's also gonna be a bank an' general store fer sale. Hey, an' a town marshal's job to fill. Got any suggestions?"

ABOUT THE AUTHOR

Each of Cotton Smith's novels brings an exciting picture of the human spirit making its way through life-changing trials, driving through physical and emotional barriers, and resurrecting itself from defeat. His stories of the West are praised for historical accuracy, unexpected plot twists, and memorable characters. They are also enjoyed for their insightful descriptions of life of that era—and for their rousing adventure.

In *Dark Trail to Dodge*, the ex-Ranger John Checker seeks a reunion with his long-separated sister, bridging a terrible childhood, and Tyrel Bannon, a Texas farm boy, undergoes a trying initiation into manhood. In *Pray for Texas*, Confederate cavalryman and pistol fighter Rule Cordell struggles to overcome not only losing the war, but the anguish of a tyrannical minister father. In *Behold a Red Horse*, we see the three Kerry brothers deal with the strongest one being blinded. In *Brothers of the Gun*, John Checker must face knowing his half brother is an evil man bent on destroying him by kidnapping their sister's children and taking them into the Indian Nations. And in *Spirit Rider*, we see a young white man challenged by white society after growing up with an Oglala stepfather holy man who talks with sacred stones. And in *Sons of Thunder*, Rule Cordell tries hard to put his days as a pistol fighter behind him but finds he can't when his friends are challenged by a cunning carpetbagger. *The Thirteenth Bullet* and *Winter Kill* both carry this fascinating psychological edge. *True West* agrees, "Although the characters in Cotton Smith's books are for the most part traditional Western men—strong, dynamic, action-driven individuals—their motivations and mannerisms definitely break the mold of traditional western novels. For one thing, they have and show far more emotion than the average man (in or out of a western novel). Characters are placed in realistic, emotionally driven situations, bringing with them souls filled with concern, fear, joy, and desire."

His love of the West came quite naturally and quite early in life, as did his gift for writing. "I rode with them all, you know," Cotton likes to say. "Roy, Gene, Hoppy, I was right there with them. Roy Rogers and Wild Bill Elliott were my favorites. Yeah, I can hold my own on western movie trivia with anyone." From the earliest he can remember, he was wearing chaps, boots, spurs, and strapping on a set of cap guns. "Like the song says, my heroes have always been cowboys."

That love affair turned into a lifelong study of the American West. "Silver screen fascination grew into an appreciation I will never grow tired of. I believe the excitement is in what really happened during this special time in our nation's history. I believe it lives on in each of us, if we simply stop long enough to let it surface. In this time of special trial, that victorious linkage will serve us well. America will win."

Cotton Smith was born in Kansas City, Missouri; some would say a century later than he should have been. He grew up enjoying both adjoining states, Kansas and Missouri, living mostly in Kansas. His ancestors fought in the Civil War, mostly for the South, as regulars and guerrillas. As a young man, he learned to ride horses from a grizzled wrangler he remembers fondly. He also learned how to roll a cigarette then, too! "Looking back on it, he taught me the right ways around a horse—and he taught me some other things too. Like swinging into the saddle with the horse loping. And springing up from the rear, like the movie stars did. Never occurred to me then that I could get hurt. Guess no young person ever does."

Cotton tells it this way: "There is much we can learn from our ancestors, perhaps today more than ever. The men and women who built this country were exceptionally strong people who overcame enormous odds to establish good families, create towns where only wilderness existed, establish businesses, and leave us with much to build upon. They loved the land and that love was returned manyfold."